GLOUCESTERMAS

649 — marco

P 351 = Guru Nut — Nirvana GE   PP 351-366
CN ≠ TM   eT.

711 — Vinniegeri

"Contemplativ Nullification
— P. 767

616 Bretelknity = Ludwig von Dorthy

360 — summary of purport of Gilgamesh text

GLOUCESTERMAS

JONATHAN BAYLISS

FONTIS PRESS
Westborough, Massachusetts

Gloucestermas belongs to the GLOUCESTERMAN series:
Gloucesterbook (ISBN 0-9625780-1-0) was published in 1992.
Gloucestertide (ISBN 0-9625780-2-9) in 1996.
Prologos (ISBN 0-9667807-0-1) in 1999.

Library of Congress Control Number: 2010929362

ISBN 978-0-9711705-1-3

Manufactured in the United States of America.

Cover by Arisman Design, Essex, Massachusetts.

Frontispiece: Etching (1969, original 11-3/4 x 12-7/8 inches) by
Celia Eldridge, entitled *Rose's Junk.* Copyright 1969 by Celia Eldridge.

This book was typeset in Adobe Garamond 3 by
Cathleen Collins, Blue Mountain Lake, New York.
Printing and binding by Sheridan Books, Inc.,
Ann Arbor, Michigan.

Produced by Eugene R. Bailey, Westborough, Massachusetts.

To my teachers, my books

This last volume of Gloucesterman is again unexpurgated of abstractions and literary anomalies. As for the temerity of my first two: Which Circle of Hell is reserved for the faintly praised? Having been unmarried, the burning can go on forever. Better than mouldering in the middens.

—M.C.

CONTENTS

CONTENTS

FIFTH MOVEMENT

1

PROFESSOR GABRIEL [1981]

[The consolidated transcription of
an unwritten personal journal]

As long as we have anything more to
do, we have done nothing.
—*Obiter dictum*: Redburn to Hawhaw

*T*he Chauvinistic Independents who planted the Word in Vinland called themselves Saints but they were scarcely self-sufficient. At first they were saved from starvation by the Irindu Naturals, successors to the pure People of the First Light. Then they depended upon uncouth Englishmen who'd preceded or accompanied them, or who had found better beachheads for less godly motives. Those barely religious Church people already surpassed them in industry and soon outnumbered them, but without demanding a share in governance. These theocrats classified such Englishmen as Strangers. Dogtown, *Ibi*, the hub of Cape Gloucester and later the temporary capital of Gloucester County, on the shore north of Botolph's bight, was the most flourishing and least deferential of Vinland settlements because, even before the Pilgrims arrived, hardy Strangers (including Irish and Norse) had been collecting fish or timber at the natural harbor ibi, latterly authorized in His Majesty's New Albion Grant stretching to the Pacific Ocean. Now almost all of us here are strangers. So at least as a retired professor of anthropology I read the history of this granite Ort-an-Sich, still productive as a working city despite the summer pilgrims and the growing number of denizens or marooners who work outside the city's nautical gating.

Dogtown is indeed a town in size, but it was incorporated as a city more than a century and a half ago without changing its name to Dog City. But here dogs have been known as saints, gulls and crows as angels and demons, cats as sinners. My Felixity is one of the sinners, redeemed from a snugly overcrowded prison maintained by charity in a Front Street storefront by volunteers unassimilated to the city government. She's dressed in fur more beautifully than any lion, tiger, leopard, or lynx—but her figure is formed as a blend of my favorite features from most of the other feline species, and she moves with all their graces—for she's said to be of the rather husky longhaired Viking Forest breed. I am told that some treacherously sentimental family retained her first litter instead of herself. After spaying by a charitable veterinarian she was formidably aloof from the other inmates, but with me she immediately adjusted to celibate luxury. Right from the beginning she tolerated my feeding and handling, and after a few months she began to seek my close company even more often than I sought hers.

Together in my renovated hillside haven we overlook to the north a basin of tidal marsh that's protected from the open Atlantic by the dunes of a beach stretched between rocky headlands. The complacent sinner has several levels of roofs and decks at her disposal, as well as a carpeted two-by-four catwalk laid diagonally from my porch roof to a bosky rockribbed garden of few flowers and some patchy grass. My house is dominated on the downhill side by two very tall blue spruce standing guard between us and a distant view of Double Digit Lights on the uninhabited reef-rock island named Pinnace Woe. Our small domain embraces saplings and trunks of several evergreen varieties. A straight young jack pine is undeterred by the great cracked whale-head of gray granite that nearly quashed its random birth to suppress its infant growth. The boulder itself is clasped by a creeping juniper bush. On a declining

slope close to the house a weeping white pine deigns not to compete for height even with enough space among its straight or
twisted cousins. Surrounded by evergreen shrubs of that loveliest of
families is a cluster of four Japanese black pines sinuously inter-
twined from ground up like gnarled Graces on a Noh stage. Better
yet, on higher ground, just a few yards from the verandahed corner
door, stands the neighborhood's wolf oak with arms of astonishing
tensile strength reaching through each other horizontally for amazing distance as well as vertically from their doughty patriarch. One
of its lofty branches has looped itself into a riverine anastomosis, as
if affectionately reluctant to part too soon in further elevation.

When clothed in half or more of our four seasons, nearly all my
plot of earth is buffered from wind and too much sun by close
stands of maple and an oak, as well as evergreens, but most of my
forestry protection is provided by deciduous woods or mature oaks
lining the potholed cul-de-sac I share with four inconspicuous
upland neighbors, whom I scarcely know by sight or by their kilroys bumping up or down our "private way", which fortunately is
snowplowed and roughly patched up by the whole city's taxpayers,
unjustly to our elite advantage, according to some forgotten ordinance long ago established by the Board of Earldermen. But right
now my dooryard pride and joy is the great wolf oak now exposing
all its naked bones. This tree is indigenously responsible for scattering this large block of hillside with the slaughtered species that
once dominated the blanket of soil that was barely thick enough for
pasturing sheep on a hill of solid granite.

The birdfeeder on my tiny lawn is out of Felixity's reach, but
all year round she's at liberty to mount a variety of superior platforms, outdoor and in, from which to survey the activity it attracts,
including the jerky arboreal histrionics of beady-eyed gray acrobats
with fluffy balancing tails less magnificent but more useful than
her own; or often from her highest hillside level, on or even above
the angelic gulls, demonic crows, and cooing paracletes. At a distance, over the irregularly hollowed meadows of the golf course, she
seems to watch seasonal flocks of honking Dominion geese as they
wheel and spiral in flawless obedience to their surveying leader,
coming or going to or from wherever he decides to take over turf as
a way-station in their uncanny migrations—generally along the
isobars of marshland and beaches fringed with greenery that don't
warn him off the erratic disturbances of saints or mobile strangers
inhospitable to loud honks and intolerable fuzzy feces.

In warm green weather Felixity hears the same sweet monotonous love-calls of our precinct's mourning paracletes that I've heard in the Old Countries, with only imperceptibly differentiated accents. At first, living here, before recurrence of the local cadence blurred foreign venues of performance, I heard each cooing call as an image in my inward eye of a different scene, surprisingly mnemonic.

So far, only twice has Felixity brought in anything like a tiny pink mouse to torment, already dead or playing dead till darting in terror, until I could confiscate the prey for wounded release out of her reach or for apologetic interment in my garbage grinder's maw. —But there was another case, when I interfered with the torture well enough to let the innocent escape in my kitchen without ever finding a trace of it again anywhere in the house! Then also, on a single occasion, Felixity regurgitated on the living room rug a horrible elongation of undigested organism in which I noticed a couple of delicate fully formed feathers no more than a quarter of an inch in length. But as far as I know my dear purring sinner is seldom motivated to stalk and pounce outside the house. That discounts her complaint that I'm cruelly undernourishing her with scientifically blended dry rations, frequently augmented with cooked fish scraps from a can or my own plate.

As for other experience and amusement, she has the freedom of many rooms (at least whenever I leave doors open for heat or ventilation), some of them furnishing comfortable chairs or beds for her, though of the latter she usually chooses mine once or twice a night. Especially in winter she has capricious exercise with golf or tennis balls, which I collect from overgrown roadsides on fairweather walks around the courts and widespread links of a club that has tastefully taken advantage of the irregular granite protruding from earth-waves down the slopes between us and the ocean. Having already forgotten her earlier shocks and terrors in and out of treacherous hands in traumatic human custody, her majesty takes for granted as her due the extraordinary prestige and privilege she's now afforded (save when I allow no exception for winter weather when it's time for her to go out and down her gangplank to scratch the earth). I respect her pride. For many years I studied selfhood in human societies.

Probably, having been kidnapped in a fell swoop as she was purring in security, without warning or explanation, after she had contentedly weaned her playful litter, I imagine she was snatched by familiar hands and thrown into a bewildering jangle of powerful giants and hostile or demeaned prisoners of her own kind, where anxiety and the threat of death prevailed even in the sleep of caged safety amid the kindliest human chatter. Or perhaps even before that rescue she'd been abandoned on city wharves, or in the wilderness of Purdeyville Commons, by the godlike hands that had brought her up as a kitten, orphaned instantly like babies in wartime. In any event her cautiously developed trust in me has grown so absolute that often now when I look at her happiness I try to comprehend all the myriad worlds of private suffering epitomized by the speechless pain and hunger of homeless cats, as a busy nun tries to feel the suffering of each among all God's children. But Felixity has now been blessed with amnesia. Her unsmiling sense of humor is revealed when she's frisky with herself and plays solo field hockey or wrestles a ball on the floor without my cooperation. I should take more time and catnip to make such fun reciprocal. One of the advantages in this my terminal rustication, not too far from Vinland's metropolis, is that I never have to leave her alone for more than a day or two at a time.

Myself at threescore and ten, I'm thinner than Felixity, skinny enough eating all I want without the exercise of hunting. Finding Oakcliff Road too steep for my bike, I must have looked like a white-topped walking stick the first summer when I went downtown twice a week on foot with a canvas shopping bag. (I soon succumbed to the convenience of using my venerable little car for such excursions.) I'm glad to be free of academic mores while living the rest of my life where I would have liked to spend every vacation I ever earned in nursing, teaching, or field work. There were always men or children, writing or penury, to avert or divert inclinations. Now, except when I'm occasionally tempted to offer the *Dogtown Daily Nous* a letter of sunny suggestion, among what kith I have, I can freely express persnickety exasperation with our culture and counterculture, yet spare myself the academic effort to reason from evidential citation.

But I'm too canny to make myself an enemy of the people in a city too small for reliable anonymity on the street. Dogtown's contrast to all the societies I've studied or inhabited is sometimes exhilarating. It's a solidarity of place (Ort-an-Sich)—not primarily of career, tribe, party, religion, or taste. It's a polity rife with bitter contention and hidden animosities that make for unintended offenses in innocent remarks, especially because so many surnames (whether difficult to remember, unhelpfully generic, or misleadingly Anglicized) result from exogenous or eccentric marriages, unadvertised divorces, or illegitimacy even unto the second or third generation. Nordic or Mediterranean names give marooners like me little hint of a person's node in the ekistical web of personal relationships. But Parson Yorick must have had a hard time here, even as early as the 17C, when the only differentiation was religious.

I don't have the guts of my late old friend Mary (or Moira) Tremont, who if she'd returned to her stamping grounds here would soon have converted most of those who encountered her from instant friends (or at least amused acquaintances) to discomfited reactionaries—though now perhaps not so actively openly hostile as their grandparents fifty years ago. That half-century of Depression, war, internationalism, divorce, advertised contraception, civil rights, expanded education, enlightening psychology, frank speech, and self-exposure has brought for the good and ill of all Atlantis a degree of tolerance to which both Protesticans and Catholicrats have accommodated their politics. Mary's cry against masculine authority was humorous: *"Women are the better people!"* But now an organized feminism, with all its benefits, denies educated women their natural sense of irony. I must be wary of exposing my distaste for the ridiculous locutions imposed upon writers and politicians of a liberal society in otiose defense of the sex that ought to be confident enough of its distinction to accept as aesthetically mandatory either the generic inclusiveness of masculine pronouns or the purely grammatical genders about which other languages make no bones. Mary would have found it hard to hold her tongue against that ridiculously clumsy feministic "he-or-she" innovation in the rhetorically cross-purposed war between men and women! Language grew to be her major weapon against any instance of bovine stupidity, piggish cupidity, or willful ignorance.

So even in these liberated times my rather discreet frankness about certain liberal misconceptions must be guarded. For me it is as much a necessary expedience to tolerate the catachrestic locutions of present parlance as it would have been for me to mouth the euphemisms of Victoria's time, when, for instance, Atlantean missionaries held the natives of Owhyee in Pauline subjugation. At Norumbega Theological School (which has sometimes invited my lectures), founded by Chauvinists not very long after Dogtown was established, they now teach "World's Religions" with an even hand; and of course I can never come right out and say that I distinguish the Classic and Apostolic Church of the Tudor Communion as closer—least objectionable—to a satisfactory religious symbol-system than any other sect of Book or theological tradition—primitive, ancient, or modern; oriental or occidental—albeit I'm known for my invidious comparison of Western civilization with certain victimized or neglected cultures under its domination. Whereas separation of church and state is pragmatically essential to liberal democracy, nowadays, amidst all the promiscuous praise of "faith", I find it necessarily polite to throttle my overt criticism—especially when I think of the extraordinarily sympathetic charity underpinning Mary's lifelong experiments with Pauline religion (acutely sensitive to the antitheses she detected between its genuine saints and its hypocrites).

I've had enough of deserts, tropical islands, and rain forests, and I crave no more of Europe either, thanks to my inheritance of this aging property (unencumbered with mortgage), more than forty years after my husband's family first let us live in it for two or three years after it was insulated for winter while I was a nurse here at the Humphrey Tybbot Hospital, making it possible for him to commute to Unabridge and get his doctorate in the Norumbega Classics Department. (My postgraduate degree in Anthropology, at Hume in Cornucopia, had to wait sixteen years.) The nearly only unselfish thing I can remember of Adam was his eventually posthumous bequest of this shelter to me, if only because his childless third wife predeceased him and the second had remarried into too much money.

Always the smart-alec philologist, Adam called this house the Crazy Castle because *crazy* means falling apart. Even before World War 2 it was hard for his parents to keep it in repair. It's far too big for me to maintain for long all by myself, but it provides plenty of space for visits by friends, children, grandchildren, or even unimaginable admirers. Unfortunately, what I really need is hermetic solitude until my magnum opus is finished. Anyway, I'm not exactly besotted with my son's kids as they progress through school and college, though I love them each as promising or unspoilt (for neither is both).

I worry more about other Atlantean children of every caste, especially those with no inkling or hope of an enlightened family. The insensitivity or abysmal ignorance of most people abusing the psyches if not the bodies of their young, and nurturing them at our common electronic hearth, savagely lacerates my heart at any sight

of an innocently trusting baby. It's only by the grace of God that
the whole population isn't overtly neurotic, psychotic, or angry.
With better-educated mothers and sympathetic nursery schools
we'd have more good teachers and attentive voters—fewer and
fewer of them misguided in each successive generation. I'm guilty
of too many abstract preoccupations to have done my full part as a
woman on the ground level of what should be our country's
common good—and the world's. I have been reserved when I
should have been generous with my time in helping to make the
culture of our nation more important than its power. But that's a
confession I must continue to repress until I've finished certain
symbolic developments of what I alone must offer posterity!

Meanwhile I'm a chatelaine without a lord. I've spent half my
capital having Mr Boxshaw install a new heating system (which alas
must contribute more than absolutely necessary to Mother Earth's
exhaustion) and restore such essentials as roofing, siding, guttering,
and window frames. When I asked him simply to make the house
last as long as I will, he tactfully replied that long before me the
shingling of my walls will start leaking. Indeed the brown-stained
cedar cladding is shabby and tattered; the cracks and curls already
reveal a pale vulnerability. The house looks massive but it was built
seventy years ago by the Morgan family merely for roomy aestiva-
tion with its servants. Subsequent patches of internal insulation
were never very effective in cold or windy weather. —That brings to
mind without pleasure the original built-in icebox with a drip pan
always neglected until it was brimmed and Adam had to carry it
cursing to the sink! I followed with a mop to clean up what he
spilled. It would have saved time and irritation for both of us if, as I
requested, he'd simply made a ritualistic habit of emptying it every
day before he sat down to the supper I cooked and cleaned up after.

Of course I could have sold this property and retired comfortably enough (if royalties from my two popular books are still in
academic demand) to any of the places I've liked between our two
oceans, or even in Britain, except for the excessively expensive settlements overlooking my native Golden Horn Bay. It was only Ishi-
matter at Hume that temporarily lured me back there to the
anthropology department, away from philosophy at Cistern here in
the laggard East. (Besides, Golden Horny Island no longer dissemi-
nates Navy men.) Yerba Buena itself still maintains some cable cars
to bemuse photographers, and keeps remodeling the elaborate
abutments and roadways of the great bridges in favor of greater and

greater kilroy traffic. The Bay's vanishing ships and piers seem to have left the western waterfront generally abandoned. Opposite the City, when facing sunsets across noticeably unattractive tides, the flat island of Londonbridge, marsupial child of Babylon Oaks, has outflanked its pleasantly shaded Bay frontage by dredging up over Jack London's old mudflats a grid of replicated houses and shrubbery scarcely above high water; and that island's eastern bank of the Oaks estuary is practically shorn of the maritime commerce and industry that used to face it on the mainland across the narrow channel. My godson Caleb who's a graduate of Hume bemoans the shipping and warehousing that has been given over to exploitation of London's popular lore.

On the northern flank of my recorded hometown, Babylon Oaks, the shady Hume campus has covered itself with much too much asphalt and concrete, replacing grassy expanses and eucalyptus trees, and peopled its environs more than ever with disgusting Blue and Gold fraternizing sororities. The Cornucopia Board of Regents now barely sustains arts and sciences, as it promotes the student chrematistics that promise richer donors in the future. So I prefer Norumbega University, on Vinland Bay, and the metropolis of Botolph, superposed by Gloucester County and the quasi-isle of Dogtown, all of which commensurate with my small scale of space and time, and to which I'm tranquilly naturalized.

But not the least of present stamping grounds is familiar old Unabridge (comfortably if not harmoniously modified), where museums theaters lectures and the Norumbega Library are easily at hand, and thanks to the Dogtown branch of the railroad no driving is required to get to and about the Garth. Still, it's a little too seasoned with recollections of the time when Adam was my only responsibility. How I admired his capability for naming things! An obsessive Classics scholar who was willing to allow us an anti-Classical year together before he got an academic job and begot upon me what at last turned out to be a remarkably self-sufficient progeny, which hasn't yet found cause to react against the influence of either of us, even unto the third generation—a rather remarkable outcome in present academic society.

After he had brilliantly defended his famous dissertation about legendary snakes and jurisprudence on the Athenian Acropolis (which I laboriously typed for him according to meticulous bibliographical conventions on a keyboard specially fitted with supplemental Greek characters, which I then barely recognized from my elementary study of that language), we joined the crew of a schooner full of cosmopolital anthropologists headed for Mardi. I signed on as combined nurse, cook, and research assistant. While serving as a brevet second mate Adam nearly mastered the language of Polynesian myth in order to estimate its psychic distance from the archaic Hellenic mentality—an adventure even today beyond my urge for unified knowledge. He could tackle any special problem except consequential matrimony. He taught himself celestial navigation, sparing the captain much anxiety about his own sobriety, after discovering that the first mate had gone native in Owhyan bars. It was just a timely fluke that Adam and I had such a honeymoon. Dogtown happened to be the home port of the research schooner *Omoo*. We couldn't have afforded any other kind of travel during the Depression, even before we had the impedimenta of a brood-nest.

That happens to be a minor co-determinant of my persuasion that Dogtown is the place in which to end my days. Several better reasons are good or real, but the most sentimental (in Yorick's original sense of the word) is my recollection of naive happiness in those early years with Adam and our first baby, Thalia, when I hardly had time to skim even the newspaper, before he took us away to junior-faculty poverty in Princedom, and before I learned not to trust for long a man's love of anybody besides his children when they are weaned, continent, and promising to get their education on scholarships.

I have returned alone in my old age to a much different but poignantly recalled Dogtown. It wasn't only the intermission of years that rendered me practically incognito here. If I'd been recognized at all by a few ancients it would have been as the scarcely assimilated figure of a young off-islander briefly employed by the hospital as an obstetric and pediatric nurse married to a condescending intellectual who had not spent much more than boyhood summer time in this his parents' house, when the paneled doors and windows were unboarded only half of every year. Anyway, as far as I know, in my elderly second sojourn I have escaped oldtimer gossip or expectation because my corrected surname has disguised my former identity with the respectable name of Morgan, which the children continue to bear. Since long before Adam's death, in order to mask the secondary status of a distinguished academic's ex-wife, I have legally and professionally established myself as Fayaway Gabriel, my maiden name, and have been copyrighted so in the academic world (which anyway in Dogtown is beyond the ken of all but a dozen or two cognoscenti). Here in Dogtown and the rest of Cape Gloucester I have not protested the honorific "Professor" because it sometimes elicits useful cooperation with delicate anthropological interests. According to local historians this was the first permanent beachhead of learning and profitable livelihood for Anglo-Atlantis.

In reverting to my proper name I imposed nothing as embarrassing upon my Morgan-children as Caleb's mother Mary had done to her parents (long before I knew her) by exchanging her patronymic Trevisa, for that of her mother, Tremont, in token of disavowing the "tyrant"—an illustriously conservative captain of fishing schooners—whom she chose to regard only as her putative father. I think that was the beginning of her public defiance, but it's very difficult to distinguish the literal truth from metaphor or exaggeration in her own accounts and confessions. I have written much about the reciprocity of autonomy and community in other cultures (in contrast for instance to archaic Greek and Roman religious ideas of property and alienation), but the contrariety in Mary's history modifies some of my formerly generalized valuation of thoroughly organic primitive societies. In my immature ethnological focus, dismissing most of Western psychology, I failed to appreciate the essential *social* value of an individual's uniquely questionable behavior (apart from crime and cruelty). How important to Geisteswissenschaften is understanding the personality of a creative and loving troublemaker whose good intentions bring vexation or anguish—or at least the shadow of shame—upon her parents, friends, compassionate benefactors, and mortified child? Nonconforming expression is often more disruptive of social amity than a common corruption of values. Mary's agape was incorruptible. Never did anyone outside a religious order take more to heart the Sermon on the Mount.

It was because of my independent name Gabriel that Caleb (who'd known *of* me after his cradling from earliest memory of his mother's anecdotes as only a Morgan) was at first unaware of my recent appearance among people we both know in Dogtown; but he might not have noticed my presence under any appellation, for I'd cautiously avoided the kind of attention that draws one into time-consuming familiarities. Anyway—though unknown to ourselves we had in common a few local acquaintances—I was not likely to be associated in his mind with what interests him at present. But when we met in accidental conversation, and it finally dawned on him what I did for my living, he excitedly recognized me as the Gabriel to whom he had written more than once in appreciation of my books and articles about the radically etiological difference between the Western mentality and that of many "primitive" cultures whose symbol-systems I all but praised. I hadn't remembered our correspondence, for he did not identify himself as anything but an enthusiastic common reader; but now I find that his ultimate allegiance, despite his admiration of what I emphasized in certain ante- or anti-rational societies, remains with the properly understood Enlightenment as an open system that we share. In the end, of course, I am a participant in the intellectual evolution that keeps me at counterentropic work in my old age. I've gotten to be a sort of metaphysical anthropologist!

A few years ago, I hear, perhaps exhibiting a strain of his mother's temperament, Caleb suddenly quit his highly respected job as some sort of an efficiency expert and technocrat at Mercator-Steelyard headquarters. That venerable old Dogtown company no longer produces the dried salt cod and canned fishcakes for which it was famous. Instead it saws to pieces and cooks compressed slabs of frozen fish (brought refrigerated by sea from various North Atlantic ports) and refreezes them as variously shaped cooked or garnished servings, which largely disguise in colorfully advertised packages the light net weight for consumption. Soon after it acquired a Cornucopia company called Stockton-Van Nuys, which I remember from my housewife days as purveying canned vegetables and tunafish, it was itself sold out to one of the multinational corporations. However, Caleb's now obviously on his own. Somewhat evasively he calls himself a freelance consultant but has no need for an office.

This middleaged Caleb Karcist—the vaguely alchemical surname ironically chosen by his mother to offset the predilection suggested by the first one she'd given him for birth certificate and baptism—is fair and slight, with her blue eyes, presumably a bit shrunken from his athletic prime (not much taller than I remember her), but energetically supple bespectacled and half bald. When he'd bemoaned his lack of a middle name to fill space on forms and official enrollments to match the gravitas of schoolmates, I remember reading in one of her amusing letters many years ago, she teased the boy by pretending to bestow upon him as a middle name the lugubrious *ichabod* as its lower case initial, which she told him he

was free to let stand for any *I* of his precocious ego. Later he made
fun of himself with *i* as the imaginary square root of minus one ("the
versor of quaternions", he now tells me), and in later years he's associated himself with both the *i*on of physics and the *Ion* of Euripides.
Yet, until he warms up, he does seem uneasy when standing around
among giants and trying to make his weak voice audible amidst the
gabble of lesser egos. He seems to have much to say. But that's one's
impression of a man only when he comes out of his den and makes
an effort to adapt himself pro tem to the commonalty of Dogtown as
an imperfectly socialized recluse formerly known for professional
ambition and power. In camera he seems cynically insensitive to the
plight of Dogtown fishermen and the insecure proletariat as taxpayers. Yet what I've heard from business people is that he deserves a
capital I for his intramural achievements.

Sometimes I can't help thinking that but for the fairness of his
complexion he might have been a son of my own. Ecclesiastically,
indeed, I happen to have been his negligent godmother for nearly
all his life. But despite my skepticism of the hyperbolically emotional ambivalence expressed in some of Mary's voluminous letters
to me, I'd been prejudiced against him (without visualizing the
baby boy as an adult) by her complaints that he'd proven not to
return her unreservedly demonstrated love. More than once she
declared that in times of especial impoverishment she'd been
taught by her pro bono female Alterian psychoanalyst to realize
that it was scandalous for her son to leave home on private school
and college scholarships instead of getting a job to support the
"aging unemployable" mother—especially in consideration of the
fact that she herself had taken extraordinary initiative in selflessly
singing his praises for the same intellectual purposes, pleading at
the highest levels his case for the best possible education as an
extraordinary sizar—just as she had sometimes personally begged
from rich parishioners of their Tudor parish or from other private
benefactors the price of new shoes, even a suit of clothes, for him as
he progressed in Unabridge and Montvert on his privileged way to
any college he liked best! That was before Atlantean society began
to benefit from revolutionary amendments of social welfare laws to
relieve adult children of financial responsibility for their parents.

So no such psychological interpretation of his independent
behavior, however selfish it might have appeared, could have been
so inconsistent with her lifelong exaltation of both his "stalwart"
character and his known or conjectured achievements, not to

mention the allowance he scheduled for her whenever he had a
salary and when she was without wages or adequate public assistance. "My Honor Boy!" for having been awarded badges, medals,
or prizes at Sunday School, summer camp, or Boy Scouts. "My
Little Oak Tree!" for his self-discipline. In her latter years she often
excused his evasions of her inquiries by convincing herself to suppose that his career was necessarily secret, either with the Strategic
Intelligence Service or less plausibly with an intelligence job in the
Bureau of Domestic Investigation. At the same time both S I S and
B D I were favorite butts of her irreverence, as if they existed only
in fantasy tales. In spite of her respect and gratitude for a Catholicratic government these secret services seemed almost to have fallen
into the same class of her mirthful bugbears as the Protestican
Party: beyond the reach of any personal contention except derisive
satire. As the cheerful advice of a political underdog whenever the
Crats lost power (as once again, this time to a smoothly reactionary
movie actor, we now have done), she loved to quote Giles Eliot her
favorite novelist: "There is strength in scorn, as there was in martial
fury by which men became insensible to wounds."

Mary (Moira Trevisa) Tremont seemed excessively creative. I
believe that most of her life, between recovery from "sleeping sickness" (encephalitis lethargica) at the age of fifteen—during the
great influenza pandemic, just after the Armistice of 1918—and
the fatal onset of medically defined senile dementia, when not occasionally suicidal she was too spontaneously critical to reflect that
her own personal insight often ignored the opposite side of what
seemed an instant's equation, as if the flood of her feeling represented a unity of its terms. If one feels an equilibrium of temper in
one's own expressed perception she can immediately induce a surge
of either faith or horror, like the outcry of a rationally irresponsible
prophet or the curse of a witch. Yet in the parsing of my present
perception she was balanced as a humorous unrecognized bard of
inexhaustible imagination and Christian goodwill. After our original acquaintance here in Dogtown, before Adam and I went to the
western Pacific, I saw her only a few times during all her remaining
years. Toward the end, at a distance, as she requested, I helped get
her admitted to the amply endowed Bishop Derwent House in
Botolph (an eleemosynary Tudor Apostolic nursing home for the
ordinary or extraordinary aged of any class, color, or creed). By then
her word was much fainter, and quite unreliable, yea or nay on
either side of memory or cherished opinion.

As might be expected, Caleb and I never happened to encounter or speak of each other on my few personal visits to Derwent House. Having vigorously protested her veritably forced removal from a snug apartment in Church-sponsored public housing to the "terminal" nursing institution solely maintained by the Diocese, as prudent charitable response to repeated instances of dangerous absentmindedness on her part, she seemed suddenly to resign herself to full dependency. According to what the staff told me by phone, or from what Caleb himself has recently told me, her waning brain insidiously undermined her robust spirit, at first with an amnesia of only irregular occurrence, saving the remnant of her mental faculties for the detection and exposure of competitive hostility in other patients (especially her successive roommates), though she was sweetly considerate of the attendants, especially the black ones, who were generally more sympathetic with her than the rest of the hierarchy was, probably recognizing her intuitive respect for their menial point of view, which underlay even her sometimes imperious manner toward those assisting her.

Still, most of a visitor's conversation was preempted by recurrent or newly articulated complaints that extinguished her memory even of the past hour, not to mention the significance of a vaguely familiar face. Past and future faded, contracted, as if symmetrically. Except for vestiges of congenital pride (which had survived degradations and humiliations unknown to privileged Black Lucies like me), the brave and hopeful poet of joys and sorrows had forgotten all her passions, ambitions, adventures, and nearly incredible toils for livelihood, as well as the exuberance of spirit that had introduced all her successive disappointments. But her refined face and wattled chin were still held high, like an aristocratic bust resting upon an amorphously stout column clothed in some sort of puffed-up dowager street clothes beneath a child's bib, defenselessly mounted upon a wheelchair that she'd grown too weak or confused to set in definite motion. At last, though most of the time she seemed to have dismissed the concerns of her lifetime, once or twice I detected the name Caleb in her spittled and dentured mouth as her blue eyes lighted up at some flicker of private imagery.

In short, there came and passed a time when only occasional flashes of humor, or snippets of phrases from her childhood, suggested what barely remained of multiply compacted life-experience; of an indomitable but tender personality that had forced itself upon everyone who knew her favorably—upon me especially; of an astute and suffering faith in the holy spirit of humanity. No one who had ever been struck by Mary (or Moira in her younger days) as no less misfitted to capitalistic society than a mendicant nun of idiosyncratic morality, with a soul of greater purity and less consistency than other creative and courageous women of service to mankind— no one who'd ever been annoyed by her healthy vitality (notwithstanding the culminating obesity of her trunk)—would have expected her to fade into oblivion as ineluctably as any ordinary woman in her dotage. Certainly not I, whom for more than four decades she'd called the best friend she ever had—perhaps because of the fact that we seldom met between her reproductive triumph and her seemingly premature invalidation before the early age of seventy-four.

The reason for her attachment to me, only slightly her elder, almost as her private counselor, is no psychological mystery. She regarded me, her briefly fortuitous nurse, as midwife and savior at the most important event of her life. She gave me the credit for saving the three babies she'd been planning since the age of twelve, even though we suspected all along that she could not survive more than one baby in her lifetime. She feared the agony of another childbirth. Caleb alone had to serve the purpose of her fervent plan for motherhood. So even before she got herself surgically sterilized a few years later he was to bear the poetic burden of being his own brother and sister as well as himself.

But she had been excessively damaged and he had nearly perished in the long and complicated labor. I happened to be on duty—scientifically speaking, an instrument of chance—as I was passing the morgue. I saw the door ajar and heard a whimper while she was still under ether in the delivery room. I had never seen her before that night shift. Later she told me that before I appeared on her scene the Humphrey Tybbot Hospital had seemed no more enlightened than Shandy Hall. She called me the White Angel, messenger of God, because I was in white R N uniform. Perhaps, contrary to other evidence I've come across, this polis is one of those societies where seeming to have saved a person's life entails the responsibility of a lifelong relationship. Caleb is still too proud to confide as much in me as most men are said to confide in bartenders, but I'm very glad to be his reconstructed godmother.

Of course my nostalgic interest in Mary's history, accidentally entwined with my own, is hardly a motive for joining this sea-moated microtopopolis as one more of its marooners, except for the degree to which she had continued by mail to vivify my memory of it, not so much by description or reference to beauty or convenience as by her personification of what's unique about its humanity. Like Mary herself I've always been attracted (like an evolutionary biologist) by tidewater marshes and presque-isles, including those contrived or undone by men. My children used to ask me for a list of all the islands I'd visited that their friends had never heard of. Once an anthropologist, always a reflexive anthropologist—especially if you're a mother interested in how your own male and female autonomists form themselves.

. . . But in my valedictory work here I haven't yet figured out how best to preserve my eremite privacy while curiously learning the disparate clans and individuals represented in this semi-isolated place. I wish I could spare time with indigenes I see on the street, before God takes back my wits. For three hundred and fifty years the populace of Dogtown has been too busy in its evolution to consider the value of its own modification by successive admixtures of extraordinary incomers and sojourners—imitative, inventive, artistic, learned, technological, scientific, adventurous, or in some other manner extraordinary—not to mention the people who actually characterize its democracy. Very few of the former who may dwell at present unobtrusively within this tiny heterogeneous polity have reason to notice my presence as anything but typical of idiosyncratic marooners, who for the most part are probably not even casually aware of each other's presence as a community of "intelligentsia"; but they share the virtue of paying their taxes to a common treasury and registering to vote. It would be good to know at least the interesting artists and scientists before I see their obituaries in the *Nous*, or before they appear in the *New Uruk Testament* for the whole world to see. That is, before they read mine.

Of those who've not long predeceased me, I've already heard from Caleb about two in particular: —1) Ipsissimus Charlemagne, a daunting but usually amiable personage, primarily an unattached dramaturge and keenly educated critic of histrionic culture, who was sometimes called a former anthropologist (as in *Doctor* Charlemagne), undoubtedly a creative genius with ideas too *sui generis* for any orthodox academy, yet recognized by ordinary locals only for his dominating stature, his shabby habitat, and his peculiar visitors from "across the Gut". Elsewhere, in avant-garde Atlantis and Britain, he was erroneously said to be the "father of Dromenology". Actually his was a specialized theatrical development of much broader ideas put forward about eighty years ago by Jane Harrison, the "Classical Anthropologist" of Newman College in Unabridge.

But not many years ago I remember being impressed by an issue of Charlemagne's irregular and unfunded journal *Dromenology*, especially because it was intelligently respectful in citing an essay of mine in *Quarterly Anthropology,* as well as of other scholars whom I've counted as influences or allies.

—And 2) Oddly enough, Father Lancelot Duncannon of Tudor holy orders, founder of the Classic Order of the Vine, who (Caleb tells me) was also an admirer of my published work (like Caleb himself). This obscure and unorthodox priest, hardly known even by Dogtown neighbors, had earned a Ph D in physics. Fourteen hundred copies of his *Theodynamics,* as well as numberless other pages published here at his own expense by the Order's monastic headquarters known as the Laboratory of Melchizedek and the Mesocosm, have been moldering almost twenty years underground in the city dump, a whited sepulchre now in the process of becoming a leveled "landfill" greened with grass as a field for sports.

Those such mortal stimulants (among all the others overlooked by the best of current bibliographies) are giving me deserved pause in my nearly thoughtless assumption that what I'm doing with the last years of my own evolving compendium will never lie shamelessly junked by the minds that succeed me. Thanks to a unique local concentration of somewhat heretical intellects, Dogtown's influence has been mutual in my case. Perhaps my godson—whose Gilgamesh plays will probably never be printed or performed—will be the only one to remember what I hope to have been lucky enough to finish as a summation and final interpretation of what I've appreciated as well as carried forward from known and unknown contributors to what I call my anthropological philosophy. At least I have the moral advantage over employed professors, now that I'm relieved of academic compunctions. I no longer need to defend my sympathy with the temerarious speculations of laymen beyond the pale, not the least of whom is Caleb himself, a creative gadfly, sometimes a very helpful Ariel.

[Poor Adam: for all his scarcely challenged brilliance, he could not abide certain opinions offered even by the most perceptive ethnologists, especially women or radical scholars like Jane Harrison. Even philologists, if they happened not to be specialists in the language of archaic Attica, were met with his silence. With all his heart he strove to further his professional reputation, his own department, and his acquisition editor at the Norumbega University Press. His graduate students, notably the self-effacing females, were a cult of epigones, but some of them began to express modestly modifying opinions after he removed himself by speeding down the tortuous road from Dikte in Candia on a motorcycle as overconfidently as usual. Until thus defeating his ultimate purposes he never lacked for travel grants. Other ghosts affiliated with Dogtown will undoubtedly turn up as I continue my finally focusing conclusions.]

On my repetitive walks in this neighborhood I continue to notice new things. Today is mild, with no snow covering broad expanses of the golf course. I passed a fascinating flock of about forty geese standing at attention on the grass in a silent and motionless formation resembling their order in flight, an unmistakable leader at their head, as if awaiting dismissal from close-order drill. A few minutes later, when after further reflection I'd reversed my direction in pure curiosity about this astonishing behavior of such notoriously noisy birds (abhorred by the greens-keepers for the squishy mess of caterpillar stools they leave as an anti-fertilizing insult to private property), some of them, without changing their relative position in the pattern, some pecking at the grass in desultory fashion, were resting on the ground as if they'd been given the "as you were" by their captain, who awaited divine signal to take to the air for a safer or more nourishing bivouac in Cape Gloucester on their longitudinal itinerary—to north or south, I don't know which! Has Universal Systems Theory come far enough to deal with the question of this singularly labile organization, an almost steady-state open system under continually replaceable leadership, consuming anabolic vegetation and leaving behind a filthy measurement of entropy? I must ask Caleb his pronouncement!

Though dutiful efforts in the tranquil company of Felixity, and other "activities of daily living", occupy much of my falsely free time for correspondence with former students and colleagues, or for writing a few of the book reviews that I'm hounded for by untenured young feminists (mainly because they pique the gentlemen), I am often tempted to take a real Dogtown vacation as the ordinary retirement deserved at an age in the seventies, just because it's probably the last comfortable time to fend off death, having finally dispensed with rigorous science as well as with men. My diversion is Dogtown itself. That's surprising, when one is reminded that the alternative is luxurious travel, new or retraced, especially to the enlightened societies of Europe that I deprecated in my reactive youth. Refreshed images of Mary Tremont, my antithetical counterpart, might illustrate what was right or wrong in my life as a preoccupied mother.

This unreasonable little city has always been famous for its fishery, and much less so for its granite industry, both of which are well recognized in published histories; but I have settled here for purposes other than a tourist's or than those having to do with the expectation to end my days right here. To be sure, I sometimes wheedle an archivist or one of our amateur historians in light-handed attempts to glean the town's living memory of remarkable souls other than Mary; but I am also professionally interested in ethnic aspects of its ekistics, which I hope not to probe as the voice of anyone but a naive reader of Dogtown's history. (I haven't yet heard of a sociologist hereabouts!)

My few informants speak no more reliably of present folk than oldtimers speak even of this century's distant past in their oral histories. The question I'd like to assign a dusky graduate student is why and how the Tuscans have almost displaced or overtaken the Lusitanians (as well as Nordic, Irish, New French, and Yankee remnants) as the fisherfolk who more than any others have come to represent Dogtown's proletarian character—at least until very recently. The Loosies (as those of my Lusitanian blood were called when tolerated as ignorant immigrants by the majority) are now assimilated as skilled workers, clerks, building-trade contractors, shopkeepers, lawyers, veterinarians, doctors, bankers, or politicians who usually can't be distinguished by their Anglicized names, though presumably more sensitive than I am to the pejorative tone of what was formerly a collective label of disparagement. Yet (unlike the Hibernians before them in Vinland's typical migratory succession) many of them are now glad to be recognized as one of Dogtown's proudest and most versatile communities, maintaining their double-towered and colorfully decorated "national" Petrine Scholastic church (with a carillon that annually attracts one or more of the world's best keyboard bell-ringers), as well as the various clubs and celebratory customs of a prosperous people, with parishioners scattered among other urban citizens in domicile.

Since childhood in the Golden Horn Bay Area I haven't confessed their religious predilections but I've always been glad to share the heritage of Camoens. Lawyers would say I have a conflict of interest if I claimed to be a dispassionate observer of Dogtown, for my mother was more than half Lusitanian. Therefore I have no doubt that my blood has a valuable fraction of the African tincture that she, in Cornucopia, like Lusitanians in Dogtown, regarded as a hereditary taint not to be acknowledged even in jest as an allusion to hereditary embarrassment.

But the secret of Dogtown's "whaling" industry (d b a "sugaring") before the Loosies immigrated from the eastern shore of the Atlantic to Vinland fisheries (but three hundred years after they'd led expeditions to the North and South Atlantis coasts) is darker and truly shameful. It's apparently never mentioned by social historians, even in censored whispers about a whitewashed era. My friend the city Librarian, Gloria Cotton (formerly Gloria Keith, as some of the people still call her by habit or in ignorance of her divorce from Dexter Keith the new mayor), tells me that some of the male "codfish aristocracy" allegedly had a secret sideline for their shipping in the Guyana trade. Not even their fiercely Abolitionist wives knew about the quick runs they made over to Africa and back with human cargo while they were down on that latitude to trade salt fish for sugar. The truth or falsity of this suppressed accusation perhaps typifies the veridicity of many a tale that contributes boastfully to the history of this place. Piracy as well as privateering, even latterday rum-running and drug-smuggling, can seem as colorful as Old Glory at historical distance.

I am romantically interested in this Cape also because of my successively admixed descent from Norselanders approximately of the kind who once served as primary labor in the granite quarries— twelve centuries after the raider Thorwald Ericsson with his dying breath (having been cut down by an arrow of the Irindu inhabitants) dubbed this whole promontory Cape-of-the-Cross in anticipation of the Christian grave marker he demanded for himself out on what's now known as Crow Point. That monument hasn't been seen by any literate witness, but much younger rock-extraction industry has left some attractive scars as well as a scattering of handsome architecture. Loosened stone is the oldest and most durable of construction materials but the business of cutting it from Lady Gloucester's bones was almost as ephemeral as Vinland whaling from a historical point of view. My father descended in part from a Squarehead who hadn't paused for long on this East Coast in his ultimate quest for legendary gold in streams of the far Western watershed, for him by way of Cape Horn.

I have also a latent political affinity with the Scandies who settled here in the "Liberties" of Taraville and North Village (nowadays more likely to be inhabited as wards of Dogtown by educators
artists musicians photographers film-makers or dancers than by
mechanics fishermen stone-cutters carpenters or cooks); on the
whole they remain advocates of the common good, and probably
are more so right now in dialectical reaction to the laissez-faire capitalism of our new President, who undoubtedly joins the present
Tory lady Prime Minister of Britain in believing that "there is no
such thing as society, only the individual and the family."

Of course no one feature of the composite Dogtown is the consummation of an ideal. The multi-villaged city's unique attraction—often catachrestically expressed as its entirety by pilgrims
aestivators and nostalgic expatriates as "beauty" (which properly
applies only to certain of its parts or elements)—is much less a
matter of sensory taste than of its composition as a peculiar amal-
gam of geography history and technology perceived as four-dimensional. That must be what has always attracted the best and worst
artists from other parts or scenes of Atlantis.

As Vinland's boldest seaward salient of rock, and the closest to
Europe by ship, buffered from mainland hegemony by its estuary,
and with an escarpment of arboreal hills as its interior, it often differs from the immediate continent in meteorological fluctuations.
When vegetation's bleakest, as it is right now, the roadside litter
(only a minor proportion of which I surmise to be cast by tourists
or quotidian visitors) is nakedly exposed; but it's also the time
when Felixity and I can best see the open scape of sea and land,
albeit at home we face away from the more interesting composition
in which the city's acropolis commands a plethora of houses and
industrial buildings overlooking the cinematic inner harbor instead
of our offshore panorama. There's little snow on the ground, but
clumps of it are captured like Christmas cotton on the fingertips of
weatherproof evergreens. At present a vernal pond, delitescent in a
hollow diagonally across the street below us where tangled shrubbery and brambles are rife, is revealed to us as a tiny dance floor of
whited ice, though still undetected by strangers driving by the
hedges in their kilroys or walking with their saints on that lower
contour of this rock-bottomed height.

Dogtown is usually but not always spared the worst of blizzards, which more often than not since I've lived in this house seem
to come from the northwest. I suppose the semi-peripheral hills of

our location tend to deflect aerial vectors above their leeward margins, which anyway in winter are tempered by the sea around us that remains warmer than the land. That small gradient of temperature may soften our sensitivities with fog, or perhaps make a critical difference when the atmosphere is close to the freezing point, and is likely to melt floating snowflakes into driven rain. (But of course, annual snow grows imperceptibly less likely everywhere, what with our cycling abuse of Mother Earth's atmosphere, which is no longer assumed as a statistically steady state of the northeast Atlantic Ocean.)

In any direction of violent wuthering, even on this usually sheltered slope, it's hard to distinguish howl of wind from roar of sea. Even in the dark, if the turbulent air is not too burdened with the moisture of its crystals, I can see the ocean's phosphorescent ranks of white-plumed cavalry assaulting the Cape's ramparts of sheer or fissured granite. Sometimes they sacrifice themselves over the top of uninhabited Half-Tide Island, a rounded hill of rock and half-starved vegetation just off the further headland of Little Harbor Beach. Beer Isle further away is a milk-foaming reef at the flood of northeast storm-tides. But when the assault is withdrawn to a few wave-lengths off Cormorant Rock, next to where Greens Heath Road descends to Back Shore Cove and makes a T at the foot of my golf-club vista, a ledge of shoals parallel to the visible coast combs the blue surface into its own contour of white foam, the rhythmic washing of a ridge that's invisible in times of peace. It reminds landlubbers like me of krakens more insidiously dangerous than crescendos of violence. Yet at times, in the retrospective abstraction of old age, those spectacular leaps of spindrift surmounting Lady Gloucester's skirts in immediate aftermath of a stormy flood tide sometimes bring to mind pleasures I've otherwise almost forgotten in the liberating tranquillity of what has grown to be my almost purely cerebral existence.

The whole populous segment of Dogtown on this side of the Namauche River (man-cut, or "Gut", of the neck that three and a half centuries ago made its island out of a peninsula), comprising all but the two sparsely "developed" wards that occupy the mainland of Cape Gloucester but about the same share of Dogtown's territory, is a self-delineated city-state, impressively conspicuous from both ship and airplane. It was probably isolated also in eons past, but after some later Ice Age disruption. Long before the arrival of primeval mankind its umbilical was fragilely reconnected to its motherland by the ocean's washed-up sediment. When the earliest Naturals arrived at their dawn the isthmian barrier at the southern end of what had been the sea's inland passage had long since created a broad marshy valley along the estuary to the northwest of it. Countless centuries later an English clergyman had the colonists dig the Gut, in effect reversing the geological procedure by providing boats with a shortcut (especially important in the winter) between the fishing grounds of John Smith's Bay (still a coastal passage to the greater Gulf of Markland) and the naturally advantageous south-facing Dogtown Harbor, the magnificent convenience of which had already determined its position as the principal northern port of famous Vinland Bay, which Frenchmen had already named Beauport. Thus was made a river that flows two ways.

Nowadays most human traffic with the mainland is by infernal consumption engines racing each other on the high arch of a highway known as Botolph's Felly, or if not, on the level drawbridge of the Esplanade at a seawalled cutting still as narrow as the locks of a 19C canal. Yet more than ever commuting wage-earners, students, and irregular travelers to the metropolis like me are hauled back and forth in self-propelling trains on a higher bascule over another very narrow waist near the dynamic middle of the facing tides, just south of the null point where the sea confronts itself.

But there's an opposite paleontology for us over here in the East Harbor Ward, which may itself be called a self-made peninsula of the greater island. It looks to me as if the salt marsh behind Little Harbor Beach was an extension of the main harbor in earliest times, when our particular rock and its seaward extension was an island off what much later became the artificial big island. After some sudden seismic shudder, or some gradual accumulation of wave-flung sand, this tiny estuary between islands small and smaller must have been clogged by ocean wash, forming an unprotected oceanic mouth while extending every yard of the inchoate weed-wracked beach between two horns of glacier-scraped granite. This blockage then scoured out behind the beach's barrier a haven for the small craft of English fishermen (or at least for Atlindu canoes before them navigating a creek directly from the sea). That put an end to the tide's salubrious flushings of the primitive Dogtown port. But the lagoon thus formed must have gradually silted up too much for anchorage even on the smallest scale, eventually finding itself a tidal marsh, which however continued also to drain the fresh water of surrounding hills. Then came the time when

men were collective landlords. For their own immediate convenience they filled the urban end of the marsh and made that level
dam a flattened passageway to the East Harbor settlement, hoping
to use what remained of the brackish basin for the hay it offered.
That nexus between the two thickly settled granite knolls of
Harbor Ward and East Harbor has since been broadened into a
complex of roadways serving as the terminus of Botolph's circumferential Felly, under fallible control of the state's automatic signal
lights.

My special interest in all this geology is the Little Harbor
Creek that in the present era defines the near end of the long broad
beach and its backing of grass-stabled dunes. Much of its course is
closely flanked by Clamdig Road, which I cross to the wooden footbridge from which on almost every one of my walks I examine the
stream and its sinuous variations on its present way from upland
banks to detached rocks that steer it to the beach's mouth under a
steep bluff of brown primeval granite. For Themis in our era (with
the lunar cooperation of Artemis in their regulation of Poseidon's
power) has found a civilized way to wash and drain that fecund
basin as a tidal marsh once more. Without piercing the beach itself
except at this boundary twice a day the land's unsalted watershed is
refreshed with penetrating brine. Yet the water flowing in either
direction under that bridge of timber is as transparent as the
potable water we're supplied by the Department of Public Works,
and its bed of fine gray sand as tempting to many a swimmer as the
beach's long wavefront in the month of August.

For centuries people have forgotten that the marsh behind
Little Harbor Beach had been a harbor for small boats, as an extension of the present Inner Harbor, itself a projection of the Outer
Harbor and Vinland Bay. Protected at its back from the open ocean
by the natural barrier that has become our beach, its passage to
commerce had been made possible only by the meddling of man,
when the neck from Harbor Ward downtown to this Joint Hill in
my East Harbor Ward had been cut away, shovel by shovel—*just*
where it's now refilled and broadened as the greatest junction of
human traffic in all of Gloucester County at the present head of all
navigation, where screaming angels wheel for the offal, for the most
part silently leaving to pure sandpipers and terns the priestlike food
to be found at the beach (when there's no call for sunning or swimming), not even mewing in transit from city center to where they
float in coves or perch on rocks for afternoon rest. The remaining

basin of marsh grass, flushed by the meandering channel of the
creek, is now bordered by lengthening and thickening lines of
houses and shopping marts indirectly protected by the windblown
beach, still perpetually in subtle reformation without the visible
hand of man.

Little Harbor Creek, at my end of the beach, is now no more
navigable than a brook, but all alone it still floods and drains the
remnant marsh of Little Harbor, which from the vantage of my
house spreads itself as an alluvial plain as a hollow stageless theater,
especially when the tide is not yet nearing or lingering at its upper
limits—a thick-piled russet carpet threaded by the wandering dark
lines of the alimentary watercourse: or a tawny meadow of sodden
uncut hay twisted but never flattened, like wracked stubble. But
when the invasive brine has its way, or hasn't yet withdrawn, the
whole field is a lake of shining blue water, or whitened frost, sometimes elevated to its brim at every road and backyard that a stormy
flood tide can reach. Yet much of the day, for passers-by in the hinterland, at most places on its pedestrian level, the surface of the
creek itself is nearly hidden by the tall marsh grass rooted all year
round in the healthiest of upstream mud.

But I've had a particularly interesting station when I often gaze
from the footbridge at this perennial state of nature's compromise
with human settlers, where between high and low tide the pellucid
water, brine or brackish, is continually advancing or receding in
one direction or the other—and all the more so when the sea is
breathing most heavily, at spring tides or neap tides, especially if in
or after northeast storms—covering or exposing half a mile of beach
the color of refined Portland cement before it's hardened by water,
not only where it's swept twice a day but also at the shifting banks
of the sandy creek itself. Sometimes the current undermines edges
of sandbanks, or almost perceptibly wears and reshapes their
smoothly tortuous lines. At various conjunctions of calendar and
weather the channeled force covers or uncovers one or all of two or
three fixed boulders deeply embedded in bathers' sand near the
bridge's abutments. They seem to alter their anchorages in a
bleached khaki desert! Here the creek is rhythmically deepened
enough to swim in. It either adds itself to your speed down to the
open waves or to like degree resists your upstream efforts, sometimes excessively in either case. You may then give up and walk to
the shallows above the bridge and wallow on the finest of brine-
bleached sand in a warmer birdbath, exposing skin to the sun's

simultaneous caresses. Once or twice last summer even I, a withered scarecrow, risked the public experiment, stepping among little kids with beach toys.

I dwell on these details because—despite the continuous cycling of tides calibrated in the solar calendar (sensibly imposed upon us by masculine science), even at nearly symmetrical times twice a day, any day of the week—almost whenever I happen to walk down there at random to ponder the phenomenon—the current is flowing seaward far more often than upstream. I've been puzzled enough by the apparent reciprocity of what is obviously an oscillation to make a point of asking for an explanation from my knowledgeable new boyfriend, a Celtic Norseman who's something of a thalassic expert. (If nothing else, as one of F D R's Former Naval Persons, he's rational!) He had no immediate answer until I dragged him down to the beach to see for himself. Sure enough, by his offhand reasoning, if I understand it (though I'm still in some doubt about the details of the hypothesis), it's obvious that I'd been stupidly assuming the bridge to be just halfway up the nearly unnoticeable gradient between mean levels of any day's high and low water.

I had also overlooked the probability that the nearly insignificant and apparently irreducible trickle of outflow at every semimonthly neap tide, especially in spring and fall, is fresh water contributed by Lady Gloucester and her natural or civilized inhabitants, bright and clear but not necessarily pure, as one can see when the creek's bed is almost as dry as a Cornucopian wadi in summer when the recessive tide leaves an extremely broad and flattened beach behind it, and when, forsooth, the low height of the dunes may misguide anyone's estimate of her relative elevation above sea level! However, I'm still in doubt, man or no man! I'm said to be a scientifically philosophical anthropologist, and I certainly subscribe to Ludwig von Denthey's general theory of systems (which I'm sure my late superorganic mentor the late Alpha Whitehead would have approved)!

. . . At this time of year my walks on the beach beyond the bridge are rare because we are visited by the cold westerly winds that take advantage of that littoral valley to abet their biting passage from the mainland through the city's center to open sea. Then, even when the temperature is bearable, a brutal Zephyr freezes your face when you return from a walk along the strand to where you have stepped off the bridge.

I should remind myself that, as the exemplary isolato Wellingborough Redburn wrote, sailing the length of the Mediterranean to
Jerusalem many years after his sojourn with the Fayaway of Mardi:
"One finds that, after all, the most noted localities are made up of
common elements of earth, air, and water." Later, when he lectured
at the Cape Gloucester Literary, Scientific, and Historical Lyceum,
even he was so propelled in ordinary 19C Atlantean maritime
appearances that he probably didn't regard Dogtown as "another
disenchanting isle", though probably even then it sheltered certain
of its marooners as worthy of curiosity as was that astronomer Mary
Mitchell on Tasheto. Anyway, like other whalesmen, in his youth
he might have scorned this the greatest *fishing* port of the continent
as too mean of spirit to risk capital and lives in building and manning ships capable of hunting the greatest of God's creatures without the comforts of port for more than a mere few weeks at a time.
Yet to sailors in men-of-war, trading vessels, and clipper ships the
whalers themselves were ugly smelly tubs. In political opinion as
well as in counting-houses there was nothing contemptible or
pusillanimous about fishermen stinking with proletarian fish.

By the way, fishing schooners are now gone, but wisps of the
old smells linger around some of the old wharves. The newer draggers are built of steel and comfortably equipped with electronic
paraphernalia for navigating safely from a comfortable seat, finding
fish like successful water-dowsers. Still, the suffering and courage of
fishermen, though seldom in ventures further than the northwest
Atlantic, have sustained the oldest industry in the country, whereas
whaling was ephemeral even by general Atlantean standards. Fishing is still the most dangerous job in the country. Proportionally
more fishermen die at work than aerial iron-workers, lumberjacks,
or miners. Nearly a thousand Dogtown vessels have been lost—and
a few still are being lost—since the town was incorporated, and
over ten thousand men, whose widows and children suffered much
longer than their men who drowned in instantly freezing seas.
Their descendants don't often move away, or at least not without
first testing military life or working the trade elsewhere. Many stay
or return only to cut or move landed seafood, or to freeze or cook or
ship or sell the mechanized harvest ashore.

But Dogtown isn't exclusively maritime, and sometimes in
exploring Cape Gloucester you can easily forget that the sea is
nearly all around you. There are components of our Lady's motionless domain perhaps older than the Atlantic, or at least much more

resistant to human exploitation, especially across the Gut in West Marsh hills. It is said that some of the forest-bound steeps of escarpment that were exposed by the logging of virgin firewood and timber a couple of centuries ago are now challenged by amateur rock-climbers in serious training. Yet I've seen for myself that some overcropping cliffs of fused cold rock serrated by jagged ravines with their own dangerous fissures are still all but totally sequestered by apparently primeval dark woods or picketed by thick undergrowths of impenetrable brambles. But in green and sunny season it's worth a persistent struggle up at least a barely traceable path that Caleb led me onto, because a smooth bald gray summit of mother-granite may prove to be one that offers an almost 360-degree panorama of the whole Cape, which in such perspective looks almost untouched by chainsaws or bulldozers. But of course most of that horizontal view is defined by the glorious arc of circumference that suddenly puts you in mind of the deep blue embracement that you'd forgotten for a few hours. Your feet stand in the elevated arms of an ocean, accompanied for as far as you can see by fleecy clouds and islets of shadow that reflect each other from left to right under the lighter blue that defines as much of your hemisphere's dome as the substantial clouds disclose. Turn around to the west and you can only guess where the railroad or buzzing Felly threads through foliaged passes to the ordinary places where you would no longer smell the sea's air or feel its irenic mood from every other direction at once.

The only fiction I read these days is Redburn's. Last night I was struck by a demigod's remonstrance to the archipelago's savant: "Babbalanya, you mortals dwell in Mardi, and it's important to get elsewhere."

2
DISENGAGEMENT
[January 1981]

1.

For the third time in the day Caleb *i* Karcist stood in his bathroom vacantly staring at a large framed photograph on the wall. A contiguous scene hung on the wall behind him. Together they mapped in aerial perspective Dogtown's crowded Harbor Ward and much of its invaginated industry. It was his unthinking habit as he relieved himself to marvel at the muscular sinuosity of Front Street, the spine of a thick waterfront familiar to innumerable scavengers on the wing or perching on the watch. His eyes were occupied by this objective view of his little native city but his subjective brain was painfully reviving a patriotic sense of disgust for the national disgrace of anti-intellectual nationalism deliberately fostered in Washington by the new President. The bitterness of suffering a Protestican administration in Washington drove him to futile personal hatred. Every word of its leaders, every gesture, struck him as gloating arrogance garnished with phoney goodwill. He was once again struggling for a bit of consolation from the future benefit of sparing himself the time-consuming distractions of political hope.

It would now be easier to concentrate properly on his word-hoarded psychic energy by heeding Thomas à Kempis: "Ask not after the news. . . ." In complying with his rationalization he would ignore all but the most succinct headlines of broadcast journalism, which however was sure to contribute to the political success of the powers that nearly extinguished his inbred hopes for the future of humanity. This was not the first time he had been depressed by an election, but President Raygun was charming even his political enemies like an amiable sorcerer. Once more Caleb resolved to abate his Weltschmerz by drastically reducing his cosmopolitan reading to as much of it that might be subsumed in the *Dogtown Daily Nous*—yet while houseworking in his kitchen every evening he was never able to keep himself from listening to the radio for the faintest trace of any organized opposition that might be filtered in the generally depressing news of sentimental solidarity. Perhaps it now was possible to become philosophical and ignore the infuriating triumph of governance by smiling demagogy.

Once or twice a year Caleb exchanged the position of these two bathroom pictures, which together made plain the inner city as it was during the latter years of the Depression more than forty years earlier, when the Fish Pier and its great freezer building were still under construction, probably when he was about four years old. By then the famous schooner fleet had been superannuated but the wooden-hulled diesel-powered trawlers moored all along the wharves still raised two stumpy masts rigged occasionally for auxiliary sails to boost the screw propeller or help keep the steering steady. Some of mankind's work shown in the photograph had since vanished, but—owing to the sempiternal subsistence of rock and sea—far more of it remained, even after teeming family tenements near the harborside as well as vestiges of brothels boarding houses and seedy taverns had been razed by federal Civic Instauration grants, which at one spot eventually provided flanks of greenery for a mercifully preserved "Atlantean Gothic" stone house on the knoll where once had stood the Liberty Tree of Revolution. Except for this tiny handsome park, most of the aged gray waterfront wharves, sail lofts, cutting sheds, salt-fish drying racks, and wooden storage sheds were superseded by the massive rectilinear concrete structures required for frozen fish storage, processing, and transport, or by maintenance facilities that served both commercial fishing vessels and leisured toyboats. Like some other conspicuous structures remaining in the photographs, two beehive kilns of the old Gas Works were demolished before he'd returned to Vinland from Cornucopia after two-score years of expatriated youth. But of the archeological monuments that had lasted a dozen years after his repatriation he especially missed the old brick powerhouse and tall chimney of the steam dynamo originally built by Cape Gloucester Power, Light, and Traction early in the century to supply the city and its environs with AC electricity, along with DC for its own proudly beloved but short-lived trolley-car routes around the Cape, connecting to mainland car-lines before the suddenly ineluctable invasion of self-propelled infernal consumption. But most of all, half a mile back from the waterfront in a neighborhood of domestic population, he mourned the buildings of the old Vinland and Markland Railroad station and its candelabra of freight sidings, prominent in supernal view, now pared down to a tiny passenger canopy without walls and little more than a single track for the self-propelled metropolitan commuter trains, apparently just to make space for an enlarged and elevated supermarket with its over-crowded parking lot.

Still, after four decades, most of the residential roofs of Harbor Ward seemed undisturbed. The clapboarded hulk of the Anabasic Church had vanished from the corner of Halibut and Pleasure to leave a small square for metered hitching posts in the immediate vicinity of Ibicity Hall. The other downtown temples in this archival perspective were as prominent as ever, especially the spacious needle-spired Church of the B V M (the Cape's largest Classic Petrine parish); the blue-capped Espirito Santo halfway up its own Lusitanian hill, with twin towers suspending a famous carillon sometimes heard as far south as Vinland Bay beyond the breakwater; and on the short level Halibut Street next door to tiny St Paul's pseudo-Gothic Church of the Tudor Communion (with its own beautiful locally relevant stained glass), the white 18C clapboarded Meetinghouse with its towering belfry whose original congregation had founded General Individualism for all Atlantean colonies and later merged with the Humanist Divinity Association, which once occupied the now converted Temple of David building two blocks nearer Ibicity Hall on the Acropolis.

. . . But before Caleb's decantation was finished off with a few twitches of the wrist his vacant vision paused as usual on the old Mercator-Steelyard office building, not far from the waterfront

Traction plant, facing inland and flush with the Front Street sidewalk. Even in his own time this dowdy 19C brick box was
crammed with offices, its mansard roof of concave slate compress-
ing a third story, almost as intimately familiar in memory as his
own living quarters. For over ten years he had spent as many
waking hours in that building as at home—and, alas, ten times as
many hours working. Many an evening or Saturday—and more
than a few Sundays—he'd spent alone within its walls. Even before
the aerial photograph was taken the next-door movie theater had
been razed. Since then the old unkempt gray frame tenements
bounding on three sides the M-S office lot remained inhabited until
gradually bought up by the Yard humanely, and swiftly razed. This
policy to make room for a wider and much longer annex of precast
concrete and glass, reoriented in the opposite direction, that is, to a
handsomely set-back main entrance on Scrod Street, a broad swath
cut through the Instauration's officially leveled neighborhood of
very weathered wood to make a thoroughfare for modern commerce
and industry, across which the company now officially faced its own
dockside plants, new and old, for receiving cutting cooking freezing packing storing and shipping of "seafood". Lighted behind
plate glass in the thoroughly modern lobby, to one side of the
transparent double doors, now hung the delicate three-foot model
of a classic Dogtown fishing schooner, meticulously imitated by a
retired naval architect who lived on the rocks over in the Village.
The sails were realistically furled because it was impossible to make
correspondingly realistic hoisted sails to the same scale without
gossamer thread spun by Titania's fairies.

As Director of Administration, and as the project's manager—
acting even as clerk-of-the-works for the de jure owner—Caleb
himself had been primarily responsible for the functional specifications and contractual supervision of this smoothly economical
structure designed by the internationally distinguished architect
Caspar Aninigo. The clean rectilinear plans and elevations of ferro-
concrete were frankly but inconspicuously coupled by a broad passageway to the deceptively humble old brick office building, which
had been built for a ships' chandlery and for a time had housed
within the reversed ogives of its top floor the immigrant Lusitanian
congregation, which soon thereafter subscribed and founded the
splendid Espirito Santo church on the hill above. As soon as the
new office building was occupied this old one was viscerally remodeled for expanding departments closely related to headquarter func-

tions, but especially for the interior taste and dignity of the company's powers, who were finally afforded such well-lighted space and furnishings as they had denied themselves as well as underlings for a hundred years inside the original box of brick and slate.

The bright beige surfaces of the new recto-parallelepiped, pierced continuously on three sides—by two rows of tawny tinted glass facing the upper parking lot and by three on the lower level (including a basement barbican slotted with agreeably detailed brickwork), to protect from prying eyes the separate bailiwicks of computer room and power supply for the building's Heating Ventilating and Air-Conditioning [H V A C]. The city's only modern office building now stood thoroughly cured and weathered, screened by maturely transplanted deciduous trees, various shrubs, and somewhat conventional flower beds. When all the razing and paving was done it took some time for the denizens of Dogtown to get used to this impressive image of the Yard's power where humble congestion had hidden it.

For nearly two years toward the end of Caleb's tenure as manager of administration, already occupied with the planning and execution of "management services", his enthusiastic supervision had nearly doubled as the architect's collaborator—almost also as an amateur's on-site student of modern commercial architecture—by instigating planning expediting inspecting correcting and generally questioning the consummation of this non-recurring project, which was much more interesting to onlooking occupants and observers than the more important mysteries of his own abstract architecture, a computer-based Central Management System [C M S]. His privileged involvement in the concrete architecture was all the greater and more interesting because the concrete project's associate architect (Caspar's field assistant and his firm's inspector) was more than busy with much grander and far more notable projects in the metropole and therefore was hard-pressed to come up to Dogtown from Unabridge as often as otherwise would have been expected in the profession. In consequence of their immediate friendship he was glad to teach, explain, and even delegate a little of his professional responsibility.

Since there was no clerk-of-the-works to scrutinize, keep punch-lists, and watch this work-in-progress, it was left to Caleb as an auctorially motivated inquisitor to deal with both usual and unusual difficulties or delays in cleaving to the specifications and sometimes imperfect shop drawings for details of the grand design at this singular site (such as the need to relocate an uncharted city sewer main—allowing for underground uncertainties), or dealing with subcontractual details, unreliable vendors, substandard materials, and the usual trivial errors or opinions expected at every level of responsibility including the architectural firm's and his own. The fourth dimensions were as critical as the first threes, since there were "critical paths" for feasible coordination of time and space, especially when in default of both intelligence and education as far as workmanship was concerned. The proleptic reasoning of the general contractor's newly acquired superintendent of construction led to the discovery that he was lying about his experience on such jobs. Yet, all in all, the white-collar theorist of abstract matters was glad to learn more than a little about the professions and trades he encountered in the effort to realize his anticipation of pleasantly efficient housing for administrative reorganization and modern office equipment of every kind, especially for the air-conditioned "mainframe" Old Homestead Manufacturing [OHM] computer, as well as his own office fitted with chalkboards and plenty of chair space for his conferences in either sphere.

Until adjudication of change-orders and final payment of all bills and contracts there was no accepted end to the frictions of misunderstanding and deliberately concealed errors. After "occupancy" was declared, with repeated and contentious adjustments of the H V A C system designed by the mechanical engineering firm, it was necessary to arrive at pragmatic compromises in correcting the calibrations and post-installation adjustments of handbook-besotted experts who were reluctant to heed the subjectivity of typical human beings, who naturally varied in degree of physical activity—by floor-compartment, gender, air-stream exposure, and basal metabolism, not to mention seasonal variations of attire—all working in a common or subdivided atmosphere determined by more or less tolerated adjustments of duct vents and thermostats, as well as by idiosyncratic susceptibilities to artificially naturalized illumination. Therefore, as an impatient soul, he grudged most of all the time it took to meet his ex officio obligation pro tem to arbitrate the hetero-regulation of atmosphere long after the building was fully operational and its social structure otherwise reformed.

But this aftermath of superficial irritations was born of the radical progress that was more or less readily recognized by the highest authorities and gradually appreciated by the grumpiest underlings. For Caleb the optimistic author and manager of momentous changes the tension was relieved only when negotiations between the conscientious architect and the scarcely competent general contractor were ended in final composite compromise of detailed expectations and the extra costs of temporal penalties. Until then most of his anxiety had arisen from the aversion of the contractor's superintendent to supervision of the subcontracting electricians, plumbers, metalworkers, painters, and other artificers whose work his firm was well paid to conduct at a fixed percentage markup according to the general contract.

This largely involved the functional details—some of them unconventional—that he himself, as an extremely intimate bureaucrat, had carefully specified for the internal spaces created (with his advice) by the architect's structure. Interrupting his attention to other responsibilities in the abstract administrative revolution, he hardly ever sat in his old office more than an hour or two without hastening out into the unfinished annex to silently approve or forestall the habitual discretion of workmen who were accustomed to the discipline of building codes but blandly inclined to be contemptuous of pedantic drawings of specified details. To some degree he was protecting his own taste or judgment—especially when he happened to be asked for decisions unanticipated by a draftsman—as much as he was defending the Yard against fraud or abuse with the change-orders that are always expected as "cost-plus" surcharges (always exceeding savings credited to the owner for detailed reductions of material or labor elsewhere), but which sometimes defy almost any expert's audit, and are sometimes the only means by which Epimethean bidders or sub-bidders can make any profit at all.

Yet this whole capital diversion had been optional in inception and non-recurrent by definition. With the expansion of business it was regarded by the financial directorate as a proleptic expansion of office work, approximately budgeted as future overhead—but left to specialists for design. This sudden loosening of knotted purse strings was prompted, in the spirit of the times, more by Caleb's non-recurrent work as the perpetuating return on investment in modernizing administration itself, which was portentous enough for a rolling revolution of unlimited management information and control. Suddenly, in the boardrooms of manufacturers, computers were now said to be de rigueur for any progressive corporation. These new costs were great and the rationale was vague, but it was said that these mysterious machines in air-conditioned rooms would eventually pay for themselves many times over by eliminating clerical errors and speeding all transactions, serving greater volumes of business without increasing payrolls. Invoices and reports were turned out much faster than ever before. The "productivity" (or "value-added") of white-collar and high-heeled workers became worth academic study. Indeed large banks and insurance companies were claiming increased efficiency even without eliminating redundance in their large-scale "data processing" for overlapping functions.

Caleb had already converted the Yard's old "unit-record" punchcard equipment to the smallest computer that OHM could provide, and had so well proven its usefulness in the old building that there was little resistance to his proposal for a much more expensive new model, incredibly faster and far more versatile in application. So it and all its peripheral equipment required large segregated temperature-controlled operating space of its own. Ergo, wasn't this a logical time to anticipate all internal architectural and atmospheric problems, as sales were already outgrowing administrative capacity, by erecting an efficient new building to meet present and future needs with one organic machine of four dimensions?

Thus Yorick's architectural leap to a new cathedral for a new liturgy and its freedom of thought, permitted in part by its provision of decent offices for the deaconry of the glamorous marketing elite, who claimed highest prestige as the company's bishops and diplomatic corps famously proselytizing the Yard's share of carnivorous converts.

Caleb asked for funds not by presenting plans for an ultimate syndrome but with a lesser argument for the profitability of equipment serving an integrated management information system based on the latest "random-access" computer as a second step based upon what he'd done with the tiny one. Most of the new floor space would be occupied by his expanding staff to serve centralized methods and procedures of human hands as well. He could not allow the building project to suspend his detailing and indirect supervision of the interlocking jobs evolved in nearly parallel or integrated transformation of many "manual" systems and procedures. He rejected the usual assumption that his computer must first of all match the input and output of existing methods and procedures, whether personal or mechanical. Thus left unsaid was the ultimate object of his supererogatory initiative in complex matters beyond the competence expected of him. The organization of the Yard's management, sheltered as half a dozen separate departments, was in his mind destined to be unified as a dynamic system, technological and social, as far as communication and cooperation were concerned. Thus few of the ostensibly secondary administrative matters should be postponed in the general evolution of efficiency.

To the depth of his leadership it would have been unconscionable to relax his personal dispatch of designs, diagrams, directions, inspections, memorandums, reports, studies, critiques, conferences, meetings, explicit instructions, tactical advice, strategic sequential plans, recruitment, interviews, and rhetorical exhortations—all of which he required of himself for reasonably swift departure from the typical acceptance of piecemeal progress in his managerial function. He taught abstractions even to his personal secretary, whom he encouraged with new ideas of her job, whose tasks and voluntary services were manifold, even as she encouraged his excessive consumption of coffee. There were always apologetic explanations of embarrassing delays to be made to peers and superiors whose own performance often depended upon the full and timely implementation of his metaphysical schemes—which anyway he didn't have time to parse for purely pragmatic colleagues. His works seemed obscurantic mainly because his cohort of executives had very little interest in the symbolic architecture of bureaucracy.

Step by step, nevertheless, almost imperceptibly in the transition from old to new culture, the whole white-collar hierarchy had found itself very anxiously trusting to a very expensive and innovative "conversion" that affected almost every former means of managerial communication inside and outside the main office, ranging from bills of lading and invoices to analytical operating reports in both physical and very fiscal terms. There was no turning back without documentary disaster, for even the simplest former journals of payables and receivables, or reports of raw and finished inventories produced by the old tabulating machines, were unavailable until the roots and trunk of Caleb's banyan tree produced its magnificent foliage—and at first that outgrowth couldn't appear as nearly instantaneously as he had promised. This his self-entitled Central Management System was so radically and comprehensively integrated that it would have been impossible to install it while the old equipment and procedures were still in operation. Many a company was known to have suffered chaos by attempting even a simple conversion from one computer to another without running "in parallel".

In what also amounted to simultaneous human occupation of the new building and convulsively cooperative disruption of all office services, largely on one weekend—risking not only his own head but also, very seriously, the reputation and prospects of his superiors—he had perhaps a little too confidently planned and sweated out the administrative transition with little support or tentative congratulation from higher levels, whether or not any of them were wise enough to be worried.

But all along he'd soft-pedaled his own worries, gratefully appreciating the provisional forbearance and unprecedented power vouchsafed him. No committee was appointed; the corporate engineer from Demeter Mills had nothing to say in disapproval of the construction. Yet for a calendar month or two Caleb continued to feel the moral and institutional pressure about the business systems, until the ebb tide of collective doubt relaxed into gradually rising satisfaction, department by department, culminating in the consensus of still somewhat grudging admiration for a computer system that changed the world of information, when departmental staffs began to praise the new resources and flexibility at their disposal. Soon, under his posthumous hand, thanks to his arcane syntheses, about everyone below the top was realizing the benefits of analyzed information.

As the new intellectual order began to exceed the company's pragmatic expectations his own ill temper mellowed, his cheerfulness revived without many interruptions, awaiting the best time to resign, seeing that the further development of C M S would take too much of his mortal impatience with the philosophical limitations of chrematistic success. Then, at a cusp of sub-ambition, he meant to enjoy as much as possible the human and technological growth of his intramural C M S, because (before quitting) he could again devote his exiguous spare time to using the computer for his own purposes in the development of operational research at a much higher level of management. He knew he would never again have at his bidding a laboratory and staff of programmers and operators for a megamachine, when routine operations were running with full efficiency in the ordinary course of progressive business at the purely administrative level.

But persuasive exposition of his general ideas (on a level of abstraction theretofore never encountered by any of his excellent programmers except the one whom he'd hired in part for having studied mathematics and some Scholastic philosophy at a Cephasite college), which lay behind the plans and devices that in numerous office conferences (often standing at his chalkboard like the leader of a seminar) he asked them to facilitate as lines of coded instructions to the computer in their own language, gradually indoctrinated his inner technical staff with an enthusiasm for their own creative solutions to the unprecedented problems demanded by his charts and diagrams. So here too he learned from experts whom he directed and admired for their capability in testing the limitation of a sophisticated machine in response to unfamiliar organic challenges. Sometimes he felt as if he could teach OHM how to take full advantage of its own new "random-access" data-storage devices—a case of exploiting finite means for infinite uses. OHM so led and dominated the business computer market that almost all programmers in the country were trained in the schools it then ran for its customers. Often at early stages of major program design there had been initial skepticism and collegial debate, but in the end he was satisfied with his magicians' technological esprit de corps, and their loyalty stood him in good stead when his own anxious superiors slyly and quietly caught them aside individually and probed for faults in his untrained command of experts without academic advice.

In those early years of economical business computers, when digital machines and their peripheral equipment were evolving far more rapidly than the thinking of their users (especially with regard to social organization and office procedures), before complicated locally customized programs could be purchased from external sources, much of Caleb's success had depended upon his recruiting and selection of programmers (or rationally intelligent young men or women clever enough to be sent to OHM courses for productivity in the near future), at a time when there was much competition from more affluent employers for the few experienced ones, especially at such a distance from the elite centers of science and electronic manufacturing.

. . . As he turned to the wash basin Caleb chuckled at this casual nostalgic reminiscence of his Yard days as an existentially tripled double agent, trumping the madness of Liam Yeats! His own obsession with the Synectic Method of Diagnostic Correlation [S M D C], as an application for C M S, was Creative Mind's vision from its False Mask—pace W B Y, who had nightmares about sewing machines still treadled by foot! For a dozen years Caleb's infatuation had blighted his unity, growing like an excited cancer, diverting Will almost exclusively to the Body of Fate's "pragmatical pig of a world", and nearly obliterating the secret solitary vision-making of his True Mask! All those day-and-night hours and weeks and months—they were not by any account wasted on the world, but they now seemed for the most part a waste of personally irretrievable energy, no more valuable than any "creation without toil"! Like rain infiltering every crack in a boulder he had eagerly allowed himself to accept every available detail of responsibility until the natural course of events and the energy of frost suddenly split open the institutional resistance to his mania for holistic efficiency. More than anywhere else among corporate controllers and managers of office systems (especially in the larger more cautious conglomerate he almost joined at its headquarters) he found himself a single practitioner of that fissive power in shaping what senior officers in manufacturing industries were still likely to regard as the necessary evil called "paperwork".

Still, everything organic or inorganic in the C M S, introduced and promulgated in the customary terms of business management, served as his own metaphors (or at least analogies) for the eventually more interesting applications of his computer! Almost from the beginning, subconsciously, it had been as if an aesthetic appreciation of what he was accomplishing, by overwork for a banausic cause, was to be privately converted into a continuum of creative ideas—too many to be fully developed by any one mind even in a tenured academic lifetime.

. . . Tom Parsons the President of Dogtown's Mercator-Steelyard had personally taken down those ambivalently mnemonic photographs from the walls of his own office in the old building the day before he left for Saint Peter on the upper Mississippi to take over as Executive V P of Demeter Mills not long after the Yard had yielded its sovereignty to the vast modern headquarters (a stately glazed parallelepiped mounted magnificently in its own bountifully isolated suburban park and with its own respectable collection of French art, as against commercialized prints of boats and fishing)—when Caleb found the opportunity to catch him alone and express the genuine sense of Dogtown's loss that heartily conflicted with congratulations for the man's extraordinarily rapid promotion, obviously making him next in line to the presidency of the whole international Corporation, famous for its leading position in the immense food manufacturing industry.

"Come on in, Caleb my boy. I'm just clearing out my junk before the new broom sweeps it away. Take these old fishtown pictures. You've always seemed more interested in them than anybody else. Out there I suppose I'll have to put up abstract French paintings and camera shots of combines mowing down the corn. They have all sorts of art out there. Worth a fortune they say. I'll have to start learning good taste from my wife." Tom knew perfectly well that Caleb was a gauche socializer and an abnormal business crony; but, as everybody knew, that did not diminish his appreciation of economic value added by certain freethinkers in the inconspicious bowels of a fiefdom.

Not much more than a year after buying up the Yard, which was one-twentieth the size of itself, the Chairman of the broadly acquisitive Mills, a retired General, had recognized the refreshingly pragmatic intelligence of this clearsighted and plainspeaking Marklander without an M B A degree who quietly ignored most of the fashionable business-school theories that were displacing the experience of commonsense among the ambitious graduates usually groomed for the top jobs. Tom had deserved this extraordinary distinction even though he had never been in a position to demonstrate its validity on a scale to compare with the major multinational responsibility of running the country's best-known "grocery manufacturer", the originator or acquisitor of twenty-nine subsidiaries or semi-autonomous divisions and thousands of edible products, especially including those made famous to children and housewives by three generations of consumer advertising (thanks to comfortable gross margins). Only a few years later, moreover, not long after Caleb himself was to leave the Yard, this sensible believer in any overhead investment that would contribute indirectly to net profit, unlike merely aesthetic display of amenities, was surprisingly advanced to the highest office, responsible for all the capital entrusted by hundreds of thousands of stockholders on the Graveyard Exchange. When that time came everybody at the Yard had long since boasted of Tom's initial elevation to Saint Peter—as honorific of this small city's crew. Almost everybody at the same time had keenly—personally—regretted the loss of his friendly hardheaded wisdom "at the fisherman's wheel of the Yard".

"I wish I could take them, Tom; but I'm afraid I don't have wall space in my office. It's all taken up with windows and chalkboards and charts. Maybe they'd be good for the new foyer near the schooner model."

"No, no. They don't belong anywhere in the new building. Would make people think of canned fishcakes, when we're trying to make them think of frozen gourmet dinners. I mean take them home. You're the one that deserves them."

Caleb was touched by this personal notice. Awkwardly he tried to avoid sentimentality in expressing his personal affection and admiration for a canny and tolerant captain of commerce whose soul had so little sympathy with his own. But casting about for distinctive expression of his genuine sentiment he could find nothing better than conventional phrases to tell Tom that the Yard division of the Mills would be worse off without him. Saint Peter's gain was Dogtown's loss. . . .

"You won't miss me for long." the Downeasterner said, as he no doubt told many others after listening to inarticulately rueful laudations like Caleb's. "No one's indispensable. Just put your fist in a bucket of water and then take it out. You'll see what I mean."

Sometime later, having firmly established himself at the Mills to the board of directors' satisfaction, Tom Parsons casually let it be known in Dogtown that Caleb might well be offered a flatteringly lucrative transfer to an important staff position in the Praetorian guard at the Saint Pete palatinate. Such a retractable trial balloon was hardly unknown in business or politics, especially at the highest levels, but it was characteristic of Tom Parsons, who hated to waste time on unnecessary deliberation, or to commit himself by any sort of formality or quotable speech until the outcome of what might have been taken as an offhand thought was swiftly tested in all but the details by existing administrative apparatus. In this manner he disposed of more propositions and decisions per day than most other chief executives did per week. He'd immediately drop any nonessential idea mooted even by himself as soon as he sensed (according to unreflective experience) that it would require too much diplomatic attention to prepare those who would be affected to accept it without resentment or embarrassment.

Even before Tom's own promotion, among less equivocal matters, Caleb had been casually mooted to headquarters during an ordinary long-distance telephone chat with the imperium in Saint

Peter. Godfrey Rodney McGrundy, Caleb's boss, when he learned of it, was hardly enthusiastic about losing the man who had contributed so much to his own reputation as the local Treasurer and Vice-President of Administration and one of the old Yard's principal stockholders (now, under the Mills, richer than ever, but more subordinate); but he was an honorable man and like any other prudent officer did not wish to seem to stand in the way of a good man's advancement for the corporate good: so in his own characteristically precipitate manner he hinted the possibility of a definite offer of an indefinite position in the middle of Atlantis.

"Think about it, Caleb. It's a great opportunity for you. Of course I can't replace you here, but you've built excellent systems to last for years to come." As a graduate of Pale in mathematical economics and its Management School, and furthermore as a Certified Public Accountant, Rod, in Caleb's opinion, never understood that what C M S planted and administered was an open system in which human organization and new ideas were more vital than brilliant programmers or speed of a random-access computer. The self-assured C P A seemed unable to imagine that C M S surpassed in efficiency and versatility the million-dollar data processing installations that were bragged about in the largest boardrooms by people who knew no more about systems than the Generally Accepted Accounting Principles [G A A P]—little dreaming of a foundation for the evolution of new managerial methods for all departmental functions, especially in marketing and logistics.

When Caleb finally understood the offer to be serious, though subject of course to specified terms and conditions, he did not wish to show enough interest even to ask about salary, or to give any other indication of bargaining. "I'd rather stay and work for you, Rod. There are a lot of things still in the works. At the Mills I'd be nothing but a maverick theorist. They've got millions of dollars commitment to the way they do things." He knew perfectly well that even with the C E O's pronounced blessing some version of C M S would take ten years to reform the "information" expertise in that huge bureaucracy, and that anyway Tom was too wise to expend any of his ultimate authority on what remained structural problems that were secondary to the "bottom line" when denied by an entrenched web of inbred experts, including two or three vice-presidents upon whom he depended for his quarterly profits. The Mills president was always fully occupied with much broader external affairs, often international, sometimes internecine or personal, and Caleb had seen enough of headquarters to know that he could have served only as a powerless internal critic dreaming up plans that would never survive collegial committees, or as the head of some segregated function irrelevant to general management.

So Caleb didn't have to "think about it". Though he was discreet enough to keep most of this insight to himself, he betrayed enough of it for an educated man of the business world like Rod McGrundy to understand his negative response to a singular opportunity. So, probably in some conversation about intra-corporate financial matters, Rod mentioned to Tom Parsons that Caleb didn't seem to want to leave Vinland. That was an attitude that Rod himself could understand. During negotiations for the sale of Mercator-Steelyard to Demeter Mills it was the reason he himself had given for deciding to stay where he was, in a provincial position. But the Mills's people were aware he was a patrician of large old-money estate in Felicity-by-the-Sea surrounded by other properties of the family that could never be equaled in the Midwest, even among richer graduates of the Laurel Amphictyony.

No more was heard of Tom's feeler as a self-made graduate of Hawthorne College in Markland. He probably gave no further thought to the assistance of an oddly energetic technician who'd started on his way up by revising clerical office forms yet was fool enough to dismiss at a glance the opportunity of a lifetime to escape a very limited industry and leap to a senior level of M B A success. Then too, though an honest salesman by nature, Tom seemed to have too much respect for men's freewill to practice cajolery even in cases that he considered exceptional. He had too little curiosity about other people's values to inquire further once he sensed lack of mercantile incentive for wealth, seeing also that retrospective understanding, like history, was useless if it had no bearing on what was yet to come for himself, his family, or his peers.

On his own part Caleb often remembered that when Dogtown was threatened with discontinuation of its passenger rail service to the metropolis this decent charitable president of Mercator-Steelyard, employer of half a thousand local citizens—an inveterate supporter of the pilgrim trade that doubled the city economy every summer and called attention to the Yard's modernized presence as the world's best-recognized seafood producer and the

Cape's largest employer for more than a century—this paternalistic friend of the people was deaf to appeals for his influence at the State House in political pleading for public funds to perpetuate a common good.

"I don't care one way or the other." Caleb had heard Tom declare offhand in his usual even tones, without emphasis or emotion, when the question was broached in the midst of a company meeting about matters of importance to public relations. "I never travel by train. I don't think any of our people commute by rail. Maybe the wrong kind of people. The Yard's business won't be affected one way or the other. God knows the depot's a disgrace to look at in the middle of a junkyard. We don't really need even rail freight service anymore. We can get along without rail freight if we have to, since there's no spur down to our plant. We have to unload our packing materials onto trucks anyway, and truck our canned goods up to the boxcars. We don't need tank cars either. What little's left of our fish-oil and meal should go by road anyway, without all that fuss and bother. Saves us overhead in the long run. T'would be much quicker to skip Botolph and have everything come and go on the Felly like all our frozen traffic. Let the gypsies handle everything. Pretty soon they'll all be eighteen-wheelers. As far as I'm concerned, railroads are antique."

Since Caleb loved railroads (especially at their sparse ramifications) he was reminded of his prejudice against hardboiled ideology. Tom was a quietly decisive leader, clearly self-confident even as a good listener, yet never loathe to change his mind for cause, nor to tersely cut off palaver to show his impatience with what he thought was verbiage or nonsense. "Get on with it!" was a locution many an advisor remembered him by.

In appearance this good man was an athletically attractive middleaged gentleman of middle size, trim and fit, with a squarish face wearing rimless glasses of similar shape, plenty of hair both forward and aft despite threads of gray on his squarish black head; neither dapper nor careless in urbane well-tailored suits, ties and socks always tasteful: clothed inconspicuously, in harmony with modest courtesy of manner and the native salt in his educated speech. His underlings and colleagues generally knew him as modest and temperate in demeanor, undemonstratively cordial, free of recreational vice, fond of provincial aphorism but free of platitude, renowned for keeping his word, adroit but honest: Caleb's impression of an innocently inbred Protestican.

Tom contributed personally as well as ex officio to nondenomi-national charities. Even after hours or in recreation with associates away from the coils of business he betrayed no shadow of anti-semitism or racial aversion. He bore no apparent malice toward the Catholicratic politicians he voted against, and served amicably among liberals as an enlightened trustee of his alma mater. He was less visible as a founding patron of the Cape Gloucester Symphony (which he attended to escort his wife). Like Marx he seemed to regard workers as assets rather than expenses. Most endearingly (though subtly embarrassing to callous do-gooders among outdoor companions), he stooped to pick up litter from company property or the public sidewalk even when engaged in serious discussion with more dignified colleagues hurrying out to lunch. But the lim-ited scope of his sympathies—self, family, friends, his own kind, and some deserving poor of his acquaintance—perfectly reflected on a personal level the nearly exclusive consciousness of supposedly traditional Atlantean conservatism.

Crat politicians subsequently saved the local train service (at least for commuters), and this ambivalent reminder of an exem-plar's moral cosmos faded from Caleb's warm feelings toward the Yard's translocated hero.

The liberal technocrat continued to immerse himself more deeply than any of his fellows in the Yard's world of business man-agement, which after all was defined more narrowly than the broader world of chrematistics, itself only a variable ingredient of the nation's truly common good.

Of course at Saint Peter in the broad Midwest, with a much larger business perspective and more responsibility, pragmatic Tom would soon have a less Downeastern view at least of railroad freight. Demeter Mills was one of the continent's principal shippers of bulk grain (its principal raw material), mostly in its own hopper cars, as well as of corn oil in tank cars, and of packaged food for supermarket chains in anybody else's boxcars (or flatcar-hauling containers)—often dominating the consists of trains much longer faster and more efficient than Tom's exclusive consciousness could have imagined earlier. (Still, hardly any salesman or executive of the Mills would consider traveling even by fast luxurious train, for fear of seeming anachronistic as travelers from Saint Peter to Washington.)

Like everyone else, Caleb admired Tom Parsons as a shrewd and fairminded C E O, and appreciated his kindly though sometimes almost sentimental tolerance of old employees close at hand, or of more distant ones whom he'd made a point of knowing by name, especially influential members of the putatively adversarial Seafood Workers Union across the street, where almost all the work was done that counted in the end. Yet Caleb, the Yard's Director of Administrative Services, found a few flaws in Tom's pragmatic sensibility besides the erasable insensitivity to Chicago's railroads. Though Caleb was anxious enough about his own ability to lead falsely pragmatic minds across abstract seas of uncertainty, he had been disappointed in the diplomatic judgment of his sovereign when he found himself set at tactical disadvantage by an obtuse indiscretion of that intentionally helpful prince. When still a newly subsidiary chief, expected to advise the high court of Saint Peter concerning the peculiarities of a frozen-food business about which the Mills knew very little, except what was reflected in the Yard's financial reports, following upon market researches for potential acquisitions in the profitably growing public self-consciousness about health and nutrition, Tom had unintentionally damaged the advancement of Caleb's cause, despite the fact that in several guided tours of the Yard's premises during preliminary negotiations, the prospective buyers of the Yard had been openly impressed by what they were shown of a uniquely comprehensive computer system, even though tiny when compared with their own lavishly expensive array of unconnected giant "mainframes".

For within weeks of the merger's consummation, like other department managers of the Yard, Caleb had been flown to Saint Peter to meet his most likely Corporate counterparts, who were condescendingly unaware that the organizational reach of his provincial Dogtown realm was far more cosmopolitan, mutatis mutandis, than their somewhat velvet-glove "coordination" of incompatible hardware and software at the immense Balkanized headquarters, as well as among the Mills's various North Atlantean subsidiaries. At first they thought he was meant to adapt the Yard's thinking to a nascent orthodoxy of federalism somehow guided or permitted, rather than dictated, by the Corporate Data Processing staff, with lip service to the Yard's administrative independence, ostensibly bowing to the local wisdom of satraps paralleling each other at least under the same general accounting of the Corporate tent.

Not only Graveyard Street analysts but also competing grocery manufacturers accepted the Mills's claim to managerial efficiency as an enlightened conglomerate, largely evinced by the magnificence of its quarters, its steady profitability, and its progressive philosophy of aggregate management, including its famously liberal investment in computers per se. Even in cocktail conversation among heads of state, at conferences of the trade association (which nourished most of the northwestern world through thicks and thins of the business cycle, as if food was always in vital demand and share-of-market was the only thing to worry about), Demeter Mills was the superficial model for complex administration. Indeed its enlightened "employee benefits" were models for progressive business, if not the modern art collection on its Corporate walls and grounds.

Now Caleb believed that during the acquisition negotiation, or soon thereafter, it was Tom who had impressed upon the Mills's people the little Yard's uniquely economical inventory control system, integrated with fast analytical sales-accounting reports produced from a common heterogeneous database generated automatically by transactions with customers, vendors, and various logistical sources. With support from the Board of Directors he warned against complacency by urging them to notice that their own admired progress depended on massive redundancy based on merely speeded-up conventions of half a dozen separate systems. And that was before Tom himself was made aware of Caleb's quietly advancing superstructural plans for C M S budgeting, forecasting, logistical simulations, and other epiphenomenal advancements into the realm of "research and development".

If the Corporate middle hierarchy of academically certified Masters of Business Administration practicing "collegial management" had then realized the oddity that a single mustang philosopher, without the advice or consent of any committee, was the yet unrealized architect of what his programmers, analysts, clerks, and operating crew were institutionalizing, the Yard's innovations would have been ignored in weighing the intangible assets that determined the premium paid for the private stock and stock options of a small rejuvenated fish-processor whose name was remembered by oldtimers all over the country for antebellum roadside signs advertising dried salt fish and canned codfish cakes, a few of which still survived in tatters along secondary rural routes that were once highways. In truth, Caleb himself had been too absorbed in the progress of his inexhaustible hopes to marvel at the largely free hand he had been allowed by Rod McGrundy, chancellor of the exchequer, who was entrusted with the jurisdiction of such matters purely on the strength of his credentials as a blueblood Certified Public Accountant with amazing ability to manipulate figures in his head. Without forethought Tom had delegated to Rod his own ultimate responsibility for an expanding investment of great risk that had begun with a newly commonplace sigh: "I guess it's about time we got one of those computers!"

Without taking time to study the technical options of feasibility, but shrewdly intuitive to "get on with" what Caleb was cooking up with Rod, this C E O Parsons had lost no sleep about the comparatively secondary movement known as "automation". For Caleb's first few years at the Yard, as its first "methods and procedures analyst", he was hardly distinguished as a face in the overcrowded first floor, no more than an "efficiency expert" assigned to rationalize the tacit knowledge of the clerks in their confusing struggle against Rod's overbearing preconceptions as the Yard's numerical genius. At first Tom knew little of Caleb's sly or openly angry resistance to Rod's interference in his improvements of clerical affairs on the first floor of the old building. His resistance to the C P A led at last to an outburst of insubordination. In light of obvious improvements, the Treasurer finally yielded to the efficiency brought by his young subaltern for all to see.

But Tom, at his greater distance from the battleground, had been only slightly aware of the clerical chaos that Rod had allowed to increase with the increase of sales. Despite sufficient office machinery, until Caleb was hired, shipping orders, bills of lading, and invoices were inconsistently or carelessly processed in a state of fluctuating tardiness fraught with anachronistically confusing codes and nomenclature. Even as a professional accountant who had directed a large office of cost-plus contracts for the Navy during the war, Godfrey Rodney McGrundy was unaware that in a single room under his command many an undeserved credit memo to customers had been issued by his machine operators, without authorization, in the effort to correct errors. Other departments were beleaguered by customer or vendor complaints about delayed transactions. Clerks themselves were docilely accustomed to almost hourly arbitration by an intimidating woman named Gert, the head billing operator, whose de facto authority had never been disputed even by Rod himself, simply because she was the only one who knew how to program the CRF punched-tape machines and who taught others to operate only according to her unreasonable habits.[1]

Q E D, Caleb's achievements had been mentioned in vague terms at the highest level in Saint Peter (of course without allusion to concepts). When he'd returned from his first visit to the Mills, with a series of escorted tours around the vast headquarters, and having been briefly looked over by the Corporate President in his

---

[1]At first Caleb's hard-won battles with various such female battleaxes and entrenched male functionaries in other habits of paperwork had only gradually checked Rod's meddling in the vital details of processing orders to the satisfaction of customers, until one of his ignorant criticisms during an impromptu inspection of the billing department in the midst of a meticulously planned realignment of facilities and procedures had provoked from his new softspoken deputy an enraged outcry at the interference that shocked the whole first floor of the old building as unprecedented lese majesty. Rod retreated upstairs without rejoinder, and thereafter was inclined to leave Caleb alone at whatever he wanted to do, usually granting his requests for personnel or other expenditures without much questioning.

Caleb's autonomy was established little by little, after the mischievous errors and systemic inefficiencies of bread-and-butter transactions were eliminated, much to the improvement of "customer relations". Thus it was that the first computer was installed with a rather free hand—at much greater risk of administrative disaster than even Caleb himself realized at the time. A more orthodox senior management would have prudently avoided the notorious hazards of changing too much at once, even if compared to what Caleb cooked up the changes had been minor. The computer would have been programmed merely to speed up normal transactions and the printed reports from punch-card tabulating machines that people were used to. Computers were in vogue also for their putative infallibility. In the business vernacular of the time a "system", new or old, meant no more than orderly procedures entailing one or more machines.

In fact it was only after he detached himself from the job altogether that he was fully struck by what a revolution he had accomplished, without much more delay or embarrassment or excruciating pressure than an ordinary parallel conversion would have caused. And in retrospect he marveled at the practical development of his systems philosophy. But of course there was no need for the Mills to be told about the inchoate struggles in Dogtown. Rod himself was glad to forget his supervision in the days before he yielded to his upstart; but he was an honorable gentleman withal, bred to noblesse oblige in a culture represented by the Laurel Amphictyony whereby credit was supposed to be given where credit was due. He encouraged Caleb's self-study of accounting principles, and went so far as to give him the title of Controller, even abetting the accounting department's acceptance of C M S ideas for analytical bookkeeping and auditing. To those above Rod did not refuse himself credit for the wisdom of employing fostering and educating such an unlikely reformer.

stately private office, and having been respectfully entertained in the luxurious Executive Dining Room by a small delegation from the confederacy of semi-independent computer experts, he was asked by Rod for his frank assessment of the Mills's uninterlocking systems. The largest of these, after almost three years of group effort by dozens of programmers and "analysts" for a giant Money-sell computer in the separately air-conditioned wing of an upper floor, was still unready for preliminary testing—with no sign of embarrassment. (Meanwhile the Mills's former secretariat of "manual" clerks with standard office machinery was occupying as much as ever of another "climate-controlled" space in the opulent palace with no significant mitigation of their paperwork. The old staff had remained almost unreduced, for a corporate V P of Finance refused to trust any of the five or six various computer installations—from three different manufacturers—until "parallel operations" were thoroughly perfected. The enormous cost of leases for computers and the payroll for their attendants had "temporarily" doubled administrative overhead, though the added fiscal burden passed almost unnoticed in the generously elastic margin of profit for a business so responsive to new ideas and costs for marketing.) During that sojourn at headquarters Caleb had tactfully asked far more about what the Millers were up to than they thought of asking him about what he'd been doing in their new little protectorate.

In answering Rod's perfectly objective and somewhat flattering invitation to comment off the record on an infrastructural charac-teristic of their adoptive parent, almost as confidentially as if Caleb was now considered part of the local "management team" vis-à-vis the awesome authority of the Mills, Caleb made too little effort to disguise his presumptuous scorn. To the best of his emotional abil-ity, however, he spoke in a judiciously openminded manner, apolo-gizing for the subjectivity of his brief and superficial inspection, truthfully emphasizing his technological ignorance of the Mills's enormous new hardware. As a spy his carefully qualified intelli-gence (or idiosyncratic opinion), expressed in impersonal terms but personal tone, was presumably well enough grasped by the Yard's chief financial officer and superficially or substantially conveyed upward to Tom, who'd undoubtedly already seen enough of the Mills's other characteristics to have formed his own skeptical opin-ion of its redundant middle-management (as distinguished from his favorable evaluation of its venerable name in the stockmarket index and general management) already tantalizing to his own macroscopic common sense. These two dissimilar minds envisioned different facets of business when they agreed on this opinion.

Anyway, perhaps having reason to know that one or two of those presently at the very highest level of the Mills already suspected manifold extravagance in the name of advanced technology in their own home office, Tom (still of Dogtown) casually mentioned Caleb by name at a Saint Peter luncheon with the operating executive committee at a lower level, which included two or three vice-presidents representing powerful sectors of the Mills's parietal bureaucracy. Without declaring himself as an advocate he told them that in acquiring the Yard the Mills had netted "a pretty smart systems man". Disavowing his own qualification to judge anything to do with computers, and assuming that all those present were as hardheaded about the new trend in "back office" mechanization as he was, he mildly wondered what they thought of Caleb's rather pertinent questions, as an unbiased outsider, of how well the Mills's own experts were taking advantage of very costly computers. He paraphrased or hinted at some of what he'd understood were his own audacious employee's generalizations in terms of centralization and integration—presumably not as criticisms but as if they somehow represented either eventual economies or simply an alternate theory for small business.

Now Demeter's President and his Corporate Controller happened to be sitting in. They were not sorry to hear pretexts for certain organizational studies they had been struggling to bring about diplomatically, but the three V Ps were instantly alert to the threat of management consultants. Of course they listened politely at that lunch but before the afternoon was half gone Caleb's name was indelibly registered for dissemination throughout their jealously mechanized duchies. In effect they warned their respective systems managers to keep the nosey fellow in as much ignorance as possible of what might be used against them when they answered his questions during visits to the Mills; and generally to keep him in his subordinate place (politely of course) when it came to asserting the euphemized centralized authority that was always downplayed even by a headquarters staff that itself hoped eventually to take over or standardize with a strong hand, according to its own wisdom, all "information processing" in the federated far-flung empire.

Therefore, thanks to Tom's surprisingly naive carelessness, on Caleb's second visit and thereafter he found himself received less cordially, more guardedly, by those instructed to "cooperate" with him, as they vainly strove for inconspicuous technological authority over every other subsidiary or division in the domain of "computerized processing". He sensed less warmth in their indoctrination of the paternalism that the Mills desired. But it wasn't until sometime later that he grasped the cause—when Rod in one of his cordial after-hours moods told him in all ingenuousness about Tom's benevolent offices. In Saint Peter the antibodies were pandemic. No matter where he might have worked in the imperial hierarchy as coach or executive, no matter what his salary or title, unless he suffered humbly in a long career he would never be able to effect a fundamental abolition of the extravagantly expensive Missouri Compromises in Saint Peter. He would have been silently branded as a troublemaking upstart, or even professional enemy, whose unspoken favor was confined to the distant top of the Corporate organization chart, perhaps as an internal consultant, doing him more harm than good in the entrenched baronial apparatus upon which the peaceful kingdom depended for its uninterrupted quarterly earnings.

Meanwhile very little more of Corporate culture would be knowingly imparted to the one who might actually shape something like a C M S. Though they continued to play the part of hosts and condescending mentors to their new second-class associate from the presumptuous fishtown, Caleb's unguarded conversation at the Saint Peter establishment was thereafter confined to a few clandestine freethinkers in feckless positions who dependently chafed at the academic bosses they served like detailing draftsmen under a partnership of independent architects. Caleb managed to have lunch with two or three of them in the underground cafeteria whenever he was able to escape eating with his official escorts in the Executive Dining Room upstairs.

Caleb himself was by no means skilled in persuasion, but (as if it mattered to him in the long run) he was astonished thus to learn of Tom's elementary insensitivity to the invidious diplomacy expected by those who alter relationships in a legion of thermometer-climbers. It struck him as such puzzling insensitivity that—if it wasn't simply a natural oversight on the part of one who had not entirely made his own way up the business ladder—it could almost have been a sly sacrifice of Caleb's advancement somehow for the benefit of Tom's own career as the very man to start a sea-change in the Mills's worried or complacent corps of M B As. Or was it that it simply didn't occur to Tom that complicitous fief-holding V Ps were at the table?

2.

. . . Mechanically washing and drying his fingers like a priest absentminded at the epistle's side of the altar, Caleb noticed nearly for the first time that the knuckles of his left hand had grown almost as wrinkled as the right's, which from infancy had borne the skin of an old man. The loosened folds of skin marked a iatrogenic burn incurred too early for his own memory but not too late to account for the sinister polarity of his manual skills and habits, most notable in his crabbed adjustment to the requirements of handwriting. This sudden reminder of a neonatal trauma impelled him to study the mirror and trace with an index finger the obstetrical scar on his forehead, stage left, where he'd been wounded by the forceps that dragged him into legal existence—the second-earliest trauma unregistered in his memory—according to his mother's consistent lore. It had long since been exposed on a conspicuous level above his forehead by the ebb of his hairline, but he found that here too the years had nearly erased a mark of distinction, which in former times he'd wryly point out to the few with whom he became intimate. Nowadays he hoped that further aging would allow him also to dismiss from his infrequent moments of dismay the incorrigible banes and blemishes of his hereditary physique as modified by fortunes of nurture.

Calling himself to attention he stepped briskly around the door jamb of his bathroom into his workplace—a living room that served as study, library bower, and reception hall—only to be reminded that in his salad days at the Yard he'd easily afforded help with the housework. Though he cleaned up the kitchenette every night, he'd done no vacuum-cleaning or bed-making for many weeks, no window-washing for a twelvemonth. He'd rather clean out the stables of Augias, or the cow stalls at Dutchkill School when his only ambition was to get into college. But his electric typewriter was not to be avoided. It awaited him all too patiently among a mess of papers and clusters of unpunched tabulating cards (imprinted on the obverse as one or another superannuated key-punching form but with reverse side up bearing penciled notes for his Gilgamesh plays). He had sequestered a lifetime's supply of

blank cards formerly sold by OHM like countless blades for any of
its razors: infinitely sortable "unit records" when perforated in a
finite variety of patterns designated more to inform machines than
humans in a manner that he thought Gilgamesh would have liked.
He always carried a supply of OHM cards in his breast pocket,
along with pen and pencil, whether in former times for the Yard or
for his amateur closet drama, as well as for private memoranda of
Immediate Exclusive Consciousness [I E C]—or at present to
relieve his overtaxed memory for anything at all except matter of
the Yard.

In September his swivelled perch at an imperfectly transparent
window on the inside second deck of Apostle's Dock in Argo Cove
had still commanded a courtyard theater of moored small boats,
less than half of them used seriously for fishing. Most of the rest
were then toyboats made of seamless plastic, generally motorized
regardless of aerodynamic shape, some with aluminum masts
against which halyard snap hooks were likely to click from any
breeze day or night. The wharf's parking lot down to his left—
stage right, above the apron of tide—was still half full of kilroys,
not yet preempted by an off-season score of cradled craft then still
afloat in the harbor or elsewhere along the eastern seaboard.

But now on a midwinter's Wednesday the ephemera were long
since hauled out or dispersed, the transhumant owners and their
children immersed in their principal occupations almost anywhere
else. Save for half a dozen local vessels meant for wuthering and
frost, the cold black theater of pilings is deserted at every lap of the
tide. Dogtown's characteristic industries are once more dominant,
most out of his view but almost all sensed by his ear. It's the worst
time of year for resident artists of light and color.

He never thinks of himself as an artist. That would be pretentious, and not sufficiently distinctive. In Dogtown parlance that
word was reserved for those who plied two or three dimensions.
Even in cosmopolitan New Uruk, magnet of all dimensions, it
would be laughing at his own joke to associate his private occupation with that of composers choreographers or writers of any recognized poetry or prose just because he's working on a couple of
unclassifiable playscripts that real theater people would dismiss as
illusionary. That is, he feels more like a hermit inventing text for
the sake of providing his own hermeneutics.

Abstracted again, still procrastinating, he stares outside at the
nearest fabricated approximation of the rare device he has chosen as

Gilgamesh's sigil. His excelsior was not with leaves of grass or tea, nor fleur-de-lis or lotus; no flame or knotted rope, no image of animal or weapon. His symbol was the static kernel of kinematic creation, the geometric germ of dynamic technology. It was not branded on the playwright's own soul, but he has devoted to Gilgamesh many of his private years, in protest not of imagination but of magic and disorder. By happenstance the isorectotetrahedron [IRTH] on the wharf below suspends from its steel frame of right triangles a swiveled boom over a salient pier in Argo Cove like the fourth vector of hyperspatial dimension. It is poised with its tackle to lower nautical props to the sunken stage of brine (where drama is rare and incidental), or to pluck them up to swing over to the horizontal flat offstage right in spots cleared of kilroys.

As anywhere inscribed in variable proportions (e g, Pythagorean), the generic right triangle served as a metaphorical calculator, not only of ideal space but also as the cipher of cyclic electricity, which was for him as substantively representative of rational civilization as water was of nature; as a continuously rotating and lengthening stylus to construct in conceptual space the double gyre of Yeats's visionary correspondences—outrigged from a construction of trigonometry and the algebra of squares and square roots, an analogical idiom of mathematics inconspicuously lodged somewhere in almost every formula or algorithm of construction navigation engineering and classical physics in the middle world of human perception. From forms or parts or motions of the right triangle came nearly all construction—masts, rigging, sails, bridges, houses, and towers—and the measurement of time. Like the poles of a circus tent even nature's trees formed right angles with the skin of Mother Earth, whose own centripetal spin rules evolution by a right angle of axis and radius in time as well as space. Despite its misappropriation by destructive forces, such as those represented in the swastika, the notion of perpendicularity informed both the Cross and the Star of David (each equilateral triangle of which combines two right triangles). Yeats's gyres were cones, and all rational curves were from conic sections. Wasn't Gilgamesh's creative talisman an anticipation of enlightenment? In the special case of the *iso*-rectotetrahedron, the IRTH's largest facet forms its only mesocosmic complement, the ideal equilateral triangle, mother of the triskelion.

But the conscious Enlightenment had failed, or at least was weakened by abuse, perhaps in irreversible decline, after two more centuries of psychical entropy. He has come to fear that time would never deliver the world from any of the faithful shortcuts to belief. Faith at any cost—as in astrological superstition, or gnostic religions—was now broadcast all over the world by the electromagnetic by-products of enlightenment itself. Though some of its technological derivatives were prostituted for force or pelf, weren't all the shortcomings and ill-usages of the Enlightenment less pernicious than most factions of anti-intellectual spirituality? If mathematics can analyze biology, reason can reconcile itself to emotion—and to mystery as well. He comforted himself with an earthy humanism—his willful ignorance of cosmology.

. . . He comes to his senses, shaking his head like a dog coming out of water. There's no avoiding the designated function of the edifice gleaming at him from his former corner office inside concrete walls, and the disappointed realization in which he had left its perpendicular surfaces. He has never renounced the principles of clerical efficiency, toward which proleptic filing is the first step—though in anchoretic life the initiative for procrastination. As for filing, Axel would have said, servants can do that for us. Baskets or stacks of sedentary indecisions were hardly ever fully cleared. Disconnected demands for thoughtful classification were even more abhorrent than the standing twisting crouching pulling scanning and pushing required in the interruption of constructive or dreamy cerebration. When it came down to filing for a one-man organization, his professional efficiency gave way to whatever was emotionally easiest.

But for a hermit's purposes the required facilities are here. He drops unenthusiastically onto the old wooden secretarial chair before his typewriter desk, which is wedged between two steel cabinets. The battered brown one on his right houses three tiers of ordinary vertical file folders above a fourth that has always concealed jumbled tools and awkward junk. The other cabinet, olive green, low enough not to block his view of the Cove above a window sill, is a rack of twenty-seven shallow drawers intended for horizontal sheaves of blank or despoiled letter-size stationery but in fact largely used for miscellaneous slips of paper and small odds and ends of possible household utility in case of any conceivable need. As he swivels to face his work the label on one of these drawers catches a usually blind corner of his preoccupied eye. It taunts him with the distracting obsession that for more than a decade led to his resignation from enthusiastic authority at the Yard.

The C M S drawer marked his sequestration of an aborted manuscript in which he'd started by demonstrating (without declaration) the mercantile value of a liberal education incorporating rudimentary math, even without mention of business, when followed by progressions of interesting office experience. The text—as far as it got before he abandoned it as a waste of existential life, no matter how lucrative it might well have been—was intended to induce truly systemic thinking in the minds of general managers who could free themselves both of M B A degrees or inherited corporate culture and of current managerial fads. But the unfinished treatise was not to have been like a couple of his case histories printed in professional journals; it was to argue the value of abstract thinking. He had been conceptually ready for the Yard's first OHM computer before it was known of or afforded, always looking for better instruments to carry out projects thitherto frustrated by lack of adequate staff and mechanical machinery, as well as by the nigh perfect blindness of his superiors to concepts of command and control beyond the double-entry accounting equation.

As tactfully as possible champing at the bit for his programmers to catch up with his block diagrams for new work in progress—meanwhile dividing his time with unavoidable requests for authority to alter the organization, preparing his arguments with carefully reasoned memos that had to omit the devilish details or positive side-affects meaningless to Rod, still less to other superiors—wreaking radical change only by a succession of apparently innocuous faits accomplis, he had challenged as stealthily as possible the expectation that the company's computer would be employed simply to speed up clerical operations and eliminate errors. His stillborn book would tell its hypothetical readers not to be deterred by infamous examples of administrative disasters when organizations had tried to introduce radically unprecedented changes without forever programming and testing the fast new machinery (crammed side-by-side with the old) to imitate more or less exactly all the old ways of performing, recording, and analyzing transactions according to the notions of each operating department head.

For years he hasn't opened that drawer half full of a rough draft outline, and he now abhors its former waste of time. Other drawers of that cabinet are each for a different Tablet of the script for his antithetical system, or notes pertaining thereto, most of them laden with corrections.

His telephone rings, in his own house a shocking intrusion.

3.

It is a voice he'd hoped not to hear again but hadn't mustered the brutality to quash unequivocately. It is the cultivated sound of a formerly exceptional body's unexceptional mentality that no longer excited his unexceptional libido. Except for political opinions there had never been cerebral correspondence—not so much as a drawbridge—between her actively benign charity and even the most humane reaches of his rectotetrahedral interests. He had no great objection to her misunderstanding of his responses to questions about his impersonal occupations—his gravitation to politics at the time he would not have considered personal—but there was simply no anteroom to any intellectual crypt that might underlie her compassionate and unostentatious devotions to political or social causes of the kind he had long since assumed worthy of his support only as a Crat voter without the time or urge to show up in meetings or marches. He had always assured her that every ballot he cast was identical with hers. How could he do justice to his concentrated life by suffering flat boredom in the wasted time of even brief and infrequent rendezvous largely taken up with repetitions of observations or social complaint that they would utter in public to anyone at all—especially with a spear-carrier devoid of autonomous critical faculties? She herself seemed satisfied with a continuity of comradeship between ephemeral ecstasies and the excellent meals she served him at her colonial hearth.

"Beni!" He feigns surprise and welcome in a voice as cordial as he can make it without inflecting either intimacy or sheepish apology for the ungallantry of having obliged her to initiate conversation after several weeks of his failure to "keep in touch" about their next assignation. He braces himself not to betray any sense of guilt, but to affect the tone of a casual friend, steering clear of gladness faked. Yet his secret sharer cringes in memory of the past in which, full of hope for cerebral sympathies, he'd gaily unaddressed this scarcely aging beauty as "Miss Pennypants".

In marriage Eric Vanderlyn the handsome wellborn father of Benilda's children had loved her far more than her lovers ever did, but never with the responsible fidelity she would have forfeited his social status and affluence to secure. Without inquiry, without volunteered accounts of herself, Caleb had sensed a lonely childhood of disappointed affection. But how could he keep trying to disguise the cruelty that she must have already detected in his evasions? Her humbly granted respect for the eccentric seclusions of his cultural hermitage, for which he had never pleaded with more than a hint (for fear of seeming to acknowledge her perception of his need for an excuse), could hardly relieve the embarrassment of clinging to him as a fortuitous lover so late in what most unattached men mistakenly presumed to be the asymptotic decline of a gentlewoman's libido. Her fragile compliance to the formula for a dowager life far from her scattered children rested in large part upon hope for his erotic participation as the independent variable.

But though from the beginning she had always accepted his implied conditions with no audible sign of injured dignity he recognized her as a shrewd reader of erotic patterns, perhaps cicatrized by slings and arrows, who was not accustomed to remaining passive. Though exquisitely loathe to wound her secret anima with one more bitter proof of what she would consider her failure to retain even an unprepossessing middleaged bachelor to whom she was generous with creature comforts, he admitted to himself that he was now immediately fearful of springing open the cage of a tigress who thus far hadn't felt familiar enough with his psyche to expose a probable stock of vulgar expletives. In the absence of temperamental affinity, he thought, she would suspend her reactive anger only as long as silken chains of sensual liaison still seemed plausible.

"I'm sorry if you were taking a nap. But I suppose it's too late to hang up now. I've finally found some Lapsang Souchong for you. When can you come to fireside tea?"

He knows that invitation: a cry for at least the motions of affection. He is ashamed to hold the upper hand over her loneliness simply by virtue of the liberty granted him by gender. How can he express his painful pity without insulting her condignity in the web of local contributors to the common good? He could never bring himself to betray the ennui he suffered at her candlelit tête-à-tête meals, kept alive only by redundant dialogue about the things they discussed in concern for the welfare of town nation and world, before or after the repetitious satisfaction of reincarnated youth and beauty in her extremely broad bed upstairs.

He'd always avoided allusion to her former aspiration as a modest creator of art. She and a friend still ran the Books and Crafts Shop in Seamark, where painters were invited to read their poetry aloud and writers to leave their pictures on consignment. For the moment he forgets that she was one of Cora Kryothermsky's best amateur dancers, as well as designer of sets for the defunct Stone Barn Company of Mummers led by Tessa Barebones (now the wife of Rafe Opsimath); nor does he immediately remind himself that a double-decade ago she deserved his admiration for co-founding the legendary Troika Arts Center, the theater's precursor, as the first in beauty among three strikingly attractive peers. Then (as now) younger than the Troika that befriended him, he had been more jealous of Eric her husband, her perfect match in beauty, an indolent photographer of or for women, than of Buck Barebones or Thad Kryothermsky, those two creative technologists who then possessed Tessa and Cora, the brilliant sisters Masterson. Beni's fine golden hair and pallor skin are now handsomely replaced by the dark complexion cultivated by sometime sailing in her own little sloop and wintertime skiing with her athletic friends. To the mature Caleb she is only inconspicuously heavier than when he'd been welcomed as anything but a hermit by Tessa's band of friends. For him the tanned face of her prime is not marred by its faint lines of palimpsest, in the bedroom her skin is as smooth as a maiden's, and her paps feel as firm as those of many a young woman who'd weathered not even one baby.

But she has no sense of humor. Yes, that is at the root of it! And I'm too old for jest or gallantry without a woman who can sense my irony.

"I love to cook for you. But come anytime when you're not bemused with writing."

It's not that I'm sitting at the typewriter eight hours a day seven days a week, he tells himself. *How can I explain the embarrassing fact that unlike literary sharks or their school fish I can't do what I renounced a rectolinear career to do unless I privately steer my psychic energy through a fecund welter of books, instantaneous interests, imaginary observations, particular political hopes, piquant journalism, vicarious spectator sport, and random amusements exciting enough to divert me from said purpose? My Immediate Exclusive Consciousness is too fatigable to be harnessed without frequent exchange of scenes for what's relevant to my calling. Yet social entanglements even when they're really fun rob me of time for the contrariant stimulations that allow me the only I E C that's worth its own time. At this age, far more than half way through the dark forest, unless or until I happen upon a woman as sympathetically exciting at least as Bice Picory was, or Lilian Cloud, or Gloria Keith, I must indulge my solitary vagaries without yielding to the impoverished entertainments of a town without theater, of a place as irreversibly saturated as any other with the broadcast advertising and political misapprehensions of a nation long molded by devilvision [DV]. Ergo the hermit I am, as I've given up trying to inform her.*

So in excusing my prayers for payless payload time, I usually plead the nonproductive demands of what occupational therapists call "Activities of Daily Living" [A D L], speaking as a bachelor with no helpmeet to shield me from mishaps or to share the nuisance of shopping, eating, and cleaning—never mentioning the lack of servants to do the living. How could I possibly justify the self-indulgence of chimeral polymathy to one who assumes the common belief that genuine laborers are exclusively dedicated to a single labor.

As they speak facelessly he envisions poor Beni in her empty house, erstwhile queen of a marriage greatly envied, a woman of independent means, mother of cosmopolitan children in impressive careers, tensely holding the phone in one hand, a glass of Scotch tremulous in the other, fearing humiliation, struggling to exclude a tone of supplication, pretending self-confidence, as she wills him to fulfill the vague promise of many weeks ago to propose a time for his next visit. A revised promise would have to be uttered still more vaguely, this time as a cri de coeur of apology for the incredible vicissitudes of creative temperament—if he could bring himself to simulate such a histrionic display of personality and thus perhaps forestall another of her invitations to recreate himself at one of her social get-togethers, or to join her at some pathetically artificial square-dance, or to attend a meeting of the Cratic City Committee: anything at all that he might have it in him to tolerate as a normal member of society—as if he didn't have his own choice of private pastimes that were much more difficult to resist! She would like him to frequent the Cape Gloucester Symphony, art shows, Lyceum lectures, and of course authors' readings (though she herself never read a book for anything but information or advice). Before and after copulation, their one common motivation, there was nothing alluring except her quiet civilized contralto voice to draw him back to her again. The burden of their friendship rested solely upon the usual atonement of root and rind (vigorously elevated to mechanical beatitude), between prologue and epilogue of conventional amenities and smalltalk, always winding up on his part with a drawn-out pretense not to be craving escape to his books. Still, only that rutting itself, a pièce de résistance for sandwiched visits, was worth to him the time away from page and print and kept him in irresolute communication.

Yet, he sometimes thought, she too probably also pretended not to notice the carnal entertainment of a singleminded association, and may have been glad enough to realize the clandestine crescendo for the fulcrum as crassly opportunistic not only on his part but also on hers as a divorced granddam wantonly outliving the choices of attractive youth. She is still a friend of Tessa, Cora, Gloria, Sally, and perhaps other women of her generation who know him. Does she confide in one or more of them a desperation as crass as his has been? No better than other men can he guess how much the sorority of college and marriage and maternity share its ultimate secrets. His sympathy with her is more gallant than his present aversion.

"I'm not getting enough work done," he tells her, "even though I've reduced my public appearances to the irreducible! There are too damned many chores and inconveniences to cope with. I'm not on an even keel the way you are! Just to go downtown for food-shopping once a week throws me out of kilter. It's an agony of disruption just to make a doctor or dentist appointment, not to mention keeping it! Haven't you noticed what a delicately balanced creature I am?" he laughs. "My equanimity is shattered just by the thought of having to take my car in for an oil change—little as I use it—or even to get gas!" He keeps trying to jolly her. "If I weren't moored to this wharf I'd call myself an anchorite!"

—Pause. No reply.

"I can't expect you to bear with me." he continues. "I'm crazy."

"If you aren't well balanced I don't know who is!"

"I used to sail on an even keel, when I dealt with the real world. Pretty soon I'll have to wake up and start looking for a job again—which I refuse to do until I finish what I'm working on. And I can't finish my work without self-discipline. I need the solitary grace of God for peace of mind to make up for lost time! Time is everything for a recluse who's squandered his youth in the debauchery of sober business! Aside from the impositions of A D L, I try not to stew over unanswered letters, neglected tax forms, and forgotten bills. I'm pretending that my Apostle's Dock is a monastic cell, where I drink my thimbleful of wine alone. For the time being my sabbatical pleasures must be postponed. You don't know what a slow reader I am: my writing is a million times slower. . . ." Too rhetorically he offers himself as her patient. But not a word of tenderness or sympathy for her side of mankind's seldomly acknowledged bargains.

He flounders, talking too much. They are good excuses, indeed imperatives, but they would certainly not have been summoned if a woman more to his taste—not necessarily younger or more intelligent—had happened to be on the other end of the line. In that case he wouldn't be demurring at invitations interesting enough to have been pursued and accompanied nearly continuously at the peril of his prime vocation. He is ashamed of himself for the simulations of spontaneity that had brought Beni to this unhappiness. She deserves a frank and open lover who enjoys community singing.

In her pathetic silence he can't help piling Ossa on Pelion in exculpation, artificially warming up in his intention to approach the bravely absolute. ". . . I'm derelict in my duties to old friends. And until too late I neglected my greatest benefactor in her nursing home—but not because I followed Jesus! That alone is guilt enough to disgust even the likes of Distard Undershot Noxin!" As if he expected her to understand that he wanted the greater guilt to excuse the lesser!

"It seems to me that you are on a very even keel." she at last replies in a surprisingly level voice. "I think you are a very sensible man. But if not, tell me how to shift the ballast." Perhaps he'd reminded her that she was sailing Eric's old sloop less and less as the years went by.

"Dear Beni, you've already been as kind and generous to a ne'er-do-well as I could ever hope for, what with food shelter and your talent in the jewel of games. But there's no way even you can do any more to strengthen my character. That's why I've finally decided that I must stay in autistic seclusion until I earn the privileges of humanity. No excursions, no entertainment; nothing but the meditative exercise of working up a sweat by forcing myself to run around Nedlaw Pond when I have the time." —Falsifying, then, he tries to palliate his declaration: "Maybe when I've recovered productive equilibrium I can even return to the world of responsibility—." —Instantly he regrets the kind of mistake in diction he'd been trying to avoid.

His faux pas does not escape her. Still in calm low voice but with new accusatory accent: "I hope you don't classify me as a responsibility."

At least his indiscretion has slightly postponed the open bitterness of erotic desolation that might put an end to the prospects of a widow-woman hoping for decades of desire, preparing her for the necessity of accepting his valediction.

"Of course not! With you it's a matter of antinomy."

"Christ almighty, what does that mean?" In a voice as low as ever, with half the grunting equivalent of a smile.

He half laughs, to show he took her lightly in making fun of himself. "In this phase of my oscillation your attraction conflicts with my vocation. If anything it was you who took responsibility for keeping me in tone. In oscillation phases repeat themselves. I hope we'll be in tune again. As a privilege, not by right."

Perhaps as her magnetism gradually faded she has learned from experience to suppress her keen sense of men's cowardly duplicity. She has learned that fierce words, though cathartic of feeling when she drinks alone, would only reverberate as antagonistic despair and present him with an easier way to sever the last thread of possibility for some future accident or impulse that might draw them together again after his unbalanced feelings (as truly stated) had clarified themselves in the putative duty of uncontested creativity. After all, she is aware from more than one long hiatus in this paramour's attention that he has wavered and dragged anchor in her direction two or three times before.

He admires the self-control that keeps her from making a fool of herself. She was instilled with caution by a family that sent her to the safest women's college, and by many years of disappointed expectations with a charmingly feckless husband full of enterprising ideas who'd never been required to supplement his hereditary annuity. Though hardly aware of her incapacity for the romance in excessive passion, she can see both sides of an ordinary equation without solving it for the value of its unknown term.

Caleb was no longer surprised by the emotional differences among women, incommensurable with their respective varieties of intelligence. None he knew or read about seemed capable of his mother's love-throes that he'd witnessed before he was old enough to sympathize, especially in her long tumultuous attachment to Tony Porter—"I'm not the marrying kind"—whose silent side of the liberation he nevertheless instinctively understood and now recalls as an unheroic veteran in a less difficult plight. His present case is nothing extraordinary, brief and ludicrous in comparison, with no such degree of intensity on either side—and fortunately less consequential than the loves of her youth before he himself was conjured into existence.

He has never known of either man or woman spared less of the living truth, provoked or imposed, than his mother. The egregious

Mary Tremont had certainly been happier and unhappier, more joyful and bitter, than wellborn well educated and well protected Benilda Vanderlyn, who therefore, uncompensated by the faculties of humor and critical clairvoyance, could not but prove mediocre by his criteria. He has always sought women unlike both.

3

DER SCHLEPPER

Atlantean Classics

*T*he Cape Gloucester Literary, Scientific, and Historical Lyceum presented a special lecture every January on the last Saturday before it closed for a month to celebrate the waxing of daylight even as atmospheric warmth continued to wane, ocean as always lagging the land. The famous Wellingborough Redburn once lectured there on Old World art, with one of his by-blows in the audience, a painter ignorant of his affiliation. In Dogtown now there wasn't much else of edifying interest to occupy a winter afternoon in public. The city's movie theaters had vanished.

A few in this audience were particularly interested beforehand, either because they sought some local echo in the speaker's name, Captain Finn Macdane, and were especially curious about the bloodlines that might be implied by that onomastic heritage, or because they were impressed by his published identification as a distinguished naval historian. But most, including those from

nearby towns in Gloucester County, were drawn by the announcement that his talk would include reference to the naval architecture
of the fishing schooners for which the Cape had once been internationally famous. As a whole the latest generations of Dogtown indigenes were too inured to repetitious insistence on that nautical
past—which seemed of value only to console the older aborigines of
the central city and even the troglodytes of the quarry wards—to
care for the bromides of maritime nostalgia. Everyone knew very
well that the lecture would not be about the few schooner *yachts*
that visited during the summer, amongst throngs of other toyboats
both local and domestic. Probably no more than a dozen common
readers attended in response to the *Dogtown Daily Nous*'s mention of
Redburn in its announcement of the event.

Unobtrusive Frank Bacon, unknown to typical denizens as
director and almoner of the cryptically influential Tybbot Foundation, was only slightly less self-effacing in his more public position
as the Lyceum's president. Mounting the shallow stage of the
assembly room, he tapped a tumbler at the podium, which stood to
one side of a white screen set further back across the center. This
deferential call to order, ten minutes late, quieted the murmuring
throng of faces, which in large part were familiar to each other if
not known by name. They were seated on folding chairs of glossy
black wood whose ranks were already pushed or hitched a little out
of alignment. The audience was divided by the beam of a slide projector aimed at the screen and controlled by a wire temporarily
hooked up to a button loosely available to a lecturer. Those doubtful of the announced subject were at least assured of having something to look at. Dogtown people of all ages were usually curious
enough to consider almost any photograph that hadn't been numb-
ingly rubbed in by the Chamber of Commercials or its advertising
members.

Mr Bacon simply welcomed everyone to the hundred and fifti-
eth anniversary Lyceum Lecture, and turned the lectern over to the
new mayor, who as a private denizen had long since publicly supported the institution. Dexter Keith, though a little enlarged in
girth after twenty years of a second marriage to an erstwhile prothonotary of the Earldermen's in Ibicity Hall, still looked as darkly
archangelic as Lucifer, and likewise charming, especially to the
League of Feminine Voters. Almost everyone in this congregation
was satisfied with his political election, for he was regarded (especially to anyone interested in art of any kind) as the most compe-

tently enlightened official ever known to have been elected to city government.

Besides a mayor the nearby clock-towered neo-Baroque landmark on the acropolis of Harbor Ward housed a public confederation of de facto fiefs closely guarded and sustained by longevity or obscure nepotism, which for the most part silently prevailed by habit over the democratic checks and balances mandated by charter or statute. These intermediate or semi-autonomous functionaries were generally more representative of voter mentality than those who were elected to govern. If there was anything the native sector of the public hated it was analytical criticism, generally stigmatized as "sarcasm". Fortunately for Keith's career as a pragmatic politician very few voters were aware that under previous administrations, as Director of Community Development and City Planner, pinned down by strings, and later as Director of the Industrial Development Economic Agency [I D E A], he had privately called the city's brick capitol Lilliput Hall.

Still, even some of the beneficiaries of past patronage, installed or retained, couldn't help hoping for at least his partial success in organizing the chaos left by the defeated opponent. Ben Nathan, the genial shopkeeper and tenement landlord, the most penny-pinching Earl on the previous Councils, had been elevated to mayoral office by singleminded taxpayers. In that position, suddenly liberal in defining his own emoluments and perquisites, though faithfully chary of official expenses for all individuals not reckoned important for his own intended reelection, he had lost control of costs for more than one special project funded by state or federal grants, to say nothing of the essential city budget borne by local taxes, thereby losing the mayoral office to the new leader.

But municipal offices being closed for the weekend, Dexter Keith had been asked to make the introductory remarks as a special admirer of the speaker. He described Finn Macdane as a naval architect and electrical engineer more widely recognized for his avocation as an independent historian of naval matters. Keith apologized for accepting the honor of appearing in the "non-political" Lyceum: he was qualified to introduce the distinguished guest only because he himself had been a junior reserve officer in one of the hollow ships that he now knew the speaker had had a hand in the design of. The Landing Ship (Tank) designated L S T 1066 in the wartime Amphibious Forces of the western Pacific Fleet was one otherwise anonymous sister in the homely chiliad invented by unprecedented necessity, launched broadside like many of the others on a tributary of the brown god that drains the fresh waters of our continent. L S Ts could carry almost any military cargo, including foot soldiers, but were designed especially to swallow armored vehicles with their cavaliers and debouch them on saltwater beaches. L S Ts were known to their crews and passengers as "Large Slow Targets". In any weather but dead calm or headwind, half a century earlier, these galumphing platforms, bristling with their own antiaircraft firepower, could have been overtaken by a Dogtown fishing schooner. But for about fourteen months, he said, many years before they'd become acquainted here in Dogtown, he and Captain Macdane, of immense disparity in seniority and experience, serving on unlike missions in ships classified at the opposite extremities of naval prestige, and of extraordinarily contrasting personal derivations, had moved about the same western Pacific Theater within a thousand miles of each other. "That's my only excuse for the honor of introducing him. I can't say I was ever his shipmate, or even knew a soul in his fighting fleet. It was all I could do to conn my little Green Dragon in plodding flotillas, or figure out how to get where we were being sent all by ourselves. But at least, like Redburn before us (in an even slower frigate), we both served under the same old Articles of War. . . .

"Questions will be welcomed by Captain Macdane at the end of his talk."

During the speaker's conventional salutations, recognizing kind sponsors and patient audience, some in the congregation realized that they'd occasionally seen the man downtown without knowing that he was the one who had established himself and his consulting business in eccentric comfort on the remodeled top floor of a former bank building where his rooftop terrace overlooked the inner harbor. His squarely trimmed graybearded face was tan, his blue eyes darkened by brows almost silver, with a gathering crease between them at the base of his smooth forehead. He was rather academically attired in khaki trousers, brown tweed jacket, and a red-striped tie; and he went about the mechanics of lowering the level of his lectern with a quick efficiency more likely with younger middle age. But in juxtaposition with his introducer he was little more impressive in voice or stature than a classic officer in mufti. In one ear he wore an unconcealed hearing aid. Only now did he don his rimless bifocal spectacles.

". . . Let me correct my young friend on two points. First, I was only a temporary wartime Captain. My highest permanent rank was Commander, and I retired from the Navy only a few years after World War Two.

"By the way, please, you need not wait till the end to ask questions. But if you interrupt me please speak up like a bos'n, because my ears are so dim that up here I can't even make out Dexter's compliments. Feel free to leave the room with a good conscience if I disappoint your expectations or get carried away on my hobby-horse like Uncle Toby—

"Second, Mr Bacon made me promise to begin by explaining the title of my address as I chose to have it printed on placards and mailings, somewhat to his dismay: *A Sailer and a Steamer: Two Classics*. So I am obliged to elucidate my spelling at the outset, instead of unnecessarily prolonging public doubt of your Lyceum's editorial dignity. I'm afraid he had to call Ms Cingani at the *Nous* to prevent her Community editor from correcting the copy sent in for our announcements in the paper. I really hadn't meant to embarrass the Lyceum by having my own way with one printed suffix of a word that was respected hereabouts more than anywhere else: *sail*. After all, Dogtown was known for over a century as the saltiest wind-driven port in the world. My classic objects are *argos*, not *argonaut*s: vessels, not crews; sail*er*s, not sail*or*s."

Though no great portion of the Cape's intellectual elite was in attendance, much of Macdane's present audience was of that aristocracy. Yet except for three or four chuckles there were no murmurs of Classical appreciation as he turned away from the lectern to move about the stage without looking at his notes. From time to time thereafter his left hand brushed the whitening hair behind his ears at the back of his well-revealed skull. When he gave deliberating thought to his words he stared at the walls or the floor, but most of the time he seemed to scrutinize the faces of his audience as he spoke, rather than look at an upper back corner of the auditorium as university lecturers are advised to do.

". . . My objects are two specialized types of complex artifact. Each took about a hundred years to reach what we may regard as its destined perfection, its summit of development—only to fall rapidly into unreproductive obsolescence. They were also ninety degrees out of phase with each other; but their shapes in certain circumstances are of similar silhouette. I trust that even the implacable humanists among you will sympathize with the loss at least of the earlier and local classic, though I do call it a machine. The main thing I ask is that you take notice of my particular instances as representing the varieties of perfected artefactual complexity that rise and fall in the welter of cultural evolution, even if you don't share my aesthetic satisfaction with them both.

"It will not surprise this particular audience that the first is Dogtown's own fishing schooner. Despite the honorable images of Cynosure Rock in Purdeyville, Double Digit Lights on Pinnace Woe Island, the Fisherman's Netting Needle, and the noble osprey, it has kept its significant place on the City Seal. You hold in awe as I do the hardiness, bravery, and suffering of this city's resourceful sailors in the world's most dangerous labor—an occupation long since acknowledged by historians, commemorated in art, fixed in the calendar of civic memorials, and manned to this day by fishermen in safer vessels but nearly as boldly. I can add nothing to everyone's respect for the griefs of schooner families almost seven generations deep. But I wonder if the old brute hardship at sea, especially in winter, and the social insecurity ashore are fully appreciated yet, considering that most history and reminiscence omits what's taken for granted in daily life both by those who live that life and by those who record it. As you know, in one forty-year period this town lost seven hundred schooners at sea, drowning thirty-eight hundred fishermen: almost twice the contemporary rate at which black men were being lost in the South! Since 1650 about five thousand Dogtown fishermen have been lost. I've heard some say as many as ten thousand.

"Yet with undisclosed returns on investment in this industry, despite material losses, and not in the North Atlantic only, the Codfish Aristocracy ashore built its wealth and culture on the ununionized hornyhanded usually unlettered men who were brought up to operate floating apparatus as beautiful at sea as soaring gulls, but as disenchanting as gulls on a pier when the payload was sold by owners, trimmed by dealers, reduced by chandlery costs, and otherwise parsimoniously distributed as the crew's share of the net profits, if any. There were as many deductions from a man's wages as if he was responsible for income tax and social security premiums withheld by the government—long before anyone in this country had dreamed of calculating for the fiscal common good.

"Schooners also served purposes of transport, even around the Horn for gold, before and after the Confederate rebellion. But the

combined hull and rig of these 'fast and able ladies' attained optimum technological and aesthetic integration only after about forty
years of post-bellum experiment in naval architecture, proximately
before the fisheries' era of mechanical power and electronic navigation that precipitated their rapid superannuation—just as the
greatest Atlantean steam locomotives were created with ultimate
beauty and power just before diesel and electric engines began their
conquest of the rails."

Signaling the janitor to dim the lights of the auditorium he
took up the electrical button that controlled the projector. ". . . So
now I must explain what I mean by *classic*. I have a few diagrams to
show. You won't be overloaded with commonplace pictures."

Most of the occasional illustrations in what followed as they
clicked into existence were abstract curves stretched out as a single
horizontal sine wave or its distortions, or as three simultaneous
phases, disappointing many a hope for interesting entertainment.
He left each successive figure on the screen for optical senses to
dwell upon until his advancing words referred to the next refreshment of attention. Plain black lines on glaring white fabric, like
textbook illustrations of geometry simple enough for high school
physics, or for Redburn's teenage Philo Logos Society, but annoying
to spectators who read only newspapers and cinematic pictures.
Only toward the end was patience rewarded by a dozen photographs of schooners or their painted pictures—and most of these
more technical than rhetorical—which he strove to display as
objects for emotional contemplation.

"The classic moment of any complex developmental species is
its phase of least disorder, when its elements are most organically
cooperative with each other, when compositional resonance is
achieved, which mathematicians might call their symmetry. My first
classic is the type realized as the great schooner *Gloucesterman*. . . ."

[*Ha, thought Caleb Karcist: possible maximum efficiency! Mercator-
Steelyard still owned or financed a fleet of their relics almost up to the day
I went to work there, when the few remaining hulls with truncated masts
had been converted into diesel draggers with deck houses, otter-trawl deck
equipment, radars, lorans, and depth-finders. Joe Rose, the last bookkeeper
in the accounting department who knew how to "settle up a trip" with individual schooners, was just retiring. Sometimes outside there was still the
whiff of odd salt-fish lots drying on vestigial flake racks, never failing to
evoke my earliest sensations of the waterfront when once or twice I had been
allowed by my mother to step aboard a schooner with furled sails moored at*

some inactive wharf, and to set foot in the lower ratlines, though forbidden
to climb any further toward what she called the crow's nest. Yet she was
always quoting me "Do great things, don't dream them all day long"! The
tensegrity of schooner rigging, along with winding towers, were always
among my daydreams. . . .]

". . . but bear in mind that an entity or species may be in its
classic phase even when its genus is in decline, or the genus itself
may be at its peak when its species are in decline, or the family
when the kingdom's breaking down. In mathematical analysis
every cyclic sine wave comprises innumerable smaller curves of
greater frequency, any one of which at any point of value may be
rising or falling in movement contrary to that of the all-inclusive
envelope—which I'll call the culture. Of course very few composite
phenomena, such as a defined culture or class if things, rise and fall
in a regular curve. Their curves of progression through time may be
very irregular—so distorted in extreme cases that they may even be
represented by segments of a straight line, like a sawtooth, as you
see in these graphs of typical shapes. But whether wiggly or
straight they can be conceptualized as an infinite number of shorter
regular waves simultaneously augmenting, diminishing, canceling,
or reinforcing each other at every moment.

"So the lifeline of one artifact may be imagined as a single small
wave within the great historical curve whose completed shape we
may not yet know. Thus the short wave of a particular technology
may be rising to approach and achieve a classic phase even as the
great curve of its civilization is in decline. . . ."

A young woman slipped away, no doubt hoping to be as inconspicuous as possible, thanking her stars that her marginal chair was
near the exit. Other auditors were grateful to her for breaking the
ice. From time to time thereafter she was followed from more disruptive positions in their rows. A few elders regretted that there
was no longer a city fire whistle to break up the boredom of lectures without the least entertainment of mild curiosity. But the
considerate majority quietly stuck it out with habitual tolerance,
looking forward to the customary compensation of wine and cheese
in an anteroom at teatime. Even if individually susceptible to irrepressible spasms of nose or throat these polite patrons or guests of
the Lyceum were embarrassed if not angered by the impatience of
their fellows pro tem. But no discourtesy seemed to faze the
speaker. He grinned at all contretemps, as if goodnaturedly implying that he had sufficiently lowered the level of his expectation.

". . . But the apex of the graph in question here—the small curve of schooner history that looms so large to us—is the integrated summation of its own components, where they attain their nearest mutual approach to god-given harmony—where the desiderata of a special naval architecture come as close as possible to the unity of diverse or conflicting interests. A classic case is the nearest one to realization of a common will for the perfection of a complex entity—as, for example, the Parthenon or the Lion Gate at Mycenae. Any evolutionary alteration or willful correction of a component will disturb this integrity, even if it improves one or more of its functions or attributes by suboptimization. If everything about a schooner had been improved at once we'd know that we'd been mistaken in calling it a classic in efficacy. A progressive design may be like the momentary conjunctions of flood tide at midnight under the full moon of a clear sky at the summer solstice—not necessarily auspicious. The noblest fishing schooner grew from the blended experiential compromises of designers, builders, owners, seamen, and home-port society in all weathers. As Redburn said of Greek Architecture,

> Not magnitude, not lavishness,
> But form—the site;
> Not innovating willfulness,
> But reverence for the archetype.

"But beware an archetype too high in the hierarchy—that is, too broad in scope—else you frieze like Egypt! When everyone agrees on a genus spanning too many species—when minds are enclosed with too many species at once—there is no further evolution. When differentiation is unnoticed there is no demand for perfection. Wills are not called to be free when they are heedlessly in unison.

"Only in an atmosphere of change—within an envelope for change, especially on a downward slope of decadence in a particular technological tradition, or genre, or society—in the disturbance of encompassing unity, is a classic recognized for what it was, not in its perfection. A new species evolves when we have the conative advantage as well as the possibility of disorder. In recovery of the freewill with which we once aspired to perfection we precipitate the freedoms of criticism and invention—but without discarding our admiration or respect for the instance of classic purity that we now leave behind in order to pursue—for better or for worse—different objects of open-ended achievement. The tradition we now hold to be obsolete, though still cherished, opens our ideas and efforts to the evolution of a different species. Amid the horrors of general decadence, when the tastes of a whole culture proliferate and its collective reason loses ground, it may tolerate genius and exception, the insecurity of new forms, new values—alongside senescent institutions and clashing beliefs, as in Athens when the *Bacchae* succeeded *Oedipus*, or in Italy when Florence exiled Dante, or in the first few decades of twentieth century Vienna when creative intellect was supreme. . . ."

"Please Mr Spengler!" Perdita Dana raised her calm and pleasant voice to call out, not with asperity, perhaps for fun, from twilight in the rear: "Since you invited interruption: Heraclitus has already taught us that the way up is the way down, and we have learned from a recent war the advantageous aftermath of decadence. I had hoped you were going to speak in ordinary Dogtown language!"

Most of the audience was shocked by this irreverence, especially those who recognized the voice of Dogtown's goodnatured white witch, a cheerful middleaged teacher in the Contemplative Nullification Movement [C N].

[*What's gotten into her? wonder her friends and clients there present.*]

But Macdane levelly matched her humor. "Presently, madame. I really haven't lost my way. I thought a few abstractions would reduce the need to elaborate context for the pith of what follows."

[*Caleb wonders why Deeta is there at all. As usual he is embarrassed by what he's learned is her veiled contempt for material objectivity. When he accidentally encounters her on the street it has become more and more difficult to disguise his painful alienation from her persisting attitude of intimacy. Neither celibate nor chaste in her private life, she was the local pundit of C N—"meditation without concentration" (as well as of generic spirituality)—she who had once eagerly taught him how to relax and clarify his central nervous system twice a day, waiving the usual fee, in consideration of a cherished friend's materialistic reluctance to withdraw from reality. But he had found C N a remarkably salutary habit, seeing that he would never be capable of being carried away by the doctrine of cosmic energy that underlay the movement, or by the claims of supernatural feats urged upon more advanced practitioners as epiphenomena of transcendence. Caleb eschewed doctrinal argument with Deeta, and he remained categorically prejudiced against extricationism (as Father Duncannon called philosophical attempts to escape social reality). He believed that Guru Nil, the*]

Hindu founder of C N, dictated a preposterously irrational metaphysics in the name of "modern science", justified solely by metaphorical abuse of terms used in scientific physics. He still admired and regularly practiced C N's basic training, a methodology of private "meditation", very different (for example) from that of Christian Cephasites—an easygoing ritualistic means to physiological refreshment that introduced him to the subjective benefits of a wandering mind when veridical requirements of rational objectivity could be put aside.

Despite the repeatedly unacknowledged failure of her international Guru Nil's predictions that collectively practiced C N would irenically influence the wider social world, by assembling and radiating the power of pacification, the movement continued without challenge or recantation to lay claims (muted in public after the disappointments in photography or scientific documentation) for such self-deceptive phenomena as bodily levitation. Only guardedly did Guru Nil's disciples reveal to their sympathizers his arcanely recidivistic astrology in which they had faith as a function of modern physics. Even the most metaphorical idea of interplanetary personal determinism had finally so appalled Caleb that he could hardly face Deeta to exchange the time of day for fear of betraying his dismay at a subculture in which an honest and intelligent benevolence like hers, active and effective in its otherwise enlightened goodwill, could remain so obscurantist after a four-hundred-year ascent of the curve commonly called empirical science. He fearfully marveled at a mental world in which excessively cultivated subjectivity could be exploited by the psyche, as if resembling one of the gnostic religions against incarnation. In a certain intimacy with Deeta he had fully realized that the human brain can transform and shape almost any information either from or to its own sensory symbols. Others in Dogtown, especially among the new generation of so-called political dissenters, adopted gnostical ideas compatible with hers, submitting their minds or bodies to her healing beauty, but none more than he was tenderly respectful of her selfless poverty.

She seemed as serene as a Buddhist beggar, as practical as a secular Christian saint. She lived by casting horoscopes, teaching yoga or C N, tutoring illiterate immigrants and children in ordinary English, gathering seaweed from the rocks or herbs from her garden, and sometimes, in necessity, as a charwoman, traveling about the Cape by bus or bike, if not on foot. She accepted no money for ministering to the sick or attending the infirm, nor from anyone who could not afford other rendered services. Meanwhile she taught herself oriental calligraphy, skillfully photographed details of natural history (generally overlooked), painted symbolic watercolors, and wrote avant-garde poetry. But she did not take kindly to strangers who

*sought her out as the formerly self-effacing housekeeping companion of the
late Ipsissimus Charlemagne, a dramaturgical anthropologist and scarcely
understood model for his national constellation of countercultural Ippies.
Perdita Dana was a pacifist but she was fearless in defense and bold in
softspoken confrontations.]*

". . . So whether or not the West is declining at the moment,"
Macdane was saying, perhaps unnecessarily laboring his point for
an audience of doubtful composition, "—and even if the universe as
a whole is in the process of irreversible decomposition, some of our
cultural elements may be improving. The river of Heraclitus forms
backwater eddies against the flow. Every life is protest against universal disintegration. During the long fall of the Roman Empire
there was some hope in two or three reigns of comparatively constructive emperors who caused perishable backwash to buck the
tide, like two or three presidents in our own single century; and
some negative regimes have provoked new countercurrents of individual liberty or stimulated particular advances in art or human
welfare. Let me put it this way: at any historical moment there are
creatures evolving to their own limited perfection while the climate
is worsening.

"For convenience, let us observe Spengler's convention in
loosely defining three segments of this universal wave . . . which
here represents an entity or type over time, purely in terms of its
intrinsic utility—nothing more remarkable than the business
cycle. Let us call *this* ascending phase of development the *primitive*
. . . and *this* descending phase the *decadent*. Between them, here at
or near the top, is the *classic* zone, corresponding to what Liam
Yeats called 'the apex of beauty'. The primitive is youthful, strong,
desirous of an improving object; the decadent is a loosening of
integration, offering the elements of perfection the vicissitudes of
separate independence—for better or for worse—after their mutual
resonance is disturbed, after unity is weakened. As time passes the
thing or its class is no longer well adapted to new conditions. Its
complex of elements grow less and less essentially related, weakening the reinforcement of each other. Only in fully classic development . . . here at the top . . . have the body's muscles been in a
synchronicity of tone.

"And so you see, madame, the way up is not the way down. I'm
sorry I can't speak the ordinary language of Dogtown. Until
recently I've known this place only as a frequent visitor."

"As long as you don't spoil for us the vision of your interesting subject!" Perdita modestly replied from her seat with a disarming laugh.

"I beg your pardon: my *object*. I'm an aesthetic technician!"

"No offence, sir!"

"None taken, ever, or I wouldn't have lasted this long without a fatal duel."

They were both laughing. Never in the long history of Lyceum lectures had such a dialogue so enlivened the proceedings. Perdita, as a guest of charity, was too poor to frequent such gatherings. But most of the regular Members bridled with pride at their tolerance of her presence. There was even a scattered bit of spontaneous clapping, though perhaps not for either of the interlocutors.

[*Fay Gabriel is beaming as she glances aside to share her approval with Caleb Karcist, the escort she'd requested after Finn invited her to attend. She already knows Perdita Dana well enough to call her Deeta, and Macdane well enough to call him dear in private. I'm beginning to love that man, she says to herself with the quizzical surprise of old age.*

She squeezed Caleb's fingers. Dogtown was so full of amateur historians and local-lyrists that save for Fay he'd never have given up an evening of reading or writing to brave the icy darkness in his old kilroy to attend any lecture he could imagine to be of interest to him now so isolated from the public. But he was enchanted by the old man's analogies, hoping that Fay would soon volunteer an introduction to the apparently new companion of her long since self-sufficient widowhood. Not quite regretting the lack of a domestic hostess and dining room of his own, he wished he could afford to invite this oddly matched couple of wise heads to a long dinner at the Windmill. He'd have liked to ask them about a Peaceable Kingdom, *presumably the apex of a composite curve that subsumes lion befriended by gazelle. But maybe that chimeral composition was a problem of high-order nominalism only in traditional taxonomy, seeing that there's no such reification in the animal kingdom.*]

"Anyway," the lecturer went on, "you'll be glad to know that I really haven't forgotten that I was talking about Dogtown's fishing schooner! I'll not discuss the decadent phase of the naval architecture that followed its beautiful apex of success. With infernal consumption engines, electricity, and new devices for detecting gathering and depleting masses of prey belonging to no one but Mother Earth, the schooner's curve dropped like a broken wave, almost as obviously in industrial evolution as mill wheels. . . ." And so in technical detail Macdane proceeded to expatiate on that famous type, before it was necessarily superseded, as many historians of fishing technology had done before him without such abstract introductions.

Most of the audience he faced was bored or puzzled, indifferent both to the principles and the details of design that were generally overlooked in the familiar journalistic lore of schooner shipwrights and seamen. Though he finally abandoned the diagrammatic analogies of high school mathematics, few of Macdane's listeners betrayed any greater interest in the ingenious hull-shaping drawings used by the builders of sailing vessels, here offered as pictorial "illustrations."

[*Fay Gabriel's thoughts lingered with his earlier generalizations. We need not despair of everything at once just because of our democracy's degradation. It's always possible that the present wave of national politics may be short enough for me to live into a following cycle of hope, before the common good yields to an irreversible corruption of the whole Atlantean civilization, or until my senile mind, like poor Mary Tremont's, gives up resistance to things as they are. . . .*]

It wouldn't have occurred to any working fisherman, even if kept ashore by a stretch of weather too sloppy for dragging, to enter the posh Lyceum and attend the lecture of an old Norman stranger about the jealous past of skills his ilk had never shared. But a few retired skippers from the Master Mariner Rooms on Pleasure Street were nostalgic enough to sit anonymously among hoi aristoi just to listen for words that might revive inherited memories of their grandfathers' generations as a diversion from dreary Saturday afternoon devilvision without games to watch. Indeed they impassively warmed with vicarious pride as the Navy man put journalistic superficialities to shame in addressing the virtue and efficiency of Dogtown's best schooners as economical machines, thanks to versatile and brave laborers who could scarcely even imagine the comforts of Workers' Compensation or life insurance, not to mention retirement benefits. Macdane reminded them that the halibut investors had risked no more than their capital to profit from unpatented construction plans, costless motive power, free raw material, and the liability for excessively dangerous operations that was charged to God. Their crews, working on contingency (like Redburn's former square-rigged whalesmen from other ports), ventured their very selves in the hope of an anxiously variable net income, the subdivided returns of a mulcting market made by shameless dealers no less tricky than money-changers. The crew was assured of nothing but room and board at sea. Both capital and labor made gains or losses largely according to the variables of weather and the wisdom of the skipper. As Macdane put it, the one constant was the sailer they sailed in. But as he also pointed out, over generations that included disastrous years swept by loss of lives and replaceable property the fisheries and whaling had hauled millions of tons of oil and protein from the loins of Father Atlantic for civic sustenance and private wealth without a farmer's invest-ment or toil in husbandry and cultivation.

Most public gatherings in Dogtown still included men or women retired from Mercator-Steelyard's office or plant, the modern aspect of "seafood". Those here present took pride in the corporate business that had owned or financed those fleets of schooners. In the hardest of times the company had spent parsimo-niously on roadside signs and billboards from coast to coast adver-tising salt fish or canned, and especially its potato fishcake mixture cherished by wistful midwestern Scandinavians and others who still knew the function of an oar, long before electrically frozen seafood sophisticated the business. *Stock Your Pantry / With Fishcakes / From Mercator*!

So from among the many likened two-masted offshore fishing sailers in the days before auxiliary engines began to corrupt the design for perfectly valid economic reasons, Macdane chose as para-digm Mercator-Steelyard's *Gloucesterman*, still famous in decadent survival even only fifty years ago. He expatiated on that schooner in its prime as the culminating creation of her architect's career, an Irishman of both Galway and Skerries descent, born and bred into the Botolph waterfront forty years before Dogtown, then the busiest fishery in the world, had greater use for his skills than any other port on the international seaboard. Terry McMahon whittled out of solid wood a maquette of all his new curves before articulat-ing them in sufficient detail to drawings for the pattern-makers, continually refining scores of previous streamlines for the various purposes of fishing or racing. He was often imitated and always admired, even by the rancorously competitive fisherfolk of Acadia and Terra Nova who claimed they had the authentic nose for North Atlantic seacraft.

McMahon had also designed excellent yachts and pilot schooners, as evolutionary variations on his theories for the hulls and rigs of working fishermen, but in his plan for a highliner bearing

the name of this cape, after decades of thoroughly tested creative
experience, with ultimate adjustments of three-dimensional curves
and triangular or trapezial shapes, he conciliated more successfully
than any of his professional colleagues the conflicting demands of
speed, maneuverability, seaworthiness, safety, stability, deck-capacity
for dories, womb-capacity for hundreds of tons of iced or salted fish,
construction cost, maintenance serviceability, and amortized return
on investment [R O I]. The works of this pragmatic naval architect,
whose heart was more concerned than his capitalistic clients' with
the loss of life at sea (which was never covered by insurance, tort law,
or contractual responsibility), were masterpieces of commercial performance and profit. As a good Petrine, and as an independent professional, he had striven without piety to realize the common good
of his economic sector. *Gloucesterman*'s knockabout bow, with an
extended convex stem and no bowsprit, replaced the clipper-type's
lethally handsome "widow-maker", from which hundreds of men
handling the forward sails of ice-clothed schooners had been swept
away by seas as they were plunged deeper than the lines they clung
to. But most of his problematic innovations, visible only on the
stocks, were below the water line, a smooth symmetry of mathless
curves more subtle than the convex swelling in Greek columns.

". . . Many a schooner was 'fast and able'", Macdane continued,
"but to my knowledge none other was so effective for its purpose
before the electromechanical age of hunting and gathering. She was
so weatherly that even in sport, especially under one of Dogtown's
highliner captains tacking back and forth in a forty-knot gale of
wind with every sail aloft, she beat schooner yachts of her size that
were extravagantly built just to race Dogtown's deep-sea fishermen."

This populist remark brought sniggers of appreciation from the
moiety of audience stirred favorably for the first time. But his personal interest carried him too far into technology for the sympathy
of psychologists, merchants, bachelors of art, lawyers, dancers,
artists, eclectic aesthetes, spiritualists, bunnylovers, goo-goos,
sportsmen, or those who loathed the small-minded details of any
discipline. It was almost too difficult for them to grasp a definition
that he carefully read from his notes on the lectern: "This design was
an optimum set of compromises among conflicting requirements
that resulted in an order of functional satisfaction and its epiphenomenal beauty." He challenged their disapproval of his jargon, as if
tossing his gauntlet before a gang of patronizing feminists, but

paused with a grin that disarmed most of those who would not have forgiven any more of his intellectual self-indulgence.

"Mister . . . !"

In truth he was less than halfway through his intended lecture, but the widow Marina Laplace of Leviathan Court, for many years a formidable champion of fisherfolk and their livelihood, chose to pretend that the speaker was already signaling himself open to final questions from the floor. Her harsh cracked voice was favorably familiar to those who attended public meetings at the Hall, for it had admirably taken upon itself to organize and represent the workers' interests in the industry that employed most of the breadwinners in her Harbor Ward. She and a few unsubservient women of the Blessed Virgin parish had persuaded the wives and daughters of the whole city's remaining Lusitanian and Yankee or Irish fishermen to join their vociferous Tuscan sodality to make it into a melted pot of victuals in speaking up for the inarticulate and disunited men of the fishery, petty proprietors and ununionized employees alike—in effect to bait them into horizontal as well as vertical unity for political purposes. She had led busloads of her indomitable sorority as far away as Washington to lobby for an inalienable birthright they claimed for the same commons that was once exploited by St Peter and his brothers. With this experience in leadership and public speaking she had long since overcome any scruple she might have felt against loudly interrupting the opinions of a superannuated stranger with what seemed a pretense to some constituency. She made no bones about her impatience with condescending gentry. Deeta had seemed genteel by comparison.

"We know you're a World War Two Navy man that has sailed a yacht of your own, and all that, but what do you know about fishing—like what the men had to do in the dories? Or what they have to do nowadays, which ain't no picnic neither!"

Except for a few hillside residents of East Harbor (which included Fay's leafy highland), who increasingly protested downwind stinks from the obsolescent rendering plant on the smelly Fish Pier where gurry was cooked into fish-oil and fish-meal for off-island transport, almost all citizens (both indigenes and incomers) extolled the fishing industry, even if only as the picturesque nucleus of attraction for pilgrims and the "needle trades" that served them. Most of the infamous stink from fish-processing was

now so abated by regulatory engineering that it was lost in the naturally tang odors of barnacled rocks and tides that usually blended
quite pleasantly with the cheerful sounds of waterfront industry.
But more than a few with interests in the fishery—personal, financial, political, or simply patriotic—were not sorry that the aging
Mrs Laplace was gradually being superseded by her intelligent and
eloquent vice-president of the ladies' sodality that stood in behalf of
its menfolk who did the actual fishing but may not have expressed
rational criticism and political demand for economic justice.

It was understood that the much younger new leader, Fiorina,
had been too busy as a housewife in the domestic tradition of
Tuscan gourmands to spare time for educational lectures irrelevant
to her household or to the present problems of commercial fishing,
but she was immediately fetched to the inward eye of most of those
who now heard the voice of her crudely goodhearted mentor. The
absent Fiorina Sanseverino was now a sturdy matron greatly experienced in public affairs, more studious and tactful than Mrs Laplace,
more educated in diplomacy; above all she was a calmly coherent
advocate in both oral and written speech, the most lucid and balanced contributor of letters to the *Nous*, as well as the fishermen's
principal tactician as drafter and editor of numerous petitions,
manifestos, and press releases. Twenty years earlier Caleb had been
present at a Hall hearing when she'd spoken in public perhaps for
the first time.

At that time everyone had been astonished by the small slim
beauty and lovely voice of a twenty-year-old newly married immigrant from Trinacria who already spoke in nearly perfect English on
the mesh size of nets as a debatable matter of fishery regulation,
ostensibly in her husband's regrettable absence, which was lucky for
her cause because otherwise it would have had no competent
spokesman at the Earldermen's public hearing. Thus she became a
leader before she finished adult high school and grew into a stout
mother of four while pursuing Atlantean citizenship and learning
all she could about the ways and means of North Atlantean fishing,
constantly urging a consensus of rational self-interested response to
fish-conservation impositions of the government's scientists, who
were regarded by her electors as stupid tyrants. She was now the
portly half-owner and fiscal manager of her husband's steel dragger,
which was not surprisingly registered as the *Fiorina Star.* In gravitas
she'd matured to the figure of a stout matriarch, hardly recognizable by one who'd seen her only in her youth. Never would she have

been so impolitic as to challenge a quizzical old gentleman for no practical reason. A number of her admirers thought she would someday become Dogtown's first female mayor, since mayors according to the older charter had no more power than that of presiding over fellow Earls.

But Macdane was equally answering Fiorina's elder, Marina the battleaxe: "I know that even today it's the most dangerous occupation in the country. But my usual playground wasn't this harbor. I did sign on a few schooner trips from here when I was a boy, and I took my turn at hand, reef, and steer. They even made me mainmastheadman before I had to go back to school. By God, I thought I was as good as Jack Chase! But not in winter, I admit. And it's true that I wasn't born in a dory, or even in Vinland. In fact, I didn't like trawling or seining. I had no objection to gutting and cleaning fish that were already dead, and I could bring myself to cut out cod tongues like scalps to tally my body-count, but I hated to bash to death the head of a live sixty-pound halibut and gaff it aboard, or to tear the hook out of a writhing haddock's eye. Still, when I eat fish I don't stop to think about how it gets to my plate, any more than I like to remind myself of the slaughterhouse when I eat beef. But at least fishermen don't first nurture and then betray victims as trusting as heifers on a Grecian urn! Fish is my regular protein, and I wear cowhide on my feet. But to this day I can't bear to see the death-throes of mackerel gasping and flopping in a kid's bucket on the pier when it's still struggling for liberty as the way back to life twenty minutes after it's been jerked up by its lips into a ghastly void. They say fish don't have feelings like us mammals but that's hard for me to believe. I'm afraid I haven't the guts to be a fisherman or a meatpacker. I'm not moralistic about it—just not as tough as I should be. That's why I'm personally not up to fishing even for brook trout. Nietzsche went mad attempting to save a street horse from a beating by its master. (For that matter, Mohammed cut away the cloth of his robe even to avoid disturbance of a sleeping cat!) I prefer to dwell upon inanimate things like iron horses that are said to feel no pain at all!

"Anyway," he smiled, "as Pascal said, 'The heart has its reasons of which the reason knows nothing.'"

The callous menfolk who took these candid remarks at face value wondered what kind of sissy this geezer had been in his youth, while the squeamish sensibilities of genteel women, to whom such adversions seemed gratuitously inappropriate, were

indefinitely irritated. Those of both genders who defensively interpreted his remarks as patronizing "sarcasm" meant to demean their
own kith and kin reacted with tight-lipped anger. But people like
Fay and Caleb were sympathetically affected by what they understood as the speaker's wryly ironic confession of anima.

[*Caleb tried to imagine Macdane saying as much to his peers during
the War, for he himself had always been too cowardly to betray his own
compassion at Boy Scout camp, or on the Dutchkill School farm where he
contrived to be working in the cowbarn or in the woods (or with books in the
study hall) when chickens or sometimes a pig were being slaughtered. He
wondered about Macdane's sympathy with live bait or snakes, or even with
a minuscule lonesome household ant suddenly swept to its inconceivable
death by the flooding swirl of a kitchen sink. On the other hand, that
thought brought to mind how grateful he and his mother were when a fisherman tossed her a dead haddock from his boat at the Botolph Fish Pier, to
which they had occasionally traveled as suppliant mimes because there was
nothing much to eat at home in Unabridge. Often she squandered transit
fares on adventurous travel that might mutely or humorously serve the function of begging as well as recreational excitement. Nearby on that waterfront they'd sometimes glean bananas when ships from Central Atlantis
were unloading on conveyor belts the fruit of private-enterprise colonialism.
(Beware tarantulas!)*

*Fish and bananas were cheap enough, but at the age of four in
Unabridge he understood that only rich kids had any money of their own.
F D R's Federal Writers Project was at that time his mother's latest economic hope—when Dogtown was for him only a frequent allusion on her
lips, associated with the dog he longed for in a picture book, before he could
remember seeing his native place for the first time—at Sacrum Square:
brick walls, cobbled streets, and a gray slice of the inner harbor, all open to
pungent tidal air much fresher than the fish-stink of a sheltered Botolph
pier.*]

Disorder threatened the hall's comity already disquieted. Even
the meek were almost emboldened to raise their hands for permission to speak. But one of the women touched by Macdane's confession was Tessa Opsimath whose husband Rafe happened to be at
her side for the first time at a Lyceum lecture. He had never been
captivated by Dogtown's local historical cult (as he called it),
though as a Norman investor of twenty years' standing he loved its
physical and commercial geography. Usually he spent the Saturday
afternoons of winter poking around the office and floor of his factory, when things were otherwise nearly deserted, often reminding

himself of interesting conversations with his late partner, Buck Barebones, Tessa's first husband, at such illuminating moments of industrial inactivity. His shop was still fabricating small machines on parts which that inventive genius of Dogtown Machine & Design Corporation had designed to meet and stimulate the market for stationary energy-exchangers. It was the "steamer" in Macdane's announced lecture title that had weakened Rafe's resistance to Tessa's request for his company at the Lyceum, so now in disgust at the disquieting manner in which the lecturer had been received, and embarrassed for the Lyceum on whose board she served, Tessa took advantage of Rafe's presence as an amiable and generally respected employer by nudging him to the speaker's relief. "Say something, Rafe!" she whispered. "Don't let women do all the talking! Make them apologize!"

Rafe, impatiently awaiting the forthcoming steamer half of Macdane's disquisition, was nothing loathe to put off the confusion with a conundrum of his own. Standing up to be seen and heard on all sides, he spoke in genial tone. "'A tear is an intellectual thing', as William Blake said. No man needs defend it. But I will have questions about your second classic. In case you're pressed for time, please don't drop part two!"

"Hear, hear!" called Huck Salter, lobsterboating sculptor from Pigeonhole Cove. "I am inured by my trade to pity for crustaceans, though not for mammals. But I'm eager to hear a sensitive man get to his talk about steamers!" *Steamers* briefly added to cognitive confusion because on the Cape it commonly meant steamed clams, which are bivalves but not crustaceans, and almost everybody's holiday treat. Huck was definitely seconded by grunts of approval from a number of other men in the audience. The bold ladies sat back in silence.

Yet this contretemps in the "sailer" discussion was as nothing compared with those about to worry the contrapuntal half of Commander Macdane's address. The majority was partly acculturated to secular relaxation of protocol in the sacred museum of polished floors and gold-framed paintings of the respectable past. Since the heckling had admitted a personal tone, however, the proceedings grew more civil, at lower pitches of interrogation, especially on the part of those who reminded themselves that they were likely to encounter the puzzling ancient face-to-face elsewhere in town.

[Tessa was already intrigued by this energetic man (no longer regarded as old) as a psychological enigma. *What could he have been doing as a technocratic sea-warrior forty years ago? Later, under casual interrogation when we met him at Fay's dinner party, he told us that he'd been known even among Reservists as a "non-reg" officer. Some of these present people would have more misgivings, she thought, if they knew his patriotism was non-militaristic even before our last undeclared war; but thank God we live where at least half the Crats would be pleased to know that much about him. He reminded me of good old "premature antifascists", who were no pacifists when it came to Hitler. He's as Euro-centric and cosmopolitan as Monsieur Voltaire, and has all the visible earmarks of having been bred by privately honorable Cans! I'm glad he and Fay have gotten acquainted. I hope it's not too late for them to have some fun together, if they ever synchronize their respites from reading, writing, or arithmetic. Fay seems especially excited by some new thoughts that she doesn't want to talk about. Half her house is a library, but I wonder if he has much to do with her kind of books. I hope to get to see his eyrie one of these days. More and more I find aged people fascinating—not for their wisdom but for their experience, if you can only get them to talk about it! I should have studied gerontology when Auto Drang was still around to suggest a special theory about it! . . . The next party will be mine . . . if that pair of ancients isn't too busy!*]

Those of speculative habit whose minds were not exclusively local probably expected Macdane to resume with something like an encomium of transatlantic ocean liners like the British *Queens*. Among others semiconscious of suspense, Caleb anticipated mention of such giant articulated 4-8-8-4 four-cylinder high-pressure locomotives as the beautiful Behemoth of the old Federal Pacific freight line. But except for president Frank Bacon, only the Mayor (veteran of L S Ts) guessed some of what was coming.

"I sing of arms, not man."

[*Though Fay almost laughed aloud at this announcement, it was not without a twinge of moral alarm. Her apprehension on behalf of the non-reg warrior was soon justified.*]

"Everyone on this cape except a *Nous* reporter knows that in the taxonomy of vessels that exclude rather than contain water, a schooner is not a ship and not a boat, nor just any sail-propelled watercraft, and especially not simply one with two masts. And a Dogtown fishing schooner is our special case among those of other size, shape, or function. But I suspect that many in Gloucester County—notably editors—do not know what's known by every child in New Port Newce Parthenia, which is not as fishy as Dogtown but very very salty and quite as old: that a battleship is not just any warship. My classic *steamer* is the *USS New Guernsey.* The Big G, BB62, is one of four sisters, all now out of commission, though still available for resuscitation before they get put to permanent rest as museums or scrap metal.

"She's a thousand times heavier than *Gloucesterman*, infinitely more powerful, and at any time twice as fast as the schooner could be on the rarest most favorable occasion for sails. Even the equally precipitous superannuation of steam locomotives by dieselized railroads has been less absolute, seeing that some puffingbillies are still serving on other continents, and even a few remain in our Hannah coal country. But whatever auxiliary service the *Guernsey* sisters may still render in renovated old age, before mummification or dismemberment, the generic history of battleships is as closed as the history of square-rigged heavy frigates represented by the *Federalist*— sister-ship of Redburn's *Atlantis*—still afloat down the line at the late lamented Charlesmouth Navy Yard. . . ."

He openly warmed to this heartfelt 19C transitional digression, using neither notes nor slides. ". . . She's still rigged with all her topside complexity, which makes it obvious that our comparatively simple schooner—no more than a fifth as large—was her superior in beating to the windward. From the highway bridge you've all seen her a hundred times, the world's oldest warship still in commission, restored to her original features for the sake of sentiment and scholarship at a plaza of gray granite space for noble buildings, parade ground, and drydock; but no longer more relevant to warfare than the museum of a national park—such at least as has been left of the nation's naval arsenal on a preciously deep waterfront by the irreversible development of opulent residential reality-estate that obstructs most of your view and lays waste irredeemable wharfage. The *Atlantis* was already obsolete when Jack Chase was captain of her sister-ship's main-top, assisted by Redburn, a hundred and forty years ago; and since then she's been nearly put out of her misery two or three times; but it's as exciting to board the reincarnated ghost of her 1812 prime as to—well, as it will be to board the *New Guernsey*, or a sister, twenty years from now, if she's still afloat at another decommissioned navy yard."

Macdane returned to his prepared matter. "At least half of culture is technology, whether pottery, knitting, church organs, kilroys, or computers—of course all kinds of watercraft, fabrics, and machinery. In the narrow band of culture under discussion here the frigate is an example of types that stand between the fishing

schooner and battleship (which now leads to the aircraft carrier).
All three displace salt water equal to themselves in weight. In
greatly differing proportions they all three have mechanical devices
operated by manpower; but only one of them is primarily propelled
and controlled by fueled machinery. At the peak of its evolution the
battleship is a masterpiece of socially organized manufacturing and
human self-discipline, a dynamically integrated megamachine . . .
something like a walled city of some self-propelled island with a
towered castle at its summit. . . ."

He then speedily consumed ten minutes on manifold details of
his most modern battleship, which for the most part was utterly
uninteresting if not repugnant even to almost every patron of an
institution whose local historical museum has been devoted to arts
and artifacts mainly nautical in ambience. As far as public rapport
was concerned, Macdane might as well have been lecturing on
Sumerian ruins. Those not bored were likely to bristle with hostility
at what they took as outmoded dyed-in-the-wool militarism. In sum:

Big guns were more accurate (as well as longer-range and more
destructive) than smaller ones. Nine sixteen-inch diameter cannon,
charged with ton-and-a quarter shells, focus on visible or invisible
enemies as far as twenty miles away, their firing usually directed
broadside in thunderously flaming harmony by a central analog
computer under the control of an officer by cybernetic means,
taking into consideration the pitch and roll of the ship, its gyroscopic course and speed relative to the moving or stationary target,
as well as atmospheric pressure, temperature, humidity, and geodetic positions (corrected for rotation and curvature of the earth)—
all automatically integrated with servomechanical indications of
the three turrets' detailed responses to the ship's fire-control system
of optical range-finders, three kinds of radar, and topside or air-
borne human observers who fed back corrections of range or bearing according to their estimated degree of accuracy in immediately
previous salvos. Dozens of smaller antiaircraft and dual-purpose
guns, primarily for defense, are also commanded with somewhat
less complex automatic computation by another fire-control officer
in an armored tower.

All such armament is protected by a five-hundred-foot internally armored vault of munitions and people. This heavily armored
space within the outer armor of the hull, as secure as possible from
enemy guns, torpedoes, and bombs, sheltered not only the ship's
supply of projectiles but also its defensive vital organs: steam boilers

and turbines for propulsion and the generation of electricity; auxiliary (for damage control) diesel generators for hydraulic steering, winches, capstans, and other machinery; redundant power supply systems for interior and exterior lighting, searchlights, communications, and all electronic devices for navigation and fire-control, as well as energy for the heating, ventilating, air-conditioning, desalinating water, cooking, refrigeration, and cinematic entertainment for a communal hierarchy of as many as three thousand temporary celibates—officers, artisans, and seamen—and for all other requirements inside or outside the ten thousand tons of inner shielding. This nearly impenetrable core, plus thirty-five thousand tons more of the ship's outer walls forward, abaft, abeam, and aloft, is buoyed, weatherproofed, domiciled, fed, and supported by a finely modeled high-speed mostly double-lined hull nearly nine hundred feet long yet slim enough to negotiate the locks between Atlantic and Pacific with a foot to spare on each side. Most of the ship's functions are as well as possible duplicated in separated compartments or conduits to provide for survival under successively damaging attacks. At a quarter of a million horsepower the whole fully loaded ship, with all its functions in operation under normally varied sea conditions, can plow through fifty-six thousand tons of undulant ocean to a depth of thirty-six feet at speeds up to nearly forty miles an hour, propelled from the stern by the brine's dense resistance to four propellers, two four-bladed screw-wheels over eighteen feet in diameter and two five-bladed ones nearly as large, turning steadily day and night like a garden of bronzed Venn flowers—for nine thousand miles if necessary (or thirty thousand at half-speed), unless that self-sufficient endurance is lessened underway by the bilateral duty to refuel smaller ships in its task force, port and starboard. . . .

At this climax of specifications Macdane bent over his notes in the dim light of the lectern to read his next sentence with the definitive care of a Scholastic theologian. "Then let's say this battleship is an intermittently independent nautical vessel of extreme size and power, a social system of highly complex artificial force and defense, controlled by disciplined technicians primarily to transport for potential or actual projection the chemical force of explosives. As a steady-state open system it can cruise for months at a time without subsuming itself to the larger social systems of a nation." He looked up with a grin of abstractive triumph over his own megalomaniacal didacticism, meaning to express his sympathy with the impatience of his audience.

[*Caleb remembered that he had been classified by his mother as a preco-cious megalomaniac when he excitedly admired the long high brick walls of the Army's mammoth Arsenal in Quinobequin Falls while on a streetcar trip to buy him a pair of factory-reject sneakers at a rubber manufacturer's retail store. Macdane's incorporation of a battleship's alimentary system at sea (distilling its potable water from the infinite supplies of its environ-ment) with its participation in the Navy's total world when being supplied or repaired in harbor or dockyard, drew an adult Caleb's ever-alert para-digm to concepts of the so-called Universal Systems Theory [U S T] of Ludwig von Denthey—who often seemed to illustrate many ideas in his own amateur web of theories!*]

Most faces remaining at the lecture remained impassive or deepened in frowns. Abstraction was less tolerable than loquacity. ". . . But a ship of this magnitude, even in old age, is too great an investment by the nation to be written off as long as it's still useful enough to justify its maintenance and minor alteration as the last of its kind. Especially for the fire-control of guns and missiles, capital ships are successively refitted with improved electronic devices for 'command and control'—navigation, detection, communication, and coordination—much of which the original naval architecture had not anticipated. Thanks to the plasticity of torched and welded steel many topside changes had been made within the characteristic profile of the *Guernsey* as she was designed before the War. I choose the year 1945 as the benchmark state of her silhouette, before sub-chemical explosives had to be considered, or ballistic missiles as their vectors—before peacetime economies and the changing expec-tations of naval strategy put an end to battleship evolution.

"Yet until the last of the species is absolutely extinct and they are scrapped, the tactical function of these fast and mighty individ-ual ships is being redefined as the headquarters of the modern task force. There is no longer any question of fighting its opponents' class of ship in traditional line-of-battle formation. Aircraft carriers, though extremely vulnerable, have become the main offensive means (except for the ultimately strategic intercontinental weapons of naval Entropy-war launched by E-powered submarines, which are now as large as cruisers). But the air-power zealots were mis-taken to pronounce the premature death of battleships themselves instead of their obsolete functions. In the last couple of years of the War, and subsequently, these few fast battleships were each very effectively assigned to command the defense or shore-bombardment as the highly flexible task forces that had replaced concentrated fleets of surface-fighting capital ships. And even today, ironically, the Marines are calling for the *Guernsey* to be converted to a so-called heavy assault or commando ship to support fast *amphibious* expeditions. Fast battleships, if active at all, are like beautiful but depopulated cities at the mercy of Civic Instauration planning boards. . . ."

Susurration of lips, twitching of extremities, impatient faces searching out each other. Who in the world nominated this man for us?

". . . But I'm not here to discuss the decadence of my model. Someday there'll probably be an entirely new surface type just as large and fast as the *Guernsey*, perhaps a sort of command-and-control cruiser with all sorts of new weapons and defenses. Electronic equipment and rocketry especially need new means of protection. The Bureau of Ships is always under pressure to add more weight for advanced inventions, every one of which requires more space and more electricity—"

"Captain Toby—" Deeta called from the dim depths.

"Unless you're mocking me, please, again: I was only a wartime captain in a vast institution of flag officers. I never had the independent authority of a Dogtown highliner captain. In the Regular Navy even a captain is beneath the College of Cardinals. When I retired I was only a Commander in the Reserve."

"Well, what did you command?"

"The closest I got to a *sea* command was in tours as executive officer of first a destroyer and then a cruiser. Most of my time in the service, by choice, was staff duty or more specialized work on temporary detached duty."

"Then—"

But this time he impatiently turned aside her softspoken harassment, raising his voice as he continued, demonstrating that he was at any rate the officer of the deck; so Deeta allowed herself to be silenced.

"'Of all fabricks a ship is the most excellent.' John Smith said, an international soldier of land and sea, who happened to be one of Cape Gloucester's most enthusiastic admirers, just from an offshore look!" Macdane was now pacing in front of two contrasting photographs. "By the same token, a couple of centuries later, John Ruskin, the great aesthete of painting and architecture, wrote: 'Taken all in all, a ship-of-the-line is the most honorable thing that man, as a gregarious animal, has produced.' Now, after another hundred years, imagine my beautiful sail*ers* side by side as classic masterpieces separated by time and space in the sea they shared. Like Smith's and Ruskin's models, neither of these species will ever regenerate. Their purposes will be achieved by new forms of function that perpetuate few of their former genes.

"Even twenty years ago in the Mother's Neck boatyard one could still see an occasional wooden dragger hauled up for caulking seams that may have been new when diesel-powered hulls were still being built under the preconscious influence of *Gloucesterman's* lines. They still retained the stubs of schooner masts for rigging vestigial sails used only to steady the steering or to save a bit of downwind fuel. A decade from now, forty-five years past its own consonance with the times, the battleship species will have no more influence on warship design than that of fishing schooners on the design of fast catamaran ferries. The *Guernsey's* elementary complications, its weight of projective and defensive equipment, its organization of managers and artificers, have already begun to seem to young navy officers as outmoded in purpose as the heavily gunned square-rigged frigate of 1812 seemed to their predecessors in 1945. . . .

[*Now even Fay was beginning to fear that her friend's cathexis would suggest, at least to women in the audience, the hobby-horse of a boy. It might seem a eulogy for instruments of force that she herself deplored. Schooners and battleships were too disparate to be worthy of comparative admiration. Would these people either approve or disapprove of him as a callow bird of prey? Indeed she asked herself if there was still something for her to acknowledge in his personality. So late in life for disappointment, she thought, I try not to suspect that like most other men he's never quite reached maturity. . . . But why should he still be too innocent to conceal his immaturity? Dear God, make him cut this short!*]

". . . But I'm not here to compare warships of different eras. I am comparing civilian and military instruments of naval architecture within my own lifetime. Boy and man, I've admired them in action. I have no other claim to the attention of those who love a past masterpiece like *Gloucesterman* than my offering of some parallels of form to a slightly later masterpiece of contrasting genre. It's interesting to see how such distinctly different fabricks, so extremely different in function, size, and power, can be compared in terms worthy of both abstract and figurative art. I assume you already appreciate the beauty of a classic schooner, especially as you see her here just off Crow Point in a fair breeze, sailing on a lee rail, close-hauled under the flattened billow of every sail. Now look at *another kind of grace, the New Guernsey* shown here in profile under way at high speed in a task force on the raid to Mardi. . . ."

Even in far-fetched analogy Deeta's sympathizers now ignored the schooners too. This time one of her male allies roused ambiguous groans of rebuke, pro and con. "Don't you think our moral blunders in southeast Asia taught us not to glorify force?"

Macdane replied with an edge of asperity. "I dislike the noise of guns and deplore nationalistic patriotism. I'm no more militaristic than George Washington. I hate to crush the tiniest insect with foot or finger. But I admire a social megamachine when it is commanded and controlled to serve a nation's common good, as certainly the mobilization you mentioned was not. But nowadays our commercial fishing also is a matter of force. Relative to size, the boats are powerhouses as forceful as battleships. Increasingly empowered, increasingly informed, they will soon be bulldozing the bottom as they dragnet the ocean, unless they are regulated for the common good of the whole world. No less than for lumberjacks with the chainsaws, it's force in fishing that makes the profit. The more force the faster the power. Power is the sine qua non of Atlantean civilization, even when it's used to fill and cap bottles of Kaka-Koma on a production line, or to assemble DV sets. The history of World War Two is not glorification. Nor is the unsentimental history of fishing, which on the whole has been for Cape Gloucester's local common good. But I'm not talking about morality when I compare as aesthetic objects a fishing vessel entirely without mechanical or electrical energy to a warship in which mechanical and electrical energy are of the essence. Try to imagine that I'm praising a piece of abstract sculpture in this museum of paintings.

". . . Now it's a comparable pair of distant offshore profiles that you have here in this next pair of slides. To me they are both more organic, abstractly speaking, than architectonic. Socially speaking, they are both organizations. Their great difference in scale is not obvious in pictures of the same size, but in all of nature differences of size necessarily entail differences in the respective ratios of surface to volume and other measurement in each. *Gloucesterman* usually carried only about twenty sailors employed as fishermen (or fishermen employed as sailors) usually of the same town and nationality, who knew almost as much as the skipper about what was going on; whereas the *Guernsey*'s company of officers and crew, over a hundred times larger, was of widely various stock and came from all parts of the country, trained in scores of different skills for specialized duties that in action kept most of them ignorant of what was happening. In a study of the homological map between schooner and battleship there's no need to emphasize the starkly contrasting ends of the spectrum between simplicity and complexity, especially when you consider what's below the main deck as well as what's above it. (The social diversity of all U S Navy ships was actually increased and greatly improved after 1946 when racial segregation was prohibited for the first time since Mr Lincoln's war—much as the individual mind may correct itself slowly through varieties of experience.)

"But in different ways our two classics are both handsome above the water line. I sometimes envision them as animated insignia: one as a spread-winged osprey taking flight from her nest; the other as a leonine Viking Shepherd dog, couchant on a long sheer hull low in the water, his forepaws outstretched to the hawse pipes as far before him as his straight tail extends behind his folded haunches to its tip at the taffrail where its tuft is the seaplane crane bending forward like the reversed hook of a scorpioid gadfly. A central citadel comprising bridge and conning tower bear the foremast, dominating the lower mainmast to its rear, which looks like not much more than the bare pole of a ketch clamped to the after funnel just forward of the secondary gun-director platform and the third turret of the main battery, at about the relative position of the schooner's mainmast—whereas the schooner's foremast, though fully rigged, is secondary to its main and at a greater distance forward of the center, reversing the dominance. In such symmetric profile, driving with all sails tightly hauled, the schooner reminds me of a parading cat with elevated tail and hindquarters high; yet strangely enough, in silhouette, hull down on the horizon, especially when there's a mist, a schooner can be mistaken for a battleship! They both seem massed at a center of gravity beneath the apex of a single triangle, visually so well balanced on midship fulcrum that under certain conditions a distant eye can sometimes be temporarily misled as to which is the direction of their movement, which is still a minor advantage for warships. An abstract painter could formally conflate them in rendering superposed their architectural elevations.

"Still, of course, the two classics are a categorical and fundamental contrast, as reflected—as symbolized, in fact—by their differing aesthetic affects upon the eye of imagination. One vessel seems to glide the waves with a lift of wings, the other looks heavily snug in ploughing the swells—signifying for the one that wind is surface motive power, for the other that it makes its own atmospheric resistance, which is merely hindered or assisted by the vectored force of natural wind. One escapes her weight in search of food, the other devotes his specific gravity—".

"Ha! Now comes the prejudice of gender!" mocked Deeta, returning to the fray.

"—to force its deep way through an incompressible fluid. Density is one of the essential differences. Mass dispersed, mass compacted. Wood and steel. But lifted models out of the water and held in your fist they are both a pleasure: as uplifting as a longbow in your left hand and as satisfying as a nine-and-a-half pound M1 rifle balanced in your right. . . ." Macdane calmly paused to wait out the rustle of protest.

[*Caleb had been struck proud by the noble image of Ibi-Roy his sainted Viking Shepherd but now he was transported much further back to his wartime love of bearing a boy's side-arms. More than anyone else in his gang, he'd collected them, displayed them, worn and carried as many of them as possible in their dismounted cavalry exercises with Rough Rider bandoleers and other accoutrements among the trees and along the banks of the Pure Pond Reservoir in Unabridge. He had carved his M1 rifle from a long scrap of oak, tacking to it as the sling a belt from somebody's ash-can, and pretending it was as heavy as hardwood-mounted steel. He wore a pair of cowboy six-shooters, hip to hip. And how he longed for the equipoised density of a slim Luger pistol in his left hand to counterbalance the rifle as he led his men on reconnaissance through the woods, up hills and down through the brush! Shots were vocalized as guttural staccato. The emotion had nothing to do with killing.*]

". . . both have fine sharp bows—unimpeded by such blunt buoyancy at the stem as a frigate's (not to put too fine a point upon it)—though most of the time *Guernsey's* upturned sheer saves her fo'c'sle from getting as wet as *Gloucesterman's*, the driest of highliners. Yet when standing a battleship watch your sensations of seamotion were usually not much different, allowing for the vessels' respective lengths relative to the pattern of swells. In either case your own rhythm of consciousness immediately harmonizes with the respiration of the organism in which you are incorporated—except when it's simply too sloppy for a schooner to dive through shortwave whitecaps without the annoying jolts and shivers seldom felt in the inertia of a fast battleship's deliberate pitch and roll.

"However, save for desultory luffs of a sail and faintly creaking blocks in the rigging, *Gloucesterman* can run with the wind in blessed silence for hours a time if the water is all blue, whereas *Guernsey* is never at sea without at least an unobtrusive aural intimation of dynamism from engines and ventilators, and the multiple songs of automotion from flags, signal halyards, aerial wires, radar antennas, and all the stiff irregularities of surfaces exposed to weather. By the same token, although the schooner has more canvas and cordage (as well as fish) to affect the nose, I must admit that even out on deck forward of the funnels, at flank speed into the wind, the pure salty atmosphere of a battleship is faintly modulated by an organoleptic trace of paint and grease. But to a sail*or* like me, even when merely observing, both sail*ers*—in motion, if not in the ultimate action for which they exist—are supremely soothing to most of the senses and therefore comforting to the fevered brain. Maybe that's enough to justify the claim that both are beautiful, whether spread in line at sea with a few of their sisters, or racing, or showing the flag in the Strait of Gibraltar.

"—But of course cutting up a ton of half-dead fish on deck is not beautiful, and neither is the damage done by the ton of a high-explosive or armor-piercing shell that hits its target. As Lessing says, the beauty of animated reality is lost in any representation of agony at its culmination."

The voice of Huck Salter (lobsterman and sculptor) put an end to the brief pause allowed by the Commander for mutual reflection. "Did you ever serve in the *New Guernsey*, sir?", hoping for a comfortably personal reply. During the War Huck had been a Coast Guardsman. He loved all ships; and he loved most dogs because he'd been intimately paired with a Jewish Shepherd to guard some coastal beaches, until he had to part with that closest of friends in order to take advantage of his statutory benefits as an art-school veteran of the War by accepting his discharge.

"I was attached to the admiral's staff aboard her for a year or so, but never officially to the *Guernsey* herself." Macdane replied. "In a pinch I was sometimes asked to take a watch or battle station for some officer in the ship's complement. For a while I had been fire-control officer in one of the smaller new battleships. Anyway I already knew the *Guernsey* quite well because I had participated in her design before as well as after the keel was laid." At the moment he seemed to be striking critics and admirers alike with ambivalent awe.

Caleb was unequivocally impressed. During the War, before he went off to the Dutchkill School, he had aspired to a Navy uniform, and was considered precocious because of what he had taught himself about ships and airplanes. Now, more than thirty-five years later, there were many technical questions he wished he could have asked this battleship man; yet he knew that such an intervention would arouse a consensus of anger at any further delay of adjournment. But the speaker's leading adversary was not so scrupulous.

"We respect the insights of a gentleman and scholar," Deeta called out, "but I'm confused about nautical pronouns. Monstrous battleships with neuter names and masculine intentions are usually, though not always, referred to as feminine, while the inoffensive and nurturing schooner, also referred to as 'she', is Gloucester*man*! Surely there's more maternal instinct in a small schooner than in a huge battleship!"

Everyone was puzzled by her tone. Although she was known as Dogtown's native sybil she still hadn't learned to beware the local suspicion of "sarcasm" aroused by ambiguous or unfathomable utterance, or perhaps by sonnets, when unaccompanied by a stock facial mask or telltale accentuation. Her pleasant flat voice was neither ironic nor jolly. To the contrary, she expected to be excused for attempting to disarm the audience as well as the masculine butt of her pleasantry. But Macdane seemed to understand that she never yielded in her cryptic scorn of typically male locutions, which she no doubt associated with a "police state" incapable of recognizing "spiritual values". Yet it was Irish humor in Irindu blood that made her witchcraft attractive to intellectuals. Only a few humorless feminists in Deeta's faction were still nettled by whatever insensitivity they could detect in the lecture of a superannuated expert in the man's world that was being challenged at last. When it came to toleration of free expression, on a spectrographic scale, this congregation fell somewhere between that of a Latin mass and that at a Dogtown public hearing on some outrageous application for a neighborhood zoning variance.

Her interlocutor still took no personal offense at her sally. "In the German navy all ships had masculine pronouns, and seamen were called soldiers. One Atlantean captain I knew wished he'd been allowed to call his battleship '*he*' and refer to his seamen as soldiers. But I stick to tradition. Masculine grammar happens to have dominated our language, though of course men are notoriously inconsistent in their metaphors for women." The hesitant laughter at this outmoded pleasantry released some of the tension imposed by the nation's new linguistic etiquette. But amusement was more problematic as he continued. "If I were a person of the biologically fundamental sex, and a gentle reader, I would be amused by the irony of gender in language, where masculine pronouns often serve for the commonplace or the impersonal, while the feminine gender is likely to be reserved for the exceptional or the precious . . . !"

[*This is a man who cleaves to his own shape despite his regimented profession, thought Rafe Opsimath, stealing a glance at Tessa, whose tolerance of old mores was sometimes sorely tested by innocent male remarks, despite the jokes she made about the war between men and women as equally waged.*]

". . . In my technical writing I avoid the cowardly barbaric locutions *he or she* and *his or hers* that nowadays rough up smooth sentences merely for the sake of disclaiming insensitivity. I detest the *him or her* that begins to befoul even our most elegant rhetoric. What will poets do? I'd rather respect the reader's or listener's intelligence by making all personal pronouns feminine or neutral.

"But I am not educated in psychological or philological matters." he continued. "My specialty is electricity. So let me talk about that. It's the most Protean element in civilized technology, and therefore inexhaustible though generally overlooked as a mother-lode of analogy that should rival the metaphors of nature— even in poetry, certainly in prose. Aside from functions now performed by computers, the engineering science of electricity, magnetism, and electromechanism can represent gender and history, morphologically or in codes: more and less, yes and no; moody dissonance of phases; cooperation and resistance; attraction and repulsion; eagerness and reluctance; loathing and reciprocation; balance and disequilibrium; fluctuation and constancy; exhibition and inhibition; continuity and hiatus; work; power; energy; pressure and volume; force and resistance; action and reaction; melody and modulation; pitch and key; velocity and direction; distance and time; intensity and attenuation; repression and expression; storage and rationing; conservation and dissipation; saving and spending; principle and compromise; inclusion and exclusion; stability and oscillation; projection and feedback; mitigation and aggravation; multiplication and division; apportionment and equalization; tugging and pushing; hesitation and haste; sensitivity and tolerance; leading and lagging; discrimination and promiscuity; mixing and filtering;

and transformation of all sorts. In short, it's a physically symbolic system. If analogies and digits help you learn and think, you could do worse than acquaint yourself with the descriptive dynamics of electricity. . . ."

Fidgeting threatened to become endemic, but his momentum was inexorable.

". . . Yet the greatest difference between *Gloucesterman* and *Guernsey* is that the schooner, like a natural organism, has no electricity of her own. In the battleship, as in a city, almost everything requires electric power or control! The inhuman commodity of electricity has become nearly as vital to society as fresh water. Long before computers and devilvision it was the most versatile of energies; and even then it was the scientific culture's kinematic medium of representation—surely an undiscovered fount of analogy for poets who seek metaphor more precise than rhetorical!"

Thus in peroration he waxed reckless, with nothing to lose of the audience's sympathy, slyly quizzing it, goading to make what it wished of a fatuous geezer. The lights came on. Polite collective applause, weak and brief, died out aborning. But Caleb and Rafe and Huck and a few others, assisted by Dexter Keith as he rejoined Macdane in the forefront, persisted in wordless bravos long enough to ignite the majority's dawning reconsideration of what had been heard, though maybe only in tribute to the speaker's stubborn effort. But it was now the normal question-time, more opportunity for indecorous disputation. So the applause seemed merely parenthetical.

Tessa Opsimath was still embarrassed by the cool reception of his cranky tropes (which she didn't try to decipher entirely). She wanted to put a stop to the baiting by diverting the line of questions. If only for the Lyceum's sake the Commander's prestige was well worth saving from degradation. She had no doubt that her first husband the late Buck Barebones, a genius in mechanical analogy, would have appreciated this lecture, and she was now sure from the facial excitement of the second husband Rafe at her side that he was very glad his usually unescorted wife had dragged him there. (Tessa believed that even cultivated intelligent men much less involved than hers with the technology of civilization never entirely transcended their apparently innate fascination with dynamic artifacts.) She readily divined that at least Fay, the Mayor, and Frank Bacon would be grateful for an attempt to alleviate members' alarm at finding a worshipper of electromechanics in their Athenian sanctum—someone who might be in favor of oil-drilling on the offshore banks, or of permitting a recreational airport to be bulldozed and paved on the Purdeyville weald. She hoped that any comments she might elicit, for the ears of those to whom Macdane was no more perceptive than any condescending Georgio (Anglo-Saxon Pauline) incomer, would somewhat mollify feminists and pacifists. In rising from her chair to ask the first anticipated question, startling Rafe with her unbecoming alacrity, she trusted that Macdane could see her well enough to recognize a congenial acquaintance. But her clearly enunciated words flowed without haste.

"Commander Macdane, your evident integration of the so-called 'two worlds'— the sciences and humanities—brings to mind the problems of higher education that interest many parents and grandparents like me. If you don't mind, I'd be interested to know where and what you studied to prepare for your remarkable career. You mentioned having been a Reserve officer. But did you attend the U S Naval Academy before your war service? I remember it was still called a liberal arts college in those days."

"When I was a boy I always wanted to. But in my last couple of years at prep school I poured over three or four other college catalogs also and discovered that my reach would exceed my grasp—and that it always would, especially in those four most ambitious years of youth, when sports and other urges conflicted with an excessive course-load. Luckily I realized in time that the Academy curriculum, much to my regret, allowed too few electives. So I applied to Norumbega instead, and signed up for the Naval Reserve Officer Training Corps [N R O T C], which kept me very busy but better suited my interests, despite the psychic conflict between Engineering Science—my field of concentration, as the university called it—and the more liberal arts. Even the engineering wasn't specialized enough for a career in naval architecture, but at least it gave me the fundamental math and physics, and a chance to study some literature and foreign languages. I had to omit a lot of interesting courses in other departments but I always thought I'd have the time to really educate myself as a common reader. . . ."

When asked by Rafe he went on to explain that he'd had the advantage of a somewhat Classics background from school years, including a little Latin and less Greek. "I had five or six years of time for reading on active duty, before the Navy sent me back to Unabridge for graduate programs in electrical and marine engineering at V I P, where I squeezed in the naval architecture. But even on that side of the seesaw I had the advantage of having been born practically on the ways of the Wight Ship Works in Markland, my first alma mater. ('Wight built is tight built' was the company motto in prose and rhyme. I hate to throw this in the face of Dogtown historians, but it's just up the Arrowsic River from where the first North Atlantean ship was built, before this cape was even a summer camp for salting and drying the catch of your fishermen.) So beware my bias, my prewar vintage, and my apparently dissonant penchants before you advise any young person as a warning."

Tessa may have succeeded in her wish to have the speaker prove he was no narrowminded militarist insensitive to the finer things in life; but she hadn't reckoned on the national protest joined by most so-called liberals (including herself) that persisted in reaction to the imperial presidency's futilely devastating war in Southeast Asia. She approved Deeta's effort to make amends with the Commander by suggesting common ground. "Aren't you proud of Norumbega for finally being honest enough to banish the N R O T C from its Garth of Veritas!"

But his reply was blunt. "No, I'm not. I'm disgusted at the faculty's lack of guts and common sense. More than ever the Navy needs as many 'Bega men as it can get. There are very few genuine liberal-arts colleges left. The Naval Academy at times has claimed to offer more of the humanities than any other engineering school, but now it's deliberately narrowing into technological professionalism. The Department of Offense seriously endangers the Republic's common good by filling the military hierarchy with poorly educated technicians nearly ignorant of international culture. Simply by attrition the officer corps is being purged of general education, critical thought, historical sensibility, and creative imagination, except insofar as these attributes survive by accidental selection of extraordinary individuals for the Academy's faculty. The eventual unification of our military services was necessary and fairly successful, but one drawback is that they are now separated from the highest civilian authority by a centralized general staff in which bold dissent is seldom revealed to Congress. More than ever, not less, this country needs exceptionally well educated officers who are not only professionally competent as technicians and leaders but also capable of rising to flag rank and proving the long-term practical benefit of intellectual versatility at the Washington level. Alumni

of the Laurel Amphictyony and other universities should be as
strongly represented in the military as in government. To read well
is to master the ages: *Bene Legere Saecla Vincere* should be on the
national seal." He paused.

"Anyway, the Navy needs officers who have some acquaintance
with literature and the history of ideas—beyond the canon of Sun
Tzu, Thucydides, Machiavelli, Clausewitz, and Albert Thayer
Mahan—if it's going to benefit fully from its recent invitation to
gentlewomen. The abolitionists of college Reserve Officer Training
Corps are shamefully confused if they think we can best encourage
world peace by leaving our naval establishment solely in the hands
of golfing warriors. It was intellectual cowardice, if not sheer stupidity, for the Norumbega syndics to give in to the howling of self-
righteously immature students who intimidated an irresolute and
misguided faculty!"

"Then are we to take it that you'd like to start up the military
draft again?" Deeta challenged. "For Pax Atlantean, I suppose!"

"Yes, at least some program of universal public service for men
and women, not necessarily military, but run by government,
defined as 'the institutional form of the people's power'. A democratic kind of youth-discipline for the common good. Not many
boys and girls have the advantageous experience of Scout camps in
the summer. Or of any other obligatory cooperation under rudiments of edifying discipline or mutual responsibility. They need
the discipline and pleasure of close-order drill even as they also
need the capabilities of independence in involuntary rigor on a par
with the autonomy of both solitary and cooperative dory-fishing:
"Pull every pound—and an ounce more!".

"You want everybody conditioned by T-square and sliderule!"
Deeta gently chaffed.

"T-squares don't draw curves and sliderules can't add anything
but logarithms." he replied with a laugh. "Civilization can begin
without design or calculation, but not without regulation, and regulation can't last without personal discipline of some kind, and discipline is the intuitional foundation of self-control, which is a basic
requirement of a decently free society. All this need not be any
more tyrannical than social agreement on the rule of law or a
scheme for keeping time without behavioral regimentation. —But
I suppose most anthropologists would quarrel with that last sentence!" [*Down in the first row, where he had asked Fay to sit, she caught
his glancing grin at her as he gathered up his papers, preparing to nod at*

whatever appreciation of his efforts might be expressed by the faces and hands about to be released from his homily.]

This closing effrontery to the Zeitgeist, following his various remarks that were probably regarded as inconsistent, gave further pause to both the Left and the Right. Some liked the difficulty of classifying him, but others were annoyed by that especially. Most were left puzzled by implications that pleased the few.

But the Mayor lost not a moment to forestall further embarrassment by cueing some decent applause with his own clapping even as he took center stage to shake hands and heartily thank the speaker for a truly memorable presentation that lacked only a tribute to the vast class of L S Ts, allowing no pause before his valedictory announcement of wine and cheese laid out in another room. In a spontaneous babble that drowned out the scrapes and squeaks of folding chairs a dozen or so people hastened to surround the speaker as he descended to the floor. Almost all the rest pressed noisily for the double doors that opened upon a table far too short and dainty for more than three or four raveners at a time.

Tessa was piqued by Finn Macdane's ruthless coda, but Fay, who liked to call him her Friendly Fenian, was only a little surprised by his impolitic candor. But as she awaited dispersal of the small cluster around him on the floor nearby so that she could introduce Caleb to him without competition, her thoughts returned with amusement to a modest omission in his reply to Deeta's question about a sea-command in his career.

*

Before Finn's sermon Fay had been aware from tête-à-têtes that he'd liked parade-ground drill and his college courses in naval science, had sailed with pleasure on summer training cruises, and had always savored the ritualistic routines of active sea duty that followed. He'd loved the ships he served in, even when he did not love all his colleagues or superiors, and had easily accustomed himself to most of the nautical ceremony largely derived from British Navy tradition (even unto ceremonial swords), though wincing whenever Holyrood's commercialized patriotism such as the strident vocalism of "God Bless Atlantis" was officially imposed in postwar days. He'd been forced by his choice to miss the Academy's professional curriculum but was willing to accept the initial disadvantages of any young Ensign commissioned in the

Reserve, especially during the Depression, before F D R was well
begun in getting Congressional appropriations for more ships, and
when promotion was still very slow even for the regulars. But, she
deduced, he made up for that deficiency in traditional training (if
not in social equality with the wardroom aristocrats) in six years of
sea duty before he was billeted ashore to get advanced degrees in
marine and electrical engineering at the V I P, having seriously
committed himself to a professional future in the Navy modernized by Admiral Symes. There in Unabridge he'd joined a few
Academy men on similarly detached educational assignments at
V I P or Norumbega graduate schools, but others were married
and lived privately, like civilian students, while he contentedly
lodged in Bachelor Officers' Quarters overlooking alternately the
bow and the stern of the venerable *USS Federalist* moored and regularly turned about to keep its waterlogging in balance at the
Charlesmouth Navy Yard, to whose Commandant they all officially reported. In those days all the Navy's rope was still being
made in one of the massive gray Dogtown-granite buildings. The
other junior officers at the B O Q were either on the First Naval
District staff, mostly for shipyard duty, or as seagoing bachelors in
the District's flotilla of destroyers.

"I've never been in bed with a Commander before." Fay had
said when they were alone.

"Better than just another anthropologist, at least! I've read your
criticisms of Western culture."

"You've already disarmed most of my attack. You don't seem to
be a martinet. Did you ever command anything?"

"I did command a Pacific Island for a while after the war, when
I was a Captain. Got a lot of reading done to prepare for European
assignments, but not much else. Later they blew up the island with
an E-bomb. But I never commanded anything afloat except a tugboat: my adjunct responsibility while I was studying at V I P. A
two-striper playing part-time skipper. An old Chief Bos'n kept the
discipline and straw-bossed most of the jobs around Botolph
Harbor without me. I took over only on special offshore jobs or ceremonials. Besides being responsible for anything that might go
wrong I really wasn't needed to be much more than an inspector.
Stepped aboard once a day for a few minutes, if I was around at all,
for the most part just to confirm general orders and sign papers for
the Chief. This was the Navy's way of keeping me in a chain of
command lest I lose my bearings among all the civilian intellectu-

als up and down the banks of the Shawmut River! But the admirals knew I was more interested in designing ships than in a peacetime bluewater career.

"But my crew and I did love that steam tug. Always kept ready to go on short notice, whether or not I was available. My cocky destroyer friends thought tugs were very funny. One of them who was trying to learn German under my tutelage called me *Der Schlepper* for my pains. Soon I was known to everyone as Schlep Macdane!"

"I can read German but I don't know that word. Sounds Yiddish."

"Maybe it's Yiddish too. But it was standard High German generic for tugboat, or suchlike grunts who kept things moving on land or sea."

"I suppose it wasn't propitious for a future distinguished captain who'd retired with three rows of service ribbons, presidential citations, and a hard flat stomach."

"I've lost all my muscle mass, most of my hair, and half my hearing. Most of my skull is exposed and I can't read without my glasses. All that's obvious to everyone. My remaining dignity requires that you with a stomach to match are the only one in present place and time who must know of the disrespect I suffered then among my peers."

"Not peers, I'm sure, but purblind drinking companions!"

"Many of them were dead within ten years, but not from alcohol. And now I may be the only one left."

"Then your secrets are a privilege I shall cherish less jealously. But has any other woman called you Herr Schlepper?"

In the dark, to her surprise, she'd felt him blush. "Only one, forty-eight years ago, here in Dogtown. When you were sailing the Pacific with your husband."

"Of course it's none of my business." she sighed. His breathing was evident again. " —Anyway, who cares about muscle mass? I'm all skin and bones myself. But I haven't been this languid for years. The later in life the sweeter its unexpected beatitude! —It's still snowing. You've trapped me here. So far, nothing but plows to be heard on a Monday morning. But I suppose a cross-grained old whitehaired anthropologist must honor indigenous mores: I can't be seen coming out of a professional building right next to the police station in the middle of town until business hours are well under way. Felixity's going to be ravenously angry."

"It's good for a cat to get irregular meals, like any wild feline. After lunch I'll take you home. Right now I'll schlep some breakfast. Then I'll show you around my working abode up here—and the harbor view you couldn't see last night. It's an honor to have you see my private eyrie. It's taken months to get these renovations done. The contractor left it to the carpenters and their helpers to balk at my 'modernistic' plans. The electricians were sullen because I cared about details. Most of the public is unaware of my penthouse because so far I've left the floors of rented offices untouched. One of my tenant lawyers hints that he's very curious about what he can see of my roof from down on Scrod Street. I hope you don't disapprove of modern architecture."

"I don't object to Western conveniences for purposes of active hospitality. But that tiny East European elevator made me a bit uneasy."

"It passes every inspection with praise. I hardly ever use it myself."

"I'm still doubtful of your permanent magnetism but I admit the causality of your electrifying oscillations."

Silent tracings of his fingertips on the whitest of skin. Then: "You know, Professor, after a lifetime of Dogtown visits I'm certain, thanks to you, that I've found my right place as a finally settled marooner. I hope you'll keep me company among the indigenes. I hate talking about 'happiness', but a lovely Fayaway brings it on!"

"I'm not lovely. Don't forget that I'm trained not to be romantic in my roaming."

"Perhaps not for similar reasons we've both done enough traveling."

This time her silence. Then: "Next time I'll do the cooking, at my house. Your short beard is nice and soft." She rehearsed a sensual moan. "I think Felixity will like you. Did you have a beard when you were schlepping?"

"In the pre-war Navy! Don't be silly! It's taken the last twenty years to liberate these bristles."

"I don't think they could ever have been rebarbative."

"You're almost too learned by half. I rejoice in that!"

"I've been reading the play of the man I want you to meet."

"When? I think you said he's looking for a job."

"He is and he isn't. He'll be my equerry at your lecture. You remind me of the time I first rode with a boy in the rumble seat of a roadster, though then my debauchery was only digital. Right now it takes an effort to remember even my own children since then. Yours is the next turn for serious hospitality. This time you'll get a good look at my beautiful cat if you don't kick her off the bed. But I warn you I'm determined to sequester myself in the meantime and afterwards for private work that has nothing to do with undignified rejuvenation."

"You sound like a solo sailor."

After the Historical's odd sermon Fay Gabriel forgot her uneasiness about the masculine ideology of cause-and-effect, force, and cybernetics on Finn Macdane's part. She would not have denied that it became a consideration in the substance of her philosophy. She was charmed by her dory-mate's image of a battleship suckling little destroyers with fuel, port and starboard, without interrupting the forceful pursuit of an enemy who'd broken the peace.

4

THE ACTS OF GILGAMESH

Forescene

[Spoken by Flavius Josephus,
né Joseph ben Mattyahu he-Cohen]

Who knows how long Gilgamesh lived? There was at least one Gilgamesh on the historical list of Sumerian kings, but I mean the original hero of the epic. Was every tradition of his fate suppressed or lost? Or was his existence simply a demigod's story that had no ending? Anyway I was never satisfied with the comic conclusion of the play Herodotus wrote about him, of which here in Rome my chief collaborator discovered a copy unknown even to the author himself. Apollonious, the best amanuensis and foremost translator of my Aramaic, major domo in my Jewish Greek and Roman scriptorium, was at the time researching other things for me in Epaphroditus's library. I gave him free rein to study it because he was already interested in the attempts made by Berosus of Babylon, a priest of Baal—or Bel, or Bel-Marduk (originally Enlil)—to discover Oriental elements in our Hellenic culture. That emigrant to the island of Cos had been inspired by Mesopotamian allusions in the known works of Herodotus to write his own history of Chaldea. Without him your Elizabethans would never have heard of Pyramus and Thisbe. But even by Berosus the search for Sumerian theater was a lost cause.

With his usual gusto my Apollonius, though only a slave, dubbed himself Apollonius of Athens because he was enthralled by the epic poetry of the Alexandrian known as Apollonius of Rhodes, preferring that deracinated Panhellenist and his circumstantial details to the latterday imperialism of our august Virgil. He admired his namesake for a somewhat reactionary independence in bucking with a long narrative poem the skeptical scholars and literati who regarded that genre as outworn discursive and unsophisticated; for a practical knowledge of ships seamanship and geography; for a plain aversion to both allegorical rationalization and sheer fantasy; yet above all for the negative capability of accepting traditional myth in an age of reason, as if a new *logos* was wanted to generate the *muthos*! (His Muse was Euripides.) He was intrigued by the idea of Jason and his Argonauts as antecedent to the heroes in Homer.

In private familiarity I called my versatile assistant Apollo for short. I can blame him for introducing or not correcting the notorious statement in my History that Roman soldiers wore their swords on the left side. Eventually in the very first clause of my last will and testament I could do nothing less by way of benison than authorize, along with a gentlemanly endowment, his absolute manumission as a Roman citizen, in Athens or elsewhere.

Apollo was always pestering me with questions about who came before the Jews: "after all, Greeks came before Romans!". And why did the Jews (as well as the Chaldeans before and after them) lack a theater, considering their famous love of drama and talent for acting throughout the succeeding Roman world?

His dry aspersion was a jest about my reputation for dissimulation in the old country. (His awareness of how much my reputation depended upon his willing cooperation rendered him a little too bold, but even as a slave he was by no means antisemitic.) My Roman friends called me "Son of Herodotus", having known that historiographer as "the father of lies" simply because he respected Egyptian and Persian traditions. But the frank simulations that make theater have always been under suspicion among the Gentiles, from Plato to your Augustine and his northern epigones, even unto Nietzsche who redoubled the Jewish connection. Jewish malleability, says the latter, provides "a world-historical arrangement for the production of actors." Listen to him: "What good actor today is *not* a Jew? The Jew as a born 'man of letters', as the true master of the European press, also exercises his power by virtue of his histrionic gifts; for the man of letters is essentially an actor. . . ." How do you like that! Were the Jews histrionic in the Second Temple (with its Corinthian columns and Greek lyres)? In the Diaspora? In the ghettoes? In hiding among Hitler's Germans? Even in the camps with chimneys?

I was indeed introduced to the Palatine by a Jewish actor after my shipwreck, but what my Roman friends chaffed me about was as nothing compared to the excoriations I suffered from my own people, especially of course the Zealots. Before High Priest and Emperor, in Galilee and Jerusalem, as general and as diplomat, on the battlefield and in the lucubrations of solitude, I have defended the factious Jews against Gentiles and barbarians—and especially against themselves! Many were the times that my life came nearly to a bloody end on their behalf. Yet it was the Romans who rewarded my profane leadership of these their most troublesome rebels.

How quarrelsome and narrowminded the Jews seemed in the days of our war! There was always an unscrupulous opposition, and opposing oppositions to both government and oppositions, orthodox and heterodox. As priests they were at best men of principle with no sense of the logical fact that high principles may conflict with each other; as fighters they ignored the political forces confronting a governor; as politicians they hardly distinguished the different functions of infantry and cavalry, to say nothing of organization, supply, or engineering. It was left to me to improvise countermeasures against the world's most effective siege army, but their thanks for my necessarily limited successes were far more than decently limited.

In Jerusalem itself I became known to the next generation as a traitorous renegade Jew—an arrogant and brutal opportunist guilty of duplicity and cowardice, serving both sides of the same war! Then as historian of the campaigns I was called boastful self-serving and tendentious, and said to be as deceitful in my writing as shifty in my actions. I was execrated by my own people as at least half pagan—at bottom a trickster and turncoat in religion too! The tactful ones called me morally ambiguous, a Janus of piety and pragmatism. Such is often the misguided infamy of a prophet who risks his life in trying to prevent a maddened beast from eating its own flesh. There were times when God really did seem to move from the Jews to the Romans. I took upon myself a high responsibility for the survival of a religious nation confused about the will of God in its rebellion against the protective power of a comparatively tolerant regime. I had warned them that resistance was folly before I reluctantly tried to make the best of their revolution. At first in command, then in thankless mediation, I served my people with devotion and grief. Along with the pride of action, the will to power, and the weight of responsibility, I felt as a private man their pain of birth, joy of life, love of family, terror of violence, doubt of intellect, loss of Temple, comfort of synagogue, and the inevitability of extinction.

Though I honored the Pantheon for its civil power and the Acropolis for its pure art, and though I revered both their languages, I was always reserved in my acceptance of Greek philosophy and Roman values. Jewish critics accused me of spiritual insensitivity, but to the very end I was teased by tolerant Romans for my unswerving loyalty to the Law and the Prophets. That didn't prevent them from erecting in Rome itself a posthumous statue of Josephus the historian.

Yet this is not the place for self-justification. I have been a public man; knowing the world, I am content with my enduring fame as a problematic but essential scholar. Without me the children of Abraham would have been mostly overlooked in secular histories. Jews, Greeks, Romans, and even Christians (whose inchoate establishment I failed to notice in my time) have used my works for almost two thousand years, at least in default of others.

Three Emperors were my benefactors and friends. In honor of my valor and skill as a former enemy, in gratitude for my diplomatic services, in admiration of my sophisticated learning, they provided me with the comfort and leisure required for mature writing (though still smiling at my personal allegiance to the lost cause of their contumacious little province). I owed them an openminded employment of the good fortune they vouchsafed me. Hence my experimental sponsorship of an Athenian bondsman's synergetic imagination.

Of course Apollo the philologist failed to discover any oriental root of Western theater for which he could claim distinct influence. The initial tributaries of almost any creation are as distant and diverse as the Mississippi's. He found no rivers Missouri Ohio or Arkansas. Perhaps a Sumerian or Akkadian drama was illiterate, or systematically suppressed. Maybe it was obviated by the arrested development of ritual, or by a precipitate decadence of liturgy that omitted its final stages entirely. An anti-theatrical prejudice probably prevailed in Mesopotamia for theological reasons. (God desires loyalty, not sacrifice, says Hosea.) But the failure of Apollo's research only kindled an enthusiasm for fabrication. This is his one and only play, intended as a complement to that of Herodotus.

With pride and trepidation he surprised me with it as a birthday present about a year before I died. You know how it is with novice poets and playwrights: they crave the praise to match their efforts. But I never could praise without perusal. Much to my eternal regret, though I made a good effort to express my gratitude and respect, I was too antipathetic toward amateur creative writers to believe that reading it would be worth preemption of precious time in my work-dominated old age. I dreaded his inexperienced challenge to the classic rules of dramatic art. I feared to find heterodoxy and sacrilege. Despite a mounting sense of guilt for hurting his feelings I kept putting him off with apologetic promises of my attention—until it was too late! Then he couldn't expect me to read it on my deathbed. Yet he declined my offer to return the manuscript neatly copied and dedicated to me in his own hand, even lovingly illuminated with symbols we had studied together. With the first tears in my eyes for half a century I asked his forgiveness, and told him sincerely that I regretted not to have adopted him as my son.

But perhaps it was not such a bad thing that not long after I was gone the original script perished with him at sea on the way home to Athens. In anachronistic comparison it is more fictitious than the *Argonautika*.

He intended it to be performed by some company of mummers that had already staged Herodotus's play about the earlier life of Gilgamesh, adding a few self-explanatory roles and dropping others, as follows.

PERSONS AND MASKS

From former play
The Tower of Gilgamesh
In *Gloucestertide*

New characters
For The Acts of Gilgamesh
In *Gloucestermas*

Lil-Amin and Inanna
Widow 1
Widow 2
Rector (High Priest)
Optimate 1
Optimate 2
Gilgamesh
Norkid
Trooper 2
Eber
Engidu

Berosus
Urshanabi
Ziusudra
Mother of All
Melchizedek
Scout 1
Scout 2
Shepherd 1 (Dumuzi)
Shepherd 2 (Peleg)
Princess Enheduanna
Villagers

5

EQUINOCTIAL GOSSIP

[Extracts from the Diary of
Tessa Opsimath, March 1981]

*I*t's a wonder how I've kept the contents of my safe-deposit box so secret all these years. My very sister Cora and my dearest friend Gloria, not to mention my two husbands, who have known that I keep an armored cache at the bank, have always assumed it's for nothing but legal documents, jewelry, and sentimental keepsakes—whereas nothing I have of such triviality requires the large dimensions of storage that I visit out of their sight. Yesterday I went to sequester with my bulky trove the latest volume of this diary. It made me realize with private embarrassment that I may have been unconsciously reflecting the narcissistic pattern of Anima Nim, the mentor of my secretarial youth in Auto Drang's office, who later made herself notorious after he died by publishing unchallengeable confessions concerning him and others, having practiced professionally under his psychoanalytic aegis. But I'm glad to say that I have never imitated her style, content, imagination, or cute self-esteem. My friends say I'm too objective about everything. Few of my secrets are about myself.

But what's more remarkable than my accumulation of commonplace books is that neither Buck nor Rafe has ever suspected that I keep the current unfinished one in such a cycle of uncommonly secret places around the house that sometimes I find myself in a panic trying to remember where I have last hidden the damn thing. I certainly have neither the time nor the habits of a journal-writer. At times I've forgotten all about it for weeks at a time.

I taught myself to write small, and only when I think there's something that will remain interesting to me before I die. That's why there are so many lacunae separating the chunks of miscellaneous observation and seemingly random selections of people or events. Some day I may find the time and get up the courage to review the chronicle of my misapprehensions. Sometimes these musings have served merely as momentary relief from the jargon of psychiatric social work. I am obliged to produce quite enough of those documents for my official locked files of professional opinion about other people's subjectivity—cases which, by and large, are too uninteresting to reward all my part-time academic study during married motherhood and business management, not to mention my vigorous avocation as the Mummer Superior and Sister Economist of what led up to the ill-fated Stone Barn Theater. Much of that time might have been more altruistically directed to Party politics.

Now there's the monotony of most psychological types! I've always feared boredom. I've never succumbed to the threat for long, but I've often had to ward it off with unwholesome novelties. If it weren't for my all-too-sincere sense of noblesse oblige to the halt and the lame I'd probably take down my shingle and save the office rent I pay skipper Macdane, now that he owns the old First Vinland Bank building where I used to have my safe-deposit box. And if it weren't for Rafe's business here I'd make him take me to big cities the world around. He's still got some Paraclete stock to sell. But thanks to him, as it turns out, I needn't have sweated for a professional diploma as anchor to windward for a breadwinning widow.

Even Melly and Miley may never make an effort to see my uninhibited cogitations. I keep waiting for the verge of senility to decide the stipulations in my will. In default, our lawyer at the time will be directed to sink them, unopened, in a big gray canvas book-bag weighted with gold doubloons, a mile off Three Griefs Reef, chartering a drug-runner's boat to get there in the dark of the moon.

*

. . . As usual this weather is a more ominous prelude to spring than the usual disappointment. I have to look to my calendar for the equinox just as encouragement—not to the sky or temperature, not to renascent vegetation. Nowadays few of our citizens remember the distinctly local significance of March 21. It used to mark the slightly variable peak of clustered birth dates nine months after the summer solstice, especially in the Great Years of Gloucestermas, like 1934, when the fixed and movable feasts of summer and spring are closest to each other and justify extended Dionysia. Every sewing circle was alert to equinoctial birth dates recorded in the *Nous* birth notices and obituaries. Throughout the year, save in clubby gossiping, people refrained from asking each other about birthdays if they weren't volunteered or otherwise known to be innocent. I can only imagine how fisherfolk speculated about quarry folk when they gathered around the town pumps. Paraclete's introduction of the Pill for women, as well as other ethological liberations of body and soul, has considerably flattened the distribution curve of natal anniversaries.

Yet I always associate mourning doves or mention of the Holy Spirit—even that trademark—with the Pentecostal years (as I vaguely understand them) in which one novena is joined to another around the summer solstice to take in the feasts of John the Baptist, Saints Peter and Paul, the annual closing of governmental books, and even the celebration of Atlantean freedom from its mother's rule. Thus Paraclete, the commercial name of the stock that made Rafe rich enough to buy and reorganize Dogtown Machine & Design Corporation, often calls to mind the enigma of Caleb Karcist's origin, which has fascinated me, on and off, for twenty years, despite the fact that it's no more of my business than the two unsolved Seamark murders that his mother thought she'd solved (to her peril) nearly half a century back in Dogtown history. For a short time I was Caleb's occasional soi-disant voice-coach and half-intimate friend twenty years ago, before I had any idea of getting into the psychology business, but he's never been a psycho-client at my mercy. Even if I offered pro bono, he'd rather die than resort to a curate of souls. Still, I've never forgotten his embarrassment at having been born precisely on the twenty-first of March.

*

. . . Last night, thinking about my independent and self-sufficient kids, I was suddenly inspired by a flash worthy of genius! I don't understand why this idea had never struck me before. It resuscitates my abandoned ambition to attack what would have been the dismal chore of a full-fledged Master's thesis! My BU [Botolph University] course-work is done: all I need is a personal incentive to overcome by sheer self-indulgent excitement my contempt for dreary orthodoxy as well as my own intellectual sloth! Auto Drang will be my unnamed patron saint and Caleb Karcist will be the presumably repressed artist (or artist-manqué?), my anonymous client—more or less! I'll learn to disguise and extrapolate my anecdotal evidence in at least semi-psycho jargon! Not a whole fictive case history, of course, but maybe an attempt to apply Drang's theories of human freewill and the artist's immortality-motive—pretty radical in such a conservative Botolph University department—with plagiarized gossip as my research data! Win or lose, the battle will be fun! I think my growing boredom with social work will be dispelled at last!!

I'm as excited as Melly was when she got accepted to Wisteria—not *too* far from Mummy and Daddy at home!

*

. . . Whereas Fay Gabriel's maternal wing is apparently offered to shelter me (if I don't encroach upon her solitary time or abuse her kindness), I hope to make up for the loss of dear old Teddi Cibber as the wise and gentle mother I always wanted. It now occurs to me that I may solicit Fay's advisory collaboration. I hope anthropologists aren't too scientific to tolerate a gossip-monger's speculations. After all, when she was a nurse here, before Hitler's war, she did know Caleb's mother, who claimed her as an exceptionally close friend! I must think about how to broach the delicate subject of Caleb's genealogy, next chance I get. After all, to some degree Fay and I share an interest in his peculiar past. Glory Keith and I haven't discussed the Karcist question since she remarried as

Mrs Cotton. Maybe, now that past sensitivities have been some-what desensitized by the distance of time, I can insinuate the sub-ject back into our rambling chats on the phone. Even into my pri-vate encounters with Caleb himself—such a "man of mystery", as he says his mother used to call him until she lost her wits and died. I must reconstruct my visits to her nursing home when she was well into senility, once when I gave Caleb a ride into Botolph and asked to be introduced, and then when I'd drop in alone two or three times on a shopping trip.

*

. . . Rafe's not the least bit interested in history of any kind, not even in mine (unless he's feministically clever at concealing his curiosity). He makes fun of what he calls "the superstition of place" that most of us share. For him Dogtown is a place sufficiently defined by contemporary geography, sociology, psychology, com-merce, religion, and the arts (both practical and fine). He faithfully participates in the Turntable and the Chamber, and seems to be everybody's friend despite his privately professed scorn of stupidity. He regards Glory and all the other historians on this Cape as super-numerary hobbyists. He's touchingly nostalgic for *other* places that he has inhabited or glimpsed, but always as if they remain as they were at the time. By the same token I suppose I myself am not attentive to all contemporaneous aspects of time's evolution (as Caleb might put it!). But in my limited temporal world Rafe's taught me more than I've taught him in his arbitrary cross-sections of time. I think my love of him has continuously advanced on that human conveyor belt since I first met him in my kitchen as Buck's new friend. But we are wise not to go around as a yoked pair all the time. That matrimonial habit is the worst part of socializing in the provinces everywhere.

*

. . . Damn my luck! I've got to find another domestic scrub-woman! Money is no object, but I can't get a new one covered by DT M & D's [Dogtown Machine & Design] commercial health-care insurance plan without leaving a felonious audit trail that Rafe quite rightly would not countenance in his defense of the corpora-tion's legal integrity, to say nothing of my honor as the firm's official treasurer! So I'll have to pester all my friends for grapevine leads. I can't wait for Raygun's economic policy to inflate Dogtown's unemployment level. Without health insurance there's such a shortage of competent trustworthy help around here that ads in the *Nous* attract only unreliable or inexperienced characters. And I don't want a female so "overqualified" that she'll ferret out this hidden journal or else inveigle me into some unreliable intimacy that I'll live to regret. The trouble is that it's not a full-time job. I'll still do some of the housework—little as it is, and much as I hate most of it that's outside the kitchen. I'd rather mow the lawn or shovel snow.

*

. . . Rafe's away at a Metalworking Manufacturers convention in Lonestar. No doubt last night while he was disingenuously charming business Cans down there I was comforting myself with congenial Crats up here. A couple of days ago Fay had me over to a nice informal dinner party that included Caleb and Commander Finn Macdane—a rather surprising liberal in politics despite his wry loyalty to the Navy. Maybe because in his Markland youth he was noticed by F D R and on occasion favored by him thereafter. Judging only by his reminiscences, I'd say Finn's a little older than Fay. I haven't yet figured out how close a couple they are, but they seem quite relaxed together. He acts more like a co-host than a dinner guest. But it's stimulating to be with old people who are still interested in past present and future alike.

Caleb's ad hoc dinner partner, despite my instinctively reflexive competition for her unassigned seat at the table, was Belle Cingani, now an important but inconspicuous figure in local public affairs as editor of the *Nous*, whom I befriended (or was befriended by) when she was a cub. Her husband Dave Wilson, a veteran professional aviator, is absent on another of his chartered expeditions, this time I suppose in Dilmun, flying archeologists in search of Gilgamesh's double-bitted axe. She has been top dog at the *Nous* for several years now but I happen to know that she still writes (besides most of the editorials) the unsigned weekly column called "The Harmless Fly", which everyone reads for vicarious eavesdropping. I'm sure she has to omit a lot of what I'd like to know from what she hears on the wall. Apparently she and Caleb hadn't seen each other for quite a while, but they obviously took up right where they'd left off, laughingly and sotto voce, like a couple of mischief-makers at a class reunion making up for having drifted apart. I had twinges of jealousy, but I've liked her ever since she interviewed me about our Troika Arts Center when she was only an ambitious cub reporter. Everyone agrees that she has greatly improved the *Nous* while remaining as cheerfully unpretentious as ever. During her elevating career I've occasionally seen her in high heels but never with a powdered face. It looks as if the gamine incomer has hardly aged in all these years. I should take more advantage of her intelligence; she must have a fund of undocumented allegations in this city of curious sources.

The *Nous* probably has a morgue going back more than a few generations. Judging by *The New Uruk Testament*, a good newspaper is always collecting data in advance of significant obituaries, with provisional revisions as the subject's maturity approaches finality. The *Nous* can't maintain much proleptic filing, I presume, but impressively detailed obits sometimes appear almost before the corpse is cold, as in Buck's case (but of course with no mention of his dipsomania): a front-page column with flattering archival photo. Anyway a journalistic morgue, even if only for printed clippings, must be a lode of misleading but telltale clues to the past in such an oddly mingled town of aborigines and marooners. With every story a reporter should be thinking ahead—but how much more does Belle personally know or care to know about the private life of Caleb Karcist?

*

. . . The main problem is Caleb himself. Long ago, when he slightly confided in me (and I in him, about my merciful adultery with Rafe when dear Buck was still alive), he gave so much credit to his mother's joyful motto WOMEN ARE THE BETTER PEOPLE that he seemed incurious about the unknown half of his lineage—in fact he betrayed nothing but aversion to speculation about paternity. It stuck in his mind, when he was too young to know what it was all about, that some magazine had printed a long letter of hers headed "The Vanquishing American Female", in response to a famous provocative article called "The Vanishing American Male". When I knew him in the days before his absorption by the Yard his psyche sometimes seemed as matrilineal as the Salic Law was not. But he claimed "negative capability" as one of his few advantages in life, and made all sorts of jests about the square root of minus one as his middle initial. His evasiveness didn't really fool me, but on the other hand I never could get a fix upon his psychological type. Maybe he's still holding out for insoluble mystery, romantic or immaculate in conception!

I mocked him with words I'd learned in Yerba Buena when I once played Yeats's Jocasta: "May you never come to know who you are, unhappy man!"

"I'm not unhappy!" he laughed. "I haven't killed anybody." And thereupon he referred me to the *Ion* of Euripides. Maybe now it's finally time that I get around to looking for it. At least I'll ask Fay what she knows about it. He's always been full of allusions that only scholars understand.

I gather that before I met Mary Tremont, in her dotage at Derwent House, she joked about the question of seeding, invariably turning it aside with variations of boasting about her pride and joy in Caleb as the realization of her childhood plan for three children, a boy a girl and a boy. His evident success as a technocrat seems at odds with that weird toleration of mystery about the other half of his fertilized brain. If one were permitted to further analyze the composite child I might find a clue to chercher le homme! At this stage the scent is otherwise stone-cold. It's evident that as a diplomatically constrained researcher I must largely rely upon clues from anecdotal history and its like. This town is thick with fictions.

*

. . . I had thought Caleb would become more sociable again after he left that self-energized job at the Yard, but since then, as a closet dramatist, he hasn't been much less evasive than an anchorite. Maybe he's still struggling to break a logjam of too many creative ideas, like other overly intellectual writers who don't belong anywhere near the real theater. Some time ago he did tell me that he's dropped the notion of a whole trilogy about Gilgamesh (who he thinks is still famous). But if Fay's gotten him out of his shell maybe he'll loosen up a bit with the poorly educated likes of me—i e, maybe his words will start flowing as freely as they did for office memos (which I'm told by my brother-in-law were considered intramural models of suasion)—so that he's no longer in a sweat to communicate his gems.

From what little I've heard of his scripts I know that no one will buy them. He must be running out of money. I can't imagine how he'll make a living without expatriating himself. No other business around here needs a compulsively creative manager of monstrous avant-garde computer systems, especially if he's frank in explaining a decade of hiatus in his curriculum vitae.

Privately he's appeared less enthusiastic about Dogtown as the Ort-an-Sich since his Viking Shepherd Ibi-Roy was killed (not long after the heartrending euthanasia of our dear old Goddy). I think it occurred about the time that apparently schizophrenic priest tried to burn down the granite Laboratory of Melchizedek and the Mesocosm (soon after Doc Charlemagne actually did burn down our Stone Barn without trying). Those were sobering times for us, presaging horrible times for the nation (though bearable enough in retrospect, compared to the whole world's present prospects). Caleb is still basically cheerful, it seems, but he likes to quote Nietzsche: "If it weren't for art, life would be unbearable." I suppose he's thinking particularly of recondite and absolutely uncommercial art untainted by consideration of an audience. Yet I don't think he'd go back elsewhere to the kind of work at which he excels, at least not without the promise of anything less satisfactory upon retirement than a theatrical production grant in Utopia.

He used to tell me that he was interested only in the legal aspect of his origin, and then only because it might affect his application for a passport, explaining that his difficulty was complicated by a B D I [Bureau of Domestic Investigation] dossier as an alleged former member of the Resistance and suspect draft-dodger. (He was too young to be stigmatized as one of us Premature Antifascists.)

. . . At one tipsy moment he allowed that he was less worried about not having a father than about discovering one, like Ion at Delphi. But he hinted that he'd found in his mother's papers a clue to some adventure on the I O M [Isle of Manannan], whence she'd returned to Dogtown in time to give birth at the good old Tybbot family hospital, where nurse Fayaway Morgan rescued him from the morgue.

But in any case, he'd said, since England prohibited the admission of any dog without six months of caged quarantine, there was no point in pursuing the question. Among all his lame excuses for not giving a damn who his father was, at least that one was later expunged: since then, without his dog, he's surely had the time and

money to achieve his indubitable heart's desire by crossing the
Atlantic to Europe. Of course now he could make the time to travel
but probably doesn't have the wherewithal. It's like going back to
frugal student days, I suppose. Even such an autonomous ego's confidence can falter with declining prospects and middle-age insecurity. There's no wife to keep him afloat. Years ago he superciliously
declared to us—in the bosom of my family—that he himself had
no use for marriage because it required coordination for more than
one or two essential functions!

*

. . . I'm still mulling over things I heard at Fay's dinner last
week. I'll probably reciprocate the hospitality, if I can gather the
same gemütlich companions. With them I'll cease to miss Doc
Charlemagne, who bemused our old gang theatrically. I hope this
new cadre will stay intact and form a coterie of private celebrations
that exclude dullards, blockheads, ignoramuses, and Cans. Though
none of us are intellectually her peers, I and my distaff friends
should take turns with our own peculiar provincial salons to share
the burden of liberation introduced by this Professor de Sevigne. In
this case the men are essential, far more important than they were
in our provincial playreading group before Rafe, Caleb, and Doc
showed up a hundred years ago. Otherwise Fay's too busy with her
work emeritus to keep bothering with us. She apparently has the
Commander to keep her company enough.

Aside from dinner parties, I do hope she can spare me a little
advisory time for my quasi-professional enterprise. Perchance her
local anthropology could benefit from my socialworking research! I
must think about how to offer that suggestion. But with or without that objective I'll do anything I can to ingratiate myself with
that self-made eupatrid old lady.

However, quite naturally, it was that astonishing Navy man's
recent lecture at the Lyceum that occasioned the main conversation.
Speaking for myself, it was hard to refrain from peppering him
with questions, especially after he remarked that the epoch of
World War 2 was like the neck of world history's hourglass. A
pretty bold simile—especially when you by-pass the year One
B C E and ignore the open end of evolution! Of course few people
are as mathematically fastidious about analogies as Caleb is, so the
topic made for some reasonably skeptical enlightenment of personal

perspectives. Caleb and Belle were children during the War, and I wasn't very much older as an immature civilian. Wartime seemed to us in New Uruk a nearly normal condition of growing up. Even to Belle, a Dominion girl, as well as to Caleb and me, F D R was virtually God's immortal viceroy. After considering the hourglass image, which I doubt Fay had heard from him before, she defended it as serious metaphor. After yielding to liberal interpretation Caleb was intrigued by the conceit, apparently because he could fit it to Yeats's gyres! Finn himself seemed gratified by that observation.

I couldn't follow all of their sophisticated allusions but I believe the general idea is that global civilization was gradually condensed by intensification of population, historical experience, and technology into a critical mass of "distilled antitheses"—the limit of integration for the human species at that stage of culture, under essentially contrarious conditions of freedom and organization.

Caleb was excited by the pessimism of what was said to have followed already. "Yes," he chimed in, as well as I can remember, "that decade must have been the center that could not hold! We who live during its earliest loosening can already see the sands of time as centrifugal, with increasing mutual aversion, repelling each other and beginning to generate from the apex of its bottom cone, which will expand over time to match whatever unimaginable base the inverted upper cone began from!"

People like him don't solemnly believe in their diagrams and figures of speech, but we're all serious about the political implications for Atlantis. Sometimes it's fun to get carried away by what Rafe would call a rationalized model. Maybe Finn was just exaggerating a tidy intuition of world history in an effort to understand the emotional cusp of his generation. His schematic was least convincing when he spoke of history's public crux according to his personal experience of its elements. It went something like the following, if I got the gist without fully grasping his definitions—something I'm rather good at, having always been a parrot-brained sort of student:

W W 2 was a single "event-system" of four dimensions involving five oceans and six continents—broader in geographical span and at the same time more concentrated than any other in human evolution: a cumulative gathering of disparate experience into the tightest possible bouquet of malevolence and goodwill—atavistic violence challenged by forceful progress, lethal efficiency implementing collective pain and suffering—a dozen years of simultaneous feckless diplomacy, antithetical leadership, political passion, brownshirt goosestepping, counter-mobilizations, murderous mass production, benign prefabrication, weapon-evolution, operations research, secret counterespionage, occult detection, mass dissimulation, specialized cruelty, vengeful torture, progressive legislation, medical invention, mathematical explosion, merciful rehabilitation, cryptographic science, Shoah camps—lethal demands of distance, altitude, depth, temperature, time, and energized matter—economic demands of agriculture, mineral extraction, fishing, manufacturing, mobile machinery, human sweat, spontaneous innovation—organization, standardization, discipline—fatigue, entertainment, housing, child-care, contraception, literacy, ignorance, training, public health, bereavement, animosity, anger, hatred, greed, theft, rape, looting, sacraments and chaplaincy, personal religion, privacy, miscommunication, domestic hardship—dearth, famine, starvation, fear, chronic misery, unassisted open-air childbirth, categorical humiliation—battlefield trauma, unstanched blood, field transfusions, surgical frustration, replacement troops—unconscionable waste, extractable resources, poisoned air, manufacturing, industrial cooperation, national debt, taxes, capital, labor, confiscation, public finance—altruism, selfishness, goodwill, frugality, friendship, treachery, loyalty, bravery, luck, solitary courage, serial grief, gratitude, memorials, tailored uniforms, military decorations, joyful dreams, immediate rewards, sentimentality, genuine patriotism, cosmopolitan behavior—statistics, logistics, railroads, machine tools, priorities and triage, experimental organization, fiscal control, managerial skill, unimaginable coordination—racial hatred, Irish distrust, the fall of France, Pearl Harbor, the fall of Bataan, the fall of Singapore, separate peace, loss of the Bismarck, total war, Gestapo, Unconditional Surrender, One World, maquis, boot camps, U-boats, nationalism, ethnic antagonism, Jewish Physics, the Final Solution, alliance, racial integration, institutional security, war crimes, bribery, contract law, courts martial, fame, glory, erotic adventure, deception, temporary love, postwar expectations, improbable coincidence—widows, orphans, lost children, maimed veterans, torture, numberless refugees, abandoned animals, ironies of chance, disillusioned hope, true sacrifice, and generally the multiple codeterminants of a surprising United Nations, followed by the Marshall Plan for reconstruction.

I've probably missed some of the items in Finn's desultory singsong muster of that decade's bandied phrases—in fact most of us chimed in with contributions—wartime's runes, emotive keywords, rising and falling in randomly associated clusters of language as they happened to come to his lips (or to my memory), his face lifted toward the ceiling, eyes closed, as if entranced in a hall of mirrors, like an awakened somnambulist trying to repossess the interrupted clairvoyance of an instant past. Then too, as his incantations drummed up those teenage times for me I'm sure I heard and added other phrases from my own experience of food and gas coupons, interpolating them God knows where in what I remember of his table-talk—not all on a single occasion—as well as of his lecture. Anyway he makes one understand why the elderly sometimes brush off our present anxieties as manageable. He speaks for authoritative cohorts of demons, victims, fools, heroes, and saints.

But that wasn't all he delivered, at our urging, in his footnotes of exegesis as we drank our wine and ate our fish, or afterwards in book-laden living rooms. He went on to say that there were never so many ways to get killed in military service as in W W 2: —so many kinds of delirium or agony, so many different degrees of awareness in dying actively or passively: unexpected, cowering, numb, defiant, careless, desperate, triumphant, welcome, or judicial deaths—so many on the land, underground, in the air, on the sea, and under the sea, or in half-frozen verminous mud under incessant thunder; and there never will be such a spectrum of human extinction again (even with meteors), no matter how magnified the radii of poisonous explosions! He started a horrible list of means: sword, knife, axe, bullet, shell, rope, garrote, superheated steam, icewater, shark, Cyclon B gas, concussion, snakebite, maggots, asphyxiation, starvation, dehydration, hypothermia, exhaustion, vermin, microbes, lynch mob, torture *following* information, deliberated dismemberment, ethnological atrocity, "friendly fire", Kamikaze suicide, iatrogenic mutilation, massive radioactive explosion, midnight torpedoes. . . . Fay sometimes had to stop him. But, he added, never were human beings—though still separated by immemorial divisions—so generally conscious of the human values likely to be lost, won, or doubted. ". . . A just war, if there ever was one, even though it didn't start with the worst injustice in mind. Or at least a necessary war on one side or other." We don't protest that statement. Nor the belief that our Squire of North River was fatally indispensable as history's counterweight to Stalin and Hitler.

But soon after hostilities ceased, Finn maintained, selfishness began to resume its inchoate or blatant precedence over the common good. While some were still hoping for more than reclamation the world of virtuous power gradually recidivated to the nearly exclusive politics of economic individualism. If I don't read into Finn's meaning what I want to hear, he had especially in mind the cultural disintegration in which our promiscuous glorification of "the Atlantean Dream"—that of a person's own property, family, and friends—has loosed many waves moving in opposite directions under a sloping envelope of society!

. . . So much for my giddy impression of what I sensed or internally interpolated.

*

. . . It looks as if Caleb is sunk in no slough of despond by his reduced circumstances, or even in no more than occasional joylessness, but surely it must be hard to reconcile himself to the lack of organizational leverage after years of security and power that endowed him with a social self-confidence he never had before Arthur Halymboyd got him that job at the Yard. He's always said that his only exceptional talent is organizational—and he hasn't had anything real to organize for ten years! But his voice is more relaxed than when I first knew him, before he was necessarily laid off at the monastery bankruptcy. I wasn't *essentially* surprised by the extroversion of his personality while he worked at the Yard— though he was so fanatically busy that we saw very little of him— because I always knew he was a cocksure little bastard; but I hope powerless obscurity hasn't enervated all branches of his libido. Perhaps we'll find out. Pretty soon he's coming over for supper with Rafe and me. I wish I knew an unattached female to help me externalize his attractiveness in a foursome. . . .

*

I haven't quite given up on my disingenuous academic project, but I am getting cold feet about it. I must summon up all my old gifts for The Method of modern mummery, screwing my courage to the sticking-point, if I'm to carry out that professional fraud in conventional *writing*! I've got to persuade myself that it's a real case, instead of an amusing detective story, and that I'm a solemn case-manager, so I can have enough faith in my capricious impulse to convince experts that I've had a real client represented by "Mr

Nought". I may lose interest in the academic objective, but I hope
not before it's sustained the energy for my game. Later I might
write a novel and make more money than any ten psychiatric social
workers. It's a purely artificial excitement of my frustrated theatrical talents. But in the worst case, one more Lost Cause for Dogtown's creative wish-list!

Ergo, let's suppose that the virtual C K has been convicted of a
crime—say, plagiarism—and has been referred to me by the court
for psychological evaluation: that will be my private fantasy, not as
a scenario for my paper but as the profile of my professional mask.
In fact, of course, the man needs no therapy just because his lost
cause scorns its only possible success. He's really a subject for Auto
Drang's "Metapsychology". I'll have to fake the kind of diagnosis
expected of me. He knows that his birth was more traumatic for his
mother than for himself. More than other men he knows his
mother-lode.

But it would help a lot if he'd let me read at least his first play.
For my academic advisors the most suspicious thing about the dissertation will be the diversity of my client's interests—the very
attribute that makes him worth my effort—but I don't know
whether it's matched by versatility in talents. He's not in the least
schizophrenic; he certainly hasn't a multiple personality. In fact it
may be said that his "personality" is singularly uninteresting! How
can I make the professors let me go ahead? I can't just make up his
confessions to satisfy a pathological profession, can I?

*

. . . The meteorologists are getting so good at forecasting that
Gretta Doloroso blames them for the weather. .

*

. . . Why doesn't somebody study the *personal* psychology of
Protesticans?

*

. . . I'm used to Rafe's overbearing manner of conversation, and
most people seem charmed by it. He's welcome everywhere. But his
interruptions are sometimes downright embarrassing when the

other interlocutors are people like Fay or Finn, who are at least his peers in intelligence, better educated, and many years superior in life-experience. Still, I'm very happy to find that they still appreciate his goodwill. I can't bear it when people I like don't like each other.

6

TABLET
EIGHT

[Uruk. Early nighttime in forum, by torch-
light, just inside a city gate.]

Berosus sits off to one side with pestle-cymbal
or darabukka drum.

Enter former Widow 2, holding a baby to whom
she is happily crooning.

WIDOW 2 Trooper 2 enters.	Sweet baby mine—coo, coo, coo! Just between us, prettier than the new queen and not a day older, nor younger either.
TROOPER 2 [Kisses her and tickles baby.]	Well, the watch is set at last. What's for supper? —Me too, tiny damsel! I want some of that teat. —So are you available for fun tonight, my dearly beloved little callipyginous wife?
WIDOW 2	Cally *what?*

TROOPER 2	Beauty-ass! That's what Norkid used to call you when you were serving in the temple.
WIDOW 2	How could he know?
TROOPER 2	He wears glasses and he has a good head for figures.
WIDOW 2	Then maybe he's a pretty nice boss after all—even though he usually keeps you out all night. Shall I ask him to put in a word for you with Gilgamesh, who always seems too preoccupied to notice what a good man you are?
TROOPER 2	Don't let me catch you talking to the Captain about *anything,* that old goat! Gilgamesh has been fair enough with all of us. I pray to Mazda he makes it back here soon. When Engidu's with him he's twice too confident. Meanwhile let's you and me pluck a young mother's rosebuds while things are still quiet around here.
WIDOW 2	The way you're plucking me, our quarters will soon be too small for a soldier's happy home.
TROOPER 2	There's no place like wherever your rose bed is.
WIDOW 2	Maybe before the Rector's old glebe is all parceled out to civilians Gilgamesh will give us a little house for my bed. With a garden and two palm trees to shade another baby-boo or two. I'll rig up a hammock for you to renew your virility in—if I can ever soften you up long enough for me to get some housework done!
TROOPER 2 [Low drumbeat.] **All actors enter** severally, from various directions, at first in unhurried curiosity, then with increasing excitement.	Gilgamesh will take care of us. God knows he's generous enough with our enemies, just to keep the peace. —Shit piss and corruption, another foolish night-alert! —Sorry, baby, got to go! We have the devil of a time recognizing shadows before moonrise. It's prob'ly a lion, or just some stray camel.
NORKID [From above.]	There are at least two out there! Sound quarters!
WIDOW 2	Oh no! I'm still afraid you'll leave me!
TROOPER 2 [Hastily, as she grasps his tunic.]	For god's sake sweetheart, I'm too busy to leave you! I've got to go to the gate!
WIDOW 2	I mean it! If it isn't Gilgamesh now, he may never return! The Rector will get back his power and all you Kassites will go back to your women in the mountains! The kings

of Ur Lagash Nippur Eridu Umma and Kish are just waiting to rape and rob us, not to mention Susa and the Hyksos raiders!

TROOPER 2 None of us will ever leave Norkid, and Norkid won't leave Uruk while Lil-Amin is queen, or her daughter. And Eber's boys are multiplying faster than your people do. That's how they count their riches, to the city's advantage. So Eber will stay when the queen asks him to, and manage everything just as he did for Gilgamesh.

WIDOW 2 But if our adventurous king *is* coming back he must have insulted the gods again. Uruk can't resist the will of heaven when its citizens are armed only with pickaxe, hod, and basket instead of bow, spear, and shield! You mercenaries alone can't man a tower and seven walls until your sons grow up, whether Gilgamesh is here or not!

TROOPER 2
[Drumbeat louder and faster. Trumpet signal.] Your people will learn how to fight, and Eber's too, not just our men, if anyone threatens the prosperity they gripe about that Gilgamesh has brought them! —Now let me go, or Norkid will put me in the guard house!

NORKID Open the gate! It's Gilgamesh and Engidu!

Enter Gilgamesh & Engidu, ragged and dusty, one with a double-bitted axe, the other his bannerstone in hand, both with bows slung across their backs.

GILGAMESH
[To Norkid, embracing him.] So it seems you've kept the city safe! How's my little daughter—and her mother?

BEROSUS
[As Norkid replies inaudibly. Mingled clamors of welcome and gestures of ambivalence. All except Berosus assemble hierarchically in the forum.] This foreign ruler of Uruk, or Erech (as the Eberews called it), might have been Sumer's Alexander two millennia before the Greeks were ever heard of if he'd cared for power more than fame, or territory more than engineering, or religion more than his own freewill. He'd rather measure the world than win it. Though this event is long after Ea sent Oannes to instruct mankind how to serve the gods it is many centuries before the Akkadians overran the lower valley of the two rivers.

Gilgamesh, said to be two-thirds god but one-third mortal man, tyrannical deliverer of the city, has won the loyalty of Engidu, the dark superman sent by the petitioned gods to overmatch him. With the twinned prowess of their friendship he means to double his feats. Now he and Engidu, looking ever more alike, have returned from an expedition

intended to disabuse the blackhaired people of their con-
viction that fiery Kumbaba, hideous guardian of the sacred
Cedar Forest at the top of the world (where nascent Tigris
and Euphrates are opposite trickles from the Lake of the
Gods), can forever deny their brickbuilt city the timber to
make it greater.

You see the pair joyfully surrounded by Norkid and his
Kassites troopers. The Eberews and most of the natives are
surprised to see the foolhardy adventurers still alive. Gilgamesh is greeted equivocally by the Rector and Optimates, but cordially by Eber his vizier who seats them
both, and calls for cups of beer. You notice Gilgamesh from
time to time peering in vain for Lil-Amin the Queen, who
remains unseen.

[Eber hands
Gilgamesh the Rod
(staff) and Ring
(crown) of kingship.]

GILGAMESH

[Addressing the
Rector and
Optimates.]

You said it could not be done. [*Brief chuckle:*] Prediction is
fiction! A fig for your solemn prophecies! Some of you
dared to murmur that I was an arrogant foreigner restless
in folly, and that Uruk has no further need of lumber for its
gates, rafters, furniture, and seaworthy boats. You've
balked at every change in trade or speech until it's made
you richer. "Enough already" even Eber sometimes said!

EBER

It's pride that I resist, not innovation. For did not Elohim
say "Let not him that girds on his armor boast himself as
he that puts it off." But now I'm glad to see your armor's
off.

GILGAMESH

The Rector wailed that I'd bring down upon Inanna's own
city the wrath of every other god because I've allowed the
words of secular life as much privilege as the language of
women. And I know that brave Norkid thought I was too
insatiable for fame to imagine my own defeat in any
matter. He believed that shape-changing Kumbaba,
unceasingly alert with flaming jaws and petrifying stare,
could detect the breath of a mile-off butterfly. Kumbaba's
roar was said to be like the sudden thunder of floodwaters
striking terror in a canyon.

Your champion, my beloved Engidu, who had lived on the
steppes and come close to the mountain of the gods, confirmed these urban fears. But he was willing to share my
fate. He overcame his dread and became my guide. He
kept watch when I was troubled by my own childish
nightmares. The time came when we had to overcome each
other's fears. Yet mortal panic would have been justified.

For any living creature—animal or man—the most distant view of that mountain touches an instinct of terror. Long before we mounted to its forest Kumbaba's aura froze our blood.

BEROSUS Before they left the city Gilgamesh and Engidu had asked Lil-Amin for sympathetic advice. But according to rumor she'd only offered intimate dismay and a vivid premonition of double grief. Gilgamesh reciprocated the love in her words but ignored their wisdom. In anger at his conceited folly she withheld her blessing and refused them even an ordinary votive sacrifice, turning her back on their leave-taking.

GILGAMESH For the city's sake, not for mine, not for Engidu's, your admirable queen execrated me with scorn for the vanity of a fastuously temerarious glory-seeking self-appointed shepherd of her people! She cursed my career of fatal sacrilege. She blamed me for corrupting Engidu—even as she tried to corrupt his loyalty to me. Neither of us laughed at the oracle. We did not deny our fear or the power of the gods. But in the end we were still refused her coldest farewell— we the sires of her daughter!

RECTOR Blasphemy! All Uruk knows that my sister the lady-priest of Inanna did not deceive the heavenly father of our baby princess with either one of them!

Storms off, thump-
ing his crook,
followed hesitantly
by **Widow 1** &
Optimate 1.

GILGAMESH That woman-mongering master of ceremonies hates all reason in the name of worship. Behind my back he spits and says my feet are clay. He has no humor for the loss of his power.

BEROSUS In those days, you see, high priests still professed their lord god Enlil to be the father in a sacred marriage. This Rector hated Gilgamesh for confiscating the temple's glebe.

NORKID He's more unreasonable since he sacrificed his orchids.

GILGAMESH Is Lil-Amin well? Has she been informed that her wisdom
[To Eber.] has proved too feminine?

EBER The queen is aware of your return. She declines to hear your story.

GILGAMESH Before morning she'll hear it from me. You may assure her that by slighting prudence I did not belittle her warnings, or yours—or yours—or yours—or all the people's. Kumbaba certainly did terrify our entrance to the sunless Cedar Forest, and did indeed guard the Tree of the Gods. We were wearied by weeks of pathfinding, of fending for ourselves on the steppes and highlands, ever half starved or parched, always awakened from brief sleep by dreams of horror, though each of us in turn guarded by his wakeful double.

OPTIMATE 2   Tell us how you found the way, alive for months in the bush, beyond the territorial endurance of our greatest hunters.

GILGAMESH   I am no storyteller, sir! I have no time to cry or crow. Perhaps you'll find Engidu more accommodating. He's learned to speak quite well.

OPTIMATE 2   As you wish. We respect the Rod and Ring of Uruk, despite taxes and conscription.

EBER   Well you might, under an administration of justice and construction that keeps you rich.

ENGIDU   When I ran with the lions I learned their fear of mountains. At first I led the way I knew, untrodden by men, between the rivers, where gazelles find water holes. Gilgamesh trusted me for forage. We ran seven times seven leagues a day, with no rest to ponder fear. But at the dark of the moon we came to drier land I did not know. I was afraid.

[In what follows Gilgamesh and Engidu step down at appropriate moments to act out the account in dance or mime, accompanied by the percussions of Berosus.]

He took the lead. The moon came round again and made shadows with his light. Then we walked—seventy times seven leagues, more days than I could count. Gilgamesh gave me heart, found food and water when I lost hope. At night I dreamed endless fears. Finally from rising foothills we saw the cloud-gathering peak of the seven mountains still far before us at the top of the world, origin of waters. Dooming thunder shook the massif as we climbed. We dodged chains of lightning bolts from the sky at our backs.

One night on an eagle's ledge we huddled wet and cold, taking counsel. All day in hail and snow we groped for the final pass. Again we took a clinging rest to study the face of rock. At moonset, undercovered by the screech of icy wind, we pulled ourselves up to the rim of Kumbaba's domain.

BEROSUS	Thus the moon has twice made its rounds before they try their strength in that forbidden crater of the gods. Gilgamesh and Engidu each lead other in fear and feat.
NORKID	You can bend his bow that none of us can string. Now can he run as fast as you?
ENGIDU: [Suddenly exuberant.]	We have a tale that will raise the hair inside your head, if I tell it right. Before his first sight of Kumbaba, in truth, the huge heart of Gilgamesh was daunted by nothing real. As we crawled up the mountainside like tandem ants on a naked slab, with no horizon to mark a level, his longbow saved us from guardian eagles only. But when into mist we climbed the crevasse that drains the valley of the gods, blind and cautious, now and then we stopped to hold our breath and listen for Kumbaba overhead, our eyes alert for the glowing nostrils and flaming mouth that had kept intact the dismal forest of the gods since earth began by blasting intruders to dust with rays of magic, or by sweeping them deathward like dry twigs by loosing torrents from the sacred lake.
GILGAMESH	I thought it would be the fight of my life, the test and fame of mortal over fate immortal.
ENGIDU	I said: "You will not die alone. Forever we are brothers. With you together I will lose the breath of human speech and my love of life; even in this newest terror, far from all things sensible, I will fight at your side as one redoubled." But at the sound of this thought my heart came nearly to a stop, as if a god was passing. It drained the swelling of my chest, numbed my legs and arms to the ends of toes and fingers. "Yet, Gilgamesh," I cried, "there is no help in me at all! Let us turn back before the whole world is overtaken by your doom!"
GILGAMESH	But I replied: "Do not imagine weakness when our strength is multiplied by each other. You have learned the devices of man and I the skill of a lion. Do not look back at the scaled abyss; do not look up at horror." So his pounding heart grew stout again; his quaking limbs were steeled.
ENGIDU	We had taken turns climbing ahead of each other, the only way to measure our ascent into the black cloud that nullified every sense of direction.

GILGAMESH
[To the others.]

Yes, yes, my friend, but cut it short.

I won't succumb to the luxury of my bed until we've mustered a crew tonight and headed it for the headwaters of Euphrates. The season will soon be too dry to fetch even secular logs afloat.

—So much for your "pillar of heaven"! Look, aren't the same old stars still up there?

—The tree will be found at the foot of the mountain where it landed, scraped almost naked of limbs I hadn't lopped off with my axe before we tipped the trunk top-first over the lip. It was still more than twice as tall as the radius of its forest.

—Please recruit some good men before Engidu and I fall sleep on our feet.

[To Eber]
[To Norkid. Hands over a small tablet. He continues to scan the assembly while only impatiently joining Engidu to dance his part in the story.]

—You must make ditch-diggers and hod-carriers into lumberjacks. Give each a double-bitted axe, tempered as I've taught you. Next year they'll find easier access to the smaller timber and start some regular felling. Here's the map I made. Later I'll tell you the details.

BEROSUS
[Soft beat.]

This is not our death-day, Gilgamesh whispers to Engidu, as they come to the top of the Achaemenian Rocks, dreading that Kumbaba should hear them too soon. Engidu prays that their lives will be spared.

[Flute.]

Suddenly the silence of blackness is shattered by a shriek. The hideous face of Kumbaba emerges above them from a white fog at the very crown of the world.

[Berosus himself dons and doffs a series of Kumbaba masks.]

Even in clearing light Kumbaba's teeth gleam ghastly yellow in a red and purple gorge spitting fury.

Suddenly a fragrant canopy of green cedars is revealed above that face beneath a pure blue sky. Gilgamesh and Engidu no longer pause. Backwards step by step, holding in the breath of death, no longer panting to keep from burning up, that wily porter of the gods feigns lessening size and rage to trap the sacrilegious invaders on the bronzed alpine floor of slippery age-old needles in the deeper forest; for Gilgamesh's purpose is already known in the lamasery of invisible dieties. But as he advances, no longer daunted by reverberating screeches, he incidentally blazes the finest tree trunks for future harvest, heedless of Engidu's warning that Kumbaba laughs in mockery while leading him into impotence where retreat will be too late and any repentance will be ignored even by those in heaven who respect his fame.

Now they find themselves at the pivot of the earth where its turning shrinks to stillness. Under the noble Cedar that lords itself above all others, pointing to the pole star of the universe, they can hear their own hearts beating in the eerie silence. At poise to strike with blazing fangs, the tensed hamadryad tortures that lull with howls and hisses, swelling to fullness with gnashes of tooth and claw, shielded by leathery wings, coiling and uncoiling in sanctioned rage around the huge cedar's base like slithering roots of chthonic muscle. But the taunted champions do not hesitate in caution. Engidu suppresses fear with reckless excitement at the apparition of Gilgamesh transfigured by his renowned battle-warp, nearly as wonderful to see as the dragon's. In a unison of the mortal powers raised by action this reckless pair attacks the preternatural defender of heaven.

GILGAMESH

[To Engidu.]

[To the others.]

Never mind the drama of it! It's not local mummery that will spread our fame beyond these walls. You can sing the feat to scribes tomorrow. Enough for now to mark the year that people from Uruk begin transhumance with an alp. Other kings and Eber's God may batten on praise for being themselves, but I want to be known for my improvement of the gods' designs. From me you have a wheel to turn your pots; bitumen that you called river dung lights the night and caulks your Sea-Land fishing boats; you trade naphtha for lapis lazuli from Kush and the people's salt from Dilmun; wood is added to the arts of stone, clay, copper, and bronze—and ciphers to your reckoning. I serve gods my own way, not by bowing down in esoteric rote. Enlil is surely not displeased that I have made seven-gated Uruk, eternal city of his daughter Inanna, proof against flood and siege. It would be too much for a soul to bear if the gods always failed to understand that canals, walls, towers, and writing too, are to their credit as creators of the people who made them—that they themselves will be magnified by the harvesting of timber for peaceful sheepfolds and temple roofs. Why should they resent my motive? Are they too orthodox to recognize my liturgies as manly worship? Anyway, I had no choice but to kill their incorrigible reptile.

ENGIDU   Gilgamesh spreads her jaws apart with the haft of his axe. I
                crack her skull with my bannerstone and hold her tail until
                he drags fifty feet of guts out by the tongue to put a stop
                to her unearthly death-wail!

OPTIMATE 1   *Her!* You still haven't learned the pronouns!

GILGAMESH   We saw her female parts. The spawn of Tiamat. Let poets
                memorize what they please. Engidu is too innocent to lie
                for the sake of a story.

EBER   The city is now returned to your hands. After the sabbath I
[Excited.]   will at last shake the dust of Chaldea from my feet. Too
                long with high office and rich reward you have dissuaded
                me. My calling is from Elohim, the One God your impiety
                cannot challenge. Let your servant's right hand wither if he
                forgets your righteousness in public justice—but excuse
                him now from listening to your creed!

GILGAMESH   I meant no disrespect to your nomad god, though more
                demanding of me than the others. Tomorrow we will
Eber goes out, reason together. You are to remain Uruk's chancellor till
motioning for   the moment of your caravan's departure, laden with the
dispersal.   city's gifts.
                —Dismiss this murmuring assembly. Uruk will never be a
                republic.

OPTIMATE 2   "Justice", forsooth! Not for Inanna's people—only for his
[Walking off, to mercenaries! I was hoping we'd seen the last of this tyrant,
Optimate 1.]   but now he'll be harder on us than ever. But I am surprised
                that lust didn't bring him and his monkey home to the
                queen much sooner.

OPTIMATE 1   Can't you guess why? All alone together like incestuous
[Replying aside, as twins? "Guarding" each other, they call it!
all except the
following speakers
go off.]

BEROSUS   Thus also did the Greeks misunderstand the poem when it
                came down to them.

GILGAMESH   Before you take your bath go tell Lil-Amin that I'll clean
[To Engidu, as they up and come to bed as soon as I can. First there are other
leave together.] things to see to.

ENGIDU   Maybe she will still be too angry.

GILGAMESH   No doubt she's at her loom.

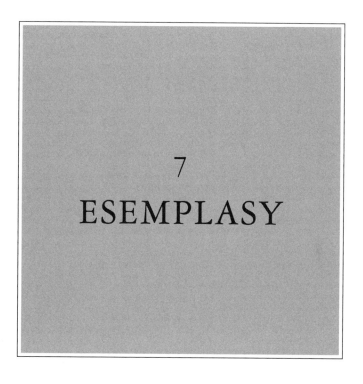

7

ESEMPLASY

[From Professor Gabriel's
thoughts in April 1981]

*T*his residency is a stimulating sort of rustication, just the place for my old age. I still can see, and I'm blessed with the security of friends and funds, but perhaps it's my Colonus. And Dogtown is still more interesting than Mardi or Ur. I've been slow to realize that for me it's a uniquely congenial locus for my cumulative valediction. Some would say that's a rationalized illusion to justify the luck that brought me here to round out what seems a happy destiny. But I think I've found the focus of my life's experience, the rare gift of productive old age. I've benefitted inordinately from chance and coincidence. But for reasons other than mine it's been noticed that sooner or later, calculating per capita of the population, more remarkable persons visit Dogtown—at least once, by land or sea, or by word or picture—than any other place in Atlantis, each one contributing to its diachronic worth a jot or

145

lump of appreciation that the inhabitants absorb among themselves as enhancements of pride at each successive anniversary of compound interest. So it sometimes seems, at least with wine and one or more of my kind new friends.

Most of the citizens, of course, don't know or care about interesting sojourners (unless they stem from Holyrood or devilvision), and half of them don't even welcome the pilgrims who disburse more and more dollars every summer. At second glance this is still in some respects a microcosm of Atlantis. I won't say that they love their neighbors as themselves; but they don't love their ethnic kinsmen as themselves either. Tribes are clubs that gain fewer members than they lose, and, as with the sodalities of military veterans, drinking and visual amusement constitutes most of the fellowship. Otherwise, except for distinctions of religion and party politics (usually a limited and periodic exception), the colons of Dogtown are no more loving or discordant than cats of every caste and color sharing a prosperous hay barn. Though this microtopopolis is not literally maternal for the residents and sojourners who've been born elsewhere, as a sometime colonist I suddenly find that for myself it's an alma mater of certain unacknowledged or undeveloped ideas that should be assimilated or contrasted with my own views before I exhaust my terminal urge to communicate what will have made my life worth living beyond its contributions to reproduction and academic education. I'm now as free as an alley cat! I can gladly appropriate others' lost causes if they affiliate with mine, which otherwise probably won't outlast this body much more than a single generation.

Only in small part can the industrious mentality of a lifetime be bequeathed even to one's children unless it's written down, not necessarily for them to understand but at least to be preserved for random explorers to read by chance. Too soon—but all at once, I hope—every symbol that has lodged in my brain from the passive or active experience of seven decades will vanish, lost to the past as well as to the future, wasted faster than a prize-winning sandcastle piled up and carved between two tides. Indeed my whole system of overt and occult consciousness will be as instantly dissipated into cosmic nothingness as the consciousness of a squashed ant, leaving behind a few pounds of ash that is itself arrested from ultimate disintegration only at the universal chemical state immediately proximate to maximum disorder. Apart from the little of what I've learned that's already recorded, or otherwise uncertainly appre-

hended (if not assimilated) by my children, students, and a few of
my colleagues, I may be able to delay my anonymous extinction
with some bruited ideas—if not bibliographically integrated and
published before I die. Like other women I deserve ordinary credit
for bearing and nurturing, but little for the self-development of my
autonomous children. I have perceptions and thoughts but I am not
an artist, I am not even an especially sensitive aesthete; I am not an
architect, I am not a public servant. Instead I am a critical savant of
a certain kind. Even the most worthy fraction of what might be
called my present oeuvre will remain largely ignored if I don't
attempt an exemplification of the conceptual anthropology I have
in mind at this salty vantage!

Before this transhumance to Cape Gloucester I had almost
given up the telling of my thoughts emeriti, which are by far more
mature—let's say philosphical—than those already printed. For the
present this little city's stimulus has offset in my head the decline
of my faculties without rejuvenating my memory, but with no
more data-gathering, no more tedious research, no more monographs or explanatory essays to issue, no more defensive polemics; I
can now rejoice in the freedom of unexplained intuitive synthesis
and emotional ideas, mine and others'—neglected, rejected, or professionally coherent—that deserve to be recognized by the purblind
intelligentsia.

*

I do not wish to have an obituary like that of poor Auto Drang.
His influence on creative laymen was faintly praised while slighting or distorting the insights for which he was damned by the
orthodox psychoanalytic establishment before he could live long
enough to finish a draft of his summa (which of course would have
been anathema to the M Ds of psychoanalysts unless it recanted his
heresy.) Like other original thinkers he is now forgotten or ignored
almost everywhere but in the mummified condescension of biographical dictionaries or historical footnotes, which list him (if at all)
as Tristram Freud's ambitious self-educated sidekick in Vienna.

Tessa Opsimath reminded me of his books. She's not a great
reader, and she doesn't grasp (as Caleb does) the philosophical
depth of his genius, but she did secretarial work for him in Ur
when she was young, and now as a psychiatric social worker she's
apparently a pragmatic beneficiary of his clinical teachings (which

were recognized and preserved by women at the University of Hannah School of Social Work in Brotherly). Tessa may be of help to me in more ways than one. She's ironically alert to the local world and cheerfully sensible about the feministic twaddle that one suffers among the misguided militants of her cohort. Anyway, I always welcome her.

So I'm now reading all the Drang things I can get my hands on. (The only ones I remember reading when I was too young are *Myth and Hero* and the posthumous *Feminine Psychology and Masculine Ideology*.) Most of his prose is hard to read. Maybe if he'd been as good a writer as Freud he'd have vanquished his hostile colleagues. But it's said he was impressive as a lecturer, despite his persistent Viennese accent, and quite charming in private, though he looked like a stunted frog. At least he had a good sense of humor, notwithstanding his alleged latterday manic-depressions (which I would say are easily explained by the objective difficulties of his life from beginning to end, but which aroused little sympathy in his professional enemies, who complained because his doctorate was in philosophy instead of medicine, thereby accounting for his outmoded belief in freewill).

Nevertheless for a time Drang was famous and successful compared to Father Lancelot Duncannon, whom Caleb personally attended for several years both as voluntary acolyte and as salaried "Business Manager" of the Laboratory of Melchizedek and the Mesocosm. That barely populated Tudor monastery on the ridge of Harbor Foreside was Duncannon's residence and his headquarters for the internationally obscure Classic Order of the Vine [COV], which he had established, as Father Founder and Father Superior, twenty years earlier in Unabridge. Almost all copies of Duncannon's books, in his own term theologically "antithetical" to his High Church in certain hermeneutic essentials—printed at the Order's expense after prudential rejection of his manuscripts by all the publishers that served the flourishing "thetical" religious market—have long since almost vanished. His followers, though intensely devoted, must have been much less numerous than Drang's, seeing that theology is less tolerant of innovation even than orthodox psychoanalysis. I dimly remember from the time I was an advisor on human rights to Mrs F D R in Ur a United Nations official from the Near East mentioning his interest in just such a classic but semi-schismatic Tudor order, so I'm sure the COV's influence wasn't totally obscured by its "socialistic" dissent.

According to Caleb some of Duncannon's concepts anticipated and rationalized the less fundamental liturgical reforms that in accordance with liberal theologians and modern attitudes toward society have recently been instituted in the classic ritual of both Rome and Canterbury without, however, a corresponding recision of their fundamental importance. Symbols can change their meanings—one Pope even grants that!

During these liberal advances I was paying no attention to the Church or its schismatic relatives because I was born into Petrine orthodoxy, only to wish escape from its Lusitanian obscurantism. Until disgracefully later it never occurred to me that Christianity could be of professional interest to an anthropologist. But Caleb sketches Duncannon's avant-garde liturgical views as pertaining, for example, to some of Eber Durkheim's ideas about "primitive" religion. The dear boy has inveigled me to promise a look at his own jealously preserved copies of the Classic Order's numerous books fascicles and leaflets, filtering out much of the traditional metaphysics and peripheral ceremony that persisted in the traditional High Church elements of Duncannon's liturgically radical doctrine, especially as represented in his ideas of *sacrifice*—which Caleb dares to say imply nothing less than an anthropological revolution in Christian theology! In his own rather intemperate opinion neither the Petrine nor the Pauline churches have ever understood themselves! By way of flattery he brazenly emphasizes that the Father Founder had owned and admired *Liberty and Responsibility*, my old book of essays on "primitive" cultures.

I must beware depending too much upon Caleb's interpretations and interpolations. I haven't much time for historical study of how the Church *has* understood itself. But I've already found that the history of Christianity is immensely ramified—exceedingly complex and subtle. But he's my only possible informant about the genius of what appears to be a radical lost cause that should be exciting historians and anthropologists today—at least a few I met when I gave some lectures on Mardian and Yahi ritual for the Comparative Religion Department at the Norumbega School of Theology, where they encourage new ideas about the relationship between religion and society, and where discussions would be more fruitful than those in philosophy departments I've glimpsed or skirted—were it not for the impenetrable curtain of suspicion that even there necessarily defends print-burdened academics from the efforts of unaccredited amateurs and cranks. If it hadn't been for the keyword *Sacrifice* in one of the titles I myself would probably have fended off Caleb's enthusiastic suggestion of this priest's relevance to my anthro-philosophy!

Not quite at first but soon enough I understood Caleb's hope for me to propose a hermeneutic linkage of the two minds, Drang and Duncannon, between two putatively separate spheres, yet both with recourse to anthropology. I rest from reading one of the minds by turning to the other. But now that association expands to the blessing of a brotherhood with two mentalities who join my cosmopolitan discoveries in Dogtown. In my researches I've always kept at least three alternatives at hand to choose from when I need temporary relief from one man's prose or another man's web of erudite allusions, which themselves usually lead to many hours of "collateral reading" anywhere in a laborious spectrum. That recreational alternating of attention-spans helps preclude the otiose temptations of journalism, fiction, cinema, and other diversions that are perfectly okay for those who haven't been through a life-cycle already. Ancillary citations themselves are often all too attractive, sometimes diverting me to generally celebrated writers (especially philosophers like Kant) whom I wish I'd had time to read before I grew so conscious of being drawn into the implacable compression of my final concentration! Allowing for one's vexatious weakening of memory and logically analytical faculties, and a reduction in neural speed of apprehension, and increasing reliance upon reference books for familiar names and terms (which I'm told is unexceptional among aged contributors to creative culture), my solitary time is happily absorbed in refreshing study and preparatory annotation.

I wish I could promise myself when I'll be finally ready to begin the literal expressed organization of what I'm still in the process of thinking with scarcely more than twenty-six standard black symbols on a blank field of all colors in the human spectrum! A swan's song of multifarious intellectual passion calls for a poet, and I'm not even a philosopher! Compared to what I vaguely envision as the delivery of what I have not yet fully conceived, my early books and peripatetic monographs were easy to write and no more difficult to communicate than a chrestomathy, because now there's a hell of a lot more of my own ideas to think about.

One of the next two fountainheads of my intellectual experience lies near the heart of anthropology, but the other is beyond my professional purview, alien to my mentality. According to Caleb my *Liberty and Responsibility* had been known and praised also by the authors of these two tributaries that join like the Chippewa and the LaBelle River to swell the mass of my momentum. (It hardly follows that I had influenced them enough to account for their present influence on me!) To wit:

About Ipsissimus Charlemagne: more is available to me from others' memoirs and Festschrifts than from his scattered and uncollected writings because, unlike Father Duncannon in person (who was hardly famous even in his native Dogtown), Ippy's life hereabouts, early and late in a semi-theatrical career, was as highly visible as histrionic. He made his commencement from anthropology courses and undergraduate drama to notoriously creative dramaturgy beyond the pale in Yerba Buena, New Uruk, and even Washington in theatrical circles, before returning to Dogtown as one more marooner disgusted with the values that define "successful" art. Here he attracted many "counterculture" Ippies before and after his death. His cultish disciples perpetuate an international Society in his name, but otherwise he is little better known to national journalists and common readers than Drang is. In his last years, voluntarily retired into poverty, Charlemagne rather unreliably coached Tessa's amateur Stone Barn Theater. My impression is that she had really believed the local public would acclaim a Dogtown version of the Abbey, even to the extent of tolerating esoteric plays like Caleb's (who nevertheless says he always knew better than to show the dramaturge his amateur script).

To locals, impressed by his polymath discourse, Ipsissimus was known as Doctor Charlemagne, a k a The Director. It was the Off-Limeway people in Ur who had dubbed him Ippy. He reluctantly accepted the functional title of Artistic Director for an unrealized Dogtown College enterprise, but according to Caleb he was a misunderstood guru. It looked as if King Lear had been a brilliant hero! In the end Tessa rebelled against his anti-box-office attitude, and of course she never forgave him for his disastrously careless smoking as an arsonist. At first in her generally alert way she (like everybody else) had been enthralled by his gigantically benignant charm as much as by his reputation for avant-garde dramaturgy, but she had no significant interest in the general theory of culture that he called Dromenology, which subsumed his special theories of theater but took little or no interest in expanding to a much larger anthropological concept. It was the latter implications of the former—the broad ideas of culture—that excited Caleb in the word invented by his friend. Naturally, at first blush, as an academically biased anthropologist, I would have waved off this Charlemagne as only an exhibitionist if Caleb hadn't already earned my respect for what I've been told of the man's intuitive genius and creative learning, which put to shame my advanced education!

So in this case again it was Caleb's infectious enthusiasm that induced me to read what's available on Charlemagne's vague phylogeny of culture—an inchoate set of speculations and ruminations calculated to raise the hackles of any responsible scholar but shot full of aperçus, fresh ideas, and original apothegms. I no sooner suspended my prejudicial defense against a crank, after just a few pages, than I was heartily moved to thank Caleb (my little godson!) for his imaginative recognition of good ideas when he sees them. I've started to read all he can give me of I C's printed works. Maybe I'll even stomach some of the posthumous idolatry in the mimeographed journal of the I C Society, which still claims international subscribers, most of whom I suspect to be irregularly educated (by I C himself, as likely as not, at White Quarry College in Montvert, from which both Tessa and her husband have their bachelor's degrees). In the name of critical promulgation the I C S pays too much obeisance to the *person* of this giant and too little attention to the scholarship and reasoning of his implicated ideas that deserve earnest development (or criticism) by specialists.

But one of the biographical details I heard from Tessa is interesting to me personally. Caleb remembers hearing part of the anecdote among his mother's many tales when he was very young, though he didn't associate it with Charlemagne's name until after he'd become a favored familiar in that maestro's kitchen. (Caleb's Viking Shepherd was favored by the man's housekeeper, Deeta Dana, who withdrew with the affectionate dog to another room as soon as those long tête-à-tête whiskey nights began.) Apparently the half of the story that he dimly remembered from his boyhood, not for an anonymous protagonist but for its histrionic technology, was about the fact that one summer back during the Prohibition era, when the young drama scholar was seasonally sojourning in Dogtown, he demonstrated his precocious self-confidence over in the Seamark liberty by getting together a horse, a wagon, a small collection of theater-students, and the permission of a gentleman farmer to use a small hayfield for his "summer school", as well as money from the same benefactor for the expenses of doing it all. For the wagon he'd made a lofty superstructure like those one used to see in circus parades, but not so gaudy, with a panel on one side that he let down and propped up on legs as a stage for open-air rehearsal or performance of his "experimental" renditions, with plenty of indigent tyros delighted to move and speak, or hammer and paint, under his command. Even with no admission charge his audience (primarily artists of modern genre who usually rented studios for the season here in the East Harbor ward) rarely exceeded the number in his company of ardent volunteers (mostly females), who were either humbly dominated or eagerly charmed as participants in a trumpeting of his briefly celebrated Theater-on-the-Wain. He literally tooted his own horn for annunciations.

But as far as my interest in Doctor Charlemagne is concerned Caleb doesn't yet know the other half of that story, which Tessa urges me to tell him about his mother Mary (or Moira) Trevisa four or five years before he was born, when she was still using her original name, according to what she herself happened to tell me much later (among floods of confessional reminiscence), after she'd pronounced me Caleb's savior and her best friend on the strength of my timely apparition as an obstetrical nurse and subsequent admirer of her courage, humor, and talent. I think that at the time of the Wain she was still living alone over in the Village and running a weekday nursery school for the kids of local aestivators. Having attended one or two of the casual daylight performances, and afterwards having hung around for a while with his stage-struck flock, she (as usual) "saw through" that "pompous ass", whose personal attention did not charm her, neither then nor later when he attempted friendship by making inquiries and calling at her door.

She still detested him a few summers later when he attempted to improve their acquaintance at a Long Rocks party where he was somewhat of a celebrity returning to Dogtown for a few days during Gloucestermas 1934. "He was such a ridiculous exhibitionist!" she once remarked to me in a detached page from "the first draft" of what she called her open-ended autobiography. Now Mary herself was never pompous, but as for the rest of her histrionic scorn, it was the pot calling the kettle black—as she frankly volunteered! She also admitted an element of creative jealousy in her proud rejection of the charmer. Of course I need not mention any more to her son than that she had known his sometime hero.

"Doc may have been an exhibitionist, but he had plenty to exhibit!" says Tessa. "And he was as intelligent as a woman. I've always wished I'd been there to see the Theater-on-the-Wain. But

then I'd be about seventy-five nowadays!" I assured her that that
would be the best time of her life. "But only if I manage to keep
my wits!"

Speaking of the Wain, the Herr Oberdichter's fame is waning
with the memory of his personal presence, whereas I'm already
inclined to celebrate his work for ideas that were never enough
developed to attract attention in cultural anthropology or the arts.
He was considered a polymath—though I'd say more of an intuitive
genius than the savant he passed for—rightly too proud to accept
the disciplines of scholarship or sustained coherence in prose. In his
latter years he was too lionized by insurgent semi-educated histri-
ones, poetasters, and other avant-garde artists—for his agragregari-
ous charm and irregular reputation as a roving intellectual—to
submit himself to the restraints of the doctoral responsibility
expected of his less imaginative peers, or even to finish reading his
first glances at the philosophical or scholarly works that he praised,
criticized, or categorized, once he'd fashioned an insight or trope to
distinguish what he had to say from the perceptions of responsible
thinkers. At least that seems to have been Caleb's slightly estranged
impression toward the end, despite his expanded enthusiasm for
Dromenology itself, by which I too shall estimate that genius, if my
first impressions are sustained by the glances I'm embarked upon in
reading. I must allow for Caleb's personal disappointment.

But he has no doubt about the anti-chrematistic purity of
Charlemagne's artistic motives. Caleb says that in that respect, as
well as in the proclivity for a sophisticated sort of exhibitionism,
and in a generously maternal alertness to the present feelings and
past experience of acquaintances who did not challenge his intellectual superiority, Doc reminded him of his mother, despite the
absolute differences in every aspect of the personal qualities in his
mystical analogy, an unconscious transcendental abstraction characteristic of his own mentality—much to his present dismay, seeing
that the resemblance he felt might simply be attributed to accidents in tone of voice, to elected political affinity, or to such trivial
parallels as the gestures and ambience of cigarette smoke.

Anyway, Charlemagne died about ten years ago, having gone
without the comfort of royalties or pension—true to his values, I
gather, and insufficiently understood—as an immensely influential
teacher and director without pensionable portfolio, famous among
the avant-garde on both sides of the Atlantic for his unlimited
"play of mind", but a procrastinator in the written word, unable to

get very far in working up for posterity at least the recorded evidence to support his insights, or perhaps an integrated summation of his two or three short paperback books that stimulated every reader of theatrical theory for promulgation by his epigones. Caleb seems to think that job is up to me! I say it's up to him!

But I'd like to be able to relate Caleb's undeveloped *General Theory of Dromenology* to certain ideas of Drang, Duncannon, and myself—psychologist, churchman, and ethnologist—and of those who inspired one or another of them, for instance Jane Harrison, the great "Classical Anthropologist" (Charlemagne's original Muse), or the sociologists Durkheim and Weber, or the monk Gregory Dix—not to mention the cosmologist Alpha Whitehead or the philosophical biologist Denthey! In my appreciation of values and beliefs in various strange societies I know I've sometimes seemed inimical to enlightened Western culture. Of course, that's not true, but I am entirely receptive to the dromenological idea that even our own Christian myth springs from distal ritual: an evolution of dance. (As I see it so far, the main task of persuasion for the General Theory is the idea that in the beginning ritual creates myth. Myth itself becomes the subject of new ritual, which in turn develops either its own myth or the myth evolved from a different ritual. Diachronistic interbreeding of ritual and myth— evolving by imagination or intellect—is (with or without a concatenation of regenerative myths) a process of linguistic, artistic, and Jesus culture, some of which is factual. (Jesus was a liturgical genius.) The time and labor required to support this proposition— indeed the labor merely to define its usually abused terms—is too much for a suggestible old woman. (Apparently the Special Theory of Drama was the only ramification of Dromenology that Charlemagne cared to pursue.) Evidence for the sweeping generalization, embracing with few exceptions all human millennia and all human places, must be largely analogical, based primarily upon Jewish, Classical, or Christian documents, only secondarily corroborated by the much fewer and less accessible works of literature or art available from other civilizations. I must leave that job to Mr Casaubon.

Extrapolations must never be trusted, but they certainly can stimulate speculation valuable enough to claim one's narrowing years of effort! I always allow for spurious errors of fact. At least in philosophical self-defense there's nothing odious about leaving boundaries or limits undefined. It would take a dozen philological anthropologists and historians a dozen years to justify Caleb's notion of Dromenology—but only if they were uncommitted to prevailing assumptions about ritual, myth, or cultural evolution. My Classical insurgent Adam would have scornfully rejected Charlemagne's presumption as the fantasy of one who couldn't even read Greek—just as nearly all academics, theologians, and psychoanalysts have summarily dismissed many of my aforementioned Muses who have presumed themselves free to peer into other people's professions. If I'm about to adopt another lost cause, I protest that it's not just because Doctor Charlemagne (as Caleb tells me) had already canonized a book of mine twenty years ago!

Still, though those names are ignored by conventional wisdom, they don't all represent lost causes. Some of their ideas, as derivatives or tardy cognates, have gradually gained anonymous respect as the Zeitgeist reflects loosening orthodoxies and various fonts of collegial intercourse. (I wish my old mentor A N W were still alive in Unabridge to test this my place in his transcendentally Platonic cosmology of what I'd now call paradoxical ideas. I myself am loathe to question his metaphysics!) The historical phenomenon of lost attribution is common enough in all the sciences, but it is especially so when original ideas (as distinguished from discoveries) contribute inconspicuously to broadly shared consciousness of a new paradigmatic Gestalt. If there's anything fundamentally progressive about our century it's in the intuition and science of systems, whether natural or artefactual.

If I'm not about to be disappointed henceforth in my reading, this is where the new key comes in, organizing for me on a higher level of abstraction the otherwise departmentalized affects of the others, and incorporating them at least by pattern or analogy with most of the concepts I've framed or accepted over the years, despite the fact that I don't know much about biology or physics. (For general scientific explanations, thanks to my recent good fortune, I can now look to my battleship man Finn Macdane, who bandies technical analogs almost as much as Caleb does.) Thus it looks as if von Denthey's Universal Systems Theory may provide my composite Weltanschauung with a symbolic language as useful as time-space-and-causality was to Kant—as well as indirect affinity to Whitehead's "organic philosophy"! Denthey actually declares a "theoretical biology" extended to physics and technology. His published works were urged upon me by Finn the electrical engineer and erstwhile leader of men, seconded by Caleb, the more abstruse author of a Synectic Method of Diagnostic Correlation and other schemes of real or virtual data. Those two systems-mongers know less than I do about biochemistry, but they've both found themselves independently enthusiastic in the cause of Denthey's general and still evolving concepts.

Like Auto Drang, he was Viennese, emigrating to Atlantis; like Drang he was opposed or ignored by most of his colleagues as soon as he deviated from the orthodoxy of his profession; like Drang he's nearly unknown because many of his ideas, or their suggestions, have been unwittingly adopted as explanations or hypotheses for research by less original collaborators in the emergent 20C Zeitgeist. But also like Drang, as far as anyone knows, he never came to Cape Gloucester in person, and nothing about Dogtown can be claimed to have stimulated their imaginations. Nor is it likely that either of them had ever even heard of my popular anthropological inseminations; so in their cases I can't be accused of congratulating myself as a feminine fertilizer!

What makes such a likely fraternity in this girl's eyes, an ignoramus in their divers special knowledge? For instance, I have no faith in psychoanalysis; I don't believe in Father Duncannon's God; I'm suspicious of independent scholars; and I ordinarily abhor attempts at mathematical Geisteswissenschaften. Perhaps this association of ideas is my figment, I the sole subject of esemplastic wish-thinking. Or is it just that my mind is at last opening to the kind of reason that I've tried to escape as a critic of the Enlightenment? Mary may have been right that women are better people, but they can be just as obtuse as men! The question remains: why do these males excite me in my studious retirement, when it's almost too late, when I still have hundreds of new books to read before I die trying to make up for years devoted to the typical concerns of my gender? Is there really enough affinity for the sympathetic vibrations of obscurity or failure that's usually the lot of unaccommodated intellectual women? Is it a shared compassion for lost causes? This ad hoc brotherhood is something of a negative catalyst, relaxing my innate resistance to the Western raft of reason.

Yet which of these causes are forever lost, which of their names will remain as obscure in the history of our century's ideas as mine has been? It sometimes seems as if Caleb is trying to use me as a genie to construct a theater for staging the antitheses of a decadent culture. His mother would have instantly divined his manipulative guile—whether she was right or not! I do miss her annoyingly unreliable clairvoyance, not least about her quasi-feminine son.

So I find myself beholden to Caleb as an evangelist for these disparate and prophetic teachers from beyond my pale of competence. He seems to promise that they will not merely enlighten me: like coefficient numerals they will expand my own reflections geometrically! Indeed I immediately understand even their abstruse passages, scarcely demanding proof or reason, as if I were a glory-clouded infant recovering eternal Forms (though what they represent is essentially anti-idealistic)! If I can fend off Father Time long enough I will either succeed at metasystemic integration or curse my irrevocable disappointment.

Anyway, my reach has always exceeded my grasp, even since no longer an impoverished housewife, especially when I've been distracted by political hopes. For one who is no poet, time is too short for "intellectual passion" to manage a contrariety of private and public intensity. And then, though I've escaped the Lusitanian Joseph's Disease, there's the decay of one's central nervous system, to be taking longer with every iota of perception and memory, not to mention gerontic decrepitude in numeric calculation. Even Finn admits that *his* analytic powers are fading with old age! More than Caleb's promptings we both already need cues from reference books, bibliographic indices, or our own foresighted notes to recollect names, even common nouns. (Of course we rationalize that we are richly compensated by the synthetic advantages of cumulative experience and skill in learning—his technological and mine humane!)

This last manuscript of mine therefore cannot be a product of thoroughgoing scholarship. I won't be able to defend my views in proper academic manner. But acting now almost as a layman, how can I present my opinions as anything much more than references and assertions? A long enough bibliography perhaps, but few specific citations. Such gloriously free discourse requires no referees or committees, and I'll have no acquisition editor to supplicate! I'll write it to please myself, like a last will and testament, and, as Hal Adams did, spend my treasure to have it printed, even knowing that most of its copies will probably end up in the Dogtown dump, like Father Duncannon's oeuvre, as yet another lost cause of a lost name.

What a relief! I haven't felt so ambitious since I cleared the decks for freedom after my girl-child safely liberated herself. The only burden of my old age is negative time! Time is life, life is time!

But here I am, anticipating my vision of conclusions whose premises I hope to find with ease, nearly abandoning the disciplined habits of a lifetime! Maybe I'm about to hack my way into the thickets of a Talmud, leaving behind me not a clearing but the mere trace of a vanishing Tir-na-Dog blueberry path to frustrate a seeker of fruit. What if there is no Cynosure Rock to discover? It may take all the time I have just to find out what is or isn't there to find!

Well I don't have to worry about antagonistic critics, because there won't be any reviews in my lifetime. Still, I'd not like to sound like a *pre*judging observer, for in fact my life's final opinions—inspired, modified, and extended by this final project—will be founded, not as Bacon would have it on facts, but on plenty of subjective inductions from vicarious discoveries! And it will be a most unacademic pleasure to trip on light fantastic toe the mores of my profession, without apology for what I must admit is an anthropological attempt at amateur philosophy!

Yet I must not live like a crone. For one thing, it's morally reprehensible to ignore politics, our human instrument sine qua non in Atlantis. Although both viable parties even at their least compromising are embedded in the degrading culture of our commercialized and anti-intellectual democracy, it is pragmatically essential for a citizen to be clear about the differences between them; for despite the advantages of our Constitution we do not have the ideological conveniences (and drawbacks) of a parliamentary system whereby factions can be more narrowly and consistently defined. So how can a culturally antithetical but fundamentally patriotic anthropologist suppress polemical emotions in a pluto-demagogic society? Religion, high culture, entertainment, sports, and mere amusement share our political continuum. How can I deal with the polity of our mesocosm, the middle world of Geisteswissenschaften, midway between astronomy and particle physics, without revealing the heart on my sleeve, without responding to humanity's dangers? Take good Tessa: she acts upon what I contemplate!

The political economy that has made Atlantis a marketing civilization (as Osbert Spengler would probably have called it) is the enveloping wave Finn speaks of, which seems ineluctably decadent as a function of rising consumption. Our ever-hopeful ever-frustrated curve of political economy, even when occasionally on the rise, is at best a momentary check to the careless corruption of our commonwealth. That's how pessimistic I am as an angry patriot, though in the serenely privileged possession of fairly healthy old age, when I'm distracted from the private life in which I have a possibility of offering ideas practically valuable in the future history of this equivocal civilization. But even if I contribute to evolution's ascendant symbol-system for readers, as my time compresses I cannot shut out the political news that adumbrates more despair than hope as a living citizen—as an integer of Christian culture and a child of the Enlightenment. I can't always resist Tessa's urge to attend her Cratic City Committee meetings, which call me all the louder as an expiatory distraction from the labor of a heavy tome.

Finn is right, that in my political involvement, which is more emotional than practical, I'm an armchair quarterback, full of suggestions, cheering on the active participants, dodging actual work for myself. I haven't knocked on doors or distributed leaflets since the lost cause of Stevenson campaigns! At best I'm tacitly excused as an oldtime liberal.

But it isn't just a higher calling, selfishness, or propitiation that makes canvassing repugnant to me. Beyond the common fellowship of dedicated Crats, locally or broadly, the effort to ignore ubiquitous prostitution of symbols and innocently pernicious degradation of language, in common information and debate, is a lost cause simply too painful. Political criticism nowadays is silenced with catchwords. Even if our party regained control of all three branches of government, we hardly would or could correct the thoughtless passivity perpetuated by mass prosperity and sanctified by a rhetorical ideology of acquisitive freedom. Where can I look in history or geography for another society so besotted with both power and narcosis? Then too, where in Melanesia, Micronesia, or Polynesia, or in Asia, Africa, Antarctica, or Hyperboreas, could I find analogy to the ordinary aggressively solipsistic drivers of insulated kilroys? Aside from a small band of intimates, who are temperamentally liberal (perhaps the one necessary qualification for my friendship), and almost except for gender itself, national partisanship for the common good sometimes seems my only cultural fellowship with more than just a few Atlantean intellectuals, despite the fact that as an effective solidarity it's based all but entirely upon collective economic values.

That's why I'm less interested in higher education than in nursery schools, where there's still a small possibility of averting or inoculating absorbent new brains against the abuse of broadcasting. The only thing more important for future society than protection of tender psyches from the saturating assaults of commercial entertainment is an enhancement and extension of enlightened maternal nurture, which, as with public education in general, probably requires at least three generations to evolve or recover, even under favorable political guidance, by unnatural selection. But how to educate the *first* educated generation?

The doubled autonomy of Mary Tremont and her only child (my godson) is a rare and inexplicable exception. I think of her, my intrepid old friend (who called me her midwife), when I'm faced with exceptional individuals in any culture. Atlanteans generally accept an unnecessarily inverse relationship between liberty and community, but she was a spurious case from both sides of that axiological equation! Of all the people I've known she dared the most, loved the most, suffered the most disappointment, endured the most variety of hardship, generally experienced the most, but remained the most hopeful—until horribly benighted by commonplace dementia.

Tessa asked me what Mary was like in her prime. (She had met her only once or twice, when accompanying Caleb on a visit to the nursing home in Botolph, or by herself, when it was too late even to imagine—in the ignominy of grouped decrepitude—the original woman's creative vitality, humor, extravagant generosity, and reckless goodwill!) Aside from a list of acts or events (mostly from her own accounts), I am unable to express her vital immediacy. I am at a loss to convey in anything better than a few conservative adjectives and gerunds what I try to remember of her actual presence. Then too I always feel as if I'm a priest or doctor when I withhold opinion that would embarrass any of the quick or the dead. There has especially been no reason to tell Tessa anything much of Mary's confidences; psychologists are particularly overweening when it comes to preternatural personalities, even about those subjects who exhibit among their characteristics certain classic symptoms such as exhibitionism, which is common enough among geniuses and fools.

Mary always wanted her death to be either instantaneous or religiously self-conscious. She had long since contracted her corpse to the Norumbega Medical School, which keeps such donations for a year. Soon now her remains will either be released for Caleb's voluntary disposal or buried in the School's own potter's field somewhere in the suburbs. (As for me, I'm afraid I can't bring myself to such altruistic self-determination. Besides, even my unsentimental children would be horrified.) The ground is thawed at last!

Digging reminds me: Felixity hates to leave her tracks in winter. Sometimes I have to shoo her out the door from under the furniture with my broom. I don't blame her, especially in high wind or blizzard; but she has such a thick fur coat and she's so courageous that she isn't fazed by the frost or rain itself. (I couldn't be bothered with a sissy hothouse cat.) When the weather's not too bad she has the endlessly interesting experience of natural liberty outdoors. I turn a blind eye to her secret life among birds, but I rescue live mice if she brings them home to play with, or I confiscate them if they're already dead. The danger of her self-confidence is that just as she readily closes her inner ear to my cacophonous radio and tolerates the suddenly piercing rings of the telephone (followed by my irrationally intermittent utterances of meaningless emotion with a lifeless gadget at my ear), she may also have become so accustomed to the doppler noise of kilroys that she assumes they are as natural as barking dogs and no more dangerous than that at a distance. I just hope she's intelligent enough not to misjudge their course and speed in simultaneous opposite directions. I grew up unaware that townspeople ordinarily kept their cats in captivity, especially when their natural predators are said to be about.

Now that I think of it—even as anthropologist, liberated widow, and fully experienced supervisor of both genders—there are many things about people (though especially men of course) that I've been unaware of. I should not claim to be better than any feminine student of the exotic or indigenous human phenomena that I behold objectively in common with males, as if invariant, but with dissimilar empathy. If it weren't for our common language there'd be double departments at every university. Nevertheless, after all these years, I'm learning some subjective as well as objective things about men from Finn. The differences we've had about education must be typical. But as he's hardened me about battleships I think I've softened him about discipline. For instance, he had dismissed nursery schooling as merely an economical convenience for parents while he attempted to interest me in his unsuccessful efforts to reform the curriculum of the Naval Academy at Port Royal, where he'd once taught electrical engineering to "illiterates" who'd perhaps one day co-determine the course of history according more to the intellectual influence of their college years than to any other formative period of their lives. But he was always rightly disgusted with the overemphasized concept of "training"—following and leading like standardized cars behind tracked locomotives—as the function of "education". He'd found that even his English and History Department colleagues at the Academy understood no such distinction when he taught there for a year.

The laugh's on me. I had taken it for granted that I could never open my mind or body to a military man! At the worst, I still think he betrays a little too much of the gentleman warrior. Sometimes his conventional politeness is irritating, even to an oldfashioned lady like me. "Funny Finny" I call him. Of course he's no more typical of the Navy, old or new, than I am of professors. Together we make intimate fun of current Offense Department jargon about "power projection" and other such phallic terms; but as an inveterate thinker of artificial systems he still has a rather puerile fascination with naval doctrine's "C^3I"—Command, Control, and Communication—plus Intelligence! The time he brought me a long rather technical naval history article, and I teased him for teaching me how to occupy my vacuous feminine time, he replied: "Even when you were still only a nurse with a single stripe through your bonnet, like a midshipman, I held a Navy "command-qualification" certificate for ships as large as a hospital! I am merely honoring you by exercising that authority for the first time on you as my capital vessel."

As a seaman at heart he probably still can't help thinking of female intellect as something like the awkward superstructure of an aircraft carrier built on the hull of a tanker. Amid his various other intriguing or hazardous duties, he tells me, he was really more interested in designing a C^3I system than in applying it. Otherwise, I believe, he'd have been a full-time man of organized action during the War, probably ending up as a battleship admiral, as he'd wanted to be when he joined the R O T C at Norumbega. Yet he abhorred and tried to ignore the unofficial social and political attitudes that prevailed in the Navy, especially among married officers. There's much to be said for establishing anthropological doctorates in technocracy just to establish what—besides nurture, nationality, and regime—so starkly distinguishes between rare birds like Finn Macdane and Albert Spree!

If I'd been endocrined with a Y gene I would have chosen the Coast Guard. Tessa would have done well in the Navy. She does a marvelous job as Chair of our Crat Committee. My social conscience weighs upon me, but it's pretty late in life for me to take on extra work, even to help save the world from Raygun's party. The only excuse for neglecting public affairs in favor of scholarship or art is an absolute dearth of time, which anyway may well be drained by demands of love or friendship, if not wasted in the usual killing of it. I've got to get over my impulses to be a hostess! Now in my "contented retirement" I have fewer amusements than ever, but my self-discipline doesn't sufficiently rise to its purpose! Mary repeatedly told young Caleb "Do great things, don't dream them all day long!"

But now I have a Finn!

8

TABLET
NINE

[Downstage right a simple cot inside a low lean-to open toward audience but initially obscured by a drop-curtain. Upstage left a small raised platform, empty at the outset.]

Berosus sitting as before. Enter upstage Gilgamesh (bloodstained), Eber, the Rector, & Norkid.

EBER	This is the wrath of Elohim!
RECTOR [Breathless.]	It's the wrath of Inanna! Her temple was spared. Never before have the gods shaken our land.
NORKID	Earthquakes are to be expected where I come from. So I suppose you think Mazda was always angry at us.
GILGAMESH	How much further damage? Have you inspected the walls? Any cracks in the tower glaze?

NORKID

No sign of that. Just a few leaks in some of the canal watergates.

EBER

Ten of the herders were killed by the cattle and about twenty of them seem to be dying. Inside the walls so many houses had collapsed that we can't yet count the dead. Most of the public wells are ruined. —But it's not the innocent gentiles that were meant to be punished!

GILGAMESH

This isn't the time to debate theodicy. Leave the dead and let the women worry about other casualties until the city is secure. Are the cattle rounded up?

NORKID

Enter Engidu downstage left, more and more slowly, attended by **Lil-Amin & Widow 1** *(unseen by the other players), limping across to the lean-to. He lies down on the bed.*

They're docile and harmless now the monster that started their stampede is dead. I must admit that such a huge aurochs was never seen where I come from. I'd like to know how he got into the stockyard before the quake! On the rampage he looked like a mammoth red-eyed lion, but he had neatsfoot hooves sharp as a gazelle's. He seemed much too canny for a wild bull that accidentally starts a domestic panic. The shaking ground may have loosened the gate but he tossed it off its hinges like an educated elephant. His horns were at least eight feet from tip to tip.

GILGAMESH

His mane was thicker than the length of my sword. That's why it took so long for Engidu and me to kill him. It was one of those horns that nicked Engidu's foot. We are very lucky not to have fared any worse.

[To Eber.]

—Send a caravan up river to get grain for the survivors' bread. We may have enough beer in your godown to tide us over till the water is cleared. Draw what you need from the treasury.

Eber leaves.
[To Rector.]

—Why aren't you ministering to your people? Are you their pastor, or just a master of ceremonies? If they think that bull was sent by Enlil you can tell them that I've turned it into the greatest sacrifice ever offered in propitiation!

RECTOR

Rector leaves.

Not sacrifice but sacrilege, out in the streets! Never has there been such profanity!

Gilgamesh & Norkid go off the opposite way upstage, conferring.

ENGIDU

[Moaning softly.]

WIDOW 1	There's no more bleeding but the smell augurs worse. He should have told you about the pain.
LIL-AMIN	He imitates Gilgamesh in every bravado. He said the puncture was nothing worse than a manly scrape. But now the polluted blood has reached his head, already too late for any medicine I know. We can do nothing but apply my herbs to keep the fever down. His life will depend upon our oblations to Inanna.
WIDOW 1	Shall I go tell Gilgamesh?
LIL-AMIN	Find him if you can. See if he'll listen to a woman. Say nothing to anyone else except Norkid. If Engidu's sickness gets out too soon the Rector will call up a riot before I can assure everyone that the earthquake was not meant for us. The people are frantic enough with grief and devastation. I must attend to the sacrifice. Those who fear I'm dead in the rubble can come and see me at the altar. But I won't leave him until you bring water and my bag of herbs.

[Widow 1 hurries off.]

ENGIDU	Why are you still here? Go away! Let your ape-man die in captivity! Better alone than watched by the one who lured him to mankind.
LIL-AMIN	I am here to help you. You need silent rest.
ENGIDU	Help me! All too well I know that woman-words have deceitful meanings! You opened your robe to reveal your snare and made me learn that I was somewhat human! You cut my hair, you dressed me in clothes, you fed me meat and gave me beer to steal my strength. You tamed me for the world that thinks of death. Bitter sorrow comes too late!
BEROSUS	Engidu drifts into delirium.
ENGIDU	You were the first I saw of wordy kin! Must you also be the last? Where is Gilgamesh? It's not his fault you led me to him and death. But why doesn't he come see me die in his dungeon? You promised I would be his brother! Why does he leave me trapped like a lion in your woman-net without the strength of a hare and my thoughts too swift to remember?
LIL-AMIN	You know I did not give you this sleeping sickness. Blame Gilgamesh for folly, not me for love! He led you into evil. I gave you dearest love. I brought you to Uruk for my people's sake. They still adore you for diverting Gilgamesh

from his most oppressive ambitions. You are their champion. Let them need not grieve for you. You will live if you try to remember the love and friendship among us.

ENGIDU

Widow 1 returns, running, with water and herbs.

The promise of that love and friendship was what made me betray the gazelles and lions who ran with me on the steppes! You charmed me into hunting their kind! Then Gilgamesh made me help him taunt the gods by killing Kumbaba and the bull of heaven! —Oh save me from the dust! [*Wailing.*]

WIDOW 1

My lady, please: I was intercepted by your brother the Rector and sent back to implore your immediate presence at the council. Gilgamesh refuses to consult the Optimates. They say the people cry out to be told what's happened to Engidu. Gilgamesh tells them it's more important right now to stop the looting and fix the gates. I'm so afraid of—

LIL-AMIN

Then I must go. Engidu can't bear the sight of me! Give him all the water he can swallow.

WIDOW 1

Oh my lady, I'm sorry for you—and for us all!

LIL-AMIN

Lil-Amin goes off.

Try singing him to sleep.

WIDOW 1

[Ministers to Engidu and draws the curtain.]

[*Wordless lullaby.*]

BEROSUS

[Plays flute.]

Engidu sleeps and dreams.
[*Gradually diminished humming.*]

WIDOW 1

Oh Inanna, do not let our savior die!

[Engidu reappears from back of lean-to, perfectly healthy, in refreshed attire, facing upstage and seen only from behind.]
Gilgamesh appears stage-left in simple dress.
Inanna appears on platform (played by Lil-Amin lightly clothed as the goddess).

INANNA

[To Gilgamesh.]

I bear the blame by Father Enlil for allowing you to contaminate my godson, and to use him against Kumbaba the warden of heaven's axis. I have defended you against the wrath of every other god. Because Uruk is my city I have also been accused of overlooking your insubordinate architecture. Yet before the council of gods I pleaded that you were a stranger ignorant of Sumerian customs. I mean to persuade my peers to withhold their righteous retribution. I will bemuse them with excuses for your effronteries and transgressions, promising each of them such favors as lie within the realm of love. For you are like no other man or god. Let us find a bed together. I promise your willing acclamation by the blackhaired people as high king of all Sumer and the Sea-Lands.

GILGAMESH As their beloved builder of walls and canals? As the gods' favorite acolyte? Or as your father's rival?

INANNA Come with me to the tower's top. I will show you the sweep of your command from mountains to the sea. You shall have the means to rule all cities. Yours will be dominion over timber forests, bitumen pits, stone quarries, herds of cattle, flocks of sheep, water wells, steppes for grazing, fields for grain, and the fruit of all blossoming—everywhere between Tigris and Euphrates, and as far as you wish beyond them! You shall harvest the reeds and fishes of the Sea-Lands and build great ships to bring gold from Ophir!

GILGAMESH Everything but liberty of will!

INANNA I will forbid you nothing, not even the continued love of Lil-Amin my servant, nor of her handmaids.

GILGAMESH Is that all that freedom calls for?
[Laughs.]

INANNA What else can you imagine? Do you know who I am? Do
[Reveals her naked you doubt my promises of power?
body.]

GILGAMESH Who could doubt the power of your promise, which is not equaled by any wish in dream. I can see that you are the goddess: you cast no shadow, your eyes do not blink, your feet do not touch the ground, and there's no sweat on your brow. I further know that a deity speaks the truth of its own desire when it offers us its body. But in this case I regret that you face numinous disappointment.

INANNA Are you too haughty to sow mortal seed in the queen of
[Covers herself heaven?
totally.]

GILGAMESH Right here in Uruk you will find such secretion otherwise available.

INANNA It's not your child I want.

GILGAMESH: Then you ought not to be worshiped for fertility. They should praise your cunicular lust. But you envy our happiest women. Even the best of your matings with a mortal cannot convert your lovelessness to bliss. You will never know the beatitude you crave from god or man. Your body is spared women's inconveniences; so it's only compensatory justice that your freer passion should never culminate as theirs often do! As you found even with sweet Dumuzi, noblest of men, best of poets, a champion in the sport. In cruel disillusion you sent him down to dust. And all the others lured by a divinity's desire. I do not intend to end my days in thrall to your uxorious caprice or as the victim of thwarted ecstasy. Content yourself with peers who never sleep, who have never built a building or thought a new thought, whose minds are blank and clothes are always clean, whose garlands never wither, who never feel the reciprocity they miss in raping too swiftly the daughters of men.

INANNA   Revolting man! You hazard sacrilegious conceits like a pretentious shaman! As if you could possibly know anything about such mysteries when you're not a female of any species!

GILGAMESH   One night nine months before I was born in the mountains my mother was visited by two gods imitating men. That truth she told me later. So I know by blood a little what it's like to be a god. My feet touch the ground but I don't sleep much. But I might claim to be nearly half human in femininity! Lil-Amin too speaks of the experience as something opposite mine when I lose my wits in battle-rage. You should become more intimate with the priestesses that serve your temple.

INANNA   May Enlil blast your impiety! I will not beseech an ephemeral worm! You have seized my city, scoffed at its laws! May you die in rubble, childless and alone, cursed by every god for insulting my generosity, for despising my accidental notice of your shape. You can't guess the devices I have to rob you of the fame you crave! If I were an earthling I'd give my life to be your assassin. But I will find a more painfully public drawn-out way to cut down your towering presumption!

GILGAMESH   Does Madam Fertility Muse threaten drought famine and
[Laughing rudely.]   pandemonium for her people? —Wait! Before you go, let

Engidu pay a changeling's tribute to his godmother! You
can have our trophy of your mammoth Bull of Heaven!

[To Engidu.]
—Flog her with the cod and pizzle! Go on, throw it in her
[Engidu throws a
lap! Even her father knows she's shameless!
knot of heavy rope
at her.]
**Inanna, Gilgamesh,
& Engidu
disappear.**
[Berosus plays
flute.]

WIDOW 1 [*Croons tenderly.*]
Gilgamesh in
former dress **comes
on running.**

GILGAMESH Where is Engidu? Is he really hurt? Where is he, woman!
Get out of my way.
[Widow 1 opens
curtain to show
Engidu tossing in
delirium.]

ENGIDU [*Moaning.*]

GILGAMESH Engidu! Why didn't anyone tell me sooner?
[To Widow 1.]
Leave those things. I'll watch tonight.
[Gilgamesh kneels
beside the bed.]

ENGIDU No! Don't come near me! Now I know your heart! Always
[Suddenly sits up in
false brotherhood with nice words! . . . When you said I
agitation.]
was your friend Eber smiled like a father and called me
Nimrod the mighty hunter. Norkid made me welcome to
the soldiers. . . . You kept me so much at your side that
because of our likeness people called me the Good Gilgamesh. Passing in the street they began to say "We are
not blind. That's the real Gilgamesh, disguised by Inanna
as barbaric Engidu!" . . . .

BEROSUS So began in Engidu's delirium the legend's amalgamation
[Widow 1 goes
of two figures. This hierodule watched and listened but she
out.]
was an imaginative witness. Afterwards she told migrant
traders disparate stories about the same personage.

GILGAMESH My dearest friend, I was pleased with the confusion. We
have not ended our feats, for yet more fame in greater
deeds than killing. You must get well soon, so that
together we can astonish the gods with acts of peace.

ENGIDU [Not listening.]	. . . Your smiles grew false with jealousy of the people's love. Yet still you used me! Without me you could do nothing great enough to keep Uruk in docile subjugation. . . . You were clever; I was just an uncouth brute, easy to deceive. . . .

GILGAMESH	Engidu, are you saying what you really mean? How did I deceive you? How could I? Why on earth should I of all men have need to play you false as twin to my own heart? I wanted the people to love you! I saved your life and you saved mine! You were afraid when I was not; I was afraid when you were not! We loved the same woman! If you had cared about kingship I would have gladly shared the Rod and Ring!

ENGIDU [Gilgamesh raises his head to give him water but then meets agitated resistance as he gently presses him down again.]	You have turned me against lions and aurochs, and even against the gods. Yet you never let me be my own man! What have I become but a savage in captivity, dying alone in this cage within the walls of a city I hate! . . . You lured me with words that never meant what people told me they said.

GILGAMESH [Lays his head against Engidu's chest.] **Lil-Amin**	You wrong me, Engidu—after all our time as loving equals! I who understand more than other men cannot guess what mistaken thought has turned you against me!

enters quickly but pauses to watch from a short distance.
When Engidu notices her she comes to stand beside Gilgamesh.

LIL-AMIN	The gods have taken his reason. We can only pray for him to sleep.

GILGAMESH [Impulsively he rises and rips from her neck the Isorecto-tetrahedron, slinging it by the lanyard into the audience.]	You pray. I cannot pray. Where is your magic now? The gods rule by doing nothing. The people prayed for him but their love cannot keep him alive! They are always answered by what they're told's the will of heaven. —This jewel I gave you is only my mnemonic symbol, not an amulet! A real rectotetrahedron changes shape in reason's nightmare! Life's edges and facets are never so neatly fixed. Our world is not a constellation in the sky! It slips away from us like an altering dream, less to be trusted than a river of moons. Let Euphrates drown every gem like this!

LIL-AMIN	You can't throttle grief by recanting your own reason! If you can't pray to gods, proud Gilgamesh, pray to yourself. Even you may be capable of that! Pray to realize the fact that Engidu is dead.

ENGIDU   I go! You stay.

[Engidu dies.]

    GILGAMESH   His eyes are clay. Inanna has killed him!

    LIL-AMIN   Your tears become you now, the only offering to gods I've
ever seen you make.

9

POWERLESS
MAYDAY

Consciousness is a variable uncertain element
which flickers uncertainly on the surface of
experience.

— Whitehead, *Adventures of Ideas*

1.

Now on the day following Walpurgis Night there is this to be told
about a solitary beardless but unshaven pedestrian under a lowering sky on the nearly deserted main street of East Harbor, even as a
sodality of Vikings in the Fifth and Sixth Parishes is gathered over
in the Seamark liberty under its Maypole in a little park by an old
millstream, preparing to intertwine on light fantastic toes the circling streamers of every color, urging fissures of blue sky to expose
the lurking sun as actually effulgent. Forty years earlier, almost
like an orphaned refugee when W W 2 was hardly started, he
learned both solar and widdershins dances around an English may-
pole out on Crow Point at the Tudor Convent of St Martha, long

since vanished as such from behind the high rusty granite walls now owned by subdivided estates of exclusively private taxpayers. The inner-harbored Georgios, Tuscans, Lusitanians, Aramites, Irish, Eberews, Marranos, Arkies, Yankees, Achaeans, and other Strangers—yet embarrassingly no full-blooded Africans, Hispanics, or East Asiatics, except for a few who commuted by weekday from the mainland to fish-packing plants, and not a single Romany or Natural—no longer celebrated with the traditional bonfire on Beltane Hill what they didn't know was their vestigial European dromena from Sumer's Bel-Enlil (Ba'al to later Semites), on the very day that Milesians drove the Tuatha De Danaan underground to fade as the twilight Sidhe of Ireland. But Perdita Dana will still be fasting and meditating after her vigil among occult burial mounds on the Purdeyville heath.

Caleb Karcist no longer runs his large daily loops for the kind of exercise that years before had delighted Ibi-Roy his royal saint. As an older man he now walks shorter ruminative excursions, usually after darkness deepens his unkempt invisibility, sustaining health well enough to prolong his longevity, hoping to clear his head of the irreducible Activities of Daily Living [A D L] that harry and infuriate his solitary freedom to read and write. The more familiar his route the easier it is to keep his thoughts on their chosen track, yet today's daylight itinerary, his favorite route, recalls objects still interesting after many years of treading it with such habitual observation that without paying attention his eyes would notice the slightest change of fact or artifact as he came to pass it. But this secondary holiday is an exception: he's looking for distractions, hoping for novelty, trying to procrastinate the unpleasant deliberation of means that he ought to be pondering in aversion to calamity. In other words, he is trying to turn a blind eye to disaster at the very time he should have been confronting it as a prudent man seeking feasible course-correction. He prefers not to remember that this existential state of mind was once all too familiar.

So for such a tour he turns to Mother's Neck and its watersides rather than East Harbor's more arboreal district of rock-surmounting hills and residential diversity (though for genuine hypnotism he would have chosen them before those of any other ward or town in New Armorica). Therefore he does not turn left from the Apostle's Dock door to Wye Square and up the sinuous Skate Street hill lined for the most part by unaltered modest white architecture intimately close to the sidewalks, including some whose lovingly preserved old clapboards of the Atlantean Gothic or Federalist styles remain uncounterfeited by vinyl or aluminum cladding (which is easier to maintain for the first forty years). But even now he wonders for an instant if he hadn't done better to go that way up to the corner house of the late widow Cibber, and turn left to the East Harbor Fire House, an anachronistic livery framed in wood, whose two double doors are open to disclose its horseless dragon-fighters, only to then remind himself that he usually regrets beginning instead of ending a long walk on its uphill leg, before his aging cartilage is well warmed up. He is not in the mood for strenuous effort so early in the season. So instead he has set out to the right after all, as intended, along the shoreline street to the causeway and its thickly settled headland, which was once an island hill with sheep grazing on it.

It has been a sullen spring and right now he feels as if he's just after being wakened by some peeler's shillelagh from a pipedream. His mother would have laughed at his predicament. A few minutes ago the parsimonious extenuation of his treasury was delivered an ultimatum by a long-dreaded notice from the apologetically embarrassed landlord of Apostle's Dock to the effect that his rent would be doubled on the first of July.

Less than a year after his mother's comatose death in some Botolph hospital—to which she had been transferred from her nursing home for acute care, where, not having understood the finality of her condition, he'd failed the conventional expectation that the next-of-kin, especially an only son, would make what amounted to a whole day's trip to witness her senseless body near or at the end of its breath, under the misapprehension that she'd sooner or later recover her former state of senility and be sent back to the Bishop Derwent House for the rest of her comparatively public life, where visits were far less inconvenient—he now personally faces the meaning of time's arrow: not the horror of her subjective death itself, for which he had been objectively prepared, but the ecocentric significance of her only child's swiftly evanescent hours remaining to finish his figment of closet drama (already reduced for artistic reasons from a trilogy to a dyad), which has justified to himself the selfishness in his dereliction of sentimentality—because once more he has to get a job!

The rent increase is fair, considering that as the Dock's longest resident he has lived there for many years at a rate that was never adjusted for Dogtown's extraordinary inflation of reality-estate and

maintenance costs, national prosperity, and thus the much higher
income now obtainable by landlords from occupants of the great
picturesque maritime barn. Indeed, Tony Estivador's generous forbearance (only partially explained by his preoccupation with the
more important management of his commercial dockyard) had been
equivalent to a considerable augmentation of Caleb's income—and
thus his savings—during the years his salary at Mercator-Steelyard
had greatly risen, with bonuses and stock options to boot. Every
spring summer and fall he's suffered the daylight boatyard voices
and noises funneled to his windows by the embracing basin. But
the sounds of others' industry and pleasure are plaintive for him
now! At the prospect of his forced banishment to some squalid
street of hustling infernal consumption engines he suddenly savors
the annoying security of wind-whipped halyards, canvas, and
molded plastic.

Working at the Yard in his salad days, when he spared much
too little leisure time for the private life he valued supremely, his
mania was that of a self-driven rationalist determined to realize his
vision of a microcosmic productive social system privately profitable to those of whom he knew very little. Gradually enthralled,
as if self-hypnotized, he'd immersed himself in the reorganization
and guidance of hands brains and machines run by alphanumeric
oghams in the service of Atlantean culture's highest values. On his
part, as a masked character, his communication both within and
without the corporation was perfectly sincere—impatient with the
imperfect devotion of others. He enlightened and empowered traditional agencies of Steelyard administration by exploiting his control
and transformation of the regular cyclic energy that empowers
modern offices. But thus engaged in his daily intramural world,
across the main inner harbor from Apostle's Dock, he had also little
by little secreted like some megamechanical hermit crab a crusta-
ceous shell to protect his private system from anyone else's. Gradually the public job had nearly absorbed all the amateur energy he
could devote to the contents of his shell.

The walls and contents of the Yard were as one, a four-dimensional organism as fascinating to him as the management of a propitious new Presidential administration for all Atlantis. His
administrative organization was an edifice of brick, prestressed
concrete, plans, elevations, symbols, men and women, systems,
promises, schematic diagrams, flow charts, writing-compiling-

testing-installing computer programs, alphanumerical coding schemes, technical writing, operating instructions, software documentation, recruiting and training various kinds of talent, job descriptions, personal performance reviews, manuals of articulated procedure, data-security measures, maintenance schedules for building and equipment, corporate operating reports, proposals, budgets, financial justifications, forecasts, sensitivity analysis, computerized matrices, safety precautions, financial controls, accounting integrations, sales analysis, logistical simulations, office equipment and supplies, inventory controls, conference agendas, charts of account, vouchers, requisitions, purchase orders, external correspondence, accounts payable and receivable, interoffice memos, staff meetings, complaints, morale fluctuations, interdepartmental diplomacy, incessant phone calls, enquiries from above, reassurances, apologies, journal entries, stupid resistance, and as much cheerful banter as time permitted—but especially whatever could not be delegated in the grand design or crucial details of the labeled "Central Management System" [C M S] architecture intended to anticipate every extension of its managerial domain for many years to come, like the counterentropic growth of a brain.

Most of Mercator-Steelyard's white-collar functions were meant to be eventually comprised in his web of substantiated abstractions. The discipline implicit in his hierarchy of tutelage educated many a retainer to higher levels of competence. In the end C M S was irreverently dubbed *Caleb's Monkey Management* by some in the crew of over fifty more or less happy vice-managers subalterns technicians and clerks who programmed and maintained it under his irritating eye for detail—and that epithet was sometimes used mockingly by peers in other departments whenever the progress of "data processing" momentarily seemed negative. But as new routines smoothed out within the office building it was rumored among simians in the highly invested processing plant across the street that abstruse "efficiency experts" and industrial engineers were about to threaten with computerization the autonomy and payroll of the Production Department, from its Vice-President's office all the way down the production lines to forklift operators on the floor of the freezer's holding room.

But it had been to the advantage of Caleb's counterentropic hypercathexis that his distant goal of cooperative enlightenment

among all the company's executives and workers gradually promised to serve the ultimate motive of the fictitious person in possession of the company as a whole. The owners' plenipotentiaries
understood (at a time of corporate prosperity) that Caleb Karcist, if
only rather indirectly, was helping them make more return on capital in the long run by inducing large investments in his kind of
overhead. Having started at a humble level, as the company's first
"efficiency expert" for trivial procedures entailing words, numbers,
and a few unconnected office machines, in less than a decade he
demonstrated that his organic mechanization would eventually
reduce the hidden costs of sales and logistics, as well as of general
administration, he fostered an ever-greater growth in "share of
market". Some of this trend was clearly justified by amazingly
quick fiscal transactions and nearly automatic accounting, by
timely financial reports, by speedy operating information, and by a
common "data bank" of details that were retrievable on demand in
an unlimited variety of quantitative relationships, made also available for budgeting, forecasting, and progressive operations research.

His greatest remaining difficulty was to overcome unimaginative resistance to new conceptions of managerial information or
simulation made possible by new computer programs. It was a
diplomatic problem (especially for one ordinarily regarded as no
more welcome to top executive time than a Goliardic beggar) to
risk animosity by suggesting to barons in their own castles a fanciful method for training their own warhorses, even though he never
presumed to mention his own past experience as an archery sergeant in the calvary of a morphologically similar business. How
could he, the worst of salesmen, persuade battle-hardened field
marshals who brought in all the revenue, and generals responsible
for communications and logistics, or costs-of-goods-sold, to take
advantage of commercial research continuously tailored to their
own jealous specialties by an acolyte? Moreover, in trying to interest them enough to consider thoughts by presenting counterfac-
tual samples of analysis designed according to his own ideas of
useful information he was all too likely to arouse their inveterate
scorn of the same sort of statistical experts or marketing consultants who had no use for Caleb's kind of conceptual commonsense.
"What the hell does he know about sales and merchandising,"
they'd think, ". . . or purchasing . . . or shipping and warehousing
. . . or standard-cost accounting . . . or anything else about the
tough world of competition? It's not just grand ideas!" —Or, on

the other hand, Professor X's exponential smoothing won't help optimize cooperative motivation between territorial salesmen and product managers!

Some supervisors he had inched unconsciously forward by reason, and the manager of "physical distribution", Waldo Cotton, had embraced his function of C M S, but most he had enlightened only by discontinuing the reports they were used to, and forcing them to get accustomed to new items and shapes of "management information" until they tacitly acknowledged his helpful improvements. Such abrupt interruptions of custom were mainly imposed, under the awesome rubric of "computerized" magic that was rising everywhere at the time, by the necessities he declared in his radical reconstruction of the Yard's systems and procedures, since there was no money or space for running "parallel systems" by keeping the Old Homestead Manufacturing Corporation [OHM] punchcard "unit record" tabulating machines and related office machinery after the initial centralized computer was delivered.

This radically irreversible conversion would have been dauntingly complex even if the company's brain heart lungs and hands could have been suspended for a whole accounting cycle to prepare for the transition; so despite all his foresight and apologetic sweat he couldn't prevent certain temporary hiatuses in reporting that was less urgent than order-writing, billing, shipping, check-printing, and payroll. Under the pressure of deliberately unprecedented circumstances he couldn't help seeming highhanded as the necessities of coordinated discontinuations jerked more than one department all at once into temporary consternation, despite all his efforts to mollify personal feelings and admit valid arguments at every level of work, to explain his concepts, to apologize for spates of inconvenience, and to mitigate the shocks of interruption with promises he couldn't always keep on time. . . .

. . . I've almost forgotten the peril in that alien world! Such accomplishment, such authority, and such anxiety seems ludicrous to a wight now dispossessed of even self-sufficiency. The fundamentals of my concepts and application haven't changed in these few years but I've willingly lost track of the accelerating advancements in technological speed and capacity. If it comes to a livelihood, I might as well be totally ignorant of the basics, because nowadays so-called office systems are little better than inorganic syntheses of ready-made programs adapted for conventional purposes according to the multiple-choice selections provided by unimaginative or bureaucratically stunted programmers. Learning to adapt ready-made

suits of software to particular managerial requirements (or vice versa)
—despite the wonderful new advantages of "real-time, on-line" display by
cathode ray tubes (instead of input and output by keyboard and punch-
cards or tape)—is no joy for me without the creative freedom I happened to
have had as an unsupervised architect and autocrat with more experience
in what was needed than in the magic. Anyway, I'm already as ignorant
of the new conveniences as a schoolchild, and more bewildered by the latest
jargon. . . .

"Hence loathed Melancholy" forms in his throat satirically,
without the poetic optimism. Not quite regretting the ambivalent
inconsequentiality of his prime years, and nearly rejoicing in what
remains of Creative Mind (as Yeats would call it), he walks
southerly on East Front Street along the edge of the Argonautic
inlet, a haven known by fishermen for its female anatomy. In prosaic brown study with lowered eyes his first object of fleetingly
Immediate Exclusive Consciousness [I E C] is a familiar small
bronze plate embedded in a single square of sidewalk concrete
introducing a short section of public works provided by the federal
government's Work Projects Administration [W P A] more than
forty years earlier. The oldest dozen-yard section of pedestrian pavement between the Dock and the Neck (or perhaps anywhere in
Dogtown), poured and finished by otherwise unemployed workers
who were demeaned as loafers by the Protestican opposition for
engaging themselves in one of the New Deal's substitutes for private enterprise, along with the Public Works Administration's
[P W A] construction of Dogtown's capacious brick high school
(including a theater and vocational shop) and such typical benefi-
cence as a neatly perduring city hall for Cornucopia's most affluent
little city, were cursed and exorcized by Protestican propaganda as
socialistically insidious "class warfare" by means of public improvements at even the lowest level. That short smooth stretch, alone in
Dogtown, has remained free of cracks, irregularities, substitutions,
or dilapidation. When thus noticed by Caleb it is always a platform
for his mother's love of F D R as an unbounded cloud of personal
affection and social passion that was not caused but confirmed by
her own stint as a writer in the W P A on a project that produced
an excellent guidebook for the tourist business of the state of
Montvert, which still consistently votes for Cans and still boasts of
the independent individualism that was said to have originated
among horse-thieves in little Allenton itself. Thus his transitory
glance summons up as usual an instantaneous précis of his child-

hood's politics, a congenital infusion of predilection that spares him, he believes, all the common misapprehensions of Atlantean democracy. At his mother's knee he was properly educated in social psychology before he learned the multiplication table in the third grade scarcely a mile beyond the pale of Norumbega University's Garth in Unabridge. The little disk embedded in the Dogtown sidewalk fetches up as political emotion a web of remembrances that could be amalgamated in a single glance without pause or review as pertinent to his new disconsolation, verging on the prediction of despair.

Instead he deliberately shifts his mind to the latest mischievous evasion of societal reasoning—the pert cliché that "what goes around comes around". Yes, but in history it never does so on the same level or at the same radius, higher or lower, represented in his own terms by Yeats's gyre. For Caleb himself it may not have symbolized what the occult poet wished, but it served him very well for his own "metaphors" and "images". And it does provide analytical geometrists with all the conic sections, including the circle, even if they have no use for analogy. Certainly, for the closeted dramaturge, it can be generated and subsumed by Gilgamesh's rectotetrahedron rotating on its vertical axis as a cinematically variable dimension; but Yeats, without its axis, cannot provide the perpendicular that makes his symbol dynamic in the real world! The symbolism of the Hermetic Order of the Golden Dawn, like much other magic, was based on the *equi*lateral triangle, which even for triune Christianity is a less meaningful symbol than the cross, both of which are subsumed by extension of their rectotetrahedron's configuration. *'Tis a pity that my character will be lost to the world forever if the theater keeps evading me. . . .*

But at the Yard C M S wasn't lost to the world! Its incarnate power (though truncated in its intended evolution by the author's withdrawal) is still wielded under the overweening aegis of Rod McGrundy, Treasurer and Chief Financial Officer, who'd hired Caleb initially for undefined duty as an analytical assistant on the strength of magnate Arthur Halymboyd's letter from his Graveyard Street office in Ur, seconding the personal recommendation of Christopher Lucey, Father Economist at the Laboratory of Melchizedek and the Mesocosm. Halymboyd's name, at least vaguely known to any regular reader of the *Graveyard Chronicle*, plus the presumably reliable character reference of a sophisticated Tudor Churchman, had been enough for Rod to waive further background inquiry beyond a single-page résumé for what appeared to be suitable for a mere office manager. There had been no particular opening at the time, and Caleb's curriculum vitae was almost pathetically idiosyncratic, but his education and experience seemed pertinent to Management's growing awareness that the Yard needed someone within the crowded lower deck full of unambitious obscurantists to do something about the known errors and delays that were beginning to threaten customer relations quite seriously. Mere "paperwork" had at last been acknowledged by Management to require as much innovative attention as methods and procedures on the production lines, though not as important as creative advertising. It was before "Management Information Systems" became de rigeur in business-school curricula. And it was before small manufacturers like the Yard were considering OHM computers for anything more than accurately speeding up their traditional clerical operations. . . .

As he walks, briskly preoccupied as usual, Caleb continues to ruminate about the past, at a time when he knows he should be thinking about his suddenly parlous future. His mind continues to dodge both the tedious housework that awaits him at home immediately and the beggary that threatens in the offing. Yet now, of all times, he happens to mull regret for having failed at the proper time to appreciate the unspoken encouragement of the man he worked for at the Yard!

. . . for a dozen years of rapid growth in the volume and distribution of frozen fish it was Rod McGrundy, a tall thin and awkward but professionally self-confident fishface wearing thick glasses, brilliant scion of old money, who tolerated a certain degree of insubordination by his protege until he grew to trust it and to accept radical innovation, as the duty of rational noblesse oblige, when it overrode his own advice or preference (even in accounting, his own Certified Public specialty). In the end he honorably accommodated himself to Caleb's wily willfulness by leaving him to his own unorthodox devices perfectly compatible with Generally Accepted Accounting Principles [G A A P] at the corporate level. Caleb's initial lack of knowledge was not held against him. Nearly all his requests for staff, equipment, or travel were granted without question. Yet as a born oligarch and alumnus of the Laurel Amphictyony, Norumbega Business School and all, Rod had been characteristically insensitive to his deputy's resentment of what seemed autocratic interferences during the first few years. At length

a tacit equilibrium smoothed their relationship and Caleb forgot
the intermittent antagonism that had sometimes flared into bitterly suppressed hatred of this snap-judging baron. Still, one such
recurrence of intervention, this time entirely within Caleb's hard-
won C M S organization, following almost a decade of peace and
growth in mutual respect, was so large a matter of protocol that as
an angry pretext it precipitated his immediate resignation. Rod had
heedlessly failed to consult him before summarily granting a
request from the Vice President of Marketing to transfer a certain
young man (who had been recruited and groomed by Caleb's Management Services for a special purpose) to the Sales Department.

For the whole building and beyond that was an astonishing
event—not Rod's highhanded insensitivity but Caleb's extravagant
response to it. It was as if the steadily enthusiastic prized quarterback had walked off the field without warning or gesture between
second and third down in a winning situation. He, of all dedicated
people at the Yard office ever known even by the oldest retainer!
This intensively devoted high-pressure technocrat, model of free-
enterprise initiative, more "aggressive" in his weak-voiced way than
any charging knight in Sales, this bachelor who seemed to ride his
plow-horse seven days a week, by all evidence too busy for normal
human interests, almost never seen without a briefcase of papers,
obviously intent upon a vision of technological power!

Yet in the interval between *terminus a quo* and *terminus ad quem*,
as Caleb fully understood only in retrospect, it was the socially purblind patrician Rod McGrundy who'd been his advocate at the
President's ear, who'd been his apologist in the Star Chamber,
who'd generously promoted and rewarded him without fuss or effu-
sion (as it were from a gentleman to his educated major domo);
who'd protected him from both praetorian guard and the lower
ranks; who'd been deferential enough to yield him full credit for
what had been accomplished under free rein—though Rod himself
had been an auditor of wartime production contracts at a very high
level in Washington, cleverly experienced in prevention and detection of fraud or waste during W W 2, himself well accustomed to
praise as a brilliant master of business finance, and later progressive
enough to have long since invested in the devices of programmed
machines to do everything already being done with OHM punchcards and paper-punch tapes for printing and counting machinery.
(His grandfather had been a Secretary of the U S Treasury and his
uncle one of only two Protesticans in F D R's cabinet, his brother

long afterwards a National Security Advisor—all of which he never
mentioned. He had finally yielded to Caleb a large measure of the
Yard's bureaucratic effectiveness for which he himself might have
taken corporate credit.)

. . . But without an iota of power, and with no further interest
in a business career, believing himself about to drop into the kind
of grubby penury that he hadn't known since childhood, free of
vain deluding expectations but not sufficiently melancholic to
waterlog his inherent cork, Caleb finds himself reflecting that he's
been goddam lucky to have had any business jobs at all, considering the odds against his resistance to Atlantean culture, not to
mention his perversely private vocation (which no one at the Yard
or any of his previous jobs had ever suspected, despite the unusual
obscurity of his bachelor life). As the only pedestrian on a street of
desultory weekend vehicles he now chuckles at the comedy of
having been a pretty good spy upon the economics he persistently
assisted with most of his energy, in his simpleminded enthusiasm
for organization.

He had been dangerously near treachery to the True Mask
beneath the visage that businessmen could see. When he'd suddenly kicked over the traces it wasn't because his burgeoning vision
of administration was frustrated of perfection—as it always must
be—by the fact that he was not a general manager or chief executive officer in a position to run everything. He never doubted that
such elevated jobs required primary attention to functions even
now more important for a nation than all the studios in which he
ever wanted to spend his stolen time, even in his most euphoric
moments of theoretically valuable public service within his ability.
With the broad responsibilities of general power rather than mere
efficiency—dealing with executives, advertisers, policies, customers, public opinion, and decisions framed by circumstances
beyond internal control at the higher levels of management—he
would have chafed at the utter lack of solitary time for research or
criticism, to say nothing of crucially detailed planning. The hurly-
burly of commonplace ad hoc contingencies would have been intolerable. One secretary would not have been enough. He would have
mourned for the solitude of entelectual imagination. No promotion
would have rewarded his soul with speculative time for serving
even a single firm's greater good, and few hours in the year could
ever again have been stolen for his secret calling (especially if there
were a woman in the picture).

Nevertheless, even in his enjoyment of nicely selected power he had sometimes been wise enough to fear the attraction of his expanding interests in organizational aspects of business that were only indirectly reflected in his administrative purview but to which it would have been easy to apply his practical knowledge. So he also had begun to be wary of the morphological aesthetic that secretly beckoned him into opinion and advice above or beyond his station. What if business or government paid attention to him on a large scale, draining him of truly creative life long before he died? C M S enlarged, or the Synectic Method of Diagnostic Correlation [S M D C] applied to every social science—in Civil Service, in the military, in academic administration?

Yet for more likely reason (as his business reputation grew) he'd worried about the ex officio social expectations of an ordinary business careerist at a normal headquarters normally situated near a normally attractive inland city. Anywhere but anomalous Dogtown, under originals like Tom Parsons the President and Rod McGrundy the Treasurer, it would have been impossible to assimilate himself to the social mores of the successful Protestican bourgeoisie when regularly released from the comparatively impersonal offices where he could join comradely conversation, which usually entailed no reference to family properties, hobbies, country clubs, Turntable charities, or Limeway musical comedies about to be enjoyed on business trips. Though humorously sociable enough in small talk within the Yard's internal atmosphere, he had never been entirely at ease with the outside ambience of acquisitive personalities. Even without playing golf, Thad Kryothermsky—an introverted scientific colleague at the Yard, Tessa Opsimath's brother-in-law (married to a former Premature Antifascist dancer), the gentle self-effacing engineer and director of the Yard's product-development laboratory in a separate building, charged also with controlling the quality of all products—was better adapted to offstage collegiality among businessmen than Caleb cared to be, save when talking shop with drinks.

On the other hand, at least in the latter years of his success, he'd grown very comfortable in leading his own crew, inspiring as much effort and loyalty as any valiant captain of a privateer. He was considerably less guarded with his subordinates than with his nominal peers, often jovial or avuncular with those susceptible to encouragement or wit, and sympathetically tutorial with the ones who wanted to learn as well as earn. Sometimes standing at the chalkboard before senior programmers and others in his corner office he allowed himself homiletic digressions hinting at abstract ideas underlying the meta-architecture of C M S, which usually required their willing cooperation or skill for its realization. To this day he remembers most of his people—women and men ranging from mail clerk to data processing manager—with personal admiration, some with affection. He heard that after he was gone some of them boasted about working under him as pioneers in the new world of managerial technology.

2.

Along the base of East Harbor's thickly populated hill of green-on-granite, from its steepest and nakedest quarter toward the thickly settled corner turn-off to Mother's Neck, he strides in wandering thought. This route is especially familiar: a few gray sheds between pavement and water, followed by small frame houses of various design, closely line the street on a lower bank of the water to his right, jealously guarding their envied segments of the shoreline at the shoal end of Argo Cove's tide. On the left, past the dominant escarpment of steep uninhabitable rock that foots the hill until reaching the shelter of trees, there is no space for an opposite sidewalk, until affording an irregular row of pleasantly crowded houses facing the neater ones on his side of the street. But one of these at the foot of the hill, partly converted into a seasonal gift shop, across from a huge oak (greatest of three) spreading over the street from the lower waterside lots, always catches his eye because twenty years earlier it once caught the eye of Ibi-Roy walking at his heel. By instinct his Viking Shepherd saint was still more wolf than sheep dog. Reflexively thoughtless, he bolted for the shop's painted silhouette of a sitting black cat, nearly killing himself in the middle of the street between two kilroys that happened to be passing each other at that instant. The dog was sheepish enough after he'd slammed up against the clapboards like a stupid puppy, and chastened almost well enough—by his master's anger, not by his own peril, at the nearly mortal violation of leashless-ness discipline—to remember for the rest of his life the folly of trusting his eyes without confirmation of ears, nose, or reason.

Nowadays whenever Caleb comes this way on foot or wheels without being too intensely preoccupied to notice the Sign of the

Cat he grieves once more at the no wiser death of his squire a few years later—when more like his knight, his shield, his steed—at a narrow dip and twist nearby on the same street, by the impact of a fourteen-wheel refrigerated semi-trailer with license plates of Whyaway as it speedily approached the delta of Wye Square from the center-city end of East Front in a heedless rush past the sign of the freezer warehouse it was seeking. But many more dog-years later, it was Ibi's chivalric fault. He'd heard and seen danger careering down to the triangular square from Skate Street: a garish dented kilroy blaring the music of youth's insolence through the intersection and steering fast upon the Jewish Shepherd bitch that the dog himself knew and loved. It was a hot day and she was following a little too far behind her mistress in crossing the nearest mouth of the delta. With a sharp bark of warning that Caleb had never heard from him before, but muffled like all other sounds by the beating noise from the car's radio, Ibi dashed to save his mate he knew not how, perhaps as a sacrifice of substitution, when the starboard headlight of the monster truck struck him with a thud, inelastically repelling him with such force against a thick hedge overgrowing the sidewalk that his body ricocheted into the gutter dead. When Caleb reached him the gore-blood in his half-opened jaws was already stiffening to resemble that of a stuffed wolf's in a natural-history showcase.

Though Ibi weighed more than anything Caleb had lifted since working on the Dutchkill School farm, he carried his lifeless dog effortlessly all the way to the other dog's doorstep at her owner's behest, which happened to be down the nearby lane. Ibi's beloved thorax was still warm and pneumatic, shaking not with the tears of a master but with the uncontrolled sobs of a brother. It was the death of a sweet prince, the pride and joy of a son, almost as the son had been the "Pride and Joy" of his mother. Ibi's beautiful longhaired consort followed them with faint whimpers, respectfully, but without understanding, knowing not what to expect of this solemnity, already doubting her lover's identity. They paused without words as Caleb knelt over the magnificent black and tawn animal. He warmed one hand and cheek with that life's last expiration of heat in the thick ruff and smooth fur of the motionless flank as his other fingers stroked the intelligent skull still clothed with the finest of hair between ears still erect with the alert sensitivity of a guardian saint. The question of obsequy was deferred as long as possible. . . .

. . . Only later did it dawn on Caleb that this stoop probably belonged to the small studio building in which his mother had lost

her female Viking Shepherd, Sycorax, in the fire of 1934 that obliterated the last drawings and paintings of her ambition in that art.
Afterwards he saw a large skylight in the other side of the roof
which at the time looked like a typical gable of a small frame
house, this one with white clapboards, crowded between two large
gray buildings and blocked behind a lower atelier half-converted
into living space with an improvised shingled-over sunporch on
legs. Beyond this cluster of arts and artisans hidden from the self-
service laundry and food shops at the Wye's level, beyond a thick-
eted ridge and a steep declivity to the waterside, is the dingle in
which Petto DaGetto, served by his own driveway down from East
Front Street, still keeps his sculpture studio and parks his welding
truck, now unregistered and rusting, overshadowed by the modern
concrete freezer-warehouse that contains the fish-packing plant of
the Yard's last surviving local competitor. Behind a screen of trees
the old man is at last retired from the industrial support of his art,
thanks not to patronage but to the Social Security system that has
survived almost half a century of Can attacks.

      . . . All these irrelevant memories are capsuled in Caleb's
glance, though immediately superposed by the present's frozen
crisis. Having long since given over the power of a *bios praktikos* he
has this day found that he is being forced to give over also the *bios
theoretikos* in sixty days—a dispossession of voluntary powerlessness.
A populace ignorant of the sophisticated management essential to
the city's contemporary prosperity is totally unaware of him and his
disused power of economic abstraction within the encompassing
chrematistic sovereignty. More than ever the Yard's competitive
plant just across the inner harbor with its five hundred workers and
logistical facilities attracts a ceaseless stream of gypsy kilroys, over-
the-road common carriers, and international seagoing freighters, as
well as the little freight and fish-oil traffic surviving by rail. Even
halfway into the present era of his hermitage the veil of public
invisibility was parted only for the notice of an otherwise unremarkable pedestrian and weekly food-shopper. His prestige was
once derived only from that conspicuous companion, the docu-
mented prince of Dogtown dogs.

      Ibi-Roy, the last of an eponymous dynasty founded by the leg-
endary Perdita's magnificent war-dog Ibi-Roi—king of the place
charted as Beauport by Samuel de Champlain, a Great White
Father beached in search of rosehips who'd shot the dog with his
harquebus in the panic of an Irindu ambush when he was mistaken

for a new kind of Viking—had been the city's public totem fortuitously in Caleb's private possession for more than a dozen years. But now further years have vanished since they last passed Champlain's historical plaque together, where one enters onto the Mother's Neck causeway. The former dog-master has become such a familiar foot-passenger of East Harbor Ward that many immovable or typically kinematic details are absorbed by the senses of both the man and resident observers in their preconscious duty as sentries to guard against unnecessary irritations. It's a score of suns since he's last stopped to read the legend of Champlain cast in painted relief by a historical commission; but now in the unaccustomed despondence cast upon his theoretical life by the late edict from his landlord, an ordinary landmarking impression of the iron commemoration's stanchion and shape again water his time-dried eyelids with the repressed sobs of an isolated country boy for the death of his only friend, an alter ego more pathetic than if he'd shared its language.

At least for a while Ibi was missed by more than a few other saints, yet among themselves none but his lady-love had mourned so much as Mephisto, the Cibbers' sweet big black Cabotland Water Dog, who didn't long survive him and whose late master's shack at the further end of the causeway Caleb now approached. If dogs don't pity the bodies of their dead friends they must be no more aware of the ultimate object of fear that motivates instinctive self-preservation than of the desire to perpetuate the genes by which biologists explain almost all animal behavior. Should we pity or envy them for having no fear of death? Let me accommodate the all-too-conscious anticipation before I die. *My mother finished her life too soon simply because she had such faith in God that her many joys and sorrows—the sheer depth and diversity of her intensely human experience—annealed without bitterness her unrequited love of humanity and the frustration of fame.*

. . . Wat Cibber was a playfully sardonic original, a kindly loyal friend whose portly ghost still sits in the rocking chair of his tool-stuffed workshop (now converted into rental space for the sale of arts and crafts) smoking a cigar under the sign HOME OF LOST PAUSES and making fun of himself as a lazy ruggedly individualistic fisherman losing money even without a helper on his forty-foot "weatherbreeder". Everyone marveled that since the War he had been married to the amazingly adaptive Teddi Cibber, a generally beloved educated gentlewoman of Anglo-Irish blood, who'd served in the Royal Navy and loved the Yankee soldier enough to follow him across the Atlantic for better or for worse—almost notoriously his opposite in temper and culture. For many years she—and their four flourishing adult children who somehow partook of both their parents—mourned him with everlastingly respectful appreciation before she was recently eulogized even more than he had been in the same Separatist church.

The causeway, defended from the outer harbor at Swanson's Cove by a concrete barrier rising five feet higher than a patch of treeless public lawn, is now doubly broadened across the street with a parking lot for pilgrims at the sheltered head of Argo Cove. Caleb slows to a saunter, hands in his pockets, as he approaches the late Wat Cibber's tiny private marine railway, which slopes down to the shallow waters of mudflats between his workshop and his personal little pier. Big thick Wat is now a grinning apparition in memory who mutters (behind the cigar smoke obscuring salt-spotted rimless eyeglasses) the one of his self-savoring aphorisms that most often comes to the fore in the amateur dramatist's mind at the brooding age of forty-six: *It's too early to predict and too late to repent.*

At this former landing on an inner edge of the primeval little island that founded the cervix of the port when the connecting shoal was blocked and filled to join it to the body of East Harbor, the street forks into the loop around which the byways, houses, and seasonal attractions of the Neck are clustered. A pedestrian or driver has the choice of port or starboard.

But first, for two seconds of hesitation, he glances to his left with a sharper pang of nostalgia, for he's also abreast the foot of a dead-end dirt lane called Swanson's Way, always attractive to his eyes despite its unaltered immobility. In a cottage on its ridge not sixty yards from where he stands his benefactor Rafe Opsimath lived for many years, in summers looking down at high tides upon a family of swans until it destroyed all the eel-grass and chose some other cove or pond for its intra-Cape migrations. Rafe had kept a barrel of North Atlantean maps in his living room, until Tessa the widow of Buck Barebones (whose collie Praisegod had been Ibi's best friend in the North Village liberty) stole him away into prosperous marriage.

Himself now an even more conspicuous pedestrian, there are still no others on foot to annoy his progress in either direction, but there are lifeless kilroys about and he can hear that the counter and tiny tables inside Spartan's lunchroom, whose front porch cleaves the walker's option of which way to open and close a circuitry of the Neck, are still thronged with men (and probably only men, except for the harried waitress) at extended midday weekend breakfasts or prolonged diversion for socializing mugups, in a de facto club still dominated in memory by Wat's fetch. It was the best customer Mr Spartan and his successor ever had. More than once Wat had lunched or refreshed with the younger Caleb, his admiring apprentice for wit, a sometime underemployed "bureau cat" in very early years whom he had two or three times charitably hired for a day's help ashore. Caleb was simply handed a pinch bar, claw hammer, and a pair of gauntlets to assist in the demolition of obsolete gray sheds on a ramshackle wharf off East Front Street that the fisherman had bought, to moor and supply his weatherbreeding *Motion* at.

On the way past it today, to Caleb's regret, that particular plot of rebuilt and undistinguished waterfront (among countless other memories of personal kindnesses associated with poverty here and elsewhere in his life) had escaped his cerebral reviews. As he passed it ten minutes ago he was not thinking of his Montvert days where he'd learned the primitive tools of carpentry. But Wat had had no real need for help with a desultory deconstruction project easily advanced at leisure, over weeks or months, with his own much larger wrecking bar. His funeral filled the city's largest Pauline church, more or less liberally orthodox. There among the congregation Caleb had been too moved to stand and blurt out more than a single cryptic sentence to second the numerous rambling testimonies of personal memorial that had become de rigeur even for ordinary folk in the age of psychology, especially where the Eucharist was missing. "Wat Cibber was a character who made and kept his own shape." Few except the widow herself understood what an extraordinary tribute that hasty mumble was meant to be.

. . . As usual he gives in to his horological custom, taking the left fork up into East Harbor's most isolated precinct: charmingly cramped old houses, tiny, modest, or ample, on very short pleasant streets shaded in summer by great chestnuts and oaks planted by the original Georgio fisherfolk who originated most of the structures now pentimentoed or mutilated by many generations of necessity or genteel taste. There's also a yellow clapboarded old hotel of four shabby stories awaiting its reality-fate, no longer expecting pilgrims, aestivators, or jazz bands; but a majority of the other buildings are still recoated with traditional white lead paint.

One nobly obscured exception is a Georgian brick mansion sequestered on its own spacious headland of private park with a palisade
of rock beetling the vestigial beach on which Champlain's shallop
had first touched the island (at least according to the prevailing
lore of local historians).

Again, without paying attention Caleb is aware in a trice of
everything in this composition that has always charmed him,
thinking, rather, of the slippery path ahead that having taken him
between two spacious houses on the ridge of the Neck will pitch
him steeply down to the crumbling roadway along the western
edge of the inner harbor channel. In another two minutes it lands
him there indeed. That level pavement six feet above mean high
tide leads on the left to the abandoned Net & Twine Manufactory
painted red (situated at the tip of what Wat called the outer
harbor's clitoris); but he turns right to reach the Simon's Point
Marine Railways in his masculine circumspection. That prospering
industrial establishment is the one uniquely magnetic attraction on
any survey of the artifactual presque-isle in the successive human
circumcisions of the maritime landmass by centuries of marooners.
Champlain had good reason to name the greater promontory in
even earlier times than his landing on the Cap-aux-Isles, seeing
that it was then (and still is) graced with several little uninhabited
calves off its rockbound shores.

. . . Speaking of that, there's still a small tincture of Gaul, represented by New France, in the local pot-pourri, though not one
drop of the quickening humor was shed here by the rather benign
chevalier whom the indigenous Perdita rejected in a rage of grief
for her dog, when he did debark, nor by the frightened crew provided him by the Chauvinist king who decided that Paris was well
worth a Mass.

So flickers and slips Caleb's bits of patriotic recollections as he
nears the shipyard owned by the Ghibellini family at the end of the
Neck, directly across vaginal Argo Cove from the home he'll soon
be forced to leave, at the lips of the innermost fractal, where twenty
years earlier his most amusing erotic friendship culminated with
the riant Bice Picory, subsequently appointed editor of the *Nous* as
Belle Cingani, whom he'd first met in the cemetery behind his
former living quarters in Harbor Ward when she admired Ibi-Roy
while laying flowers upon the grave of the wonderful woman Isopel
Berners arcanely immortalized by *Romany Rye*. She immediately
formed a close relationship with Caleb's susceptible Urhund. It was

she, not Caleb the master, who jealously discovered that the Viking
Shepherd was enamored of the Jewish Shepherd; it was she, while
pleading access to the city's stud book, who searched the Hall
archives on Caleb's behalf to confirm that John Doe Karcist was his
"unknown" father, proving him as much of a bastard as she herself
was. Belle is now quite respectable and contentedly married without issue to the first and last of many a lover, the aging aviator
Dave Wilson, who serves her like an excellent pair of bookends for
a long shelf between door and hearth. She had hoped to get one of
the longhaired queen's puppies, but apparently the lovely bitch
remained as nulliparous as herself.

. . . Wandering in mind, walking by rote—an unprepossessing fugitive from power, long bereft of royal protection, close to
the end of his fiscal hoard, without the prospect of acceptable
employment, and soon to be searching for a home, yet under the
supreme vocational demand to do his best in the swiftly shortening time of unremunerative leisure, he strives against his nature
to remind himself that he verges on what he wishes to think
about no more than about the steadily magnifying horizon of
aging inability: irresponsible poverty far less bearable than that of
which he was blithely conscious during most of his peculiarly
shielded childhood. He forbids himself prudence until he finishes
going for broke, as improvident as never before! In his struggling
craft he's never before had the advantage of a deadline. *How can I
conjure and cudgel creative madness for sixty days or less, too much coffee
and little sleep notwithstanding? I'm a slow writer and in the best of
times a clumsy typist.*

What a laugh the powerful bureaucrat was that he'd been taken
for when working with secretaries, ambitious assistants, and genii-
machines! He frames a promise to let drop all social defenses
against humiliation until he makes his own deadline and has the
common world finally forced upon him, dodging former colleagues
in the street simply out of self-respect—as "an executive in transition", or as an "overqualified" applicant to "entry-level" office jobs,
or even as a competitor for some bagging job at a supermarket.
Granting that stipulation, he refuses to anticipate recourse to debt
or failure of wherewithal to pay anybody any rent at all for any
dwelling unit on Cape Gloucester or anywhere else! He tries to
smile like a brave young devil at the prospect of any circumstances
in which his singular proofs of practical ability may be suspect or
incredible to employers wary of alcoholics and frauds (though of

course more gracious about rejection than off-island producers of drama on or off Limeway).

Yet standing now on the outermost pier of the Railways, quietly alone with the unguarded and innocent boats awaiting workday attention in or out of the water, he gazes across the inner harbor at the conspicuously modern office building he had brought into functional existence—at this distance its clean horizontal lines of beige concrete and glass still gleaming in rectilinear contrast to its setting among the city's jumbled shapes and weathered colors compressed in time by space, from acropolis to waterside—reflecting that his angry resignation from the Yard went for naught as far as his dimly remembered secondary motive of justification was concerned. According to the Demeter Corporation's rules for its subsidiaries all changes of important personnel were to be reported and explained to headquarters in St Peter. Rod McGrundy had been skeptical of what he considered Caleb's "over-reaction" to the unexceptional transfer of an employee from one departmental supervisor to another simply because he himself (Rod) had forgotten to mention that the V P of Marketing had his eye on a bright young clerk that Caleb's people were educating for promotion.

Of course there must have been a *real* reason for Caleb's astonishing reaction as a mature and prudent executive, obviously appreciated at the highest levels of the Corporation and destined for future promotion somewhere in the national corporation. It would have been detrimental to Rod's own invitation to St Peter as a possible Corporate Chief Financial Officer if his highhanded carelessness as a manager and motivator of people had blotted his scutcheon among corporate cardinals with any managerial flaw that might have justified Caleb's professional suicide—otherwise unaccountable on the part of an enthusiastically valuable figure for the Mills's future growth. Despite Rod's obtuse psychology it must have been his intelligent suspicion that Caleb's emotional reaction to a minor breach of protocol was a pretext or a final straw of some much deeper cause for criticism of his performance as the Yard's administrative V P. He therefore avoided further unpleasantness by disingenuously reporting to national headquarters that Caleb's reason for abruptly quitting the job of a lifetime was a "lack of a further creative challenge in merely managing systems essentially completed". Roughly speaking this was ironically true. But it was only the final cause, not the efficient or proximate cause that made him decisively angry on the spot.

Though Caleb had no wish to contradict the lie he allowed himself to be deprived of the vengeful satisfaction he deserved for Rod's riding roughshod over an organizational plan already promulgated within his own department. Because he himself had half falsely accounted for the defection after his professional surprise had subsided, and because all along he'd been waiting for the most effective occasion to decide the conflict between the contrarieties of his True and False Masks, he wasn't entirely sorry that his petard had been a dud. Even now in distant retrospect he's discomforted by a twinge of guilt about his watered-down statement of resignation face to face with Rod, his merely obtuse benefactor who had never himself suffered as a non-com from upstairs authority.

Nevertheless Rod's prevarication was teleologically correct in his belief that C M S was indeed "essentially completed"! That brilliant master of chrematistic mathematics had still failed to understand that the C M S had so far been functioning almost only as the routine core of a system open to a whole new world of analysis. He would have prevented Caleb from realizing its more innovative development. In fact, several programs of unprecedented managerial information were in his conceptual pipeline at the time. He'd known that sooner or later Rod would order them aborted or starved as unnecessary for further sophistication of the high-speed calculation and reporting required for G A A P. Rod could then get credit for reducing the creative staff and increasing the productivity of clerical jobs as the routine functions of C M S's learning curve flattened out at maximum efficiency. By simply using a hot-shot consulting firm with sharp young M B As to buy and install off-the-shelf programs he thought he could keep everything up to date with fewer clerks under an office manager. By the resignation Caleb's vision was truncated at a stump of applied science sooner than later. In fact he was spared the agony of false hopes too late, gaining *proper* time for *proper* life, at the mercy of what Yeats calls "malign externality".

So now—as he paces more slowly the briny ambience of two hauled-up boats (as it happens), a local dragger and a tug from Botolph whose deep up-tilted bows tower above the yard's pavement like the fore-bodies of scaffolded whales, their keels and rudders visible under their spines in the open air at the bottom of their inclines between sheltering piers—he laughs to remember that he still occasionally dreams of being hired as an efficiency expert to overhaul some totally imagined mis-en-scènes (or "messy scenes" in

Wat's terminology) of some perfectly realistic unenlightened administrative headquarters and finding that without the promised support of higher authorities he's persisting in his usual visionary determination to turn typical people and departments with a central computer into his ideal model of organically systematic business—always to be awakened in frustration by entrenched clerical resistance or shortsighted bureaucracy! Then, senses still alive to the totally imaginary situation, genuine consciousness comes slowly to the fore as it repossesses the wonderful fact that for years Liam's Will has actually been relieved of its false Body of Fate, and that the dream has been concocted by his hermetic brain contriving to warn him that such counterentropic struggle of practical reason is a Sisyphusian delusion without hope of catharsis. He is grateful to his unconscious mind for its backhanded reminders that in the real world his conscious Creative Mind is true to his Will only when building castles in the air.

. . . Yet for all his pessimism about the present life-cycle phase of Atlantean civilization—which swallows its own tail like the Uroboros, as both cause and effect in the educational degradation of democratic dogma—Caleb's temperament reflects half his mother's. As if a man of cork he can always take a breath long enough to ebulliate, no matter how deep he sinks or dives before and after. He's usually convinced that his buoyancy is less natural than nurtural. It's the insensitivity of having been cicatrized in his youth by what he'd felt or witnessed of that "father, mother, and Winnie the breadwinner" (as she often boasted in introducing herself) when within her reach of hand, voice, or pen during manic-depressions, not least of which was her scarcely equivocal attempt to kill him with her in a double suicide. As he once told Tessa (whom he'd still regarded a sincerely sympathetic and confidential friend) when she pumped him with ostensibly casual inquiries, his bizarre childhood of intimate witness to extreme feminine emotion explained the unresponsive mask that at an early age had become his defensive mein in facing unanswerable demands, but that had been imperceptibly grafted into an unconsciously defensive physiognomy at the first blush of any alarming occasion, as if it was likely to pass without permanent augmentation of the condition before him that he already understood unfeelingly. He's sometimes sorry that in ordinary circumstances the scarring of emotion dulls his interest in poetry or charity, and that even when it's a matter of someone's physical pain or mortal fear it sometimes makes his undemonstrative sympathy seem callous.

That's one reason he hesitates to call himself a Christian. It was of his own generally cool charity that he'd suspected—finally to the point of separation and disguised estrangement—his revered Father Duncannon, whose adult life was devoted to teaching the social essence of religion. As Christians both he and Father Dun were the obverse of Mary Tremont, who would give her only pair of sneakers to a foot-sore tramp, and when herself a pauper would send dollars to United Nations relief agencies before she'd also contribute dimes to Mrs Roosevelt's campaigns for social justice. His admiration of Fay is founded upon recognition of *feeling* as the origin of all concepts.

. . . There's no wellspring of melancholy in Caleb's nature. He blesses his own exceptional luck in nurture, education, and work. (And as far as the common good is concerned he's still too much of a meliorist. Even so soon after the election of Roland Raygun he's gathering hope for the next election!) Indeed, at this moment in his treading of Mother's Neck he's estimating that with a burst of rigorous self-discipline he can free himself of his theatrical pre-Chaldean fantasies in forty days and forty nights, with almost three weeks to spare thereafter for improvising future shelter and livelihood. Best not waste time in extraneous worry until he comes to face the drawbridge that must in any case be crossed. *If I need a living Muse to finish my work betimes, let her be Fayaway Gabriel! Not Inanna but Themis! And, futile closet drama or not, it's the sole expiation, though too little and too late, for my selfish life as the son of an unrewarded mother. My Lady of Disappointments spent her life for me, her three-in-one child, her greatest "Gift of God", more precious than her futile art.*

. . . What about his own love and loves? His sensorium may spin many visions, mostly too evanescent to lodge in memory at all; but in sleep, to his knowledge, it seldom resurrected his dog—and never at all "the mother who bored him" (one of her merry locutions), nor even paraphrased his uncommunicative neglect of her whom he's always loved and appreciated as his embarrassing advantage in a life requiring escape from her supervision. Despite the shrouding of loyalty to the omphalic bond that originates and nourishes human sympathy in all its categories of transmutation, his oxymoronic love and delinquency were surely obvious to Tessa Opsimath after her few curiously charitable visits to the Bishop

Derwent House nursing home during her shopping or professional trips to Botolph, when she introduced herself as a casual Dogtown friend of Caleb's who happened to be on a round of errands in the big city, dropping in to see if she could be of any service, at first without identifying herself as a psychiatric social worker.

Tessa's second visit was greatly extended, he gathered, when she took advantage of her professional credentials to enquire behind the scenes about the welfare case, making friends with the lady social worker in charge of all the patients, who was particularly well informed about the "marvelous but sometimes unruly" Mary Tremont—as was the Bishop himself, who had especially befriended this erstwhile active member of his See. His Grace had long since been aware of her lively contributions to the fellowship of several diocesan parishes or missions in the metropolitan area when all her faculties of unofficial leadership and entertainment were still extroverted. Caleb was grateful for Tessa's active interest, which he had taken as his excuse for at least two of the visits a dutiful son would have made to an ordinary demented mother despite the preciosity of time, money, or patience. But for him each actual visit did amount to a day's expensive excursion, disconcerting his eremitic routine, more than commensurately robbing him of the priceless sequestration for which he'd traded power and social confidence.

But now, in effect, he faces self-eviction at the June 30 close of Gloucestermas, which also starts and ends the fiscal year of the city and other political entities that are regulated by the rational solar mentality (whereas Mercator-Steelyard's fiscal year began and ended four months earlier, when the inventory of saleable fish was at its minimum, according to the lunar logic that determined Lent and Christian abstinence from meat, key to the nearly feminine fiscal year of thirteen usefully comparable four-week periods—long ago cleverly introduced by Rod McGrundy or a family predecessor, along with standard-cost accounting for all operations of the plant—which with minor adjustments was locally more logical than Caesar's irregular duodenary scheme, until the Yard yielded its sovereignty to Demeter Mills and was forced to convert its accounting rhythms to those of a conventional empire). Even at the present level of rent he would not have the wherewithal to remain much longer in the maritime lodge to which Belle had steered him twenty years afore.

But the deadline is a goad to respect! In dubious aristocratic leisure he's dallied long enough in liberal pursuit of interesting knowledge and etymological perfection. Hereupon he swears it will allow just enough time to top off his catch, clear the deck, batten down the hatch, wash his hands, and breathe with relief before he toots for the drawbridge to let him out. Or, as if the connecting roads were washed out, and it's like a footbridge to cross from islet to main isle by the rickety wooden one at Little Harbor Creek, when in the dark after winter and storms you can't be sure the beach isn't washed away to trap you in a wet hole at the opposite abutment. *At best a menial job may avail me; at worst some sort of temporary "public assistance", if there's still any such public charity for an undeserving able-bodied ne'er-do-well who's guided himself into homeless improvidence. —But homeless without my files, and practically bookless too! From whence to whither? Much to think about later of course, when I'll have to face a Cuchulain or Kumbaba.*

But of course it isn't a Ragnarok that I'll encounter! Consider lilies of the field, she always said; behold yonder fowls of the air. . . . Take therefore no thought for the morrow, for the Lord will provide! So I shall. It's a negative imperative, at least until the rent's past due! —Meanwhile let my devil take the hindermost: it would be joyful to finish with Gilgamesh on any terms. Only incompetence can stop me now! I'll go for broke, he laughs, with no one to hear or see. For a negative jackpot!

So broods the postgraduate of enthusiasm who has in the past either freely or none too gladly impressed everyone who knew his organizational ability for both common and novel purposes— known for such remarkable foresight and originality, for "critical path" planning, for theorized innovation, and sometimes with nearly overbearing certainty—none of which are required for closet drama. Well, laugh again. His mother often teased or encouraged him with proverbs: item, in this case, "Pride goeth before a fall!"— a lesson long since learned or relearned. Yet lost in thought it's exhilarating still to be free of vulgar prudence. For seven weeks he will double his consumption of coffee, paying no attention to news or entertainment if it isn't party politics.

But that means I should be at work right now! No more coffee today, just tea. Until I've done my Nullification and returned to the typewriter refreshing myself with a parsimonious glass of beer. Then make the simplest possible supper while listening to no more than the radio headlines, now that the Cans are in a position to brag about their popularity and mesmerize even liberal journalists. Perhaps, if I hit it right, some uncommercial music as I wash the dishes. Then at last allow myself to read for mental nutrition, in no more than three different books, saving fiction for sleepy-time in bed, swearing off history and philosophy until I've minded my own business.

Yet that routine doesn't always work, though coffee always helps. I'll drink a lot more of it if I must—but only for my teleological purpose, not to stimulate food-shopping or housework, and never for mere pleasure. My nerves would soon tolerate too much caffeinated agitation as the tonic abused the independence of Creative Mind, much as the gestation with tobacco did that made me the runt of a litter before I was pulled into the world like Tristram Shandy. Otherwise I'll burn the double-ended candle cautiously— at least until a week before I take up my axe. Nowadays my only Muse is a wise old lady. I'll keep my nose to the grindstone, but how best to hone my psyche? My imagination is a stubborn donkey with spindly legs. Still, for forty-two days or less I can ignore conservation of the earth's energy and help myself to hot water for an Archimedes three nights a week instead of only one. Plus showers every other morning to awaken the flesh and invigor- ate the mind, simply to arouse the energetic impatience from which I some- times benefit during twenty minutes of inert subjectivity in Contemplative Nullification before wasting thought on the invariable fast I'm about to break. C N's negative discipline is usually relaxing and clarifying but not often enough does it seem to float me just the kind of image or idea that happens to loosen a Gordian knot of imagination without having cast my bread upon the waters I otherwise soak in. The nearly total submersion of my parasympathetic nervous system in uterine warmth is less determinative than turning a hungry mind out to graze in a meadow of mixed metaphors. —But all too often, alas, in bath or trance, I've forgotten my Eureka before I could get to pencil and paper. I must try that chandlery at the Fish Pier for a waterproof notebook such as used by yachtsmen to keep track of racing time, or by fishermen to mark the inshore or offshore spots of lucrative hauls. I'm not yet down and out. I've had the inestimably lucky benefit of excep- tional teachers, mentor, friends, and at least one imaginative parent.

As his ambulating eyes and feet are wandering he cudgels his brain just to start thinking about the half-blank page that awaits him at his desk, actually procrastinating in the critical pleasure of undeciding among varieties of simultaneous shapes in a spectrum of unrealized possibilities—all the while listening to quietened sounds (even the hoot of a train) from far more of the cityscape than he can see, and absently scanning the decks of tethered unmanned boats awaiting their turns to expose pungent barnacles or underwa- ter damage, or those seeking repairs afloat. On this visit to the apex of his course he hasn't lingered before the familiarly mysterious whale's vertebra, a yard in diameter, centered like a horse collar on

the great calcified vagus that threaded its column of intelligence
and pain; nor before the slender six-foot wrought-iron anchor from
a previous century: weathering trophies carelessly decorating an
edge of the Point's open asphalt parking lot. Hardly less familiar to
him than his own apartment is the whole unfenced yard of successive investments in its submerging tracks and piers, hoary with
countless moons, that wade motionless in the breathing tide. The
modernized shed for materials, machine shop, and railhead-hauling
winches—a hangar clad in metal—has displaced a wooden building
that had long since ended its original fishermen's function by housing a summer-stock theater until local art-lovers and stage-struck
aestivators failed to support it after the War.

This the City's most active industrial boatyard is best inspected
when inactive, deserted by workers and clients on off-season weekends. So Caleb now pauses for a fondly multifaceted minute to gaze
upward at the main attraction of his tour, the frame and vertex of a
figure he can also see at mid-distance from his desk window just
across the mouth of Argonaut Cove. It matches the one under his
closer supervision at Apostle's Dock. Until now on his stroll he's
been looking downward most of the time, that is to say (according
to pseudo-Aristotle) into the past; but now he thinks of the future
as well as the past. This nearly isotetrahedral skeleton, like its
opposite, supports and serves as a derrick-crane, though its purpose
here is to lift machinery and maritime materials more than small
boats. This structure has always been for him the Point's principal
lure. Just as he has done countless times before, he stands for a
moment on its pier to contemplate the symbolic geometry that
always focuses his peculiarly metaphysical world as a thought-
experiment theatrically unrealized. Gilgamesh's gem is a reiterated
Eureka from any angle!

But glancing across to Apostle's Dock, from Magog to Gog (as
Wat Cibber dubbed the two cranes), as from foot to foot of a minor
Colossus, it strikes him for the first time that from both harnessed
frameworks the steel booms swivel idly like maypoles waiting half-
erected for boys and girls with gaudy streamers, hesitant in view of
the lowering sky. This conceit may have been prompted by the
faint sound of a brass band now wafting through the ceaseless continuo of the harbor's mechanized sounds, for he is mindful of the
minor parade now forming at the gates of Acorn Pasture Cemetery
in Harbor Ward close under the windows of a house whose garret
he had inhabited in his youth as an untrustworthy tenant.

It's a vestigial celebration of May Day that over the years has condensed into a pleonastic dress rehearsal for the solemnly expanded Memorial Day march four weeks hence. For Dogtown's commonalty in this century the words "May Day" are more likely to signal emergency distress at sea, or perhaps the street threats of International Communism, than a perpetuated salutation to the joys of spring. Yet to Caleb the steel edges that delineate the shapes from which the derricked spar-boom, rigged like a motionless gaff, represents rotation in an angular continuum, suggest as well an infinitely variable vector in more than three dimensions. The descriptive geometry of this symbol-subsystem is more than twice as versatile as W B Y's double cones, not to mention the ideal but inferior equilateral Trinity and its double the Magen David, or the fixed pentagonal star of Inanna.

Yeats was the greatest poet of modern times, much more dramatically exciting than I could ever approach for exquisite souls who despise the very notion of dynamic right-angled symmetry, I acknowledge, but the gyre limits imagination of generalized analogical and digital relationships that as a function of infinitely varied right triangles can describe the middle world we've made. My idiomesocosmopolitan mapping promotes a sense of trichotomy in decision trees and other determinations of the mind. —But I must admit that right now it's my recurrent mathematical diversion from the deeper demands of fresh poesis. If all is vanity, this is probably the vanity of vanities. Too often it tempts me to elaborate my practical abstractions, stifling the negative capability that half of me was born with.

Thus self-chastised he ceases to linger. But turning back to complete his circuit of the cervix he must pass the Railways' long spindle of flowered "wheels" (in Dogtown lingo), mostly bronze, varying in diameters more or less to about four feet, strung like a Brobdingnagian necklace along twenty feet of a horizontally suspended pipe: screw propellers of two, four, and even five blades— almost every favorite number except i —though most of those in this spare-parts inventory display the three lobes in fundamental conflict with simply paired conceptions. Still, nothing's more biological than normal human gender, he points out to himself, heading down from the cusp of the Point to resume his way from the end to the beginning of Mother's Neck Avenue. Thus he is about to pass south along an inner thigh of Argonaut Cove, where the "needle trades" of pilgrim business under the rubrics of art, cuisine, and companionship expect their owners to prepare for seasonal customers.

3.

Suddenly his solitude is hailed by a level feminine voice of the rare quality that he prefers whenever occasionally at his limited opportunities to consider rejoining the evolution of our species.

"Hello, grandpa! You look a bit seedy."

Its breathtaking apparition stands in the half-opened doorway of the otherwise boarded-up Starboard Gangway to his port, a waterside lobster house and piano bar a step or two below street level. He's avoided Lilian (née Cloud) Algo as a matter of honor ever since her husband Gilbert appeared at the Yard as OHM's very competent and cooperative "Customer Service Engineer" for both tabulating unit-record machines and the new computers. In those days of authority Caleb's embarrassment evaporated as soon as it became evident that the man knew nothing to associate him with his wife, especially since the fellow turned out to be anything but the forceful brute he'd imagined from Lilian's hints at irascible masculine violence and passionate anger. He and Gil Algo then had many a cordially impersonal lunch together. Owing to his intramural preoccupation at the Yard and his nearly furtive citizenship thereafter since Lilian's last clandestine kisses he's never encountered her unaccompanied or mutually acknowledgeable as friends. Even now he glances around reflexively to be sure that they're alone.

"Moonfeather! It's been a dog's age! But you look as lissom and ageless as ever in that smock."

"Don't look too closely. I'm an old squaw now."

Many years have already evaporated between past and present, though he can't remember what she looked like as the melancholic halfbreed art student from the High Cordillera whom he had met as a frequenting customer of the bookstore in Hume where she'd worked, and from whom he had departed only half a year before her maternity, followed by her lengthy adventures on the way to Cape Gloucester with her mother and a young daughter, finally more or less under Gil's protection over in the western hinterland of Prudence Cove. Her second apparition then, presumably less accidental than this late tête-à-tête, was lighterfooted than the first, and (as he now finds) more ironically intellectual with the confidence of her veritable establishment. He presumes no third intimacy, but he must make an effort to conceal the autonomic excitement in his breast—in his solar plexus, perhaps incipient in his loins—at the

harmonic intelligence of her mind and body as so abruptly correlative to memory by his eyes. Yet "What a stranger!" was all he could
summon colloquially from embarrassed surprise and confusion as he
rubs his chin. He feels deprived of dignity as well as power, like
little John Smith before Pocahontas, though he wondered what the
reacquaintance with this semi-Yahi could do to his dignity under
present circumstances.

"But still half a paleface, only a half savage. Come in and have a
Beltane muffin and a cup of coffee! This is my first day here this
year, to start getting things ready for our opening before Memorial
Day weekend."

On the spot, in a surge of impulse, almost a thoughtless rein-
statement of love that rendered his voice infirm, he could not refuse
her cordial summons, despite the warnings of history (rather than
conscience) against intempestive arousal. Inside, having shut the
door, she sat him down in the kitchen and rummaged a cupboard
for another mug to scald and pour his coffee into. She obviously
didn't expect a middleaged kiss.

The uninsulated former fishery house—its peaked frontage
remodeled to suggest a charmingly warm tavern of yesteryear, built
half upon pilings whereby a summer float offers transient mooring
to toyboat customers a few at a time for joining the usual crowded
merriment of the landbound patrons—is still dark and cold from
winter, most of its fixtures and furnishings still shrouded or
stacked. Lilian has just begun to think about what to attack first, a
question now postponed by her exploration of this illuminating
diversion. "I hope we still taste palate to palate about drinking
coffee black. There's no milk of human kindness here yet. Maybe
only a little sweet talk."

"I hope we still agree in a few other tastes, like Caesar salad and
Scotch at suppertime. I'm still slightly civilized."

"It's nice to see that you no longer look it. I've never before had
the privilege of seeing you so unshaven."

"Or old."

"You seem to be in good shape. Gil used to talk a lot about
your inventions at the Yard."

"That sort of scheming was my only talent. I didn't do any of
the programming. I still wish I were a dramatic poet."

"He said OHM flew you to the Homestead headquarters in a
company plane to talk about an article you'd written. He said
they'd reprinted it and sent it to their offices all over the world. He

obviously benefitted from his cooperation with you. He was really shocked when you quit so suddenly. I was surprised at your unlikely career, but not that you gave it up."

"I never mentioned you to him."

"Nor I you. Just listened without expression. I usually didn't let on that I was interested in any of his clients for fear of having to listen to what almost always bores me. Later he made so much money from his OHM-employee stock options and your ideas that he's started his own business in Bethsalem and I've been able to buy half of this one."

"I may have seen a notice in the *Nous* about some new management for this liberal hostelry." Sitting across from each other at the table as they sipped an uncommonly good strong brew he soon noticed that when her cup was at rest she absently twisted the gold wedding band on her left hand—evidently a habit formed since his time. She caught his glance and they both laughed, struck by the same funny memory. "How many times have you lost it since 1961?"

"Not once! You cured me of carelessness. I started doing this after I finally quit smoking. I hardly ever think of cigarettes by now. I think I've passed the stage of overeating. I'm glad you're too late to catch me chewing gum. I'll soon be a scrawny squaw again, but weaker in the knees and with a lot of wrinkles elsewhere."

"I don't know why women worry about wrinkles. They're a sign of wisdom and kindness."

"Don't you wish it! Not on the belly!"

"Then I'm wiser now. Who's your business partner?"

"I'll tell you all about her in a minute. First, guess why I called you grandpa."

"Because it looks as if I'm growing a beard?"

"Come on, Caleb: you're more prolific than that!"

"In wit, or on my face?" For ten seconds as she watched with a patient smile he wracked his memory for joke or event to orient his spinning gyroscope, until that compass abruptly fixed upon the lodestar in her mind when she added: "Surely you haven't forgotten that you're a father?"

Pause. "Yes, I suppose I had." And indeed he had. "But isn't that what you preferred?"

"You know perfectly well that I didn't even want you to know after I got here. But with wisdom comes inconsistency! Gil and Mooney both have always been told that the male in question was a masked anonymous incubus at that Annunciator Lab in Hume."

"As well she might have been!"

"Waive my preference just long enough to have some fun with the thought of being a mysterious grandfather, beyond the ken of future scholars! I never thought I'd take delight in a grandmother's hood." she smiled, looking away.

"So Mooney's a mother already? My God, I hope she's married!" They burst into laughter like old cronies, but without dispelling Caleb's undefined alarm.

"She is. Well off, with her own law degree. Don't worry, she's happily settled in the Baby Oaks hills with a very nice black civil engineer on his way up. They have a view of the Bay when it isn't too hazy."

"Still not too far from the High Cordillera!"

"Yes, by proxy I'm relieved of loyalty to my native mountains. Mooney inherits the burden of Yahi duty. I'm going out there to see them again for a few days before we open here. Your granddaughter's name is Monica."

Caleb's unprecedented heart-pang yielded to calculation. "From Monday—Mooney—to Monica! Was that your idea? Mother of Saint Augustine. I hope she doesn't have a son!"

"It's not surprising that Mooney's a very smart young woman. Second in her class at the Hume School of Jurisprudence. Time off to get maternity out of the way."

"With genes like yours she'll probably make it to the Supreme Court."

"May the Crat tribe recover power soon enough to appoint her!"

"Let's shake on that!" And so they touch again, slowly, prolonging with affectionate pressure their honorable reunion. Then a coffee toast to their child's child. And like any ordinary granny Lilian must fish a photo of the mature Mooney from her handbag. Caleb isn't stirred by the face of his opaque daughter (of whom he had been unaware until her childhood was well advanced and whom he's hardly glimpsed since then). She's not even a key to memories of her mother; but it's nice to think of her on the Supreme Court! He's learned to learn nothing from the present color of any woman's hair. As he glances back and forth between the present matron and what's hardly even an anachroromantic spit-and-image in the young quadroon, or an opportunity suggested by his sympathetic nerves, he's momentarily overtaken by a revival of his perfectly normal binary instinct to take up an old chase. But at the same time he's grateful to his wiser nerves for immediately dampening that inappropriate flare of interest in the grandmother long ago lusted for mind and body. Still, there's no harm in recalling like Tristram his Yseult as he contemplates the erotic significations of her finely molded physiognomy and only slightly thicker shape. As an armchair adventurer he himself has yielded time much more of his own youth, especially in scalp and muscle. It's good enough if their faded love persists in retrospect.

Looking away as she returns the picture to her wallet, his Lil-Amin adds: "But that's not the only reason I called you granddad!"

"I never got the chance to be blamed a second time!"

"Not by me. I never had another baby. But somebody else has a granddaughter. Funny that just last night I was thinking of that joke—and then you turn up, of all people! It never rains but it pours."

Bracing himself but mystified, he stalls with one of his redundant remarks. "I'm ready for a coincidence. Per capita, Dogtown is the locus of more coincidences than any other place in Atlantis." He's beginning to feel uncomfortable again. She gives him no time to propound and solve enigmas, let alone pairs of biography. She'd always been swifter than he in her tactics.

"My not-so-silent partner is from Babylon Oaks. Don't you remember that one either?"

He began to squirm. All he could think of was his secret contributions to the Annunciator Laboratories of Cornucopia. But how could she know about how he earned that part of his way through college? It would take a judicial injunction to unseal those records for either mother or donor!

"Has there been some sort of lawsuit?" He was vaguely alarmed.

"Don't be silly, Caleb. You must remember Mrs Argent."

"No, I never heard of a Mrs Argent!"

"Mrs Fox-Argent, to be exact. Known then, I suppose, as Mrs Fox. Do you remember the generous impresario?"

"Who in the world are you talking about?"

"Miss Jones, then. Hecuba Jones!"

Ah! Stunned, but scanning his brain to beat the band. "But that was never proved!" He admitted at least knowledge of the question.

"Certainly not to Mr Fox. He never got as far as suspicion. Hecuba herself never doubted. And apparently you didn't dispute her. The old fox left her a lot of money, much to his own daughter's dismay. Hecky moved down to Holyrood Hills and changed her name to Argent to escape his underworld entanglements. As long as you were in Baby Oaks she'd feared for your life."

Caleb expressed all the air in his lungs between pressed lips. "I'll be damned!" First he frowned, then he laughed. "I'd forgotten all about that!"

"I believe you. You're an absentminded confessor—preoccupied with the Will, Mask, Body of Fate, and Creative Mind of Gilgamesh! That's a lovable thing about you."

"What I love about you is your fathomless intelligence agency!" Now they are both laughing. "How in hell did you happen to get in touch with Hecuba, three thousand miles away, after all these years?"

"After her kid named Wednesday grew up and left home Hecky gave up her job in Yerba Buena and decided to indulge her curiosity about the reality-estate market elsewhere in the country. So she sought me out, after asking Dave Wilson where I'd finally landed up here in the East. Of course she already knew you'd gravitated to your origins in Dogtown. At first sight she loved this town, but she didn't move here until recently." Lillian paused for him to reply.

"Did she suspect us of living together or something like that?"

"I doubt it. She's always been confidential with me. By that time I was married and you had changed your masks."

"Well I remember that partner of yours was an inimitable financial manager in those days. Also a very resourceful gatekeeper." He paused for imagination.

"You've got the restaurant experience. Let her do the accounting, but at all costs keep her away from the written word! You're the Starboard, she must be the gangway!"

"Don't worry: Hecky's the silent partner, at least until she's had enough of her new granddaughter in Chicago, the magical metropolis of her childhood in the Labelle coalfields. Yes, I'm the manager and she's the sometime comedian. She's now very good on the piano." Lillian drops Caleb's gratuitous advice, and in a lower voice changes the subject: *"Her Wenny was born about the same time as my Monday."*

Caleb sobers up as she smiles generously, patting his hand. "Right now you look more ewish than ramish. But there's no such coincidence about your granddaughters' birthdays. Monica's husband wasn't as eager for paternity as Wenny's was. They say Jewish men usually do make good fathers, especially when they're from banking families. My granddaughter is three years younger than Hecuba's, but they're both yours, willy-nilly. But I wonder why you're the only male in this patrilineal genealogy. I hope you haven't found your Y-chromosome weakened by this decantation. . . .

"Nevertheless," she resumed, "Hecky and I are both grateful for having been chosen by the Lord. Without telling anybody about that we'll welcome you to a meal here, on the house, any time we're open, until it gets too cold for business, which is usually in October—as long as you're not with another woman! You are free and clear of all obligations. She and I have always insisted upon that, though for differing reasons."

"I'm alone these days, and I'm going to be hungry." says Caleb facetiously. "I may want big helpings, plus leftovers to take home. I wish I could sing for every supper all year round."

She doesn't realize that he's only half-serious about the bachelor's burden of A D L. "Hecuba's a loud accompanist. You're bound to run into her. I'll probably have to listen from here in the kitchen, but this is where the plates are loaded."

They part as good friends as if without thought of their next meeting, but Caleb is troubled on his way home. Hecuba might be embarrassing even after twenty-five years. Lilian is sensibly humorous and discreet, as always; philosophical about eccentricities. Yet he suddenly recalls that she had once fallen under his immediately suppressed suspicion for a plagiarism of some brilliant words in what she'd written for her junior-college teachers long before he knew her, shown him as her own at his behest, evoking his astonished praise; but there is no doubt of the intelligence and sensibility that stimulated his passionately intellectual romance. She seems not at all coarsened by all her years of different occupations.

Was she disappointed to find him worn down? Again it's on the tip of his tongue to find out, by suggesting a future for the friendship, but Body of Fate insists that Creative Mind give way before the exigency of his social plight. Besides, at this time of life he's already spent too much of his allotment seeking women— most of them intellectually interesting only by virtue of possible experience or knowledge of something or someone interesting, few of them worth expenditure of the waning libido in his jaded years. He's not sorry to have lost any renewed prospect of Belle's body, or Gloria (Keith) Cotton's, or as well Lilian's herself, not to mention those of merely opportunistic gratification. He's glad to have arrived at an age that relieves him of masculine pursuit as the highest instinctive imperative. For an olympiad, it now seems to him, the intertwining of polaric limbs has ceased to predominate in his spontaneous visions.

Withal, he starts home in sensory oblivion, cautiously elated, as if tasting the salt of her tongue. He is so accustomed to a typical gloomy April that until now he hasn't noticed the few daffodil heads lifting on the sheltered edges of dismal lawns, or the nascent tips of jejune forsythia buds, except to commiserate them for having ventured into weather too cold for joy if not for survival, while other trees and shrubs still procrastinate in dressing themselves. Everyone on this chilly side of the Cape resents the temperature of the sea wind, much below seasonal norm, keeping Dogtown's exfoliation a week or two behind most of Vinland's vernal greening. So the alewife and herring are running late hereabouts, too "broody" (as his mother used to call the spawning urge) to feel other meteorological influences. There's no breeze at the moment; rain is beginning to rebuff it.

The paracletes also seem to be late this year—or else it's just their mournful declaration of love that I've missed. Not even mourning over their marriably state! Weather forecasts are now so reliable that my radio no longer predicts: It "calls for" atmospheric conditions so confidently that I'm beginning to blame it for the bad stuff! It may be that women are more intelligent than men—certainly the converse is not true—but why is it so hard for them to discern a young man's authentic attitude toward procreation? Superego and prosperity seem to have weakened the defenses of normal men against reproductive responsibilities. At least I'm glad of that.

This time the painted black cat, now on his right, recalls Lilian's mention of Beltane. Besides Deeta Dana, the white witch of Purdeyville (and his own teacher of C N), few marooners old or new are learned enough to associate that name with this year's May Day, still less with Walburga Eve on the Brocken of Purdeyville a generation ago when Ibi-Roy was chosen as Doge of the Thing at Cynosure Rock, the Marking Stone. Then for twelve hours not a single dog was to be seen in town, and for forty-eight hours Caleb thought his Viking Shepherd king was stolen or dead. Like an anti-corona the mist of his dog's face for a moment fogs up the glass lenses with which his eyes struggle in the truest of love.

Well it isn't good for drama to write in an optimistic mood! On the other hand, Wat's motto was right: Sufficient unto the day are the anxieties thereof. *In thirty days will come Dogtown's most communal ritual, his own earliest, as a very little boy in his mother's hand at the end of a magnificently assembled parade of brassy red white and blue that he remembered not at all, as a flotilla of green wreaths for the five thousand fishermen drowned at sea in the last two centuries. Out through the Gut, from under the open drawbridge, they floated on an ebb tide to their solemn disappearance toward the distant breakwater, carried of their own accord through decorated boats at anchor and a fully flag-dressed Navy destroyer to the ocean he wasn't tall enough to see. He never again has attended that celebration, so fearful he was to feel the decadence of historic sensitivity even where grief began.*

But now the oaks are about to hang out their greenish yellow parasols of gauze.

10

TABLET

TEN

[The queen's reception chamber. Two formal chairs side by side upstage somewhat right of center. One is occupied by **Lil-Amin,** motionless and apparently listless in mourning; the other is empty. **Norkid** stands or paces upstage like a self-effacing bodyguard. **Gilgamesh**, unkempt, his back turned to the chairs, as if in an inner room downstage left, is working awkwardly on an inchoate stone statue, little more shapely than a stele, of about his own height mounted on a sculptor's swivelled stand. A few apparently cuneiform characters are lightly visible on its base. Engidu's bannerstone serves clumsily as both mallet and chisel. His own double-bitted axe lies nearby. **Berosus** sits as narrator and musician in his usual place on the right side.]

[Without interrupting his work Gilgamesh beckons to Norkid, who advances stiffly toward him.]

GILGAMESH	Has Eber at last left me?
NORKID	With his people and his chattels.
GILGAMESH	I thought he might postpone his departure until the obsequies were over. More than ever I need him now. That is to say the city does.
NORKID	Yes sir.

GILGAMESH   You saw him off?

NORKID   He was my friend.

GILGAMESH   He at least didn't die.

NORKID   We are vulnerable without those Traders and their cara-
             vans.

GILGAMESH   But especially without his management. Had he no com-
             punction about leaving us at exactly our weakest moment?
             Even gravediggers are distraught by women keening with
             lacerated lips and clawing at their own eyes to enlarge the
             flow of tears. I wish I were able to console myself by howl-
             ing with them. Did Eber express no regret at giving up his
             power here?

NORKID   He'll remember that loss when he's at last shaken all our
             dust from his feet and his fear abates.

GILGAMESH   It's absurd to fear another earthquake here, any more than
             he might have feared one before now. All along he's need-
             lessly feared the wrath of his God for serving me. Is there
             something new in his usual displeasure with my lack of
             policy? There has been no ominous death in his family.
             Perhaps I've stayed too long in seclusion. Did he leave any
             explanation or apology?

NORKID   He only kept repeating "Pride goes before a fall, and a
[Gilgamesh stops   haughty spirit before destruction." Referring to what he
work without   calls your murder of Engidu.
looking at Norkid.]

Rector enters ceremoniously carrying an abstract iconic figure
representing the god Enlil, which he places in the seat of the empty chair.
He is accompanied by Optimates & Widows.
Norkid turns back to stand behind Lil-Amin. Flute music by Berosus.]

GILGAMESH   Is this new ceremony of yours meant to remind me that
[Looks over his   Engidu once sat there? Or is it an attempt to usurp the
shoulder; slowly   kingship by reclaiming the rod and ring for yourself? If
drops his tools and you weren't the queen's brother you would have been
moves to center   removed even from your present office for clandestine
stage. He speaks   resistance to my assumption of sovereignty. As magus and
wearily.]   pontifex maximus you must stop meddling in affairs of
             state. Don't dare take advantage of my mourning.

RECTOR   You have killed Engidu, sent by the gods to relieve us of
[Boldly.]   your tyranny! The Lord God Enlil is our only king.

GILGAMESH	I saved your city from the Elamites, built its walls above the highest floods, and bonded it to gods with an imperishable tower as a ladder down from heaven. I have made Uruk preeminent in prosperity and power under a rule of reason and justice. Yet you continue to instigate the seething disparagement of me as a godless rebel against heaven, a savage northman civilized only by the people he subjugates. I am weary of engineering the excellence of a city that denies me credit. With Engidu's death I have outlived the satisfaction of public works and the pleasure of invention. I am ready to renounce the hope of constructive adventures. But who will make a better shepherd for this people? I vow that you will not succeed me!
RECTOR	And now you have prevented Engidu from doing so. Whoever is chosen by the queen must be a king that banishes strangers with foreign words and what they mean; one who will not destroy or scorn our rites. I speak for the temple, I speak for the people, I speak for the queen herself!
LIL-AMIN [Apathetically.]	I speak for myself, brother.

She and Norkid remain impassive as
Rector, Optimates, & Widows walk off ceremoniously.

GILGAMESH	Norkid, for whom do you speak?
NORKID	I am loyal to the queen.
GILGAMESH	And no longer to me?
NORKID	The death of Engidu absolves me, except as she may direct me.
GILGAMESH	You really believe I killed him?
NORKID	You caused him to die in the prime of innocent strength. Even as your old dog I howl with the people at such unnatural death.
GILGAMESH	Wisest of soldiers, old Kassite friend, how can you be so blind? Are you so affected by their religion?
NORKID	Too much invention is intolerable to anybody's gods. Your kingship was too defiant.
GILGAMESH [Ironic tone.]	*Was!* Do you and the Council consider me deposed? With the troopers in my pay? No doubt incited by the effeminate priest and ratified by his puppets. It's strange that no one has dared a word of mutiny until I now pry it from my

oldest friend! Of course I can remain the shah if I pretend not to notice the honest tense of his speech. Or are you simply anticipating my assassination? —But if retribution comes from gods, why haven't they long since killed me?

NORKID

Perhaps they waited to strike with a blow that's harder to bear.

GILGAMESH

[Turning back and forth.]

Then they are perceptive after all. The nothingness that follows life of course knows nothing of its loss. But for me the loss of another's uniquely beating heart, which you say I myself have caused, forever feels the extinction of a life as precious as my own. My tardy wisdom comes with grief and dirge. My lifeless works have gone for naught as far as I'm concerned.

—But for the gods' sake, as well as the people's, it would be stupid to neglect canals and walls now that they exist. They serve both species. Teach the people you've joined to consider them monuments to Engidu, the creature sent by heaven to destroy my pride. That's all I still ask of you.

—Without you and your Kassites at my side this city would still be little more than a disputed place for fording the river. Together you and I liberated from Elamite vandals the ruins these new wonders of the world are built upon. Without you, for that matter, I'd still have been wandering the world for something to do like an impoverished knight. And without you, as staunch older brother, I never would have mated with this queen and found my twin! For me the sorrow broadened by the threat of your defection would belittle the loss of all that we have constructed. You now deprive me of whatever solace I might have found in mourning.

—But no more foolish speculation about eliminating me! With or without you, I remain king, much the wiser.

Norkid runs off, doubled over, covering his face. [Gilgamesh removes the idol of Enlil, setting it behind the chairs, and sits in its place beside Lil-Amin.]

LIL-AMIN

Have pity on that good man's unhappiness. His thoughts hurt him more than the wounds of torture. He will never betray either of us.

GILGAMESH   Does displeasure with me drown your lamentations? And is denunciation easier for you than it is for Norkid?

LIL-AMIN   My allegiance is to Enlil and Inanna. I wish I had told you
[Indicates the chair.   before their patience ended that I could no longer allow
He jumps up and   you in that place by me.
steps aside.]   I don't need anybody's chair or bed!

GILGAMESH   —Then it's true that even you blame Engidu's death on my impiety?

LIL-AMIN   I shall not darken the enlightenment of your rule or defame your arts, but I was wrong to let you loosen my religion in gratitude for your liberation of this city and in bemusement with the distinction of your manhood. But you were not willing to defy the Tablets of Fate without enlisting guileless Engidu to share your guilt. As your mirror, an actor of your will, he was damned.

GILGAMESH   It's true that I gave not much thought to his soul. But—

LIL-AMIN   Nor to anyone else's!

GILGAMESH   I spared you implication in most of my transgressions.

LIL-AMIN   Because to you the royal priestess of Inanna was but a cap-
[Suddenly   tive yoni, otherwise distinguished as nothing more than a
animated.]   weaver of indoor pictures. I was for sporadic recreation from your daily operation of a public labor machine, or for carrying whoever's child might win the game!

GILGAMESH   The art of weaving is higher than any of mine. And in your absurd indictment you don't mention that our recreation has always been in a bed of love.

LIL-AMIN   I've learned from you a manly silence. At first I thought of you as the mildest of kings, gentlest to women, boyishly besotted by the lure of glory. Now I'm not content with occasional addresses of the consort thigh and solemn advice on how to manage the state in its absence. I can't believe I ever thought of love! For a woman of my kind it brings the unhappiness that exceeds all others. The people deserve a competent queen—to honor their cult and conduct herself as a regal mother. My daughter needs the love that surpasses the love of unhappiness.
                   —Yet maybe she will inherit and esteem much of what I did love you for.

BEROSUS [Aside.]	My history reports that the princess later did so, married elsewhere to imperial power, a harder woman than her mother.
GILGAMESH [Returns to his work downstage.]	I hardly recognize you as the person I have loved. Is it motherhood that's made you inimical to me? Or was your soul cured by the shaman's behest to "know yourself"—pernicious counsel to anatomize your heart and cloud your reason? Don't you even remember your past feelings? Do you really deny our matchless affinity?
LIL-AMIN	Yes, matchless by any two others but not a match for us! I repudiate my illusion without forgetting it. You are replaced by my proper responsibilities.
GILGAMESH	Engidu was witness to my loyalty when I spurned your goddess. She promised me chariots of gold and lapis lazuli, and gave assurance that my goats would multiply in triplicate! I might have thought that in your heart you would recognize my fidelity to love and value in refusing the carnal Muse herself.
LIL-AMIN	I am the servant of Inanna, not her rival.
GILGAMESH	Yet your disaffection is colder than I thought possible for the chief priestess of her temple. No wonder your people and my own soldiers have joined your brother and his puppets in execrating my alliance with Engidu.
LIL-AMIN	Not the alliance but your fatal abuse of it! You still fail to understand the city's solidarity of hope—and how you doomed it.
GILGAMESH	Yes, I fail to understand why I'm blamed for the first death I've ever felt—I who part even with you, and dismiss a whole life's famous accomplishments, to contemplate Engidu's extinction! I for whom he was loving and beloved brother! I whose life was many a time hazarded with his and thereby doubled! Am I so untutored in sympathy that I cannot understand the public's mourning for a champion hardly to be distinguished from myself at our usual distance from the common eye? I did not seek to learn compassion by the pain of a loss wholly beyond the imagination of keening women. —What can causes matter after death?
LIL-AMIN	You are cruel to include me in the public. Or Captain Norkid, without whose excellence you'd still be a vagrant privateer.

GILGAMESH	Never mind *Norkid* and me! You're the one who cannot understand the many-knotted bond of service and command. Speak only of Engidu and me.

—I do not think of you in any class of beings, but you have joined the commons in holding me at fault for the first despair in my life. Until the final adventure with my peer, most of my thoughts were hopeful and active, never disappointed. I was as innocent of compassion as a lion. My foresight was for worthy public things, my heart a bobbing cork of innovation, unanchored to the bottom of life. Then came Engidu to complement the private unity I thought I had with you. With him I could undertake benign expeditions and glorious feats too difficult for a single champion. But the extinction of culminating hopes has awakened my heart to the vanity of those I'd realized. I'm a plummeted bust of stone staring groundward from the floor of the sea,

[Indicates the stele.] with no more ambition than this lifeless matter, which I can hardly see in a sea of tears when I look at what I'm doing!

LIL-AMIN It would be a truer image of Engidu if you let me make it
[Softly.] of clay on my potter's wheel. Fired in your kiln, it would endure as long as stone.

GILGAMESH No clay, never never clay! I saw his eyes fade to clay. He no longer heard my voice. His face was white, his lips were pale, his chest was hard. I thought we'd always be together, but I saw him petrify in revulsion from life's oven. Yet not too cold to incubate the worms that before my very eyes began to crawl from his ear, then from his nose and mouth! If mad I am, that's the horror that drove me mad. So I limn his effigy now in colorless rock, the precious last piece of Elamite stone stockpiled for my towering vainglory. Worms cannot live in faces made of granite.

LIL-AMIN There would have been no worms if you hadn't kept his body from the tomb so long. Ungodly mourning has disturbed the people more than godless deeds of the past. It was madness to prolong your weird dirge—without considering public, priest, or queen—in your transport of newfound pity for a living creature because he might have been yourself! As always, too enraptured with your own excesses to heed any nation's law or custom!

GILGAMESH [Loosing his anger.]	How can the lady soul-doctor open her mouth with such infuriating exaggerations? I won't listen to such asinine clairvoyance about me! —Only fire could have killed those loathsome maggots! But Norkid threatened tripartisan sedition if I tried to cremate Engidu's corruption! Even the best-educated Kassite really believes that sacred fire must not be polluted by a dead body! I have no covenant with gods but in affiliation I do address the all-burning sun. Utu does not scruple to burn parched fields and their vermin! But your people abetted Norkid's opposition by clamoring for the wormy ditch. Even before Engidu was dead the Optimates ordered his grave, and citizens were sent out to glean bricks and shards, as if to hide a midden!
LIL-AMIN	The tomb was properly ready long before you let go of the corpse. I promised that the chamber would not be closed until you laid your imperishable effigy by the body's side, but for fear of plague the sepulture's sealing can be postponed no longer.
GILGAMESH [Turns back to his work with renewed energy.]	I'll soon be finished! Neither worms nor fire will disintegrate this apparition of the mighty hunter they call Nimrod, Gilgamesh's only partner.
LIL-AMIN	The commonwealth cannot continue to indulge your nobly morbid lamentations, which I think express more than anguish for your best friend.
GILGAMESH	Now don't tell me to know myself! May Utu curse all feminine divinations!
LIL-AMIN	In any case there's no more time for pity. We well know that misery comes at last to the healthiest of men. Deer and lions weep; wild asses too; priests, widows, farmers, and servants weep. Our river weeps, the other river echoes. It is said that "Every man must give up the days that are lent him, and take up his dwelling elsewhere." Engidu's house is large enough to add Semiramis and me: but stuff it with what you wish!
GILGAMESH	I curse your superstitious custom! Engidu's pyre would have been atop my tower, filling the night sky with solar glory. That beacon would have been remembered unto the last generation by all the wild creatures of the steppes and by the gods who love high sacrifice but do not notice the puny mounds that keep mankind's memory alive between

dust storms. But at least this stone, half formed by an insane artificer, will never die!

LIL-AMIN   Since you can't infuse the breath of life.

GILGAMESH   When I was young, thinking forward and outward only, seldom lingering in reflective meditation, naturally the death of self, or of my mother, did on occasion cross my mind; but it would instantly dissipate into the stream of my appetites and plans—even as I saw more of violent death than most men did, and certainly reckoned on it for many who opposed me. I'd been told, and never thought of questioning, that I was two-thirds god. So I was never curious about how it feels to die.

—I suppose you believe that even in my present hopelessness I'm still too armored with congenital hope to contemplate an end to the one who hopes—that I have too long claimed the fame of defying necessity. In part you are right. But the shock of Engidu's death and an unfamiliar numinous fear has awakened me from the sleep of reason. Never more shall I ignore the mystery I share with every animal and human. Yet not for me is soul without a living body!
—All my designing here is done. You must finish what's begun.

LIL-AMIN   Gods themselves weep for the death of mortals who serve them, some of whom are children of their own. But you think it's the fear of death I see in you, when I know your thinking has a nobler cast.

GILGAMESH   How can I trace the path of time?

Dropping his tools,
**Gilgamesh lifts the heavy statue to his shoulder,
takes up his axe, and carries them off stage,**
accompanied by Berosus's darabukka drum.

LIL-AMIN   Here, take Engidu's own axe for the grave!

Picks up Engidu's
bannerstone. Calls   Lady Inanna, spare the people. The fault is mine alone for
after Gilgamesh.   weakening to the sacrilege of an overlord. And keep safe
Then stops to pray   my daughter, your father's child, to live out her destiny in
before **following**   a city that honors the laws handed down from heaven.
him off.

11

SPRINGTIME
DIARY

[Extracts from Tessa's Diary
and an Exegesis Thereof]

1.

. . . Tomorrow I'm having lunch with Glory, my very dear old
friend Gloria Keith, whom I haven't seen much of (though we frequently talk on the phone) since divorces have inhibited socializa-
tion among some members of our old circle. Her native Montvert
husband Dexter is now our saltwater Mayor, married to the former
Protonotary of the Board of Earlders, who was the local wife of
midwestern Waldo Cotton, Glory's own present husband. It's sometimes also embarrassing (to her, at least, when we're not alone) that
Waldo now works for my second husband Rafe (from the Pacific
Coast) as production manager for our Dogtown Machine & Design,
on whose board of directors I serve ex officio as the corporation's
nominal treasurer, hatched in the Lagash of New Uruk City.

Waldo made his first Dogtown connection as a gypsy (owner-operator of an unregulated semi-trailer kilroy) hauling frozen meat eastward and frozen fish westward or southward. Belle Cingani, who once covered the seafood beat for the *Nous*, told me his big spotless black tractor with cosy bunk and "fifth wheel" that hauled his trailer-loads was christened the Romany Rye. But as a critical thinker he studied the whole national transportation industry, including the much larger parts that were outside the realm of his own experience, especially the regulated freight and public ware-housing businesses for products of all kinds. He became so helpful with sophisticated suggestions to his acquaintances at the Yard that he was hired first as traffic manager and later (despite lack of college education!) as director of all logistics. As such he made himself Caleb's only creative colleague and crony, and they collaborated in many of the interdepartmental innovations. So later he came to Rafe highly recommended by our systemizing friend, even though he'd had no direct experience in manufacturing. But he'd been a Fire-Control petty officer in the Navy and knew a great deal about electromechanical equipment. "A vigorous manager with intellectual curiosity can run anything," says Rafe, "especially if he's a mustang." Before Waldo left the Yard he'd made a reputation among materials-handling experts in the Grocery Manufacturers Association for his work in promoting and standardizing "four-way" wooden pallets (to replace the traditional two-way ones) for forklift trucks, and did a lot of unpaid work urging "containerization" in steel boxcar units by land and sea. He's certainly proven himself as production manager of our little company. Thanks to his competence, Rafe will soon be free to take me on a geographical vacation to Europe. For me it will be historical. I'm very curious to find out what drew Mary Trevisa to the Isle of Manannan—of all places!—as a refuge for her pregnancy in 1934.

So that's Waldo, Glory's sensible man (albeit with a Chauvinist religious background), who used to be the husband of the mayor's wife! He's not very comfortable among "intellectuals" (as she says he calls the likes of us), but on the job as a manager he's invaluable, as Rafe makes clear to him with exceptional salary and bonus. But no doubt he's content to stay in this oldfashioned milieu also in deference to her wishes as a naturalized marooner who loves her job as Head Librarian. (She never expected to have to deal with her ex-husband at least indirectly in public budget negotiations! Otherwise Dexter's run for the mayoralty has pleased us all immensely.)

I'm going to take Glory to the Windmill as a special treat, where hoi polloi won't be clattering. (It may be the last chance. I've heard it's being sold for conversion to a conference center.) She deserves a two-hour lunchtime once or twice a year. Everyone knows she's as busy as a mother squirrel, working longer and faster than any hidden hand could have driven her.

She has ingratiated hoi aristoi by persuading the Library Board to let her give the Lyceum (with display space) its greatest and most unappreciated treasure, Alfred Blackburn Walkyr's cracked *Tir-na-Dog*, which for almost a century had been stored undisplayed on a basement wall. Thank God she was disingenuous enough not to mention that Walkyr was the secretly spurious son of Wellingborough Redburn, though probably even that's a name underappreciated by the "main stream" panel of our public-spirited elite. But after all, the Atheneum is supposed to be a *Free* Library! . . .

*

[The truth is that Tessa Opsimath herself, with more freedom, more leisure, and more resources, was nevertheless more pressed for time than her resolute friend in public service, who now could spare very few of her office hours in pursuit of her official ancillary interests as City Historian, for Gloria was first and foremost chief of a legally independent "charitable corporation" originally endowed by J P Morganatic, expanded with capital donations from Richard Tybbot, the late "Duke of Dogtown", and otherwise improved by its own private fund-raising, but dependent upon the state and especially upon the city for its operating expenses. For all practical purposes, at least at budgeting time once a year, it was regarded as a department of the city. Sometimes before the Budget and Finance Committee, and occasionally in open meetings before the entire Board of Earls, having already defended and negotiated provisions for the Library in the mayor's proposed budget, she (the first woman ever appointed to that post) was obliged to support with details or argument the parsimony of her requests for little more than a continuation of previous appropriations (which Ben Nathan the previous mayor had refused to adjust for inflation). There wouldn't have been any public library at all if it hadn't been for the Commonwealth's statutory recognition of what 19C philanthropy had contributed to the common good even of an anti-intellectual nation. The appropriation for book-acquisition was regressively constrained by the more readily granted proportion of funds for the cinematic devices of the popular culture that the Library was now expected to accommodate in justification for the maintenance of its handsome new wing of modern glass framed by brick painted white to match the wooden sidings of the original Halibut Street mother of books, which continued to serve administrative, archival, and research purposes, including Gloria's old high-ceilinged office with a close view of towering Ibicity Hall just across Whale Avenue.

Tessa, leaner and darker than Gloria, was not even on the Library's board. Her private interests, though ultimately no less contributory to the local common good, were conspicuously partisan in politics. In any event, as a public servant of nonpartisan city government, still a freckled blonde embodiment of selflessly attractive energy (though a little heavier than when she'd been Caleb's landlady), not a whit unhappy with her own more difficult career, Gloria cheerfully envied Tessa the privileges of choice.

Tessa made no effort to solicit private clients in her registered profession. Most of those who consulted her were referred by teachers or public welfare agencies. She had a rented office in Finn Macdane's recently acquired building (which still bore on its weathered cornice the name of the bank that had formerly sequestered her diary in its basement vault). Still as nervous from tobacco-abstention and nearly continuous activity as a theatrically ambitious college girl, black hair cut short as ever, she made time for a plethora of other pursuits that invigorated her slim body as a graduated matron well satisfied with two independently careering children elsewhere who were still busily uninterested in propagation on their own part. Her second husband Rafe's distantly erstwhile family in Cornucopia, entirely separate from hers in everybody's consciousness, was of his own unnecessary concern.]

*

. . . I have never been able to follow Glory's historical imagination, which once greatly excited Doc Charlemagne, who knew enough about the past to appreciate her researches and speculations in Dogtown's legendary prehistory, which persuaded him (and other imaginative scholars) that the earliest developers of this place were interracial as well as intercontinental. I simply don't know enough to evaluate her hobby-horses, much as I've always admired them. Doc called her Goody Keith, Dogtown's Clio, and compared her to Hesiod! She has always said that it was her students' Gloucesterbooks and Legends that inspired her when she was a teacher in the Dogtown schools. But I'm sure it was she who most stimulated and enamored hundreds of kids, especially ones like Inez Canary whose own imaginative research in the lore has considerably expanded the scope of our poets and other artists.

But at first that background had nothing to do with the lively conversation at our lunch today. I plied her and myself with unaccustomed amounts of wine, to the degree that she was really worried about returning to her work in respectable sobriety. (She insisted on walking back to her office. I'm too inured to be affected in my driving.) Quite apart from my ulterior motive, we had more than enough other things to catch up on, and she was almost as effervescent as ever in the nearly thirty years I've known her. I've never loved a friend so much!

We looked out over the peacefully traversed plain of an outer harbor embraced by greenery. The gossip started with one of those rare pauses in which most Dogtowners remind themselves of how greatly their city has been changing ashore, for better or worse, in the aggregated consequence of alarming insipid or horrible building and demolition permits, or of vegetation's less perceptible incorrigible alterations. Our beautiful purview from that table of wineglasses tended to ameliorate our mental visualization of the hills and cityscape behind our backs. This smelly old Beauport has been rediscovered by off-island Philistines, and in twenty years it will be largely gentrified either tastefully, distastefully, or tastelessly. We agreed that at least it will be some interesting combination of all three aesthetic levels, ranging from that of prefabrication to that of ostentatious custom-design by the most fashionable architects. (Two of the exceptions are by Aninigo: the Yard's office downtown and my own house across the Gut.)

Meanwhile the plastic stinkertoy boats will be getting bigger, faster, and far more numerous. But, Glory characteristically reminds me, we've got to take the bitter with the better. The center city is cleaner and neater than it was in our early days, with more urban plantings, thanks partly to federal grants, partly to civic volunteers, with less shuttered commercial buildings and more interesting shops. Civic Instauration has already removed most of the inner harbor's lofts and shacks. When we're in no mood to mourn or complain we don't speak of the junk and litter still to be found on roadsides and under hedges where kilroys roam unchecked outside the center-city precincts, to say nothing of lovely elevated terrain despoiled by chainsaws, dynamite, and bulldozers. It would be unbearable to take daily stock of the incessant changes that appear to be individual exceptions to one's memory of unfamiliar neighborhoods or along the many many roads one hasn't taken in a dog's age when displaying our Eden to visitors.

But I'm originally from the world's densest city, and Glory's from a Montvert village: I wonder how differing pentimentos affect our personal palimpsests of memory in this mutable town. As a new marooner, once you plant children here you're almost as dedicated to the whole as to the parts you know, no matter how little you share the conditioning of aborigines. On this cape it's the place, not your tribe or origin, that seems to make for civic loyalty and historical pride. Even my geographical (anti-historical) husband partakes of that, after participating in a whole generation here without locally schooled children of his own.

Since time's long-distance arrow (short of "history") was the leitmotiv of our lunch, Glory and I spoke also of the dead—with the pleasure of forgotten pain—and I believe with similar mental images, if not with equally sympathetic memories of what now is considered a kind of a golden age, when the streets were messier and the city government more primitive in both concept and management. At the time Rafe showed up in search of Doctor Charlemagne, hiring Caleb to help him with his White Quarry College correspondence-school homework (which later led me to the same matriculation and unimpressive degree), he picked the brain of my dear old husband Buck Barebones, father of my children, and later became his partner. It was an era of the local past when sculptors outnumbered painters and we were dreaming of our own theater and Doc's foundation of a Dogtown College. I think I remember that all the draggers were still made of wood. Most people took the flourishing fishery for granted as the city's lifeblood. Most of our gang—the women at least—knew it only from Wat Cibber's humorously grumpy point of view. He complained that there were always at least two Dominion or European freighters tied up to unload compressed blocks of frozen fish for the Yard or for one of the other packing plants, as if they were stealing the livelihood of his little one-man day-tripping fresh-fish *Motion* (built for a crew of two or three). The city's chronic problem was to find enough overnight parking spaces for all the gypsy reefers that clogged the streets, waiting to load our refrozen and packaged finished products for retail distribution.

She and I rehearsed the ghosts of our almost forgotten prime as matrons: For instance, Shelly and Edie Schlossberg, long-lived with all their wits, made immortal almost coterminously, both spared the ignominy of nursing homes, are faded in our memories as peripheral friends. They died not long before their CaraVANsary Hotel, with its basement Main-Top Bar and his furnace-room sculpture studio, was swept away like the nearby Alma Mater department store, Great Aristotle & Plato Coffee Company chain store, and whole waterfront tenement blocks by federal grants for Civic Instauration—along with piers, sail lofts, chandleries, taverns, and the city's steam-whistling power plant—in favor of a shopping plaza and a broad-swathed thoroughfare along the waterfront between the Yard's office and its wharf-side production plant. Rafe and Caleb knew the Schlossbergs much better than we did, but at this reminiscing lunch we recalled them first because they were commemorated in the Atheneum for their many years of financial support while Glory was still teaching at the high school. I think it was the boiled lobster that reminded us of Shelly's woodworking imagination of a living model. Which in turn fetched up our notice that Petto DaGetto, the iron-working sculptor, was still alive and shouting, though seldom encountered in our separated worlds. She and I each have minor works of his in our houses, though no longer as prominently displayed as his ferric Brazen Head now in my living room.

One memory leads to another, at first in fits and starts but then in spates of recollection, interrupted only by the sips, bites, chews, or swallows of us the interlocutors. I began to worry about making a scene of two overly mature women chattering like nubile girls. Fortunately the Windmill is better padded for sound than any other cookhouse in town, despite the high ceiling and two walls of plate glass. Looking out and down upon the sea serpent's parterre between us and the breakwater must have made us appear supercilious!

And thus was brought to mind our old theatrical visions, and the huge warm revenant of His Imperial Majesty (H I M). Doc Charlemagne was lost to self-indulgent cancer, from who knows what comforting ingestions, when he was not much older than we are now, long before his mind could have failed or bitted. Glory recalled the dismay of ourselves and some of our well-housed friends when he'd suddenly show up for a dinner or to ask for the use of bathtub and linen. His mooching always seemed funny to those who were spared, and made us wonder how Deeta Dana bathed who was then his housekeeper. She has always seemed as fresh and clean as a golden Nordic princess. Nowadays she has her own little converted summer cottage, but perhaps it too lacks a full complement of hot-water plumbing; maybe she washes at one of her secret springs up in Tir-na-Dog, or in a Taraville quarry, if not as a mermaid in one of the tidal pools alive with barnacles periwinkles anemones and sea urchins when she's collecting seaweed out of sight. But as a spiritualistic person she had nothing to do with our cluster of theatrical disciples. She always withdrew to the bedroom when Doc started to hold forth to several of us for half the night in his kitchen, but especially addressing Caleb (the only one with temerity enough to question some of the dicta but by far the last to leave). It was drama's place in Dromenology that intensely interested that young dog, rather than the real theater's place in drama, which Cora and I were always trying to get Doc's practical thoughts about. Glory, for her part, and most of the others who were interested in such matters, barely had time even to attend Stone Barn planning sessions or rehearsals.

The exciting leap from bourgeois playreading group to avantgarde theater company had been a flare of priceless enthusiasm set off and then carelessly extinguished by the great self-absorbed Director who beguiled audiences with his alert interest in everything outside himself. Aside from national politics, our long attempt at artistic and civic cooperation about Stone Barn and Dogtown College was the greatest and most valuable lost cause of all the lost causes I've been party to, hopefully impossible from the start.

Caleb never participated in any of our actual projects, but we heard that sometimes he briefly crossed swords in theoretical discussion when alone with Doc at the Leviathan Court quaffing table. When we were at the Barn my sister Cora would occasionally insist upon professional aspects of dance or music; but my part as de facto impresario, when it got down from general theory to stagecraft, was only to question feasibilities of time, place, and action. Cora and I had debated dance, voice, and design all our lives. Despite my openminded collaboration I was considered the reactionary champion of Stanislavsky's *pereshivanie* (which the rebels called "psychopathology") when it came to propounding the "synthetic theater". (I would have done much better in Holyrood or on DV.) As far as drama was concerned Cora was of course for Meyerhold. Insofar as he would admit to influences, Doc argued for Tairov. No one could be less poetical than Caleb, but he wanted Yeats's Abbey bred to Tairov's Kamerny, soft-pedaling the music and recommending sculpture—abstract of course!

The other members of our pick-up company just wanted to act, on or off the boards, waiting for us dramaturges to select, cast, assign, decide, direct, and judge. As a housewife, mother, teacher, historian, and librarian, Glory had too many other things to manage, so she was one of those willing to be docile in this matter. As such she was the best of our heroines, especially as the Maid of Fressingfield in our one popular production, *Friar Bacon and Friar Bungay*, for which Petto provided a masterpiece of imagination as the Brazen Head. In that train of associations at lunch we both at once remembered the same lines and attracted unseemly attention by nearly screeching in unison "Time is . . . Time was . . . Time is past!" How hard I had coached Huck Salter's deep voice for the hollow tone of fate!

That one success encouraged us to overreach with a yet unscripted plan to put on one of the legends that Glory's student Inez Canary had unearthed about how a Captain Hood (of the Sea Fencibles in 1776), in tribute to the Reverend Merry Sterne of the previous century, had been the one who instituted Dogtown's octave of solar festivity known as Gloucestermas. Our failure vindicated Caleb's opinion (vs Tairov's) that the dramatic theater always needs above all a playwright! He holds that all the other dramatic arts advocated, from Hume to Saint Petersburg, follow upon some writing. For my part, I've grown sick of all the feckless debates. At the culminating point in Tairov's early career as a *pereshivanie* (emotionally living-through Stanislavsky Method) actor he "cured" himself of the theater and took up the practice of law; but later he recidivated, only to coruscate with theory from a position in which he could practice what he preached.

It comes back to me, how Doc warned us: theater has so many actual as well as conceivable elements of architecture, design, actors, and skills that any one set of imaginations can never be *fully* satisfying to anyone—that is to say, perfect—because the artistic collaboration is limited to one experiment at a time. Any performance is made of many worlds! And the literal perspectives of critics vary both with their theories and with the vantages of their seats, not to mention their irrelevant moods at various performances. So likewise in regard to the creative fundamentals. Caleb told me that his second Gilgamesh play—even his one-man world—differs entirely from the first!

Of course, to the expectation and despair of the Director Charlemagne himself, as well as of Caleb the opinionated armchair amateur, all of us were dilettantes, except Cora of course, our exacting Muse of dance, with whose sardonic permission we managed to wrest her Rock Dance into a musical comedy at the high school auditorium so that we could pay our bills after the demise of our Stone Barn fantasy. She got so tired of Dogtown dreams, her opaque husband, and me (her conniving little sister) that she's gone back to Ur-town and found a job directing real professionals in serious experiments with the dance element of "synthetic theater". And as far as I, Glory, Sally Salter, Beni Vanderlyn, and other mothers in our band were concerned, once our children or favorite pupils graduated from high school and left the local scene it was hard to take much further personal interest in the abuses of public education. We no longer wonder which the kids have chosen for the Senior Play, whether *Midsummer Night's Dream* or *Romeo and Juliet*. (Maybe nowadays they don't even recognize Shakespearean titles when they vote.) We've nearly forgotten the wonderful Arts Festival that Dexter organized for all ages and genres in those days when Dogtown was so redolent of fish and he was only the City Planner.

Every now and then I wonder if Cora envies me her niece and nephew. Poor gentle ex-husband Thad does, I'm sure, living alone over there across the Gut on verge of retirement from the Yard to which he has devoted his whole career in "food technology". Every year he sends Miley and Melly a Christmas present. I wish I could bring myself to invite him to dinner more often. . . .

. . . But how that man Charlemagne could talk! Invited to our houses he came to sing seminars for his supper. Beyond that he was our unreliable Artistic Director and irresponsible arsonist. But the experience of listening to him, and learning from him, was worth our investment in that predictable Dogtown disappointment. Now even the last movie theater is gone to asphalt, and private devilvision provides the substitute for public entertainment. That's why when I tease Caleb about his arcane drama he claims he's writing for an even less public and less commercial "virtual theater", in which he must experiment by thought alone with stagings of his scripts, dealing airily with problems and opportunities, imagining

whole systems and procedures for realization, including the coopta-
tion of skills and talents outside any of his worlds. . . .

*

[In truth, save for the stimulus of conversation with her old
friend, Gloria recalled far less about the days of the Hoof and
Mouth School at the Troika Arts Center, the Stone Barn Company
of Mummers, and high school theatricals under her own leadership,
than tendentious Tessa did. The private memories that Gloria associated with those distinctive years were best dismissed as expiated
or forgiven by remarriage, usually even forgotten in casual conversation with Dexter, Caleb, or Deirdre (her own daughter's very
namesake and the Ibicity Hall beauty for a whole generation), with
whom she had exchanged matronal surnames, as if in the revirgina-
tion of a chalkboard. But she hadn't forgotten an iota of Lady
Gloucester's history—true, speculative, or merely legendary;
demotic or arcane.]

"Oh Tess, guess what! I'm so tipsy I almost forgot!"

"You've been declared Woman of the Year by the Turntable
Club? Or you're a granny?"

"You remember my student Inez Canary. After she worked her
way through Bethsalem State she got a clerical job with Octavo
Alden the publisher over in South Parish where he put out literary
and historical hardbound reprints, mostly for library replacements
all over the world. Alden moved up here from New Uruk years ago,
and for a while was in an old garage building on Depot Avenue,
but now his shop has a storefront—"

"Oh yes, Peter Wright's daughter was a neighbor of ours when
we lived in the North Village. Her husband is an architect in
Caspar Aninigo's firm."

"Well, she's inherited the business and Inez runs the office for her
now. Inez still lives at home taking care of her old mother but seems
perfectly happy to have avoided marriage in her obsession with colonial history. She's been to Yorkshire twice on her vacations and she's
read everything about the 17C and 18C over there, trying to track
down Merry Sterne's lost manuscripts. Scholars are still hoping to
find his ditty box, which they think contained, among other things,
his *Fallacie of Attributive Substance*, some of his sermons, his account of
the lost Cavalcanti brothers, his *True Historie of the Naturals Found at*

Cape Gloucester in the Drogeo Plantations, and what he cared most to preserve, his recommended revisions of the Holy Communion section of the *Book of Common Prayer*, which would probably have been as incriminating in the eyes of rigid old Archbishop Laud as the May-pole was in the eyes of straightlaced Chauvinists separated by an ocean from his Church. Seeing that she's a papist herself, I think she's pretty liberal about heresies within schisms!"

"Well, old girl, it's your fault if poor Inez has sacrificed normal life for offbeat history."

"I almost feel responsible for that. But at least she's happy with her job. And now she thinks she has a clue about where to look for the casket of Sterne's lost manuscripts!"

"Lo these many centuries we've been hearing what to look for!"

"Well she's been clever enough to worm a hint out of Deeta Dana, the end of the Sterne line on this side of the Atlantic. Deeta's the last Perdita of Purdeyville, and apparently she's finally begin-ning to worry about the extinction of that lineage, which she used to pretend was a mere fairy tale."

Gloria explained that when Inez went to see Deeta for help with some small detail in a colonial allusion to Merry Sterne, the goodnatured white witch took to her (as anybody with an eye for energetic intelligence would have done), and seemed to have decided that it was time to accept an apprentice who might at least foster the gossamer legend of her matrilineal Irindu tribe, and that it was better to take on a very bright disinterested Lusitanian, proven to be full of sympathetic initiative and still in her prime, than to hope fantastically that some unbigoted young Irish girl with the same qualities would turn up at the last minute, just when aging demanded a link for posterity.

As it happened, to boot, Deeta herself had recently found in one of the cellar holes of Purdeyville overgrown with crab-apple trees and brambles, behind a frost-loosened stone inside the founda-tion, a jagged slab of slate still faintly scored by a tool with an irregular diagram that could easily be taken for an unlabeled map. It was not unusual to find artifacts on or under that deserted village heath, but this one was exceptionally intriguing in its defiance of archeological classification. Inez was invited to copy the drawing in her notebook, and she eagerly promised to study it at home. A number of naturally accidental runes scraped on rock by crawling glacier or shifts of bone in Mother Earth along coastal New Armor-ica had been erroneously advertised as the uncanny work of Atlindus, Irishmen, or Vikings—but never one that looked to Deeta so much like directions drawn in sand between tides. But without landmarks it was impossible to fix a point of reference. Deeta had been unable to find any correspondence with trails, boulders, or ruins in the vicinity of its cellar hole.

Decipherment without monument or marker seemed more hopeless than guessing at the transactions recorded by cuneiformed symbols on clay tablets in Sumer, as Tess remarked when Gloria drew a pocket notebook from her purse to display a sketch she had penciled from Inez's copy of the stone. It struck the skeptic as some remaining fragment of a spider web torn from its corner of a ceiling by the broom of a horrified housewife like herself. "What makes Deeta think this is a map?"

"Because, of course, that's what she's been looking for most of her life! I suppose she has reasonable promptings. Everyone knows that Merry Sterne buried his papers in an oaken 'casket'."

"You mean everyone is supposed to think they know, my dear."

"Well, all we have to do is find it—then you'll know that we were right!" But already Gloria was beginning to smile, giggle in fact, and now she burst into her glory of freckled blonde laughter. "Well, it's worth thinking about! Inez is no fool. She's respected as a Camoens scholar."

"But you know how Deeta loves magic. Meriwether Sterne was a rational cleric, if there ever was one in the 17C. They didn't call him the Anglican Rabelais for nothing."

"There's nothing irrational about burying treasure for your wife to retrieve when you know you're about to be ridden out of town on a rail, by order of an Inquisition, and shipped back across the Atlantic Ocean for assignment to some impoverished vicarage on the wuthering moors—or in a forested enclosure where the parishioners aren't much more joyful than the settlers here. If any drop of unreason had diluted his blood it couldn't have transmitted such pure ratiocination to his great-grandson's humor."

"But by the same token Merry's Irindu wife Perdita, hereditary native of eponymous Purdeyville, should get just as much credit for the first generation, and no less than Merry Sterne himself for the 18C genius. But don't get me wrong: you and Inez can dig up our land all you like. We know that there was nothing hidden on the hilltop because we dug deep for our foundation and didn't find so much as the rotted roots of a pine. But I suppose the map may have been drawn from that point of view. . . ."

Tessa's children had taken over the sea-level Powerhouse in North Village when she and Rafe moved to a new house of Caspar Aninigo's design on Old Bethsalem Road in West Parish, across the Gut on the mainland, aligned for easterly and southern prospects on the summit of a drumlin said to be that upon which Merry Sterne had stripped one of the King's most noble pines to raise his last defiance of the town's Chauvinist magistrates by hoisting a yardarm to make a naked Maypole serve as a blatant Cross. A rabble of Separatists had been instructed by the true believers to chop it down before razing his log-cabin vicarage and preparing Merrymount Hill for Puritanical exorcism.

Quoting Caleb, Tessa took mischievous pleasure in reminding Glory the historian that this case differed from that of Isaac Newton's metal box, which was lost for a couple of hundred years in the Trinity College library, a trove perhaps not heated but at least protected from earth and sky. Nevertheless: "As Rafe tells me, always attack a muddle in the middle. You and Waldo come to dinner on Saturday, and bring Inez if she's willing to abandon her mother. They must have the world's best view of the inner harbor from their perch up on Espiritu Sanctu Hill. Our remote area is not so interesting. Come a couple of hours early if you like, and bring your shovels! We'll do anything we can to help Inez find—"

"—El Moro's lost manuscript along with Sterne's own *Book of Armorican Exiles*, or at least his sequel to the *Kings of Britain*. I'm hoping especially for Sterne's *Prologos To A Historie Of The Dogtowne Plantation*!" Gloria shrieked with glee.

*

. . . Glory inquired about my "academic" work-in-progress (a secret known in Dogtown only to Belle Cingani, Fay, and herself, if they haven't betrayed me to their men). I told her that as City Historian it was her turn to help me in my research. Belle has scoured the *Nous*'s lousy morgue to very little effect as far as collating 1934-1935 events is concerned. Her predecessors (when Richard Tybbot the Duke of Dogtown was owner of the paper) didn't regularly keep physical copies of every day's edition for more than a few years, so she has no way of finding anything that wasn't specially clipped and filed for possible obituaries. Thus searching the paper's files by name revealed little more than what I'd already been given to understand about the significant contemporaries of Mary Tremont (née Trevisa). She was the kind of troublemaker or whistle-blower that officials and local editors prefer not to recognize. Probably fearing the Police Chief, especially after the loss of her dog and studio artwork as well as much else in a devastating fire, her public utterances were in self-conscious remission. So we've found nothing about the private years of her life that led to the conception and gestation of our Tristram. I seldom see Caleb these days but when I do (or hear of him from my spies) it seems that since her death he hasn't loosened up much for my ostensibly casual inquiries about his preformative history, which he may know less about than I do. But about his epigenetic memories he's grown a little more frank, as if willing to reveal pride in his mother only after the embarrassment of her presence is no longer threatening.

He too has a casket of papers—neither oaken nor metal, but foldered in fibrous or plastic for storage. I'm inclined to believe him when he murmurs that he still hasn't read all of the voluminous holographs and disordered enclosures simply because the task is prohibitively eye-straining and time-consuming, sometimes even upon arrival. He says it's hard enough to face the endless queue of clearly perusable print that he *must needs* read for nourishment of his *objective* wisdom, or at least for the basal metabolism of his own Creative Mind (à la Yeats), which itself is in excruciating rivalry for the time it takes to be a common reader, especially for a compulsively deliberative writer of no extraordinary talent. He declares that he will attend to her *subjective* matters after he's through with his own Gilgamesh.

For my project, as far as psycho-*objectivity* is concerned, I should know more about Cape Gloucester bootlegging before Restoration, and its echoes of recrimination during the immediately subsequent years of the Depression. Dogtown had always been notorious for smuggling of tea or other evasive commodities, because (until recently) its variety of small undeveloped beaches and inconspicuous coves has been hardly appreciated by speculative reality agents. It seems likely that Mary (as Trevisa) was right in believing that the two infamously unsolved murders in Seamark's North Village liberty could be traced to the son of the rum-running marshal of police, who threatened her with violence for jeopardizing his life-tenure by arousing democratic political action, as well as for seeming to threaten *him* with publicly plausible suspicion of his own son's autonomous crimes. But without known evidence the accusation seems highly improbable except as fiction—right up my alley!

As I told Glory, it was not because I wanted to solve the murder cases or bring anyone to tardy justice but because I wanted to know more about Caleb's origin that I asked her to see if in spare moments she could scan some of her Library's old bound copies of the *Nous* (which are now stored in the archival vault because acid has reduced their newsprint to a fragility that can't be trusted to anyone who isn't specially authorized as a scholar or detective) to look for mention of the names or events in question during the Depression years centering at Gloucestermas 1934, the inchoate New Deal period of her own historical interests. I asked her to watch also for such names in the news of that era as Ozone, Nathan, Morgan, Weatherly, Charlemagne, Duncannon, Halymboyd, and Macdane. Whereupon she laughed, and promised to report back to me before the end of Raygun's second term. . . .

2.

[Tessa was hardly ever more candid than she should have been with anyone, even with her best friend, to say nothing of her husband. She had always behaved rather as confessor than confesser. It was now time to drop a few hints about the personal past in question that she'd casually picked up from the dowager Teddi Cibber, Wat's incongruous wife, not long before her death. At every infrequent encounter for three decades Tessa had tenderly embraced that graciously stalwart gentlewoman as an incarnation of the understanding mother she'd longed for in her disappointment at the limited one she was born to. Tessa thinks she has now happened upon genetic clues to the peculiarly ambivalent psyche of Caleb as theoretical artist, her peculiar protagonist, no less than half of whose mentality prior to the conditionings of post-natal environment and freewill might be accounted for by his mother's chromosomes.

As a licensed social worker, Tessa Masterson (her maiden name) had contracted to advise and assist the management of Merriwether Hall, a luxurious "retirement center", in its assiduous efforts to forestall, diagnose, remedy, or cover up discontentment within its resident gerontocracy, and to offer unhappy souls as much counsel as they would accept. The large main building of half-timbered stone, situated by a shortcut forest footpath only half a mile from her house near the city's artificially elevated West Marsh reservoir, had been built early in the century by a patrician enamored of the theater to accommodate and entertain limited numbers of rich or illustrious acquaintances visiting by yacht, private railroad car, or limousine. Its built-in stage, designed for Limeway professionals and their special patrons, was modernized by the corporation that purchased the estate from his heirs, but as far as the comfort of an audience was concerned it had needed little improvement for appropriate plays, films, musical dances, or lectures. It reminded Tessa of the ocean liner she had once explored when seeing off Dr Drang at a Westside Ur-island pier before the War.

Her duties were not as difficult as one might have expected because the paying residents were free to come and go, or absent themselves in hospitalization or travel, and even the disabled ones had all kinds of personal service in their private suites, in common rooms of the Hall itself, or in nearby "modern cottages" that matched the central architecture in outward style. No resident was obliged to put up with any other individual. For some of them the only social difficulty was to tolerate certain accidental ensembles at table in the main dining room; but even this vexation was mitigated by the fact that single as well as double, large, and larger tables were served, and save except upon request no places were assigned. The menu, there and for room service at all hours, was fulsome enough to earn the respect of any gourmet in Vinland. Even so, compared to the owners' high-flying payroll, maintenance, and debt service, food was not a major variable expense for the resourceful entrepreneurs whose total overhead (except for room service liquor) was practically fixed in proportion to the number of guests.

Every week without announcement or name tag Tessa attended an afternoon tea or cocktail party in the lounge, distinguished in dress from the normal rich only by her relative youth and social initiative. Her quiet charm in any company was a fusion of vocal moderation, unhurried slender carriage, calmly tactful address, and sympathetic unpainted aquilinity. By inconspicuously circulating in this elect community at teatime, and in other rooms at other occasions, she'd soon introduced herself to almost all the residents as a professional communicator and personal advocate at their service in any matter, public or private, that might affect their comfort or satisfaction. In other words, she conducted herself as a soi-disant hostess and entertainment manager, coordinator of personal care, or confidential (if not spiritual) companion.

But among those she hadn't yet met and logged into the official register of her contacts until a few days before her lunch with

Gloria was the single V I P occupying suite Number One, a ground floor annex of the main building, equipped with its own garage. He had recently returned from a trip to Europe, she learned from the Manager, but he'd hardly been missed because he was often absent, and in any case was inclined to keep to himself in the usual course of events, though he was no curmudgeon and made no difficulties for the staff. His name had sounded vaguely familiar to her before she phoned him for permission to introduce herself at his convenience. So one afternoon she had rung his bell like a new female curate completing her first round of parish calls.

In the meantime, because of what little she remembered hearing the name Halymboyd in the distant past, she'd consulted her husband, who immediately recognized it with avid interest. Rafe was curious enough about the man's surprising local presence to give some deliberate thought to her question, hoping to hear whatever information she might obtain about the erstwhile magnate's latter years.

"You see how interesting history can be!" Tessa had teased her geographical husband, who affected to belittle Clio.

"I don't regard contemporary biography as history. But I advise you to be skeptical of anything Arthur Halymboyd tells you of his past, which he probably thinks the world has forgotten because he knows that on Graveyard Street any time longer than the living memory of young traders and analysts is treated as irrelevant to the present, seeing that nowadays more investors are too impatient for the future to give a damn about retrospective fundamentals. It's a good thing you do business under your own name. He may not remember mine, but he might clam up if you call his attention to it. I think I actually met him only once or twice but he knew I was associated with those priests at the Laboratory. . . . Assuming, of course, that he's the same King Arthur!" Rafe had added. "It's a name unlikely to be duplicated."

So Tessa was curiously excited when a healthy Mr Halymboyd graciously responded by inviting her into his apartment, as if with the paternalistic understanding that he was making it as pleasant as possible for her to do her duty once and for all, presumably dismissing any need for her personal services. But of course like many men of any age he found himself charmed by this lady young enough to have been his daughter. She could see that he had shrunk in both length and breadth from a stocky prime, but he wore no glasses on his prominent nose, he still had plenty of white hair, and the loosened skin of fading fuscous complexion had hardly lost or never suspended the telltale double chin of superfluous victualage. Many books and journals were lying about this his sitting room, but from her quick distant glances she recognized only the day's *New Uruk Testament* and a bookmarked copy of *Democracy in Atlantis*. Even before they sat down to talk near his empty fireplace he ordered by home-phone wine and tea-things of her choice, leaving little time for her to inspect.

Tessa wondered what kept him so alertly occupied, especially after she began to believe that he had outlived any further personal interest in chrematistics, about which his four-score age was usually measured. He seemed to have launched himself onto a centrifugal tangent, readily telling her that he had already divided most of his estate between "socially responsible progeny" and the philanthropic trust established in Washington by his late wife, reserving for himself only as much as he could spend if he lived in the world's most expensive resorts and most scientific hospitals for another fifty years or happened to take on an extravagant mistress. He professed to loathe the idea of possessing any real property besides a German car in the garage that he did not own, in all cases preferring hired people and facilities to personal responsibility or demeaning negotiation.

But he was provisionally courteous as he in turn sounded the intelligence of her social work, and kept her at it longer than she had hoped. Only after she got home, without having overstayed her welcome, did it dawn on her that the old rascal had gained more information than he had given. Was this a case of mutually attempted seduction started in mutual suspicion? Or merely ended as such?

Yet she was satisfied with having picked up an unexpected scent. She told Rafe some of what Mr Halymboyd had said, but the prior engagement for her academic degree would have to take precedence over whatever surprise her research might unearth to expand or substantiate what she would call her novel. In any case she was determined to play the cards close to her vest with both her faculty advisor and her intimates (in their respective understandings of the story) lest she make a fool of herself with erroneous speculation or spoil the drama with premature and piecemeal clues; and to herself she could plead quasi-professional confidentiality for omitting mention to Rafe of some other things she had elicited or detected in her conversation with a possibly pertinent witness of the Gloucestermas '34 era.

"Mr Halymboyd," she asked after the diplomatic preliminaries, "I can't help wondering when I meet everyone who has come from the greater world to settle here in this mainland half of such a peculiar place as Dogtown. When you have the unlimited choice of an independent retirement, why Cape Gloucester?"

"Viking Shepherd dogs, Maxwell Gulls, things like that. From Dogtown I can easily get to anywhere, whenever I wish—especially Botolph and Unabridge. And from this side of the Gut it's even easier than from the Little Rock (as I call it), where I spend most of my time without the slightest inconvenience—except of course when the drawbridge is up! No one in London, Paris, Berlin, or Ur can get to an international airport as fast as I can. Yet except for the nostalgic train whistles there's nothing as quiet as this on the island. I want peace and seclusion."

"Dogtown's center city is not always very peaceful, when one gets to know it. But it can bore those who are used to living close to entertainments and famous events. Our angels have flat feet and they waddle in digital jerks. Our saints are dwindling. We don't even have a movie theater now."

"Well nothing is more graceful than angels aloft. I am not interested in theater. I'm no longer involved in ephemeral excitement. I can read as well here as anywhere in the cosmos. Dogtown reminds me of Saint James's in the Big Rock I came from, but it's neither so remote from 'events', as you put it, nor so desolate in winter. Terra Nova, except for its one city, where I no longer have relatives, is all a vast cold emptiness fringed with ugly forlorn villages scattered among bare and melancholy cliffs. It's only Saint Jim's harbor, and the magnificent bays, that make that big island worth visiting for anyone who isn't attached to it by nativity. All the rest is unchanging wilderness—the trees are dwarfs and they're all alike. This little Cape is a garden of trees by comparison! Trees are my flowers! I hope you appreciate them, young lady. Summer and winter, what can match these green mansions by the sea? Have you ever contemplated the twisted strength of a great oak or beech? —I'm a thoroughly naturalized citizen of this country. I never did consider myself an alien, thanks to the English and the codfish that we shared: I simply want to be able to get away from the hectic world of my middle age without losing at least mental access to the worlds that flank it."

"Then you are in just the right place. Most of us marooners feel the same way, in our own terms. Dogtown is a colony of allopatric historians, and one history leads to another, and all histories are connected sooner or later, especially, I suppose, because of languages with a lot of history. What better hub of history than where you are most welcome!"

"Well no one can fight off history, Ms Masterson." he smiled. "And I was a Marrano before I became a marooner. Before the War I was called to Dogtown on international business and later I lived over on the Foreside for a few years. I may be a luxuriating recluse now but I'm not exactly a stranger."

He was drinking Scotch as Tessa sipped sherry. With difficulty she held more of her tongue, for fear of arousing the witness's suspicion by naming names with a concatenation of questions. But she did let go one arrow in the reversal of time. "I'm an incomer myself, from Lagash, after Dogtown's golden age. I try to imagine what it was like when there were gas-works and trolley cars, before there were plastic toyboats and a high-rise Felly bridge. My kids and I pored over photos of the circus parade at Gloucestermas, especially the Great Year of Gloucestermas 1934. Were you here then by any chance? The Fleet anchored for days in the outer harbor and Navy sailors filled the streets, they say."

"I was just a poor young lawyer then."

As a cautious professional herself she was tactful enough not to ask a lawyer what his business was at a certain time and place, especially because she now knew from Rafe that he had represented the legendary Arnheim family in its preparation for Jewish refugees at its Stonyhurst estate on the Point at Kracken Cove.

"I had to go back to Charter Oak before the festival was over." he added. "That was one of the years that Roosevelt stopped here, I think."

Nor did she mention her knowledge of his visits to the priests at the Laboratory of Melchizedec and the Mesocosm a quarter of a century later.

"I seem to remember being told that this estate later belonged to a ham actor who read the Lessons at St Paul's Church on Halibut Street." he said. Was it an emerging association of ideas that began to furrow his brow with vague recollections of very different import? Somehow connected to Christianity: he never saw or had any reason to see a young analyst he'd recommended for a local job at Mercator-Steelyard after his own offer of a great ambitious opportunity in his own headquarters or some subsidiary of his own galactic Parity Investment Trust had been rather surprisingly declined? . . . Something to do with an unusual organization chart?

As Tessa rose to leave, handing him her card, he invited her to visit again and gave her his own private phone number. "They serve nice meals here. —And bring someone else along, if you like." he'd added, without emphasis, to allay any suspicion of himself as an old lecher.

It meanwhile occurred to her that she was presented with the possibility of a shortcut to her purpose. It was still too early for an actual scheme of exploitation, but she intended to approach Fay-away (Morgan) Gabriel, who was said to be Mary (Trevisa) Tremont's oldest known friend, though they had not met each other until the hour of Caleb's birth in 1935. Tessa was aware that from the beginning that relationship had been asymmetrical in temperament and intensity, and increasingly unbalanced in culture as well as in almost everything else but mutual respect for their reciprocal personalities. It appeared that after a very few years of contemporary residence in Dogtown the friendship was maintained almost exclusively in writing, overwhelmingly epistolary on Mary's side. Apparently in loneliness or enormous enthusiasm her letters were voluminous, compulsive, impulsive, and therefore exceptionally confessional. So perhaps Fay knew her, at various distances over nearly fifty years, more comprehensively than anyone except her son. Though her younger by five years, Fay was always the patient objective philosopher in Mary's eyes, naturally more reserved and immensely respected for her learning, spared any of Mary's critical attitude that sooner or later found its way like seeping water through the masonry of other figures initially held by her as high in estimation or affection as paragons of friendship. By virtue of temperament, marriage, education, and academic intelligence Fay was forgiven for having joined a world assumed to be less emotional than that of a lonely woman deranged by sleeping sickness during the 1918 influenza epidemic. Unless Fay was too unsentimental—too selective in her scholarship—Tessa speculated, she might have saved at least the most extraordinary of Mary's letters among her own family baggage. But even that much weight of paper may have been prohibitively inconvenient for an itinerant scholar surviving motherhood, widowhood, and scholarly fame—besieged by books, too swamped with printed pages and her own A D L to have enough time for *all* the thoughts she'd like to chase—not to mention writing!

*

. . . Where can I find an earlier contemporary of Mary hereabouts? I'm too late for Teddi Cibber by not much more than a year. She was never in favor of pejorative gossip but she had befriended Mary and still had her own insightful wits. Why didn't I think of combining my amateur curiosity with this professional research a long time ago? It must have been only in the aftermath of addiction to cigarettes that my lazy brain was finally clarified. How many other good ideas escaped me in the thirty years of my prime under the demand of a stupid vice? Mary herself told Caleb that it was tobacco that stunted his growth in her womb, and he thinks his reach would not have exceeded his grasp if his underdeveloped memory had been equal to his learning. But he speculates that his mental limitations may be attributed also to the mechanical advantage of the forceps by which he was delivered. (Thank God, from what I've heard, he's been spared Tristram Shandy's mutilation!)

Anyway, in this project my last resource will have to be the child himself. I'm sure his subjective memories—whether or not he chooses to interpret them—are more reliable than his psychological scholarship. Even his indifferent scraps of uncertain recollection give me clues to the relevant life of that "single mother". He can't keep holding out against my skills, no matter how busily he's absorbed with his theatrical will-o'-the-wisp. A man's a man for all that, and I think he likes my type of older woman! Surely he can be brought to bring himself to be both object and subject? When he finishes with Gilgamesh he may be ready to liberate his reservations! But I mustn't discompose his preoccupations prematurely, lest it prolong even unto my *really* old age his achievement of the theatrical vision that averts my psychological curiosity.

12

TABLET
ELEVEN

[Upper edge of an island's flat beach. **Urshanabi** squats looking down at **Gilgamesh**, who is prone on the beach before him, axe in hand. (He wears not much more than the small Isorectotetrahedron slung from his neck on a thong.) On the sand in a transverse row between them are seven loaves of bread. Nearby lies a gourd of water. **Berosus** as usual sits off to one side.]

[Gilgamesh raises
his head to look at
the loaves.]

URSHANABI	Can you stay awake now?
GILGAMESH	It was miraculous to recover breath enough for sleeping! I dreamt there were seven giant stone men above my brow to keep me from getting off the beach!
URSHANABI	Eat the bread. There's sweet water. I thought you were a dead man.
GILGAMESH	So did I.

URSHANABI   How did you get ashore with that axe? Even when you were sleeping I couldn't get it out of your hand. It's something that may be useful on this island.

GILGAMESH   I swam with one hand. That axe is all I have. No use landing without it.

URSHANABI   Well now the Mother of All Living has proved The Ancient of Days wrong. He said you must be some demigod, since Enlil has drowned all mankind for being too troublesome and noisy. But gods don't sleep. She baked a loaf every day you lay there to show how long you slept. She expected you to want the truth.

GILGAMESH   I'll never sleep when I reach the sunrise. I fell asleep while she was talking, but I thought it was in the dream. An old man and an old woman were droning over my head.

URSHANABI   The surf was up. They came to watch and noticed you tossed by the breaker. There's not much of a tide here, but it left you high enough to be hauled the rest of the way up the beach when they called me to help. You were very lucky to be washed through the western passage in the reef.

GILGAMESH   My boat had been once too often patched. In fact I didn't think it would last that long. The reeds were waterlogged and finally the pitch gave way. I was paddling with the axe head. That at least was no dream. And I don't think I've dreamt you up.

URSHANABI   I'm just a carpenter who's lost his tools.

GILGAMESH   I'd prefer to address you by name.

URSHANABI   Urshanabi, but Ziusudra still calls me Sailor sometimes.

GILGAMESH   Who is this worthy Ziusudra?
[Still dazed.]

URSHANABI   Was. King of Shuruppak, he claims; also originator of sacrifice and auspicy. The wisest and most virtuous of soothsayers, his wife says: therefore entitled to the honorific Atrahasis. He told me he was warned of a flood by the voice of a god. But it was I and my raft that saved him and his woman. We found that our river had no mouth: we were swept out to sea before I could pick up something to steer with. What we haven't salvaged for the fire is rotted driftwood now. —Well then, who are you?

GILGAMESH [Gets to his feet and stretches. Peers at the bread.]	I hardly know. Give me time to think my way back out of dreams. But I must thank the lady for my daily bread and pay my respects to the governor. I think I remember seeing their faces.
URSHANABI	There's no one here to be governed but me.
GILGAMESH [Points to the sky.]	So I surmised. —Which way is sunrise? Is the sky always so overcast?
URSHANABI	Aside from typhoons, very seldom. I suppose it's a sign you've brought us bad luck. But I would have been glad to see any human being, though a young woman would have been more welcome.
GILGAMESH [Drinks water and starts eating bread.]	I am no enemy. But where are Ziusudra and his lady now?
URSHANABI [Points landward.]	The Ancient of Days and the Mother of All Living are off in the bush for their daily attempt to breed a new race. Since your avatar they've shunned this beach as wanting in privacy. He told Ziusudra to sire four sons, each to start his own new tribe. I am to be midwife. So those two survivors have been going at it three times a day ever since the Lord God Enlil amended his curse on the teeming world. All the other gods had raised a clamor for the restoration of public services and earthy women's favors.
GILGAMESH	In his ire Enlil sometimes forgets that without human work there would be no canals to water fields of grain, and no altars for the sacrifice of flesh. There'd be no leisure in heaven. Gods would be laborers, or go naked and hungry. —What will Ziusudra do for daughters-in-law to bear fecund grandchildren?
URSHANABI	It is said that Inanna will produce them from this island's clay, all in good time. But the question is moot because Mother of All doesn't tell the Wise One that she's too old for babies. I suppose she likes his efforts. Meanwhile she spares him the burden of any other work if I can't do it. She is convinced that an archiflamen who studies gods' messages in the night sky can't be expected to pick coconuts, gather seaweed, or go fishing.
GILGAMESH	The gods chose a friend of mine for death, and it didn't require a flood. What about livestock and all the other creatures living on each other to feed or clothe those who served the gods? Such a flood must also have rid the earth

of snakes and cats. Ospreys and their like might survive on fish, but the other birds must have perished.

URSHANABI Ziusudra made pictures of all the birds and beasts, male and female, to preserve the species. He grieves more for the animal kingdom than for his comforts and servants.

GILGAMESH If I had thought life could be preserved by pictures I'd not have taken the trouble to fix words with writing. How did he save so many tablets on a raft, or even cylinder seals?

URSHANABI For one who counts the stars and communicates with gods it is not difficult: he stored the pictures in his head. He's learned everything that I don't understand.

GILGAMESH You can see in the stars what takes your fancy. I have seen a raging bull.

URSHANABI It's not his wisdom that makes me glad to serve him. Nor the riches that will be my reward if his expectations come to pass.

GILGAMESH
[Finishes eating bread.]
I'll ask his advice, and yours. But if this ocean is an ephemeral inundation, when will it subside?

URSHANABI He watches the irregular reach of waves on the sand for hours at a time, and chases the retreating surf to reclaim the margin of its undertow. And as the tide ebbs he follows it patiently with hope. When he can no longer deny its return he says it's still just practicing for the ultimate revelation of basic earth. He declares that it tastes less bitter every day, and that when it's sweet enough to drink our shoreline will begin enlargement. We shall find ourselves on a mountain peak.

GILGAMESH That reasoning is not unsound. He sounds like a patient prophet.

URSHANABI
Enter Ziusudra
& Mother of All
Living.
[Urshanabi hastily
busies himself.]
Here they come. Maybe he'll have the pleasure of finding out who you are! He may even answer some of your questions. —I must get ready for cooking.

ZIUSUDRA Speak, apparition! You look alive at last.

GILGAMESH Thanks to your kind lady and this affable sailor.

ZIUSUDRA	It looked as if the flood had drowned you, but we couldn't let a survivor starve. How did you escape the common fate? I wonder if you are one of my descendants. If so, you must have heard of me: Ziusudra, sometimes Utnapishtim in legend: secretary astronomical, master of ceremonies, royal Atrahasis in any case, so entitled by the gods. Why do you disturb the proper succession of things?
GILGAMESH	I journey east on Utu's road. But always sunrise seems as far ahead as ever.
ZIUSUDRA [Points inland.]	The sun rises over there and beyond. From the other side of this island you can look toward the world's east edge, but it's still too far to see.
BEROSUS [Aside.]	I don't know distances by sea, and I'm not a scholar of time.
MOTHER OF ALL [To her husband.]	No one can get there. —Even to find his father a stranded son would be suicidal to waste his salvation by ignoring the facts.
GILGAMESH	Madam, your words betray some clairvoyance—but no mortal has ever wished more than I to stay alive. In youth I paid no heed to time until I found that my friend Engidu had not had his share of it. He was seized by the earth like some creature of a day. Now he's curled in that black womb, disintegrating in slime that turns to dust, uncohering from unique personality into a million common atoms less alive than the seed of fossils. Now I always face the morning sun and put the afternoon behind me, striving to see time's arrow at the bow.
ZIUSUDRA	You may as well search for the winds. Time is the gods' mystery. Can you be so privileged? If not, you will go blind seeking such light. You are speaking to a seer.
GILGAMESH	I have no wish for second sight. The very simplest knowledge of here and now is what I want. Let come what may. Prophecy is fiction. I leave that to you. Time was before the Tablets of Fate. Even your gods themselves can't overcome what doesn't come by necessity unless it's already here.
ZIUSUDRA	May I ask by what name such a polemical monotheist distinguishes himself from slender-witted madmen?
GILGAMESH	Call me Noman. I hope for advice that only you as a scholar of the skies can give. As long as I'm learning I'll teach in return.

ZIUSUDRA   I'm intrigued by the offer if you're as clever as you sound.
                  But Mardi is my kingdom now. This is the end of the rain-
                  bow. You must do my bidding.

GILGAMESH   As long as you are just. I wasn't born to be subjected.

ZIUSUDRA   This is an island of no return.

GILGAMESH   There is nothing I wish to return to.

ZIUSUDRA   Where do you come from? Who really was your father?
                  How did you escape the flood?

MOTHER OF ALL   No no, my dear. Let Noman tell us as he wishes, a little
                  now, a little later. Everyone's story reveals its causes, and
                  when pieced together anyone's story is worth waiting for.
                  That way he'll tell us much more than what you can think
                  of asking. You won't have to speculate so much. A friendly
                  way is always best. Let him take his time. He's suffered
                  much in getting here. Any tale is better than none.

ZIUSUDRA   All right. I am tired of my own news.

[All except
Gilgamesh sit down
opposite Berosus to listen.]

GILGAMESH   I may have strayed off course. This is the same earth I've
                  always lived on but the stars here are new, or too low to
                  recognize. —How much do I remember? Certainly not my
                  two fathers. I'm not even sure how many of my memories
                  may be dreams.

MOTHER OF ALL   Please don't worry about needless distinctions. Sometimes
                  we too confuse one kind of memory with another, and some
                  are false perforce. Just as you and I forget some of the truth
                  that we used to remember.

GILGAMESH   For me there's often too much to remember. At times in
                  stress I forgot to stay on a straight course to the sunrise by
[He accompanies   keeping the pole star on my left without crossing the eclip-
much of his narra- tic to my right. But there was no way to observe both those
tive with dance or marks at any one point unless I stopped for a night and a
pantomime, moving day. But when I sojourned for a while, repossessed by
from point to point, habitual interests and pleasures, I was likely to forget the
with his axe, in   purpose that drove me.
illustration of his
travels.]   —Yet I do remember the greatest challenge to what was
                  still my youthfresh strength. Two lions tried to deny me
                  water and a share of their kill at an isolated spring. They
                  may have been former companions of Engidu who held

against me his decadence and wormy death. Of necessity I killed them both, each with one blade of this axe.
—Then trekking an immense plain eastward, I was daunted by the barrier of an endless mountain range gradually rising in the east. The massif of unscalable cliffs was surmounted exactly in the center of my direction by two broad-based peaks like upright fangs of heaven guarding the nativity of time.

BEROSUS
[Aside.]

Thus his memory.

GILGAMESH

That night two giant scorpion-men stood guard over the pass between the peaks. They seemed to see both ends of time. I hailed them. They conferred together, bending across the alpine space that separated them. I held up the axe to show my only weapon, calling up to them my name and purpose. Again they whispered through the void of stars. Then they turned again and pointed down into the recess that separated them, one with his left hand and the other with his right. Accordingly I advanced and beheld that I had been deceived in perspective. The scorpions had been standing on two separate mountains overlapping like crooked teeth, split apart by a bending canyon no wider than my shoulders. For seven nights and seven days I groped and wended through that deep fissure, dark as a cave, ever fearful of wedging myself into a jointure of sheer walls as parallel as a frost-crack's, where my skeleton would stand upright till the end of the world. But at last, as I was about to succumb to thirst, I was revived by an errant ray of the risen sun briefly penetrating the twisted darkness ahead. I forced enough hope from a kindred spark of life to claw myself many hours later out upon the gentle eastern slope of that sierra, next to a purling brook, just as the day was ending

BEROSUS
[Aside.]

Thus his dream.

GILGAMESH

When I awoke the sun was rising as far away as I'd ever seen it. But my feet were cold and a beautiful girl was rubbing them. For many days she kept my attention. I recovered my strength. She had been lonely. She had been yearning for someone worthy of her first love, and she was well prepared by imagination to make me forget for a time everything that she had no interest in. She diverted me with reciprocal usages she wished to learn. For a long time I gave myself up to the pleasures of tawny skin like the lion of a pride. I lingered in her pleasure garden with amber beer, among the peaceful people of that broad valley.

BEROSUS
[Aside.]

Memory of the Harappa flood plain.

GILGAMESH

Day and night, nothing—no one in the circle dance—was denied me. A black panther was my bodyguard, purring at the foot of my generous bed. No strife, no jealousy, among that moonlit people! I had bells for my toes and elephants to ride on—but a ring on my nose! So when I paused from idle recreations my mind began to recall old motives. They allowed me to make plans and build a city safely on the river bank, with watered fields and gated canals to carry their freight. I also taught them how to write and reckon. The ring had fallen from my nose, but still for too long I was distracted by constructive pleasures—as if I was seizing the chance to build a greater Uruk with an exotic labyrinthine tower! It took seven years and more for me to be learn that public improvements are always in progress and decay, never finished. . . .

MOTHER OF ALL

Sir, you lose us in your memories!

GILGAMESH

Anyway I noticed that I had forgotten both the bitterness of private loss and my essential quest. I had forgotten myself in the bemusements of dalliance and engineering! To my horror I woke to the understanding that I was still captive to a gratitude greater than any I had known before, and to a young woman's instinct for godlike babies, threatening to lift her skirt to the wind as my mother did.

ZIUSUDRA

I can understand that.

GILGAMESH

But the east was still barricaded against me by a serrated range of mountains arrayed in snow-laden thickets from end to end of the horizon, their myriad peaks as entangled with each other as with the clouds that never ceased to rake the highest sky. Only by turning south could I hope to get past around them. To make a clean escape I had to steal away without warning, apology, or pity. I made the best river boat I could secretly contrive and cut myself fifty punting poles to get through the marshes and off the shallows down to the open sea, by which I reasoned the whole continental barrier might be skirted. Then I could again travel as close as possible to Utu's daily path while keeping the pole star on my left by night. With a bolt of lady's cloth I hoped a breeze would ease my way. But the small winds were against me and the big winds tore it away with my mast.

—If I had another cloth I'd now know how to make it work to my advantage in any weather. Here at least I can cut a mast and spar.

MOTHER OF ALL I'll not weave your shroud! I've lost too many sons to trust men's confidence.

GILGAMESH

[Indicates his axe.]

Half of every day afloat I faced the blinding sun to fix my course. I ate and drank undigested fish from the fluid bellies of occasional sea birds, always defending myself from curious sharks with this handy invention of mine. At intervals on every island sojourn in my eastering—deflected by wind or current but always between the Crab and the Goat—I bartered knowledge or invention for my keep, but never again, no matter how long I tarried, did I forget my purpose. I do not forget it here, but I shall leave you the better for my visit.

ZIUSUDRA

[Suddenly rises and begins to pace about excitedly. Mother of All and Urshanabi stand up reflexively.]

Now wait a minute, Mister Noman! This will be your last stop if you don't parley in good faith! You've been informed that I am wise! I will not be deceived! Double-bitted axe—tower—walls—canals—Uruk—Engidu! I am not ignorant of what the world hears! Are you a poet or an actor?

GILGAMESH I cannot sing. But I sometimes take action.

ZIUSUDRA You pretend to be Nimrod!

GILGAMESH No, Engidu was Nimrod. I am Gilgamesh. I had hoped for the advantage of anonymity; but I have been too transparent in telling my story to a student of every science.

ZIUSUDRA Then prove that you are Gilgamesh.

GILGAMESH My seal, the Isorectotetrahedron, a four-pointed jackstone.

ZIUSUDRA I have heard of that amulet! But you may have stolen it from Gilgamesh.

GILGAMESH Do you know the legend that I'm two-thirds god, only one third human?

ZIUSUDRA Every human must have at least a trace of the gods that made his race.

GILGAMESH	My mother confessed that I was conceived under Utu's eclipse of Sine at a moment when her loves were equally divided. I had to choose between them for my god when I corrected Uruk's calendar.
ZIUSUDRA	Identity is never absolute, but the scope of your replies is sufficient. We shall have plenty of time to debate the heinous errors in your infamous measurement of years. —If you are Gilgamesh you can teach me how to write and read.
GILGAMESH	Then Urshanabi must help me build a boat, advise me of the local currents, and chart the eastern opening of this atoll.
MOTHER OF ALL	If Ziusudra agrees to that I'll weave your sail despite my warning. But I fear you're no less apt to kill yourself than any woman's reckless son.
URSHANABI	I'll show you how we fish the lagoon without an axe!
GILGAMESH [To Ziusudra.] [Points to the Isorectotetrahedron on his neck.]	At half ebb tide the sand will be smooth and firm. Every day with a stick on the hard beach you will draw from your head some of the pictures you hoard. With this stylus I will write their names for you to compare before the tide returns to wash them out. All the words and pictures can then be inscribed on clay outside your head to work the thaumaturgy with at any time. Posterity will know forever the acts of resurrection by which you will have restored all living creatures to the earth.
ZIUSUDRA [Bends to examine it.]	Fame is not my motive. Is that the talisman that's said to reconcile three with four?
GILGAMESH	Also with the degrees of every azimuth. And with much else in reckoning. At your leisure I will decipher its many meanings.
ZIUSUDRA	If you were once a king, why now such a generous tutor?
GILGAMESH	I have no responsibility to keep religious secrets or vows of obedience like those that burden you. I have relieved myself of works. I've renounced my interest in power. I harbor no arcane jealousy. I exercise no wish either to know myself or to empty my mind of the pragmatical world. My mania is now confined to retrogression, leaving me in all else disinterested.

ZIUSUDRA   I pity your derangement. You are not the thoughtless brute of your reputation. But you cannot reach the meeting place of earth and sky without the vitalizing herb I shall give you to round out our interesting covenant. You must guard it for your life from diving albatross and breaching giant squid. They can sniff it at a hundred fathoms.

MOTHER OF ALL   Come, my dear. We must leave this brave guest for a while to gather incense for our meditation. We'll pray for him to acquire a taste for my palm wine that will at least prolong his holiday with us. —Urshanabi, let's celebrate with a new fish tonight. It goes without saying that there'll be yams, coconuts, and bananas for the other courses. Please sound the conch when everything's ready.

Mother of All leads Ziusudra off stage left.

URSHANABI   I must go fishing now. But tell me about this boat you have in mind.

GILGAMESH   The tide looks about right: come on down and I'll draw a plan. —What's this herb the shaman has in mind for me?

[Picks up his axe by the head, handle downward.]

URSHANABI   Brier roses grow all along the shore. If you mind the thorns you can chop yourself a bushel of their hips.

Gilgamesh & Urshanabi go off stage right.

BEROSUS   In Babylon those thorny flowers are known as dog roses. Pyramus picked them for Thisbe.

[Aside.]

13

PILLOW
THOUGHTS

It is by no means enough that a Naval Officer
be a capable mariner. He must be that of
course, but he should be as well a gentleman of
refined manners, liberal education, punctilious
courtesy and the nicest sense of personal honor.

—John Paul Jones

*A*t last the people were no longer being fooled by flowers and foliage as harbingers of spring; their trust in
proper weather was no longer threatened by collective
memory of a Colonial cold snap that killed all buds for the
"summer-that-never-was".

As Caleb was reading the *Nous* and finishing his ocean-catfish
supper he was startled by a ringing of the telephone that he'd
seldom lifted from its cradle since his graduated withdrawals from
ordinary human communication—he who a few years ago almost

261

every day during office hours had juggled without surprise or hesitation a stream of nearly simultaneous unarticulated business matters with an instrument operated by five push-buttons. So different were his old and new lives, and thus so hypersensitive to intrusion upon anyone else's time, that these days he was even hesitant to make calls of his own to people who were always glad to hear from him.

"Caleb, my dear, I hate to interrupt your work, but for me this is somewhat of an emergency. I need your advice while it's still daylight." said Fay Gabriel. "If you can spare—"

"Don't worry about that. What is it?"

"I wouldn't bother you if Finn weren't at sea on a Navy cruiser shakedown for the Wight yard in Markland. He swore it was the last time he'd take on one of those— . . . Do you remember my cat Felixity?"

"Of course. She has a magnificent tail. I think she likes me."

"Oh she did! But now she's disappeared! I'm afraid she's gotten too adventurous because of this warm weather and full moon. Sometimes the little glutton stays out overnight but it's not like her to go more than one day without her main courses at home." The cat had gone missing for more than three days, she told Caleb.

"Many house-cats stay away longer than that once in a while. But she's spayed, isn't she?"

"Yes, but she's very attractive! On my deck I sometimes see a wickedly handsome black gentleman with a white badge hanging around the kitchen window, looking for her aesthetically I suppose, and a few times I've heard her snarl-singing at him through the glass. I call him Minalouche. He's got a guilty conscience and as soon as he sees me he flashes out of sight two stories down to the ground. He must be a platonic seducer. . . ."

"That's why our saints chase felines as sinners. Fascinating creatures but categorically unelect." Despite his facetiousness Caleb hadn't forgotten the excruciating distress he'd suffered at the prolonged Walpurgis Night absence of his own Ibi-Roy, elect Viking Shepherd as king of the Dogtown saints. He was not deceived by Fay's fluctuating assumption of a reasonably sanguine tone intended to mask a trembling dread of ultimate despair about a merely subhuman life that would be publicly regarded as unbecoming in a venerable scholar of human kind, cicatrized by long experience of the wholly personal vicissitudes she was presumably thought to have suffered without complaint in a long life of detached objectivity. For lack of reciprocating language even the transitory love of a solitary person's household animal is likely to be more anxious about casual absences than the communicating kinship of a parent or sibling. He was aware that this muted evidence of his godmother's love, perhaps as suddenly piercing as his love and fear when Ibi disappeared to lead the saints of Dogtown, and no less irrational, was all the more endearing because of her formidably unsentimental character, before any speculative sympathy for the poor cat itself began to disturb his imagination of its ignorant pain and terror. He was struck with love for the kernel femininity of a venerable lady so enormously more informed about life than himself. At the same time her softly adiaphanous voice served no more than a negligée to forestall the subtle excitement of her womanhood in relation to himself. He had already inferred a certain quality of mercy from overhearing that her two children were graduates of the Laurel Amphictyony without having taken to reactive irresponsibility or libertarianism; and he had laughed to himself at his jealousy of the brilliant husband who must have been fortunate to die before knowing any fear of anachronistic courtly love. But now she's apparently giving herself to the Commander! If she's susceptible to the blandishments of a technocratic old knight, why not excessive love for a typical self-absorbed female cat whose beauty has millions of precedents and replications?

". . . Longhaired dark-brownish tabby with gray bars, and a plumed tail as black as crow-feathers, not one of those silly gossamer fluffs! Finn says she looks like a Gothic question mark when seen from the port side. From my side I say a bishop's crosier."

"Yes, I remember." he said, cheerfully trying to divert the worst of speculation. "I love well-formed domestic cats. The shapes and proportions of cats like Felixity are ideally beautiful composites of the zoo-cats I've worshipped from afar since my first story-book. But in grownup times I've noticed imperfections in each of them, such as rounded ears, or faint shadowy spots beneath supposedly pure black coats, incongruous bellies, or ludicrously elevated hindquarters, or heads the wrong size for their bodies! But she's as perfect as Bagheera. She jumped onto my lap at the first invitation!"

"That's a sign of her clairvoyance. As a Norseland Forest Cat, you know, she's wary of Finn the Celt! But perhaps she's really a Markland Viking mischling. She has a lot of feathers between her paws and isn't afraid of snow. Her claws frighten me at times. She keeps moving my scatter-rugs around because she doesn't like my floor configuration. I don't believe that's just for sharpening her claws, as they always say about calisthenic cats. She's exercising her sinews, testing her grasp."

"All the more reason she might be up a tree. That's a climbing breed. It's said some even climb rocks, like snow leopards."

"I didn't think of looking in the trees!" Fay exclaimed.

"Cats' claws curve only one way, so it's easy for them to go up but hard for them to get down if they've gone too high up on a limbless stretch to slide or jump down. A cat's been known to stay up in a tree for as much as eighteen days before rescue."

"Probably a male, too proud to call attention to his foolishness." she chuckled, grasping at the momentary reprieve. ". . . But I don't dare go out to look around again because I have to stay at the phone in case there's an answer to the ad I put in the paper, or a call from the lady-catchpoll, whom police and the Public Works people notify of all the animal reports they get, fatal or not. Felixity refused to keep wearing an identity-collar. Feminine vanity, no doubt. It disturbed her ruff."

"I'll be up in an hour or so, the long way around, to scan the streets of your neighborhood. My mother used to call our cats *Come kitty, kitty, kitty* in soprano, which I'll try now in my falsetto. That wasn't as mortifying as when she called *me* in from some street-game. It had the piercing trill of a tongue vibrating at the roof of her mouth. No name or epithet was necessary to distinguish me in the vocative case. It made me the butt of every nationality in the neighborhood—especially in the pidgin Yankee element of it who understood the catcall in terms of native English."

"Felixity never answers my calls." Fay rejoined in the seriousness of this topic. "But she plays with my apron strings when I'm getting supper and unties my shoes when I leave them on the floor. That's why I call her *Kitchen cat with cupboard love*! She degrades herself with piercingly raucous screeches, shedding all dignity and affection, when she's under my feet demanding food. . . . But I haven't yet analyzed her pace—does she walk like a camel or a horse, sometimes cantering, sometimes galloping, or in some sort of augenblicklich legerdemain? She's too self-satisfied to listen to me. Our family dogs always did. Finn says it's a waste of breath to call any cat. . . ."

Caleb was trying to envision the various city or village cats in his domestic childhood. Now that he thought of it, he couldn't remember the fate of any one of them. Not that his mother, who urged upon him the experiences of life, would have concealed any facts he didn't witness. How could I have been so callous? The first one, in Unabridge, acquired from a woman who lived near the apartment house in which Alpha Whitehead dwelt (that name his mother impressed upon him with awe when he had no idea of why) was dubbed Missus Bissus and coaxed by his mother to deliver her kittens as frankly as possible in the back of a closet, much to his distaste.

"At twilight, when things quiet down, I'll be better able to hear her if she responds to my catcall from overhead. But anyway, while there's still daylight I'll try to look at every telephone pole and tree, especially in the woods across from your house."

"Oh Caleb, I hate to ask that of you. But don't forget she's camouflaged!"

"Not as much as our Bagheera, the black cat we once had. In the shadows if he didn't open his eyes you couldn't see him."

"I thought my sentimental days were over!" Fay sounded apologetic.

"I'm glad they're not. I call it sentiment, not sentimentality."

"If I only knew definitely what happened to her! She may have been catnipped."

"Kidnapped."

"Yes of course, I must be ridiculously distraught. When there were kids around the loss of a cat wasn't excessively grievous. Burkes and O'Hairs for vivisection laboratories never occurred to us—I hope Finn will be back soon. —You are an angel!"

"No, not a gull just a saint, tracking down a sinner for my godmother." Caleb himself wasn't yet much more affected by the loss of her cat than by the extinction of a benign spider crawling across his floor. His imagery was occupied by the pale olive face of the cat's mistress half a mile away at a telephone held in slender wrinkled fingers near thin refined lips and smoothly hollowed chin, its cerebral beauty accented more by quotidian anxiety than by crease or blemish of age.

"Then look for golden eyes. She might not be exactly a Norselander. —When your mother was staying on the Isle of Manannan she wrote some poems about interbred migrant cats."

Caleb hastily sheered off from the landfall of that topic. "Allow time for me to cover all the blocks and roadsides on foot, especially in bushes around the golf course, as I circle my way up the hill." Not for the first time he wondered if Fay knew his mother's only secret.

But as a transitory relief of aching anxiety Fay was yielding to amusement in an association of objective ideas. "Mary was so afraid of snakes! I'll never forget: she wrote me enthusiastically that the native Manx cats were said by some to have been bred without tails in order to avoid the snake bites that came from stepping on a cat's tail! Others said that the original pair had been so busy copulating that they were the last to get aboard the Ark—so late that Noah had closed the hatch on their tails! She had some funny little poems about that. She seemed to compose and write long informative letters without hesitation or effort—always in legible longhand! . . .

"—Oh Caleb, alone in this old house in the middle of the night I hear thumps like the sound of a cat jumping down to the floor from my bed or some forbidden surface, or the mews of a cat downstairs, but she's never there! If it isn't entirely delusion it's just the usual mysterious creaking of old timber or the expansion of metal pipes, or angels on the roof. In the morning I wake up from the anodyne of sleep with no more than five seconds of peace before her absence knocks me back into devastating reality! I'm afraid of what the neighbors tell me about predators around here. It seems absurd, but there's talk of house cats having been killed by a fisher cat or a coyote! A fox is often mentioned. I saw one myself in a neighboring yard last year! I've been a fool to think that Felixity could take care of herself from local fauna. But nobody's reported her carcass on the kilroy streets, so what else is more likely than such a feral death in a denatured habitat, in the thickets where her pelt and bones would never be found? I can't believe she'd adopt another owner just for the sake of tastier food! Or that she could be lured into any cat-fancier's car, or captured by a roving experimental biologist! And there'd be no outdoor population of cats at all in the neighborhood if anyone had been poisoning. . . ."

"Let me make my search before you reconcile yourself to the law of the jungle."

"It's the uncertainty that's harder than the worst fact. I didn't realize how devoted I'd become to serving her simply in return for her ladyship's company, almost as if she were a grandchild. I still find myself going through the reflexive motions of opening doors to let her in or out, or automatically starting to reach for her food and water at feeding time when I'm thinking of something during my A D L routines. It still seems unnatural to be able to open a can without her pestering response to the sound and scent from wherever she's asleep or waiting. The bedtime routine is now too simple. I feel the presence of her absence. . . . From now on my daily schedule is going to be more monastic. Nobody's hunger to take priority over my own. No more traumatic caging for trips to the vet. More time to work. Nothing to disturb my concentration! Better than having kids leave home because I won't have to worry about what she's up to on her own. Love versus liberty. . . . But then, no placid aristocratic beauty spread on bed or chair to lift my heart when I walk into a room! She would open her eyes and trill at the sight of me. Sometimes at night, when she'd been draped upon my ankles like a heavy sack of birdseed cutting off the circulation to my feet, while still sitting up in bed, I'd pause before putting aside my book and turning off the light so that we could gaze at each other for a couple of minutes for no other purpose than reciprocal contemplation. But I'm afraid it was her wild curiosity that—" It seemed to Caleb that she'd resigned herself to absolute loss.

"Wait a while! Don't assume the worst. I wish you'd called me sooner."

"Psychologists talk about 'closure'. I hate that term. Her purr sounds like a lobster boat. She turns it on in anticipation. —And off, in sudden displeasure."

*

Commander Finn Macdane (U S N, Ret.), engineering systems consultant, had finished his final shakedown cruise inspection report to the Navy on the propulsion and electrical performance of the Wight Yard's latest destroyer, the first of a new class. She was as large as some of the cruisers that fought in his own war, but a hundred times as lethal for both attack and defense. In these new warships electronically guided missiles had replaced almost all the guns, the only conspicuous one of which was even to himself all but incredibly advanced in range, rapidity, and accuracy—controlled by a remote computer, its single barrel fired from an unmanned streamlined turret all alone on an open forward deck. But at least these powerful destroyers with clipper bow and handsomely centralized superstructure—conning tower integrated with masts and funnels—still looked like classic ships in distant silhouette, worthy of reminiscence! But he did not wish to follow their evolution any further.

The previous year, as a former consultant in her design, he'd
been present at her perilous launching, when she'd balked at sliding down the ways without extraordinary prompting, seriously
alarming the hundreds of souls responsible for building or using
the product being conditionally purchased by the nation's taxpayers. As champagne dribbled down the flared stem of the motionless
ship in the drama watched by several thousand hosts and guests in
a noisy open-air auditorium framed by towering cranes, a sudden
silence defined the moment of horror. But few besides the Launch
Master and his assistants at the Works (along with a cadre of the
Navy's future crew) understood that a hesitant launching, if accomplished by jolting force, especially into a small river after the
proper stage of the tide and near a major bridge, is enough at the
very least to get a ship jinxed. Of course no such superstition had
taken root after the highly successful sea-trials, probably the last
time he'd tread a deck of steel. In the event, prodded by dwarfs
with sledgehammers, the great hull, destined to displace almost ten
thousand tons of brine, began to obey the will of human beings
with its expected dignity by accelerating its proper way down the
inclined plane of thickly greased rails in a cradle of wood. He supposed that he wouldn't have the heart to take his absolute leave of
ships until he had gone down to New Port Newce for the commis-
sioning in honor of the late intellectual warrior lamentably overlooked in public fame, the Admiral on whose staff he'd most happily served toward the end of the War.

He was driving home to Cape Gloucester from the "downeast"
Wight Works (a k a *The Best Fabricators in the World),* where as a
summertime loblolly-boy and apprentice shipwright during World
War 1 he'd had his first paid job, when his father was the company's shipbuilding Superintendent. But now almost at last, as if to
put aside childish toys and renounce a lifetime of immature entertainment, he was determined not only to free himself of occasional
jobs for the Navy (instinctively more defensive of its hierarchical
authority than of the common good and characteristically inimical
to the most disciplined and respectful internal criticism of its traditions) from which he had long since officially retired, but also to
close his ears forever to the other applied sciences that had diverted
him from a normal living. One of the alleged benefits of modern
technology is that it has taught people not to bat an eyelash at
sleight-of-hand. The benefits of electrical engineering have brought
electronic magic for those who merely operate its products without

knowing the distinction between volt and ampere, in nearly total ignorance of basic Newtonian principles.

But this veteran engineer now rejoices in complete freedom to resume his education among liberal Geisteswissenschaften. The humanly imperfectible compromises in naval architecture and the ultimately imperfectible knowledge of the cosmos are now less interesting to the old pensioner, and far less important in authentic life than history and politics, especially in decadent Atlantis as the vainglorious leader of progressive civilization. He is now definitely acknowledging that for himself philosophy, from which he was sorry to have allowed himself to advance no further than the Greeks during his artifactual career with real and virtual machinery, was even more interesting than efforts to predict the infinitely incorrigible posterity in which he had no personal stake.

As whenever possible, he is driving the old slow route along the coast because its seascape rehearsed a succession of random memories from much of his formative life, including some that were of his cerebral yearnings for adventure in other tracts of the globe. Yet now most of his thoughts are about the anchor of this concave maritime arc, his destined bourne by choice. His affection for Dogtown wasn't quite inborn, but during most of his youth it had been a favorite port of call for sail or steam. This afternoon, however, there is a sea-fog, and on his starboard side of the southeasterly road there now isn't much of diachronistic interest.

At first, speeding along the familiar curves and modernized reaches of straightaway in the familiar route (probably for the last time), slowing down only to thread the towns that seemed hardly to have changed during his lifetime, he ruminates about having finally determined his all but absolute withdrawal from gainfully attractive employment: no more of the fees or honoraria that he'd pick and choose for personal satisfaction, or out of curiosity. He finds himself at absolute liberty to renounce even cursory glances at the dwindling number of professional journals and newsletters that have not yet expired for lack of his reciprocation. He would no longer be inveigled even into domestic architectural conception or criticism by his old friend Caspar Aninigo because Caspar had retired soon after his own delayed retirement from the firm he had founded. At least for the present, in short, Finn Macdane believes himself absolutely free of interest in the advancement of aesthetic technology. Instead he is anticipating his terminal liberty as a marooner in Dogtown.

*

What had drawn him to settle down for good in that insular little city-state with only three vehicular gateways but no ramparts or moats that were not natural, obviously not to be compared with Valletta, Rhodes, Lucca, Galway, Kirkwall, Visby, or any other town it fetched to memory at the moment, save perhaps Peel on the Isle of Manannan? There were many answers but he never could muster them all at once. Certainly his purpose had been to spend his time reading and reflecting on whatever he pleased, unhindered by past social obligations or outlived memories, while easily available to people he liked. Except for books he hadn't yet brought much impedimenta from his several caches of personal property. Save for Dogtown he might well have kept on the move of discovery, according to wind or whim. Or invested himself almost anywhere else in the world of places he had considered testing. Nowadays friends and temporary attractions were almost equally available from nearly anywhere else. As for his estate, he had no wife, no mistress, no possible heirs to be worth evaluating before it was too late for options. His true loves had been few, mostly fleeting in wartime, sophisticating but undamaging his general admiration of women. His closest shipmates and colleagues were dead or lost to the kind of communication that he would now welcome. So as he drove the last half of his nearly effortless way home in a soothing soundproof kilroy (his main indulgence of luxury), without once turning on his radio for news or music, his second thoughts were converging upon the terminal bachelor quarters to which he was returning. He now realized that his first thought was captured by Fay Gabriel, only ten years his junior.

But hours later when his objective consciousness reawakened from perfectly alert autonomic driving by familiar roadside navigation buoys and atmospheric whiffs of his destined headland, as he finished skirting the Cape Gloucester marshes and crossed the Felly highway's elevated steel-arch bridge over the Namauche estuary, thrilling with its chorological perspective (which had never been afforded travelers before Eisenhower's postwar highway program), he reminded himself of the parking problem, preparing himself for enragement at someone's car occupying the space he'd leased from the landlord of an alley jammed between two office buildings that flanked his spot just across Pleasure Street from his own corner of granite-faced bricks and mortar facing Morality Square, the vital center of a twisted city. He had bought this former bank building so that he could design his own penthouse above two floors of rented offices that yielded enough to justify his only uncharacteristic entrepreneurial investment.

Steering into twilight traffic, his soul at a distance from everything he saw or heard through the glass of his insulated vessel, he'd been lost in reverie throughout narrow bends and habitually cautious intersections, mechanically anticipating evidence of imprudence in the opposing stream of less alert automata. Could it have really been so long by clock and miles that he'd parsed his recollections and speculations about realized and unrealized possibilities as a visitor to Dogtown dimmed or distorted by a half-century of extrinsic life in war and peace before pledging it his allegiance as a taxpayer? Perhaps original experience itself was molded by his own obtuse misunderstanding. Until recently, except maybe in unnoticed fragments of kaleidoscopic dream, elements of the early past that he now recalled as certainly undeceiving memories had been forgotten for years on end, having been too easily dismissed as nonrecurrent adventure insignificant at a time followed by the events and dangers of history's greatest war and its aftermath. If so, it was only natural that those rising to consciousness now would have preconsciously influenced—even overdetermined—his choice of Dogtown as the site of his first and last reality-estate. The place to which he was drawn by its uniqueness had revived for his psyche a few virtual seedlings and saplings that had never grown to exfoliation in his subsequent history. Nostalgia, piquant memory, was a pleasure of his old age in which the spending of action and passion hadn't quite ceased to spread its wake of tumultuous perceptions in a telescoped reversal of time's broad arrow. . . .

*

. . . It was the eve of Gloucestermas in the Great Year of 1934. Our flotilla of six W W 1 four-stack destroyers was anchored in the outer harbor roadstead. After their anchor-holds had been tested, their topsides dressed with signal flags from stem to stern, and their liberty boats launched to start ferrying ashore throngs of exuberantly neat sailors clad in white dress uniforms with hats initially squared according to regulations, soon to be exchanged for loads of civilian visitors during the best part of

every day for nearly a week, my tug, having done its precautionary escort duty, tied up in the north channel of the inner harbor, at a wharf that now after slum-clearance and other demolitions might have been very near the foot of that crowded alley, within view of my present superposed studio.

This tug served only for contingencies, as a sort of porter for the real ships of war, which seemed a gaily decorated pack of thin grey wolves come to protect fishermen and landlubbers from threat of Viking dragonships or British privateers, commanded by senior officers of whom I was still in awe. Such a sight of even these the smallest of warships dominating the usually unobstructed harbor that now embraced them with arms of tranquil hills— pointing at anchor in unison like a band of seabirds alighted against a wind—was even then a thrill for me, and its like still is, as much as if they were battleships at anchor in the Statue of Liberty's vast roadstead preparing for a parade up the North River under the eyes of F D R, or, for that matter, the victorious fleet I saw in Tokyo Bay. (As a matter of fact, as I was later told, about that local time in 1934 the President was secretly visiting for a couple of days within half a mile of where I was then a guest.) I was almost as much an aesthetic spectator as civilian spectators on Navy Day, which used to be distinctly celebrated in the national patriotic calendar, mainly perhaps to glamorize the recruitment of young men when there were no other jobs and the Navy itself was still languishing for funds to pay them. . . .

I came ashore in my two-striped Lieutenant's white dress uniform, much like all the other gentlemen paying official tribute to New Armorica's oldest port at the commencement of its midsummer celebration, fraternizing not at all with their far more numerous and less mannerly subordinates, then much less educated even in their specialties than they have been since the technological War. I had been invited to a dance for the following night and my tug was due back at the Navy Yard the day after that, seeing that the D Ds would probably need no further assistance from us by then. My Chief Bosun and I gave our tiny crew unrestrained liberty to join the other sailors and local celebrations or to go wherever they could be reached in emergency, while he and I took turns as the sole watch aboard, alternating each other for civilian meals ashore. He was a married man with many service stripes, a seadog long since purged of carousing and suchlike adventure on the beach, as glad as I for some leisurely solitude, as long as he could listen to Big League baseball games on the boat's excitedly articulating radio. So he was content to watch the fireworks alone and glad enough to negotiate quid pro quos largely in my chronological favor, knowing that he would come out ahead sooner or later in our future mutually respectful relationship. He must have been too old for overseas duty in the war ahead.

I simply cannot remember that man's name, though many others of less significance pop into my head from time to time for no particular reason.

Anyway thanks to our trade-offs I could stay out on the Foreside for a couple of days with the family of Admiral Symes where it had lived for more than twenty years of his retirement. I owed them my affection and every courtesy because that great navigator, gunnery guru, and W W 1 analytical anti-U-boat C-in-C of the Atlantic Fleet (though he knew next to nothing about designing ships) had been a friend of my father in Markland, and my honorary uncle long before I went away to school or had any serious thought of a naval career for myself. . . .

*

Finn was relieved to find his parking space unoccupied. It was only a few steps up to Front Street and around through the communal door to a tiny elevator that he used only when he carried baggage. No office tenant or janitor was usually in the building long after business hours. As he turned his master key and reached back to lift his bags off the sidewalk, glancing diagonally across the sparsely peopled square at the corner rummage shop which had been Pound's Drug Store for three or four generations, he suddenly remembered for the first time that it was at the soda fountain counter therein that he had met the artistic woman to whom he was heartily grateful for having diverted his vision (before too late) from the prospect of lifetime matrimony with some respectable beauty known for grace, intelligence, wit, and humor of the kind to be found in a Navy wife without audacity or guts. Beneath his other thoughts since crossing the Dogtown line he'd been trying to remember her name also, for she was the idea he associated with his general impression of the living past that had lately attracted him to this peculiar city even after the modern Felly's steel-arch gateway had successfully urged the mainland to trade, invest, or immigrate despite the vestigial smell of an oldtime fishery. After that meeting his many tests had never led to more than momentary illusion.

It had been on a pure green and blue June day immediately after he'd left the Chief in charge of the tug and walked up the hill to the rectangled hub of this smelly old port-of-call, intending to find a taxi, or at least to get aboard the trolley car to East Harbor, after he'd found a sandwich to fortify himself against the excessive midday hospitality of Admiral Symes's womenfolk, including the enviable daughter.

*

Despite Cape Gloucester's uncouth peculiarities it harbored a few features of mainland Atlantis, such as a private tap-dance school and edifying etiquette columns in the Nous. *Still, that recently modernized drugstore lunch counter was an unlikely spot to meet a Yankee Bohemian female obviously indifferent to the disapproval of Mrs Grundy as well as of any other model in the stew of heterogeneous marooners. I wish I could remember her immediately attractive apparition (or anything at all about what she wore at a time when all sorts of clothes now look ridiculous to us in photos), instead of only its general affect upon my selective nerves. When she sat down beside me on the last open stool at the crowded counter, though she seemed grimly absentminded, I had noticed out of the corner of my eye (as any man would) the short loosely gathered dark-blonde pigtail that would have struck anyone as peculiar behind the ears of a well-bred maturely young woman with intelligent blue eyes and small patrician nose in a smooth fair-skinned face, every natural and unadorned feature in classic proportion—at least so it must have struck me at first blush: perhaps a vaguely clad Rima, last and most refined of the lost Amazons. How would she look to me now? Even without the faintest notion of her clothes I guessed from a sidelong glance that her body was likely to be as well formed as her head. She was no taller than most women in those days of coal gas and other public contaminations, when doctors of medicine knew as little as Doctor Slop did about pediatric nutrition. She clearly was neither a fishwife nor a flat-chested bobbed-hair flapper from a metropolis of contemporary art. At first glance as a fairly experienced man of thirty-four I assessed her as perhaps an aestivating peregrine from the biggest city of all. As it turned out, she was younger than I but a little older than she looked. I'd write a novel if only I could remember the sequence of events during the next twenty-four hours in and out of her company!*

Even in a span of many years, once one knows the outcome of acquaintance it's impossible to trace the graduations of perception; but when its brief advancement is truncated too suddenly for guesses to mature in reflecting rumination, everything about it, except for immediate fact and act, with very little aftermath, remains as nothing much more than hypothetical nescience clouding with age. But by the same token my adventure was so transitory—and even as a comparatively romantic albeit footloose quasi-puritan I had reason to hope for repetition of my less exceptional affairs—that afterwards it didn't take me long to sublimate the pleroma of that particular experience. Yet given the supersession of exciting and exacting professional duties during twenty years of planning with steel, steam, elec-

tricity, and guns—navigation, inspection, intelligence, diplomacy, and operations research in the Navy, followed by twenty-five more of related self-employment—that mnemonic woman has started to reappear as a landmark in my unwritten autobiography.

After my career of chafing against much of the prevailing off-duty naval culture, as well as the frustrations of an innovator beholden both to flag officers like Hotspur Halsey and to the Bureau of Ships, not to mention other Washington establishments that adjudicated my criticisms as well as my constructive ideas, to say nothing of the obstacles raised by conservative diplomats or industrial lobbyists—prevented by Articles of War from appealing to the presumed wisdom of highest authority—I more than ever sympathize not only with the brilliant Jews in early days among my friends in the illiberal officer corps, who were more dedicated and radically more important to the Navy's future than I ever have been, despite the prejudicial adversities and humiliations they had to overcome—just as nowadays the blacks and women in the service (and in most civilian jobs too) must work harder than white men without ostentation or complaint, and moreover do everything so well by the book that in any organization with the slightest pretense to supervisory justice it can't be denied, to earn even an equal level of recognition, whether or not they're geniuses benefitting only from the interference of liberals on the Armed Services Committees of Congress.

With broadening social sympathy I later found myself appreciating in private life the subjective liberty that's inhibited by too much devotion to impersonal things of only three dimensions; and though I've never cottoned either to psychoanalysis or to French existentialism by way of introspection, I tardily began to reflect upon the myriad inner worlds of people who did not share my exterior fascinations with desirable objects of intellect. Too late, as a chivalrous libertine primarily concerned with myself and the objects of what might be called my selfless lust—virtual or real, artificial or human—thanks to the memory of her I finally understood enough to be less jealous of how much I'd missed with an ordinary variety of women. Only at the age of about fifty, even as I slowly opened my mind for heartbreaking politics, did I begin to taste the loss of opportunities—for better or for worse—of sacramental marriage. Is it possible, then, at the age of eighty, before new experience of every kind is foreclosed, that I may now be able to share the equivalent manifestations of selflessness with an opposite kind of exceptional woman, my senior in culture?

Anyway, as to the savor of what I'd missed until 1934, after a few minutes of pretending not to be aware of each other side by side at the quieter end of a fully populated "luncheonette" counter in Pound's modish apothecary, which anticipated the general-merchandising of nearly every *town's omnium gatherum in a Depression, I asked her to pass the salt and pepper, having timed my sandwich and coffee to finish up about when she sucked the bottom of her double-chocolate ice-cream soda. Later she explained that chocolate was her puerile anodyne for every sorrow—in this case for the recent devastating fire that in her absence had charred all her artwork and asphyxiated the regal dog she loved more than a sister. Her grief was hardly past its nadir. But before learning that, in my ignorance of her psyche and its world, I contrived so well that we chanced to swing face to face as we left our stools at the same moment.*

Just then the dopplered sound of a marching band approaching down Pleasure Street from the Ibicity Hall burst upon us from the outside world. The adult solemnity of her face broke into the smile and gladness of a special treat. "It's the circus parade!" she exclaimed. "That's why I'm here. Let's see if we can get a good place at the curb! It's the beginning of Gloucestermas!" I liked her voice as well as the ingenuous boldness of her manner. Maybe my white uniform reminded her of someone else.

I had been mildly surprised by the number of people idling on the sidewalks all about Pound's corner in Morality Square, especially down along both sides of Front Street's westward dip where much of the city's shopping was done. She tugged on my sleeve and with five minutes to spare she found us a frontline position only a few feet further than the parade route's sharp right turn. Everyone's excitement was rising, even my grownup boy's in uniform! Soon the marching music and its animated train would be upon us; but before I could think of how to express my thanks to her for this contretemps (when I felt like jumping with joy) she had a cigarette in her mouth and was rummaging in her purse for matches. Along with carefully concealed condoms I always carried two or three of the least distastefully decorated paper matchbooks I came across in the Officer's Club or elsewhere for just such an eventuality, and I gallantly lighted the tobacco as she puffed an aroma that always pleased me when wafted in outdoor air, though I myself never smoked the stuff for fear of shortening my athletic breath. In Vinland at the time one still seldom saw a woman smoking on the street, but her audacity seemed utterly unselfconscious.

"I can see why you don't smoke" she said—or something like that. "Those lovely Eastertide vestments must be hard to keep clean. I can never wear a white smock without burning holes in it."

Further conversation was deferred by deafening brass and percussion wheeling at the corner, to the applause and irregular cheers of the spectators they so closely divided in the narrow old streets. I doubt that any of the nearby children surpassed her in suddenly jolly enthusiasm as we first awaited and then gazed at the prisoners she'd come from East Harbor to worship as they were displayed on a route from the railroad yard where they'd been unloaded from garishly painted boxcars, thence all along the customary circuitous way through the winding brick canyon of western Front Street, across Sacrum Square, down to the Esplanade and across the Gut drawbridge to the fairground on Tansy Hill in Salt Cod Park. Because the streets were narrow the parade was thin, and because so thin it took a long time to pass.

Seeing that the city's downtown traffic had been detoured or immobilized for half the day, I understood that there'd be no cab or trolleycar for me. But I also couldn't inoffensively cross the street to escape the rest of the pageant even if I'd wished to—a tacit excuse for prolonging our casual introduction and proposing to escort her on the east walk home insofar as we shared that common route. The scheme proved to be successful, but in the meantime her enchantment with the animals seemed to have interrupted her awareness of my existence, save for a few exchanges of somnambulistic remarks. For I too was enthralled by most of the beasts that walked with attendants or rode in open cages, sometimes nearly forgetting my ulterior motive for standing where I was, touching clothed shoulders.

First, venerable toothless Asiatic elephants headdressed with spangles and pompoms but docilely superior to the puny slave-masters who kept them in line linked tail-to-trunk by mere reminder of the pricking hooks carried alongside below each sad starboard cheek. (It's always hard to imagine any of these pathetically defanged beasts with delicate ears trumpeting in rage or rut like an African bull.) Then came caparisoned show horses and feathered ponies, prancing as if they were painfully tender-footed Cherokee Walkers, followed by teams of decorated Flems or Gauls double their size, harnessed in multiple pairs to haul separated ponderous wagons bearing unhappily popular mammals in one long gaudy train. Visibly torn between joy to see and sorrow to feel, the "girl" (as I thought of her) sometimes touched my forearm, glancing up to appraise my brotherly understanding of her empathy with the captives on display, ursine (lethargic), feline (melancholy), or primate (histrionic)—but especially canine (wistful). The cage of wolves thus brought her instantly to tears. I sensed her stifled sobs—which awakened my own memories of an Irish Wolfhound I had loved in Markland, threatening my resplendent composure. I stared straight ahead with tightened gut to keep from looking at her as she clutched my hand. For a few minutes my solipsistic propensity for young women (which I now recall only as an objective abstraction) was succeeded by an almost altruistic charity. I was tenderly surprised by the unsophisticated selflessness revealed beneath an ingenuous manner suggesting her indifference if not challenge to public sentiment as well as to the censures of

Mrs Grundy, who in Dogtown even at that time before the War seemed tolerant enough of the society I was used to.

As I later learned, most of the materiel and personnel of the circus had been loaded beforehand onto vans at the freight yard for transport by a direct route to the Salt Cod Park hill overlooking the outer harbor, but half a dozen garish clowns with bulbous noses served as caboose for the majestic train we watched like kids at a railroad crossing. Bravely they cavorted to meet the usual expectations of childish entertainment, at which she was no more amused than I. With me trailing behind her she tacked northeasterly across the square through the dispersing crowd to the vacated sidewalk not far beyond the northeast sidewall of the very building that I now possess, which then was typically formidable as a bank in accordance with the brick architecture granite facade, a perfectly respectable false front.

She apologized for her tearful "breakdown" by explaining that the dog she had lost was more beautiful than any the wolves could have elected as their queen. When I offered my starchly ironed white handkerchief to dry her eyes she asked to keep it as a souvenir to match my pristine raiment of all colors according to scientists who knew nothing about pigments. She asked if I didn't fear that my cloth was too good for Dogtown, vulnerable to the stink of codfish drying in the open air nearby. I replied that the air was bracing. I didn't know whether she was teasing or really awestruck by what she saw in me—or rather on me. Especially after I later knew of her nearly satirical familiarity with the Foreside Yacht Club and other venues of hoi aristoi I did not believe that I was the first such splendid officer to weather her equivocal inspection.

Still, as a commissioned officer of a traditional navy I was uncomfortable about being seen in my nearly most solemn uniform (almost all but the ceremonial sword) with an informally attired woman walking some rather shabby streets that were about to be filled with liberated enlisted men seeking bars and cat houses on the eve of a notorious town's annual Dionysia, while more or less welcomed by both nubile amateurs and the latest cohort of curious innocents still celebrating their own liberties from school, with or without diplomas, who were accustomed to the sight and sound of drunken fishermen or lumpers in disorderly clothes. But at least I was glad she walked fast with chin held high as we got acquainted between puffs of her cigarette (until she stamped it out behind me on the curb) as we got to inform ourselves of not much more than gross identifications and immediate destinations. (For God's sake, when is at least one of her names going to pop back into my head?) However I think it was then I found out that she had occasionally nannied in summertime for the Symes grandchildren, which somewhat reassured me as to her reputation. It's hard to remember how much my rather straightlaced defensive attitudes have relaxed with the times. We've lived through a social revolution that began with the War and continues to expand by the broadcasting of pictures, even as it cultivates the seed of reactionary theology by its pandemic dissipation of intellectual energy. As my gentle anthropologist has already noticed, civilian life may have loosened me up but in liberal terms I'm still a selective puritan. The girl whose name I'm trying to remember said I was too polite. But for all her boldness and indiscretion there was nothing coarse or mean or cynical in her freshening manner.

I do remember that she wanted to talk about what was going on in Germany. More than anyone else I knew at the time she was aware of the danger to Jews in Hitler's assumption of power, and wanted to know what I thought about European affairs in general. That was not long before I served ashore over there. I think that was only a few days before the Night of the Long Knives in Berlin! While she was hoping to get my opinions about F D R's personal attitude I was trying to divert the conversation to second-person intelligence relevant to my immediate prospects.

Yet she was curious about my name: was I a Fenian? Or indeed did I myself have a son named Oisin? I told her my ancestor was only a Celtic Viking mischling, come to Vinland with yonder long ships on full flood tide.

*

PROFESSOR FAYAWAY GABRIEL: My family almost always had cats. We usually took one or two with us when we moved. But I've never before lived alone with one, and children long gone. That's a much more intimate situation. It makes you examine the details of symbiosis that you'd taken for granted. Where's the line between extremely gratified affection and human love? Is it only at the proportional difference between the length of time one grieves for a cat and the length of kinship mourning?

COMMANDER FINN MACDANE: I had to part from my short-lived Wolfhound when I went away to college and the Navy. His name was Cuchulain. But I don't remember our cats.

FAY: I never wore long fur; she never took hers off. But she spent the first part of most nights purring in my armpit. I still find myself starting to stoop and fill her water dish at the beginning of dinner routine. And something still seems missing if I don't have to feed her twice a day. I didn't realize how trained I was to her service. I still feel the presence of her absence. But I know that soon

I'll be living a totally introverted life again, totally forgetting my effort to imagine her pain at sudden death; remembering the pleasure she gave me by accepting the luxury of my room and board, and how readily she purred and kneaded blanket or pillow with exquisite pleasure as audibly and rhythmically as an eight-day clock; but forgetting how shamelessly twice a day this perfectly dignified regal beast fit for a scutcheon demanded service, zigzagging underfoot, leading me into the kitchen with her streaming banner of a tail, yet with the piercing squeaks of a dying banshee unlike any supplicating mew, or like an angrily chirping ghost in the Inferno—so unpleasantly distracting my unfocused thoughts from what I was supposed to be doing in my menial routine that I'd sometimes end up yelling at her to shut up. That unladylike behavior on my part, a breach of her trust in my servile responsibility, would shock her into five seconds of silence. But she always forgave me without a grudge the instant she got her dish.

FINN: Even if it was only a case of *kitchen-cat, cupboard-love*, you can be sure your Felixity trusted you. You never betrayed her like a milkmaid bringing up her own beef calf. It's the slaughterhouses that perpetuate absolute human treachery. That systematic death is said to be quick and humane, but feeding-and-killing is harder on my soul than hunting-and-killing in the wild, even with agonizing spear or arrow that at least is nearer to the screams of natural predation. Don't blame yourself for granting her the odds of freewill that all healthy cats want. If she'd belonged to someone else she might have pined away in frustration, watching her own natural prey from inside the glass, or else lost her senses in malignant obesity. She preferred the risks of liberty to the confinement and boredom of safety.

FAY: I need that cold comfort. —I gave her everything she wanted except fancy foods, but after testing my discipline she contentedly reconciled herself to a healthy diet with only occasional fresh fish. I turned a blind eye to whatever she might have tasted on her own initiative elsewhere. Here indoors she knew many ways to make herself comfortable—complacent enough to be worshipped for grace and beauty. That's the only thing that ever softened me to the cruel Egyptians. I've read that in case of fire their cats were the first to be saved. When one died the whole household went into mourning. No wonder the cats of their royalty and the priesthood were honored by mummification. Mohammed once cut the sleeve off his robe rather than disturb the sleep of his cat, and God knows

I took great pains to avoid disturbing Felixity when I slipped in or out of bed. Yet she herself had no compunction about suddenly breaking off ecstatic relations without warning or apology, just to sit on the floor and nonchalantly wash her face. By the same token she wasn't in the least surprised by the most sudden interruptions of her felicity; she'd simply leap to the floor and go about her business as if nothing ever took her off guard. Her nerves and muscles were always as instantly reflexive as a self-supporting leopard's in tiger territory. She didn't even blink when I'd suddenly turn on the electric light at night, as if photons were no faster than the earth's rotation at dawn. Except when food was concerned, irregularities never seemed to bother her.

FINN: Your sympathy is more proprioceptive then empirical.

FAY: Oh Finny, you are too intuitive for a technical man! None of the *Felis silvestris catus* individuals, ancient or modern, sanctified or not, were as beautiful or more affectionate than my Felixity! Maybe it wasn't true love, but it was more sensuous than commonplace cupboard love. At her leisure between meals she loved me for my hands. Food was just the daily animal right that happened to be my human duty, but she deeply appreciated as supererogatory my daily curry of coat, ruff, and tail with her personal comb, which she came begging for if I forgot it. She never smiled but she had a deadpan sense of humor. She would probe household crevices for amusement, and move my rugs around for fun. And you should have seen her playing field hockey with a golf ball on my dining room floor! I collected lost balls from the roadsides around the links. Oh, and tennis balls! I'd roll them in a saucer of catnip and she'd hug them to her belly as she writhed in ecstasy and you could hear her purring all across the room.

FINN: It sounds like an empathetic friendship.

FAY: Yet three days after giving up hope I couldn't help feeling relieved of inconvenient duties and anxieties. Things I no longer have to consider, surfaces that I don't have to keep clean or keep clear of with my feet, habits I no longer need! And my inclination to accept out-of-town invitations is no longer complicated by anyone but my own convenience!

FINN: Don't feel guilty, my dear! Her consciousness was simply extinguished, as ours will be, with no more or less unknowable posthumous distress than civilization is built upon, of which I've seen almost as much as our species can. Death is the loss of subjectivity. She crossed the line of demarcation and became an object only, a disintegrating object. I wish there weren't so many subjective cats and children in the world, so there'd be less cruelty, less starvation, less human treachery, less suffering from insensitive abuse. The hordes of feral cats, very conspicuous in Greek cities—and even on islands like Rhodes, which was once infamous for its infestation of snakes—are especially heartrending because of their innocence. They swarm all over street trash bins. They look like walking skeletons without reproach. You can see every bone in their bodies.

FAY: Cats have more bones than we do. That's why they can twist up in all sorts of luxury and land on their feet when they fall. But the more bones the more pains, I should think. After all other searches failed we looked for at least some bones, or shreds of her pelt, in roadside grass. I was told that coyotes usually leave some bones. No one I talked to knew about the eating habits of foxes or what they called fisher cats. But of course I couldn't expect Caleb to beat about all the shrubbery and brier patches in East Harbor for evidence of her fate, especially under a lowering raw sky with expectation of dismal rain. He said that his dog had made him love all dogs but that a black panther hadn't made him love all cats—only Felixity! Before I got the call from that thoughtful woman who'd seen my ad in the paper he worked hard to cheer me up when there was no evidence of any kind. I must admit that I submitted more readily to the idea of her death by natural predation than to any mysteriously unsupported presumption of anthropological accident, or of stupid wandering to another home or a distant neighborhood on her part like some mercenary tomcat. Coyote, fox, or fisher cat might well have carried her body off to a hidden den. No more nights did I feel I must wait up for her possible return as I had more than once for a delinquent boy or girl of my own. No more mornings did I have to wake up trembling with hope not to be disappointed when I went to the door. Before my eyes opened I would be preparing for miserable solitude.

FINN: But I thought you and Caleb had both inspected that street without seeing her there.

FAY: Can't explain it. Perhaps it was because of her beautiful Darwinian camouflage, if she was there all along, especially to the bleary eyes of one who's almost given up hope after hours of scanning both margins of similar pavements. When Caleb went to look for the spot described by the woman he immediately found her body nearly conspicuous in long grass just off the pavement, under the wild underbrush that lines the vernal pond not two hundred yards from this house! Her coat was superficially whole but she was stiff and cold, her mouth open, obviously dead of internal injury for more than a day—though not much longer—from something consistent (as detectives would say) with a speeding rubber tire.

FINN: Maybe she was hit after a night or two hunting and eating on her own.

FAY: That's the conjecture Caleb and I came to. I'd rather have had her devoured by some hungry mammal of an endangered species. And so would she. There's a certain justice to that. She had the native courage to match her curiosity. If we hadn't deprived her of kittens she would have taught them how to hunt. Somehow I don't feel as sorry for birds or mice as I should.

FINN: At least you can be sure there was no abduction for neurological or pharmaceutical research. She wasn't burned alive by sadistic kids or superstitious Puritans. No torture unto death. You know, one ironic thing is that the Nazis imposed all sorts of laws to protect animals from mistreatment. They saved their most agonizing *individual and personal* tortures for pure useless vengeance, not just for information, and even made films of their fiendish vindictiveness for Hitler's private satisfaction. I heard about them from some of the friends of Admiral Canaris and Count von Stauffenberg when we were interrogating Albert Spree after the War.

FAY: Oh I know how silly my effusions are about the quick and maybe painless death of a happy cat lacking self-consciousness—

FINN: Not silly at all! Just the opposite. At our age we're naturally curious about the subjective side of death. How will we *feel* when we're overtaken, we who are as self-conscious as Prometheus? We may try to be sympathetic but we can't be empathetic. I suppose funerals and other memorials are meant by objectification to divert us from trying to feel what it would be like if we were the victim. —Weddings too! Like everyone else, atheists and cynics have funerals and weddings. Generally speaking, people elaborate their commiseration with the surviving kinfolk because it's impossible to imagine what death is like. Do any of your academic colleagues study ants from the ants' point of view—I mean not their collective behavior but their individual consciousness? Do they feel pain when I'm obliged to snuff them out with my thumb on the kitchen counter or wash them down the drain? They are brave hardworking cooperative little bastards, always toiling for the common good. Death may never be too unexpectedly instantaneous

not to feel it. That is the question! Do they have any nerves for feeling at all? Certainly they have invented no religion to console
themselves beforehand.

FAY: Then each has its own world? So speculates the rogue
Viking!

FINN: Or recalcitrant Celt. Enlightened just enough to decode
ceremonies, military or religious. Once at parade rest during a
burial service in the National Cemetery I was entranced by an ant
carrying in its proboscis the wing of a moth many times its own
size. It threaded its roundabout route through obstructive blades of
grass, erratically dodging and swaying, zigzagging this way and
that, sometimes even backing up to correct a decision, with its
bulky burden but never forgetting some definite goal, like a quartermaster's mate sweating to keep on course amid the yaws and
buffets of a typhoon: all the two-dimensional movements of what
game-theorists call a random walk, yet with a selfless purpose in
mind! Most remarkable was the fact that ants of larger species were
coming and going in all directions paying no attention to it! Without listening to the murmured eulogy of a human object whom I'd
known and liked, it was a queerly subjective experience!

FAY: You are a tender technocrat. I don't go to bed with big-
game hunters.

FINN: Next time can we lie side by side and gaze into each
other's souls before you turn on the light?

FAY: No offense taken. —You know, Finny, sometimes I felt
like a man when I caressed and massaged that warm muscular body
under the fluffy fur. Whenever I headed toward this room she'd
leap before me and fling herself wantonly outspread on the bed,
purring in abandoned expectation—foreclaws rhythmically expanding and curling like ecstatic fingers—before I even touched her. Do
you think I might have homoerotic leanings?

FINN: I tell you what we can do to find out. You come up to
my place when I've got Deeta Dana there. I bet she's uninhibited.
—Ouch! I'm still too ticklish in my old age! —Now, how do you
like it?

FAY:—No! Stop right there! I take it back. But don't you want
to play another funeral game for poor Felixity? . . . Aren't you used
to being tickled, Commander Sobersides?

FINN: Oh I remember the functions of touch. In my schooldays artful fingering seemed the only means to seduction. In fact
for a few years digital touch was the end as well as the means. At

first girls seemed to have the upper hand. But touch always came in handy.

FAY: Sometimes, believe it or not, girls were deceived by hope. —It's sweet of you to cheer me up by diverting me from Felixity's lesbian erotics before I get back to my books and papers, forgetting how it feels to be killed as a cat. But a cat's world is bigger than an ant's. I cried at Adam's death, though I no longer loved him; and never again at a funeral until Caleb and I buried Felixity, whom I did love and will sooner forget. I'd be a better man in love than war. But I think Caleb was weeping as he filled in the grave, though he hardly knew the cat he covered with dirt.

FINN: He was probably weeping in sympathy for you. Didn't you say he's your godson? There are more tears in the world for the living than for the dead.

FAY: I think he was weeping for the final feelings of the dog he told me he and a friend had buried illegally twenty years ago, at night in a windrow of dry dunes above the beach at Dilemma Cove. He said his Ibi-Roy had many kitten friends. Caleb's been my working angel these past few days. His time is rightly more precious to him than any moneymaker's, but he's given me a lot of it by listening, searching, and digging in my rocky dooryard with a pickaxe and shovel that he rummaged around under the porch to find when I didn't even know I had them. Up on this nob of a solid granite ridge that was scraped clean by the last glacier it's not easy to find deep topsoil. It took half a million years for the earth tremors and atmospheric ice to open cracks for wind and birds to fill with dust and seeds rich enough for the trees to embed and proliferate. I love to see gray whalebacks still exposed as lawns or sequestered in the greenery of rock gardens all around on this amazing hill.

FINN: Yes. On the ridge less than half a mile away Admiral Symes's old house is on the top of a naked granite glacier frozen by reflected sunlight. Down its face there's a steep cascade of weathered terraces overlooking the golf course and the whole eastern shore. But it's even harder to build on the hills across the river where I've been Caspar's engineering consultant for a couple of his private houses.

FAY: I thought he consulted you on your passenger ship concept non realisée.

FINN: Turnabout is fair play. That was just for recreation at a magazine's behest. It got him into the habit of asking my opinion about his ideas. —But residents—once they have their own land—naturally deplore this age of construction, when ledges can't defend themselves against the new combination of dynamite, pneumatic drills, and merciless bulldozers. I've grown almost as horrified by mechanical force as you and your political friends. Goethe said that the man of action is always ruthless and that no one but an observer has a conscience. That's why I gave up action and became a liberal!

FAY: Well Caleb is now a man of action. After some unsuccessful probing with the crowbar he found a grave spot next to my big whale of a cracked boulder that the last glacier dragged here.

FINN: If I'd come back from Markland any earlier I would have been put to shame, because you probably would have had to call on him anyway, for the pick-and-shovel work at least. Just because I can still get around as well as Ariel on my feet, I keep forgetting how much muscle mass and stamina I've lost. My spine has shrunk so much that there's no space for a belt between my rib cage and my hip bones. I'm going to have to start wearing suspenders. Despite his sedentary career, Caleb looks in trim and nimble for his age; but in my prime I could have knocked him out of the ring, though probably he'd have outrun me cross-country.

FAY: His mother called him the runt of her litter.

FINN: What a lousy mother, starting him out in life with that blessing!

FAY: Just her way to praise him for overcoming his adversities, especially her smoking while pregnant. That child is as mad as his mother—in Hegelian dialectic. He has a new handicap now: very soon he must find a new place to live, and a job to pay for it, yet he refuses to do anything about it until he's finished what my friend Tessa says is very alien drama.

FINN: He seems to have misdirected his talents. As far as I can see, if he'd stuck to his systems work he could have been very well off by now, as a genuine pioneer in the new arts of bureaucracy, like Mr Pepys. It appears that he has plenty of practical ideas. If I weren't retired and bored with the business side of consulting I'd be inclined to invest in a start-up company to develop especially his Synectic Method of Diagnostic Correlation—under some less ludicrous name of name, of course—which I think could be used effectively in dozens of different professions, and especially in the Navy. He's no mathematician but I think he has good mathematical ideas of what can be done with simple statistics. Anyway I believe it's practical for computerized operations research. If I thought he'd cooperate I'd connect him with some venture capitalists I know. But I already know him well enough to see he'd balk at that, from what you tell me, at least until he gets esoteric play-writing out of his head.

FAY: I think he'll have more in the back of his mind than that, whether or not he gets a job to keep him busy in what he says Yeats called "this pragmatical pig of a world". You should read Caleb's theory of tragedy! He calls tragedy the culminating category of what he calls the apex of Dromenology!

FINN: Well, *The Mind of Man is the Man Himself*, as Pepys my favorite parvenu in British history had in a Latin motto for his coat of arms. I'd like to help your fair-haired godson somehow, even if it's only to lead the life of a half-starving artist with no prospect of success in the marketplace. But I think he's wasting his practical abilities. He could have been the Pepys of our Navy! God knows we always needed one. It's too bad he didn't have the benefit of some military discipline when he was young.

FAY: That would have been a silver spoon. He had the discipline of childhood poverty and the self-discipline of good education.

FINN: Do you think *drugs* explain his disconnections?

FAY: He's as puritanical as you about feeling good artificially. Of course he makes exceptions for caffeine, as natural and necessary for his kind of work, and he's not averse to alcohol, seeing that even Jesus drank wine! But otherwise he scorns stimulants, sedatives, and desserts—almost! He refuses even the delusive comfort of aspirin.

FINN: Then I guess he's a good Scout. He apparently did learn business from the ground up, and he obviously understands systems. It won't do any harm if I speak to the Mayor about him. From what I hear, Dexter's elected himself to a bureaucratic chaos!

FAY: I'm glad you got back in time to stay for supper while he was still here tonight. Thanks for taking my mind off Felixity for a while. Caleb said your presence was his reward.

FINN: As a superannuated man of action?

FAY: Quite active enough for the present occasion.

FINN: Thanks for rewakening the old beast.

FAY: Thanks for freshening the well. Good night, sweet prince. But don't shuffle off this mortal coil before I do. It's hard to think of you as a raffish puritan.

FINN: Only a romantic bachelor. In marriage *every*thing must be coordinated, not just the one thing. I've always wanted gauntlets, not a switch.

FAY: Is that electrical vernacular jargon?

FINN: Older than that. Railroading.

FAY: Well it sounds nicer than turntables.

14

TABLET

TWELVE

Column One

[**Melchizedek**, tall, bearded, vested in white and gold, stands burning incense at a field-stone altar outside his tent. Berosus sits with music instruments in his usual place.]

BEROSUS

Enter Gilgamesh,
stage right, escorted
by two of
Melchizedek's armed
scouts.

This is Melchizedek, Amorite king of Canaan, priest of Elohim, come down from Shechem to the hills near Bethel.

MELCHIZEDEK   A prisoner from the west?

SCOUT 1   A pirate called Noman, captured at sea off the coast of Kittim. Your ship's captain sends us to you with him.

MELCHIZEDEK   Well, another disappointment. I was hoping otherwise when I saw you coming. I'm awaiting the rich son of Shem who built this altar long ago. —You have no retainers or possessions at all?

GILGAMESH   A single free traveler, relieved of power but not a pirate.

SCOUT 2   He was carrying this axe.
[Hands over
Gilgamesh's axe.]

GILGAMESH   It has saved my life on land and sea, but not as a weapon.

MELCHIZEDEK   You look as if you were once strong enough not to need one. But obviously you're not the shepherd warrior I've been looking for. You may keep your ambivalent axe. Let me see that jewel on your neck.

GILGAMESH   Just a piece of baked clay of no value to anyone but me.
[Exchanging the
Isorectotetrahedron
for the axe.]

MELCHIZEDEK   What image is this? No god that I have seen before. It's an
[Examines the   ugly naked figure.
IRTH intently
before distastefully
handing it back.]

GILGAMESH   It's not to idolize but to bring to mind some thoughts.

MELCHIZEDEK   I'd like to hear those thoughts. We must converse at length before I let you go. Are you a wandering song-stitcher then, with a poor memory and no harp?

GILGAMESH   I'm sorry that I can't sing you my story. I was an autocrat,
[Points in the   and will be again, but now I am alone. Almost twenty
direction from   times with the polestar on my left I saw the sun veer to the
which he'd been   Crab and fall back to the Goat. Then after three oceans my
brought.]   course narrowed through two mountains into a narrow sea of stepping-stone islands—Trinacria, where they offered to worship my amulet; Caphtor, where they copied my axe; Kittim, where I taught them to draw plans; and others in between like even the Isle of Snakes where I found cordial haven in return for my advice. After all my previous solitary struggles, these heartening sojourns led me on a sea-path to these brine-ending forest-clad hills so sweetly watered by the clearest springs I have ever tasted. I hope that I have at last put angry waves behind me. What a discovery, this whole unbeknownst anti-world! The land of the rising sun! Already, in approaching, I have marveled at the outreach of its skills; now I have been brought to face the sovereign of its wisdom and power!

MELCHIZEDEK   What might you want of my goodwill?

GILGAMESH

Perhaps when I return from the further end of this land I may be allowed to fell some of these great trees to build a dragon ship for my voyage home. Down on the beach I would gather a crew of young sailors who'd like to see the old world and bear back to you more precious tokens of its glories than a humble axe. Meanwhile in gratitude for your generosity and friendship, as well as opening my mind to your ears I will open my mouth with navigational and military intelligence about how you can plant greater colonies along your landlocked western sea. —But how much further is the *eastermost*? Will I at last face Utu rising on the other side of those majestic heights, surely the last barrier to my goal?

[Points off stage left.]

MELCHIZEDEK

No one knows the end of that land across the valley. I can tell you only that there is a mountain pass to the steppes before you come to an endless river. Even now I am awaiting word of a great sheikh who comes with his tribe from somewhere down its banks. If you will wait with me for his account we may amplify each other's science.

GILGAMESH

At this stage of life I cannot linger. I must first find my half-father, the progenitor of time. The horizon has disappointed me so many times over these years that I am apt to be overtaken by weakness and irresolution before I can return to regain my strength. Until then I dare not sleep again, for fear of never waking.

MELCHIZEDEK

Your half-god Utu is but the Creator's creature! Speak of your other half.

GILGAMESH

My other half is human. My other third is lunar. Sine is my moon-father. I am not a worshiper of any other.

MELCHIZEDEK

Two at least approaches unity. It will not be entirely a sin to make you my guest for a day or two and hear all I can about a fabulous old world!

[To Scout 2.]
Both Scouts enter the tent and return with bread and wine, which they place before the altar. [Melchizedek blesses the bread and wine at the altar and brings it to a low table center stage, at which

—Fetch the bread and wine.

—At my table you will eat and drink nothing better or worse than what is offered servants of the One God—he who has taken this fertile land from the perfidious Nephilim and given it to his righteous people.

—Humble bread from labor in the fields is holier than bloody meat, and I think you'll find the wine made from our grapes a more wholesome refreshment than the crude beer of idolaters. Let us celebrate the joining of two worlds

they place two seats | under one God! Eat and drink in peace, stranger, and then
on either side. | ask for more. At least for a few hours shed your travail and
Gilgamesh sits | favor me with the pleasure of your company.
facing east (stage
right), opposite Melchizedek, each with a Scout nearby as servant. The
axe is propped against the downstage center of the table, helve down, its
head above the surface. As Gilgamesh and Melchizedek speak more
confidentially the Scouts finish their own portions and discreetly bring
another (unblessed) jar of wine to the table.]

GILGAMESH   A most welcome meal. Never have I tasted with such
gusto!

MELCHIZEDEK   But, my friend, only an eagle can fly to the sun. No longer
afloat with your gear, you won't be spared the stumbling
blocks of gravity. You will be footsore and slow, girded
with impediments, a pack on your back. And your axe
can't feed you where game is rare and swift. You will need
the distal weapon of a hunter. You shall have a longbow
and its quiver of arrows if you are able to use them, won
from a rock-slain giant. It is of no use here because none of
our archers is strong enough to draw the string. Try it!

[Scouts fetch the   —Bring it out to him.
bow and arrows
from the tent, stay
just long enough to
watch in awe as
Gilgamesh draws
and shoots in a high
arc eastward.]

GILGAMESH   I think I still have the strength to draw anyone's bow!

Scouts disappear.

MELCHIZEDEK   For your sustenance and safety on the eastern heaths—
according to the will of God, if I'm not mistaken.

GILGAMESH   Then I thank you and Him for a timely gift. In my youth I
was a bowman. And thanks to you for sharing the lordly
purple-lipped invention of this draught! It warms my heart
when I need rejuvenation. Vagrancy wearies the body more
than manic battle does. I age with little aches and pains I
never had before, none as definite or serious as sickness or
wound. I used to hold a lion in my arms as easily as a cat;
now even my legs don't recover all their strength when I'm
fully rested in cloudless humor, charged with proleptic
zest, and rejoicing in a spirit almost as clear and buoyant as
when I had my dearest friend to double every muscle! I
refrained from resisting your sailors only because I was
loathe to test myself. Sometimes reason seems futile.

MELCHIZEDEK	Every mortal ages.
GILGAMESH	But I've survived the sea-world's fury only to face what I fear will be yet another continent of hazards! Is the orient endless? The sun is always rising or setting, constantly inviting, forever inaccessible! I feel no closer to the morning of the world than I did long ago in Dilmun. Has time no youth?
MELCHIZEDEK	Even youth grows old.
GILGAMESH	Even on a course against the sun's? Why shouldn't I be gaining time? Instead, fevers of thirst and starvation have left me weaker, though I stopped at every landing to recuperate and gather hips of roses. It's a sapping of lungs and sinew too subtle to notice in a month or year, enfeebling the very memory of full strength and wit—even of love and hope itself. Yet these swallows of your vine-juice call up pristine the idea of my end in view!
MELCHIZEDEK	Which I now perceive.
GILGAMESH	No, no, you mistake me! I have no wish for everlasting life. Better even to die without fame than live forever ruled by fate! It's more interesting before infirmity of mind to learn the mystery of time! The very thought of that success invigorates me! Too often now I sleep when I used to need no rest. —Ah that recalls the last dream I can remember: I spent many weeks on an island with the astrologer Ziusudra who had notions of the future. I had long since left him when he appeared at sea, standing in the stern to wake me from a sitting sleep within that dream. He warned me that even a god can die if he attacks another god (not to mention a demigod's mortality). He said: "Utu and Sine will eat up each other's light, one after the other. One must not watch his fathers fight!" Still dreaming, I was about to ask his meaning when suddenly with a downward surge both gunwales were seized by four raptorial limbs of a single loathsome intelligence I felt rising from beneath me as its other lurid arms groped like snakes for my basket of dogrose fruit. With my axe, left and right, I tried to free myself of the horror, terrified by underwater thrashing and bloody foam, but the boat of reeds was swamped, its length severed by my own blows. I saw Ziusudra's head calmly sinking as he continued to advise me. "Look, here comes a white whale to feed on the monster, and a dolphin to save you. Take your axe, but don't lose your life diving for the emptied basket."

I awoke on a shore I'd never seen before. Are you an inter-
preter of illusions? What did the old sage mean? What did
the dream mean within which he meant it?

[Long silence as
Melchizedek ponders.
He suddenly rises in
alarm.]

MELCHIZEDEK   —Noman, tell me your real name!

GILGAMESH   —Is that important?
[Taken aback,
hesitates.]

MELCHIZEDEK   If you expect my neutrality.

GILGAMESH   Well then: I'm generally called Nimrod.

MELCHIZEDEK   What made me dread to ask? A strange name I've heard
before. What could have already carried it here?

GILGAMESH   Perhaps it echoes some indistinct word you've dreamt.

MELCHIZEDEK   No, there is only one cause of all things. It must have been
an old warning among the words of God when I was dis-
tracted by immediate difficulties.

[Abruptly.]   —Now the sun is down. I am disquieted by intimations of
my indiscretion. I must leave you now—for special pray
alone, higher on the hill. In the morning we may not part
as friends.

[To the Scouts.]   —Take your prisoner to the guest tent and see that he is
provided for.
—Under my hospitality you need not fear to sleep. The
bow is yours to keep. The Scouts will make you up a pack
of food and water for sustenance on your way. But your
quest is an impiety that I cannot countenance. A man
might more easily try to watch one of God's oaks turning
into the acorn that fathered it.

Melchizedek leaves.
For a moment **Gilgamesh** stands still looking
after him before he is escorted off by the Scouts.

Column Two

[**Gilgamesh** is prone on the ground, facing upstage center, drinking awkwardly from a
river. His axe and bow are lying beside him. As he twists to cast the Isorectotetrahedron
off his neck he notices that a young **Shepherd** with a crook, spear, slingshot, and short
sword (slung on a baldric) is watching him from stage left; but after a brief hesitation,

driven by thirst, he bends again to drink with one arm behind him groping for the handle of his axe. **Berosus** is in his usual place with music instruments.]

BEROSUS   Gilgamesh is desperately drinking from a river. The bank is steep. He must take off the Isorectotetrahedron lest he lose it in the water.

SHEPHERD 1

[Takes a cup from his belt, which Gilgamesh turns to accept. The Shepherd then gestures to someone behind him.]

Here, use this. If you drink too much all at once you'll get sick. Don't worry about the river running dry. You were lucky to get here before our flock muddied it all up. I won't let them come this far. Go ahead and take your fill. —That's far enough. Water them down there by that double palm tree. Then we can pitch the tents up here. Send Peleg to tell the master.

[To Gilgamesh again.]   —I've been watching you come down from the desert. It looked as if you wouldn't make it this far. You must be a stranger to these parts. So are we, but we know enough to stay near the river, even when it turns north. Take your time. There are a thousand sheep, three hundred goats, a hundred asses, and all kinds of cattle to slow the camels down. They're still two or three miles behind. With all our men, women, children, and chattels, sometimes that takes a whole day. Thank God we don't keep swine!

[Gilgamesh finishes drinking with a sigh and hands back the cup.]

—Whatever possessed you to cross the desert? I suppose a desert's as deserted in the mountains as on the flats, and maybe harder going. I hope the Amorites aren't after you.

GILGAMESH   Thank you, my friend. I feel much better now. No one's chasing me. I've been heading east from the west the straightest way I can find. Down here it's hard to believe how cold I've been up among those rocks. I'm a stranger.

SHEPHERD 1   That's obvious. We're both strangers here.

GILGAMESH   Where are your people going with all those flocks and herds?

SHEPHERD 1   Going west from east, in a roundabout way. We must follow the fodder. The chief says we're going to settle in greener pastures somewhere over there. Did you see a land of milk and honey?

GILGAMESH   It's indeed a land of plenty.

SHEPHERD 1   More to the point: we lost a ewe, two lambs, and a kid last night. Did you see any wolves or lions on your way here?

GILGAMESH   Sorry, I haven't been looking for them these days—just hoppers or hoofers that I can eat. I haven't had a shot at one of those for the last five days. Nor even private property.

SHEPHERD 1   Oh I'm not accusing you! Here, have some figs. Not too

[Gives figs.   many all at once!
Gilgamesh eats
voraciously as
Shepherd watches
him closely.]

GILGAMESH   Where are you people from? Did you live by yourselves with all that livestock at the end of the earth?

SHEPHERD 1   With more people than you can imagine! At least from

[Laughing.]   what I've heard. I don't know much about it. I was born on the trek. My mother was one of the chief's favorites. All I know is that we usually give cities a wide berth, and even when we don't I have to stay outside with the sheep. I wouldn't know how to deal with a mess of people penned like cattle, even if they sacrificed to our God. I suppose they swarm and bleat like hind-legged goats and sheep! Not only the noise: I imagine cities stink to high heaven! But the chief and his wives don't seem to mind. He's just spent almost a month feasting and trading inside the biggest one yet. It's a relief to get moving again.

GILGAMESH   Cities! When I came over the ridge today I saw something

[Bowed in thought.]   that looked like a city in the haze down there, but I thought it was a mirage. I've been having so many dreams and delusions that I was surprised to find there really was water quickening under the greenery I saw! —What's this river called?

SHEPHERD 1   The River. What else? The desert is the desert. The river is the river. I think cities have names, because there are more than one. But that's no concern of mine.

GILGAMESH   Where does the river go? Where's its mouth?

SHEPHERD 1   Mouth! Where's its nose? Where's its toes? You *are* an odd

[Laughing again.]   one, the way you talk! Maybe the sun's too hot for you here. You must be some kind of a poet. What do you mean by "mouth"?

GILGAMESH   Where does it flow to? Where does the water go?

SHEPHERD 1   How should I know? Where does the land go? Where does the sun rise? You do ask strange questions!

GILGAMESH Do you know of another river?

SHEPHERD 1 Another river! There you go again! I hope you don't read from the stars like some daft minstrel singing to sunstruck camel-drivers about another world in the north or suchlike fantasies of the fireside!

GILGAMESH You did say there are several cities. So they must have names to tell them apart. What's that one called?

SHEPHERD 1 I never heard the name. Fishes don't have names. I don't know why cities need names. You can never be at more than one at a time. A city's just a big village, isn't it? All I've heard is that the king of this one is sometimes a woman.

GILGAMESH Have you ever come across any holes of black water?

SHEPHERD 1 Oh, here and there. Even sheep are smart enough not to drink it. Where it's as thick as honey I've heard there are gentiles who even burn it! I once saw a gazelle get stuck in the devilish stuff. It took an hour to disappear. I wouldn't touch those stinking pits with a ten-foot pole, but last year I watched a city man smearing some of it on his boat with a stick. Maybe he was a wizard. Believe me, I didn't stick around to find out!

GILGAMESH Well all people are not alike, since some live in cities. What are your folks called, or the people you work for?

SHEPHERD 1 They just call us Eber's tribe. I think he was my chief's great-great-great-grandfather somewhere down to the east or south of here. If I knew where that was I'd have answered your question about where the river goes to!

GILGAMESH What has disconnected the pieces of my mind? This bewil-
[Aside.] derment of old age frightens me! It's as if this boy is at the wrong end of things. Was my dear Eber a ghostly name-sake five generations removed, across three oceans and a sea? But if New World names and migrations may repeat themselves by chance, is there another Lil-Amin to be found—or Engidu?

SHEPHERD 1 You might ask the chief all your questions. He'll feed anyone who comes with knowledge of the west.

GILGAMESH I thought I knew the world! What am I about to learn? — Some day, when I return to power, you will be rewarded. You may be opening my eyes to a wonder I cannot yet grasp.

SHEPHERD 1   There are lots of things no one ever understands. Why does water move? They tell me what difference does it make, say your prayers, that's all you have to know. But of course I can see that you're no ordinary old fellow. My chief understands everything. He may give you a good dinner just to hear your story. I'll have Peleg take you to him when he's settled in his tent. I appreciate your gratitude but I don't count on your goodwill to better my lot. As for the refreshment, it's only the common courtesy we're all taught. You must have already learned a lot from me by the process of elimination. For all I know, you may be a spy.

[Gilgamesh betrays increasing agitation.]

GILGAMESH   I begin to think I'm a spy from the world of dreams! But you and your help are real enough!
—Does the world repeat itself? Or is it merely accidental that the easternmost looks like the westernmost, their rivers and landscapes so much alike? The end of the journey remains to prove that east is west and west is east!

[Laughs, but no longer addressing the Shepherd, he throws himself again prone upon the river bank to see his reflection in the water, talking to himself. The Shepherd cocks his ear to listen.]

Yet I don't look any younger. The dog-rose saved my life at sea but does not erase the additions of time. It's not mere emaciation that unstrings my legs and shrinks my shoulders. It isn't the river's ripples that lays lines upon my face. Will I still be welcomed anywhere for the strengths of my prime? I've never relied on brawn as much as brain, but will that soon fail me too?

[To Shepherd.]

—It's impossible to get to the west by going to the east. Does the sun reverse and the pole star shift, and the zodiac too, to make me travel in a circle when I go straight toward a rim of the world that I can never reach? Do Utu and Sine deceive my senses in order to nullify this pursuit of reason? Or do I misinterpret my eyes with rash imagination?
Maybe this terrestrial expanse and its weird transhumance goes on forever, dismissing the question of sunrise anywhere. Has mankind always been deceived by reasoned facts?
—Does your leader retain a sagacious master of paradox? You think I'm old and crazy, but this is the first time in my life that I've been bereft of commonsense.

SHEPHERD 1   He is himself our savant. God speaks only to him. It's a
[Laughs.]   poet you should ask for! You make it sound as if the world's a turning hornet's nest!

GILGAMESH   But if time's an arrow in the air, could one find himself about to be where he began—yet older? You who know the sky at dawn so well, what keeps the sunrise out of reach?

SHEPHERD 1	It's just too far away. Like the stars, which I've given up trying to count. Girls are more interesting.

GILGAMESH	Nevertheless I wish I could take you with me.

SHEPHERD 1 [Laughing.]	I'm willing. You've got me curious about why and what the river flows to. Ask the chief. But what could you trade him for me?

GILGAMESH	Knowledge of the Old World. He'd find it useful.

The younger
Shepherd 2, less
well armed but
carrying a flute, enters from stage left.

SHEPHERD 1 [Laughing again.]	He'd listen to the proposition if not forbidden by Elohim the One. He doesn't seem to value my services very highly. —Peleg, stand on that rock and watch for you know what. I'm taking this gentleman to the chief. If you see anything, skirl on your pipe right loud. No need for you to fight a lion! If I don't come back to save your life, sooner or later somebody else will be sent to relieve your anxiety!
Peleg leaves stage right.	—Did you have horses in the old world? I don't much like herding camels and dromedaries. They're haughty and mean. But I'm sure I would be too if I had them for my masters! Asses can be difficult but at least you can feel sorry for them. I should think horses would be the best for an army.

GILGAMESH [Aside.]	Norkid could make this clever fellow his understudy! He's a bold cadet and probably brave to boot. If my dreamy way back to Uruk is not the path of a mirage he'll be a good messenger and companion—if I can teach him a spy's discretion.
[To Shepherd.]	—You are confident enough. If we ever stop long enough I'll teach you how to make a bow from the finest wood and bone. You'll soon be strong enough to bend it. With string at ear, it will hum like a purring paramour!

SHEPHERD 1 [He tries unsuccess- fully to draw Gilgamesh's bow, first with one hand and then with the other.]	And I'm now old enough to have one! I can already imagine . . . all kinds of love! . . . . If you show me how to handle bow and axe, on both sides of my nose, I'll teach you the javelin and sling, sinister or dexter!

GILGAMESH	I have no time left for superfluous skills, but you have enough for them all. If you're as bright as you sound, and

[Points to his
pendant.]

not too impatient, you'll do best for yourself by mastering
this stylus to scratch the words of patrons and carry them
to distant places for honorable reward. You will have no
competition.

SHEPHERD 1   I've always had a secret yen for magic! So on second
thought, if you really hope to be my new master without
promising so much as my keep, we should stay out of the
old sheik's way. We'll avoid the hospitality of his righteous
feast-bowl by skirting the camp and coming back to the
river further downstream, out of sight behind his back. I
begin to doubt that he'd willingly give me up for the
bemusing stories of a scarcely clothed vagabond! We must
show ourselves only in territory he's left forever. Then I can
do your bidding without hindrance. I'm tired of sheep;
they're all the same. I'd like to learn new work and see
strange gods. But I won't mind if friendly girls are all
alike!

GILGAMESH   I have weathered enough in plains as well as mountains.
Let's hope you too will learn to cherish city walls for the
advantages of civil enclosure! Every fleece in one fold—
princess, priestess, and milkmaid!

[Aside, musing.]   —According to one of my dreams I am about to transplant
a green twig to an orchard in the past. I seem to have lost
the idea of what I thought I sought—something that's
made by all the changes of sky and earth and living creatures. Or was it what buoys all hope and doing? Am I
losing more than I thought to gain? Is it living or unliving
to trace an arrow against its motion?

SHEPHERD 1   Never mind my motives. —Hey, what wants to be filled
when it's empty and wants to be emptied when it's full?

GILGAMESH   Your belly.

SHEPHERD 1   I was thinking of girls, but that's a good guess! You *are*
worthy to be my master—even without wages or food. But
on to our first bivouac! What shall I call you?

GILGAMESH   Noman is good enough for the present. What's your name?

SHEPHERD 1   Ha! For the present I will answer to "Dumuzi". I'm an
ambitious shepherd-boy risking longevity for adventure.
What kind of dislodged beggar are you, whom I desert my
tribe to serve? A fugitive for murder?

GILGAMESH   I'm a Sicani who has killed many men who were trying to kill me, and was made captain of fighting ships for the king of Caphtor, an island that rules half a middle sea. By war and bride-raids I won him fabled wealth, of which I was allowed a share. But I do not murder, and never before have I been a suppliant. I lost all my men and treasure, some to Phoenicians, some to the deep. This bow is the only gift I was able to save from my last whirlwind at sea. The Canaanites on shore drove me into the desert because they regard all seamen as Caphtors and all Caphtors as pirates.

SHEPHERD 1   I know what islands are, in the river; but what exactly is a sea?

GILGAMESH   The sea is an eternally restless flood of irritable bitter water, green or gray or blue, that only fish can drink. It invests all continents and enlarges every breach with many-fingered hands. It heaves to the breath of Father Sine like an immense desert perpetually in motion. Though you sail for many moons in chaotic winds and currents you may never see a place. Except for Sine and Utu the gods themselves avoid it.

SHEPHERD 1   I'm skeptical of whatever you may tell me, but, as you seem to think necessary, I'll accept your stories and definitions for the convenience in understanding each other. You've let slip that you know mountains; and you seem familiar with river-land: between us, I think you're a Kassite straggler trying to get back home through enemy lines much deeper than you'd expected!

GILGAMESH   What do you know about Kassites?

SHEPHERD 1   Kassites are gentile freebooters who live by cruel rapine— fierce and cruel barbarians who toss babies on their swords and put villages to the torch. They are enemies of God! Nimrod was their khan.

GILGAMESH   Is that the lore of your tribe?

SHEPHERD 1   That's what everybody says. I've always wondered how people hate what they don't learn for themselves. My mother told me the secret that her father was a Kassite prisoner. The people around here share most of that opinion, and they don't spare suspicious strangers by merely driving them into the desert. They'd assume you were a Kassite even if you weren't. We must disguise ourselves.

GILGAMESH   Maybe the reason you don't think like a shepherd is that you're half sheik by blood.

SHEPHERD 1   But only one of many!

GILGAMESH   When we repossess my walls and tower I'll give you a job to your liking. Maybe my daughter's equerry. Meanwhile I intend to keep your attention with assignments and thoughts interesting enough to occupy whatever attention can be spared from your hereditary lust, which nevertheless I'll aid and abet with nostalgia.

SHEPHERD 1   With all respect, to test that promise as we search for a safe spot to pitch our imaginary tent, I'll thank you for a fuller version of your outlandish story.

GILGAMESH   Then go keep your word to poor Peleg, and pack your kit. I'm sure you can find for us some useful artifacts too common in your camp to be missed, while I try to start a hare or something bigger. When we rejoin, and get a night of rest, I'll tell you how to teach yourself the ways of a city by going into the bazaars with your eyes and ears open until you find out who's wise among the foolish, and whom you can trust to answer a foreign trader's harmless questions. Then you can test yourself as a mummer. After a few days of taking in the local customs you'll know your way to the palace and where to hang around until you get access to the inside market.

SHEPHERD 1   Market for what, our camel-load of golden fleeces?

GILGAMESH   You are no longer a shepherd or wool merchant: you are apprentice to a Phoenician arms trader who wishes to sell one of the best battle-bows ever wrought by famous Caphtor craftsmen of well laminated wood and ivory, too stiff for ordinary men-at-arms to flex but destined for lords of the sea. It's worth an argosy, you may say in truth, and fit for some strong king who in his own chariot would lead the conquest of these riverine plains. Someone at the court will invite a display and demonstration of our uniquely precious treasure. Whatever the price they bargain for, it will buy a boat and all necessities for our escape down Euphrates—if that happens to be the gentile name of yonder river—to find what is where down there! Until you have elicited a royal summons this treasure will be the tool to provide us with flesh from field or stream.

[Aside.]
**Gilgamesh &
Shepherd 1 leave,**
stage left.

—He's no Engidu, but in this dream he stabs my heart like memories of young Lil-Amin! This clever Dumuzi serves well as an only son.

Column Three

[Young princess **Enheduanna** sitting in her simple reception chamber. Elderly **Widow 1**, heavily veiled, and a couple of palace **guards** attend. **Berosus** stage right as usual.]

BEROSUS

This is Babylon when it was newly civilized, many centuries before I was born and educated there. It has not yet occurred to Sargon that he could overcome the southern cities on the river that were vaguely acknowledged to be the sources of all culture.

Shepherd 1 enters, carrying
a rolled carpet on his shoulder,
followed by Gilgamesh.]

ENHEDUANNA

[Shepherd 1 unrolls
the carpet on the
floor and reveals the
bow, which is then
handled as implied
by the dialogue.]

You are sure that no one knows what you have inside that carpet? It must be a surprise for my father when he returns from driving off the Elamites. I hope it will be on his birthday! I'm always looking for such exotic presents as he'd never win in ordinary battle or get as tribute. On pain of death, it's a secret to be kept from his court and all the local merchants until after he's surprised by it—and before he can surprise *me* as usual with something in gold or lapis lazuli.

[She indicates
Shepherd 1.]

—The king loves me all too well, but he knows I find grown-up men too coarse and hairy. He's never thought of bringing me a beautiful young slave like this one!

SHEPHERD 1

I'm a student, Madam, not a slave!

ENHEDUANNA

You're not any older than I am! I'm glad you're free. Your legs look sturdy and hairless.
—Anyway, the surprise is as important as the bow itself. In a high king's life any novelty is rare, especially from a sheltered daughter! It has to be something I can meanwhile hide even from nosey chambermaids. Of course I trust my life and reputation with these three dears, but if your slimly curved machine is as manly as you claim, and I give you what you've asked for it, how can I be sure you'll refrain from boasting about my patronage until it's in my father's hands and you're a thousand miles away? Everyone knows that the Elamites and Kassites have spies out there in the plaza, and they'd love to spoil my fun!

GILGAMESH   No one could see that he carried anything but a carpet. You can trust me as a cautious trader who has every reason to earn your continued protection, and to be at your future service from near or far. It is everywhere known that even rumor can't outdistance the effects of your displeasure.

ENHEDUANNA   Woe betide any betrayal of my condescension! If word gets out too soon I'll have every person now in this room garroted and thrown to the river sharks without a scruple of injustice. I mean it too! I have more power than any of my brothers because I'm the favorite, and my father loves to see me exert his authority. When I'm just a little older I shall be the chief priestess of Inanna and Sine for his empire. He promised me!

              —So you are the master of this lovely boy? Where do you hail from? You're better looking than other men your age.

GILGAMESH   I am Noman of Caphtor in the Middle Sea where this bow was made for me from the finest materials in the king's arsenal. I had saved his country from famine with shiploads of Sicani grain. No other bow can shoot so far, if one's strong enough to draw the string.

ENHEDUANNA   My father is the strongest man in the world!

GILGAMESH   Then he will value it for more than the surprise.

ENHEDUANNA   Try it, soldier.

[She gets up from her chair to handle the bow with feckless childlessness.
              —You too.

              —How can an old merchant be nearly as strong as my father!

Then the soldiers try without success to draw it.
Gilgamesh finally shows them how easily he can do it.]

GILGAMESH   It's not strength but understanding. I have lived with this bow so long that I can feel its breathing. I know how to make it joyful.

ENHEDUANNA   Do you think I could make it laugh? I am a poet. With the words of my mouth I can make men laugh or cry.

GILGAMESH   Accept this royal weapon and on my return I shall bring you as a gift my tablet of runes with all the kennings that can be knotted among themselves a thousand ways to bring on smiles or tears, as you may choose to use them.

ENHEDUANNA [Laughs and claps.]	What, do you trade in poetry too? Will your tablet tell me the story of Nimrod? I get nothing here but scraps or rumors about legends of what elders may have said when someone was too young to understand the words. The Eberews wouldn't tell me anything because of our religion! —Do bards in the west sing of Nimrod?
GILGAMESH	In Canaan I think I heard that name used for a dragon to terrify children with.
ENHEDUANNA	Well I know he was a cruel tyrant! He betrayed his city to the Elamites and killed his own brother.
WIDOW 1 [Wailing.]	. . . his own brother. No! Giszax loved him! . . . Elamites again! Call Norkid! . . . Father's soaking blood . . . cry my Kassite babies also dead! . . . Lil-Amin hates Gilgamesh gone from bed. . . . Enkidu lies in mother earth. . . . Mother Lil-Amin carries Semiramis to die a mother. . . . All mothers gone but one who flirts to be one. . . . No, no, no—not yet! . . . My eyes still hurt, hurt, hurt. . . .
ENHEDUANNA	Quiet, you crazy old fool! You tell me nothing! Such tantalizing gibberish, always the same! That's all I ever get out of her when she hears Nimrod mentioned—crooning repetitious unpoetic syllables! I hate her! Every now and then she falls into that agony of trance and torments me with her meaningless staccato screeches!
WIDOW 1	. . . screeches.
GILGAMESH	But every lamentation has its causes!
ENHEDUANNA	So of course I do love this half-crazed woman, alone of all those who wait on me in their own interest. They say she had served my grandmother, whose child she brought to the king my father. That child—whom she adored more than gods, to whom she devoted every breath of her life—grew up to be my father's queen, young enough to be his daughter, and even in her youth ruled Babylon as his regent during endless foreign wars. Her I killed, my mother, by getting born too late. This shattered ancient, unable to tell her woe and no more useful to me than a mute as far as my mother is concerned, still loves me as much as she loved her—but sometimes when angry she makes me feel the guilt. Noman of the world, am I a murderer? Should I cast off my mother's savior and accord

myself some peace of mind? Or should I keep her here in hope that someday her memory of the years before my birth will return? She must have been far braver and more loyal than I can even try to be. I cringe at the thought of looking at her bloody eye-sockets.

WIDOW 1   . . . bloody eye-sockets.

ENHEDUANNA   Her memory is gone forever. —But why am I telling all this to a wandering merchant? . . . —Oh I know why! As a learned adventurer you can help me with the poem I mean to write about my mysterious origins. I'll reward you with jewels of your choice, or even private hugs and kisses, old as you are! —Now that would really give the palace some-

[Bursting into a peal of laughter.]   thing astonishing for their gossip!

WIDOW 1   . . . their gossip.

GILGAMESH   Forgive me, but I can accept none of the gauds or kisses

[With signs of impatience.]   deserved by youth. You cannot give me time. I have heard enough to understand your wishes for intelligence of the past. For that purpose, and for mine, there's no need for me to linger here. If you provide us with a safe-conduct to your father's frontiers I will search the stuff of legend in every place along my way. Please let us take our leave with-out delay. If all goes well I'll stop here when I retrace my journey. Or at least Dumuzi here will carry you the story for your poem. Meanwhile you must study the art.

ENHEDUANNA   I'll make beautiful verses of what you find! Someday you'll

[Merrily clapping her hands.]   hear how clever I am. My brothers don't even understand the stars, but I know how to interpret dreams! I can almost figure out the little marks that stand for acts and things on seals in my mother's jewel box. My father will depend on me for reading all kinds of signs! He wants me to learn for him, so I can keep accounts and make a lot of tablets to perpetuate his glory. What could be more interesting to future priests than stories? So find out for me all you can about that terrible Nimrod who hated the gods and made slaves of his own people. —If only women could be as free as men! I'd ride my barge all the way down the river to see for myself if there really is a tower almost touching heaven! But I can become famous right here by entertaining travel-ers who are not prevented from seeing elephants and giraffes, or mountains and sea-monsters, or shining walls!

WIDOW 1   . . . shining walls.

ENHEDUANNA   But this boy is not dismissed quite yet.
—I notice you did not try the bow, Dumuzi. Maybe you
and I could do the trick together, before I let you go and
keep the secret of my purchase—or tell the tale and make
yourself the enemy of all my vengeful suitors. I'm still
almost a virgin, but I know how to overcome your trembling in my presence. Such a body is nothing for a princess
to disdain. You may learn something especially delightful
and still get back to Noman before the gates close. —But
you are free to spurn the simple curiosity of an imperial
princess. I am not vindictive.

WIDOW 1   . . . not vindictive.

ENHEDUANNA   —In any case, Noman, here's payment for the bow, and
[Hands Gilgamesh a   something more in anticipation. In this city even my pri-
purse.]   vate affairs can't be kept secret for more than one turn of
the sky. You have time to buy a boat, but you must cast off
before dawn if you wish to stay afloat alive. Sometime soon
this innocent messenger will take you safe-conduct tokens
that can get a boat off and past the reach of jealous assassins.
—Well, do you choose to stay with me a while, my fresh
darling?

WIDOW 1   . . . fresh darling.

**Preceded by the
guards,
Enheduanna** takes
up the bow and
leaves, tenderly guiding Widow 1 but
glancing back over her shoulder at **Shepherd 1,**
who hesitates, looking back and forth,
before **following her out.**

GILGAMESH   Does the tongue of that old woman foretell? Or does it let
Gilgamesh circles   loose fantastic nightmares of the past? Do I seek past or
the stage in   future? In the name of Utu, in the name of Sine: who is,
agitation before   who was, or who will be that New World Nimrod? —
he **leaves.**   Time's deception deepens. How can I know which way the
arrow flies?

15

GRETTA
DOLOROSO

"**O**ld age is the time to consolidate, assess, review, and tie up the package before it's posted for disintegration." said the widowed Endicott Krebs, attorney-at-law, lounging in his office, to Commander Finn Macdane, his terminal landlord. Some years ago the old lawyer had retired from the respected Botolph firm of O'Grady, Krebs, & O'Grady to selective personal practice as much for the leisure and convenience of Dogtown's center-city haven as for keeping his glass-cased law books and legal files out of his house. But now he was making the final move after all. It was the Memorial Day holiday afternoon; the old bank building, which he had sold to Macdane, was deserted except for themselves. Finn had stepped down one flight of stairs from his penthouse for casual conversation. In the course of their amicable discussions they had discovered common interests in the war they were both veterans of. Now they were celebrating with Scotch and water the commencement of the last month of a lease

Krebs had negotiated as one quid pro quo of the sale that marked his anticipation of full retirement to the great house on the Foreside where he and his late wife had lived from time immemorial. "Here's to two old geezers!" they drank.

"You were damned decent putting up with all the construction noise over your head." said Finn, referring to the installation of his modern suite in the superstructure. "I owe you at least a case of the best single-malt for every month that you've made no complaint."

"I haven't been in here enough to be bothered much. It's a good excuse to take my round-the-world cruise. That will be my indolent stimulus—easy sleeping, easy learning—gliding past beautifully exotic dangers in comfort and safety, with social entertainment whenever I wish. But first I've got to buckle down and clean out my files. Have you lined up a new tenant yet?"

"I've been procrastinating." said Macdane, new to the reality business. "Of course I'll have to do some renovation down here. Gretta may have put up with the frosted glass in the ante-room as something of her own vintage but another tenant and his secretaries will expect modernization. I don't seem to care enough."

"I'm glad it's such good timing for Gretta's retirement. I've fixed up an annuity for her. I may ask her to move in with me, as housekeeper or wife! She's the best accountant I've ever had, and she's always seemed to know my local clients' business affairs as well as they do. If we'd had her in Botolph I'd have made her the whole firm's office manager."

"I suppose I'll have to entirely renovate this dark oldfashioned den of yours. Fortunately it's right under most of my apartment. The electricians and plumbers will be able to use the same chases. Even from only these three windows the view of at least the inner harbor is almost as good as mine."

"I didn't have to *live* here." the lawyer said. "I needed wall space for books and pictures more than inspiration or solar enlightenment. Look at all these legal-file cabinets that I've got to empty and get rid of. That's the main reason I've been postponing my absolute retirement for so long. When I left Botolph I could turn everything over to my partners. Here I'm stuck without succession. I've had my eye on all the relatively young lawyers around here who might want to take over my Cape Gloucester files—mostly just archives of the dead, a few clients whose estates or reputations I want to protect from legal beagles and mooncussers. I've never liked probate law, and still don't know much about it. It's still too much like Bleak House. —The hardest thing you'll have to do is get rid of my smoke. Better not try to salvage any of the permeated paneling or carpeting."

Mr Krebs, Esq., was somewhat portly in his old age, no longer quick in his movements, but jovial enough with a slim cigar that he delicately tasted at each puff but never rolled in his mouth. He hadn't lost interest in the world's professions, and he had no intention to retire to Poncedeleon or Cornucopia for the sake of weather. The unbusinesslike new landlord thought the veteran counselor-at-law might be content to serve out his charitable days with the meditative comfort of his Jewish wisdom in the world of Christians. Krebs had done very well for himself in his lucrative specialty of corporate law, but he seemed not to have had the driving ambition of a prosecutor, nor the intellectual purity that had driven such exceptional Jewish professionals as the engineers who had done so much to reform the Navy without financial incentive

The amateur new owner of the old brick building with a stately facade of granite was always warmed by the presence of this reasonably gemütlich gentleman who reminded him of his own erstwhile colleague at the Bureau of Ships, Admiral Hyman Windhover, who had been kept in the Navy for sixty-three years (long after mandatory retirement) by a special act of Congress, largely to the distaste of his nominal peers. And also the heroically versatile salvager, his early mentor and friend, Captain Ned Ellsworth, who had finally retired to Markland as a private political conservative never socially recognized by the conservative Navy. Then too, in Finn's historical recollection of brilliant Jews in the country's service there had been the compassionately "pushy" Commodore Uriah Phillips, in youth the victor of a fatal duel about the honor of his religion, who, by the way, was barred by the antisemitic naval aristocracy from commanding the frigate in which ordinary seaman Wellingborough Redburn later enlisted. That Commodore, but for an unusual implementation of the U S Constitution, would have suffered as much malicious injustice as Captain Dreyfus did in the avowed land of liberty, equality, and fraternity a generation later. He'd finally proved his aggressive patriotism by salvaging Monticello, which he owned, before presenting it to the people as his legacy. Probably none of these ambitious and no doubt often irritating Jews (like their scientific counterparts in 20C Europe), Finn thought, shared with the genial Endicott Krebs much more in temperament and initial proclivity than an innate urge to develop the racial heritage of cerebral enterprise; none ever so much at peace in the objective wisdom of retirement as this liberal squire of obscure wealth who seemed to tolerate death without famous accomplishment.

Until now the two men had been acquainted only at arm's length as cordial negotiators and daytime neighbors. But that night for the first time the new landlord invited the older one for dinner across the street at the Doghouse (which with successive changes of proprietor had never managed to escape its name), having discovered that neither of them cared much about fancy food or extraspecial wine. Finn wanted to hear more about what the lawyer had been doing with the S I S in Europe during the War, and at the war-crimes indictments thereafter.

*

The more modest office of Tessa Masterson (Ms Opsimath) was on the second floor with no view of the water. She had known Krebs quite well on the board of Dogtown Machine & Design, for which he had served as the firm's lawyer while he was still a partner in the Botolph firm of O K & O. For a few years thereafter, as a personal favor, before giving up his open Dogtown practice nearly absolutely, he had handled perfunctory legal matters for Rafe Opsimath and herself as a couple of private citizens in the aftermath of previous marriages and for their future estate, while remaining on the board of their corporation. So he was an old professional friend, hitherto more objective and reserved than intimate. She nevertheless guessed that, soberly approached, his habitually supererogatory confidentiality would somewhat relax as his professional concerns finally approached an end—when he began to enjoy liberty of leisure and contemplate the satisfaction of uninterrupted retrospection, as well as of South Seas travel and certain pro bono or other eleemosynary pleasures here at home, usually anonymous and for the common good.

In her pursuit of the past for hints of Caleb's origin as evidence for her diagnosis of the nameless "client" whom she was to synthesize for her academic thesis, Tessa remembered that her husband had remarked, at the time that she was installing her office, that Krebs the landlord had been the corporate lawyer for the religious society that twenty years earlier had intimately employed Caleb as "business manager". Krebs had also been the one secular Trustee of the three who legally supervised the Laboratory of Melchizedec and the Mesocosm, the monastic East Harbor chapter house of the international Classic Order of the Vine, whose legal existence survived only a few years after Lancelot Duncannon the Father Founder and Superior expired by pulmonary embolism in Tybbot Hospital. Hence, she reasoned to herself, Mr Krebs must have known, directly or indirectly, Arthur Halymboyd the Chairman of the galactic Parity Corporation, a holding company with which the Reverend Christopher Lucey, the Order's Father Economist, had done a great deal of Street business in securities as a Registered Representative of Weatherglass, Neatherd & Co. of Botolph and New Uruk. Accordingly she decided to take advantage of long acquaintance by occasionally calling upon her D M & D associate during one of his half-day stints on the premises. Surely he remembered some private impressions of Caleb's relationship with those two Members Regular, both long since dead and generally forgotten by the few Dogtowners who knew them.

It was scant but unsuppressed public knowledge that "Dun's Farm"—a large tract of overgrown and overgrowing open land of scrub and brambles, more or less elevated on a ruggedly irrupted eminence of chthonic rock and vegetation within an irregular open field, the whole of which in the last century had still been a dairy farm, later providing a ground for drying fishermen's nets—had been preserved by Father Duncannon's family and bequeathed to him. Having taken the monastic oath of personal poverty, he had donated it to the assets of the legally incorporated Laboratory, for the City's limited athletic use and generally for the public's right of passage as unenclosed "open space", protected from what is called development. But when the Lab's own property—the great house and its own land—went quietly bankrupt and the exterritorial loosely centered Members Secular of the Society of Classic Order of the Vine began to understand what was happening, soon after the Father Superior's own death, despite forbearingly gentle treatment by the bank at its mortgage foreclosure, Endicott Krebs contrived permission for the creation and sale of some peripheral subdivisions of the Farm, for the sake of preserving the rest. Thus a few lots were auctioned (with certain restrictive covenants) to a local reality-estate magnate by the name of Mooncusser, who was thus enabled to build half a dozen modish "mansions" on flats where the soil was deep and level enough to require no dynamite or heavy equipment. This entire intricately protracted compromise among probate law, city ordinances, municipal mercy, and private avarice—thanks largely to the public-spirited attitude of the late Jason Anacoluther (the banker), along with a residual tendency of City officials to negotiate for the higher moiety of common good—was Krebs's enormously patient work, who would never have taken a quiet part in such local affairs before his penultimate retirement but for his kindly memory of Father Duncannon and his general dismay at the irreversible depredation of Lady Gloucester's domain.

Of course the public was not privy to the financial scandal—or the internal devolution of the COV despite the saintly efforts of Father Lloyd Davy, a parish priest in Markland who survived Father Duncannon as the final Father Superior elect of a weakened cause, not long before Chris Lucey the loyally troublesome Father Economist had killed himself while a patient at the stately Norumbega Psychiatric Institution in parkland Walden, over the stipulated expense of escrow assets left him by his late distressed father in the state of Cherokee during a suspended prosecution for arson and insurance fraud.

There was no obituary of Father Christopher Lucey in the *Dogtown Nous* simply because at that stage of the affair nobody in Cape Gloucester was recorded by the hospital for visiting rights or notification. Even Caleb, his former close friend and educator in the financial world of capitalism, preternaturally absorbed as he was in the utterly different job at the Yard that Chris had vouched him for, had heard nothing of that lovingly neurotic socialworker and stockbroker until several years later when he was called upon by a young Dominion divinity school graduate who was researching facts for a biography of Father Duncannon, inspired by fortuitous reading of his works, having approached a former member of COV with a literal enthusiasm that rekindled Caleb's own dromenological excitement in the figurative terms of Theodynamics. Taking the young man to dinner, like Eckermann with some distant disciple of Goethe, he poured forth discreet information about his revered Father Duncannon, from memory and from a few notes he had once taken with a like object in mind. But he never heard any more from that provincial apostle of the lost cause. It was in return for his encouragement of the project that he learned the cryptic fact of a penitential suicide. It had been Chris's devotion to Father Dun, as the only other monastic Member Regular of the COV, that had kept Chris alive that long.

Because of Tessa's interest in Caleb her attention to what little she knew about the rather mysterious "High Church" Laboratory, from him and from her late friend the devout Teddi Cibber who had often attended its weekly Anamnesis (a k a Eucharist) without much interest in the radical theology more or less embedded in the traditional Tudor sound and shape of its Mass, her attention to news and rumor, and from some gardening she'd done for the Lab as a sort of religious offering to supplement the bread and wine, had greatly exceeded that of casual readers or rumor-mongers. Tessa vaguely remembered the dramatic *Nous* reports of a September late-night emergency in which Chris, Father Lucey, rescued the Father Superior from their dormitory end of the Lab by carrying him down to ground before the Fire Department engines and ambulance arrived. Awakened by the smell of smoke, according to the *Nous*, he'd traced its eruption to the distant basement stairs before deciding it was too serious to investigate further without first telephoning the alarm. Having done so, he'd rushed back to the second floor bedroom to rouse and wrap his Superior in his own bathrobe and had carried the frail old man out onto a rock ledge by the one French casement still accessible, thereby escaping the thick oily smoke that was already filling the house and threatening to burst into open flames from the boiler room. The *Nous* printed no more about the story. Fires in Dogtown were commonplace.

As a matter of fact it was extinguished in less than half an hour, with very little obvious external damage. Both uninjured priests were examined and accommodated at the hospital for the rest of the night. But the internal smoke damage to the heating system, the woodwork, the books, the antique furnishings, original works of art, the sacristy and its vestments (perhaps the biggest dry-cleaning bill of all) left most of the house discolored with acrid soot, if not charred or destroyed. Fortunately Chris had everything fully insured for both replacement and salvage costs. Most of the valuables had once been Father Duncannon's personal property, collected or inherited, before they were conveyed to the Laboratory's "charitable corporation". Father Dun had saved for himself only his pectoral cross and the personal clothing that supposedly did not belong to him.

The Lab was promptly indemnified in full by the insurance company. A goodly sum of cash was funded for the purpose of paying step-by-step for replacements and rehabilitation over the course of a few months. Meanwhile, Tessa was told, Father Duncannon went to stay in Markland with the stocky and deceptively easygoing bachelor Father Lloyd Davy (the elected successor of Father

Superior in any case) in his commodious parish rectory, while Chris Lucey was fixing up conditions for his spiritual father's heartbroken return to the Lab while it was still pungent with smoke and unfinished in the limited restoration of such amenities as money could buy. The sacristy's vestments and altar cloths were more or less successfully cleaned at great expense by a local dry-cleaner, and the sacred communion ware was eventually polished, but much of what had furnished or ornamented the chapel, library, and great hall was irreplaceable.

Soon after the two Fathers had returned to the Lab, toward the end of the State Fire Marshal's long subtle investigation (which had begun as a routine but not mandatory procedure at the request of the local Fire Inspector, an intelligent and conscientious but tolerantly unreligious officer who had personally risked his own life fighting many a Dogtown fire in years of national Total Abstinence), Father Dun was heart-stricken and died as he was listening on the radio to the favorite opera of his pre-ecclesiastical youth as an exquisitely aesthetical physicist, while Father Chris sat in continuous attendance. It was he who asked for the autopsy.

As for what Tessa had heard from Gretta Doloroso about the fate of the Order, she knew from Caleb only that the new Father Superior, though still unwilling to take the monastic oaths of a Regular, had grown discontented with his undemanding secular duties to a suburban middle-class congregation predominantly impervious to new ideas, in a diocese cohesive by very reason of its expectation that Tudor liturgy and theology would never change in the changing world. He was increasingly unhappy about his failure to inspire more than two or three half-comprehending parishioners with Father Duncannon's radical interpretation of the Eucharist as a social sacrament. Soon after his mentor's death he gave up his comfortable salary and rectory to take on a nearly impecunious rural parish, practically without perquisites and emoluments, up in the marginal wilds of the Dominion's New Westphalia. He dubbed his new little rectory the Paraclete (after Abelard's final retreat) because it was purchased with the last scrap of Paraclete Biochemical Corp [PARA] contraceptive stock remaining to the Lab after its liquidation in Dogtown. Caleb once visited Father Davy there on the bank of a burbling salmon river along which his host had spent all his vacations. There was no more than a small sagging frame house next door to the white clapboard church, which itself was hardly large enough to seat its tiny congregation of aging dairy

farmers gradually yielding their pastures and hayfields to the evergreen forests of vast timber-harvesting and paper-pulping corporations. There at his leisure the good man could revel in his creative
hobby: tying flies for his rods and wicker basket.

But that oddly sorted final leader of the Order (as Caleb and
most Members of COV appreciated) was not for nothing a pragmatic native of Brotherly in the U S A, a Doctor of Philosophy
from Norumbega, and an ardent disciple of the Father Founder.
His only stipend came now from a part-time celibate secular professorship in Divinity at the Provincial University an hour's drive
from his ichthyological home, next to which he preached and celebrated the Eucharist on Sundays, and from which he exercised as
much cure of souls as the few poverty-stricken bodies available to
him would otherwise accept, save for baptism marriage and death.
He told Caleb that he felt more like a missionary than a pastor.
But he often drove his battered car to see the Bishop, and elsewhere in the Province to visit sympathetic peers, urging upon the
diocese his beautifully spare version of Father Duncannon's *Anamnesis* (which in no way literally violated the international Book of
Common Prayer) and its rectified meaning of social Offertory and ·
Sacrifice. His concise functional tract, cautiously discussed and
approved by the Bishop as an experimental option for the core of a
liberal litany, was eventually adopted and published by a Provincial synod. Nobody could predict the eventual acceptance of this
reform of Archbishop Cranmer's reform, Caleb had told Tessa, but
there in an obscure presumably conservative see of North Atlantis
it was the only ecclesiastical consequence of Lancelot Duncannon's
life-work as far as he knew. It was far more likely to fall as a withered leaf of the Vine than as a planted acorn for the subtle new
mutation in cultural evolution as it deserved—unless windblown
seeds of the Order sown by its secular priests and their wives in
Cipango, Chosen, and South Hindustan had taken isolated root
among other obscure communities since the Father Founder's
death, when it had taken no root in Dogtown itself, save in Caleb
Karcist's private anthropology while merely a nominal member of
St Paul's Tudor parish.

Little of this recollected information in itself advanced Tessa's
interest in Caleb's immediate ancestry, mainly because it had
seemed to her that with the exception of Fay who had known his
mother only at and after his birth, none of her own acquaintances
lived on the Cape before 1935. But she now reconsidered her

habitual identification of Endicott Krebs as a postwar corporate lawyer in Botolph who incidentally may have been privately domiciled in Dogtown when she took notice of his new status emeritus at an age of eighty or more. Of course he had a youth! Was he indigenous? Where did he spend his youth? Was he practicing law here or elsewhere before the War?

In any case, did a retired lawyer ever keep papers of the dead? —personal papers that were not transferred to successors in a client's legal representation or filed exclusively with the Probate Court: letters, briefs, notes, diaries, or printed matter, perhaps thrust upon him by intestate estates, by heirs or by survivors who themselves were carelessly uninterested, dead, or only too glad to escape archival responsibility by vanishing without trace? What were the professional ethics of postmortem confidentiality when there was no one left alive to care? For that matter, was there a statute of limitations for the exhumation of a pauper's grave? She was afraid to ask such questions—as a friend, not as a client. Not as a private detective. Not as an investigative reporter. Not as a busybody gossip. Could she dare imply that Caleb wanted her to discover the lesser half of his parentage? She admitted to herself that she was unscrupulous enough to do just that, but for fear of being exposed, humiliated, ostracized by Fay's community, even scolded by her all-too-tolerant husband who otherwise admired her adroit social ethic and heard whatever she confessed with cosmopolitan equanimity.

Softly, softly. Surely dear old Endicott would have no objection to respectful inquiry about his distinguished career! A little female flattery was never amiss to a lonely geezer who has memories to be proud of! Even if he'd known nothing of Dogtown before the pleasure of wealth had attracted his wife and himself, as a member of the local bar then or later, he must have a headful of rum-running and Restoration stories. For instance, gossip about the two mysterious murders that Caleb's mother thought she'd solved at the peril of her life. I must tread softly, said Tessa to herself.

*

Tessa did tread softly, as you might expect. She began as a casual visitor to his office, an old friend, dropping in for old times' sake to offer congratulations, having heard that he was finally yielding to a bachelor's continuity of leisure, and inviting him to dinner sometime before the world cruise she'd heard he would be embarking upon.

Krebs chuckled. He remembered old Tessa very well, and was not much surprised when after some persiflage she told him a little common knowledge about her new career as a private L I C S W, asking for consideration of referral if he still came across any appeals for help of that nature. "I'm afraid I'm too superannuated for that; but I'll keep you in mind if any of my grandchildren are driven to counseling or I myself go crazy with boredom." He wasn't fooled that this was the kind of motive for her first visit to his office since she'd moved hers downstairs.

She mentioned research for her academic thesis. Sure enough, this was getting closer to the mark. But he was not mistaken that it was no more than one step closer to her ulterior motive when she mentioned as relative to her new academic ambition the pair of unsolved murders in Seamark half a century a earlier. More than once over the years he'd been sounded for his confidential opinion about that case. "I suppose you've heard of it at least." she said. "I don't remember ever asking you if you lived here then. I've been told it was in all the Bot papers for a long time. Lots of fruitless investigation by the State Police. Wasn't that before the B D I Feds were called in to help with technical forensics? Maybe they were too busy chasing down the rum-runners."

"I was an incomer with my own family from Novantum after the Second War, but my father had had a summer place in Seamark where I spent part of my carefree vacations until I went off to college just as the First War ended, only a few seasonal visits in between. You're talking about a Depression year, when I was working for the Department of Justice in Washington. In those days it was a long train trip all the way up here. My sister gave up the summer house after our parents were dead. My wife and I knew just enough about Cape Gloucester to head here when we could afford a permanent establishment near the water. Until they built the Felly and the Eisenhower bridge I rode the rattling V & M commuter train almost every business day to my office. . . ." And so he mused about the discomforts even for rich lawyers in the good old days that he knew she wasn't interested in hearing about while she weighed her next leading remark—circuitous question or provocative comment?

But with an indulgent smile, still leaning back in his swivel chair across the desk from his attractive interlocutor, he interrupted his own temporizing patter. "I assume that your disguised client in this hypothetical case history is forty years old at a minimum?"

"More than that." she laughed as a charming trace of blood appeared in her cool ivory cheeks. "But also less than that. One might say it's a matter for family counseling."

"The proper framing for all psychotherapy, I've always thought."

"Then you've been ahead of the times, sir."

"Why don't you tell me what you're driving at, Madam? I'm a very discreet uncle, and there is no charge for this conference because I'm sure it isn't legal. After all, we're old business colleagues, I've always admired your insights, and I've known your very interesting second husband at less than arm's length since before he took over Dogtown Machine & Design and yourself, after the death of that mechanical genius you were first married to. Everyone liked that generous man but I never got the chance to know him very well when he was my client. —By the way," he said, momentarily turning in his seat to look away from her gaze and pointing to his file cabinets, "all my local files not otherwise disposed of were long ago turned over to your Weatherly, with my blessing, a brave young attorney, along with the D M & D documents, correspondence, briefs, notes, and scrap paper. I gather from the Board meetings that he's doing a good job for us. I know he's trustworthy and well educated in business law. You're pretty lucky to have a Norumbega Law School man willing to practice here full-time. Those file drawers", he pointed to, "are now all empty. It's kind of you to call on me. I'm very glad to see you. But I no longer exist as a repository of information or advice. My professional cupboard's bare and my memory of my career is obliterated to make brain-space for common reading and uncommon traveling. I may even buy a stinkertoy and learn how to pilot it up and down the coast."

For an instant Tessa felt almost insulted by his presumptuous geniality, as if he'd implied something inappropriate or even lewd in her unescorted visit to him; but she was so inured to that sort of possibility even with impeccably elderly gentlemen when she called upon them alone that she immediately dismissed the suspicion of disrespect as the faintest echo of her own forgotten fantasies of double entendre at other times and places, reasonably passing his words off as an old man's casual joke about his professional innocence. It was his masculine gestures more than his irony or benign countenance.

But by the same token her feminine self-consciousness evoked sympathetic imagination of what the heroine of her therapeutic "family" case must have suffered as a comely unprotected young woman like Moira Trevisa trying to call to account a whole town of nefarious male authorities and timid witnesses fearful of partaking in knowledge brought to light by what she thought she knew about politically protected individuals. Tessa regarded herself as less vulnerable to intimidation than most women, but she easily imagined the fear of prominent men in those earlier times when it was taken for granted in all critical or executive initiatives.

Krebs smiled like a favorite grandfather. "Look, I still have another cupboard with a little something left in it. Help me finish this last bottle of sherry. You used to like sherry." He produced two stemless wineglasses that looked clean enough. "It always reminds me of Father Duncannon. Every afternoon. Did you know him?"

Alert to this unexpected opening, Tessa relaxed, careless of conceivable innuendos or personal advances. The complacent old man seemed to have an old woman's intuition. With sherry he seemed to her avuncular, almost maternal. "I met him several times at the L M M's financial Board meetings. Our friend Caleb Karcist was Father Duncannon's so-called business manager and acolyte in his chapel."

"I think I remember seeing a couple of organization charts produced by someone with a name like that. Wasn't he the one who assisted that remarkable Father Lucey with their investments? I was one of the three Trustees but only at more than arm's length distance, from my office in Bot. The only time I ever saw their place inside was a few years earlier, before the Order moved up here from Unabridge. It was a messy business at the end. Very sad all around. You seldom see two such different colleagues, even in law firms such as my own—not just because it was two Irishmen and a Jew! —Prosit, to two interesting Christians!" he laughed. "I suppose they wanted a Jew on the board to keep them honest. But you might say that even here I was too far away to protect Father Duncannon from his half-crazy Father Economist who meant all too well. You must have known about all that."

"Not all. Only what I read in the paper, plus a little that my husband and Caleb have mentioned."

"Come now Tessa, a little birdie tells me that you have an ulterior motive for this civil and very welcome visit. Surely you're not doing research for a detective story!"

Having been the only other woman privy to her tearfully honest friend Gloria's brief liaison with Caleb (as a tenant in her house) not long before the end of her marriage to Dexter Keith the present Mayor (who unknown to Gloria had been equally adulterous with herself as Mrs Barebones many years earlier), a quid pro quo for her own confession of lovemaking with Rafe Opsimath (her then unexpected future husband) before the alcoholic death of her first husband, his friend and partner, Tessa had not been embarrassed to enlist Gloria in sinless assistance and harmless curiosity about the prenatal life of her one and only illicit love, if merely to help explain a virtuous wife's fascination by the interesting young man at the time.

Tessa guessed that her energetic friend Gloria willingly joined the fictive game because in advancing middle age she was beginning to find domestic word and touch a little boring at home even with an intelligent and immensely competent, personally honorable self-made executive, whose admirably objective professional initiatives were eventually narrowed to his own resourceful ideas about materials-handling, purchasing, manufacturing, systemic logistics, and shop-floor management, all of which greatly benefited the Opsimaths as profit-seeking owners but didn't do much to enrich the life of a liberal librarian waiting for him to come home to bed, uxorious as he was by common standards of bed and board. No doubt Gloria had spent many more than one night waiting for her "family man" to come home from an unanticipated business meeting—not to mention multi-day trade conventions at almost any city or conference resort on the continent. Though Tessa herself was too contentedly preoccupied to pay attention to her own involuntarily imaginative recreation of Gloria's bed-and-graveyard experiment many summers past as a romantic rite of passage into matronly maturity, from her own experience she still sympathized with the unexpressed feelings of her friend, coolly remembering the biomechanical reason for the queenly Deirdre (Keith) Cotton to have successfully coveted Dexter in what at length turned out to be to Gloria Cotton's disadvantage in an asynchronistic swap of legally contracted lovers, rather too Atlantean serious for Roman comedy.

But Tessa's relationship with this old lawyer was far too tenuous to permit the liberties she took—the kind of sympathies she could trust—with such an intimate old friend as Gloria; or such an elder new doyenne as Fay (after Teddi Cibber was gone), or even any remaining players of the Hoof and Mouth or Theater on the

Rocks gang who might at least have known Caleb after he'd returned to Dogtown at the age of twenty-five. Her husband Rafe Opsimath, who'd been Caleb's enthusiastic employer for a time, seemed like most men to protect the private life of other men in tacit disapproval of women's curiosity, a product of social evolution, whether or not they knew of anything to embarrass their fraternity. She had learned not to test his impatience with what he called historical gossip. In any case he knew nothing about Dogtown before Caleb's return to his birthplace. But she still thought that if anyone among her surviving Dogtown acquaintances might remember something objective about Mary Tremont it was this canny lawyer, though he'd spent his main professional career outside Dogtown.

But there was at least one person she hadn't thought of: just then came a quick soft double knock on the door and with Krebs's voiced assent Gretta Doloroso poked her head through the doorway. "Sorry to intrude, Mr Krebs. I've finished today's work up with Mr Macdane and I wondered if there's anything you might want me to do before I go home."

"Gretta! Just the one to help for a minute. Come in and sit down. Have some sherry, or luse if you prefer."

"Luse, I suppose. I'm always more for red than white. —Hello Tessa! This is how I still dabble in what's called my retirement. At home I sometimes get tired of sitting at my beloved loom."

As Krebs rose to fiddle around with bottle and another glass he made fun of Tessa over his shoulder. "Tessa's here for ancient history. Maybe you can help in her confidential research about a period known as The Great Depression, so far back that she has to come to me for the secret story. Just between us, please, she's writing a detective novel. Or else she's counseling Seamark's repentant murderer. —You don't mind if I'm frank with Gretta, do you, Tessa? Maybe she can help, but she's barely old enough to hear us old folks speak of it."

"I was old enough to keep secrets—at least until everyone concerned has died. So maybe it's still too soon for any Dogtown history later than the Roaring Twenties, because around here families never die, and it's a rare happening that doesn't have a family of friends or enemies behind or ahead of it—sometimes when you'd least expect it. It's like the truth about cannibalism in a lifeboat. You can't just read a log book."

As Tessa knew, creative weaving had become more serious than a pastime for D M & D's retired accountant, in which position from early times on she'd been invaluable to Buck Barebones, Rafe Opsimath, and herself. Until her retirement Gretta had taught herself enough to become de facto comptroller of the flourishing factory that had grown from a tiny job-shop owned by the late Buck Barebones to a sophisticated manufacturing corporation under the presidency of Rafe with Waldo Cotton (Gloria's second husband) as the Vice President of production. Like a sturdy cob horse without affectation her simply bunched black hair had turned grey without changing the color or lines of her dusky semi-semitic Tuscan face, part and parcel with a short broad body, still generously applying the experience of poverty, maternity, bereavement, self-education, loyalty, and humor from a lifetime of subordinate work. Now ostensibly out to pasture, save when she chooses to turn some furrows for a handful of corn when a friend is at the loss of a mule, she has devoted herself to an industrious craft in the small house that the Opsimaths had afforded her at the edge of some woods across the Gut, relieved by many an evening attendance at charitable or political gatherings more active than passive.

Tessa had an inkling that the hue of Gretta's manner had been slightly heightened by a few thimblefuls of something upstairs with Mr Macdane while finishing one of her irregular stints with him in the penthouse apartment above. The Commander had proved himself unexpectedly convivial with all ranks, adjusting himself to the temper of local mores.

But after Gretta had been told that only the years before 1935 were in question she shrugged off the possibility of being very useful to a writer. "I was only a child then."

But now Tessa sniffed a new breeze, and encouraged Gretta's thirst by accepting a second glass for herself, as if Krebs had his feet up on the desk like the host of an office tea party laced with hard liquor just before Christmas. Why hadn't she already thought of Gretta for her research? She had to suppress the impulse to tap her temple with the palm of her hand—not just once, but soon again in her gossipy probing—when Gretta suggested that she ask her questions of Huck Salter, a member of the old playreading group and to this day Rafe's favorite chum when there was time for poker or boating. Huck the resounding troglodytic sculptor, erstwhile mason and lobsterman, sometime Ward representative of the Village on the Board of Earldermen, was a little younger than Gretta, but he and she were both aborigines of the Cape old enough to be aware of public events leading up to Midsummer 1934. And

Huck's wife Sally, the beautiful poet from the Eastern Shore of Magdalene, had been one of the dancers in Tessa's own Troika and a principal figure in the Stone Barn Theater—an intimate friend in the old days before they had gradually drifted apart in the general degeneration of Dogtown's autonomous culture, reflecting the nation's devilvisionary entertainments as well as the individual discouragements of age, inactivity, and family dispersion. Tessa immediately determined to arrange a spur-of-the-moment reunion dinner dragging half a night to net whatever tidbits might further her ulterior motive. Unfortunately there was no way to avoid invitations that included spouses. She believed that often people's lips were not as loose when accompanied by persons most likely to detect borrowed locutions or unacknowledged interests as when freed of critical attention and in a confidential mood for liberal expression of private memories or suspicions.

"After all," Gretta was saying, "Huck's lived most of his life, before and after the War, over there among the Scandies, and the first victim of the murders was an elder relative of his."

Finally, here and now overcoming her prudent hesitation, but still uneasy with the guilt of her own disingenuous tactics—though after all, Tessa thought, many people intended to write impossible books without being blamed for not producing them, and in any case it would be easy to deny the misunderstanding if she should be obliged to—Tessa asked her interlocutors if they remembered the name Moira Trevisa.

Krebs slowly shook his head, rubbing his chin for the wisp of a memory that he tried to unearth, if only to test his faculties. But he was piqued enough to get up and doubtfully open a drawer full of vertical files that remained as his residual miscellaneous or personal papers meant for transport to his office of retirement at home. "This is my geniza, you see." With furrowed brow he slowly closed the drawer and sat down again, as if cudgeling his brain for something vague, without scanning the tabs of manila folders of intermixed letter and legal sizes. "It's too much of a mess to go through now." His voice trailed off. "Most of this I'll take home with me, where it's always belonged. I haven't looked in here for years. Maybe I should cull it before I get out of here." Talking to himself with his free left hand he waved behind him at the row of file cabinets across the room. "Those cabinets are already empty. It's almost hopeless. I've been a martinet with secretaries in my day, but always sloppy as my own file-clerk." He intoned through fifty years of reminiscence. "Anyway, I can't remember names these days. I can remember the essences and analogies of laws, cases, briefs, maxims, and juridical dicta but I can't remember personal names. Sooner or later by reading or putting aside the question I can *recall* them vividly. Once I have an accidental clue, or a random inspiration when I'm absorbed in something else—but I can't remember them *immediately*! In my personal files you can't find much. If I've filed by subject which I do when I don't have a full-time file-clerk, you'll have a hopeless cross-filing problem. And if I've dabbled in one of my idiosyncratic classification schemes that have appeared intuitively obvious according to my concerns at the time, in the stream of my later experience you'll soon find that I can't remember the logic of it. It's like my home library in which I've shelved books by author or by name, or only by subject—sometimes inconsistently. Any of my categories can split or merge! And I can't even use a simple chronological method because most books and files have an indeterminate history of beginning middle or end significant at the moments you have need of them.

"Anyway, all this confusion started after Gretta retired." He winked at his former secretary, who was about to resume that function under domestic circumstances. With a contented laugh she returned the wink.

"I'm told that computers will eliminate the problem." Tessa remarked sympathetically.

"Then after I'm dead let a giant brain catalogue the books in my house! —Now Ms Psychologist, don't try to reassure me about my failing memory."

"You're no worse off as a common reader who loves to browse his own books for nostalgic entertainment." Tessa replied. "The pleasure of recollection proves you have kept the neurotransmitters as available reserve. That's the important thing." Tessa replied.

"Then you *have* reassured me, my dear. I am no longer dialectical but I'm not *necessarily* on the verge of senility. At least I'll appreciate my British cruise aesthetically. The ship will have a reference library.

"Gretta, do you have a few hours to spare here with Mrs Opsimath, if she wants to look at stuff when I'm not in the way— maybe this afternoon to start? I have to be out of here by the end of the week. Perhaps you could separate the wheat from the chaff for an empty drawer in my study. I wouldn't trust anyone else. . . . Hire someone with a van to do the heavy lifting."

Tessa listened at her exciting good luck as arrangements were begun.

"Please look for Mary Tremont too." she ventured.

"Oh I remember Mary Tremont!" Gretta exclaimed. "How could anyone forget her? My very first paying job, when I was still in school, soon after she had a baby. I was so innocent, even though I had half a dozen brothers and sisters! She told me the facts of life! I learned a lot of other things from her. She was very kind to me, and very generous even though she hardly had enough money to pay me. I loved to hear her stories about the newspaper business, New Uruk Times and all. And a lot about art. I'd probably have dropped out of school and never read books or gone to museums if it weren't for her. Apparently the city authorities didn't like her. But she was religious in her own way. She left town after I got a full-time job at the bank—right here in this building! I've often wondered what happened to her."

Swearing Gretta and Krebs to secrecy, Tessa told them a little of what she did know, without mentioning Mary Tremont's child. She shrugged off her inquiry as obviously irrelevant to the recondite murders written off as a closed case by the police long ago. She felt dangerously close to needlessly embarrassing Fay's godson, her own anonymous protagonist, associating his unlikely name with his mother's; and in any case time's arrow could lead postpartum events only in a direction opposite to that of the annunciation she was seeking to fathom.

But as the visitors descended to the street after taking their leave of the residual law office Tessa invited Gretta to lunch at the Windmill on the morrow. A few days after that Gretta managed to move Mr Krebs out his office, lock stock and barrel, thereafter finding herself reunited as a pro tem confidential secretary and housekeeper for a valedictorian eager to get rid of a lifetime's supererogatory superannuated or supernatural paper. She was in effect assuming the functions of a domestic major domo, so that he could feel as free and lawless as his own Holyrood son-in-law. Then Gretta would wish him Godspeed by driving him down to the Ur pier for his carefree round-the-world cruise, whether or not his heart gave out before she returned him his power-of-attorney for quotidian affairs.

"I trust your judgment, Gretta." he'd added complacently, putting out his unobjectionable cigar. He was glad to pay her much more than she asked. "Don't save mail for me unless you find some good cartoons or uncashed checks, or think I *should* see it for any reason. Pay the usual bills that keep coming. Call my daughter in Cornucopia if there are any minor questions, bearing in mind that she's never had my full confidence since she married that actor. Anything urgent, send me a radiogram and I'll call back as soon as possible, but I won't blame you for making any reasonable decision instead. The bank has my will and all the essential documents that you won't have to worry about, if all goes well. —And while you're at it, if you've got spare time, reorganize my books! Perhaps this lady would give you some advice. She's married to a man of practical wisdom. —But don't neglect your weaving on any account. Delegate as much as you can to the maid and gardener, or any help you need. I'd love to take one of your beautiful shawls with me. I measure by my peace of mind. What a relief! I've been worried about returning to three months of aggravated disarray. It made me feel guilty for taking a leave of absence from an idleness that I'm not accustomed to. Now I can come home with a good conscience, and read the fiction I missed as a man of selfish law. . . ."

And so without disclosure of her motives Tessa won a curiously resourceful recruit. It turned out that stout Gretta had also been to some degree a confidant of the late Teddi Cibber, as well as a witness in propinquity to what Caleb saw through his mother's navel after her return from the Isle of Manannan.

A quarter of a century later she had also known Caleb by his unassociated name, and others (including Tessa's husband) who attended the Father Superior in advance of what proved to be the Order's last Chapter.

*

As Finn Macdane grew more and more comfortable with his situation in Dogtown, and especially with Fay Gabriel, whose intimate friendship was precious for the stability and mutual respect that were deepened by their variable but self-regulating distance between freedom and obligation, he was gradually absorbed by the living history of life on primevally clothed granite supervised by gulls. It was hard to recall most of his earlier impressions as an incidental visitor, especially those before the War, but scenes of pine needles on grass-fringed rock rekindled the pleasure of summer visits in his youth. One pastime led to another in an idle process that he wasn't used to—until he turned to a gradually intensifying rumination upon the Dogtown event that had awakened his emotional life for a few years after the great Gloucestermas of 1934, only to be forgotten under subsequent layers of wartime and postwar adventure both erotic and professional.

He began to question Fay particularly about her memories of the town as nurse and wife before her anthropological schooner-cruise to Western Pacific islands dominated by the sinister Land of the Rising Sun, at a time when, but for the extended absence in exploration with her husband and their scientific or nautical shipmates, it was possible for him to have crossed her path somehow on his official Gloucestermas 1934 visit to the altered presque-isle they now inhabited almost as a naturalized couple.

Meanwhile, expecting at last no more translocation of domicile, he was sporadically collecting his lifetime's scattered corporeal and incorporeal hereditaments in order to sort, negotiate, donate, discard, or preserve them for legacy, worthless or not to persons or institutions stipulated in his last will and testament. He had already sold off the real property in Markland that he'd inherited by lineage, so that aside from the building he now owned in Dogtown all his assets were easily marketable. That conservative treasure he left more or less to the management of his age-old Norumbega Bank & Trust in Norumbega Square just outside the walls of Norumbega University, where he had opened a small checking account at the age of sixteen as a college freshman. His safe-deposit box in Norumbega at the Trust had been successively enlarged in size and value after the War but the contents of it he had recently transferred to a large drawer in the vault of Cape Gloucester Security Trust half a block away. There too, in the late Jason Anacoluther's bank, he now did his ordinary financial business, with liquid or fungible assets and liabilities. The massive steel vaults on two levels of his own ghostly bank building had been disabled and converted into inconvenient and inefficient storage space for his tenants, their thick doors removed or fixed open like the breeches of giant guns in a museum of technological fantasies. Little by little, sometimes dreamily or capriciously, he had collected words, pictures, or mnemonic talismans of interest only to himself—of "sentimental value" in insurance jargon—to a locked "fire-proofed" four-drawer cabinet in his penthouse study near the position he usually took when standing at his sliding-glass balcony with drawn curtain, to gaze down upon the city's throbbing waterfront. Gretta was not ordinarily invited into this

outer sanctum of professional implements and symbols; but sometimes she was asked to assist in the disposition of unembarrassing
items that he gradually organized in intermittent reveries about a
nearly completed life.

But one day after a dream that he could not remember except
for its mood he excitedly began to dig with vigor, like a dog that
suddenly takes it into his head to find something in a particular
spot of tide-washed sand on the beach. Has it noticed the almost
imperceptible squirt of an embedded clam? It had occurred to him,
as he was reminded of his old steam tugboat by its puny diesel sim-
ulacrum that served as the trailing pilot boat for a reefer ship
making its way to sea through Dogtown's outer harbor, to search
the annual "little black books" he had accumulated before the series
of them had been interrupted by his wartime service.

As a Norumbega student with no important restraint upon his
personal expenditures the young Finn had signed up for lifetime
membership in the academically specialized retail establishment
known as the Norumbega Cooperative Society, or "The Bega
Coop", whose compact department store dominated Norumbega
Square, and whose policy was to distribute profits (if any) to its
members after automatically issuing to all of them an annual
pocket diary with all sorts of guiding information about the ensuing academic year, which loosely paralleled and overlapped the
Society's fiscal cycle, along with its main body of unused spaces for
anticipating and logging daily events, beginning and ending with
blank pages for distant anticipations or significant phone numbers
and addresses, or occasional ad lib remarks about anything at all.
Thus before he was commissioned in the Navy he'd grown progressively accustomed to relying on this little black book for quotidian
convenience. But once on the move and obliged to travel light,
with no permanent desk on land or sea—not even in a Bachelor
Officer Quarters [B O Q] when he came back to Unabridge for his
postgraduate studies at the Vinland Institute of Polytechnics
[V I P]—the little black book had become indispensable. To the
verge of absurdity he maintained the names and addresses he
needed or might need during each ensuing year, especially for
affairs or potential affairs of the accelerated heart. He dreaded the
annual chore of chirological transposition because he was of such
sanguine temperament that one might have called him a perennial
Boy Scout of Eagle rank. So with many years of experience in
almost continuous lightfooted or unpredictable peregrination and

numerous transitory personal communications, some of them at times officially confidential, he found it impracticable to maintain a bulky perennial address book; he'd devised and habituated himself to depend almost solely upon a single little black book for his shirt pocket and a series of predecessors in his impedimenting footlockers ashore. With this foresight he hoped to reconstruct data of the past, even if seldom earlier than a year or two beyond those in his current baggage.

This set of uniform booklets, each 4 inches in length × 2½ inches in width × ⅜ inch in thickness of storage space, was usually kept as the latest two or three years of condensely coded experience with him, but even before the War was over there were twenty years of mnemonic treasure in 72 square inches of safe-deposit drawer of half a dozen times that capacity for souvenir letters and flat legal documents, but after the War in which Finn lost several of his little black books with the sinking of a cruiser he grew far less faithful to the full practice of this idiosyncratic routine because in a series of offices ashore he usually had electromechanical conveniences for security.

. . . She invited me in for a cup of tea, apparently unaware that it was not a very attractive brew even for gentlemen of the Navy. She defended her embarrassment at the contrast between my neat attire and her Bohemian atmosphere by talking continuously with her back to me in the kitchen as she got going with the teakettle while according to her directions I sat with my head uncovered in the single easy chair of the skylighted studio. In the dimmest corner was a wide bed whose disordered covers she had hastily rolled over the open triangle of sheets. My heart sank as I noticed a man's necktie that she had overlooked on a bed post. The place still smelled of wood smoke, and the tidied-up aftermath of her recent fire was evident. Much of the woodwork and furniture—mainly a bookcase, a large all-purpose table, and a few wooden chairs—was smudged with carbon. Thanks to the painter's northerly fenestration, on midsummer's afternoon— abetted by large windows at the gable's far end, with interesting glimpses of the inner harbor close by—this airy living space was cheerful without a glare, a studio swept bright withal. Considering her recent fire I could see that she was not a sloppy housekeeper characteristically. But I was chastened by envy of the neck that wore the tie. At first it took an effort not to betray the sullen self within what she called my resplendent raiment.

Conversation and admiration soon drove away my instinctive jealousy. I forget what started it all, but she sounded religious at heart, or at least romantic, even as she cheerfully expressed fears for her safety. "The Lord

*will provide." she said. She believed that someone had broken into her base-
ment to start the fire in a coal bin next to the furnace. I couldn't quite make
out whom she suspected but she clearly didn't trust the police or the fire
inspector who'd recorded the fire as an accident, with what she called the
implication that she was an irresponsible tenant—"an untenable tenet", she
laughed, because her reputation among friends was that of a conscientious
and self-sufficient artist, allowing for the fact that she was a bold single
woman generally misunderstood for her independent criticism of authority,
at least as I read between the lines.. At that time I was still too susceptible
to the frisson of piquant Bohemian company, and in those days I must have
shared some of society's shock at a woman's simple frankness. Yet her voice
was low and temperate, her critical intelligence seemed rationally conciliatory, her beautiful unpainted Anglo-Celtic face was aristocratically
refined, and her very slightly plump blonde body was very nearly as ideal
as any platonic man could wish. I remember regretting that I had to take
the Admiral's tall daughter to the Gloucestermas dance that very night.*

*"This must have been a fine place for painting!" I said, or some bro-
mide to that sincere affect it had upon me.*

*Then I think I heard her say, with my encouragement: "I'm no painter
now! Never really was. Only a miserable illustrator. I was clever as a
child, making pretty pictures for my poems and stories, and it went to my
head. After art school started painting for money. Knew in my heart the
vanity of selling meretricious talent is a sin against the Holy Ghost!
Angered God. He sent the fire to finally get it through my head that I'm no
visual artist. He hates false art. But this IS a good studio for writing,
now that I've cleared out all the colorful junk." She laughed to make me
think she wasn't serious. "Last week I finished giving all my undamaged
art materials—paints, stretchers, canvas, and all to the high school, and
sent all the useless junk to the city dump. I've been scrubbing up ever since.
But now it's exhilarating to have a clear creative conscience! My imagination is fully liberated for the first time since school graduation!"*

*At first I had seemed to strike her as some sort of unimaginative Spar-
tan, but her polite questions about me were genuinely curious after she heard
that my distant paternal forebears were Manx, and that I'd visited the Isle
of Manannan itself, her legendary "navel of the British archipelago", out
of genealogical curiosity when my ship was docked in Liverpool for some
exercises with the British fleet. She identified that Isle as King Arthur's
Avalon, and offered her opinion that he'd died there in Lancelot's Castle of
the Holy Grail! Of course I didn't believe that, if only because I'd actually
visited half a dozen of Arthur's burial spots, but at that time I was as
chronologically vague as she was in conflating Geoffrey of Monmouth's his-*

torical King Arthur with the Arthur in Chrétien de Troyes's age of the romances, to say nothing of our uncertainty about the date of the Romance of the Rose *(that I have since read as a great algebra of analogy), an English edition of which lay upon her table under a Chaucer anthology among her writing materials and dictionaries of French and English. In both languages at least I recognized the names and titles!*

It was one of the early occasions on which I blessed my stars for having chosen to educate myself in elective liberal arts at Norumbega instead of close-order drill at the Port Royal Naval Academy or arbalests and mangonels at Vinland Polytechnic. I don't mean to say that's because classical poetry was handy for ensorcelling fair readers—though sometimes I've found it so—or because of sweet nostalgia for my sophomoric youth, but because it reminded me that it was not too late to recover, simply by reading, my interest in the literature I had had to curtail when I chose discipline, organization, ships, electricity, power, and masculine adventure. When I was a student of engineering science at Norumbega, after some secondary schooling in Classics, I understood from compeers in its cultivated milieu that the teaching of their English Literature practically left off with Milton.. At sea I had read nothing but modern novels now often considered classic and soon forgotten, but after that unforgettable encounter in 1934 I began to make up some time as a common reader.

Suddenly I wanted to plunge with her into talk of Chaucer, Shakespeare, and all the rest that I'd tasted only in "survey course" smatterings! She infused me for the first time in my life with a curious longing for the imaginative matter that was driving her in exaltation or desperation—I couldn't tell which—to abandon a career in commercial art for the much greater insecurity—the very hopelessness—of narrative poetry, which she apparently now believed to have been her authentic talent from early youth when she had filled notebooks with poems about the lost lands of Arthur and Lancelot. But she was exuberantly realistic enough not to expect a livelihood from what she intended to call her first Dogtown Cycle! As an autodidact she had never been coached in a college at all, and I the semi-Norseman remembered just enough of the professor's histrionic recitation of bits from the Canterbury Tales *to be able to speak of meter with feminine endings (much to my suppressed amusement at the term) and to help her translate the printed Middle English words to approximately rhythmic sound—after halting in some laughing attempts at* The Parliament of Fowls *and* The Legend of Good Women, *which at the time were what most interested her as models. She was very pleased with my apologetic promptings.*

I discovered that her romanticism was critically ambivalent—sometimes as ironic and comic as Chaucer's. It was my spontaneous response to her enthusiastic touch on my wrist as we sat opposite each other laughing at animation that grounded our sublimations in unison.

Though by then I'd judged that she was no prude, I needn't have hesitated for fear of seeming to take unfair advantage of her cerebral preoccupation, or of her presumed loyalty to an absent Troilus. But Resistance, as Guillaume de Lorris might have said, was sound asleep; Jealousy had evidently left his post early that morning. . . . I was relieved to notice how much care she took even in our awakened lust not to let my lily-whites get wrinkled or soiled. She took the time to hang them carefully in her closet as I surreptitiously kicked the green-striped crimson necktie out of sight under the bed. . . .

After the two-backed beast's artfully prolonged ascent to reciprocal crescendo and another half-hour's contented aftermath of dreamily subsiding beatitude she suddenly stiffened in my arms as she remembered that she had to dash out to the corner to get some shampoo for washing her hair before she expected to be escorted by a "scientific divinity student" to the Gloucestermas costume dance at Long Rocks (which I was also slated to attend with the beautiful boring daughter of the Admiral). Promising to be back in a few minutes she was soon on her way in a whirlwind, leaving me to spruce up in the bathroom. There, as I turned to find a towel after washing my hands, my eye was caught among the clutter on a shelf by a brown bakelite casing of size and shape associated in my inward eye with prospective reassurance. But when I impulsively shed my conventional compunction as an anointed gentleman and opened the cartridge I found to my alarm that it was not empty. It was snugly occupied by a flexibly rimmed elliptical membrane of fuscous color and dimensions that I judged designed for a nulliparous conic section, neatly packed and dried with powder according to the usual directions for such storage. Of course I've never been one to knowingly enter the nettled Garden of Nature after visiting the Garden of Inanna. The need for my "precaution" had been casually waved off when I'd paused to reach for my secret pocket as I handed over my clothes for hanging up before we'd joined in bed. "Don't worry," she'd said. "I hate those ungodly things!"

*

One day Finn Macdane gives lunch to Fay Gabriel and Tessa Opsimath, prepared and joined by Gretta Doloroso in the spacious kitchen of his penthouse. In order to avoid attracting too much attention to her exploitation of friendship Tessa has resolved to refrain everywhere from mentioning the year 1934 or the name

Mary (or Moira or Trevisa or Tremont), but of course as a sleuth she's hardly disinterested when Caleb's economic insecurity is brought up by Fay, who's been discreetly worried about his prospects for housing and livelihood as his domestic terminus ad quem approaches. The unspoken but mistaken sense of his friends is that he himself worries as little about such personal matters as he does about selling his Gilgamesh script.

Now Finn by virtue of heritage nurture and career is rarely sensitive to the ecomonic anxieties of ordinary strugglers, and is likely to consider the question absurd in a case such as Caleb's whose experience and abilities are so evident that one takes for granted that it's just a matter of choice among the world's offers—even without a degree in Business Administration or some kind of engineering. But Finn has been interested in the man's Synectic Method of Diagnostic Correlation as an idea perhaps worthy of being worked into the Universal Systems Theory movement. He has also weighed the possibility of contributing to both technological and social progress by helping Caleb get some sort of grant or subsidy for the leisure to pursue his ideas independently right here in Dogtown. Finn understands Caleb's weakness at tooting his own horn to complacent specialists, and as the sympathetic elder he respects that handicap. He has lived long enough not to fight the crotchets and maggots of creative or erudite friends whose idiosyncracies justify his toleration of their stubborn resistance to rational suggestions for their own advantage. But he himself is interested in the prospect of personal collaboration, once the absurd Sumerian chimera is laid to rest.

Gretta has no notion of such an abstruse subject, and Tessa cares little for the mystification of numbers; but Finn is confident that Fay, though at some higher level of generalization, appreciates his own appreciation of Caleb's abstractions. Even if Fay were to laugh at the concept of applying S M D C matrices to fictional systems as a means of examining the causal relativity of a real entity's real elements, he thinks, once Caleb's analytical technique is demonstrated and explained she will surely understand at least its potential advantages in a metaphysical study of social entities.

After mulling this possibility with expanding speculation as the wine and lobster are consumed—during reciprocally commiserating conversation about their dismal expectations of the new regime in Washington (which delights in virtuous attacks upon the common good), and trying somehow, by agreeing in grievance, to

comfort each other in face of the extravagance with which Atlantis
is exploiting the body and air of Mother Earth, seeing that despair
lacks Promethean governance to moderate the culture of advertising that continues more than ever to corrupt or starve the cultivation of education, notwithstanding their own civic hopes for
Dogtown—Finn waits for a relevant interstice in the ladies' conversation to change the subject.

Addressing Tessa he says: "If you'd like to move to a nicer
vacancy on the ground floor for your clients I've thought of turning
Endicott Krebs's suite into an apartment, assuming I can get the
necessary permits. The reality-estate management service takes care
of cleaning and all that, but landlording still takes too much of my
time. It ties me down. This building needs a whole cycle of repair
and improvement. So I'd like to get an occupying superintendent
who won't have many time-consuming duties but will take responsibility for the whole establishment as major domo and night
watchman—in return for free living quarters. Do you think Caleb
is too stiff-necked to accept the job after he finishes his play?"

Tessa smoothly considers the idea. "Apparently he had a job on
a lower level of something like that when he quit graduate school
in Hume."

"I thought he was a willing worker when he worked for Father
Duncannon." says Gretta. "He certainly did a lot of indoor office
jobs!"

Tessa bethinks herself. "But he'd still need some income to live
on. If he had to get another job elsewhere too I don't think he'd
want to live here. All he wants is productive leisure!"

"Yes, I suppose you're right. Maybe I'll ask the Mayor if there's
some little advisory contract he could provide."

"What good would that do?" Fay asks. "Caleb would only
engross himself in that, like a dog hungry to manage everything in
sight."

"Well, I won't give up on the idea. I'm still learning the ropes
of civilian management myself. He'd love a little bit of the most
interesting view in Dogtown."

It strikes Finn that he himself frequently exchanges even his
superior view of the harbor for Fay's ninety-degree horizon of the
Foreside where not only fishing boats but also passing tugs, barges,
and seagoing ships pass the Cape day and night—sometimes even a
sleek small Coast Guard cutter imitating Navy small craft. Lost
again in reverie, Finn gazes out through the double sliding doors of

double-paned glass to his fire escape balcony (which he admits he does not deserve as long as any painter goes without a studio) as the women admire his urban vantage. He is half aware that Fay and Tessa both speak with the kind of low intelligent voice that has almost first attracted him to almost all the women he'd admired. (He's usually agreed with Caleb's such generalized opinions.)

His eyes pause at the lantern of the stubby lighthouse on Parliament Island just beyond the Net & Twine on the shoals at the tongue's lip of the inner harbor. At the moment there's not a bird in sight on the uninhabited island but its frequent cacophony of colonial sea-beards always brings to mind Chaucer's ambivalent Parliament of Fowls, which the islet had been named for (according to what that imaginative woman of Gloucestermas 1934 had told him) by the liberally educated 17C Tudor clergyman who slyly stole a march on the pious dissenters who later exiled him forcefully, seeing that he'd already affixed other names for the King's Atlantean cartographer. Nowadays in foggy weather it's from that deserted bit of rock and grass and human ruins that he hears like a voice from Avalon the mournful diaphone of compressed air emitting "a strong note of low tone ending with a definite grunt", which many indigines resented as the replacement of the traditional warning bell that he heard in 1934. No living person is now required there to operate either bell or light, which are automatically controlled from the Cape's one remaining manned lighthouse on Crow Point far out by the breakwater. Even in 1934 the Coast Guard base for "flying boats" on the island had been abandoned, for they hadn't been effective in enforcing the law of Total Abstinence.

The ghostly moan also reminds him that he and Caleb shared a lifelong inability to sing.

16

TABLET

THIRTEEN

[Badly damaged]

[An open space suggesting buried ruins on a truncated hill. **Widow 2** (as a ragged crone) kneels with a fire-drill and a piece of socketed soapstone before an open fireplace and cooking pot, upstage left, near the inchoate statue of Engidu made by Gilgamesh in Tablet 10, now chipped and discolored beyond casual recognition. Engidu's bannerstone is set before it. Nearby stands the stone gnomon of a primitive sundial. **Berosus** in his usual position.]

BEROSUS	This high dune has been piled up and flattened by winds of sand swirling in contention. There is no evidence of the forlorn hamlet below it. The old woman formerly served as a priestess in the temple of Inanna (now known as Ishtar). She performs as a sacristine, preparing for a special liturgy of intercession as she addresses the effigy.
WIDOW 2 [As if meditating aloud.]	Nimrod, you were once our mighty hunter. If this day we are spared the bolts of heaven save us from slow starvation. We have served Inanna with the utmost means of our destitution. Humble offerings cannot measure our devotion. Listen to the frail voices of our faltering dance. Do not

scorn the sacrificial tithes of our withered sustenance. Not a sheep or goat is left to offer. Instead the Optimates will bring seed cakes made with the sweepings of our barley. Dust is the only flour for bread we eat. The sun has sucked dry our well. A wineskin of river water is our libation.

*Gilgamesh, nearly unrecognizable in desert dress, carrying his axe, **enters** from downstage right. [Until he speaks the Widow is unaware of his presence.]*

—Let Inanna lay her hands upon your head as savior of her people. Plead that our sins have been thrust upon us. We always disavowed the sacrilege attributed to your name in error, but have too long suffered for. Only she can petition the Lord Enlil to absolve our submission to alien power and rescind impending doom.

—Pity the infirmity of our priest and the confusion of ancient Optimates; forgive the decline of women and the ignorance of men born too late to know how far we have fallen.

—I myself have barely strength enough to make this tinder hot. My husband used to say that I could inflame a rock.

GILGAMESH Madam, do not be afraid. Can you tell me where I am? I am out of place in this naked landscape, and in time as well!

WIDOW 2 Well, you did startle me; it's been a long time since we've seen a stranger. But I can no longer fear any whispering man or daylight wraith. Speak up! I can still hear with one ear.

GILGAMESH Why do you live in arid desolation?
[Louder.]

WIDOW 2 I stay on this sand hill to haunt it. You can't call it living, under the pitiless sky of a second widowhood, surviving much too long both daughters born to a soldier of fortune. They put a stop to happy memory.

GILGAMESH Who, your own children?

WIDOW 2 The Elamites who raped them to death.

GILGAMESH Why did they attack a godforsaken place like this? They are known to sack for riches.

WIDOW 2 For revenge. Once before they had seized this place but were driven out by others.

GILGAMESH So, wreaking vengeance on your gods?

WIDOW 2 On us, for calling Kassites to displace them as our masters.

GILGAMESH All for a knoll of sand half a mile from the river!

WIDOW 2	Euphrates was so angry about our canals and watergates that he changed his course.
GILGAMESH	I see no trace of irrigation works.
WIDOW 2	When fields are parched the floods level dikes and fill canals.
GILGAMESH	So famine was the bane?
WIDOW 2	The gods don't like artificial plenty. The farmers had to dig according to a dictator's plans. After he was gone our crops grew feeble, but it wasn't because they had failed to maintain the works. They discovered that the gods had sterilized their irrigated fields with salt.
GILGAMESH	Why do you stay up here without shade or shelter? Haven't you a village?
WIDOW 2 [Grunts a bitter laugh and points stage left.]	"Village" is a term too noble! Our hovels are down below. This windy summit is the sunken crown of a citadel that once gathered clouds. Sandstorms spun this tumulus over rubble. You now stand where stood a nuptial bed lifted to the Lord God who has long since cursed us.
GILGAMESH	I grieve for every one of mankind's losses. Some day, if I can in this dream of mine, I'll help you recover—if I find my own city translated to the New World. But my memory of landscape is confused by too much travel. What do you call this place?
WIDOW 2	It's known as Warka to the caravans that now avoid it.
GILGAMESH	A name I never heard.
WIDOW 2	Naturally; since you're a stranger, like almost every other man on earth.
GILGAMESH	I thought I could get a better view by beaching my boat and climbing this hill, but the horizon doesn't seem any different from up here. Have you ever heard of Erech? If it's in this dream at all it must be further downstream than I estimated.
WIDOW 2 [Looking at him narrowly and hesitating.]	Oh, the nomads used to call this Erech! . . . The real name was Uruk, as women named it when the earth was young.
GILGAMESH [Laughs.]	Your folks must have copied that lore. It's not surprising as a common kind of ekistic echo. Uruk is a famous city, emulated everywhere. A place to be celebrated with namesakes!

WIDOW 2
[Snorting. She
labors with fire-
drill on soapstone
socket.]

I doubt that, mister. A name reviled everywhere between the great two rivers! Disowned by our own Inanna and blighted by the highest god! We don't boast of names that label discord. You are a remarkably hapless traveler to find yourself here on the day of judgment. I am making ready for the liturgy by kindling pure new fire, as my husband was taught in his religion. I'll never be too inured by the fate of women to tremble at what anyone's gods still have in store.

GILGAMESH

What distinguishes today for fear?

WIDOW 2

Our priest's oracle has warned that the moon will come like cancer to eat our sun at noon today, in retribution for the night this month when the sun stole upon the moon to suppress our brightest light. When gods dispute each other the catastrophe is always human.

GILGAMESH

Everywhere, even in ages of famine and sorrow, both such prodigies have always been idle threats, followed by neither gain nor loss. But your priest is a very good astrologer if he can predict of the omens themselves. They at least can have nothing to do with the sins of a single spot in the wilderness!

WIDOW 2

I remember that kind of unbelief when we were ruled by a godless khan. I tell you, this is no ordinary pile of crumbled clay!

GILGAMESH

You are remembering other people's dreams of another place. I know very well how that can be. I too find myself old. In fact I may be dreaming what you say! But I hope I can provide for you after I find my way back to the real Uruk. Didn't I hear you say that river is Euphrates? —But I can't understand why it would be so hard to see a tile-clad tower stepping halfway up to heaven even from as far away as Tigris is.

WIDOW 2
[Squinting up from
her work.]

You now stand upon that landmark, old dreamer! On this dilapidated platform the priestess of Inanna was dedicated queen by the Lord of heaven. The blows of gods and follies of men have reduced it to the dust of clay that once elevated it to the bottom of heaven. From fields that once fed a wealth of trade you have climbed a skirt of windblown dirt!

GILGAMESH
[Peering in all
directions.]

Can it be? And a whole city in this ruins too? You can't bewitch me, woman!

WIDOW 2   The walls were first to fail, undermined by floods no longer controlled to our advantage. Temple and palace crumbled. Then all our houses dissolved in mud. Our false prosperity left us desiccated ruins after the waters withdrew. When I was a little girl, before the khan and his northmen forced us to build those great monuments and gates, we were content with powerless rounds of toil and custom. By delivering us from enemies and raising us to glory he brought upon us grief and shambles!

GILGAMESH   This cannot be a lifetime's dream!

WIDOW 2   I was once a happy mother, but one affliction after another has humbled me to the state you see. Yet my widowhood and child-bereavement was no worse than the loss of our queen to the raiders who carried her off for a ransom that only Babylon might afford.

GILGAMESH   Had she no protection? Where were the Kassites then!

WIDOW 2
[Leaves her work to look more closely at his face, just as he takes sudden interest in the statue and bannerstone, walking across diagonally and dropping his axe to examine them on his knees. But with face averted he stops to listen closely.]

They were loyal palatines, but when we all began to believe that the tyrant who bound them to Uruk would never return they lost confidence in their waning power. He was no longer here to inspire general respect for foreign mercenaries. Off duty they were tormented by the people. Most of them were past their prime. By then their captain Norkid had become the queen's beloved consort, her source of secular power—her brave and just advisor, always guided by what he thought Gilgamesh would have wished; but his sword was no match for a hundred pitchforks in an alley of assassins while his few warriors were defending us at the walls. My husband was one of those devoted martyrs.

GILGAMESH   So Norkid's loyalty had as many edges as my axe! He occupied in full the place of his khan!

WIDOW 2
[Gets up to pace about the stage behind him with increasing interest.]

Why do you try to conceal your knowledge of our former times.

GILGAMESH   I remember you. Your man was Norkid's bravest.
—This numinous stone is Engidu! By the hand of Gilgamesh. Uncorrupted by worms or suppuration, free of posthumous filth! No carrion to mourn!

WIDOW 2

Enter Shepherd 1,
downstage right
from below, out of
breath, standing
still to listen
unseen, armed with
slingshot and
javelin.

Engidu is a name forgotten. This is Nimrod the hunter, protector of my people, resurrected from his grave. —But I grieve no more for this dead Nimrod than for that vanished Nimrod who buried this one. It was he who led my husband to me and all my sorrows. So tell me no more! I want to guess nothing about you! But I warn you to go back to your boat before it's too late. You are imperilled by people who abominate all strangers, fixed in the hatred of fatal heresies implanted by foreigners who flouted their sacred law. The remaining citizens are old, but they are fierce, with too many stones and pitchforks even for a demigod. Save yourself from ignominious death. Then at least you may keep alive for humankind the memory of—whatever causes your quest.

GILGAMESH
[Looking up at her.]

Is reason a false shadow of the world we really live in?

WIDOW 2

The people here may now have forgotten that I left the service of Inanna to marry a Kassite, but when there were no Troopers left they would have murdered my children if the Elamites hadn't speared them first. In folk memory the name Nimrod has come to mean either Gilgamesh or Engidu. But our implacable Rector isn't confused. He doesn't forget the details of humiliation under the regime that usurped his authority. What's left of my barren life, which I cherish only to remember its few truncated years of fruit, depends more upon his spark of charity for me than upon my sacerdotal craft. —Unlike our former king you appear to have no army to implement your offers of protection.

GILGAMESH

My latest army seems to have immolated himself to Inanna in Babylon.

WIDOW 2

I dare not speak well of Gilgamesh within local earshot, but I will say to you it was not his fault that my people refused to see the common good in which he left them. He broke the Tablets of Fate for the sake of liberating those who now remember nothing of him but their hatred. I am so used to the cumulating weight of terror and sorrow that I could not bear even an ounce of illusive hope, but if you should find that Gilgamesh is still alive somewhere in a world that I cannot imagine, tell him that at least two of Uruk's women, one high, the other low, did appreciate his reign.

GILGAMESH   You and the queen?

WIDOW 2   Lil-Amin and I. —Go to your boat, I say, before someone steals it! —I do not recognize you, but the priest's eyesight is not quite gone, and his enmity is enriched by four decades of vitriolic brooding. —So hurry down the way you came, stranger! He will soon be up here with the congregation. Even in this shrunken parish he can rile a plethora of fanatic men and ignorant sons to overpower an unprotected interloper, not to mention his gang of pious women with a bottomless supply of ceramic shards. If you haven't entirely lost your senses, sir, don't stand here and reminisce. Turn back while the day is still young. Get to your boat before someone steals it. —I can say no more! I cannot listen to you! I have no more wish to share the curse upon a man's head than I had to bring it down upon him!

GILGAMESH   I am very sorry that you've suffered so much for what seemed a heartless regime. —Perhaps it really was.

WIDOW 2
[Points upward.]   There's the first kite crossing the sun! Hurry, or you're lost indeed!

SHEPHERD 1
[Showing himself.]   No, an eagle! Good omen.

GILGAMESH   Dumuzi! You restore my faith in Eber's tribe! Has the princess of Babylon already had enough of your innocence?

SHEPHERD 1   No. Enheduanna sent me to learn the story for her poem. I was only a day behind your wake and spoor. This morning I found your empty boat and saw you in the distance clambering up this hill like a goat-hunter.

GILGAMESH   How long have you been standing there?

SHEPHERD 1   Long enough to hear what my mistress thought might be concealed by a mysterious trader. Apparently I'm as good at choosing a hero as I am at making love. Those are the two reasons she wants me back.

WIDOW 2
[She indicates stage right.]   Quiet, boy! I hear the procession coming up from the village! I won't give you away if you lie down and listen behind that pile of rubble. No matter what happens, don't look up at the sky! Perhaps you at least will be spared as witness of our doom. The story will be all that's left of us, and should be told in Babylon.

GILGAMESH

[Shepherd 1
crouches in hiding.
Gilgamesh passes
him the IRTH to
wear on his neck.]

Not the end of us, but another beginning! Engidu has been restored to me because I have breasted the arrow of time. In former life I broke up the council of gods and altered fate, but I have never despised them—only their submission to fate. I can face mutiny without your help. Yet if in my pursuit I've been mistaking death for time, you must save yourself to save my life as legend. Take my Isorectotetrahedron as proof to Enheduanna that you were here to verify the transfiguration of Uruk!

BEROSUS

Rector enters
stage left, solemnly
but nearsightedly, **with Optimates leading a number of men and women.** His clothes are shabby but he is still a powerful figure, wearing some shabby remains of ecclesiastical vestments. He carries the royal Rod and Ring.
[They do not notice Gilgamesh but form behind the Rector in a semicircle as he stands and genuflects to the Nimrod idol. Music by Berosus.]

The priest shows himself, rising head first from the hillside, followed by Optimates and people.

RECTOR

[He drops the Rod
and Ring to take up
the axe. Quickly
peers about but sees
neither the banner-
stone nor
Gilgamesh.]

Ahh! . . . A sinful omen to portend this hour's judgment of our fate? My eyes are half-burnt by study of the sun but I can see what I feel in my hand! What was Engidu's bannerstone is now the hateful axe that I know as well as my daily prayer even after forty years! —Woman—defrocked Widow—is this the deed of a god? Or some nefarious trick of yours? I've never trusted the renewal of your vows!

WIDOW 2

Your Grace! The axe was here when I arrived this morning. I thought you had done magic during the night. I dared not touch that strange axe.

RECTOR

[Turns to point
immediately at
Gilgamesh before
the others follow his
gaze.]

That axe is no stranger to me than Nimrod himself! I can smell his aura better than you can see the sky. There's been a change of air up here! Is this abomination a sign he's out of my reach in death? Or can it be that I'm to have my life's revenge before it ends?

—Look around, all you fools! This axe wasn't dropped from heaven!

—There he is, usurper of my glebe! Defiler of the temple and enemy of the gods! Murderer of godgiven Engidu!

—But look, now he has no Traders or Troopers for schemers and bodyguards! No Eber to dispense invented law, no Norkid to execute decrees by force! Can't you see he's helpless? There are no longer any Eberews or Kassites to corrupt our language and defy the customs handed down by Inanna!

Several men hurry off, after some hesitation. [He draws a knife and hands it to Widow 2. Gilgamesh is surrounded by the remaining people.]

—Quick, some of you, fetch the hunting net! We may be spared at the last moment! Hurry! The unavenged gods themselves have led their enemy to us for immolation. In this last hour of doomsday we have in our hands the offering to expiate the pollution that has brought our city to the verge of extinction.

—Here, this is work for a female priest. It's long since we've had flesh of any kind to sacrifice! The gods could not ask for better!

WIDOW 2

But that is human blood! And if it's Gilgamesh's, said to be mingled with the blood of gods! The oldest laws forbid sacrifice of any victim that can plead in language!

RECTOR

Don't argue, woman! It's nearly noontime! The Lord Enlil grants sacerdotal discretion to carry out his will. Demigod or antigod, Gilgamesh has attacked the gods we serve. But our atonement will fail if we don't work swiftly!

—Strike once and collect his blood. I'll do the rest. Meanwhile stoke the fire to illuminate our Nimrod in the dark of the sun. Remember that this is the tyrant who violated our queen Lil-Amin, my lost sister. —At last he faces me without the powers of force!

GILGAMESH

[Suddenly steps forward and seizes the Rod and Ring.]

Yes, my implacable adversary, I am alone, no longer tireless or confident in my body's strength, but I do not plead. You are unfit for government, even in its service to your gods. Against your will I built up Uruk, made it a ladder halfway up to heaven, taught it record-keeping and how to plan. I left the city famous for its prosperous peace. You have let it fall to ruin amidst fields of poisoned soil that once fed flocks and herds as well as populations through good years and bad. Always in the name of a religion made hateful you mouthed abhorrence of reason and harbored conspiracy against the sovereignty I earned by driving out those who had actually enslaved your people. For Lil-Amin's sake I was too forgiving of your vengeful sedition, ignoring Eber's advice to scotch you at the roots.

—I did not set out to retrieve the Rod and Ring of a polity that's been poisoned by your pious hatred of changes made for the common good, but now that I find the beginning of my journey at its end I must do exactly that. I resume kingship over the ruins of my works wiser in the mystery of time. I have been at fault for pursuing my private thoughts and absenting myself from the constructive government of a discontented and selfish public that prefers the servitude of rote religion. I will begin again by sharing the wretched poverty to which you have reduced your congregation, but with less confidence in time the carrier of hope.

RECTOR

[Indicating the sundial.]

Time! There's no time now to hear more of your conceited folly! When that shadow passes zenith the Tablets of Fate you smashed in ostentation will be at last fulfilled! You will be dead before the sky grows dark.

GILGAMESH

[Addressing all the people.]

Without me, if heaven spares you the desert will not. There's only lingering death in your feeble efforts to survive. I'll make a softened calendar to strengthen and protect your—

RECTOR

No doubt with softened plans to pacify the gods! With the imposition of barbarous new tongues! With softened kilns of stinking naphtha from the devil's jakes to fire godsent clay! With softened rules and regulations, softened tolerance in specifications, and softened work-orders for the human machine! All under a haughty despot's softened lash!

GILGAMESH

Despot, perhaps—but no longer haughty, if I ever was.

RECTOR

You've trapped yourself on the apex of your orgulous architecture!

GILGAMESH

Time's circle ends where it begins—if this is really Uruk that I stand upon, if reason is disproved by fact, if the cosmos is irrational, or if logic's altered in duration! I now reset my mind. But I do not find the queen to whom I delegated power, only you her dissenting brother. That royal priestess was of more worth than all the power and glory of a shining tower, impregnable walls, elite archers, productive treasury, regulated canals, public granaries, and every art but those she made her own. You still claim leadership of the people and the sanction of heaven, so you I blame for the greatest loss of all.

RECTOR

[Incensed.]

You abandoned her! Your guards failed to protect her! I had no men-at-arms. Do not claim her love!

GILGAMESH

Men return with a gathered net. [With the help of others, directed by the Rector's gestures, they close in on Gilgamesh.]

I left this kingship to the queen, not to a narrow-minded clergyman. I need claim nothing more. This woman, here, who served in her temple may remember that Lil-Amin and I were of one mind. Even Engidu could not share that!

RECTOR	Now I'd like to see your nostrils flare! The late Captain Norkid said the air around you used to glow in battle warp. Show us the red corona of your reputed fury!
WIDOW 2 [Gilgamesh exchanges the Rod and Ring for the knife.]	Here, take this knife! It's not for me to kill a hero. Cut the net and run!
OPTIMATES & PEOPLE	[Hostile commotion of voice and gesture as they manage to throw the net over Gilgamesh.]

[The eclipse begins, gradually darkening the scene. Shepherd [Bewildered uproar. Cries of consternation and confusion at what may have seemed an unseen bolt from the sky.]
1 slings a bit of shard at a sector of the circle furthest from the Rector (who stands upstage right) and **kills Optimate 1**, thus diverting all attention from himself as he comes out of hiding to strike the Rector with his hurled javelin. **Optimate 2 seizes the axe.**]

RECTOR Rector dies.	Kill Gilgamesh!
SHEPHERD 1	Master, cut the net!
GILGAMESH [Shouts, gasping, as he futilely attempts to cut his way out of the net. The Opti- mates and people surround him in a spiral dance as the men tighten the net around Gilgamesh and the women batter him with shards, bricks, or staves.]	Run, Dumuzi! . . . I'm all right! —My life began with thunder in mountains far away. . . . These are not my gods . . . the people do not love me . . . but I have made this my place! . . . —Go make yours in Babylon! —If you disobey me, my head and heart will feed the kites and suffer common worms in vain! —My sempiternal public works have failed to last the lifetime of a man, but don't let my efforts vanish in the dust! . . . —I tell you, go! . . . Correct the memory of my love for Engidu! —Escape this mob. . . . —I don't claim fame for madcap feats . . . or for the love of Lil-Amin . . . but there will be space enough in time between my extinction and the world's . . . for arts not handed down from heaven! . . . —Don't let thoughts be lost to time. . . . You must be my voice until Enheduanna writes her poem. . . . Give the poet your words of mouth. . . .

—If you perish, I fail . . . but if you live, so shall I. . . .

[**Optimate 2 chops at Gilgamesh with the axe.**]
Shepherd 1 hesitates until the eclipse is total; then,
as Gilgamesh is hopelessly silenced, **runs off downstage** into the audience.

Gilgamesh dies. [Illumination slowly returns. As Optimates gather around
the Rector's body the people, jeering, heap dirt and shards upon Gilgamesh's body.]

WIDOW 2

[Plants the Rod, Ring, bannerstone, and axe (head upright) in or upon the burial mound.]

He did not die in exile. Some day they will mourn their king. Unless our dance is broken I am only the first to decorate his tomb. Here the rainbow ends. Not all things change: this hill will last forever.

BEROSUS

[As full light returns.]

Three millennia have inherited an illiterate boy's witness. Let the world's remaining centuries preserve this version of the legend.

17

CACHALOT POINT

Memorial Day

1.

on TM

[8:00–8:30 AM, Caleb's Contemplative Nullification,
fasting, shades drawn, in his straight-back chair,
ankles crossed, fingers loosely knitted, eyes closed]

Granting from his own experience the physiological benefits of basic
Contemplative Nullification [C N], Caleb no longer troubled himself with objections to the symbol-system upon which it was
founded. Deeta Dana had introduced him as a private practitioner
even after he'd made it clear that he was simply a persuaded empiri-
cist who had no intention to pursue the Science of Cosmic
Consciousness either physically or spiritually. In open honesty the
Movement's recruiters ordinarily expected as much of its skeptical
initiates, asking them to believe no more than that it was possible to
clear their minds in learning how to relax and improve their health.
They themselves were commissioned as believers—teachers and ini-
tiators—to make the most of enquirers' motives. The benefits of

daily C N at the beginning level would continue as long as one continued the self-rewarding practice of the primary procedure. Before initiation (with its several refreshing lessons) it was considered not necessary to tell catechumens that further steps toward Indian Enlightenment, to be led by teachers at any of many C N Centers, at further cost, would be proposed by mail with printed matter and free lectures. Otherwise the quasi-religious metaphysics of Guru Nil's doctrine remained undisclosed to those who did not seek participation in the Unified Field of Pure Knowledge by mastering the advanced techniques that facilitated such collegiate experience as levitation or by such perfect unity of meditative fellowship that discordant urban masses could be discernibly pacified unaware.

The Unified Field of consciousness was what Caleb called a continuum of subject, awareness, and object—equivalent, it was claimed, to the scientifically accepted unified field theory of quantum physics, if not indeed an aspect of it!

Deeta herself was an advanced student and teacher of C N, well qualified to initiate Caleb as a personal friend, waiving the considerable fee. He would have given short shrift to anyone else who'd offered scientific spirituality. For him this anti-thermodynamic cosmology derived from a Vedic "inner Self" was not only a reasonably paradigmatic version of what Father Duncannon had criticized in Christianity as deliberate "extrication" of the psyche from the troubles and uncertainties of objective reality, ignoring or misunderstanding religion's social origin, as well as discrediting Guru Nil's own socially benign objective as an affect of radically subjective individualism; but even as reified metaphor drawn from physics it was a meretricious "fallacy of misplaced concreteness" (as Whitehead would have called it), presenting a modishly acceptable adaptation—even improvement—of certain practices and doctrines in genuine Vedic traditions directed to mystic personal enlightenment in a system like Yeats's, which was refuted by the cosmic Second Law of thermodynamics, since it did not account for the irreversible arrow of time flying toward shapeless disorder, despite all counterentropic eddies of form or evolution by subsytems—as well as the Third Law that will finally tax unto death all the available energy of creation like a tiny undetected leak in the hull of a ship's lifetime at sea, driven either by wind or by steam, each in its own manner. *I'm a free radical in church and state, charged with counterentropy, too excited to be a good spy in the realm of Nullification, I hope—until I die!*

Yet isn't it remarkable that both the Guru and Father Dun were once physical science students of Mark Planck in Berlin!

Nevertheless, as a respectful but unambitious undergraduate in the neurophysiology of a Unified Field, the value of its tolerable discipline lay for Caleb in the degree to which it served as a private substitute for what he regarded as the flywheel of social ritual, but more or less according to circumstances of the moment. For him—as what Yeats (and Shakespeare) called a "mechanical" man whose spiritual sensibility was limited by a willfully rationalistic (or comical) sensorium—Guru Nil's freely associative method of meditation, as distinguished from the preceptive training of anagogic nullification by other Eastern methods such as those requiring exclusive concentration, and from such Western programs of spiritual insistence and regulation as those of the Cephasites, the brain's routine relaxation of flesh and muscle, relieved of obtrusive and reflexive objects without loss of attention to those that happened to present themselves as representations or ideas, and at liberty to explore considerations banal or sublime (even to visualize or wander), almost always rested his body and clarified his ensuing consciousness. C N was especially salutary in preparing—in making way indirectly to preparing—plans or decisions in the fully conscious objective world. Sometimes it seems to have afforded him ideas that would have escaped his play of mind in either wakefulness or dream.

For these reasons he remained grateful to Deeta his sincere proselyte and still attractive adept. Though his spiritual opposite, at one time she had been carnally active without reference to her practices in Eastern modes of poetry and painting subservient to varieties of yoga, shamanism, or other arcane doctrines. As the late Charlemagne's housekeeper she had captured Caleb's affection by her love of his dog Ibi-Roy, with whom she'd roamed Purdeyville many a day or even night with what seemed to transcend Western courage. No ethic of renunciation was required of man or dog, no striving for transcendence or belief.

But Caleb had not been disappointed in her modest assurances about C N. Now at a time when he still wholly refused the ideology of secular and religious extricationism, after having lost communication with the "Movement" in which Deeta had then earned much of her livelihood, as he steered clear of ulterior spiritual motives, he faithfully (though not always conveniently) continued twice-a-day C N as a practicable and mainly pleasant habit for the benefit of his psychosomatic health, though he had no confidence in the hint that all other things being equal it would extend the length of his life. Yet this skeptic of "spirituality" as any more than an epiphenomenon of mentality was one of very few among the years of seekers from all over North Atlantis who neither invested more in postgraduate advancement nor lapsed into permanent neglect of the primary practice of solitary C N after a few months of disappointed metanoia. For many initiates the regularity of it became a boring discipline that interfered with A D L [Activities of Daily Living] or curtailed time for entertainment. Privately he deplored the delinquents' misguided pursuit of heresy, magic, salvation, or psychotherapy. Most of those who'd paid the substantial fee in hope of the blissfully effortless Cosmic Subjectification cultivated by millennia of genuine Eastern genius soon found that the nuisance of observing a semi-diurnal schedule all by themselves without so much as music to ease their half-hours at it wasn't worth further investment in Sisyphean self-improvement. He guessed that only the vocational elite went on to higher levels of beneficent self-discipline, at great but apparently satisfactory cost in life's time and money, much of it in graduated residential courses of communal training and spiritual edification at the prosperous new Guru Nil University in the Corn Belt, which accumulated its handsome reality-estate capitol by providing, along with its own occult doctrines of cosmic intelligence, strictly virtuous tuition charges for degrees in Business Administration, as well as in everything else in the banausic world that it takes to be accredited as an institution of higher learning in the U S A. After all, in his opinion, the well-coached ability of brains to persuade themselves of almost any proposition, positive or negative (as in the West to believe in the categorical perniciousness of Jews or in the East to overlook man's inhumanity to man, or in the expectation of a Second Coming), sometimes under the suasion of charismatic liars, has also philosophized illusions no less true than faith in God as the purpose rather than the grace of Western Christianity, which in its usual election of individual immortality ignores human society as both the historical matrix and the proper entelechy of our orthodox religion. Over and over again sentimental patriotism has deceived our liberal democracy simply by way of diversion from perplexing uncertainties that otherwise demand cosmopolitan consideration of the common good.

As a persistent groundling in C N repetitions twice a day according to instructions Caleb made no attempt to control the object of his subjectivity in its reveries of relaxation. In this case, scarcely touching upon his assigned mantra to mark the transition of consciousness under his breath, his thought wandered from meditation upon C N itself to a general subject that was often the object of his diurnal speculations in ordinary life. The idea of Immediate Exclusive Consciousness [I E C]—his term for a useful but dangerous faculty of all brains—recurred in his rational speculations as a perfectly appropriate object for this especially subjective state of detached consciousness. *How the devil can you distinguish subject from object in this apperceptive conundrum?* So his daimon began to take advantage of this recurrently unlimited process by pondering an epistemology of limited consciousness, individual or collective, in the all-too-familiar temporal world wherein many different levels of scope and intensity conditioned action, habit, belief, criticism, imagination, peace, love, folly, or powerful response—especially when driven by the urge for expansion of its sphere. He remembered the Victorian maxim passed down to him by his mother as pedagogic parody:

> Good, better, best—
> Never let it rest
> 'Til your good is better,
> And your better best!

Bonus, melior, optimus.

The best for a group of cancer cells is bad for its flesh; excessively developed organs are not good for the whole body. Self-aggrandizement is detrimental to a family, a selfish class to a society. The optimization of wealth for one nation among many comes at the world's expense. The cost of perfection, like that of any counterentropic organism in the entropic universe, is a slightly more than equivalent dissipation of free energy from the subsystem in which it is embedded, which is itself another subsystem, in a series of larger and larger subsystems, closed only as the universe (assuming no God is larger). Every imaginary utopia would have been humanity's suboptimization, nourished by its global environment, just as a farmer's field of corn depletes its environment of soil unless its available energy is replaced from the region's nutrients, absorbing its water from the earth's ambience. As long as one political economy is unsatisfied with meliorization, allowing for the same in others, the global imbalance caused by optimization will malnourish the life of all flora and fauna except for those that also optimize themselves and disturb the existence of other species on Mother Earth, causing a slow loss of net-total usable energy to the nebular quanta of absolutely irrecoverable energy in a universal sinkhole. Caleb had to concede that our personal subsystems—symbols and artifacts, such as the dead-ending subsystem of his own life's experience *(one good drift of thought for C N!)*—can continue their virtual counterentropic optimizing defiance only as long as human society survives thermodynamic destiny by the meliorating grace of God!

Thus it has occurred to him that the spheres of Immediate Exclusive Consciousness may correspond to spheres of hierarchical subsystems. Ranging from the concentrated attention of a new mother, a laboratory microbiologist, a studio etcher, track-sprinter, or a lone low-tide clamdigger, a journalist, mayor, governor, president, Secretary of the United Nations, a batter at home plate with the bases loaded, or astronomer at her mountaintop telescope— judgments, decisions, actions, or new ideas are occasionally focused narrowly on limited circles within the spheres of all these brains, like a spotlight defined by utter darkness. *I've seen it in cats!* Each such circle or slit may enclose a virtual quasi-subsystem, perhaps too brief or limited in focus for history or philosophy—a reciprocal to the whole raft of reason, if not simply unreasonable!

Still, he sighed with amusement, *I've just demonstrated that reason as well as intuition may be at liberty in a receptive state of consciousness between pure nullification and exclusive objectivity. . . ! . . . This is not a bad reverie to expatiate in C N, to alternate with I E C. I haven't been dedicating passages of my arrow's flight twice a day these last few years without such intellectual compensation. . . . My schematics may be internally inconsistent—I'll think more on it when this trance is over—but the ontological hierarchy of systems and the epistemological hierarchy of consciousness seem to be unified in a metaphysics worth further testing—unlike an emotion recollected in tranquillity—if I don't forget these fugitive thoughts when I'm brutally conscious!*

That is, when his meditations were not occupied with randomly unrelated images from memory, plans for the day, grocery lists, political speculation, personal hopes for the future, betterment of sentences, or numerical recollections. His mantra itself was never an I E C. Thus, one way or another, aside from dreams in ordinary sleep, Caleb never reached the liberal limit of disembodiment.

Yet from the echoed obiter dicta and authorized publications of Guru Nil he was uncomfortably aware of the fact—since nothing is but the central nervous system makes it so—that artfully indirect management of the brain, even if not under coercion by external authority, could create its own sensations, its own reality, to the extent of faith in a virtual world. A certain kind of leader could make human beings believe themselves to be flying; and collectives of gnostic practitioners could persuade themselves even of their irenic effect upon exoteric urban populations who lacked the grace to keep peace among themselves. Guru Nil's paradoxical recognition of reality's common sense in his interpretation of Hindu tradition offered the view that the veil of Maya could well be expressed as a cosmology of the relativity and quantum physics established by empirical rafts of reason, as if subject determined object. It was in such willful or pathetic subversion of natural science, Caleb believed, that the supernatural or irrational elements of any religion or collective persuasion were both propagated and accepted as true, hopefully or hatefully.

Notwithstanding his longstanding awareness that the scandal of his own freewill was the difficulty not of knowing himself but of managing himself—mind body and habits—so that his I E C would be properly concentrated at times of proper importance when faced with too many interesting distractions, but allowing for enough rest and recreation to compensate for weaknesses of character and deficiencies of talent, Caleb had never doubted that his kicking of objects refuted Hindus as well as Berkeley. As a general rule, object determined subject. Yeats would have called him a "mechanical" man in more ways than one. He was interested in the transcendental phenomena of illusion only as foil to the excessive extensions of reason's rigid rafts—in particular to the spectrum of science between what we call the subjective and the objective in common language.

In memorable infancy, unknowingly on the verge of learning the moves and gestures of Father Pole's acolyte at the chapel altar, as the most teachable boy in the Convent to start serving its priest at the altar (without ever adequately mastering his rote responses at the whispered Introit prayer) he'd been the subject of a mystical experience outdoors in which a palpable firmament was unveiled lowered and absorbed as a pulsating visual sensation. On a clear moonless night, he had looked skyward in wonder as he was left alone for a moment just outside the house that was to be his first dormitory at Saint Martha's, about to enter a new life that he seemed to have accepted without protest as not particularly unexpected or alarming, perhaps a normal discovery. [He was then unaware that his mother was confined elsewhere in an institution of less kindly alienation, suffering for him more than herself.] As the stars vanished in their own pleroma he was possessed by the pulsating universe of an ether almost tangibly quilted with uniformly distributed spangles of thicknesses in space. From time to time thereafter, in his dormitory cot at night, or elsewhere, long after his return to domestic life a year later, even with closed eyes in daylight, but with gradually diminishing frequency, he'd been able to summon up that image of anagogical matter. Afterwards in his youth he was sometimes willfully able to recall a fainter and fainter echo of that experience, merely out of introspective curiosity, when he was old enough to have heard about psychology without dismissing it as an uninteresting field of enquiry into the madness of crowds or the legerdemain of mind-reading.

Later, in searching the history of certain ideas, he'd read with spates of sympathy a few of the Western mystics like Boethius, Thomas à Kempis, or Yeats's friend A E, to trace their influence on theology or literature that animated his polemics—not always merely to delimit his own notions of essential religion. After some time under the spell of Father Duncannon and his radical revision of the Offertory's meaning, which accepted many supernatural assumptions as matters of irreducible orthodoxy (such as Original Sin, the validity of ordinary Intercession, the Ascension, and even the Immaculate Conception in two successive generations), Caleb had briefly tried to believe, if not in miracles, at least in the afflatus of prayer. He'd finally reconciled himself to prayer only as hopefully directed meditation (albeit without disavowing his belief in the church as humanity's immemorial need for the epiphenomenal grace of society by liturgical means). Thus in truth he could hardly tell the difference between enlightened intellectual insight and the spirituality of love, whether in hope or despair for the telluric planet. He was aware that his insensitivity to the transcendent varieties of religious experience was part and parcel with his prosaic imagination; that he was fundamentally unpoetic in thought; that compared (for example) with the metaphorical diagrams in Yeats's *Vision* his own analogical geometry was more electrical than mechanical, strictly speaking in a middle class between the banal and the sublime, but responsible for them both, like a peacekeeper in arms!

It was with this latter wisp of thought that after a few gentle repetitions of his unspelled and unuttered mantra, the thoughtless thought of an internalized sound—a basso continuo involuntarily synchronized with respiration every now and then—he momentarily emptied his mind of all but the monotonous spondean rhythm of normal breathing. The mantra served as a whispering gyroscope, a road's central guideline, to remind his inward eye of the quiescent course when he wandered into cogent thought. Re-emerging consciousness of the mantra suggested that any thought at all tended to keep him from the null. Generally speaking, he had conscious recourse to the mantra whenever his cortical busyness, trivial or profound, lapsed of itself—on some occasions, when he was tired or sleepy, but seldom between the beginning and end of a concept, never in the midst of an emotional syntagm—except when interrupted by noise or mishap. In this particular case, intent upon nothing (not even the coffee toast and eggs to follow), drifting within the prescribed limit of time in his daily approach to Nullity—a relaxation of the weariness, the fever, and the fret which otherwise he made no dedicated attempt to oppose—Caleb readily afforded further visitations of aleatory and eleutherian reflection, passive or active (aesthetic or poetic), inseminating or gestating images and ideas arising from objective consciousness (quite unlike the expression of irrational dreams), under the liberating condition that somewhat resembled the more symbolicalistic moods "between sleeping and waking" in which his one modern poet had often found paraphrase or metaphor without the benefit of Guru Nil's enhanced meditation of an Eastern tradition. Caleb was more easily able than Liam Yeats to loosen the grip of "malign externality" without appreciating its existence.

But for him both real systems and symbol-systems—everything in the universe—were subsumed by his one modern philosopher's cosmic "Receptacle", the Void and matrix of ultimate objectivity. That was part of Alpha Whitehead's trick for trumping the fallacy of misplaced concreteness as well as all other ultimate misconceptions while professing platonism. However, as a mature laborer in the anthropological arts Caleb was not interested in the pleroma, which his metaphysics stopped short of. Therefore it's no wonder that his less comprehensive rumination gave way to immediacy as he complemented this short interval of retreat from life's long hours of active or passive engagement by mulling the present phase of his personal destiny.

He was just after coming to the end of his Gilgamesh text! Following that rough-hewn provisional externalization of intellectual heroism he faced a painful period of attention to his true external world. The urgent difficulties of his *bios praktikos*, whose solutions he'd been procrastinating as a multitude of troublesome distractions, but all that stood between design and realization even of a merely unrealized plan for an art, called for the semi-independence of some steady income with enough free time, perhaps halfway down the decline of his neurological faculties, to make the most of his own unperfected symbol-systems. He could no longer ignore the dreadful necessity for bread and shelter while he smoothed his clay for the first half-baking. It was painful enough to remind himself that even when that was finished (after hours) it would be just the beginning of probable disappointment in a series of hopes that he had no ability to fulfill in the Atlantean world of theater, which was almost as inimical as other kinds of marketing, commercial or academic.

An unperformed playscript from the *bios theoretikos*, even if designed exclusively for an art that can exist only on the choral stage, imagined by a well-qualified dramaturge of complex bureaucracy, was a plinth for the collaboration of artists in every dimension that contributes to the action. As Caleb told himself, that imagination was no closer to realized drama than Father Duncannon's fascicles were to his liturgy in a new edition of the Book of Common Prayer for optional practice anywhere in the Tudor Communion. Still, he'd sometimes congratulate himself on the limited proof of his unrealized (not to mention unperfected) vision, the skeletal pages of which offered producers such a wide range of artistic possibilities. There was plenty of leeway for all sorts of unconventional excitement that wasn't his responsibility to create unless he had plenary power to train, select, hire, fire, spend, experiment, and learn at every level of organization, without political or commercial interference! But perhaps he was better off not to get involved in realization with any less authority than that of an owner-architect-general contractor founding his own polis. Poor Yeats, who got the Noble Prize for his autonomous poetry now practically forgotten for his transcendent theater!

My playscript is simply a new fiction extrapolated from the oldest myth, unhindered by the inertia of institutions and taste: fundamentally unpopular. With only three-fifths of our senses Ellen Keller wrote that "The bulk of the world's knowledge is an imaginary construction." Though with-

out making a theater for anyone but myself, I think that as sprung-prose of eolithic myth my sketch for a staged drama is something more than mere fictive communication. But until it's finely refined on archival vellum I fear for even its virtual existence. I'm like Goethe struggling to finish Part Two before he dies! Do I manage my object as well as Deeta does her visions?

In my life so far I've divagated too much into privately extraneous excitements. Long ago I should have stopped reading. For me it's an excessive stimulus, a distraction, and an inhibition. Now every minute counts. In my earliest schooldays, when edifying apothegms were still commonplace, I chose "The pen is mightier than the sword" as my favorite, long before I had any interest in writing, when I would have vehemently protested any suggestion that I was under the influence of my mother's literary values. At the age of eight she offered me the astonishing amount of fifty cents (to be credited to my elusive domestic savings account—a notorious "three eighty-five" accumulated by nickels and dimes from bottle-redemptions, gutter or sidewalk gleanings, snow-shoveling solicitations, errand-running for neighbors, and random gratuities for being such a deserving little kid, the Coins of which were debited or credited to the fund for Christmas or birthday presents from Yuleworth's in Norumbega Square)—if I would read Bernard Russell's The Educated Woman's Guide to Capitalism and Socialism! I refused to try, because my only interest in political economy was its vague element in F D R's New Deal, and because I wasn't a woman. At that early time she had been busy with her newspaper job in Bot. Two or three years later, when we had the good luck to find a ground-floor fireplace in the last of five or six Unabridge tenements from which I attended four different public schools, she began to read aloud famous novels of presumed interest to us both. My grasp of the texts was usually limited to passages that would pique the fascinations of a fatherless boy disdainful of the distaff—stories of wise and powerful animals, masculine adventures, or military details that I associated with technological leadership. She gave way to my vehemently bored rebellion against George Borrow's murky peregrinations; but after reading me Kipling Carroll Hudson and Dickens she grew impatient with my pleas that I had better things to do. Finally, disgusted at my lackluster response to her educational scheme, she made me do the vocal reading, thereby intensifying the maternal discipline but sparing herself the effort, while still getting to hear some fiction she'd loved in her youth or perhaps had never read at all. I hated the task. With my voice it was so onerous that it prevented me from understanding what I was supposed to concentrate on. I particularly remember sitting before a coal fire as I sulkily complied more than once. Then I had a bright idea for negating her will. It was difficult for me—it definitely occluded any understanding I *might have had about the subject matter, it thwarted any benefit she might have expected from my punishment, and it slowed things up intolerably for both of us. I demonstrated my rebellion simply by prefixing every word with the syllable un-! At first she just laughed, but before the session was over it angered her so much that all reading aloud came to an end—much to my ambivalent relief, and probably to hers. "From now on you'll have to fill your own knowledge box!" she said, using one of her favorite Manx expressions. "Surly dog, I've had enough of your insolence! Go out and play with your sister and brother!"*

That is to say, Dectora and Luke, whom she'd named, along with Caleb, even before her own menarche. I turned out to be the Dogfaced Boy, the one and only one to materialize. The triad burdened me as the total redemption of her disappointment, alleviated by jest, spurring me with expectations of talent and sensibility, male and female, that I was never expected to take seriously and never did—unless she was really angry! It was understood as a substitute for preceptive discipline, while also the funny framework for invidious chastisement, or as a complement of players for various games. I was dubbed head of the family. The younger Dectora was a beautiful redhaired browneyed daughter, meant to be the loyal staff and comfort of her mother's old age, herself mother of joyous grandchildren. The youngest Luke was a sweet darkeyed brunet genius of the family, whose altruistic brilliance would serve humanity in church or medicine. As far as complexion was concerned, I had begun as ordered in the maternal dreams of her girlhood, with fair hair and blue eyes, though handicapped in development (as she apologetically explained to me) by her cigarette-smoking during gestation; but that disadvantage, she pointed out, only proved me all the more remarkable as her self-made Honor Boy against the odds. I now suspect that she'd always had a narrative poem in mind about the triumphs and sorrows of an independent mother in the man's world. That's why my siblings could be mentioned so playfully, or as allegorical foils to disappointment in my behavior, either to stimulate her poetic imagination or to dissipate her anger. For they too, my sister and brother, were sometimes scolded according to their characteristic personalities: e g, Dectora for ill-tempered "flubbing" when we were all out for walks together; brilliant Luke for his "negativistic" attitude toward tooth-brushing and other salubrious self-disciplines or social conventions. Yet as the only survivor of that subjunctive family I retain the indicative advantage of having had no paternal fostering as a coefficient expressed by n-squared minus n over two: because n was four instead of five. As a single child this calculation reduces my psychopathic vulnerability by almost half—at the very least according to a certain reductive way of thinking about family relationships. Thanks to my brother and sister I am anything but a spoiled child.

Though I was her incarnate Pride and Joy, she always insisted, and I believed, that she praised and criticized the three of us with equal love. At a certain moment of self-preservation she had chosen to live for me alone, but my opportunity for freedom from the "mother bond", by way of education and self-reliance, always prevailed in her selfless initiatives and decisions. She trusted in my love when after the age of twelve I was too embarrassed to express it, though at night the thought of her death was my greatest fundamental fear. Despite the "I love you my pride and joy", and all the praise that made me basically self-confident even when I was most aware of my deficiencies, I was unable to return the words of reassurance she deserved. I couldn't even call her "Mummie" as she wished, not even "Mother", which I thought an affectation imbued in the academic kids of Unabridge; all my life I could bring myself only to say "Ma", for lack of anything less distasteful in unavoidable concession to the common denominator of common folk who were undoubtedly never embarrassed in any such linguistic predicament. Yet all the while I was absorbing most of her critical discriminations in diction. I've always been too wary of political, literary, or social claims upon my communicative freedom.

But my major embarrassments were far more public: for example being stopped in the middle of Norumbega Square to have a previously unnoticed spot of egg yolk scrubbed off my cheek with spit on the corner of her handkerchief. That I eventually put an end to, but I had a hard time outgrowing the mortification of my incongruous surname and the humiliation of poverty, both of which she seemed to expose deliberately, perhaps simply to exhibit her exhilarating martyrdom to Mrs Grundy's tyranny, but I think mainly to prepare affluent acquaintances for her begging, explained by unpaid bills and the need to keep me in respectable clothing. I was very careful to avoid familiar routes on the few occasions that I had to go on foot all the way to Unabridge City Hall by inconspicuously circuitous back streets and stand in line with shabby adults to collect the weekly welfare dole when she was too sick to get out of bed. But I was especially embarrassed by anything that exposed not only our poverty among the "rich kids" with whom I often found myself associated (first in Unabridge public schools and church, later at my Dutchkill boarding school in Montvert), but also, among the bigoted Irish and French Petrines who dominated our tenement neighborhoods, her all-too-courageous disrespect of their tribal ignorance.

It was only after many years of my dependency that the absolute fear of her death had faded, my nearly subconscious love surviving that dread, an existential foundation obscured at great distances from her by the competing preoccupations of my adult times, or by the embarrassments of occasional propinquity, especially when she tried to make herself known in institutions I served with dignity (when it was already hard enough to conceal my private conditions from professional colleagues who assumed I shared their security). Yet never, ever, did my considered gratitude for her prodigious nurture fail or falter—yes, except for once when I was four: I accused her of being a lion, not a mother, when she fiercely reprimanded me for building a fire against a side of the house we lived in, the same one in which she tried to kill us both by turning on the gas with our heads in the oven! (At that time I didn't know that maneless mother lions are the heroes of their kingdom. Singly they feed, teach, and protect their cubs among dangers from their own kind as well as from other natural predators, environmental irregularities, and humanity.) She never taught me the fakery of Santa Claus as anything but a merry symbol for true Christmas cheer, but added a "Damned Easter Rabbit" to our own cycle of celebrations. His testy generosity could be reported at any time of year.

. . . So after being forced into stories by print I had to get books for myself from the tiny Astronomy Hill storefront branch of the Unabridge public library (across the street from a little shop with a picture of F D R on the wall, where two-cent three-cent and four-cent paper cups of orange sherbet were sold in the summer) and read to myself. At first I looked for pictures as my lure, especially photographs. But I've never forgotten ideas and visual images I had formed from a few of her fireside readings, such as the Alice *stories, the* Just So Stories, *and the* Green Mansions *story (which I only partially understood at the time). The* Jungle Books *I still cherish too much as I visualized them to risk disabuse by rereading. Since those early days I've hated illustrated novels and movies from novels, and especially animated cartoons' opinionated dictation of imagination by their own scenery, physiognomy, and style. But even after beginning my age of print I continued to admire her own water-colored visualizations of the hand-lettered stories in her tattered manuscripts made for me or her friends. In her high school years she had proliferated illustrations of her poems and fictions for classmates and anyone else who admired her talents.*

One story in particular, evolved by successive amplifications, luckily survived among the manuscripts that were lugged along with our few sticks of furniture every time we moved. It was about the Cellaneous family whose adventurous heroine was Miss Cellaneous. Under its dining room table lived an undepicted pet known as Mulligin the Mitten-mender. That favorite series always made me laugh. As for poetry, her memorized songs and poems by others seemed limitless—Irish from her mother, English from her reading, or smutty limericks at second hand from men she'd known. I didn't know the difference between folk poetry and literature until a decade later. Almost the only whole lyric I still know by heart, involuntarily memorized simply from hearing it repeated so often when my clay was still soft, is Allingham's two pages beginning with

> *Up the airy mountain,*
> *Down the rushy glen,*
> *We daren't go a-hunting*
> *For fear of little men;*
> *Wee folk, good folk,*
> *Trooping all together;*
> *Green jacket, red cap,*
> *And white owl's feather!*

I never heard her mention Yeats (whom she probably would have hated in person, as would I, for an "effete supercilious la-de-da"); but he put that poem first in his collection of native Irish lore. The one poet she most loved and reread all her life was FitzGerald's Omar Khayyam. "This is PERFECT POETRY (not dribble)" was inked inside the cover of her last heavily underlined FitzGerald edition. I can still hear a few of her favorite lines, such as

> *And, as the cock crew, those who stood before*
> *The Tavern shouted "Open then the Door. . . .*

which she usually recited in cheerful melancholy, but sometimes with gentle irony, even as lately as her early days in the nursing home, before being overtaken by advanced dementia. Only to the Bible (many chapters double-underlined) did she return more often. She was also an inveterate household singer. She sang innumerable popular songs of Civil War vintage, like "The minstrel boy to the war has gone" and "Swing low, sweet chariot", or of her own participation in popular songs of the Roaring Twenties. She also sang Apostolic choir-hymns, such as "Onward Christian Soldiers" as she strode field or path in the countryside picking apples from private trees; or "A Mighty Fortress is our God" when trying to rally the spirits of lesser souls around her. Her contralto was soft and clear.

Therefore in my insolent trove of prejudices for a long time all singing lodged itself as feminine. Indeed for decades I thought all male singers were sissies, and I'm still a little surprised that women fall for crooners. But that was only part of my invidious attitude, even then, toward what was too popular. At this same mother's knee, despite her gender, all unaware, I was inculcated with her respect for the intelligentsia despite her wrathful scorn of the numerous individuals she knew or read in that class whom she could immediately "see through" as stupid, second-rate, supercilious, ostentatiously overeducated, or politically vicious. She often repeated the Manx adage that "Learning is fine clothes to the rich, and riches to the poor one."

Yet it was largely in consequence of her goliardic mentality, I'm sure, that instead of totally devoting myself to the main road I've allowed myself to be continually distracted much less by the annoying conditions of my insecurity and quixotic mania than by the saturating news of our society: the country's prevalent derangement of popular opinion and the apparently ineluctable destiny of its self-destructive democracy, corrupted by the influence of wealth stemming from religion of selfishness in the name of individual liberty. In the living presence of Raygun and his party—the triumphant prophets of perverted ideas, blind despoilers of Mother Earth, worshipers of force, magnifiers of self-interest, unscrupulous enemies not of tyranny but of any government that seems to threaten the optimization of private aggrandizement—how hard it is for me to summon the tranquility of Negative Capability! How can a moral voter suspend objective consciousness of amenable history in its very process? It becomes an agony to train oneself for sustained detachment.

But at least thank God and Perdita Dana for Contemplative Nullification, which, as promised, often alleviates Weltschmerz and tension. I can sleep well at night; I am spared continuous stomach knots and otherwise uninterrupted rage at the meanness and dishonesty of our unscrupulous oligarchy as it exploits our uncritical culture. —Even though C N sometimes leaves me irritable when I'm too impatient to have composed myself properly, too excited by something in the outer or inner world to relax my diaphragm—or when I've been interrupted by the malign externality of doorbell or telephone! After a few years of forming this contemplative habit I don't feel healthy when there's any hiatus in its daily null or rhythm, as if I haven't brushed my teeth in the morning. . . .

A desperate search for new shelter would serve as his first vacation from internal tension in many a year; but next month he would be faced with external rent he couldn't pay, seeing that he's failed to give his landlord notice for fear of disrupting the increasingly exclusive consciousness required for the culmination of his life's principal project, the virtual charette of his strictly private career in middle-aged dramatic illusion. Anyway, short of earthquake or starvation, he had no wish to hasten his re-entry into "the pragmatical pig of a world" that he had once engaged from the raft of reason as anything but alien. But now in his transmigration by

mantra and ritualistic breathing from observation and will into
contemplative passivity the retina of his inward eye began to entertain recollections of the penurious anxiety that he'd been all but
spared as a child by his mother's courage and encouragement,
before she'd seen to it that he would be delivered from their
poverty by a scholarship boy's unique education, at her cost of his
presence: the apple of her eye, her own flesh and blood, the only
maternal substantiation of her lifelong dream.

   Ur-van. . . . Ur-van, he continued his mantric rune, breathing
in and out . . . *Ur-van . . . Ur-van. . . .* As always, the lip-less,
throat-less sound gently lifted and loosened—sometimes submerged or entirely forgotten until the floated thoughts that hardly
resembled dream yielded their places in consciousness—but now
risen more often to the mind's surface in his motionless ablution,
until a calculating daimon cued him to lift his languid eyelids
barely far enough to see by the clock whether or not the prescribed
time of sense-displacement was yet fulfilled. Sometimes he impatiently awaited that signal; at other times he was surprised by the
physical dispatch of his dutiful retreat; but often, as in this
instance, the entire withdrawal and return was a smooth envelope
of satisfaction.

   Ur-van . . . Ur-van. . . . The mantra's flywheel of heart and
lungs kept cycling his viscera as it faded into thought or vision.
When perfected the cadence was effortless, with all organs in
unconstrained coordination, and often (in his experience at least)
with memorable stimulus as an outcome. Sometimes the process
following the first two or three repetitions of the mantra seemed a
single long algorithm of synthesis or speculation precious enough
to be carried forward out into the world of pencil and paper if he
could succeed in keeping his grasp of its novelty or complexity
during the gradual return to normal consciousness that reversed the
simile of a diver's decompression. But now the subjective "receptacle", in its untraceable succession of ideas, limited only by the standard allotment of twenty minutes, finds itself admitting thoughts
more directly relevant to the first person's actual life.

   *. . . Ur-van. . . . I must apologetically refuse Finn Macdane's tantaliz-
ing offer. Literally under his roof! It was uncomfortable enough to be working for Father Duncannon, serving only during business hours a cause
worth the devotion of a lifetime. I got to know too well its author's secondary
qualities before he died, leaving me slightly estranged from some of the
merely aesthetic ceremonials and secondary traditions of High Church ritual*

*in which he clothed his essential Theodynamic version of the liturgy as an
organic offertory, sacrifice, and reciprocal communion. Considering both the
self-serving piety and the social altruism that motivate slightly interpene-
trating demographic sects of our population (variably overlapping each other
in elections but mainly Pauline and Petrine), the* Anamnesis—*his concept
of the Mass as an ever-renewable inspiration of the supernatural grace without which human society cannot sustain its liberal possibilities—cannot
remain the ultimate counterentropic hope of the planet—I still believe is the
fundamentally reversed sacrament fatally missing from orthodox church doctrine using the same legomena. Furthermore, the hope for communal charity
is thwarted without the Holy Spirit's consequent grace in polity.*

    *But in the end it was Father Dun's inhibited personality—the emo-
tional limitations of his genius—that divided my unreserved affection from
intellectual enthusiasm. It's a good thing my mother never met him: she
might have disturbed my judgment. (After she once said in passing that her
sister was a "grasping" woman, for whom I felt nothing but gratitude for
generosity and kindness in hard times, the admiration of my aunt's character was tempered by my mother's subtle insight.) Never hesitant in her clairvoyance, if she had ever attended his fastidious High Church eucharist
without hearing him preach—or his tea table, knowing nothing of his scientific career, or his creative erudition, or his ecclesiastical courage—my
mother would have pronounced him a sheltered aesthete without the guts to
face a bottle of beer, not to mention the facts of femininity. I can't help comparing and contrasting her with any male or female who's impressed me
with knowledge talent intellectual achievement, the heroes I've had from
books or history, or even my godmother! For existential strength of character
and weakness in education her integration of love joy sorrow suffering
humor courage initiative generosity ebullience intuition imagination and
sheer variety of insecure experience was idiosyncratically firm; and on this
reckoning, at least when I knew him in his old age, Father Duncannon
seemed ultimately infirm as a leader. Yet he once told me in amusement at
his own innocence—during the East London deaconry of his rather late conversion from physics to Tudor holy orders, at a time of troubles after the
great stockmarket Crash, not long before his creative metanoia at the age of
nearly forty, when clubs of Hitler Youth were forming in Berlin (where
he'd been befriended by Mark Planck), and when Arthur Halymboyd as a
lawyer for the Arnheim family was arranging Atlantean refuge for European Jews out on the Point right here in Dogtown, when antisemitism was
rife from sea to shining sea in the land of the free and the home of the brave,
and lynch mobs were still running free in its South (right when the sands of
time were entering Finn Macdane's neck of history's hourglass)—he had*

tried to organize for the Antidisestablishmentarian bishop one of the pious Sir Galahad Boys Clubs among the stunted young ruffians who terrorized the half-starving dockyards of the Isle of Dogs where bobbies feared to tread! But even this Lancelot's theory of art, which excited me almost as much as his Theodynamics, was marred by its negative reaction to Bohemians of the time! He thought he had known too many of them on both sides of the Atlantic. Mutatis mutandis, however, this Knight served Caleb as Ipsissimus Charlemagne's counterbalancing demonstration of Dromenology as preeminent in the history and prospects of Christianity—which even Alpha Whitehead misinterpreted as basically spiritual (perhaps unsurprisingly, seeing that his father and brother were Tudor clergymen in the old country). Though religion and art are not consanguineous, both Christian hierophant and histrionic artist are comprised by my genus of culture. No matter how much their values may overlap, their souls come down to different motives.

So also, though Finn Macdane is a composite of my boyhood's ideal men of action, uniformed or half-clad, and the nearest likeness to a heroic master of the technics that still interest me as far as my retirement from the world's service, I don't want to know him well enough to learn too well where his authority balks the kind of autonomy he will never fully approve. If I allowed myself to fall beholden to his generous seniority I would no longer remain his equal in freewill. Though for no particular object, he too would naturally expect me to sing for my supper, not his praises, to be sure, but in deference to a wisdom it would be cruel to question in any of its implications for matters I happen to have better ideas about, if only because his remaining time is too short to revise his life's investments. It's much easier to talk to Fay. Therefore I'd come to resent his hegemony and we too would grow uneasy with each other's temperament. Ur-van. . . .

Ur-van. . . . I almost (but not quite) wish I could take back at least those years in Hume and use them for the theater. Twenty-five years ago I was quite right to renegate an academic career for the relative freedom of a common reader; I was right to fear my propensity for the "imponderables" generally loathed and ignored in English Department philology, and to recognize my lack of the oral ability to defend them in competition for the liberty of professorial tenure. But that negative decision gone for naught, most of my life diverted, after producing no more than one or two manuscript drafts of my theory of tragedy, without the agents resources or time to realize them in so much as a "workshop", if I now give in to a humble security that devours whatever time I have for a corrigible fourth dimension? Of course it would be very nice to live in that insulated brick and granite castle above the harbor at the very core of my city. It might even be comfortable and stimulating to have Finn Macdane as benefactor and mentor, perhaps (he hinted) as a partner and successor in his consulting business—as soon as I could justify the hiring of someone to take over my A D L with janitorial duties to boot! But [as our Controller would ask in *Prologos*] *with my Side Adjacent at least two-thirds spent, to what Side Opposite should I thus reduce my Hypotenuse? My Isorectotetrahedron would be bent out of shape! Will lamplighted expatiation of dromenological theory, or ephemeral essays on Atlantean politics, be the only things for Creative Mind to write about when my True Mask is removed, when I'm too old to sustain even a feckless double life? Ur-van. . . .*

. . . Ur-Van. . . . Ur-Van. . . . The continents I haven't seen I can study; in faithful imagery I can see a lot; in words I can examine; from paper I can plan itineraries: but except for train rides from coast to coast, excursions from hereabouts or Hume, and moments of hurried freedom on aerial business jumps from point to point, I've feasted or set foot upon very few of the scenes and pavements I long for in the Western heritage of islands, duchies, coasts, dockyards, rivers, cities, capitols, bridges, mountains, tunnels, ancient architecture, railroads, universities, museums, industries, theaters, and historical or literary locales at the disposal of a solvent and anticipating traveler. My virtual Wanderlust began when we lived without money or kilroy outside the walls of Norumbega in Unabridge and hadn't yet crossed even the nearby state line of Montblanc. The church's summer camp did take me in a truckload of kids across that line to an Animal Farm, which I'll never forget for its bareback elephant ride and the impenetrable hedges of a thrilling maze. When I was little older, before we moved to Montvert, I remember that my mother splurged on a very small number of Welfare dollarbills for the traveling expenses of two or three exploratory hitchhiking trips, one night sleeping with farmer's permission in his hay barn in return for a single greenback; and another night in a tiny musty "tourist cabin" for the same (after some beggarly pleading that I turned away from in aristocratic embarrassment). But even those jaunts couldn't be afforded more than once a year. But there were always a few day-trips up here from Unabridge by train to visit old friends of Ma's, and one overnight jaunt on Purdeyville commons when we slept very comfortably under the stars, each in blankets spread over juniper bushes, supported by pillows in their centers. For breakfast we made a fire and cooked strips of bacon that were folded in slices of fresh snow-white store-bought bread, even more delicious than the marshmallows we'd toasted on green sticks the night before. I regarded that as a genuinely masculine adventure. More often were our daytime picnic jaunts by connected subway lines and a streetcar ride to the marvelous 19C fort in Bot's outer harbor on a former island, reached by

a park and causeway. I clambered the ramparts (built of granite quarried and shipped from our North Village), exploring every unbarred nook, and gazed with a desire I've never outgrown for the sailing-yachts anchored with openly displayed proprietors idly lunching on their decks or diving to tread cool clear brine in the cove below, half-circled by sweaty proletarian promenades, redolent with more hotdogs and popcorn than we could afford. . . .

Ur-van. . . . Oh yes, going further back—I can barely recall the adventure: so vaguely early on that it hardly counts as travel, there was a long bus trip to New Uruk (of which I remember hardly more than heavy street traffic deeply shadowed under a thundering El that bore twice as many tracks as the one in Bot) when she could find no one to take care of me at home. I don't know how she scraped up enough for that. I did know that the much more exciting boat or train was far too expensive. I don't remember asking any questions or getting any explanations, but it had something to do with seeing a publisher or agent who'd showed a little long-distance interest in her work. (It was only one of the infinite series of disappointments I grew more resigned to than my mother ever did.) Somewhere in downtown Ur we stayed overnight with an old acquaintance of hers, a deafened Scot novelist who'd been a Chief Engineer in the British merchant marine. . . . I don't remember noticing anything more about the sleeping arrangements there than I did when there were occasional such visitors at home in Unabridge, at least until I was older and Tony Porter often spent the night with her in the room closest to my bed on the sunporch outside. With him as lover her discretion with me must have faded. She had always told me more than I wanted to know about what was concealed from other children, not only her desires but even the distasteful mystery of feminine hygiene and her allusions to protracted agony in the childbirth that had left on my head a scar from the forceps. . . .

Ur-Van. . . . She was a serious reader of Tristram Freud, or at least of his popular interpreters. Unlike Einstein or Whitehead, and a few literary figures, he was the one of her intellectual heroes whom she admired with the confident knowledge and intelligence of her own experience. His expulsion from Austria by the Nazis, to which she was as alert as any Atlantean intellectual, immediately excited her written protest against Hitler through the German Consulate in Botolph and the Embassy in Washington. She later believed the act recorded her name on the B D I's domestic blacklist, at a time when it classified "Premature Antifascists" as enemies of both church and state, which was still the policy when she told me about it a few years afterwards, when I was old enough to understand the fall of France and Britain as something vastly more ominous than our personal danger from

*the B D I or the Dogtown Police Chief. (In her loneliness she often
expressed herself to me—in prose or rhyme—as I would speak to my dog
when we were alone, or Kafka to a cockroach in his cell. But I think that
at other times she expected me to understand by tone alone or by the sound of
proper names. I felt her transpired fear of Nazi storm troopers as early as
Kristallnacht, no more than a doubtful harbinger of the mass exter-
minations that became generally known only much later in the War.
Weltschmerz, more than Hard Times, drove her patriotism, her hatred of
reactionary isolationism and her contempt for the Atlantean (mostly Protestican) politicians and journalists who encouraged or tolerated the elements
of native fascism that nearly thwarted Roosevelt's leadership before 1941.)
Except for what I heard afterwards, still in my early years of schooling, I
don't remember much about the War years. I was aware of food rationing
and scrap-metal collections only as aspects of normally continuous graduations in background experience, as if in normal evolution from the ghastly
Depression, not in the foreground like that of learning fractions or parts of
speech. (We had no interest in the gasoline coupons that worried many
wage-earning families as well as the affluent.) Nevertheless I did understand by necessity the dire housing shortage around the war-production
industries in the cities where she worked, when we lived in quarters like the
subdivided living room of a paneled mansion in Charter Oak, or a single
furnished room sharing the cockroaches and elevator of six or eight stories in
downtown Ur, or the faded sitting room of an erstwhile railroad flat in
New Warka—each usually for just a few months at a time, while she was
getting losing or quitting in indignation some ill-matched mechanical or
menial factory job, but never (she insisted and I believe) for incompetence—
always for critical insubordination, unionizing agitation, whistle-blowing
patriotic complaints of inefficiency, or inability to sustain the fatigue of
overtime on second-shift hours with lengthy commuting by overcrowded
public transport, always measured by the time and energy of which was
deprived for writing as well as for me (who always came first in her joy,
despair, and feelings of guilt). Accepting the way of the world without
question, like a kitten taken from mother to human masters, I submitted
without resentment or memorable distress to a blurred series of female care-
takers, some too old to remember childhood, sometimes others requiring me to
pass whole daytimes with their own congenitally stupid children in smelly
tenements, fed with foreign dishes. Before migratory stints of war my
strictly regulated year's experience at Saint Martha's Convent here on the
edge of the outer harbor had been an educational pleasure, especially when
chosen as Father Pole's acolyte apprentice, learning a few words of first-
grade French, living in a boys' dormitory of parallel cots aligned in two*

columns, monitored around the clock for speech and behavior acceptable to the good Sisters. . . .

Ur—Van. . . . It would have been something like living under the wise and gentle Sister Dominica the Mother Superior's benevolent restraint, a discipline of emulation and aspiration, if with all my baggage and paraphenalia I'd accepted Fay's offer of separate household facilities in exchange for a little outdoor care-taking, despite her utmost efforts to steer clear of my private life. And it would have been awkward in my heart to keep from feeling like the libidinous suitor of my own godmother—my mother's midwife, you might say—who's also equivalent to a Muse in my pantheon. I have grown too proud to serve as altar boy in any temple or as anybody's fair-haired dependent. Even only slightly disappointed adoration of her would have made me more nervous than marriage, which as far as I can see is much less delicate. For instance, Fay who knew Mary Tremont before I existed in my own right hasn't enough experience of the down-and-out, or of professional failure, to match my intelligence of Mary Tremont's peculiar psyche, which was apparently afflicted by adolescent encephalitis lethargica *(perhaps further disturbed by an incident of mild sexual molestation) and almost continuously altered or distorted by extravagant imagination, subjective social oppression, superabundant love, unmatched passion, optimism, disappointment, despair, generosity, humor, courage, energy, loyalty, and Christian faith—the causes and effects of a personality that together (or sometimes singly) composed her variably happy and scornful exuberance, both before and after certain cusps of suicidal hopelessness. It's not that I can expect anyone to know what only I can know and judge; it's just that it's a matter of my privileged superiority to everybody else in understanding this otherwise necessarily misunderstood mother of myself who determined all except freewill in my formative nurture (though of course I still can't empathize with the anticipatory instinct of storge which her half of the population is born with to some large degree, regardless of anguish, even without her precocious stipulations and disappointed expectations in my special case). Thus I would have to make allowance even for Fay's necessary underestimation of the woman we'd be bound to discuss, and in my heart that disequilibrium of wisdom would limit the idealization of my Muse, who may have saved her life (as well as my own) in the hospital as a complementarity of subject and object. I already sense that she has presumptive opinions about my mother—minor animadversions, to be sure, perhaps rationally and humanely justified in her view as the asymmetrical benefactor in their distant relationship, having kept her affectionate admiration at a prudent distance—the only possible manner in which to remain a friend of the difficult Mary Tremont for so many years, which reminds me of*

Natty Hawhaw fending off Redburn's overburdening hope for total friend-
ship. . . . Ur—Van. . . .

2.

Though Caleb was often somewhat impatient to get to the
chronological end of his mantric exercise, the span of this morning's C N was possible because of the extraordinarily seamless
swiftness with which it came to the ritualistically determined
peripeteia in his return to the objective world. He always found
this delicate reawakening to the real world a more difficult transition of consciousness than that of beginning the contemplation.
But (like the decompression of a deep-sea diver) that process of only
gradually opening his eyes to the objective world in not less than
three minutes of patience was crucial to successful practice, as if
calmly awakening with the dawn from perfectly clear and reasonable sleep. Failure to obey that rule could spoil the beneficial seren-
ity of meditation and threaten to leave him irritable for the rest of
the day. So now it was slowly and conscientiously that his disclos-
ing gaze, in transition from twilight to heavy-lidded vision, came
to rest straight before him on the seat of an opposite chair bearing
the small brown carton of his mother's ashes. They had been
occluded, or not entirely envisioned—perhaps only postponed—by
the intrusive queue of thoughts closely or distantly related to that
strange capsule of her exuberant life.

Without so much as an autopsy report he had been obliged to
take on faith that after a year of evisceration, pickling, dismemberment, and nominal reassembly the Norumbega Medical School had
delivered her mutilated cadaver to an economical Unabridge under-
taker for transmission to the crematorium of the Mount Olive
Cemetery, which had finally presented him two of these cardboard
caskets. The putative content of the first had then been clandes-
tinely interred when the public gates of the cemetery were closed,
according to its policy in such cases, in the last small corner of her
maternal ancestors' burial plot, maintained in perpetuity according
to an endowment by one of its founding Corporators a century earlier. These preliminaries were carried out at Caleb's discretion, substantially according also to the corpse's written wishes of long
standing anent her ancestors on her mother's side. He had been able
to pay for the cremation and a small headstone from the coffer of a

fund somewhat more than an order of magnitude larger than three dollars eighty-five cents, which he'd legally inherited as the balance of her uncharacteristically hoarded public welfare "personal care" allowances, thanks to the political philosophy of F D R's Party.

In absentia, however, a whole year earlier special weekday memorial Eucharist and eulogy had been arranged and earnestly conducted by Father Daniel, her priest and friend at Saint Elizabeth's mission church in Botolph, but performed on this occasion in fashionable St George's of Unabridge, George Washington's Pauline Apostolic house of worship during the Siege of Botolph, where she and especially Caleb himself had found a center of faith hope charity and social edification during his primary and grammar school days, when they were living in civic discomfort a mile or two away in the marches of abject slums among bigoted Irish, New French, Lusitanian, Tuscan, Armenian, and other parishioners of the huge Petrine Scholastic church on Astronomy Hill.

St George's Low Church pulpit had then been the mother's magnet of joy and admiration for the "gentle, beautiful, eloquent, unassuming" rector at the time (a former civil engineer) to whom she sent personal but spiritualized love poems; its Parish House the boy's center of social athletic and Sunday School education, where or whence he took earnest (sometimes competitive) pleasure in organized sports, picnic excursions, and the like—especially Cub Scouts and the arcane Sir Galahad Club—all under the encouraging subaltern leadership of congenial tutors such as junior curates or Divinity School students in elective avocation. It was in that socially generous society that he had won various badges and a gold medal, which his mother never let him forget, sometimes in praise, sometimes in mockery, by calling him her Honor Boy—the special case of "My Pride and Joy, me own flesh and blood". It was also through the good offices of that parish that for several years he had greatly improved his abilities and eager experience with the inestimable advantage of two weeks around the clock under communal regulations at a multifarious summer camp, in the country among kids more secure than many in his urban schooling.

Except for Tessa Opsimath, who had accompanied him to the memorial service at St George's, and Father Daniel himself, Caleb had known none of the surprisingly numerous people clustered in forward pews at the choir end of the gray and white Colonial nave, which in his present eye was considerably shrunken as a boxed emptiness from the awe that had silenced him when filled with

organ music and overshadowed by the adult congregations of his
childhood. The priest and "mourners" were there to celebrate with
humor and gratitude not the death but the life of Mary Tremont,
by whom they'd all been befriended or otherwise appreciated by her
boldly eccentric old age as a faithful and tangibly helpful communicant of their unique Tudor "High Church" Mission located in a
shabby neighborhood of the dominantly Papist city.

Before this minority of a minority joined at the altar rail for
Communion the tone of the company had been set by Father Dan's
cheerfully authentic praise of Mary's creative contributions to integrated Christian fellowship with her talent for personal friendship,
social energy, and unladylike teasing of the complacent. That
gentle priest's thoughtfully delivered (sometimes stuttering)
eulogy was no conventional panegyric: standing with no notes on
the step to the choir, his eyes staring upward into space as he
mused, when not searching those of the individuals before him
who shared his familiarity, he inverted dirge by celebrating with
anecdotes the mortal life of a party. He spoke of her merry performance at his own family dinner table before babysitting for the
evening as his kids' new granny, boasting with a funny book of her
own colored pictures about how sternly she'd treated her own
three children; and of how he and his wife were teased by their
young ones for not being funny enough. Without attempting to
mimic her silliness he alluded to a few of her little childishly
entertaining acts that Caleb himself had witnessed too often over
the years before and after her South Atlantean sojourn but were
fresh and amazing to him and his congregation: for instance, with
head bent down, mincing and twisting, forefinger in mouth, *My
name is Lorraine Tilly-i-o, and I'm the cutest little girl in North
Atlantis!* Or as a nanny, with her hands full and unwitnessed by
critics, to quieten babies or make young kids laugh, with her
tongue she'd suddenly project ugly false teeth to the forefront of
her lower jaw's handsome grandmotherly face. . . .

Then, according to latterday custom in mourning, he invited
tributes and reminiscences from the smiling laity looking up at
him from below the floor of the choir. Before he could finally get to
his celebration of the requiem (Tudor-communal "in both kinds")
the minutes flew past with a dozen more delicate traces of the
deceased in absentia—subjective, objective, redundant, or too long
drawn out. Despite the recollections of the priest, Caleb gathered
from the appreciations of other speakers that his mother had some-

what mellowed as a social critic before succumbing to the premature disease of old age that prevailed in his own last few impressions of her, without however having entirely rid herself of the exhibitionist traits to which he'd always been more sensitive than her audience was—as he now remembered, for example in his mother's jocular demand to be called the "dear old thing" of the Diocese even by her arm's-length friend the Bishop. Caleb tried to conceal his tears from Tessa as he heard of the egregious goodwill that had seasoned a religious melting pot of several races—immigrants, indigents, daily wage-earners, shopkeepers, artists, and learned professionals—in the absence unto death of her three children. In tears he was unable to rise and say so much as a single word of thanks to those who had loved his own mother amid the penultimate satisfactions of her Christian life.

[9:30 AM on the same day: Tessa at home gets a phone call from Caleb]

"Today is a good time to do it. It may not be very warm, but there's no wind, at least down in this cove. Clear sky. Blue as my mother's eyes. It's low tide at 10:32. She wanted it on the rise so that I wouldn't slip on wet rocks and the laving waves wouldn't wash her away before she was ready to leave home forever. I don't think we'll be disturbed. Most people will be over on the other side of town. I can already hear the brass bands warming up over at Acorn Pasture cemetery where they start the parade. But again, don't feel obliged, if you have plans with Rafe or anything."

"Good! Fay and I asked to be invited, didn't we? You need observers, in case you slip on the rocks. I'll pick her up, and then you, at twelve-thirty. She says she's a lucky anthropologist to be invited. She's making us lunch at her house afterwards."

[To the rocks of Cachalot Point, a little before
the Daylight Savings meridian]

Sitting with the second little box of ashes on his lap in the back seat of Tessa's elegant kilroy, Caleb asked her to divagate here and there on the way to North Village, so that he could recall bits of landscape and architecture in which he had been inculcated by his mother in various phenomena of memory or dream or conjecture.

Very few of them could be claimed in his own first-person experience, seeing that his exile had begun in infancy. Most of the sites
and their related anecdotes were retained as personal memory of his
own imagination of what he had been told in imaginative language, often sweetly associated with sad or funny singing from her
repertory of songs popular in the decade of her romantic maiden-
hood, including a few nostalgically echoed from half a century
before the first Great War. In his musty knowledge box these were
mingled or modified with accidentally acute local images from
almost furtive visits to Dogtown when they were living in urban
Unabridge:

   . . . A certain thrilling bump in the rumble seat of a roadster
crossing a culvert for Little Harbor Creek on the shore road from
Harbor Ward to Seamark—a sensation still noticeable on the nearly
flattened gradings of 1981. (Who was the man giving them a ride
in his rattling Model A Ford?) . . . A fragmentary memory of
having been taken to a mock wedding of small children in tuxedo
and bridal gown at a community center or church hall in a side
street of the Village, when he hardly knew what such ceremonies
were about. . . . The scene of a distressed coal barge being pumped
out of water alongside T-Wharf in Seamark Harbor. . . . Still vesti-
gially rigged with enormous masts braced by steel cables: a granite
quarry brimming with fresh water that lapped smooth flat ledges,
below and above the surface, upon which women in full black
bathing suits stand or from which they launch themselves like
placid amphibians, until remaining visible only as rubber-capped
heads. . . . A red and yellow tugboat chained to a green barge in the
corner window of what was still Seamark's toy store. . . . But most
nostalgic of all, a steam-snorting Boanerges simmering and sighing
at rest, its bumper, peering over the street like a benevolent monster, at the end of its line from Botolph without a turntable.

   When not excused by excessive inconvenience of route, Tessa
drove by or near the more or less revised sources of these faded
images according to Caleb's quietly diffident suggestions, as well
as other resurrections along the way that happened to be silently
dragged in his net. On the northeast sector of the Cape's circumferential Cod Street, high above Tessa Barebones's former Power
House down on the water's edge, between the center of Seamark
and the Village, they crossed the New Stone Bridge, an old arch of
rusty granite blocks that spanned the abandoned track which
beneath it had connected a vast quarry with its quay. This passage

had opened the busiest seascape of their route. Admiring the view to their right Fay remarked that it was a halcyon day. "No surf. The horizon is a blue line between slightly lighter and slightly darker hues."

"The house I live in now across the Gut" Tessa replied, "is much higher up than this but most of our view of the 'gull's bath and the fish's commons' is cut off for me by hills and trees." Seeing that there were no impatient cars behind on the narrow road, she slowed down. "I also miss most of the gulls themselves. You're lucky to have them both: the sea *and* its angels!"

"The ocean's still our unenclosed commons, not yet over-grazed." Fay mused. "Apparently no one in Dogtown has more than one of the best views. You can see the lighthouse and breakwater in the outer harbor; Caleb's view must be the best for the innermost harbor. I wish we could rotate scenes every day like the supercilious angels. I watch them enviously when they fly, coasting and wheeling above and below my house, when they dip and soar and twist to catch the western sun lighting up the undersides of their pure white wings, especially the Maxwells with aristocratic black capes. When squabbling in a swarm after the gurry from a fishing boat on its way back to the harbor they are not very attractive, but in the upper air, on patrol alone or with two or three others, they take my breath away. Nothing on earth seems so beautiful as their principle of least action in coasting on the breeze. When there's no interesting boat passing or collecting lobster pots, when as far as I can tell the angels are not expecting picnickers on the beach in their inspection of our Little Harbor valley, they often rise so high and cut so many intentional figures, skylarking higher still and higher from the earth, riding the air like joyous souls on vacation that I can't believe they've got food in mind! —*But* not the lonely one who comes every day to perch on the pipe railing of my kitchen balcony, patiently awaiting crumbs from my table. I try hard to refrain from tossing her something more than once a day, which I do in order to watch her through the sliding window while she hops down upon the deck to peck up the pieces not three feet away, letting her get used to me now that Felixity's no longer there to threaten through the glass. Little by little I'll venture outside to see if she'll let me get closer. But I don't want her to get so familiar that she hangs around long enough to drop white splotches on my boards! So far she's been a lady in that respect."

"Why do you say 'she'?" Tessa asked.

Fay hesitated. "I suppose because she's cultivating a last resort for chicks? I don't really know why I assumed her feminine sympathy. Maybe one of the flatfooted creatures that stamp around on my roof from time to time, but she strikes me as an outcast accused of witchcraft."

"Or honest adultery!" Tessa suggested. "Isn't there a spot of scarlet on her beak?"

"Anyway she singled me out as a grandmother even before I started to compensate her for the visitations. She definitely seems lonely, like the widowed halcyon who has to fend for herself. I often wonder if she has a nest on Half-Tide Island. But she never seems to be in a hurry to get back to a nest."

This last bit of talk drew Caleb out of his brooding back-seat inattention to the womenfolk. "Is she really just a Cosmo? Grayback or blackback?" He reminded the Dogtown immigrants that graybacked Cosmos were common angels, souls of ordinary saints. They were ubiquitous, perhaps universal in maritime climes. But twenty years earlier the blackbacked Maxwells, Cape Gloucester's hybrid contribution to the heavens, had seemed to be gaining ascendance in the mixed population. It had then been predicted that they, a species of slightly greater physique, more striking in appearance, almost like eagles when high in the sky, would first outnumber the local and eventually survive the whole eastern Atlantean population of Cosmos. "Yet these souls of local Viking Shepherd stirp seemed to have failed in evolutionary competition— after the death of my king. I hardly ever see one nowadays."

Caleb referred to his saddened Just So story.

"'AS DOGS GO, SO GO THEIR SOULS'. Up in Purdeyville that's carved in stone." Tessa remarked to Fay.

"In the end Maxwell's demon always loses ground." Caleb added to his tale. "Yet people think they dominate!"

"Well," said Fay, "this one will be less disappointed. She has black only at the tip of her feathers. As a grounded suppliant my angel is awkward and looks brainless, with mechanical eyes, matchstick legs like articulated stilts, swollen knees, and big liver-colored feet more like ridged rubber flaps than 'the dark webs' of Leda's swan. When she occasionally cracks her mouth open to utter something her jaw is longer than her yellow blood-spotted beak and reaches into half her head, which moves like a clumsy robot's. When she drops down to the deck she waddles and lunges on those clumsy feet. You get the thrill of her slender beauty only when she turns her back, unfolds her amazing wings, launches downward, and retracts her landing gear, as she gracefully soars off and up. I wonder if windhovers are just as disillusioning when grounded."

"Or osprey and albatross." Caleb suggested.

Caleb was grateful for the women's unnecessary attempt to distract him from resurrected grief. The longer he knew them the more he trusted their affection. He believed that their love of dogs equaled his own, and of children naturally much more. Fay's intellectual sympathy, heart and soul, he hoped was that of a Godmother Superior in objective wisdom.

. . . Then came the horizontally corrugated sidings of a great shed housing the works of Cape Gloucester Forge encroaching upon the sidewalk to their right. The factory's steel sheets were rolled down as a holiday facade in blessed silence for the Villagers, concealing the workplaces within a lofty steaming cavern of coordinated smiths, now taking time off for Memorial Day. Usually in the work-week this inferno resounded in deep gloom with the thumping cacophony of almost as many autotelic hydraulic hammers as the dozen or two carbon-streaked operators serving the foundry's entire floor of furnaces and machines, which even in normally vigorous operation were apparently as loud and hostile to sunlighted pedestrians as angry devils in hell. Caleb remembered hastening on foot past the opened wall of sweltering pandemonium as a dark vastness crowded with brute machinery and blackened attendants, only an outer few of whom were fleetingly visible from the sidewalk at its very threshold of open air, having been advised to cover his ears against the rhythmic earth-stamping bangs of mechanical force. He'd dared stop to glimpse no more of the frightening depths than the mouths of two or three open furnace doors brighter than the glare of a ninety-degree sun outside.

But now on a silent day more than half a century later, borne in much swifter passage, and swifter yet in thought, the steady conflagrations re-envisioned in that thumping tomb of ovens touched off other memories and epi-memories reciprocating with each other as if they were each a reverberating existential or vicariously true experience, even mere analogues drawn from fictional recollection. Like an electronic capacitor his mind oscillated and distorted, irregularly back and forth in the surviving circuit of all his years from infancy to the present: from Sunday School, the attempted cremation of Shadrach, Meshach, and Abednego; kids scaring themselves in Mount Olive Cemetery by peering through the cobwebbed apertures of dark dynastic mausoleums to see the drawers of coffin-ends stacked to the size of furnace doors; walking past such monuments in those same hills and dingles, amid the beautifully designed flora of an inland green and blue Mother's Day, wrapped in exhilarating hope for Lilian Cloud beside him on the way to be shown his mother's favorite landmark the Princess Tower.

. . . There were no angels in sight when, by "right of customary passage" (despite notices of exclusion posted by the latest generation of landowners), Caleb Fay and Tessa now stood on the bare rocks of Cachalot Point under that translocated clear blue sky, fortunately warmed at a midday zenith stirred by no noticeable onshore breeze. Even at the end of May it was an unusually pleasant day for lagging springtime on this tip of Cape Gloucester. Tessa had been drawing attention to the general similarity between this stretch of the outer shore and that of Fay's own Foreside further down the coast, which had inspired the unforgettable Rock Dance choreographed by Tessa's own sister for the old Hoof and Mouth company, and in which—believe it or not, after all these years (pointing to her legs)—Tessa herself had danced!

All angels seemed to have been drawn to floating siesta elsewhere in coves or marshes, if not in the distant harbor where odorous fishing boats were tied up among small yachts for holiday tribute to centuries of drowned fishermen, as well as to sailors and soldiers of war, where the crowds of bipeds signaled artificial refuse of all varieties, and where in any case the band music attracted casual inspection.

Thus no white-winged angels were left singly or as whirling constellations above Cachalot Point in hope or curiosity over these three nearly motionless figures on the rockscape smoothed or blunted by thousands of years of glacier, waves, and salted wind. They stood on a randomly stepped slope of naked granite between the softly laving sea and a headland of dark green behind them, which at their level hid from sight all but the outermost of venerably spacious summer houses with broad porches and cozy old coach houses, most of which were now internally remodeled for "all-year-round summer folks".

It was in one of them that most of Mary Trevisa's maiden poetry and watercolors had been formed. It was in this isolated aestivating neighborhood that after release from the school year's genteel curriculum she had read the Matter of Britain and memorized Omar Khayyam. It was hereabout in one summer night of 1920

that her early romanticism had been consummated with one Todd
Elton, as Caleb was told long before he paid attention to her reminiscences, beginning, according to the biographical confessions of
middle age, a forty- or fifty-year span of betrayals or disappointments in the spiritual aspects of carnal love, requited or not. In her
last tattered copy of *The Rubaiyat*, at the lines

> *You know how little while we have to stay,*
> *And, once departed, may return no more.*

she had inscribed, before neural deterioration made handwriting
impossible, but not for the first time, the reminder now being
acted as her final obsequy. These and almost every other verse of the
"Fifth Version" of FitzGerald's translation, which Caleb had recovered from the Botolph nursing home, had been underlined or
doubly underlined in ink, like many whole chapters in her latest
echoes of the Bible. The title page of the *Rubaiyat* bore in her bold
round hand her rating "when poetry *was* POETRY!".

Cachalot Point was named to commemorate the sighting of an
alleged sperm whale—long before there was any possible conception of a mistaken U-Boat, even before the Sea Serpent had
appeared in these waters—but soon thereafter pronounced
"Catch-a-Lot", according to the careless etymology of fisherfolk.
The base of the irregular slope on which the long-deferred request
of Mary Tremont's silent threnody took place was blackened and
weedy from a millennium of tides, but the fuscous bedrock that
Caleb carefully descended, followed part of the way less confidently by Fay and Tessa where washed by no normal tides,
bleached by sun and storm, was here and there encumbered with
worn-down and rounded baggage left by the glacier; but the few
obstructions, vertically jagged and obliquely creased with seams
of basalt, were eruptions of seismic granite weathered long
enough to have acquired, like the whole shore of open rock (as
young Mary Trevisa had noticed in poems) the color of a classic
lioness, nothing like the weatherbeaten gray exposures of Dogtown's interior palisades and whalebacks of the same ingredients.
The hue grew darker as the slope steepened below the indefinite
line of mean high tide in descent through the increasingly slippery intertidal zone to greenly black seaweed hiding its fruit of
blackened green hips, the beaded hem of Mother Earth's skirts
loosely responsive to motion.

But it was also true that the broad exposure of Lady Gloucester's upper thigh, unhindered by vegetation, had been occasionally
raped by men with hardened tools, to carve their shoreline kind of
"motions" when blocks were needed for domestic structure. In a
later instance though, probably to please their aestivating girls and
ladies, they'd hired a sculptural quarryman to cut and finish out of
naked mother rock at its most elevated level of vantage, as best he
could without a studio, the solid block of a somewhat shallow
straightbacked bench hardly long enough for more than two. Caleb
had pointed this out to his companions before climbing down alone
to the uniquely rounded tidal pool that he well remembered from
his infancy. "Sit there. I won't be long. The edge is sharp but the
seat is smooth enough." Of one accord however they'd preferred to
stand and watch considerably closer to the lapping waves, seeing
that this man's personal ceremony belonged more to church than
theater. When he slid down to reach his chosen spot of dry footing
they followed as far as they dared without offending his nearly
motionless privacy or endangering the elder.

The softly stirred wavefront made no sound that could not have
been over-risen by a mumbled prayer; the easterly breeze was so
mild that no murmured words could not have been heard by sharp-
eared Tessa if Caleb had expressed any. Nor was there any furtive
signing of the cross that baptized Fay could have detected—any gesture except the hesitant movement with which they both saw him
slowly pour and scatter the powdery gray ashes on the frontier of
licking motion, followed by suddenly vigorous flips of his left wrist
as he shook from the cardboard cube his mother's last grains of dust,
putting an end to the brief solemnity of his seed-sowing rhythm. At
first the spreaded granules floated on an imperceptibly rising surface
of the naturally gated pool, like the lethargic filling of a canal lock
with no other aperture—soon to be inundated and left behind by
the ocean's face. In Caleb's eyes, from time immemorial it had been a
clean font of immersion for mothers and children who were privileged to spend summers near enough for walking a shady distance in
bathing clothes to wade or sit in the tub with very few barnacles,
safely between dangerously slippery walls of weedy rock. Having
inhaled more than it could hold of clear transparent brine over the
seaward lip of its elliptical rim the pool was now waist-deep, with
living water's sweetly salted breath lazily welcomed and soon
released to the cold progressive tide's hidden undertow.

Caleb's timing was propitious, for in a few more minutes the bath-basin for children of many generations would be indistinguishable from a thousand other gaps in Mother Earth's tumultuous first line of defense against Father Ocean on this Cape. The ashes of Caleb's particular mother, symbols or samples, swirled in a last eddy of pure brine valediction before they sucked down and forever out to dissolve without distinction, as she had wished, in God's ocean primeval. Caleb's mouth never moved. His stationed feet were wetted by the irregular advance of cadenced sea-licks. . . .

Then he simply climbed behind his stumbling escort in the recessional to the upper margin of masoned seawall and wild grass, turning with satisfaction for a last look at the aqueous entrance to his mother's global tomb where the tide would rise for another few hours and then fall for twice as many, to allow the final grains of disintegration to bathe as long as possible in the embrace of her native foundation. He thought of Augustine's mother Monica, who said "It does not matter where you bury my body." He wondered if death was the moment of maximum subjectivity.

[That afternoon at Fay's house]

On the shortest way back to East Ward the women had been silent in deference to Caleb, not pretending to empathy in a loss that only he could refresh, but awaiting evidence of the attitude that would best accord with his preference for either consolation or diversion and thereby set the course for conversation. But during those twelve minutes he too had been more objective than they suspected, pondering the best manner in which to make them comfortable in the aftermath as unsentimental mourners. It wasn't until Fay was unlocking her front door that in a somewhat strained tone of conventional heartiness he simply thanked them for their kindness. Then as they entered the house they all seemed to break into speech at once, as if ready to celebrate a wake with Irish whiskey.

The fare was wine and lobster salad, the conversation quietly irreverent, in cheerful exploration of their friendship, especially when Caleb tipsily mentioned that the postprandial tawny luse he toasted to was just the thing in which his mother had taken most pleasure before she was deprived of it by her medical regime. He became fully aware of its effect upon himself only when he was

walking home down the inner harbor slope of Joint Hill in a condition that precluded his usual afternoon clarification in C N, the
time for which he'd casually intended to occupy with doubts about
the degree of veridical correspondence between history and symbol-
systems like Yeats's within a thermodynamic scheme of reality as
the one and only really closed system. . . .

 *At last Tessa made me talk too much. Damn psychologists! Half-
truths are less informative than no truths. I've been an obscurantist with
almost everybody here in Dogtown all these years. Quite apart from social
secrecy as anyone's pragmatic policy, I know it's also my ingrained self-
defense against excessive insertion of factual truth in childhood, to which I
owe the benefits I derived from most of my other education, but it made me
chary of self-expression and inept at public speaking. (Is that why I've
never immersed myself in poetry? Does that account for all my impersonal
abstractions?) What else could Tessa and Fay have expected of me at
today's vestigial funeral, a year after my mother's death, three or four years
after her remaining self-consciousness became so unintelligible to me as well
as to herself, in the premature senility precipitated according to her doctors
by some occult residual affect of the* encephalitis lethargica *from which
she'd ostensibly recovered during the influenza epidemic at the end of WW1
when she was fifteen?*

 *The last words of recognition I had from her, dragged with saliva
through false teeth no longer fitting gums or cheeks, at first directed to me as
a stranger, came forth as her blue eyes suddenly brightened with an echo of
her old joy as she declared that she didn't know why but I looked like her
father! That meant the stalwart highliner captain Trevisa, loyal husband
of her mother Hannah (née Tremont), born in Galway of Petrine Celtic
stock. His prosperous family of chandlers in Botolph had emigrated from the
Skerries on the eastern side of Ireland as opposite hers in the specialties of
fishing as Dogtown from San Ricardo in the U S A. Coming from the
Fingal coast of Pauline Anglo-Nordic genes that name seems a bit odd, but
apparently it was respected there for at least two hundred years, reputedly
derived from an Iberian survivor of the Armada, said to have been first
beached on the Isle of Manannan. Attracted as a boy to Dogtown by its
fishery of four hundred schooners, the first Trevisa in New Armorica had
earned great respect as a highly successful seaman and leader in our famous
industry—the man whom much of her life Mary had privately acknowledged only as her "putative father", cuckolded by the rich unprincipled electronic engineer Prosper Ozone, known as the Cathode King, titular Baron
of the New Albion land grant, who'd later shared the military honorific
"Captain" by virtue of his secret service and torture by Nazis during*

*W W 2, but who unwillingly expiated his reactionary politics by succumb-
ing to consequent blindness long before his death, of which she was never
aware in thirty years of slowly moderating fearful and defiant self-banish-
ment from Dogtown at work in dozens of other North or South Atlantis
places, as well as in ships at sea, because it never occurred to Teddi Cibber
or any other remaining local friend to write her about that mysterious
figure, and because I never reported to her about him for fear of arousing old
demons when she was struggling to devote the rest of her life to The Brotherhood of the Peaceable Kingdom or some other Pauline community by overcoming her own "sins of self and ego". As far as I could see, the only evidence against the inventor of the sexode tube and the dynatron seems to be
that she was the firstborn child of her mother Hannah who had been
employed for many years by Captain Ozone as chief housekeeper of his
Joyous Gard. As Hannah's recalcitrant daughter, Moira acted out an
instinctive ingratitude for the conscientious filial support and protection of
the steady schooner captain. Perhaps her critical animosity was simply an
unusually prolonged symptom of normal adolescent rebellion against reasonable regulation rather than substantiated contempt for his horns, either the
cause or the effect (as she believed) of a feverish experience she remembered
from an interval in the deliriums of sleeping sickness when she'd felt his
hand exploring her fresh new breasts beneath a loosened nightgown. During
my childhood after this father's death she may have grown less censorious of
"attempted incest", ambivalently fluctuating between forgiveness for
molestation and apology for what may have been a guilty dream. Figmented
memory of a forbidden sensation? or precocious clairvoyance of the poor
man's instinctive thoughts as recollected by her in an age of psychology?
. . . After that last flare of sensibility in my presence at the nursing
home her deterioration seemed smoothly asymptotic to death, and the intervals of my inconvenient and uncomfortable Botolph visits lengthened accordingly. The burden of my conscience was gradually abated by the rationalization of hopelessness and her frequent spells of filial oblivion. Now the
meticulously obedient casting of her ashes has left me less "defensive"—a
leveling term of psychotherapeutic condescension that often finds itself in
Tessa's conversation.
. . . But it's a good thing that I've had only one parent to love, learn
from, and mourn! Without psychic bifurcation I can concentrate and integrate. I was lucky in the conditional advantage of unadulterated incunabula in an extraordinary case of strong femininity, leaving me plenty of room
for the freewill of ignorance in the masculine half—sparing me the commonplace conflicts between male and female progenitors, leaving me at liberty to grow up in simple antithetical dialectic with a mother whose*

escutcheoned motto in Bradamante's time would have been Amo ergo sum. *Considering that I've managed to survive, without dissatisfaction, the parental and circumstantial disadvantages that even a courageously intro-spective, talented, energetic, resourceful, and nearly indefatigable mother could not forfend all by herself, it's clear that the unselfishness of her love shielded me from the usual subjective difficulties of an only-child or "mother's boy"!*

Still, now that all embarrassment is over, now that the outcome is inal-terable, it would do no harm to know the one important secret she kept from me. I can hardly object to the curiosity of my friend Tessa, or deny my awakening appetite for diachronic ironies. Wherefrom the masculine strands of my fundamentally feminine genesis? I certainly didn't inherit through Trevisa-Tremont molecules my proclivity for abstraction, my managerial temperament, or my technological bents. My stiff lips and monotonous voice seem to derive from accidents of nurture or circumstance. My stature is explained by unforeseen toxicity in utero, *my sinistrality by mishap in infancy. That leaves the normal complex (though unknown) coefficients to account for everything except my own freewill. Perhaps when I've finished with Gilgamesh I should at last take the time to search for clues or revela-tion in all the papers I've inconsistently retained in my mother-files—or even to offer Tessa a look at them the next time she drops one of her casual hints about wishing she had known that "remarkable" woman much sooner.*

*

Fay stood beside Tessa out in the warm sun of her upper deck on the other side of Joint Hill after Caleb had left. Thoughtfully staring down into the basin of the large Little Harbor Beach and the marsh behind its dunes, half rimmed with green hills invested and adorned by human nests and commerce, she told her remaining guest that Caleb was right. "I noticed it again when we were driv-ing along the open curves of the coast out to the Point. Now and then", she smiled, "he reminds me how our lovely landscapes are jarred by rows of houses against the background, especially from offshore. I agree that on many streets and hillsides we have a remarkable variety of domestic architecture spoiled only by poor taste in combinations of color. There are hundreds of old houses and a few new ones that I'd prefer to this one for design, comfort, con-venience, or outlook; but almost all of them, whatever their basic color, wear their clothes inside out! The nearly universal white trim disconcerts me—except on white clapboard houses of course—once

one stops to figure out why most of the Cape's ekistical scenery
isn't as beautiful as it could be. You see bold seams for lines that
would be recessed as shadow in any decent rendering. I don't categorically deplore houses of any color or material—red, pink, yellow,
green, blue, violet, brown, brick like yours (which is genuinely
modern), or wood-shingled like this one (which is too shabby for
current consideration)—but thank God for the trees and rock gardens on this side of the Hill—"

"But there are some recent exceptions, Fay. Especially, that all-
gray hilltop cluster of new condominiums I see over there across
your marsh. Across the valley they look a little like some Tuscan
hilltop town. It seems to me as perfectly in modern harmony with
their landscape as those shaded old Cachalot Point summer houses
we saw with their own antebellum time and place. Residential
development is inevitable when people and riches multiply while
space doesn't budge, especially an island or a peninsula. Rafe and I
are now glad to see how well the condominiums turned out. But of
course we still protest the zoning ordinances that allowed the loss
of that beautiful rocky tract in particular, which used to be a wonderful farm of rocky pasture for free-ranging pigs! But at least the
City insisted on all the open upland around the rather artful concentration of wooden houses, which I think blend very well with
plenty of undisturbed granite ledges. —Thanks to Dexter Keith,
now the Mayor! You may not know that when he was City Planner
he fought like a prophet for professionally aesthetic approval of
plans. —Not that anyone would ever dream of banning white trim
by law!

"But aesthetics are not just visual, and that ranch for pigs was
unsavory to say the least. Under certain meteorological conditions
it really did stink of happy hogs! At that time very few people lived
near enough to make a public health fuss when half of those around
here were screaming about fishery smells. There above the Little
Harbor marsh it was the first rural scene that struck Rafe when he
visited Dogtown mainly on business, especially in his capacity as
chief executive of the Cornucopia company that made his new
steam-cleaning machine for cooking the garbage that the farmer
fed his pigs, as required by a transitory state law to prevent the
human trichinosis caused by eating improperly nurtured swine.
That was before the whole Commonwealth was forbidden to feed
garbage to any animal not eating in a restaurant, the final resolution of what was called a swill debate! It also relieved my first

husband Buck of his protracted and impracticable promise to adapt Rafe's standard equipment to that "special application problem". Mr Murphy's land soon became much more valuable than his livestock. We were very distressed when that last bit of local animal husbandry was turned into such tempting reality-estate."

Tessa made no further reply because she was too honest to pretend that she hadn't sometimes advised friends in favor of white trim for dark houses.

But Fay had returned to her own rumination. "When we were watching the tide climb those rocks today I thought about how much faster it marks its rise or fall on our beach—though even there the progression is imperceptible, especially along the mouth of the creek that fills and drains the marsh. Yet twice a day within just a few hours the stream flows like a river, in either direction, or trickles like a brook. I was wondering if Mary's dust will dissipate this far down the shore and enrich the basin I admire every day. I think she hates to trade Lady Gloucester's love for Poseidon's impartiality." Fay laughed at her own whimsy. "She always seemed more interested in the mire of fertilization and fecundation than Classical conceptions! But of course I knew her mainly from her wonderful letters after we moved away. I see her young and you see her old, but most of her life came in between. Apart from the usual pettiness of nursing-home senility, do you think she had many recollections at the time you knew her?"

"Probably by then only fragments of what she'd memorized of poetry or what the Bible took in place of concepts." Tessa mused. "I had the impression that the comfort of Christian faith outlasted all its meaning except the existence of God. But, at least with me, she didn't talk about religion, which she took for granted. Except for one or two momentary flares of petulance when she thought she was being jostled in her wheelchair by one of her mean-spirited peers, or was unnecessarily reminded about something by one of the aides, she was very attentive and friendly. She ignored the ordinary sentimentalities of visiting hours. She would have scorned a Teddy Bear in her room but I'm sure she'd have loved a dog on her bed."

Fay was again struck with humbling embarrassment by the contrast between her old friend's excessively superior experience of life as creative suffering and her own secure good fortune: healthy longevity, satisfaction with a small variety of children and occasional grandchildren, and the freshly hopeful faculties to undertake new adventures in ideas without academic diplomacy. "Even before

Adam and I left Dogtown she spoke with joy of her 'great sin' and her baby 'born *from* sin'. I refrained from inquiry because my own difficulties seemed quite enough and I didn't want to be burdened with the expectations of attention or help implied in most confessions. Later, from a cowardly distance, I regretted my reservation. But the same sort of phrases appeared several times in her long descriptively interesting letters, most of which I never had time to answer properly. As I got older I'm afraid I grew progressively callous. Maybe that's inevitable in book-bound life." As if apologetically she touched the hand of the thin dark-haired woman at her side who might have been presumed her daughter.

"Well I'm in the confession trade myself." Tessa replied with reciprocating affection. But neither was thinking of herself. "I just wish I'd known her when she was in her famous prime."

As the table was cleared and the dishes were washed after Caleb had left, it was evident that the good cheer of lunch had loosened Tessa's discretion as a sleuth-hound recovering a faded scent, and Fay had opened the discussion about him with her remark that "He seems to boast about having no patrimony and no patronymic— certainly not because he's leery like Ion at Delphi fearing to discover some shameful origin. I like his fanciful claim to the lower case *i* that represents an imaginary number for his middle initial! I think it was those years in business that jaded his view of Dogtown culture, but more fiercely than anyone else I've met he defends this town as a locus of ideas. I love him for that!"

Now Tessa didn't know or particularly care to know who Ion was, nor what an imaginary number might be in academic locutions—so she tacitly agreed, in order to make the most of her time with her beloved Fay by getting on with the interesting facts of the case. But she was still careful not to let Fay guess her foxy collusion with Gloria, Endicott Krebs, and Gretta Doloroso from whom she spun intelligence for her web of speculation. She said nothing to Fay about the academic pretext in her therapeutic profession. As a decently educated actress, mother, businesswoman, and psychologist slightly uncomfortable with some of the erudite allusions passed back and forth between Caleb and their Athena, she was able to hold her own among common readers. But she had incautiously allowed herself to take advantage of wine and friendship by probing the personal experience of a peculiar unattached man more than his godmother does as the real mother's face-to-face confidant in 1935 and intermittent correspondent thereafter. Yet Fay was the best

possible judge of hypotheses. For the indicted mystery was Mary
Trevisa-Tremont's, after all, not Caleb's, whether or not he cared to
know the truth.

In her youthful salad days of Ur among sophisticated theatrical
people Tessa had heard of an undefined medieval Court of Love,
knowing nothing of its factual or fictional context. It was an
intriguing allusion. It now occurred to her that the titular phrase
might apply to her script ironically. Chatting with Fay she entertained an inchoate notion of eventually asking her to preside over
some such coded tribunal of a European kind in which magistrates
would conduct investigation and prosecution. For then (under
Napoleonic Law?) she herself could hardly serve even as one of the
trial judges. *But it might be fun to recruit the panel and start a charade,
if Caleb continues to pay his nonchalant attitude toward the question—
only among friends of course. Besides Fay of course I'd want Gloria: I'd
need her to present the inquiry. Who else? We can't have three women judging a female in absentia. Or would we be charging the man? That would
make a model witch hunt! Maybe Endicott Krebs as magistrate—no, not a
man! I know: let Fay be the only judge. —But her wisdom must not be
compromised. —Of course we can't expect Caleb to do anything but testify
as an accessory after the fact. —Still, none of this would work without me
as prosecutor! Who then should represent Mary in absentia? But if she's
not the defendant anyway—only an imaginary material witness! —Yet
the whole point is that we don't know who should be on trial! The court's
very purpose would be to find the accomplice of a deceased woman! —Under
the circumstances I should not be blamed for having anticipated the magisterial assignment in my fishing expedition as a professional investigator pro
bono! —How does all that sound, you clever little actress?*

Tessa's laughing head is full of tawny luse going round and
round with these silly questions about her pipe dream. She is well
aware of the foolishness but she is too pleased with her fancy to dismiss it before sober consideration at such time as the rational function of her brain could be recovered to deal with the obvious difficulty that she was unable even to invoke an assize without more
help than she already had from the one who might be called the
victim of the crime, who even today has hardly been any more
forthcoming than he has recently been to her the author of the outcome! It now seems that he's been playing dumb to all her hints.
But even with his new air of openness about half his parentage at
the cheerful lunch this afternoon he spoke as if he never heard of
either insemination or the Incarnation! How to elicit the other half

of his own *self*-interest, Tessa wonders? *Once he tossed off to me the remark that "Know Thyself" is for platonists and other spiritual people. Even Oedipus hesitated! Ion stalled!*

"Well I love him for at last showing some of his feelings!" she replied to something Fay was saying. "Why is it that men find it so hard to say *I love you* when it isn't a matter of lust?"

"I wondered if he had any regrets especially when he told us he was thinking about the ashes of Rima in Veradana as he was scattering Mary's ashes. She read him *Green Mansions* at her knee but he read it for himself when he was a teenager, he told me as his godmother the other day. He read it again after coming back to live here on the Cape and noticing a grove of seemingly primeval pines on the way up to Purdeyville that he'd always dimly envisioned with Rima's death-leap into the fire. That book was one of the few favorites they shared, like *The Jungle Book,* despite the instinctive fear of snakes that he inherited from her in infancy. He thinks one of her motives for joining the Brotherhood of the Peaceable Kingdom was to see Rima's tropical mansions. Besides Hudson and Kipling another writer they both continued to cherish especially was George Borrow. Did you ever read him?"

"Never heard of him." Tessa replied without much curiosity. "Irish I suppose."

"English. A self-educated linguist. His greatest character, generally taken to be fabulous, was an astonishing woman called Isopel Berners, the Artemis of Mumpers' Dingle, a creature after Mary's own heart, who subsequently emigrated to Atlantis and is buried here at the untended back of Acorn Pasture Cemetery. Borrow wrote a lot about Gypsies, but I'm told that none of the modern Atlantean ones who drive their trailer-kilroys in and out of Dogtown have ever heard of her. Until Caleb got enough education in college to read it for himself he apparently never appreciated his mother's heroines, but now he boasts that Isopel landed here in the end. Like many a lesser-known marooner who's vanished from history, by the way, the Playboy of the Western World also landed here, directly from Aran, according to your marvelous friend Gloria at the Library. I like her special shelf of favorites from her own youth—just below Yeats and Redburn!"

Playboy, at least, was a name familiar to Tessa, who'd once had a part in the play. She apologized to herself for human interests more personal than the anthropologist's. "I'm glad Caleb gave us a whiff of his mother's bawdy repertoire. Gretta didn't quote any, but when

she was still in school she worked part-time with Mary's housework
and the baby until they left Dogtown. She was delighted to have
been shocked out of her innocence by the plain speaking of her
Bohemian employer, enlightening about what a girl should have
been told at home. In the process she heard Mary's casual confession
of having had seven admirers (at the age of twenty-nine), and the
normal 20C implication of those words had to be explained. She
also heard a collection of dirty jokes, which I dare say Caleb heard
in later repetitions. Gretta still remembers one about the Jewish
butcher's wife. But she also heard many of Mary's creative tales, like
the one about a little New Uruk Irish boy who was always being
tormented by his redheaded sister. One hot summer's day when the
two were squabbling in the kitchen that mischievous young colleen
cried out Oh listen Danny, I hear the fire engines coming up the
avenue, run to the parlor and look out the window; so Danny ran
into the other room and stuck his head out the window; that divil
of a girl came up behind him and slammed the sash down on his
neck and begod if it didn't cut off his head and let it fall rolling
down the street; and damned if the kid didn't run back into the
kitchen screechin *Ma, Ma look what she doon to me now!*" Tessa knew
how to read stage-Irish lines, and Fay responded beneath her dignity as much to the performance as to Mary's scenario. It called for
another round of tawny luse.

Tessa resumed: "So you can imagine how much Caleb was
exposed to his mother's sin and fun right from the cradle, and probably began to get the gist of carnality and fiction before he was old
enough for nursery school! He knew enough to be embarrassed
when Mary had his handsome statuesque whitehaired fifth-grade
teacher to dinner whom she teased for looking like a Madam! He's
probably always been knowledgeable beyond his years! He must
have heard or overheard all the jokes and jingles his mother picked
up in her hundred-and-one jobs, or from men-friends, e g,

> *If you can't find a woman*
> *Get a clean old man!*

An eight-year-old kid gets used to hearing his mother singing
songs like that in the kitchen! When he told me he couldn't
remember many of the others I took it as the innuendo of a gentleman! Whenever possible she explained to him the erotic or scato-

logical derivations of words currently used in all innocence as publicly respectable."

"I've never heard him follow suit. He seems to avoid Atlantean diction, at least when he's with me."

"That smut was apparently a minor ingredient in his household brewing, but it helped make him sensitive to words! Years ago he told me that the Irish poetry she recited and the Civil War songs she sang were mostly learned from her own mother, as Victorian legacies that were already lost from popular entertainment. They must have been important in his head, even though he thought he was paying little heed to them at the time. Mary loved to sing and she knew countless songs and poems by heart. He didn't mind hearing them, but that's why, as he said today, he always thought male singers were sissies, and why he resisted or skipped efforts to memorize or vocalize in grammar school as feminine skills—a bias to his disadvantage ever since. Of course there's also his half-strangled throat. I used to think I could teach him to control his voice, but he didn't really care enough to work at it. That may be why he's driven to abstractions! He seems to think he's rounded enough to get by in a world of pure ideas!"

Fay laughed at the innuendos and exaggerations, and she didn't expect Tessa to appreciate her own scholarly sympathy with Caleb in that regard, but she'd become very respectful of the social worker's practical competence in all things that did interest her in the application of "abstractions"; and as godmother she was especially fond of Tessa for having taken such a remarkable interest in her godson, even though her obliquely persistent curiosity about Caleb's personal life did seem to have left her oddly indifferent to the value of his lucubrations. Could their common allegiance to the Cratic party have distinguished him so strongly for adoption as a younger brother, though he did not attend the valiant little meetings over which Tessa presided once a month. After the last catastrophic Raygun election was decided they could never have commiserated or encouraged each other any more than other of their friends in political abjection.

Then might such distinct personal interest for twenty years in the midst of very busy occupations be explained by Caleb's great admiration for her late first husband, whose mechanical engineering talents weren't fully appreciated by her other friends, and by his directly related gratitude to her present husband Rafe for getting him started with his first Dogtown job? As the latest marooner in their small circle Fay still felt in the dark where Dogtown was deep. Perhaps that was the magisterial moral advantage.

For after Caleb's tipsy departure Fay was surprised to have heard from Tessa to what lengths she had gone as an unofficial but bona fide colleague of the social worker at the Bishop's nursing home to look at the records after the old lady's derangement was written off as all but post mortem. Before that finality was reached Mary Tremont had tried to be the life of her sour classification as well as the leading troublemaker of the whole Second Floor. Perhaps the quasi-medical supervisor had taken too literally the tales of nurses and aides about what occurred in the daily course of social events, as accepted for diagnosis by the medical doctor on his generally euphemistic or sanguine rounds. Fay guessed that Mary's imaginative humor was never fathomed either by her fellow inmates or by her attendants. Weren't her stories, at least originally in her incarceration, simply figments of creative recreation to amuse herself, challenging the incessant nursing-home banalities of devilvision and cooped-up animosities, perhaps no more insane than the entertainments that had always made her popular with children. It should be no surprise that in mental decline her merrily ironic inventions had crystalized to outlast mortal reason.

Thus for example, in those closing years, according to Tessa, Mary claimed three children, totally forgetting or disbelieving the tubal ligature she had undergone at her own request during Caleb's early childhood: the eldest and factual technocrat who'd abandoned his mother; whose fictitious schoolteaching sister had loyally remained her mother's helper until her husband had dragged her off to Cornucopia; and his concocted brilliant little brother who was now a neurological professor at the foremost training hospital in Parthenia. She boasted of six grandchildren, though she offered none of their names and couldn't remember where even their parents had gone to college.

"From girlhood to middle age she'd yearned and described those three—or at least two of them!" Tessa laughed. "Children came before lovers, religion, or art. The remarkable thing, the noble thing, is that she let the three-in-one first-born 'break the mother bond' when he reached manhood at the age of twelve!"

"Do you think Caleb ever regretted his ghostly siblings?" Fay mused with a faraway smile. "From all I've heard he seems to have had a happily solitary childhood, never aware of hardship or desti-

tution except as the spur of ambition. Always interested in school
and play and reading, always building or drawing what he wanted
and never expected to possess, probably never bored. His mother
took him on little adventures whenever they had sixpence for car-
fare. Everything interesting, like yachts or horses or guns or uniforms, as he told us, could be put on paper somehow. Maybe he
missed having a brother and sister to tell his stories to, but I should
guess that he was never lonely. Before he could read Mary praised
him for the things he built with blocks or salvaged from rubbish.
In her letters to me she was always boasting about him. That irritated me a bit when my husband and I were a little worried about
the talents of our own academic brats. Caleb may have inherited
from her his penchant for exceptional friends to share his exceptional admirations. But from what he told us today I think her
undisguised disappointments with unimaginative people taught
him more caution with his associates than she had with hers. Some
friends she made instantly, often losing them almost as quickly, in
enmity or disgust, but sometimes, as with me, kept forever. But
that's because I was almost always at a safe distance from her! She
never had a chance to see me looking snug and smug in academia!"
Fay paused with a glance into Tessa's eyes.

". . . For his first twelve years she must have been his absolutely
trustful but unconscious foundation—with no permanent nest to
confuse mother with place—until he was independent enough to
go anywhere without her if he had the money to do so! How many
a single mother of one child would have had such reciprocal confidence? In advance she had named him as her dog—Caleb who
would see the promised land, the Caliban of this island—but
meanwhile her only domestic companion, with no expectation of
any response except love and understanding at his own distance. He
must have learned to filter her words and anecdotes according to a
little boy's natural indifference to the world of grownup women, all
the while with his thoughts on what fascinated him in the masculine world beyond her ken."

"Yes," said Tessa, "and now he's counting up as much as he can
of the treasured impressions, true or mistaken, that had never been
assigned to his conscience! Or partly right and partly wrong. So he
prematured! Advantage or inhibition?"

"Probably both, don't you think?" Fay answered, looking again
in the face of her younger friend, a surprisingly earnest psychiatric
social worker. "You know him better than I do."

Tessa smiled and relaxed, regarding Fay as a sympathetic mother superior. "It's you and the wine that loosened his tongue today. He suspects me of being a crypto-Freudian. I must admit that sometimes I'm under the influence. But Fay, don't I understand his mother better than any man could, Viennese or not except maybe Auto Drang, who himself was too profound to be understood. My hard times have been hardly an iota of hers—no destitution, no isolation, no lack of protection; but I was married to a kindly alcoholic much older than myself who was immersed in his mechanical work day and night. It was better than being alone but the loneliness at night after my kids were born sometimes seemed unbearable, much as I loved poor Buck and pitied his evasive embarrassment. It came to the point that I hid a dildo with the underwear in my dresser drawer. I suppose she did as much."

"I got hints of something like that in one of her long letters. I pretended not to have noticed that aspect of her tribulations when I finally had time to respond. For instance when she was in love with her numinous and virtuous Rector in Unabridge. . . . I too led a sheltered life, as she often contrived to remind me!"

Maybe Fay was more like an elder sister than a mother, Tessa thought. *In spite of all our intrigues and collaborations I've never trusted Cora as much as this.* "It's hard to have lovers in a small town. Before my wonderful Rafe appeared on the scene I had a few brief affairs, but they were too dangerous or too disappointing to be any relief as soon as the beatitudes subsided—if they were that good. After Buck died even my lingering guilt vanished. So both Moira Trevisa and Mary Tremont have my excruciating sympathy. But I don't believe she was promiscuous. It sounds as if she wanted love more than lovers—until after Caleb flew the coop in Montvert, leaving her to fight it out with a village dame for the treacherous company of Tony Porter."

"That must have been her 'world's greatest lover', the Loosie taxi man from Dogtown she referred to for years. It sometimes seemed that she was teasing me. I was never quite sure of the grammatical tense or mood in which she mentioned him—indicative or subjunctive. Despite her troubles, most of her letters were good-humored and hopeful. Sometimes the narratives of her work and religious experience in South Atlantis were professionally interesting to me in the cities as much as in the hinterland. She had enviable adventures and described them lucidly. I wasn't comfortable with her Pauline kind of emotional faith but I must say that I ben-

efited from her geographical anthropology! Her critically enthusiastic descriptions of people and places would have enriched subjective ethnography! I think she was too avid with agape or suffering
in loneliness—and at the same time too devoted to the common
good—to have been anything like a nymphomaniac."

"Well," Tessa ventured, "none of what we've learned from Caleb
today has given us more than a jot or tittle about Caleb's other
half—assuming there's no such thing as immaculate conception—
during the portentous Gloucestermas of 1934. Mother and nurture
don't account for everything. Except for his mother, he claims too
much for chance and freewill to account for himself! He pretends to
know nothing about chromosomes."

Fay seldom allowed herself to participate in personal gossip,
but she was dutifully concerned with the peculiar constitution of
her godson. Forty-five years before, as a nominal Petrine Scholastic
from her earliest years but partaking in the Tudor Classic sacrament
of baptism at the font of little Saint Martha's Convent chapel out
on Crow Point, to please Mary she had come up from Unabridge to
accept indefinite responsibility for her son's spiritual future, only to
do nothing about the promise thereafter. In fact, until recently she
had forgotten her pledge, as even Mary herself the religious mother
probably had in her old age. Having lately consulted the Apostolic
Book of Common Prayer she now found that it had called for two
godfathers. None had appeared. Alone with single parent and child,
Fay had all too casually pledged as Caleb's attorney to see that he
would be taught to renounce "the devil and all his works, the vain
pomp and glory of the world, with all covetous desires of the same,
and the sinful desires of the flesh". She now believed that Caleb had
instinctively complied with the first three of those four unconsid-
ered commitments, but she was an empirical skeptic about the
fourth. And she had shamelessly failed even to enquire about the
remainder of her ecclesiastical obligation: to ensure the babe's religious education and eventual presentation to a bishop for Confirmation, his license to the Eucharist he practiced. In most of the
primitive cultures with which she'd sympathetically spent her
career, such dereliction, mutatis mutandis, would have been shocking. Indeed, she reflected, if anything, Caleb had been instructing
her in heretical Christian anthropology. The least she could now do
to expiate her venial sin was to give rein to maternal curiosity
about the infant's father! Since the beginning, and ever since, she
had tactfully refrained from blunt questioning. Now that Tessa,

bless her, had broken the ice, she could remark "I wonder about that conspicuous dramaturge Ipsissimus Charlemagne, whom I remember hearing about in those days. He called himself an anthropologist. Apparently he inspired some of Caleb's theories. Didn't he start the Dromenology cult?"

"Oh my god, by all accounts Mary detested him!" Tessa laughed. "I knew the Director many years later, but I can easily imagine why she would. When I knew him he was a histrionic exhibitionist if ever there was one! Rafe tells me that the two like charges repelled each other. Even in those early days, before he went away to become famous, when he was lanky as well as tall, behind his back Mary Trevisa was calling Charlemagne fatuous. Maybe she was the one who originally dubbed him Ipsissimus. She must have recognized in him her own temperamental affliction, though she granted his superior genius. Gretta told me that Mary claimed to have taunted him as 'obviously an only child'. — Remember, that was B C, Before Caleb in some of her diaries! She seems to have laughed about her own humbler and less learned propensity to entertain company she found herself in, but no doubt Ippy resented public teasing—maybe disrespect—from a half-educated girl five years younger than himself. I gather that having spent some time among New Uruk Bohemians and other cosmopolitans she detected cracks in his feet of clay and did not conceal her scorn of his 'avant-garde airs'.

"All her life, as far as I can see from scraps of evidence, she ridiculed whatever she interpreted as aesthetic preciosity. She could hardly avoid him in Dogtown's little universe of art. I suppose it's possible that at first he was briefly one of her 'suitors' but it's highly unlikely that he ever got to be one of her 'admirers' at the time, especially since she may have had a regular year-round visitor during some of the time before Doc Charlemagne gave up the summer Theater-on-the-Wain and went down to Limeway for crusts of bread as an apprentice. Then too according to the *Nous,* for much of 1934 he had a grant to visit the British Isles and study the Abbey Theater and Yeats's dramaturgy—who, by the way, I hear was no slouch at displaying his own personality. When I knew Doc he was no clown. Always warm and gentle in his condescension, not a trace of humbug, but his kind of exhibitionism was so personalistic that I doubt he was incapable of self-consciousness. But I found it much more charming in his case than in lesser men."

Fay had already been surprised at Tessa's unintentional exposure of her rather peculiar interest in the depth to which she had delved for Caleb's past; but every now and then the social worker herself was sober enough to notice her own lubricated indiscretion and bite her tongue. But the temptation to confess her motive as a frank and open devotee of her venerable Athena was still hard to resist. So she continued with an obliquity tending toward the reckless truth of her investigation and its staff of innocents. At the same time she regarded herself as all but scrupulous in avoiding improper influence of her own imagination upon the impartiality of the queen who would be asked to preside over a Court of Love that might be assembled to settle the paternity case.

Fay's thin lips tightened. "Are you compiling a list of the men she knew?"

Tessa felt a possible rebuke in the words of her superior, but she made no apology, resolving to abate the usually latent tension between their two generations of ethos despite sympathetic enlightenment both forward and backward. She thought that it was the temporal stratification that made Fay such an excellent choice for presiding magistrate in any courtroom. After a pause neither too short nor too long to express natural delight in Tessa's surprise at what happened to catch her attention in the immediate scenery: "—Oh look at those two squirrels chasing each other up and down one tree after another!"

"I never get tired of watching them. Sometimes there are three of them. Felixity was tantalized by their acrobatics. Squirrels are more astonishing than gulls." Fay followed the eyes of her alert younger friend, as thin as herself, with black hair and complexion almost as olive as her own at an earlier age, but perhaps slightly disingenuous in morality. Then she looked up through her kitchen window at the sky. "This has been our only perfect day in May." To Dogtown's usual surprise it had been a spring of the ocean's choosing—overcast, nondescript, and generally disappointing; but, as if suddenly, a taller thicker landscape of foliage was obscuring neighbors, marsh, beach, opposite hills, Memorial Day flags, and the level blue horizon more than ever before. Fay estimated the summer's ensuing growth by the stiff pale-yellow stamens, already over half a foot high, erect from seed pods like Christmas tree candles at every extremity of her Japanese black pines. She smiled at the torches of youth. *I think I understand the lust of men. It's not rockgut.*

18
ISLE OF MAN
[Mid-June]

1.

One morning Fay Gabriel rode the commuter train into Botolph to join a colloquium on the anthropological philosophy of religion at the Norumbega Theological School in Unabridge. An ample honorarium provided by the Arnheim Foundation had overcome her reluctance to waste time in her preciously remaining intellectual life for the mere honor of representing heterodoxy within an obscure "interdisciplinary" profession. Her retirement's disposable income was wholly absorbed by the debtless equanimity of the steady state she had chosen, which provided for reasonable contingencies, all necessary insurance included, in a convenient situation on an interesting Joint Hill; but still it was a "fixed income" with no margin for extravagance. Non-recurrent honorariums offered occasional liberalities.

Sorties to the mainland, by rail, were rare for her nowadays. Even when she'd lived in Dogtown half a century earlier as a married hospital nurse, and for a short time before the birth of her first child, it was her husband who'd done the regular shuttling to Botolph for classrooms in the Norumbega Garth. Probably she alone among the jaded or constitutionally incurious passengers who would eventually board this train en route had never worn out her appreciation of the Dogtown Branch's scenery, though even she took no pleasure with her return ticket when it was dark and the poorly lighted hardly heated bumpy cars seemed dangerously decrepit or sullenly slow in the intervals between drawn-out debarkations of ravenous students and weary office workers, while chattering was impatiently silenced. Especially on the last pro-tracted inland stretch before Dogtown's central station in unavoid-able journeys home after dark in a coach all but emptied she would find herself shivering almost alone with nameless apprehension as she gathered her things and rose from her seat too soon and stood at the vestibule door as if she might miss the stop and a last taxi, only to be swept helplessly past her destination on the coda of the Dog-town Branch, a single track curving north through the hills to its absolute terminal at Land's End, usually with no more than two or three other lorn souls in a rattling capsule of safely evacuated ghosts and their litter. But the morning ride into the metropolis was otherwise in mood. As much as possible she therefore planned her round-trip errands and appointments for a repetition of the eastern seascape views, sitting to the starboard ("Eastbound" northerly to home) in the P M, leaving the glare of descending suns to passengers across the aisle, instead of sitting on the port side as she now did in the A M ("Westbound" to the south), as she adjusted with her left hand any necessary shading of the warmly ascendant sun that lighted her side of the aisle through a tolerably functional window, dirty or merely scratched, as its angle fluctuated with the sinuous course of the tracks. But in either direction, whatever the time of day—since steam engines had long since been retired and passenger windows sealed for nominal air-conditioning—she some-times still tried to recall the acrid scent of cinders borne with the smoke of coal and wafted lubrication oil.

On her right as the train cautiously approached the Dogtown Draw it passed the modern low brick building of the *Daily Nous* plant and its parking lot, which had displaced a coal yard with many pockets, served by railroad hopper cars on a side track that no longer existed, and then the gutted and abandoned walls of the Dogtown Smithy & Iron Works on the deserted bank of the Namauche estuary below, to gather speed on the straightaway across salt marshes to West Parish. But in half a century not much had changed for the rich or the poor, or for industrial architecture, in Fay's view from the left side of the righthand track on a lovely green and blue day on the way to Botolph's North Station. Yet the route was still so familiar from the distant past that she no longer watched at every minute of motion along landscape seascape and shabby urban walls beside above or beneath aged public superstructures.

Early in the journey she opened her morning *Botolph Orb* as the train entered the longest uninteresting passage of the Dogtown Branch, through nearly uninhabited backwood hills to the open coastline and its offshore islets beginning at Felicity-by-the Sea. There she no longer could bear to read news of Roland Raygun's re-rooted Protestican power, but her eye was caught on an inner page by the cryptic report of a young youth-club leader in one of the suburbs who'd set fire to a seagull, insisting that his young followers pay attention to his feat. There was no report of the aftermath. The newspaper dropped to her lap and for much of the rest of the one-hour trip she stared out her window, scarcely conscious of what she saw, or looked for by the habits she had so readily resumed, ignoring the long-armed "young man on the way up" in a bow tie who got on at Felicity and carelessly elbowed her as he incessantly folded and unfolded the *Graveyard Chronicle* folios already distributed from New Uruk.

A subliminal relic of the Christian polity, in this basically Pauline country as well as in Petrine Europe, that burned domesticated cats alive and tortured even captured wolves, but without the excuse of superstition. Such Manichean vengeance must have been suppressed—or abolished in tamed and civil Wales when George Borrow found that a whole village of Chapel "Calvinistic Methodists" had been deliberately starving a black cat by banishment simply because it had once belonged to the former vicar of their Tudor English Church. That behavioral anachronism in a society can at least be rationalized as a collective practice of apotropaic innocence. But personally sadistic torture of a harmless bird—even as a man's unconscious retribution for childhood mistreatment, or even under evil orders—is a polar antithesis of instinctive humanity when hunger or foresight plays no part, as precisely outlawed by Hitler's regime in Germany. Its gratuitous cruelty is not excused by any iota of Hegelian degree as a resultant between conflicting moral urgencies such as torture inflicted to extort information necessary to prevent the slaughter of a million innocents; or as Tessa, unlike Finn, might construe as confounding love with hate, if only she knew how to diagram conflicting forces, seeing that she's perfectly right to dismiss the

dialectical simplicity of opposites in ordinary psychological contrarieties.
. . . Compassion, literally at least, is empathy—a nearly solipsistic intu-
ition, however brief—whereas even the purest sympathy is only a selected or
otherwise limited resonance with another creature, a consonance of certain
affects rather than a sharing of subjectivity, reserving the innate selfishness
that's naturally irreducible even in all but saintly altruism. But there are
continuous degrees of understanding between the first person and the second
or third, and the vectors that represent them are seldom in such polar opposi-
tion as in this vicious case of senseless torture, a rarity of pure dialectal
antithesis among higher forms of life. . . . But the idea of human love, in
all degrees of its various ends and means, moves me to Mary Tremont's arcs
of synthesis. The many faces of her clock, ranging from nearly selfless altru-
ism to nearly selfish lust, each resolved for a time or for a moment one of the
hundred and eighty degrees of love between two pairs of arrows. But for me
the configurations that outlasted all the rest—from what I knew of her in
person or by her own writing, before the hardest struggles and religious con-
solations of her later life—were the epitome of human storge. Every living
thing, normally, whether victim or predator, begins with motherhood. Like
many women, poor Mary Tremont, longing for love and God, may never
have been compassionate enough with men to understand even the most sym-
pathetic ones. . . . Lovers, forsooth, never quite get to the bottom of us. But
if for nothing else I'd love my Viking Finn for his surprising sympathies.
Perhaps Whitehead, so famous for his mathematical metaphysics, expressed
the ground for sympathy better than any other philosopher with his casual
remark that "Concernedness is of the essence of perception." That kind of
thinking was what first drew me to that philosopher's Unabridge soirées.
There's no personal separation of ontology and epistemology. Yet commonly
there's so much misunderstanding, especially by wives of men who have mar-
ried them without sharing reproductive motives and do not dare to make it
clear that they fail to sympathize with what Mary called women's "brood-
ing". At the beginning of marriage a husband may imagine satisfaction
with children after the difficult years are over, but women are astonished
when they hear of mindless infanticide by a debt-ridden young man, left
alone with a baby, its bottle empty and its diapers loaded, who in an explo-
sion of fury to stop its bawling with his own screams, shakes and flings the
tender brain to death, when all he craves at the ebb of his humiliating
workday is relief from domestic responsibility, soothed with beer and passive
sport in an easy chair before the DV screen—or else the peace to get his
night-school homework done, if not even the peace to write a poem that's been
evolving in his head all day as he's served others in the clamor of his
shop—before the exhausted mother comes home a little late with her arms

full of groceries from the one supermarket that stays open at night. But his crime of passion, whether or not simply pathological, is a violation of trust, not torture, not vengeance, not meant as castigation of the mother, and not necessarily a revelation of God's will. Even when Adam and I were seeking out Mardians at the Equator before assuming the burden of a real family, though I'd already earned my stripe as an experienced nurse, I didn't fully understand my perfectly decent and apparently devoted husband. Still, I instinctively spared him the worst of our nesting enterprise because I was never as innocent of compassionate suspicion as Mary was before her repeated disillusions of perfected erotic union even without the spurs of marriage. . . . I'm as ignorant of her existential suffering as she was innocent of my "intellectual passion" (as her son calls his own most elevated feelings). Yet the theodicean problem is that I am considered a successful woman in the man's world while Mary died as a social and poetic failure! The least I can do for her sake is my duty as Caleb's godmother, the nearly forgotten pledge that I now must try to honor. My own successful children have to worry more about my "success" than I do about theirs. It was far easier for me than for Mary to be a good mother, considering how sheltered my life was in marriage and security. At least my kids were brought up to absorb the axioms of mathematics and the fundamental definitions of science as touchstones for discriminating among the tropes of art and religion that seem irrational. . . . I didn't quite realize that by myself I had lacked that appreciation as an advantage for what's called truth in my wholly "relativistic" profession. Reason needs an anchorage. That's how enlightenment, no matter how divergent from physical science in its humanities, can appreciate the varieties of experience. I'm alert to axiological definitions for the metaphors and analogies in Caleb's interpretations of Charlemagne's Dromenology and Father Duncannon's dynamic sacramentalism. It's almost as if the priest thought that mankind, represented by the Jews, evolved sacrifice to the point of intrinsic definition so that an expectant God would be able to appropriate an Incarnation in order to enable his own divinity! It might just as well have been that the liturgical Incarnation produced the God that Jews had not imagined, not unlike the boy passing through a graveyard at night who is scared because he finds himself running. . . . Years ago what I wrote too exclusively of Mardian mental "patterns", which served them for navigation as well as causality, seems naturally to serve us (if only as foil to theology and quantum theory) in framing either empirical or supernatural truth. Hemispheres of understanding seemed essentially meaningless to each other. Anyway, indeterminism doesn't necessarily imply freewill; but when it does, is the will free of its own causality or free for causal action? Right now, for the sake of country and all humanity, especially with our new President, I fear more than anything else a popular contempt for reason, a faith in willful ignorance of evidence. Of course fate has many options, but especially in democratic politics there is no point at which you can disengage the practically infinite decision-tree of causality or escape from the web of circumstance into what Father Duncannon called the "social stagnation" of totally spiritual Eastern religions. For the last hundred years we've been liberating the emotional elements of our psyches: Caleb is right that now's the time to divert psychic energy to the extrication of reason from the moil of electoral culture. I wouldn't take back much of what I've published but I'd like to say more for the West's enlightened analysis of reality. My political hope springs eternal only because almost all my friends and colleagues either disbelieve in effects without causes or are hypothetically reasonable in reconciling whatever they conjecture about truth or probability (as others otherwise did in the Middle Ages), and The New Uruk Testament *tries to be on our side. Yet dear old Alphie Whitehead admitted negative capability even in systemic cosmology with his kind of idealist realism, and so did Mary Tremont with her own emotionally realistic consistency of religious faith throughout all her battles against powerful ignorance and stupidity. Caleb too, the rationalist regarding faith and mystery from the opposite direction, seems sufficiently capable of negativity in his esemplastic fusion of Charlemagne's inchoate Dromenology with Father Duncannon's "metacosmesis", as well as in playful symbol-systems far less plausible than his rationally synectic correlations of truth and supposition! Who could be more rational and more faithful than Anselm? In the end it's the options of axiology that make us human. . . .*

When the car was nearly filled at a few irregular intervals that seemed as natural in rhythm as the linear variations of littoral scenery more or less according to the indented shoreline of beaches headlands and enviable old estates, even to one who'd ridden the line only half a dozen times two-score years after returning to her foster home as a terminal marooner (still connected to an impersonal terminal by filaments of speed too familiar to have interrupted vacant stare at what occupied her eyes), Fay's reverie was broken at the ancient midpoint of commuting, the Dogtown Branch's junction with a single-track spur line that survived in kilroy civilization as obsolescent outreach to a few remaining inland manufacturers from what used to be its roundhouse and turntable for steam locomotives—just before the commuters are rushed through a short antiquated tunnel lined with smoke-stained granite blocks beneath the main streets of Bethsalem, a city at least two hundred years older than its cavern. In less than a minute the train emerged from its dark swift noise to the sunken open-air concrete platform that had taken the place of a lofty steam-filled barrel vault of glass on the busy County seat's station at street level, which she remembered from before the War as continuously sheltering far more human and mechanical activity than the narrow sporadic bustle of students now getting off and on, with hardly a working man to be seen among them. Nearly every empty seat was suddenly filled, discomposing all those who spread open their newspapers.

For a few moments the new rustling and chatter reduced the speed of her consciousness to that of the common present, which as always drew her attention to the sudden change of scene as the fully loaded train climbed out of its concrete vale onto the open commercial and industrial flats of what once was an important manufacturing city. A broad rail yard was surrounded by a neighborhood earnestly attempting to sustain its waning district with inventive small businesses, but among those newer buildings was the dominant older one that Caleb had once pointed out to her as an illustration for his curriculum vitae. It had housed his last job, as a "Sales Analyst", before turning to work in his birthplace and finding less recognitial employment first with Tessa's husband Rafe and then with Father Duncannon's Laboratory of Melchizedek and the Mesocosm, the most curious of all! This symmetrically fenestrated factory and office structure of reinforced concrete fifty years old and five stories high, crowned with a clock tower, had long remained one of Bethsalem's paternalistic institutions, but since Caleb's time it had been bought out, emptied of machinery, and temporarily used for storage by the international Arnheim conglomerate (subsequently admired by Caleb when as the Lab's "business manager" he studied its part in Arthur Halymboyd's intricate stockmarket webbing), only to be spun off not long afterwards to an Atlantean leviathan willing to pay a great deal for the further reduction of its former competition in the mass production of incandescent and fluorescent devices of electrical enlightenment (having given up on radio tubes prematurely, just before the forward-looking profits of wartime electronics).

Dear me, do I get his story right? What a bizarre counterpart to his mother's career! Tessa's ad hominem gossip must not be allowed to distract me from my own critical synthesis of certain systemic ideas in a culture that Caleb modestly assures me can be ultimately evaluated only by a philosophy that is beyond theistic or even deistic capability, with or without the divine grace that makes possible any progressive evolution of mankind's superorganic social subsystems. His compliment to me! I have sometimes been accused of "cultural relativism"; but I believe more than I once did that an equality of values does not necessarily follow from their incommensurability. Yet until I write my last will and testament I must stick to my professional last, which keeps a stamp book of values, including that of men's managerial technology. But the mischievous sentimentality in Atlantean "patriotism"—is that a value to be classified as corrupted enlightenment or as secular expression of a nebulous religion? How do you distinguish the authentic emotion that Sterne called sentimental from the feelings of rational religion or the love in a family? Sometimes in the transposed commemorative or aesthetic sentiment of a sympathetic reader or spectator there's nothing any less genuine than the tranquility transposed from original compassion by the poet. Still, meanwhile, not by nature, not by nurture, I seem to find myself a rational counterweight to the maternal in Caleb's adult psyche! Let Tessa worry about the genes. Finn never stops calling me that boy's fairy godmother! With Finn's advice I find benefit in the metaphors of Caleb's technology. It's interesting discipline to describe an equilateral triangle as the face of Gilgamesh's "isorectotetrahedron", or a regular pyramid as the womb of a cube; but I'm afraid he verges upon the very kind of "symbullisticism" that he scorns in the mystic occult, despite his insistence that it's as functional as the analogical quaternion rotated by the square root of minus one in electrical engineering!

There came a long inland stretch of "undeveloped" hills and swampy bottom land in a heath between colonial Bethsalem and obsolescent Liverpool, a city once famous for acres and acres of narrow streets darkened by tier upon tier of shoemaking floors filled with locally manufactured machines for men and women to operate (Tuscan, Irish, or even Canuck): great redbrick blocks pierced with rows and columns of dingy windowpanes—but now either dismally empty or converted to public housing, if not entirely replaced in open air by kilroy-parking conveniences, macadam or concrete, at one level or another, to serve more sunnily the purposes of a renovated downtown shopping center. At new platforms on the remaining old rail bed that crossed the semi-sunny canyons of the city's nevertheless overshadowed central square, this coastal Liverpool without port or dock was the last stop for Fay's consist of six self-propelled commute coaches before its final braking at the line's southern terminal twenty minutes later. But she happened to remember that it was the proletarian birthplace and cradle of

Gepetto DaGetto, one of Dogtown's oldest living marooners, the ebullient old sculptor whose twisted and welded "Ironry", having shocked to life the traditional arts and tastes of Dogtown, now represented in Tessa's house as well as her own (a present from Finn) by table-top pieces from his proliferated *Nude Teiresias* series, which she had heard was inspired by the youthful Belle Cingani, present capable editor of the *D T Daily Nous* but then known as Bice Picory, spontaneously marooned from Acadia in the Dominion of North Atlantis before she'd qualified as a cub reporter. Petto signed his ferrous copper granite or driftwood pieces as Simplicissimus, or simplified as *S-s*, his industrial welding trademark.

Among the quasi-lettered citizenry, she ruminated, Petto was considered a lunatic doyen of all the arts, though accepted as a sort of atheistic saint by virtue of the patent fact that he'd always worked with his hands for a living and was no richer in his reclusive retirement than when he'd begun thirty years earlier by wangling a second-hand welding rig to take him all about the Cape like a gypsy tinker doing commercial odd jobs in situ. Others generally agreed that his passion for beauty and truth never waned, or that he never grew less guileless in enthusiasms or denunciations, though waxing in confidence of his pontifications as a prophet with overweening insight into the soullessness of public affairs. As a local celebrity he embarrassed the Trinacrians and other fisherfolk who knew of his family's origins among the peasantry of mainland Etruria or of their humble capitulation as cobblers in the Atlantean factories down here among urban landlubbers, as well as many of the local aborigines and troglodytes of other blood who suffered egregious art and radical personalities about as gladly as most continental Atlanteans did. Yet nowadays most of the Cape had grown accustomed to the gadfly of artistic liberty, and the venerably uninhibited old prophet had a purely voluntary claque of both sophisticated and naive admirers, who loved him either for his art or for his self, if not for both. Under their influence he was invited to attend or speak at many "cultural events" and at all private parties of the like.

Fay had already come to regard Petto with impersonal affection, having been spoken of him by Normans who preceded her as marooners, though not without the reservations of a prudent scholar. Caleb for instance was only one in a manifold circle of Dogtowners who cherished the intuitive skill and imagination of the sculptor, now also emergent as a vatic poet of genuine insights in a language he had gradually taught himself to use in his own right, whose work sprang more from tender sympathies than from thirst for the satisfactions of a theatrical role as the clarion of existential courage in a mechanized culture saturated with hostility to sui generis art and the traditional fishing industry. Fay had been told by Tessa that in his earlier old age, before Doc Charlemagne's careless arson of her Stone Barn Theater, Petto had tried to study mime in order to lead a few women (among the many who were susceptible to ostentations of artistic virility) in performances illustrating his abstract sculpture, purportedly to challenge the best of French cinema. And Caleb had told her that Petto once returned his selective praise with an offer to agree enthusiastically that modern religion, like modern art, should turn to the primitive for fresh inspiration. For Caleb himself, as a friendly savant responding with his usual reach for abstractions, that artist's spiritualistic opposition to all Christian churches warranted analogical comparison in which one formula serves isomorphically for two or more ontologically unrelated expressions. For Fay his rather tiresome example of that equation, which she didn't bother to distrust, was the same esoteric expression used in measuring information as the one that represented thermodynamic negative entropy (which Caleb persisted in calling counterentropy). Rather than attempting to disabuse Petto of his most ingenuously passionate vaticinations with argument or gently countervailing citations, or else with the pretense of taking them in as solemn food for thought, Caleb always tried to reply in words that were ostensibly satisfactory to them both, sometimes in the process opening the trope to new associations in his own mind—as if, behold, the conversation itself was suddenly revelatory to a listener like himself. (It occurred to Fay that she might have smiled and said the poem was only Petto's!) But usually Caleb let his encounters with Petto remain at that level of cross-purposes, as by the same token Petto reciprocated Caleb's tributes without mentioning that despite his interest in stage sculpture he was not fascinated by the Gilgamesh playscripts he'd read!

. . . Thus Fay's wandering meditations recalled random particulars of vicarious knowledge in this brief insulated passage through a city in which she had never alighted when her own distracted eyes were in transit with a preoccupied husband and two cranky small children on the way to Unabridge, though it always summoned her imagination of its namesake in Redburn's excruciating book about his first landing in Britain. The place now so named in Vinland was

known to her only for idle exhumation as a vaguely recalled mile-
stone in the curriculum vitae of Caleb Karcist, now glimpsed south
of the city center as a flat industrial structure nearly undistinguish-
able from others in its truck-ridden neighborhood except for the
large sign on its roof, VINLAND SUPPLY COMPANY. It was
there that Caleb had once been Sales Analyst, learning something
about wholesale groceries, frozen food, paper products, and other
chandlery for retailers to landsmen, broadening his previous experience with automotive jobbers in the sales of industrial machinery to
garages and construction equipment dealers when he worked for a
manufacturers' representative.

*I believe him when he says that what possessed him in those early years
was not interest or ambition but necessity. As a student of literature he'd
been in no position to "choose a career" in the vocational manner of current
college graduates. At that point every job was only the means for living
without servants, he swears, seeing that he chose not to qualify for journalism advertising or teaching. But I'm not sure he's sufficiently aware that
even with his record of apolaustic college education he had the inestimable
advantages of an ableminded male free of demands from anyone but himself—for his mother usually absolved him of guilt! Poor unguided Mary,
despite occasional anger at his selfishness, had never been more mercenary
than Saint Francis even in her commercialized ambitions, and long after
these wherewithals failed she would give hoboes or beggars her next-to-last
sneakers or pence, or F D R's party her next-to-last disposable dollar. In her
later years she called Caleb a miser, but his excuse is that it was only in
reaction to her characteristic improvidence. As a boy he sometimes stood in
weekly welfare lines when she was too sick to act as head of the family. He
confessed to us that two or three times before he got his final job at the Yard
he'd suffered, like Wellingborough Redburn or some shabby Gissing character, the humiliation of an unclassed gentleman's son when he'd had to wait
on foot in a public room to collect unemployment insurance among people who
seemed to witness his degradation with Schadenfreude as if they'd known
him personally; and that even in prosperity his parsimony is scarcely
relaxed, for he's always shocked by the prices in a store whenever he remembers what prices seemed to have been in some previous decade! Now of course
he wishes he'd been more of a miser. Patrician sympathy with life in the
lower ranks is more altruistic than the self-centered empathy of Crats like
Caleb to whom it isn't foreclosed by inexperience. . . . Besides teasing me for
my easy life above stairs, Mary was inclined to remind benefactors of their
advantageous lack of her experience. Maybe there's an inverted analogy on a
technological level when Caleb's sympathetic imagination of warship life in*

wartime is distinguished from the feelings of that engineering and intelligence officer whose hardship it was to undergo the sinking of his cruiser. But here's where the communicative abstraction of general ideas can help salvage Enlightenment: two men so different in age temperament and experience are able to share such interests as "general systems theory"—though certainly not so remarkably as men and women communicate in the linguistic and mathematical sympathy that normally demands nothing of personal fortitude. Mary deliberately disturbed all ranks of the gentry by challenging in unladylike terms a putative type of pretty common gutless males, especially the mealy-mouthed arbiters of female speech. In one of her letters she made fun of a neighboring widow in Montvert, brought up on a dairy farm, who primly distinguished bulls from cows by their "tassel". In those days of Mrs Grundy's rule no one else outside the medical professions would publicly utter words like cancer, menopause, *or* rape. *And even to this day nearly all speakers and writers* perspire *instead of* sweat. *Then too, not just words: Caleb tells us that in his embarrassed presence (and God knows how often without it) she'd sometimes ostentatiously shock adult witnesses when she was entertaining young children with the lower shelf of her teeth. More often, even unto old age (when dentures are no joke to old people), she'd stand head-on with arms akimbo and legs apart like a sailor braced for the roll of a deck, a stocky comedian of God's truth, and rehearse her chant that "Women are the better people!"—ostensibly meant to be taken as a prophetic joke. In many ways she was a harbinger of the present generation, which is so tolerant of itself that it shouldn't object to any form of clowning. . . . But what was she really like before I met her at the very breaching of Caleb's life? Was that event a metanoia on her part, a mere graduation, or simply the histological continuation of an adolescent dream even before idiopathic sleeping sickness? I know little about her earlier life than what she told me of Caleb's neonatal years or wrote me on postcards if not as narrative descriptions in her many long letters thereafter—some of which were damaged in transit when I got them, or were otherwise left unread in their entirety because I lacked the time to read any but immediately interesting passages until a more convenient time, which seldom came, I'm sorry to say, as in the case of many a philosophy book on my professional shelves. (After all, even polymath Whitehead confessed he never got around to reading Hegel, whose special kind of idealism in opposition to his own he had grasped vicariously for his debates with other Apostles—and never afterwards either!) But with a loyal sense of guilt I kept lugging along a carton of everything she ever sent me, hardly studied and never reviewed, with all my other impedimenta, from post to post, among all my own papers and books, with or without husband children or furniture, along with many lesser dust-bound treasures of the past. Now that my own granite ceiling is approaching apace, with my last work still left to do, and no secretaries or office machines to help, as well as no appointed executor, I'm as pressed as ever for time to read what I currently need; so the decision to lend my Mary-trove to Tessa was an equivocal relief of conscience. I can't do Mary's life the justice it deserves more than most of the stuff I must read. Caleb has years ahead to repent in, but he sounded as glad as I am to have lightened his more rightful treasure by likewise turning over to Tessa the batch of her South Atlantean papers. They are probably too interesting to be destroyed or left to the archival dangers of cheap acidic paper. Perhaps we are responsible for one of posthumous fame's most hopeless losses, for none of us have children at leisure, nor is there likely to be any such genealogical interest among the grandchildren. Besides her feministic cry in one long-forgotten little magazine she had nothing in known print either to record her adventures, to suggest her uniquely creative joy and suffering, or to mention her immediate effects upon those she encountered in so many walks of life. Even the mad John Clare was known in his lifetime. A life's experience lost by death is a far greater loss to the world than that of mere disclosed knowledge, which can be heuristically recovered by other human brains. "Different is the condition of everyone, and different the nature of each place." was the Rule of Saint Carthage, Sister Brigit told us in the eighth grade. She also said "A man is better than his descent", which I now take to mean that the individual soul is not limited by parentage or tribe. Thus from Trevisa to Tremont to Karcist! Will Caleb put an end to that line of biography? Tessa's curious about the missing half of his lineage, but even that much of his blood may be irrelevant, seeing that nurture alone usually conditions one's response to the environmental contingencies that make up what Yeats seems to mean by* Body of Fate, *the composite objective instrument of experience to which the genetic constitution and will have been subjected. Father Duncannon held that history is substance: likewise, then, experience is the substance of personal history. We know enough of her little oak tree's roots to throw up our hands at a degree of complexity that is already sufficient—at least that's what Caleb himself seems to be tongue-tied in telling us. I'll leave the generalizations of psychology to Tessa. My adventures are in ideas—like old Alphie's, but of course much more modest, being limited to the middle world of humanity. How many different thinkers, generally approved or disapproved by publishers and professionals, famous, lost, or never known outside a cult, have inspired* Creative Mind *in Caleb. As a godmother—not even a foster mother—I try to distinguish his original technological thoughts from those of the other C Ms, as integrated with what I assimilate from them, which altogether have drawn me to the final test of a valediction. Without any child would she have lived in my mind at all—if he had been miscarried? . . .*

It's all to be expressed with lettered abstractions no more satisfactory to human understanding than the "inherited conglomerate" of intellectual history—not by direct derivation from anyone's living experience but my own! It's for the literature of imagined experience to invent or suggest by tralatitious tropes cut loose of rigorous definitions or etymons. Yet as Whitehead says, though ideas modify practice, practice usually precedes thought—the essential dynamic in Charlemagne's "general dromenology"!—and for the most part thought is summoned to justify or criticize existing apprehensions. In the old days of my youth when I had the chance to attend Alphie's soirées I resisted his urge for the "acceleration of civilized thought". . . . Mary knew his fame, nothing about his philosophy; but I gather that she had somehow with her usual bold initiative befriended and visited his spinster daughter, the eccentric mountain climber who'd recovered from a broken neck. On the strength of that charitable acquaintance, but of course without that woman's leave, Caleb thinks he remembers, his mother took him along (because she had no one else to take care of him) when with characteristic bumptiousness she barged in on the good old man's flat in a posh riverside part of Unabridge to ask his help in getting her some job, or perhaps in seeing to it that her poems were published. But for all his personal kindliness and love of novelty, he was still a proper Englishman, and his wife a counterpart or better. Just before their teatime! What a comic scene it would make on the stage! But Mrs Whitehead must have intercepted the intruder in the vestibule; Caleb remembers no further mention of the incident, else he would have heard its echo for years afterward. Unlike her many successful or amusing anecdotes such rebuffs were best forgotten, especially by the little boy to whom—as to a dog—she continually disburdened most of what she had on her mind, and not especially to prepare him for the school of life.

—I was wrong to protest too much of the Enlightenment, just as Caleb—the idea man!—is wrong to dismiss too much of the platonism that Whitehead sees in his own metaphysics. But am I foolish, as at least a social scientist by profession, to spend my last years in gratuitous examination of what I value? For God's sake, I'm no more of a philosopher than a psychologist! Of course Philosophy is the Queen of Thought, but she doesn't address herself to all her subjects. I hope I've taken up the material of intellectual biography simply to test an integration of interesting but disparate ideas that happened to have been borne to me by a single human vector whose mother happened to have been an interesting but rather distant friend. Lord save me from irrelevant entanglements! . . . But I must admit that at the moment Caleb does seem more interesting than my own son in Cornucopia,

who's so successful that he verges upon complacency and needs no further bol-
stering from me. Olly is quite content in his profession of unadventurous
Sociology, which nowadays (since Weber and Durkheim are dead) I can't
help thinking of as one of the dismal extractive industries. It's the best he
can do to free himself of parental influence. Whereas I'm afraid that
Caleb—in his own terms—had the makings of a creative scholar, not a
playwright. Maybe his originality owes too much to hermeneutics, a bent
that in some degree impedes the kind of imagination he wants to contrive. If
it isn't an oxymoron to say so, his imagination is mainly for the unimag-
ined world we are born into. His spirit, like mine, is not inclined to ascend.
It's hard for him to accept religion without his own symbols, having cut the
mother bond at the umbilical cord, the trauma that I can testify was hers
more than his! When I tried to comfort her she would have nothing of my
assurance that her agony couldn't have been as bad as that of Schopen-
hauer's mother whose late-term gravidity was jolted by the roughest of coach
rides all across Europe from London to Danzig with one unlikely mishap
after another (instead of a lonely sojourn on the tiny pretty Isle of Man),
only to deliver "an ill-tempered pessimist", whereas her own eventually
delivered and resuscitated baby was obviously as happy as she was—despite
all her agony—to find himself alive and well enough. I could always make
her laugh eventually. That reminded her of Tristram Shandy, making sure
to have Caleb safely circumcised. She called me the village midwife. I called
her the Manx Witch, who seemed to be a prominent figure in her expatriate
legends. But I know nothing about her life before the Dogtown "lying-in"
except what little she told me then or later, or what Chief Inspector Tessa
Opsimath cares to offer me in terms commoner than those of social workers'
jargon that I've asked her to spare me—pace Auto Drang's "feminine psy-
chology and masculine ideology", which does make sense. . . .

2.

Had Fayaway Gabriel's time been slow or fast compared with
the timetable's standard of an hour? She blinked and rubbed her
chin, hardly aware that she'd been lost in so many autonomously
linked ruminations. To her the scroll of a Grecian urn seemed to
have unrolled too fast for reading. A minute or two before the train
began its cautious creep toward a buffered safety bumper at the end
of a sheltered slot chosen for its rest by an invisible master of many
switches she was reminded that the Dogtown Branch was not an
exclusive public utility. Two or three other commuter lines

converged on northwesterly suburbs of no great distinction, first
cusping into a broad rail yard, then more narrowly joining her line
in a six-tracked drawbridge over the Shawmut River at its tidal
locks, finally to spread once again into the candelabra of maternalistic platforms. As Caleb had vehemently lectured her, for Botolph
itself North Station was a gateway blocking entrance to the city.
From time immemorial to the latest generation it had interrupted
the continuity of railroad itineraries to the rest of the continent, as
far as passengers from the entire forehead of New Armorica were
concerned, as well as an entrance to all other points within the
metropolis. A crowd was already standing in the aisle of the coach
to squeeze out one side of the forward vestibule and join the competitive rush ahead of as many fellow passengers as possible to
scattered connections afoot—mostly only to find other wheels for
local transport!

Fay herself was in no hurry but she stood up to take a polite
position in the train's straightened spine rather than waste time
waiting in her seat with nothing to look at but passengers hustling
past her window who'd already debarked from the coaches behind
her. But soon after the debouched queues began to disperse inside
the station's doors—swiftly left and right—halfway across the heel-
clicking concourse she was overtaken in the throng by a joyful hand
on her arm.

Tessa Opsimath had been riding farther back in the same train!
It was a delightful surprise for them both to continue side by side,
though sometimes jostled by the undelighted crowd, on the way
out to the street. These two striking women would have deserved
the pleasure of curious contemplation for any civil man who'd been
calm enough to look about in the swarming herd: both faintly olive
faces suggestive of aquiline intelligence, both figures thin and
effortlessly vigorous. The elder and taller, adjusting her stride to
the quicker steps of the younger, wore an outmodishly flowing
black skirt belted beneath a knitted blue cardigan sweater that
opened upon a charcoal-gray blouse and a single strand of small
turquoise beads. Except for odds and ends in her unfashionable side
pockets she carried slung on her back by one hand only a well-
stuffed green baize book-bag; she bore neither finger rings nor ear-
rings, no color on her nails, though her long gray hair was tied
behind her neck with a tightly bowed blue ribbon.

In small particulars the svelte and modish Tessa complemented
Fay with inconspicuous cosmetic contrasts; though her wedding

band was simply gold she was dressed in a manner scarcely behind the latest businesslike Ur-fashion, for her few small ornaments were of plain abstract shapes, bits of silver as highlights to a few gleams of flesh and black fabric; her equally dark hair, short and uncurled, was shaped close to her head and neck like a loosened helmet. Here and elsewhere when Tessa left behind her domestic and casual comforts she appeared altogether a tastefully appropriate public dame in this or another tailored two-piece, usually black; on this occasion her baggage likewise was solid black, a black leather purse loosely strapped over one shoulder and a slim matching briefcase in her opposite hand. Women in the Botolph crowd would have guessed them mother and daughter.

Even before they reached the stairs to overhead rails for the streetcar that was to take them underground to the junction of their divergent courses—Tessa on to Botolph University and Fay to Norumbega in Unabridge back across the river—they had agreed to meet later in the day, looking as if they anticipated an unexpected holiday. To double the happy improbability of their meeting in the metropolis it happened that both Rafe Opsimath and Finn Macdane were away from home on business that very night.

3.

Late that afternoon, before the colloquium was officially disbanded, Tessa crept into a back row of the small lecture theater in the main neo-gothic building of the Divinity School campus on an outer march of Norumbega University less than half a mile from its Garth. She had arrived from a distasteful personal conference at one of Botolph University's sub-institutions, downstream on the opposite side of the Shawmut River. She was still deeply breathing in exasperation at the professor of psychiatric social work who supervised the Master's program for nonresident students. For one thing, the pallid twitching pompous obtuse sententious ninny-man hadn't even heard of Auto Drang! That was bad enough! She blessed her stars that Fay was the one person in the world who would most readily understand and sympathize with her particular rebellious disgust at the insensitive fatuity of narrowly professionalized bureaucracy. Thus preoccupied, Tessa Opsimath was in an almost humorous mood of anger affection thirst and hunger as she heard without listening the last few minutes of the discussion on the stage, which seemed to have nothing to do with anybody's religion or private psyche; and in any case it was too late for more than unintelligible echoes of Fay's contribution to whatever the issues were. Tessa hoped that her venerable friend would also have something to complain about today!

Tessa had found Botolph University far more demanding of obedience than the all-too-liberal bachelor's degree program of White Quarry College in Montvert in which she had enrolled primarily as a correspondence student under the guidance of Adjunct Professor Ipsissimus Charlemagne while her first husband Buck Barebones was still alive and the kids were young, before she married Rafe Opsimath, an alumnus of the same inconspicuously accredited institution. She had finished her undergraduate education and some advanced courses at BU while Miles and Melissa were getting sounder educations and thereafter liberating themselves from everything but their joint ownership and irregular occupation of the granite homestead in Powerhouse Cove from which they'd fledged. It had been conveyed to them when she and Rafe had moved away to their new house in the hills across the Namauche River from Dogtown island at a distance far too great for walking or casual visitations—not that the second generation had much to fear from a mother as discreet as herself or a stepfather as busy as Rafe whose surname they did not bear.

Tessa waited for the audience to evaporate, lingering peripherally until the small congregation of participants and sponsors put an end to conversations or congratulations and began to break away. When she saw that Fay was looking about for her she came down to the floor and was courteously introduced to a few departing doctors of philosophy anthropology or religion as if she was assumed to be a peer in some other discipline. But it was past teatime, and the two friends were soon walking by themselves to the Faculty Club at the very edge of the Garth.

"My Courtesy Membership soon expires." Fay said. "It's too expensive to renew, and I use it very seldom. Tonight for once I want to take advantage of its only real benefit for a hardly encouraged outsider. I can still get a 'Bega library card, but I no longer require even that, since by now I've accumulated most of the books I'll need, which I usually want to mark up and keep for reference anyway. The Vinland public interlibrary loan system is good enough for most exceptions. At least your good friend Gloria makes it work for Dogtown borrowers like me.

"We'll have a drink or two in the lounge before we go to the dining room. I'll show you the downstairs lunchroom that boasts academic wistfulness with theatrical posters from all over Europe and Atlantis, which I prefer when it's open. Then it's usually more congenial than the solemn cenacle because it's used by junior faculty and Noble Prize winners in dungarees, as well academic ladies and gentlemen in ordinary professional clothes who don't especially mind their manners. Anyway, however, your unexpected company makes this an occasion to celebrate like gentry, quietly but not too quietly, at whatever length you can tolerate without boredom. We can take the last train home if we choose to. I'm sure that will give you enough time to get sober before you drive me home from the station."

"I'll accept your invitation if you'll accept mine next time I get you cornered like this away from home. But you must let me pay for this meal. My husband is a prosperous industrialist."

"Not at all. I've had a windfall, and now you've shown up to alleviate the rather disheartening manner in which I've earned it."

"That can't have been as disheartened as the outcome of my hopes today. So I'll be glad to drink you under the table."

"Allow me a handicap for old age."

"Just take smaller and slower sips and don't count mine!"

First, between teatime and dinner time at the Faculty Club, they had coffee in a quiet corner of the lounge. The side tables were lavishly spread with newspapers, magazines, and journals for almost all piques of interest, and the beverage urns were kept alive like westernized samovars of stainless steel, flanked by delicate crockery, starched linen, and gleaming English cruets. Because it was the beginning of a week most of the senior professors had either stayed home or gone home or would arrive appropriately dressed for the dining room no sooner than it opened. Few of the younger less tenured scholars, or postulant Members of even more various origins races and sexes, could afford the luxury of time and expense for the prandial facility just across the reception hall. But for an ironic social worker who was no stranger to the most ostentatious recreations of country clubs and five-star hotels it was an interesting experience just to get an inside glimpse and whiff of an elite institution that represented the burden of an intellectual aristocracy in the pelf-seeking democracy of Atlantis.

Even for the anthropological septuagenarian (once a registered nurse) this indulgent visitation was a bemused rehearsal of such times elsewhere in the academic world, which hadn't always been so easygoing for her. She smiled to remember Caleb's account of his stint as a fastidious busboy in the faculty club at Hume, which he declared was contaminated by its tolerance of rudeness and arrogance on the part of those he guessed to be uncultivated nuclear engineers, even physicists, from the Cyclotracropolis, or tenured celebrities from learned departments on the Campus down the hill—whether blowhards in gourmand argument or fluent arrivistes in the upper class of academic lordship. She believed Caleb was inclined to be an intellectual snob even at the age of sixteen.

While both women were making up their minds about what they most wanted to talk about on this specially precious occasion they naturally temporized, with the most recently sapid topics reverberating in the forefront of political news as fresh grist for criticism or dismay (with tiny rays of hope) among devoted all-year-round Catholicrats half a year after losing the Presidency by a landslide, hoping that the outcome (from an unsentimentally patriotic point of view) would at least teach Atlantean voters a lesson by the time that the rebarbative Protestican came up for reelection. But by this time, for such earnestly inveterate Crats, inured to their heightened Weltschmerz, commiseration tinged with Schadenfreude had gradually given way to the immediate social comfort of glasses held high with mutual cheer, implying their perpetual hope for a more enlightened electorate before the evolutionary course of F D R's legacy was irrevocably reversed, lost to the perverted individualism of selfishness in the name of religious virtue.

". . . I hope I live long enough for that!" Fay was saying. "It's nice here, for a lark, but the ramshackled Crat Party is the only club for me. It's still the largest club in the world. As a losing cause it tends to be purified of the inconsistencies that F D R had to cope with, like a reformer turning a blind eye for the sake of imperfect progress, leaving to his brave wife the leadership for acceleration. But the Party still manages to rally around all the ingredients of commonwealth. All it needs is some simple catch-phraseology to express the common good as a whole, to trump the Cans' glorification of selfishness in the name of virtuous freedom."

"I remember hearing of Crat social clubs when I was a girl in New Uruk." Tessa replied. "They were benevolent societies with an open eye for loyal votes! Caleb says that in Unabridge the Jefferson-Jackson political club always delivered a turkey and its fixings a day or two before Thanksgiving and Christmas for his mother to cook for a family, which in her case meant Caleb and one or two of her pick-up guests from the Poor House, or presumably lonely 'Bega graduate students from Law or Divinity. Apparently she was always looking for ways to do her part! It was only when they moved to Can country in Montvert that he became aware of hunger as a possible hardship for themselves at any time of year. Allenton of course had no welfare department and the dying Tudor church was as helpless as its unattended 18C graveyard. It has prospered since then, like most of the country—perhaps a little too pretty—thanks to postwar Crat policies. Now even in the cities we're losing second-generation voters to the sacred new 'middle class' ".

"Maybe now there are other motives to join a fellowship for the common good." Fay suggested. "In fact there are so many different ones that voters should have a sociable way of fusing them as the more congenial half of an imprecisely abstracted general attitude about final wishes rather than just particular policies. Under our Constitution in such a diverse country we are supposed to be forbidden government by religion, praise be to the Lord! We can't get along with a separate political party for every faction like where a parliament is the whole government; but a natural coalition of friends from reasonably compatible factions can have broad unification of spirit against the forces of social entropy! No membership dues, no admission requirements, no exclusions, no obligations, no oaths! One oak tree, from root to branch, even in the leafless winters of our discontent! —Cheers!" Fay laid a hand on Tessa's wrist, knowing that she would recognize this political homily as a compliment to her young friend's accomplishments as a leader in awakening Dogtown's voters to the practical importance of party politics by mustering volunteers, at great expense of her personal labor, time, money, and unremitting energy as Chair of the local committee. Tessa gladly *Prosited* with two cocktails to Fay's one pint of English bitter.

But Fay couldn't help feeling like a slacker because her contribution to political education was no more direct or useful than a few theoretical words, heeded nowhere, about conflicting religious ideas that were gradually detached from their provenance, secularized, traded with each other, and applied to political doctrine on the balancing scales of *freedom* and *organization*. Nevertheless she knew that Tessa was not much interested in the history of ideas, especially those of religious derivation—to say nothing of the generalized proposition that all religion was itself social in origin, *before* it developed magic, gods, or private souls. In Tessa's association with Doc Charlemagne and Caleb the theoretical derivation of Dromenology had concerned her acute interest in their personalities no more than their allusion to symbolic logic, howsoever graciously she may have listened to them with gemütlich attention or ulterior motive, silently making up her own mind about the human relationship. From Fay alone she would have readily accepted the idea that the diachronic and chiasmal religious connections between Cans and Crats in unnoticed metastasis were more ironic than anything else in Atlantean exceptionalism, but it added no excitement to the political dedication of her generously efficient, intelligently sensitive, actively altruistic influence upon one who regarded herself as more of a performer than a writer. So Professor Gabriel steered clear of political history with what she thought was a timely remark about the reactionary essence of their common enemies. "Whitehead said that 'the pure conservative is fighting against the universe'—which consists of 'becoming and perishing' novelty."

Yet Tessa meanwhile mused that she was thinking of writing a novel. *It might solve my problem. I'll make up my mind before we get home tonight. For the moment I'm sick and tired of laborious politics. Right now it will help to talk about the disastrous thesis conference I had this afternoon.*

But she had resolved not to waste time by indulging in petty complaints that would do her no credit with a true mentor, whose opinion was worth more than any other's since the death of wise old Teddi Cibber, faithful Anglo-Irish "Friend" of Father Duncannon's Order and of everyone else who knew her and her husband Wat the eccentric fisherman. Instead, with fewer misgivings about a confession of the extraordinary investigation she'd been conducting to satisfy her ostensibly casual interest in the private origins of their friend Caleb, she decided first to broach the novelty of what she proposed to do about her anger at the pompous twerp who blocked her academic novelty. It still wasn't too late to alter her new intention, if Fay dissuaded her, as she cooled down in the friendly warmth of this evening's wonderfully opportune tête-à-tête. So in order to discuss the effect of this afternoon's BU interview like a mature counselor in her own right, she sheered off from any petty account of what had caused her subsequent rebellious mood in the bus ride across the river between BU and Norumbega.

Fay was saying with a laugh ". . . I wonder if Whitehead spent much time in this room. I've been more fortified by him than by anyone else generally considered to be outside the Geisteswissenschaften. But I'm glad I was never his formal student because I came to him with ideas from my own experience that made it easier for me than for most people to appreciate his obiter dicta without knowing any principia mathematica. He said the Greeks 'invented logic in order to be consistent'. How much simpler can you get without the figurative talent of a poet? This afternoon when one of my religious interlocutors in his pejoration of the Enlightenment invoked Keats's 'negative capability' as the dismissal of '*any*' interest in 'fact and reason' I suddenly realized that the dichotomy between negative capability and reason is falsified by the *any*. Those terms are not symmetrical! But Keats just dashed it off in a personal letter to his brother, and I think he'd otherwise have deleted it. Neither he nor his poetic idol Shakespeare was unenlightened by 'fact and reason'—and neither was I in my radical essays long ago." She paused, recalling from previous conversations that Tessa had never made sense of the Keats quotation to which Caleb all too often alluded; but it was too late to undo what might irritate Tessa as unnecessarily arcane literary babble. Yet a little alcohol had loosened even Fay's tongue, and it seemed to her unfriendly to suppress an active thought about something important.

"I did say something of that kind in appreciation of either the Mardian or Yahi intellect. But now I find myself citing Whitehead's enlightenment! He—greatest of rationalists!—allowed for the uncertainties of Shakespeare and Keats; and I should have allowed for *reason* as a universal value even if it was alien to the native people I loved and respected for some of their other values that the Enlightenment disrespected. I was too intent upon my criticism of anthropological orthodoxy of the time, as Keats too was over-reacting when he scribbled the adjective *any*. A liberal synthesis is in order here, as it was in Shakespeare's intuition, who was probably at least half a cryptic Scholastic Petrine anyway. Reason does not necessarily imply logic. And facts are not necessarily empirical."

As Tessa sometimes surmised, Fay was struggling to suggest to her, the demi-educated junior, at least the spirit of intellectual interest in her godson's history that accounted for her somewhat reserved countenance of speculations nearly indistinguishable from biographical gossip, which seemed to be excused only as the professional curiosity of a friendly psychological therapist; whereas said junior for her part was always trying as tactfully as possible to

convey her own respectful indifference to "philosophic" speculations—especially religious doctrines—that had nothing to do with
the lives of their individual human subjects beyond the formal cause
of their excitement about any ideas. But at least in personal loyalty to
Auto Drang's short career she hoped to assure Fay, as she had always
hoped to assure Caleb, Doctor Charlemagne, and her opsimathemati-
cal husband, that far from despising the elite sphere of printable culture as an aesthetic complement to socially useful education, she
wished in late middle age she could spare the time from business and
profession to acquire the learning of a common reader, who presumably would grasp the allusions that inconsiderately spiced Fay's rather
academic speech in her presence, even if Caleb's theory of tragedy, his
Synectic Method of Diagnostic Correlation, Isorectotetrahedron, and
other of his cerebral idiosyncracies occasionally mentioned within the
inner sanctum of her Dogtown circle—though unreported at its very
center of private but separate conversations between the youth and
his two late mentors, the irreconcilable Reverend Duncannon and the
dramaturgical Doctor Charlemagne—were hardly worth further
studies. In her unattached New Uruk youth she had wrestled enough
with the gratuitously Classical references of her old boss Doctor (of
Philosophy) Auto Drang. Doc, in contrast, had embedded his esoterica in the latest argot, except for proper names that popped up in the
magisterial stuttering which were meaningful only to people like Fay
and Caleb, who seemed to hardly know the practical almost commonsense terms of psychiatry.

Yet these two ladies, senior and junior, being women, never
doubted that they understood each other well enough to negotiate
any uncertainties and continue to improve their mutual affection.
By the time they got to the gleaming white-tabled dining room
next to a French window overlooking its garden to the first modern
architecture of the country's oldest university—an Art Center of
Swiss design—they were on a second round of aperitifs and Tessa
was ready to express the excitement she'd been cautiously suppressing. But first she had to confess the former intention that her exciting new plan (not three hours old) now abandoned, whether or not
even that one would have been disapproved by her revered advisor.
But if Fay should veto the first plan, which had not yet been
revealed to her, it would simply have been canceled with an apology for not having consulted her earlier; whereas if the new one
were also disapproved there was a whole world of possibilities for
diverting her psychic energy to another course altogether. Tessa had

no financial or emotional compunction about quitting or changing a career, thanks to the sympathetic Goodman Opsimath who had plenty of money to support her.

Fay had known as others did that Tessa was enrolled in a Master's program that required a final thesis-paper, but this student had always equivocated as if in doubt when questioned about her chosen subject of it, implying that there was still plenty of time to decide on one. Her replies had diverted attention to the course-study she still had on her program, without mentioning that she'd already breezed her way through that part of the dismal ordeal first required for a diploma. Blithely ignoring how odd the repeated evasiveness must have seemed to experienced tutors, to an exceptionally liberal confessor who rarely inquired about personal matters unless asked to do so Tessa now briefly explained—by way of introducing the reason for her obvious excitement—what she had intended to draft for Fay's approval or veto as a fake case history loosely based on the bastard Caleb's deprivation of a parent, which happened to interest her personally in connection with Auto Drang's theories of mythopoetic therapy.

To Tessa's great relief Fay smiled, expressing neither shock nor censure, as she might have done if the proposal hadn't been cleverly framed for its negation. This anthropology professor anyway was not one to jump to conclusions or to otherwise react prematurely. "Drang's ideas or your personal curiosity?"

"I knew you'd call it gossip. But I wouldn't have tried to use him to advance my brilliant academic career—." Instantly struck with dismay at the possibility that her last jocular words might be misconstrued as a jibe at what she knew of Fay's own special interest in Caleb, Tessa hurried on, distinctly laughing and raising her voice to abate the sound of what she'd uttered inadvertently. But Fay had never been driven into hypersensitivity even by antagonistic colleagues; to Tessa she seemed more amused than offended. "Of course my motives were ambivalent. I don't mind making merry about that. Caleb is not demonstrative, to say the least. That's what piques me as much as anything."

"But he's usually worth understanding. You're primarily interested in the subject of various nugatory objects, whereas to me those intangibles are what make the tangible subject interesting!"

"That's a crossword puzzle!"

"Well, I'm a little tipsy. What is it that you were going to tell me before I won't remember it? —Oh, yes, after we've ordered some sobering food." A tall dark and handsome young man in white-jacket uniform, no doubt a precociously urbane student, was suavely at their service, part-timing for his bread and butter. "First choose us a bottle of wine." said Fay to Tessa.

Thus loosened in tongue and awaiting their fluently described dishes, they resumed with Tessa's tentatively enthusiastic revelation of her day's peripeteia. "It's a metanoia! I've discovered my negative capability for a mystery story! Unlike like the B V M's case, it takes more than parthenogenesis to breed such a Caliban as Caleb."

Fay was still smiling. "How so? And did that surprise you? What are you so happy about?"

"This afternoon I was so mad at all the objections restrictions and pedantic obstructions to the idea of how I wanted to deviate ever so slightly from the standard beginning-middle-and-end template of that parrot-brained windbag of a fool—a paper padded with citations and swollen with bibliography, no doubt featuring his own publications—that I stomped out of that pretentious little office covered with framed diplomas for everything from kindergarten to his last award for pure orthodoxy, for the privilege of seeing which he'd kept me waiting an hour to begin with!"

Even allowing for choleric retrospective distortion or inebriated poetic license, Fay easily imagined the scene from her own experience in divers educational institutions, sympathetically amused at Tessa's uncharacteristically vehement outburst—she who was locally famous for her cool equanimity within or without closed doors. Though Tessa at this remove from the scene of her account was laughing all the while, Fay wondered if the emotion was occultly exacerbated by the probable fact that the offensive professor was much younger than the student; but of course that was a question maybe too delicate to be raised even in the fully shared amiability of this liberating salon, which after all nowadays was only slightly too elegant for a fully uninhibited letting down of hair.

"So I've thrown up my hands at the whole idea of getting a higher ticket for therapy! I'll keep my present clients as long as they want me, but my professional ambition is kaput."

"And leave Caleb to stew unconsciously in his own juice? My oh my, negative capability with a vengeance! But has respect for psycho-dogma survived your huffing rejection of just one disagreeably puny young puppy among the dogmatists?"

"Oh no! Psychotherapy is my only learned ministry. I shall draw upon that experience in my new apprenticeship. I've decided to write a novel!" Tessa laughed, looking Fay in the face.

"Well that *is* a surprise!" Fay paused, curling one eyebrow. "May I ask if your new métier will draw upon that particular professional disappointment?"

"No, just beginning to think about it, I imagine something between detective story and mystery. Just for you and our friends. I don't want to lie by disclaiming resemblance to actual persons or places living or dead. Names themselves are too significant to be faked."

"So it will be an outrageous novelty? True fiction."

"But the mystery may remain beyond the grasp of truth. I don't yet know the plot."

"Cheers to Keats!"

After a few thoughtful sips and bites Tessa added "I do have a title."

Seeing that it was not offered, Fay hesitated to guess or probe, in superstitious fear of either spoiling the pleasure of surprise for herself or prematurely draining the writer's zest to substantiate a feckless ambition. In her long life among intellectuals she had witnessed the unspoken death of many such ephemeral enthusiasms, especially from beginners emboldened by proficiency in some superficially similar vocation. Seeing that novels in any case (as Whiteheadean "receptacles") were vulnerable to future experience, she excused Tessa's reticence as a playful rhetorical device and repressed her own casual curiosity while waiting to be told what the virtual author wanted to tell her.

Tessa chewed a bit more and slowly sipped a taste of wine, then looked up again at Fay with a hesitant grin. "*Court of Love.*"

Fay was delighted. "That's an intriguing title for anyone who's heard of troubadours. Prosit!"

"Or due process of law!" Tessa laughed in response with disburdened pleasure.

"Is the protagonist male or female?"

"Female of course."

"Don't tell me! Mary Tremont?"

"Mary Trevisa. How'd you guess?"

"You're a sly gamine, to get at Caleb that way!" Fay laughed. "More power to science fiction!"

"I don't want the clues I've gathered to go to waste." Tessa truthfully admitted.

"I admire your chutzpah. I won't criticize your creative imagination. But please keep it secret, at least until I see your manuscript. I'll turn over to you any evidence of mine that you may not have. It's about the penultimate Tremont effect of the Trevisa cause. You must not make clear to your readers the distinction between art and scholarship that will distinguish our work!"

"But we can pool our royalties!" Whereupon a shake of slender hands across the table, and another toast to each other.

Nevertheless Fay soon found herself in spirited collaboration as one of the few secondary historical sources of suggestion for Tessa's fiction, simply as "a friend of the court".

For almost an hour as they lingered over fancy dessert and liqueur she haphazardly contributed in commonly understood language whatever she could add to Tessa's rapidly gestating brainchild from the Karcist era, which began nine months after the mysterious event in question. As Tessa knew, some of the random anecdota were recalled by Fay's special interest in the mental development of her godson after she'd learned by letter early in Caleb's nonage that Mary, marveling at her child, often couldn't help assuring the boy that he was "not a stupid bastard", perhaps the earliest of her vocative praises that he might now remember. At present that was the kind of detail that suited both his guardian angels. But for Tessa, a lapsed Petrine since her early Confirmation in the Lagash borough of New Uruk, Father Duncannon's influence upon the mature man was of no more interest than Yeats's. The clinical social worker was for once intent upon genetic enigma. By the time they left the Faculty Club's lounge toward dusk Fay had tacitly accepted Tessa's whimsy as at least amusing. Thus they agreed that in a particular dearth of evidence it was perfectly rational to start one's imagination working backwards from Mary Trevisa's delivery on the vernal equinox of 1935 pointing to the octave of 1934's Great Year, Dogtown's summer solstice.

Why then does so much of the gestation take place on the Isle of Man? Tessa believed the answer to that question would be the best lead to the paternal mystery—before Fay could get around to asking point blank for her unenumerated clues or scraps of inference along other lines of investigation. Fay was puzzled more about Tessa's interest in the case than about the mystery itself; but she was content to let her go about her own way of amusing herself as they rode back to the Dogtown station by subway streetcar and evening commuter train without noticing the punctuated darkness outside the reflecting windows. The elder listened to the younger with an opening mind as she heard about suggestive intelligence already garnered or surmised in an imaginatively coherent note-book. But Fay was likely to be more helpful than anyone else alive when considering Mary's gravid trip abroad.

Fay asked "But still, why the fiction? The Isle of Man is real enough, and so was Mary."

"Because everything I know or can guess without negative capa-bility is not enough to settle the question that every mother is sup-posed to know the answer to. The secret has been lost or kept so well! Despite what I've read of the thoughts and experiences Mary wrote about to you after the spring equinox of 1935 or sent to Caleb himself in various forms after she'd 'cut the mother-bond' by releas-ing him to boarding school at the age of twelve, I think—having twice been pregnant myself, and also seasick on the Atlantic—that Mary's reproductive anxiety was the most likely time for contempla-tive regret and resentment, not to mention the desolate fears of absolute loneliness without friend or lover or relative, probably without much money, on an alien island, three thousand sea-miles from the origin of all her memories. If I can imagine her feelings then I could at least hope to guess the cause peculiar to her case!"

Fay responded with a gentlewomanly grunt of mildly skeptical respect for Tessa's authentic sensibility as partial explanation of her virtual interference in Caleb's private life—which however, like chicken and fertilized egg, had probably been motivated before the Isle of Man had swum into her ken. Impatience with stultifying aca-demic discipline was evidently meant to justify gossipy curiosity in the form of fiction. But the real scholar was getting too interested in her own role as god-sip to impartially disapprove of her junior's thought-experiment. Fay even wondered if she herself had been too incurious in her respect for sexual privacy within her own studies of culture! Besides, a hypothetical procedure for seeking necessary cause from empirical effect was not necessarily unscientific!

"If you don't mind," Tessa leaned over to whisper in the white noise of the clattering coach to announce in a humorous manner of genuine apprehension, "I will ask you to preside over a Court of Love."

For an instant Fay was nonplussed. Then she laughed from bottom up, irresistibly coughing in the effort to control her reply,

especially because Tessa was infected with the same affect of her
own absurd words. But they were sitting side by side on a train still
half full of passengers. They had to stifle their undignified mirth
like giggling girls before they were simultaneously struck like
imaginative young virgins by the possibilities of Pandora's box.
"What, as a wrinkled old schoolmarm?" Fay whispered back at last,
re-endangering their composure with another attack of causeless
hilarity. "Because I adjudicated quarrels between my kids? Because
I've forgotten the pains and inconveniences (though not the joys) of
gender and am therefore a disinterested diplomat in the war
between men and women? Because I'm not biased by a life of
poverty or frustration? Or just because between here and the
antipodes I've seen too many a happy Child of Melchizedek to be
anything but disinterested in your calling up from the vasty deep
an unnecessary parent for my accidental and involuntary godson?"

"Because you are reserved and fair with all varieties of
mankind."

"You can't really believe that. My children wouldn't!"

"Everyone respects your opinion." Tessa declared aloud, sitting
back in the aisle seat.

"That doesn't mean that a dozen Dutchmen can't be wrong. I
am deeply prejudiced in cases of law! —Your mystery should be
staged as a play, not disembodied in a novel. I'll be Morgan le Fay,
and you can find someone less sinister to play the queen."

"The play must open with the protagonist as a lorn expatriate
almost thirty years old taking refuge on the Isle of Man. Did she
think she was pregnant only after she got there? She may have hoped
she was enceinte even before she left Dogtown, soon after Gloucestermas. Before that, having no child to protect, she wasn't frightened
enough of Chief McCarthy to run away. She must have been miser-
ably anxious about having a baby that obviously belonged in Dogtown as an Atlantean citizen. She was determined not to be a coward,
and it was the sorrow of her life, later, when she believed she had to
flee for two lives, like the B V M without a Joseph. She loved this
'microtopopolis of dogs and gulls' (as Doc Charlemagne called it) but
was finally worried that it did not love *her*.

"Caleb himself remembers having been told more than once
during his early childhood in Unabridge that through the porthole
of her navel he'd shared sight and sound of the exotic Isle of Man.
But long ago he told me that he grew up usually with no interest
in whatever interested her as a female, even that charming refuge,

notwithstanding his dawning fascination with the whole British Archipelago and its people, including the Irish."

By then Fay was sobering into her thoughtful self. "I do remember that she told me she had learned more about writing narrative verse from the Manx poet T E Brown, whom I'd never heard of, than from Homer Virgil Ariosto or any of her favorite Victorians. But she wanted her lying-in at the hospital here. She trusted her local doctor, and I was in a position to know that he was a good gynecologist. She was lucky to have him for her delivery, which was really just as difficult, objectively speaking, as she thereafter spoke of it."

Arriving in Dogtown center at the messy dimly lighted parking lot of what little remained from a century of the erstwhile V & M Railroad's business properties, they slipped into Tessa's elegant car. On the ten-minute trip to Fay's hill in East Harbor they rescinded their assumption that Fay would be left on her doorstep. They were both still in a mood for convivial refreshment. Tessa had expected a solitary night at her own house in remote isolation protected only by supersensitive burglar alarms; and Fay, though more accustomed to solitude, and more secure in her plenary neighborhood, was now so jovially imbued with Tessa's hobby-horse that she'd almost forgotten her ingrained vocation: so they immediately agreed that Tessa would stay overnight in one of the guest bedrooms—but only after exhausting their renewed thirst in a discussion of Tessa's initial evidence for some possible plea against a John Doe or Richard Roe in the Court of Love on behalf of her indifferent client as plaintiff, the sole surviving victim, who was not yet ready to lay aside his supercilious insouciance about one of the world's most universal questions. So almost like mother and daughter they took off their shoes and sat at the kitchen table in dressing gowns from the wardrobe upstairs.

"But again, why the Isle of Man in particular?" Tessa asked. "Moira, or Mary, had considered many others across the ocean for her isolation. If we can imagine her reasons for that choice we might be able to guess the *precise* 'great sin' she lamented but never regretted for the rest of her self-conscious Christian life."

Secure in social and emotional confidence, with occupations in profession business and politics to keep her busy, yet with energy and leisure to spare, Tessa was now as tetched with busybody excavations as Uncle Toby with his hobby-horsical entrenchments, though nobody but Fay or Rafe was likely to notice the seriousness of this infatuation beneath her mask of civil composure. Directly or indirectly she had assembled more than a few shapelessly conceivable bits of the puzzle (now cheerfully envisioned as her own work of art) from Caleb the protagonist; from Gloria Cotton, the Librarian and curator of legends; from the retired corporate lawyer Endicott Krebs and his retained secretary Gretta Doloroso; from the late Teddi Cibber or her children; or from other sources, private or public, that slipped her mind for the moment. She hoped that Fay could remember, as obstetric nurse, any scraps of conversation following Mary's recovery from an indelible "four days of agonizing labor"; or, as epistolary confidant over many years, clues that presumably hadn't yet been gleaned from a bale of surviving letters. In any event it was to be expected that a veteran critical scholar could help stimulate the editing of what wasn't dismissed and remained to make the most of—once she was willing to hear evidence and propositions offered by the dramatic detective. Still, the astute instigator was not yet prepared to mention *all* the desultory suspicions or leading questions that were probably to be found in her own secret diaries over the past twenty years, especially at the time of Caleb's connection with Father Duncannon's Laboratory of Melchizedek and the Mesocosm.

4.

> The following is a composite summary of Tessa's findings, interpolations, and reasonable conjectures, to which Fay conditionally assented or tolerated as informant and tactful literary advisor, in so far as their conversations (well begun before the overnight guest departed for home the next forenoon) were relevant to Moira Trevisa's sojourn on the Isle of Man. By way of third-person gloss it incorporates objective information about an existing mise-en-scène never witnessed by themselves. In truth, much of the text is lifted from Moira's surviving letters or diaries.

The Isle of Man (Manannan Mac Lir, god of the Irish Sea) was known to the Romans as Mona (not to be confused with its namesake in Wales), after it had long since been settled and civilized by

successive and overlapping waves of Celts and Norsemen. To a child
named Moira the similarity was intriguing, attracting her attention
or inflating her canny curiosity whenever encountered. Later in life
she read about the island in a family encyclopedia, and learned that
its cultural composition of Celtic language (from Ireland), Norse
political institutions (from Viking predations and settlements), and
Anglo-Saxon sovereignty (from the earliest British imperialism)
had ended it up, like the Channel Islands, as a nominally independent protectorate under the English Crown without being legally
incorporated into the United Kingdom. Its formerly dubitable
independence of the British Parliament seemed to her as vaguely
traditional as Britain's unwritten constitution—based upon laws of
precedence and modified by the trade negotiations of civil servants
educated by English universities. This weak and resilient hegemony was one of the I O M's attractions for wily British taxpayers
and pensioners, who boasted more openly about the fused beauty of
its misty mountain and its spine of monticles, sensational sea-cliffs,
quaint fishing coves, undulant green valleys, tawny moors, lus-
ciously forested glens, charming towns, a well-preserved medieval
castle, and various remains of even older architecture. Its natives
prided themselves on their preservation of such serviceable artifacts
as a Victorian steam railway and several small granite-built fishing
ports that were now only beginning to yield the fishery's moorings
and shingle-space to the yachts of new residents.

In Mary's year of 1934 the lawfully struggling fishers of herring
were still in spirit the equivalent to the traditionally honorable
smugglers of whatever was due as a protective tariff or was wholly
banned by the Crown. Cottage-farm laborers working in slate quarries and lead mines had had their counterparts in Purdeyville quarries. Troglodytes and aborigines on both islands alike dispraised the
marooners aestivators and pilgrims who would bring business to
their decaying economies even during the Depression.

But as a visitor who at that time had never gone hungry she
knew and cared little more about the Man micro-economy than her
subsistence on the remnants of her inheritance from the father
whose conservative but forbearing tolerance Moira regretted having
misunderstood in the overweening rebelliousness of her youth, and
of whom she prayed forgiveness for the private accusation that he'd
been cuckolded by Prosper Ozone the Cathode King and therefore
had no paternal authority over her. What pain she must also have
caused her sainted mother Hannah Tremont (née Trevisa) with that

shocking insinuation! She loved the God to whom she made solitary confession before the Manx Crosses that clasped to their heart
the surreptitious circle of the Vikings' pagan sun.

She had briefly considered the island of Guernsey, the I O M's
most likely counterpart in size and status, but in her research she
had found unprepossessing its expense and dignity. She was disgusted by Victor Hugo's absurd *Toilers of the Sea* as inauthentic
romance, and she definitely preferred George Borrow's taste in
exploring the I O M in the Irish Sea for truthful fiction. For her
refuge from Dogtown enemies she had thought of other islands—
such as the Faroes, Gotland, Rhodes, Corsica, or the Baleares—all
of which she rejected for their lack of English language and literature—ignoring Malta, Scillies, Orkneys, Shetlands, and Hebrides
as too limited in size, population, or her own reading. She had also
dismissed larger islands such as Crete, Sicily, Sardinia, and Cyprus
as too large for any intimate sense of place, if not for difficulties of
communication, travel expense, or personal safety.

As her search had narrowed, anyone she discovered to have traveled in the Archipelago was likely to be sounded for possible whiffs
of the I O M, or at least of the Irish Sea, which to her on a map was
a womb symbolic of her initial uncertainty about its content. In
high school years this instinct for maternal interpretation was usually preconscious, but it had drawn her to Arthurian romance and
its spiritually erotic sagas. Before she ever hoped to see the I O M
she was prepared to know it as Lancelot's Avalon as well as Svein's
proudest conquest, and its Castle Rushen as the schoolyard of Galahad, son of Elaine the Grail King's daughter. It was Merlin's Isle in
the Lady's Lake as well as Arthur's Isle of the Dead. With watercolors she had illustrated for her high school friends the poems she
wrote about Sir Gawain in the precincts of a Grail Castle still
standing on Saint Patrick's islet at Peel, and the Green Chapel near
Tynwald Hill where the oldest continuous parliament in the world
is still convened every Midsummer for a day of oldfashioned military ceremony and archaic legal pomp under personal sanction of
the Crown's Lieutenant Governor, even as a bustling commercial
fair takes place behind the grandstand. These and similar associations in her mind were to be reinforced by the prospective comfort
of her native language and Tudor religion, at least within the
island's ruling class. Thus upon her arrival familiar subjects would
be wholly absorbed by unfamiliar objects—altogether the pleasure
she had hoped for.

Her adventure began at a pier on the west side of Ur when she boarded one of the aging British ocean liners that among others of various European flags had been glamorized by two generations of Atlantic crossings by steam. As a third-class passenger, she shunned as much as possible her cabin below the water line, which she shared with a grumpy Swiss nanny, but during the long drawn out departure she was as excited on open deck as any Great Plains schoolboy by every harborside sight and nautical event, and increasingly angry about the class barriers on upper decks that kept her from the best vantages for taking in both the paraded skyscrapers on the port side as they were gradually illuminated in the twilight, as if turned on seriatim by the ship's stately progression down the river, and the torch of the comforting Statue of Liberty to the starboard, already lighted under the darkling blue of a clear day at the end of July. But mainly she was busy, hither and yon, as permitted by unequivocal class-discrimination, with everything that was possibly visible from her frustrated vantages; principally the tugboats tooting abreast or butting alongside as the ship blasted her own signals with puffs of white steam against the nearly vertical columns of black smoke from two of the four tall funnels as she was eased out into the stream and conducted down the long harbor past a score of anchored freighters and out through the rapidly benighting Narrows, until the pilot was dropped to his puny boat at the verge of a stirring void. In a third-class pen of open deck under the trailed smoke (now of all four funnels) she thought of Wellingborough Redburn on his first voyage, when ten years younger than herself, without the smoke but on anxious alert as a postulant seaman with a hundred times as much to fear.

About eight days later (less than half the time of Redburn's initiation as an apprentice seaman), after Moira's one brief bout of mal de mer (soon forgotten), the *Mauritania* crept past the Scilly Isles and the Isle of Wight into Southhampton. Struggling with two huge leather suitcases and declining the help of porters, Moira took the train to a recommended women's hotel near Victoria Station in London, where she lingered for two nights—walking and walking and walking, as far as Saint Paul's and back, or taking long rides on the tops of buses, wasting none of her time or money underground.

The next day, softly permeated with occasional precipitation from a solidly gray sky, she arrived at Liverpool's James Street Station, as excited as if she expected to find Redburn's *Highlander* in Prince's Dock—somehow as hopefully as he had looked for his

father's ghost. The following morning, a Sunday, temporarily disen-
cumbered of baggage while awaiting the afternoon Isle of Man
Steam Packet, she spent nearly three hours in yellow Dogtown oil-
skins on epicene walking shoes, sporadically opening and folding
her umbrella with the whims of a dismal sky, pacing as much as
time allowed on the granite masonry that lined the waterfront of the
Empire's largest port on a Sunday's eigenstate of trade and transport
in intercontinental Depression. Long after Liverpool was registered
in the Doomsday Book, she'd read, these were surely the world's
first wet docks, preceding those in London at the Isle of Dogs. The
massively continuous seawall outstretched along the river, bearing
the stone superstructures that hoisted stored and protected all sorts
of imported and exported cargo, most of which was moved about by
steam on imbedded rails when there was work to be done. The vast
elongated precinct was also protected and largely concealed from the
city itself by an endless wall of granite masonry, a bailey at present
defending from citizens the sabbath inactivity of rusty merchant
steamers and work boats moored in gangs idly afloat within water-
gated granite-blocked pens, which in level interconnection above
the river's ebb tides had reminded Redburn of the Atlantean Great
Lakes, and which brought to Moira's inward eye the scarcely comparable tiny quarry piers and wharves of her provincial Cape six hours
westward by the sun. This system of basic civil engineering had
needed few basic alterations in two hundred years; and only a century earlier in Redburn's eyes, when slave-traders still shared the
maritime agora, this unsung wonder of the world had put to shame
the sagging timber wharves and piers of Ur's Hell River waterfront,
which now in 1934 illustrated the degenerate state of Atlantic trade
more truthfully than Liverpool's far older infrastructure.

   She was so determined to make the most of her opportunity to
realize Redburn's experience that for once to save time she refrained
from her habit of boldly accosting workmen with naive questions.
The sabbath's few visible shipkeepers or deputy dock-masters who
might have been addressed with the kind of feminine appeal to
masculine authority, which in Vinland usually responded condescendingly to the flattery of a pretty face, were passed without a
glance for fear of being detained with largely incomprehensible
redundant or irrelevant misinformation, if not with leers clumsily
disguised as flirting tribute to her solitary audacity. Lest they suspect her of whoring she strode in view of those few idlers with what
she hoped was the air of a gentleman's respectably eccentric wife

scanning the distantly opposite shorescape of the Mersey to mag-
nify or translate it at home, in picture or word, taking advantage of
the infrequent fact that there were no anchored ships in the riverine
scene to obstruct an imaginative scene. She believed that in
miming this role her garments and uninterrupted gait were more
noticeable than her out-turned face.

Later that afternoon, under way aboard the Liverpool Packet,
planted on the open foredeck with legs apart, beneath solid gray
sky in the misty aftermath of a gentle drizzle, she peered with disappointment at the flattened shores that opened into the seemingly
infinite mouth of the Mersey estuary, measured by an interminable
line of navigation buoys, with no definite landmarks to distinguish
the slowly divergent eastern shore from a colorless asymptotic horizon. But not long after the seascape had been swept clear of everything but two or three cargo vessels bucking the whitecaps up or
down the Irish Sea, there was no need for seabirds to presage Land
Ho! Observing her anticipation, a young deckhand pointed where
to look for the rising peak of Snaefell, Man's distinctive mountain
at the northern head of a spinal massif, at that very moment about
to rise from the horizon as majestically as an atoll peak five thousand feet loftier seen from a whaleship's masthead ten times as distant. (She remembered Redburn saying that the three peaks of
Tahiti can be seen ninety miles away, but of course they were nearly
9,000 feet higher than the I O M's peak. The boy quoted George
Borrow, his favorite writer: ". . . in sight of Man—a lofty ridge of
mountains rising to the cloud . . . an island smoothed by wind and
watered by a close sky of clouds.")

An hour later, impatiently, with all her rain gear packed, she
landed on the pier of a manmade harbor, the port of Douglas, the
Manannan's modern capital. The rain had let up entirely, but still
without promising not to resume before one could find new shelter.
From here on its eastern coast, two-thirds of the way down the
island's thirty-three miles stretched to the south, only low green
hills were visible behind the Promenade's contiguously decorated
row of garishly similar bed-and-breakfast hotels and houses of
working-class holiday entertainments, averaging four or five stories
in height, seasonally full of English city-dwellers taking advantage
of the Gulf Stream, which moderates the atmospheric temperature
all year round at a level almost as subtropical as that of the Scillies
(where palm trees grow, whence daffodils are shipped to London all
winter long).

But the next day was blue green and joyous. An honest taxi driver had taken her to a satisfactory B & B with its own pub in a plain unexceptional neighborhood two blocks up the hill behind the glittering Promenade but conveniently close to the obscure little I O M National Museum. She was one of the few new visitors who bypassed all the holiday advertising by beginning her explorations with its kindly and scholarly guidance to the island's unique history and geodesy. Nevertheless, as she wasn't yet assured of the personal condition she hoped to be in, she wanted to make the best of her present athletic vigor by postponing most of her daytime literary and historical studies until she'd simply seen the whole island's land and seascape as thoroughly as possible by the network of public transport and footpaths—soon enough, she hoped, to have able-bodied time remaining to get some sort of temporary job, even in a time of bitterly excessive local unemployment, to ease the drain of her transatlantic funds, whether or not her hope for annunciation on this island would be fulfilled with inalienable delivery among friends and enemies back in Dogtown. Otherwise she would need as much money as possible to afford an extended lead to the hygienic fertility devoutly to be wished in some other venue of interesting refuge—if not a possible full year's loss of ultimate satisfaction by remaining on the I O M for its 1935 Tynwald, a perhaps too formal and official analogue of its approximate solar counterpart at Dogtown's Midsummer dionysia; though in any case it seemed to her that this particular island was a likely international crossroads for poets novelists explorers aviators athletes motorcyclists actors artists musicians scholars philosophers diplomats and priests, as well as for lawyers scientists engineers and various uniformed officers: possible chromosome-vectors of intelligence talent or physique worth considering, even unto the unlikely yoke of marriage with an alien passport.

She would soon have reason to forget any such outlandish contingencies. Meanwhile, bracing herself for a prospect of morning sickness and an eventual display of belly, she made as merry as possible with her invigorating dearth of company. Her first trip was by electric tram to the peak of Snaefell, an exciting ride through trackside Manx sheep, horned like aggressive goats; but an upper shroud of fog frustrated a panoramic view of Northern Ireland, Scotland, and Cumbria. That was the one tourist spot to which she returned a week later when she was gloriously satisfied with nearly three hundred and sixty degrees of the island's horizontal azimuth.

On another day she took the Victorian steam train down to Port Erin and signed up for a tourist open-air fishing boat excursion to the steep little Calf of Man, the peak of a seismic fragment separated from its mother by a tidal race, exposing high above the sea irregular hillocks of its rocky core above or around hollowed pastures reclaimed from natural banks of gorse or other salt-air flora when it had been continuously inhabited by monks or cottagers living off the surface soil. Moira was delighted that the islet bore two very important lighthouses and their keepers, as well as a few summer sheep. Most impressive of all, seen and heard almost within arm's reach of the bobbing boat, were the cacophonic throngs of breeding seabirds nesting at almost every level in the laminated striations of slate-and-limestone cliffs, also faulted vertically by eons of Mother Earth's fractured emergence. Yet, for all Moira's awe, she did not feel out of place with boatmen and terrain like this. There were so many different dialects of Gaelic or English in the constellation of the Irish Sea and its visiting derivatives that she was usually not distinguished as a Brother Jonathan unless put to the question by her slightly problematical Yankee accent. In this instance—exuberantly breathing with the rise and fall of sea-swells so close to familiarly unfamiliar sea-rock birds, nostalgic with the briny waft of barnacles and cockle shells—she took pride in an exotically dramatic expansion of her native environment, as if it was for the Manx an anticlockwise and civilizing fulfillment of topical kinship. Rising and falling with the swells that lapped the base of this perforated precipice, when her face wasn't twisted upward as much as neck and spine could bend to see the seawall's zenith, she made brave show of dipping her hand over the open side and licking off the droplets of brine as a seafaring connoisseur—just as, wherever occasion offered anywhere else on the island she made known her sympathetic appreciation or envy of its inhabitants, though perhaps with less affectation than she sometimes did with humble folks at home, where her demonstrative sympathies were often misunderstood.

Soon she had accomplished her plan to ride every mile of the island's public transport—steam train, electric trolley, motorbus, even a short sentimental carriage along the paved tracks of the esplanade, at which she publicly made much of her affection for the docile velvet-lipped draft horses who were said to be gratefully aware of the charitable retirement that awaited them until natural death on the island's farm of lush green meadows and pastures dedicated exclusively to superannuated members of their guild, sparing them the unspeakably treacherous butchery that immediately ended the useful lives of draft horses almost everywhere else in the world simply to avoid mankind's unproductive costs and gain a bit of revenue from bloody knackers. There was nothing insincere about her especially compassionate love for all members of the species that had been represented in her emotional life, and most of all those who trustfully served mankind. For her the face of any horse, compared to a dog's, was enough to prove the humane intelligence of its sensitivity to the domestic awkwardness of its inhuman body.

It was the individual cruelty and love, together with the general fortitude of the Manx ethos, and the tender endurance of all the living things that were treated in Manx literature—more than its romantic art, its idyllic geographical matter, or its uniquely amalgamed history—that had long since begun and now reinforced her affection for the former little kingdom, which was contented well enough with its present democratic semi-sovereignty. She had no interest in learning or preserving the Celtic language that the East Anglican George Borrow (one of her favorite writers for other reasons) had explored on foot to supplement his wild investigative walks in Celtic Cymru. (She loved his imaginative appreciations.) And so she had been led to read the bitterly realistic tales of Hall Caine, whose long suspenseful Victorian novels were probably truer to Manx history than any of its subsequent fiction.

Browsing in catalogs and bibliographies at Dogtown's Atheneum Free Library she had also discovered with great excitement the poetic works of one Tom Edward Brown, a native of the I O M and its preeminent celebrant as a peer among Englishmen of letters during his long academic career in Oxfordshire and Gloucestershire. He'd first struck his bright light as a scholarship boy (son of an impecunious local curate with many children) when he was on menial probation at the King William's College "public school", the island's own highest level of education, which was well respected as an institution of preparation for the great English universities, attracting superior students from wherever the sun never set. The Isle of Man thus seemed in the powerful second tier of those who would finally get to rule from the seat of Empire. After rising from a foundation of Victorian learning with a Classical First at Unaford's Oriel College to the venerated supervisor of pedagogy at his Manx alma mater, Brown further proved his collegiate leadership as an admired poet, nominal clergyman, and perhaps beloved

teacher, culminating his educational career in Bristol as the celebrated provost and all but headmaster of Clifton, a school worthily
as exclusive as Harrow or Eton, but apparently more liberal, or at
least more congenial with creative literature.

At first blush, with her habitual prejudice, practically as a
matter of course, Moira Trevisa had scornfully ignored the poetry of
such a genteel character—presumably an epitome of Mrs Grundy's
ideal intellectual. She hardly softened even when she learned of his
humble origins in a lower-class Tudor parish, or of his childhood
humiliation as a "servitor" on charity in earning his brilliant university reputation without the usual advancement in academic rank
that would otherwise be taken for granted by a born gentleman of
lesser capability. She had assumed from Victorian sources that there
were always ambitious parrot-brained parvenus like him among
genteel clerics and boring poets; but she began to reconsider that
after learning from the Museum's literary exhibits that this Tom
Brown was acknowledged as a peer by the likes of Henley, often
mentioned in comparison with Browning and Tennyson as well as
with the earlier Romantics. Chastening herself for narrowminded
arrogance, she opened his collected poems and was immediately
convinced she'd found at least a quasi-kindred spirit.

She was soon enthusiastically immersed in Brown's long utterly
unVictorian and often humorously disrespectful stories in vernacular verse. In the manner of legendary and imaginary I O M folk, his
"Fo'c's'le Yarns" worked out surprising, even shocking, plots substantially free of sentimentality, though introduced with an external apology in conventional literary terms as meant "to unlock the
treasures of the Island heart" in "old familiar speech". Save for
explicit reference to unconcealed sexual motives and events (no
more sanitized than Redburn's contemporary sojourn with Fayaway
in the Marquesas) his narratives were as honest as Hall Caine's
novels or anyone else's at the time in dealing with the tenderness of
unselfish love, loyalty, devotion, joyous innocence, and incessant
hard work, in a context of lust, brutality, treachery, deception,
poverty, crime, drunkenness, old age, and domestic cruelty, especially from the personal perspective of underclass women. Moira the
rebel was won over by the poet's equivocal mirth and unobtrusive
irony, as well as by his sensitivity to injustice suffered and rarely
overcome, yet never without hope.

The stories were set before the inroads of commercial moder-
nity, but she read avidly for both the interesting plots and her

fellow feelings, hardly caring about the unevenness of his almost
reckless independence in prosody, braving every poetic convention
in her ken. She no more than glanced at the author's lyric poems in
standard English that seemed to have nothing to do with his
beloved island, but she admitted to herself that she hadn't yet
begun her efforts to learn as much as necessary of prosody generally
known to literary college students if she was to convert her fundamental imaginative talent from the commercialized art of eye and
hand to what she now believed was her innate calling of ear and
mouth—without the benefit of advanced education in anything at
all. Romantically or psychologically, instead of perusing Homer
Virgil Dante Camoens Chaucer Spenser Boiardo Ariosto or Tasso for
narrative verse in translation, she had cottoned to the nearly plain
English of Byron Browning Coleridge Tennyson Frost and Jeffers
for their stories or characters without much notice of the means by
which they'd held her interest at first reading; but now, practically
for the first time, as if ensorcelled with a share of Brown's energetic
wellspring, she was inspired to read narrative poetry with less
impatient attention to the methods by which impulsive verse can
achieve subtle ends with complex stories. Inspired by his sort of
romantic realism she pondered poetic means to realize her own
inchoate art of experience and imagination as virtual events in the
arrow of common time.

   The learned poet's vitally engaging poems lay before Moira's
eyes in irregular and apparently careless lines, where the printed
display strove rather for appropriate respiratory response than for
immediate intellectual resonance, sometimes rollicking with
ambivalent amusement or inoffensive expletives, each almost
always as the long uninterrupted voice of a kindly but uneducated
and illiberal native, who by inference alone, when the reading was
over and she remembered whose tale it was, excited her even more
than the men and women of his narrative with whom she keenly
sympathized. It was fair enough that the first time through his
books she depended upon Prologues or Dedications, in the usual
literary English manner, to frame and tint all the levels of bias
beneath the author's own, thereby benefitting from his creative
experience with the deepest classical and romantic traditions of his
orthodox poems when he wrote in a mainly intelligible English
worn down or superposed by Manx works of settlement on soil and
sea, successively infused with Irish and Scandinavian argot, in an
alloy of Anglo-Saxon more or less compositely analogous to the

Scottish dialect of Robert Burns. Moira entertained this wealth of integrated imagination in such a tiny insular city-state as an objective correlative to her emotional foundations, in such manner that it inspired hope for success in her own new métier as an authentic constructor of realistic fiction in 20C verse.

Anyway, poring over Brown's volume whenever not roaming outdoors in daylight, she was happy to be deeply moved, as a new reader, as a restless woman, as a kindred critic of injustice, as an essentially Christian optimist. Though scornful of the island's persistently puritanical and sometimes self-righteous religious doctrine in Brown's uncensorious work (which embraced many genuine exceptions of tolerance charity and sensible goodwill), she vividly imagined the feelings of his Bella Gorry and Mary Quayle, and sympathized even with the avariciousness of a maternal Witch. She especially appreciated Brown's apparently intimate knowledge of male and female work in the lives of fishermen and tenant farmers. She was so absorbed by her unexpected discovery of his treasure in her exile that she seriously hoped to find for herself, right on the island, a latterday Tudor priest as wise and generous as the self-effacing parson, called the pazon, who appeared in both levels of narrative below the poet's own.

Generally, more objectively—despite the I O M's dearth of good beaches and modern art and Cape Gloucester's absence of mountains and Gulf Stream—she was eagerly preparing to stretch and fertilize her correlations of this 19C Shakespearean island with her own native 20C presque-isle. To the extent of her knowledge she related I O M's inshore herring fisheries to the North Atlantic ground-fishing of Dogtown schooners, its former mineral and slate mines to her hometown's open-air granite quarries, its sheep-downs to dairy-farming meadows, its diminishing arable land to her counterpart's deforestation—while she read in Manx its histories of degenerate crime, including the unsolved murders that she easily associated anachronistically with Dogtown's colonial contraband trade, Federalist privateering, and recent bootlegging—all of which were likewise obscured by pseudo-historical legends, misrepresented on police blotters, or deliberately ignored by the timid press. She contrived to equate Celtic barrows, Neolithic burial circles, and ogham-scribed menhirs with 17C Colonial gravestones and a few randomly scattered boulders of terminal moraine recently indited with the block-lettered maxims of a native Pauline underwriter known as the Duke of Dogtown who was immediately

famous for having sold short in time to capitalize on the disastrous
Graveyard Street Crash. She was reminded of Purdeyville's dilapidated fieldstone foundations of tiny wooden cottages left open no
more than a century and a half earlier in upland pastures, abandoned by witches and dogs.

But in Moira's hope for local comfort from an insular representative of the Tudor Communion she was disappointed. According to
the illogically effective pragmatism in British hegemony over pro-
tectorates and autonomous duchies in the Archipelago, the Church's
large minority of parishioners on Man were under the spiritual jurisdiction of an archdeaconate subsumed by the smallest diocese of the
United Kingdom, whose bishop seemed to serve as ecclesiastical
assistant to the Archbishop of Yorick, second most distinguished
among the highest of English equals, as established by Parliament
in the name of the Crown! As a confirmed communicant with this
Old World settlement between Petrine and Pauline institutions she
was not especially surprised to find that the insular Church, resting
on its quasi-governmental authority and immemorial properties,
had lost much of its practicing membership in the outlying parishes
after it was divorced by the Chapel faction of spiritual independence
known as Wesleyan, which she found had quietly grown to become
the island's plurality in a quietly religious population, even after
shedding its own dissidents and tolerating other Pauline sects. To
anyone as insignificant as herself the bishop of course was inaccessible, but she soon had reason to guess that his dozen or two clergy on
the island offered no objection to the ecclesiastical tradition he passively perpetuated, which was equally impervious to the High
Church Unaford Movement of liturgical theology and to the liberal
Low Church evangelism of social justice as charity. Without great
surprise she saw herself as a questionable questioner whose only
comfort from the local Church was perfunctory rehearsal of the
familiar words and rites of the Book of Common Prayer and its
adjunct hymnal, celebrated hardly more than once a month with
Eucharistic bread and wine; but it was the no less perfunctory
preaching by biblical text that kept her from any effort to repeat her
attendance at any one of the Church's cold and dusty little outposts
of unadorned stone. Simply as a stranger, many weeks before her
gravid condition betrayed her as a lost woman, she felt unwelcomed
by the parsons and congregations who were kindly and sometimes
even friendly as random secular acquaintances outside a system
closed especially to the likes of herself. She never discovered how

much of that daunting attitude might have been due simply to the shyness of charitable souls, or to the inertial custom of earlier times; nor, she told herself, did she care to test it with patience. Yet with impersonal and almost romantic satisfaction she continued to read richly animated histories about the Manx Church before its 19C stagnation, as if also putting to shame the bland immaturity in her Atlantean Apostolic branch of the same stem.

Thus at more than half the Tudor churches, though obstinately without wish for absolution, she found no cheer or succor with the kind of sympathetic pazon she'd hoped to discuss the "exceptional sin" that she believed deserving of more spiritual attention than the ordinary scarlet letter that was soon to be made visible by any curator of souls on an island comparatively tolerant of Victorian impurity by the practically common-law standards of an established Church whose vestigial jurisdiction shared the government's responsibility for irreducible public welfare. For once she was silenced and tethered by circumstance—but not without a sense of relief from the shame of resorting even to a private confession without penitence that would amount to admission of regret. After all, it was better not to alleviate her moiled conscience at all than to equivocate her extraordinary breach of civil society in an offstage aside to the unimaginative curate of some musty almost candle-less little stone-cold chapel nearly deprived of cloth and color. The publicly leveling effect of sacramental guilt was humiliating enough in the collective recital of General Confession prescribed by Archbishop Cranmer, which was no better than a dogmatic apology for being a run-of-the-mill human being, without the satisfaction of revealing anything about one's individual attitude toward ineluctable guilt. She wished and yet did not wish to abuse either her integrity or God's personal commandment. Sometimes she was pleased to flagellate her soul with the unflinching awareness of anomie in her moods between flaunting and flouting, between appetite and nausea, between extravagance and parsimony, between exhibition and secrecy, between friendliness and hostility, between sweating and shivering, between optimistic hope and pessimistic faith, or simply between the urges of common womanhood and any kind of creative art, because the libration itself summoned her courage as both blatant poet and liminal mother—as at last definitely expected!

"Alone here in Douglas with my one friend and protector, the formidably tactful landlady and cafe manager Mrs Kermanner, who is allowing me to encourage her young son Francis in his literary reading (when everybody else in the family who recognized his intelligence thinks he should study bookkeeping)," she wrote in October to her sage counselor Teddi Cibber back in Dogtown (long before the apparition of Father Duncannon), the charitably tolerant yet far from intimate gentlewoman with whom she had grown all but unreserved, "whenever I see one of the Manx sheep dogs I mourn the lung-choked death of poor loyal loving Sycorax, who was rumored to be the victim of my own smoking in bed—I hope YOU never believed that of me even as you so generously took me into your house and family for nearly a week while my studio was being rehabilitated, and collected from your friends and neighbors all those practically unused garments to replace my charred or sooted old clothes! [God knows I have reason enough to know that smoking wasn't the officially "unknown" cause of the fire! But from here I dread the pains of childbirth more than I fear the Chief of Police and his pyromaniacal scion.]

"Half the time, when I'm depressed, I do blame myself for the loss of a clever charming and devoted part-time lover by unjustly accusing him of subordinating love to crass ambition dissimulated as service of humanity. But I know that what I want is right in God's eyes. Even the great Tristram Freud thinks women don't know what they want. I've always known what we want, whether we know it or not. We want babies, even if we don't always realize that we want them!

"—With all respect for your immense kindness and selfless Christian values (which also tear at my heart), this comes from Dogtown's unrepentant feminist, its half-liberated ultramodern witch! So pray for me to overcome the fear of pain that has never daunted you in the family way. I want *and* fear more than other women do.

"But on this lovely mist-or-sun island, full of toiling modest uncomplaining poverty-stricken quietly goodnatured (at least among their own kind) child-sowers and child-bearers, I often forget for hours or days my fears and homesickness, and sometimes even what I want! Tomorrow I'm taking the Dublin ferry for a few days of Irish exploration, to get an overnight glimpse from Galway of your poetic West Country domain, after first, especially, feeding my ancestral imagination with a contrasting day-trip north on the east coast to Skerries, which I heard so much about, as distinctly more identified with the English, when I was growing up in the aura of highliners. I hope to be sailing from Cork when I return to Dogtown, temporarily, for the presumptive event in March.

"I think you once told me that as a young child with your family you once visited the I O M (en route from Ireland to England on holiday?) when the Manx poor all wore clogs. A few still do, but because of the Depression this government (finally urged by the Church) has begun to concern itself with public welfare, under pressure from a population awakening to democratic possibilities. (Even they have already heard enough to admire Franklin Roosevelt, as 'traitor to his class'!) You may remember enough here to visualize the varieties of rural beauty and archeology presiding over or under everything else that interests me as a 'visitor' viewed askance by almost everybody, especially now that the seasonal tourists have left less bankrupt the diverse attractions of Douglas, Ramsey, Peel, Port Saint Mary, and Castletown (the historical capital with a small medieval castle still standing, which you may have seen, as stoutly weatherproof as ever). In my next letter I can tell you more about what I've liked about this truly green and pleasant island.

"Meanwhile Mrs Kermanner, my landlady, apparently an orphaned farm girl of independent mind, though oddly reticent about her early life, who married into a humble but respectable family here in Douglas, the capital town of the island, has been my guardian angel—without offering to penetrate my own reticence, even after I told her that a doctor at the hospital has confirmed what you may have guessed, that I am indeed with child. She asks no questions but her tacit sympathy will help protect me from public embarrassment for some time to come. At least for the present, she's my solicitous accomplice in respectability. Francis, her bespectacled somewhat fastidious fifteen-year-old, rather clumsy and diffident, the quiet ugly duckling of the household, otiose in his father's opinion but admired for intellectual curiosity by his mother, has been assigned by her to escort me to the movies or elsewhere as required, when his time permits from schoolwork or his summer job, as long as when I'm with him I don't smoke in public. She thinks that if he copies my cultivated diction and learning he can pass as a gentleman's son! Imagine that—from ME!—as a sort of governess in the arts!

Francis cautiously confesses to nobody but his mother and me his apostate hope to 'cross' from the island for an expatriate life in England—not (as she wishes) in order to rise above his class, and

not primarily to escape from the tempora and mores of Man to
Liverpool's notorious liberties of deportment, but simply for British
education, to begin some sort of learned occupation in the cosmopolitan world to prepare for coming home with professional authority. (Despite all our parallels, in this respect the I O M is generally
unlike Dogtown, where few college students seem expected ever to
earn their livings among relatives and playmates.) Of course he
doesn't yet know my condition, but he may not be too innocent (as
his mother seems to believe) to be prepared for my revelation by
some of the novels I'm getting him to read. In any case Mrs Kermanner is certainly an exception to all this island's native types, her
uneducated dignity and humble competence to the contrary
notwithstanding! I thank God for that! It's more than I deserve."

It was also by letter to Teddi Cibber that Moira first announced
the intention to change her name from Moira Trevisa to Mary
Tremont.

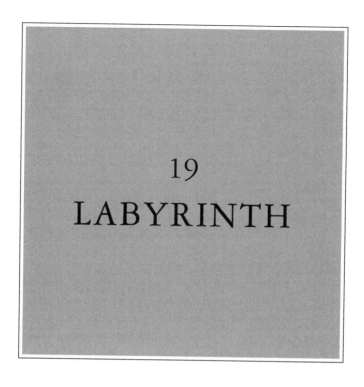

19
LABYRINTH

1.

Tessa found *creative* writing harder than she had anticipated it to be, having relied upon her facility with the simple expository syntax in school, business, and profession. Anyway it became obvious that she couldn't be sure of Fay's collaboration as a judiciously disinterested observer who lived across the Gut on the island side and had her own infinitely more difficult swan song to imagine write and sing before it was forever too late in her life. Fay said nothing about infringement upon her time but Tessa was diplomatically sensitive about taking advantage of her precious friendship, still hoping for her active participation in as much as two or three days of judicial mummery. She therefore temporarily put aside the manuscripting aspect of her hobby-horse and continued to pursue its objective by other means. Without accepting new clients in her professional practice she was determined not to let the present ones out of her hands until they no longer really needed her. She had no intention of resigning from her adjunct performance at Merriwether Hall despite her opinion that none of its inhabitants or managers deserved her skillful attention. Nor did she neglect her interest, as a member of the Board of Directors and occasional duty as corporate Treasurer, in her husband's Dogtown Machine & Design business. Of course it was out of the question to resign or moderate her regular activity as elected and successful leader of the local Catholicratic Party. Anyway, none of these occupations seemed entirely irrelevant to this her virtual leisure, which Rafe called "Pump-House History", referring to the house of her first marriage.

The beginning of her manuscript was not consigned to her secret cache in the house, or to the bank's safe-deposit where she stored her earlier diaries, but it was kept handy in a desk drawer of her office at home, along with her sheaf of accumulating notes, where occasionally she sat down to draft a sentence or two. But she hadn't the slightest intention to leave her curiosity unsatisfied by succumbing to the inertia of unassisted literary procedure. Faced with disappointment in the generative process of her own writing, and well aware that her recreational mystery required historical as well as merely speculative clues to form a coherent hypothesis from her random bits of anecdotal and imaginative documental suggestion, she decided to change her medium from those of an archival detective to those of an investigative screenwriter. She was suddenly pleased with herself for that idea. It pleasantly comported with her social talents. The strategy was to cultivate as *separately* and *leisurely* as possible the *unguarded* memories of those people she already knew (or might learn to know) who were possibly able to shed light on the case from any position contemporaneous with the personal existence of Moira or Mary in Dogtown circa 1934. This was not the unsophisticated diplomacy of an intelligence attaché simply asking for truth! Was it not more like obliquely eliciting experience from the collective unconscious? That was less exciting than writing plausible fiction. But she did not fool herself that she had much more than the method itself to go on—at least until she resorted to the familiar mode of a theatrical script!

It was essentially the technique of tête-à-tête lunches or dinners, though sometimes formally facilitated by her husband as a third person who usually had good reason to apologize for excusing himself halfway through an afternoon or evening—or maybe, with old chums, described simply as potluck suppers to follow up details. The trick was to get all her friends used to the notion that no one was preferred to another as a casual guest in her own house. She tried not to disrupt her usual turn in the familiarly irregular round of dinner parties for more or less half a dozen friends, but Fay was not to be further disturbed despite a standing invitation. None of her own familiar guests were to be inhibited by the presence of anyone else from the intimate circle of friends for what Rafe called "Gossip by Musical Chairs". He'd let it be known to her that he had no wish to know or join her machinations until they were perfected!

But first she decided to give a special garden party for the "New Deal seniority" among those who wished to have seen Dogtown in F D R's time. This select collocation was planned for a week or two before the city's crowded jamboree of public events in the Gloucestermas octave, to make sure that every one of her invitations would be accepted for the event well before Endicott Krebs was too distracted by preparations for his six-month world cruise, which was scheduled to begin only two weeks after the midsummer Dionysia.

The most difficult stratagem in gathering her personae at the same point in time place and action was to lure Arthur Halymboyd from his comfortable seclusion at the Merriwether Hall Retirement Center to even such a quietly exclusive collation on the strength of a convenient opportunity to attend very nearby a private viewing of the literally spectacular hilltop house designed by Caspar Aninigo, a name bruited among the unconventional rich with whom Arthur's late wife in Duke County had been internationally associated. With a wry smile she admitted to herself that she hadn't done everything possible to discourage the typical old man's ulterior attraction to her particular sort of femininity, which no doubt was what overcame his nearly cynical aversion to the kind of social affairs upon which he'd wasted too much of his spare time in the best years of his metropolitan life. But for a healthy octogenarian it was an easy walk through the woods in daylight, in case he didn't want to call an IXAT cab or drive a mile and more roundabout, risking the consequences of a tipsy return. The guests would not be given to understand that the date was deliberately chosen in her husband's absence at the Association of Fabricators convention in Washington.

However, she managed with neat success to stage her first act of crafty inclusion and exclusion in the aleatory experiment, meant only to play itself out, come what may as her own success or frustration, in what she could not foresee, and hardly expected to oversee, as a speculative observer. At times she was reminded of Fay's cryptic remark that "writing makes you think and thinking makes you write; sometimes you have to start with the egg." But she had replied that the chicken was always female and the egg may not be.

Endicott Krebs was pleased to come, with Gretta Doloroso, now more than ever his sine qua non, whose entire family had vitally benefited from the New Deal at the nearly lowest level of the common good. Fay came readily enough, escorted by Finn Macdane who was always glad to converse with his friend Krebs. Fay, to whom nothing about the inchoate scheme had been divulged except the ostensibly casual invitations, was surreptitiously amused with undefined suspicions, which she did not share with Finn, who nowadays was automatically invited as her gentleman consort.

Caleb, Gloria, and other friends were uninvited, as nowhere to have been seen in Dogtown on or before 1934. Tessa herself was the one necessary exception to that criterion, as the only one who could serve King Arthur as both hostess and equerry in her home, perfecting her arcane hexagram. But she was quite aware that even on the stage no witch can be omniscient about the consequences of her own magic after the dice are cast.

Indeed, to the extent that social communications had been opened between all points of her star, Tessa's wily party transpired as a manifest success, howsoever doubtful tantalizing and nebulous as far as she would be able to see its outcome. But for a long time the motile clusters of talk were about her house and its magnificent view of the outer harbor as well as some of the horizon beyond it, or about Endicott's prospective itinerary through and beyond the Panama Canal, avoiding Japanese islands, but touching most of the subsidiary British Commonwealth. In the shade of the higher hills behind them, conversation finally settled into chairs on the terrace, dwelling far more upon the second phase of F D R's simultaneity with Hitler's Third Reich than upon the first, still less upon his first term in 1934. That historical imbalance disappointed Tessa, but she was not surprised, seeing that men were almost always more interested in war than public welfare (as she remarked to Fay sotto voce while they refilled glasses at the sideboard).

2.

At Tessa's reception the retired industrialist and the retired naval engineer were comfortable in each other's aged society during the course of a bantering argument about the best kind of place for a single man to live as a base for his leisure, in effect reassuring themselves about the peculiarly contrasting designs they had already realized for their terminal freedom and independence. Any talk of happy bachelor life is insensitive in the presence of women, as they were soon reminded, so at the time they had confined their brief otious debate to aesthetic and utilitarian ideas about locations. They both had chosen Cape Gloucester, of course, but Arthur Halymboyd, a recently dedicated defender of nature's environment, wanted the quiet greenery of inviolable rustication (with unnotice- able personal services), whereas Finn Macdane wanted to take care of himself at the very center of conveniences in a town where the street traffic disappeared at night amid the sights and soothing sounds of maritime industry. But each was curious about the other's peculiar solution of the retirement experience. Finn had called on Arthur to see how unlimited wealth was spent for a uniquely pri- vate wing of the Merriwether Center mansion, and had been pleased to find himself served lunch in the educated quarters of an amateur intellectual who seemed to be hoarding his remaining time to make up for the ruthless lifetime of a captain of industry (who'd served the government throughout W W 2 in the European Theater). That rival in ideal leisure had then come by taxi one afternoon to return the visit at the penthouse of an amateur reality- estate investor who cherished many histories in his one wall of books atop his casual source of income from bricks and mortar, which would make up for capital expenditure otherwise beyond the prudent means of a professional career largely in public service, a veteran of the same war, still never caring more about invested money than the rich man finally did about any single component of his estate finally overdetermined by a very conservative Ur firm he no longer bothered to talk to.

Side by side in reunion at the Opsimath house, behind a tea table laden with Scotch and ice, they gazed up at the frank blue sky clear of air lanes to and from the Guy Winthrop International Air- port in Botolph, and down to Parliament Island in the open harbor, or farther over at the wharf-and-shed-fringed inner harbor, much of which was out of their sight behind Casbah Point, from which the annual seine boats race by oars, as if in competition for whales just off the open harbor's Esplanade Beach, was soon to take place. What they saw as they contemplated very different things with their respective inward eyes was the silent resting holiday heart of an indefatigable melting pot, dear to all marooners like themselves, who for lack of anchored lineage or local progeny could never fully assimilate though perfectly comfortable. At least Finn the sailor did so feel now, after more than fifty years of movement at large; and Arthur felt he might soon find himself willingly dedicated to Dogtown soil as that same kind of second-chance patriotism for a place more proper than the Wandering Jew's ports-of-call half a century earlier.

Next to the more athletic Finn Macdane (still with the respectably residual hair and skin of a much younger man), Arthur Halymboyd's somewhat shrunken spine and the prominent crags of a creased face and high freckled forehead made him seem older and frailer than his spruce and taller companion of equal age, as if he'd traded vigor for wisdom, with a hearing aid in one ear (but with no eyeglasses except, like Finn's, for reading and writing), notwithstanding his brisk gait and self-confident gestures.

"It was just this time of year that Rathenau was assassinated in Munich," said the Jew to the Aryan, "only ten years before Hitler finally came to power. Even as a Jew he was mourned by all Germans except the nationalists: the one statesman of the new German Republic who might have forestalled the Nazi Third Reich. At the obsequies his wife was invited by the Reichstag to take the German Emperor's empty seat. I had just finished college and was lucky to get into a graduate school that didn't discourage us too much—even North Atlantean nonreligious ones like me—but it isn't surprising that I'd hardly heard of him, though I was to learn sooner than almost everyone over here. Even many German Jews didn't believe what was happening to them until long after Kristallnacht."

"Yes, Count Kessler, who died three years before I went to Berlin—when I was innocent of the worst—still vilified by the Nazis for having called Rathenau a John the Baptist for international liberalism cut short. I'd read about Kessler's hope for the Weimar Republic and the League of Nations."

"But the other day when Krebs was talking about his forthcoming trip through the Canal you said your battleship had even fewer inches to spare in getting through the locks, so I suppose your Navy service was mostly in the Pacific. But did you ever have sea duty in the European Theater?"

"Except for European jaunts as a teenager and a few show-the-flag training tours on sea duty", said Finn, "I got to know much more about the German world than the Japanese *after* the German surrender. But because I knew the language pretty well almost all my shore duty over there was before Hitler made his vital mistake in declaring war on us, just as I was ending my assignment as a technical intelligence attaché, first in Berlin and then in London. And afterwards, when he was dead. And I read some history to extrapolate from what I witnessed, because soon after *Yamato* was sunk the Navy sent me back to Germany to help interview surviving Kriegsmarine officers—not so much for their technology as for their personal attitudes in the War—when they were prisoners of war in Flensburg and thereabout in horrible British army camps. Royal Navy Intelligence couldn't get much cooperation from the prisoners because they were all sticking with the unofficial disclaimers of Dönitz their commander-in-chief and Hitler's official successor, who took advantage of his gentlemanly treatment as captive head of state to coordinate their separate replies to interrogation at several separated locations.

"He seems to have used coded extramural messages carried mainly by the permitted family visitors and other P O W rights of communication. Then one of the public school Brits came up with the wonderful idea of inviting each of the staff admirals to write an essay about the course of the War from his own personal point of view. One of them at least had some very critical opinions about the strategic blunders of Hitler and his Army-dominated General Staff, but that admiral had been serving as liaison officer to the Italian navy, so far from Berlin and General Staff that he could plead he had nothing to do with Germany's great blunders and internal rivalries. I was up there particularly because I had known quite a bit about the *Bismarck*'s design and performance, and I interviewed a few of its available survivors; but of course by that time my technical intelligence was no longer of interest to the top brass because battleships had been demoted as obsolescent, especially after Halsey's fiasco at Leyte Gulf. (I admit that I dislike aircraft carriers simply because they're flat and don't look seaworthy!) But I was interested in the German admirals for how they differed from the generals in mentality—."

"They didn't! They were all Nazis." Halymboyd hoarsely interrupted, tense in his chair, finding himself instantly disputatious before he could listen to another word, involuntarily anticipating any exculpatory notion that he couldn't help fearing would be resurrected anent any charge in the forgetful distance between 1932 and the 1967 Nuremberg Trials despite the liberal opinion that

Atlantis had finally learned the moral lesson of tolerating misplaced forgiveness. Too many Nazis had escaped prosecution and
many were still protected by the S I S itself, as known war criminals putatively useful to Western power as experts like rocket engineers against the former ally now generally considered more sinister
than the Reich that animated an intuition of hatred for Jews as a
moral *principle* of civilization. He almost immediately checked his
prosecutorial reaction, chiding himself for betraying his prejudice
against postwar Germans, which he had hardly accustomed himself
to concealing when he wasn't caught off guard.

Finn at once recognized this worthily saturnine Jewish sensitivity to his cosmopolitan topic, which he would not have expected in
a former magnate of such evident worldly experience; but before he
could try to set Arthur straight about his historical interest in a
matter of first importance to all Jews and Mischlings, the tone of
his new friend's premature response, or rather interruption, seemed
nearly a threat to get up and stumble downstairs to the street without waiting for the creepy little elevator or calling a cab. Sensing
his companion's self-chastening regret on the instant, he was about
to continue as if he hadn't noticed the hypersensitive reaction to
words unintentionally evocative of history's most systematically
deliberate collective horror, when Arthur apologized for his uncharacteristic intolerance by uncharacteristically raising his palm and
explaining himself.

"During the War Crimes Trial investigations I worked as an
S I S officer on the Albert Spree case. Maybe he was a tolerable kind
of exception. I'd say his ex post facto remorse was sincere enough,
and certainly he was extremely competent as an architect and planner in the broadest ancient sense of public service. If it hadn't been
for his insubordinate industrial countermeasures to the Führer's
scorched-earth orders on the eve of his suicide, Germany—and
therefore Europe—could never have recovered enough infrastructure from needless devastation to benefit from the Marshall Plan
and the United Nations."

Finn nodded. "Some blame the Allied blanket bombings of
German cities up to that point on F D R and Churchill for having
insisted upon unconditional surrender; but if Hitler or another
Nazi had lived to negotiate a peace the whole pattern of World
War One's disastrous aftermath might have been repeated, especially considering Roosevelt's death. At least there'd have been
little justice at all."

"That's true." Arthur replied. "Anyway, I saw so many Nazis get away with murder, and sometimes get restored to officialdom, or attain it for the first time, ostensibly as having been secretly humanitarian advocates of democracy or underground defenders of Jews, that I could hardly trust anything I heard from either military or civilian Germans as anything but barefaced lies or self-delusion. Even when F D R's Secretary of the Treasury was a Jew you could easily imagine the anti-New Deal demagogues joining our reactionary manufacturers and Graveyard Street Cans who had quietly done business with Nazi connections by ignoring courts and Constitution, marshaling the unemployed, and persuading much of the electorate that they were saving our democracy from Jewish Communist conspiracy, just as Hitler did.

"I suppose I grew too skeptical of gentile goodwill after F D R was gone. At Nuremberg I learned to suppress legal bias, but for decades afterwards my prejudice against Germans was always revived by pictures and accounts of the death camps manned in the shrouded East by ordinary Germans and their antisemitic local recruits, even as they celebrated Christmas, tenderly cherished their families, and embraced laws against cruelty to animals. I still assume the moral guilt of even the generals and aristocrats who tried to assassinate Hitler for noble or ignoble reasons that had little to do with their own lesser degree of inbred antisemitism, not unlike that of many respectable Atlanteans, including some of our diplomatic gentry, before the war was started against us. I had come up against some of them on both sides of the Atlantic when I was a young lawyer working for the Arnheim Electric family in Holland to transfer European assets to Atlantis while getting as many Jews out of Germany as possible by hook or by crook, starting in '31, long before the Night of the Long Knives, when the old man of the firm foresaw Hitler's politic cabal with other industrialists and the Junkers who definitely ended the German Republic. Before that I had still hoped for the progress of a democratic Germany in politics as well as science. So by '45 I must have been deliberately ignoring any evidence to the contrary of my personal experience." He paused.

"I still can't help being faintly skeptical about German redemption. Again, if genuine and permanent it's only because Roosevelt and Churchill, in disingenuous agreement with Stalin, required *unconditional* surrender. With any armistice less than that the bargaining and procrastination would have obfuscated all important exposure of individual culpability. There probably would have been no serious War Crimes Tribunal at all, let alone indictments for genocide. How many of our own financiers or regulators have gone to jail for their sins after the 1929 Crash? Can you imagine the hopeless task of making a criminal case against every guilty Nazi as an individual according to pre-war law? Neither Hitler nor any head of the German government (except maybe Spree) would have given up without the assurance of his personal security, for everyone in the world had finally recognized that the inhumane transgressions of the Third Reich were no merely excessive repetitions of ruthless Wilhelminian aggression. This time the French weren't allowed much opportunity for such unilateral postwar threats and shortsighted obstructionism as when they vengefully or jealously resisted the German Republic's membership in the League of Nations and stifled its economic recovery in the '20s—but of course I don't blame France alone for the rise of Hitler," Arthur chuckled, "as you may guess from my previous hints! It was only half as antisemitic."

Finn relaxed at this last light touch of accommodation from an authority he'd begun to fear was too sardonic and cynical for reliable congeniality, and decided to continue with the subject he'd hoped to discuss as a matter of naval history.

"I'm puzzled by a certain Admiral Günther Lütjens, the austere and highly professional Fleet Commander aboard the *Bismarck* in that sortie into the mid-Atlantic intending, as you probably remember, to play havoc with the crucial supply lines of the British Empire. (It wasn't much less reckless than the suicidal mission of the *Yamato*, the greatest battleship ever built, four years later in Japan.) I was officially interested in the construction of that marvelous German battleship, finally sunk more than six months before we were in the War, when long before that I was an attaché in Berlin. Lütjens was known for his courage, intelligence, sea-fighting experience, personal reserve, and classic aristocratic qualities, like most of the German senior naval officers in no way (except Fatherland patriotism) resembling Hitler's original thugs. I remembered what I'd heard of his intellectual professionalism a few years later when I served under Admiral Spruance, my own hero in the Pacific. Lütjens took the oath of loyalty to Der Führer that was administered to all officers but was said to stay aloof of 'politics' as much as possible, which was easier to do in the German navy than the army, which was much closer to Hitler's

heart and power, who'd ordinarily looked askance at his Kriegsmarine, apart from the U-Boat fleet, as a necessarily expensive but
untrustworthy military institution."

"Pretty ironic," Arthur remarked, "considering that Hitler was
finally forced to appoint *Admiral* Dönitz his apocalyptic successor!"

"It's just such ironies that intrigue me. For instance, the
German naval aristocracy—insensate to the common good save for
the internal ranks of the Kriegsmarine, which was perpetuated and
perhaps socially improved between the wars, during all the tur-
moils of incipient revolution and counterrevolution, attempted
putsches, and actual assassinations (mostly by the fascists)—tolerated off-duty fraternization with enlisted men to a degree that
shocked the Prussianistic army officers—maybe more than we and
the Japanese did, in very different ways of course, because we were
never allowed to strike our men—either with or without a baton!
But more to the point, it was a navy mutiny that started the revolutionary downfall of the German Empire, and it was those com-
munistic sailors who early on came inland to the streets of Berlin
and saved for a while the frail new Weimar Republic from right-
wing nationalists eventually represented by Hitler. Yet just a few
years later the esprit de corps of the Kriegsmarine under Raeder
and Dönitz, and Fleet Commander Lütjens in particular, seemed
excellent. It's true that the navy was generally believed to be less
enthusiastic about Hitler than the army (which bore the main
burden of purely professional resistance to Hitler's meddling), but
they all overtly took the sacred oath of loyalty to him *personally* as
the present lawful embodiment of their country's honor, however
they may have privately interpreted the signification of their *Heil
Hitler!* salutes. It was said to have been noticeable that Lütjens
especially was no stickler for practicing that protocol of word and
gesture, at least when not under the eyes of Party members."

"Yet we were told that just before he went down with the ship
he radioed Hitler his consummate fealty!" Arthur protested.
"Surely that would have been gratuitous for an anti-Nazi! Don't
tell me it was a sarcastic valediction!"

"No, but maybe it fit in with the narrow honor of Nibelung
chivalry in literal fulfillment of personal allegiance to *a* Führer,
according to irrevocable oath, for better or for worse, falling on his
sword—what Count Kessler called the ideal of 'purposeless death
in the shape of self-sacrifice'. Yet as a doomed foray it was more
successful in battle against the British than the futile *Yamato*'s

maiden sally was with the world's greatest guns intended against
us! But now they say Lütjens had a Jewish grandmother!"
"Everybody has a Jewish grandmother, if the truth be known!"
Arthur snorted.
"But what if he *did* know that?" Finn proposed.
"Probably was never told." Arthur chuckled. "I never told my
wife or children that I had a Scottish grandfather! Germany was
full of oblivious Mischlings, many of them blue-eyed blonds in
uniform and all of them as antisemitic as everyone else. How many
in this country's Ku Klux Klan know their full bloodlines? Under
Hitler, negative genealogy was a cottage industry, just the opposite
of all the usual searches for noble bloodlines. Noble, ignoble—who
cares?—even the Cans, as long as we all get rich together, without
government interference? The Great Atlantean Dream! And what
Tocqueville called our 'perpetual utterance of self-applause.'"

Finn had heard enough about this erstwhile captain of industrial
conglomeration to have no doubt about the tone of those words
from one of the Crats' most reliable financial supporters, especially
since he'd withdrawn from all activity in the financial marketplace.
*But does he still suspect that I was trying to exculpate or rehabilitate battle-
ship Nazis just because they shared much of their professional symbols and
practices with Anglo-Atlantean naval aristocrats, as well as pre-war "non-
political" technocratic colleagues in the service of Cipango?*

*Am I naive, even today, to believe in Germany's re-enlightened demotic
metanoia—its sincere reversion to the best intentions of Count Kessler's
Weimar—to separate "Germany" from the "Third Reich"? In the eyes of
the world will we be able to distinguish the national society "Atlantis"
from their Can regimes in peace or war? It's much easier for me than my
non-Aryan friend to do so. And it's easier for him than for me to imagine
gullible and sentimental Atlanteans, in case of imperial war or another
Depression, warbling "God bless Atlantis" under the stars and stripes of
devilvision, as they elect or accept all three branches of a corrupted Constitution. Fay's fears are not misplaced.*

"In codfishland's Saint James, Terra Nova, where I was born,"
Arthur was saying, "my family talked so much about our 'cultural
heritage', as if what you call the Old Testament was an encyclopedia of history, that I hardly heard of Torah Midrash or Talmud,
simply because that big isolated island of religion in an isolated
province, being what I was stuck in, couldn't be of interest to a
young rebel like me. Not that my parents were what are called religious Jews. They certainly weren't practicing Jews. In fact as nomi-

nal New Christians they had me baptized by the Tudor Church. My father was all but an atheist. But they were historical Jews. It was I who insisted no bar mitzvah for me! I just wanted to get a civilized start as a freethinking cosmopolitan without history—and in Atlantis! Still, I vaguely admired the mysterious Wandering Jew, who sounded as interesting to me as perhaps Robin Hood or Prester John did to you at that age. My belief has remained in *Either the Or and the Holy Both!*"

"I'm with you there, even as a confirmed Tudor!"

"It turned out that my first real job, as a lawyer, was for the old patriarch of Arnheim Electrical Industries in Frisia, the most powerful and maybe atheistic Jew that Europe had ever tolerated—the one who personally put me to work extricating from Germany as many as possible Jews smart enough to believe his warnings before it was too late. That's what first brought me to this Cape, because he put his Stonyhurst House estate on Kracken Point at the temporary disposal of the scientists, intellectuals, artists, politicians, or anyone else, religious or not to any degree, who qualified as a refugee deserving safety for the good of Western civilization, with or without enough money for travel tickets. I managed to include qualified Mischlings and goyim in that humanitarian process while I was helping the Arnheims transfer or liquidate as much as possible of their Frisian holdings on the Continent.

"Only lately, since I came across the old Midrash social idea of an ethical will, I've been mulling over my life before and after the not very admirable decades of overreaching ambition on the Street, which left me with nothing but the success of money. At present I find myself wondering if it's the right time to write this message to posterity as my Jewish sort of traditional tikkun. Your mention of the essays by German admirals suddenly made me think of that as my only proper pastime until I reach the granite ceiling!" He stirred in his chair to help himself to more Scotch and ice from the low mahogany table in front of them.

"Well," mused Finn, "only one of those unrepentant Germans invited to assess the War came anywhere close to what I think you mean to do, and he did so in the form of sharp professional criticism of his peers' strategic blunders in failing to understand what they should have preached to the General Staff in Berlin, as he had pleaded from his post as liaison officer to the high command of the feckless Tuscan fleet: his theory for the Third Reich's effective use of *global* sea power! He sounded like a poor Teutonic epigone of

our venerated 19C Captain Mahan. I know you don't mean a
screed like that, but I do see the poetically ironic parallel!
—Prosit!"

"My Graveyard Street contemporaries would laugh to hear me
spoken of as charitable! But they'd laugh twice as much—even those
who never believed the rumors about my devious manner in small-
scale empire-building—to be told that my life's testament was going
to be *ethical*! Most people could truly believe that I was much more
interested in the power to build an organization of industrial relationships than in the money I personally made. As the president of
our central holding company my reputation was mistakenly tar-
nished by association with the sly maneuvers of a bland gentile
investment banker by the name of Zane Capstick—a name known
hereabout—who was for a long time my collaborator. He liked his
work for nothing *but* money. He had started before the War as a professor of dentistry who took a fancy to managing his own investments, discovering his own genius during hostilities when he was a
dental general in the Army Medical Corps. Even before Hitler's
demise he was very involved in forensic investigation of Nazi atroci-
ties. And then—presto!—he became one of the Allies' most important field officers in the recovery of art treasures mainly belonging to
aesthetic Jews! He never told me much about that part of his Army
career, and I didn't want to ask; but in retrospect, since we finally
split up our joint empire according to our heartfelt shares of the
industrial network I'd been forming with him, on the banking side
of things, my suspicion has grown that he got on well with a few of
the culture-mongering Nazis who evaded postwar prosecution. Does
that sort of thing deserve mention in my ethical will? Come to think
of it, he and I lived here in Dogtown at different times, and I think
someone told me that his daughter married a local shark named
Mooncusser in the ethical profession of reality-estate."

"Oh? I know the name!"

"As I understand it, ethical wills are supposed to enlighten
your progeny with what they've never asked about during your lifetime, as well as with contemplative wisdom that for one reason or
another it has never occurred to you to urge upon them the
common good. And often they're meant also for anyone to read. Is
this the time for a demon to write about his hellish experience?
God knows I would have to write very fast! It was much easier to
dictate my legal will and testament, edited by a probate specialist,
and no surprises to spring, no advices to impart."

"Talk to Endicott Krebs. He's my lawyer now. See if he knew your man. He's an oldtime marooner. They may have crossed paths here, or even when he was practicing in Botolph. The other day he mentioned that he was an Army attorney under the Judge Advocate General in Germany after the fighting was over, though he had nothing particular to do with the Nuremberg trials as far as I know. But he'll be out of reach soon after Gloucestermas. His office is right under my apartment. He must know about ethical wills."

"Not a bad idea, if I decide to wax autobiographical in an ethical will. That's an idea that first popped into my head when I was thinking about what has transpired in my life to determine my almost involuntary attraction to Dogtown, the locus of my ending! My last brief stint on the scene, about twenty years ago, publicly incognito for business reasons, was to visit for the day a Tudor priest, the late Father Superior of a small religious society, who surely was the most remarkable stockholder we or any other charitable corporation ever had. I came to warn him of some difficulties with his assistant priest, called the Father Economist of his tiny monastery, a registered broker who had managed all their funds. I never met their other trustee, who was said to be a Jew, and of course I remember very few names of the corporate lawyers associated even with our largest stockholders, but I wouldn't be greatly surprised to find that Krebs was one of them. Just out of curiosity about that I'll try to catch him before he sails around the world—a wandering way for a Jew to wind up his life, it seems to me. I've met his genial companion Gretta, but I couldn't figure out whether she's a housekeeper, girlfriend, or common-law wife."

"For all I know they may be secretly married." said Finn. "But she's certainly an extremely capable managing secretary, too valuable to be taken away from her rather powerful station in life! He doesn't appear to be pedantically reticent in answering questions. —By the way, it's too bad the Opsimaths don't provide enough ashtrays! I often forget how I used to languish for lack of tobacco. But Krebs has lots of Havanas!"

"To tell you the truth I've long since hardly missed the weed, trying to be abstemious for the sake of longevity. I've gotten to the point that I scorn puny cigarettes and find I can't be bothered with messy pipes. I'll have my daily cigar after dinner tonight."

"But what impressed you about the High Church priest," Finn asked with a hesitant smile, "aside from his commerce with respectable usurers?"

"It didn't take long to dispatch my warning of his man's indiscretions, and he cordially answered my questions about his Society. I knew his Members deplored legal usury almost as much as money-changing in the Temple, but like Cephasites they had somehow rationalized their definition of it. This country may soon need a lot more excuse for trimming its computerized plowshares into the profits of borrowing and lending. What interested me at that time were his remarks that made me more comfortable with serious Christianity than I'd ever been before, especially his criticism of most of it for omitting attention to the so-called social gospel of Jesus—ethical if anything is—*between* his all-too-famous birth and exploited death, the Jewish core for which he was our prophet! At least that's as much of his theology as I could understand. Of course he was just diplomatically avoiding his belief between those two bookends, but, though I didn't grasp his ideas very well, he had a more persuasive explanation of what he called sacramentalism than I ever heard in Judaism for a distinction between mere ritual and *essential* liturgy. At the time I was too preoccupied with my secular vocation to read his tracts or otherwise pursue the intriguing possibility of a modern social religion, without God if necessary, or at least without too much faith. I remember that even your Saint Paul mentioned the importance of hope, which is enough for me.

"I didn't show my skeptical attitude toward both Christian and Jewish orthodoxy, of course, but, now that I have so much time on my hands and am in danger of getting pseudo-philosophical, I wish I could talk to him about his semi-Marxian ideas of political economy as a primary concern of—shall we say—Biblical religion! It's a pity that I'm too old to go back to Norumbega and catch up in liberal education!"

"I've heard about that priest. Caleb Karcist can tell you about him. His name was Duncannon. Ask Fay. She's been reading his books from her anthropological point of view. Would you come to dinner at her house sometime? I can't cook for anybody but myself because I still live by Navy standards—without the Philippino stewards—but Fay sometimes likes to cook for recreation. Father Duncannon was a scientist, and I've heard told that he studied under Mark Planck in Berlin before World War One. He was one of Dogtown's few native intellectuals. According to Dogtown historians, his father managed the Cape's first electric power system, for everything, including streetcar lines."

"This new Dogtown is beginning to seem really gemütlich!"

3.

A few days later Arthur Halymboyd was in Finn Macdane's penthouse surveying the inner harbor as if with a magnifying glass. After a bachelor lunch of cold-cut comestibles and beer the host was to show his guest the center city. "Let's go see what we can from my car of today's Gloucestermas festivity, where the streets aren't blocked off. The boat races must be over by now and we might be able to drive to the Windmill and park there for the best view of the outer harbor. In fact, unless you're expected back at your place, let's have a warm-up dinner there tonight!"

Arthur was nothing loathe. They went downstairs to find Finn's parking space just around the corner from Morality Square, which the host remarked was where the circus parade used to make the right turn onto Front Street. "You know, I never got to see that famous event when I spent so much time on and off here before the War. I was too busy going and coming on business and other matters, and anyway I suppose that then I regarded it as too childish for a serious international lawyer. I never quite liked the smell of drying codfish. The last year I had the chance I was called away the morning before I had promised to watch it. As it is now, I'd give anything to see live horses and elephants marching anywhere!"

"That was the one I did see." said Finn. "It was a stirring sight. Especially at the Gloucestermas of a Great Depression!"

A few hours later they would find themselves at the vantage of the restaurant, having dodged temporary barriers while cruising or waiting within sight of minor processions or festive bands, which competed with a commercial carnival camped in Sacrum Square at the other end of Front Street, gradually reducing the radius of their approach to the city's great white mansion that served as the city's preeminent inn, still the one place to dine in a muted spacious grandeur transparent to sky and sea, without necessarily being confined to the huddled architecture of artificial light. In the old center of the city Arthur had already noticed that Redburn's Needle CaraVANsary hotel for traveling salesmen, in which he'd stayed overnight twenty years earlier, separated by only a block downhill from Finn's rehabilitated building, had vanished, as well as the large department store between them, which was ruthlessly demolished to make flat pavement for a kilroy parking space ended on both flanks by single-level shops designed in ubiquitous mainland style. On their streetscaping route up Beltane Hill and down dales of obscured sightseeing, much of it new to them both, they passed the brick high school on the near bank of the Namauche, which by aestivators and incomers was usually landmarked at a distance for its homely square bell tower raised by the W P A as a modern structure forty years earlier. Its parking lot was already filling with the kilroys of participants in preparation for what Finn had seen announced in the *Nous* (of which he had already become a habitual reader) as the senior class performance of *Romeo and Juliet*.

The two gentlemen extended their evening at a table walled by one of the great spotless plate-glass windows, overlooking as much as one could take in from a single point among the city's numberless perspectives of its singular character, each of which represented a different admiration of its person. In this instance, the eye's arc outward from a peripheral point of its streets was the broad outer harbor of its actual inner port now behind the diners' gaze. Their southerly panorama was an irregular open circle imperceptibly interrupted to their left by the channel to the inner working waterfront, beyond the beach and commercial buildings of the internal Casbah's Watch House Point; and to their right by the artificial and much narrower drawbridged Gut of the Namauche estuary, which was busily navigable all the way across the Cape to fishing grounds in the great John Smith's Bay opening into the North Atlantic.

But what held their conscious or absentminded admiration, as shadows of their small promontory grew upon the spit of sand that invited a creeping tide beneath the cliff of rock on which the inn's predecessor, a historic windmill, had been mounted, were the long embracing arms of the harbor brightened or flashed with flames reflected from the sun's gradually leveling beams on quiet waters, on navigation lenses, and on the mirrored glass of reflecting houses scattered among green hills and margins like eyes cheerfully winking open from privacy to join the common gratitude for a laminated pink and blue departure behind the mainland after almost flawlessly lighting and warming the seashore's holiday. The last of the small craft that had nearly filled the vast open vale all day, darting cruising or tacking in various and varying directions, had ceased their hooting and tooting and were now individually dispersing, each with its own goal ashore, at sea, or at anchor, with discernible riding lights or with sails glorified by the western valediction. The white Crow Point lighthouse and its ancillary low red light on the other end of the long breakwater were already drawing attention to their horizontal against the dusking ocean of Vinland Bight to the south. The green ridge of East Harbor Ward was beginning to loom as a range of fully outlined hills; and far across the water the giant rocks and picnic grounds of Salt Cod Park, dwarfing the grassy ramparts of old Salt Fort at its sandy foot, were reluctantly evacuating from tables fireplaces and lawns most of their families, clans, teams, and fraternal congregations, about to leave the premises for the most part to lovers and the few who intended to set off some unofficial rockets a couple of nights before the official fireworks that would set the whole Gloucestermas firmament amazingly ablaze above the harbor, its waterborne spectators much diminished by a gaudy dome of supernatural shooting stars in every transitory color.

Linking their candles, in the quietly clinking Windmill dining room with postprandial glasses of luse, to the Park was a row of white lights lining the Esplanade and drawbridge at a lower level, face to face along the full straight segment of the harbor facing the frontier lighthouse and far beyond it the whited glow of the great metropolis across Vinland Bay down the curving coast (and now emerging from the twilighting horizon) where it incessantly attracted or propelled the streaking or circling red and white lights that traced North Atlantic air lanes beginning or ending at the Guy Winthrop International Airport, most of their present vectors far enough from Dogtown to seem as silent and harmless as comets growing visible in the star-scape of a planetarium when its base lights are dimmed.

Finn by now had found his formerly sober companion rather thoughtfully loquacious, as if the idea of an ethical will had fecundated his private memories and at last liberated him from wealth's dignity emeritus. "When we—Judy and I with the young kids— had a house out on the Point for a few years after the War," Arthur was puffing on his choice Havana, "I had very little time to get reacquainted with much of the town but I'm pretty sure that high school was already built, long before I was married, during the Depression, when I'd spent a lot of time here on the refugee business. I remember the massive old high school was opposite Ibicity Hall on Whale Avenue—probably the shortest and most important street in town! There was no call for a children's parking lot in those days, but I bet they had a Latin teacher! I'd have hated law school if I hadn't known some Latin. If there's anything I abhor in education it's blind memorization of words that suggest nothing of their derivations."

"Yes, nowadays I think there are even more parrot brains in medical school, because they have to master the agglutinated words of biochemistry, which irritate me no end when I'm wrestling with pharmaceutical labels. I also can't abide the contradictory instructions of obfuscated prescriptions and patent medicines, which have at last permanently entered my daily routine. I used to get along very well with just brushing my teeth." Finn's tactful intention in this offhand remark was to discount an apparent superiority in the contrast between his own apparently healthy vigor—for he had never spent more than a single night in any hospital—and the aged appearance of his sedentary new friend—shorter heavier seamier and nearly hairless, who had suffered several bouts of surgery and at least one heart attack, though in fact his junior by a year (as he had gathered from incidentals in their retrospective discussions of public events during the last half-century).

They both expected to rub along very well together by virtue of the interesting differences with which they had experienced the same war, its advent and its aftermath, almost as if they were comrades in arms, seeing that Arthur for his part tactfully deprecated the obvious advantage of personal power extended by earned wealth spoken plainly, personally unembarrassed, about what to do with the uncommitted segment of his legacy, as if rather than a superannuated magnate he was an arm's-length arbiter for a Royal Arthur's eleemosynary court.

"I wouldn't want to be a Polonius in my ethical will. I'd rather make it for some sort of foundation related to my own experience. I might perhaps join other donors before I die. My late wife Judy, as an Arnheim much richer than I, helped fund a number of good causes in the arts or elsewhere for the common good, but I'd like to leave something for a special purpose even if nobody else contributes. Maybe just to convince myself that I haven't wasted my life since the Nuremberg Trials. Isn't that what an ethical will should do? For many unlucky Jews, in final desperation, it was enough if they could register their name with scratches on a cell wall, or on a slab of smoked wood to be found under the rubble of a synagogue—or anywhere for an archeologist to find in the next millennium. I owe their posterity something more commensurate with my better luck."

"Reminds me of Ozymandias." said Finn impulsively—at once biting his tongue for possibility of offensive banter in his ironic tone. But Arthur didn't know who Ozymandias was, and he let the remark pass as some sympathetic expression from a strain of Atlantean culture less worldly than his new friend was accustomed to.

"My progeny need nothing much from my estate—except perhaps some advice they'd never have liked."

"Have you thought of something like the endowment of a professorship?" Finn asked.

"I wouldn't trust committees for selecting the beneficiaries à la academic mode, especially considering this generation of misguiding educators in departments I know something about. This country is saturated with centuries of legally unenforced clauses and slackened or forgotten definitions after the generations go by. Reminds me of our controversial Constitution! Anyway I don't think much of probate judges either."

"You'd have to narrow down the criteria in some specially lucid way, with a preamble to explain your purpose with a portolan of bearings to narrow down the leeway of interpretations! That would be fun! Almost like engineering specifications. But of course the next difficulty is how to set your personal standard when the committee holds its first election of candidates for your eleemosymary legacy!"

"But look how abused the Constitution's Preamble is!"

Finn laughed. "It doesn't have the retrospection of an ethical will! I wonder if Dogtown's city charter has a preamble. Ask Endicott Krebs when you see him."

"I've been thinking that I'd like to have you with me, if you agree, when I write that codicil—without calling it ethical!"

"Let's have a little stag party for three World War Two vets!"

"Good enough! At my place. Come in a taxi so you don't have to drive home! I'll invite Krebs, but urge you to urge him to come before he goes away."

On both sides a thoughtful silence ensued, until Arthur Halymboyd resumed. "Meanwhile, as an alternative, what occurs to me now: When I visited that priest long ago he showed me a diagrammatic chart—intelligently colored shaped and annotated with numbers—of my leveraged indirect and interrelated shareholdings that one of his office workers who had lunch with us had constructed as well as any outsider possibly could from all the various quarterly reports each one of our companies had to file with the Securities and Exchange Commission or the stock exchanges. This was before computers mechanized such research and discouraged the imaginative usefulness of relational diagrams. Naturally it couldn't keep up with the trading or other deals that were going on all the time, but it did marvelously clarify the structure of what was labeled as "King Arthur's Empire". It made me laugh, but I'm glad the S E C lawyers never got hold of it, because it clarified all the complexities that we depended upon for the continually evolving design of our 'spider's web' as the industrially organized low-priced stock holdings of a bland closed-end investment trust company, which was called the Parity corporation—P A R on the Big Board. As Chairman and President my motives were mysterious simply because I was more interested in quiet small-scale empire-building than in increasing the market value of our immediate portfolio, according to certain generally overlooked provisions of the Act we were governed by."

"Why did you call it 'Parity'? I've found that to be a word of too many meanings!"

"Capstick and I originally meant it as equality in access to ownership of the public company, which merged the original investments of our personal private trusts. That's why I picked a double-bitted axe for the icon in our corporate seal. Only later did I learn from the guy who made that chart that in Greek it was called a *labys*, the symbol applied to the labyrinth in Crete. Recently in my retirement I've visited some archeological museums during my travels and discovered how unique the axe was until it was reinvented as a very practical tool by Atlantean woodsmen in the 18C or 19C. The only place I found an artifact closely resembling the symmetrical design of the axe—despite all the picks and pikes and axes in history—was in an obscure museum's archeological showcase in Sardinia, and even then it didn't quite match what you'd expect to be a universal development. He thought it originated in Sumer, in Eber's time! Isn't it remarkable that in all the magical iconology, heraldry, kabbalahistic masonry, and psychologized esoterica that has shown up in my sporadic little archeological hobby, the efficiently balanced double-bitted image seems to skip from the beginning to the middle to the end of manual civilization? Should I endow a Norumbega fellowship dedicated to a professional search? At least it would fit with the vogue for cross-cultural studies!"

Finn was warming to the man's good humor. "And with the history of technology, working backwards from the northern Big Lake woods of Paul Bunyan! Chain saws have put an end to its leaps. —Anyway it's still a good symbol for what sounds like your labyrinthine life. What better device for King Arthur's ethical will?"

"Unambiguously ambiguous, eh? Constantly equivocal. But diachronistically anachronistic!"

"Maybe we'd both better call for an IXAT cab to get home tonight!"

"But not quite yet. Since you listened to me so much, I want to tell you more! Or ask you. Maybe you wonder why I don't just leave my ethical estate to some of Mother Earth's great causes. Urged by my late wife, an Arnheim heiress who was able to give much more, I am already pledged to many of them with money: geological protection, global conservation, international human rights, social justice, human rights, education, global poverty relief, and the arts. As for political donations, I'm a Catholicrat because my criterion has always been the composite common good—even," he smiled, "even when I thought F D R, though he meant well, didn't understand the difference between conspiracy and monopoly in all his antitrust regulations and tax policies that were obstacles to certain of my schemes. He only laughed when I told him that, without even trying to read my mind for self-interest. He knew well enough that Parity was small potatoes in the national scheme of things. He was dead before I had the chance to make him believe that what I wanted to do with holding company investments was an exception in *motive*. But he was usually right about the common good.

"Still, none of these affairs are peculiar to my life or particular in my personal motives. Nor was the Shoah personally distinctive of my life, even after I learned more about the mechanical engineers of Zyklon B ducts than any intelligence agent did when I testified in Nuremberg cases, though Auschwitz or Buchenwald or Treblinka or boxcars or death marches must have exterminated hundreds of my own blood whose existence my family never even heard of, and millions more of my kind who suffered in the convolutions of Hitler's rectilinear labyrinth, both his architectural maze and his involuted spiral of the whirlwind sigil he sowed in his psyche and reaped with his power. His legacy of German self-destruction, by reversing the direction of common good, the spindle of evolution in reverse, to glorify the common evil from the cold dust of unwound cerecloth, may have marked the historical center of humanity's career, since nothing in our future can be more evil in principle. There have been hopeful signs, for Jews and blacks together, for Irish Petrines and Paulines, even for international justice.

"Besides, I should think that ethical wills are bequests of values—not of assets, not of debt, financial or moral. I'm not indulging in confession. But I do have money available for a small legacy or instrument, you might say, to help perpetuate whatever distinctive value my banausic life would like to have left behind without having contributed any work of art or new idea or social innovation or political leadership or mentionable good works, or even a child promising enough to take and do what I ought to have done!"

Finn was too humbled—spiritually—by this apparently impulsive confession not to suppress his skepticism of a conscience in this armored man of the world. But before he could think of how to express his honest admiration he was spared a response by the long puff of smoke that accounted for the pause.

[*It seems that Dogtown, after all, may be the true center of his winding and unwinding labyrinth, the natural kind of labyrinth, finally dissolving his clever maze of artificial decisions and cul de sacs? Has Daedalus— the name, by the way, of his private personal trust for controlling Parity's investments—has his contemplative retirement drawn him to an authentic labyrinth of his inner life—whether it's continuous winding or unwinding, clockwise or counterclockwise—into a center of engendering compression or out to an unlimited tangent in escape from the prison of a womb? What was the last point of Arthur's first irrevocable twist in the selfish direction? Fay believes that instead of claiming Moira Trevisa he let her disclaim him!*]

Finn was not confident that he remembered what he'd dimly dreamed a few blocks away; but less dimly now he pondered his 1934 Knighthood at anchor in Dogtown. Indeed he'd found enough of the remaining mystery to laugh at his curiosity as he finally agreed to leave his car overnight and staggered out of the Windmill parking lot. As he awoke from dream with a headache the next morning, under the glaring skylight of his own bachelor quarters, the form of a memory without retrievable content somehow seemed to have clarified an extrapolation of consciousness relevant to poor Arthur's.

4.

Arthur Halymboyd had no headache when he ordered breakfast in the paneled sitting room of his digs, earlier than usual. His head was clear, clarified by sleep, which seemed to have enlightened and shaped matitudinal memory of the greatest passion of mature youth. He recalled Finn's presence as the catalyst for dissolving the compacted sediment that had nearly hardened and shielded from himself the prehension of his years before the all-but-successful Holocaust and all his successes in Atlantis thereafter.

Moira was unreasonable, but she was wrong and she was right. It was my good fortune, and my loss, to have been right to heed the summons of Arnheim not just to keep my lucky job. I was wrong and I was right. I was lucky—though not as fatally lucky as Romeo, seeing as I would never actually die just to keep a promise—to have escaped domestic husbandry, and so was she to escape matrimony simply in the desire for three preordained children. More than once she said she'd heard that Jewish men made good husbands, and I don't think—as she assured me that crack of dawn in her tearful whisper trumping my temporary departure with her irrevocable dismissal—I don't think she was faking in her praise for my part in our physical foundation for a happy marriage. Perhaps she read my mind long before I did. It would have been disastrous for us both. Not until much later was I grateful to her for causing me the immediate grief from which only the threat of doomsday's ultimatum could divert me—none too soon, for it quickly proved that my two years of nearly slavish love had not been strong enough to survive the obsessions of service to the state and the elation of private power, which I tried to believe was in my case as creative as her pictures and poems, not to mention her blind urge for the creativity of reproduction. Romeo wasn't yearning for kids. But what else is marriage really for? We'd never again had such wonderful times as we'd had when we were male and female bachelors living separately except on small travels from time to time at social liberty.

But she was also right to silently accuse me of selfishness for not undertaking to support her totally, though I wouldn't have had the salary to do so without devoting myself to the very kind of poverty-shunning that she sometimes chided me for, even if she'd agreed to keep using her rubber oval. But no other woman has so much deserved my admiration sympathy and respect—even now, from what little I've known of her in half a century of perspective and all passion spent.

Maybe she married that unworldly slightly effeminate-looking scientist I was beginning to get jealous of, when she had once callously remarked after seeing him play tennis that it might be interesting to spend a weekend with such a gentle gentleman—as if absentmindedly expressing how much she missed my attentions when as often as not I was down in Charter Oak or elsewhere on business for the Arnheim charity which I was "not at liberty to talk about", much to her disgust, especially since I couldn't take her to

my little apartment over at Kracken Cove, where I spent fewer of my Dog-
town nights than in hers. I hadn't been suspicious, because she said that
epicene paleface lived in England and was here only for a few weeks in
summertime to visit his mother, and because she and I were so closely paired,
even in public amusements, we were so devoted to pleasing each other every
moment I was free of my active preoccupation with Weltschmerz (which she
shared empathetically as a Gentile more prescient even than most European
Jews). I managed to take what she'd said as frivolous musing about an
innocent pipe dream meant not to be in the realm of nature—as an artistic
fantasy with not the slightest consideration of disloyalty to me, her unques-
tionably destined soul-mate lover—though not without a virtual teasing to
goad my awareness of the luck I enjoyed in having won her preemption in
the existent phase of her erotic maturity, almost too late to serve the purpose
that I then realized she had silently harbored all along, whether or not it
was respectable—whereas I was stupidly contented with things exactly as
they were! She called me Honey Cat when I was in bed with her, King
Arthur whenever I had to leave on a trip. She knew by heart a hundred old
songs and poems, and a lot from the Bible (especially about Jesus in the
Temple with the money-changers). But countless times when she was happy
I heard Omar Khayyam, sitting down to eat in her kitchen, "A book of
verses underneath the bough / A jug of wine, a loaf of bread—And Thou /
Beside me singing in the wilderness— / Oh, Wilderness were Paradise
enow!" The one poem I remember by heart. My beer and wine, her own
simple recipes, the most delicious meals I ever had. She almost made a lib-
eral Christian of me! She said it was my lovely circumcision that almost
made a Jew of her.

But with really dangerous worldly things so much on my mind I was so
insensitive to the things she didn't say that they took me by surprise in retro-
spect. She was courageous and ebullient, and wanted more emotional expres-
sion from me, even scolding me for being too conventional, too staid, too polite.
But her sense of humor, and mine, saved many a day and night. I told her
that when she was good she was very very good but when she was bad she
was horrid! She was the one with imagination; I was only the wise man.
Yet she was too religious to be a Bohemian artist after all! Then again, she
sometimes thought that my occupation "saving the Jews" was an excuse for
not living together! It was uncomfortable enough when she lightly referred to
herself as neither maid nor wife nor widow; but in our perfected two-backed
beast that last dawn, before I had to leave for what had been planned to be
only one of my usual trips of unspecified but urgent leaves of absence from her
bed, when I remember especially thanking my stars that our love left nothing
to be desired, and that I had nothing to fear in our fundamental devotions to

each other, with a suddenly bitter renewal of strength with fingers clutching my shoulder blades she called me Aeneas, and herself Dido, as if the absolute parting she'd just declared was my *idea!*

Yet back at my base in Charter Oak, before I could brood over the finality of my nearly incredulous shock, I was whirled away by ominous events in Germany to which it was my job, always aspiring to obedience. And perhaps I'm not sorry to admit I remained so until I had some power. I do remember, soon after we'd first met, a cloudless autumn picnic one azure afternoon when everyone else was at school or work, when we sat against a cliff of solid granite in Salt Cod Park looking across the outer and inner harbors, and the city in between, toward the East Harbor ridge from which we'd come, its foliage garnished with the descending sun out of reach behind the western hills, as she fed me from her basket between the ravenous bites of lobster rolls that for us were expensive even in the Depression, when our fresh love was as pure as the halcyon air. In fact it was the purist romantic day of my life. At my age it is very hard to do justice to a love hardly remembered as more than a category of experience, yet still specific in admiration and sympathy—those elements of any love worth recalling—and actually enhanced in the clarified history of a lifetime. If only as a matter for nostalgic valediction, before my final heart attack back here in Carthage, I wonder if Endicott Krebs ever heard of her in those days of universal insecurity.

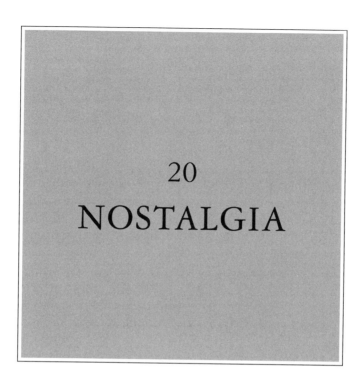

20
NOSTALGIA

1.

[Athur Halymboyd's paneled and padded private sitting room in his attached "coach house" at the Merriwether Hall retirement center, where he is giving Finn Macdane and Endicott Krebs a long lunch after the end of the Gloucestermas octave. At first one or two waiters are still coming and going at their silent duties but they soon disappear, leaving his private bar on the sideboard well stocked with water, ice, a variety of bottles, etc, to which each of the three freely help themselves when the host's suggestions grow familiarly unnecessary. Without too much emphasis the collation has been designated as a farewell party for Krebs, who is unexpectedly leaving for his global cruise a few days earlier than he intended in order to attend the wedding of a granddaughter in New Uruk who altered her own calendar solely for his sake as soon as she heard of his sailing.]

"Fortunately," he sighed, "I had already packed formal clothes to satisfy British expectations of first-class travelers in any of their seagoing hotels. But it's hard on poor Gretta, to be left with so much to sort out and dispose of."

"There's no need for her to evacuate the office in too much of a hurry." commented the former temporary Captain in Navy rank, who had outranked the Army's Reserve Captain Krebs in mufti without crossing the other's path, as far as they knew, in immediate postwar Germany. Nor had either of them knowingly encountered their present host of the same nearly subaltern rank as a temporary member of the Strategic Intelligence Service by virtue of his extraordinary European experience before the War. But the three new comrades were within a year or so of the same advanced age, now haply united more by intellectual perspective of the War (during which they'd seldom met former acquaintances, East or West) than by others who'd shared the same oath, if not the same uniform. "I have no new tenant in the offing, and there's a lot of renovation to be done first in any case. Let her take as much time as she needs. I wouldn't charge an old vet like you another month's rent!"

"Thanks, but we want to get out of your way right on time," said Krebs, "even if it requires all her ingenuity to deal with more complexity and perplexity to face at leisure whatever's hauled over to my house. She actually welcomes that kind of responsibility! Let her decide what needs shredding or burning. She's the one that's got to do it. My personal financial and family stuff is already in my safe at home.

"And by the same token, Arthur," Krebs continued, turning to the host, "much as I appreciate this very kind invitation, I'm afraid I must get back to the office even today, almost for the last time, before she locks up. She's always standing there with a list of small decisions for me to make, most of which I'd much rather leave to her. Doesn't speak well for my reputation as a lawyer, does it? Well, I'm no longer a mere lawyer. I'm Chief of the Supreme Court, supervising one Clerk!"

"Please don't retire absolutely!", Halymboyd replied, "I was hoping that when you get back—if I don't have a heart attack for another three months—to get your billable advice about setting up an ethical will with some sort of charitable trust pertinent to Dogtown. Just for general consultation. You wouldn't have to do the details. You're the indigenous Solomon, from what I've been told."

[*By now the dining table has been removed.*]

KREBS: I'll be glad to help if I come back with all my wits, as long as I don't have to consult a lawbook, open a file drawer, or write a formal document. If it's for the good of Cape Gloucester I don't charge, of course. There's a young lawyer here who does detailed odds and ends for me.

FINN: And without leaving Irish pennants: I can vouch for that.

ARTHUR [*To Krebs*]: I heard from Mrs Opsimath that you've done a lot in helping to preserve public land.

KREBS: She's probably thinking of Duncan's Farm, mostly many years ago, practically my only professional work here in Dogtown, as a Trustee. As far as I can remember all the rest has been small pro bono stuff after I retired. Much less demanding of my peace of mind than volunteering for one of the city boards, and getting involved in Ibicity Hall battles. One mayor wanted to appoint me to at least five different commissions. I admire the people who do serve. It requires tough skin and a lot of patience.

FINN: Poor Dexter Keith! He seems to have inherited a primitive mess of disorganized amateurs. I still don't understand Robert's Rules of Order for the Board of Earldermen from what I read in the *Nous*.

KREBS: It's just rules for the elected council, designed to fight the mayor! Our new Charter, which by the way is actually an improved constitution, attempts to impose modern municipal management—much constrained by Vinland's General Laws—upon the old Colonial conceptions of self-government by independent amateurs who pride themselves on dissent! So we end up with Venetian kinds of "checks and balances". But at least we have a good Doge now, who campaigned for reform.

But he's frustrated by the totally incompetent lord of members, defender of the status quo, who was supposed to know more about what needed to be done inside Ibicity Hall and the outlying departments, not to mention the inside powers that be, than anyone else could possibly learn in a dog's age, simply because he's been kept on by the Earls as the mystically authoritative "Auditor" (by 18C charter definition) for twenty years.

ARTHUR: Did you ever know the priests that ran a monastery over on a hill in the Point?

KREBS: Alas, I knew them well. I was their secular Trustee for quite a while. The Laboratory of Melchizedek and the Mesocosm! A sad case. I miss Father Duncannon. Duncan's Farm would have belonged to him if he hadn't taken the vow of poverty when he gave his own estate to the Charitable Trust as such. His life's work seems to have been destroyed by his loyal assistant, the stock-market priest—

ARTHUR: Now I remember why your name sounded familiar!

KREBS: I remembered yours. I knew something of your Parity Corporation. I didn't say so because I couldn't help feeling the vestigial compunction of my former fiduciary duty—but since everybody involved except Gretta is dead, and you the first to mention the matter: It's no secret that I was one of the three Trustees, their Old Testament check and balance!

FINN: One of their people is still around. He may not have been a member of the Society but he was a privileged hired hand. I've heard about those Anglican priests! [*To Arthur:*] That was Caleb Karcist. He must be the one who made the diagram of your empire!

ARTHUR: Ah! I certainly remember one of his charts! It put everything in an elephant's nutshell. I think the Fathers asked me to recommend him for some job at Mercator-Steelyard after they had to let him go.

KREBS: I heard about him, but he was never present at the Trustees' meetings. I didn't know he was still around. But Father Lucey, the Registered Representative of stock exchanges, scion of an antebellum Nashdom plantation, graduate of Princedom, and a certified social worker—an original character to be sure—was absolutely devoted to his Father Superior and told me a lot about *him.* Lancelot Duncannon was a native son of Dogtown, but somewhat sheltered from the uncouth elements, even though his father, an electrical engineer, was general manager of the all-powerful Cape Gloucester Power, Light, and Traction Company. After being sent to Grottlesex prep school and his father's V I P [Vinland Institute of Polytechnics], young Lance wanted to get *really* away from home.

He went to Germany and England to study everything that he didn't already know about physics and cosmopolitan culture, with the advantage of having already learned Greek and Latin as well as French, German, and Italian! However, I have the impression that he was even then too delicate and sensitive, as well as too independent financially, to show much academic ambition in physics until he got more interested in the Tudor Church when he lived in London. But apparently even then, at the beginning of middle age, he was an excellent otherworldly tennis player and ballroom dancer, an elusive bachelor, who still evoked speculations by the gentry and the artists when he was at home visiting his mother out on the Point in time for Gloucestermas at the start of almost every summer. He must have been a familiar face in half a dozen ocean liners commuting to Southampton from Botolph. I take it that here he was some sort of an occasional Levite cherished by the local Tudor congregation for reading scripture or helping with the music and ritual, or otherwise assisting at whatever they do on Sundays. I imagine that to women he must have seemed a blond angel in his temple costume. I've never been inside a Christian church except for weddings and funerals where a stranger has to guess at how its basic liturgy, if any, compares with ours.

I suppose his friends were even then a little in awe of him for his secular learnedness, which obscured his achievement, if any, as I was after the War, especially after I saw his former library and connoisseur's chattel in Unabridge, before his mother died and left him the family house up here, when he had me turn all his property into an institution. That was before Father Lucey met him among intellectuals as the Society was being formed. By that time Duncannon was an ordained priest, with a small following of religious leftwingers down there who were excited about his social interpretation of Christianity, you might say from an anthropological point of view, which, from what little I knew of it, seemed closer to some kinds of Judaism than to the Pilgrim Fathers or the Petrines. He was trying to start an ecclesiastical revolution even as he stuck to the basic orthodoxy and ceremonial symbolism of the conservative Tudor High Church, as imported from the Unaford Movement in England, generally considered as all but papal in its Scholasticism, which I heard a lot about when I was an undergraduate reading English history. From within his church he was almost defying the Bishop of Vinland. But in person he was calm and modest. He swore that for all his docile learning he'd never thought for himself until he was forty!

FINN: Sounds a far cry from most of the scientists or inventors who have new ideas. Of course all the greatest of the geniuses, like Einstein, are exceptions in one way or another. I don't know how you two fare in law and business, but judging by myself I think most technical men do their best thinking early on, losing analytic ability as they age, even while getting better at some kinds of synthetic ideas, which may improve or at least hold their own in intuitive judgment. At least that's my comfort in wishful thinking—as my memory betrays me!

ARTHUR: Cheers for three old stags!

[*Exit Krebs, reluctantly departing to his office downtown at Gretta's behest.*]

FINN: Duncannon sounds to me like a guy I once saw at a Gloucestermas dance. You might say he stole my girl—only because I was already stuck with escorting the Admiral's daughter.

ARTHUR: What year was that?

FINN: Must have been '34, when I had a little yard tug.

ARTHUR: That was fifty years ago. I wonder if it was a guy they used to call the Holy Ghost. . . .

2.

That evening Arthur Halymboyd, again avoiding the common dining room of Merriwether Hall, sipped his luse alone. He had gone for a walk halfway along the faint path to the Opsimaths' hilltop before hesitating and turning back to order dinner in the privacy that had become more and more valuable as time itself was growing uncertainly short. He liked to think that he never ruminated or planned about his death because he was too occupied with the recollected immensity of seventy years past, as they might be reflected in an ethical glass as small as his thumbnail, so difficult, so pleasant: the choice for framing the good kind of power with which a will might endow something deathless, not by its money or name but by its conceivable symbol of his ceaselessly interesting life, whether or not anyone else cared. He had not felt this powerful even when he was King Arthur of a productive organization, driven—contrary to the assumptions of investors and enemies—not by lust for wealth or fame but by an instinct for vitality in honest manufacturing of useful materials with ethical efficiency by happily rewarded people.

Maybe I should invite Gretta to lunch after he's gone. No, better yet: Tessa. She'll know everything Gretta does, and a lot more, I bet. Yet, again, Gretta may have been young and innocent at the time, but she's the only one now available to me who actually knew Moira in those days. She might even have noticed the traces of me in that studio. So why not have them both to lunch at once, right here? At least it might allay Tessa's suspicion of me as a lecherous old spider. On the other hand, whether in my web, or else in any of the noisy restaurants, either of them would probably be inhibited by self-consciousness with a third party present. I'll have to think on it.

3.

[*Meanwhile Finn Macdane was having supper with Fay in the kitchen of her patched-up old house that looked out from its heights upon a hundred and twenty degrees of the Atlantic horizon, over and beyond less than half a mile of green-carpeted hollows and rounded ridges, now nearly emptied of golfers within the irregular perimeter of more variegated hedges and trees deeply shading its neighborhood of roads and often enviable houses. Hidden from their present view by the highest ridge of rock-borne turf linking two of the gracefully extended meadows, the fairway likewise exposed a few scattered gray whalebacks or breaching heads of chthonic granite in its long slope to the lowest corner, nearly to the shore road, as the least artificial hillside of sport that Finn (himself never a golfer) had ever seen. Ending just short of the sea rocks, it made a sharp elbow across a road to the Club's newest reclamation of Lady Gloucester's integument, civilizing with another green for shots a strip between the backs of shore motels and the rockiest ridge of all, from which in the Admiral's house before the War he had looked down upon it as a much wider and rougher pasture of the original Duncan's farm, then crowded by scrub oak, sumac, and brambles, as well as by a surface boulder shrouded two stories high that happened to rest upon an accidental spot of unconnected subterranean granite.*]

FINN: I've never wanted to play golf, but this course is even more tempting than the famous one in San Ricardo. It's a silly pastime, like chess, but lovely to trespass when no one's in sight. Yet inland, elsewhere, I wouldn't give it a glance.

FAY: If I were as biased as you I would have chosen theology instead of anthropology. But I like some of your prejudices, now that I'm retired and almost fancy-free.

FINN: At least we're both Catholicrats. Every time I think of this last election I'm dismayed that the Party seems uninterested in expressing its political philosophy, which I hope is at least inchoate in think-tanks somewhere! The Cans win by concealing theirs. Even as a naval imperialist, born into a family of Protestican virtue, drinking with mother's milk all the prudential precepts and adages of Franklin's and Emerson's self-reliance as embedded in the Bible, I'm a Crat because I'm half Petrine and half Pauline in what you might call the Roosevelt settlement of the political symbol-system.

FAY: Pray, sir, what does that mean?

FINN: The rigidly graduated common good that originated with the inequalities of Petrine feudalism was like the societies we have in whole navies—and in their subsystems, especially great capital ships like *Bismarck* and *Yamato*, full of social unequals who die or survive as nationalistic patriots symbolized by demi-gods; while in our ships, insisting upon practically the same hierarchy and discipline, we regard ourselves as free individuals within a democracy derived from Pauline ideas of spiritual self-salvation— liberally affected by each other in a secular commonwealth! F D R's "Four Freedoms" weren't meant to distinguish the Crats as a party from the Cans in national pragmatic political terms. Like Queen Elizabeth he represented both Petrines and Paulines under the same flag. Our party's political philosophy is silent because it has only a preconscious and vague understanding of the historical dialectic. The Preamble to our Constitution, which speaks of the General Welfare, was made possible by the coaching of deists. We usually lack the concepts of organic abstraction that could succinctly integrate our various "issues" and "policies" without overdetermining the details. Crats seem to have no comprehensive offensive against Raygun's antisocial Chauvinism. I wish at least they'd challenge the polemical meanings of words like *conservative, morality, values, freedom,* or *liberty* that are so twisted out of history in Protestican propaganda.

FAY: My dear Viking, you should be an architectural sociologist in the next Crat cabinet, if we ever get back the White House. I can see why you love systems theory. All systems, as you've said before, are ultimately organic. I'm sure Alphie Whitehead would have appreciated what you're saying. Even though a theoretically Platonic philosopher in British terms, he was uncanny in his pragmatic perceptions of what's wrong with Atlantean politics.

FINN: I'm under the impression that he'd agree with me about chess and golf. Maybe Caleb told me that. My memory about things disappears as soon as they're understood! I now spend a lot of time trying to recover what I've learned! As often as not I overreach my object and the process deceives me. Psychologists speak of false memory. That's false synthesis, I suppose. Like dreams? Reversing that process drives me back to what I'm now no good at—analysis of what I can remember when I cudgel my brains. For instance—

FAY: Finn dear, I didn't know you to be so introspective! What a wonderful husband you would have been according to family psychologists!

FINN: Don't talk about family! I'm getting to dislike the word. —For instance, the other day I was trying to dis-absorb the name of a Dogtown woman I met in 1934. It must have been when you were working at the hospital. I seem to have recollected her name as Moira. True or false, after fifty years it came back to me after I heard you and Tessa mention your old friend.

FAY: In 1934 I was on an anthropological expedition with my husband in the South Pacific. I didn't meet Moira Trevisa until 1935, when I was back here working in obstetrics, when she was changing her name to Mary Tremont.

FINN: But weren't you a married woman then?

FAY: Would that have stopped you, a dashing officer and gentleman, from gallantry with an undereducated provincial nurse with a husband commuting by train schedule almost forty miles to Unabridge practically every day? I would have looked up to you as an older man of the utmost responsibility and kindness, much less selfish than an egotistical graduate student making his name in the Classics Department. But even if I hadn't been married, and had been a scholar, I don't think you'd ever have married me—or anyone else. Besides, I wanted children.

FINN: You must remember the old Depression song [*crude recitativo*]:

It costs three times as much for two
To live as cheap as one.

FAY: Is that why you never married? I didn't think you were in danger of penury or some job in vulgar commerce. I know you are parsimonious about Mother Earth's resources, but not for the money it saves you.

FINN: That ditty's a metaphor for my outgrown bent for selfish intolerance. It may not be too late for remorse but it certainly *is* much too late for reversal. If I had married and sired I'd never have found you.

FAY: I'm still a widow. Is that taboo in your godless religion? We're compatible enough as social Catholicrats.

FINN: Then will you go to the Hall with me tomorrow?

FAY: No. I don't have time, and I prefer my independence.

FINN: Then we're half too much alike. I've never wanted kids. Will you move in with me?

FAY: Never. No room for my books. No room with a view I want. No silence for my concentration. Assuming you continue to make me happy as you do now, I can always get another cat to keep me company if my Maxwell gull ceases to visit. I need a lot more space than you have. Would you like to move in with me?

FINN: Haven't I already—more or less? Occasionally. Maybe more board than room.

FAY: Thus you gallantly decline my impetuous invitation. Good! Maybe I'll get my work done before I die.

[*Both laugh outright.*]

4.

[*After clearing up the kitchen, but before the sun's aura was entirely withdrawn from the open valley of the marsh, the two spry ancients had walked briskly side by side down to the footbridge of the tidal creek, taking care to keep on the left side of roadways lacking sidewalks, at Finn's elbow-guiding reminder, in order to face the kilroy traffic and trust their own nimbleness to confound the drivers who thoughtlessly assumed in moments of blinding glare or unbraked kinetic energy that familiar deserted-looking thoroughfares were always uninhabited by pedestrians in dark clothes at shady spots, or around blind curves that had never appeared in public accident reports, or which bore warning signs too familiar to notice. But that took only ten minutes. Whenever they walked together in town or country, Fay was tacitly pleased by her gentleman's apparently autonomic habit of keeping himself between her and the traffic—an anachronous custom that annoyed the independent pride of modern women like Tessa.*

Crossing the creek's strong ebb tide, silently enjoying as if in summation of separate lives the extension of their harmony to their respectively unspoken nostalgia for itemized loves and friendships (which to feel at this culmination it had been unnecessary or impossible to recall in enumeration, visualization, or analysis) they'd then taken their usual turn half a mile down and back the length of hard-packed sand. The day's lifeguard and bathers were gone, but they passed dozens of native or aestivating strollers and almost as many newly amnestied dogs elated with freedom to chase and play, or at least to run—sorely envied by the law-abiding ones still on leash. At that hour, with no in-shore fishing boats still in sight, no seabirds called themselves to attention alow or aloft. The sun's valediction had been reduced to a single flame in the highest windowpane of a summer mansion on the summit of a dominant sea-bluff as they faced to the east on the return lap. But a summery day on Cape Gloucester was hardly ever any warmer than a warning of the heat expected late in August, so most sleeves were rolled down and nobody was in a sweat, except two or three self-conscious runners who usually had the beach to themselves in opposite seasons.

As the two veteran walkers climbed home in the twilight without much loss of nisus or breath, a lone angel might have observed that more than their wont, contented though they were, and much as they admired every azimuth of their ability to be walking there when past their prime, too absorbed with memory to glance at each other, both had rested their eyes on the ground in front of them, their brows slightly contracted, the closed mouths in their aged faces occasionally tightening at the corners of their lips in recollection or anticipation.

Finally, at a moment when an angel could have fully viewed them only through a tiny skylight installed long before Fay's solitary occupation of the old house, they sat lightly clothed side by side against the great mahogany headboard of her oldfashioned bed, each staring without comprehension at an open book in hand under doubly incandescent reading lights. As soon as Fay resumed speech Finn closed his book and reached to turn off his light, and she instantly followed suit. Like twins they had recognized in each other the same mood of quizzing rumination, naturally from their oppositely engendered points of view, which this time kept them stretched flat on their backs, almost comically aware that they were motionless toward each other, all passion suspended. The evening's wine and wisdom had advanced their conversation to this point of curiosity.]

FAY: What do you mean, you *met* her?

FINN: [*Chuckling.*] Just casually, downtown at the circus parade. Actually at the soda fountain of the drug store. I walked back to East Harbor with her.

FAY: And?

FINN: She showed me her studio. I didn't know her more than eight hours altogether.

FAY: That's a long time to see some pictures *casually*. She lived in her studio, I suppose.

FINN: The pictures I saw had been damaged by fire, and then I wasn't particularly interested in art. We had tea. In those days there were a lot of Bohemians around there.

FAY: I was aware of that, while faithfully married and eight thousand knots away.

FINN: A knot marks speed, not distance.

FAY: You were a sailor on liberty.

FINN: Loosely speaking.

FAY: Yes indeed. Forty-seven years later it's a cosmopolitan bachelor's casually unforgettable eight hours. I'm very glad to know that you're in no danger of Alzheimer's senility.

FINN: I was overwhelmed. But I was slated to escort the Admiral's daughter to the Midsummer's Dance that night, and there it was that Moira eluded me. End of adventure.

FAY: I'm not going for trade secrets.

FINN: Just for auld lang syne?

FAY: Anyway, it doesn't much bother me that you were a casual opportunist. It's better than some oily Casanova earnestly devoted to collecting scalps. I hate men who are always on the prowl.

FINN: Even you can be fooled!

FAY: I've never been jealous of men's freedom.

FINN: As far as I'm concerned it takes two to be free. I certainly wasn't anticipating.

FAY: I don't think my friend Mary who lived over that way in 1935 was casual about men. No doubt you were exceptionally attractive to an honest woman. You must have been dazzling in your white uniform and ample head of Nordic hair. But I didn't know either of you at the time. Are you sure it was 1934?

FINN: Oh yes. It was the *Great* Gloucestermas of 1934. I have good reason to believe that she had a steady lover at the time. But I don't think it was the Holy Ghost she vanished with at the dance.

FAY: [*With a short scissor-kick under the covers.*] I'm about to turn my back on you.

FINN: I'll roll you over if you do. And that might arouse my libido. —Are you too aloof even as an anthropologist to be interested in ethological anecdotes?

FAY: Of course I'm an unbiased judge of humanity!

FINN: Then swear in Arthur Halymboyd and me as the only eye-witnesses.

FAY: What's he got to do with it?

FINN: Ask Tessa Opsimath. She's been pumping him.

FAY: Just for fiction.

FINN: Fictitious fiction, maybe?

FAY: Like the Holy Ghost?

FINN: Don't tell Tessa that I know anything about her inquisitive imagination. Give her enough fiction to hang by. But you apparently knew more about the Mary one than anyone else we know.

FAY: A lot I've already told Tessa. I knew Mary in person after Caleb was delivered, but mostly afterwards from her letters.

FINN: Why was the Moira-Mary already so interested in islands when I met her? Was she already planning to leave Cape Gloucester?

FAY: Maybe it'll be explained in Tessa's novel.

FINN: Especially the Isle of Man, I remember she questioned me about it.

FAY: Ask Tessa.

FINN: I think I may know who the Holy Ghost was.

FAY: I'll be interested to find out when I get to read her fiction.

FINN: Do you know Caleb's birthday?

FAY: I told you: about spring equinox. Don't pester me. It isn't good manners, for a man of the world.

FINN: I admit that. Why should I care about anything like this for the first time in my life? Did that scholarly husband of yours ever get you to read the generally overlooked plays of Euripides—in English I mean?

FAY: I remember *Medea* and *The Bachae*, from early days, when I was trying to keep up with Adam's expectations of a child-bearer, though he scorned the opinion of anyone who didn't read the Classics in Greek. Of course as a young nurse I disliked Euripides. Why, do you recommend any of his other plays?

FINN: In the Navy, especially at sea, I had time to read a lot of things that I'd had to skip in college, though without attempting the Classics in my smattering of prep school Greek. But in translations I was prejudiced against Euripides, simply taking sides against him as the decadent opposite of Sophocles, or of Aeschylus as in *Prometheus Bound*, just the way I've paid attention to rivalry in football or baseball only after I've found a hero to anchor my loyalty in one team as the enemy of every rival! I still admit that attitude in politics, but I finally got over it in aesthetic matters. For instance, without compromising my apotheosis of Yeats I now admit that T S Chittering was a great poet too. So also, at least when I disregard quite a few plays in the Euripides repertory, I find him in my good graces. Forty or fifty years ago his *Ion* left no impression on me. Now that I've learned my lesson I elevate it to a very interesting comparison with *Oedipus*, my touchstone. Will you read a readable translation of *Ion* if I leave it with you? I'd like your opinion.

FAY: I'll find the time. Your request is an honor, not at all like one of Adam's condescending demands. —But now, my sensitive sapient Schlepper, perchance to dream about your battleships or the last book I'm hoping to finish before I die. After you kiss me tonight as gently as if I were your sister.

FINN: Get Tessa to read it too. She reads plays, I'm told. It's an enigma. [*He complies with her request. The kiss is reciprocated and extended.*]

21

HOLY GHOST

1.

Endicott Krebs stood in the center of his evacuating office as he warded off the reasonable last-minute questions and reminders of his secretary-housekeeper Gretta, confessing himself more bewildered than he'd been since beginning his first S I S field assignment, when he found himself unharnessing a parachute near the wrong farmyard in Occupied France, too late to avoid moonlight and already too far from the rendezvous to meet the Maquis expecting him five kilometers away, just as headlights of a German patrol were coming along the road in both directions! Such a contingency was by no means unexpected, and he was dutifully trained in feasible alternatives of escape.

Now in Dogtown more than a generation later, except for the fact that he carried no capsule of cyanide, the consequence of failure was unlikely to be fatal; and the cause of trembling at his fingertips was not fear but normal old age. Gretta had tactfully noticed that it was often hard for him to separate pages of paper as he turned

them. But his brain was muddled by haste under a multiplicity of
exciting pressures without exactly relevant training or previous
experience. There were too many things to think about all at once.
A date for action had been moved forward a few days by an unexpected event in the scheme of things—not weather over the Channel, or an appearance before the Supreme Court, but an inconsiderately announced wedding in New Uruk. In old age one's executive
self-confidence can be shattered even after thirty-five years of civilian practice, rationally arbitrating or scheming under the literal
rule of contract law. All he wanted to do now was finally bow out
of his profession, make the exotic trip of his dreams, and let his
trusted deputy tie up what his landlord called the Irish pennants of
his evacuation from the Dogtown office to which he had long since
resorted from the Vinland metropolis. For years, right here, he had
collected odds and ends of personal accoutrements away from his
domicile much neater in the quiet Namauche Plantation.

In particular, among his professional documents and furniture,
Gretta was urging him to look over the contents of a dusty battered
brown expanding file jacket designed to contain legal-size file folders and their contents. Its winged flap was tied down with a bow-
knotted ribbon. She had discovered it behind a follow-up block in
back of the bottom drawer of a cabinet that had been used for
unclassified miscellaneous drafts and memoranda. She was holding
the gap open before him, the cord dangling, to reveal financial
papers, pamphlets of various size and shape, a few smaller letter-
size standard folders, and about half a ream of hardbound typed
manuscript, the cover of which was paper-and-candlewax sealed
with the flowing handwritten label: "LD, Personal", double-underlined in black ink, superposing the emotional block letters "DO
NOT OPEN BEFORE 1975!"

"I took a quick look at a few of the papers and most of them
appear to be notes or correspondence about the financial affairs of
that religious Laboratory that was out on the Point. Some of the
stuff may be personal."

"Yes, yes, I remember that mortgage-business mess. I thought
we'd archived those files. I can't be bothered now. This is probably
the stuff that that crazy Father Lucey imposed upon me before he
finally left town."

"But Endicott, maybe some of it is important, or at least
secret!"

"All the more reason I'll leave it to you! Help yourself! Ditch it, cull it, or otherwise deal with it, if law permits, before I get back if you possibly can! I won't hold you responsible for reasonable mistakes, which in any case would be less numerous than mine. As my executor you have my power of attorney for anything that isn't quite properly in that young attorney's hands—my God, I can't even remember his name! He has copies of my will of course. I've told him to consult you on any doubtful matters. If I die, don't forget to notify *all* the names on that list I gave you. I might as well be buried by the Rabbi. Pay the usual bills; anything unusual, do what you think's best. You might dun a few of those moribund accounts receivable unless they're too poor to pay. Not everything I've done in Dogtown was supposed to be pro bono!

"But try to spare me any more decisions in my old age! I don't think you'll find any secrets in Father Lucey's mess, which he foisted on me 'for temporary safekeeping' before he shook this dust off his feet and got sent to that elegant psycho-suicidal booby hatch; so I must have seen some of it years ago. —Come to think of it, the Laboratory's Trust probably owed me some expense reimbursements when it dissolved, and now they're both dead, God bless at least one of them. I can't think straight—all this trivial stuff at once—just because I kept procrastinating with my new friends even after my granddaughter threw a monkey wrench into the family calendar by getting married in Ur!

"—Is all my travel stuff packed at home? Are you sure you'll be ready to drive me into the city tomorrow soon enough to catch the train even if we get caught in a traffic jam? Do you have the radiogram address I gave you to reach me on the boat—or rather ship, as Finn insists? When . . . Passport . . . tickets . . . ? Big ships wait for no man. —If you still need any practical help, consult Tessa Opsimath, almost no matter what it's about. She's very resourceful, as well as curious, but she keeps her mouth shut, even, I believe, with her husband Rafe, unless it has something to do with their business. Social workers can be very useful about things that are none of anybody's business! I have an inkling of her 'research' that you're abetting. It's harmless enough, as long as everyone involved is dead and it's not relevant to my reputation—as to which I trust you implicitly. Tell her I intended to say goodby to Rafe and herself. . . . Jesus Christ, my old Colonel would twirl in his grave if he knew what a wreck I've become when there's nothing to face that's

any more dangerous than luxury travel! I think it's because I've
been *too* long *too* retired from the real world, thanks mainly to you,
my dear. You make me feel like a protected old lady!"

"You can always fly down to New Uruk if we miss the train—
which, God willing, won't be your fault or my fault if we do."

"I don't like to fly without a parachute."

2.

[*Meanwhile, more or less, Tessa tested as context for her text every tes-*
tament that she hoped would cohere with her untested text, singing cheer-
fully to herself. Much to her surprise it was less difficult than playwright-
ing, which, as a sometime actress and stage director, she'd always affected to
dismiss as secondary in the dramatic arts. And now as a convert to fictional
investigation (for the sake of an organic hypothesis) she reveled in her
corvine talent for gathering novel bits and pieces she didn't understand in
order to make a plausible nest. Then too, she imagined, her silhouette from
behind the scrim sometimes reminded one of an intelligently amoral magpie.
Thus, without renouncing her social dedication to the common good, she
wondered if the individual freedom of a novelist wasn't full compensation
for the contrapositive frustrations intrinsic to social work. Watching
Gretta's prize-winning craft at the loom that had been moved from her
little house in the woods to the Krebs manor, Tessa began to feel confident of
understanding (at least with an anthropologist's permission and Gretta's
assistance) even religious or scientific people warping and wefting at right
angles to each other in her own new fabricating art well enough to weave
bits of ribbon and jewels with the skein of her own distaff. Although she
hadn't yet solved even her own idiosyncratic mystery she was sometimes
momentarily tempted to guess the much greater liberty she'd have in positing
a solution to Caleb's. God knows she had enough case histories to stimulate
her creativity. In her youth, after all, she'd deftly helped Auto Drang write
his books when she didn't understand much of his brilliant theories.

The following partial first draft, as casually corrected or interpreted by
Fay Gabriel (where she was offered extraneous matter inessential to Tessa's
insights), directly or indirectly incorporates extracts from letters, other docu-
ments, or scraps of evidence in the possession of Caleb, Fay, Gretta, or her-
self, whether or not found in office file drawers or Caleb's unexpectedly dis-
covered foot locker. Among them they include evidence in the handwriting of
Mary Tremont and Father Christopher Lucey; but these two individuals
had known nothing of each other between the years that connected them with

Caleb's life respectively, and Tessa herself was no great practitioner of either graphology or difficult exegesis.]

Father Christopher Lucey, all but officially self-defrocked, had awaited the appropriate moment for suicide by attempting to write a biographical tribute to his late Father Superior, Lancelot Duncannon. He knew himself to be a dunce at writing (though he had gotten through Princedom and endured the literary requirements for a master's degree in social work), and he never wrote out the few sermons he was called upon to deliver; but he was not too humble (in his mastery of the spoken word as a salesman) to make the most important documentary effort of his life when he found that he alone was in a position to serve posterity with intimate personal biography of his beloved Father Superior. He had not given up hope that someday an exceptionally alert scholar browsing in the stacks of an ecclesiastical library would discover by chance or God's will the radical originality of Father Duncannon's Christianity, long after the failure of the attempt to establish as its secular wellspring a tiny religious institution which was cold-shouldered by his own Tudor Church as apparently too Petrine in its liturgy and too socialistic in its political philosophy. Gentle Lancelot Duncannon was vehemently opposed by most of the clergy for "dangerous materialism", to the detriment of "spirituality", despite the essential orthodoxy of his theology and practice in his symbolism of traditional actions and vestments as performed, High or Low, at every Tudor altar.

But neither the theory nor the practice of this rational "Metacosmesis", which Father Lucey loyally embraced, was of nearly as much concern to him as his personal devotion to the person of his discovered Father Superior, the creative scholar, his confessor, who had taken the place of his own father as the object of his will to live. In the two-man monastery he had been this father's medical attendant as well as resident acolyte and assisting priest, as a strong and skillful nurse preventing his mentor's sudden death in the latter years of their close but sometimes difficult companionship. Christopher Lucey was the only follower of Father Duncannon in the Classic Order of the Vine who chose to take the oath of poverty, chastity, and obedience to become a Member Regular and thus inhabit the Laboratory of Melchizedic and the Mesocosm with the Superior.

Early in his priesthood Father Christopher Lucey had occasionally been Father Duncannon's own confessor, but that aspect of their sacerdotal relationship had proven uncomfortable, and after the Laboratory moved up to Dogtown from Unabridge, for a permanent institution as the headquarters of about six dozen international followers, priests or laymen, married or not, visitors or not, the Superior's spiritual privacy called for him to drive alone up to Markland in the Laboratory's little Autotod to make periodic confessions to Father Davy, a parish priest, the Member Secular elected as his successor and representative of the whole Classic Order of the Vine. But Chris Lucey never forgot the advantage of what he'd learned or earned, ex officio, about his mentor's earlier life. Thus wrote the greatly junior priest from a mental hospital not long before his suicide:

None of this my memorial is a violation of the Confessional, even though by leaving to posterity my witness of his anguished scruples I am acting in my knowledge of it [he wrote with green ink in his sprawling hand on the first page of a copy book], because I'm pretty sure he told me, or led me to believe, one way or another, even once or twice by briefly fragmented utterance in his sleep near my own bed, what I now offer as the scrupulous anguish of an ultimately pure sinner whom I was privileged to serve as perhaps the closest confidant of his entire life, though I knew him only during the last fifteen years of it. He died prematurely, when he was not yet seventy—a loss much greater to me than any other I've ever felt or feared in my own tortuous life. [His punctuation was obviously the guesswork of tortuous emotion.]

Anyway, that I was partly the cause of his death, by disappointing his trust in me, by my own sinful deception, only reinforces the demands of Conscience that ultimately override all the Church's commandments and vows of Melchizedek forever. I'm a lousy writer, I no longer have files to consult, and my memory for facts is faulty; but it would be a far greater sin against humanity for me to omit anything the world should know of what I happened to know of this radical genius who should have been recognized as the prophet of a liberal Church. . . . No one in my luckily privileged position would in good conscience let such an extraordinary man fade into the obscurity of professional rejection, especially no one as much as I in need of penance for the miscarriage of his seminal institution. I have betrayed his faith and hope in the dramatizing delusions of my unforgivable personality—a suffering man of comity and peace, abhorring violence, but condemned to the other two-thirds of the same Seventh Circle. . . .

When I could no longer cope with my financial difficulties as the presumptuous Father Economist for our "charitable corporation", I allowed a fire to start in the boiler room—and, worse, got credit in the Dogtown Daily Nous for carrying Father Duncannon to safety—before our insur-

ance lapsed. But of course we didn't collect enough to pay off my recent ill-considered "temporary mortgage" as well as cover the costs of rehabilitation. By the time Father returned from his Markland refuge with Lloyd Davy the Classic Order of the Vine had faded to nothing but an occasional membership bulletin produced by the correspondence secretary in England. When that ceased altogether, reduced to not much more than someone's obsolete membership list, its enthusiasm was sapped by Father Dun's death, soon followed by undeclared dissolution of the secular Order, which had always been legally independent of the monastic headquarters Lab reality-estate, which I had worked to sustain financially, mainly by investments in the stock market. No more than the two of us, as both monks and priests, had been free and willing to take the vows of religious life. But we were in no way alike in age, intellect, temperament, personal desires, aesthetic judgment, or will power.

Under those peculiar circumstances my Father Superior was uncomfortably expected to report occasionally to a latitudinarian Low Church bishop in Botolph, an expert in music and fund-raising, who had little or no interest in the perplexing purpose of our infinitesimal Order, which he and most of the other Tudor clergy cautiously respected only for the anachronistic use of ceremonial incense blended with the civil right to exude a homolitic strong whiff of socialism. So the obedience was left to me, the poverty was theoretical, and the chastity remained difficult for sacramental confession on my part—for on Father's part it had been questionable only before taking holy orders long ago as an ordinary secular deacon. . . .

Thus Chris Lucey, who had escaped prosecution for altruistic fraud only by the forbearance of his betrayed Superior and of his two fellow Trustees of the Laboratory, one of whom was Endicott Krebs, the Order's skillful corporate lawyer, began his apology and narrowed his purpose to what was most interesting in the personal life of his beloved teacher, spiritual advisor, ecclesiastical protector, and at times fussy old maid in the character of an insistently aesthetic boss. Apparently without a qualm the junior admitted that in tears he had broken a sacred promise to the master by wresting from his coffin the black silver-framed pectoral cross, the elder's only personal possession in canonical poverty, sparing it from flames to preserve it for posterity as that holy life's only relic. It was said to have been found among personal effects accompanying Christopher Lucey's final violence to himself.

The rightful owner of that rectangular talisman had worn it under his clothes ever since he'd taken special vows of religious life in Unabridge (having been ordained as a secular priest in

England only a few years earlier) to mark the founding of his
unorthodox Order, and the nominal establishment of his first
"monastery" in a private house not far from the Norumbega
Garth. For himself, privately, it also especially reaffirmed his penitence for the one great sin of fornication that in his own terms
had blemished the brilliant and holy life of Anselm (and Abelard
too of course), but the Saint's secret sin had been committed in
early youth, whereas his own he considered far less excusable
because it had occurred nearly at the end of youth, having privately sworn himself to chastity in dedication of the spiritual
purity he believed was required to make the most of his orthodox
persuasions, which were still inchoate as his religious calling. By
then he had learned that his ultimate enthusiasm was in neither
science nor philosophy nor poetry. After some oscillation between
Maxwell and Whitehead, Cardinal Newman and Dom Gregory
Dix, British Museum and Tate, James Maynard Keynes and T S
Chittering, or Planck and Bohr, hoping for synthesis of learning
and faith, Lancelot Duncannon eventually found his own ideas in
a systemic vision of Christianity radically differing from the
gospel that had faltered within both Petrine and Pauline
churches. Experience as a Tudor deacon in the brutal dockside
slums of the Isle of Dogs was one source of his enlightenment,
after returning to London from the signal culmination of his Midsummer 1934 in Dogtown. Thus having broken his much earlier
private vow of chastity—undertaken not in fear of sex or in lack
of desire but in hope of unclouded self-discipline—his humbled
psyche, avoiding repetition of the most natural sin, began its creative liberation from what had been an essentially moral attitude
toward all of humanity. A contrariety of feelings was positively
awakened in an intellect already fortified with a remarkable spectrum of studied knowledge, yet he continually reminded himself
that his renewed vow of chastity was not yet selfless, not yet fully
responsive to God's particular gifts.

As a mature man of the cloth he remained professionally con-
versant with scientists and scholars, and selectively attentive to theological debate; but, except for his own followers, he comported
best with philosophers anthropologists and historians, especially of
course those who were interested in the idea of religion. He loved
classical music but approved of very few contemporary artists, especially the proliferating poets. He had known few of those after the
War.

3.

In the early '30s, before the death of his already widowed mother and his fifteen years of primary residence in Europe, Lance Duncannon had been locally regarded as a harmless gentleman of perfect behavior, reputed for his academic successes, his tennis, his devotion to the Tudor Church, and his ballroom dancing—held somewhat in awe by indigenes and aestivators alike, identified especially by his charming manners and his penchant for white clothing in the summer. Behind his back some of the Bohemians made friendly fun of him as the Holy Ghost.

One of them, Moira Trevisa, he had often seen at the Communion rail, and occasionally noticed walking with her Jewish Shepherd on the streets or strands of his East Harbor precinct, coming up to Wye Square from her studio. But his gentle austerity wasn't breached until he showed up as a stag to help celebrate at a tea dance the great 1934 Gloucestermas, when the fixed and movable feasts of the Christian calendar came nearest to very rare synchronisticity, solar and lunar. This special social event was offered in open ad hoc partnership by East Harbor's mutually askant Yacht Club and Art Association in the latter's Barn of Art-on-the-Wharf at the very edge of Argo Cove, close to Moira Trevisa's unfortunate place. This amicable "mixer" of summertime tolerance and defensive solidarity was goodhumoredly supposed to betoken a melting pot of "all-year-round summerfolk" and artists, with their local friends, amid the common good's cruelest Depression lately encouraged by the nascent New Deal.

This gathered elite was an informal mixture of attire: most of the dancers wore ordinary summer street clothes, according to the quality and manner of their immediate intention for a Gloucestermas evening as eaters, providers, watchers, acters, or just ordinary people; but among them were a few in costumes or decorations as disguise or distinction for a later dinner party at a private house mounted in the brow of an extended steep bluff of naked granite well known to navigators of the outer harbor since the times of Champlain and John Smith and charted as Long Rocks, for which the present residence was named but which would be overshadowed and concealed from spectators of the public Beltane Hill bonfire high over its roof and chimneys that same night.

As a favored dancer Lance Duncannon had promised several ladies to show up at the Barn, presumably dressed in some version of

his usual white-trousered tennis garments, as East Harbor's summertime matinee idol, much to his amusement, when he returned
from England for the usual extended visit to his mother. Moira Trevisa, in an equal and opposite sort of Bohemian category, had also
been committed to two or three on an unwritten and unscheduled
dance card, but she showed up somewhat later. After that Lieutenant
Finn Macdane dropped in, on his preordained way to the Yacht Club
dinner with Admiral Symes's daughter, who herself had promised a
proletarian sculptor a turn or two, before her family knew that the
Navy tug would be calling at this port with its familiar commander
available off duty. Unhappily he'd wasted his bargain with the Chief
Boatswain to have this night off for the sake of his little crew's most
possible liberty. In his slightly wrinkled white uniform Finn suddenly found himself hot under the collar with unaccountable jealousy of the man in white who happened to be the one with whom
he was obliged to exchange partners by the most untimely spring of
a lock, in the casual manner of recreational dancing. Despite this
normally insignificant transaction, portending no more than a few
minutes of disappointment, the transaction of this particular female
mind and body, unparalleled in his experience or imagination, was
too valuable to take for granted even for his temporary possession. It
was too late to catch her eye before she and the man in white had
disappeared, leaving him to curse his luck with a boring conservative on his hands, perhaps until he could repair to the reserved bed
where he was always welcomed to the family room and board of his
great naval mentor in bachelor's retirement.

His intuition was not mistaken. At a pause in the fox trot,
Moira's dance had been cut in by the civilian man in white, as gently
and politely as could have been expected in the chastest chivalry of
Catharism, despite her mildly mocking dress in the role of an eman-
cipated flapper with a milkmaid's blue-eyed complexion, bobbed
hair, and a rakish black beret. Her manner was languidly quizzical in
their mutual recognizing introduction—faces known only by smiles
at church—as she responded to his inquiries during their subsequently uninterrupted round of flings and glides, while she seemed
remarkably calm in her account of the studio fire, which a few days
before had started in the kitchen of her landlady on the floor below,
destroying or damaging most of her unfinished or unsold paintings,
and consuming or devastating much of her habitat and personal possessions when the firemen had wound up their hoses too soon (as they
seemed too often to do in Dogtown), for they failed to notify the

police for defense against vandals, or to quench more than just the flames, allowing her to reoccupy her initially untouched sleeping quarters between their first and second appearance, whereby the occult embers were rekindled to neglected flames, from the lethal smoke of which she had awakened just in time to survive, but not soon enough to save her dog Sycorax from the fatal fumes.

"It's a good thing it didn't happen during the circus parade." she mused. "The fire engines would all have been tied up! And most people wouldn't have noticed the fire-whistle signals." All this was expressed before she dared to show her curiosity about his semi-sacred self.

Lance remembered having heard the actual fire whistles that night and morning, but since there was nothing spectacular to observe from a mile away, and since as usual he'd had no reason to associate rather ordinary civic sounds with the woman he now embraced on a public dance floor as a member of the church he'd noticed in the choir when he read the Lessons.

Persistently, despite his modest evasions, she was soon interjecting her own eager questions, trying to make the most of an unexpected opportunity to gratify her own more purposeful curiosity. He was so little conscious of the melodies and rhythms that guided their extraordinary unity of movement, so absorbed by her bold intelligence, that it took some time for him to understand that she was appealing to him not for sympathy or help but for his blessing of something that she had already determined.

Thus in semi-comical fashion she extorted from a semi-man-of-God the confirmation of her exasperating decision to renounce the commercial plastic art that had diverted her soul from the only real talent He had blessed her with—poetic imagination. But there was nothing playful about God's demand for the burnt offering of her best friend on earth as punishment for failing in her girlhood pledge to put before anything else in her life the blessed duty of motherhood, now that it was nearly too late to have the three children she had righteously promised herself. At least so he was amused to suspect the meaning of her cheerful remarks. She did not scruple to turn their acquaintance into a test of priestly confession.

If not, what was he to make of this cheerfully frightening talk, which might well be meant to tease him about the profession she had heard he was considering? He didn't especially relish the pastoral aspect of priesthood; despite his authentic cerebral sympathy with individual human suffering, he found it difficult, even when personally interested, to face the call for the ecclesiastical cure of souls or comfort of the afflicted, to say nothing of improper conversations like this one. But at the same time he was fascinated by the thrilling irony of agape emanating from the natural blonde Celtic beauty associated with carnal folk tales. He was embarrassed but not put off by his inexperience with unclassified women.

In the end it was God's will to find that they were both free to head for the Long Rocks party as partners, for though streetcars ran nearly all night during Gloucestermas, they were only once an hour. He was as elated as a yachtsman sailing his sloop with a single damsel in the moonlight to find her beside him in his roadster when he drove across town with its top down in the balmy dusk already lighted by Silene after parting respectively for an hour to dress for a very different occasion.

But at first Moira's thoughts didn't seem romantic. ". . . and I've always been so obsessively careful to prevent fires!" She raised her voice above the engine noise and chassis squeaks to make sure he understood the proximate cause of her misfortune. "It wasn't my own fault on that level! The firemen meant well. My friends were wonderful. They went out and collected for me a big basket full of donated clothes, and all sorts of comforting food. . . ."

4.

[*Father Lucey's nearly illegible divulgence gradually lapsed into chirographical and syntactical incoherence as it shed his posthumous light on a secret that Father Duncannon had kept for half his life, long before they'd met in Unabridge when the Superior was middleaged and the proselyte about half as old. But Tessa perused it all, as well as all her other scraps of corroborating or suggestive evidence, in continuation of her aggregated synthesis, as follows.*]

This year's Gloucestermas celebration was held at the old capaciously framed white house three-and-a-half stories high on spacious grounds above the bluff of Long Rocks—as if a Yankee parody of Dun Aengus—having been assumed with the estate's purchase from Richard Tybbot (the "Duke of Dogtown"), along with its name. This landlord had finally moved into a massive chateau with high walls of rough-hewn but tightly fitted granite, recently built a hundred yards away for a million dollars or so from a domestic fund originally invested on the Graveyard Exchange by anticipating and selling short just before the Crash. But the large comparatively humble Long Rocks house was said to have been acquired during Total Abstinence anticipation of the recent Restoration. Though this present buyer of the Rocks was known to few of his guests, he had nominated most of them from his own list of friends unknown to the locals.

Moira, known as a cosmopolitan, was invited "with companion", but she had assumed the festivity was a sort of bourgeois affectation, devoutly to be avoided, especially in her mourning for Sycorax—until she'd seen Lance Duncannon at the tea dance, who was obviously not the kind of aestivator who would have been invited to this mysterious game of identity and theme for Gloucestermas insiders; but he was as curious as any man would have been to escort this Tudor woman anywhere, dressed in any reasonable manner.

Neither of them saw reason at first not to take it all in as the overture to a quasi-comical ball congruous with their costumes based upon his tennis-white trousers and black eye mask and her flapper's version of a Victorian hearth-maid.

But it was soon discernible that the hospitable host—a whip-in-hand wrangler calling himself Balaam in a cultivated voice—was basing his party here on an extravagant bar still echoing the Restoration, as if trying to get rid of the fortune he'd amassed when it had been illegal as long as the Coast Guard was patrolling at sea with flying boats launched from Parliament Island half a mile from where he stood. A three-piece jazz band and piano were quietly warming up in a dark corner with the pianist, seated next to a painted figure apparently awaiting the set-piece directions of a painted cabaret female with a cigarette holder in her mouth looking to Balaam to signal a change of the soft and soothing dance music to the beginning of their Weimar interpretation of Atlantean speakeasers making the most of freedom from want as soon as twelve pairs of guests had arrived and been to the bar to get numbered badges with whispered options and gestures to the lavish buffet further inside—my "ever normal granary" (said the host) open all night—and thence the black-curtained stairway to a dozen bedrooms upstairs. "My whole family has gone to Europe." explained the genial mooncusser with a wink of his one uncovered eye.

Lance was immune to thimblefuls of red wine, and Moira did not care to drink anything stronger than that (remembering her younger indiscretions at parties in the Village of Ur). Instead of indulging even that much on this occasion they took to the introductory sparsely occupied dance floor, rather than joining the line of presumably erotic or dipsomaniac revelers picking up fungible keys at Balaam's counter for random or calculated use during the expected afteraffects of sensual music, munching, matchings, and movements.

Lance was not immediately fazed. He had survived the Roaring Twenties among sophisticates of many types in Europe—but so had Anselm and Abelard, whom he felt strong enough to outdo, simply by gradually hardening himself against waves of desire by denigrating the vascular system of God's gift to human nature. Yet sometimes red wine seemed a complement to the Creator's testings. At this stage, anyway, there'd be no harm in learning more about the real character of this native enthusiastic Tudor Apostolic woman who now told him she'd been a "Modern Woman" of the Roaring Twenties.

"It's too dark." she laughed as they stayed swaying to the suasive music almost by themselves. "This ridiculous decor has nothing to do with Gloucestermas or Dogtown except the obvious allusion to our erstwhile rum-running! I don't have many good words for Duke Tybbot, in spite of all his eleemosynary paternalism. All his gold came from moneychange in the Graveyard Street temple. According to what I've heard, he had absolutely no need to sell this house, which he was brought up in, to a dubious marooner just so that he could elevate himself to a lord of the pretentious castle made of local granite right next door, to illustrate as impressively as possible his rag-to-riches autobiography! This house used to be pretty shabby and a lot smaller."

Allowing for her poetic exaggerations (to which he was already accustomed), Lance took a closer look over her shoulder at the doubly artificial ambience. But at the same time he wasn't sure whether or not she was making fun of the prudish kind of man she might think him to be. He could now sense that she was fathoming his social experience. He decided to risk the revelation of his innocence. "It's a much different atmosphere from the Long Rocks when I envied its situation from my stuffy house out on the Foreside. Now it's sinister. On a beautiful evening, with a view of the whole outer harbor, the curtains are all drawn!" The minimal truth of this observation was his tentative defense against her possible scorn of his apparently genteel gullibility.

But she was serious. "It makes me shiver. Anyway I don't like the way they play this kind of music. And I'm the one they call

Bohemian! Really, I'm an oldfashioned romantic, and I hate surrealism!"

"Your voice is very sweet. I've noticed it when you sing. I wish I could hear it now. But even lovelier is your speaking voice."

"I would like to hear more of yours. If you were to take me home right now, before things get too obviously embarrassing, we could watch the fireworks from Nedlaw Beach and talk more about what you think of cabbages and kings. Then with apples, red wine, and cheese, and coffee at my studio, if you like. But of course if you'd rather stay I can easily take the trolley at the bottom of the hill, which is due in about twenty minutes."

"Of course! This isn't what the old Long Rocks were mentioned for when I steered my little cat boat by this landmark. I'm not any more pleased with this incipient Dionysia than you are. But don't let me spoil any of your plans."

"Let's go. We might not miss an illegal bonfire before we get off this hill!"

And so they did, as the evening passed—alighting here and there, like innocent excited tourists, according to lack of spaces for his car, talking of many things on the way—finally under the sky-light of her studio apartment. She had listened intensely, as if required by the full moon. He found her a common reader with significant questions, even about physics. But at her urging he spoke of his long sojourns in England, with an especially favorable description of his one visit to the Isle of Man, as compared to the other European islands she asked about. Some of the time she sat looking up at him from her footstool, wringing information and advice from his smiles. To his relief, her remarks boded nothing about his moral opinions or absolution.

But she evaded talk about the commercialized art she'd recently renounced, the surviving remains of which she had penitently—perhaps (he wondered) fiercely—destroyed; they were not unblemished victims worthy of sacrifice to God's fire. But "just for fun" she recited from memory a poem she'd written in her girlhood about Sir Lancelot looking out over his submerged Lyonesse between Cornwall and the Scilly Isles. It was that sort of poetry that brought them together from the English culture of their unconnected youths that seemed almost incredibly coexistent on this tiny heterogeneous cape.

"Nowadays that's a so-called Victorian subject for painting. So is Pyramus-and-Thisbe. But when I was a schoolgirl here my great ambition was to write an epic poem about Maid Marion and Robin Hood. Now that we know she was really neither maid nor wife nor widow, maybe this is the time for me to start on that with some hope of getting it into print!"

He the elder sat in the only armchair admiring her candid vitality, gazing down into her bright-blue eyes and the humorously highlighted face. He resisted an urge to caress with the fingers of both hands the darkened roots of her girlishly twisted hair beneath its taper at the back of her neck. He delighted in her quick wit and literary taste, and especially the mellifluous low pitch of her voice, which more than anything else moved him to heartquake. They at last lost track of which of them tipped the red wine bottle into unmatched glasses (his chalice was the larger). He grew oblivious to her unladylike improprieties despite his upbringing as a critic of vulgarity. The unconscious frisson of her close presence might have been represented in his scientific mind as the thermodynamic burst of heat-of-vaporization that prompted him to move, when she kissed him on the cheek as he suddenly stood up, much to her surprise, as if to leave abruptly. Whatever his intention, her impulsive affection unlocked a strange fit of passion that overcame his lifetime of gentle constraint. She was astonished by his athletic strength as he forced her (hardly protesting) to the broad couch nearby, while with one hand (in touching consideration of housekeeping inconveniences) he swept back the neatly stretched crimson corduroy bedspread and its embroidered cushions which served whenever she tidied up to pretend that this article of furniture was only a studio sofa. Sensing her inclination, as tenderly as possible, without the haste she would have expected, he compelled her submission to the liberation in himself of a diffident but unequivocal power. His reading and imagination had prepared him to consider with sufficient restraint her reciprocating sensitivity. Until the end his anagogic passion was less blind than hers.

And then, at peace together, she marveled at the purity of his omniverous reading! It seemed clear that he had never been of Sir Thomas Browne's ilk—or Saint Anselm's—who "never yet cast a true affection on a woman". The compelling force of his inexperience was Moira's divine afflatus. She hadn't yet come to wonder about divine punishment for allowing herself to be stormed by a man of God against his own will, when she herself that day had been twice appeased already.

5.

[Here follows a redaction of Tessa's amateur scholarship, intensely reasoned with alacritous imagination of M T's retreat on the I O M more than half a year later, founded upon numerous items of evidence for her subject's thoughts and feelings, which were indicated mainly in guarded letters to Teddi Cibber at the time, if not otherwhile to her distant friend Fay, but also nostalgically to Caleb her scarcely responsive pride and joy. The writer's construction of a biographical fragment, a plausible composite of M T's letters and diary bits (quite unlike her objective literary style with her second-hand portable typewriter) that happened to pertain to her maternity, was not hindered by M T's fluently rounded handwriting freely punctuated for emphasis or other marks of redundant emotion, sometimes reinforced by lines of her own or someone's quoted verse.]

On the god-blessed sea-lashed wind-rounded isle of Manannan, the only rock for dead reckoning in the many-weathered waters of vindication fought and shared by Celtic Viking and Anglo-Saxon navigators, omphalos of the British Archipelago in its very belly, Moira Trevisa's moods alternated between joyful optimism and nearly suicidal despair, with not much neutral time in between; but such was her nature that the preponderance of her time was in the former, and the latter usually came on the verge of sleep. From the beginning her greatest objective pleasure lay in discriminating the interbred yet distinct bloods subtly reflected in the island's traditional temperament and culture. Taken all together, the towns and villages, not much more than the size of Cape Gloucester, the island seemed very much like the prehistoric entirety she'd anticipated from her reading, half a year of personal experience sometimes to the contrary notwithstanding.

At first she was little more than an ordinary client of the depressed "visiting industry", almost forgetting the possibility of her own fecundation. But even before she was assured of it by the local doctor, when she wasn't occupied with the knowledge or pleasure of her objective senses she pondered one by one the remarkably disparate men who might have assisted in her wish. Not one of them—"A", "F", or "L"—Jew, Viking, or Anglo-Saxon—would have been displeasing as a virtual mate.

If cohabitation had been thrust upon her, A, whom she had loved to begin with and knew infinitely better than the other two, would have made the most loyal husband or protector. But F, the perfect model of an accomplished gentleman, had the makings of a hero. And L was a learned genius reserved by God to be carnally enlightened by herself the principal sinner. Each, under the same sun, to her astonishment, had bestowed beatitude she believed worth never to be forgotten, each by his own quality—one in passionate farewell, one in dazzling excitement, one in divine afflatus. Thus lasted each in memory of her own turpitude in bringing about her essential purpose as a coefficient woman.

The day after Long Rocks she had awakened in superb contentment, every nerve and sinew pleased with itself, her exquisitely mature brain presiding over distal organs and limbs as naturally as the pelvic brain from which her beatitude had emanated in a series of languid waves. Rising with the midsummer sun, long before she turned her brain to the eventual aftereffect, she had found herself singing irrelevant words in careless volume (now that the downstairs apartment had been emptied by the outright flames), intermittently suppressing the traumatic thought of her dog. Even trivial relief had dissipated in irritation at her own geometrical stupidity as she stood before her bathroom mirror impatiently trying to paint for fun on her forehead with costume-party lipstick a mirrored face caricature, branding in scarlet her trumping of chastity, to see for herself what it would look like in public: **A F L.** Her failure to manage the legerdemain of optics had then awakened the basic ambivalence in her soul, and, before the longest day of the year was half over, her sense of security in everything was reversed. Having gradually lost her sensual tranquility, a triplicated ecstasy from viscera to tangents was impossible to formulate—or even to differentiate—as even its objective experience sensations faded in the late morning art-light that reawakened her practical reason.

Here in her transatlantic alienation, she was sometimes amused by the workings of her unconscious, or frightened by her own metaphors, into recognizing her own predicament as the living correlative of the image that symbolized the Isle of Man's unique sovereignty. Its famous icon on official flag and in civic seal seemed to flaunt her flight from Dogtown's Chief of Police, or the real social complications, and her own guilt, according to God's oxymoronic disapproval and encouragement. Perhaps obscurely cognate in armory with the Viking occupation of Trinacria, this variation of Aryan device, peacefully blazoned on land and sea for recognition disproportionate to the tiny island's geopolitical insignificance, was

displayed as a chivalrous scutcheon proclaiming the valor of a city-
state more independent in security than the Hanseatic League or
the Channel Islands. Moira took to heart the symbolism of her private triplicity, as distinguished from the various archetypes of rectilinear swastikas, for seeming to challenge all logic and geometry (as
when a calendar year of three seasons would set at odds the axial
mechanism of our spinning globe) in its most elaborate version
with the heraldic design of three armored legs and articulated
feet—jambeau, cuisse, greaves, spurs, and all—knees bent with feet
running clockwise in the same rotary direction (supposedly following the sun from a northern point of view), three steel-clad thighs
pivoting together on a center spot that she couldn't help seeing as
female. In spite of her better self, she could not help being
reminded of her amusement in London at the spectral chant that
sounded in the Underground whenever the straight carriage doors
were opened at a concavely curved platform, like a foghorn warning
the passengers of the vacancy of footing between the floor of the
train and the platform: "Mind the gap!" All men do, was the vulgar
thought that now came to mind willy-nilly. But for her in prevailing moods the essential emblem in all its simple or elaborated versions was a seriously interesting reflection of some nearly heretical
modification of Christianity that was otherwise expressed in Manx
churchyard sculpture by the pagan "sun-disk" of shorter radius
than the arms but centered at the same intersection, sometimes
with Viking runes carved in the stele. In her notebook she often
sketched her attempt to combine the themes, in some versions of
which Christianity was reflected only as three cross-handled swords
whose points touched at the center—sometimes even interwoven
with a pair of oppositely directed regular triangles superposed as
the hexagonal Star of David—as if working up various designs for
her own gravestone.

The traditionally tinctured armorial bearings (curiously indifferent to the posture of the feet) are specified as "Gules, three legs
armed, conjoined in fesse at the upper part of the thighs, flexed in
triangle, proper, garnished and spurred, or." But the most interesting thing she felt about the Manx triskelion was the translation of
its subsumed motto *Quocunque jeceris stabit*: "It will stand up where-
soever you may throw it". It represented in two dimensions a tripo-
dal three-dimensional version (too difficult to visualize) of the
quadrangular jackstones she had cast on pavement in East Harbor
schoolyard competition! Had there *ever* been a *three*-legged god?

Always alert to such literary heroism as that of the Royal
Navy's rebellious first mate Fletcher Christian—scion of three
centuries of Manx deemsters, shipowners, magnates, and politicians—Moira eagerly pursued connections between the island and
the *Bounty*'s mutiny against Captain Bligh, who not only had married into a Manx family on its own ground but had recruited one of
the local boys, Peter Heywood, as his midshipman. At his unjust
trial as one of the mutineers (before he was sentenced to death,
reprieved, and eventually elevated for excellent performance to the
rank of Captain, R N) Peter was identified as "much tattooed, on
his right leg by the 'three legs of Man'".

During the early months of her expectancy, except when misty
drizzle fell as outright rain, having hardly noticed morning sickness,
she developed a craving for Manx apples and grapes as she pedaled
many of the island's paved roads on a hired bicycle—until the
doctor at the infirmary warned her of risk to her fetus. But she was
less obedient to the old witches' tale to which he seemed to subscribe when he advised her to stop smoking cigarettes, even as she
noticed the ashtray on his desk. She believed the old boy's counsel
was biased as a typically disguised attack upon her unconcealed feminism, which she had learned to temper when at large among a quietly conservative citizenry that tactfully disguised its own disapproval of her gravid condition, notwithstanding that it plainly
invited the suspicion of egregious sin. On the other hand her prejudice against Manxmen was mollified by the fact that they had anticipated most of the Western World in granting women "parliamentary suffrage" for the House of Keys, and recently had elected the
first female to that two-thousand-year-old democratic institution.

As far as her lesser eccentricities were concerned, she cultivated
the rather dramatic habit of excusing them with the offhand
remark that in her childhood she'd suffered an acute case of sleeping sickness (*encephalitis lethargica* to her more educated interlocutors) during the great postwar influenza epidemic of 1918, which
(she told shopkeepers) had left her so counter-mathematical, hoping
to check unpleasant reaction to her practically irrepressible blunders in transactions. Even in Dogtown she'd never made bones
about that. For years, in embarrassment or chagrin, she had
repeated to herself the comforting words of St Paul to the Corinthi-
ans that "God has chosen the foolish things of the world to confound the wise, and God has chosen the weak things of the world to
confound those who are mighty."

But this cheery boldness was antithetical to much of her solitary introversion, whether emotional or rational—gynecological, religious, or poetically creative. Often her hopes were of she knew not what, her dread of what she thought she knew. Yet this admission of syncopated competence was hardly ever obvious to animated beings because she loved them all, as if they were flora, unless or until an inimical motive presented itself. She never for long ceased to feel the vulnerability of Ruth *without a husband* in the alien land—despite the lovely sense of temporary freedom from the fear for herself and her conceivable conception that had haunted her nether consciousness. The present growth within her was taking place as her last vacation, the greatest pleasures of which were Mrs Kermanner's famous kippers that she consumed every day, along with "fastidious Francis" the Kermanner boy and a few transient guests, with no intention of ever putting the dietary question to her doctor! She believed that she sufficiently compensated for this typical option in a Manx breakfast by eating as many green "potherbs" as possible during the rest of the day.

In the autumn Moira spent a Quarter Day of Michaelmas in an excursion on the Victorian steam train from Douglas down to Castletown and its small but perfectly preserved Castle Rushen, the original keep of which was built very soon after William landed at Hastings, and even its curtain wall went back to the time of Chaucer. It passed from Viking to Scottish hands before the English perfected it according to classic Norman architecture. She had no interest in its military function but she was impressed by its subsequent series of civil functions, as capitol of the island, as hall of justice, as prison, and as lunatic asylum, before it was purified as an extraordinarily authentic museum-in-the-making.

That night she dreamt that she was passing through an ageless limestone kitchen of the castle as if in conversation with a faceless attendant planning her commissioned occupation of the living quarters. In the dream she had already settled upon the tower for a studio (thinking of Montaigne's) where, after everything below was running smoothly, she would design and learn how to weave a modern tapestry of Arthurian motifs for each of the principal stone chambers to make them more habitable during a coming winter of snow and stormy ice; and she was now inspecting all small chambers to choose the warmest for a nursery, which would determine the selection of her own bedroom. But she was frustrated by the stupidity of the answers she got from the person who was supposed to know the castle's practical idiosyncrasies better than anyone else. She tried to conceal her irritation by changing the subject: asking how she could send a telegram to Hall Caine and post a copy to T E Brown at King William's College, because she wished to give a dinner in the Great Hall for them as guests of honor, with Mrs Kermanner (who had promised to sew baby clothes), her son Francis, and perhaps her husband, before the Keys changed their minds about her own appointment as the island's publicity director. But the stubborn old witch at her elbow kept interrupting with harshly whispered howls of warning that cooking and all the rest must be put off until some way had been found to dig out of the basement and its dungeons a century of muck and decomposed German corpses from secret torture at Knockaloe (the late war's English internment camp), in order to get rid of all the snakes. "You don't need to worry about fires, Miss American!" the woman hissed.

That voice was what awakened her with a shudder. But in this instance it wasn't her innate horror of snakes within the dream that shocked her, a fear that was with her whenever she paused instantaneously to envision the meaning of a word whose sound she wasn't inured to. In the dream she hadn't missed the fear, but in the immediate virtually objective memory of the dream it was screened by her detection of the irony in worrying about *German* victims in a concentration camp! Even in Atlantis her sensitivity to limited information about the Nazi Swastika had been clairvoyant in its dread. To double the irony, many of the internees sent to this island during that war may have been German *Jews* loyal to the Kaiser! In Dogtown, especially because of her intimacy with Arthur Halymboyd, she had been one of the earliest Aryans to understand the international seriousness of Hitler's rise to power—as F D R's anti-Christ.

Moira had read more books than anyone else in Dogtown High School, and kept up with "current events" better than the teachers did, leading her classes in English and history, despite the fact that she failed graduation because of flunking algebra and geometry; and ever since then she'd held her own with a literary moiety of the intelligentsia: so, for lack of the social stimulus to which she was accustomed in Dogtown, she made good use of the Manx Museum and the public library, more for local archeology and history than for news of any mesocosm in which she might expect to address the rest of her life as a mother—whether for livelihood, for the common good, or for poetic fame.

The least personal and most objective of her random interests in the I O M were archeological structures and grave sites; yet even thus absorbed it struck her, especially on Spanish Head (opposite the Calf), that the triangle-and-circle concept had prevailed before there was any Christian cross or bilateral sword-hilt, not to mention the most primitive triskelion. Near the summit of Mull Hill were embedded traces of neolithic burial tumuli arranged in "tritaphs". They were called "three-armed graves", found nowhere else in the British Archipelago, because together they formed circles of stone graves made with chambers built in the local slate-stone in the horizontal shapes of an equilateral tan cross with its stem radiated outward. Moira guessed that the apertures between these tombs were oriented to the same solstice in which she was implanted, before she too ran on two legs against the sun. Similar barrows on the island were nearly obliterated by more than a millennium of Celtic or Viking (if not Sicilian) inhabitants in search of construction material or in retaliation for resistance.

Moira visited some of the other sites of excavation or speculation—and the island was full of amateur archeologists to keep the inexhaustible general subject at the forefront of local culture—but she soon grew weary of looking or listening to redundant opinions and pedantic erudition that had no present bearing on her existentially religious or poetic concerns (to say nothing of politics). Before long archeology dropped almost as far from her list of daily pursuits as the possibility of learning the Manx language that nowadays was never learned by most of the population and was forgotten by all the scholars who didn't make it their specialty. And as she approached the mild but often unpleasant winter (with not enough snow to obliterate the mood of dismal days), which was naturally announced by the homesickness of exile during the Atlantean holiday of Thanksgiving and the less avoidable celebrations of British Father Christmas, her days of rumination grew less active and more melancholy—except when irrational hope and joy leapt up with the sun at glorious intervals in the weather, or with inexplicable surges of psychic energy, bestowed by the Paraclete in Holy Communion or springing sui generis from her own God-forgiven optimism. And naturally in both the alternating moods she dwelt more often on her memory of the day of Long Rocks than on any other mark of time in the past.

Little by little she paid less attention to immediate experience, narrowing her meditation and wandering thought to foresight of

homeland exigencies peripheral to the essential brooding of expectant motherhood. For instance, celebrations of the new year 1935
suggested the calendar, and the calendar suggested objective time,
and objective time suggested proleptic time, and proleptic time
reminded her that there was no time to be lost in implementing
her intention to change her name at a favorable opportunity to start
the process for doing so, in Dogtown, with the least possible public
notice of that particular defection before the spring equinox when
her major transgression was expected to be recorded. It would be
her private rite of passage into a state of ultimate anomaly.

With the assistance of Teddi Cibber, who provided her with
local addresses, Moira applied for advice, with unnecessary explanation of the circumstances, to Endicott Krebs (with whom she had
casually conversed a few times at cultural events). As a metropolitan corporation lawyer, who only happened to live in Dogtown, he
politely referred her, if legal advice should be necessary, to one of
the struggling young attorneys in Dogtown, hinting without formality as a kindly pro bono suggestion that there was no need to
bare her soul to anyone else, since there was a standard procedure
administered by the City Clerk and the Gloucester County Court
requiring no personal explanation of motive. Thus, after a further
inquiry, by the time she was starting to pack up for her return to
Dogtown she knew what had to be done to change her legal identity and announce it to friends before her lying-in.

But her own altered identity—reasonable enough, seeing that
Moira=Mary and Trevisa=Tremont (her mother's Anglo-Irish
maiden name)—was not all. She was assured by her I O M doctor
that she wasn't carrying triplets (whose names she had planned fifteen years earlier, though not seriatim); but she was too superstitious to tempt Providence by anticipating the survival or the
sex—and therefore the name—of her first child. But she was also
determined for symbolic reasons not to burden it with any surname from the past. She humbly resolved to leave that choice to
the voice of God at the proper time, meanwhile attempting to
suppress her creative urge to assemble a list of suggestions that
suited her imagination.

So she did her best to avoid proleptic meditation, and to prolong what she thought of as her last vacation from reality—that is,
to make the best of a journey back to Dogtown by way of Ireland,
both Skerries and Galway, for embarkation at Cork. For she was
disappointed not to have found more overt Celtic tradition on the

island, at least displays of step-dancing, which from books and hearsay she regarded as a fascinating and subtle expression of the primitive urge for social expression of sex under all but absolute puritanical oppression of natural woman by the most reactionary national hierarchy in the whole Classic Petrine world of dogmatic anti-feminism. As it had been described to her, exactly how could women dance like handicapped puppets, without locomotion on stage or threshing floor, spine stiff upright, face impassive, seeming not to breathe, without movement of thorax or hips, almost without bending knees, yielding all animation to the sound and motion of heavy clogs ringing all the changes of rhythm and clangor possible at a single spot, exciting eager crowds with the delicacies of putatively unconscious repression? She somehow believed that this restrained art of motility was best demonstrated, because most needed, in the West of Ireland where even the feelings of men were most closely shackled by Petrine suppression of human nature.

She was too far along in the most feminine of all natural functions to learn from anyone else what she hoped to find was an ironically constrained skill—or at least, if disappointed, to see how to write about it as the combined decadence of matriarchy and the combative passion of warriors like Aoife! Either way, as performer or as critic, she sought sympathetic inspiration for her own all-too-liberal métier. Whether in buoyant optimism or in falsified joy, her phantasmagoria of daylight moods and nighttime dreams more and more referred to her belly, the one true self of trust and dedication. Her centrifugal dreams nevertheless quickened as independent and inscrutable exegesis that usually vanished with its correlatives before it could be snatched into her memory. But she did remember bits of a few smokescreens.

In one dream (as she made sense of its verbal fragments and dimly remembered images) she was walking along the outer quay leading to the Douglas passenger terminal at half-tide when she was passed by a dozen or more merchant sailors cheerfully swarming ashore over the sea wall from the invisible main deck of a large seagoing tugboat that had just tied up. Just as she reached the top of a rusty iron tide ladder affixed to the concrete, the head and torso of Finn Macdane arose, about to follow his men for a pint somewhere on the Promenade of entertainments that she had left behind. Like them he was dressed in casual dungarees but he wore cocked at an angle the visored cap of a master merchant mariner, and his sleeves were rolled up to show muscular arms darkened with deeper tan than the hue of his smiling insouciant face, for while she was astonished he hardly seemed surprised. Side by side they turned to look past the superstructure of his ship to the great headland of solid rock across the open harbor. "God has nothing to do with this," he said, "even if he started the universe, as Einstein apparently believes. He merely hoped that people would evolve rationally, perhaps in order to establish a Kingdom of Heaven, but in any case to create something for him to admire. Our freewill was his selfless gift, not a demand for worship. There's never been a fallen world or a golden age." "I don't care!", she replied without knowing what she meant. They walked together toward the Promenade. She made every backboned effort not to betray her burden (which was larger than she thought it should have been) by her shape or her stride, pretending to stroll as a dancer on aimless holiday; but he showed no evidence of interest in her person besides what she had to say. Yet even with that she could not hold her own in conversation—until she relaxed all pretension when he remarked that Arthur Halymboyd—"Did you ever know him?"—had been arrested in Berlin by the Nazis. "Most of the men you saw are secret agents I'm taking to Hamburg so they can join German labor unions before Nazis take them over completely."

Before she could pour out unguarded questions she awoke, trembling with fear and remorse, instantly believing that she never dreamed of Arthur Halymboyd because he brought up memories of unrequited kindness, unjust quarrels, and love that was recalled only on the Isle of Man—her imagination still blurred by truth.

Another night it was Lance that she more easily brought to light. She had indeed attended Sunday services at a few of the Pauline churches in the Douglas area, including both Church and Chapel, primarily for sake of opportunity to sing with people famous for their singing, always glad to hear the Bible readings but usually closing her ears to the other prose. Even at this Tudor ritual of her own kind, as familiar as nursery rhymes, she found nothing; when she was most conscious of her singularly irreducible immorality according to any variety of deism, she was unable to approach contrition. Humbly enough she remained no more than contrite in her prayers, not as a sinner—as much as possible she eschewed the word *sin*—but as one who caused the burden of sin on the part of another who did believe in the sin of violating his own specialized oath to God. The corruption of which she was guilty in her own eyes had been in itself transcendental, mystical rather than evil. Yet she had been aware of her feminine attractions, and, according to her own mores, she had been shamefully venial. Most of all she could not dismiss her new fear of God's retribution at one step removed from herself, more precious than herself, either before or after the forthcoming season of vernal equinox.

Hence in another dream she had been continually searching newspaper listings and the latest postings of Church signboards for announcement of Lancelot Duncannon as guest preacher and celebrant of Holy Communion, or even as a new curate in one of the island parishes, when walking on the street very near her lodging she noticed for the first time a narrow thickly shaded tributary mews that invited one of her usual explorations. From the urban hillside on which she stood it ran higher still before curving out of sight. Effortlessly climbing the slight acclivity she found it anciently walled higher than her head to sequester what seemed to be a bit of primeval forest on the left, blankly facing, on her right, an uninterrupted row of what appeared to be bankrupted small livery stables, private horse barns, or competing blacksmith shops, all emptied and padlocked by the Depression. She hated to retrace her steps on such expeditions but she was about to turn back when the alley curved to the left and the wall abruptly ended, revealing a small stone church of typical pseudo-Gothic style, with a simple open bell tower over the entrance. The forest behind it was now revealed to her as two or three centuries of unattended churchyard overgrowth that obviously protested the vanity of all exceptional commemorations. She saw no trace of the remnant tombstones among the great dark trunks under a solid canopy of deciduous green. What astonished her was a brisk gathering of worshipers funneling themselves through the diminutive double doors of a sunken foundation in a century of undrained ground.

There was no cross to be seen in this dream, and no signboard to hint its denomination, but despite her inbred Tudor culture she felt comfortable praying with most Pauline variations so long as good hymns were sung and the preaching wasn't by a "stuffed shirt" or a "reactionary Chauvinist". But in her uncharacteristic diffidence as a stranger, not knowing whether or not pew rents or other seating protocols were in practice, she quietly made her way as primly as possible among the congregation of self-effacing women to a place in the back row, beneath a choir loft, where she could most easily imitate the common posture in habit or response to mysterious rubrics. In the rack before her hardwood seat she found no book but tattered hymnals. The women on either side of her were so silent and impalpable that it seemed most considerate to pretend she didn't see them, and her view of the sanctuary was so obscured by the heads and hats between herself and the chancel that she couldn't see whether or not there was even an altar. But she was suddenly aware of a man standing in the low but much closer pulpit on her side of the stone-cold narrow nave, his figure thoroughly sanctified in white green and gold Anglican—almost Petrine—High Mass vestments. With furrowed brow, squinting her eyes and flogging her memory, cautiously testing her first impression, admonishing her impulsive imagination, attempting unmathematical calculation of irrational probabilities, she decided to leave at once, so as not to seem to these good people a spying witch, but to take her protest to the *Mona Herald*. It was in that newspaper that the preaching of Lancelot Duncannon, right here and now, had been promised! It was outright deception, obviously deliberate, to steer her away from the small dark bare five-hundred-year-old church with a well-tended graveyard to which the new young curate had actually been called. No wonder the I O M visiting industry was in decline! No wonder the island needed a full-time professional as director of publicity! As she rose apologetically, disguising her fury from the parishioners whose knees she had to knock on her way to the aisle, she woke up with a laugh.

"So much for penitence!" she said to herself aloud. She still hadn't contrived to hear any of the ecclesiasticized carvals that distinguished the island's music from the rest of the world. In a certain sense its choirs were the last modern counterpart to the medieval miracle plays in England, though more secular in matter and without wagons for mobile staging.

For Moira was determined to make the most of her I O M sojourn as grist for her creative mill, no matter how long it would have to be stored before she could use it, as a mother with enough relief from the most demanding stages of motherhood to work on the kind of long narratives she had in mind for her poems. The romantic subjects of her schooldays writing, after almost a decade of commercially plastic art, had given way in her head to the possibilities of correlative matter in the art of actual experience. She found that she had chosen well for her temporary expatriation. This living Avalon, far exceeding her expectations, was a unique crossroads of imagination and reality accessible in the English language.

When she was looking for parallels with Cape Gloucester, which best represented her own understanding of "experience", her sporadically amateur interests in its archeology, history, folklore, superstition, government, trade, agriculture, fishing, and other industries extended even into research of its recorded murders, which, though rare, were as brutal, and perhaps as poorly investigated (though more compassionately), as any in Atlantis. But she could be carefree and almost condescending in her own experience on the island because here she had no more to fear from a guilty chief of police than from the public genealogies by which Manx folk exposed the true origins of natives who put on airs of social superiority on the strength of banausic success or inheritance. In the interest of earning money, before wearily giving up that hope under present economic conditions, she had considered the idea of writing articles about the island for readers of the *Dogtown Daily Nous,* or about Dogtown for readers of the *Mona Herald*, if not both. To that end, as well as in pursuit of her own interest and pleasure, she spent much of the winter's wuthering in the hospitable museum, whose elderly cosmopolitan librarian, himself a "come-over" from the sin-city of Liverpool, had befriended her on the strength of their common interest in encouraging the intellectual appetites of young Francis Kermanner, her remarkable landlady's misfitting son.

Mr Stanley's unobtrusive kindness in answering all her questions, even when they required research on his part, greatly magnified Moira's knowledge of local society, probably sparing her many a blunder, perhaps the most perilous of which was that of drawing inferences from surnames. There had been so many generations of intermarriage within each parish that those who shared namesakes were often not relatives, and relatives were likely to have different names. To avoid giving offence with any derogative comment about a third person, Mr Stanley warned Moira, "One must heed the Manx adage *Same name, no relation; different name, probably a cousin.* And anyone from outside the parish, like me, is a foreigner. They listen patiently, even to long sermons, without swallowing anything whole, and seldom offer their own unasked opinion. I've learned to love their modest humor, but it's too literal for irony or wit."

"It's not very different in my Dogtown." said Moira, always alert to the significant parallels and differences between the two

maritime polities of very different ages but similar aura. "Here I
miss our squirrels but am very glad there are no snakes! Our thirty
thousand are not quite as Celtic and Viking as this island but we've
had our witches, and English overlords. Our Gloucestermas homo-
logue is your Midsummer Day and Night, bonfire and all! Our
fishermen are just as superstitious. Our autumn trees are more colorful than yours, but yours make me homesick. I suppose we both
have about the same share of insular drunkenness and insanity. You
have mountains and headlands that put our hills and glens to
shame but we have hundreds of great North Atlantic fishing
schooners that dwarf your fishery, and granite quarries that supply a
whole continent—but nothing like your beautiful lanes and pastures, nothing political like your civilized Tynwald, nothing like
your stone circles and castles! But still, I say, we're alike!"

"I wish I could claim some of the prize," said the librarian. "I'm
still an enamored stranger, though my children were born here.
King William's College brought me over to teach, mainly because I
was one of their old boys. My parents had sent me there to prepare
for University. I'm from Norwich originally."

"George Borrow's Norwich?"

Yes indeed he very proudly was! Moira was so delighted to
have found an objective literary guide to the island who happened
to share a special interest in that peculiarly anti-genteel avatar of
John Bull (whom she liked to astonish sophisticated readers by
comparing with Brother Jonathan, Wellingborough Redburn) that
she made an unprecedented effort to avoid rebarbative enthusiasm
by moderating her impulse to abuse the bounds of a friendship
meant to be professional; and in this case she was successful. The
questions she asked of Mr Stanley, whom she saw only within the
cordial walls of his institution, were never more than very slightly
personal, nor of course meant to be by either of them; yet they
were impersonally frank and sometimes bold in objective examination of the island and its peoples. She had to force herself to keep
from visiting his office too often or too long when she was haunt-
ing the whole building of displays, always hoping that it was he
who noticed her of his own accord. Consequently, as the cicerone
and Virgil of her learning he became the mentor of her explorations, the guardian angel who distracted her from fears and
turned her away from the subjective aspect of a loneliness ranging
sometimes wildly in vicissitudes of feeling between alert gladness
and black depression.

She was sorry only that Mr Stanley himself, like a good Daddy, had not offered to take her to see the stone circles, prehistoric graves, and the dancing grounds of witches; or sheep-sustaining massifs, moorlands, dunes, farms, woodland, gloomy glens, chasms, deserted mines, abandoned stone quarries, salt pans, smugglers' coves, precipitous sea-bluffs, pastoral downs, treacherous curraghs, and turf huts with thatched roofs that echoed in tales of the Celtic Little People (especially in the south of the island), and of giants (preferred in the more Viking north), heartless landowners, and illicit passions of fisherfolk farmers who amalgamated their own kind of Viking and Celtic lore in gentle resistance to Christian hegemony, "the same with graz'in on the commons, the same with fish'in ground", white herring or red herring. She needed Mr Stanley all the more as polymath tutor because she was ignorant not only of local law but also of much natural history that seemed to make amateur botanists ornithologists and mineralogists of every otherwise uneducated Manx man woman and child. Nothing natural on the island seemed to her exotic or distasteful, but she was unable to remember most of the names and identifications she was informed of. In this regard she felt herself a stupid helpless ignoramus; but she sometimes thought that was a blessing, for it tempered the benign self-confidence that she was tardily aware often turned aside possible friends or sympathizers. She had to speak of flowers trees and birds in her own limited categories, using such terms as *seagull, oak,* or *wildflower* as well as she could to express her appreciation of the Manx ecology, which they seemed to master effortlessly in the natural course of growing up.

Yet with Mr Stanley, confident of their common ecclesiastical heritage, and trusting him as a broadminded man of the world without a whiff either of old-age lechery or of condescending censure, she believed herself free to question without risk of offense or personal insult about any sensitive topic in Manx society (such as inbreeding or incest, as in Dogtown) that was normally taboo in the presence of incomers and unmentionable in religion, whether manic or depressive of her curiosity. One of her inquiries was about the treatment of its few Jews. Was there any vestigial superstition—perhaps revived by the fact that some of them were among the German internees in the Knockaloe prison camp with which the British made the island prosperous during their first World War—of the old pandemic canard that they sowed the Black Death? On the one occasion that she and Mr Stanley drank a Manx

bitter together, in his favorite pub on a quiet rainy afternoon, when
she had ambivalently booked her gibbously gravid return to the
younger land of more heterogeneous prejudice, she felt free enough
with this disinterested friend to remark that if she were in Germany right now "I'd be paraded naked through the streets with a
sign saying I GAVE MYSELF TO A JEW." But he asked no question. She had been given to understand that notwithstanding the
mild mistrust of unfamiliar Jews in Jewish-seeming occupations
the people of Man were less antisemitic than most Atlanteans, who
shared much more of their culture with Petrines, the Irish or
French especially.

All in all, at least when under Mr Stanley's enlightenment, she
had found it hard to believe not only the hardships but also the sui
generis cruelties that had participated in the formation of this
apparently gentle citizenry. In her preoccupation with inchoate
feminism she was most distressed by one of the less heinous practices in the 18C: the flight of its all-too-virile men from their
womenfolk, especially those expectant of reproduction, when times
were unbearably bleak, became so common that a law was passed to
require of any male a license to leave the island (including many a
frustrated smuggler or pirate)—not in sympathy with the abandoned women or in moral discipline of their deceivers but because
they would be left to become "a burden upon the parish"!

It occurred to Moira with wry amusement that her naval
Apollo, Finn Macdane, had no such scruple on her smaller quasi-
isle; but Mr Stanley was musing aloud on the world in which they
now sat. "Kindly or not, Manx folks have never neglected their
poor, but at last this Depression (which I blame on your country)
has forced the government to assume decent 20C public responsibility. But the Manx, though personally generous, have always been
a bit smug about their personal thrift, and very interested in *Other
People's Money,* the regular listing of financial statements and testa-
ments that you may have noticed in the *Herald*—if necessary to
take genteel neighbors down a peg. That's one reason why George
Borrow liked them so much. They never were oppressed as peasants
or serfs, but they have needed no thorn in the flesh to keep them
from being too elated."

"In Dogtown our paper prints the names of everyone delinquent in tax payments, sometimes many years old if they're for
vacant lots."

"Well, it's in other matters that the Manx tend to procrastinate in deciding things, and especially in finishing jobs they're working on. *Traa-dy-liooar—there's time enough—*is their motto. They can be stubborn under bosses, but there's no tergiversation and they pride themselves on always being careful."

"Our fishermen aren't famous for carefulness, especially if their boat's well insured. North Atlantic schooners recklessly race each other home to get the best price." She spoke of Captain Trevisa as her father.

"Here's cheers to all fishermen—pelagic there, weeks at a time, I believe; only herring in the nasty Irish Sea for us—but both losing more lives than any other class of labor. Visitors don't come over here to see fishermen. Many of them just want to see our tail-less cats."

"Not I! That's like going to a circus to see a sideshow of hunchbacked monstrosities. I've seen pictures of those poor misbegotten and misshapen creatures! I'm too sorry for them to stare at their deformity!"

Mr Stanley wasn't enough of a naturalized Manxman to miss the levity in her words, or the amusement in her clear blue eyes as she leaned back and patted the great mound of her belly. But he tilted back his head with a smile and looked at the ceiling. "Maybe that's why our witches prefer to inhabit hares!"

"I wouldn't want one of them to cross my path before I get home. My baby may be more susceptible than others because I had sleeping sickness when I was a girl. I have practically stopped smoking. I hope this half-pint won't be noticed. But I love this island so much that I'm a little afraid of returning to my own island—if it really qualifies as one—without scales over my eyes. Maybe it's not fair to compare two such different places. Yet the I O M is just as real as Dogtown, which is going to look shabby and corrupt. Here I've seen no slums or brothels. But I'll see myself shabbier than when I left."

"Thomas à Kempis said 'They who travel seldom come home holy.'"

"I left home *un*holy, but I feel less so, thanks to your kindness and enlightenment—as far as I'm concerned, a man sent from God. You should have been a bishop!"

"Just because I've lived here so long. It makes me defend the place against its reputation in England as nothing but a cheap holiday resort for the lower classes. Many visitors don't get a mile beyond the Promenade. But as one of my favorite writers says, 'Man can follow reason against pleasure, and pleasure against reason, but when the two combine they are irresistible.' So what, that 'No man is an island.'? Neither is a city. But a city-state is, and that's what we are, poetically speaking at least, even though we're officially a 'dependency' of the Crown. A small island, to be sure, integrated, almost self-sufficient (with harbors and a certain amount of trade), but not overpopulated like the gormless island of Ur celebrated by your barbaric Whitman. But this is a civilized place, with a limit to things. Yet large enough to be a whole society of reasonably unredundant genes, and cosmopolitan in its own historical way. Our fairies are as likely to have been Norman French as Irish, and our mummers used to perform *Saint George and the Dragon.* Our seals are Scandinavian mermaids. Not without reason our central valley is called the Plains of Heaven! And if you look closely you can see a lot of tropical plants! Moreover, don't forget that King Arthur's sword Excalibur was forged here in Avalon!"

Moira laughed with him at their shared infatuation. But she remembered with a pang that she had called her Arthur the other version of what that sword was called, something like Caliburn. She wondered how different her present conscience would be if she hadn't sent him away without definite explanation, despite the mutual ecstasy they repeated the very morning of his final departure, as if sensuality excluded all other considerations, perhaps leaving him with the sense that he had somehow failed to perpetuate her love, perhaps having innocently irritated him with her accidental notices of the man in white! Neither A nor F nor L wanted to understand what it was of them she essentially craved, deprivation of which at times of introspection she thought underlay her anger at the best of men. How can you distinguish freedom from selfishness? Selfishness in the name of one calling or another.

"I never told you" she said to Mr Stanley "that soon after I got here, before I became fully aware of the unemployment conditions, I thought I ought to be thrifty, according to my father's incessant advice, which I respect more after his death than I did in my rebellious years. He lost quite a lot of money in the Crash (despite all the warnings of our own nationally famous financier whom we call the Duke of Dogtown), but I was left with enough—after Mama died, as my share of our summer house and some other property, with what I got by selling my sister half of it—to take a couple of years off from job-hunting. But when I saw the hard times here, and tried to imagine how bad they could get at home for an unmarried mother, I thought I'd try to save a little money by earning it. It was a romantic notion to apply for anything available at King William's College, which I ought to have known was the least likely place to be hiring my kind, on the strength of my admiration for T E Brown's poetry, but I did. At that time I didn't look immoral. In my interview I was so enthusiastic that I made the mistake of saying I was willing to do anything, no matter how low the pay. Hoisted by my own petard, I found myself working in the scullery for room and board and little else. Even working down there and living up in a miserable garret among nearly illiterate gossips supervised by a harridan who naturally resented having an alien like me imposed upon her, for one horrible week of very long days, with my hands all rough and red, I did learn a great deal about boys and masters imprisoned in the English Public School tradition, which seems stupidly cruel to a freedom-loving Yankee like me."

"You are quite right. The only thing that justifies that school of mine for intelligent students is now and then an exceptional teacher with a sense of humor who loves his subjects, as Brown seems to have been. But I haven't been near the place since I retired."

"You were surely one of the exceptions. I would have stuck it out until my stomach did, because I could see it was good discipline for my egregious character, and I started to make friends. But I felt like a dog in the manger. I couldn't bear to deprive some loyal scullery maid of the job who really desperately needed it to fend off utter destitution or a fate worse than death.

"I had already applied to the *Weekly Adventurer* for a temporary 'Copy Boy' opening, based on my overqualified curriculum vitae, but they're obviously afraid of women. I even offered to write on my own time an article about the busiest fishing on the Atlantic Ocean!"

All the while, sad to be parting from Mr Stanley in this most suitable refuge before her fruition, she was anxious for a perfectly formed child.

22

OPEN VERDICT

1.

[Tessa's manuscript remained a secret in her bank's safe-deposit box. She no longer even mentioned it to Fay, whose probable ignorance of her own paramour's part in the story was best left undisturbed for the time being, especially from the hands of a younger social worker who had no wish to distract the all-important last years of exceptionally creative scholarship. As Chair of the Crat City Committee Tessa was also busy with her voluntary duty to sustain only two years after an annus horribilis the morale and incentives of her diligently cultivated constituency after the national catastrophe of defeat by the dismaying popularity of a President-elect determined to reverse F D R's New Deal, at a moment in the political cycle when liberals had sunk into self-piteous lethargy. But she was also so diverted from her private project, and so often troubled by other contemporary events relevant to her life in Dogtown, many of them overlapping as impingements upon each other in the cinematic welter of claims upon her active attention or sympathy (usually in

public or private response to the expectations of others), that more
important pressures of the present and immediate future now submerged the hobby of tracing a particular past that was nothing of
her business, except as spurious matter for a new bent in her professional career. Besides, by now her etiological question of Caleb had
been overtaken by admiration of his mother. A mother can largely
cause a man, but a man cannot cause his mother, especially one more
sensitive than himself.]

Anyway, Tessa thought, time enough to continue after things
calm down—if the case then still seems intriguing enough to
pursue, if Arthur Halymboyd survives his impending heart by-
pass surgery, if Endicott Krebs (the one who *did* fear a heart attack)
returns from his world cruise loosened up in his habitual defense
of professional confidentiality for both lawyers and priests, if my
dear mentor Fay broaches the subject to Finn without reproach, if
she relaxes her honorably withheld memories of Mary Tremont's
retrospective confidences in later years, if Caleb himself gets over
his hypersensitive aversion to pedigree, and if I ever have time to
examine all the irregular shapes of envelopes and sizes of paper—
acidly fragile, tattered, carelessly creased, or stiff with clumsy photography in a few colors out of mutual registration or backed by
the cryptic handwriting of anonymous souls (such as Teddi
Cibber's hodgepodge of memorabilia). I abhor the prospect of
spending the necessary hours of patient boredom in panning for
grains of gold like a textual scholar—not to mention searching
public or ecclesiastical records, and interviewing local oldtimers
with very small probability of catching anything edible in my
mesh, as if I had a futility-grant from the Arnheim Foundation to
do so, all expenses paid! Anyway, for the present I've my clients to
serve, and duties as treasurer of my husband's corporation, which
considers selling out very profitably to the leviathan that's been
buying some of our stock, in which case I'll have no need for a
grant or a shingle to hang out for my profession, Rafe and I will
no longer live in envy of those who cruise around the world at
will, and Caleb's baroque conceits will fade to stardust in the
cosmos of our carefree retirement. Once again Rafe will have time
to be my ardent lover!

Nevertheless I'll keep pondering the sanity—apparently benevolent, ambivalent, and ambient—of that brilliant sophist Father
Christopher Lucey, who seems to have convinced himself that he
was not violating the confessional (before he did violate the

Church's prohibition of suicide) when he artfully permitted the
posthumous revelation, to me, by amazing chance, of his beloved
Superior's venial infraction of his own supererogatory and premature vow of chastity, perhaps believing it a salutary religious experience for an unchallenged Father Superior hearing others' confession,
more reminiscent of the heroic Saint Anselm than of Augustine,
who even our Irish nuns in Lagash admitted to knowing had spent
a whole youth anything but celibate and promised God to be so but
not quite yet. Of course neither of our two priests ever knew Moira
Trevisa, a Dogtown shadow of the Lost Generation; but I'd give my
psychiatric certification to have been able to set her loose at the
Laboratory! At least with Father Lucey it might have started and
ended an instant friendship, they being exhibitionists of goodwill
by opposite means—as different as if the connection were between
a gently unstable curate and (by that time) a boldly mistaken
seeker of love.

I try to imagine her at that age, long after Caleb had flown her
wings. After a few weeks of her enthusiastically friendly diagnosis
of the psyche that animated Father Lucey's courteous tolerance and
his double career as priest and stockbroker, no punches pulled, he
would have run for his life, unable to deal with her presumptuous
imagination. (I myself could never have analyzed or counseled that
ecclesiastical experiment.) Having briefly met her only in her insti-
tutionalized senility, and witnessing only the gerontological cast of
her calm years, I can hardly trust even the facts I do know about
her tumultuous life after the birth of Caleb, let alone the fully
candid recollections of her mature child (allowing for the natural
misapprehensions and distortion in time's passage).

If there were any altering interruptions of the continuity in
Mary's womanhood (such as tubal ligation) it would be even less
possible for anyone in my remote position at a perspective earlier
than the middle of her active life to fathom the ultimate personality of her namesake the B V M. I had heard from Caleb twenty
years ago when he still casually trusted me with some of his personal lore that as a probational member of the Brotherhood of the
Peacable Kingdom in equatorial Orellana at the age of fifty-five her
futilely happy wish for permanent acceptance had been denied with
the explanation that she had failed in quelling her one distinguished disqualification for communal life, namely the "modification of ego"! But of what interest would she have been without her
loving and selfless version of exhibitionism? Does one best estimate

a human being's essential personality by its manifestation early, late, or in the middle of its proof?

So I've lost my appetite not only for further pursuit of the maternal half of Caleb's consubstantiation, but also for any attempt to analyze (as my dear old Auto Drang might have wished to undertake) the man's own peculiar self. At least in my present mood, what remains of interest to me, besides a few other professional questions such as the basis of truth in Mary's immature attitude toward the apparently generous and tolerant highliner captain whom she regarded as a false father (at least during her years of filial rebellion), which seems to have been typical of many clairvoyant opinions throughout her life, is the question of her son's paternal half, where biological fact takes precedence over anyone's psychological speculations. Otherwise this is just a shaggy dog story. I seem to be going round and round!

2.

[*Late Saturday afternoon.*] Caleb's C N meditation was shattered by the ring of the telephone necessarily located across the room in his kitchen. He was now accustomed to having very few calls. For the most part those he did get were infuriatingly obnoxious advertisements, but he couldn't ignore the piercing sounds without allowing them to continue; and in any case it was always possible that the call would be important or welcome. He staggered from his desk snarling to the pitiless instrument. —Hello?

"Cubie boy, you can't have forgotten me!"

"Age cannot wither, nor custom stale your infinite variety!"

It was Belle Cingani, perhaps all alone next to the otherwise emptied offices of the newspaper. He was pleased and astonished. "Not as long as you're the illustrious Editor of the *Nous*! Besides, there's no other enunciating diction like yours. But I was the last one to hear that you'd married Dave Wilson. Are you still with him?"

"Of course. I've never been flighty."

"Well I thought he was. Or has he given up his wings?" She giggled, as she probably hadn't often done since she was a cub reporter and writing a weekly "Fly on the Wall" column to prove her youthful zest for journalism, never mentioning to the publisher the poems she'd like to write. "Nowadays he doesn't do the flying:

he gets flown, for his advice. He's a tough old eagle but he's about to retire. Just one last look for the bones of Lil-Amin at Warka."

Caleb calculated that the former Bice Picory must now be about forty-five, still his junior but very hard to remember as a humorously coruscating black-eyed beauty of the Gypsy type. He visualized her tanned young breasts, maidenly domed and shaped never to sag. A constellation of images with words ignited an instantaneously flickering constellation in the echoes of his cranium, emblematic bits of irretrievable feeling. But in respect to emotion he felt safe enough, despite the pangs. "What brought me into your silky little head after all these years?"

"I think about you all the time, for old times' sake! It's just that I try not to be a nuisance. I happened to hear that the mayor's firing his feckless administrator. I wondered if you knew that."

"How should I know? And if so, why? I'm not a fly on anyone's wall to corroborate your tip."

"I've also heard that you're looking for a job."

"Who could have told you that?" But his suspects were few and his repartee was irritated—not by Belle, because he was touched by her resurrected friendship—but at Dogtown's ghoulish grapevine.

"I'd sooner go to jail than reveal my sources."

"I wouldn't want you to lose your liberty."

"It's my duty to be alert but not to trust unconfirmed rumors. I have to put two and two together and keep ahead of the pitch, as my sports writer likes to say."

"What's *your* pitch?

"Was your mother's name Moira Trevisa? How do you spell it?"

"Are you cooking up my obit in advance?" He hoped to sustain a different conversation, but now an impersonal sort of anger was also kindled.

"Are you now a legal citizen of Atlantis? How do you spell Bice Picory? Did you write poetry in your youth? Was your father an honorable gentleman?" In particular, before he checked himself, he was ungallantly recalling her confessional walk with him one night on the beach of Dilemma Cove. "I know a thing or two about the arbiter of public opinion."

"Look, Caleb, we're both bastards. I have no intention to violate your secrets, and I trust you as the only one alive who knows about my only trauma."

His conciliatory tone was gentler. "The Magic Mountain, as far as I know, has been dismantled. I'm sorry, I shouldn't have said that."

"And my father no longer exists to remind me of it." A pause.
—"I had hoped you'd have forgotten what I told you in my ingenuous youth. Even as an inviolable secret it's been more destructive of my aptitude for a happy life than anything I could possibly do to damage you in public. Just your cruel mention of it may bring it back to my dreams the way reminders of Hiroshima still sometimes summon up David's nightmares about flying in the War. I know you don't mean to blackmail me, but you've hit below the belt."

Her suddenly serious tone surprised and punished his brutality. Belle's steady tone had hardly changed but, as he feared, it was now too late to ward off painful tears of anger invisible to him across the city. In his rather tentative experience with her seemingly invulnerable youth tears had been totally uncharacteristic, despite her precociously urbane frankness about what was then the past. She could never play the hardboiled newspaper editor after all. "I'm truly *truly* sorry, my little Beatrice." he whispered. "I've been too callous lately. I would never betray your friendship, which was very important to me, and still is, more than I ever told you. I'm your loving brother, when all is said and done!"

He tried to envision the face he'd hardly seen for years. All at once he recalled and confirmed his tender feelings for the recalcitrant young Dominion girl exiled by her preoccupied mother to the puritanical Tudor convent where her only sympathizer was a wistful nun who gently explained the truth about what was natural for girls. He remembered more compassionately what the older Bice Picory told him about her emotionally wretched background than he did his own experience of her goodnatured freedom when she sparkled like a sophisticated Carmen. With tears in his own eyes, for a moment like the brother she had always longed for, he obliterated all memory of the little cultural flaws, some of them innocently vulgar, which alone had given him just enough pause to forfend the fatuity of competition with countless admirers at their first or last sight, though he noticed that all the apparently successful ones he knew about or suspected were in some manner distinguishable from the commonalty of rovers or poets. She was still neither acquisitive nor otherwise selfish. He was very glad to have known that after all her libations she had settled with equipoise into a cheerfully professional gravitas as the independent wife of the same David who had been her first choice on the Magic Mountain of Terra Nova, spanning the distance from one Codfishland to another.

"I'm sorry too, for my tactless intrusion." she was saying. "I just want to avoid embarrassing you if and when the *Nous* is obliged to report your appointment to the ultimately key executive post in this Venetian government. I can't avoid writing a paragraph or two as soon as it's no longer merely hypothetical. I'd be fired if I let the *New Uruk Testament* scoop me!"

"Thanks" he snorted.

"What I'm trying to say is that you are going to have to run the gauntlet of self-important Earls if you are to be confirmed by them. The mayor's recruitment is only half the public process. And you've got to prepare yourself for a kind of traditional governance that's little else than the oxymoronic management of aged democracy. It's less rational and more vulnerable to public interference than what you knew in corporate business. Even more so than the arbitrary business I'm in! State law and municipal accounting are nothing like what you've been used to. There will be a lot of doubt about your lack of specifically appropriate experience. Most of these people have learned their own work only on the job and they can't imagine the advantage of a first-class liberal education like yours in quickly understanding something new or different. And you'll still be facing a bench of nine popularly elected personalities, at least six of them probably skeptical of your competence as the city government's executive and financial officer, simply because you've never had such a job or awe-inspiring degree. In their own private occupations the majority six are likely to fear 'efficiency experts' as much as city employees do. I know what it's like in the newspaper business when the management calls in hotshot consultants to break us of our troglodytic habits! —I may even cover the story myself!"

"But since the mayor can make a ninety-day interim appointment without the Board of Earldermen's approval—"

"Aha! So you must have been reading the Charter! Where there's smoke there's fire! This would be very newsworthy for anyone who was aware of your essential part in the Yard's 'pioneering information technology', as the *OHM Bulletin* article called it. Besides, with peasants and shopkeepers your appointment may be taken as an enormous financial demotion for a really exalted technocrat like you, or so it would seem to those who don't know that by right of primogeniture you have inherited your mother's contempt for wealth."

Caleb grunted a laugh, and he was about to ask her how she'd come across that great corporation's publication; but he was too nettled by her continued arrogation of an outworn intimacy, exploiting (as Tessa did) private remarks that he'd since forgotten, though she'd never met his almost legendary mother.

"I'm beginning to trust my hunch!" Belle continued after meeting with some silence. "After another three months in the temporary office your ordeal would be worse. The Earls will still not have understood what it takes to undo present mismanagement before new systems are actually installed. You'd have embarrassed the poor mayor with attempts at administrative changes that go against the grain of traditional sinecures or union rules—brought on by reckless concessions in previous contract bargaining—or even by promulgating protocols for the distribution of mail!

"No doubt Dexter will stand behind you, but you'd better start making a few friends on the Board. It's likely that the newly elected ones will still be feeling their oats and will give you the most trouble simply because you don't respond with sympathy for their enlightened managerial suggestions. These new incumbents all have their own half-baked fixations on how to 'modernize' the city with an internal telephone system, a certain copying machine, or a well-advertised computer. The veteran Earls on the Board, conservative or liberal, are wiser about the difficulty of getting anything done without raising taxes or otherwise riling one faction or another of the voters whose relatives or friends are on the city payroll."

Caleb appreciated her well-meant warnings but he remained silent lest he offend her by seeming to doubt her oracle. "Dexter Keith has already shown that he'll be the best of mayors," Belle went on, "but checks and balances impede him every step of the way, and he doesn't know much more about well-organized general management than he did when he got out of the Navy as a Junior Grade Lieutenant line officer thirty-five years ago. Ever since then he's worked as an architect or city planner. No doubt he's learned a lot about how things actually work in local government, thank God, and he's serious about radical reform; but I don't think he's creative in his thinking about bureaucratic problems. He really needs an eminence gris like you! I don't want to print anything that will make your oral exams any harder than necessary. And maybe I can be of some indirect help—as long as we're not seen together, though my face is even more unknown down the street than yours."

Even in warning him she questioned the professional dignity he must needs recover if he was to perform in a life far more public than almost anyone's in a private industry managed with an essential semi-secrecy. But he had been battle-scarred enough in flexible private corporations to be wryly amused at her own naive notion of responsibility for management without the authority and staff of a Cardinal. Yet at the same time he was prospectively stimulated both by a nearly pro bono salary he hadn't yet been offered by the job market in Dogtown, and by the moral frisson of working for an admirable and congenial man with whose wife at the time (the librarian Gloria Keith now married to Rafe Opsimath's plant manager Waldo Cotton) he had been recklessly conflagrated very briefly before he was eased out of his apartment in the Keith house, a former Rectory next to Acorn Pasture Cemetery on Cod Street close to the railroad station, whether or not Dexter (then the City Planner) had suspected that accident, or learned of it later by the research librarian's confession, or had been guilty enough of exploiting his own outstanding attraction for women (especially Waldo Cotton's then wife) to erase or cover up any resentment he might have harbored against the young tenant and his dog (pander in the cuckoldry by the name of Ibi-Roy), both of whom had been taken into the bosom of the Keith family. *After twenty years it was not to be forgotten*, he said to himself, *that the enthusiastic blonde librarian Gloria, once a popular high school teacher, who now knew a generation and a half of Dogtown citizens, was at least then the closest friend of Tessa Opsimath, who's been prying into my life ever since I came to work for Rafe Opsimath her second husband. What a tangled web everyone interweaves on this magnetic little island!*

Finally he replied with an intentionally audible sigh. "Well, you've tricked me into admitting that I may be offered the job. Please note that it's still supposed to be a secret possibility until after Dexter gives the present administrative manager his notice. Your paper has never mentioned that inside the Hall that fellow's said to be over his head in chaos. You must be suppressing that gossip as impossible because he can boast a master's degree in Public Administration! Could he be complaining about not getting an immediate raise? No matter where or how he gets another job— if the rest of your gossip is true—his pay will be much higher."

"My purpose in talking to you now comes down to this: send me a private copy of the probably doctored résumé that you'll be submitting to the Board, so that my announcements in the paper will be consistent with your wishes. And with it, after due consideration, jot down any subject I should particularly avoid or boast in print, or in tips to the female reporter I'll send to interview you—that is, if this turns out to be real!"

Resorting again to his chair of meditation in order to begin again his interrupted attempt to withdraw from objectivity, Caleb found himself grinning in satisfaction with the mutual infatuation that had condensed and solidified as a peaceful friendship, occasional twinges of jealousy by both parties to the contrary notwithstanding.

Soon after he was resettled in Belle's absence the phone demanded him again. He anticipated a postscript from Belle, but this second nearly simultaneous call to his hermitage, nowadays seldom invaded by anyone but advertisers, redoubled his suspicion of trouble. It was Gretta Doloroso, Endicott Krebs's major domo, whom he hadn't seen for years, asking whether his mother used the name Moira or Mary when he was growing up. He replied to this docile old bookkeeper and amanuensis politely and truly, but tersely. Obviously Tessa Barebones Opsimath was up to mischief unintended for his ears. He therefore swore to have no more to do with Tessa, and even his affection for Fay was marred by suspicion of benign conspiracy. Yet Finn Macdane was the one who'd urged the Mayor to provisionally offer him a job that he certainly needed and had begun to sound interesting.

3.

It was the Mayor who made it sound interesting. At home as landlord and host at many a meal, Dexter, as Dogtown's city planner, had shown intelligent appreciation of Caleb's potentially useful Synectic Method of Diagnostic Correlation [S M D C] (eventually worthy of investment as the foundation of a specialized data processing corporation), which as its author he had invented experimentally for work with Father Lucey in stockmarket analysis before there were computers to relieve him of the unassisted personal labor of compilations and calculations at his desk that were required for its practical application. But at Mercator-Steelyard, he'd finally had a random-access computer and skilled programmers at his disposal (but before satellite workstations were available for input and output without keypunched OHM cards or tape), in his obsessive drive to complete a comprehensive information system for a whole corporation of departmental functions and other basic operational needs which were at all times in higher priority than enlarged computing capacity for research. Brushing aside Belle's sagacious warnings, his old technocratic blood was up to overreaching the Mayor's simple mandate to "install an economical computer system" in the Hall's tiny organization as he saw fit—assuming that the Earls authorized its operating budget.

"Mainframe" computers with remote personal workstations were now coming onto the market, with ready-made programs supposed easily adaptable for a city's separately managed functions—hardware, software, engineering, and maintenance all provided by one or more outside "service bureaus" in monthly leases without touching the capital budget! Most of the white-collar workers in the Hall quaked at the prospect of labor-saving efficiency, but the Board itself no longer resisted an immediate increase in administrative expenses that promised much faster and more accurate collection of revenue as well as improved control of all expenditures and better response to taxpayers' gripes. The Earls hoped to get as much credit as the Mayor for publicly urging the progress (rather than "reform") implied by "computerization". Hadn't the magic of "digital" electronics finally proven itself all over the country? Most of these legislators envisioned the simple plugging-in of a gaggle of cathode ray tubes resembling devilvision sets! The Mayor was better informed, but at least half as broadly as Caleb in his vague grasp of what he hoped could be accomplished in his first administration with just the routine information of basic municipal accountancy.

Besides his obscure reputation as an occult architect of business abstractions, Caleb's one subjective advantage as an innovative administrator was that he had no electoral ambitions, no other political or managerial position to covet, and no wish for longevity of employment—not to mention an almost supercilious confidence that he could easily pick up what he needed to know about the patchwork of municipal finance and the Commonwealth's law. Yet even before he set up his office in a gloomy but spacious corner that had been a conference room, sharing one of the Mayor's two secretaries, he began to excite himself by the hope of creating a model for all municipal governments, large and small, and eventually earning the opportunity to apply his innovations in data analysis unimagined in the conventions of either academic or business practice—especially when finally extended into the solid geometry of rectangular parallelepiped for annals of data in simultaneous array! This would be his last chance to have even the smallest institutional resources required to produce the kind of small pilot demonstration that would be necessary for an approach to any government agency or research institution for the means to a large-scale practical demonstration of social or economic research. In the end it would prove the possibility of finding truth or determining policy by the interpretation of facts, estimates, opinions, goals, and/or fiction in imaginary closed systems! Pie in the sky! Or Hamiltonian quarternions with $\sqrt{-1}$?

He wasn't fool enough to have *faith* in this recrudescence of an almost forgotten pipe dream from his palmy days, because he well knew that S M D C et al were severely limited by the necessity of a perfected foundation in regularly collected rectangular sets of data: no small matter—especially in an anachronistic organization erratically evolved from practically autonomous entities of freemen defined by Colonial notions of self-government!

Yet he couldn't suppress—even as a mockery of religious theory—the *hope* for something to look forward to in default of his virtually dromenological theater. In invention, as in art and in social leadership, even false hope is of great value in cultural evolution if it comes in a discrete series of short steps without too much foresight in the process. He needed a job anyway, and he had no money to return to Cornucopia or to emigrate elsewhere therewith. A taste of wanderlust was less possible, at the age of six-and-twoscore, than a creative career in public service starting at the anti-intellectually parsimonious local level, with no assurance of security, not to mention ascent.

Resigned, at least for the present, to the vivification of a nearly outworn hope that diverted from supremacy his highest creative aspiration, Caleb shook off the existential angst to await the Mayor's social decision. In his last interview the Mayor had assured him that he was his first, but not necessarily only, choice, pending final deliberation, and he had no doubt that Dexter Keith was an exceptionally honest politician who had no fear of educated intellectuals. Still, there was some slight chance that an experienced city manager from out of town might turn up who might accept half a normal salary simply because the Dogtown challenge was so interesting! Or who had successfully concealed his professional blacklisting for dipsomania malfeasance or congenital incompetence—more or less the defects that had led to the sudden departure of the first incumbent of this newly created position under a radically new city charter that had been earnestly adopted by popular vote (in striking parallel to the adoption by the thirteen quasi-republics of an enlightened Constitution to replace the ineffective Articles of Confederation almost two hundred years earlier).

In the back of Caleb's mind his artistic conscience still claimed as a tiny anchor to windward his ruggedly individualistic patch of destitution if the job fell through. He had no other iron in the fire, and maybe no claim to unemployment insurance. But it didn't come to serious fears of penurious independence as long as he continued to have sub rosa support (to which Caleb himself was not substantially privy) from Commander Finn Macdane, a new resident of Dogtown hardly known to the public but already the senior member of the Mayor's unofficial brain trust, who had privately instigated, on the one hand, a summary dismissal of the incumbent administrator, and, on the other, an astonishingly unlikely application by this exceptionally qualified dark horse in the city's midst as the best successor, hastily justifiable to the Board as an interim three-month appointment, according to the Charter, subject to permanent confirmation if he'd proved his reputation, though lacking previous experience in "the public sector", as a modernizing technocrat whom Dogtown was damn lucky to have in managing the transition from the 18C to the 20C!

In public Dexter was too shrewd a veteran of municipal wars to display more enthusiasm for Caleb than was necessary to get by on this provisional basis, because though he had long since been impressed by Caleb's ideas he had no way of assuring the man's ability to get the cooperation he'd need from city employees who were excessively protected from removal by Civil Service law and otherwise resistant to "efficiency experts". Any mayor would be devastatingly embarrassed if for the second time he were forced to renounce his own chosen chief of staff and most intimate colleague, the constructor of budgets and coordinator of all his semi-autonomous chieftains as well as leader of radical administrative innovations. And in this instance Dexter was slightly uneasy, despite Caleb's illustrious performance at the Yard in the half-distant past, that his urgent need to fill the position had obliged both Finn and himself to omit further "background checks" of his nominee. They were charitably remiss (since they almost alone among the public were

aware of his secretly virtual vocation) in failing to ask him (as the
Earls would have done in interviewing for a permanent appointment) w*hy* he had left the Yard, voluntarily or otherwise; and if on
his own initiative, what was his motive, since he'd taken no other
job for several years thereafter? As a matter of fact, as neither of his
protectors knew, if they'd pedantically used official channels to
search poor Caleb's personal past, as would have been done for a government job at the federal level, they might have been given pause
(though only from the public opinion point of view) to learn that he
had once been stigmatized by the Bureau of Domestic Investigation
[B D I] as a "Premature Antifascist", and long ago in Cornucopia
been listed by Selective Service as a military draft evader on suspicious grounds, as well as recognized in the Hall's own dusty archives
as a bastard in alias at birth! But fortunately by now—the Red-scare
fading, other doubts not yet pandemic—almost all non-elected
public or private officials were hired in lazy trust of self-composed
curricula vitae and a few personal references.

Nevertheless Caleb was bitterly sorry that in his ingenuous
days he had lent Tessa a carton of Mary's letters (only lately
returned, presumably with nothing missing), not to assist an investigation of himself but to verify his boasts about that woman who
put to shame in imagination, courage, generosity, charity, love, and
life-experience any respectable mother of the century. His trust had
been meant as an expression of sympathetic feminism. Despite his
gratitude to Finn, with whom his bond was their common appreciation of such abstract ideas as systems theory, Caleb was now
almost sullen in his uncommunicative attitude toward Tessa and
others he deemed involved with her detective agency, and so
ashamed of his own hesitancy to challenge or chide her that he
avoided even her mentor Fay, his own godmother.

So he made himself scarce to friends and resolved to attend no
more Crat meetings or social events, making the best of what
would probably be his last few weeks of intellectual freedom. He
stayed at home, studied the City Charter, read Vinland's municipal
laws, postponed the bore of perusing uncodified and probably
inconsistent local ordinances, longingly aware of all the other-world
books that had to remain unread on his shelves, unable to goad him
into thinking about another quasi-archeological play to write in his
distantly pensioned retirement. He realized that he would have
hardly the leisure to read more than the daily N U *Testament* and
DT *Nous,* if he had personal time at all as an obsessively bureau-

cratic technocrat, regretting but betting on the very modest financial salvation he had been driven to consider, rejoicing only in the
fact that it would be for public service instead of private profit—a
local contribution to the common good.

Know thyself! Caleb jeered. *My middle name is Ion!* Of course he
did not know of Tessa's writing, which still lacked any reader to
find fault with it. Furthermore, he had no brother and sister to stir
his curiosity. Strangely enough, considering dialectical differences,
he thought his genes were too much like his mother's to have
required a holy ghost. Yet as far as her exhibitionism, religious
faith, emotional thinking, and open-hearted charitableness were
concerned, he was her antienantiomorph—although in adventur-
ousness (though frustrated), hope, political emotion, and vulnerability to heterosexual love he was perhaps her spit and image,
mutatis mutandis. He believed that the other influences on his constitution were intellectual acquisitions of his own choosing, or else
environmental accidents in his biological development. Most of his
amazingly good luck in circumstances was made possible by the
blessed Mary who was his mother.

4.

[If Caleb was not of the notebook-writer or diarist type it was
because he liked to sort items or units in various piles or file folders bearing his observations or intentions so as to find them when
the categorical was more important than the chronological (as it
usually was). He jotted his notes on sortable cards, usually the
blank side of those intended for input to the old "unit-record"
OHM tabulating machines. But the following passage more or less
represents the sequential rumination that a diarist might have dictated instantly by preternaturally cud-like thought-waves on the
long walk of a third person tracing a map of nearly all the pavement on Mother's Neck.]

In this hiatus of his life-stream Caleb postulated and hypothe-
sized the outcome of the next week's all-but-certain offer of objective livelihood (as Finn had assured him on the phone), preceded by
a public announcement of the present administrator's removal; he
fell to brooding about what he had immediately suspected was
Tessa's active opposition to the freewill with which he chose to
defend himself from her psycho-therapeutic friendship. In any

event, he grumbled, she might have skipped the genealogical research which exceeded the objective inquiries of full-fledged psychoanalysts about their clients. He wondered if it wasn't a vulgar case of the private sleuth finding herself more interested in the accomplice before a fact than in her unguarded patient.

But if so, that's exactly what he, the exhausted subject himself, had preconsciously encouraged, casually, passim: Mary Tremont was the protagonist and hero of his existence. He had always assumed that her mate—if any!—was no more to be questioned in his case than in Ion's. Hadn't she teased him with the middle initial *I* when (striving for respect with kids in school) he'd asked for one? Usable for playground distinction—anything but Ichabod—preferably commonplace. After the early years he always avoided the father-topic in aversion to being pinned down as to existential reality, especially when she was angry at him. As he grew more educated he had conjured a disdain of the *Know Thyself* preachment, in favor of freewill's vagary, such as the imaginary *i*. Thereafter he continued to fend off anyone's presumption to detect the half of his nature that he could manage on his own terms. This inchoate comedy sustained an unstated theory, and the theory his habitual autonomy in both betterment and folly.

I beget from Gilgamesh my Y *chromosome. I don't need the trouble of a father. My mother was usually my only nurturer until she sent me to the Dutchkill School. Books and bookkeeping have served for the rest, along with my teachers. That's probably why I've never wanted children. Or perhaps it's for that indecency that I have no right to question my paternal cause, even as I don't accept responsibility for my own two or three unintentional deposits of humanity, and fortunately am never invited to meet them. I hardly ever think of their existence. —But I am beginning to wonder if old age will chastise me with wistful human curiosity. —It's selfishness, to be sure. I was selfish about the claims upon me by the mother I boast about from increasing distances. I had no interest in her evangelical brand of Pauline ideas. Roughly speaking at the highest level of abstraction to the contrary, I'm in the Petrine half of Atlantean theology. We voted the same way, both venerated F D R and his kind of politics; but she was all humane and I was all technical. I was selfish, or so I seemed, for the sake of my free time or the money that paid for time, when she was still not old, and afterwards too. If it weren't for New Deal Social Security, and toward the end her initiatives in finding lodgings with the admiring assistance of the Tudor mission church in Botolph where she worked as a much appreciated volunteer in old age, I wouldn't have been allowed by law to act self-*

ishly in avoiding the normal devotion to an indigent parent who deserved my gratitude more than any social worker could imagine. So thanks to the Catholicratic Party and Christianity she was never in the danger of homelessness, as we had been—mother and baby—before the War that provided her with jobs earning enough to pay for my day-care. What I did send her, when I had my own jobs, she knew was stingy, until she no longer knew anything at all about my livelihood and expected nothing. . . .

As this Great Year Gloucestermas was again ending in conjunction with the summer solstice, the modernized festivals and celebrations about to be outdone by the most Dionysiac fireworks of all, the city's new fiscal year would mark its beginning: a logical moment for the budget-master to begin his work: most logical but perhaps the most difficult for a stranger in Vinland's unsystematic world of municipal organization and finance. Caleb the neophyte had been privately warned by Dexter the most subjective insider as well as by Belle the most objective outsider, neither of whom was capable of doing what he was expected to do, to say nothing of advising him how to get ready. So Caleb, like Boethius (the metasystematic philosopher as well as Magister Officiorum of the Western Empire), was making the most of his final time for one more metanoia. The job ahead—like paternal Salvation—did not faze him; what he contemplated or dreamed was about his past—for him nearly a novelty in the distribution of his time. In fine, he was almost humbly beginning to have second thoughts about knowing himself—as if by a personal history of ideas, the evolutionary half of his present constitution.

It was impossible to construct a genealogical chart of the influential teachers and books, remembered or not, that had contributed to his mentality as now purged or purified of entropic losses. *Wherefrom my disposition to select and improve special insights and my disrespect for others? Most of them (including many or most from the minds of women) of no attraction to my mother. Though from her I inherited the habit of reading and critical effrontery, can it be entirely the difference in our institutional educations? Mine she urged upon me, fought for my scholarships, and praised my achievements for their own sake, without regard for professional or chrematistic success. Her Irish respect for learning was almost Jewish, with no pretension of her own. Whence Gilgamesh? Whence Dromenology and Theodynamics? S M D C? Central Management System and Systems Theory? Whence my drive to organize? Whence the love of engineering and architecture? Whence my absurd theory of freewill and tragedy? My search for heroes according to the criteria of prowess in sports, politics, arts, technology, or any academic category? Why such as Sterne, Redburn, Harrison, Drang, or Whitehead among all to choose from? In short, why wasn't I a biologist, physician, psychologist, actor, teacher, priest, lawyer, philosopher, veterinarian, novelist, politician, architect, or even poet?*

—But wait! Maybe some of the ions she weaned me on were filtered from her psyche like recessive traits from him who passed his genes to her! Know myself *must mean* know thy father too: *that's something to dwell upon in my respite from otherwise incessant counter-negative capability, between solitary phantom playwrighting and probably a new obsession with painfully intimate social engineering!*

Thus Caleb, with nothing else to engage his immediate energy, approached middleaged self-anagnorisis after all, having worked himself by abstractions from pigheaded aversion to something like enthusiasm for self-knowledge. He felt with a laugh as if like Boethius he had reconciled Aristotle to Plato! He began to feel more kindly toward Tessa, as long as she made public nothing of what she learned about him. Perhaps he would let down his guard and join her as the introspective member of her gang—with a joyous new sense of liberated privacy!

How to tell her so is only your first problem, my boy. Don't get carried away by euphoria during this brief hiatus in your career. You won't be able to drop the subject afterwards.

If only he had questioned his mother, even long after she herself had probably forgotten there was such a commonplace thing to question!

23
MENTORS

Literature in my opinion is almost the only
resort of a man who wishes to render his
enjoyments independent of others.
                                        —Lemuel Shaw

1.

At first Finn Macdane had paid no attention to local names in the
Depression era that were mentioned in what he happened to hear
among the womenfolk of his closest acquaintance, but some of
them were repeated more than others; and after his friendship with
Arthur Halymboyd became closer, inevitably rife with reminiscences about the decades associated with the War in all the minds
of his generation, naturally with special interest in places or experiences they might have known in common, he realized (without
saying so at once) that they'd both been in Dogtown during the
Great Year Gloucestermas of 1934. In pillow talk with Fay Gabriel,
having suddenly been prompted to remember the name Moira, he

asked her if it had anything to do with the name Mary Trevisa that he'd overheard a few times in the conversations of Tessa Opsimath.

It was after a dinner party given by fifty-five-year-old Tessa for eighty-year-old Finn and a few local pairs of congenial elders—who toward the end of it, after all these years, permitted the conversation to drift toward the delicate aspect of wartime dread when tacit mutual (though usually unequal) suspicions of infidelity had carked in the hearts of men and women during their mandatory separations—that, finally trusting in Fay's broadmindedly weathered outlook, he imparted to her, without ingenuous detail, an offhand digest of his 1934 Gloucestermas liberty as a bachelor Navy officer in part-time command of a seagoing tug on harbor duty.

For a moment, beside him, she seemed to hold her breath. But it was not in disapproval, nor in jealousy half a century out of phase. For three seconds she thought at the speed of a billion synapses; then she chuckled, pinching his neighboring biceps. "A minor incident in your swashbuckling career, I suppose."

"I've been wondering." he ventured, revealing nothing about what Arthur Halymboyd the day before had told him about the sudden breach of his first implanted love—when a woman named Moira had impetuously banished him forever on the very morning of his sudden summons to help save some prominent Jews in their last chance to get out of Germany before they were arrested on false charges of treason. So it was with nearly negative probability that Finn found he'd discovered the owner of the necktie he once wryly noticed in a hazily remembered art studio. Of course he'd never suggest to Arthur the possibility of having once quite innocently trumped him in all innocence. And neither to Arthur, nor now to Fay, with suddenly accelerating heartbeat—recalling the unmistakably vehement letter Moira had written him the next day to nip in the bud any necessarily imperfect continuation of their perfectly consummated idyll—did he reveal his astounding suspicion of the Holy Ghost with whom that same evening at the Long Rocks tea dance he had seen her disappear, apparently enthralled.

"I know you are fond of my godson." Fay teased in a humorous whisper which was not lost upon the brute beside her. "Don't worry. You are already his de facto godfather, but that's likely to be as far as it goes. There's no reason to think you bear any responsibility! As my god-husband you're expected only to make him memorize the Nicene Creed. That's all there is to *my* claim upon your kinship!"

Fay at once felt a little ashamed for having so obviously pretended to mistake the principal significance of Finn's anecdote as a disclaimer of what was supposed to be the typical motive of a widow. She had found that Finn was hardly ever obtuse, and sensed that he was estimating the odds pertaining to Caleb's birthday. The very idea was amusing. "He was born at the spring equinox. Last year I think he really wanted us to forget his birthday. I had been told that the term 'immaculate conception' was a local joke, apparently even among most of the Petrine clergy."

And here she dropped the subject, lifting his arm to kiss the back of a hand that she admired as that of an ageless athlete. She wished she had time to cudgel her memories of all the letters in which Caleb's mother had intimated but never elucidated a one "inexpiable sin" clearly distinguished from the venial transgressions or indiscretions of her friend's passionate and susceptible years as (by her own estimation) a loving Christian with all sorts of undisguised regret and penitence for sins that in the sinner's conscience never rose to this one's level of glorification too Satanic for moral classification! At least in one of Mary's recurrent moods—usually when isolated and lonely at great distance from all her sympathetic friends, neglected by her coldhearted son—that hint, made somewhere in one of her compulsive screeds, had for lack of explanation seemed nothing else than an ultimately reserved limit of exhibitionism that sends a certain kind of witch to the stake in a theocratic society, its threat of reverse defiance contrasting with her obverse coin: an open, ebullient, humorous, respectful, friendly, courageous, and generous personality as a confidently religious "single mother".

As an adjunct lecturer of comparative religion Fay differed from most savants and journalists in her recognition that the distinctions within denominated factions were often in some respects more significant than the categorical divisions of faith, especially within the Pauline statistics of Christianity, which as often as not seemed unified only as a collegiality in opposition to the Petrine monolith. As far as the basic sociology of religion was concerned, a few colors in the Pauline spectrum were more closely matched by factions of Jews or Moslems than by some of their fellow Christians. She saw Mary Tremont's life as an illustration of the misleading tendency to understand "varieties of religious experience" as theological criteria. Mary was born and died in the Tudor church, essentially the least unsettled or separatistic of the Pauline denominations, but between adolescence and aging equilibrium she had several times been a wholehearted participant in Pauline evangelism in the rainbow of anti-papist practices, such as baptism by immersion, as her letters made clear. Having given up all ambition in the professional poetry of an outmoded genre, her last years in Botolph as a Social Security pensioner were spent (until overtaken by mental incapacity) as a Pauline Apostolic volunteer in the social-welfare activities of the Tudor diocese, appreciated by the Bishop himself, as well as admired in the local affairs of her beloved Father Daniel's congregation of diverse races, givers and receivers as an inner-city parish, substantially interfused by educated nonresidents united as liberals of a High Church mission.

Scanning her faded recollection of cryptic allusions to a peculiar sin, Fay was reminded of Mary's middleaged span between her uncertain Tudor allegiance and her self-correcting postulancy at the self-sufficient community of the Brotherhood of the Peaceable Kingdom in equatorial South Atlantis, when her exceptionally long letters had been devoted not only to remarkably interesting descriptions and narratives of her solitary journeys to get there, but mainly to the kind of individualistic ego-introspection that the self-disciplined commune of Brotherhood was expected to cure her of. In some of her letters Mary had also reflected upon her earlier travels and sojourns—before taking the stewardess job on a Viking freighter in which she found apparently mutual love with the Chief Engineer who never denied that he would have to return at last to retirement with his steadfast wife in Norseland—when, recently immersed up to her neck as a "born-again Christian", she had earned a stretch of happiness as an itinerant chapwoman selling Bibles all over northern Cornucopia (though probably not proselytizing as effectively as George Borrow in Spain). By her own account that anabaptism, though not explicit in subjectivity, was an occasion for the frankest kind of public confession, ostensibly to God, among strangers as incapable of fathoming her semantic expression as Anglophone savages hearing a Scholastic sermon on Realism vs. Nominalism in the Middle Ages, though there was never anything academic or esoteric about her diction, which was never as passive as speaking with tongues.

All at once Fay recalled, though vaguely and without detail, that she had been so impressed by one of Mary's letters on the ecclesiastical subject that instead of saving it as usual in her "M T" carton she had filed it somewhere among her professional notes related to the famous *Varieties of Religious Experience*. The anthropologist seemed to remember that it was distinguished from Mary's other letters by its omission of Sin, a reification which she herself had otherwise never found very interesting, even when the Sisters in her own parochial school were obviously euphemising its substantives. *Maybe I should dig it up for Tessa—at least to see if it's a good thing for memorials of Mary that I have not handed it over for quotation!*

How much our dear psychologist misses in assuming that poor Mary never recovered from undulant afteraffects of encephalitis lethargica.

2.

Caleb was now so far along in existence that he was too accustomed to the perpetual postponement of a Wanderjahre in Europe to notice the irony that the present hiatus in his career would have been an opportunity to visit at least England and the Isle of Man (which as a child he was frequently told that he'd seen through the porthole of his mother's belly), if only he'd arrived at middle age having saved enough money to take advantage of his lifelong heart's desire. But some of his other realms of desired gold were readily available at home. Halting before a week or two of suspended motivation while waiting for the Mayor to act decisively, he at first almost forgot the pleasure of a common reader in surveying his great dusty wall of books with an eye to resuming one or more of the collateral enthusiasms that he had been forced to set aside by the demand of concurrent occupations, always among themselves conflicting in time and energy, no matter which one was primary, like an agricultural monk with no time to pray.

Yet in this situation his deepening association with Finn Macdane was indeed a godsend. As Caleb soon realized, the elder reciprocated in the friendship, for after fourscore suns of versatility he had nothing exciting to anticipate except adventures in ideas that happened to interest them both. Finn was glad to complement with his cosmopolitan experience the virtual extension of a younger hungry brain. For his part, without saying so, he was as hopeful for equality in friendship as Fay's godson was.

Often they met for long lunches at the Windmill, for which Finn insisted upon paying. Neither of them liked to waste time figuring out how to make a meal at home for more than one mouth. After one messy attempt at efficient victualing by having a dinner

for two delivered up to the third floor of his office building Finn
was as impatient as Caleb with any sort of fussy hospitality for
anyone but Fay (who anyway had little leisure for the time-consuming experience). But one afternoon when he was first invited to
Caleb's humble "studio apartment" for a drink—at Apostle's Dock
in Argo Cove, for a much more intimate odor of boats and tides
than from Finn's own spacious view of the whole inner harbor—he
was immediately pleased by the specific gravity of Caleb's small
wall of close-packed books. That library seemed almost devoid of
fiction; but more than one brick of its masonry was often in Finn's
inward eye when they discussed common interests, walking or sitting somewhere on the Cape.

As an amphibiously itinerant naval architect, engineer, and
consultant, until now without a permanent base, the bachelor
Commander had not been able to retain more than a handful of the
books he had read or wished to read; but the time had come to
build the conveniences of a common reader's personal library—
scholarly lexicons as well as technical reference volumes, recollected
classics read or long ago recommended as a student of liberal arts at
Norumbega, and hundreds of others on watch-lists he had compiled over half a century in anticipation of retirement, largely from
particularly interesting leads in *The New Ur Review of Books* or such
journals as *Technology and Culture*. He knew he wouldn't live long
enough to use many of the books on his new shelves but he wanted
to have a maximum range of immediate options when he followed
his impulses with the assistance of indices. He asked for Caleb's
advice about the eternal question of how best to organize his horde.
He was aware that the Dewey Decimal System was of little use in
the service of the one small personal collection of any one mind
who had more than one thing to think about but didn't want to
waste space and time on anything just to disagree.

Caleb laughed. "I wish I knew how to classify my own books!
What seems logical in one decade seems stupid in the next, when I
don't have time to dust them off, study the contingencies, and reorganize them according to my latest enthusiasm—which is much
more important than being systematic in time of need!"

"Then what about the other kind of 'subject'? Is the basic division by author or by subject?"

"Sometimes one and sometimes the other, depending upon your
latest cross-sections of memory! One of the problems is that some
authors or titles are valuable to you for biography or idea, but you

may find yourself looking by shelf locations or color for something uppermost in your sympathetic nervous system! At least in my case! But if you've managed all that when reaching for a book, you may still have trouble deciding where to insert a book entirely new to you in both name and subject. You may place it on the top of a horizontal pile hoping to read it when you have time to open it for assistance in deciding where it belongs whenever you get more shelf space or come across a new set of coordinates for your multi-dimensional imagination. I usually end up with random order within my own impulsive syncretion of genus and species. Of course I'm just talking about a tiny narrowminded library for someone like me, not a doctoral student's."

"Well", said Finn, "That's good enough for me. Sometimes I remember a book by its cover. Up in my place I don't have much more wall space than you have."

"I'm often wrong about the color to look for, because my system is prejudicial and often misleads me when it comes to something I'm looking for, something perhaps I haven't opened for years. When I first place a book the whole mnemonic situation seems unforgettably logical! But I've never been any good at memorization of any kind. In the end it all comes down to your idiosyncrasies!"

"At my age that's really serious!" Finn chuckled. "I rely on notes and experiential analogues when I read history or politics, but I've lost my analytical capability, even with numbers. Like most students today I rely on slide rule or desk calculator. It's a good thing I don't have to navigate anymore!"

Nevertheless Caleb was in humble awe of Finn's much superior mathematics, hesitant to advance any of his own ideas that might be confounded by a keenly intelligent practitioner of engineering; so it was much to his surprise that he found his new mentor interested in hearing the essence of his purely numeric coding system, which interpreted every iota of information in the computerized Central Management System at the Yard, regardless of function or identification, without any detailed correspondence between numbers and their meanings. "But that was an objective problem. The arranging of books must be arbitrary, no matter how methodical." Explaining a little more of the C M S coding concept he began to love and fear the man's appreciation of undereducated ideas.

After that, returning to bibliography: "So I suppose, for lack of art in introspection, I'll start by just tossing my books onto the shelf as they come to hand for a First-In-Last-Out inventory!"

"They'll make a wall just as colorful as any other. Just don't forget that there's always the question of whether or not, in a 'by author' system, it may be important to batch a great creative scholar with *her* work, as translator, critic, or exegete of someone else of equal or greater importance as another author in *his* own rightful place elsewhere."

Thus such kind of abstract discussion, with Fay Gabriel always in mind, making possible the friendship of two such respectful generations, which Caleb was rarely privileged to enjoy. This was not typical of their conviviality, as Caleb delicately pressed Finn for expanding detail of experience in kinds of world beyond the reach of his Immediate Exclusive Consciousness [I E C]. It was musing in that vein that he was eventually struck by their congenial relationship as an undeclared cosmology shared to great degree in the same sector of the ontological spectrum despite their unspoken reservations in metaphysics. When this felicity manifested itself Caleb's excitement was less reserved than Finn's, but it soon proved an intellectual companionship of common emotional value, setting aside their shadowed differences like two cultures overlapping each other as lobes of a Venn diagram.

Caleb was already delighted to have had a hearing responsive to his peculiar abstractions, especially after Finn's reading of his Gilgamesh plays with unmistakable respect. He hadn't felt so satisfied with a male interlocutor since his exciting days with Father Duncannon, the intellectual father of theodynamic liturgy in dromenological culture, whose posthumous remainder of self-published books had ended up in the city's landfill dump. But Caleb had begun to collect details for a possible biography from that slightly older priest of Finn's generation. He had already been estranged by much familiarity with the unheroic weakness of the Father Superior's private manner in failing to control his intimate assistant the wayward Father Economist.

Finn was a different order of mentor, impressive at first for his "outer experience" as a former man of action, but soon found to be no less attractive for his versatility in the true realms of gold, a liberal mind that was readily engaged in ideas and opinions about what Caleb had personally encountered within as well as without academic constituencies. Not long before his prospect of the City job rose over his own vague economic horizon he and Finn had been invited to dinner with Arthur Halymboyd in his private quarters at Merriwether Hall. The host had heard enough about Caleb from

Tessa and Endicott Krebs to recall the young man's service to that
junior Father Economist Christopher Lucey and his Superior as the
draftsman of an annotated chart unofficially titled "King Arthur's
Empire", which purported to trace the intricate investment relationships that constituted an industrial conglomerate, the erstwhile
Parity Corporation—which even Arthur himself as its architect had
found useful for compendious contemplation. Once prompted, the
magnate dimly recalled that it had been on the strength of this
convenience that he (as a weighty personage in the Graveyard Street
Market) had recommended Caleb for employment by the Mercator-
Steelyard corporate management in Dogtown, without the slightest
recollection of that young man's appearance. Caleb for his part
would have been more likely to recognize his awe-inspiring benefactor if it hadn't been for the wrinkles and shrinkage that mask the
powerful history of many octogenarian geezers.

   Yet confirmed acquaintance on less unequal terms at Arthur
Halymboyd's table, after his retirement, was easily accomplished,
though Caleb continued to behave with much of the deference due
both his formidable elders at the distance of three and a half
decades in age. He listened without speaking for far more than
two-thirds of the conversation, but ate and drank much more than
a third of what was consumed at the table without impairing his
acute attention to the names and places that were touched upon
like random footnotes to nearly half a century of history. From
time to time one of the two would turn to him in apology for
being carried away by the recollections they shared, but he assured
them of his keen interest, especially in the significant wartime
years of which he remembered little more beyond his unfledged
ken than civilian food rationing and some banner headlines. With
such encouragement the old gentlemen had sometimes found
themselves reminiscing expressly for the edification of this young
Samuel. Both had known famous places and exceptional persons,
some of whom though obscure to the ordinary public were venerated by Caleb.

   One of the thrilling names that happened to arise precisely at
this opportune lacuna in his usual line of work—despite some economic anxiety and a rare relaxation of psychic tension—was mentioned by Finn as that of a pre-war Norumbega graduate Classics
student with whom he'd hobnobbed while he himself was a Navy
postgraduate student of engineering at V I P, after they'd met in
Unabridge about the time Total Abstinence was being repealed by

amendment of the Constitution—that is to say, a year or two before Caleb was born: Harold Ore. Finn was the elder of the two, seeing that he'd already served several years of sea duty, but it turned out that they had both taken some of the same undergraduate Classics courses at 'Bega. Then, as now, Finn regretted that it had been impossible to pursue further study of Ancient Greece while following his career in marine technology. The next remarkable coincidence was that Arthur had crossed paths with Harry Ore a decade later, during and immediately after the War, when they were both S I S [Strategic Intelligence Service] officers operating in Europe, though their language specialties and assignments were quite different.

"Ore was actually commissioned as a Reserve officer in the Marines, more military than most of us in the S I S." said Arthur. "Maybe that explains his special reputation for bravery among a lot of brave men. Of course I didn't know what he was doing except that it was behind the lines on dark and stormy nights in the Balkans. I never volunteered for roughing it like that!"

It was also a probable coincidence, Caleb had thought, that Fay's late husband, then an S I S agent too, would have known Harold Ore in Greece; but he'd felt it would be indiscreet to mention her outlived private life, especially since he knew hardly anything about it. Anyway it wasn't surprising to know that the S I S especially recruited scholars who had devoted themselves as detectives and explorers to deciphering cryptic languages, perhaps—as students of heroism—more inspired for dangerous missions by the bravery or peril of the figures in their professional imagination than were their overtly brave peers in the uniformed services by patriotic camaraderie.

Caleb at the time said little about the greatest and almost incredible coincidence, except to express his recognition of Ore's name as present department head at the University of Whyaway, recent author of an innovative study in Greek tragedy that radically corrected prevailing theories of its origins. His arguments, with few modifications, very neatly solved certain secondary problems in Caleb's own presumptuous theory as an amateur common reader who knew no more of the language than an almost forgotten smattering of its elementary grammar and a few ubiquitous idioms. He'd had several thought-heroes in Classical scholarship, but Ore had excelled them all in his tendentious estimation since the first radically brilliant savant of archaic ritual and myth of the present century, Jane Harrison, who (unlike Ore) had worked primarily on the matter much earlier than the period of cultural innovation during the supremacy of Athens.

"I wish somebody would write *his* intellectual biography!" Caleb interposed. But of course for himself by now the virtual appearance of any such genius within one's personal reach by association—in this case a figure in the least noticeable department of an academy that would not have been supported by a public otherwise indifferent to its disappearance if it hadn't had imposed upon it the curricular responsibility for teaching someone the Biblical languages that were given lip service by representatives of the state's farmers and factory workers (Pauline, Petrine, and Jewish alike)—was not entirely astonishing in marvelous Dogtown, the intersection of many peripatetic paths from the wider world, like so many additional dimensions as unseen rectangles at the corner of his Isorectotetrahedron! That overdetermination of this polis made his cerebral neurons resonate with abstracted solidarity! Indeed, what made the name Ore uniquely coincidental for him, the voice of a deus ex machina, was the fact that Caleb happened at the moment to have been just about to clarify, stimulate, and relieve his own equivocally suspended occupations by turning to the suddenly tantalizing section of his book-wall which had more than once dominated his reading for weeks or months of available time.

Gradually, after his first enlightening acquaintance with Jane Harrison's works he had sporadically (in discontinuous batches of enthusiasm) acquired a score or two of scholarly volumes in a cluster that concentrated exegesis and criticism of the Classical literature itself as limited to English translations on which he depended even more than he depended on elementary geometry for his tropes. It was the philologically most valuable collection in his overstuffed little varsity, most of it out of print, some of it heavily marked with his own pencil, and the rest of it simply awaiting an ever-disappointed leisure to pursue research that might justify his preconceived opinions—which usually trusted to an echelon of acceptable or contentious predecessors. This same Harold Ore was the one with whom he had left off in his last stint of theoretical dromenology! In this inconclusive hiatus of productive reading he made up his mind to plunge back into the crucial midpoint of human civilization by reaching for Ore's fascinating thin little blue-covered paperback easily overlooked among much larger volumes—somewhere within the span of his treasure.

The Athenian Invention of Greek Tragedy was an exceedingly compendious work with many meticulous footnotes and citations. It boldly but graciously dissolved the etiological hypotheses of the subject's generally accepted scholarship (anchored in Aristotle if not Nietzsche), against which Don Karcist also had privately tilted without credentials or new evidence. As unqualified critic of the academic aristocracy he gladly welcomed even Ore's corrections of some inessentials in his own dromenological idea of tragedy as the rarest and highest product of eternal conflict between absolute values. It was exactly the book with which to recall, stimulate, and improve upon his avid appreciation of literature in the political art of seventh and sixth century Athens. With enthusiasm renewed by this chance opportunity to re-ignite his psychic energy, he afterwards plucked this elixir-stone from its sequestered hibernation and plunged into a second reading at his kitchen table, this time wiser by a few more years of self-education—approving, erasing, or adding his own penciled marginalia—and a little chastened by a few traces of earlier fatuity, but rejoicing in the company of old and new ideas still brewing.

Would this excitement eventually urge him to write essays in defense or apology for his life of abstractions, as represented in particular by a theoretical approach to the scarcest art by surveying chiliads of dromenological evolution between Harrison and Ore— between primitive ritual and consummate tragedy—eliminating the monkeywrenched issue of George Murray's Dionysian school (which remained pertinent to Comedy) and incorporating Ore's insight into the creative genius of Athens—always having in mind the hope that scholars of more than one department (especially Anthropology and Near Eastern Archeology) would advance the overlooked proposition that it was the Sumerians who had originally inseminated (perhaps with negative capability for kingship) coeval ideas of both society and hero finally realized only across the Aegean Sea, in the public art of Classical Athens, midway between Mesopotamia and the British Archipelago? He wouldn't dare mention such a fantasy to Finn; but neither would he let slip the lifetime-rare opportunity to talk about Else's ideas with one who had learned some Greek and now served as the irresponsible thinker's technocratic symbol of a hero in the decadence of civilization! At this perilous moment in his nondescript career Caleb was irrepressibly happy in one of the improbable illusions that kept him from despair of the culture he lived in.

But since the excitements of fiction in boyhood he'd hardly ever been able to read the same book passively for hours at a time. The more interesting, the greater urge for action—if only that of reading something else! In this case the somethings else (besides dreadful political news) were from the same shelf: Classical reference books and cheaply available editions of scholars who had been his eastward stepping stones—toward the origin of dromena and legomena that suited his aesthetic prejudice against mummified ideas. It was exciting to find imaginative liberty proportional to its distance from the overdetermined present. Ore (as taken to represent the crossroads of East and West) rekindled his appetite for the Greek poets and historians (if not for Plato), and especially for Aeschylus, whom he'd been slighting in his crescent appreciation of Euripides at the opposite end of tragedy's Athenian spectrum, though in his nakedly romantic youth the *Prometheus* had been his touchstone for pure tragedy.

Thus while temporarily idle in both organizational management and dramatic art Caleb kept his mind off personal necessity by re-reading Ore, Aristotle's *Poetics*, and a few of the tragedies, testing his most mature opinions. This amateur student reinforced his presumptuous confidence as a Greekless judge of comparative translations, reinforced by rusty linguistic advice from Finn, the worldly man of modern technics who had once known the vital dead language better than anyone else at hand. It helped that Finn was also fluent in the foreign tongues to which Caleb, biting off more than he could learn in undergraduate years, had deliberately given shrift too short. When he'd retired from the Navy, after years at sea as a common reader, Finn was as learned in Caleb's eye as any Atlantean engineer could be, especially in historical perspective. It happened that in this full retirement the old man, in critical review of his still questionably satisfied life (missing he knew not what before he died), hoped to study philosophy and history. The Commander had begun to think more about what *Die Geisteswissenschaften* might do to resist the accelerating entropy of his country's polity. His tastes enjoined Caleb's resistance to the decline of Atlantean language and its political mischief.

But most of all Caleb and Finn found similar interests— another coincidence (as if without two generations to separate them)—in their appreciation of a rather recondite advancement in the philosophy of organization named by the founders of Universal Systems Theory [U S T], ultimately derived from the Second Law of Thermodynamics by its leader, the Austrian developmental biologist Ludwig von Denthey. Finn was an official member of its small international society. That alone would have made him a demigod in the eyes of Caleb, who was an expert in nothing but bureaucracy, who could hardly refrain from bursting out with the subsequent suggestion that every member of U S T would naturally appreciate the organic metaphysics of Alpha Whitehead. The younger common reader now referred Finn to all the other metaphors of thermodynamics (a science founded on engineering, now applied to economics by George Roegen and to physical chemistry by Igor Prigogine). Thus did U S T fuel the younger's intellectual libido, which was susceptible to re-ignition anywhere halfway around the particular northern hemisphere to which he advisedly confined his virtual wanderlust in mind if not body. As either Samuel or Telemachus, this middleaged boy was rarely impartial in these adventures. Knowing that Finn had been brought up in the Tudor church, he hoped for the opportunity to elicit his interest in the dromenological Theodynamics of Father Duncannon (but as symbol-systems rather than articles of faith), the most original hero in his personal *Argo*; for Finn was the most experienced of the ship's company, travel being the least of his adventures.

3.

Finn thought Caleb somewhat precipitate in his judgments, and more buoyant—less melancholic—than he was likely to be before soon enough, if he went to work in Dexter's Lilliput Hall. But Caleb's energies were infectious. Also he was fair-haired and blue-eyed, as well as smaller and thinner than Finn himself had been at that age. It was only in those respects that his young friend seemed to resemble the woman he remembered so uncertainly from his Dogtown adventure five and forty years before. She had been anything but a learned technocrat, and he suspected excessively melancholic otherwhiles, judging by her frantic letter of unexplained apology and absolute dismissal—for which in retrospect he had blessed his lucky stars as a warning against any further complicity in what would have been an embarrassing liaison. But, despite an ambivalent sense of relief at the time, it had been hard to suppress his urge to extend, if only by satisfying his rueful curiosity about its context, the uniquely erotic event that was never to be forgotten in vacant or in pensive mood—at least during sea duty in the War. Now despite some typical secondary infirmities, without medical prescriptions, he congratulated himself on the emotional and sapient advantages of healthy old age—one of which was the tranquility of his love for the very different friend of that deceased woman, while missing none of his pleasures between those two poles of extraordinary femininity, though he could scarcely remember what it was like even after the age of thirty-four to be possessed with a totality of complex desire.

But it was wryly interesting to speculate about the seminal cause of Caleb's hybrid constitution, which he would have been very glad to have had under his command as an exceptional officer, though probably not a popular one in the wardroom, thanks (probably) to his precise respect for Regulations and his meticulous attention to details, and probably also to his scrupulous criticism of the enlisted Chiefs who bossed the crew. He laughed at the thought of Caleb doing his job at sea rather than where he really belonged on some admiral's staff (like himself) where he would have been more appreciated as a critic of the ship's design and maintenance. In wartime there was necessarily more tolerance of intellectuals, fussy or not, than in spit-and-polish peacetime. *All the more reason that Caleb would have done the Navy good—if only he could have gotten himself promoted to Washington by the fitness reports of his superiors! On my part, I'm very glad he got me to read* White Jacket. *Apparently even Wellingborough Redburn wasn't a particularly good harpooner or boat-steerer in whaling before he proved himself as a valorous topsman under Navy discipline when reform had to come (if at all) for the lower deck.*

Finn was disinclined to ask Tessa much about Caleb, because he didn't like to hear anything filtered even by the most unopinionated psychology, and of course Fay wasn't able to tell him as much about Caleb as about the mother (herself usually the last one to know much about a man's independent life). He wondered why his own gentlemanly reserved inquiries of Caleb about anything personal (besides his enthusiasms) were nearly always answered briefly, as if of no real interest to a man of the world, while welcoming opportunities to put forth much more important questions of his own about interesting experience above his own civilian station in life. Yet even with friends Finn too was generally taciturn about his career in peacetime—not in modesty but usually in the belief either that no one was actually interested in what he might have related as significant to himself, or else a waste of time to articulate the technical or the ineffable. But he had come to feel that Caleb was sometimes too curious about subjects both before and after his Navy career, like a slyly deferential biographer concealing his mission.

Know thyself, Finn now thought for the first time directed toward his own life. *That I have not. This is my last chance at posterity. I'd hate to leave behind nothing of my unique experience. Not that I want a biography. Why should all my counterentropic energy go to waste? I'm not an artist, I'm not a scholar. Nearly all my battleships have given way to ugly asymmetrical beehive boxes with yawing flat roofs to load and unload swarms of artificial geese that screech on and off without propellers yet more beautiful than their heaving fields! Like almost everything else nowadays, they drive a seaman to history. The only promising thing about this new Administration is that it will increase the Navy budget and perhaps retard the decommissioning of capital ships that still are ships! Now that I'm finally retired I can admit to myself that I'm an old fogey, to everyone else calling myself an objective historian of technology! But that seems to delight Caleb, who so far seems to be almost as inconclusive as I am when it comes to leadership.*

Finn gradually convinced himself that Caleb sincerely wished to learn as much as possible about the extraordinary professional career of this old man, most of which was of little intrinsic interest to women or savants as far as its aesthetics was concerned. Caleb's casual remark, one evening at Fay's table early on, that "literature is the art of experience" had not escaped his attention. At that time it had seemed to the engineer rather superciliously sententious, but now that he knew the younger man better it struck him as an explanation of the bond that was forming between them. Not that he himself hadn't for a lifetime seriously appreciated the liberal arts, or that Caleb wasn't experienced in many kinds of technological design and management; but rather that they traded to each other some of their negative capabilities—their available energy as specially counterentropic human beings—for experiential information that would otherwise dissipate at their own lives without proceeding "down the endless dale of posterity" (in Redburn's term) to benefit even in some microscopic and all but evanescent way their civilization's resistance to cosmic entropy. It was as if they were exchanging naval *projets non raisonné* for closet drama.

[Finn laughed to himself, wondering how different life would have been if he hadn't been stuck that singular night with the insipid daughter of the Admiral whom he'd been tacitly expected to marry. *She was amorous glamorous and dulcet enough, with the huckle-bones of a sylph, but her only imagination was domestic. Our son would have been the captain of an aircraft carrier by now, our daughter the wife of one of Raygun's ambassadors. And I'd have divorced her for intellectual inanition as soon I met someone with half the brain of Fay. —But if I hadn't already been ticketed to her for the Yacht Club dance I wouldn't have let Moira Trevisa disappear with the Holy Ghost that night. Then I would have been in an emotional mess, for God knows how long! I might have washed out for my Master's at V I P. Or what if she was already pregnant? Or just about to be? I've always been a lucky man about things like that. —I wonder if that priest was left-handed. I just noticed that Caleb is. Was Moira? Could I have told, from the way she served the tea? She was certainly as symmetrical as any man could wish! But I think her eyes were brighter blue than his.*]

Caleb so well earned Finn's trust—with tropes and parallels of sympathetic technical understanding (usually on the basis of no more than what they shared in common of elementary classical physics and the penchant to clarify ideas with diagrams), sometimes with excessive persistence, like an emboldened student in office conferences pestering his revered professor with questions having nothing to do with the cataloged course except suboptimization—that he learned or deduced more about the Commander's career than Fay Gabriel did, especially by taking impertinent advantage of his visits to the bachelor's well-furnished quarters nobly above the city's center of social transactions. As a self-appointed surrogate Telemachus, Caleb took the liberty of fingering books and examining wartime photographs as he probed for he knew not what in the casual manner of idle curiosity, one inquiry leading to the next. Finn pretended not to notice these elementary tactics in espionage because he was touched by the intellectual motives, and, at last, because he was beginning to think of himself as the exceptionally worthy mentor of a humble Socrates who wasn't trying to trap him in banal axiology. Why shouldn't a man learn to appreciate the ego in himself, as well as recall the horrors of war, while disarming many a suspicion of the false modesty bred into a military gentleman of the old school, since the process began as a sort of smiling game further softened by wine, beer, or Scotch? Certainly they drank cheers to the proposition that "pictures are worth a thousand words, and one diagram is worth a thousand pictures!"

Finn's somewhat naively aroused introspection, awakened from
the sleep of reason by Caleb as well as Fay, was never spiritual, not
even Platonic. Instead it progressed by partnership with the sudden
consciousness of rock-bound aging brought upon him by multilat-
eral retirement from the objective world he'd always lived in. It was
only imperceptibly that he'd accumulated an alarming variety of
trivial medicines, with a calendar to keep track of medical appointments, rarely doubting his fundamental health. Until now he had
felt and assumed that he appeared young for his age, trim and reasonably indefatigable. But just the other day Fay affectionately
teased him by stroking the smooth skin on the top of his head,
which he'd never suspected or searched in the mirror by which he
shaved and inspected a face which had never before struck him as
older than it had been since he wore a couple of stripes. He was
startled to notice that his remaining hair (which in his daily front
views seemed normal for a man of much earlier retirement) was
more silvery than respectable gray, and much higher on his forehead than he had felt it to be. But nothing to brood about, he
chuckled. *I still have no trouble keeping up with Caleb on our walks, and
the creaking little pains in my lower back every morning when I bend over
the wash basin disappear without further notice as soon as I straighten my
spine and warm it up with the activity of dressing, exercising arm muscles
for five minutes, and boiling my eggs. I'm almost as thin as ever, but I'm
annoyed to admit that the shrinkage of backbone keeps narrowing the gap
between my hip bones and my ribs, so that none of my belts are narrow
enough to get at my waist between them. What a nuisance it will be to wear
suspenders! Still, I feel so fit when I'm out of the house that I must keep
reminding myself to sheer off invidious comparisons when I'm with Arthur
and forget his cardiac infirmity. He still makes no attempt to lose weight,
smokes as many cigars as he shouldn't, and talks as if death is still to be
invented. He tells me he's been discussing his ethical will with Tessa. His
respect for her seems excessive.*
Nevertheless he conscientiously took almost daily walks about
the city or its edges, occasionally with Caleb downtown or Fay on
the outer seacoast, at odd times after daily ablutions scrupulously
attending to teeth and tongue, bathing his eyelids for blepharitis,
and swallowing the pills said to be appropriate for his mildly aging
condition. At meals he took vitamin supplements that were currently recommended for gaffers. When he occasionally watched his
DV screen he did not sit down, but limbered with fanciful calisthenics and dancing with small weighted dumbbells in hand. Yet

he couldn't help noticing that it was often difficult for him to separate pages that stuck together when he tried to turn them, notwithstanding that he could discern no other trembling in his fingers,
and that he always passed standard neurological tests by his "primary care" internist.

Finn still shrugged off what he regarded as more ominous
symptoms of his destined helplessness. For instance, Caleb had a
Greek-to-English lexicon, but because he could not find one for
English-to-Greek he sometime had recourse to Finn for guidance to
a word or phrase he wanted. It wasn't surprising that Finn's assistance was limited, considering the lifetime since he'd perused a
Classical text, and half that time since he'd been to Delphi, but his
efforts embarrassed him by calling inward attention not only to his
fading memory for familiar proper names but also—in suppressed
dismay—to his waning grasp for common English words on the tip
of his tongue, like stage-fright at his own thoughts. Sometimes he
felt like a juggler with words, always losing one or two to catch
another, no longer able to think by Aristotelian standards, his
verbal alacrity no better than an autumnal tree of rusty switches
which by themselves picked and chose a slow route through the
four-dimensional thesaurus of his experience. He comforted himself
with the flimsy speculation that his kind of memory loss was just a
reminder of normal longevity, seeing that the simple lengthening
of experience logically increased the number of things to be stored
in the brain, thus (as one reached maximum cranial capacity) displacing earlier mental inhabitants; or, more plausibly, with the
physiological reasoning that he was only temporarily weakened in
the neural *connection* to a word's residence, for always (he liked to
believe) the word came back to him in a flash, sooner or later, when
thinking of something else, or after applying rational mnemonic
searches such as alphabetized review of initial letters since, once
found, he always—almost always—recognized the word and knew
its meanings, even if he had to call upon his limited etymology for
analytical reminders. So the word was no more lost than a wandering child who reappears at the front door, as he remembered himself once to have been seventy-five years earlier, in Markland woods,
before his dawning sense of self-preservation! He also believed that
he had spent so much of his life reading or writing technical communications and other rational efforts at literal clarification that he
hadn't developed ordinary habits in even simple journalistic diction, not to mention the contemporary jargon or poetic locutions of

ordinary language. That was one of the several reasons that he was devoting the rest of his life to savoring the experience of art in history and fiction. He had bought a bundle of 4-by-6 note pads to take the place of moribund cerebral neurons, though he deplored their retardation of the time for actual reading and thinking.

But he had no such library as Fay's to look up whatever evaded his homespun lexicology. Worst of all, nothing he could deny or devise would long suppress the frightful fact that more and more often he was unable to entertain more than one idea at a time in his slowing mind. He was failing Aristotle's criterion of mental competence. Sometimes in the very formation of a mental (not to mention oral) sentence he could not remember the predicate of his subject without stopping to review his motive! And he was far too easily distracted even from his quotidian procedures in the kitchen! As he unenthusiastically divined himself he became aware that he was instinctively concealing from everybody his hitherto subliminal fear of losing dignity more than his lightfooted vigor, especially in the eyes of acquaintances who didn't know or remember that he was more than eighty!

Yet he was cheerfully far from despair because, like many before and after him who preferred rational illusion to irrational delusion, he had privately jubilated at the possibility of at least a preamble to his autobiography, which germinated from nothing else than Caleb's casual remark that experience should claim its own art. Personal experience was versatility's greatest reward, and versatility made possible the greatest experience. He was the only one in the world who could know the otherwise unconsolidated content of his extraordinary sea-chest in shipshape and Bristol fashion. *But it would be well not to mention the idea to anyone, sorting and pondering all alone, lest I find Pandora. Anyway, the value of that treasure would not be enhanced by an unseemly publishing contract in advance, or book-signing travel plans—at least not until I have in mind a chart of the scheme to justify my presumptuous self-satisfaction. The pressure of time must be my only excuse for the amateur's haste. This would be no ethical will to influence the lives of others, or simply to tell my tales and commemorate what I've witnessed in history as a particular life in the making, or of the people I've known who were other makers of it.*

The gift I'll make to posterity, if I can, should be a consolation of philosophy for technology's posterity who are naturally indifferent to "salvation" as well as everything else supernatural and will die unnoticed without asking themselves the ridiculous question "what does it all mean?" It may touch upon the meaning of meaning! The meaning of meaning is functional, the intention of intention; when that is love or sympathy—personal or social or zoological—in the very end. Various experiences may each be intentional or unintentional in the beginning; but, unless your life has been generally motivated by self-aggrandizing ambition, or unless you've devoted it to the common good as an intended benefactor of life in public or private service, your experience of life as a whole is not intentional—no matter what its actual outcome. But lack of meaning—lack of ultimate intention, whether or not consciously articulated—only proves the Third Law of Thermodynamics. Value an Sich is a Ding an Sich! At least so it is that I justify my life as a curiously traveling battleship man. In those terms just to know that of myself at the time of death is as good as having saved a soul!

Of course, though modest, the untutored philosopher knew he wasn't as pure as a technological saint, and could hardly be expected to pretend total self-effacement when questioned by an intimate friend about the service ribbons or four sleeve stripes visible on his uniform (at its apex) as one of two or more figures in photographic snapshots or official pictures he'd saved in memory of befriended scientists, professional colleagues, statesmen, or shipmates (even Philippino wardroom stewards), or by someone who merely visited men of war in navy yards, or who belonged to the Universe Club in D C, if not to the White House or Whitehall.

His memory was refreshed by what he found in his sea-chest. The only picture on his Dogtown "study-office" wall, among a few of the *U S S New Guernsey*, which he had loved both in the making and in the manning, was a press photo of President Trueheart sitting at his desk in a press conference during the nation's stormy outcry after he'd deftly relieved, for military insubordination, a very popular histrionic five-star national hero of his wartime Asian command in a subsequent smaller war. Finn, who happened to be standing in the background as an aide to the Secretary of Offense among a dozen admirals or generals, was not very tall but obviously more athletic than anyone else on the scene. He now explained to anyone who for the first time noticed that picture on his Dogtown wall that it ironically represented one of the most politically courageous decisions an Atlantean President had ever made, at little less than a constitutional crisis, when that majestically fake hero (already with boulevards named after him from coast to coast) had advisedly provoked and was still instigating, possibly to the point of a Protestican *coup d'état*, a tide of public opinion in the name of patriotism which still kept alive the sentimentality that had carried away even many of the civilian Commander-in-Chief's own Catholicrats—some who even now failed to remember the arrogant Generalissimo's long record of authoritarian arrogance. That modest President of all the people was wisely braver than his constituency.

So it was that the notion of experience as having its own art had inspired Finn with the implication that it could be in itself of some worth even without expository artists to celebrate it. That enlightenment of a self—seldom seen by the oldest of men—suggested that broad life-experience brought with it the great advantage in thought (and even expression) of being able to draw upon the broadest possibilities for metaphor when society's reason fails! *At least until outright dementia one can always remember analogical shapes and patterns, without recalling names faces places or causes! One can instantly associate flower with machine, or woman with event. Most of all, the aged have diachronistic superiority in discerning, when there are no heeded warnings or proofs, the parallels between past present and future, and not the least in recognizing political motives or other psychological types in public persons. I don't say that a great reservoir of new tropology is necessarily what I need in writing, for there are more than enough images and analogies at large; in old age (up to a point) the supply is reliable enough until senility to keep us in the running when half of them are forgotten!*

This is none of Caleb's business, but, after all, I think I'll see what Fay thinks about my incipient philosophy without giving Caleb credit for my new ambition.

Finn's tropology was not merely literary. It included fractional equations like $a/b=c/d$ [a is to b as c is to d] and the little sine waves that shape a big sine wave. In his mind's eye, diagrams were more fecund than figures on grounds! Analogical metaphor, he thought, wasn't just for poets or math students or draftsmen or oscilloscope electronics. *Mutatis mutandis* it was also availed for a mind's whole meaning of combined personal and vicarious experience, which at its best includes not only all manner of learning and doing but also (supremely) the written art of other people's experience, ancient and modern, foreign and domestic. Those were the things to study. . . .

So we come down to words! According to degree of experience and intelligence, without predicting the future and without communication to any other mind, one can challenge young geniuses sages savants and holy prophets by recognizing the shapes not only of one's own life but of all history at its various curves of suggestion. The words of open systems and subsystems that transcend their diagrams! Only words can express disastrous suboptimization in the very making, when economy and democracy are in as much peril as dinosaurs, drug-fixed body-builders, or peace. But also of organic super-systems when the bodies politic are intelligent enough to integrate self-interests for the common good! Caleb has some crotchets and eccentricities, and so have I, but typologically we understand each other and the people we admire, especially women like Fay, and critically alike see our society's hypersuboptimizing pharmacology and sentimentalist politics of the Stars and Stripes, however we may diverge in existential interests.

But what is experience more than just the assimilation of events? Much of my experience has been endowed or complicated with women yet responsible only as the experiments of a bachelor physiologist. As incentives they were of course essential also to most of my learning at every level and every distance of language or art, some as heroic as any man, usually sight unseen. But whether or not by touch, virtual or live, known by circumstances or inaccessible to my person in thought or deed, they've been perhaps my most valuable experience in present perspective—the best people, as Mary is said to have preached long after I met Moira. In no more than half the light of a single day I learned that she was the x in my equations, the last of which is x to the nth after forty-seven years of irregularly pertinent experience, the dance from modern to ballet yet the feeling I'd lacked in Caleb's advantage of me since his earliest childhood, where he and I may someday match as bookends.

This private and almost delirious state of gerontological self-examination—though discontinuous—made Finn lighthearted in mood with Caleb or Fay when face to face, sustaining confidence in his longevity notwithstanding the warning signs of ineluctable mental regression. Death be damned, it was the self-consciousness of experience that mattered! If the truth were told, he was training himself to jot down every snippet of such thoughts, and many of the words he wanted to keep at his immediate disposal. He pondered methods to use the blank backs of OHM punchcards to annotate and shuffle by hand, hoping that the symbols of language, if only in the act of writing them down, would add or renew elusive connections to his retrievable word-hoard, fishing up the predicates of subjects that were now all too often forgotten even as they were summoned.

He replaced his typewriter with a "word-processor", looking forward to the day when he could rely on some such device as the "personal computer" that was promised for the elite by futurists in Caleb's lines of work. But then in one of his dreams he was warned of the time it would take to learn how to take advantage of its speed and super-human capacities for information! There would be too much for a busy pensioner to learn—*like having to take over a four-engine jet plane with no more than a dim memory of piloting the stately old flying boats I earned my Navy wings in, which were meant for usually placid long-range patrolling (with co-pilot and a crew to help), supposedly a skill to enhance my profession as a designer of hulls or even as a commander of airmen at sea. I never got to use one in earnest; but flight school was no more wasted than many another collateral effort in what I now see was my innate ambition for versatility* an Sich—*at the expense of suboptimized achievement in specialties (even after the fortuitous assignments of war were over)—though without optimizing a lifetime's career that might have assisted the counterentropic struggle for the common good at its international level. Jack of all trades. "John in the morning, Jack at night!" as they say in Wales. Still, the Wings looked good on my lapel and in my service record. Nevertheless that experience with P B Ys was a godsend when I got the last of us aboard the one that a very brave young j.g. picked us up in. He rescued us in very dangerous waves five days after the* Atlindopolis *went down in poetic justice for having delivered the E-bomb to its island take-off base.*

That had been his most absolute experience in the War—between the first totally unexpected torpedo hit and the eventual rescue of the few floating survivors who happened to find Macdane the oil-blackened senior officer floating among themselves as the life-jacketed prey of sharks, still in fear of the lingering enemy submarine, trusting only in radio distress signals that they did not know were never sent, or in the initial air-searches from land that were never launched according to standard practice simply because of negligence by their own unreliably disciplined Navy base ashore. Now nearly forty years later it seemed to him that for all his athletic versatility in college—cross-country track, infield baseball, backfield football, boxing, fencing, and tennis—it was only his superiority as a 'Bega swimmer that proved to have been worth the time of practicing that precluded the extra courses he had wanted to cram into his Homeric undergraduate program—to make time for the supererogatory Naval Reserve Officer training that finally put him in harm's way during the War!

In short, he did not regret anything he'd chosen or been obliged to do in the program of his life; but in melancholy moods, like most other embattled veterans, he despaired of expressing the experience in its essence. Few Atlantean civilians without poetry were able to know what he had witnessed or suffered and survived

so short of horrible death—especially, besides the bloody dismem-
bered bodies on tilted decks in the dark, followed by the suddenly
truncated shrieks of men around him bobbing and soaking with
the swells of grease as they awaited in terror or resignation the
invisible jaws looking for bodies to snatch and drag out of the
world without instantly putting an end to the pain. But it had
been even worse to imagine the men already burnt alive in greater
torment, perhaps barely reaching an open deck from the engine
room with skin already peeled from their faces by superheated
steam. Was it any easier to compare the pain of officers and men in
the North Atlantic winter hemisphere with both legs so frozen
black that they had to be amputated by numb Hospital Corpsmen
the moment they were hauled aboard a rocking life raft even as
they rejoiced in being rescued many hours after a night alone
brushed by floating ice? Or Petrine priests publicly tortured to
death by Queen Elizabeth's?

Still, though no less than ever despising psychoanalysis and
most of the other indignities of guided soul-searching, Finn's aging
on the whole was rather cheerfully entertained by the self-findings
that Caleb provoked with his persistently exhibited admiration.
The elder was amused to find the envious younger technocrat
(who'd never commanded more than fifty subordinates) curiously
impressed by the temporary Captain's tour of duty immediately
after the War at leisurely well-served private quarters in consistent
tropical weather as absolute Commanding Officer of a flat mile-
long Pacific island and its calf, originally (and eventually) a nesting
habitat of guano producers. It was then nothing less than a naval
air station on an island manned by three hundred souls as a refueling airfield for the military transport service, but subsequently—as
cargo planes improved enough in range to dispense with Pacific
stepping stones (and anyway needing longer runways)—sacrificed
as long as possible to Zeus as a testing target for E-weapons.

Thus Finn reflected that versatility (nowadays continued for the
most part in literary and historical realms of vicarious experience)
was as satisfying as fame or categorical honors, and required less
therapy than did his reveille of brief untreated arthritis or the blepharitis that was kept under control and also forgotten till every
morning with a couple of over-the-counter eye drops. What did
cause some concern were his hitherto controllable cases of heart-
burn and "benign" prostate hyperplasia [B P H]. They were no
immediate threat to his essential faculties but they too might more

than metaphorically presage further deterioration of wit, judgment, and memory. He still walked vigorously, and occasionally swam in public, and performed some private calisthenics, but it was his eyes, now with reading glasses, that sustained the struggle against time for all the things to learn or love or pity until he could no longer overcome the vulgar instinct to quit training when there would be nothing more to hope for.

Meanwhile, aside from his intimate association on the one hand with Fay and on the other with Caleb, and his hobnobbing with Arthur Halymboyd, his principal solitary motive was to read or reread the works of Wellingborough Redburn, and to become (as far as longevity permitted) an amateur critic of the man himself, who'd briefly enlisted as a Navy sailor before the mast, whose schooling had lacked both Norumbega and Pale, the original writer *par excellence* whom he considered a greater representative, body and soul, of Atlantean originality, than any hero in his own experience: taro roots worth digging at the end of one's life. During the War he had glimpsed Redburn's beach of cruel escape from his savage Juliet. And Fayaway was now his pet name for the anthropological woman he teased, who, but for the prewar hostile Cipangese, would have beached in Mardi ten years earlier. For the sake of his own mnemonic infirmity he resolved to work out his own simplification of the laborious Index Rerum, the method that served so well the rhetorical purposes of the young Redburn's amazingly protective elder brother, without whom the junior writer probably would have remained merely the inexpressive and unknown Prometheus of opposition to Atlantean Transcendentalism.

The longer I live, as history continues, the more often I can regale myself with "That reminds me of . . . !" But I must learn to suppress such boasts every time someone remarks upon the news!

Without sensing this private exultation of Commander Finn Macdane, Caleb had devoted himself to Father Lancelot Duncannon's idea of *history as substance,* for it suggested the idea of *experience as substance*; but by this time there was apparently little hope for him to arouse the naval architect's curiosity about a priest's theodynamic branch of dromenology, an unrecognized component of what he called an anti-thetical loyalty to the thetical Church. Nor did Caleb have the nerve to risk Finn's quizzical smiles by broaching in earnest the metaphorically abstract symbolism of his own recto-triangular system. It was also too soon to broach his wishful conjectures about the Sumer-Attica axis (via Semitic sea-people), or related thought-experiments with his exhilaratingly spurious Gilgamesh. (Only Fay, he hoped, might appreciate such esoteric fancy, some day, God willing, when the far more important preoccupation of work on her own *summa* no longer forestalled her personally perfected sympathy with Caleb's irresponsible ideas.) He was already sensitive enough to Finn's unspoken opinion that his much younger admirer trusted too much to intuition, with more wit than judgment. But when ordinary conversation between Finn and Caleb failed to reach unanimity they were almost always able to communicate amiably with the higher abstractions of Universal Systems Theory.

24

SS PETER
AND PAUL

And a marvelous effect did it have, in
dissolving the crystallization of the brain,
leaving nothing but precious little drops of
good humor, beading round the bowl of the
cranium.

Redburn in *Mardi*

1.

June's Pentecost and Trinity Sunday having not been generally
observed for a century or more, the City's alloyed celebration of the
like for church and state had gradually gathered momentum for
this year's particularly recurring conjunction of these and other
fixed or moveable feasts. Nowadays even the Midsummer's solstice,
which began the extended octave of Gloucestermas, had lost all
traces of its hilltop bonfire, and other such solar or lunar revels, to
the Christian demands of the secular calendar, which no longer
included public recognition of John the Baptist's feast three days

later than the longest day of the year. For Petrine fisherfolk, who
ruled Dogtown's one famously combined sacred and profane fiesta,
the annual cycle of life began and ended with the last day of June,
as if the whole country's government and all businesses followed
fiscal suit.

The Lusitanians had begun the religious feast in their parish
but the Tuscan Trinacrians superposed their own European traditions with a later and larger fishing population, joined in the end
(at least as celebrants) by various other nationalities of seamen,
workers, and bourgeoisie. All manner of citizens shared the festivities especially when itinerant commercial carnivals drew peripheral
crowds to Sacrum Square, after an open-air block dance in front of
the lofty temporary altar, electrically lighted in several colors,
where Mass was also celebrated al fresco with the statue of Saint
Peter, who was borne on a shouldered litter to and from the
sequestered clubhouse and temporary reredos at the beginning and
end of his novena.

But, on the other hand, as Caleb had learned to appreciate, 20C
generations of Yankee magnates and their shrewd navigators at the
Mercator-Steelyard fish-packing headquarters had ruled their operations with a four-week thirteen-month fiscal year (synchronized
annually with the universal hebdomad weeks of solar derivation).
Approximately with the lunar ecclesiastical year they had conveniently planned the near-exhaustion of frozen-fish inventories
immediately after the pre-Lenten peak of sales, the easiest time of
year to close the books, shut down production, and perform maintenance procedures—when shipments were down to a trickle, like
the Little Harbor Beach creek at neap tide. Unfortunately this idiosyncratically efficient calendar could not be tolerated by the Demeter Mills conglomerate, which of course had to operate all its component parts on the same fiscal year according to a commonly
accepted pair of bookends. By the same token Caleb's computerized
Central Management System, much to the surprise of his internal
clientele, took the earth-quaking change in stride as the Yard
joined the consensus of organizations whose operational years began
with the first of July—including state and local governments as
well as educational institutions, the most pertinent of which was
the City of Dogtown itself—as the best moment for any financial
officer's least difficult introduction to the peculiarities of municipal
management in Vinland, the budget accordingly settled between
Mayor and Earls (and approved under the state's golden dome in

Botolph) for better or for worse, by the skin its teeth, which he would have to administer without responsibility for its practicable shortcomings.

On the feast day of Peter and Paul, however, the day before the fiscal-year closing on June 30, a special event took place that had no bearing on any saint for Dexter Keith the Mayor or his senior Navy friend Finn Macdane, who had both been keenly looking forward to it for nostalgic reasons. A band of old sailors or their sons and nautical friends from the Bay Area of Cornucopia had incorporated as a charitable organization to take over from the Greek navy as no longer useful one of the U S Navy's own long since decommissioned and diplomatically donated Neriads. She had first been worn out (like an old Dogtown fishing schooner converted for trade among the Azores, no less unsung than Napoleon's artillery horses) in the unparalleled sea war that these two Reserve officers had separately experienced without knowledge of each other. L S T 1066, one of a myriad Landing Ships Tank without the dignity of proper names, tied up at Dogtown's Coast Guard station. She was the only one of her sisters still alive, the last of her kind—relinquished by the Navy when she was still serviceable to penurious sovereignty in inland seas. Like a body donated to a medical school for revivification she was now in the hands of superannuated Atlantean veterans and their active sympathizers, the bravest and most technologically proficient of whom had then formed an ad hoc crew to weather several near-death experiences in open ocean, sailing her back to the Middle Atlantic coast of her native land where, at various unadvertised port facilities, thousands of hours of pro bono advice and labor by nautical antiquarians, male and female, young and old, had been gladly invested in welding, cutting, patching, sandblasting, steam cleaning, and painting, to restore her afterlife to a reasonable semblance of her defensive and aggressive prime. Much was still left to do in the interest especially of below-deck authenticity, but she was now fully seaworthy and sufficiently equipped with the latest navigational and safety devices to start a protracted public tour wherever her offer was welcomed from East Coast to West Coast between venerably enthusiastic Dogtown and permanent mooring somewhere yet to be determined on the shores of Golden Horn Bay, preferably Babylon Oaks—assuming that she would be able to earn her way on the nostalgia or curiosity of men women and children in a generation that seemed almost as distant from her obsolescence as the replica of a Viking long ship.

But her operating expenses depended upon the turnover of pertinent publications and souvenirs in the shop that also collected alms. It was so stuffed with merchandise and picture books that Dexter Keith could hardly recognize the compartment as his junior place in the original wardroom. Dogtown was chosen as one of her first ports-of-call because it was known that many fishermen had served in various of her long-gone sister ships in the amphibious forces, Atlantean, Mediterranean, and Pacific. Perhaps the 1066 alone had weathered forty years of postwar vicissitude because she hadn't been sent with a few of her already obsolete sisters to any of the Offence Department's hostilities thereafter. Anyway, she was said to have been one of those last assembled and launched broadside into a Midwest river, a year or two before the amphibious forces in Europe were released to augment those intended to finish off the Pacific Theater with an invasion of Cipango. It was necessary to sprinkle cadres of experienced L S T sailors from those earlier invasions to guide and steady the newer and younger crews, especially because many of the junior officers known as "ninety-day wonders" had had no more than three months of shore training in seamanship navigation gunnery and even scantier engineering, having previously qualified for commissions by little more than a few years of indifferently respected college education. Dexter Keith had earned a solid degree in Montvert, but he was one of these half-educated freshmen as far as naval sciences were concerned. Thereafter he simply happened to be dubbed the Communications Officer of this nearly indistinguishable little ship in this very successful wartime class.

That astonishing coincidence was beyond the dreams of any promoter among the civilian enthusiasts who manned this all-steel ghost of a "Large Slow Target" as she slipped into Dogtown's inner harbor to meet relays of swarming Cape Gloucester boarders with less than a week's notice. Furthermore, as it was later discovered, more than a dozen in the volunteer crew—and more than that among its greeters—were veteran enlisted men of the 1066's beach-landing sisterhood, genetic clones of a design to which the Mayor's senior friend had contributed some electrical engineering advice at the drawing-board stage when he happened to have been on battleship task at the Bureau of Ships in Washington.

What grand capital warship has ever held such a significant reunion with such a proportional sample of human attachments to its few quasi-siblings, when the mayor of a famous city led the official welcome? At the start of a public trek back to its destination it was a serendipitous event to enter into the 1066's logbook and haply initiate for national publicity and sales from the ship's ever-normal granary of mementos. Like the tail of a comet, for half a week after the L S T had cast off for southerly coasting to the West, Belle Cingani at the *Nous* made sure that Dexter Keith, the tall dark and handsome giant of Lilliput Hall on the modest acropolis, was written up and photographed with the Commander, our new city-center marooner, as an important figure in Washington's W W 2 Navy.

Aboard the little ship at its mooring, in private conversation with the civilian skipper (who had been a Chief Quartermaster in the Navy on greater ships in lesser wars), together with his even younger mates, Dexter, accompanied by Finn, who was embarrassed by his unintentional part in the *Nous*'s publicity, said all he could to divert this public attention to the W W 2 matters of design and mass production that had distinguished the L S Ts themselves as a heroic class—like Dogtown's former fishing schooners less worthy only than the men who'd sailed them.

Not a word did Finn think of speaking for the business bonanza suddenly delighting the Chamber of Commerce. This battered ship's own people (men and women), as well as the impromptu crowd attracted from all over Cape Gloucester, spent plenty of money ashore after visiting hours were over, unexpectedly enjoying the charm of their busy little port. Finn was glad to notice Dexter's refusal to exploit the political advantage of his position as the official representative of extraordinary nautical patriotism, which was particularly marked in this little city of famous fishermen, who in war never hesitated to join a dangerous Navy needing their seamanship, especially in the war against submarines.

Crammed into an L S T compartment with its major officers, Dexter and Finn both asked many questions about the crew and the few passengers who, like gypsies or dispossessed Vikings, were carried aboard on this East Coast stint of the mendicant cruise. Cape Gloucester was probably the most sympathetic port-of-call between the beginning and end of the voyage, which was tentatively planned for a year or more of financial improvisation, with continually changing personae, actors or supercargoes, save for the cadre of devoted mariners.

Dogtown's praiseworthy news for the national wire services was all the more remarkable in that the pick-up crew from Cornucopia had crossed the Atlantic by air to rescue the rusty ship from the scrap yards of the Greek navy, to which it was donated for a posthumous decade of active service among our European allies—long after it had been originally decommissioned and dissolved by the U S Navy at a floating graveyard in the northern reaches of Golden Horn Bay for rehabilitation in case of a third world war before new ships and tactics could be commissioned. Yet not until on the shore of Attica, not far from Athens, had she been dignified with her only proper name *Argo*, by these Argonauts who'd come from Atlantis by a plane-load to accept and man the obsolete but resuscitated and self-serving gift from Uncle Sam, Greece's ally in resistance to Communism. She had then been sailed back to Atlantis, this time in an exceedingly aged shell full of old and young salts, nautical mechanics, electricians, and electronic navigators, who patched her up as best they might, removing many of the Greek alterations found inside the hull, and bravely navigated her back at more than a little peril in storms without having renovated her steering gear. After further repairs and repainting in Magdalene's Mother of God Bay, hard by New Port Newce, they had brought her up the coast to Vinland, aiming to reverse direction and begin their patriotic publicity tour of hospitable ports down the eastern shore of Atlantis until, once more through the Canal, up the Pacific's east to her mortuary mooring as a floating museum in the Londonbridge estuary.

That it was that after public visiting hours at the Coast Guard station the Mayor and his distinguished guest, Finn Macdane, the naval constructor and battleship man, found themselves invited to simple chow and common beer in a still-unredecorated compartment that brooked no social distinction between officers and men, for quiet discussion of the naval war, the varieties of amphibious craft cargoes, and anecdotal particulars of the many differing services performed by numbers of these intensely short-lived sisters they happened to have known, or known of, notably those old enough to have been embattled in both Theaters of the war, especially on beaches.

That privileged confabulation on the second day did not break up until after midnight, hardly eight hours before the 1066 was to cast off like a hollow whale in pursuit of broader fame, having well profited at Gloucestermas from admission fees and souvenir sales at the fiesta of what was once said to be the greatest fishing port in the world, regretting that they hadn't scheduled more time with such friendly and generous people, even those too old or infirm to take the guided tours up or down from the long open deck surveyed from the forward bulkhead of the conning tower, namely the bridge. The same gnarled but beefy whiter-haired veteran who'd been the principal guide of visitors, a loud-voiced former First Class Boatswain professing to have been one of those classic L S T sailors who'd never conformed to the Navy's "chickenshit" regulations but who in retirement from a civilian tugboat job had learned the navigation skills of a certified first mate in the legitimate merchant marine, bossed the motley crew next morning in casting off from the especially sympathetic Coast Guardsmen with spontaneous cries of "Buona fiesta" and "Viva San Pietro!". Most of the departing sailors (including a couple of middleaged wives) had had a late evening ashore at the carnival in its crowded candy village of garish amusements and assorted Tuscan refreshments, while Dexter and Finn were still immersed in fellowship as the only two commissioned officers (and therefore authentic scholars) in the original victorious War—though in Finn's case aboard ships profoundly unlike this vessel in speed, weight, size, safety, function, and investment (more like a metropolis than a village). The differences in former rank were ostensibly disregarded, but on all counts (save L S T adventures) he was deferred to, not only as expert in history and technology but also as the markedly senior guest of His Honor the Mayor, himself the amiable regent of Dogtown who proudly escorted the old man over whom he towered, but who had some war stories of his own, albeit as no more than an untested junior L S T officer toward and after the end of the "Pacific war", without having experienced the heat of set-piece battle but weathering many perilous months of danger in preparation for the worst, slated for the bloodiest of all history's beachings, which was averted only in the nick of time by the air power of redundant E-Bombs.

But that shabby little refectory, whose steel bulkheads and crannied angles still betrayed the rust beneath the slaps and dabs of white paint to which the Greeks (or indeed their subsequently anxious repossessors) contributed, had been altered or maintained by partitioning the original gift. On many inessentially weathered surfaces outside—such as deck gear or gun mounts—even the latest gray paint was inconspicuously flaking or peeling for lack of labor or money. But the ship's great empty womb, like a basketball court with clamshell-shaped portals closed at the bow, still looked and smelled ever-ready as a garage for the squat or lofty

bulk of rolling cargo, whether for immediate battle, for landing
construction materials, or simply for the transport of troops and
supplies. Once it had served as a windowless campground for hundreds of Cipangese prisoners repatriating from Mardi after hostilities were over.

So Dexter and Finn had both been welcomed to an impromptu
confabulation of special brothers who'd had their fill of revels and
blessings and were delighted with their opportunity to learn what
ordinary military mariners never knew about the origin of things
they operated, seeing that Finn, as a sometime Naval Constructor,
had often been consulted on certain engineering problems by his
close friend the chief civilian designer at the Bureau of Ships who
(not Winston Churchill said to be the conceiver himself) had made
practicable with freehand sketches solutions to most of the major
problems entailed in a new concept of naval architecture designed
to meet the demands of W S C and F D R, both of them proud
"naval persons" by background. Finn's then superior Constructor at
the Bureau of Ships, who was ordinarily preoccupied with capital
ships, had consulted the young Ned Ellsworth (now a Captain),
Finn's personal friend and technological colleague, whom he'd
admired (and still did) as the hard-driving genius, later famous for
having personally led to salvatory success, sometimes under fire,
creatively solving many nautical problems as the world's preeminent salvager of submarines, ships, and docks—deservedly popular
as a writer of lucidly exciting fiction relative to his experience as a
deep-sea rescue diver and surgical doctor of ships—to the chagrin
of many in the officer corps who despised him as a Jew, if not
merely as a tactless ego-eccentric maniac who'd been number one in
his class at the Naval Academy.

How can versatility trump a man like that? If that hero hadn't
been protected by the admiral who finally became Chief of Naval
Operations, and by certain influential members of Congress,
Ellsworth would never have been promoted at all, even after being
recalled from retirement to repair several unprecedented disasters
and urgently summoned back into service more than once, when
there was no one to match him in brain and stamina as a leader of
men in engineering emergencies. To this day Finn had kept in
touch with his old technological friend, who had finally been honored by a tardily grateful Navy as a Rear Admiral emeritus, all but
post mortem, thanks in part to the urging of Finn's own unofficial
choice as historian and laureate, only latterly retired to the Reserve

as full Admiral. Ellsworth's reputation had greatly benefitted from the unexceptionable opinion of that indefatigable scholar— returned after the War to his place in the Norumbega faculty— who had benefitted over the years from technical advice about ships and electricity from Finn himself, whose father on the faculty of Hawthorne College in earlier days had been a lifelong professor, often visited during Markland vacations. To Finn's fleeting new friends in dungarees and peaked caps he of course said nothing about those personal interconnections, and he had never said much more of them to Dexter; but they were vividly brought to mind and cherished by Caleb, an uncommon reader without the benefit of such social relationships, to be counted for vicarious experience.

Huddled in that bare and windowless little L S T cabin full of abhorrent tobacco smoke, Finn, scarcely noticed in the five-course banquet of his wandering mind, bemused by the concatenated memories touched off in the narrowed conversation of rather commonplace male nostalgia, notwithstanding its remarkable coincidences—was all at once moonstruck, as if in transcendental afflatus, by the significance for *himself* of the ethical-will idea that had suddenly captivated Arthur Halymboyd, a fellow war veteran, at an age shorter by a year than his own. It was suddenly clear, existentially obvious, that the only way to prevent the world's absolute loss of one's cerebral treasure—one's uniquely integrated experience in an extraordinary lifetime, all at once in the instantaneously unconscionable loss of one's only life—was to write whatever could be expressed before too late, especially that which no one else had ever shared in his perspective. For his personal history to survive as more than an ordinary autographic public memoir it was not necessary to have it printed and distributed, or accidentally searched posthumously by a scholar of 20C technology history. *Even if cremated, the solid geometry of an unfleshed skull would have sufficed to make Hamlet sniff the cavity as a reliquary of information in my lingering dispute with entropy!*

But mere information, I'm afraid. Not a cell in my body is Shakespearean. That's the rub: even if I filled a time capsule of ethical will for the Norumbega Library it would be too literal. It's too late to reform my ingrained habits of writing to clarify—officially, or at best journalistically, too rationally for the negative capability required to express the feelings of experience before they expire absolutely. Nor is there any hope to be alive and alert long enough with Fay (alive and alert with her own definitely important public contribution to culture) to convey to her whatever it is that I seem to be hoping to say about the quintessence of the last experience per se? —But of course a reader or two is devoutly to be wished, just for the thrill of having made a little contribution to the dust in posterity's consciousness, if only at my penultimate instant to wonder if another skull will someday take interest in my delinquent coherence. —Come what may, I must stay alive long enough to observe this counterentropic responsibility of the ego! My late start is a sprint with weakened faculties. I already begin to forget common nouns as well as proper ones. My Fayaway is no younger, but she does not suffer dizzy spells, she's never lightheaded or confused in her own kitchen, and her experience, even though feminine, even though totally civilian, even though more vicarious, is broader than mine, and certainly more important to posterity by virtue of her learning in a Venn diagram of spheres far more numerous than mine. There are her children to be left behind, and a multiplying heritage of intellectual colleagues and students around the world. I have neither time nor craft to write a book, nor the will to trifle with acceptable articles of professional opinion, nor the urge to educate anyone in anything but government—and that's too democratic for an "elitist" like me to influence with more than one vote on behalf of the common good. Tessa knows how to do that more effectively than any of the rest of us. . . .

Experience—not just memory and thought— is exclusively personal, no matter how much distilled from what's abstract, technical, theoretical, social, or historical—but surely worth some sort of living perpetuation even when it's worth no more than the thought of having put a particular life to its test. Isn't mine of value only for my appreciation of the people I have known, whether famous, infamous, quietly prophetic, or simply clever and generally ignored. So perhaps at worst my lucubrations might be worth something to Fay, or Fay's intellectual heir, whose intelligence and influence may benefit as my characteristics entail. After all, seeing that the rest of humanity, especially its female moiety, lacks my experience, it should be the job of a cultural anthropologist to make room (aside from her legal estate) for peculiarities without being psychoanalysed—executed simply, by a private letter!

But how can I discuss what I have in mind without interrupting her anthropological amendments to scientific philosophy that we believe to be a truly counterentropic development of cultural evolution unless I lure her at last, if only for a few weeks, to the Mardi that she and her husband's crew were warded off by the Cipangese before the actual war started! —Speaking of experience that isn't mine, that's hers, in no more than a topsail schooner out of Dogtown! —Which reminds me that I have been in all but seventy-five degrees of meridians in the northern hemisphere though it hap-

pened that even in the War I never got below the equator. Maybe I should propose marriage—eloping without public announcement, impatient for that honeymoon! . . . Then I could reasonably plan my ethical will!

—At this age how could I even want to produce a narrative autobiography, with an index methodical enough to make it of interest to educated browsers? I'm probably on the verge of senility and perhaps can no longer distinguish significant ideas from what were accidental thoughts about apparent cause and effect; or otherwise inconsequential in my allotment of life, but taking as much time to write as I'd rather spend re-reading Dante's idea of counterentropic comedy. Maybe technology served me only as an incentive not to lapse, like most other men of exceptional good fortune, into the many effortless pleasures of healthy unimbecile longevity, with no sense of incompletion and no anticipation of extinction at the end—which of course is unimaginable anyway. —I'd have to forego most of the reading or re-reading that has awaited my exciting leisure—life's time that I haven't had in which to finish my liberal education, without which my experiential substance is deprived of its fully inferential expansion into the greater experience of myriad men and women.

What in literature would do that best for an old man with no time to waste for redundancy or lightweight specific gravity? Caleb, imagining himself thirty years ahead, suggests, as obvious, Shakespeare; as less obvious and new to me, the oeuvre of Yeats; and as a world of the more imaginable experience that always intrigues me with Redburn's samples of it: the Analects of Babbalanja as the beginning of an always deeper dive. Fay's list defers to his, but it's too daunting at this late date to fill the yawning philosophical gap in my liberal education. Yet they both have listened to me! Quid pro quo! At least we are now as harmonized at the metaphorical level as a three-leaf clover in accepting the concepts of Ludwig von Denthey that I have promulgated to them, though in the process I had to learn a few words, and a page or two of modern metaphysics, when I came to Dogtown and caught myself reflecting on the ultimate thermodynamics of technical systems. . . .

. . . Thus for the first time, after his several conversations with Arthur Halymboyd about "ethical wills", Finn was struck with the obvious idea that the only way to prevent the world's absolute loss of one's putatively absolute experience at the instant of death was to write a fragmented memoir ahead of time as his ethical will, not for printing and distribution but for his private transaction with the future of time that required very little exegesis regarding the fungibles in his last will and testament. Rather it was to be a *communication* to those in the part of his orthodox Markland legacy that belonged in Dogtown as of the essence in his valediction. *In principle, my whole unique past, including whatever I have known, done, learned, remembered, guessed, or felt, will no longer satisfy the subjective component of what I've called experience—not even as strands of feeling of what I've forgotten! —If the Royal Navy was ingenious enough to wind a red thread into the core of all its cordage for hundreds of years just to prove Royalty's legal possession—then, in my case, in whose reading list shall I invest my twine before it's snipped? This will be a very late start in economy, especially as the last in an old family name, thanks to all the marriages in my dissipating lineage. If only Fay and I were as young as Mardi's Fayaway to plant in Vinland! —Can I live long enough, after all, to write articles of interest to historians, not of myself but of the people I've escaped? There at least might lie a journalistic incentive to take up the robust labor of a quill, and by sheer momentum stretch the limits of unimbecilic longevity—provided that I'd be willing to give up most of the reading I have in mind to extend exponentially the power of experience I hope to discover just for the love of life!*

Meanwhile Dexter the Mayor in their ad hoc museum kept alive the genial reminiscences like a charming self-effacing god with plenty of laughs; but he never mentioned what might have been the most fascinating event among all the far more important or typical anecdotes exchanged by L S T veterans: a bizarre manslaughtering 1945 duel by two 1066 sailors with bayonets in the otherwise empty garage that served as payload space in this very ship while she was anchored in the somber lagoon of Mardi awaiting the load of Cipangese prisoners and their open-air cauldrons of rice for return to Wakayama several months after the Emperor's surrender. That night he himself, now the Chiron of Ibicity Hall, had been a shaken young Officer of the Deck, the authority-of-first-response pretending to be equal to the shock until his First Lieutenant took over. The killer was 1066's blatantly muscular brute, a sometime third-class Gunner's Mate born with the face of a Greek god.

2.

The seine boat races and the greasy pole-climbing-and-falling contest were over, and so was the climactic Blessing of the Fleet by the Archbishop up from St Botolph with full canonicals, following and preceding the days and nights of the Mass in Sacrum Square with its statue-bearing processions of introit and withdrawal, where the loud flood-lighted block dance had taken place as introduction to these central celebrations of the usual solar Gloucestermas within this year's Greater Gloucestermas for sun and moon together, absorbing as its lunar harbinger the utmost movable limit of the ecclesiastical feast known either as Whitsuntide or Pentecost to commemorate the foundation of the Church (as well as almost unbeknownst to Christians in Dogtown the Feast of Weeks after Passover). The religious observations were over; the secular fireworks of the city scintillations, alow and aloft, were awaited a few days hence, when Gloucestermas was also to reach its highest distinction in celebrating with all Atlantis and millions of military and civilian expatriates its competitive zenith on the Fourth of July, when the whole sky of the outer harbor would be tented with a cinematic dome of contrasting colors and shapes for the best part of an hour, culminating in a crescendo that sends skyward in terror all the resident seabirds that have innocently trusted the city's normal nocturnal noises.

Thus from beginning to end, with all the other elements of more than a gaudy fortnight, the emotional Petrine octave (or novena) extended its generously heterodox embrace to Dogtown's democratic festivity for a patriotic community rejoicing in its Independence of a king. It therefore embraced, though it did not represent, the self-serving Pauline spirit that had founded and still dominated the body politic of Atlantean culture insofar as it imbued or reflected its hyper-hybrid religious miscegenations, Cans and Crats alike. Here the whole Cape's common good was also represented in the individual clouds of families and clans who centrifuged themselves in the outer swirls of the Petrine Mass. Most of these spectators or players would have amicably attended any Lusitanian or Trinacrian celebration. The fiesta's clothing in ubiquitous Stars and Stripes—flying or worn in unintentional desecration of official patriotic ornament that especially irritated the ritualistic orthodoxy of Commander Macdane—testified to the civic scene's melting pot as the admixture of non-Papist theism, deism, agnosticism, and atheism under red white and blue banners according to the degree in which they differed from the unified cult of Saint Peter in actually honoring his statue. As in national Atlantean politics, religious roots and concepts had been so confused or distorted in transfiguration, back and forth between theology and politics, or between faith and science, that few of the clergy knew enough of historical philosophy to educate citizens about how their votes or donations ultimately contributed to freedom or organization. For purposes of Dogtown discussion, let the term "Pauline" represent most of what was not simply Petrine in the western world, stemming from unreliably amorphous ideas of freedom with the suboptimized best of intentions, à la Hector Thoreau.

However, on the last day of the fiscal year, before a late afternoon meditative retreat into the "alternative state of consciousness" usually attainable in Contemplative Nullification, at a time across the inner harbor in the precinct of Sacrum Square when the most sociable citizens of Dogtown were gathering for the night's solemn recessional parade of Saint Peter around the loop of the Casbah on a litter shouldered by fishermen, the climactic torch-lighted return to rest in the Trinacrian clubhouse that bore his holy name, Caleb found himself accosted on Mother's Neck by a revenant from the dawn of his manhood. On this side of the inner harbor people less than faithful to Rome were still at home getting ready to join the sun in winding down the midsummer superfortnight of games and masques in less traditional fashion, intending to cool off among the shops and bistros of what once deserved the fame of East Harbor's art colony, among which the small-scale Starboard Gangway was still shuttered for the day against its particular clientele of eaters and drinkers.

But he should have known better if he wanted a better time and place to brood about the shock that he knew was before him two days hence, no matter how imaginatively he girded his loins in anticipation of brutal extroversion after some stolen years of unremunerative liberty. It had been painful enough once a week to force upon himself the vital interruption of introverted struggles and tranquil satisfactions by driving to the supermarket or food cooperative (sometimes stopping at a liquor locker) merely to remain a frugal hermit, quite apart from the nagging necessity of irregular laundry and other vulgar A D L, to say nothing of the less objectional but more time-consuming routines of his crude cuisine.

The emergent recluse thus dreaded his actual commitment to what the Mayor privately called "Lilliput Hall on the Acropolis", now announced to and by Belle as the *Nous*'s clarion, much to her personal glee. She had immediately phoned Caleb to assure him that the paper would treat him with due respect and suspicion, but warning him that she and her reporters would monitor his office to the negligible degree in which its readers gave a damn about his arcane performance as the City's backstage bureaucrat, while privately advising him that certain pompous arrogant or narrow-minded Earls would do their best to make his innovations difficult, some of them with spies nominally under his command, including those in virtual sinecures protected by Civil Service law, all of whom seemed to have been aware of Dexter Keith's decision to hire Caleb before Caleb himself was!

"Don't expect anyone to understand the importance of what you long ago did at the Yard." she had said. "It's the city's largest industry but its office building might as well be a castle in the air as far as local government is concerned. To ordinary citizens Mercator-Steelyard means boats, fish, freezer, industrial ovens, packing lines, and gypsy trucks—not much else. They don't even know who owns the company now! It's a fixture in the economy that they take for granted as immemorial. . . ."

Only a few minutes before leaving Apostle's Dock to calm himself on a ruminating circuit of nearly daily habit, Caleb had been informed by the Mayor himself on the phone that the risky die was cast. Dexter Keith had never doubted that he wanted Caleb on the job as his executive officer. The announced decision had been a matter of political tactics in overcoming what obviously would be the skepticism of an individualistic plurality in Earldom that typically constituted his variable "non-partisan" opposition, some of them in the old guard and full of themselves as canny politicians by virtue of their infinite personal connections with the native electorate even unto the third generation, but also two young turks who prided themselves on their "across the Gut" experience in what they called modern business methods. This opinionated minority interpreted the Charter narrowly in holding its specification that the office be occupied by someone with both experience in municipal management and a related Master's Degree from some institution. But Dexter was banking on the liberal codicil "or the equivalent thereof".

His politic decision also was to postpone the battle for a "permanent confirmation" of Caleb's appointment by making a mayoral "ninety-day interim appointment", as permitted by the Charter without the Board's objection, lest the city's business be interrupted by a difficult recruiting search on the mainland at such a stupidly low salary. Above all Dexter wanted to avoid a battle royal about anyone he didn't ask for from the island's shallow pool of politically touted incompetents based on local consanguinity.

It wasn't lost on Caleb, though still innocent of strings that were pulled behind the scene in the Hall, that Dexter was deliberately putting at risk his success as a re-electable mayor in less than two years by demonstrating his confidence in an almost unknown "efficiency expert" as a systematic reformer of the Dickensian city government that was supposed to have been sufficiently reformed by the new city constitution under which the office of a "weak" mayor, chosen from its own Board, was replaced by a directly elected "strong" mayor, eliminating the "professional City Manager" previously hired by the Earls as their autonomous C E O. But the new popularly elected mayor was already weakened politically for having disastrously misjudged the curriculum vitae of a stupid "professionally experienced municipal administrator" commuting from the town of Newessexport until fired (to everyone's relief) after six months of feckless floundering in aversion to every purpose or procedure that he hadn't previously learned by rote in townships (not cities) under very different local constitutions.

With a reputation based solely on little-known functions in private business, Caleb (who had previously paid little attention to city politics) would have three months to learn what he had to know about the Commonwealth's general municipal law, as well as Dogtown's self-designed new charter (a well-intentioned but managerially naive construction of "checks and balances"), along with its dusty heritage of uncodified city ordinances and unwritten but inflexible administrative habits. Caleb now feared that he had been inadequately prepared for the vexations of custom, public opinion, and petty personal interests in a government of Dogtown's people for its people and by its people. He must appreciate the talents and goodwill as well as the incapacities of various complacent or jealous city officials acting by ordinance or custom under divided or ambiguous authority, but also, worst of all, face the burden of many uninteresting and festering responsibilities of a general manager (especially when expected to respond to complaints directly from Earls or individual constituents about such boring subjects as taxes and potholes). When one is overworked and understaffed with critical or progressive fundamentals, what is the best manner in which to ward off time-consuming trivialities that are of personal concern to individual citizens or their enemies? Despite Dexter's best efforts to absorb or divert their attention from his engine room, that administrator was bound to answer the phone call of any voter or voter's representative who couldn't be put off or mollified by a harried secretary when His Honor was away from the office. And how can an unelected bureaucrat earn the trust of at least a majority in the augustly discordant Board of Earldermen without attending at least a few of their long tedious or unruly meetings late into the night when they have nothing on the agenda that has much to do with his functional management?

Caleb's tardy patriotic motives would thus be limited to his prospects in the inconspicuous bailiwick of municipal administration that determines the synergy of departments, largely as measured in financial terms. Without that genuine hope in mind the job of implementing highly resisted changes—above all in organization (at least where local "checks and balances" are officially abused)—would have been intolerable. According to the gentlemen's agreement with Dexter, Caleb's first willful objective was a logical revamping of the piecemeal budget, and thereto the interdepartmental organization itself, so that future budgets could be rationally created with the horse before the cart and correspond to the *actual* performance of the City's services. His second major project was to plan a centralized computer system, and perhaps actually begin its installation if he, with the assistance of the Mayor and his political allies, could persuade the legislative body to authorize an appropriation or other funding to pay for the "automation" that would eventually save administrative costs many times over, to the benefit of all operations, ad infinitum!

But Caleb's covenant with Dexter made it clear that in return for the trust placed in his administrative navigation under His Honor's shield in all appropriate aspects of an adjuvant's detailed responsibility for the efficiency of apparatus, he must not embarrass or question any of the mayoral policies or political assessments without specific authorization. Having been educated and first employed as an architect, for many years as a city planner, Dexter had been occupied with land use, industrial development, public health, public works, public safety, educational finance, social justice, taxation, and other external civic affairs; and these remained the communal preoccupations of his psyche. But what Caleb most admired in his new boss was an ultimate purpose that could never be overt in the politics of Atlantean democracy: cultivation of all the arts as a flowering of the common good. It was his prior knowledge of Dexter's history that would anchor Caleb's cooperation with

the charming handsome giant who had never distrusted their
friendship since serving as city planner in Dogtown and elsewhere.
This mayor would have been far less confident in his judgment of
men if he had had to understand that petty details of method and
procedure, as well as of minor inventions in facilitation, were as
necessary for the systemic integration of nearly autonomous administrative entities as were detail drawings specifications and bid-
forms for all levels of contracting in public architectural projects—
all of which especially required enormous personal time when a
designer has no staff assistance! Without the prospective ends of
these means Caleb would rather have served as a docile Ion sweeping Delphi's steps and driving birds away from its temple doors
merely to earn his Social Security after retirement.

3.

. . . Assuming that Lilian Cloud-Algo would not yet have
arrived to open her Starboard Gangway, or else would already be
far too busy in her sunken kitchen helping the chef prepare for the
holiday evening's usual crowd (more or less Pauline schismatics by
default, assimilated Jews, or liberal Petrines, if not atheists) to
notice the passing feet of an old boyfriend among those of a few
wandering pilgrims who were naively attracted by the neighboring art-shops or simply avoiding the gaudy festivities across the
harbor, Caleb had passed that select cookhouse (as well as two
larger seasonal restaurants half abuzz with daytime drinkers) and
was about to enter the open shipyard on the tip of Mother's Neck
to inspect in detail the two boats whose sterns he'd seen lofted
high and dry on the marine railways directly across the mouth of
the cove from his own windows. One of them was a steel dragger
painted the usual black and green; the other, unfamiliar, a sturdy
black and red tugboat too large to be stationed at Dogtown, no
doubt sent up or down the coast from one of the big seaports for
economical overhaul, whose name and origin he hoped to read
from the wharf that supported the yard's portable machinery, now
idle, which sandblasted, steam-cleaned, or painted such hulls,
sometimes raising ladders for the men who overhauled conditions
from the deck above.

"Hello, Mister City Manager!" came an unhurried voice, soft
contralto, from a mouth not much lower than his own.

He turned to see the apparition: a comely rather plump woman, bleached-blonde, who looked active and friendly at an attractive age anywhere between fifty and sixty, whose eyes were artificially accentuated by black trim, with lips painted as crimson as a hostess in devilvision.

"What did you say?" was his temporizing reply to her quizzical expression. She seemed to be expecting recognition, probably with reciprocating intelligence. At this startling stage of regressive metamorphosis the shell of his introversion was cracked by almost any introduction, as if already held to public accountability.

"Can't I talk to you for a few minutes? I'm on the Administration and Finance Committee. I don't mean to jump the gunnery, but I may not get the chance after everyone knows you're in Publicity Hall." She paused with a doubtful smile, as if gazing at his face she might have made an impossible mistake. "I'm now the Earl of Ward 5 Liberty, which you can guess is not the kind of place I was used to. Most people down here at the Harbor don't even know my name, because this is only my second term on the Board." Again a pause, puzzled but still smiling. "Well then, I'm Mrs Fox-Argent." She offered her hand, which was firm, spangled at the wrist. Her brown eyes were frank, but her brows and lips now flickered with confident amusement, suggesting that he should understand some ellipsis in her communication. "I hear you've become a commuter expert. Automatic conformation and stuff like that."

"I'm not exactly an expert in anything except paperwork. I'm just an old bureaucrat from what nowadays they call the private sector. It will take me a while to get the hang of things up on the hill. I'm glad to meet you, but I'm not in office yet." *Very, very vaguely—long ago—had he so gently heard lines like that, but not from a perfumed stage.*

"You will be in a couple of days." She laughed. "I can already give you a few tips!"

Caleb hoped not to disengage himself too clumsily from this curious impertinence. It was a warning against endless embarrassments before him until he was established as an authoritative leader. But how does an unclassed gentleman ever deal with presumptuous commoners in the seat of power? It seemed a lifetime since he had lived long enough in Dogtown, especially as a former tenant of the mayor's family—even before he was comfortably obscure at the Yard—to be nervously aware that some of the citizens felt free to exercise freedom of speech with a city's officials, as

if Dogtown were still run by the immediate unpaid democracy of
Colonial town meetings. His protector the Mayor had promised
that in his specific capacity as chief executive, the elected representative of all the sovereign people, he would personally handle
public relations, as well as the political negotiations with the
coequal legislature, save only when his administrator might be particularly requested to opine or explain technical matters of purely
managerial nature. Dexter compared Caleb's position to that of the
chief executive officer in a Navy ship, who has no formal contact
with the higher hierarchy of its flotilla.

The lady persisted with her guessing game. "We hope you'll
show up at our weekly Committee meetings more than the first
and last guy did under the new Magna Carta. He said he already
had a full-time job and did not expect to work overtime at night. I
could sympathize with that, but he was a ninny-goat to say so. I
summarize that you won't blab like that. I'll do my best to exculpate you."

Caleb's heart continued to sink at the prospect of being so
direly accessible to the people's familiar representatives. Having
been accustomed to the nearly total secrecy of corporate business
affairs, he was hardly prepared for the impediments to efficient
management that were entailed by the law that all but personnel
and labor negotiations in city government were public in principle.
Still, in order to do his bureaucratic work with any measure of
effect, he hoped that matters of purely internal administration
(aside from the reasoning of reality-tax Assessors) were traditionally
shielded from inspection and objection as too arcane for common-
folk, at least as the purely technical methodology of public business, unless or until they were legally stipulated in formal reports,
or specifically investigated by some committee of the Board according to due process or rules of order in open meetings. Thus to some
extent he would soon be sympathizing with his ex officio enemy
the City Auditor who enjoyed no rational Generally Accepted
Accounting Principles to rule his bookkeeping by any accounting
equation he'd heard of at any level of Atlantean government despite
its immemorial traditions.

Still, the liberties taken by the people who bypassed their
elected representatives in complaint or inquiry were as nothing to
the Earls' own unofficial interference with management of the executive branch, during office hours or at any other time, by phone or

in person, by speaking directly with subordinate City employees, especially the semi-autonomous department heads (like the Chief of Police, the Fire Chief, or the Director of Public Works) who knew it prudent to appease their legislators, all of whom participated in the approval of budgets and personal emoluments. Of course there were always some of the Earls who also strutted their political power for its own sake; or those of condescending civilian dignity as knowledgeable experts in some profession or trade beyond the grasp of anyone humble enough to be a civil servant.

But besides her probably characteristic officiousness, what special motive could be prompting this busybody to get at him even before he had a desk in Ibicity Hall? He prejudicially imagined her cosmetic eye-shadow and scent as a typically ironic counterpart to the white trim that no doubt delineated the red yellow green blue or gray clapboards of houses along many a picturesque old street of shops admired by pilgrims all around Seamark's picturesque harbor, the center of her constituency. Still, her candid curiosity aroused his own. Perhaps it wouldn't hurt to glean a hint or two of the types he would have to get along with, whether or not they sufficiently appreciated the complexity of municipal management.

"I hope you and your colleagues will bear with me for the first few weeks. I first have to study the budget and get acquainted with all the departments." By this time they were slowly pacing toward the canted rails laden with the unmatched pair of loftily inclined fully exposed vessels, which must have looked curiously down upon them with about the kind of attention they themselves awaited on the morrow. The two strollers also paused for half a minute, their thoughts elsewhere, to stare vacantly at a whale's yellow-weathered vertebrae, three feet in diameter, that was carelessly displayed as an amusing surprise to any one who guessed what it was as an alien oddity in this strictly functional workplace that had never served the locally clandestine whaling industry. "What do you think the City's most urgent problems are?" he asked in softened resistance, glancing sideways at her with his first expression of genuine respect for whatever she might think about anything.

Suddenly he was struck by the unsubstantiated tone of masculine superiority, as it might seem to her by virtue of education, when actually attributed for the nonce to an unfamiliar peasantry— though really in his own defense. He warmed with contrition, considering the frank benignity of the woman's self-confidence. Of the four humors, he thought, earth must be her prevailing element. For the first time he made an effort to recall the name by which she had identified herself. Didn't it sound French? As usual in his abstractive grasp of an unanticipated social situation, one in which he expected no further personal entanglement, the introductory name had gone in one ear and out the other as some unnecessary identification. He glanced again at the amused mouth between neatly folded wings of yellow coiffeur, noticing a tiny skin-colored knob plugged in her right ear as a muted diacritical knot for the silver pendant that hung free in the shape of an embossed *psi* [ψ].

Just then she laughed outright: "Jesus Joseph and Mary! Am I so decrepit that Cubicle the bachelor fugitive from Baby Oaks doesn't remember his old Hecky?"

Instantly there came upon him a similarity of vision and memory, united like a zenith's bolt of lightning and its own simultaneous thunder, but recognizing from weather of a forgotten year exactly who she was! The flash touched off a name he'd overlooked as surd!

"Hecuba! I'm flabbergasted!" Indeed, he was simultaneously flustered and delighted by a conflated abstraction comically mustered as atonements and beatitudes. Without the slightest lust he was tempted to hug and kiss her, but just wary enough to refrain from emotional trouble, momentarily offering to leave her the next step toward equilibrium as he cudgeled his brain about the consequences of his possibly having missed some such implication in the information that Lilian had openly offered two months earlier. This second stroke of enlightenment warned him of complications far more than twice as delicate as his more joyful stroke of intelligence at first, especially because the second apparition was a widow and the first was married. "But Lilian didn't tell me you were a politician!"

"Just for fun she wanted to surprise you! I was hoping she'd be a witness when our wires crossed."

She stood still and they faced each other as she summed up the history of their coincidence. "Hecuba Jones Fox-Argent, mother of a bastard daughter, now noisy partner of another mother with also such a lucky daughter. Lil told me she'd seen you, and we drank to that for old times' sake. This is like Mother's Day! Naturally you've been voiding us, but you can't ignore me in the Hall now that you'll be working for the City good!"

Would she dangerously complicate his new career? How well would she wear as a political friend on the acropolis? But anyway she must give the Board a fillip too! At best, until she's re-elected or he himself gives up, voluntarily or otherwise, the frisson of their secret will probably be either fun or unbearable!

"She's the chief and I'm sometimes the camelion behind the bar." Hecuba was saying. "I've learned to play the piano, and sometimes people ask me to. But I don't want to be too conscious in the Gangway and ruin my political refutation."

. . . Like a wise old drama critic attending a play he hasn't seen since he was a college freshman, he was watching the footlights of a proscenium stage gradually brighten, yielding to the floods and spots on a pair of oddly cheerful characters who think their meetings are secret. All at once he was experiencing in only one dimension, uncertainly and inaudibly, what led up to his opinion that the ultimately harmless chicanery turned out to be an adventure highly significant to others. He rapidly read the story on this colorless screen but his consciousness reassembled it as a codex of superposed two dimensions with the denouement on top, vivified not by the action but by the syntax of an exceptionally numerate bookkeeper who'd been his governess when he was a janitor, now opening a floodgate of vaguer memories, an almost ludicrous reconstruction of the course in which, just out of college, his sophistication had been praised and brought to ground. In this waking dream the revenant broke open for him the ever-potential anastomosis of hips and heels. That hazily distant farce was now just someone else's fiction, yet still nostalgically fabulous!

. . . "It seems from the curricula I saw that you're now a lizard at electricals." she was saying in past and present. "I'll prolly be asking you to come to our committee meetings at least once—just to get seen as an official cohort. But let me know if you ever want time on our addenda. Our budget leaves nothing to be desired. The guy that just got kicked out thought it was the cat's pajamas because he'd figured it all the way down to the penny! . . . I hope you're not still too insidious about sailor-talk. There's shuttlebut going around that you're a secret arthur. But don't worry: I'm not setting my sail for you again, and my lips are peeled. I won't tell anyone else about our sacristies. Lilian already knows them well enough, I can insure you." She laughed, with a forefinger at her nose. "No one but us smells a cat!

A whistling girl and a crowing hen
Always come to some bad en'!

Anyway I turned over a new fig leaf before I got to Dogtown! You're not harassed by my wagon. Whatever you think, I've never been a nymphochondriac."

He took no offense at her sympathetic innuendo. As far as his past was concerned he had to trust both grandmothers in the secret fiction. But, as a matter of prudence, Hecuba especially.

In the story that he fondly remembered she had been a boon to the Chapman family, as cookie-maker, babysitter, and procurer of free tickets to the Yerba Buena Opera House. As he and she now found themselves, as if by instinct, wandering side by side toward Magog, the rectotetrahedral crane on the extremity of its wharf, Caleb restrained the impulse to clasp her to his chest—even to kiss her on the mouth incestuously—in acknowledgment of his libidinal retrospection at meeting again an extraordinarily double-bosomed dream sister, buxom blithe and debonair, in an enthusiastically grimy episode of his exploratory youth. So instead of embracing and bussing her he signified his shameless celebration of that brief but consequential liaison at an immeasurably earlier time by laying a hand on her shoulder, bowing his head in reminiscent laughter as he visualized scenes alternating especially between the boiler room where he'd worked and the rabbit warren where he'd lived. As she turned with a girlish giggle, one hand brushing back her hair, he noticed again in her right ear the all but concealed nub of her electronic hearing aid, which (as almost instantaneous revelation) sent him into a deeper bend of mirth, the other hand on his belly, seeing that he had never before suspected that the underlying cause of her faulty elocution was not just dyslexia, for he certainly remembered respecting her former intelligence in transmission of speech and writing as well as her excellence with numbers.

Soon, yielding to Hecuba's bottomless altruism, he recklessly accepted the standing invitation to eat and drink a meal in the restaurant of his two erstwhile lovers—indeed, to sit by them this very night, without so much as a change of clothes—as their guest before and after they opened to the public, Lilian running kitchen and dining room; Hecuba, the bar, as publican and impromptu entertainer; relieving each other at the cash register, whoever was the more convenient one to it. This particular night in Gloucestermas, the peripheral patrons were perfectly happy to pay a fair price for the good cheer and unostentatiously first-class menu (which listed but was not limited to local lobster and fish) in the little rustic dockside house owned by a pair of cheerful Petrines liberally lapsed. No less than half Pauline himself, the occasion would serve well as a valediction to his liberty. The Starboard Gangway was famous as a unique nightspot for summertime merriment, but frequented mostly by couples.

Thus he skipped his afternoon C N meditation, and staggered home after dark ringing in his ears Hecuba's last word in reply to his redundant thanks: "Better more of you than less." By that time she was all decked out in fabric envisioned as her mantra, making very bright eye contact.

25

MICHAELMAS

The variety of motions in man are equal to
the variety of accidents or thoughts affecting
the mind, and each of these thoughts, or
accidents, will operate more or less according
to the temper and age of the subject; for the
same cause will in the actions of youth, or of
old age, produce very different effects.

Leonardo da Vinci, *A Treatise on Painting*

*I*n most cultures on our spinning globe the annual calendar has been a
quaternion of calculated seasons, usually based upon combined celestial and terrestrial evidence. The time of each quarter has been variously defined by solar or lunar considerations, sometimes by both.
Even settled customs have been complicated over the millennia by intercala-
tions stemming from the pragmatic need to keep seasonal characteristics from
ultimately slipping out of synchronization with the twenty-five thousand
eight hundred year cycle of equinoctial precession caused by a circular
wobble of the earth's axis, as well as with the subdivisions necessary for

rhythmically repetitious patterns of social hope and endeavor, in lunar if not solar terms, twelve or thirteen cycles, with minor adjustments to add up as precisely as possible to the proper end of every year, as if to reconcile religion and science, if not human reproduction. Even the days of a standard work-week sometimes affect holy calendars. .

Historically, some priests watch the sunrise, some the sky, to measure their quarterly anticipation of what the sun will do within the dome of stars in order to approximate nature in celebrating the demarcations of solar quarters—two solstices and two equinoxes—as moved or extended from their astronomical date in fixed calendar time for revelry or sacred liturgy. The lunar and therefore movable Easter day has given its name to a continuum of religious weeks known as Eastertide. The winter solstice now anticipates the instituted Christmas by several days, and Christmas itself has been conventionally expanded to at least twelve days of Yuletide, but it still represents the longest night of the year. So also with its opposite, Gloucestermas, the inordinate expansion of Midsummer's Night, which by itself represents the longest day of the year ten days or more after that solar event. That day in the artificial calendar opens and closes Dogtown's fiscal year (as it does for many public and private entities), nearly in phase with the natural rise and fall of hope. Thus for good or sufficient social reasons the dial of the calendar clock has always been ruled by synchronizing twists of artful wrists, one way or the other, without seriously confusing customary zeniths with those of more or less scientifically annualized chronology. Even without Cape Gloucester's peculiarities, consider the complexity of the Missal or the Tudor Book of Common Prayer.

But however one numbers the quarters in, say, clockwise rotation, the autumn equinox, as a dialectical vector conceived as halfway between Gloucestermas and Christmastide—between summer and winter—immemorially representing harvest time, there is a day, and long span of days (even a whole season) still known liturgically and academically in the Anglo-Saxon world as Michaelmas, though practically anachronistic in modern secular parlance. Its anchor date September 22–23 is hardly noticed under skies palliated by electric light, but it's still represented on September 29 in the churches as a feast of Saint Michael the Archangel, who "fought against the dragon . . . that old serpent called the Devil, and Satan, which deceiveth the whole world. . . ." Save in tidal meteorology, Michaelmas has probably never been any more celebrated than spring equinox in the vernacular of Dogtown fishermen—whose only respite it is, even nowadays, from ten or more days at sea with only three-day layovers, hardly acquainting themselves with their own children between the octaves of Gloucestermas and Christmas until they retire and delight themselves with grandchildren—since the fading of Colonial Chauvinism as the local fleet's dominant religion.

According to Caroline Chapman, a rather new marooner in "this foul island of dogs and gulls", Michaelmas is her father's birthday as well as the archangelic name-day. Michael Chapman, one of Cape Gloucester's permanent expatriates since childhood, known as the Controller of this book, is our author in absentia. She and her older brothers were born in the Golden Horn area of Cornucopia when her father, as a veteran of W W 2, was beginning his business career as chief petty officer of a small bookstore in Hume. Much later he became an executive of the Tubalcain Manufacturing Company in Babylon Oaks, and eventually the well-compensated Controller of Thanatron Rectification Company when it was still indirectly owned by Arthur Halymboyd's Parity Corporation, a closed-end New Uruk investment trust. His bachelor daughter Caroline has an important but inconspicuous job as Personnel Manager at the modernized Mercator-Steelyard seafood headquarters in Dogtown. She had hoped that her father would at last return to this his birthplace, perhaps to celebrate some Michaelmas; but he insisted that it was a prematurely discouraging time for him to marvel at the discrepancies between his fiction and the truth. The year for that was not yet, he'd told her. A painful visit would be too early before it was too late to repent.

1.

Late on Friday afternoon, after Caleb left what the Mayor privately called Lilliput Hall, when it was already emptied of everybody else but the janitor, he stopped two blocks away on his way home to visit Finn Macdane in his eyrie as response to a standing invitation. In his determination to get what exercise was possible— as also when his self-driven tasks would drive him back absolutely alone to the echoing umbrageous Hall at least one more day in the fatiguing but hopeful week—he briskly climbed all the dimly lighted levels of stair, past varnished brown corridor offices of the commercial building's opaque "professional" tenants, ignoring a contemptible little box of an elevator that wasn't too slow or suspicious for habitually lazy people much younger than himself. In this respect he gladly emulated his mentoring host, the new owner and restorer of the erstwhile bank building, who was his athletic senior by more than a whole generation. Finn, sometimes called Mac, had recently completed his transformation of the top floor into his personal penthouse apartment. It was designed and furnished in a lofty modern style of architecture, half of it largely lighted by the easterly sky as favorably for his office as any studio artist could ask for northern light. The view from its windows was more interesting to both of them than any other urbanly maritime scene north of Botolph.

Caleb's ice-clicking glass of nearly undiluted Scotch was an exhilarating relief from his deskbound time-pressed toil—an immediately delightful recreation! His appreciation was a reciprocal pleasure for Commander Macdane in his nearly total retirement from the consultative practice of naval architecture or electrical engineering (as well as various kinds of naval intelligence). As an amateur domestic designer he was glad to share the concepts and details of his radically realized domicile with this civilian bureaucrat so remarkably experienced in the aesthetic practicabilities of functional office construction. Gazing down upon Dogtown's inner harbor, and out upon the spacious outer harbor, as they sipped and mused, the senior host and junior guest enjoyed the warmth of a growing friendship based in large measure upon systematic analogies of opinion, as well as upon their personal respect for Fay Gabriel and her academically recognized philosophical writings about symbol-systems at a deeper and higher level of civilization than technology. They were now casually discussing Dogtown's pride in its unique contribution to nautical evolution. They gazed down at the salty matrix that had conceived, shaped, gestated, delivered, and progressively educated competitive generations of schooners for both efficiency and spiritual satisfaction in international deep-sea fishing, famous in their heyday for profit and organic beauty, as well as for many an injudicious or unlucky loss of men and fortunes.

"Of course the later spoon-bowed knockabouts saved hundreds of lives," Finn was saying, "but the fairest to see with all sails set in a decent breeze, now as rare as a white sperm whale, had clipper bows."

"Even as beautiful as BB *New Guernsey* under way in a task force at sea?" Caleb teased. He refrained from commenting that as a very young native of the city he'd loved to see and hear about schooners only from the very feminine point of view of an inquisitive daughter who'd fled from her father, a highline skipper of more than one such vessel—possibly (he wondered) even this one in its prime. Anyway, Finn's shadow of the past was cast in the light of more professional history.

"Let's just say that a man's delight has many mansions." Finn toasted Caleb's thoughts. "Even in the bonanza era of schooners, these races, squeezed into a few days between grim all-year-round commercial fishing trips, provided sporting challenges to seamanship and fostered local pride by sailing gala yachts designed and built in imitation of Cape Gloucester's commercial success. The money-making hunt of public wildlife has called for a form and content of deadly earnestness so beautiful in everyone's eyes that to certain sailors of the leisured class it was worth large investment that returned none of itself, thus to assert both noble skills and disinterested wealth. It was like condescending to compete against horn-hearted farmers once a year with their own teams of immaculate draft horses; or like striving to win society's praise for being hauled up Mount Everest at great expense by veteran Sherpa guides. Perhaps they were not embarrassed by the fact that with the best naval architects and elite crews at their disposal, for speed and seaworthiness alone, they could only imitate with ballast the large freight they were designed for. Even so, they rarely equaled in races the class of swift and handsome mercenary vessels that had to hunt and fill the fat payload of ice-packed fish!"

"Unblemished imitation as art!" said Caleb, rather rudely raising his glass to ask for more. He was already a bit giddy in his surrender to diurnal exhaustion, trusting that he would recover gravity on his walk home to Apostle's Dock in East Harbor.

Finn smiled sympathetically, as he stepped aside to refill the glass emptied of everything but the ice. He remembered the thirsts of compulsive and prolonged immersions in his own career.

"Still, those two classes of skipper respected each other in cup-races handicapped for equivalent loads and rigs. But even with much of the year available for preparation and practice at any cost, the amateur commodores could seldom beat Dogtown schooners' speed and seamanship, crewed with experience honed to land tons of fish from the Banks in very serious competition to land first for the best price—which sometimes could make the difference between momentary riches and no profit at all—if not a financially disastrous 'broken trip'. But to win a race, as if offhand, for one whose theatrical reputation was at stake, must have been the greatest public pleasure of any summer. For him the silver trophy cup was enough to boast about in a glass case at Ibicity Hall after a night or two of extra-special carousal, wryly forgotten that it happened to be in a Dominion rival built to one of Dogtown's plans."

The taut and tanned youthful old Commander paused to replenish his own shot of whiskey. "Nowadays this weekend is also occasion for the long and the short and the tall of any two-masted sailing rig, between twenty feet in length to over a hundred and twenty, about forty small ones tomorrow, a dozen big ones the next day; but all of them, even the phony replicas of obsolete designs, are comparatively more authentic and thrilling to see under sail than any kind of motor yacht. I hope you'll get to see *Gloucesterman* moving with all her angles of canvas tightly hollowed by half a breeze! But any two-masted gaff-rig is a dozen times more interesting than the over-simplified pointed Marconi mainsails of a Tuscan sloop, which is nearly as objectionable to me as a toyboat stinkpot. Of course the profile of any reasonable schooner, large or small, is more satisfying than the competition of a yawl or ketch, which as far as I know have never been handy for serious deep-sea fishing in this country. . . ."

Caleb's mind drifted back to his earliest boyhood impressions of the waterfront, and then after the emigration from Dogtown to Unabridge when he was much more than an infant observer, he had pasted into scavenged greeting-card albums countless newspaper and magazine pictures of schooners, along with those of his favorite battleships, warplanes, locomotives, and many extraordinary products of civil engineering. As he grew in size and selective curiosity he'd increasingly devoted his indoor time to rendering in pencil the two-dimensional visions of his own military or civilian ideals, consolidating or suggesting what he hoped for in past or future realization of blended superiorities in both function and form. His axiological opinions were thus mainly committed to drawing, not to writing. Almost all his only humanistic drawings before mother and son moved to Montvert were of oak trees or of heroic leaders standing at attention in full-dress uniform of his own design.

"I always longed to sail—and rock and roll afoot in subway cars—without the *danger* of going to sea!—in one of the Dogtown schooners that tied up here two or three abreast when I was a kid under my mother's orders," he said. "I was vividly scared at the prospect of seasickness or storms! It was thrill enough just to climb a little way up into the rigging when no one else was looking. I liked the salt-fish smell that kept most of the gentry from settling anywhere near the harbor. I never minded climbing worthy ascents!"

"That lady now slipping into the inner harbor," Finn continued, "was the original *Gloucesterman* (of course without an engine) that won many of the Ozone Cups for racing before the War. She's joining the climax of what's the latest revival of this town's greatest inshore regatta." Caleb politely refrained from protesting that he was not as ignorant of local nautical matter as the newly marooned expert addressing him seemed to assume, but it was true enough that he regretted having had much to learn about the design of hulls and rigging. He knew nothing at all about the contributions of Ireland's and Botolph's naval architecture to Dogtown's consummate artifacts. Yet he was vaguely conscious of much that the distinguished aficionado continued to tell him as if reviving his own satisfaction with having come to end his days in the heart of Cape Gloucester.

The greatest event, whose culmination wouldn't be known by radio until hours after it departed from its origin in Dogtown, was reserved for half a dozen competent crews in vessels of the largest schooner class, which were either restorations of relics or confidently improved replicas of great highliners, if not modern versions of those ghosts adapted to the functions of luxurious yachting, designed and built at great cost primarily to participate in this majestic jousting, the last of which had occurred (before the War) when participants could qualify as *fishing* schooners only by having spent at least one season in commercial hunting and gathering. They were now all equipped with auxiliary engines, modern navigational and safety devices, some with suspiciously mechanical advantages in the management of sails. The race to be won was a one-way northerly course across the open Gulf of Markland ("Down East" by the usual wind) to Selenburg, Dogtown's traditional archrival on the Acadian coast of the Dominion.

". . . Her immediately previous owner made her seaworthy enough for the Coast Guard to permit sallies without a professional crew among inshore islands up and down the coast of Markland as summertime passenger cruises or as vacation training schools for sea-scouts; but down here now she's Briney Nedlaw's sailing museum. At this time of year most of his itinerant crew goes south to work on yachts. He takes over when he can get away for a while from running the *Nous*. Somehow he seems to have acquired a skipper's ticket, maybe on the strength of his record as C O of a corvette during the War. —I suppose he couldn't afford to own, maintain, repair, and operate such a treasure if he didn't own the *Nous*."

"I'd be surprised if the paper contributes much to his family wealth. For such a tiny circulation it seems to have a pretty expensive plant and staff." Caleb remarked. "Besides, he has plenty of other interests. He's probably the saltiest lecturer on local history the Lyceum has had since Howard Blackwell! I hear he's the sustaining money-raiser behind that museum too. He writes very well, and I think he's a good unacademic scholar—allowing for his blind eye to old codfish aristocracy's exploitation of seagoing labor, not to mention Dogtown's phantom whaling trade."

"Oh? He told me he was a radical reformer and traitor to his class in younger days as a working reporter in Botolph and New Uruk. He certainly doesn't put on airs, and he supports good causes."

"Yes, it's a good man who can publish his own books!"

"A little town like this is very lucky to have him."

"If you please, sir, *he's* lucky to have this little *city* for his circulation!"

"Aside from my worries about his seamanship, we are indeed fortunate—I especially, as an interloper-come-lately, trying to catch up with a few centuries of patriotism. But it's pure luck that the City now has Dexter and you to run it!"

"My part is thanks to you!"

"Apparently the Earls confirmed you without a public murmur."

"But there were murmurs all right. They suspended judgment, and gave me ninety days of probation, as allowed by the Charter. Come confirmation time I'll be the lure of Dexter's opposition on the Board!"

2.

Some days later Caleb and Fay remember that it was still hurricane season when, under pure blue sky, everyone was wondering if there was enough wind to sustain exciting competition in any of the day-races. The outer harbor was populated with two-masted boats of every size and configuration, arrived from yachting ports all along the East Coast, some of them owned by skippers who were more alert to the possibility of bad weather where they came from. These yachting visitors, as well as Cape participants in correspon-

ding classes, were distracted by the annoying or sometimes dangerous buzzing and darting of malapert little plastic sailing craft and
mahogany-varnished plastic stinkertoys that seemed deliberately to
make a nuisance of themselves by appealing to the eyes of a thousand cameras during all the official efforts to form dignified parades
of sail, much to the interest of angels from every reach of the sky,
wheeling, gliding, sweeping, soaring overhead.

In ruminating reconstruction, godmother and godson envision
Finn Macdane descending to the waterfront from his own eminent
pilot house to remind a throng of exuberant buffs that weather
forecasting still left something to be desired. Caleb, frequently on
foot along the inner harbor, had already begun to guess that the
battleship man, despite his restrained courtesy, had shown reason to
feel himself getting to be known as a well-meaning irritant from an
anachronistic background, whose opinion deserved no more respect
due to an ordinary superannuated Polonius of historical wars than
that accorded any ordinary technocrat out of his depth this far from
the Hexagon in Washington.

But now, as long after the day of Michaelmas as before the
festal half-day race open to schooners of all sizes rigs and owners,
Caleb is standing with Fay in her kitchen looking distantly down
over tortuous carpets and tapestries of greenery's blazing autumnal
hues, the same vantage from which they had watched the northern
leg of that ladies' train irregularly attenuated behind *Gloucesterman*
and her few rival peers. With all sails set and slightly bellied, near
and far at her heels, some gray profiles sliding silently past others,
and still others trailing along for the sheer honor of being officially
seen with royalty, actually a flotilla of heterogeneous stragglers, this
finally impressive pageant for Dogtown's stationary eyes had only
hinted at what would not be seen of the full-blown open-sea competition among aristocrats by themselves, dramatically emulating
in earnest their authentic passages to oftenly bitter North Atlantis
fishing grounds without using even the auxiliary engines or air-
waves that had been of some avail fifty years earlier.

In that finale of the two-day local inshore sailing rally, before
landbound spectators dispersed to their various livelihoods in a
new week, the venerable queen called *Gloucesterman,* though calmly
confident of her own sex, was thus closely trailed by well-
respected schooners of later and much more expensive launching,
close-hauled in a breeze barely strong enough to form concavities

in the sheeted sails between booms and gaffs to flatter the tacking skills of calculating yachtsmen. The largest wings of canvas were already returning from the northern marker buoy, in an irregularly segmented line, while many of the out-bound laggards (some of them in miniature) were still emerging for the first time into the seascape visible from Fay's house, long before they would get far enough to reverse course counterclockwise and proceed back out of sight again behind most of the Foreside to the finish line at the end of the long breakwater in the mouth of the outer harbor, thereby opening for themselves splendid views to the west of where the race began: the city's architectural landmarks on the urban hills, which, but for the Namauche River's cut to John Smith Bay, connected the fells of variegated autumnal greenery that embraces the broad haven with both arms like maternal mountains keeping their distance. On a glorious late afternoon that panorama alone was reward enough for tedious hours of bringing up the rear of goodsportsmanship.

But long before any of the winged craft had beaten their windward return to the harbor, which was hidden from the view of Fay and Caleb, though a very short gull-flight, by Joint Hills' granite-grounded hump of climbing streets, shaded or exposed, lined with dry-walled yards of ingeniously naturalized ledges or boulders of gray granite rock gardens shaped snugly beside or behind white or colored houses made with Atlantean timber, more than angular or not according to personal taste (what angels enjoyed with aerial motion), the sea's vista from the opposite slope of the hill, at a breathlessly silent distance, soothed the affect of classic races for the human companions. At their lower level the schooners seemed to glide past each other like revenants passing in the same file of opposite directions. It was a staged cinema played by gentle knights white or gray, each partly shielded by her own overlapping of jibs and staysails, each modestly displaying at masthead her own hardly noticed strip of flying scutcheon as the wind's own vane, which always served as a variable gyroscope pointing the prime mover of a redoubling race that from the upland's perspective slipped toward either goal to double its speed when the sails passed on opposite courses.

"They remind me of the pulleyed clotheslines loading and unloading laundry on the second or third floor of Unabridge tenements!" said Caleb.

*

But on another day, from the same vantage, in contemplative gaze of the same seascape emptied of sails, nearly emptied of mankind's less beautiful creations, the thin old gray-haired lady and her lightweight frailer-haired godson, both seeing everything through framed lenses, remark to each other that the visible sea-rim will soon be getting longer than it has been all summer—longer and bleaker with the loss of leaves. Many of the treetops, and then whole deciduous trees, will lose even their golden resistance to the odes of cooler wind, at more northern degrees with which to present hill-dwellers the ghosts of vanished nobility that never gave off a whiff of its slaughtered fish. The winter anger of the sea would be much easier to scold, with or without snow to match its cold white surf.

They tie the arms of sweaters around their necks and descend from Fay's kitchen windows to start her fair-weather route by foot down to an intimately magnified edge of the shore. Most sightseers have faded away, children are in school, breadwinners are at work, but the remaining pilgrim kilroys—this far from stores and high-ways, while most of the shoreline hotels are preparing to hiber-nate—venture upon the scenic roadways closest to the Atlantic's confrontation with Lady Gloucester's autochthonic basement. These days weekenders and city folk are primarily in search of her seasonal valediction displayed on interior slopes and avenues in glorious gra-dients of a few gaudy colors where the ephemeral contrasts of foliage are less vulnerable to the ocean's alien passions. Once in a while the sudden whistle blast or melancholy wail of a Botolph commuter train pierces the Dopplered ether from its distant valley through the City's center to its six lonely miles to or from its silenced end of the Cape in Seamark, where the track is single.

And here, now, not a single golfer disturbs a green ignored on either hand of their flattened pavement toward the sea. Thus, having steered straight down the public arborway dividing the downhill landscape of our bedrocked Lady, without glancing at the bourgeois sport, Fay and Caleb almost immediately face on level pavement the deepening edge of open bare rocks above my Lady's ambiguous but never absolutely rejected suitor. Otherwise the bas-tion at the Cape's rim, where the confrontation of land and sea is never interrupted, was to be seen by other human beings only from

behind a string of seaside inns or rather majestic family houses on
the shoreline road that crosses the T at which the two quiet companions will turn to the left, skirting the chasms then on their
right, footed and kneed by Mother Earth's restless adorer, as if for
Lady Gloucester alone, proving his attempts at the pools he left
behind him when obliged to apply his strength attacking up or
down the coast, leaving as his living spoor of black seaweed the
promise of his returning desire—or even joy—for her naked escarpment bared for sun or air.

   To the extent that this local cove is remarkable as a barrier it's a
theater of waves and their recessions—an auditorium's broad con-
cavity. It's at its greatest depth when the tide is out and its floor is
a tiny poppled beach. The surges of sea within the steep hollow are
met with an immemorially passive rampart for defense against the
whole Atlantic cavalry, whose charges aspire to the Back Shore
Foreside Road, made for people walking on a narrow sidewalk protected from passing vehicles and the threat of exceptional storms by
a low buffer of steel fence planted in concrete very firmly. Here,
unlike Lady Gloucester's more typical contours elsewhere among
her promontories and frontages between her coves and beaches, still
looking down at the chaotic cove bestriding or bracing the precipitous dangers there is a continuous range of pale amber granite
smoothly weathered into convex surfaces swept by successive eons
of ocean and glacier facing suns and storms of intermittent violence. For these rocks the exposure of telluric slopes predominate as
barriers, some of it veined with basalt lava, openly tracing volcanic
eruption in one of the unimaginable eras.

   Fay has not said much and Caleb has made none of his usual
efforts to sustain a conversation with his venerated godmother. It is
not an occasion even to remember—still less to express—any of the
themes that animate his deferentially opinionated enthusiasms in
the company of Athene. The old lady matches his unabated pace as
easily as she does the unusual silence of his presence, which is as
sensitive of hers as hers of his. He does not doubt that their
thoughts somehow reflect each other's. Yet he readily apperceives
that his conscience is peripherally evasive of absolute sympathy;
that she has reason to put to shame his almost callow feelings about
what she feels.

   In fact, Caleb is thinking in retrospect—of what they've put
only a few minutes behind them—yet still in sympathetic preoccupation with speculation about the feelings within the uncharacter-

istically taciturn woman walking so quickly beside him. At the same time he finds himself banally straying into rumination about an optimal habit chosen by only a few of Dogtown's excursive foot-passengers, all others in that category being regarded by him as either stupid, unschooled, or blatantly as ignorant as sheep or idiots, if not simply excused for having been deprived of infantile nurture (like certain criminals exonerated by virtue of insanity or childhood neglect). His opinion, recently strengthened by the support of Commander Finn Macdane, with whom he advanced it, was that it should be no trivial matter for Dogtown's public-spirited leaders to promulgate. Teachers, scoutmasters, mothers, and saucy youth should pay attention to details. No Earl, Police Chief, Director of Public Works, Superintendent of Schools, or Board of Health member is rightfully too lofty or busy to heed "micro-management" for the common good. But they laugh at our last President for trying to save electricity in the White House lighting. Even Mayor Keith would be uncomfortable if his fanatic lieutenant sent out an interdepartment memo on the subject, and Caleb's own office would lose its initial prestige as an authority to reckon with. He admits that he worries too much about pedestrians while everyone else bows to the democratic supremacy of kilroy-drivers and cares very much about the tax money devoted to wheeled automotion. But even he himself, right now, can't help wanly smiling at his own crotchets, or rather at his own awareness of the suppressed amusement of friends who've more than once or twice heard his opinions as serious complaints about Atlantean culture! Still, it *is* a simple statement that persons walking on the left of any roadway without sidewalks, facing the closer lane of traffic, have more than half a chance to anticipate and dodge a careless driver, whereas fools walking in the other lane with their backs to traffic—especially if they are wearing musical earphones, or are pushing perambulators accompanied by other children or dogs—are always tempting Providence. Finn too, right from the beginning of his local residence, voiced notice of the stupid anarchy exhibited by Dogtown foot-passengers in old residential areas of the City who should know better, even educated bird-watchers and grimly sweating runners who should have learned better in Scouts or summer camps, not to mention callow boys wheeling in self-absorbed unconsciousness of any society but their own! Friends too sometimes laugh also behind Finn's back about his "militaristic" dictums, but, as Caleb has some reason to appreciate, that elder is generally respected as a respecter of his junior's opinions. At least there was a tacit alliance in despair of the rationally ritualistic discipline generally wanting in Atlantean habits.

But now, for the first time—his Immediate Exclusive Consciousness [I E C] of the *highest* authority thinking and feeling at his side nearly in silence, interrupted perhaps only by a reflexive lurch in negotiating an unexpected pothole at the pavement's edge—by an occult bit of logic in tonal association of ideas, Caleb's inner ear suddenly echoes a special significance of the spoken word *left* in this accidental context. Aside from its political meaning, it's an all-too-commonplace sound of multiple meanings. He himself is sinister by almost congenital accident in the cradle—but only just the other day did he discover by chance the same physiological predilection in dynamic expression of Finn's natal character. The old man's surprisingly emotional activity on an exceptionally animated waterfront was first suggested by the way he grasped and gestured with the double-bitted axe borrowed from Caleb himself. It was handed over on hasty delivery from its sequestration in an overstuffed closet at Apostle's Dock across the inner harbor.

All at once, as if on the road to Damascus, it strikes Fay's godson that it has taken such a long time to notice that commonplace and sometimes gifted abnormality as preponderant among others with whom he's been closely acquainted. (In truth, he has rarely noticed so much as the color of anyone's eyes.) Was the word *left*, all by itself, the catalyst for ending a fifty-year lapse in his sensory observations of human beings for a particularity of women? There is certainly nothing unpleasant in the tardily discovered homology. In retrospect it occurs to Caleb that he has seldom regarded as distinctive his own kind among anentiomorphic fellows, seeing that their gesture and reach seemed as natural as his own.

This randomly distributed predilection happened to be shared in habitual traits by the otherwise dialectically contrasting characters of Father Duncannon and the magnate Arthur Halymboyd, neither of whom betrayed the slightest trace of clumsiness or alienation, yet for the first time it now struck Caleb that he happened never to have seen either of them writing by hand, nor had he ever had occasion to see the slant of their signatures or checkmarks. He'd simply failed to remark the right hand of a firstbaseman or an antithetical stance at home plate, or even the particular asymmetry of left-handed limbs on a tennis court. Yet he did remember that he himself had sometimes been annoyed during exams when a desper-

ate student to his right tried to take advantage of their relative configuration by exploiting his contiguity within the honor system.
But long before that stage of maturity, when he still strove for
public conformity, as the child of a notorious nonconformist, rival-
ing his peers in all possible achievements, he instinctively admired
the ambidexterity of certain playground heroes. His mother had
laughed when once in boyhood he had complained that his sinister
affliction (of which she herself had been spared) was as serious as
that of a homely redhaired girl in a school of conventional blondes
and brunettes.

Thus wandering in his cranium as he walks straight downhill
with a person surely less vagrant in her own wonderfully capricious
world he asks himself what fractal has been released from the
depths of his psyche, disguised as idle digression from serious emotion, excused by his self-assured workload in a part of his world
that she did not share. His fickle mind he knows is all but always
too busy with reasons and intentions to make way either for merely
distractive entertainment or for the humility of true self-examination, to say nothing of vacuously drifting amusement. On any other
occasion he might have asked his godmother her view of the theoretical association of ideas that might still be embedded in the
orthodoxies of her professional territory. But despite his fitting diffidence in her solemn company this day he can hardly inhibit the
twist of his lips formed by an inward smile at the oddity of such a
long delay in apperception of three behavioral nonconformists
among his mature life's most influential figures at this stage of his
wisdom. In entirely different manners they were each an accidental
stimulant of interests he had scarcely considered as exciting or valuable for academic pursuit but whose influence was now integrated
with that of his personally unacquainted heroes in self-education as
a common reader. . . . An open-ended list flashes through his
immediately accessible experience in random order, unsorted by
history alphabet or aspiration, to wit: Ezra Schrödinger, Jane Harrison, Sorri Kierkegaard, Ludwig von Denthey, Alpha Whitehead,
Wellingborough Redburn, Eber, Durkheim, Liam Yeats, Jean-Louis
Bartaud, Auto Drang . . . —Only Fay Gabriel belonged with the
sinister three higher than this impersonal list!

. . . There was no reason to think that the said three spurious
left-handers known to him should have deviated from the norm any
more than those among historians or lumpers unknown. This coincidence of sinistrations on his tiny intersection of lives now strikes

Caleb as stochastically egregious anent the obvious criticism that his eisegesic *Iso*-rectotetrahedron failed to express all the possible shapes of an *irregular* rectotetrahedron! For each of his southpaw pitchers was no more of a kind with the others than he was himself—in weight, extension, fractal, or symbolic representation: *Father* Lancelot Duncannon; an industrial magnate, *King* Arthur Halymboyd; and a cosmopolitan man-of-war, *Commander* Finn MacDane. Still, all three of them were once and perhaps forever discredited here or there in Washington's dossiers or unofficial annotations as Premature Antifascists at least temperamentally at odds with conventional exegesis. Welcomed by a small minority of their colleagues, respected by many, but their proper influence unfulfilled, they were scarcely known in the history that leaves originality undistinguished from common learning or successes. To Caleb's mind their inventions or skills were best evaluated in systems either social or symbolic.

. . . So at least, as is his wont, Caleb drifts into and out of vaguely speculative abstractions, as if unconsciously in the magnetic field of Fay Morgan's anthropological philosophy, or of Ludwig von Denthey's Universal Systems Theory in its promising philosophical development of all the sciences! But at her side he now reawakens to the by no means simple phenomena of saltwater, granite, and basic life.

Foreconsciously grateful for the privilege of living where their counterclockwise excursion is freely public and refreshingly familiar, they'd turn left on the shore road's righthand sidewalk provided for pedestrians, brushing the low aluminum barriers that hinder them as well as wheeled vehicles from climbing and falling upon the parlous rocks. Though never tiring of the scene from which this time their sublime attention is absented, hardly looking at what their eyes present, lost in the sparse conversation that hardly represents their differing facets of the ultimate preoccupation they share side by side—wherever possible without stepping down into kilroy space when dodging overgrowths of seaside rosehip bushes—they walk along the seaward edge of Back Shore Drive, Caleb insisting whenever possible upon an oldfashioned gentleman's position of protection against the muck of traffic according to an obsolete custom to which Fay had no objection. Skirting the maw of the ebbed cove, looking without thinking of the smoothly worn seastones in the interminable process of grinding themselves to the sand they cover, strewn with flotsam and jetsam, largely the wrack of lobster traps, their eyes lowered to their feet, only seldom elevated to the sky or its few wheeling inhabitants, pacing sometimes hands behind their backs, ignoring the distantly naked view of the Double Digit Lights, they at length mount the road's bulging acclivity of the neck to a lofty headland spaciously mounting to a very few large old houses of timber, built for the worst of storms, enviably conspicuous from both land and sea, one view commanding much of the rockbound coast beyond the way they've come, the other looking down upon Little Harbor Beach at the mouth of its creek immediately below them as they are about to descend from the neck in a landward curve of the weathered asphalt road shaded by privately owned oaks.

The highest and furthest house of the promontory, on a bluff above the beach, with no streamlined or buttressed attachments to compromise its frankly vulnerable stories framed in right angles, looked as if wuthering had shorn it of verandas and balconies in its original design. Its romantic brown wood-shingled architecture was otherwise invented along Victorian lines for the great panoramas viewed from its generously squared tower meant for spyglasses in any direction. Though its lofty bulk looks too flimsy for daring the elements, from his inferior level of wealth and satisfaction Caleb surmises that when there is no fog it must be exhilarating to survey from one's desk in the cupola everything in and around the theater of marsh and sand, along with the level offshore distances beyond lesser promontories to the north, flanked by three islands and two lighthouses. He covets the tower more than any man's wife, with even less probability of satisfaction, invisibly anchored to a baldly unclothed monticle of solid granite within threatening reach of surf only at the very worst.

Descending to the road's sidewalk alongside the creek on its barrier wall, where passengers to the beach footbridge are not allowed to park their cars in high season, they scan from a widening angle the background and full length of the vastly expanded beach not yet visible from the descending walkers, its nearly flattened bed left wrinkled gray by recession of the tide, draining from behind its dunes the marsh basin's trickle, feebly ramified from a sinuous course to a delta as shallow as the imprint of an old bamboo rake lying on its back. As a formerly full-time mother alert to every danger in any child's situation, Fay at other times enjoys this ambulating cinema in the nearly two-mile loop beginning and ending at her house on the wooded upland of Joint Hill, especially

Little Harbor Beach for its latest banks and surfaces—its hollows of sand, and its relative exposures (or apparent transmigration) of two or three bottomless boulders at this end of the otherwise stoneless strand sometimes invisibly embedded like tightly tethered buoys that sometimes disappear entirely but usually show themselves to some degree. The creek's wandering rocks and those that more or less naturally form the raised seawall perpetuated by the Department of Public Works are each day separated once or twice by a strong current of lucent brine delightfully tempting for a summertime swimmer for floating or speeding in either direction; but they are nuisance attractions to children who mistakenly think they know how to swim with or without the support of flotation toys. But the worst of it (as Fay involuntarily remembers even on this preoccupied off-season occasion) is that many children's guardians are themselves deceived of the danger by the innocent appearance of such cool swift power within close earshot of a hundred totally relaxed familiars at their most confident leisure, eating hot dogs and drinking Kaka-Koma under colorful sunshades.

This afternoon the creek's gross or refined readjustments of bends, contours, and opened palm at the ocean's edge were forcefully configured in elastic cooperation with the morning tide's bullish intrusion. These finishing corrective details of a sculptor's model for civil engineers are now as sentient as the fingertips of Poseidon because in the distance, almost half a mile to the opposite headland on a cool September weekday, the windswept field, save for abandoned lifeguard pulpits and a circus of four or five unleashed dogs amicably testing their speed and friendship on an unobstructed flat of moist gray sand between its dried-out inertia and its restless frontier, is all but voided of human walkers and trashers. Bathing in either sun or water is the last desideratum brought to mind in one's unavoidable anticipation of November. The dormant surf scarcely laves the ripples and cross-ripples of fine gray sand that borders the somnolent blue sea, worth no visit by any fanatic rubber-suited man or girlfriend with a pedal pontoon hoping for surf.

Pausing by habit halfway across the footbridge, but turning away from her favorite walk on the beach, Fay gazes vacantly down at the pellucid rill of shallow brackish water still flowing seaward from what remains of a flood tide in the hinterland of marsh, subconsciously estimating as usual its opposite phase, when the beach is again ineluctably narrowed by compression until the ocean's broad salient looks as if its endless ranks of aggression mean at last to undermine the marsh grasses mounted on a low sierra of nearly uncohesive sand, which would have no character or substance without the adhesion of such rooting grips as pale green hair. Not now, but always before, when a swarming phalanx of cavalry in her presence further defies gravity, threatening the sand soil and plants inside the barrier beach, once more intending to inundate and undermine the concrete abutments of the bridge itself as the brine rushes to spawn in the arms of Mother Earth, it supersedes all Fay's other subjects—feminine, masculine, or neuter—not least the frail thread of current conversation, suspending speculation about the mystical object known as Little Harbor's internal marsh, about which both Finn and Caleb lovingly tease her for persistent curiosity, yet never with quite enough certainty to answer her questions. Always she has to rely upon her own hypotheses, like a patient with a history of more than a few doctors and nurses who is slightly skeptical of medicine as a science.

Thus on her last excursion with Caleb alone, under different circumstances, free of Finn's usual aversion to hyperbole (though not without humor) and to evidence of careless margins of error for ordinary resolution of questions that interested him (in this case even to the point of deciding to read up on geology, one of the boring subjects he had skipped in his liberal education), Fay felt free to express some of her casually inconclusive musing, relieved of the scholarly burden of "discipline" essential to her work at home. She never wished to be considered an arbiter of what she called "reflexive polymathematicalistic" investigation. (It was in part for this reason that she had separated her maiden surname Gabriel from that of the widowed Morgan under which her works were published and by which she was remembered, if at all, by her legal identity as a nurse or young mother once married to a commuting Classics scholar before the war that was generally accepted as an epoch.) Then, for psychic freedom from the greater truth of the present, anachronistically dressed, with loosened gray hair, half smiling at what she thought gazing back and forth from the scenery to his face, she seemed to Caleb more like a modestly precocious undergraduate than a retired professor, a girl of the unpainted kind he had always looked for as beautifully lean for romantic eyes: blonde or brunette or auburn (though of course his specifications of attraction were easily modified by creatural chance).

So as Caleb listens to what she now is saying about the Little Harbor Beach he altogether recalls as a single wrapped-up scene the passage of a private conversation in which Finn Macdane had surprised him with some confidential expressions of feeling as they'd

found themselves side by side slowly walking down to their distantly parked cars after departing from one of Tessa Opsimath's
hilltop soirées across the Gut while there was still enough daylight
to see where they were going, as if they were conscientious locker-
room comrades in the same statistical cohort, leaving behind them
the guests who felt no fear of inebriation on the roads. But in fact it
was a preternaturally congenial geezer, bending forward with glee,
one hand on Caleb's back, who said "I tell you, that erudite old
godmother of yours surpasses all other women for beauty as refined
by intellect and knowledge. From now on, whenever I read her
stuff in half-baked awe, I'll picture her with what we saw and heard
right here tonight, with more of an appreciative crowd than I've
seen her with before. That's one good thing about political commiseration! Everyone started to listen in on her conversation with
the firebrands and the bitter pessimists who wanted to howl like
beaten dogs, or vent their distribution of personal blame on our
own side, which they can't forget even half a year into the tipping
point of our empire's decline and fall—which seems attributed at
best to a gullible electorate miseducated by devilvision and broadcast advertising, forever inculcating a vernacular degradation of
English accepted by teachers taught to do so by teachers trained
before them, who themselves were only slow innocent steps before
them in the negative evolution of selfishness without discipline or
self-reliance. . . ."

"At least there are a few who care about such things." Caleb
had said inanely as he cautiously treaded water to fathom the man's
tone, dreading the prospect of needless alienation, respectfully
guarding against a slightly flushed hard-bitten commanding officer's tenets when at least half a sheet to the wind. But, though still
puzzled, he was glad at last to find himself in political agreement
as Finn continued, searching the face of his junior officer in expectation of infectious enthusiasm for what was about to explain this
anomaly of behavior in mufti.

"She didn't bother with denying or endorsing the obvious," the
Commander had continued, "as she quietly sat there in Tessa's
undeclared chair of honor, not as we usually see her when she's at
home doing service as a cook without wardroom stewards. —Those
are the times when I try to help without vouchsafing housekeeping
advice." he chuckled. "But she doesn't need my help with math or
Greek or Latin."

Nor obviously with German, French, or Iberian, Caleb thought, who couldn't help begrudging him Fay's intimacy. Finn's laugh seemed to him callously ignorant of his subaltern's christening and elective affinity.

"I knew she was a philosophical anthropologist because I've read her book about the Mardian islanders, but here she enthralled everyone as a personification of political savvy—even the goddam so-called Independents who regard themselves as virtuously above the partisan fray, or else as smugly too leftist to join any party as pragmatically diplomatic as ours. She unintentionally silenced all the usual cocktail chatter, political or not. Everyone gravitated to her corner, where she never raised her voice or spoke about the so-called issues current in the *New Uruk Testament* or *Washington Advisor*, not to mention DV journalism. . . ."

Caleb clearly remembers his own impression of what Finn's lengthy encomium in such a tone of astonishment was intended to convey, as if marveling at its own emotional metanoia. Finn had always been a liberal by Navy standards. It was perhaps no great exaggeration to say that Fay was attended by many an enchanted servitor trying to spare her the trouble of approaching bar and side-board to select her solid and liquid viands—indeed that they wouldn't even give her a chance to stand up.

To the usual blaming and mourning of defeated Crats, shocked and shocked again by Roland Raygun's initial words and actions as the irrevocable President of the new universe, she softly replied, her thin wrinkled neck somewhat stretched like an alert bird's, to take in with openly searching eyes the minds of her audience while inwardly occupied with discourse unrehearsed for such an occasion. Her unadorned face and swept-back silvered hair were those of a devoted unselfconscious teacher whose bright black eyes were meant for the intense transmission of the intellect that paled her long lips, which, if one hadn't heard her speak, might have been suggested by a slightly arched predatory nose. But her sympathetic nods, unlike any bird's, suggested that she substantially agreed with every reasonable fear or opinion registered by Tessa and her whole Catholicratic City Committee (as well as most of their national counterparts in politics and journalism) after their Party's shattering loss to the cumulative elevation of Protestican re-reaction (in the name of conservatism) to half a century of F D R's Crat legacy. However, she wasn't fully understood in pointing out the tangled religious roots of our political history that conflated or transferred ideas stemming from Pauline and Petrine seeds, which accounted for the ironically appropriate names of the two great parties generally insensitive to religious appellations in the basic political dichotomy of Atlantis. The public's heralds gave no more thought to the religious muddle embedded in Atlantean politics than to the proscribed derivations of euphemistic words in common cursing. Very few, even at Tessa's cocktail party, were capable of sophisticated interest in the historical algebra: Protestican is to individual as Catholicrat is to society—as freedom is to organization, as selfishness is to commonwealth, as—

But Fay was a surprisingly patient old teacher. She tested a practical proposal that even her studious godson and her actively passionate friend Tessa hadn't yet heard, and that of course had never been brought up in pillow talk with Finn, whose epiphanic outburst of clarity now revealed to Caleb an outright enthusiasm for the noetic bedmate half a decade younger than himself. She suddenly made Finn understand his lifetime instinct to support the Crat cause despite having been brought up in a family and class of inveterate Markland Cans, despite his career's institutional and fraternal loyalty to "conservative" ideas, despite his manifold abhorrence of disreputable Crat politicians prominently featured in the press, despite his initial aversion to F D R ("That Man, Traitor to His Class") and the proletarian New Deal administered by radical and opportunistic henchmen, and despite his occasional votes for some honestly superior Can individual running against a personally despicable Crat when the outcome of an election hadn't seemed to matter much as a Party matter—until, on his Washington tours of duty, it had turned out that there was nothing disingenuous about That Man's love and patriotic support for a Navy worthy of the New Empire! All at once Finn realized that the calm tone of his paramour concealed her fervid hope for some Crat leader to introduce a political philosophy as the Party's leit motiv, in common language, the compendious concept of the Common Good. That simple idea, or its rhetorical equivalent, had been sorely missing in recent Crat campaigns against the Grand Old Party of selfism in the guise of liberty.

But as a matter of tactical philosophy what struck both Finn and Caleb was her simply innovative referral to the single sentence of the Preamble of the Constitution that mentioned "the General Welfare" as succinct expression of the Founding Fathers' composite

doctrine. As equivalent to the "Common Good" concept in historical Christianity it would have been a simple fulcrum for political
polemics that obviously favored Catholicrats when challenging the
Protestican valorization of extended selfism. It was also the core of
an oath sworn by all commissioned officers of the U S Navy (and
others) to the People's government—not to those of the several
semi-independent States. Only the Catholicratic Party could win
argument for the Common Good, notwithstanding all the rightly
preserved values of personal liberty and private rights. The General
Welfare should be repeatedly advanced as the touchstone—the very
foundation—of Atlantean debate.

Fay explicitly pointed out that she meant only the extended
Preamble (which also emphasized the "Blessings of Liberty"), as
distinguished from the implementary body of the Constitution
itself, which fully satisfied none of its framers (to say nothing of the
very large minority of antifederalist citizens) as an unavoidable
system of bitter compromises presented to the People for pragmatic
ratification as a flexible beginning of evolutionary dialectic between
national society, states' rights, and individual rights—contrarieties
too inconsistent for rational or poetic approval. She proposed that
incessant iterations of the Founding Fathers' unity of this generalized theme (regardless of subservient disagreements among themselves) would force the Cans to defend even their purist philosophical values that underlay their deliberately obscured reaction to the
nation's social and economic progress stemming from liberal
administrations since Roosevelt's election had offset Deutschland's
installation of Hitler. In the same level contralto voice that had
enamored Finn, Caleb, and probably many other gentlemen in private conversation, Fay seemed to express no doubt that such exposure of Protestican origins and motives, if skillfully challenged, in
terms of the country's general welfare, would be greatly to the
advantage of the party that best represented the majority of
Atlanteans if analysis were simply begun with the Preamble—
words understandable by any voter, or indeed by anyone who failed
to vote for lack of hero or cynosure.

Her simple idea was to win over the electorate in gross affinity
as a perfectly honest union of composite diversities—just as the
Preamble abstracted the will of all the people, not of independently
colonized states and primarily local interests. The various and
sometimes conflicting desiderata of any party's politics are not consistently represented by a selective list of currently lively issues and

policies any more than the Union Jack symbolizes every historical hope and despair of a Celt or Anglo-Saxon still waving the Union Jack of Empire. A party only loses votes when it unnecessarily itemizes its properly internecine discomforts. Few voters are permanently incapable of seeing that the whole is more than the sum of its positive and negative parts even when certain topics are more personally emotional than rationally social; yet it's only gratuitous to risk all debate upon "issues" and "policies" or on narrower emotions possibly detected as poisonous ingredients by analytical chemists in their partisan staff of life. Both major parties stand for some values too disturbing within their own sub-parliaments to thrash out as embarrassing compromises or persistent grudges in the semi-finals of elected power. Especially in our de facto two-party system the very existence of both broad factions was determined by pragmatic need at the highest level of organization. They need a single umbrella, convertible to a parasol, that serves their true or false motives as well as objectives in the broadest possible defense or purpose—especially, for example, when it comes to getting and spending!

Thus the gentle anthropologist urged the Preamble as an introductory précis for the aggregating and converging ideas latent in the unwritten constitution of the Crat Party. It might liberally educate by unexceptionable deduction the largely anti-intellectual Atlantean majority without relying upon self-interest as its armature of intentions, thereby preserving a stable and robust majority in the body politic, practicable for the whole country and therefore, at least in substantial part, for the democratically conversible interconnected globe.

Caleb immediately shared the hopeful prospect of shaving his Party's prospects with Occam's Razor; and the Union Jack of the Atlantean Common Good (a k a the "General Welfare") that intoxicated Caleb's naval mentor with the tactful suasion of his ordinarily unopinionated lady-friend seemed to strike upon Finn for the first time as her astute common sense. But at the end of the day both he and Caleb had to admit that few of the other listeners (including Tessa the political leader) grasped much of the historical significance in what they heard in her apparently idiosyncratic fellowship. In the unending and redundantly persistent determination to exorcize F D R's ghost, President Raygun stood for the whole Protestican reaction to the liberal progress they were heretofore accustomed to expect more often than not. Hitherto Finn's political specifications would have been much the same as those of Tessa and nearly everyone present when the labile chatter of the occasion had at once instinctively returned to political commiseration and excited execration, half of which were readily pontifical complaints about the tactics of this or that individual or group on their own side of the battle.

The guests in search of refreshment gravitating to the lady in a long gray skirt, ensconced in the unupholstered seat generically known in New Armorica as a Captain's Chair, reminded Caleb of students on the first day of a term looking in on the initial lecture of a new course to make up their minds whether or not to enroll in this one; but to the Commander (who even at 'Bega had had no such option in his academic days) the scene was curiously exhilarating. Ignoring the precedent even of civilian rank, the rejuvenated bachelor officer hinted to his junior companion something more of what underlay the knighthood of his tailored suits.

". . . Until now," in frankly joyful tones said Finn, "I've been a little embarrassed by Tessa Opsimath's brand of liberalism, but if she would take up Fay's ideas about teaching everyone that 'general Welfare' doesn't mean the 'social welfare' that Raygun hates, I'll tell the world that the oath I took for my commission in the 'common defense' was directed to the Constitution and the Congress, not to any President or Department of Offense, even though I swore to obey legitimate orders in the chain of command, according to the Articles of War."

—"Which once drove Redburn nearly to suicidal murder in the chain of command!" Caleb ventured to interrupt his own virtual commanding officer.

"I now find myself about to be a much less cautious Crat. I'll donate more money and even some of my remaining time to her Committee, as well as all the way up to the Washington level! What better use of legacy! I've no family to placate!

"By God," he continued, "I'll study exactly what Fay means by the miscegenated blood of Petrine Catholicrats and Pauline Protesticans, which I suppose is too complicated and socially taboo for public discussion. *History is substance* you tell me your old Father Duncannon used to say. 'History is to the nation as memory is to the individual.' says a young 'Bega professor I met in the Faculty Club. —Oh boy, my memory for names is getting more and more faulty; and much worse, I'm afraid, for common nouns. . . ."

The exuberant old man paused again to dignify his breath. "I wish I knew more about the *history* of our Constitution! And political science. And George Roegen's entropic economics! Fay knows how to answer Raygun's girlfriend over in the old country—that Tory Prime Minister who says 'There's no such thing as society, only the individual and the family.' —Maybe it's too bad Fay doesn't concentrate on politics in her writing."

Thus Finn kept returning to his own noetically expanded enchantment, as if he and Fay had shed two- or three-score decades of body without losing the wisdom of longevity. He was too animated to expect any reply from his adventitious sidekick. "I've never seen her in such a diplomatic setting! I've been damned lucky to last this far without getting married! For a short time after the War, before all the temporary ranks were reduced, I was still a Captain and they made me C O of the Gooneybird Island refueling base for Pacific air-hops—a mile long and a quarter of a mile wide, guarded by huge sting-rays—before it was abandoned as one of the targets testing E-Bomb Squared—maybe to keep me away from attached and uncommitted women in other officers clubs! My housing and boarding were luxurious, the house a good distance from the raucous off-duty camaraderie of bibulous time-killing gentlemen, but anyway traditionally segregated from a ship's skipper, who suppressed whatever evidence they admitted of scholarship, even in technology. But the temporary celibacy was short enough to be no hardship because I had plenty of books."

But he was sober enough to sense that Caleb wasn't sure of getting his drift. "—Until too late, I was fortunate enough to invest in this particular town of yours." Once again, but more sensitively, he laid his palm on Caleb's back, though still in the manner of a Norman or stage-Irish drunk, without noticing that his young friend was holding his peace. ". . . Not that I'm going to ask her to marry me now that I'm learning how to use my own kitchen! For the Common Good no genius should be distracted before her masterpiece is in print. That's something that I think worries her. . . . Caleb, my boy, genuflect when you serve her! Or else write a part for her that no actress could play! What an astonishing mind and memory!

". . . I haven't heard her *public* sense of humor before, with such calm purity of speech, yielding nothing to language or to clothes less than ten years in vogue. And with such a sly sense of humor! . . . Even the way she sips her wine! I bet she's never left lipstick on a rim of a glass—or worn high heels, for that matter! She'd never have mouthed the latest slang, at least not without knowing its derivation (except when genuinely poetic), or just to otherwise fill a semantic void! Jesus Christ, come to think of it, wouldn't she have dampened my shaky popularity if I'd taken her to a Navy cocktail party!"

He stopped to laugh louder than ever, while careful to keep his footing where there was no pavement on their path downhill, yet still not *entirely* loosened of the polite restraint that Caleb was accustomed to expect in his deportment as a former Gentleman and Scholar in the Reserves, reluctantly accepted by the illiberal officer corps of the regular Navy long before F D R's prolific expansion of the Fleet. "With her as a wife, even after the War, the admirals would have assigned me to a tour of duty advising the Swiss Navy on new ideas for their future battleships!"

Caleb softened. Having already appreciated the Commander's admiration of Fay's uninsistent care about manners and speech in their appropriate settings, Caleb wryly refrained from mentioning that he sometimes wondered how his sagacious godmother must have behaved with squalling young kids underfoot in her kitchen while trying as cook to hear herself think exactly about the next motion to attend one of the cooking vessels and maybe make sure that all the ingredients of dinner would simultaneously reach their thermostatic perfection at the moment of optimum synthesis, minimizing the irritation of her hungry and thirsty academic husband hardly waiting to begin eating exactly at the appointed time, after his martini and her toast to his list of professional successes, when all along she was expected to welcome him home with delighted smiles to a civilized dinner with well-behaved kids at which everyone's gustatory and intellectual interests were reasonably and respectfully discussed if they did not interrupt the head of the house—after she has finally exiled the piercing high-pitched screeches of a cat, probably called Catullus, who has left his allotted food almost untouched to demand instead a share of the table's purest protein prey, of which a feline could not be organoleptically deceived simply because it has been hidden from his eyes.

In those early days the talents of both Fay and Caleb's mother Mary (who had only one child in the flesh but less than one husband to share expenses) had been starved of private time, for poetry or learning, the frustration of which naturally accounted for extraordinary explosions of anger, much less at its immediate objects than at

the conflict of unequalized male and female interests even when situations and temperaments greatly differed. Ladylike Fay must have
done her own caterwauling at the creatural willfulness of wholly
beloved and codeterminate variable dependents, at least once in a
while, Caleb conjectured in the light of his own experience of a very
different mother, though his smaller scenes were those of a fatherless
only-child. But he had deservedly absorbed the suddenly furious
yells of an unassisted breadwinner responding in many a shabby
kitchen to petty or irrelevant complaints from himself about his
housekeeping chores or his disappointed hopes for greater liberty or
postponed repayment of pocket money.

Thus from his own very different childhood he humorously
extrapolated the proposition that a well-sheltered intellectual kind
of goddess, harried yet unbound, would never have burst out with
undignified curses or violent threats in regrettable expletives
totally out of the ordinary. Generalizing for the fun of it, he mused
that even the most ladylike debutante from one of the finest finishing schools, innocent of locker room and street, or the most contented old lady without dependent children on her hands, must at
least once or twice a year regurgitate forbidden high-pitched scatol-
ogy or sexual smut formed by her tongue but frozen from her ears,
in the patois of a fishwife, somehow echoing from she knew not
where or when, particularly in its etymological derivation. —But it
would have been disrespectful for Caleb to abuse Finn's tipsy fellowship by offering a naive old bachelor some precociously distasteful history of usually unmentionable femininity.

Anyway, the startling exposure of Finn's youthful feeling when
delivering with loosened tongue his tribute to Fay, unmistakably
devoid of parity, was never to Caleb repeated or amplified, presumably because his drinking (at least in Dogtown) was comparatively
abstemious, in keeping with his most unostentatious practice of
keeping fit with prudential eating and unusually vigorous exercise
for the sake of optimum longevity (though nevertheless comfortable with the temperately relaxed mores of their inner circle). The
next morning he was bound to be retrospectively embarrassed at his
sublime indiscretion with Caleb that night.

Perhaps he'd allowed too much familiarity in his instrumental
assistance to Caleb's livelihood, who after all was no man's famulus,
but whose gratitude for such favor sometimes seemed excessive,
their meeting of minds in many reciprocating conversations
notwithstanding. Primarily they were both fascinated by the func-

tional abstraction of systems, according to their respective realms of technological experience—even as they grew cautious of each other's ostensibly insignificant differences, beyond those of age, while taking pains to make the most of other common interests, some of which were nothing less than enthusiastic, such as Redburn's book about the world as a heavy frigate (the 19C analogy of a modern heavy cruiser) when the U S A had no ship-of-the-line analogous to a new class of battleships last readied for W W 2.

Even though he was a legal evader of conscription in a later generation, Caleb's nautical interest in the Bureau of Ships, the center of Finn's career, was historically familiar as an institution of vicarious experience begun as a schoolboy full of longing to become a Navy officer by way of the Port Royal Academy. Even now, as much as anything else of the kind he envied the cosmopolitan experience of his newfound hero's exceedingly diverse stations in the Navy, including unofficial liberties that were scarcely alluded to in casual remarks about traveling in Europe or continental Atlantis as a bachelor in or out of uniform. Fay's sojourns within the Pacific Rim were only of special literary attraction. And even she, whose academically privileged life he counted as cosmopolitan, had never been as far as Finn north of the Alps and Dolomites.

". . . She certainly knows more than I do about everything except *may*be marine engineering!" Finn was concluding his encomium. "Athene in person! But her writings are harder for me than for you to fathom, especially when she's so oh-so-surely criticizing epistemological scientists or ontological metaphysicians from the ground up!"

—Recently Fay herself it was with Caleb on a happier walk to the beach who said "I've been down here at apparent high tide when that rocky cove back there seemed little more than two-thirds full, only to find that here at the creek it looked almost as high as normal; and when I walked down along the beach I was sure the water was still advancing on the sand in one place while it was clearly receding at others. I thought the beach itself, generally appearing straight and level, was continually amusing itself by reforming hollows and interesting little ridges just to dissuade people from contenting themselves with the regular beauty of freshwater wavefronts. Or maybe it's mocking the big petrified fractals all along the Fore Shore."

"The shore's friction is what causes every town on the North Shore its own distinctive tide-table." replied the sapient Caleb who sometimes can't help sounding rather didactic when flattered by being asked for his views, momentarily forgetting that many years before she had lived in Dogtown more than long enough to learn of its irregularities, including his own birth. But immediately recovering from his suppressed embarrassment, he went on in a diffident tone: "I suppose the tide creeps up along its occasional unobstructed perpendicular to the beach, which probably isn't typical, but that otherwise it comes in at an imperceptibly changing slant, unless the wind-driven waves come in strong enough from another direction to ignore friction entirely in our whole part of the irregular New Armorican coastline. —I haven't thought of it before, on the other hand, but some weather must make for higher relative friction right here in particular, rather than neutralizing it. Let's ask Finn. He told me, if I rightly understood him, that along the beaches of the British Archipelago (all inferior to ours) they try to keep surf and sand squared with each other by dividing whole strands into small parcels bordered by berms of knee-high timber to form hedgerows pointing openly in the direction from which they are individually most likely to confront the waves at a right angle. It sounded to me like differential calculus! Have you seen those in Britain or Brittany?"

"Yes!" she replied. "And I remember wondering why anyone would want to further spoil even one of their pathetically shingled beaches. I probably guessed that those barriers had something to do with abating storm damage."

"Well, I've glimpsed them only in the movies. That's the only explanation I can think of. I may be all wet." They smiled in familiar unison: she was invited to continue; it was a companionship in autonomous association of sensed ideas.

"It's good we don't need such contraptions spoiling this lovely bleak deserted beach with not so much as a single sandpiper in sight." Fay wondered. "I don't know where my lone-ranging blackback Maxwell does her socializing, but right now most of the raucous gull federation is probably darkening the sky over at the State Fish Pier while some boats are unloading, shrieking and squabbling at the densely populated center of what you call a microtopopolis within three blocks of where you're so busy abstracting symbols for a common good in the center of things! —Look, at the very foot of that eel-grassed ridge of sand I've seen a Cosmo angel dart down through a canopy of close-packed family paraphernalia to snatch half a roll of mustard-and-relish hot dog already fingered on the way to the mouth of a little boy from his paper plate to a flapping vortex of aerial competition. I didn't think the gull had path enough through the bunched sunshades and crowded parents to open his wings, but it came and went before the boy's amazement could turn into a howl. I didn't stop squeezing my passage that happened to be through that cluster until the enraged parents and grandparents couldn't see my laugh. It was no laughing matter to anyone not brought up, begging your pardon, in a Cellaneous Family. Your unpsychological mother would have made the hungriest of them see a delightful joke as the imperative!"

"Embellished with a fairy tale of her own making." Caleb laughed. "Tessa thinks I should try to remember my traumas."

"You must have been happily inured to disappointed expectations of fun!"

—But now, surveying the broad Little Harbor Beach, this time in solemn mood, as observers or readers in random association of ideas suggested by the vast theater again emptied of angels, Fay Gabriel and Caleb Karcist are almost similarly somnambulistic at equal levels of consciousness while naturally differing in perspective. Fay's utterances are unusually disengaged in tone and meaning, for she whispers anachronistically, irrelevantly, "That time I thought the bird deserved it." as they turn around to ascend for ten or fifteen minutes a lattice of nearly deserted asphalt pavements to regain her elevated but delitescent house above the intersection where, by a shabby patched-up lane of asphalt negligently lined by overgrowth of brambles and shrubbery, they finally approach the pentagonal locus of the spinal Oakcliff thoroughfare, joined as if with three tributaries. They are emerging from the one opposite the dead-end "private way" she officially lives on.

But before they make the main road's crossing (very cautiously looking both ways) neither of them can refrain from glancing exactly at the spot on a shoulder of untended grass where he had found the dead body of her cat. Without glancing at each other, without a word, they mutually acknowledge the fatal trauma of her kilroy-stricken Felixity, tiny jaws locked open. For Fay it's an instant of recapitulation, an extension of their affined preoccupation; for Caleb it's more like a metaphorical equation, which for him is natural enough when comparing two kinds of human beings in technological terms: a is to b as x is to y: with nearly watering eyes he feels something of his part in Fay's grief for a female cat he'd hardly met, and he particularly tries without success to feel the commonplace death-stroke in sudden agony by any innocent creature abroad. He remembers Finn trying to empathize with gasping fish in a waterless bucket, a Viking who readily apologizes for his insensitivity to Mother Earth's uneducated humanity as consumers—disconnected from his own experience of suffering in the Pacific War and its excruciating aftermath in Europe, having never been personally underprivileged or handicapped at a psychological disadvantage of an early life too sheltered.

—*Sheltered*: Caleb is no longer astonished by elective affinity when his godmother remarks, as if out of the blue, when he happened to be speaking of his admiration for Finn, that "If F D R, as Traitor to His Class, had not been stricken with polio, maybe the New Deal would not have made of humane tenderness an active force in the political economy, even as he was being pressed instead to assume an emergency dictatorship."

"But his crippling came late in life." Caleb replies on her level. "Without that chastening disability and its endless physical therapy I think he might have done as well for the common good—just as highborn, yet of a better mother, perhaps some kind-hearted intelligent woman with *guts* (as my mother always put it), willing and capable of common experience. The mother he did have, or rather had him, was neither lion nor daughter of lions who feed their children by hunting and killing, in a sense at least for a time altruistically. Mother lions also do the teaching, as well as the nursing. His mother was not one to teach what was outside the shelter of wealth and finishing schools. At least that's what *my* mother scoffed at! How would she know or care anything about *real* society, still less feel the uneducated feelings of the people at the bottom of Aquinas's pyramid? Yet my mother especially loved F D R for overcoming the handicap of having been a momma's boy."

"Your mother was a sage of maturity, dear boy. But it's a pity she didn't have those other two she'd planned for, especially your sister, to assist her motherhood; or at least a little brother smarter than you to marry and produce a teachable granddaughter to start the perpetuation of the maternalistic feminism I read so much about in her marvelous letters!" Fay smiles as Caleb smiled at her rebuke. "But unless there's something you've never told me, you're putting a genealogical end to what would have been the world's most radical matriarchy!"

This tone of familiar persiflage was but a shadow of the kind of non-elective affinity still inquisitively pursued by Private Detective

Inspector Tessa Opsimath on behalf of Caleb but without his wish or continued cooperation. The uninquisitive godmother also thinks that Tessa's recent ostensibly casual remarks have grown less candid, as if to prevent that judge from recusing herself from a Court of Law. But the defendant himself, though wishing for the first time to discuss with his otherwise omniscient Athene (a k a Minerva, patroness of quarrymen) the case in which he himself is the ultimate subject, is aware of his guilt in allowing his thoughts to wander at all selfward in the mood they tacitly shared on this excursion meant to divert the deepest thoughts they shared in this instance. But impersonal images and reflections are always invading the echo chamber of his materially psychosomatic head without distinct curiosity about the process of semantic association. (Psychologists might call the process an evasion of truth.)

Crossing the thoroughfare, at the bottom of the leafy dead end maintained by the five residents, they turn uphill toward the majestic wolf oak that shades Fay's front door, closely next to a massive whale-rock, whence they had begun their circuit. Still an untraceable network of Caleb's synapses offers elusive excuses from feelings of grief that continue to slip back into wisps of guilt—like aesthetical visions of the faintly bubbling but pellucid eddies he's sometimes studied from the footbridge and elsewhere at the edges of flooding or ebbing tide, when the creek behaves like some of a river's molecular conscripts making up their minds whether to keep going with the flow, or like volunteers regretting the direction taken by their motives, especially when the momentum (mass times velocity) drops to outright nullification. Objective thoughts of his usual kind are still lagging behind the thoughts he should be feeling, even without contrary wind to deceive the eye by making ambivalent ripples or wavelets on the creek's surface as prima facie evidence of prevalent power. Even when the direction of its vector is obvious without dropping a twig to float one way or the other from the bridge, either bank is always irritated to some degree, if only as defensive resentment of the main stream. Tiny eddies protest and curl wherever there is marginal friction of sand, dune grass, rock, or weed—as if stirred by hope for abrasive foothold against either anabasis or catabasis, with or without the prospect of premature death.

Thus also in the two-minute ascent to the grandfather tree he finds his broader thoughts continue in a few seconds to concatenate from the creek's diurnal rhythm to symmetrical tidal streams like those of the city's own Namauche River or (from what he'd never seen) the large and larger Straits of Menai and Magellan, in which the tide confronts itself twice a day somewhere within the length of its channel, according to the frontier of ebb and flow due to friction or obstruction along the coast in reaching or retreating from its two mouths, ever under lunar influence. The reversible river named Namauche by Irindians has remained almost the same (*pace* Heraclitus) ever since the Gut was opened to isolate the town three hundred and fifty years ago. Yet—yet, as always, irreversible time measures irreversible losses of eddied energy even when the dual momentum is equal and opposite in reversal more than twice three hundred and fifty times a year. . . .

—At home in the kitchen Fay pats Caleb's arm. "You can go into the living room and do your contemplation while I rustle up a meal. Nothing fancy: only fish, potatoes, and greens."

"Fish, potatoes, and greens are what I fancy most. But I've already taken up too much of your time!"

"I'm trying to be a hermit, as far as society is concerned, but I more than fancy your helpful presence, dear Caleb. Especially right now I'm very glad you're here to keep me company. More than anyone else you are connected to the work that makes me a nun again. Let's dust off a bottle or two of my dark red wine, and make the best of melancholy. This is one occasion when you and I can lay down pens and put aside books without wasting an iota of our time. We both need a pause to think about our loss without sentimentality. You help keep me balanced. At my age of course the granite ceiling looms, not in fear but in haste. I almost forget my scattered children but I often wish I could claim more of *your* time to talk about my presumptuous work-in-progress, as I could not do even with a brilliant daughter who knows me too well. My natural son is too undereducated to be treated as an intellectual peer, or at least too refractory to open his mind to the suggestion that he and his family come to Dogtown, even to visit in this nearly empty house—if only to remember that this is where they both spent the happiest summers of their early lives. He'll never stop living off fellowships or expense accounts in Europe, Eyerup, or Syrup!"

That last phrase is Fay's affectionate recognition of his mother's merriment, who'd picked up that portable bit of burlesque from the straw boss of a construction crew rebuilding a storm-wrecked bridge over the broad trout stream in Montvert near their tiny pro tem cottage on the edge of Allenton village when Caleb was still an inattentive listener to explanations of men who took her fancy. The man in this instance gave him his first socially responsible job: filling portable red lamps with kerosene, lighting them at sunset, blowing them out in the morning, and recharging them to warn drivers of temporary barriers in the road. When not at public school by day he studied the methods of reconstruction and was sorry when the project was finished and the jovial contractor disappeared for the last time, leaving not a single lamp behind.

—In a suddenly uninhibited impulse, hugging Fay's almost fleshless armature, he kisses the palely olive cheek drawn smoothly hollow by the stretching of brow and chin. Then, bowing, he kisses her skinny tapered right hand, pressed in both his own, with the warm impertinence he's hitherto restrained in awe of her polymath superiority to the ordinary intelligentsia—so remarkably did she complement rather than offset the humanity of Mary Tremont's self-educated exuberance of imagination and emotion in poverty and independence, in suffering excesses of both eros and agape, in Christian charity as both giver and receiver, in mystical joy, humility and doubt, in hopeless courage, in self-chastisement, and in self-dramatization. He has chosen not to test his assumptions about the godmother because she has become a Muse who with all his filial values infuses a symbol-system that integrates nearly everything that excites his private energy.

Of her own influence upon himself he believes Fay is scarcely aware, but at a time in which he is dragged away from active intellectual passion to public service her model keeps alive his vainglorious vision in dramaturgy, even as he reckons his diminishing prospect of recognizable achievement in guild or craft. But now at least it is plain to him that both his affinities—one congenital and the other elective, dead mother and live Muse—were founded upon reciprocally acquired feminine emotion in different realms. Therefore he does not reckon as necessarily advantageous the envied economic and cultural privileges of Fay's own children, with a father to teach them Greek when they were still innocent enough to learn it for fun. He tells himself that he the mundane rational technologist, his fragmentary postgraduate learning too late for academic affiliation or for the development of any extraordinary talent, was the one who benefitted from a precious kind of negative capability. Fair enough, when a man can also love his teachers.

—Teachers! Comfortably settled alone in the armchair of a musty room, inert fingers interlaced in his lap, starting with his

mantra's breath, Caleb recalls his most formative years with personal mentors in church or school, before the impersonal college
tutelage that became the foundation of self-education, setting first
and foremost the firmly married and honorable owner and headmaster of the private Dutchkill boarding school in isolated
Dutchkill Falls. That tiny institution was almost unknown among
well-off parents searching to place their boys in private secondary
education for a leg-up to college which Dwight Northstone, dedicated to teaching the Latin language and English poesy, whose own
father had been a highly respected headmaster at elite Grottlesex,
had perilously established as a semi-classical preparatory school on
his wife's inherited hardscrabble dairy farm, initiating a new kind
of liberal education for boys who might be capable of work on more
levels than one. In his struggle to make the farm-school solvent and
more or less harmonious—without letting up either on his own
down-to-earth handling of the core Latin and English classes, his
necessitous leadership in physical labor and pedagogy on the part of
a few half-paid but initially enthusiastic young catechumens in an
iconoclastic version of teaching, to say nothing of supporting and
encouraging the wife who supported and encouraged himself with
German and French, teaching conventionally enough between her
menial labors behind the scene in an understaffed kitchen—within
six or seven years he had inconspicuously fallen into beer-can alco-
holism (imbibed largely while laboring in the woods or fields) by
way of bearing up under the otherwise impossible stress of keeping
alive an increasingly penurious effort to sustain an innovative ideal.
This he shared with his equally dedicated but preternaturally
equable and abstemious wife who as a factotum, with her own children also to nurture, lacked most of the praise and admiration he
was accorded by observers. Her two boys and two girls, younger
than the other students, she knew, suffered perforce "at home"
amongst youths of older growth (some of whom she also tutored
and disciplined without favoring her own pupils). Their apparently
tireless mother, furthermore, not only filled in wherever academic
subjects or household labor were short-handed but also performed
as guardian nurse and foster-comforter for all the students, most of
whom were discontented or misfitted for traditional education, private or public.

   Caleb will never forget the chores he learned and with which
he was sooner or later entrusted as a specialist or leader—not as
the extra work of a charity boy to earn his keep but as a student

who was always glad to take responsibilities, starting as a stable boy for the team of draft horses Daisy and Dandy, and later as one of the two pre-dawn cow-milkers and colporteurs for the same barn half a mile from the manor house where everything was churned or directly consumed, and eventually as the point man for a few boys his own age in otherwise hardly supervised woodlots. Most of these coppices were second- or nth-growth, in patches of hardwood that had once been laboriously cleared of stony forest to become pasture land, before it was reclaimed by descendants of the forest-primeval's seeds.

But in winter his most important job was to fuel the school's central furnace, of which he was sole custodian and operator (pretending to himself that he was in charge of a nautical engine room) in the cellar of the former farmhouse. Thus for a time he steam-heated air and water for everyone who wasn't bunked or worked indoors about or above the great cast-iron kitchen, or in rooms inefficiently warmed by a brick fireplace or a stovepipe wood stove meant (without much confidence) to keep the water pipes from freezing in weather of thirty Fahrenheit degrees below zero. But the system stoked and maintained by him had reached its B T U limit when its asbestos-wrapped arteries were extended to heat the annexed "barn" built by earlier faculty and students to serve as dining room and study hall, with an upper story of classrooms and small dormitories. In season, the boiler was voracious, and its fire tubes were nearly choked with stenching creosote if the split logs were still too green, as all too often they were. In dry weather a dozen or more team of students, faculty, and the black hired hand, as well as the headmaster himself, often spent most of whatever non-academic afternoon and Saturday time permitted (as counterpart to the sports customary in other secondary schools) trying to maintain a proper inventory of firewood; so his semi-autonomous weekday assignment to the woods was supplemented alone by taking charge of the split cordwood logs that were put to use at the house, seasoned or not too soon, sometimes from almost no stacked inventory at all. His peers liked to blame him for the stink. Once or twice every winter Dwight had to cancel classes when the supply of carbon energy capsules fell dangerously low outside the cellar door, or elsewhere in the usual piles of small buzz-sawed stove wood. Winters were either bitterly cold or thickly covered with exciting depths of snow—or even both—until the thick ice muffling the big brook in its vertiginous plunges more than a hundred feet to a forested chasm suddenly thawed, once on Caleb's birthday, and broke open the season of equinoctial hope with an alarming roar, about when the sap for maple sugar was promising to rise in trees still naked.

Caleb loved the gentle and tolerant horses whose pungent manure he had forked and swept and whose glossy flanks he had curried as a city-bred boy's introduction to animal husbandry. That chore soon followed as his regular early-morning preprandial duty, often lighted only by the kerosene lamps they needed to see their way to get to the barn across hill and brook and pasture, while most of the students did miscellaneous work only in the afternoons. After a year or so with horses he did much the same, but in sweetly contrasting smells, in the basement of the barn, assisted by a few other boys, with a small herd of milk cows, calling them in from pasture (when there was green grass to find), draining them as they munched grain or hay, and scraping up after them. By hand on a three-legged stool he rhythmically squirted their generous milk (humanly extorted as the prolonged aftermath of calving) into a stainless steel bucket between his knees. Their loyalty and contentment were essential to the school's economy. Most of them were large rangy black and white Holsteins. His favorite was Ruth. In winter she warmed his cold fingers on the skin of her silky udder, looking back in thanks for not going immediately to her naked teats. This grasping exercise strengthened the muscles of both his forearms as even forestry could not.

Yet his fifteen-year-old pride lay in the development of his biceps as he improved his balancing skills with the double-bladed axe and its complement of other tools, especially a long crosscut saw with wooden handles and another boy at the opposite end. Two artificers worked as reciprocating functions like an old single-cylinder steam engine, one man exerting force, the other more lightly drawing the machine back to its re-potentiality, both operators in the delicately rhythmic sweat required to fell and dismember, say, a noble silver beech crowded by less mature stands of hardwood amid undergrowth of sapling scrub. The execution took place on a slippery carpet of green seedlings sprouted from manifold layers of brown leaves from untold previous autumns.

The other implements were three or more steel wedges and a maul to drive them, as called for, into the slot behind the saw to keep it from pinching by the cut, and to prevent the still-living tree's weight and center of gravity from tipping or twisting in the wrong direction, or from crashing with too many upright splinters left on the stump. Later in the immemorial algorithm wedges were also meant to be driven into longitudinal cracks, neatly marked and started with a single carefully considered blow by an axe's blunter blade at the uppermost edge of an eighteen- or twenty-inch diameter rim.

But the main action, the thrill, came between these two phases as the felling itself, usually performed by the boy playing hero. He has already notched with his thinner blade a gleaming white throat opposite the course of the sawyers but on a slightly lower plane, awaiting their progress, then vigorously chopping a larger and deeper angle of invitation, until the saw's cut, well past half the tree's diameter, prodded by the wedges, makes the great tree groan and start to sway on its intended hinge of valiantly diminished resistance reduced to a small horizontal semi-circle, approaching like a maw the powerfully accelerated strokes of the momentously undercutting headsman's axe. When the beech gives up and lies flat in a resounding crash, taking with it all the lesser growth in its path, its beautiful gray trunk and useful limbs are trimmed of all branches from butt to apex, making way for the saws applied at regular three-foot intervals of slicing, felled trunk now lying in pieces like a vandalized Classical column reduced on the ground to its disjointed components. Wedges and maul are again required, this time to split the segments down the middle, and yet again to split the halves and quarters until they are of a size to fit through Caleb's furnace door after being carted off and stacked in the hope of long enough weathering. What Grottlesex or Botolph Latin schooling could have been more valuable experience for a managerial technocrat to assimilate before finding himself at an electronic forefront of action?

Thus at Mary Tremont's behest—at first by mail alone—a generously hopeful reformer of masculine education had been persuaded to accept her yet-unseen son by the name of Caleb Karcist as a pupil without charge for tuition, board, or room if he was willing and able to profit from a truly Atlantean version of the best in British tradition (except for Greek and most of science)—as if a pubescent midshipman in a seagoing ship of scholars.

It was only years later, to Caleb's excruciating embarrassment, that his mother confessed to him by expiating letter a contemptible sin known only to herself, Mrs Northstone, and Dwight Northstone *himself* at her first visit to the school, that she had been passionately struck by the heroic manner, mein, and body of the blond and blue-eyed headmaster. No doubt many a visiting mother had suffered the same afflatus at noble prep schools. Having recently been at last definitely betrayed and abandoned by a dark Loosey taxi driver, the gently uneducated but classically handsome Tony Porter—as it was to turn out, her life's most persistently adored lover, who among his passengers was likewise desired by women of every class in many places—she pursued this unlikely lost cause with more than one unacknowledged poetically honest letter to the genuinely literary teacher. Thanks to the kindly discretion of both this ruggedly handsome Anglo-Saxon headmaster romantically dressed as a farmer and his graciously welcoming wife, not a whit of the secret was hinted to Caleb or anyone else, nor did it prejudice their affectionate guardianship of her son, whom they treated just as if he was a scion of some rich family seeking a solution to certain problems in education.

Thanks only to his mother's written persuasion Caleb had been invited to test her confidence in him. He was quartered as a peer among five other boys ensconced in the dormered "Garret" above the common room of the Colonial wing that linked the main house by space or communication to various dormitories for older boys, some in outlying buildings where he later had more congenial roommates, some of impressive origins, among whom a few may have understood a scholarship status when they saw one, according not so much to his academic achievements as to the quality of his jacket-and-tie dinner outfit, which otherwise was mandatory only on a truckload of Sunday attendance in a tiny village church where almost the entire student body constituted the choir under the headmaster's voluntary direction, still (for bucolic or diplomatic reasons) wearing as foundation the uniform of dungarees and laced boots, a leveling of no particular denomination. Thus the school's two-dozen pupils or teachers dominated a representative Pauline society. The village's only Petrines were the family who ran the little general store next door which was quite active on Sundays.

Like more than a few clergymen of poetic or chivalric manner elsewhere in large fashionable parishes or academies, Dwight Northstone probably evoked erotic emotions in half the women who saw, or especially, heard him speak, whether or not they had anything to do with any kind of education, and presumably he was little more overwhelmed or even surprised by Mary Tremont's A-plus romantic poetry than his lovely sensible wife Charlotte had

MICHAELMAS 641

been or was. These pro tem foster parents of Caleb in Montvert were experienced in cheerful and delicate ways to avoid encouragement without recourse to incivility or scandal. Nevertheless it would have been a disaster if Mary had had her own means of transportation around the mountain to exacerbate or repent her one visit. Anyway, for Caleb in his ignorance it was one of the advantages of poverty and maternal misbehavior that she had neither car nor license nor bicycle, as well as cash, for access to his situation. Soon she told herself as much.

So no one at Dutchkill School privy to the fact or suspicious of it ever held his mother's blatant indiscretion as a blot on his history, and even in the summer, when there were no classes or students, he was a modestly hired hand living almost as if within a family and meeting its cosmopolitan visitors, many of whom were former students or colleagues from the famous academia against which the Northstones had respectfully reacted. While working at his various tasks on the hundred-and-sixty acres of manor, barns, pasture, hayfields, vegetable garden, farm machinery, forest, workshops, and carpentry projects he was treated as a son of their own, including the opportunity to get his driver's license and drive the truck. In three summers he had enough liberty to become (he thought) one of the whole county's best Saturday night square-dancers, enjoying also other entertainments with nominally sophisticated daughters of professional summer folk as well as with one or two local lasses.

At the end of his third academic year, as his early graduation-diploma and prize for academic honors, he was awarded the school's binary symbol, a pristine double-bitted axe with a gleaming hickory haft exactly replicating the ones he had had to wield and sharpen in cold and heat, each of the blades for its different purpose in shaping wood, even at the inferior level of the kitchenyard where the stationed tractor was rigged up with a drive-belt to rotate the screaming circular buzz saw that cut the smallest pieces of firewood for domestic stoves and hearths. It was up to him with grindstone wheel and finer hand-files to distinguish a new axe's blades by precisely concaving the one he preferred, which now in retrospect had reminded him of schooners built with beautiful but dangerous clipper bows amazingly delicately suggesting those of the fast Atlantean battleships under Finn Macdane's influence, as compared with the bluffer spoon-bows of a knockabout fisherman or, for that matter, with an L S T's drawbridge shielded by a pair of clamshell

doors to push the waves. He preferred grinding that slightly concave cleavage to the slightly gibbous blade meant for cutting brush
at the grubbing level of roots and rocks, or any object too hard for
deep penetration. He had kept his academic talisman almost
untouched during the intervening years as the scutcheon of his
most important alma mater—except for once when used in the
High Cordillera of Cornucopia on one very brief summer job with a
Hume friend (Dave Wilson, now at last married to Belle Cingani
here in Dogtown) when he was too afraid of rattlesnakes to spare
much attention for swinging at anything but the ground at his feet,
seeing that the haft of the axe was too short for any broader defense
against a serpent of any stripe.

The axe had betokened singular honor as well as graduate's
godspeed, something far more precious than his gold-key from
Hume a few years later. It represented his beloved schoolmaster's
disinterested devotion to the liberal education of many others at the
expense of his own orthodox career among the elite of pedagogy.
For Caleb it tacitly symbolized his gratitude for all the education
he'd been awarded also thereafter by openminded officers almost of
Dutchkill's ilk under very different circumstances. He congratulated parents who tried to choose the unconventional best for either
maladjusted or peculiarly gifted children, as Dwight Northstone
did, who demonstrated the value of his personal recommendation
to colleges by showing no A on any of the academic courses he
himself had taught, but without mentioning on the record what he
always told his Latin and English pupils: that he never gave such a
mark unless it was for what he himself could have done as their
teacher. Off the record, he was especially critical in Caleb's
advanced English class, as when he wrote in the margin of a paper
submitted by the sophisticated and clever grandson of J. P. Morgan
(and Caleb's older and cosmopolitan political enemy): "A lot of
[picture of a barn shovel] very well expressed. . . ." He never tolerated bullshit, but always recognized the worthiness of unintellec-
tual talents.

For his own satisfying and exceptional experience in mind and
body, afterwards expressed by mail, Caleb could offer no financial
return to such a frail and microscopic institution. After his departure the school survived only a few more years, as the postwar
nation flowered with liberality and innovation, before its bankruptcy, which, thanks to a loyal and affectionate number of affluent
alumni and former colleagues, left the Northstones with possession

of their dwellings, the renowned Falls, and most of their land. Neither these benefactors nor most of the alumnied parents resented
the disappointment of their trust in the Northstone experiment in
uniquely complementary education—nor did Mary Tremont, for
this was exactly what she had sought for him whose only alternative had been a rural "consolidated" public school designed primarily for "vocational" education. Yet even a little of the latter had not
been lost on Caleb when he got to Dutchkill, for in his brief attendance among Allenton children in Montvert he had learned the
breeds of horses, cows, and chickens, and how to write a check
(though he was to have none of his own until he became a semi-
selfsufficient student three thousand miles to the west).

Thus to this day with his eyes closed the middleaged boy happens to find himself coming to the end of his C N meditation in
Fay Gabriel's house, for some unknown reason awakening simultaneously from his unpayable debt-without-price to the late headmaster and the much greater perpetual obligation to his vanished
mother. For three more minutes he slowly opens his visions of the
anima mundi, wondering how his selection of mentated experience
had been intuited with his mantra. Was it because of remembering
the fear that in a visit to Dutchkill she'd try to be the immediate
life of the party by comically simpering her then latest personation?

Little tee-wee went to sea.
Out in an open boat,
And while afloat,
Her little boat bended.
Now my story's ended.   .

3.

Supper with his supreme tutor is solemn but pleasant. Caleb
marvels at the casual competence of cultural anthropology's independent philosopher, as if her duty as housewife to a Classical
scholar was long ago learned once and for all (having already earned
her stripe and pin as a Nightingale nurse with manifold skills
under many a male superior), needing no further thought about
how to get things done and out of the way, like riding a bicycle
while instinctively using her head at a higher level of existence—of
course saving her guest the time spent in shifting for himself back

at Apostle's Dock without such competence. But even without
thinking of what she was doing to make and serve the meal, he
shamefully realizes, her priceless old age is being spent on him who
still needs his own remainder of life much less urgently. Yet without dwelling upon his admiration (which she shortly forbids), the
generous substance and easy manner at her kitchen table is exactly
attuned both to his taste and to the mood they seem to share
almost at the same depth. They are treading water, with much left
unsaid about dispirited swimming. On the surface her life-work is
left aside; his present occupation with the city's common good is
forgotten. In his eyes her aging face is beautiful. In his thoughts no
man, not even the late Alpha Whitehead her own final tutor, has
ever equaled her integrated perceptions of humanity. She has complemented in intellectual scale his mother's actual experience of
Atlantean mankind.

"... but how did Arthur Halymboyd die?" Caleb asks. "There
was very little in the paper. I don't have time to read *The New Uruk
Testament*. I don't dare: it's too much of a distraction, especially now
when election hopes are in abeyance—as if forever."

"I don't either. But Tessa has heard a little about its obituary
from Belle, which of course can't be copied in the *Nous*. Even if that
were permitted, it's hardly a matter of much interest up here.
Who's ever heard of him as the off-island resident of a practically
secret old people's retreat for the rich? People of this generation
never knew who he was, or why, when they saw Sam Craigie driving him around town every so often in that big car, just an old fat
cat looking like some curmudgeon living in that secluded luxury
across the Gut. Anyway, Tessa says, in cases of outside wealth it's
remarkable how a deceased marooner's charity or madness, or possibly senile attachments, seem never to acknowledge Dogtown as a
place. Before we know what's happened the body has been legally
whisked away by its distant clan. Apparently in some way probate
lawyers who know nothing of Dogtown are alert to every locus of
beneficiaries mentioned in wills before anyone else gets to know
what's in them, in order to immediately forestall by swift action
anything that might be disputed or otherwise misunderstood even
at an unattended coffin or eulogy, which might be more like a
pauper's than a benefactor's." she faintly snorted.

"But of course, even without riches or metropolitan obituaries
and unseen lawyers", Caleb replied, "many important marooners
plant themselves for decades without special notice or appreciation

by citizens, with their own family lawyers or clergymen right here in town, expecting no claim on a great estate to be overlooked or revivified. Arthur Halymboyd was a bold magnate of corporations on Graveyard Street who according to some outlived his unworthy personal ambition, escaped legal reprimand, and never became a Whig!"

"Well, in the end I admired him" said Fay. "As an alumnus on Hawthorne's Board of Syndics in Markland, Tessa tells me, he seems to have managed with his transplanted heart arteries long enough to get up to Nassau and negotiate with the college attorney his last-minute 'ethical endowment', as an annual four-year scholarship for a Dogtown boy or girl (if each year one can be found to meet Hawthorne standards), with no strings attached except that it was to be named in memorial to a professor of history who had befriended and encouraged him as a sixteen-year-old insecure young Jew from the colony of Terra Nova before it became a province of the Dominion. It wasn't until Arthur was up there, just before his last heart attack, that he happened to learn his beloved benefactor had been an uncle of Finn's, whose father, the professor's brother, had managed the shipyard nearby in Wight!"

Caleb was puzzled by his venerable godmother's interest in this subject as he gazed at her unusually animated face.

"I did hear that Arthur intended to surprise Finn about the ceremony," she continued, "but they planned to go up to downeast Markland together, so that a healthy friend could keep the heart-frail one company on the trip, as well as share the driving, and then while that legal business was going on at the College also take a side trip to see Finn's stamping grounds."

"I think he was wanted to help the Works and the Navy inspectors evaluate the condition of his last destroyer when it was due for final approval of its first extended duty with the Fleet." Caleb offered. "Finn probably planned to do *all* the driving in order to avoid risking both their lives!"

"I have the impression that Finn was always restless," Fay nodded, "not just officially but also on his Navy leaves by himself. He told me that until he settled down here he was always carrying around in his head a list of places still to visit or revisit. But it turns out that Dogtown retirement reduced the radius of Wanderlust to include only the vicinities of his origin! *I've* never been so slightly adventurous." she added with a smile.

"But he didn't go!"

"That's why old Sam Craigie—you know him, I think, as Dogtown's official Poet Laureate, and Arthur's usual taxi driver—drove
him up there instead. He had to suffer the shock of witnessing his
employer's death on the way from the hotel to the Nassau Hospital, which otherwise would have been Finn's role in that week's
fatalities."

"So Finn changed his mind at the last minute?"

"Belle is still Tessa's Fly on the Wall as well as editor of the
Nous with a waterfront reporter at her disposal, and I suppose
plenty of volunteer spies. As a new marooner and landlubber, all
I've been able to make of it from Tessa, whether or not printable as
either fact or gossip, is that at the last minute Finn couldn't stand
what Brian Nedlaw was about to do with the irreplaceable old
Gloucesterman in the deep-sea race."

In the halting monotone of one recounting a discomposed
dream Fay tells Caleb her third-hand reconstruction of the event
that he has hitherto known only from the *Nous*'s publicly reported
facts or a few overheard conjectures in the Hall, where he was far
too busy to cultivate hypotheses, still very sensitive to insiders' suspicion of himself as an insidious outsider with occult influence
beyond what might meet the eye in Dogtown's City Charter.
Anyway, everyone already knew that Dexter the Mayor, unlike his
predecessors, tolerated no gossip or prejudice. Furthermore, with
his own friends (especially Tessa and Fay herself) he wished to avoid
the appearance of intimate curiosity before the facts in question
were remote enough to be regarded as more or less emotionally
objective. He especially wanted not to be seen with overt interest in
anyone's speculations.

Finn was worried about Briney Nedlaw's overconfidence as a
nominal captain (hardly provided with the proper Master Mariner's
certificate); about the weather (albeit still predicted by the Weather
Bureau to be clear and mild enough this far north in approaching
the Maritimes); but mainly about the fifty-six-year-old schooner's
own seaworthy condition, which was so doubtful in the private
estimate of the grizzled professional sailing master as ostensible
mate with the private understanding that Briney, though owner,
was to be the actual understudy of himself as the authoritative
seaman in case of need. That stranger had been hired, with half a
dozen college volunteers under his supervision, to serve as the experienced cadre of *Gloucesterman*'s more or less familiar racing crew.
But this wary consultant quietly quit after one thorough inspec-

tion, even though the Coast Guard's last cursory look at the vessel had voiced no objection, and took his two sailors back to the New Uruk Yacht Club three days before the widely publicized celebration of the one truly aged fishing schooner participating in the famously resurrected race of dory-loaded highliners. *Gloucesterman* had recently been sold to Nedlaw by one Captain Jim in Markland who'd rehabilitated her for ten years of dawdling summer cruises (in safely truncated rig) for adventurous vacationers among the sheltered islands of an idyllic downeast coast where she'd never been re-tested under stress.

Under the threat of passionate disappointment Nedlaw seemed to those aware of the crisis that he felt personally insulted by doubts of *Gloucesterman's* seaworthiness, especially when his old friend Finn, the naval architect, seconded the pragmatic sailing master's prudential anxiety by breaking his professional engagement at its very commencement. But overnight Nedlaw was excitedly provided with experienced deckhands by a gathering of off-island or neighboring adventurers who were free enough to take off a week of schooling or earning without income or penalty; however, none were officially qualified as mates or skippers of large sailing vessels. He was beside himself with stubborn determination, resolved to set sail illegally, against all reason, as an inexperienced captain without proper officers, with whom he might slip out of the harbor unnoticed by the Coast Guard. That underfunded federal body stationed in Dogtown was busy inspecting all the unfamiliar schooners and observing smaller craft from all over the East Coast, now claiming space in the harbor if only in order to trumpet the crowning race from as near as possible to the breakwater vantage of its starting line. Others posted themselves offshore to the north in the promised breeze like knights and squires gathered to royalty as far as they were able on the march of a rivalry beyond their class, just for closest possible view of aristocratic sails in collective motion.

Finn was personally incited by his uninvited inspection of the superficially refurbished hull and rigging of *Gloucesterman*. In fear for the schooner herself, as well as for the people who trusted her rejuvenation, especially the innocents among her enthusiastic crew, after looking below the main deck with his flashlight, especially at the depth of her bilge water, probing with his jackknife the inelasticity of planks and frames and mast-butts, but particularly examining what was visible of the metal controls and lubricants of the cramped steering gear and her auxiliary engine, he was heard to mention that the acid-encrusted storage batteries boded ill for any occult Coast Guard examination. At first he spoke calmly, as if casually understating his opinions as a passing-by consultant who just happened to be on hand as an old man of iron-clad days, confining most of his open criticism to a remark that he'd noticed a vulnerable seam at a frame near the stem. True enough, said Briney, but we'll have no gale in the next week: the Weather Bureau said so.

Then Finn began to raise his voice in argument. "That may be right, if they know more than I can feel," he was rumored to have yelled, "but your rigging is worn and slack, your engine is a greasy mess, with batteries that I'm sure are long past their warranty, and you don't have navigation equipment good enough for these times! The last skipper of safely adventurous landlubbers no doubt knew his inshore daylight piloting—with familiar charts, if he needed any at all. No doubt he did a taut job keeping things shipshape with paint and polish wherever accessible to passengers. But otherwise his maintenance looks forgotten!"

Buyers don't like hearing that they've been deceived by appearance, no matter what the price. It appeared that as Finn fumed with warnings he told Briney what little could be done immediately to reduce what he called a temptation of Providence. The festival's day-race would present no difficulties, her speed and panoply untested by real weather. It was in the days afterwards that the long seagoing competition would endanger her beauty. But he must have decided that such deterrence had little effect upon his pig-headed friend. Finn must have believed that skilled seamanship was the only amenable recourse to the carelessness of her masters, and that on such short notice it was his instinctive duty to insist upon himself as the managing mate and principal helmsman.

By then Nedlaw was probably intimidated enough to feel relieved of full responsibility for conducting an excursion so susceptible to authoritative criticism by a surprisingly emotional peer, when a cabal of command seemed the only alternative to scandalous withdrawal from what was certainly the nation's last possible revival of unique competition among obsolete or replicated models sailing with seagoing payloads by wind-power alone, in which for years he'd hoped to satisfy the almost libidinous desire of his lifetime. Not that he took Finn's meticulous worries very seriously. Indeed, he was comforted by the thought of being in this thing

together. Finn was known as a sometime yachtsman and professional ship-designer brought up with his mother's milk on the
Markland coast, long before his fully accredited naval navigation at
sea more than half the world round. No point in consulting the
Coast Guard only a few hours before the starting gun. Again, there
was no tolerable alternative in this trap of gentlemanly honor.

Briney Nedlaw apparently did not resent the general belief that
Finn was more worried about *Gloucesterman* than about him and his
pick-up impressment of a partially substituted crew—salty men,
larking boys, and earnest girls, plus an ancient sea-cook. "They
could be saved, if a disastrous storm overtook them," Finn told
him, "but the vessel herself would not survive any serious damage.
You might open at least one of those neglected seams; some of her
spars look cracked; much of her cordage is all but rotted with old
tar; your electrical pumps will probably fail under stress, and in any
case you're not likely to get any emergency power from a diesel
engine that was installed in 1926 and I bet hasn't been overhauled
since then." His tone grew almost sarcastic. "The batteries look as
if they've never been replaced, let alone tested and recharged. In
short, if you take on water in an emergency you'll rely on an auxiliary power system as old as the oldest strakes. Worst of all, the
steering gear creaks as if it's never been greased. None of these
defects imperceptible to casual inspection blinded by beauty and
legend are likely to show up and mar her history on a day's shore
parade, and her hull's as fast as ever in normal superficially shipshape condition."

"Well," Finn must have also said, "I may be too skeptical of the
official weather-forecast parameters at this time of year, and *Gloucesterman* may well make port safely on the long race under ordinary
conditions at reasonable speed, but don't push her too hard just for
the sake of beating some of those hotshot highliner replicas that
were built yesterday according to architectural draftsmen's specifications, sparing no expense for all kinds of new material and
modern equipment, almost for the *sole* purpose of winning the
glory of a baroque gold cup, here or elsewhere, that can't be sold
and must be yielded eventually—if this race is ever run again.
Remember, our lady will be the moral winner if she finishes at all,
and as famous as ever. She should at least make it as a dignified
leader of replicas and little fellows."

But puffed with more confidence than ever, having already won
the local race on those grounds, Briney laughed at such a sorry

compromise with ambition, paying little attention to the latest qualifications in the weather forecast, making friendly fun of Finn as an inveterate perfectionist molded by Navy regulations and other books who had been much more of a cruising yachtsman than a racer in all his two-masted sailing experience as a boy. Yet Finn did not even pretend to reciprocate in manner or mood. He made it clear that he was suspicious of the vessel's recent log and maintenance records. But he sarcastically assured the new owner that he should not be disappointed at the absence of a timid yachting skipper who had made his unimpressive reputation mainly with imitation oyster schooners in the shallows of Mother of God Bay along the inner shores of Magdalene.

But there on the pier in Dogtown, comforted by whiskey and some immediately added (but untested) electronic equipment, Briney watched final preparations with a twisted smile, thinking that he would not disappoint all these kids and older enthusiasts who'd cut a week's classes or annual vacation time just to re-enact the international glory of *Gloucesterman* in 1937. Why all this pedantic commotion about imperceptibly slack rigging and the hull of a whited sepulcher? Everyone else thinks she looks as taut and shipshape and Bristol fashion trim as she did back then. He reminded himself that the only real ship his old friend had ever actually commanded as a Reserve officer after the War, and then only as a very brief substitute, was the oldest one in anybody's navy, permanently moored in the Navy Yard, all sails stowed, as a patriotic museum famous for poetry as well as for battles.

Pacing back and forth Finn pondered possibilities like a frustrated panther, within earshot of *Gloucesterman*'s people awaiting the outcome of a disconcerting last-minute defection. He was about to shout with unconcealed anger when he finally decided to throw in his lot by imposing himself as the most rational leader in personal participation, reconfirming his offer to act like an all-but-absolute captain, insisting unequivocally on his function as the master mariner. "I can't let you go without me!" he shouted in Briney's ear. "Sign me on as your mate, and let me take the wheel for as many watches as I can stay awake if a hurricane catches us." For the sake of appearances the captain-owner would have someone to take the helm who remembered more about how to weather a warship's gale than a boy's small sloop danger in a little breeze before the first World War.

MICHAELMAS 651

From that point on, whatever his feelings, Finn probably spoke with equivocal authority, dividing most of the final night between assistance to Briney in vetting the crew, supervising the stowage of baggage and victuals, counting life-jackets or insisting upon a plethora of collective safety equipment, begging or borrowing tools missing from the disgraceful tool locker, and rushing like a gray-haired youth up and down pavements and stairs between his bunk in the schooner and the eyrie from which he could see her masts while he packed his bags and telephoned his anxious apologies to Arthur Halymboyd for suddenly withdrawing from the automotive trip to Markland. He'd recruited for special duty the amiably poetic Sam Craigie (his usual IXAT-dispatched chauffeur) who as well as being an excellent driver would be far more useful than himself in a medical emergency, as a Navy veteran with plenty of wartime experience as a Pharmacist's Mate—a k a Hospital Corpsman—for a man still convalescing from triple-bypass heart surgery. By telephone he briefly explained to Fay as well as he could the anguished rationale for his obviously quixotic reaction to something that was none of his business except as a lofty new observer of the Dogtown maritime. He'd joked that he'd made Hal promise to have the English Department at Hawthorne arrange for Sam, as bonus, a solo reading of his Dogtown poetry.

He hoped that at worst, before returning with or without having reached their goal, he could scare Briney enough to have the schooner hauled up for repairs at some oldtime shipyard in Markland or Acadia and come home chastened, with the whole crew, by public transport.

Fay had been a little surprised at Finn's inexplicable concern for *Gloucesterman* the vessel herself, maybe among the loves he'd never mentioned in table-talk or on a pillow. Otherwise her pragmatic thought about that female was that she'd get more of her own work done for a while. But she now murmurs to Caleb "It was the last time I heard Finn's voice."

A hurricane internationally named Miriam indeed played itself out too far eastward to overtake the racers, but its aftereffects exacerbated a violent northeastern storm, and it may have been a rogue wave that finally separated *Gloucesterman* from the last of the successfully laden rubber rafts awaiting with Finn's place—just as her bow dove down to the deepest yet, felling her foremast with an anomalous broadside to a cross wind, the wreckage of which dragged her over on her beam ends, holding her helpless as she was swept toward wreck-haunted Black Island, far off course, long after it was possible for Finn to steer from the stern with broken linkage to the rudder. His body submerged, with one arm clinging to the horizontal stub of the mast, he was last seen still chopping at cables and ropes to free himself from the tangled rigging with a forrester's double axe held by its neck in his left hand. It was also said that he had confidently waved off the survivors just before they were washed out of sight in another implacable lunge of the twenty-foot sea, carrying away the raft saving Nedlaw, who was hardly conscious with a broken leg. In the end no one but Finn was lost, after the survivors' two nights of hardship and pain, before being sighted and rescued by the Dominion Coast Guard.

According to the scattered evidence found afloat or washed ashore on the island's beach in the next few days, the marvel was that Finn later must have succeeded in cutting free the foremast's tangled rigging, then chopping clear the felled foremast and jib with their entangled flotsam in a broken pyramid of snarled stays and halyards that soon dragged over the mainmast and its heavier mass, preventing the hull from righting itself with counter-heaving waves. There were various conjectures, all of them uncertain in face of the maelstrom; but the consensus of veteran seamen was that, perhaps with the assistance of a lucky swell, but no doubt thanks in part to the ballast and stowage that Finn had thanklessly insisted upon having shifted before departure, the devastated hull, stripped to the cluttered deck without masts or top hamper, returned to rolling equilibrium, no longer guided by human intelligence relative to the wind. She must have been buffeted back and forth broadside before her prow was spun by the more massive stern to face the wind that drove her. The expert speculation was that the wind shifted and that just before she struck the reef that killed her it was the bow that touched land first, as Finn clung to it in his effort to leap ashore in crashing surf onto great rocks awash at the fore-foot of the stern under a dark cliff that he could not have recognized.

In replying to Caleb's questions Fay was forced once more to imagine cinematically these knowledgeable speculations in order to accept the bleak fact that for the second time in her life she was stricken with violently absolute disseverance from a man, though this time it was insulated from the first by most of her lifetime in motherhood, a few other loves, and a peaceful profession. In this case it was more difficult to visualize the circumstances. For herself this loss was tempered by the insulating layers of vicarious experience and imaginative learning, this time for a man she had only begun to know. At the same time, however, she was still alive in empathy with fresh shock and pain of the brutal death suffered by the youth of love in early development at his and her same age. Her young husband's death on a motorcycle had been irresponsibly reckless and practically instantaneous, at a peak of his academic self-satisfaction. This slower extermination of an extraordinary life was in a voluntary cause, with the body at an age that forbids extreme exertion.

Were Finn's multiply distinguished but comparatively undecorated achievements in peace and war—sometimes as a lone wolf serving organization and discipline, as a creative master of selfless technology for the common good, as a private traveler in goodly books and places, and as a restless reader of adventures often parallel with ideas of her own—was this mind's unrecorded experience totally lost to humanity in gratuitously dangerous service to a superannuated artifact of somewhat feminine technology which had never before occupied much of his attention? Had he simply risked his life in an exultation of some madness that overcame the fatigue of muscle and many decades of regulation—perhaps even in ironic demonstration of his inchoate wish to marry her, to prove himself by leaving behind no scraps or dregs of unexpended energy? She could not envision this knight as Cuchulain in a warp-spasm.

One of the investigators searching for his body two or three days after both wind and tide had withdrawn from extremes, Belle says, is rumored to have discovered blood on a tattered shred of canvas bound to a snagged tip of wood in the fissure of a bluff a hundred yards from the sloping field of slimy boulders where the battered and already eviscerated hull shivered when groaning with seaweed in the absence of high surf. Had the Viking Celt blamed himself for allowing the wreck as an acting skipper, perhaps believing that Briney and his crew were about to be drowned as the wind drove them leeward in their cockleshells? What does fighting a prolonged death feel like in ignorance of all else? Was it worse than floating for many days of war among sharks with a collection of screaming or moribund sailors who'd readily trusted to him for leadership? How do fatal wounds from petroleum fire resemble or differ from the prolonged labor of a nulliparous young woman pleading for her own death if the pain is going to waste? . . . Yet

maybe even Finn the warrior, before his last chance to float away
with his crew, simply chose under the circumstances to forestall
senility, if only by less than half a dozen years, thinking or not
thinking of Fayaway? . . . But she knew that there wasn't a suicidal
molecule in all his agile virility. . . . Yet again, she wondered if he'd
have been glad that so little trace of his body would ever be found.

But Caleb's mourning for Finn was no more sentimental than
Emerson's philosophical grief. As he told himself, for lack of the
moral strength to review the depth of his shock, *there goes my old
Dutchkill School diploma-axe that I last found occasion for one postgraduate use thirty-five years later. I would never have lent it to anyone but
Finn. I took it as a symbol of our technological affinity, though we didn't
share much practical experience, seeing that I was never in the Navy and I
didn't choose 'Bega. But as a symbol of our common interest in various
kinds of mechanical electrical and architectural counter-poetics—ships
bridges and railroads come to mind—the axe offered a peculiarly
Atlantean blazon. Finn said he had searched most of the archeological
museums and libraries of Europe without finding a single instance of any
such simply balanced binary axe except the ceremonial one pictured in
Minoan Crete. In fact, recently he spoke of his hope to go up to Markland
next spring and cut with it some firewood for his widowed cousin at her
summer place. So I'm not sorry he coveted my obsolete artifact, and in a way
I'm honored that he lost it for me, at sea. He'd remembered the model and
trademark as well as if an earlier one of them had been the silver spoon that
got him into Norumbega in 1920.*

*But for me there was more to this tool than that. My own generally
beloved headmaster at Dutchkill Falls—despite the help of wife children
pupils and teachers for almost all the labor of sustaining fundamental operations and maintenance of the investment made in the properties of a small
dairy farm by the Northstone family and two or three affluent academic
friends who wished him well in realizing his pedagogical ideas for a new
kind of private secondary school; despite his mounting debts; despite his
gradual addiction to beer for outdoor refreshment in doing more than his
own exemplary part as truck driver farmer and woodsman away from his
academic study, with the eventual consequence that it became harder and
harder for him to conceal or suppress in sudden unreasonable angry frustration at the stupidity or obviously unintentional recalcitrance of some pupil
or teaching assistant, all of which some of us understood only in our retrospective maturity as the efficient cause of growing irascibility in the firmly
authoritative yet humorous temperament and evenhanded boss; and despite
the nearly imperceptible degradation of optimistic demeanor, owing basically*

to the secret shadow of bankruptcy and the threatened failure of his life's one great creative ambition before he'd reached the age of forty—this hero remained courageously true to his liberal philosophy of education, a faith from which he never defected, whether or not in his own hands: for even at proportional great financial cost he included in the curricula craftsmanship and vocational skills beyond the fine arts (especially music), which his wife and the tiny resident faculty had wished more time or knowledge to teach and for which he had longing with his own viola. Necessary facilities were prepared or purchased, and a few artificers or mechanics were hired for certain afternoons, when interested boys who would otherwise be at compulsory labor for the school's common good in woods or fields or housework learned some rudiments of one or another métier that had nothing to do with Classics poetry or chamber music. The language and jargon learned was as technical as practice required.

Thus under the aegis of his symbol Caleb had avidly learned, much less by theory than by observation, trial, and error, how to rehabilitate and restore to self-starting automobility a junked prewar Buick eight-cylinder in-line engine and its whole wheeled carriage, as well as how to shape and weld glowing iron at a forge, and how to advance his skills in carpentry. All in all, he learned or taught himself enough tin-smithy and electrical wiring to get blessing and material support to string up and operate (in his own free time) at very low voltage a battery-powered direct current five-hundred-yard aerial telegraph line to the main house, with voluntary assistance from his three roommates on the second floor, across a brook's tree-obscured glen from the recently built outlying "garage" (still redolent of rough-cut sheathing of spruce). This utility was offered, under his supervision, for the recreational efforts of anyone willing to memorize dots and dashes of Morse code, starting with S O S.

So it was that Caleb's altruistically dedicated educator, as he often reminded himself, had afforded him an ideal liberal curriculum for the development of his secondary fascination with engineering, thitherto (as the fatherless son of a discalced mother) pretty much limited to his own paper and pencil for masculine desiderata, usually of imaginary designs concocted from favorite elements in his scrapbook of newspaper pictures. Then his primary interest in artifacts was railroads, and his principal interest in railroads was the locomotives, and one of his greatest interests in locomotives was the generation of steam, and his even preferred though never witnessed application of steam itself (except on the train trips

to Dogtown) was the marine engineering alluded to in unillus-
trated fiction handed him by his mother or read for himself in magazines. He vaguely remembered once or twice in Unabridge when
he had been too tongue-tied to speak at all to a former rather deaf
but still heroic Chief Engineer formerly in the British merchant
marine, then an aged novelist whose career was often described as
resembling that of Jim Konrad's in a previous generation of square-
rigged ships that in port depended upon tugboats (which at the
time were dark satanic mills in the eyes of literary seamen), who
stayed overnight to discuss prosaic matters with the hostess after
her son went to bed.

Twenty years later, on the west coasts of North and South
Atlantis, she was for a really long time the truly loving shore-wife
of an active Chief Engineer in the international merchant marine,
until upon retirement he was obliged, she believed, for the sake of
collecting his pension, to return to his native wife and family in
Norseland. It seemed to have been the most contented liaison of
both their aging lives, spending all passion. Soon afterwards she
began her celibate sojourn with The Brotherhood of the Peaceable
Kingdom at its ranch in the Rio Orellana basin.

Fay Gabriel is glad that Caleb does not pretend a grief greatly
deeper than that he'd immediately felt for her cat Felixity's categorically violent death. He'd known their technological Viking Finn
only half a year. Nonetheless she believes that his objective and
intellectual sorrow for such a liege is abstractly so profound that it
transcends existential emotion. She knows that respect and gratitude were not rare in Caleb's loyal history of thanks to the gods of
chance, even when the lines and colors of his overlapping paragons
failed to register perfectly in all parts of their portraits. She sensed
that this slightly emerging misalignment of prints composing
Caleb's final monotype of Finn were blessedly halted, if not fully
readjusted, by the irreducible imperfection at this death. Her intuition of his actual feeling she thinks is sound, but she doesn't know
exactly how. She believes that the foreshadow of alienation between
those two men had been halted by a sunset that had little to do
with the axe, which, as if Caleb's outright oblation, had almost
sanctified an attitude that must be accounted for by the difference
between their generations.

Fay herself now sometimes felt like half a Gordian knot after
the cleaving.

4.

Early the next morning, in his own quarters, before making breakfast and getting to the Hall ahead of everyone but the janitor—anticipating the discomposure of trivial interruptions after office hours began—Caleb found his C N meditation totally occupied in recollection of the conversation with his godmother. As often happened in this his substitute for godless prayer or more sleep (without visual or aural object to rule the consciousness) it took no more than one or two breaths of his mantra to start a clarification of the subject that he had all but willed to be his object. If the matter had been floated by the content of a dream he did not know so; for scarcely ever did he remember more of his dreams than their physiological sensation of intense activity stricken off the record by the opening of his eyes, leaving it devoid of substance. But anything properly evoked from preconsciousness in this supposedly will-less evacuation of the objective mind might attract and cause him to ponder with pure reason a kind of problematic memory, from the ridiculous to the sublime, funny or profound: e g, what to buy at the grocery store, how he should have phrased his curriculum vitae to impress the Earls, what he said to a certain woman who seemed especially congenial, or the relationship between 1, 2, 3, and 4 in the tetractys as symbolizing the decimal significance of his Isorectotetrahedron. But in this instance it was the sudden recollection of a rather obvious mental association that he had missed, which was a flash of hitherto unapplied memory more than five years old, which both reason and dream had overlooked. Fay was the unwitting catalyst:

In his natural mother's protected old age (afforded by the Catholicratic social insurance and the Tudor Church), before she was obliged to submit to institutional sheltering, and when she was living in her independent Botolph apartment, she had parsimoniously saved enough pennies from her Social Security check (earned a hundred ways for many years at minimum wages) to treat herself, perhaps for the first time in an adult life of a hundred jobs and half a hundred addresses, to a summer week of vacation.

Three or four times, claiming to be a worthy old salt by virtue of her former service as a freighter stewardess in the South Atlantis merchant marine trade, she'd joined an annual "Windjammer Cruise" along the shore of Markland. Of course she struck up a

great friendship with a genuine old salt, the proprietor, Captain
Jim Wheeler—since he had her company no more than one week
out of fifty-two, when she was as happy, ebullient, and as liberal in
expression as a comedian could be without offending more than a
few of her temporary shipmates, usually middleaged or older. Her
free speech relieved Jim of the obligation to entertain everyone in
her batch all by himself, though at the risk of troubling Mrs
Grundys as listeners to liberal speech, even unto the bawdry merely
implicit in humor nearly matched by his own cheerful vulgarity as
a normally jocular seaman, from earnest boyhood to kindly cap-
taincy though hardly in the tone of calloused sailors hunting fish or
lugging freight. Caleb had no doubt that lean old Jim and older
Mary (by then obesely jolly) had hit it off as innocent old troopers,
even after more than once a week she had entertained his payload
guests with her falsetto performance of "Lorraine Tilly-i-o"—simpering, eyes downcast, with a finger to her lower lip as she twisted
demurely from side to side, as if waiting for a lollipop—"the cutest
little girl in North Atlantis!" But sociably or demonstratively she
also whipped up oldfashioned community singing with sweet and
sad folk songs or solo recitations of purely Victorian poetry. She was
always ready for joking repartee with the boldest of her companions—especially with Jim himself when the prudes were out of
sight below or stepping ashore to buy souvenirs. One of the last
poems she wrote in her "diary", before she gave up all writing (and
all reading except for the nearly continuous doubly or triply underlined New Testament), was in praise of Captain Jim's "Sea-Blue
Eyes", which Caleb recognized as habitually associated in her
mind's eye with the Dutchkill headmaster.

In retirement from his typical career, but with a mind to commercial enterprise, new in his experience, the canny skipper Jim
had bought for a swan song in the downeast harbor of Pembrocks
the all but abandoned schooner, last named *Explorer*, little known
and last forgotten for her year of arctic exploration by scientists,
her strakes reinforced with an extra layer of oak planking, her
engine compartment endowed with a quieter diesel, and her rigging reduced to a sturdy minimum. Before that, after her long
career in fishing, she had been sold across the Atlantic to ferry
freight and passengers among the Flemish Islands, owned and
sailed by Lusitanians, registered as *Alcacovas*. But all her regular
Atlantic fishing had been *out* of Dogtown—her christening,
launching, building *in* Dogtown.

It was thus that Caleb had learned from Captain Jim that to his mother's delight and insistence her geriatric pleasure was aboard the once illustrious highliner called *Gloucesterman,* which she claimed had once been commanded by her father! She was a life-long student of nominatives. But for Jim's sake she must have shared that commercial secret as far as naive landlubbing aestivators in Markland were concerned. Those two also suppressed the truth that the advertising term "Windjammer" was, to say the least, a puffed solecism even in slang itself, properly meant to be reserved for fully square-rigged ships, especially clippers that sped around the Horn from Botolph to Cornucopia in three months, from Bensalem to the Celestial Empire for tea, or from Haiphong to the Isle of Dogs, if not for even slower and less shapely merchantmen from Liverpool to Sydney downunder.

The first time Caleb himself had driven Mary up to Pembrocks to save her the discomfort of bus trips, and there, awaiting the dozen or so other passengers (most of them previously satisfied customers), before he took his leave (having sustained the embarrassment of her maternal introduction to the proprietor) he had sounded Captain Jim, who (aside, man to man as he was about to cast off with his full complement of less boldly expressive clients of lesser age) had already expressed his special delight in her refreshingly irreverent kind of response to his wanderlusty classified advertisements. But Caleb gathered everything more he knew of these annually repeated cruises from his mother herself, much of it extrapolated according to her pattern of merry friendships he assumed endured largely in her interruptions and imagined goodwill in her absences.

Explorer was after all a fairer name for the partially restored schooner in Pembrocks than *Gloucesterman* would have been before she was fully restored and identified by Briney Nedlaw in Dogtown when he was tracing the history of that particular schooner in his yearning for nautical fulfillment. Afterwards, as in clarified contemplation, Caleb now recalled from the welter of uncertain memories and conjectures about Mary Tremont's admirable and mortifying life—as an unmarried woman of odd jobs and countless places, most of it without the protection or help of himself the older son she had lived for, having hoped since childhood for two sibling children—she had almost convinced him of the plausible conjecture that *Explorer*—né *Gloucesterman*—had really been owned and perhaps personally sometimes skippered by Captain Trevisa, her estranged but loving father—or (in her own indefinite opinion most of the time) *putative* father. This questionable latter persuasion had immeasurably excited her remaining summer cruises and perhaps intrigued Captain Jim too. Indeed this forgotten recollection now excited Caleb's retrospection enough to mention it later to Fay as a new curiosity in his lymph or blood, perhaps worth some anthropological hypothesis. But she had no reason to pass it along in her conversation with Tessa or anyone else.

And Caleb soon forgot it again, as he had forgotten it before, while he implicated himself further in the city of his birth, or rather in the government of that city as such. In earning a livelihood defensively his fascination with the problems and possibilities of municipal management grew obsessive. Every aspect led to another facet, and local history was one of them; but accounting and financial controls were basic, immediate, and more important to his boss the democratically elected mayor, if not immediately to the personnel involved, whose families' votes were important to some of the Earls who had no compunction about using their legislative influence to interfere with the kind of progress that was too abstract or complex to be appreciated until it had enough time to be realized in the Annual Report. Though the City Charter seemed at first glance to reflect the national Constitution, the separation of powers was actually more like the interlocking authorities in the Venetian Republic. Caleb marveled, sometimes with hope, otherwise in dismay, at the model he envisioned when he had moments of clarity in Contemplative Nullification, or at least at a few unwelcomed dark dawns before he got out of bed when he faced with clairvoyance his whole absurdly divided life. Nevertheless, his concatenation of discoveries between Vinland's municipal law and Dogtown's immemorial legislation helped him understand the problems of federal government in Washington, where the accounting system was almost equally irrational in comparison with the standard accounting practices he had learned in business.

Meanwhile, though he was careful to consult Dexter before every overtly important proposition, the Mayor left him to his own devices—provisionally, sometimes with a blind eye—in the little things that might reconcile improvement in the City's organizational efficiency with the administrative architecture fixed by statutes of the higher-level governments. Many of the local ordinances, enforced or suppressed, were dear to the hearts of Earldermen as biannual representatives of Dogtown's sovereign people.

Meanwhile, after there was no further possibility of finding Finn's body, amid all the national news about the wreck and various heroic rescues of Captain Nedlaw and the rest of his crew by strangers in the Gulf of Markland, apparently no one on Cape Gloucester was informed of any obsequies that might have been arranged by Finn Macdane's relatives on his native ground in Markland, as if they'd looked askance at his retirement down in this fishy gull-ridden melting pot of disreputable Bohemian artists, stolid squareheads, and screaming Mediterranean immigrants. As far as the local public was informed it was only Belle's obituary (borrowing more than she ought to have from the *New Uruk Testament*) that awakened Dogtown to the great distinction of this particular loss, until his friend the Mayor urged the Earls to pass a resolution of mourning on behalf of the City at large. By that time the communal A D L had lapsed into nearly normal conversation.

In Fay's presence, when Finn was mentioned, remarks were objectively curious, as toast or praise for what was gradually discovered of things of which the Commander had never boasted as an exceptionally experienced man of the world. She herself, a person unknown to the public, had already been trying to calculate the unknown coefficient of her own death, as the negative factor to be fended off until her work was done. She wasted as little time as possible, behaving even as a tough old bird in her cage should, mourning as a reticent common-law widow. She wondered if Finn too had been pressed by haste on his own less focused way to the resolution of all forces. She thought he'd have laughed with her about the march he'd stolen on her. But he didn't really need the time for anything more important than the present. She'd hardly even mentioned Finn to her presumably indifferent children, who now she assumed would not have been particularly sorry for the stranger's outcome. And she was indeed tough enough to tell herself that if she'd grown senile before he did, he would not have taken care of her, whereas that if he'd succumbed first she would have been expected to take care of him. She was sure he'd have especially laughed at that inequation. Fay tried to think less about the loss of her paramour's instantaneous feelings at a death infinitely more prolonged than Felixity's in all innocence, or her self-absorbed husband's in defying for a few seconds the centrifugal force, probably with life and family out of the picture. What are the parts of agony and terror in the common good?

The recovery from genuine shock and objective mourning by Caleb's small circle of other friends relieved his conscience of its uneasiness about the subjective shallowness of his grief. Like every other extinct person to whom he was indebted for his own philosophical existence, this one deserved far less heartfelt sorrow on his part than the selflessly heroic mother of his insufficiently sensitive psyche, from the trauma of his birth to her mindless unattended expiration in a pauper's hospital.

He was almost glad that Finn had died before some inchoate disaffection was exposed, or before recourse to the excuses of a difficult new job were finally given way to an overt breach in their intellectual relationship for lack of long clarifying discussions. Finn, the elder authority on inorganic matters, had begun to seem obtuse in understanding certain organic applications of systems theory that were supposed to unite them in Geisteswissenschaften, in grasping the negative capability of art and artists, and especially in fully appreciating the extraordinary symbolic facultation of the Isorectotetrahedron.

Furthermore, to Finn a work of art *meant* something, whereas to Caleb himself it *was* something. Fay understood the difference; but, Caleb was quite aware, ridiculous as that theoretical discordance might seem to anyone else as an excessively emotional misunderstanding, at that level of intimacy it represented a blemish in the spectrum of their broad community of interests, an inoculation early enough to ward off such disappointments as Redburn suffered by investing his soul with Natty Hawhaw, or many times over as his mother's hope for a perfect husband—perhaps even with the all but dispassionate Professor Gabriel herself, all sympathy and perception notwithstanding. Did the fault lie in his own ego? Caleb was sometimes critical of his own scorn for flaws in the intelligence of brilliant or creative persons, an almost contemptuous proclivity imbued in him by his sole parent, through thick and thin, in the joy and suffering of one disappointment after another as a "failed poet" even from her own ambitious point of view. Infrequently, however, this critical characteristic also delivered him from quick prejudice to studious appreciation.

But such more or less modest reflections were kept at bay in days and weeks and months of public service, and even in the end he took back very little of his feckless self-confidence, especially with regard to the unsurprising death of Arthur Halymboyd. When Caleb occasionally went to the early Sunday morning

Eucharist at St Paul's (vainly hoping for a homily that might reflect the subliminal influence of the theodynamics long since offered the Tudor Church by Father Duncannon, or that might at least recognize the anthropological basis of the Eucharist), on his way to half a day of solitary lucubrations in his corner of the great hollow Ibicity Hall at the opposite end of Halibut Street, he recalled less regret for having missed reconciliation of merely tacit estrangement (perhaps unilateral on his own part) in the last few months of the late priest's life than for half a world-religion's loss of radical reinterpretation of liturgy that would have enlightened and emboldened both High Church and Low in a new understanding of the currently inadequate "social gospel". Still, he couldn't help being glad that in his own way he was as far out of registration in the particolored map of his unclassed culture as Mary Tremont had been in hers.

5.

The loss of Finn was not so simple for Fay, who occupied no public position that demanded distraction from her private work. Especially when cooking her meals and washing her dishes she found herself ruminating on the last and best man who would ever share her bed or open her more to the technical mind, after she thought she'd had enough of both subjects. That conative man who hated to have to drown a valiant bug struggling to the last before being swept to hell in the vortex of a kitchen sink, who steadfastly jeopardized his competitive Navy career as a known "intellectual" and "Jew-lover", had softened her secret anthropological prejudices with many revealing offhand remarks that conflicted with the simply convivial orectic zodiac she had naturally cast for him at first. In the mainly serene satisfaction of her emotional and economic security there had not yet arisen any need to recognize the love of him that was not yet declared even to herself, if only to spare him the embarrassment of a forced reply, whatever it might have been, though she had been cheerfully confident that whatever he felt would not have been rude. But now, a few weeks later, she realized that his unexpected death in heroic circumstances was tightening rather than relieving the compression of her life's finale, sometimes obliterating consciousness of her self-sufficient children, who had been keys to the personal anthropology that unlocked her philosophy. As Finn's survivor her brain now seemed nearly as androgynous as Merlin's. Caleb, who she sensed had begrudged Finn her most intimate affection, was the only one in Dogtown with whom she wanted to talk about the work that sustained her longevity. Though she was not deaf to any mention of Finn's name she didn't join much in the conversation of others in their circle; she was intuitively aware that Tessa was mistaking her unusual reticence as an unnatural suppression of normal mourning.

But Fay still believed that Tessa would not have been wrong if she had guessed that Caleb's recent silence of emotion was an element of irritation at her own indiscretion in showing Finn without permission the scripts of the plays that had been intended only for the eyes of his godmother. The closet playwright had correctly expected that the naval engineer would have nothing encouraging to say about Gilgamesh's use of a double axe in connection with an absurd Isorectotetrahedron, which with a kindly laugh out of Caleb's earshot he had brushed off as some kind of Sumerian fetish. Caleb had regretted having once before tentatively offered a proposition at which his usually courteous and openminded superior had nearly snorted and scoffed outright, when hearing from his protege that God finally justified the creation of humanity, with man's inhumanity to man, only by its own creations of art. Even Finn's cordial interest in Universal Systems Theory, and in Caleb's own abstract device called the Synectic Method of Diagnostic Correlation, had not been enough to assure a completed circle of affinities.

Nevertheless Caleb's hearty gratitude for Finn's solicitude and generosity in economic assistance was enduring proof of their reciprocated all-but-perfect friendship. Above all, they'd shared an extraordinary enthusiasm for the oeuvre of Wellingborough Redburn, especially *White Jacket*, at any mention of which they both visualized the nocturnal population of a heavy frigate's berth deck packed with half a thousand sailors hanging cheek-by-jowl with unity of motion in the roll of swinging hammocks. It reminded them both (sometimes to the point of chanting it with what they drank together) the alleged old ditty:

> Fourteen men in a boarding house bed
> *Roll over, roll over*
> Would all roll over when anyone said
> *Roll over, roll over.*
> One little fellow thought he'd get smart
> *Roll over, roll over*

Not to roll over when someone said
Roll over, roll over.
In the tussle his neck was broke!
Roll over, roll over.
That's the moral of my little joke.
Roll over, *roll over!*

26

IBICITY HALL

[Winter Quarter 1981–1982]

To be abused and misunderstood by political
friends of worth is not pleasant, but the
great question in all those things is: Did you
perform your duty, and did you, as far as you
were able, promote the public good? For,
worldly as you think me, rest assured that,
however I may prize public opinion, it is not
there that I seek for a reward.

—Albert Gallatin
U S Secretary of Treasury for Thomas Jefferson

*I*f you drive out through private wealth along the eastern shore of
the harbor to Crow Point and its public lot at the Foreside Light
and Coast Guard Station, whitewashed stout and stalwart upon a
tawny knoll of sea-sculpted granite, you can get out and walk a
third of a way across the distance to the opposite shore on a mole built and
defended by roughly shaped and fitted gray granite blocks stacked as an elevated path to reach and mount a raised red beacon controlled by the Coast

Guard base ashore at the bottom of the tower you have skirted, which is the last humanly quartered lighthouse of Dogtown's half-dozen such towered beacons still projecting in rotation the marvelous white light from its capitol. Its beams both focus and sweep the vast stretches of the azimuth in a dome of darkness, rhythmically circulating sky and sea-space with flashes of unbearably tense white electricity without thunder that silhouettes certain sectors of landscape like the black-on-white figure of Prince Achmed in silent cartoons in the cinema at its first discovery of mankind's most comforting artifiction.

By standing out beneath the beacon's constant red lamp in daylight on the end of the breakwater and turning your back on Vinland Bay you can scan the center of Dogtown and its skylines a little more than two miles along the harbor's northeastern axis, the farthest half-mile of which may be imagined as through the throat and lips of the City's most densely occupied land. Only because of urban ridges as the background will you see nothing of the city's complexity from your distant vantage. If you were able to continue on this the 18C Sea Serpent's approximate course another two and a half times as a seabird you would fly over the uninhabited Purdeyville highlands to Cachalot Point, the very tip of Cape Gloucester, well on the seaway to Markland.

What you do *see from the outermost harbor to the center of the city is its acropolis, or at least the tops of buildings and even the tips of trees surrounding it on the four or five streets that define its geological platform— an unnoticed almost Euclidian practically flattened shelf, amidst irregularly crowded acclivities declivities and sinuosities that underlie or overlook the urban jumble of the Harbor Ward neighborhoods—which at your distance is visually obstructed by all sorts of roofs or spires signifying church and state, several of them (or their fetches) much as they may have looked to helmsmen for more than a hundred years. But just west of the acropolis you will easily perceive the tallest and most conspicuous as well as oldest of the remaining sacred erections. It is the whole Cape's noblest piece of architecture, belonging to the parish founded sui generis by a sect of 18C Protesticans who are credited with having introduced and ultimately won for all northern Atlanteans the constitutional protection of individual liberty both within and without churches, and who soon afterward led secular ideas about the desiderata of equality for women. The towering steeple of this fane is perhaps disproportionately a little too tall and heavy for the plainer clapboarded Meetinghouse upon which it rests, but it aesthetically diverts your studied maritime attention from other ecclesiastical steeples not yet razed or converted to secular purpose—particularly, at present, a disappointingly slender fleche attached to the square tower of the massive granite basilica dedicated to the Blessed Virgin Mary, only two blocks more distant, housing and blessing a congregation that outnumbers all the Pauline parishes together, though it shares the Petrine population with three lesser parishes commanded by the same birdseye flying low in surveillance.*

But the largest and most spectacular landmark is based in the acropolis, dominantly secular: the venue of Dogtown's politics; a meetinghouse for successes and failures in true and false attempts to advance the common good at its sovereign level of democracy. Of this peculiar and unmistakable edifice, an almost nondescript headquarters intended to represent the citizenry, there are too many impressions to be described with an adverb for its thousand adjectives. Our ibi-polis acropolis has no Lion's Gate to introduce its granite steps, nor one for Ishtar, but every time out there you glance this way (without seeing much lower than the angular French roofing of the functional Hall itself) you will be vaguely pleased to accept as somehow traditional—indeed respectably familiar in other cities—the top half of its engaged and illuminated round-arched lantern, suggestive of Baroque if that style is stripped of unnecessary decoration.

In color this granite-founded and gray-granite-trimmed Hall is externally walled with not quite unobjectionable brick and mortar as its sufficiently subtle contribution to the symbolic miscegenation of umbilical bloods and brains. Thanks to fine workmanship at quoins windows and other cortical surfaces, which of course you can't see from where you are at any one moment, there is only slight overemphasis of architectural details. But wood that can be repainted makes possible, for better or for worse, small chromatic changes of great importance in any building's aesthetic affect. In fact, according to the City Charter, there is a pro bono committee of variously cultivated advocates for the "public arts" appointed by a mayor to make judgments about this and much more heralded issues.

The question of changing trim-color was hardly raised even after the de rigueur trim of white lead on the lower floors had been replaced by a hue to match the lovely beige that has always traditionally been painted on wooden segments of the tower without applying that change to the white decoration below. We are lucky now to have a mayor who's packed the committee with artists or critics of his private acquaintance. Budget permitting for a new paint job, there will soon no longer remain conspicuously incongruous white trim at different altitudes below the tower against the red brick of all external walls. Instead, Caleb and his friends hope, the same shade of lineations will carry one's eyes from the dignified color at ground to the proper purpose of its acceptable style as a squared tower with clocks and cupola. That monument is unfortunately guarded by fantastically pointed chimneys. But with your binoculars on the breakwater you can ignore the upper structure's discontinuity of taste without objecting to its kind of nobility. The conical roof of the Renaissance tower, with its own delicately detailed balustrade, above clocks and bells, is always colored copper-tarnished green, and is surmounted by a finial weathervane of gold (nowadays concealing the police radio antenna). Under certain meteorological conditions, this aerial trunk of the edifice, painted with proper beige, may be what first attracts a seaborne eye. For you its grotesque shoulders are out of sight.

Bear in mind that the Hall as we see it from the streets has sometimes been called the Phoenix because soon after the Civil War it rose from the granite foundation ashes of a Town Hall built essentially according to the same eclectic Yankee design and which was burned down to a few standing bricks the night after an itinerant minstrel show in its great auditorium not much more than a year after it was built in celebration of the Town's incorporation as a City. The replacement we now see is superficially taller and more classically decorated—much less nude, less economical in civic pretension; but despite the semi-nondescripting aggregation of earlier conventional Euro-Atlantean styles the Phoenix was obviously an evolutionary bird before it died. Long before its present descendant became so ambivalently comfortable for its inhabitants on the short narrow Whale Street (next door to some journeyman architect's Depression-era light ashlar granite Post Office, catercorner to a vast redbrick Victorian high school, then yielded as a grammar school for many years, until finally remodeled and abandoned to pensioners directly beside the all-white recently modernized and extended Atheneum Free Library)—in fact even longer before that, when the acropolis was not yet regarded as the public nest of a phoenix, especially when steeples were fewer shorter or otherwise, there was no breakwater for you to stand on at the outer mouth of the great harbor.

For centuries, however, the principal landmark for mariners had been private property, slightly to the port of your course down the harbor, as the brow of an escarpment closer and higher to the Gut. And so it remains, less central than the acropolis, though much obscured by denser private settlement by great white clapboard or granite properties still defending the aboral cultivation of a residual Codfish Aristocracy which no longer searches for sails on the horizon—the sails of their own property—from the hill's private octagonal cupolas now outmoded. The greatest of them, called Long Rocks, owned below its edges a long and lofty palisade of almost vertically sheer weatherbeaten dark stone, the unmistakably natural landmark formerly to steer by. And so it was called by word or chart by many a thousand who knew or cared nothing of what a Long Rocks Trust consisted. These owners never conceived that their unelectric beacon might be dyna-

mited for reality-estate development or painted with advertising, no longer associated with the Long Rocks in Athens.

1.

His Honor the Mayor, Dexter Keith, had been provisionally and hesitantly warned by Caleb Karcist his new chief administrator, apparently by way of proleptic apology, that he Caleb himself as an erstwhile resident of Babylon Oaks in Cornucopia was embarrassed by his totally unexpected apparition of the clever Earlderdam named Hecuba Fox-Argent as an old acquaintance on the West Coast, now serving her second two-year term on the Board representing Seamark. Dexter had reasons of his own to avoid or suppress reference to private life that never appears on anyone's curriculum vitae, especially in this case, as Caleb's former landlord.

But, as far the Mayor could discern, it turned out that Hecuba had been less indiscreet than all too many legislators and employees of the City. In fact she had made no trouble at all by never even quietly voting against the administration's unsentimental commonsense. Nor yet did she seem personally to favor Caleb's name in the usual lingerings of pleasant fellowship between their meetings or after their Board meetings—sometimes boisterous on the way down to drinks at the Doghouse, especially when members of "The Mayor's Office" or other departmental representatives of City government, having been summoned to testify or inform at the Phoenix according to Rubber Rules of Order, were in an affable or politic mood to give up much of the sleep they presumably deserved for unofficial association with the legislators at their own expense, often when Hecuba was the vocal life of the party (even without a piano). The small committee meetings and their aftermaths were of course two or three times more numerous and less inhibited than those of the voting Board as a committee of the whole.

"How did she manage to get appointed chairlady of the Administration and Finance Committee so soon, after only her first term? Just because the seniors found her so smart and energetic?" the present Mayor Dexter Keith asked Ben(levi) Nathan the last one in his seat, who under the former charter had been for many years a bull on the Board when the Mayor's office was more ceremonial than managerial and most executive functions were left to a hired City Manager—and when Dexter himself was also new to that aspect of municipal government. They were dining together like alien conspirators, away from Dogtown, as unrecognized as possible, down the line in posh Felicity-by-the-Sea, the old Falstaff's ultimate hideout, accompanied by the impressively tall aristocrat in a sportsman's clothes.

Dexter had never erased his Navy maxims, and he'd been influenced by their genus of wisdom since the recent appearance of his new friend the late Commander Finn Macdane as a model. Like a prudent captain the Mayor generally tried to avoid fraternization more than politely cordial with his civic officers, not to mention his ship's company altogether. Still, after all, as he well knew, the chief of a democratic commune has to be a good politician and therefore must cultivate a good ear for intra-caste gossip as well as for public opinion, which he gauged mainly from the talk of friends not necessarily representative of the electorate, including intelligence from his back-channel connection with the press, namely Belle Cingani, editor of the daily *Nous*.

[*By and large the rest of his private associates had hardly ever even opened the portals of Ibicity Hall, even for personal business, before Caleb's appointment awakened merely curious interest in what went on behind the inner doors usually unused by the public, though at one time or another almost every citizen had at least once climbed the venerably rounded broad staircase to the lofty balconied auditorium on the second floor for a civic performance of some kind—political, patriotic, edifying, amusing, artistic, merely aesthetic, or boringly educational—probably oblivious of that atrium's tin-ceilinged acoustical reverberations as ghostly echoes of the space in which the Phoenix had committed its youthful immolation within different walls of very similar brick according to the same plan a century ago.*]

At the least Dexter had compensated for this honorable disadvantage of social rank by striking up a comfortably informant friendship with his immediate predecessor, now retired from both business and politics, all but certainly out of public news until what would be an interesting obituary if Belle had anything to do with it. A usually amicable opponent in the latest mayoral election more than a year ago that no doubt was to have been his Falstaffian swan song, Benlevi Nathan exhibited such diplomatic incompetence under the then-introduced new charter that it had withered his popularity as a rival to Dexter's handsome person with excellent credentials, said to be running as a "born leader". The older and heavier man was still sometimes affectionately labeled the "Leviathan". He had several times held the city's highest de facto rank as the presiding Margrave Earl of the Board under the old Home Rule "weak mayor" constitution, led with the complimentary title of its chair. His political machine had always been little more than himself, fat jovial canny and often narrowmindedly selfish—as for instance an inveterate transcontinental gambler—when his almost candid self-interest wasn't otherwise sincerely altruistic in concern for the common good of Dogtown in terms of the individuals he knew. But Ben was both jolly and worried as a useful fountainhead of oral history and retail reminiscence.

"The Margrave put her on that committee, and then the other two voted her the chair," Ben replied to Dexter, "because she was obviously so goddam smart at accounting and seemed friendly with everyone. Besides, the old bull of finance had given up the ghost after twelve terms of bossing most of the whole Board's votes. For me he was always a pain in the ass. It was the chance of a lifetime to get some new blood, in money matters especially, and to rid ourselves of that cock-of-the-roost so-called city *manager*! Until you showed up I thought I was going to be the new charter's *"strong"* mayor. But I guess that would have bitten off more than I could chew. You saved me a lot of trouble I'd have gotten into." He cordially raised his glass of bourbon, a comedian who never smiled at his own pleasantries.

"Hell, not as much as you're saving me now, right here!" Dexter replied with the broad smile that still at nearly detectably corpulent late middle age helped make him so popular, reciprocally raising his barely half equivalent alcohol as white wine. "I never thought this job would be so hard until I *really* realized what it's like to be only a naturalized marooner after living here twenty-five years. The commuting I've done, from here as a voter when I wasn't working as a simple city planner long ago, prepared me less for this job than having been an off-islander by birth."

"I can see that." Ben sighed with a grunt. "I've spent plenty of time long ways across the Gut in business and pleasure. Can't travel much now."

"I remember that I used to see you cruising around town in the biggest car that Frontenac can make!"

"Couldn't fit in anything smaller. Still can't. No more airplanes, for sure. But it gives me plenty of time to see things about the old days on our rock." With a thumb over his shoulder Ben gestured northward toward Dogtown.

"But you seem to keep up with what's going on *now* better than anyone else."

"My hobby, I suppose. Or just putting on years. Don't expect me to tell you all my good wife could tell you when it's none of your business—unless it's not about anyone's family further back than my family. I don't know any more than you do about the Dogtown in history books or *Nous* stories. Your ex-wife is better at that than all the historians."

But that *was* a mayor's business—and probably Ben well knew too much of it. So Dexter quickly returned to what was on his professional mind that day, less troubling than puzzling. "Belle Cingani seems to know more than she lets her reporters print."

"She'll always know more than those college kids think they know." Ben snorted. "She's as good at what she's paid to do as old Flash Silver did half drunk with his camera outdoors. I miss him. His pictures should have been in *See Magazine,* without many words. The *New Uruk* cartoonists used to try to copy him. Belle was a pain in the ass until I got to know her, and more than once she's done me the favor of leaving something out. She may be sophisticated but she means well, and so do I, believe it or not. She's not like those dumb sob-sisters that used to do all the female assignments for the *Botolph Orb.*"

"I'll tell you something that I bet you didn't know—trivial but confidential. Promise?"

"Sure."

"Our Caleb Karcist's mother was once a sob-sister there. And here too maybe, before the War."

"No offense meant." Ben mumbled.

"No offense taken. He and his mother were both born here."

"That's funny: I never heard of that name until you hired him. Must have been a bastard case or something. Might be one of our Jews, if not Greek. Maybe before I started listening to my father. Might have been one of his tenants, unless they were rich. Maybe one of our deadbeats. It might be worth my time to go through our old rent books."

"No, no. I'm not asking for anything like that. He's a good man. The City needs him especially right now, with all this rage for computers. I hope you won't undermine his permanent confirmation. I know you've still got a lot of underground influence on the Board, perhaps a majority."

"Don't you wish it!" the fat man sighed with another grunt, grinning for the first time, still not as old as he looked. "Mooncusser's the one on the Board to watch out for. Biggest landholder and reality-estate shark on the Cape. He's pretty smooth in public but he wants to be the next chief Margrave and will do anything to put a stick in your spokes. He's hated me for years and he's hated you since you were City Planner, before you started commuting to your big Liverpool job. I think that son-of-a-bitch is now in cahoots with Danny Protocol, supposed to be the most honest and public-spirited City Clerk we've ever had, very fair to the Jews as well as the Aramites in my father's time. He used to be my best buddy after hours. But he controls all the City papers, and it could be that high-class Norumbega shark got some private tidbit from him to use sometime against you by way of your guy. Mooncusser's not above gossip for blackmail. He's given me some hard times. But my face is red that I don't know that name Karcist! At least I may be able find out where I've made a mistake—just to let my wife take me down a peg. I've still got a friend or two in the City Clerk's office." The Leviathan chuckled with his belly.

"No, no, please leave Caleb himself out of it." Dexter smiled: "I promise never to ask what you've *missed* on me. I really only want your opinion on things, because you know the widths and depths of Dogtown—"

"You bet it, the width at least!" To which they both raised their glasses with almost brotherly love, Walrus and Carpenter.

After a sipping pause for thought on both sides, Dexter continued: "I'm not interested in the depths right now. I'm thinking about the best way to reform the *efficiency* of this crazy government you left us. It's just that he knew Hecuba Argent in Cornucopia. I need her votes on the Board, but more than that her experience in bookkeeping with office machinery. She seems to understand better than anyone else what all the clerks are going to have to go through—nothing less than teaching their bosses! You know all the people, and practically all their families in every department. She'll be a godsend on the Board if she takes official notice of their point of view. She can also help a lot by teaching the Earls and department heads to be sympathetic and patient. Caleb can't go into this storm waving magic wands for me."

"You're the elected one: you'll get the whole blame for hiring Karcist if anything goes wrong, but if it all goes without too much of a hitch you won't get any of the credit—the Board will claim praise for including a computer in the budget when I was still the Mayor. Our last City Manager wouldn't have begun to know how to handle the Board's screeches for a magic machine without a magic wand. I retired from this rat race just soon enough not to make myself a damn fool. But I'll help you from the pigheaded underground if you tell me what I can do or undo as an *invisible* man." He actually laughed at the word "invisible".

"Deirdre's expecting me home now. Next Wednesday, same time, same place?"

"Unless someone spots us here or I split a gut. Dexter, Your Honor, I'm glad you're the one I lost the election to."

"Well I'm still a greenhorn, but I'm from Montvert, so you can trust me more than you think I can trust you!"

Driving home in his modest private car (almost too small for his frame), Dexter thought that the most surprising thing about the altruistic aspect of the superannuated self-indulgent Benlevi Nathan was that he was still alive despite all his eating drinking and trips to Esmeralda, where he was known to be such a regular high-rolling gambler that he was given free airplane tickets and hotel accommodations by one of the casinos, presumably for the class of customers he attracted without going broke or winning too much.

But smoking, never one of Dexter's own vices, was what would kill this codger and tentative new friend. Ben calmly allowed that smoking was pernicious, and he was selfless enough not to hold against the giant new mayor a do-gooding fait accompli in banning the use of tobacco throughout the Hall; but that ordinance was enacted only after the former mayor had little need to visit the goddam Hall. Defeat had given even him good reason to avoid smoke more visibly pungent than the worst in crowded bars on Front Street, or in his own permitted smoking room at home. Most of the people in Dogtown—even those who suffered outright deprivation of tobacco, even the enemies of public health, even his most bitterly disgusted opponents who loved him least for what he was or what he did in private life—respected Dexter for the guts it had taken to anticipate medical science for the common good at least within the Hall's dismal walls. Which, with some small housekeeping improvements, became positively inviting to ordinary citizens, though still far from the spit-and-polish satisfaction of the former naval officer now its skipper.

Dexter knew, as Ben had told him, that he wouldn't get off easy as far as matters of public taste were concerned when he'd find the right time to persuade the volunteer Arts Committee to paint over white Corinthian columns, balustrades, and all the other trim the historically artistic color, even if they had to raise money to pay for the less popular paint by private prescription. Such were the kind of "overeducated elite" who quietly formed most of his personally nebulous "nonpartisan" political communion—supporters of the Library, or one of the museums, or the amateur Symphony, perhaps even creatively participating in the most obscure or inchoate local arts—whether or not they individually joined in the overwhelming public opinion that fishing and athletic public education deserved the highest civic priority.

Ben, however, apparently totally indifferent to what he called "culture", had been a somewhat disappointing scion of Ur's Lower East Side Ashkenazim, after its mercantile ascent to Dogtown, as his literate family's merely arithmetical proprietor of the City's long-since vanished ramshackle Factory Outlet for "Dry Goods at Bargains" practically on the waterfront. He nevertheless admired and befriended the theatrical Doctor Charlemagne (one of his father's nearly deadbeat tenants) as a man of unquestionable cultural authority. More than a majority of Ben's political constituency around Harbor Ward—though politically augmented by most of the affluent or educated congregation scattered among all the other parishes and liberties whose people met each other at the synagogue on the acropolis just around a corner from the Hall—judged people's motives or values by their localized genealogy. This sense of humanity's anchorage, not of its ventures, was the key to Ben's unreliable but usefully peculiar friendship.

Was Ben now Silenus or Balaam, lingering with one more drink while awaiting the check, or heaving himself onto the spacious driver's seat of his infamous ass in which to post home as he thought of all the Dogtown people he knew or knew about? For Ben (Dexter thought) there seemed to be no arbitrarily labeled cohorts of generations. Each family had its own unique calendric origin and subsequent ramifications anywhere in the common grid of time, privately lumped in its unanchored common present tense. But anyone of that world who stays in this place is aware of each other's positions in terms careless of the universal fourth dimension. On the street Ben sometimes recognizes a son as the son's father, or a woman's face as her cousin's: over the generations a relativity

often transcending by intermarriage (or its physiological equivalent) in blood or religion, perhaps even in race. A man of certain
age must be careful in attempting familiarity with a woman whom
he takes to be the girl who sat ahead of him in the eighth grade.
But even if Ben did make that kind of mistake in the web occasionally, he seems never to forget that his own ward's counts aren't half
as important as the city-wide votes for the Board that made or
broke his responsible administration.

Dexter's interest in civics was of course broader than that of
Ben, the pejorative "local politician". This mayor found himself
still troubled by the fact that a national candidate can win the Electoral College for the Presidency while still losing the total popular
vote. But he knew that without that flaw the national Constitution
could not have been ratified in Brotherly's Independence Hall, and
without that irrational synthesis of unity. But wasn't it characteristic of almost all functional democracy, which is based upon the
assumption of compromise at every level of society, verbally if not
mathematically? Architectural compromises were a political necessity for our town's democratic adoption of a classic Atlantean
model. It was an inspiration for the present Hall's infernalized
replica, symbolizing its more or less contemporaneous municipal
promotion from Town to City in the 19C, no longer to be run
directly at the ground level of "town hall" democracy. More than
fourscore years later the sovereign people adopted the charter under
the latter part of which Ben had served merely as the nominal
republican leader of powerful legislators actually elected, individually, to represent the people democratically. But then, under a
revised charter, all plenipotential executive power had not long ago
been relegated to a "professional" City Manager, according to popular referendum in hope of efficiency, subject only to the Board's particular outright veto of the person who'd been hired at its pleasure,
if only to overrule a single substantial decision. But recently, yet
again, this charter had been rescinded by the sovereign people, led
by the citizens for counter-reformation who blamed the city's thus-
tested constitutional interregnum for the Earls' incompetent selection of a particular incompetent C E O as the sole executive of a
new constitution constructed by a voluntary commission of compromising citizens charged with amateur ideas of sound management. Thus the City finally graduated to the "Home Rule" plan for
a "strong mayor", in a faulty attempt to adopt the "separation of
powers" emphasized in the national Constitution.

As Dogtown's City Planner under an earlier charter and the same professional function elsewhere, after youthful jobs with an architectural firm in the metropolis, but as a continuous local resident, Dexter had known more about how the administration was affecting public time space and causality outside Ibicity Hall than about its inside headquarters for administration, where Caleb's work was now usually confined out of public sight in a corner office, converted from a conference room in the Mayor's first-floor suite. This central level of power was reached from either of two rectangularly cornered streets by great bold flights of granite steps to a classical porch, or suggestion thereof, and from a third facade at the end (darkened by a windowless wall of the granite Post Office), similar in theme but with many fewer steps and without any overhang at all. The three rectangular approaches met centrally in a marble-floored circle tiled at its center as a compass card. Where there was space on the walls they bore ibi-painted murals, or public notices wherever the various offices were not penetrated by varnished brown doors with titles. (The great balconied and staged theater upstairs was used primarily for public political assemblies and other performers, especially at occasional civic activities or displays.)

Across the long main corridor opposite the functions of Mayor and Treasurer was, among other offices, a room of obsolete or obsolescent office machinery and operators, now designated as the future Computer Room, whose equipment was yet to be installed. Since it seemed out of the question for the City to make a capital investment, then design its own staff and train its own technician, in response to the loud demand for "computerization", which Caleb pronounced strategically premature—it being logically secondary to the initial implementation of extraneously fixed procedures and communications—the Board had approved his plan to advertise for competitive proposals from various firms in the business of leasing by long-term contract some appropriately modest computer "system", including its maintenance and all the prescriptive software needed by a municipality (save payroll, which in Dogtown's case was already served as a specialty by an existing service bureau nearby).

After narrowing seven competitors in Gloucester County down to three proposals, visiting their offices and those of certain existing users of the packaged system (suggested or not by the salesman himself), studying both financial and functional factors, and getting nominal approval from the City's bewildered Purchasing Agent, Caleb had recommended to Hecuba's Admin and Finance Committee, with an unprecedented presentation of documentary evidence and pragmatic reasoning, the Algorithmic Data Service based in North Bethsalem, owned and managed by Gilbert Algo, though not the *lowest* bidder, certainly offering the most in hardware, software, reputation, and financial stability. It was of no disadvantage to Gil's proposal that he lived as a local taxpayer on Folly Road in Taraville, not five miles from the Hall.

In discussing his proposal with Dexter (in whose name it was to be presented first to the Committee and then to the entire Board), Caleb confided that for two reasons he had unnecessarily taken too much of his available time and efforts to argue for a rather indisputable selection. The first was that he wanted to ease any future appeal for the Board's trust in the professional quality of his objective judgment. The second was that he wanted to avoid any "conflict of interest" suspicion, for Gil Algo had once been his OHM Field Engineer at the Yard representing the world's most illustrious computer firm, who had much admired and even disseminated some of his unprecedented C M S ideas for the Yard. But he admitted to Dexter that he had also known Algo's present wife—the kind of relationship that sometimes troubled the personal memories of Dexter himself.

Gil's pragmatic and comparatively ready-made leasing system for the standard municipal practice in Vinland's small towns— though in Caleb's mind unsatisfying in its "software" programs— could be adapted to present ways and means and therefore only delay rather than powerfully resist the undeniable future nuisance of fighting for his own development of radical improvement in both efficiency and information. He hoped eventually to have a tiny municipal C M S relieving him personally of extensive detailed planning, as well as of budgetary pleading for a programmer in fiscal exchange for clerical help in his own analytical applications of the computer's capability—perhaps with such devices as his S M D C—all of which were pipe dreams at this stage of Dogtown's evolution, as he explained to Dexter at a hurried lunch counter early on in Harry's Delicatessen, just down Front Street from Morality Square.

Dexter told him to relax and take his share of time-off; there were plenty of managerial problems other than organized efficiency for both of them to deal with. "Efficiency isn't everything. By all means, keep in mind your hope to eventually make Dogtown a model for all Vinland cities, but let that develop in due course. Washington wasn't built in a day, and by the time you've got what you want with technology I think you'll have found the broad field of government as interesting as I do, at least philosophically speaking!"

"I know you're right." Caleb laughed with his mouth half full of a hot dog. "It helps to know that you understand my mania as the long haul. I hope the Earls will be no less patient."

"Don't let them get you down. You should have been here when the young Turks were getting elected by yelling for us to replace the Browning Chancellor copy machine with the Photon model! Battle cries come and go, especially around election time. Most of the new ones have to display their own expert opinions about something. Pretty soon one of them will be pontificating on the so-called 'personal computers' that the futurists are promising! Those guys remind me of radio hams in the old days, the ones who would work for hours to raise anybody in Australia just to ask 'How do you hear me? . . . I hear you three by four' [if not 'five by five']! But sometimes they save lives with useful messages. There was a young Radio Technician in our L S T who fixed the wardroom shortwave radio so we could listen to shards of stateside music all the way from Truk— pretty remarkable then, when radar and Loran were new, before anyone had devilvision. But Public DV at least seems to be worth the rise of popular electronics. I'm not a Luddite. Maybe midget electronic fanatics will turn out to be our personal Ariels."

After lunch Dexter liked to tease his junior with a tall hand on the back when there was no particular emergency known to be awaiting them on their return to the acropolis. But it was not often that they chanced upon such a simultaneous interlude in their obscure efforts for the local common good. Dexter sometimes scheduled private conferences in his office as an important element of his duty as a courteously sociable and openminded skipper who tried not to interfere with the special work of his less conspicuous first lieutenant.

2.

The night of Dexter's return to Dogtown after his private lunch with Benlevi on the mainland of Cape Gloucester he was obliged to attend a meeting as ex officio chairman of the semi-autonomous

School Committee, but the semi-educated and highly accredited
Superintendent of Schools was so pompous and boring about
minor bricks-and-mortar matters totally within the man's own
administrative bailiwick that he (Dexter) hardly listened to the
unremarkable proceedings. As Mayor, used to acrimony at budget
agendas, he was preoccupied with his leadership of everything in
City government except the intellectual edification of its future
citizens. By law he was not allowed to interfere with the mandated
profession of education—only to provide the local tax money to
meet its demands! Only ex officio was he a member of the School
Committee.

Afterwards, having remained taciturn at the headquartered
school of modern brick and glass design and spaciously luxurious
administrative offices (compared to all the City properties under his
direct jurisdiction, including the one he worked in), he lay ruminating in a very large bed beside his slumbering wife number two,
namesake of his daughter Deirdre ("Deedee") engendered with wife
number one, the one who'd long ago been his schoolmate named
Gloria in rural Montvert, now the city's public Librarian and pro
bono Historian. Typically in Dogtown pattern that former wife was
married to Waldo Cotton, the Production Manager of Rafe Opsimath's Dogtown Machine & Design; whereas the wife beside him,
formerly Mrs Waldo Cotton, the most beautiful woman in the city's
public service, a perfect match for Dexter himself when he was the
City Planner, had long ago, in his present house, served as the
Board's prothonotary, taking coherent notes and writing them up as
official record of their questions, statements, and answers (but
omitting any comments that might be personally embarrassing or
otherwise inappropriate in print) in her own fluently succinct
prose. Besides advising the Margrave on points of order, she drafted
and corrected even substance for ratification all the legislation she
had helped the Board to articulate. With this former experience she
was privately of great help to her present husband when at home he
invited advice or uttered an exacerbation related to his functions in
Lilliput Hall. He blessed his lucky stars when she was awake and at
his disposal of her memory and acute commonsense. But under the
immediate circumstances he couldn't avail himself of her knowledge as a thoroughly local woman at every graduation of education
diachronistically parallel to Ben's mnemonic web of intergenera-
tional miscegenation known to his opposite gender. He, unlike his
former wife, remained a stranger to the Dogtown psyche, from a

rustic almost inbred inland little valley with castes and animosities of its own at a time two or three generations in the past.

Pondering advice to himself as a managing leader, though in a career long since diverted (with Gloria, the first Deirdre, and Robert the younger child) from architecture, the one creative art in which he'd hoped to find a promising place, he now congratulated himself on the possibility of further expanding satisfaction in politics as the best way for anyone to advance the common good defined by what had been his undefined religion. At one time, during the War at sea, long before he'd met the late Finn Macdane here in Dogtown, he had thought of staying in the Navy (God willing his survival), if it would accept him with a Regular commission. That would have promised his betrothed Gloria the financial security that everyone worried about before the specter of Depression finally vanished on V-Day—a narrow lifetime path in special service to the General Welfare of his country.

As a very young Ensign about to become a Lieutenant (jg), a subaltern without much liberty or incentive to fraternize with enlisted subordinates almost all his senior in age, but serving with largely semi-literate wardroom officers from many unimpressive levels of life or academy older than himself, under a lawfully grouchy skipper—and with no money or L S T cabin space for a drawing board or sketchbook, or for the large tomes of his aspired civilian profession—Dexter took advantage of free paperbound double-columned Armed Forces Editions (and Navy Base lending libraries) to expand his limited college background in the literature that had stimulated many an architect or artist. Thus his moving situation in the Pacific Ocean steered him especially to Wellingborough Redburn, whose famous leviathan led him step by step to realize that that story was but the central zenith of a single book with the seven tomes that altogether founded the later fiction and poetry (as Caleb had pointed out long ago when his garret tenant). From that base Dexter had turned to study what was available to him at sea about the author's literary or philosophical allusions, thereby greatly expanding his scope in the background itself, thus enhancing his appreciation of literature as the sum of lives, unlike the plastic arts.

I think by now it has amorphously enlarged my democratic grasp of a small city's General Welfare: Ben's people, and Hecuba and Deeta Dana, plus Caleb and those like myself and Deirdre and Glory and Fay and Finn and Arthur Halymboyd and Endicott Krebs and Belle and Rafe

Opsimath, and Tessa Barebones, and all the other-minded voters on our side in politics who must not be omitted from the ultimate credit for political goodwill. Amid the clamors in Lilliput Hall for public safety, public works, the Chamber of Commercials, and diplomatic relations with the State House I see very little of most of them (though naturally sometimes because of perfectly understandable embarrassments arising from our internecine divorces or suspected intrigues).

In the lonely lumbering L S T (hardly ever assigned to a flotilla), a thousand miles from the nearest flagship, most of the ship's company, from captain to second-class Fireman, went "by the book" in their own way; they were all as subject to the Articles of War as Redburn had been under the famous Commodore in his frigate. The lanky young Dexter was the one who had believed in going by the regulations. He still did. But in democratic Dogtown it was almost impossible, from bottom to top, even in the Police or Fire Departments, to say nothing of the Public Works hierarchy. Any standards of procedure and communication were too much like discipline.

He'd begun to notice that distinctly Atlantean proclivity in war as well as peace while he was conning the ship as she placidly plowed the bright blue Pacific with none other in sight, with no clouds except those always accompanying the traveler's center like a circumferant sierra of snow at the utmost distance of the whole horizon's rim, especially when he gazed down at the postwar pay-load of his elephantine amphibious craft: the long open deck full of cheerful but orderly repatriating prisoners who went about their much simplified A D L in the open air, cooking, eating, cleaning, and relieving themselves, in three apparently autonomic shifts, ascending and descending hatches from the tank deck below, two or three orderly times a day without discernible supervision except for that of the serenely goodnatured Cipangese army major who occasionally came up out of his cabin to sit on an ammunition locker outside the wheelhouse with his legs drawn up and crossed like a Buddha's, sometimes exchanging smiles or English words with an off-watch sailor or officer who liked his exotic company. How much did he differ from the same man who commanded the same men ashore in Truk when they had awaited a deadly invasion or had already fought in one elsewhere on another island, or even earlier on a much larger island when one of his class had beheaded with his sword many more than one Atlantean or British prisoner of war? Or perhaps his men were all young replacements in atrocious carnage that he himself had survived at a lower rank? It was hard to assume that he was of the same brutal officer corps.

The prematurely authoritative "ninety-day-wonder" from the hills of Montvert, a graduate of the North River training ship tied up for the rest of its existence as a greatly hastened naval academy for civilians scarcely old enough to vote, was still eagerly learning varieties of society that he hadn't yet even read about, aside from desire for women, which was neither social nor selfish. Now, much heavier in chin and belly, full of years, he remembered that in those days he hadn't forgotten Sunday School and certain phrases of Pauline sermons, especially those associated with Job, whom he'd never liked, even without his boils, whose name had often been repeated by the meek and kindly Separatist pastor in his weekday role as interdenominational Scout Master, meeting in a vestibule of the framed white parish house attached to the church. The figure Dexter had found most interesting was the Old Testament Joseph. But what brought that little rural scene into the present Mayor of Dogtown's cranium when his reservoir of sleep was as parched as any political C E O's?

Having vainly cudgeled his restlessly recollective brain for both boyhood and its military maturity, without knowing why, he crept downstairs in his bathrobe to dusty old books in his study, ironically aware that this his many-altered house next to the Acorn Pasture Cemetery on Cod Street, main thoroughfare for monstrous trucks from land to sea, and from seaside to land, was sometimes still called The Rectory because it had originally been the residence of St Paul's Tudor Apostolic Antidisestablishmentarian parish priest and family. One glance at the table of contents in his worn and spine-cracked Standard Version dismissed the need for any further reference than the Bible's text itself. In his Sunday School days he'd been obliged to memorize and recite in sequence the names of all its chapters, and his tongue had remembered just enough of them to mumble the name of Job, further blocked by Psalms, of which he learned by heart only its twenty-third, simply from sheer congregational repetition while trying to distinguish the voice of Gloria in a nearby pew across the aisle. With such a divided mind he found what he thought he must have been looking for as a link to fragmented memories of something very different from standing watch silently with a silent steersman at night likewise dividing more than one leitmotiv with the perpetual preoccupation of all young celibates at sea, in his case with lust tenderly betrothed to

the same sweetheart, who'd faithfully kept pace with his educational years, together or apart, but never forced to doubt each other
half the world away. . . .

*What why and where—after a morning of reasonable paperwork and
phone calls, until I had that odd lunch with Ben, immediately followed by
a full day's worth of typically aggravating petty politics, too busy to think
about anything else, until I got home to Deirdre long after we had dinner
out separately—did apparently unrelated wisps of theme and variations
start up forgotten bits of religion flickering in my head, dialectically or
chronologically, to agnostic speculation? Redburn seems congenitally fascinated by the Bible in his own way. I suppose it has to do with what Caleb
would call my own "complex symbol-system".*

For half the remainder of that night, engrossed in chunks of
Job, puzzling over the ambiguities of irony and tone in the translation of "bless" as "curse" (or vice versa), which he remembered
being warned of by his surprisingly liberal Scout Master, or leafing
about from here to there in the Bible according to referential footnotes, Dexter searched to recall bits of language he might have
remembered on his night watches at sea, but sometimes pausing to
read with interest passages that he was sure he'd never read before,
whether or not he'd heard them from a pulpit. As soon as he
became aware that he quickened like a weakening pendulum
between Old and New he thought extraneously of the mechanics
he'd learned without enthusiasm in an elementary physics course,
with which he associated the esoteric metaphors bandied about by
Caleb when off guard. Thus with half a smile Dexter recalled what
little he understood of *entropy vs counterentropy* in that poor boy's theoretical effusions that were sometimes interesting but which had
practically nothing to do with his job in the Lilliputian scene.

—Practically *true, yes, but perhaps not* essentially *nothing!*

*Right now I'm trying to remember what Caleb told me about entropy
more than once in this very house a very long time ago, after the rest of the
family had left our dinner table, when I was the non-political City Planner (at least an architect without political responsibilities) and young
Caleb was the tenant who lived in our attic apartment, when he was
making his living as Father Duncannon's business manager and religious
factotum over in East Ward at The Laboratory Something-or-Other. I was
never sure where his science left off and his imagination began to abuse it. I
miss Finn's opinion of technical metaphors! Anyway, for a layman like me,
even orthodox thermodynamics needs a poet, and that definitely is what
Caleb is not, God bless him! As far as I'm concerned, he talks the jargon of*

"systems theory", which only puts the cart before his horse! . . . What he seems to be trying to say is that although our universe as a whole is ulti-mately doomed to a chaos of utterly useless energy and irreversible meaning-lessness, everything that lives or otherwise gets made must buck the trend—whether just for self-preservation from deformity or death, for growth or organization, or for creative art—must borrow positive energy from its immediate environment. Every urban planner should know that even the best-governed loveliest and most prosperous great city has its peripheral or internal byproduct of disorder, mainly poverty and crime (not to mention disease, public fiscal folly, unenforced building codes, general corruption, or obvious bad taste). That much in physical or social science applies to greater Dogtown as a whole, as well as to my Ibicity Hall and each of its organi-zational or architectural parts at variously scattered functions of my central responsibility. Except for justice, what more should I worry about for the local common good? . . . Obviously neither money nor rank are measures of the unstable counterentropy that presumably integrates the sum of its less stable contributors. It's impossible of course to record or calculate any of this for the manager of good government—but still a usefully amorphous way to think things through in intuitive judgment of what's helping or hurting, especially with only a primitive accounting system to reason from. . . . So far, so good. But what gives me pause in Caleb's reasoning is about who pays the piper. He almost claims to have the composite answer by intuition, though he admits it's probably impossible to prove anything without a theo-retically modeled closed system in an extremely sophisticated physics lab. But he thinks theoretical physics favors him anyway.

So is it true in practice what may be true in theory, that the cost of local perfection may only be a dissemination of the entropy exiled somewhere else by counterentropy, as in Caleb's concentration upon efficiency? Job says "If you would learn more, ask the cattle." Why did the Creator install this bias against civilization? "Speak to the earth and it will teach you." Listen even to the Sea Serpent, or to Leviathan, or to the people! Even to the good fish: that's what Ben himself would go tell the saints and angels to do. Forget the cats! Even with Saint Paul's charity—even his Christian kind of love? Is Ben's attitude the wise one, in due course of time, for a mayor who believes in the possibility of optimum balances. —But aha, that would get me a bit of a bite off the hook! I could relax for the common good, almost like Ben, and forget about achieving all my objectives before next year's elec-tion. Let Caleb take his time drawing order and information from disorder and ignorance, spreading his improvements gradually, so that the environ-ment's attenuated debit entries won't be noticed as his system secretly draws its energy of counterentropy or information from outside the Hall, maybe

even from across the Gut and everywhere else from all but harmlessly dissi-
pated anima mundi? So in the end—that is, at least the end of each
chronological universe—what real difference does efficiency really make for
society and culture as far as the larger system outside ours is concerned,
where humanity plays no part? Danger deferred always seems safe enough
for the present. But should I let the sly playwright perfect all his works all
the faster—right here at home? I'll be more popular if I take things easy.
As long as there are no emergencies or local injustices. . . . Deirdre will like
me better too.

Thus Dexter amused himself, and went back upstairs to bed
without disturbing her. They were both immunized to the sporadic
rumble of eighteen-wheelers, a noise that even their tallest experiments with fences and hedges had never much muffled in their
second-floor bedroom minimally close to the kilroy artery where it
approached the railroad crossing and its diesel-shrieks from a
ninety-degree angle in either direction, nowadays almost always to
carry only human passengers.

3.

[The Osprey Function Room of the renovated Doghouse.
Knights of the national Turntable Club in what they call their
Reunion Room at their final local Luncheon Meeting of 1981, providing the mandatory Seven Round Tables altogether nominally
expected for a total of 84 members and guests. The very few already
on the scene are taking advantage of early-bird time with drinks
while leisurely awaiting the first gavel of Slim Willard Boxshaw,
the continually re-elected Knight Commander, to be followed (after
matters of business, charitable edification, and announcements of
the Knight Victualler) by the occasion's Roundhouse Knight, who
in this case happens to be the Thirteenth (new) Knight, Earlderdam Hecuba Fox-Argent, the first female ever invited or admitted
to this venerable brotherhood, thanks to recently adjudicated interpretations of Constitutional law. The speaker tonight will be the
Honorary Knight, Dexter Keith, Mayor of Dogtown and formerly
its City Planner.]

RAFE OPSIMATH [*Chairman and CEO of Dogtown Machine &*
Design, husband of Tessa Barebones, finding Dexter about to sit down alone next
to the podium, intending to scan a palm-full of note cards as inconspicuously as

possible. They are obviously old friends, though accustomed to each other mainly by telephone, but Rafe joins him without hesitation]: Dex, you look good! I'm sorry I've missed the last two meetings. I've been shuttling back and forth to Baby Oaks where we're now occupying the new subsidiary, for better or for worse—Wind Power Manufacturing! I'm sure you'll approve of it, even if it reduces your dividend for the next twenty years or so. But you'll see all about it in our Annual Report.

DEXTER [*Rising to clap him on the back like Chiron welcoming home the only reliable Centaur he could talk to*]: Money is no object for a public servant, you shameless old gold-coaster! But it's Dogtown that needs more of your industrial development. Why can't the City sell you a few more acres up on the hill? No reality taxes for the first ninety-nine years!

RAFE: Too much opposition by locals and too far from where people really care about the conservation of energy. Couldn't you persuade Waldo Cotton to move out West? We need a man like him out there where we now need him even more than we do here in Dogtown now that he's got our shop running like clockwork! He doesn't know much about generating electricity, but that's okay because he'll quickly learn what we're about to get into. He made himself a First Class Fire Control Man in the Navy, you know. Then from solo gypsy kilroy owner-driver to the Yard's Distribution Manager with new ideas.

DEXTER: Oh, I've heard a lot about him. I think it was Caleb who got him hired at the Yard. They collaborated in computerizing all the Yard's shipping and warehousing. The staid old mossbacks referred to Caleb and Waldo as the Tweedledum and Tweedledee of inventory control. Isn't Waldo Cotton the one who got everybody in logistics to use four-way instead of two-way wood pallets for forklift trucks? Reminds me of Casterbridge staddles!

RAFE: Something like that. He went from local development to a big part in urging the international movement for standardized container-shipping by land and sea. When the Yard promoted him he was well known in the frozen-food industry for his sophisticated coordination of raw material supply, transport, production, and distribution to customers. But never went to college; a self-made man if there ever was one. No matter what he doesn't know at beginning something, Caleb and I both know he doggedly learns and immediately improves it, and ends up with better concepts entirely. When I first hired him he hadn't much more than peeked into a machine shop in his life, but he's got our production going very efficiently. I know you haven't tried to dissuade him from moving for his own sake, but apparently he just won't leave this Rock at any price.

DEXTER: You mean his wife wouldn't. I should know! This town is small.

RAFE: Well that's none of my business. —Another glass? —What I've been trying to find out is what our pretty-boy, that repugnant reality-shark Hastings Mooncusser, still the Norumbega Norman, is now up to. From what I hear it sounds as if after all these centuries of international litigation he's still claiming the title (if not the property) of the Lord of New Albion. After twenty years to be seen through in this intimate democracy how did such an insidious salesman become your de facto enemy? Just when we get the best of nonpartisan mayors you're apparently being opposed by a sly gang of sappers.

DEXTER: Shussh! It's a fishy democracy. Thou shalt not speak against a brother Knight. Especially if he shows up today. I think you're exaggerating my danger. I'm not terribly worried about the "nonpartisan" opposition. He may have gotten the Board's majority to make him the chief Margrave but he still doesn't have his own way very often, thanks mainly to Hecuba Argent in all important votes, because her heart and mind are ultimately in the right place, once we make sure she understands our words. She's very astute with numbers. Except for Mooncusser, who's scared of her intelligence, most of his cronies find her company very amiable, whether they vote with her or not. What I like about her is that she's personally as partisan as I am extra mural. Of course it's no secret from anyone who cares to step into the City Clerk's office to look at the register of voters. But too many people in Vinland think it virtuous to register as nonpartisan even when they vote just as we do in final elections. That attitude is the bane of fundamentally sound progressive government in Botolph and Washington—

RAFE: —Dex! Tess's whole gang have been hoping you'd run for something bigger, after you've had your fill of this petty boot camp!

DEXTER: Rafe, it may be small but it isn't petty! It's Dogtown, Atlantis writ typical! But I tell you, government is *interesting* [*sotto voce*]. As long as Caleb stays with me I can skip most of the bureaucratic stuff. He says that he'll stick in the Hall as long as I support him. It's a good thing he's looking more for power and a secretary of his own than for the going rate of pay for the kind of work he does at a discount even by small-town standards—not to mention private business salaries. Don't forget, he and I are public *servants*! We can't or won't organize a union and threaten to strike for fair wages!

RAFE: Of course Dogtown's never been rational in the past. You can't expect commensurability all at once. The mainland's gain would be Dogtown's loss of its windfall if you left to become a governor or congressman. When we urge you on to higher levels we're just being unselfishly proud of you for the whole country's sake! One thing I like about this smaller cape is that it counterbalances my hometown on the Pacific side as it gets too rich and luxurious, losing its fishery. Dogtown's an unostentatious magnet for marooners of all kinds, noticed or not, from Merry Sterne to Doctor Ipsissimus Charlemagne, in almost as many as San Ricardo's three and a half centuries; from the aboriginal Irindian witch Deeta Dana to the likes of Caleb, Fay, and Finn Macdane—you, me, and most of our womenfolk. —Oh, oh! Methinks there's one in a red dress with her eye on you right now. Please introduce me to this character if she gets this far. —Meanwhile I was going to finish my point by saying that we stay in a pretty steady state only because many of our bright kids sacrifice themselves in a continental diaspora, successfully or nostalgically, leaving room for replacements in a continual immigration of new marooners to help keep this place in a steady state of vitality. This librating seesaw has kept the name of Cape Gloucester in famous pictures and less famous print, but as geography more than history in my opinion. Which of our friends can or will have children or grandchildren to boast of names in their telephone directory? —Here comes the new marooner to bear me out, I believe.

DEXTER: It sounds as if you're trying to bear Caleb out. You're the one who should run for mayor!

RAFE: By the way, Gretta Doloroso—you know, Elliott Krebs's aged major domo and secretarial factotum, who's known a lot of unknown legal secrets over countless years and won't die until he does—she told my dear wife Tessa that the City should have given Caleb a medal long ago for keeping the Yard headquarters here after Demeter Mills took it over, instead of centralizing all the office administration themselves in St Peter and shutting down all but the production plants here and elsewhere. That's why the Yard keeps its name as a semi-autonomous subsidiary, not just as a local division of the parent company.

DEXTER: I'll ask Belle Cingani. If the editor of our *Dogtown Daily Nous*, who's been writing the "A Fly on the Wall" column for twenty years, doesn't corroborate that I won't take it seriously. Business administrators at high levels, unlike public officials, don't have much trouble keeping their secrets, and Caleb himself would be the last one they'd confide in at that level. But I suppose it may have been one factor among other independent variables. At least it's plausible, as a factor among others. She and Tessa have always been interested in his private life, but they know nothing about big business.

—Hello, Hecuba! Congratulations from Table Seven to our First Lady! [*He and Rafe rise and the introduction is made. The Mayor gestures her to a seat facing them on either wing like the pupil of an alert eye between the two men as they settle themselves to her left and right from the vantage where they too can watch the field of six other tables, which are being slowly occupied, one two three or four seats at a time, as if the newcomers always gather piecemeal rather than in elementary Pythagorean numbers. Slim Boxshaw can already be seen sauntering from the door, greeting and buttonholing his way in genial goodfellowship, never glancing at his watch, on his meandering way toward the rostrum hard by the trio's somewhat daunting Table Seven, which he must eventually share according to immemorial protocol at least with by-law speakers and guests, as well as with any indefinite oversufficiency of mufti-Knights for seventy-two chairs at six Round Tables. Even Table Seven will at last be nearly complemented with curious or lagging Knights, most of whom are familiar comrades in business or politics. Hecuba is now obviously the day's peculiar attraction, as much to those who voted categorically against her membership as to those who welcomed the law on behalf of even an ordinary female. They are all used to having women on the purely public Board of Earldermen, which two or three times under the former weak-mayor "home rule" charter had chosen a woman to head the city's government as its presiding Margrave and titular mayor ex officio. But most of the Knights are resigned to the fact that their old world is giving way to new times and mores, for better or for worse, notably in the public attitude toward fraternization. Immemorial cycles of weather are at last splitting open harmless cracks in the largest whales of the moraine.*]

HECUBA: I'm still not used to pubic speaking. It makes me nervous about saying my say up there [*glancing at the podium*]—all these serious men—especially when I have to go up on a rooster to do it. It makes me talk too fast! But I don't mean to interrogate your conversion, Mr Mayor. I like the cut of your bib. Right now, if you don't kind, I just want to warm up for my ideal by taking advance of this lonesome opportune to ask for a date after your office hours. I'm not being nosey—I know how hard it is for you to have a stitch in time.

DEXTER: An appointment would be my pleasure. If you don't mind, please call Inez at my office and see if she can find an open-ended one for you, at my request, so we wouldn't be rushed like a doctor in whatever you'd like to discuss. She knows much better than I do what I'm supposed to be doing every day in the week. If there's any difficulty let me know. I've wanted to get better acquainted.

HECUBA: A city's work is never fun. But if we rest at our fours the dory will drift!

DEXTER: Please join us with a drink. There's no hurry. Even according to schedule there's still a quarter of any hour before they start and they never start on time. [*She chooses Welsh ale on draft, which Rafe goes to fetch. Meanwhile:*]

HECUBA: Thanks. That'll slow me down, when I'm still smacking my lips up there on the scaffold. Makes me feel at home. Off season I'm always thirsty. Bring your wife over to the Starboard Gangway when we open this spring, on the house. That goes for Mr Optimist and his wife too. My father was a Welsh coal-minor in Labelle, before we moved to Cornucopia. He heard somebody reading Shakesear and he thought Hecuba was a magic witch. How about your name?

DEXTER: It means I'm righthanded.

HECUBA: That's why you have a southpaw as your righthand man?

DEXTER: You're very observant. I didn't notice that until I asked him to sign a staff Christmas card.

HECUBA: Oh I knew him back in Baby Oaks. We both worked for the same landlord. I brought him his paychecks. He was the *night*time coal-burner. He said Caleb meant dog. My daughter still lives out there. Her name is Wednesday, short for Wenny. What's your wife's name?

DEXTER: Deirdre. Irish. Nobody knows what it meant originally. [*Rafe brings her ale. Three glasses of liquid are cheered.*]

RAFE: Here's for your maiden speech to all the Knights!

HECUBA: Oh don't call it that! I'm a polygrot woman!

RAFE: I wish I could vote for you, but I live across the Gut. I'm hoping we'll change the charter to have some Earls at Large, so I can vote for people like you.

HECUBA: Oh, I like having my own nest! I bet Hasty Mooncuster won't come to hear me on this menu. He seemed to hate my guts from the first vote I dared in preposition. He doesn't live in Seamark, my ward, but he got his friends who are there to spread tumors about me at our ridiculous "town-meeting" caucasian— such a useless waste of time, left over from the Railroad War of 1848 when they surrendered. But it's a damn good thing that they did. Dogtown squashed the little buggers. But it wasn't the old people who elected me! Most of my constitutions think it's no immortal sin to follow an admiral mayor where my own vote counts, especially when it comes to physical affairs. I can tell you what I worry about when I see you at the Hall. —Your Honor, what's Mooncusser got against you?

DEXTER: My opinions. Taxes. A Margrave doesn't have the power he wants. Especially the veto. Call him just a rugged individualist. In itself, nothing wrong with that.

RAFE: Without the honesty. Everyone knows he's a selfish kind of Can, much as he may disguise his motives.

HECUBA: That's the ungarnished truth!

DEXTER: Well, I don't call attention to the Cratic company I keep. There's something to be said for "nonpartisan" government and against "factionalism" at our charter's ground level, but [*turning to Rafe*] as Hecuba understands better than most of the so-called independents, including many of our virtuous friends, even as so-called nonpartisan voters, we're indirect supporters of people we don't personally want at higher levels of effectively partisan government. You and I can't officially talk about that tree of power, but it's more or less what this man's wife Tessa has been making the underlying theme of her canvassing campaigns to enroll Crats without disputing nonpartisan ideals locally. It's a scandal how careless most Atlanteans are about political roots, [*lowering his mouth*] even in this clever microtopolis. But I think, Hecuba, that you have tipped the majority to her side against the rich and charming Mooncusser. That's why some say he's desperate, because it means he probably won't be Mayor after the next year's election unless Caleb and I make a mess of it! Which depends very much on the cooperation of the Margraves.

HECUBA: It's a very precocious balance. The five guys now usually on my side are not to be reliable on, especially when your man Caleb is making his first budget—after all, the season of sisters and brotherly love are past! Until budget time I think half my male collegiates will keep our meetings too short by apostate trouble, until they finally get down to brass facts by having too many of them at the last minute. That's when Mooncusser can get tricky. Anyhow you'll have plenty of crickets when there's any little bubble. They admire figures decorated to the penny. But you can inspect much worse evolutions than round dollars from a philosophical like Mr K. Even I may have to cribble about some things. But in the whole, present company suspected, I hope as Mayor you'll stack him up! —Oh oh, [*whispering not far from the nearest curious Knights on Table Seven*] they're going to call me on the rug in a minute!

4.

Deirdre [Cotton] Keith, Dexter's present wife—not his daughter Deirdre, intimately known as Deedee, who was brought up within the same Rectory—matches him to a remarkable degree, with nearly black Celtic hair and leadership's height. As much as possible in a small city she diplomatically avoids those who don't avoid Gloria Cotton the present Librarian, her much smaller but still blonde predecessor as chatelaine of Dexter's residence. In two decades, however, this tall slim Deirdre has put on no weight while Gloria has put on only a little. Deirdre the second does not mind that Dexter's jowls and belly have perceptibly expanded, owing to political eating and drinking—just enough so that the women in town have begun to notice a growing imperfection, sometimes referring in visionary fashion to past rather than present appearance.

Nor did he himself worry much about his supererogatory gravitas, partly because he wanted men to trust him as tamely harmless among womenfolk as well as old enough to refrain, wisely reciprocating the exclusive loyalty of his final outstanding and understanding mate. Without complicating his political career—though in friendly society she is sometimes teased as the new First Lady of Dogtown—she has long since withdrawn from Hall politics.

Instead she's bought out and greatly expanded old Bill Babwell's secretarial services and personnel employment agency d b a PER-SONS LIMITED (which he himself had often laughingly called LIMITED PERSONS). In fact she did so well that she had moved the business from a storefront on Cod Street to a spacious modern office in the hilltop "industrial park" that Dexter himself had instigated on the city's behalf many years ago when he was City Planner and ex officio Director of the Industrial Development Economic Agency [I D E A]. She has a battery of the latest copy machines, as well as stenographers and other respectable "human services". The Park's variety of manufacturing and other industrial services (except for railroad freight) has steadily attracted major capital investment, little of it having anything to do with Dogtown as a seaport, to say nothing of enriching its culture. It is tacitly accepted that Deirdre is the independent star of this industrial acropolis, like Atalanta when the only female in *Argo*'s crew, as if she'd ascended from boring public service to sovereignty in the exclusive aura of free enterprise. But so, in her own view. She renounces nothing in her civic interests, even deeper than Benlevi Nathan's by virtue of gender, religion, and self-education. She knows more about Dogtown than her unassimilated husband doesn't want to know, or at least has no business knowing.

After many years she feels no instinctive aversion or reflective rancor toward either Gloria Keith or Waldo Cotton, simply because she considers herself without doubt the emotional beneficiary of both divorces, which have embarrassed herself, she believes, more on Dexter's part than on her own. More important, on the other hand, she does try to steer clear especially of Gloria for her more embarrassing part than Waldo's, actively or passively, in the story of that couple. Deirdre herself was not blameless of course, and she openly admires Gloria. In the underground sensorium Dexter alone had once been known as secretly bold, and was therefore inured to microtopolitan gossip sub rosa.

Anyway, the mayor's second wife, Deirdre Dexter, has heard that Gloria Cotton his first wife is to be away for a week at the annual conference of the National Public Librarian Association in Chicago and therefore would be unable to attend the annual Advent celebration of Christmas and Hanukkah by a liberal caucus of the Business and Professional Women's Sodality. Besides, Deirdre already knows that Dexter's secretary Inez Canary—Gloria Keith's former high school student and subsequent bibliophilic protege, an amateur scholar of history whose presence would inhibit loose conversation even more than her own—always uses her two-week vacation at this time of the year by taking her widowed mother back to the Fortunate Isles—thereby abating suspicion of at least double agency in contemporary gossip. So the First Lady herself will have the pleasure of showing up without excessively reminding this sub-sorority of the nearly faded scandal of "wife-swapping", despite which her husband has been elected by a large overall majority, though only by the skin of his teeth in Harbor Ward, where female voters prevailed over masculine obedience to the Petrine clergy despite their husbands' flawless registration of piety. It is said that most voters would have been bemused by Dexter Keith even if he'd been proven a tither to the Latterday Church of Cenogenetic Prophets.

This liberal coterie of mostly middleaged women could not entirely avoid the men's Roundtable venue in the Doghouse because all the modest hostelry with small private dining rooms like the Starboard Gangway are closed for the winter. The ladies' male cynosure, their single guest and speaker, is a harmless-looking man of their generation who enjoys the advantage of being centrally seated in the semi-circle of his audience in the restaurant's back room. Belle Cingani has conjured up Tim Scriabin, a national Book-of-the-Week celebrity whose novels are founded on a very successful career in printed journalism, recently culminated with the *New Uruk Testament* as an Arts editor and general columnist, following steady advancement in stints as investigative reporter for the *Botolph Orb*. He is toasted here as a former Dogtown figure. It had been as a small bespectacled young man just out of Hawthorne College, a secret aspirant to creative writing, that because of his meek and unassuming appearance he had been turned down elsewhere for jobs he wanted, as well as because he lacked a degree in Journalism. He'd been interviewed by more than ten New Armorica newspaper editors before he was finally hired at an apprentice wage to become a cub reporter for the *DT Daily Nous*. (That paper was then still owned by autocratic penny-pinching philanthropist Richard Tybbot, the "Duke of Dogtown", a financier once internationally famous for having made many millions by sagely anticipating the great Graveyard Crash of 1929.)

At first glance Tim seems as vaguely unassuming as ever, though now neatly bearded and obviously confident. He always attributes his success to an assumed timidity; but, since the child is father to the man, one surmises that he had indeed been shy enough as a child to get to know what sometimes puts him in a position to listen for clues to secular truth—subsequently leaving most of the professional news to personalities fearless or loud and clear. It is no wonder that he avoids performing on both radio and devilvision. Belle has already made known to her sorority that he's just taken early self-sufficient retirement from New Uruk to return and settle on this fair Cape, living comfortably on steadily mounting fiction royalties. Occasionally he still writes Opinion pieces for the national press to express his liberal emotions.

He marvels at the damaging changes wrought in Dogtown since his initiation, especially by the federally financed Civic Instauration projects that have promiscuously swept away most of the gray old wooden structures of the waterfront fishery that had attracted visual artists, along with the residue of 19C slums and quietly vicious labor practices that had been declining well into the 20C. Even after most of the shoreline swath cut for an electrically refrigerated modern fishery had become neatly lined by decently functional brick and concrete housing the best of industrial machinery between harbor wharves and kilroy loading docks, he grudgingly accepts or deplores many smaller ekistical improvements, public or private, whether or not harmonious with their environing circumstances, in retrospective comparison to his original implicit satisfaction with the cityscape of his first job in this nevertheless peculiarly immutable topos of history and artifact. Now and then he condemns a suddenly realized change on a street or corner, large or small, only to delight almost instantly in its revelation of structure or space formerly hidden from a personal exposure whose objective "beauty" is problematic. Aside from eating and drinking, such tendentious opinions are the first topics of hearty and humorous conversation between the following unorganized ladies as an impromptu holiday muster and their quietly captured guest, Dogtown's latest marooner of renown—with personal eye and ear guessing at his future fame.

His unintimidated talk at this little ad hoc banquet offers nearly a dozen uninhibited amateur critics the suffrage they hardly ever get to exercise in fraternal places. They have jotted place cards to identify all the man's hosts, large enough for his framed glasses, thick and bifocal, at no great distance for intimacy with these hopeful Ladies of Misrule. Viz,

Deirdre Keith: wife of Mayor Keith (formerly m. Waldo Cotton).

Lilian (Cloud) Algo: wife of Gil(bert) Algo, proprietor of Algorithmic Data Service.

Tessa (Barebones) Opsimath: wife of Rafe Opsimath, CEO of Dogtown Machine & Design.

Belle Cingani (formerly Bice Picory; wife of a Dave Wilson), editor of the DT *Daily Nous*.

Gretta (Gretchen) Doloroso: senior factotum for Attorney Endicott Krebs, friend of the Opsimaths.

Hecuba Fox-Argent (formerly Hecuba Jones of Yerba Buena): Earlderdam representing Seamark the Fifth Parish, a newcomer.

Fiorina Sanseverino: native spokeswoman for fishermen.

Deeta (Perdita) Dana: poet of Tir-na-Dog (Purdeyville), purveyor of seaweed and meditation.

Beni (Benilda) Vanderlyn (widow of art-photographer Eric): member of the former Troika.

Caroline Chapman: Steelyard's Personnel Manager, an inconspicuous newcomer, little yet known outside her business office.

The unusual omnium gatherum in Advent happens to take place in a back room typically decorated at Yuletide for the Chamber of Commercials, before the Doghouse summons its busiest weekday night shift. For most of the conscientious women here it's a couple of hours for unguarded independence, before daylight's baubling two-faced Feast of Fools imposes upon them the holiday duties assigned largely as the natural burden of people generally designed for motherhood.

BELLE: Tim, I've been trying to think of the interesting things you've missed these twenty years. For instance, since the death of Doctor Ipsissimus Charlemagne there's been a steadily increasing trickle of Ippy pilgrims to see his personal mise-en-scène, school fish following the ghost of their whale, as someone has called it. Also some of the offbeat intelligentsia that he used to curse. His "dromenology" means something, after all. It's a pity that most of Doc's writing is so antagonizingly idiosyncratic that only one guy can make something important of it.

TIM: I remember seeing him on the street, but I was warned not to beard the lion in his den. Ms Opsimath, weren't you the manager of his little theater?

TESSA: Something like that. An outgrowth of our Troika dance company. But the Stone Barn Company of Mummers was struck stone dead when the stone barn burned down. Anyway, by that time Doc was too damned cantankerous to direct anything that wasn't all about the director. Besides, he was getting too preoccupied with his *Dromenology* magazine and its critics. As Caleb Karcist later put it, Ippy seemed more interested in showing off to his avant-garde rivals in the treetop foliage than in the trunk and forks of theatrical culture.

My husband and I both knew him well. To tell you the truth, I thought he was a bit too much of an overbearing and confusing director—on paper, more like an arbitrary smart-alec. He's the one who burned down our theater with his almost deliberate carelessness about smoking. He wouldn't even condescend to vote like the real Catholicrats he professed to urge.

LILIAN: Caleb said Charlemagne was intuitively brilliant, getting either plausible or improbable essences in such a way that he could confidently allude like a 'Bega professor to the history of ideas, or anything else—as if he'd already lived long enough to have read everything in the varsity library, when actually, for the most part, he'd probed like a water witch. According to Caleb, in those days Doc seemed a wizard partly because he thought he'd found the key to every culture in the books he'd really understood at a glance, and partly because he was simply too formidable to be argued with. I suppose that has much to do with why so many people were fascinated and charmed even when they knew nothing about the subjects of his rambling conversation! —Of course I'm not one to talk: I'm not even a common reader. My grasp is woefully less than my reach. I've never read more than random samples of philosophy.—But Deeta, you knew far more about him than we did?

DEETA: You want to hear my *present* feelings about him? Overlording personality. Maximum presence. Had never been overlooked by anyone. Knew himself born to be the center of attention, even when animals diverted attention from it. Therefore naturally self-indulgent. But alert to everything and extremely perceptive of other people's responses to himself. Couldn't help being lionized. But gentle and generous with words of praise when he was nice. Except for the animals, he was as generous as a Saint Francis. Usually dressed like a voluntary bum. Yet sometimes cruelly insensitive, as with Petto the iron sculptor, his oldest and most loyal friend in town. He liked to get information of all kinds by fathoming all sorts of inferiors in interesting conversations—or drinking and talking the night away with his quasi-peers—as long as they didn't dispute his opinions. Egocentric, you might say, but not egotistical. Or vice versa, I sometimes think. —Working for him was like testing religious vocation. I've been asked so many times what he was like that I've practically memorized my spiel! Sometimes I modify it in one direction or the other, but I always feel as if I'm not quite doing him justice. Maybe he was just above all of us. — But please, I'm talking only about Ipsissimus the person. I know very little about his work, except that like many spiritualists I have faith in his genius. He claimed that F D R personally tried to keep him in the O W I [Office of War Information].

LILIAN: Well for me he's too hard to read, but he must have been a creative volcano if Caleb says so.

HECUBA: I never heard of him here, but I used to conversate with Caleb in Baby Oaks.

BELLE: But there's no denying the charm of his dominating personality, as an unkempt but almost motherly friend. Yet when he wasn't glowering at something he always seemed to want to talk to *someone,* like a profound comedian, when he wandered around the acropolis like Socrates waiting for his daily mail! I think Caleb Karcist was the only one around here who had really dialectical conversations with him in Deeta's kitchen. —Is that right?

DEETA: Yes, while I cuddled up in the bedroom with Caleb's dog Ibi-Roy.

TIM: Are you talking about that efficiency expert that's ruffling feathers in the Hall?

DEETA: Yes, but not the dog. [*Laughter.*] Belle can tell you how everyone in town, including the Dog Officer, admired that Viking Shepherd. No one would have noticed Caleb if he hadn't had that grand bodyguard.

BELLE: I was jealous of anyone else who stroked *his* feathers, including Deeta.

HECUBA: It's quite a surmise to find Caleb here bossing bureaucats. In Baby Oaks he was physiological. But I hear he's rifling more than fetters now!

DEIRDRE: Commander Macdane, God rest his soul, recommended him. He's been a tremendous help to Dexter. People don't like changes and they're scared of computers. The only trouble is that he can't do all he wants to do by himself. He's not getting any help! The Mayor's whole staff consists of two secretaries, which he and Caleb have to share until they're lucky enough to find an unemployed yet qualified assistant in the New Works Project Administration [N W P A] pool of applicants. That's a temporary fund from federal coffers that Caleb himself managed to get from Washington for various City departments. Now he's responsible for managing the program for the whole City of job-placements and oversight—just one more set of tasks equivalent to an ordinary full-time job of supervision, when most of the workers are assigned to jobs outside the Hall and under the jurisdiction of nearly autonomous department heads, such as the Director of Public Works or the Chief of Police!

FIORINA: The D P W naturally gets most of the benefit.

DEIRDRE: The one that has the most voting families on the City's payroll! All the departments are screaming for labor or clerical help—even the Clam Warden and the Library, not to mention the Arts and Culture Project that Caleb has created with Dexter's sup-port to employ qualified creatures who happen to be out of work.

DEETA: I'm eligible myself! And lots of my friends!

BENI: I might apply too. I'm an unemployed widow. I hope they don't exclude property owners!

GRETTA: Judging just by what the *Nous* prints, even under the new charter, I've always wondered how mayors without a Caleb have time for any of the so-called details that make or break administration.

DEIRDRE: They don't have. For instance, in business practi-cally everything can be kept private, but in public service practi-cally nothing except labor and other contract negotiations must be secret—not the *results,* just the *process.* Salaries and costs (at least in theory) are supposed to be open to the public. There are perfectly legal tricks, or historical accidents of tradition, as Caleb is unoffi-cially known to have discovered, in getting around public knowl-edge simply by keeping certain emoluments or functional fees off the general personnel payroll, for lack of functional cross-coding. Now he's reorganized all city funds and expenses into one parallel deck of cards, budgeted or not. For instance, that's why the tradi-tionally colonial City Clerk and City Auditor who earn certain stipends ex officio, like running the employees' pension fund "off-budget", will now have their incomes for all to see in addition to their salaries. They are far from the more important D P W and Public Safety chiefs who are going to resent Caleb's computerized reforms.

TIM: Too bad I didn't know all this when I was the cub reporter! But they wouldn't let me investigate anything anyway.

BELLE: I never thought about anything like that. But don't think I'm "The Fly on the Wall" for nothing! What I write really isn't for investigative reporting if it's legal. I'd be fired, if not also burned at the stake by firefighters or persecuted by the police, if I printed anything that seemed unnecessarily prosecutorial, seeing that as far as I know legally these perquisites are no more questionable in municipal practice than "trivial" entries missing from the police blotter as "unenforceable laws," too unpopular to prosecute for almost all departments.

FIORINA: In Trinacria we say public money is like holy water: everybody helps himself to it. Isn't that worse?

TESSA: Noxin said "When the President does it, that means that it's not illegal."

HECUBA: What's new? Yerba Buena and the Oaks are far worse when it comes to parking tickets!

TESSA: At least they can vote Catholicrat. But you can't trust dogs even in Dogtown. [*To Tim:*] Did you come across our sardonic Wat Cibber, the truly rugged individualist?

TIM: Oh yes! The one-man Yankee dragger with his Cabotland Water Dog! He took me out on a few of his trips and let me steer while he was hauling nets. That's when I met dogfish face to face!

TESSA: He had a whole bag of aphorisms, most of them original. Caleb's favorite was *It's too early to predict and too late to repent.* Wat liked to tell his highly educated Anglo-Celtic wife Teddi that she would be the smartest one in the cemetery. They were both very kind to Caleb when he was out of gainful work and working on his play. Wat used to sit in his rocky chair and tease him for "making book". But he said it with genuine respect.

HECUBA: So those were the old days I missed. I think Mr Inscriber wants to know what's going on right now. I'd say Caleb is shipping on black ice. I inspect that Mooncutter is out to get the Mayor by way of dissipating Caleb. That man has no scrapple! He may be up to some cahoots with the City Clerk who's a good guy but doesn't know the motif. It's the Auditor that's got the most to lose if the Board calls in a dispassionate instigator.

TESSA: Yes, Hecky's on the right track!

BELLE: According to my sources—

[*Led by Gretta, everyone laughs.*]

BELLE: —allright, according to my *informants*, it's got to do with the past—something just short of blackmail. It doesn't take much to ignite either sentimental or anti-sentimental symbols, like a forgotten scandal revived.

TIM: It's obvious that you ladies aren't going to tell me everything you know—and quite right you are. But it does sound as if you've hinted at material for my first Dogtown novel! [*Merry applause.*]

HECUBA: Anyway, it would take a philanthropist to read Mooncusser's swarthy mind. But his political contention is no anagram. Present company accepted, I think this mayor is exactly what we need! [*Discerning smiles and nods all around the table.*] Even with a Caleb to do all the logical stuff, and a wife as smart and beautiful as Deirdre, just think how much has to be on his mind all around the clock, poor commander-of-chief! Too many crooks would spoil his bath. He's not a humbled guy like Napoleon or Caleb!

TIM: As a matter of fact, that's what I wish you all would tell me! According to this strong-mayor charter, what *is* politically problematic for or against the executive branch? I've read the new charter. It's supposed to be based on the separation of powers, and it is a basic improvement, but it seems to me that it's inconsistent in that idea. What keeps a mayor awake at night.

HECUBA: Always attack a fiddle in the muddle!

BELLE: Yes, Deirdre, you're the insider for outsiders, if there is one. What are the public affairs that keep a mayor busy within or without the Hall's doors so briefly unlocked?

FIORINA: Yeah, [*humorously jeering*] that work-week sticks in the craw of all *real* workers! We should pay this mayor ten times what those thirty-five-hour Civil Service clerks do.

DEIRDRE: I'm all for that! We could spend the winter in Poncedeleon, with a private line to check what's going on back here in Ibicity Hall.

HECUBA: In business Dexter could earn a million, but he believes in serving the good commonplace.

BELLE: He certainly believes in power! [*Snickering laughter.*]

HECUBA: Hold your dogs! I'm serious. Don't you believe the strictures? The law and the profits couldn't do any better. Under the circumcisions that he's inherited, just try to revision all the officious problems that a mayor sustains. For instance, getting our proper share of money from the Feds and the state when we're stirrupt with a Canned governor and Canned President. There's that invidious Mooncutter to foreclose, but no one can veto everything counterversial and still stay in power long enough to be benefectual. The Dogtown voters don't realize that the Cans want to starve the feast! —Let's just ask Deirdre what it's like to be convinced for everything that goes astray. [*General murmur of assent.*]

DEIRDRE: Let me see: —Investigating, proposing, energetically working for, quietly supporting, quietly opposing, actively promoting, or losing support on such topics as whether or not, with the state's cooperation, we should install on the beautiful 325-foot span Eisenhower steel-arch bridge over the famous Namauche estuary with its splendid 100-foot high view of the center City's western hills and northern marshes, as well as of the two much lower-level drawbridges, one for the railroad, one for people and kilroys, and of the outer harbor beyond them, to stop native suicides, a high chain-link fence on top of the handsome pedestrian railings, thereby spoiling the scenery for both walkers and riders, not only pilgrims assiduously attracted by the Chamber of Commercials but also all the aborigines, Normans, and other marooners whose aesthetic sensibility overcomes their sympathy for those who think life isn't worth living, the chief defenders of whom, Police and Fire, are very sensitive to the various pathologies of human behavior that end up in public rescue or death, whether accidental or deliberate in occurrence, always under the Mayor's jurisdiction— directly by moral persuasion, indirectly behind the scene, by evasive procrastination, by appointing a citizens' committee, or courageously by a veto of the buck that he has passed to the Board under pressure from the Vinland bureaucracy! [*General laughing and applause.*]

DEETA: That's a pretty good example of democratic dilemma.

BELLE: But it's still only a special case. What are some more common difficulties for the Mayor to handle? I know many of them professionally, but in fact almost exclusively from the outside. Much of the inside stuff that I do know is a newspaper's moral dilemma! And we can't afford an investigative reporter! But it would be helpful if we could hear a sort of checklist to keep us on our toes. Maybe Tim's novel will spill the beans!

DEIRDRE: Well, I'll do my best to reel off just the topics—not the decisions or nuisances or impossibilities—which come to mind in random order. Let's see: Bond issues; separating sewage from rain water run-off; Fire Department's selected closing of certain outlying

substations because of depleted funds due to previously unforesee-
able arsons or blizzards, or voters' general opposition to tax
increases while demanding improvements in public safety; harborside occupation of waterfront land by business that has nothing to
do with fishing or port activity; the nuisance of "pothole Earls"
interfering with Public Works schedules and priorities to favor particular repairs or to plow particular streets out of rational order,
motivated by Ward reelections rather than by the common good;
the highly significant selection of a new Chief of Police from among
existing officers and their respective underground lobbies, if not in
competition with a stranger from the mainland; ditto for Fire
Department Chiefs or other appointed officials; fighting the cherished lucrative practice of allowing police officers of any rank short
of the Chief himself to take on primitive entry-level extracurricular
duties immediately before or after their normal hours of highly
prime policing for much higher pay, thereby performing their regular duties in sheer fatigue, reducing their already none too alert
service as protectors of the public with responses somewhat less
than clear-witted; adjudicating the nasty Loosey-sensitive case of
"disparate treatment" brought by the City's one black policeman;
settling a front-page dispute about the state's recommended installation of an unprecedented traffic light at some busy junction dangerously used by schoolchildren near his own house despite the
unanimous howls of everyone who uses that overburdened trunk-
line to drive practically the only way back and forth between the
Massachusetts Felly and Dogtown center, already cursing the stop-
and-go interruptions made by the traffic itself as first-come first-
serve; choosing a professionally qualified Director of Public Works
to command by far the largest number of sinecured employees
whose voting families want no internal shake-ups or prosecution of
delinquents that are now overlooked or defended by the union or
ludicrous Civil Service regulations; persuading the Graveyard Street
municipal credit bureaus to classify Dogtown's bond-issue rating
favorably so that the city can borrow economically for capital expenditures, either to maintain essential public facilities or to create desperately needed new ones, such as waterworks or sewer expansions
long since demanded by state or federal law; then to persuade those
state or federal authorities that we deserve to be allowed postponements of deadlines on the strength of our goodwill and managerial
competence despite our history to the contrary notwithstanding;
issue permits for private extensions of the City's sewer system;

deciding to buy or lease major D P W, Firefighting, or Police equipment; answering bitter complaints about the kilroy gypsy tractor-trailers with four or five axles and as much as fourteen or eighteen wheels, each preempting several parking places on public streets meant for local citizens' use by day, and often leaving them there all night with their refrigerator motors running, loudly disturbing to neighboring families even when recognized as essential to the city's economy; demolishing as obsolete and dangerously dilapidated the noble brick Poor House, an architectural gem; propose any tax increase at all and urge personal donations to qualify for matching funds, or plead for state funds to build a large and modernized wing of the Atheneum Free Library, which does not belong to the City but is half supported by its functions, on the acropolis just across Whale Avenue from his office window; represent in Botolph and Washington the city's quarreling lobstermen and fishermen who are generally more concerned with their livelihoods than with conservation of their patronymic industries even to the benefit of their immediate descendants; attempt to revive a summertime open-air Farmers' Market in Sacrum Square, or an Arts Festival that the City Planner had once organized twenty years ago; praise the Cape Gloucester Food Cooperative at the risk of seeming to complain about the three supermarkets locally employed by international capitalism; find and encourage some entrepreneur to provide a downtown movie theater to replace the two that have been demolished; sign an ordinance to leash or unlock unpopular saints; preserve all thirty-six hundred acres of watershed and unenclosed parkland of Purdeyville from further abuse—

DEETA: Hurray! [*All the women clap and Tim smiles.*]

DEIRDRE: —diplomatically order the pragmatic Police Chief to see that his people hand out parking tickets consistently and equitably, while rigorously supervising the individuals who collect and bank-deposit the coins gathered from parking meters; bemoan the sloth of malingering D P W workers under straw bosses who themselves are unsupervised when behind sight from the managing desk, which itself is located far from the Hall and without regular interoffice mail service, thereby discouraging written records of higher-level communication; failure of the Treasurer to examine and approve the line-items of the warrant submitted by the so-called Auditor for payment—but wait, I'm getting into Caleb's administrative territory! Remember, city government in Vinland is internally as much a federation as the whole country is, and our city is in practice a federation of departments, inasmuch as many of our functionaries are answerable to state offices even though appointed, paid, and directed by us. Add to all that, every person covered by general Civil Service rules—and even many who belong only to a union—is very hard to fire, even for the worst performances or absences. Some old crustaceans regard their own seats as interminable—even though their jobs may have none of the moral defense that protects the expediencies of free enterprise! —So, all in all, nobody but God will ever cure most of a good mayor's pains.

—Well, I can't keep babbling on about even half of the pains that occur to me at the moment as typical of what a strong mayor has to think about, whether or not they can be prudently handled on Dexter's watch, or even mentioned to the Earls—present company excepted!

BELLE: Hecky is one of us!

TESSA: Most of these items certainly are not Caleb's cup of tea. He'd rather write up a three-inch looseleaf binder full of procedures for every department, even the Mayor's Office, which includes himself!

HECUBA: From what I hear stooping around to the clerks, he'd make sure there's a three-tier paper casket on every desk; and every machine should be dust-covered after hours! But it's all to the good—if he didn't have bigger things to do. It makes the girls rumble!

GRETTA: Well, most of us are on the wiser side of mid-life. We know how to separate the wheat from the chaff. . . .

TIM: [*To Caroline.*] Then what say you, Miss Chapman? You look like a young woman on the way up.

CAROLINE: [*Covering her mouth.*] New to Dogtown. Just trying to learn. My father was born here.

5.

"When the cat's away the mice will play!" said Tessa to Belle as she turned the key in her front door.

"Maybe Hecuba would say 'When the rats are away the cat will stay.' You're a damned nice cat. Every weekend I'm exhausted. Good thing we don't have a Sunday edition."

"As soon as I turn up the thermostat we'll have our first drinks. Let's celebrate what we'll call the last snow of the year. Even with double-paned glass and accordion tapestry you can't keep this hill-top barn warm if you're a patriotic conservationist. Which I am, but I'm not as much of an aesthete as Rafe is, especially when he's under the influence of a modernist architect like Caspar Aninigo, who's dauntingly famous to defer to even in the furnishing details."

Soon the two modern women were in the large and faultlessly efficient kitchen, slowly or intermittently getting ready a cooperative meal of merely habitual interest to them both, each more occupied with her wineglass. Tessa for the most part stood at the long rectangular console for culinary operations, which had plenty of room for at least two servants, Belle for the most part sitting on a stool as required with the tools of raw material on the same level beneath a wall cabinet or another naked cutting board, occasionally rising to do other kitchen errands almost as readily as her hostess. They were not indifferent to the food they will eat, but they were as one in keeping it plain and simple to satisfy the healthy appetite of two pragmatic women unaccustomed to notice the prices or routines subsumed by their preoccupied careers, even, as now, when their lucky stars were crossed at a fortuitous conjunction of absent husbands.

Tessa had continued: "It was only a lucky fluke that Caspar took us on as a minuscule client, thanks to having known Caleb when he was managing the Yard headquarters building."

BELLE: I've been worried about Caleb's predicament. Margie, the computer operator who used to run the bookkeeping machines for the Auditor, seems to be the only clerk in that department who understands and doesn't resent what he's trying to accomplish. Those who aren't directly involved with his radical changes, especially those with some office experience elsewhere, apparently like him for his sense of humor and consideration of their feelings. But I seldom show my face there, and of course most people used to petty tyranny are on their guard against saying anything that might be quoted or misunderstood in a newspaper.

TESSA: Well I've hardly ever darkened those doorways, so it's only the Mayor or Caleb himself that would know me from Eve, but I do get some second- or third-hand hints, especially from Gretta, who knows a lot about what you and I know in Karcist history, that he's going to meet some opposition from the Board when he goes up before it for something or other. Without saying anything in public that snake Mooncusser I suspect really is trying to ruin Dexter by discrediting Caleb. I told Dexter that, but he just laughed it off, saying that Finn Macdane had known a good man when he saw one, and that's generally considered the best reference anyone in Dogtown could claim. "On and off I've known him myself for twenty years or more." he said. "So has Endicott Krebs also, who remembers good things about him."

BELLE: Look, Hastings Mooncusser is the masked landlord of half the rented property in center City, as well as silent owner of his ubiquitous residential and industrial reality-estate agency; and as president of the largest local bank, he is suddenly elected president of the Chamber of Commercials too, not to mention his ascent as the top Margrave. He can't wait to be Mayor. Did you know that he was born into Mooncusser, Coneycatcher & Company, Graveyard Street's largest fur-trading firm? You're the psychologist: what do you think he's gunning for in the end? Just money? You should see his house already!

TESSA: He's a typically disingenuous business-power politician, but with the voice and manner of hereditary 'Bega aristoi. What does an aging pretty-boy like that want if he can't be governor of all Vinland? He knows how hard it is to beat a tall dark and handsome popular hero like Dexter. —But I know very little about public administration. I'm mainly concerned with Caleb's security. Dexter can take care of himself, and as long as he remains a Crat I'll do what I can to help him graduate into a partisan career if he doesn't love Dogtown enough to put up with Lilliputians forever. Aside from making a living, Dexter's in this for the power to do some civic good—I do believe that; for Caleb that's secondary: he wants just enough power to create a model system of systems for its own sake! With him it's about a pragmatically aesthetic endeavor! If he isn't defended from enemies, and isn't willing to make a career of the kind of politics that's against all reason—especially if Dexter doesn't stay as Mayor—he'll probably await some defiant opportunity to quit, just as he did at the Yard. If I knew more about the inside bureaucratic issues maybe I could somehow help keep both these guys doing what should be done to and for our restive Dogtown. Tell me a few examples of what the Hall reactionaries have against our besotted friend! In all other matters, of course, we know more about him than his enemies could dream of.

BELLE: Before I get too drunk to forget some of the scuttlebutt: in our newsroom—most of it probably stemming from the Hall grapevine—Caleb's cartoon would make him look like Saint Paul: short, bandy-legged, and bald. That's a goodnatured one. On the other hand, he's not color-blind, and that's not how he dodged the draft. He's an atheist, I guess, and a liberal. As City Budget Director he goes to lunch studying a textbook about municipal accounting and he freely admits that when he started the job he hadn't realized that City budgets are equivalent to legal appropriations, like definite laws, not just operational guidelines or goals.

TESSA: Most Hall inhabitants evidently believe that their bosses should have weathered previous experience exactly matched to any new employment unless they have a magic academic degree assumed to be relevant to the position's expected ambition! —Oh, the sacred degrees: no questions asked! —But of course they aren't the only ones who don't believe in education at all if it's called liberal! One of Caleb's sweeping gripes about Atlantean culture! He and Fay trump each other on that subject!

BELLE: Caleb's jeopardy in Lilliput Hall is not just educated names—it's sticks and stones after being on the job. Do you remember when "zero-based budgeting" was all the rage in schools of management? It was a war-cry that helped elect the young-Turk Earls on this latest Board. It was an exciting motto supposed to represent enlightenment and efficiency.

TESSA: When I noticed the term in your paper it sounded too technical for an ignorant psychiatric social worker. Rafe scoffed at it and told me not to worry my pretty little head.

BELLE: Well I have to pencil-out more of the ephemeral than the perennial. The zero-based-budgeting consultants made the great discovery that C E Os and government budget-makers should examine *every* item in making their annual budgets! Accept no financial need as obvious just because it has always been allowed in the past as axiomatic! It's a familiar subject that should be studied and predicated like any other line-item. That sounds and *is* a perfectly rational rule. The only problem is that fresh analysis requires more time and attention than any analyst has—especially when there's no analyst on the staff! In practice most new budgets are simply tinkered editions of the preceding one in terms of dollars only: adding or reducing this and that item in turn. Controversial items are normally debated, to be sure, but others are perpetuated automatically, as if handed down by Moses—unless you insist upon considering all the variables of circumstance in fiscal terms. So it seems to me at least in the newspaper business as well as in city government.

[*By this time the two women are cleaning up sideboards and utensils, about to retire to the coffee table in the living room with customary esculents and bottles but comfortably disburdened of masculine opinions, and not a bit hesitant to stay up late by starting with coffee.*]

So the subject of our zero-based boys is rational and promising: even Caleb is glad to assume it's in the heads of those who speak it. But for him the oxymoronic devil is in the details, which are tripping on the tongue as if not much more than a wave of the wrist to him the budget director—who is not free of other responsibilities. He is assisted with neither the capable sort of staff nor the sufficient supply of midnight oil. He tells me that at first he readily accepted the mandate of Z B B as a perfect invitation to eventually demonstrate the need for mechanized cost accounting and basic financial controls. But suddenly he discovered that Mooncusser had slyly persuaded his Earls that the Board's official request for its implementation in budget-building was required almost immediately for the forthcoming fiscal year! That ridiculous demand was of course ignored by the Mayor and Caleb as simply impossible. Most of the Earls listened to reason. But the budgeteer himself didn't want to let that idea die (as he knew it would without his continuing enthusiasm for the principle as part and parcel of his ultimately integrated system for municipal *management* as broader than mere budgeting). Therefore he promised to start by zero-basing a few of the small line-item departments this year as part of the computer project, thanks to Margie's beginning to take less of his time for basic mechanization.

BELLE: . . . But, as I see it, Mooncusser has been trying to plant his seed in the bureaucracy's psyche for the purpose of spreading kinships in the electorate. At opportune moments, gradually growing less subtle and more often, he'll make it known that as a naive dreamer Caleb has resisted and obstructed the practical intentions of the people's down-to-earth representatives.

TESSA: It never occurred to me that it's that bad! But is Caleb interested in diplomatic cooperation with his opponents at all? Does he know he has this enemy?

BELLE: As I understand it. [*In tentatively thoughtful words of her own, interspersed with bits of ordinary digressive rumination, or affectionate compliments to each other, the following is a summary of her journalistic grasp of these questions in terms of the city government's internal culture, which was discussed until the tipsy laughing end of the long evening when Tessa finally directs Belle to the second bedroom, prepared for her with its private bathroom in the west wing.*]

6.

Armed with a unanimous request from the Board and consequent orders from the Mayor, Caleb could apologetically ask certain department heads or minor budgeted officials to justify or explain the amount indicated in each line-item of the ensuing budgets. Even without resistance to the very idea of such a shock, or when not taken as gratuitous insult, it would be much to ask of anyone overworked or understaffed. It would call for detailed justification of items that had never before been questioned! Above all, as far as Caleb was concerned after this pilot project, it would bring to light the internal incompetence or needs of internal departmental operations—hence, eventually, of the City's overall organization (his ultimate purpose, surpassing in importance even the creation of a properly computerized information system).

But Caleb had never mentioned to Belle in any of their very few casual meetings since he'd taken his hectic job—partly because no one inside the Hall except Hecuba (an acute accountant), not even Dexter, thought it was merely a refinement of little importance compared to all the other advice or correction that was vital for the City's management, and partly because his thoughts about it would take too long to explain, especially to one whose knowledge of civic finance was only intuitively aggregated—his most philosophically interesting ambition, viz, to eliminate fiscal lies by beheading the snake that bites its own tail. Every City expenditure must be identified and matched by code number to a line in the budget, but no one can expect that all a department's individual line-item needs will end the year exactly as circumstances have required. In practice, as long as the department as a whole does not exceed its budget, the money actually spent for some line-items may have remained coded and charged by its manager though actually used for the purposes of a different account. In theory the coded expenditures should be altered accordingly, by offsetting debits and credits so that the accounting reports at the end of the year will represent the functional truth. Therefore some departments (typically Public Works which must operate under extremely variable demands) often rob Peter to pay Paul by simply mis-coding what they spend money on. If you run out of Peter's winter road sand, by taking some of Paul's unneeded money for motor oil you in effect still report the expense as Paul's. In the present accounting system,

Caleb declares, your white lies (and no doubt a few black lies about major expenses) perpetuate themselves by final expenditure reports that distort the truth, which inevitably (even in an ideal zero-based system) will misguide the figures used in construction of the following year's budget, thereby biasing appropriations for the following year, perhaps seriously distorting facts upon which new judgments are based.

But how do you describe all that to a journalist who hated algebra in her childhood nunnery and consequently either avoided civic economics or trusted it to reporters no more numeral than herself? Yet the problem, for lack of systemic controls, apparently never occurred more to Dogtown's bookkeepers than it did to any Earl but the one who understood Caleb but talked funny.

7.

[*Particular excerpts from Caleb the ghost-writer's first draft of Dexter's budget message for the next fiscal year (before most of the final figures are determined) to be submitted as soon as possible to the Board of Earls in lengthy detail for debate, modification, or approval, subject to the Mayor's acceptance, further compromise, or preliminary veto, until a final document can be agreed upon and eventually presented to the state authorities, as required by laws of the Commonwealth, before the end of June.*]

1. Introduction

. . . In my constant effort to hold the tax rate level in face of understandable pressures for better city services and improved public safety, I have been emphasizing organization and control. This budget shows substantial changes in accountability. It will be impossible to control taxes if we don't recognize the importance of municipal organization. The productivity of talented and dedicated public servants must not be frustrated by poor allocation of the City's workload. With good organization we can improve our services without adding to the payroll. I also believe that people are happier at any work when they can be confident that it is contributing to the common good without confusion of efforts.

In this next fiscal year I intend to implement the reorganization and changes in accounting for which we've been preparing during the present year. But of course these cautious innovations are only the beginning of radical reform. Management is an endless process, just as problems faced by the City are endless.

Policies and programs will get nowhere if we fail to create and control a flexible and inexpensive organization that can carry them out. The accounting I speak of is a matter of fundamentals. A football team must master blocking and tackling before it can expect a winning season of long runs and touchdown passes.

This budget itself reflects changes in both method and substance. The gross expenditures herein projected are 6.7% above this present year's original appropriations. However, aside from capital equipment expenditures, which will soon be recommended to the Board for separate financing by bond issue, I expect fewer supplemental appropriation requests during the coming fiscal year than have been necessary in this one, due to a more comprehensive reach of the budgeting process. . . .

. . . This year I have introduced the first phase of our own practical version of what is known as "zero-based budgeting". It is a method of building up fiscal requirements, as if brick by brick or day by day, analyzing actual departmental costs in terms of their component costs. As much as possible we will refuse to take for granted present budgetary figures as the foundation of our new projections simply by adding or subtracting from the latest budgetary line-items. Our first procedures have been imperfect, for lack of time, but we have learned enough to be quite sure to improve our methods as we progress from the small departments to the large ones. Being without a staff analyst, it will probably take another year to complete this departure from the traditional budgeting based upon lump sums or past patterns, whereby imbalances or untested assumptions have often been carried forward from year to year without critical examination.

However, there is no question about the fact that program budgeting is far more difficult—for my office as well as for the Board, but especially for the department heads. I am emphasizing year-round attention to the proper identification (numerical coding) of all expenditures, since mistaken allocations of costs directly distort our consequent operating reports. This is especially the problem when departments "rob Peter to pay Paul" without official transfer of authorization. . . .

. . . The Administration and Finance Committee has been most patient in helping me fulfill the Board's mandate for zero-based budgeting. With its continued cooperation I am sure to deserve less of its rightful criticism next year. This year's managerial developments were much strained by snow emergencies, which affect all communications as well as operations, especially as our comparatively small Department of Public Works has four hundred miles of roads and 62 miles of coastline to protect, much of it just when the usual year-end office work is approaching its peak. . . .

2. Budget Structure

The new structure of the budget shows redefined organizational responsibilities. The departments and divisions are clearly segregated for purposes of managerial control. All accounting and reporting, as well as plans for the computer systems, are based upon this concept.

Meanwhile the new chart of accounts has been published. It is a flexible scheme that can be expanded during the remaining course of this year for overall application beginning on July 1. The new coding system will integrate identification of organizational units, categories of fiscal accounting, and cross-classification of functions. . . .

3. Personnel

Wages, salaries, and personal contracts constitute 58% of our total requirements. . . .

*

. . . 6. Significant Departmental Changes

. . . I have also established in principle as a function of general management an administrative services division, which is intended eventually to have a separate manager, even though at present it is staffed only by a (federal) New Works Progress Administration [N W P A] mail clerk, who provides an interoffice collection, delivery, and mailing service (previously performed very uneconomically by catch-as-catch-can between buildings of various departments by unscheduled personnel), and by a single machine operator transferred from the Treasurer's Department according to my reorganization plan.

I hope that in time we will be able to staff this general function with other duties that are common to departments, boards, commissions, and specialized offices, such as typing and stenographic services or their modernized equivalents . . . for the most important function of this new division will soon be computerized data processing. . . .

. . . Strengthening the analytical function of the extremely important Purchasing Department. . . .

. . . The Assessors Department, at federal expense, has been assigned half a dozen N W P A employees for a reality-estate inspection program that will greatly reduce the cost of property revaluation now required by the state. . . .

. . . City Auditor's Department. . . .

. . . City Clerk's Department. . . .

. . . Most important of all, anticipation of a Public Safety Department comprising Police, Fire, Harbor, and Civil Defense divisions—unified with centralized communications. . . . Most public utility and inspection functions, perhaps including Parking and Animal Controls. . . .

. . . Public Health Agency. . . .

. . . Community Development Department, including Planning; Industrial Development; Tourist Commission; Conservation Commission; Fisheries Commission; Downtown Development Commission; Community Development (Federal) Block Grant and Revenue Sharing parallel managements; and the Engineering Division (to be transferred from the D P W for purposes of professional services and independent inspection). . . .

. . . Public Works (more than a quarter of the total budget), by far the largest Department, as mentioned above, including Sewer, Water, Solid Waste, and general construction operations, as well as custody and maintenance of all City vehicles and heavy equipment except for those of the Public Safety Department. Here internal organization will be the principal problem. . . .

. . . The School Department, according to equivocal state law, is practically our responsibility only as brick-and-mortar landlord and umbrella for the City's overall budget supported by Dogtown taxpayers. I believe we can reduce the school part of the budget by efficiently consolidating with the city's budgets and operations our facilities for purchasing, janitorial services, and vehicle maintenance (including school buses). But we must await full development of our computer system and other changes to be able to argue the case successfully. . . .

. . . My office is also responsible for administration of all the funds and functions financed by federal, state, and other external sources. These parallel funds will now be incorporated in our financial controls and reports as recognizing the City's management of itself, wherever the money comes from.

8.

Gloria Cotton the librarian and Caleb Karcist the City's administrator have fallen into a modus vivendi—at times nothing more than ordinary forgetfulness of any special relationship older than their current public service—which hardly ever recalled even the coolest history of anything to do with mutual passion twenty years in the past. But now as Dogtown's official Historian as well as managing Librarian, still his unlikely senior in age but no longer so unguardedly ebullient, perhaps slightly heavier but more efficient in the expenditure of apparently inexhaustible energy, her dignity is enhanced by the fading and conservative training of her basically blonde hair, freckles and all. In her earlier Dogtown times she had been very successfully demanded for the role of "A Keeper's Daughter, the Fair Maid of Fressingfield", when the Stone Barn Theater staged *Friar Bacon and Friar Bungay.* Now she sits at her swiveled armchair, fingers on the edge of her large heavily laden oaken desk wanly smiling in memory of Gepetto DaGetto's Bronze Head rehearsing "Time is. . . . Time was. . . . Time is past." She awaits the Mayor's new deputy carrying documents to compare with her own.

—Oh there he is now, framed in her open door, having been admitted to the official sanctum within the original building that had once housed an entire legacy of books but now serves as an obsolescent wooden wing of a larger modern structure, which will never be large enough for Dogtown's satisfied Atheneum, right across the street from Ibicity Hall, which occupies most of the view through the many windowpanes of her lofty old office window trimmed with cracked white paint. Caleb takes his seat opposite her. The door has been left open, to her left and his right, where the initially self-conscious innocents can be easily seen as businesslike public servants by those of lower rank descending or ascending the nearby stairs to the storage vault. It's the Library's turn to be zero-based, as a simple pilot model.

The uncertainties of relationship between politicians and schools are as nothing compared to the ambiguous connections of the City and its semi-independent Library, which is actually owned by a private nonprofit charitable corporation but is staffed and maintained by the City's budgeted General Fund. Its "off-budget" capital expenditures, except for very infrequent special bonds issued by the Hall and repaid from general property taxes in debt-service installments for years ahead, are funded by state or federal grants, from private foundations, or from voluntary contributions (which compete with those to the private Historical Lyceum nearby). This the Free Library legally functions as a philanthropic trust called the Dogtown Library Board, the president and chief financial private owner of which is Briney Nedlaw (co-owner of the *DT Daily Nous*). This individual, ex officio as well as pro bono, is Gloria's direct superior, though hardly showing himself in the building off-hours between quarterly meetings of the Executive Committee.

"Of course this is just for the budget of the City's General Fund, so it won't take long to go over what you're asking for as far as operating money is concerned. What's going to take much more discussion is the organizational change I'm proposing for the City's cultural benefit."

By this time Gloria's an adept veteran of B Bs [budget battles], and she's never been a fool as far as money is concerned—not even at home when she impulsively decides to replace all the curtains in the house. "I've heard something about what you're trying to do. Sounds good to me in general, and may make good sense for the Library." Lowering her voice: "But it's going to be B B royal with Mr Nedlaw when he sees what you're up to. And so with our poor old janitors, who think they know all the groans and tricks that minimize their work and amplify their comfort. But those two men are otherwise honest and loyal, and they don't want to join the Public Works union. All the people on our board probably will take their side."

She speaks almost mechanically because her feelings are on an uncertain lower level of feeling. "Anyway, whatever, we really need more money for buying books and subscriptions."

"That's what we're both here to defend. But recorded movies are what the general public wants even more than computerized

Interlibrary Loan systems and unliterary music discs. I'll do the best I can for the books item. —Remember when Doc Charlemagne used to call you the Clio of Dogtown's 'legendary prehistory', with the 'historical imagination' of Herodotus, a k a Goody Keith?"

"I'm no longer a Keith, thank you." she smiles ironically. "I'm happily married and much wiser."

"Then how are DeeDee and Robert?"

She brightens, almost as much as if she were only an excitable research librarian with a couple of bright school kids, the apples of her eye. Caleb is so stirred by his unspoken recollections that he hardly listens to her success as a mother: DeeDee was now an assistant professor of English out at Hume and the boy was now a senior-grade Navy lieutenant attached to the Atlantean Embassy in Kenya.

"I haven't seen Waldo for a long time." he says. "Please hug him for me. He was my best friend and collaborator at the Yard. Neither of us is taller than the other but he was the stocky muscle man. I'm not surprised to hear he's Rafe's righthand man, much in demand from coast to coast. He's probably just as good in production as he always has been in logistics."

"He's putting on a little weight but it seems to broaden his shoulders. I still marvel at his husbandry." It seems to Caleb that she nearly blushes. "He still speaks of you, too."

He brings himself up short. "We can't do this whole budget of yours today." he says, handing her a paper copied from a sheet in his provisional master-binder of all the departmental budgets. "Here's a draft of what I hope will serve as an explanation of the figures that the Mayor will finally deliver to the big Board. Your budget happens to be small enough, simple enough, and shocking enough to be my best sample of the radical reorganization that this budget format reflects."

To his surprise, instead of laying the page on her desk for dignified consideration, she playfully snatches it from his fingers to demand immediate perusal, shushing up his inchoate response with the spread fingers of her right hand. With an open mouth of astonishment he watches her read with substantial comprehension from top to bottom as without looking she accepts on her desktop the stapled sheaf of worksheet forms that follow.

"You're crazy, Caleb!" Now with both elbows on the desk she seriously looks up at him with absently widened eyes. "More power to you! Personally I'm with you. But you'll never get away with it. I hope Dex has approved all this you're putting in his mouth. He must be mesmerized by your rationality! And I thought he was getting to be a good politician!"

"We'll see." he mutters, somewhat taken aback by her tone of certainty.

Ignoring the man before her, she takes up the first paper and scans it again, reading rapidly with her lips, parts of it out loud, not as if in doubt or scorn but simply for changes, naturally comparing new figures or line-items with the old or missing ones, quickly grasping for the bottom line that pleased her—before realizing the radical changes she is being asked to accept.

The Library is one of the city's most efficient institutions, speaking well for the contributions donated by many individual citizens. However, Caleb points out that its historical development as a private nonprofit corporation has resulted in certain duplications of expenses as well as separate incomes. "If we can organically consolidate money efficiently we should be willing to spend it efficiently to save enough to provide for things or amounts that we are otherwise unlikely to get, competing as every department does for its share of the City's whole bottom line.

"Here, read this sheet, the Mayor's rationale for this his part of the budget. Several other departments will get similar notices, but this one leads the way in its own terms."

I [*says the Mayor*] am therefore integrating the Library's itemized accounts, payroll, and ordinary procurement functions into corresponding clerical operations for the budgeted General Fund. (Thus, for example, Library employees will be paid by way of the computerized payroll). I believe that under present economic pressure, when new methods and procedures must be developed in all departments, these measures can sufficiently relieve the professional Library staff of purely administrative matters to justify elimination of the Assistant Cataloger's position. The incumbent will be transferred to a centralized clerical position in Ibicity Hall [*aside: perhaps in the Mayor's Office where the whole city will benefit from her ample skills!*]. I will thereupon appropriate money for subscription to a cataloging service, thereby reducing the human workload in this library function at the front desk.

By the same token, maintenance costs, including custodial and janitorial services, will be assigned to the Public Property division of the Department of Public Works.

These moves are intended to enhance professional specialization of the Library's educational and recreational services as far as the City's limited fiscal resources are concerned. I carefully guard a distinction between the administrative support of a library (which has much in common with that of certain other departments) and its unique cultural service, which must be protected as well as possible from political and economic pressure ["*you don't say!*"]. I am especially sensitive to the rightful prerogatives of a Library that has voluntarily contributed so much to the quality of Dogtown life. Its authority is not always consistent with my responsibilities as the executor of public funds, but I believe that the Library will benefit on its own terms if it willingly cooperates in this efficient consolidation of certain hitherto redundant services. . . .

"Obviously neither Dex nor Inez wrote this."

"He went over it all. Help me make it a model for reorganizational quid pro quos!"

"I'll cooperate, if you wangle some money also to fix up the abandoned old third-floor attic. I think it has a lot to do with the City's horrendous insurance premiums. It could be good for much-needed storage space but now it's languishing as nothing but a rotting roof for the leaky second-floor conference rooms. It's from right here in these hidden old quarters that the public gets its impression of our working conditions! I've tried to get our board up there to see for themselves, but they're always too busy even to visualize my song. I'm only an ex officio member of that senate—almost all of them literate, kind, and generous, but never rude enough to challenge Nedlaw's understanding of distributive justice. He's got the eleemosynary money that keeps us in existence, and sometimes he thinks Dex is practically a communist. Belle could no more print as much against his genuinely good intentions than she can publicly complain about his sporadic interferences in the newsroom—even if she understood ego-motives better than Dex does." She pauses, then drops her tone. "I hate to see you enmeshed in petty diplomacy. —What would Ibi-Roy have thought to see you dragged into the common good at this level? He was your Engidu; you were his Gilgamesh!"

"I still miss him. Do you still have time to write new poems?"

"Occasionally I get something into one of the little magazines. Waldo insists that I take time for poetic inspiration. Meanwhile he'd do our cooking!"

"Good old Waldo! You couldn't do better for brains and strength. Unbeknownst to me he once personally changed a tire for me in the Yard parking lot—in his business clothes—while I was in a meeting, before I even knew it was flat."

"I've never regretted divorcing Dex, but he seriously means well for the common good, and he's what's rightly called a leader. When he was City Planner years ago he pleaded with the City Manager and the Earls to anticipate all the things that should have been done to avoid most of the troubles we've since had with the roads and streets, sewer and water projects, electricity blackouts, fire alarm systems, police communications, and God knows how many other capital projects called infrastructure, as well as the long-term decadence of public property in general. Planting trees for future generations! Taking care of playgrounds and cemeteries! But not just actions that cost money, like building the Purdeyville Reservoir (which he instigated), but also in simply recognizing and trying to enforce all the neglected rules of land use. It's still disgusting to see how people get away with encroaching upon public ways or building on wetlands, or usurping public landings that happen to be next door, or deliberately constructing something else forbidden. You'll find that many laws are ignored unless there's a public outcry. But who's got time to search out violations and organize public-spirited posses when it's more than you can personally do to keep private hedges from blocking a public sidewalk by disabling any passageway inside the gutter? 'Of course we can't raise taxes just to obey the law'— unwritten laws until someone gets killed!" Gloria takes a deep breath and laughs, her palms at ears inside saffron hair finely threaded with the silver adumbrations of a young grandmother.

And an obverse echo in Caleb's mnemonic heart. For a few seconds of both their silences she restores her dignity as a senior civil servant while his motionless eyes stare at a composite vision of events that would not have been recovered without this unspoken stimulus to his nostalgic brain. It is a gentle jolt of joy to be reminded of dormant sensations. "You sound like a pedestrian and you look as athletic as ever. You are the city's curator of legends. Are many of them private?"

"Don't worry. My poems are cryptic. Out of town I have a pen name and a fake origin out of state. Why are you so enthusiastic about earning your living this way, badgering those like me who keep the books?"

"What's the matter with that? Napoleon quoted Goethe as saying 'The name of fate is politics.'"

Quickly she replies "Yeats quotes Goethe as also saying that the Irish were like yapping hounds that always drag down their noble stags. Dogtown was founded by Irindus; aside from the primeval English, most of our first fishermen were Irish; your mother was Irish; and like me Dex is Scotch-Irish from immigrants to Montvert. Irish blood sustains our official history—along with some casual Viking energy. I'm afraid Dexter is Dogtown's noble stag, sometimes like Metatron tallest of angels, other times like wise and gentle Chiron the Centaur. But you're more like Gilgamesh the city-builder after all!" Glancing at the door she suppresses a shriek of laughter. "Not fit to be a bookkeeping politician!"

"I'm not in the race. Accounting intrigues me, like an opened closed system of labile weathervanes freely suspended in equilibrium by a single string, all separately twisting in the breeze!"

"Your poetic expression I suppose."

"At the Yard I didn't know anything about it until after I knew *how* to do it; here I understand what it should be by learning what it shouldn't be, so that ours can be much more useful. Our present accounting is probably no worse than the federal government's, but it can be much easier to replace radically. The budget you and I are talking about now represents only part of the City's finance. Don't forget the rest is an unorganized jumble of independently scattered accounts that are supposedly gathered coherently by our City Auditor (who works for the legislative branch instead of for the Treasurer, who works for the Mayor). —You've made me defend myself, Gloriana!

"Visualize a pack of cards. Sort them into four suits laid out side by side. It's the very improbable completion of a solitaire game my mother used to play, without any wild cards, king down to ace in parallel numbers. It starts with thoroughly shuffled cards, the highest probability, according to the Third Law of Thermodynamics—but I can't remember how the game of moving cards gets started! In our so-called Budgetary accounting method we have at best only one suit complete; all the other cards remain in off-budget fragments of the real deck (assuming there are enough to make room for all possible items). What I'm preaching is a whole matrix for maximum counterentropy—order from disorder, including the virtual realism of accrual accounting in the equation—but for as many suits as there are, including parallel Enterprise Funds that take in and spend their own money—Beach revenue for instance, or Landfill fees—and any other money the City or its employees collect—but especially the federal Block Grants we get for special purposes, sometimes intended to provide employment, as you know."

"—Wow! [*Almost choking with laughter.*] Don't make me dizzy with visualizations. The longest budget column looks like the best of marriages. Altogether your scheme sounds as if it needs naming like the latest fad I see on the business magazine covers: *Total Quality Control*! Good old zero-based budgeting is as much as this librarian can understand—unless I conceive a chessboard!"

By this time Caleb too is bending over and choking on his breath. Fortunately there isn't any traffic up or down the staircase to the vault, thanks to the need for all Library hands elsewhere in the bustling after-school crowd.

"So do you see how much more interesting accounting is than cataloging or psychoanalysis?" Caleb asks. "Or political diplomacy. Or Dexter's 'ekistical topology', as Ippy called the City Planner's preoccupation when we lived in that Rectory manse on the edge of a cemetery. —Besides, I like hoping for a microcosmic society that may soon welcome black people. We had one at the Yard, a foreman in the plant, who was affectionately respected, but he felt he had to commute from Liverpool because he knew it would be socially unpleasant to live here with his family. I wouldn't work for Dexter if I didn't know that he tacitly wants to do something about that ingrained but not actually hostile injustice."

They are both solemn Crats again, yet still skirting their old intimacy. "I think we'll make some progress, even if it has to be led by the example of us naturalized Green Mountaineers. We need both you and Dex." says Gloria. "You got through the confirmation of your temporary appointment fairly easily because the Board doesn't like to be seen as rude to a Mayor with veto power, but it's going to be much tougher for your permanent confirmation when they realize what an invidious revolutionary you are."

"It amounts to nothing more than a new chart of accounts!"

"I'd call it nothing more than writing out the U S Constitution as a second edition of the Articles of Confederation!"

Caleb can't help rising from his chair and turning doubled up 360 degrees to suppress as many as possible decibels of an immature outburst. It was extremely difficult to restore self-discipline. But with a nearly whispered belly moan he manages to blurt out his reply, word by word: "I . learned . . at my . . mother's . . . knee . . . that the . . . pen is . . . mightier . . . than the sword!" Then pulling himself together: "The first of her adages that I paid much attention to, I suppose because it sounded at least half-masculine."

Now the librarian gets up to face the book-laden shelves behind her desk, handkerchief at her nose, her shoulders quivering. But mutual silence through the open door might be incriminating. That dawns on both of them almost at once. As she returns to her chair with a smiling sniffle he fumbles with his briefcase, making moves of preparation to take his leave, their unstraitened faces averted from each other as they struggle for composure. Gloria is the first to achieve it.

She is resourceful, pertinent, and relevant when she raises her voice to challenge him professionally. "You efficiency experts may be right about the great 'computer revolution' after the great age of steam, but I think that the most influential boon for ordinary paperwork has been copy machines! I bet that the quick evolution from blueprints to high-speed automatic-sorting copiers has multiplied clerical productivity more than your glorified word-processors ever will!"

"What are the odds? Ten thousand bags of air without the bags? You remind me of my maiden years with dictating machines. My ambitions here are really just eddies of resistance to subsystemic entropy!"

"You certainly know the excited jargon I see on book jackets or back covers! 'Operations Research', 'Exponential Smoothing', 'Sensitivity Analysis', 'Decision Theory', 'Game Theory'—"

"That's not my stuff. Systems Theory is something else, more like philosophy! Anyway all that argot goes by the board in the primitive government that I'm reveling in as a result of Finn Macdane's encouragement. I'm not enthusiastic about learning technology that I'm not in a position to practice. I'm heartily, even humbly, impressed by some of the unobtrusively dedicated and resourceful City workers, like the clam warden, the Fire Inspector, the electrician, the part-time City Solicitor, the Police Boat Patrolman, as well as my Margie and half a dozen of the women who work with her on my floor of the Hall—especially Inez of course. I only wish Sergeant Proctor and Mrs Sirius were still alive with Ibi to love."

"So do I. What if the next mayor doesn't want you around?"

"I'll be forced back to some vocation that may not be of my own design—unnoticed for lack of a tunable voice with scant hair, bow legs, and splayed feet. Except that when venturing into society as a vagrant I shall be put to shame as a vainglorious pauper."

"What if you have to be fired before that to save you-know-who's career, for Dogtown's sake? It's inauspicious to talk so much like Alec Hamilton!"

"Well, I'd go back to my thankless knitting if I had some income. I won't pass away in a duel! —One thing I'll leave behind for you, as well as for the Mayor, that will be appreciated sooner or later, though now scarcely noticed: your Arts and Culture project in the New Works Project Administration. It helps a lot that you volunteered its meeting place downstairs. You don't lean on your shovel. That impressed the Fed lady (who thinks her own job won't last much longer under Raygun) when I asked for an overhead allowance that would tend to be locally perpetuated after the national recession is over and the Cans in Washington cut off this penny from heaven as typical Crat largesse. You've invited a way into our hearts by re-seeding the cultured 'private sector' meant by J P Morganatic et al, as well as by Duke Tybbot and a few of the local philanthropists like Nedlaw. (It's a good thing he likes you so much!)

"Unfortunately some of the departments won't know how to use the subsidized people I assign to them, seeing that they don't make the best of the crews they already have on their payrolls. I'll see that you get up to twenty or so people for the Library if there are enough jobless applicants who really claim to be artists or writers or rhapsodes of some kind or other, or who seriously want to be, or who at least have some related ideas you find interesting—such as tape-recording oral histories. The hard part will be disappointing amateurs in the Seamark kind of public art! I already know that some of them want to paint or repaint copies of the W P A historical murals we have in the Hall. We may be allowed to spend some of our overhead allowance on improvising studios or workshops, or at least let real artists work at home. The Feds won't realize how much freedom they've given us until it's too late to withdraw. That's one good case for risking what Cans call fraud. Remember, though: *everything produced becomes the City's property.* You may get a masterpiece or two for your walls."

Gloria muses. "I've got plenty of research projects in mind—
and qualified jobless friends. I'd like to produce a scholarly
N W P A Guide to Dogtown History and Legends, *To the Memory of
Ibi-Roy.*"

"Don't let on that he was mine! —Do you remember that
astonishing Arts Festival that Dexter put on when he was City
Planner and got the high school at his disposal? Amid all the
kitsch, grotesque, pastiche, and sentimentality of Cape Gloucester
there's unrecognized talent and taste of all degrees—off-budget, so
to speak. Besides, you may even influence the Downtown Development Commission, hence also the Chamber of Commercials!"

27

CENOTAPH

[From Tim Scriabin's unwritten work diary as he considers writing a book of exposition or fiction based upon current events in Dogtown, where he is now a prominent resident, having returned to it after his stint there as a cub reporter before he'd earned fame and fortune as a novelist for the literary middle class. Until deciding to settle there for the sake of a sequestered family life, he'd given no thought to the prospect of finding the place itself a contemporary locale of interest to his readers. The fishermen, painters, and poets had already saturated that sort of his market. But now, having lived here for a while, it occurs to him that he may find more than enough grist in this place for a few short stories in *The Newurker*, which will readily print anything he tenders, even as a serial if necessary.]

1.

What makes this case a stimulant for fiction is that it's the germ of an idea about just such an unprecedented event in a President's cabinet at the beginning of a new administration in Washington. But I must stick to my resolution not to let my imagination exceed its technocratic grasp, and that is what this political matter is all about. The Vice President resigns in the middle of a private meeting when the President suddenly buckles under the open anger of his party's own Treasury secretary. —Of course my parallels are somewhat askew, but this is the feeling that excites me. . . .

The outcome is as public as public can be in a respectable local paper, but only after the Mayor tips his hand to the Board by adumbrating his proffered budget as now drafted. As a matter of courtesy and pragmatic psychology this more or less traditional diplomacy anticipates a mayor's line-item negotiations and other possible changes that would be acceptable without his veto, although by this time it's ordinarily too late for structural or organizational alteration of more than sentimental significance. Something like this procedure, it seems to me, is the climax of what I've learned or guessed in retrospect. The anticlimax comes when the Mayor's only recourse is to copy the old format for the present budget, merely changing or keeping dollar amounts and perhaps realizing categorical innovations that the majority of voters and legislators, together with the executive branch, have wanted all along—especially when involving legislation or positive opportunities from higher up in the food chain of government.

In this case, by far the most important upshot from the new mayor's startled point of view seems to be the deep political embarrassment of his first-term administration by trusting to the persuasions of his essential friend. Each had relied on the other—one for the ideas of the other, and the other for the power and political courage of the principal. They had known each other uncertainly from twenty years back!

*

. . . Lest I defeat my harmless purpose—again, for fictional fact or factual fiction—I do not claim to be more than incidentally informed of this event as a bewildered newcomer to the City. But I gather indirectly from Belle Cingani, my old colleague (when she was Bice Picory), and a few others (by way of bits here and there) from their friend the effervescent but very discreet librarian who witnessed the scene) that the Mayor's hyper-energetic administrative lieutenant—even if I only read between the lines of gossip— had sneaked radical organizational changes into play under the rubric of "zero-based budgeting", for which the innocent Earldermen had been clamoring as some sophisticated way of keeping up with the times. Z B B seems to be a newly fashionable slogan emanating from one of the business schools a year or two ago, hardly intended as a sweeping excuse for surreptitious reorganization.

I don't need to know the technological problems, but shortly before the Mayor's proposed budget was to be released, fortunately or unfortunately, somebody leaked the alarm about what all the numbers were embedded in. The call to arms began from the Library, a minor financial element of the City's finances, a very small adjunct of debate under normal conditions, something like a public donation to charity. But its tiny appropriation demanded premature explanation of what "the Mayor's Office" had in mind (or might have had in mind) for the fiefdoms of great barons—who usually had to worry only about their shares of money. Apparently this scare had to do with the redistribution of authority, personal prestige, and encrusted traditions. Even without change in its normal size, the budget came with an unusual manifesto to explain the financial plan for an extraordinary fiscal year. There simply had not been time for "the Mayor's Office" to fully explain such progress without spending another year for the political preparation that would have been preferred even by the one-man producer of "computerization". I must bear in mind the state's deadline for last-minute final approval of a city's legal appropriations, effective the day after the end of June. Now I have to learn some names and dig for the dramatic details, perhaps as Konrad tried to do with easterners under western eyes.

. . . I now think, after two weeks of sleuth-hounding, that Karcist took for granted the Mayor's belief in the value of what the drafted budget would have put before him to sign after discussing and accepting the substance of it, familiarizing himself enough with its concepts to defend them when it came to facing skeptical Earls. —Not that the ghost-writer of his text expected his boss to share all its component parts, including the author's enthusiastic ambitions. The Mayor, after all, is a politician who prefers reason to tradition but is not very studious of methodical bureaucracy. They were both taken by surprise when Nedlaw, the president of the Library Board, almost without notice demanded a meeting with them in the Mayor's office. This locally philanthropic V I P (also owner of the *Nous)* insisted that the City's Librarian (Gloria Cotton) accompany him, as the only one with all the facts—much to her consternation. I've heard the rumor that for "indefinite

reasons", instead of jumping to help her professional cause with
her characteristic alacrity, she is said to have instantly considered
quitting the job she loved because of his irascibly precipitous
response at first glance of a line or two of the drafted budget; but
that as a conscientious pillar of Dogtown's popular culture she was
given no time to point out the pros that more than outweighed
the small matters that he took to injure his ego as de facto chairman of the board for an institution maintained by the taxpayers'
democracy without his permission. I gather that she said hardly a
word in the parley of three men that followed his premature
outburst.

Nedlaw was so beside himself with crimson indignation that he
ignored the Mayor's extended hand. They knew each other well
enough, most recently as fellow mourners at a memorial for the late
Commander Macdane, a name I hear respected everywhere. It was
well known that Nedlaw—generally a kind and generous Crat
without bias against individual Cans who opposed him politically—had contributed to Keith's mayoral campaign with quiet
munificence; but now he was steamed up to hostility because in his
eyes the Mayor was proposing to annex a free library whose charter
guaranteed its sacred independence.

The Mayor explained that he was only trying to relieve the
Library of janitorial costs and a particular clerical redundancy by
assigning those services and costs to the D P W's centralized
municipal functions, while actually increasing the City's total contribution to the Library by way of adding more funds than ever
before to the book-buying fund, as well as providing money to
join the computerized regional interlibrary service, which would
lighten the purely clerical workload of the Library's own overburdened staff, especially by relieving it of existing costs for three janitors who served no other departments, vacations and emergencies
notwithstanding. They would now join the D P W's payroll as
part of the City's flexible pool for such janitorial coverage, come
hell or high water. To that reasoning of benefits—which would
also give the Library a larger professional staff and greater appropriations for its books and equipment—Nedlaw paid no attention.
He was too agitated about losing his relative autonomy to think of
turning to Ms Cotton herself for her professional opinion of Karcist's Z B B suppositions.

Nedlaw began to threaten Keith with resistance on a much
larger scale, as well he might, since the giant battles for the Mayor's

Office would be with the same concepts of reciprocating efficiency with the Director of Public Works and the (worst of all) Superintendent of Schools! Compared to them the quid pro quos with the powerful Police and Fire difficulties would be cooperative pieces of cake! Despite the idea that the Library-vis-à-vis Public Works plan was the only one not to be installed until the following fiscal year, Nedlaw angrily raised a sledgehammer above Keith's head as he scowled at Caleb and tried to catch the Librarian's eye.

Then, a little cooler, less directly, more insidiously, without mentioning his membership on the boards of more than one Dogtown bank, before the Mayor or his guilty assistant could make logical rejoinder, the uncharacteristically loud flush-faced white head leaned closer to the Mayor's. Yet it was almost with a mumble that he hinted his disapproval that the City Collector-Treasurer (with Karcist's approval) was investing all his short-term Certificates of Deposit in "financial institutions out of town", a supposed disservice to local prosperity, just for the sake of minor differences in the interest rates. But before the City's chief financial officer could offer to defend his thrifty free-market policy of investment regardless of local relationships, Nedlaw withdrew the angle of his spine, perhaps in slight embarrassment at his own ethical solecism, for he was not the kind of man who cared for the kind of pressure he was about to apply for the first time in his rather innocent life. Instead, I'm supposing, he gave his friend Dexter Keith, no fool, five seconds to think. Karcist must be no fool either, glancing without response at the Librarian, who must have been holding her breath.

Karcist was holding his, but in rising anger that there was going to be no chance for reasonable discussion. No debate. With caving expectation of support from his superior, who no doubt assumed that the baron of Public Works had already been informed of the scheme suspiciously forthcoming from the Mayor's Office. And of course the Police and Fire chiefs were probably already in an uproar about how they would fare if this nose under their tents cunning kind of budget were to be approved—all mistakenly adduced to "smart-ass computerization"!

I can only imagine the scenario for this climax. The Mayor suddenly realizes that as a pragmatically progressive politician he has failed to take this bureaucratic reform seriously enough. Thus, until now it has seemed merely a logical step in the progress of civic enlightenment for a populace that would know little or nothing about it. Did he only dream about telling the barons what was coming? Was he a subconscious coward in putting off the first psychological step, only casually tossing the subject offhand when talking about urgent or commonplace matters? But he did encourage Karcist by leading him astray about political priorities. That amounts to betraying him.

And so he did, as the easiest way out of this peculiar modernization of an old city. But by others who may be interested in the contents of Ibicity Hall this Karcist is said to be a misplaced fanatic, too much of a critic. Anyway the Mayor backed off before the furious old philanthropist, allowing that maybe this revision of the ambiguous separation between the City's management and its extracurricular culture needed more profound discussion with all parties concerned, etc—or in words to that compromising effect. Or we'll take it easy this time around, without interrupting the present continuity of tradition. We'll have more than a year for you to join a committee representing all City departments. . . .

"Like hell I will!" the complainer growls, jumping from his seat. "Come along Gloria. We are our own damn committee already. We'll tell the public about this outrage! . . ."

But Keith must have already turned to his perpetrator. "Okay, Caleb? Briney has a point. Switch back to the old chart of accounts and plug in the new numbers. Can you do that in a week?"

Just for a second, before Gloria has moved, the attacker pauses at the door to look back for the impression he'd made, with his hand on the doorknob. Karcist takes a deep breath, looking at the floor. "Yes, I can do that, while you look around for my replacement. I'm resigning at your earliest convenience. I've been wasting too much of my time."

At least something like that, a bombshell that echoes in all city phones almost within the hour. The Mayor was shocked of course, and especially irritated by the inevitable public knowledge of this event via his inner sanctum at Ms Canary's confidential command post. But as a sincere and talented charmer, although somewhat embarrassed, he was mistaken when he thought he could talk his meticulous friend out of an extremely intempestive and self-destructive decision as soon as they had a private conversation.

However, he'd forgotten that Karcist was known to have resigned from Mercator-Steelyard under similar circumstances for the same sort of reason, except for the fact that the Mayor was a longstanding personal friend.

2.

It's hard for anyone my size to be conspicuous, and so too for Karcist. When I was a journalist I found that to be advantageous. And again in Dogtown it helps to be inconspicuous for a while, now that I've decided to look no further than this incomparable town for my next best-seller plot. My real name is associated with my pen name only by the sort of people who read such books and the informative reviewers thereof, like those women who wined and dined me about a month ago. They swore not to let the cat out of the bag until I'm here on a commercial book-signing tour! That's a frail bargain, to be sure, but at least it may last long enough to keep the local intelligentsia from staring me down before I've learned more about them, not to mention hoi polloi who care nothing at all about the printed page. —If only I can just make up my mind which scent to pursue as a starter for the story. Whatever it is will branch in half a dozen different directions (except for the fishing that's so well gone over in print and picture for a couple of centuries), wherewith I expect to have my hands fuller than I've ever had in simpler places. It's a good thing Annie and the kids love to be living here. They're well trained to keep their mouths shut in embarrassment at some of the stuff that's de rigueur in my usual stories. I'm pretty sure it will have to be very fictitious in its final form, if only for the fun of allegory! Meanwhile I hope I can be as inconspicuous in person to the general public as Karcist seems to have been until now. It was only just the other day that he was at last pointed out to me as he waited to cross Cod Street and enter the state's employment office, presumably to line up for the dole. You don't find white-collar jobs in *that* outfit.

My old friend *Isopel* Cingani, who knows I remember her as the beautiful young loose fish Bice Picory before she started her ascendant career at the *Nous*, when we found in common a great interest in the books of George Borrow and his gypsy people, is now cordial enough; but she doesn't trust me with more than vague allusion to any present fans among local readers. However, she did introduce me to Gloria Cotton, the librarian, a less suspicious soul who still lights up at the mention of Borrowsing.

I frequent the Library, and once I couldn't refrain from bearding her in the inner sanctum—just enough so that her assistants regard me as almost officially reputable. I suppose they come across

my name in their work. It could be that they're a little thrilled to
find me here in person and to help me in my unexplained Cape
Gloucester research. I pretend to be mainly interested in the history
of local journalism. Indirectly, I benefit most from Karcist's
N W P A project assigned to the Library's personnel and overhead
funded by Dogtown's broad allocation of the Crats' national "New
Works Project Administration". Even the extraordinarily well-
educated or artistically recognized of otherwise unemployed
N W P A beneficiaries (for at least a federal fiscal year) are as glad to
assist or enlighten me as privileged children at a summer art camp,
most of them having already devoted themselves to hopes or careers
in a creative or studious realm of the Muses; but many of them seriously needed a job of any kind, as people did in the days of F D R
when their counterparts painted the Hall's still-admired murals, or
staged plays, or built new sidewalks and public buildings when
accused by Cans as loafers "at taxpayer expense". The Library's
detachment includes a straw boss, one of their kind, usually out of
sight making the Library's priceless oral recordings of Dogtown citizens before it's too late. He delivers paychecks and takes attendance,
but the Librarian herself is practically the only supervisor, de facto,
because, as far as I can see—unlike the other cadre leaders of
N W P A help—she's intently interested in taking advantage of
what is produced besides labor, seeing that it all belongs to the City,
much of which belongs under her custody, where it can be displayed
and perhaps appreciated. For Gloria Cotton, ex-wife of the Mayor,
N W P A has been a permanent political godsend.

Of course the Library has always kept files of newspapers,
recent ones hanging in racks, ancient ones available to patrons in
the vault (where certain precious paintings are also stored), as well
as especially valuable books and papers. She's an excellent local historian as well as an amazing archivist, and she's trained her very
competent senior assistant as reference librarian. . . .

. . . So at last my vacillation is over, as far as a tentative protagonist is concerned: narrowed down from all the characters I've been
considering for subject, object, and worthwhile predicate. Dogtown
has had a very recent hero, much more interesting to me than their
legendary Captain Hood or one of the famous fishing captains.
After probing for weeks my zest is revived: Maybe I now have a
biographical beacon! No need now to avoid or disguise any of my
inquiries. Quite to the contrary, I expect encouragement, at least
from common folk, now that he's dead.

3.

. . . When I was with the *Botolph Orb* I once covered an interesting Navy Day celebration on the open deck of the frigate *U S S*
Federalist moored at the Charlesmouth Navy Yard, where I learned
that she was the (barely) surviving sister-ship of the *Atlantis* that
Wellingborough Redburn and Jack Chase had served in. Ever since
then I've been a Navy partisan, though I know nothing about its
modern ships except what I'm beginning to know in this amateur
research about an officer coated in many colors. Before W W 2
Finn Macdane was qualified to fly P B Y amphibious patrol planes,
but that was just a sort of elective extracurricular course in his own
unofficial mind, which apparently was always dedicated to versatility. He wasn't crazy about aircraft carriers, which he called "fast
barges" or "eggshell platforms". He liked cruisers as the modern
successors of these 19C Atlantis-class frigates, but battleships were
the loves of his special career as electrical engineer, constructor, and
active navigator—in short, a naval architect with what seems to
have been mastery of all the technology required to design, build,
and operate the most advanced capital ships in the times they were
most needed. But even before the War he was urging future task-
force tactics with individual B Bs as centralized command of carriers and all other ships required in one or more formations, which
eventually were called a fast "strike force". His span of knowledge
and experience became so well recognized in Washington that he
was several times assigned to diplomatic or intelligence duty
requiring diplomatic communication with ally or enemy. . . .

Macdane rose to the temporary rank of Captain (one step below
Rear Admiral) during wartime but later had to retire, according to
regulations, as a peacetime Commander. Nevertheless, there have
been special exceptions to that rule, and I suspect that I'm going to
find how and why he actually preferred criticism to promotions
when he turned down a sea command in favor of a history professorship at the Naval War College. That's an attitude probably never
forgotten in the admiralty. I suppose the fact that he'd never been
the skipper of a ship (despite his successful stints as C E O in the
Pacific) blackballed him at the highest levels, and he pretty clearly
displayed either too much versatility or too much initiative—either
way indicating too much liberal education for an institution run by
graduates of the Port Royal Academy (no matter how many graduate degrees the Navy authorized at universities). And I suspect that

he couldn't avoid the resentment of some peers in the regular competition for the best personal composite ratings in his rank, which
are taken very seriously by the brass in Washington I believe. . . .
    . . . My enthusiasm is rising with good luck. My perseverance
earned an interview with the Mayor, who obviously loved that man,
and probably knows more about him—at least as far as the Navy
was concerned—than anyone else except the local intelligentsia,
with whom the Mayor himself has always been friendly, and whom
I'll have to search out before I'm through. Now, more and more,
I'm leaning toward the freedom a novel. . . .
    . . . I know that it was this F M who persuaded D K to appoint
C K for his administrator! And I've learned that the Librarian used
to be D K's wife! So C K turns out to be one of the inconspicuous
intellectuals! So the plot thickens, or at least a spider web emerges!
It spices all the public obits and news stories about F M's death—
body still missing like the missing source of the old DT's sea serpent—which I've been clipping or copying. Pretty soon I'll have a
dozen folders next to my marvelous new word-processor. How can I
get to talk to F M's exclusive cronies without cringing before them
as a mercenary middle-brow? I think I'll start with B N [Brine
Nedlaw] who spoiled D K's reformation of the City's government.
Briney, he's called—the man who's whispered on the waterfront to
have been ultimately responsible for F M's death without the
slightest sense of guilt. . . .
    . . . According to G C [Gloria Cotton], City Historian as well
as Librarian, the speech F M gave at the Museum only a year or so
ago was soon after he came to live in DT. He's no more of a native
marooner than I am. Therefore he was less known in depth even
than his lady-friend, F G [Fay Gabriel], the East Harbor professor
living alone in a ghostly house, who is generally venerated by those
who interest themselves in "intellectual life". She is a recently repa-
triated naturalized nurse formerly married into academic summer
folk a couple of generations ago. I've made friends with Slim
Boxshaw, her carpentry and maintenance contractor, who's a big
wheel in the Turntable Club and knows everybody in town. He's
the one who introduced me to Ben Nathan the former mayor, an
amiable font of personal remarks, who goes gambling for a week in
Esmeralda but says he never lied unless he had to.
    In the short time he lived here Captain F M naturally got
acquainted with quite a few movers and shakers by way of reality-
estate business when he bought the old First Vinland Bank build-

ing and remodeled the whole top floor for his own residence, which served also as the office for his consulting business. For a healthy old nautical bachelor, who is said to have looked not much more than half his age and needed no eyeglasses or hearing aid, with excellent credit, there was no better way to live than right over the inner harbor, and close to the acropolis withal. He was an almost daily object of inquiry, if not of familiarity, at the very hub of this Cape. I've actually been stopped on the street by people to encourage my open interest in that residence.

By this time everyone of that mind has assimilated most of the published obits and journalistic comments, from Markland to Parthenia, from which I'll try to extract by memory without the labor of synopsis for this notebook, which is meant to be my heap of common ore. The extractions of a private or critical nature, hardly revealing personal or anecdotal matter, I'll expatiate with fictive imagination. The Navy Historical Museum in Washington seems to forbid anything that should be read between the lines. But even without my insights this Commander man was uniquely unique. Never married but probably especially attractive to women, reciprocally. Nevertheless, off duty he seems to have preferred solitary reading and travel to socialized leisure—perhaps until he got to DT. His inclinations were European, culturally and geographically. He once explained it to the Librarian, she tells me, by quoting Socrates as saying that Athens was his mother. Yet he used to laugh that despite all his travel westward from the Levant to the Far East shores he'd never crossed Asia or entered the southern hemisphere at all, not even at sea during the War, where many of his ships or shipmates had fought much of the Pacific war. —W W 2: that seems to be less the backcloth than the wings of my prospective two dimensions, judging by everyone I talk to about him!

I suspect that before that international epoch, as child and man, even after he was still a postgraduate student in part-time command of an inshore Navy tugboat, he was still something of a benign imperialist, who wouldn't have minded if Atlantis took over the Dominion, as well as the Greater Antilles and the Manila Archipelago, et al, for their own good, as our "manifest destiny". —Well, maybe I'm overstating that aspect of his character; but he certainly was a gentleman who liked to march with the flag. Yet he chose (as it turned out for the Navy's good) Norumbega's liberal arts Naval Reserve Officer Training Corps rather than the Port Royal Academy for Regular officers (with its asinine hazing but

much better career prospects); and he told his civilian friends that
our flag—much as it stirred him as the historically established
symbol for the patriotism he fundamentally approved (especially
when he saw it flying in a foreign country)—was aesthetically far
inferior to the Union Jack, not to mention some dozens of others. I
was told by Ms Opsimath [T O] that he retired earlier than necessary from his formerly beloved Navy because of its increasingly arid
culture in the age of "civilian electronics"—whatever that may
mean! In sum, he regretted the fall of the British Empire more than
Atlantean liberals do.

Yet in politics a liberal is what he always had been since the
election of F D R. And even before that he had been openly sympathetic with (and admiring of) Jews in the officer corps, his contemporaries as well as those before him in history, e g, when Uriah
Phillips fought (with Redburn's unofficial help in public opinion)
to eliminate flogging in the Navy. Later, in 1860, Phillips was
commodore of our Mediterranean Squadron. In F M's own cohort
Eli Edwards, the brilliant and indefatigable engineering officer in
the Construction Corps, famous for rescue and salvage operations,
as well as for being the author of naval fiction that I remember
reading avidly in best-selling books and magazines, was Macdane's
closest friend in the Navy, and F M stood by him in all the fraternal furor about his overweening "unprofessional personality". F M
was likewise a friend and defender of Hyman Windhover, who
only under pressure from Congress in the publically fearful nuclear
age has eventually been promoted as an Admiral for his radical
development of Entropy-driven submarines. They had served
together in the the Bureau of Construction and Repair before the
War while F M was a designer and engineer of battleships (when
F D R wisely decided to put no more money in thin-skinned
battle cruisers, partly because of the sad experience the Brits had
had with capital ships that preferred speed to armor). Both those
two unorthodox Jews apparently were dear to the heart of this
unorthodox Christian, who perhaps was more cultivated from a
goy point of view but probably much cherished by themselves as
an openminded Yankee polymath who promoted their ideas without caring that he was suspected by their Regular class of more
Reserve scholarship than aristocracy. Yet, though not one of the
Port Royal alumni, F M was more saturated with the Navy than
almost any of them, mainly because of Markland family and forebears in the military shipbuilding industry, but especially because

he grew up under the summertime tutelage and companionship of Admiral Ulysses Snowdon Symes (known by insiders as Old U S S), "perhaps the most influential officer in the history of the U S Navy", who had retired with his family to spacious comfort on a high granite ledge in East Harbor, not far from where I live now. It was partly in memory of visits there, I suppose, that Macdane at last chose this town for his own valediction. It was with that famous old man over there that F M, already shaped by his ship-building family, had become interested in electrical engineering, fleet tactics, continuous-aim gunnery, precise navigation, and all facets of seamanship—as well as nautical exercises with the British and Allies. But he was concurrently prepared for diplomatic duty overseas, and for other cosmopolitan posts, with an education where students learned to be critical of custom and brass. Yet sea duty was the alphabetical recreation for every rank, like nature for Darwin! So I think U S S was F M's model (except for domestic matters), even in his advanced studies of the latest electronic fire-control and communications. (I have learned some of this jargon, as in other professional matters, without being much the wiser. Anti-technological and anti-Classical fictioneers are expected to settle for respectful ignorance.). . .

. . . Didn't someone say that, in any realm, only history satisfies broad minds like F M's? But he had more than one field, even within the Navy where most officers of the intellectual type were primarily classified for staff or liaison posts. Much to his surprise, as a naval constructor, he was chosen to be Admiral Solomon Spruce's representative practically at the elbow of Hotspur Halsey on the bridge of *New Guernsey* when that subordinate admiral ruined a well-founded plan of great importance in the Pacific Theater by chasing off in pursuit of a Cipangese decoy to the north when he'd been ordered to stay his hand in order to bottle up for long-sought destruction the powerful enemy fleet at an eastern mouth of Magellan Bay, possibly to end the war before President Trueheart deemed it necessary to let loose the E-Bomb. (Halsey's precipitous misjudgment was contrary to a personal agreement with his oceanic Commander-in-Chief superior, who happened to be F M's own personal Solon and Solomon by choice and position as his highly trusted liaison officer. Spruce had ordered another fleet up from the south to reinforce the trap. It was only by godly luck that the great Cipangese battle group was prevented from breaking out to devastate hundreds of lightly armed Atlantean ships and kill thousands of sailors and troops who were meant to augment and supply our direly endangered land army. So at least it seems now to be the historical consensus for a layman like me who was a child at the time.)

But much more to my purpose I have before me the study of something later in the War. I gather that F M himself nearly drowned when a senior "passenger" on a cruiser that was sunk on its way back from delivering the first E-bomb to its launching point in the Chamorro Islands not very far from Mardi. B C the DT D N editor told me that her husband Dave Wilson, an Army pilot much older than she, had flown to Hiroshima from that same island airfield on the same day. . . .

. . . Ms Opsimath and her friends think F M's broad experience rapidly evolved without much redundancy. One rogue wave at sea in a destroyer was enough; one turn as executive officer in each of two cruisers was enough; and even his participation in the one design of a whole battleship class! The sea and its ships were efficiently assimilated, and so were most of his private travels. (Unlike many of us, I presume, he didn't need DV to repeat cherished visits abroad, expecting never to set foot there again.) As a 'Bega alumnus looking back on the luxury of his student days before the War, when beds were made by servants and meals were served with the menu options, as if handed to gentlemen in restaurants, at times and tables of their choice, F M must have retained lots of separately unimportant experiences that he had no wish to rehearse by repetition, just as he attended lectures or tutoring by a professor or family friend such as the one who later became an admiral as the officially academic historian of the Navy's war in all oceans before and after his own wartime appearance in all theaters. In Europe, both before and after hostilities, F M was ostensibly an intelligence officer, usually in the uniform of a diplomatic attaché in London or Berlin, but actually was a multifaceted technician who spoke German as well as anyone in our Navy, was far more versed in German culture than any Port Royal graduate. Before the War in mufti he managed to see Germany's secret battleship *Bismarck* under construction, and later while we were still diplomatically neutral he was vitally helpful to the British by secretly warning them that that extremely powerful battleship had finished her shakedown cruise in the Baltic and was taking on a very comprehensive supply of Atlantic sea charts at Gotenhafen, obviously intended for a long foray into the Atlantic as an insuperable raider of the British supply line from Atlantis. After the War he was deeply involved in debriefing valuable information from imprisoned officers of the German navy's high command. He was particularly useful in discussions with Hitler's civilian industrial boss, the very thoughtful man in a War Crimes prison. . . .

. . . Though F M had circumvented Port Royal to get his commission on the strength of his Reserve Officer training while spending most of his Norumbega time on the engineering science curriculum then allowed for his liberal arts bachelor's degree, he had already learned how to educate himself with cultivated teachers at the best of classical private schools, and no doubt was further edified by summer travel or interesting jobs in preparation for college. Therefore, following the War Crimes Trials and their immediate aftereffects in Germany, he was perfectly qualified for a tour of duty as a professor at the new Naval Postgraduate School in Cornucopia on the beautiful San Ricardo campus. In wartime its luxurious buildings and grounds had been occupied by enlisted men as a school for specialists in radio and radar; but it was thereafter devoted to postgraduate studies for officers in all relevant branches of professional government service for advanced degrees in naval architecture, marine and electrical engineering, electronics, communications, intelligence, and other semi-military sciences, as well as history, government, diplomacy, et al—many of which he had studied before the War at Vinland Institute of Technology or the Naval War College in Island Roads. In this sort of academic atmosphere F M was invaluable as an instructor or professor with practical experience. It takes years to recruit Ph Ds and mature civilian professors while still shaking down various experiments with academic research. He declined the Navy's offer of permanent teaching with time to pursue a doctorate for himself, either there or back at Unabridge, in almost any subject at all. But he preferred the other offer of Admiral Prince, the Navy's highest voice of all, known as a difficult man to work for: namely to learn more and have greater influence as a member of the C N O's own staff in Washington— whence eventually he took early retirement to ad lib as a civilian consultant to government and industry, while sometimes writing articles of suggestion or criticism for professional journals and occasionally the most serious public periodicals.

. . . Yet above all, more to my interest, he apparently continued his self-education with learning what he could of humble Dogtown itself, starting with its quintessential fisheries and distinctive granite quarries. It was discovered after his death he had been studying the present development of commercial boats by reading technical books and papers and walking the waterfront, and the geology of granite by reading up in a science he regretted having dismissed in his youth as best left to those who couldn't master the geometric disciplines of artefact. Who knows what else he might have done for DT culture or industry if he'd lived a few years longer?

Nevertheless, his Trustee and executor—the retired lawyer Endicott Krebs—found on F M's word-processor that just a few days before the fatal schooner race he had begun a memorial eulogy of Professor-emeritus Giles Frank, said to be the most respected and amiable Classicist in the world nowadays, whose work about Aristotle and Greek tragedy is supposed to be revisionary in his field. Though I know nothing about the subject matter of what I *did* grasp when Krebs showed me this interrupted manuscript, I sensed reference to certain issues with which Frank had singlehandedly disputed the old conventional wisdom about Aristotle and the origin of tragedy, thereby establishing some new set of paradigms which has excited an academic revolution against instantiated authority. Despite the genuine deference and affection with all due respect among tenured fogies who repeat their lectures by rote and make the most of linguistic memorization, Frank's new ideas (which do not happen to attract my interest), in F M's amateur opinion, must be recognized if modern civilization is to survive its anti-intellectual faith with no raven in sight of its ark! That's how important the Classics were to him in the age of electronic culture that had scrapped or mothballed all his own triremed castles of steel!

In these later days, I'm told, even the dwindling liberal arts students have little or no interest in ancient literature, especially under professors who insist upon teaching from the bottom up. Frank knew well enough that nowadays even just the grammar of Greek (or at least Latin) would have to be learned under contemporary academic conditions that left no time for dreary memorization of chickens by rote without the etymological eggs that would have made the chore much easier. F M himself at 'Bega, even having had a little Latin and less Greek from prep school, with no slack between his elective courses to complement those required by the Navy, was befriended by Frank for skipping what he'd already learned, to squeeze in a tutorial opportunity to add some functional Greek for its own sake. They hit it off exceptionally because both student and professor believed, beyond their own interests, in the

universal advantage of this historical terminology in any art or profession within the Western World of reading writing and arithmetic—from math to chemistry, from medicine to law, from
Ensign to Combined Chief of General Staff, from typesetters to editors, from programmers to philosophers, from diners to chefs—
assisting all sorts of common readers to grasp as quickly as possible
almost any word they have to stupidly guess at or look for. I'm very
glad my own little college infused me with a little bit of it for a
cub reporter!

Later, in wartime and its immediate aftermath, Frank himself
became a Captain in the Marine Corps Reserves, assigned to the
Secret Intelligence Service in western Europe, where Krebs thinks
they might easily have encountered each other, if not at Delphi
itself. —But I must be careful not to get sucked into a spy story.
I'm only trying to get clues to F M's life in this fantastic town—in
which I now expect to pay taxes for the rest of my life, to the benefit of my children. . . .

. . . The Librarian in her Atheneum mentioned that F M had
delivered a lecture at the [Cape Gloucester Literary, Scientific, &
Historical] *Lyceum* on the opposite side of her acropolis. This originally small private "charitable institution", rather famous for its
mainly maritime paintings and related artifacts, has been much
enlarged and conceptually modernized since I worked at the *Nous*
in my youth. I wonder if the school kids still call it "The *Lice*"! It
was on the 19C lecture circuits. Its podium had drawn (besides
military and political figures) such literary celebrities as Orestes
Emerson, Natty Hawhaw, Hector Doolittle Thoreau, Lincoln
Irving, Charles Pickens, Redburn, and even Liam Yeats.

I found out that, except for a brief and superficial description of
the event, no one seems to have recorded or summarized F M's words
when he recently spoke here. Now I ask everyone who seems a possible member if s/he happened to have been in that somewhat distinctive audience. I'm gradually winnowing my catch down to a list of a
few dozen people intelligent or educated enough to remember the
event. So far, when that's recalled, the one word that's common to
them all is "battleship". However, as a responsible journalist, I had to
explain to most of them that in the official and universal nomenclature the term "battleship" is restricted to royalty as one awesomely
narrow class within the carelessly employed genus "warship", which
one often finds referring to all naval vessels painted gray and obviously armed, just as schooners elsewhere are sometimes heard to be

called sailboats by landlubbers because they're boats with sails. Battleships for a line-of-battle used to be the measure of sea power before air power was invented. I guess the old guy lecturing there in Redburn's footsteps would have agreed that this edification in his lecture reminds our language of many other solecisms, as well as misread ironies, in our present generation of the nation's fourth estate. I've always wondered why ladies *and* gentlemen of the press who cover military matters are so ignorant of fundamental discriminations in the ranks and organizations of power.

. . . "he seemed obsessive!" whispered more than one voice to that effect, I'm sure. Fair enough, I should think, seeing that Macdane had just spent ten minutes in recitation of *New Guernsey's* numerically comparative specifications of naval architecture, artillery, and performance, all in great detail without using the slide projection on his blank screen. Even feministic housewives might have tolerated his boring enthusiasm if he'd given them a condescending still life of lilies to look at! All his statistics, and a hell of a lot more, are available in the Library, in case I need them for realism in my story; but what I really want to know is this: if sailors love ships they serve in, do they love even more the ships they've built; and even more than that, the evolution of designs and specifications which determined their construction? More to the point, when they lose or transfer to other ships are they widowers or bigamists? Or do they simply dilute their mourning? For all his intimacy with the lives of ships and seamanship, F M served as "ship's company" in only a few, which are long gone to seabed or scrap furnace. Yet he was certainly most proud of the *Guernsey* as his patriotic integration of symbolic "systems".

Or am I reading too much into an accidental but analogical story of battleship and schooner as merely a facile diode? Did he have the makings of a new Dogtown legend? The solitary death of Commander Macdane naturally evoked less mourning on the part of a majority in a city that had mourned more than five thousand fishermen at sea in no less than four hundred years; nor are all but one of the various minorities especially interested in memorializing someone hardly known during the two years he'd lived here without attending any church or joining any other sodality. But G C as Librarian and City Historian has now proposed that her Arminian church hold a memorial service liberally invited (as always) to the public in which everyone would be encouraged "to share appreciations or sympathetic recollections of Commander Macdane half a year after his heroic death." Her practically agnostic minister, a really lovely middleaged woman, and her liberal congregation were pleased to comply. Belle's *Nous* announced it on the front page as a civic event in the "non-denominational" church. I've already wanted to see inside this towering white edifice known historically as the birthplace of religious freedom in Atlantis. I have heard that at present its national affiliation is an amalgamation of Divine and General Individualism, whose origins were Colonial dissenters. In architecture it overshadows the friendly little Tudor Apostolic Church next door; but together in secular persuasion they represent Dogtown's Enlightenment, most of which stays home on Sunday.

Anyway it's a godsend to me. I'll try to be inconspicuous with my notebook. But it's worth risking who why and what I have in ulterior mind if I can hear more about F M from various angles, doing my best to scribble only quotes, direct or indirect, as inconspicuously as possible, without lowering my face to the pad more than necessary. But Ms T O warns me that sometimes these newly customary "Memorials", free speaking, open to surprising rhetorical and histrionic talent, can last as much as three hours! . . . I'll close my eyes or work my lips at any prayer-reading that isn't worthy of Dogtown. I won't have time to take down any names even if I make out a few I know. . . .

4.

Each speech among congregation, below, is expected to be delivered standing up in one of the amply cushioned pews that form a shallow concave arc focused somewhere beyond the elevated mahogany structure upon which organ music and vocal ministry are regularly mounted in humanistic leadership. For this special secular occasion, however, the minister herself stands most of the time on a step halfway down to the floor. She is a pleasantly informal interlocutor and catalyst apparently without so much as a stole for vestment to adorn her nonsectarian (if not nonpartisan) civilian attire. After her cheerful welcoming introduction, she calls upon the Mayor to speak first, then points in turn, sometimes having to bend in reach for a particular face in the multitude of raised hands, which at first are few and hesitant but soon proliferate in communal warmth, one idea or exclamation concatenating to another, most of them modestly brief, but a few longwinded. Some she recognizes by Christian name, occasionally as familiar in this her own collegial auditorium. Of course she is equally hospitable in encouraging faces new or nameless to herself. A surprisingly large majority of the full house includes many of her local ecumenical colleagues in mufti, even unto a rabbi and a Petrine priest—all of whom are friendly mockers of her theology. In fact she is especially encouraged by the smiles, even winks, of the Tudor Rector of St Paul's next door with whom she and his wife have many a good time together.

As the presiding minister she occasionally offers her own secular observation or anecdote to keep the pot boiling democratically. Once in a while she acts as referee when speakers unintentionally require contradiction, or when enthusiastic voices overlap each other, presumably because of impaired hearing or impulsive excitement. But with skillful diplomatic patience she distinguishes wheat from chaff—of poetry or prose delivered in a pompous or touching delivery that's otherwise sincerely concordant with the collective self-effacing eulogy. Without seeming to notice she keeps almost everyone from leaving before the unlimited wake of opinions is ended with her perfectly timed reading of a poem by Yeats. Most of these dry-eyed mourners wouldn't have been drawn here at all if they hadn't already been familiar with locally pertinent stories about the deceased in one way or another as a very admirable marooner.

"'A time to weep, and a time to laugh; a time to mourn, and a time to dance.' I hope you are not tired of Ecclesiastes. Today in fellowship we share our memories of an extraordinary man. Let us tell what we know or what we ask, even if only in curiosity, about things that haven't been mentioned in the press, or need more mentioning, whether trivial or not. . . . I've invited the Mayor to tell us a little about the part of Commander Macdane's life that most of us probably would appreciate to hear—even if only to correct or modify things that may have been said about him, especially in light of our prevailing public attitude toward the latest peacetime war. At first some of our friends, who now appreciate his final settlement here, were a little wary of his influence.

—"Please, Mr Mayor. . . ."

"I am speaking first not as a mayor but as the recollecting veteran of a very young Navy reservist in the World War 2 Pacific in the humblest of ships. I never met or heard of Finn Macdane before he came to Cape Gloucester as much my senior citizen in all respects, having built and then served in the greatest of ships and on a variety of the highest staffs. After the War ended and I returned to civilian life in the Reserve for another twenty years of inactive fealty to the Navy I subscribed to its professional journal that was devoted mainly to history. I probably read something by or about him without noticing the name because I wasn't much interested in preventive warfare after I became absorbed in domestic architecture and city planning. But when he came to Dogtown about two years ago I found that we had common interests of that peaceful kind. I hope that from you tonight I can learn some of what I did not get to know before his valiant death.

"I'll just start the ball rolling with a bit of impersonal background pertaining to his astonishing versatility. After I sit down perhaps we'll hear things great and small—amusing or grim anecdotes or opinions, about him as a humane officer and gentleman as well as conscientious citizen. But not superhumanly correct or unemotional! So please listen or think sympathetically with each other. There are bound to be differences among us, and I hope there will be some because we're talking about a complex man in a complex city. I think that's what we're here for, not just for the genuine praise and glorification we've absorbed in the months since we lost him. I suggest the word 'appreciation', whatever it is in Greek or Latin, as the key word to describe our meeting as the wreath of this cenotaph until the proper granite is designed.

"Or at least let's say he was a remarkable fellow with an exceptional gift for diversified experience. That's my general impression. But no doubt some of you knew him better than I did. We can mix and balance our bits of knowledge and conjecture. We've had half a season to reflect, when the deepest mourning has naturally disseminated—a good time to continue as best we can the life he lived among no small number of others who reciprocated his goodwill. In his short time as a Dogtown marooner he became one of our honorary leaders as a representative of the whole outer world. Now, just to get you started, here are a few suggestive examples of what might occur to you:

"While combat-testing for the Bureau of Ships he was praised by the austere Admiral Spruce, no small distinction! During the Pacific war Spruce allowed no chairs in his office. You might say he appreciated standing intellectuals on his staff! That's why he made Macdane his liaison officer with Admiral Halsey's battle group, to urge tactical caution—as well as to observe objectively the official and necessary request of the Bureau of Ships to study the sea-keeping and electromechanical condition of that flagship, and as much as possible its collective fast task-force performance in terms of hull design, propulsion engineering, communications, and fire-control, reporting especially any structural or navigational imperfections or defects, together with his technological suggestions of any kind, particularly relating to performance in battle. At the same time he was also supposed to compare this Halsey's performance with Spruce's own previously successful attack on the atoll of Mardi. Despite Halsey's willful mistake in missing the tactical part of this strategic task—in its disgraceful aftermath of wardroom opinion—Macdane was a little less censorious than his colleagues and seniors (including Admirals Spruce and Prince), though of course concurring in the professional opinion of Halsey's appalling insubordination and misjudgment. With the eyes and ears of a witness on the man's own bridge Macdane nevertheless sympathetically defended Hotspur's value to the Navy, refusing to join in sweeping discredit of a great leader known for decisive courage in situations at which timing and guesswork were of the essence. . . .

"Yes?"

[Male] "Where can I get a list of Macdane's decorations? Did the Navy give him specific credit for what he did to keep so many men alive among the sharks after the cruiser was sunk, when the Navy bases didn't even know the ship was missing? I think it was only several days later that the pilot of a P B Y flyingboat on routine patrol passing many miles away happened to notice something odd on the very distant crest of a wave. That was a very brave and skillful young aviator! Did he also get credit for that? Without orders he risked himself and his crew in those rough waters to rescue as many men as he could under very unfavorable conditions without waiting for reply to his radioman from their headquarters. Afterwards Macdane always seemed to divert inquiry about the ship's disaster from the fact that he himself was the senior officer still alive—hardly recognizable as he floated in a waterlogged life-jacket in the thick black oil on the heaving surface—without insignia of rank but with the instinctive tone of pronounced leadership and exemplary courage when keeping as many as possible heads gathered above water as they were being decimated day and night by sharks. Without him the men would probably have been praying for the enemy submarine to return to the scene with its vindictive machine guns to finish its job!"

[Male] "I can vouch for some of that, at least second-hand from books! A raggedly floating field of live and dead heads bobbing in and out of sight under a starless black night, rising and falling in blackened life-jackets, hoping not to be the next one dragged under in a sudden flurry by one or more of the invisible sharks darting in a lethal game of chance."

[Male] "Yes! Macdane insisted on being the last man saved on the day when one of our destroyers collected the final survivors, risking final disaster if the Cipangese sub returned to get our rescue ship; but always afterwards in responding to questions about the breathtaking rescue he mentioned only the intelligent eyes and bravery of the pilot who performed the opening act of the amazing rescue. . . ."

[Female] "He was the handsomest old man I ever incurred— and very digilent all his life. He was an Osprey Boy Scout. In the Navy he was a sticker for regimentation, which a lot of people didn't like, but he was always right. He told me the Navy was cleaner than most housebreakers. —By the way, maybe he was a little too smart. He thought women washed the outside of a glass only to see if there was any dirt on the inside! Everybody should extricate the inside of his goblet before he gets forlorn! . . . But it doesn't matter what church he extricated from."

[Male] "He was no war monger. If he loved battleships, what- ever you call them, it was for a different kind of power, just as many of us loved the great articulated steam locomotives that hauled long freight trains over the mountains, or a hundred freight cars across the prairies at a hundred miles an hour! It was the age of steam with mechanical ingenuity! Most ships are still marvels of electricity made by steam. He was renowned even outside the Navy for his electrical engineering. I used to see his name in our journal when he worked in the secret Office of Preliminary Design, espe- cially with turbines for prime mover. F D R's 'two-ocean navy' was meant for defense. . . . Radar, you know, and all the command-and- control systems that go with it—not just what they used to call "communication"—began for protection. But, defense or offense started, he hit it off with Lord Mountbatten in 1941, who wanted to make floating air strips out of self-frozen sea water!"

[Male] "The funny thing is that a lot of our fisherman—maybe I'm the only one here—took him to be against fishing altogether just because he wanted scientific conservation of the living fish and admitted that he didn't like to see the fish dying. There was a silly rumor that he'd never drown a mouse or sweep a bug down the

garbage-disposal sink of his kitchen. He couldn't stand seeing lob-
sters being boiled alive. They couldn't believe he was warrior
against anything but our industry."

[Female] "But he liked to quote Jim Konrad: 'Man is a worker,
or he is nothing!'"

[Male] "Well he had a great sense of humor!"

[Female] "Did he ever get married?"

[Male] "He'd just smile and chant the old song: *It costs three
times as much for two to live as cheap as one.*"

[Female] "Somebody told me that he never got married because
he wanted time to read. That may or may not be true, but the
thing about him that impressed me as a librarian was how much he
used the Interlibrary Loan service beyond a common reader. Serious
books that we can't afford to have here. Yet he swore he was a slow
reader. I can never be sure when a gentleman isn't kidding, but he
once told me that he joined the Navy to see the books. That accords
with his love of Wellingborough Redburn. I think he's almost the
only one I've known who's read everything Redburn ever published, poetry and all— he swears our greatest Atlantean writer! He
especially recommended *White Jacket*, the wonderful quasi-fiction
about serving in the Navy that helped so much to abolish ship-
board flogging before the Civil War. Anyway, Commander Macdane apparently could read at least a little Greek, Latin, French,
German, and Italian! . . ."

[Male] "That's probably one of the reasons why he was sent to
Europe to see the remains of the Holocaust and help intelligence
officers or lawyers interrogate the imprisoned Reich admirals, who
of course pretended to know nothing about Hitler's civilian
killings. —By the way, it was Macdane's idea to have each of those
gold braids write his own account of the War as well as what led up
to it from his own point of view. Macdane must have been a good
psychologist because each of those prisoners—supposedly without
collaboration behind their bars—was very glad to explain extenuat-
ing circumstances in the manner of double agents caught in an
Embassy at a sudden moment of surrender! This was free speech,
writing in comfortable cells, to exonerate themselves, and their
innocent frustrations, sometimes at the expense of guilty colleagues
as they were about to face the War Crimes Tribunal with their tangled web unsealing. One of our prosecutors said that in the end
none of them expressed regret for anything done by the German
navy; they 'only sought to evade personal responsibility'. They pro-

fessed to have known nothing about what the German experimental 'selectors' were doing for doctors on land, who finally got off almost scot-free, assisted in some instances by ex-Nazis or clergy or the Red Cross after hostilities were over. But those devious autobiographies provided our intelligent services and historians with a lot of collateral material that otherwise would never have been brought out in the trials (defending themselves by implicating each other). I have a doctoral candidate working on the Deutschland's naval war plans right now, for a second look. I'll make sure that Mac's in the bibliography. We'll see plenty of parallels in our own less lethal political wars every decade or so."

[Female] "From his youth, learning how to learn, he was wise enough to take advantage of a rich family for his education—the best of private schools from kindergarten to Norumbega and V I P! And a lot more after the War as an occasional research professor. I'm not against that kind of inequality! I only wish he'd spent his life teaching humanistic subjects."

[Male] "Well you might be interested to know that the Office of Naval Intelligence had a dossier on him as a 'Premature Antifascist' in 1938 because of something he said in Berlin when he was a naval attaché. He might have been kicked out of the Navy if Admiral Prince hadn't protected him—along with the brilliant Jews who were modernizing the Navy in spite of itself. He was also called an atheist because he showed interest in some church like the one we're sitting in! . . ."

[Minister] "They used to call us the Humanistic Humanists— H H for short! It's the Big Bang theory that barely saved us and Alpha Einstein from the stake. . . ."

[Female] "He had no sympathy with civilian hunters, or the gun lobby's false interpretation of the Second Amendment. He admitted to me that he liked to have power but didn't like to depend upon it. He said there were times when he didn't have *faith* in our democracy but that he always *hoped* for it, and certainly never preferred any alternative to it. . . ."

[Male] "I'm not a fisherman but I know he helped a friend of mine who works here at the government Fisheries Lab make some contacts in Washington on behalf of fishermen, who are unfairly blamed for the overfishing. Macdane wondered how much truth there may be in a scientific explanation of falling catches that it's from an irregular cyclic season under certain conditions in which the predatory fish naturally exchange vertical positions en mass in the water column and therefore block bottom fish from rising to their usual habitat. It's apparently an extremely complex process that's fully understood only by mathematical scientists working with systems theory. So Macdane must have been sympathetic with fishermen as well as fish! . . ."

[Female] "What was his political attitude in general? Is it true that he said Raygun is the apotheosis of selfishness, or was it one of his friends who did? It doesn't sound patriotic! He probably was an atheist. . . ."

[Male] "He was always glad to see our flag when he was abroad, and was always glad to salute it at what he thought were appropriate times. In fact, he loved close-order marching and authentic ceremony—which he called 'protocol ritual'. But he was disgusted to see the flag abused—flying in all weather, day and night, or folded carelessly, or as pieces of clothing or commercial streamers as decoration. He knew a lot about symbolic orthodoxy! Maybe that's as close as he came to religion! . . ."

[Male] "Well it's not a matter of sentimentality. He said a flag without its proper symbol is nothing but a sail without its sheet! —But you could never be sure he wasn't playful. Sometimes he was ironic—"

[Female] "But he was never cynical. . . ."

[Male] "He was no iconoclast in his discomfort with some things about the Navy. Like Redburn before him, he allowed for some decent and effective high commanders—ours or British—like Admiral Prince, who'd kept antisemitic slander out of personnel evaluation records."

[Male] "Macdane was generally called a spit-and-polish officer, like Spruce, when I was in the War, the bane of swabbies like me— you know, the 'bellbottom-trousers-and-coats-of-navy-blue' type. But he always knew the good reasons for keeping decks spotless and all steel dry, or whatever else we had to do. Here he still hated to see floors being washed without being swept first! He was always against a lick and a promise in anything! His cleaning lady told me that he said a bachelor who leaves his cuffs unbuttoned is a bull in his own china inventory, and function follows form!"

[Male] "Well I was a Fireman when he was a young engineering officer before the War. He went out of his way to get me into Port Royal. After I got my commission we lost touch. But he was always my model for helping good men get promoted."

[Female] "He told me he'd thought people should always be training themselves for something or other! But Mr Karcist said that the Commander's motto was 'Nothing Doesn't Matter!'. At first I thought it was a joke! He could say things with a straight face. I heard him say that you can't square the circle but you can circle the square! So he was pretty sensible."

[Female] "He thought everyone should have to take a physics course to get a driver's license!"

[Male] "But is it true that he believed in free love? I heard that in India after the War when Lord Mountbatten was the last Viceroy he sympathetically granted his wife her notorious life at home in England. Now Macdane greatly admired Mountbatten for many talents and achievements, as a British model—but with or without feet of clay? Some people around here thought our Commander was sort of puritanical—"

[Female] "You don't know how the other half gives! That's a crazy minuendo against Commander Macdane! Just because he liked the Brits for their deficiency! I know a waitress who got big tips from our man for brushing crumbs off the table cloth between courses! He laughed at himself for his morale. He was liberal to the hilt, a perfect gentleman. He reminded me the opera Dildo and Aeneas! Thereby hangs a trail! But he was as polite a they come! I don't think he should be prostituted for using their mannerisms! To think, when I first saw Mr Macdane I resumed that he'd be a Can!" . . .

[Male] "Konrad says 'A train of thought is never false.'"

[Male] "Let's get back to the details of the War. A lot of people want to know more about it before it's too late to remember. I was always struck by his interest in personal stories of it before during and after the experience of them. I heard him say that if Admiral Prince had been in command of the Pacific fleet in 1941 there probably would have been no Pearl Harbor disaster, and Hitler would not have declared war on us, and therefore F D R could not have persuaded Congress to declare war and save Britain from the Germans, who then would have been able to defeat the British soon enough to turn the tables in Europe which would help the Cipangese neutralize us and win all the territory they wanted between Owhyee and the Suez Canal, and who would already have won all the shores of the Mediterrean. Maybe the Australians. . . . ."

[Male] . . . "Or else the Protestican isolationists would have made a treaty with the Germans. . . ."

[Female] . . . "And there would have been an Auschwitz in Texas."

[Female] "He said that his worst experience of the War was just to see one of those camps right after the Germans abandoned it. It made him feel guilty for speaking German, for not being a Jew, for being excused the ultimate suffering in a continuum of mind and body. He also said that the prisons on the Isle of Man for Germans and Italians living in Allied rest-camps, by comparison—"

[Male] "He also saw Coventry, London, and Amsterdam early on, as well as Cologne, Hamburg, Dresden, and Berlin later. All he could have asked of man's inhumanity to man! He seemed almost apologetic for never having suffered like infantrymen or sub-mariners or flying tail gunners! His love of battleships was for them as architecture for swift community, meant to save civilization *from* war. He laughed as he told me that Lion's Gate in Mycene reminded him of seapower! . . ."

[Female] "Well I remember that he hated to hear Navy men calling battleships 'battle wagons', I guess because it made them seem old and clumsy. It was a swagger of sophistication by sailors who also called destroyers 'tin cans', and who had lot of other unmentionable epithets de rigueur to prove themselves old salts."

[Male] "He made up for himself two or three condescending nicknames for aircraft carriers!"

[Female] "'A manned ship is a roving place.' he said. 'The better the ship, the better the place.' So is the dory then a family—or a roving predator?"

[Male] "Long before he knew Lord Mountbatten he'd studied the history of the British navy, especially in the 17C, and one of his heroes who didn't fight at all was the self-educated commoner named Samuel Pepys, starting as a clerk, who as a brilliantly honest manager became Secretary of the Royal Navy and thus First Lord of the Admiralty (in modern parlance) from a political desk job, between King and Parliament. Finn told me Pepys had built many of his ships with the King's pines—twenty-four or more inches in diameter—and other timber from this our very own Cape Gloucester for many battleships of his day! Masts were crucial. Pepys believed that they grew better here than in Britain because our winters were cold and long, our summers shorter! See the kind of things that he picked up from all kinds of reading! How he was ahead of his time! . . ."

[Female] "But did this hero of ours believe in God any more than he did free love?"

[Minister] "He believed in church, he told me. But I don't know which one. —It's not hard to imagine in this one."

[*Laughter led by the minister.*]

He said he believed in reason, but added that *faith* wasn't necessarily a virtue. It all depended on what the faith was *in*. He deplored a medical culture devoted more to symptoms than to causes."

[Female] "I invited him to my church too. I never heard such whole independent sentences stuffed between parentheses inside a larger sentence. In all my years of teaching English I've never had a colleague or textbook so precise in classical grammar! But he wasn't just an ordinary atheist! He didn't mind any evolution or novelty that was compatible with some of the Bible in such-and-such translation!" . . .

[Male] "What I liked about all that stuff with him was that he knew the aesthetic wasn't always the best. His example was the old Iron Sides still down the line at the Navy Yard. In her day she was called ugly for being down at the head when under way at sea, yet she was the fastest frigate of them all! . . ."

[Female] . . . "You've never seen such a conservationist! He hated to see anything thrown away unless it could be consumed by animal or vegetable, or salvaged for the mineral. He'd waste time in the process of disposal. Even in old age he admitted that! —But, as a matter of fact, his straight-faced sense of humor was as laconic as the late Wat Cibber's. It excused all his technology!" . . .

[Female] "I once asked him if he was going to do any more traveling. He said 'Only once more: to Delphi!'" . . .

[Female] "More than anything else in our society he detested the fact that our Atlantean "feel good" commercial economy has engendered and sustained relief from freewill in the painless face of indulgence. . . ."

[Female] "That double-bladed axe he took down with him: I wonder if it was some oldfashioned kind from the Middle Ages?"

[Male] "Abraham Lincoln's axe was so old that it had had three new handles and two new heads before he died, like the Greek river that wasn't ever the same one. It could no longer be identified! It must have been the epiphany of a concept! Much less real than the organism of a fishing schooner, Aristotle would have said—or the organic township of a battleship. The difference between them is that one is propelled by the environment and the other by its own temporary willpower, using its brain to dodge independent torpedoes. . . ."

28

FOURTH
QUARTER

I do not seek to understand in order to believe,
but I believe in order to understand.

—Anselm

1. Raphael Opsimath

"Eastward Ho forever! From decadence to enlightenment, pioneering in reverse! Pacific to Atlantic! San Ricardo to Dogtown! From
Bay Area to the Great Vinland Bight! From Peninsula to Cape!
From sardines to mackerel! From self-indulgence to self-discipline!
But it's that harbor down there that makes the biggest difference!
—Well no, a lot more than that has won me over, not to mention
you! From now on, in this avant-garde house, I eat leisurely breakfasts with you up on our little hilltop spot, right here in earliest
possible Social Security retirement, expecting you soon to join my
demographic class! —With all the money we'll ever need, fully
insured against everything!"

759

"Except Protesticans. They're just as antisocial in Vinland as in Cornucopia!" replies Tessa to her husband in almost absentminded good humor as she ponders the best way to make the social use she had in mind for his immediate magnanimous metanoia, meanwhile bantering in her familiar tone: "Yes, we'll have to get a full-time maid or houseboy, lolling in all this supposedly laborless equipment by operating electronics I'll never understand, devising youthful amusements for elderly bones. But let me take care of the self-discipline." They sit with postprandial dishes before a large insulating double pane of glass overlooking the outer harbor on the morning after his return from the funeral of his distantly erstwhile partner in Tubalcain Manufacturing Company, a very profitable small firm in Babylon Oaks that fabricated and distributed industrial steam-cleaners of its own design, which had drawn him peripherally to Vinland from Cornucopia for the first time twenty years ago. The funeral was in San Ricardo, whence both Walter Edenfield and Raphael Opsimath himself originated (from very different domestic backgrounds), a hundred miles down the coast from Golden Horn Bay.

But without utterance the respectively engendered thoughts of Rafe and Tessa naturally converge from irreducibly different memories even of their love's shared experience on Cape Gloucester (or in its New Armorican reaches), beginning before she became the widow of the benevolent alcoholic Buck Barebones, a mechanical genius, the proprietor who'd founded Dogtown Machine & Design, which Rafe had greatly admired as a mutually affectionate visitor on a business trip. He'd soon thereafter joined the Barebones couple and their prosperous job-shop in a manufacturing corporation in which, eventually, all three (as well as a few of their friends) successfully exploited Rafe's diverse managerial talent as well as Buck's practicable ideas in creative imagination. Dogtown Machine & Design, Inc. rapidly became a diversified metalworking facility for mechanical research and development, together with specialized prototype manufacturing (notably for the frozen-food industry). With many propitious investments in highly specialized machine tools, its most lucrative orders were from large contractors or subcontractors for the Offense Department and related civilian industries which needed small quantities of small uniquely designed component parts or small subassemblies, some of which were jealously patented. DT M & D itself became far enough up in the great chain of assembly to let contracts or pur-

chase orders, if possible to machine shops or purveyors in Gloucester County. A few of those were occupants of the new City-spon-
sored Industrial Park built of concrete and asphalt high on the hill
that had once been the loveliest of Colonial pasture lands according to the cultural critic Caleb Karcist.

A modern DT M & D headquarters office and expansive shop
had been built within comparatively easy reach of the railroad (not
far from the hill on which the Opsimaths' new private house was
built), amid the woods on the mainland side of the Namauche estuary; but the nature of the plant's materials and products, and of
much easier rubber-tired conveniences, was such (also to Caleb's disappointment) that no spur track had ever been called for. The Felly
bridge and interstate highway, prolific with all sorts and sizes of
available trucking, now obviated steel rails for continuous linkage to
the continental network of Atlantean history, though still occasionally economical for single carloads in or out of the city's shrunken
and moribund rail yards (one of its tracks extending to a forked dead
end of the passenger line) used for boxcars of packing materials or
canned fish, or even a tank car of fish-oil. This still called for trucks
to communicate freight with the inner harbor. In short, the railroad
drawbridge nowadays rarely connected the presque-isle to the
greater world for anything but people sitting either way on metropolitan schedule up and down thirty miles of the coast.

The growth of industrial commerce on both sides of the Gut
had been inconspicuously accelerated by Rafe's little corporate
enterprise; but now it had been sold outright to an international
conglomerate, which itself had already been alienated (among many
other enterprises around the country) from his ideal of industrial
integrity, as once nearly realized by the open-ended investment
trust formerly traded on the Ur Curb Exchange as the late Arthur
Halymboyd's Parity Corporation, which he believed had always
been more interested in growth than acquisition.

For a moment Rafe lays his hand on Tess's as they remind
themselves of all the water under other bridges since his Cornucopian divorce and liberally pledged alimony when dwelling near
the banks of the Babylon Oaks estuary. The family of which he was
otherwise legally relieved had finally scattered in apparent random
across the country, he hardly knew why, in various degrees of successful independence. Yet he still kept an affectionate eye on his
three children—without much alarm or regret, relying on the
maternal competence of his first wife (with Tessa's sympathetic

approval)—none of whom loved their second father with disaffection for himself. Tessa knew he was as generous to that family as he was to hers. It was a typically satisfactory Cornucopian settlement.

His nearly congenital penchant for experiential geography has now been directed toward Europe, though definitely based in Dogtown with Tessa in a remarkable house. He can hardly wait to start planning for a dozen concatenated sojourns with her the following year, after promising a twelvemonth to her preferences and preparations on this cape as anchor to windward. He and she keep no secrets from each other about their reasonably differing ideas of geriatric pleasure. They never have to read each other's mind when a fresh travel is out of question for either the retired businessman or the practicing psychiatric social worker, each of whom by now has earned plenty of freely available time to make up for unanticipated cancellations or postponements. These two professionals had looked forward to being amateurs before it was too late to resume their divergent careers, or new ones, for the extraordinary recreations of old age. So now is a time, with enough time—with enough sleep— to talk to each other about what they haven't had enough time for: discursive colloquy about wishes, opinions, deeds, or even honest disagreements hitherto accepted without rational or psychological examination as an unavoidable duty of marriage intelligently satisfied with reciprocating senses of humor.

On his part their love had strengthened more in bed than in board, thanks to his long business hours at Dogtown Machine & Design—and sometimes hers too as part-time Treasurer of that corporation. But she too, more in bed than in his undressed domesticity and scarce society together, due almost as much to her own irregularly onerous practice of professional consultation, as well as her major dedication to Atlantean party politics at the local oaktree level. (She is even frequently called out of town for two or three days as a member of the Vinland State Catholicratic Committee.)

"Maybe I'll get a boat." he's saying, absentmindedly warning himself to be careful about merely drifting into commitments of actual retirement. A diver avoids the bends by returning to the surface slowly. The metastasis of valorization from ophelimity to poetry is still my pipe dream! He chuckles and shivers. Unlike most other managerial retirees he had intended to pursue at least the putative satisfactions of a poet. He hoped for twenty years to catch up without too much loss of his salient imagination. But now he finds that he can barely remember any of the poetic ideas that have trespassed and faded in the interstices of executive action and sleep. Until now he's had hardly any proper conjunctions of time and mood as much as to glance at others' poems in the *Newurker Magazine*. But perhaps, to be honest, he tells himself, he's been afraid not to know the meaning of what he reads. Have I been too confident that my geographical conceits and unique existential perspicuity are enough to prove that I can learn more than the tentative craft of poetry so late in life?

"Dear Rafe," he hears Tessa saying, "you've always said boats take up too much time, even if you pay for maintenance and a crew; ultimately boring; creating nothing; basically more passive than banking; et cetera. However, it wouldn't hurt either of us to be more athletic. I'm short-winded from smoking and you're heavier than you used to be."

"Yes, you're as thin as a rail and I'm as fat as a Can. I'm going to walk all the streets and paths of this cape that I've never had time to find or fully appreciate—as much as you'd like in your company; otherwise just to gather past and present thoughts for a new life. I'd like to muse Lady Gloucester's nooks and crannies."

"Never mind nooks and crannies away from home! Maybe I'll think of some honorable Muses for my all-too-attractive husband. Not just conscientious Cratic meetings once a month. I wish we still had Stone Barn theatricals, or even playreadings like the ones we had way back before that."

"You know, I was just remembering those old days, when I was still married in Baby Oaks and you were still Mrs Barebones, trying to resuscitate that moribund political committee, and I was acquiring mechanical ideas from open-hearted Buck Barebones the forefather of our present wealth. —By the way, how are the Barebones kids these days? I often think of asking you when or where you're not available—one of the numberless faults I regret in my disgraceful cohabitation."

"You've always been graceful in private, better than catch-as-catch-can. Outdoing your harem last night! —All my kids seem to talk about is my grandchildren, which I'm not yet enthusiastic about. But I'll tell you about everything you want to know when we've caught our breath. Plenty of other things you'll rather hear about that I've been sparing you these last few weeks of your business consummations."

"I haven't even glanced at Belle's front page for local news that can't be suppressed until tomorrow."

"Before the next cock crow I'll get you up to date in a few nutshells of import to me." says Tessa more thoughtfully. "I've been shielding our court from you on the pretext that everyone's probably busy filing certifications of the bottom lines. Everybody wants to see more of you, but with no reason to plan a surprise. The cat's been out of your bag. Meanwhile—"

"I know you, Tessa the Confesser, when you're up to something that's something else. It's not my birthday, and I know it isn't yours. I don't remember any sentimental or ironic anniversary that you'd be likely to remind me of."

"Okay. I have a present for you." She rises from the table to fetch from under a sofa pillow in the next room a small soft-covered black book, holding it over his coffee cup just long enough for him to see the title.

"*Law Dictionary*! I hope you're not thinking of divorce—after last night! And just when I'm finished ahead of time with the alimony of my last case! With no ill-will to be heard from coast to coast, and no hardship in sight! —Or are you trying to teach me the Latin you need for me to read your professional jargon—whatever it is that you're up to?"

"The law has many mansions. But I have the day planned for us. I need your help and advice, especially after a wonderful dream I had early this morning when you were flat on your back."

"You want a divorce because I was snoring—for the first time in ten years?"

"Stop clowning, you incorrigible old late-learner! You are going to help us solve an interesting mystery that will test your good humor, which usually prevails."

"So far there's no reason to worry particularly about that, as long as it doesn't require hard labor. I haven't been fit for that since I walloped oil drums on the shipping dock in San Ricardo." For no particular reason Rafe is happy to interrupt as nostalgia (in every sense of the word) the retrospective mood that's a backdrop for his perfectly contented withdrawal. He loves Tessa for her brains and supple backbone. He believes she's preparing him for something seriously amusing without yet figuring out how to frame it.

"Finish reading the paper: satisfy your news of the world." she says. "Here's more coffee. I'm going to make you a holiday lunch. Then take a nap or do as you please while I write down my dream and gather my thoughts. Tonight we're taking Fay to dinner at that fancy new cosmopolitan restaurant on Front Street."

"As usual, you know better than I do what I want. There's no one else I'd rather see first. But I'll miss the old Windmill building at the top of that street. I hear it's remodeled for office spaces."

"And conferences. Or charades. Dogtown's up and coming, for better or for worse. Largely thanks to you, my dear, for attracting all the new industry with little old DT M & D by getting so many specialized contracts and subcontracts from all over the country that need local subcontracts and supplies from you. It hasn't yet dawned on most Dogtown people that it isn't just your investments or the hundreds of good new jobs you've added but also all the work you've done gratis for the I D E A in developing the industrial park that has brought all sorts of tax-paying investment from national and international firms, as well as from a dozen small businesses! I'm asking Belle to play that up in the *Nous*."

"Bless you, old girl: you've never taken me for granted, and that has helped immensely. I was just thinking about things that I couldn't have done without you and your recognition as a leader for the common good of Dogtown. I wouldn't have stayed on Cape Gloucester or learned to care about its history without your advice and hard work when I didn't appreciate this town's complexities. I never forget also that we've both been Fellows with Highest Honors from old Doc Charlemagne's evanescent White Quarry College! Those medals are few indeed! Both of us have always been opsimaths! But what are you driving at? I'm through with business, while I still have a little time for its opposites!"

As he rises with a yawn that belies his curiosity she bends down to hug and kiss her husband's tonsure fringed with gray. "You're my one and only middleaged man. But to save you from distraction I've concealed my fascination with a younger one. I'll confess more on our way to Fay's. She's my confess*or*."

"From you I'll listen or obey to reason, as long as we're ready for foreign geography next year. Until then I hope no one bids me to Roundtable meetings or public good causes. Tell your Crats that I'm a doddering hermit, recuperating from a nervous breakdown, giving a little money but less time—at least until the next national election. Or say I'm just an old grouch who refers all communication to you."

"Of course our inner circle is excepted! Perhaps starting tonight."

"I'm all ears for the clerisy! What's left of it. Charlemagne long gone! Ditto, Father Duncannon and Chris Lucey! Now the philanthropic King Arthur also caput mortuum! And Mac too, the healthy new one that I wanted to know much better. Isn't he the one who said *Nothing doesn't matter*? Caspar thought a lot of him for that maxim. Any architect would. He also thought we were the best domestic clients he ever had. I always hoped to get him on our DT M & D Board. So I'd gladly join your friends in some sort of cheerful memorial en mass."

2. Now Fay's Bank and Shoal of Time

This is no way to use up my morning's coffee quota sine qua non, just gazing out at the land and its reflective mate, when I should be cudgeling the "word-processor" that Finn insisted I replace my faithful electric typewriter with, just when I had drawn the line at our pompous "electronic revolution"! He predicted there'll be "on-line, real-time computers" for everyone able to pay the price! How I loathe that prospect, if only for its jargon! But I'll be lost if I don't finish my book before "programs" take over all the "machine language"! Isn't that what he said? —I should be working right now, instead of staring at tranquil nature when my forward motion is irresistibly distracted by my own dear Thalia. She tells me that Yeats said "all things are from antithesis." But mine is no simple contrariety of motives in the race against death. If I'm in this dream it's not as a segment but as its parallel! In essence even Tessa's dream should be divisible only by twos. Caleb is right that even Yeats lacks trichotomy. "I'm an engineer at heart, and so is Gilgamesh." Caleb once told me. "Yeats was a poet, the supreme artist": something like "yet he and I both think with systematic diagrams as racks for symbols—sometimes the same symbols—for different meanings." But he's really a six-shooter, in the way his symbols factor two and three according to his argument!

Still, he rightly propounds that commemorative liturgy is the architecture of religion, symbolically understood. Maybe it was with that understanding on his part that Father Duncannon was enthusiastically served by him as acolyte and business manager—of course with reservations, even unto the present day.

But Tessa is right: reservations are always to be understood in Caleb's vainglory! As an ambivalent quasi-metapsychologist I'm intrigued by her socio-psychological fascination with his background, mainly because I too lightly promised his mother to oversee his character as it formed after baptism! For more than forty-five years I never even saw him again. Now I'm an apologetic godmother from whom he sometimes seems to think I learn as much as he learns from me. I suppose I'm thermostatic instead of thermodynamic in his vision. Yet he may be the most appreciating reader I've ever had! . . .

But Tessa and Rafe have also excited me in spite of myself, and I can't say that won't stimulate my own work, now that I'm past my concentration on the exemplary diversity of Polynesia. Besides, I've never paid enough attention to the French Middle Ages.

—Wouldn't it be ironic if, for lack of the peace that passes all understanding when distractions vanish, I should borrow even more time to go to Deeta and learn Contemplative Nullification, keeping in mind that learning its kind of meditation is of little worth unless I keep up a regular practice of it—considered as if a solitary ritual—robbing me of an hour a day altogether! Fine—if even in old age it would compensate for the loss by adding more than three hundred and sixty-five hours to each year of my longevity with *cumulative* mind intact! All the odds are against me. Besides, even if I could be sure of that, I'd need a deadline just to keep my book from getting endlessly stuffed. I think the 'Bega Press suspects just that. Otherwise there's no reason for the diplomatic hints I get about my E T A. As it happens this has been one of the most expansive surges of my mind, right here in peculiar Dogtown, sequestered from laureates, high tables, and garths. And I can't be rushed just when I have the most to say! . . .

Yet still I stand at the window simply looking at familiar changing things—trying to remember the gobs of dazzling snow at thirty-two degrees gradually absorbing the heat of fusion as they relieve the spruce trees of their beautiful weight, left under a quiet bright blue sky, gradually slipping off the wingtips in recovery of the healthy green of my unreliable hoped-for spring between the last two storms. But otherwise my eyes gaze at familiar attractions in rapid and jerky movements that always astonish me with action that is all but motionless relative to me if I blink. The reversing climbs and flying leaps of these gray rodents, usually hastening or chasing in pairs, make them into self-conscious acrobats. They amuse me especially when they jump weightlessly from twigs to twigs of trees that hardly touch each other in a breeze. Straight up,

straight down, through all the yards of maple or oak, by light fantastic claw, often thievish, they hesitate at nothing, paying no
attention to us who mean to feed only the little birds. With their
curled fifth limb, the extremely subtle interrogative figure is much
more functional than a human's horizontal pole on a perilous
tightrope, which they put to shame in versatility seeming almost as
light as an eyelash feather, without chit-chat, yet propelling themselves with the multidimensional agility of fish—vociferous mon-
keys that flaunt their skills as a superior race if only for the zigzag
distance they can cover. . . .

I remember when most of the trees were still naked in the
spring, with not so much as a promising bud to be seen, these
squirrels of all weather made me think of studio dancers in
rehearsal; but their instantly articulated movements are too abrupt
for dancing even as acrobats can dance (at least with their heads) in
a rope-rigged circus tent. I'm very glad they're vegetarians, for I
actually congratulate their ingenious successes upside down on the
hanging birdfeeder in my yard to steal from presumably innocent
beaks that are apparently dependent upon me and my charitable
neighbors to survive indigenous winters. They make the squirrels
seem indifferent to our weather. Is this anthropology, geography, or
sociology? . . .

. . . In the counterentropic season of stirred-up hope even the
greenish lichen spread like splotches of whited cancer along the
upper surfaces of the trees—especially on my noble wolf oak, still
in its timeless prime, the grandfather of all the others in my
purlieu (and they say great-grand-uncle of the maples). By Bacon-
ian induction over a few moons I took that ghastly fungal-looking
epidermis as a dynamic harbinger of time at its best—the ironic
pattern of growth by what I saw from the infinitesimal movement
of the sun climbing northerly day by day, whether or not plainly
visible at the horizon. Such inferential curiosity by abstraction is
my advantage as a human animal! . . . At the next vernal equinox I
must try to remember that: the lichen's reversibly opposite motion
within the same reversible lifetimes. Maybe it's a hopefully protesting organic wheel within all the larger unaligned wheels within
wheels. I should have taken a course in botany, instead of that one
in geology! . . .

Denthey's Universal Systems Theory seems ultimately not
about any or all systems: I think it applies only to what prove to be
systems! It comprehends the special cases of Caleb's Synectic

Method of Diagnostic Correlation, of course, but I think he would agree that it can never explain what he calls pure tragedy, his most special of cases in all the arts. Finn never accepted that one. Nor, as far as I can gather, would Father Duncannon as a theodynamic physicist have done so in his radicalized yet still supernatural Christian symbol-system. Must it remain for me before I die to propose a dromenological metaphysics that allows for the supernatural only in art! But I think I can—think I could write about that (with my houseful of books and other intellectual conveniences) if I can buck the entropy of a dementia that's slow enough in its certainty. When Finn was alive I never gave such thought to what's irreversible. He seemed to rejuvenate me, and I him. . . .

. . . For my own sake I'm pathetically glad that Caleb is free of his unnatural obsession with organization in this "pragmatical pig of a world"! He belongs with Yeats only in his *kind* of symbols, not in his own correlatives attitudes or meanings! In his devoted chrematistic and liturgical service to Father Duncannon's Laboratory of Melchizedek and the Mesocosm he apparently found an intellectual mentor of stimulating satisfaction, initially bonded upon the recollection of his early childhood training at the altar of the High Church chaplain of a Tudor convent.

Strangely enough, long after the Father Superior's Classic Order of the Vine was disbanded, following his death and an embarrassing legacy that I know little about, I've been almost as delighted as Caleb himself to know that it's an entirely different kind of character, known among us as King Arthur Halymboyd, who has left my godson an entirely unexpected posthumous annuity—modest but secure—with the ironic proviso that he accept no other income unless or until he ceases to devote himself exclusively to the reading writing or arithmetic he's properly destined for, perhaps playwriting, "successful" or otherwise.

Furthermore, Caleb's to be protected from poverty by an annually upward adjustment for the national cost of living! In effect, Caleb has now retired with Jewish social security not many years before it'll be augmented by his long-earned Social Security checks from the public melting pot. I gather that anyone (even a close friend) who'd known Caleb in his Quixotic career trying just to earn his living without boredom, as a candidly fascinated spy on the religious and political economy, would have expected no angel on his behalf. Anyway, he may not be as heroically independent as we thought when he quit his short job in the Hall. . . .

But the semi-retired Endicott Krebs is our practically charitable legal Ubermensch (after bowing out from his marvelous practice of corporate law as a commuter to the metropolis), apparently
just for his love of civic complexity in the common good. Now that
I stop to think, he didn't get back from his world cruise until a
month after Finn's death. As he happens to still be the Dogtown
number one attorney for several of us, including what's left of
Finn's Dogtown estate, directing our casual or routine legal service
or providing communication with other lawyers in Markland or Ur,
not to mention his own young independent surrogate on Front
Street who handles most of his pro bono or minor billings that we
know nothing about, it never occurred to me that my name might
be mentioned in any of the surprising probate, despite the shrewd
simplicity of his cy-pres will when he probably assumed he'd have
at least a decade more for altering it. . . . After my own astonishingly munificent legacy from Finn, I suspected that Endicott, our
Jewish Merlin, coached Finn in the cy-pres and other particular
provisions in his will that no other lawyer would have suggested for
my particular assistance when I had not the slightest knowledge of
such a document's existence—especially after being with Finn such
a short time.

Anyway, as to the Merlin function on Endicott's part, I suppose
as no longer a competitive octogenarian member of the greater bar,
he's as persuasively benign with other lawyers and judges as he is
with us. Now, for his own moral entertainment, he's treating me as
the widow Sheba of Christian wisdom, little imagining my struggle to sustain, let alone finish, my all but desperate contribution to
social science, just when my memory is beginning to depend more
and more upon thousands of my scarcely sorted notes and hundreds
of books without detailed indexes! I've submitted my tentative outline, which after all was only a pleasurable draft, without claiming
to myself that I can reduce my debt to individual human life like
that of Caleb's mother, my counterpart in experience—hoping it'll
somehow infuse my philosophical anthropology with what's really
expressed only in her kind of poetry. . . .

This morning I have a nice sky and a sharp purple line to
deceive me as a straightened edge of my hundred-degree horizon.
It's almost time, with neither leaves nor snow, to imagine Lady
Gloucester's naked body at the melting of our last glacier, a disrob-
ing that Finn liked to talk about, looking left and right for granite
moraine like my cracked whale-head outside the other windows,

taller than a man. The side of that domestic boulder is pressed by an evergreen juniper, rubbing its side by a straight young white pine two or three times higher, which seems grateful for its leeward protection as a seedling from its amazingly recent birth. If you keep walking about this extraordinary hill as appareled with mankind at this time of year, sooner or later in the fragmentary of copses or woods you'll discover one or two detrial boulders almost as high as that young pine, though the impressive rock that you more commonly see is embedded in the earth as a protrusion of unfathomable granite rock, whatever its atmospheric extent or elevation, stunted or rounded from lava. . . .

Finn made me look around at all the dry walls of lichened gray stone, tumbled or fitted, usually with traces of purposeful mortar. He said with a smile that he was about to start a geodetic study of the geology that was omitted in the superficial oceanography of his naval R O T C—no doubt equally irrelevant to supercilious studies like mine! He remarked that all the weathered rocks of the seashore (like the great palisades of inland quarries in Seamark and Taraville) were various shades of rustic brown, just as those of the same granite magma exposed in a landscape of breaching whales may be weathered to tan either with or without the greenish maculations of lichen, just as a living whale, it's said, may or may not be landed with barnacles.

But I made him look at the anthropological housing on the other side of our hill: a variety almost entirely with angular wood-framed houses of different shapes and colors, many with idiosyncratic displays of very limited grass, some with—but usually without—cunning little spaces for trees or rock gardens, which may be sunken or hidden, often freshly striking me as differentiated similarities to my own taste—but which Finn sometimes couldn't help regarding as *too* humble on some streets or boringly commonplace on a few others—if not vulgarly misplaced in pretentious situation or style, such as a few in the Key South style, with verandas—two or three at least which I actually liked! Where the terrain is precipitous the yards are ingenious. Yet on this end of the Joint Hill ridge there are only two houses built of stone, one a converted coach house, the other a massive chateau. At this lingering passage of the solar year the sun exposes in certain yards some of the sides or patches of immeasurable rock that most of the time overshadow tiny chthonic gardens tilled by meticulous men or women—at least where residue of greenery or flowers don't still hide smooth flanks

or clefts of some master ledge as high or higher than a modest
house in front of them but set lower than the pavement of a street
above. Or else there may be a few feet of naked rock escarpment
above them that invisibly retains the earthen basin of an inconspicuous vernal pond raggedly obscured by the wild hedges and brambles which obscure the houses that guard it at the higher level.

Except for those, the vales of most neighborhoods are afoot at
lower levels. I thank Caleb for leading me to peer deeper. But at
hesitation between summer and winter, to say nothing of wary
spring, this hill founded in solid granite everywhere underfoot—
shaped or finished and stacked as side walls—makes me curiously
sympathetic with the rows of small houses that line without interruption both sides of the steepest streets, occupying all the human
shelter above their basements with wood and shingles, almost sharing single parking spaces as ingenious boundaries. I do love Caleb
for appreciating this catalog page of Atlantean tastes—or anyway
necessities—in our local kind of closely packed ekistics without
rows of brick, challenging each other for homely individuality
where there was once a cliff too precipitous for goats or trees.

But of course these particular streets are only one short face of
a hill that spreads many slopes and categories of reality-estate from
the ridge that divides its outlook, in part like my own, of the
ocean's horizon without many ostentatious vantages nearby. Even
the Fore Shore promontory, where great houses of tightly fitted
stone and cleanly troweled mortar still predominate, is chastened
by the lighthouse and breakwater naturally sought by exploring
tourists with guidebooks as good as the best for domestic geography in England—at least so suggests Caleb who's never been
there! He points out gratuitously that my hillside house happens
to be barely on the outside of an elevation that could be claimed
by several differing populations. To be sure, he's annoyingly careless with many of his analogies: videlicet, comparing our Joint
Hill with the Observatory Hill in Unabridge—when "reminds me
of" is uttered as "like"—upon which he and his mother lived
during the Depression on a hump between town and gown, not far
from where we Morgans lived in private academia. Unknown to
us, on his way to school he crossed that hump from various decent
apartments little more expensive than slums to mix his poloi as
public children with those of the public aristoi. He's properly
proud of that experience. Strangely enough, though, it was not
entirely unlike my own, many years earlier on the other coast in a

parochial school much like the one on his Observatory Hill. But my observatory was not surrounded by a Norumbega to defend the Cornucopian intelligentsia! . . .

I still sometimes try to imagine a young Finn marveling at flesh or granite as he explored or reviewed these slopes of Lady Gloucester before the War, where he spent some time with an admiral and a certain daughter when he was visiting them from his home in Markland, or when he was stationed at the Botolph Navy Yard. I was already married when he had someone else's Fayaway. . . . When I brood or speculate about our simultaneous chronologies I wonder. Maybe that's what he too wished before he lived long enough to fully trust my love and its satisfaction. Whenever I asked too many sly questions he'd make fun of me as his favorite angel by pointing up at the sky to indicate my sense of time in "the great hinged capacitor for clouds". —Now I try to visualize his deep blue eyes— alive or dead, open or closed, full fathom five, anything but pearls. Or the purple wispy mounted majesty of our eastern cordillera that he and I would fancy as Redburn's when sailing north along the western coast of South Atlantis. . . . But now I've no such company at my side as an independent variable when I look upon my oak tree's lichen to remind me of the death that oscillates in space— bringing to mind non sequitur that Redburn said (as if to explain himself to deserted Fayaway) that he himself did not oscillate in Emerson's transcendental rainbow. . . . I know exactly where the sun rose this morning, and I know approximately where it rose a couple of days ago: ergo, I know we're tilting toward the north. As Caleb would say, winter will be icumen in! —But what boots all that to sanction the fatal quantum mechanics of the parallel dreams I've created by myself without Finn's wakeful existence? . . .

I don't even yet know whether or not the Court I've agreed to join is the masque of a somnambular tribunal. Is it worth the interruption of what I would better do without tears in the swan song of my study? Am I demeaning my profession?

3. Caleb the Dreamer

Finn was both trained and educated. I could have been *his* acolyte. Once I almost wished to be King Arthur's chief of staff in Ur. But they were only two of the three-phase watts I've needed for the alternating energies that have both diverted and stimulated my half-starved calling! I couldn't hear Finn as he waved against the wind with Gilgamesh's axe in his left fist, holding to a slackened shroud with the other, but I knew in my dream that he was yelling to me that I didn't need to know Greek or quantum physics or "present value" calculation of investments, as long as I knew myself—taunting me with a wink! But before waking I didn't know that he had asked King Halymboyd to provide the livelihood that gives me a chance to finally do what I ought to be doing around the clock, responding to the vocation I think I was indirectly born to without the wrong kind of talent. After excellent schooling my principal benefactors were each creative in his own way—but none were artists.

My mother had the imagination and motivation of an artist but she lacked the ongoing education that she started me off with, as if maternity was the sacred duty of her life, even in the retrospection of an old age in penitential or enthusiastic society progressively distant from the religion of her one real baby among the three seriatim that she'd yearned for as a child herself. Yet her highly variable self-confident selflessness was my unconscious heritage despite our obvious difference in temperament. With a wretched aptitude for numerical education, and for such training as that required to drive a kilroy, her literary and artistic mind was probably far more sophisticated than her classmates' in high school on the way to college. Her feckless calculations were more than counterbalanced by what she herself claimed were both the positive and negative intuitions said to excel in femininity—probably, by her own account, because of lengthy deliriums in her nearly fatal teenage sleeping sickness as the first World War was ending. Yet, of all my exceptional teachers and mentors whom she indirectly or unwittingly urged upon me, she was my prime mover in unique development— not the lion that I once accused her of being when she angrily scolded me for lighting a house fire when I was four years old, but the lioness who does all the hunting (and other teaching) to keep us both alive with books and hopes and curiosities, overcoming her continual disappointments with lions who rule and lions who rove. I hardly missed imagined siblings, but she continued to make no secret of her hope to be found by the finest kind of a shaggy king. I don't think all mothers are that courageous. Only with the self-reliance that she bred in me could I have become her happy independent cub in poverty. But alas for humanity, her inverted cone of influence came to its vanishing point, unless I also do more to claim her prowess in climes beyond her savannah! With far less than half my life left to do it in!

The trouble is that I haven't concentrated my gyre on the dromenon. For me drama no more exists without action than I recognize a religion without the action of a societal mass. It isn't enough just to persuade my godmother of dromenological Muses. For lack of dropping everything else to make myself a scholar, criticism may be my wan hope for a place in the philosophical perpetuation of Fay's Summa Anthropologica. That comes of my being a quack of all tirades and a beggar of some. All my causes and those of my heroes lost. But such is tolerable and reasonable, seeing that I haven't the eloquence or poetic imagination to express what can be conveyed only in art—what it would take to amalgamate my disparities of excitement. I've had too many secondary interests, too many truncated curiosities. Konrad was wise to stick to his lathe, once he gave up seamanship. . . .

Ergo, for me, too much technology with too little math, not enough poetry—in fact none at all of my own. Nevertheless, past my prime while still priming my pump, I suddenly seem to have time to spare for the energy to write the Gilgamesh play I thought I had to skip when I thought I'd never have time to finish the middle and then rewrite the whole damned cycle without a stage for my technological epic!

. . . Yet, still, I can't say that I regret any of my diversions. I was an acolyte but not an apprentice. If I'd had the talent and skill—the so-called "gift" of a quicker and more capacious brain—I might have taken and done everything I did take and do with plenty of time to try poetry, or at least attempt criticism thereof, without renouncing any of my symbol-systems as analogies to whatever art my brain may harbor in store. The great architects today seem determined to show themselves off as sculptors by shunning display of the right angles that hold them off the ground and in their chambers, essential to their profession on drawing boards and in the entablature of columns. My Gilgamesh was an Ur-architect of the squared circle as the unwinding gyre on the vertical axis of a thinking man, whereas Egyptians mistook their monuments for ideas.

. . . How to make the most of my present hiatus, with dear friends so curious about ideas in what I am supposed to be made of, but not—thank god—in what I don't yet know about what I next might try to do? For the nonce I'll let them cast me in their masque. However:

. . . God forbid that we should give out a dream
of our own imagination for a pattern of the world.
Francis Bacon

This is not a matter of "natural knowledge". Finn would have laughed it off as "symbullisticism". When I dreamt that I told Tessa—and then did tell her—that I no longer gave a damn when she and the others as usual pretended not to notice that the spring equinox was my birthday, I seemed no longer embarrassed by its local implication of gestation begun in Dionysian Gloucestermas, by all odds the classic presumption of ludicrous bastardy. It took a while for them to understand that it was as if I'd just been liberated from the lingering echo of Mrs Grundy's lingering disapprobation. In those days it was a blot on the copy book for both present and future to ignore the economic demands of any independent connections—if I could be branded in this residually Puritanical colony as oriented to spurious genesis. Now can I actually celebrate Tessa's exposition of my ultimate privacy! To Arthur the king—the only chrematistic of all my benefactors whom I scarcely knew in person (mainly in memory of his short friendship with Father Duncannon), and the least I'd have thought sympathetic with my spurious axiology—I owe my sudden escape from the normal society in which I've been swimming upstream for my minimum standard of living. This annuity will triple my longevity for years ahead doing only what I want to do with my time! Who wouldn't jump for joy— while swearing freewill with self-discipline? Not to worry about the price of everything I'll need to extend second-class travel for suboptimizing experience! God willing, with good health and continued inspiration, all I'll have to lack is women, if not *a* woman! Never mind a *dream* woman! This is a time to re-exfoliate myself, not just my ideas, opening my maturity (for all it may be worth) to psychological histrionics. I'll risk getting half as curious about myself as my surviving friends are. Though worth it for some comedy, I still hold that "Know thyself" is degrading. Let Coleridge—as clergyman, not as philosopher—appeal to "the dread watch-tower of man's absolute self".

4. Impresario and Bailiff

Raphael Opsimath has no such sensitivity. Appointed by the Magistrate Gabriel at the request of his instigating wife, he finds his assignment as just the kind of interesting occupation to segue from private enterprise to rapidly concentrated community development as convenient means of reacquaintance with the Ort an sich, from which he had been diverted for years by his practically semi-isolated preoccupations outside the city's center to its great economic benefit only indirectly, known hardly at all to the present public by name, still less by sight. He'd been sparing his wife most of the relevant preoccupations she is now about to release at the sluice-gate of a small dam unknown to hoi polloi and most aristoi.

Voluntarily he's taking on a packet of related tasks with his ascending interest in a newly discovered facet of microtopolitan Dogtown's uniquely shaped diamond among all the mines in his geographic album of North Atlantis, as if recovering his youthful zest for travel as required for business without the slightest personal expense. Thus elsewhere as a recreational traveler he has found many favorable surprises, as well as some of the usual vulgar ones that even this city has not consistently shunned; but this possible intimacy with select personnel is worth harmless exploration in the tiny dimensions of his own geodesy.

Rafe's immediately ensuing explorations, however, aim primarily for fantastic form that must be caused by quotidian function: viz, he must rent for a few days at least either a small sound-absorbing "function room" with a stage or "private theatrical space" of some kind, available at all hours. The interior space and external situation were to be considered for aesthetic or physical comfort only in the unlikely event of finding more than one offer of functional satisfaction. He insists that money is a minor factor in the decision, seeing that he will not divulge the comparative costs until after the project's undisclosed "executive committee" approves the final selection, since he reserves for himself the honor of paying the bill, whatever it can reasonably be.

Though a distinguished figure on the Chamber of Commercials' roster he has been forgiven his absence for many more than once (save more than one or two appearances at annual meetings when everyone expects his strategic or financial opinions), just as he is tacitly excused because of his business from the Round Table's

monthly convocations of the whole. Thus, due to the previously
patterned scarcity of his civic appearances, he is now rather practiced—by all manner of means, such as evasively alluding to major
plans for global travel with his wife—in avoiding the socially
attractive mention of "retirement" and its typical predication of
genial conversation in a man's search for something to do with his
time, if not in golfing or sailboat racing, especially for certain kinds
of honorific charity. To the contrary, right now, he's ready to walk
the streets and alleys as a scout, stranger (by sight) to almost everyone downtown, dressed unexceptionally, sometimes like one returning in a daze from years within a distant military hospital—not
quite in disguise until he chooses a door to knock on.

 As if that were actually the case, he couldn't have been more
astonished than he is at the challenges to his memory of the earlier
city when as a Cornucopian he was a correspondent-course student
of Charlemagne, who then represented White Quarry College in
Montvert. After only two days of much walking, climbing stairs,
and some prudential inquiries by telephone from Tessa's office—
looking much, listening more, riding on wheels hardly at all except
to get back and forth across the Gut drawbridge between his
remote hilltop home and one of the downtown parking lots—thus
always on or near the inner waterfront, from the Windmill building at the outer harbor's demarcating landmark near the end of the
Esplanade, along the inner harbor's thickly used or settled water's
edge, over the foot of Joint Hill and Wye Square, past Apostle's
Dock on the eastern inner shore of Argo Cove. He was sorry he
hadn't the time to extend his walk to the neighborhood end of the
cove where he had once lived alone with his barrel of rolled-up
maps and geodetic charts. Anyway he knew it was still too late in
the season for shuttered restaurants conceivably available for the
kind of arrangements he might have envisioned. His beloved Starboard Gangway was far too cramped and rickety.

 After all, its opposite number, at the other end of this great
curve, out of sight and unavailable, the Windmill, abutting a
narrow shingled beach above a concrete-patched granite seawall,
would have been quite suitable for his present purpose, internally
spacious enough for all sorts of movable seats and other furniture
for scenery if it hadn't recently been turned into a great gleaming
white clapboarded barn of glazed office spaces and conference
rooms, a polished hardwood dance floor and two or three "formal"
dining rooms with magnificent views of the outer harbor, repellant

by its new external ostentation and internal decor, all of which declared a general aura meant for sales meetings or the commercial equivalents of a high school prom. But he was looking for the arrow to his bowstring.

Between these two notches of his nostalgic bow, as he told Tessa, he was pleasantly surprised to discover several interesting modern brick buildings at which to aim inquiries, as well as half a dozen restaurants in clear and sturdy structures of unweatherbeaten wood on or near Front Street, if only to empty his quiver with personal curiosities or ingeniously possible purposes less peculiar than the one he now pursues. A few of the available spaces on upper floors of business buildings—such as the former quarters of the *DT Daily Nous* and its press, the large room of a former dance studio above it, or various empty spaces in forlorn locations above the city's spinal street—seemed to him exact satisfactions of nonexistent demands, tempting to rent for oneself as a diurnal den for appointments or downtown storage or dressing room, never to sublet but perhaps to occupy as a place for reading or telephoning while waiting for his wife in her nearby office with a client. It was pleasant to look down at Dogtown's oldest and narrowest street for shopping, eating, and drinking.

At last, following a train of vague or merely suggestive replies to his vague or merely suggestive questions, he was directed to the manager and daytime bartender at the Triage Tavern, in the city's oldest brick structure (survivor of the street's great 19C fire), right at the pentagonal conjunction of vehicular pavements known as Sacrum Square, stemmed or stopped where Cod Street begins in an abrupt hump on what Hecuba calls its circumcision of the island. He had a long lunch close to the bar of the Triage on the ground level of Front Street, after which he followed the manager outside and up a flight of outdoor granite steps to the main floor door that conducts patrons or tenants up an indoor wooden staircase to the dimmed branches of a stoutly timbered third floor.

In two hours of aroused ideas he negotiated a whole month's rent, with an option for longer leasing, simply because it was (besides its suite of necessary rooms and separated functions) a tiny experimental theater that had been going to waste for lack of the current public's enthusiasm for unprofitable histrionics, good, bad, or indifferent. He knew this discovery would resuscitate his wife's dramaturgical senses, which over the years had several times been disappointed either by socially anti-theatrical circumstances or by

the faithlessness of amateur mummers, not to mention the absence
of financial facilities, especially after Charlemagne had eviscerated
by fire the granite walls of her Stone Barn theater.

—But will she kiss him for this successful service—at his own
personal expense? Or will it just revive bitter memories of the
waste of leadership in the one art within her reach? (Her sister Cora
is now a senior choreographer in the arts of Ur.) Or would she
cheerfully accept as amusement the architectural morphology from
Little Theater and Lecture Room to an exercise of Private Law? He
whistled on the way home, instead of turning on the car radio to
hear the dismal news from Raygun's Washington.

The landlord had promised to have the high-ceilinged chamber,
its green room, and its ancillary spaces thoroughly cleaned and
refreshed within the week. He'd also assured Rafe that the legal
premises included emergency exits, as well as the suite's separate
entrance lobby with a tiny anteroom opposite the main entrance
similar to the functions of a box office for the theater above. There
would be up to six keys at his disposal for use at any time, though
necessarily according to his regular or irregular permit, tacit or
enunciated, by Police, Fire, and Building inspectors (who'd naturally have the right of both moral and legal verification of the
owner's guaranteed prepaid contract, whether or not notified by the
tenant). However, with a smile, Rafe was warned of the certainty
that traffic for entrances and exits was bound to be noticed on the
city's most publicly used pavements, day or night, on foot or
wheels, even when the streets are nearest their irreducible activity,
when the city expresses its alert life only in the rhythmic pulsations
of waterfront sounds. In other words, any irregular internal proceedings with so much as irregularly lighted windows, or irregular
passages of human beings, would draw remarkable attention—with
or without police objections.

Anyway, thinks Rafael Opsimath, recklessly disregarding other
possible usages at his disposal in the weeks ahead, the accommodations would come in handy for highly specialized lectures or poetry
readings! The capacity of the little theater, at best, was about right
for something or other. No need for microphones. No squeals. No
echoes. Cozy. Yet easy therein to move platforms and seats. All
kinds of staging equipment were at his disposal from rack and
stacks abandoned in the storeroom. Lighting equipment too. Distances quite suitable for personal photography or stage whispers!

. . . It's a bargain if you ask me! Call me Lorenzo de Facto, impresario and manager of an Atlantean idea we can call a masque for the court of our Eleanor from Unabridge, open to untold thoughts, though unempowered and unrecognized in advance for the space time and causality of unforeseen nightmares! —Though, come to think of it, I'm told the judge's daughter is now coming from Aquitaine to stay with her at least through Christmastide. That mortal must have inherited enough of her parents' culture to help me translate my dictionary of law into cultivated locutions that are really nobody's business but Caleb's. Her Majesty must lead a new kind of anthropology for our courtroom.

—Tessy always anticipates my needs, if not all my wishes. She knows I like suspended surprises if they're harmless. But will my ignorance of what she and Fay actually have in mind for filling that spectral forum of mine help or hinder my preparations? If not, it serves them right for keeping me in the dark about their expectations. Yet it's fun not to know in advance what may be exciting when I'm called upon to signal any syllable of protocol as a stage manager. And as the gentle Queen Fay's supervisor of ritual I hope I won't be opened to ridicule by bearing a shepherd's staff! . . . Is this just the beginning of dramaturgy for a few days of Tessa's Mid-quarter's Night confusion?

5. Natural Law

. . . time is . . . time was . . . time is past
ROBERT GREENE

"Listen, my child," says Fay to her daughter as they clean up the kitchen after dinner together, "this job I'm drafted into by my friends has nothing to do with 'rith and mitual', as our friend Hecuba had it when referring to my awesome profession of 'anthroology'. Perhaps nowadays there's a taxonomy of law courts to specify the ironic masques of Comus. I'll tell you more about it tomorrow. Meanwhile look upon this contretemps as Tessa Opsimath's thought-experiment in the category of 'dromenological' jurisprudence!"

They are preparing to relax in the living room with dainty comestibles that Thalia has brought with celebratory wine, after

doing a week's worth of shopping with her own car on her first day
home—if once more it may be nostalgically called home while
making up her mind about the next one. With most of her personal
effects she has driven alone across the country from Hume to see
her mother—from sea to shining sea—for the first time in Dogtown since before the family's summer house of her childhood had
been renovated for all-year-round retirement of the intense scholar
who had always loved her children but spared them the vulgar sentimentality of inessential propinquity. There is now no brother in
Atlantis, for he and two grandchildren live wherever the United
Nations sends them (so far) in Europe.

Fay guesses easily enough that Thalia Morgan is tactfully waiting to hear about the late Finn Macdane, of whom she'd heard little
more than his name. For once she is prepared to talk about him as
if with a daughter already familiar in her past. Fayaway Gabriel,
the mother, was a legal Morgan too, by marriage and profession,
before resorting to her maiden name mainly to avoid unwelcome
communications, which are the bane of an old well-known scholar
still full of unpublished ideas, in the struggle against normal
dementia with fresh ideas, and trying before it's too late to make up
for the child-demanding time lost in deference to her late husband's
academic career, as well as to the happiness of children that she'd
carefully wished before she'd become fully aware of her own intellectual potentiality, yet without a qualm as to the eventual advantage of maternal experience for any anthropologist—even as a
philosopher—whether or not she or her two grandchildren overseas
would ever live to see her name recognized for its worth by the
deepest of philosophical thinkers in more than a single department.

Yet as Fay's own two children had grown more than normally
independent of her personal attention she'd eased her conscience
about how much less time she'd devoted to ordinary maternity than
the best of good mothers do, self-driven as she was to compress
time for her studies and teaching as well as her external duties, first
as a nurse while her husband was busy getting his advanced degrees
(commuting from Dogtown to Unabridge) and then as a double-
duty housewife determined to make up for that initial handicap in
education for the learning and skills of postgraduate research and
teaching—until the two kids precociously cooperated with both
mother and father to leave home with undiminished love, independent in all but expenses and gifts. There was little sense of
rebellion or deprivation on anyone's part in the fairly steady but

well-anchored evacuation of the childhood nests except for many of their easily accessible possessions. Communications were usually happy at both ends of the line even after the parental divorce. Both children appreciated their head starts in common schooling, and they were grateful for their self-confidence as first the girl then the boy matured among educated peers and advanced into self-education. They thought of Caleb as a sort of distant second cousin whom they'd never met in infancy as their mother's godson.

But Fay's lingering sense of maternal parsimony still constrains exuberant expression of what might be called the normal feelings of a girl-child—even about facts—now a grownup self-reliant woman assumed to be of broader experience than herself. Hitherto the mother is old enough to have twinges of conscience about her limited knowledge of her distant son's progeny. She hardly expects a reciprocating affection with the grandchildren whom she vaguely hopes to meet once more before she dies—before she's finished her last book—having more or less evaded opportunities to become mutual admirers from overseas. Any possible teenage discord that might have stemmed from the father's attitude toward the mother, or the mother's attitude toward the father, would have evaporated and long since been forgotten.

Yet now in this Dogtown reunion, Thalia is satisfied with the latest news of her own "little brother", who still called her "Lia". More than he she had responded earnestly to most of the trivium and quadrivium of the seven liberal arts in Unabridged public education, before and after picture books or abridged editions with outgrown cartoons of fairytale adventures and random legends from international mythology—geography, history, and comparative religion encouraging spontaneity of critical response; but both had developed sensible imagination of the good and the bad as they often gathered at the mother's hearth for the pleasure of books and maps that were unimaginable at school, usually while the head of the family was teaching Greek nearby in the Garth. The boy and girl, Thalia and Oliver, only thirteen months apart in naming, learned or absorbed in simple or paraphrased English much of what the mother offered, which was chosen and sometimes rehearsed at various levels of the animal kingdom. Kipling's contributions led them all—assimilated as deeply as the Lord's Prayer in Sunday School.

However, for a few years later than her son such evanescent home-schooling as the *Jungle Books* when read aloud for pleasure was of special interest to her daughter in the "sea-born" *Lusiads,* as presented in various English redactions. This epic served as a referential core for all sorts of edification and cerebral games in occasional family huddles, especially for winter conversation and charades, the holiday time of year for recreational respite from official teaching and learning. Fay's literary affection for the quaint nationalism of the "old country" (in the modern perspective of competitive imperialism), told in steady quiet tones, inviting intelligent interruptions of her exegesis or opinion—sometimes offering evaluations as models for their own elsewhere in the narrative—led both girl and boy (severally) to think about the general human comedy and its struggles from west to east more than half way across the world's longitudes (and back again) with astonishing bravery in the service of greedy kings, as traced on maps of conjecture amazingly verified by patient hardship above and below the equator. In these little seminars the two pupils learned to respect the Lusitanian part of their blood with names and stories about as fictitious as those in fairy tales.

As if anticipating Wellingborough Redburn and Jack Chase in the future readings of her most cherished pupils, but without warning of her namesake in forthcoming allusions, Ma-mai had imparted to her incunabula a complex imagery of Camoens himself as a poetic hero in a geography and history more truthful than Vasco da Gama's in his own foreign language. At least Lia, for one, subconsciously absorbed tolerance for the idea of a quasi-autobiographical kind of fiction as dreamed up by an author from unsavory facts! She'd never tried, with young Olly at her side, to make unwanted distinctions between reports and real adventures.

Even in those early days, the mother herself took care not to praise the Lusitanian epic as a work of the highest literary—still less as history—art compared to Greek or Roman antecedents whom he'd soon enough encounter as a properly educated student when he got to the Classics that dominated this family's culture. Later, with unemphatic smiles, Fay would occasionally observe that nowadays this rambling derivative of Classics and neo-Classics, ingrained with Mediterranean romances, was revered by nobody but nostalgic Loosies like herself. Yet it would help children break the ice when they got to history and geography classes in school. Meanwhile they were free to ask about anything in the facts of life or fictions, relevant or not, especially when funny or otherwise relating to extraneous myths less respectfully than those of Sunday School.

Thus, for example, her children's inoculation with the serum of critical thinking, as she reminded them all along in the progressive part of their outside schooling. To Thalia she had often mentioned as critical in her own torch of enlightenment the name of her unfortunate old friend Mary Tremont who never got to college.

Adam Morgan the renowned Classics professor, who'd never gotten along very well with Mary during his wife's very brief overlap of their lives in Dogtown, had not minded that his kids were getting acquainted with the epic genre in chronological and pedagogical order reversed, along with their early exposure to the undisciplined readings of modern Geisteswissenschaften in English. After all, as he'd teased his wife at the family dinner table, far better Loosey tales than Holyrood and DV dramas, even if the hearthside readings were about magically overblown exploration for the greed of bloody imperialism, or harmless episodes of modern romance from the songs of a seagoing poet who's a sardonic critic of his own unrewarded enthusiasm for Lusitania's glory under a God supernaturally more powerful than the divinities of Moslems, Hindus, or savages! Better practice literary criticism than mangle ancient alphabets! At least for getting to know India's, it's one step better than absurd Kipling stories! Yes, he told them, I grant that Camoens also prepares young minds for the likes of Robert Greene in England, along with Campion's horrors!

Thalia remembers that Fay had stood her ground with good humor. The girl never doubted that the mother knew better than the sardonic father how to plant and multiply a child's—at least a girl-child's—inchoate thoughts as descriptions of feelings that would lead to the understandable expression of her own chosen pursuits without unnecessary distress at ignorance of what she'll be as a woman. At the hearth her full admiration of the father she always loved was yet to come, when she'd enter the factual education outside, both before and after her teenage stint at odds with the father's wife, following which, at college and beyond, she appreciated that person—now clicking wineglasses with her—more than anyone else in the world. But having paused without plans at this undirected plateau in her mainly uninterrupted emotional independence as successful in her solitary career, she's silently reviewing her particular gratitude for the early benefit of her vicarious experience from books that prepared her fairly easily to choose or expand, if not to miss, a happy childless life at middle age, all disappointments softened from grade school on. Again, Thalia thanks her mother for thereby vaccinating herself and Olly (as far as she knows) against Platonic neurosis or fear of dreams. She remarks to her mother with a laugh that just the other day she was reminded of her sensible kind of childhood by reading that historians had until recently suppressed as unmentionable the fact that the cleanly Atlindu natives in Parthenia suffered from the characteristic *stink* of "civilized" English colonists, from never bathing—gentlemen, artisans, and indentured toilers alike! Now in the cognitive flash of association it brought to mind from childhood the memories of red bricks and fire screen where her Ma-mai was willing to converse about anything years ahead in physiological stages, perhaps especially when her brother Oliver happened not to be present! How times have changed!

Yet it's only the next morning at breakfast that the daughter finally broached her one urgent curiosity: the whole story of her mother's natural but uncharacteristic reticence about her recent sudden gain and catastrophic loss of an elderly lover—which collaterally led to the strangely questionable story of private dramaturgy meant to settle by law a local mystery! The daughter was of course invited to judge the judge's judgment, at least for fun. Fay smiled but Thalia laughed at the prospect of her mother playing the presiding role at a Court of Love! Not the kind of diversion one would expect in the midst of her struggle to complete a very long swan song with the energy of youth!

The mother had pledged only a weekend from her immense work, but she secretly began to justify the foolishness by luring her daughter to settle at what would become her proper home. Fay didn't try very hard to hide her all-too-human hope that Thalia as a godsend would participate as a spectator in such pastimes at least as a sojourner until after Christmas. Even thereafter Lia might have nothing else in mind, and might be inveigled, as if incidentally charmed by Dogtown's motley charms, to settle nearby in a house of her own.

Considering family history, Fay believed that her daughter could not be crassly bribed into stagnation. But she herself was patently aging in anticipation of the wish for casual supervision by compatible minds. It was not lost on this intellectually preoccupied mother, so sensitive to the speed of intelligent mortality, that (as Camoens wrote, according to Finn) "fear treads hard on the heels of hope". Fay and Finn had both been tacitly aware that, though living together in Fay's roomy house would save combined expense, it would not save time for them individually unless they confined their cooperative organization and schedules to the irritations of eating and cleaning—to the nearly impossible coordination of time's two extraordinary freewills with plenty of things to do as they each listened for the narrowing of a pendulum in a separate pit. That would have been quite a different matter from the comparatively simple cohabitation of a mother and daughter who'd almost never been at odds, and with only one of them under absolute pressure from fatherless time.

Fay has increasingly irritable objections to the time demanded by A D L [Activities of Daily Living], the domestic, commercial, social, and medical interstices of her solitude in reading and writing toward the end of an inevitably truncated physique, hardly recovered from the shocking reversal of her contented happiness in only two years with the love of Finn—this twist of fate had already begun by age to retard the cognitive efficiency of the preciously counterentropic axons of both the acquisition and use of memory that's usually expected late in life. She's become increasingly dependent upon her immediately available books and prescient notes. She by no means despises the wisest of diets and exercises, but like all the other A D L they swallow impatient hours of the functional longevity for sticking to her last. She says to herself that she's never before been so sensitive to the fourth dimension that Caleb so glibly commensurates with space and causality. Thus even the ambient presence of Thalia would abate the wish for a new cat, with its reciprocating A D L attention. She doesn't know or ask Thalia's income except that it's ample for wants as well as independent needs, which no doubt demand freedom for opportunity and travel. She would gladly allow her daughter that much freedom—if only the old girl anchored her baggage here at home! So with quiet smiles Fay plans to lecture her visitor daughter that for any undetermined outcomes there are numberless efficient causes, material causes, formal causes, and final causes for all sorts of living.

Meanwhile she leads the subject to what she knows Thalia has primarily come to visit for: information about an apparently self-sufficient mother's private life, not to take upon herself the care of her spry future. "I'll tell you all you want to know about Finn. There's never been his equal as an Atlantean gentleman of the world. He was always surprising me with his knowledge and intelligence. He even helped me with Greek and Latin and German! I'd known him a very short time to call it love, but that's what it was, at first or second consideration. He was both engineer and common reader—in fact, far more than common! Also very kind and generous.

"Of course after he gave up his life I was nearly incredulous when Mr Krebs announced that Finn had left me his office building downtown. Not that I ever wanted any property or business to worry about: so I'm looking for a manager. But it's worth a lot, with no mortgage strings attached, and it gives me additional income for all the A D L help I can find without more time than it's worth to teach. If I don't sell it, you and Olly of course will eventually have to deal with the whole business. I may buy a safer car and make some more improvements in the house. I may ask you and Mr Krebs to invest some for me. Anyway I'll give you power of attorney. I don't want to keep thinking about money. I'll have enough to travel first-class—if after or when I finish this endless book, which I could keep expanding and improving ad infinitum without being a perfectionist!"

"Ma-mai, I know what that's like! But no one believes it of your other books already!"

"I don't want to waste another minute learning about business." Fay continued. "What do you think? I wish one could buy time! I had hoped that Finn would do this sort of thing for my estate! He was an unofficial architect of many things besides battleships! —That reminds me: tomorrow I'll show you the wonderful penthouse he made for himself above all the rented offices. I'm saving it for you to try out for as long as you like, especially for the view, if you don't mind the daytime noise of downtown traffic. It would make a good studio for anything at all. It would be safe for the rooftop of a curious cat, over the harbor and next to the new Police Station!"

"Okay Ma-mai, let me think awhile. But even when I was pinching your obols in Athens I loved the mother I was blessed with for her infinitely more important attention to what I was learning as her spoiled brat!"

6. Prosecutor

Tessa the amateur fictioneering professional dreamer is privately licking her lips with glee even as she reminds herself that pride goeth before a fall. But Caleb as appellant-by-writ is the dependent variable in her problematic cinema. Yet now that she has Fay's reluctant acquiescence as an honorable godmother—nearly to the point of recusing herself for conflict of interest as presiding magistrate—Tessa secretly shares a similar scruple as the master-minding prosecutor about to draft rules for a moot court in case she fails one or more quantum meruits for an unprecedented masque.

Lately she and Caleb have been on exceptionally good terms—partly because she saw so little of him while he was, in her opinion, horribly possessed with what she called his thankless public service job in the Hall. Meanwhile, she knew, he still had every reason to remain annoyed at what seemed her intrusive interest in his life. This curiosity had long ago begun in her brief role as his kindly overweening voice-therapist, simply owing to the fact that she was his senior and they happened to find friends in common. Indeed he'd once worked for her second husband Rafe, having been befriended by Buck Barebones her first. Later more than once he was stifled with anger by what seemed to him her presumptuous interest in his origin—which was now at last to be actively infused with the history of his life that she was definitely trying to explain on a level of frankness that he'd hitherto dodged. But at this point they both have become fascinated by the categorical uncertainties of a court in theatrical mode without which neither can rest without at least a semblance of thought-experiments performed in four dimensions, if not five. At present she knows no more than he about obscuranted *commedia erudita* in the brain of Michael our Archangel.

But at her daytime office desk, awaiting an uninteresting client (charged in this case to a Public Welfare account) as she struggles to banish Platonic dreams for the nonce, Tessa starts an Aristotelian checklist of common or proper nouns, and underlined verbs espe-cially, to remind her of the facts she and her husband must attend to, very soon, in the real world of fiction. These words engender separate slips of paper, eventually numerous almost to despair of ever getting read. Saved only by her doorbell, she laughs at the shrinking leeway for absurdity in her weird theatrical miscegena-tion of Fay's anthropological genres—or at least Caleb's. Not to mention her preparation of briefs with absurd resources. Aside from the challenge of initiatives brought upon herself, against all her real psychology, how can she organize and promote a production of uncertain objective?

For a one and only stage performance two nights long, without a script to go by!

It's getting so that I don't always know what world I'm in! —*Better than itemizing what's still amorphous in four dimensions, I should spend my putative free time by going to the bank safe-deposit vault and reading through all the post-1960 diaries that may be relevant to the case I'm supposed to be the prosecutor of,* right now—*and all the more so when Rafe must never know of the diaries' existence! If I'm seen at that bank I'll have to let it be known that I'm renewing in all sorts of ways my B U academic work for a Doctor's degree, which I'd actually almost forgotten about. Do fictions ever lead to truth?*

Meanwhile I'll encourage my ingenuously astute husband to list the necessaries, and as major domo to participate in provision or management thereof. He's already fascinated by the novelty of keeping himself in suspense about what I'm up to. He's not one to look for pastime on a golf course, or in any competitive series of spectator sport more than minimally required to keep up a conversation. Once we know more of the virtual particulars he'll be excellent at recruiting spectators and substitutes, impaneling a shadow of jurors, furnishing props, keeping order, scheduling the use of borrowed facilities, purveying refreshments, dealing well and ill with the landlord, handling anti-public relations in general and the DT Nous's negative cooperation in suppressing our news (as long as he and Belle don't collaborate too much with each other!), though I have sworn her to general secrecy as one of the mummers to be coached in person. But if Rafe doesn't or can't befriend the police she can at least promise not to print a notice of our delitescence that might be maliciously interpreted on the blotter as gross immorality or witchcraft in the suspicious third-floor chamber of an underground Resistance by invitation only. . . .

But the native surname Opsimath is not for nothing as an onomastic impressario—else I wouldn't have married him! He can size up things heard in the real world better than anyone else. And I think Gretta Doloroso will gladly help in any way. She's a granary of local intelligence, professional or demotic, and of course a veteran of solemn law courts. My canny cranium may be psychologically deeper than Rafe's like half a decorticated walnut, but it's too specialized. I can trust Gretta as my paid private secretary at DT M & D not to let my left hand be visible to my right, yet even her I can't let in on my big personal safe-deposit box in my other bank. Of course I don't doubt her oath of confidentiality to Krebs as far as our normal privacy is concerned. After all, in this case even he doesn't yet know that either of them will be called under subpoena! They'll have to make up more than they've seen fit to reveal about secret local history.

But of course the crucial question is whether or not Endicott will be willing to show his face at all in our company—to say nothing of letting me draft him as an expert witness for fragments of the fiction that still are missing in my story. He's a wise man. At the very least I'll consult him as a recusant friend. As far as categories of dromena are concerned, court martial is one kind of tribunal that we definitely exclude. Not so with pageants and tableau. . . .

But no matter what turns up in the drifting fog of dreams, an initial scenario is for me to set forth. I might first pique my mummers by hinting at this delicate question: How much, if anything, did Finn tell Fay about his Dogtown visit during the Great Gloucestermas of 1934?

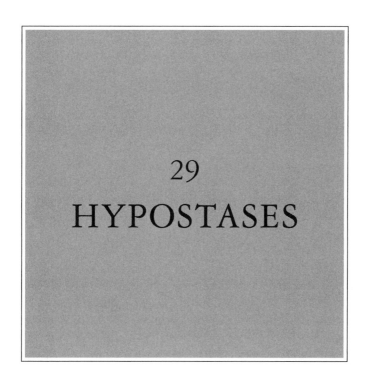

29
HYPOSTASES

You have often
Begun to tell me what I am; but stopp'd
And left me to a bootless inquisition,
Concluding, 'Stay! Not yet!'

THE TEMPEST

1. Caleb Musing in His Bed after the First Day of the Court

They seem to think that this is a dream of Virgineola the Isle of
Devils! Or of God knows how many other fabulous cases, like Ion's
at Delphi! On the other hand, this *is* an island, and fictional questions *do* arise! If it weren't for that I'd just let the cases drop as
uninteresting. Dogtown has always been peculiar, never commonplace, even as a representative of everything one can think about.
That's why Fay, by common consent, was drafted to be the judge in
our court. My sainted mother, the only comprehensive witness,
would have been an emotional misfit for that job—very hard to
concoct even for science fiction! That thought makes me wonder if

793

it was a mistake to let the thought-experiment get beyond mere
merrymaking about an ordinary by-blow in a simple unsolved set
of simultaneous equations, no different from millions of others that
don't get chalked up on a docket—if it weren't for the peculiarity
of the lady established as the vital coefficient, half of whom she and
I have answered to! Sometimes when she was mad at me—or
laughing at me—she called me Caliban.

Fay was generous and prudent to insist upon extending the trial
to more than one day. Rafe hopes it will be only two. But it took all
of the first day for Tessa to boil it down from a suggestion of seven
"suitors" to the plausibly synchronous three, considering the date
certain. I'm amazed at the volume of evidence (or clues a k a reasonable conjectures) that as prosecutor she has amassed, having cultivated the friendship of Gretta for testimony as the single living
soul of relevance in 1934, according to the advice of Gloria, the
expert in municipal as well as historical archives. I must admire
Tessa's annoying persistence in bringing my origin out into the
open among friends. Within limits, it provides me with an excuse
for half my flaws! Much as she's irritated me at times, I can't help
believing that she loves me almost as a little brother, not to mention her original intention to model me as a fictional case history in
psychology. But there were few questions from the jury. Even our
dear judge didn't have much to say in enquiry about what Tessa
had thoroughly disarmed in anticipation, though of course the
elder has been no stranger to Tessa's detective work on me over the
years as putative fact, not fiction! But I won't be surprised if as
prosecutor Tessa springs something newly old on me, before final
deliberations, as accessory after the fact.

As far as the immediate aftermath of 3-21-35 is concerned, the
records—official and unofficial—have not been in dispute: birth
certificate in the City Clerk's custody: mother's name Mary
Tremont (formerly altered from Moira Trevisa; given name Caleb
(deliberately from the Bible); surname poetically imagined by the
mother believing it to echo the occult tradition whence Villiers de
L'Isle-Adam invented the *Axël* in his romantic German castle. Soon
afterwards, for God's sake, a certificate of baptism (corroborated by
ecclesiastical archives) was signed by Father Pole (founder of the
Tudor Order of Saint Agatha in Unabridge) at the former Convent
of Saint Martha here in Dogtown out on Crow Point! Attending
that long-deferred and uninflated ceremony at the baptistry of the
chapel (after Sunday Eucharist, I think) the only registered witness

was the godmother, one Fayaway Morgan, herself not quite yet a young mother, an obstetric witness of my birth.

But of course in this crazy Court of Love I'm not sure who could be defined as either defendant or plaintiff. In a certain sense I suppose that's the main purpose of the whole trial itself. There certainly doesn't seem to be any living criminal or victim—unless it's myself. Nor any complaint, nor any claim—unless it's the absence of an attorney for all women! The latter I positively deny a need for. No one speaks of rape or deception. I consider myself the nominal protagonist of this Chapman saga—at least in whatever life is ahead of me in print before he dies. You must look to readers for proper uncertainties—if you disregard the demented segment of Moira's vigorous faith in existence long after the era of her suicidal emotion. Anyway, she's the star of whatever heroism there may be in my Karcisistic genre.

Then what about the three sainted Wise Men after turning around their camels? Unless it was the trump of simple superfetation, there must have been a dizzy dance of two or three homosexual admixtures around the cervix, either vying with each other or fusing as a single fluid headed for the egg, which was the only biological fact we can be sure of. We can't even surmise parthenogenesis because if we rely upon the norms of gestation, and upon precircumstantial evidence, Moira could not have been called a virgin. Thus I, certainly her son, am inclined to look for the *uniquely* coefficient cause that's neither material nor formal nor efficient nor final for my synthetic existence. However, tomorrow's trial is intended to determine something missing from *evolutionary* biology.

So unless forensic *bio*chemistry is further advanced and retroactively applied to some imaginary imprint of the established date in question more than half a century ago—considering that all suspects are now dead and inaccessible as sampled remains—the various hypotheses are fairly clear. Whatever the initial etiology, I feel like the centrifugal vector of my mother's whirl on the Isle of Man—or else the lucky Ion of Delphi, who's spared the true knowledge of himself! In any case, for my purposes, a mortal female was my superior parent. Truth to tell, my interest in this trial boils down to amusing curiosity. After that is satisfied for naught I'll content myself with the wisdom shouted by the tough kids when we lived on Astronomy Hill, when they saw me coming and going to or from the little storefront branch of the Unabridge Public Library with books: "The best part of you ran down your mother's leg!"

I'll consider myself well enough served by any finding of the court's first day, summarized as follows. I contributed to the Court's colloquies about matters of ignorance and legal fiction from my unique vantage as what some have referred to as the frustrating outcome, others as the "biological beneficiary", as well as excused "expert-witness-once-removed".

X. The Late Arthur Halymboyd

For most commentators he turned out to be the prime suspect, seeing that he was shown to have been my mother's lover for a couple of years before he happened to have been obliged to leave on a clandestine mission to Europe as legal agent of the Arnheim family in its foresighted rescue operations for German Jews; that by chance the date of his early morning departure from Dogtown was that of Gloucestermas Day 1934, shortly before Finn Macdane and Lancelot Duncannon happened to appear in Moira Trevisa's presence, seriatim, on the same longest day of the year; and that, though unknown to the court, he has recently been to me the donor of an annuity that will nearly free me of occupations antithetical to Creative Mind.

The Prosecutor and her so-called witnesses drew attention to the probability that he and she sincerely loved each other but had spent their last night together in mutual erotic passion as their hardly unexpected valedictory separation, at her unsurprising insistence—with his painful reluctance—apparently because of his firm aversion to procreation, even without marriage. He apparently understood (without sympathy) her long-deferred determination at the age of thirty to have two sons and a daughter on almost any terms with someone she could admire enough to love for a lifetime. Despite the promise of F D R's salvaging election, the Great Depression and rise of Hitler justified many such ambivalent partings among the professions: she was an artist; he was a graduate of both the Norumbega schools, Law and Business, who was lucky to be employed by an international family for a humane cause perhaps more important than any other in their concern for future civilization. In his private life thereafter, according to Tessa, he remembered Moira as the least selfish love of his life.

Twenty-five years later, when she would have been fifty-five and he about sixty, they couldn't have lived more different lives in the same hemisphere, or perhaps have had less knowledge of each other's present existence. Indeed they never met again. In our times she was, among many less altruistic workers, a resident scullery-maid postulant-member of a self-sustaining commune established by the Brotherhood of the Peaceable Kingdom, surrounded by the green mansions near the headwater divide between Hispanic and Lusitanian South Atlantis, in the northern reach of Amazonia—while he was a rather idiosyncratic magnate of an industrial conglomerate built of controlling stock gradually acquired when undervalued as solitary investments hardly suspected by traders for anything but random speculation on Graveyard Street or Smart Avenue in New Uruk according to the market's behavior. His final industrial holding, Parity Corp, just before his retirement, had grown to professional fame, at a very lucrative time for selling out to a very large company, which spun off various smaller firms, one of which one happened to own the little one that ended up in the hands of Rafe Opsimath here in Dogtown.

Halymboyd had sometimes been an object of suspicion by lawyers of the Security and Exchange Commission for technically ingenious trading in his unorthodox financial means to integrate his functional investments; but (as far as I ever wanted to know) his movements were not to the discredit of contemporary leveraged capitalism. Even more than his acumen in analyzing and acquiring control of corporations that were worth more than the market's "conventional wisdom", I admired what seemed to be his grasp of unprecedented relationships between independent firms from a managerial point of view (as opposed to quarterly or annual appeasement of stockholders, including himself). At arm's length this captain of industry seemed to me more interested in the *Ding an sich* of a little empire of cooperatively intercommercial manufacturers or the like—as was I, who had no investments at all, and very little ecclesiastical salary! But finance and industry have much changed since then, and I'm sure they're about to change even faster as the country's industrial economy yields ambagiously to the sophistications of usury and electronics. At his peak, that man, as king, was alone on one end of a seesaw with his foot on the ground, riding in the air a very complex gang of disparate businessmen.

Of course, as an inexperienced and untutored analyst who actually *decided* none of the investments made by the Father Economist for the Laboratory of Melchizedek and the Mesocosm, which paid my salary, I was emotionally intrigued by the corporate seal of Halymboyd's Parity Corporation (PAR as listed on the tickertape), an Atlantean bannerstone that resembled a double-bitted axe, the *labys* of Halymboyd's corporate labyrinth. "A symbol is as a symbol does." I said. The whole court laughed.

In truth, I still believe, Arthur was less interested in making money for himself than in his power to gather an almost organic party of specialized manufacturers worth on the market far more by leverage than by his personal equity—a prime mover I sometimes imagine as the inverse of mechanical advantage in physics. When I was working for Father Lucey, the Order's Economist, he let me spend a great deal of time investigating Parity's public but obscure records in Ur and Washington. From them I constructed a particolored molecular-looking diagram on a large sheet of folded graph paper. It showed the extremely complex cross-connections of holdings, which included his cooperation with a shadowy financier by the name of Zane Capstick, a "private banker". The diagram, imposed upon the paper's green reticulation of right angles, consisted of severally sized circles linked with each other by straight lines at any feasible angle and labeled with numerical shares or percentages compiled or calculated from multifarious reports of information generally missed by investors or regulators before being filed in nominally public vaults, as of their respective approximate dates, more or less quarterly (but hardly synchronous enough for purposes of arbitrage trading). At first glance it might have been taken as an analogical map of the Roman Empire at the point of Byzantium's schism, especially as Halymboyd and Capstick were still cooperating.

Armed with that schematic map, the Reverend Christopher Lucey—not a grubbing analyst or statistician of the market, but doing well as the Order's investor in his ancillary sideline as the very convenient private Father Economist—was a Registered Representative of Weatherglass, Neatherd & Company. He thus could immediately review (or envision) more about Parity's movements than anyone else outside its innermost executive headquarters on Smart Avenue in N U. This annotated diagram was worth thousands of words! This was made plain even to Arthur himself when he paid his visit to Father Duncannon at the Lab, having been shown my picture of his own web which is what it was! Later, though he'd hardly seen me in person, when I needed a new job I declined his offer of some splendid position at his PAR office; yet he went out of his way to please the two Fathers by using his influence to get me hired at Mercator-Steelyard just when it had begun to realize that it needed someone like me in its Dogtown headquarters. (Previously I had drawn a different kind of chart—as if for choreography—of the Father Founder's creation: his revision of word and action for the sacramental ritual at the altar of his Mass, that is Eucharist, which he called the Anamnesis, and which I, his studious acolyte, learned to assist in his metabolic liturgy of Theodynamics.) We never did learn anything about Arthur's connections with the political powers in Washington, except that he was on the Crat side, and knew more from his wartime intelligence service than many politicians concerned with foreign affairs, as well as S E C regulators.

Whereas, in this fantastic court, with pride or concession (or perhaps with what Fay tells me modern Greeks call *entrope*), I am the one most concerned with the genetic funnel of love's most consequential excited action, I am now entitled to illuminate as much as I wish of the unfinished product—myself—with clues to half my genesis. There's no better time to display my traits than as my part in the collective whirl! It's a matter of justice that this miracular comedy has equalized my mother's three maculations. All three of the attorneys-at-love will have the same apparition, my same character as both subject and object. Think of them as three masked doctors huddled over me in an operating room while awaiting judgment by a bevy of anesthesiologists. I don't want to offer or withhold any psychosomatic evidence in my ether-dream that may bias for or against any of these specialists, none of whom I know to be either Freudian or Alterian by training. As far as psychology is concerned, if I trust anyone it's the Drangian prosecutor herself, as equably chided by our anthropological judge. I am the only one assigned to defend my mother against any possibility, and I do not tolerate the canard that first come's first's serve.

Twenty years ago, in a solitary supererogatory visit from N U City to the Lab as one of Parity's largest stockholders, to warn the Father Superior about some of Father Lucey's strange behavior as a Registered Representative of the Order's shares, the Jewish King Arthur befriended the Tudor Father Superior. No doubt he was needlessly prompted from Graveyard Street to do so because he liked to give free rein to his goodhumored intellectual curiosity about more than money. But of course he'd never forgotten his lengthy sojourns in Dogtown. At first sight, before climbing the granite steps to the Great Hall of the Laboratory, he had played tennis-ball with my great Viking Shepherd dog Ibi-Roy. "Ah-ha,"

he said to the clergyman awaiting that diversion at the door, "This
dog gives a good Return on Investment!"

At second sight, half an hour later, inside the Lab, on that unofficially personable trip in his diplomatic effort to forestall scandal
for the Classic Order of the Vine by nullifying before it was too late
an indiscreet visit by Chris Lucey the Father Economist to himself
at Parity's headquarters, he exceedingly pleased me (as limited
onlooker) with the great man's response to the Father Founder as a
gemütlich gentile sage, formerly a doctoral scientist. I guess that
afterwards Arthur Halymboyd never ceased expanding his odd
interest in such *Dings an sich* after liquidating his banausic holding
company and devoting most of his leisure to pro bono back channels of the unwritten political philosophy of the common good
upon which Atlantean culture depends for its enchorial degree of
moral decency. He'd accepted a copy of Father Duncannon's most
secular book to be read at the level of Judeo-Christianity, though it
was tacitly understood that his vision of epinician capitalism was
rather less regulated than the radical priest's socialistic version of a
"social gospel"!

Yesterday we were told by Attorney Krebs that later, not long
after the death of this secular friend of the late priest (as the last
of Dogtown's long line of Duncannon patrons), he was nearly pen-
niless in personal sacerdotal poverty after the family's residual
legacy had been donated to his Order of the Vine and funded for
its M & M monastic Laboratory (with chapel), eventually to be
lost to Jason Anacoluther's bank after its reluctant foreclosure of a
large mortgage that had been duplicitously hypothecated by his
own devoted Father Economist—rashly speculating far too much
on the initial public offering of a new birth-control stock trade-
marked as Paraclete on the Street—without prior approval by the
Lab's more cautious Trustees. Yet very few local people have ever
heard of Father Lancelot Duncannon, if only as an ecclesiastically
ostracized Tudor priest, still less of Arthur Halymboyd, a silently
philanthropic Jew, whose roots in the Maritime Dominion, and
successful stamping grounds in the world's greatest island-city,
were not on *this* island.

That one time I met Halymboyd, early on, at the lunch with
Father Dun, King Arthur remarked "After all, it was only the accusation of bringing the first Black Plague that started Europeans to
hate us. It was not our Gospel, not our circumcision, not our disingenuous defense of usury, that originally prevented them from

leaving us to our devices." He and Father Duncannon had been discussing the fundamental idea of liturgy as "public works", at least
in ancient Rome.

To my mind, though not to faithful Father Duncannon's Christianity, nor to my brave mother's, faith is not the essence of
religion.

Y. The Late Finn Macdane

I knew the Commander not much more than a year before he
died with my actual double-bitted axe in his hand after saving an
entire crew from drowning. Everyone around here knows the story.
It was mentioned in his New Uruk and Washington obituaries, as
well as in several professional journals. He deserves a Navy biographer. Unfortunately his technical colleagues are almost all dead or
medically incommunicado, and, since he had no siblings and never
married, so are his distant relatives in Markland. Much of his so-
called "diplomatic" work in Germany (before and after his sea duty
in the Pacific) remains officially secret, though I know he happened
to cross intelligence agencies with Arthur Halymboyd's once or
twice in Europe. But in theoretical matters, he and I found much in
common, despite the paucity of my experience. In certain ways, as a
naval architect and electrical engineer, as well as a line officer, his
career lived the dreams of my fatherless boyhood, except for stories,
which before I knew him I had in a certain sense weirdly adum-
brated with my construction of Gilgamesh. Finn was a liberally
learned technocrat who commanded men when required.

And therefore only gently mocking, if not seriously skeptical,
about some of my abstract notions, he took seriously my Synectic
Method of Diagnostic Correlation, and was even considering an
attempt to interest the Navy in using it (with its systematically
existing operating data) to analyze the efficiency of individual ships
as both to design and to its manuals for operation. Each according
to our own vision we were excited by Ludwig von Denthey's Universal Systems Theory, an interdisciplinary approach to applied science (including biology by way of philosophy). Finn was far more
mathematically competent than I am to justify my enthusiasm for
its biological significance. To Finn I also had grateful recourse to
philological questions of Latin or Greek.

On the other hand, though he appreciated military drill and
naval ceremony well enough and had little sympathy with those

who might loudly object to altered meanings of symbolic Eucharistic bread and wine—inculcated by his Tudor origins, only a little
less comfortable with Classic or Byzantine culture in cosmopolitan
experience—to him it was "all just ritual", and therefore harmlessly
comfortable as properly observed. He had no broad interest in the
historically anthropological concept of "dromenology" even after
his dear friend Fayaway began to consider it. Nor except for playful
amusement did he pay any gratifying attention to my symbolic
Isorectotetrahedron except as a mildly interesting stage prop for
choruses. All the rest was classified as "a sort of engineering for
people like Yeats!" But he appreciated what I'd done with my computerized Central Management System at the Yard, and it was he as
a friend of Dexter Keith the Mayor who got me the timely job
against untimely odds in Ibicity Hall, despite my utter lack of
knowledge or experience in municipal government.

This versatile "battleship man" might have been my closest
friend for the rest of my life if he'd lived this long. I admit that I
needed his kind of paternal knowledge. That would have been of
the command-and-control kind. But he hated to kill insects or see
fish gasping for breath. He was said to have been a good horseman,
but he would never have joined fox-hunts when he was a naval
attaché in Britain. He was indelibly sorry for the tram horses on the
Isle of Man, which he'd visited at least once on a weekend liberty in
Liverpool during his first summer's cruise with the Norumbega
R O T C in 1920, which, according to the prosecutor's circumstantial evidence, hitherto withheld from me, seems to have especially
interested Moira Trevisa the first and only time he met her, here on
a long day of the Great Gloucestermas 1934.

Fay introduced me to Finn after his talk at the Lyceum, when
he still had his gray beard and moustache, looking much older than
when I knew him thereafter. Maybe Fay liked him smoother. He
told me privately that it had been a nuisance and didn't belong on
both Morality Square and the waterfront (where he was called Mac).
At the lecture I liked his appearance without giving it a thought.
Almost from the beginning I was fascinated by his presentation,
particularly the diagrams. Besides battleships and schooners he
mentioned or suggested to me dozens of my own parallel interests
in other subjects that had excited me for years without having
anyone with whom to discuss what I read in books. I listened
between his lines—or put words in his mouth.

But after we were better acquainted I found that we were both critics of what passes for "systems analysis" in commerce and industry. At something of a philosophical level, though from rather different perspectives, we were each an intent admirer of von Denthey's Universal Systems Theory at its speculative as well as pragmatic levels. Indeed it would have pleased Alpha Whitehead as an "organistic" philosophy for any science, founded upon the various concepts of closed and homeostatic open systems—essentially indeterministic and anti-reductive. Before its evolution to deductive theory its inductive originators had proceeded from experience and imagination in experimental biology and physics, broadened by insights of Geisteswissenschaften, including, I must believe, certain confirmations in literature and art. Of course it's resisted and mocked by the main bodies of scientists and academics, but I think some of its ideas are unconsciously beginning to infuse such scientific professions as medicine—or any other that literally respects the ancient idea of analogy, the highest of abstractions. But I don't think Finn took me seriously on that proposal as anything much more than one of my metaphysical fancies. Yet Finn knew I'm also practical. He saw evidence of my works; called me Samuel Pepys; and firmly recommended me to the Mayor for the most managerial of jobs.

The last time I had a long talk with Finn, up in his exhilarating eyrie enviable especially for its glass and bracing drinks, when I forgot all about my preprandial contemplation at home, I think the conversation began with my request for a little tutoring about Fourier analysis, which I hadn't fully appreciated when I found that it underlay one of the computer programs I used for forecasting and inventory control in my C M S a few years ago at the Yard. I wish he'd been my math teacher at Hume before I switched to English, trading my physics rifle for a scattering shotgun!

But to my excited satisfaction that evening his leit motiv was essentially political: our country's "infrastructure", the term for design, construction, maintenance, and interconnections of public or private institutions and services, especially for transportation, water, sanitation, energy supply and conservation, as well as recreation. In Atlantis at present most of these matters, already in various states of shortsighted neglect, are now facing at least one Raygun presidential administration, which will accelerate the degradation or removal and general opposition to what should be

for the common good, fundamentally because his party has no
emotional interest in what the Constitution calls our "general
Welfare" except when expressly justified in the name of "liberty".
That tacit political philosophy may prevail for a long time in this
country founded by Protesticans, he and I agreed. All the more
reason, he said, that we Crats must not wait for some overwhelming disaster to demonstrate a political philosophy of more than a
stack of contemporary issues. We should take advantage of such
devastating delay by working out in as much detail as possible the
restorations, corrections, resuscitations, alternatives, expansions,
finances, coordinations, etc—but especially the most time-consuming integrated plans to have immediately on hand what's
needed for a feasible Atlantean Renaissance.

Finn had joined a liberal nonprofit foundation as a consultant
to work on concepts for the continent's network of steel rails and all
their purposes as a primary component of the greater infrastructure
from seas to shining seas, for people or for freight, back and forth
among and circumscribed by international borders and ships afloat.
How joyful could a boy get, to have a friend like that, who's actually traveled all over Europe to compare with what is left of our
former railway glory! I was glad to hear that Finn's colleagues may
be able, during the interval, to prove to the electorate that too
many kilroys on the roads and bridges will stifle our economy by
ruining the roads and bridges themselves, unless we increase and
modernize our truly vital railroad tracks—as handsome creatures
for a more efficient future than they were for our famous past: perhaps the ancillary backbone for a global purification before a mil-
lennial knight! I cheered Finn on with patriotic enthusiasm, postponing food (except for popcorn) with jovial drink, despite the
nation's present prospects of false prosperity as the nourishment of
selfishness at every level of society. Characteristically, he emphasized the needless deaths from auto accidents caused by congestion
or poor highway designs or neglected maintenance, not to mention
the lack of mutual discipline in ordinary driving—or the solipsistic
carelessness of locomotive drivers when they don't have automatic
track signals to make them see when to stop.

Anyhow, even Finn as an occasional visitor to Dogtown was
nostalgic about Railway Express where it used to be active at the
spacious railroad station, with its telegraph key and a candelabra of
tracks outside in the middle of town as the resting places for boxcars, fish-oil or other tank cars, coal cars, or flat cars for maintain-

ing double tracks this far from the metropolis, leaving only a single line for our Seamark terminal, with its own smaller fork of tracks for commuters and local industry, where my mother used to put her ear to a rail, pretending to hear all the way to Botolph. When I was grown I liked to imagine the rails as my electrical contact with all points of continuous steel in the U S A. You get no such unity in airplanes or buses. In bigger cities I still delight in doublets or triplets in streetcar consists. But Finn disliked underground trains of any length, even in Europe, unless they climbed to the surface somewhere along their lines.

At first I hadn't liked the idea of container-loaded trucks riding on flat cars as their own bundled containers, each with or without its own driverless diesel tractor, but he won me over with their amazing long-haul speed and efficiency off the roads, especially considering the very important relief of traffic on the roads. Even now these miscegenous interchanges can occasionally be seen as the hundred-mile-an-hour dance of a hundred dancers, at least where the stage is more or less level—another thing that can't be done up in the air. And even with old rolling stock the future electrification of locomotives won't require dragging huge amounts of their own fuel! And they won't pollute the atmosphere they traverse! With electric current from windmills or bobbing sea-tides, or even from the friction of their own passage through the air, they will eventually draw proportionally less from the main cross-country grids that must be further developed and integrated by various sources of usable power that's as clean as possible. Electrical power is actually generated by freight trains running downhill to offset some of the power required to make the opposite climb to new peaks.

Thus he elaborated with hope as he enlightened me with possibilities for truly rational progress—as we encouraged ourselves with dreams of political success—without diving into the public and private finance for the wherewithal, leaving to our brothers and sisters the competition for investments even more in radical revision of public health and education. A very stimulating interlocution, basically of an unwritten political philosophy that our party seems afraid to abstract from our pragmatic particulars. Finn still deferred to me for worrying about that side of our merry brains.

When we spoke of Finn's propensity for systematic technology he'd mentioned significantly that von Denthey's father had been a railroad manager. Yet I was a little surprised at this Captain's vehemence in political opinion. I fully realized the humanistic

type of his psyche, no matter what category of occupation he
addressed, apparently without a specialized bone in his body. In
this discussion he'd been talking about the means to his ends—i e
politics, a broader category than the one or ones of his various
experience. Perhaps he was never made an admiral, which he
deserved to be, because his naval career was like that of an industrial director of manufacturing who, despite his broader competence, has no personal interest in the marketing that sells the
famous products and is certain not to be the next C E O, unlike
the treasurer who gets to be the chairman of the board simply
because he's essential to every element of making the product. He
called himself the nuts and bolts of his jobs when explaining himself to ignorant journalists.

In the business "models" at every level he would have recognized and evaluated marketing economics as the prime mover for
personal wealth rather than material to promote the General Welfare. In his heart he was no uncertain promoter of the common
good, however many systems must be reconciled in the making.
Almost as well as he understood the motives of F D R's New Deal,
he *felt* them! He and I both understood that the project he'd joined,
though an optimum entity in concept, would at best be socially
realized as a suboptimization of a political Newer Deal conceived
by a fully dominant party in Washington. Within hypothetical
limits assumed between small and large entities, the apparently
optimized (and thus almost always suboptimized at a higher level)
are picked according to the relative perspective most pertinent to
what one has in mind for synthesis or ultimate criticism. But
beware Jonathan Swift's naturalists! Their descending order of fleas
is but a single hive of piecemeal bites—ad infinitum!

But I'm not interested in physical chemistry or entomology, and
I'm only an unqualified layman in most subjects that now interest
me, which accounts for my hope to find a method of criticism to fit
all my suboptimized conceptions before I drive myself back toward
the theater where I don't belong, my A D L financially alleviated, no
longer subject to anxiety by the threat of poverty or excused by my
privileged companionship with the incomparable Finn Macdane, a
savant of technological naturalism!

What's wrong with optimization—which we see or predict
every day, on all sides, and in the endless dismays of history—is
simply that it spoils the system or systems that contain or accom-

pany it. By perfecting one's self one spoils someone else's, above you
or around you. Optimization epitomizes the ironies of history and
the grief of innovations. It may wreck the world that it tries to
serve, or the world it's not aware of. I should write a list of examples before I get pessimistic about every project that I see, every
leader, every proposal that matters to me! And it's not because I'm
the "perfectionist" some people call me. (How could I be, anyway,
without so much as a master's degree or a talent for speech?) . . .

Whether or not there's consciousness of a systematic relationship between the concepts of optimization and suboptimization,
the criterion of analysis is the point on which you ground your
analytical relationships, resembling the bull's eye of immediate
boundaries which in theory define an area as small as your ego or
as large as the cosmos, the limits respectively of optimization and
suboptimization. Normally one starts with the latter as the question at hand. Unless you optimize your subject in a single step to
ultimate satisfaction, you will recognize that your scope is only
enlarged, and you therefore find yourself at another level of suboptimization, and so forth. You may even proceed at a series of good,
better, and bests, as Anselm did, to the last suboptimization before
God.

Suboptimization is the curse of a democratic government like
ours as the rich grow richer, which is made possible at the relative
expense of the populace. It is the curse of a regime that favors "freedom" as a coded term for selfishness. It is also the effect of most
human lives at the lower level that corresponds with what the Rus-
sians used to call "rich peasants". Likewise there is an axiology of
popular art, the pontoon of culture at its better and best. We need
to elevate good subsystems without impeding or disorganizing the
system as a whole. Yet this we do by wasting energy that does not
serve a purpose morally useful at the higher levels of the human
universe—or a theoretically closed system. Finn's plan calls for
reduction and elimination even as he adds new matter.

He and I both took pleasure in playing with the conceptual
possibility of perfected systems, save for what humans can never do
much to realize even in erudite realms of the supernatural. We were
both pragmatists—until it came to analogy, or equations of ratios:
a is to b whatever c is to d. Without arguing about it, there we
diverged! I think of impoverished boys who try to build their own
cities around a score of electric train-tracks and some blocks of

wood. It's more than a hopeless pastime. So I loved Finn, who knew nothing of poverty, for his innocently penultimate hopes. I secretly liked to think of him as my discovered common-law godfather. . . .

. . . even as we discussed the modernized rail backpacked container freight from north to south along the East Coast that must be very inconveniently rerouted westward because a mid-19C tunnel under the city of Port Campion has an unaltered granite ceiling too low for any train much higher than passenger engines! This pinch (just the opposite of Chicago the far greater railroad "choke point" as the historically planted hub of rolling steel originally centralized by national laissez-faire competition for unregulated investments) is typical of our comparable infrastructure as nationalized in Europe, even in Alpine engineering! Atlantean respect for efficiency is usually secondary to return-on-investment, which makes it all the more difficult to serve the General Welfare when voters are unwilling to trust government and pay taxes for its appropriate infrastructure (and its functional parallels like education and public health) instead of trusting and paying for personal luxury, lazy ignorance, and vastly unequalized suffering. But of course in the case of plans like Finn's you must expect the implementation and management of them to be carried out by capable and disinterested executives at every level of thought and labor— who instead in Atlantis are for the most part intellectual products of what's often wrong with our kind of peasants getting rich or careless. Finn understood in his own hopeful manner that politics is the central means for democratic hope. In fact, if or when we ever displace the big Cans in Washington, all radicals and liberals will have to learn that studious eggs are as important as hens in the various reciprocations of a common good. Otherwise our rare victories will lay rotten eggs until we lose again. But that last night Finn and I talked little about the irritations we'd sometimes incurred while being mildly teased for our "passionate" interest in systematic efficiency.

Our conversation was mainly focused on interesting subjects from the abstract vantage of systems theory, according to what we knew about it as illustrated without the biological knowledge and statistical methodology in which it originated. I'd have to say that he talked in terms of elementary classical physics:—mechanical and electrical, at least enough for me to grasp analogies and suggest more of them in my effort to develop a limited Critical Philosophy. As an engineer he wasn't interested in analogy per se, as I am—as I hoped, alas, to explain in an unsatisfied but promising continuation of our discussions, especially because for me the U S T leads a metaphysical mind above a naturalist's notice of mere "patterns" that happen to be repeated in entities that only accidentally seem to occur in superficially unrelated entities.

Still, even anachronistically suboptimized embarrassments due to lack of coordination in time rather than space, typical of the costs that will forever impede the realization of our creative energy when efficiency is feasible, are the curse of acting as well as planning. It is one of life's repetitive disappointments, even when not recognized as such, a loss especially at low levels of personal experience, but also in political science. It's obvious in the heating of a familiar house in wintertime when your universe is small enough to consider local atmosphere as fully optimized, as either a matter of home economics or some pragmatic consciousness of immediate social satisfaction.

All these concepts expand the enveloping or overlapping layers that we systematically define as either extant or purely conceptual—for instance, if the U S T itself were to be postulated as a particular abstract entity, cybernetics would be regarded as suboptimized in philosophical adventures! The very laws of science have their own suboptimizations, though perhaps not of the kind that necessarily increase the entropy of their immediate supersystem— as energy wears itself down one way or another.

But the suboptimization that happens to annoy me most in my kitchen is banal, typical of food packaging for consumers. The package engineers who work on the product (e g crackers) for its inside lining, a plastic capsule (usually with others of its kind in the same package) within the boxed container, are apparently in a separate department from those who design the process near the end of the production line where the capsules are sealed. When you go to open them on the kitchen table you find that you must tear the plastic cortex that's meant to protect your remaining entities. Even if that makes you fall for the manufacturer's trick by eating more crackers than you wanted, to save the balance from open air, and even if you don't mind the inconvenience of ripping bladders open by force or scissors, what benefits are there from the research and development of a glue that's so much stronger than what's to be protected? . . .

Well, I must admit when Finn laughed at me, it's theoretically possible that there's no more efficient way to make the sealing less porous than the plastic that's not supposed to be porous at all! What's suboptimized for me may be optimized for Demeter Mills, like most *branded* food manufacturers, to protect the public. Thus it is that systems analysis can be either subjective or objective, depending upon the perspective. . . . But now I'm too sleepy to think about all the other kinds of subsystems conceptually suited to ideas or events in time, whether or not metaphysical. . . . Almost everything I read these days makes me think like that, when I should be thinking of what I have left to do with Gilgamesh, to say nothing of my philosophical criticism if I never write another play!

. . . Cross my heart and hope to die, I've got to shut up my wearisome abstractions of analogy. I can't write a bible. Finn and Fay very kindly thought that the notions I live by are those of a semi-educated amateur in everything from management to metaphysics, and as a common reader of anything I know enough to comprehend maturely. I don't think they jeered at me as others probably do, but they listened skeptically to some of my flippant opinions of suboptimizations ranging down from God's millions to the individual! I've been too glib in skimming past the congeries of closed to open systems, which would be a central concern of a truly analogical critic, either functionally or symbolically. . . . Finn rightly looked askance at some of my sub-enthusiasms. . . . Nevertheless, we were both excited by the exponential ideas of U S T in abstractions as well as experience. It's not too poetic to say that electricity was our lingua franca for almost all we thought in common.

So we seemed to reach provisional congruity that evening on which I was treated to one of the most exciting conversations of my life, like more than one with Father Dun about Theodynamic liturgy for the common good. After all, *liturgy* means *public works*. National public works, for the most part, are a foundation for the world's service: mankind's very life.

*

—But there is one new idea from that last supper with Finn Macdane that I hope I can remember till morning and cherish thereafter! It probably would never have struck me while we were talking if I hadn't happened *not* to have staggered home to my own cooking. I refer to what wouldn't have won the favor of Finn as anything more significant than my "metaphysics". Viz, I was struck (as one standard model) that the little sine waves of our alternating current in electronics are to the big sine waves that constitute our waves of electric power what ordinary regular suboptimizations are to their ultimately optimized system. I now find this analogy everywhere I look, even for heterogeneous meanings of their symbols!

. . . Still, it's the *irregular* relationship of entities that is significant at higher orders of abstraction—as in poetry and other arts, as well as in cultural anthropology or other parallels such as other branches of mathematics—that I'm grasping for at the moment even as my inspiration fades! . . . I'd hate to lose overnight what I think is an insight. . . . But all this is better than dwelling upon my origins. . . . I wish I still had poor old Ibi at my bedside. . . .

Z. The Late Lancelot Duncannon

. . . But it wasn't Ibi-Roy that I dreamt about last night. It was Father Dun. Maybe because he loved Ibi, gave him food and water, not just tidbits. He let the dog frequent his sunporch at the Lab, even along with COV visitors who were of the same mind. I wish I could remember what the dream was about, except that people were whispering about Theodynamics when they should have been listening to Father's homily at the chapel altar. It may be an underground sense in my psyche—yes, I must have a neglected moral psyche, the semblance of a soul, almost with a sense of disloyalty to the temporal roots of my insensitive ramifications under a low firmament. That super-priest had been the scientific Maxwell's Demon of my thermodynamic excitements—a stimulus revived by Finn many years later. Even though I never joined the Order, when Father Dun's sympathetic attention was not directly focused on religion it was a joy to discuss almost anything as we sat facing his great wall of astonishingly eclectic books. Neither then nor in the chapel or in the refectory saying grace with my sacerdotal responses as his acolyte did he hint at catechism or the cure of my soul. He knew that I had been trained for much of the ceremony in a convent for children. I was never expected to explain my meanings, as I offered and accepted bread and wine according to his own revision of the High Church manual called Action at the Altar, the formation of his Laboratory. So I think we understood each other in what might be called analogical abstractions of most of the things that we discussed without mentioning faith. Senior and junior—typically early in the morning once a week, alone in the chapel like vested dancers with lines to speak, without music or homily—we

practiced the basic Anamnesis, more often than not with no other
soul to bring forward the Offertory wafers.

Usually five afternoons in my five-day work-week, with sherry
on the sunporch, with Ibi dreaming nearby, talking about such
things as physics or anthropology or history and politics, he was my
most influential postgraduate tutor, who sometimes personally
cooked me meals, as if I were his private secretary (while I was
actually doing almost all my Mesocosm work for Chris Lucey the
Father Economist, by whom I was tutored in the Vine's putatively
necessary chrematistic section of the world). Thus, now, after Finn's
death, as well as Arthur's, I still owe to Lancelot Duncannon my
most educated and most philosophical stimulus, even in my nostalgic maturity. I should reread everything he and his academic followers wrote in the effort to make known, among other insights,
his rational integration of Christianity and the agnostic common
good.

There is much about Lancelot Duncannon in Michael Chapman's earlier books, but not nearly enough to properly expatiate on
his radical ideas, such as a nearly unprecedented anthropological
analysis of religious sacrifice, which still refreshes my enthusiasm
for an analogical oak tree in its seasons.

The book that Arthur Halymboyd accepted from Father Duncannon is titled *Sacrifice: A Doctrinal Allocution*, imprinted with the
Classic Order of the Vine's *Metacosmesis Mundi Per Incarnationem*
[M M P I}. The word *sacrifice*—promiscuously abused in ordinary
secular diction (like my peculiar meaning of *tragedy*) in our broader
vernacular—is hideous in New Testament context for most
Paulines. It was understood at a glance (though not adopted) by the
visiting Jew. Alas, this small volume never got to the eyes of Pope
John XXIII for consideration in Vatican Two, nor of any prelate in
the papacy at any other time. Indeed, Father Duncannon was
heeded little less in the Apostolic hierarchy of his own Atlantean
Communion, mainly for conservative political reasons. It might
since have eased many liberal efforts to reduce some of the theological differences between the churches that are characterized more by
institutional liturgy than by preaching evangelism. Hence, in my
lexicon *sacrifice* is a particular act in Christian liturgy in unique
dromenon, though partially comparable with several other religions'.

So one can share Father Dun's symbol-system without relin-
quishing the liberty of one's own allegorical hermeneutic acceptance of Scripture's symbols, or his faith as one's hopes. Religion is

culture and our Western culture is full of connotations in our denotations without philosophical discussion. So I say about everything *I* say! Is that as liberal as the *Inferno*? But better yet: neither he nor Father Lucey, nor any of the Members of his Classic Order of the Vine whom I talked with at the Lab about their Christian doctrine, seemed to assume—as if by intuition, despite my voluntary service at the altar and our convivial conversations in the refectory or on the congenial sunporch with sherry, as well as my obvious affection for the Order—that I had any more qualifying interest in becoming a Member Secular than a typically confirmed but irregular visitor to the local Tudor Apostolic church named after Saint Paul on Halibut Street, which is playfully said to be used by most of its members only for "hatching matching or dispatching". Officially at the Lab I was only a hired "Business Manager", as if a temporary landscape gardener or amanuensis. In all that time I spent as occasional assistant to Father Dun, the former physicist—when I wasn't spending the much greater amount of my time assisting Father Lucey's economy, the former social worker but then a very active participant in stock exchanges on behalf of the COV's monastic headquarters here at its Laboratory—Father Dun and I between ourselves never bothered with the concept of Faith or the XXXIX Articles of Religion in the Book of Common Prayer, even in conversation about the likes of Abelard, Mark Planck, or the High Church poet T S Chittering. The latter two had been Lancelot Duncannon's intellectual friends in Europe before he was struck by God with new ideas of the cogwheel that drives all the other wheels within the greater wheels of the Lord's church, which called him to undertake his studies for the Tudor priesthood in England when he was already almost thirty.

As far as I can remember, aside from the memorization of my words and actions as an acolyte for his revision of the High Church mass (which I'd learned as an infant altar boy in a convent) that he called the Anamnesis, the most religious person we talked about was Saint Anselm, not for his youthful sin against chastity but for the sake of his Ontological Proof, which is to a certain degree easily analogized, or at least worth comparing, with modern cosmological naturalism, especially in consideration of Bohr's principle of complementarity.

"The pen is mightier than the sword!" my mother chided me whenever she saw my military drawings, even before I was old enough for Sunday School. Then came her aphorisms adages and

apothegms about fools or sages, before I was specialized by my own
toy models and eventually my own designs of floating ships, warplanes, and canyon bridges—even human uniforms—hoping to get
my advanced education at the Port Royal Naval Academy, if not at
the Vinland Institute of Polytechnics [V I P]. But, as it turned out,
I found enough math for me at Hume! I got more interested in liberal studies (which may lead anywhere) than in the necessary disciplines in math and physics or biology, *mutatis mutandis*, perhaps
Lancelot Duncannon's path to the arts of imagination, the *sine qua
non* dromena essential to his refined ritual and my general concept
of legomena, subsuming Huizinga's theme of *Homo Ludens*, as eventually ramified (among other kinematics of society) in *law* and
theater from their origin in primitive dance, according to Jane
Harrison, my goddess of scholarship. (Only the prosecutor and
supreme judge of the court will have suspected how much I think
about too much for my capacity.) My insistent point has been that
the liberal arts should have precedence over all other education,
even when they omit opera with its Urim and Thummin, and art
history with its endlessly refined aesthetics, both of which I've
silently avoided, despite those recreational electives of Father Duncannon as a rather conventional aesthete. He tacitly avoided interest
in "modern art". His mother had wanted him to be an art historian.
    Anyway, he always disclaimed qualification as a theologian,
though he knew a lot about the history and philosophy relevant to
Christian divinity as the anthropological evolutionary background
of his social ideas. If theology is said to be "thinking about faith",
his Theodynamics was thinking about society's access to God and
vice versa. He proclaimed it as antithetical to the "thetical" *church*
as the cure of private souls. (He also cited Huizinga for writing that
law is "orderly, antithetical play".)
    . . . Tonight I'll tell this tribunal whatever it wants to know
about my few and very vague after-affects of the procreative actions
in question. But one can hardly call me a witness in this case by the
birth in flagrante delicto. Ask the judge herself! You want the baby
to say to the mother: "I'm flattered to have so much of your attention! My trivalence—or rather half my bivalence—is at your service, Ma'am."
    When I'm called to the box I'll ask Gretta Doloroso and the
Bailiff to testify that in fact, according to my dream, what Lancelot
Duncannon must have looked like in 1934 was a winning tennis
player on his annual summer vacation, visiting his widowed mother

in her hereditary mansion on the Foreside. He must have been little taller or heavier than he was when I knew him at the age of sixty-five two decades ago. Then he wore rimlessly squared glasses, and though his hair was gray, he gave the impression of once having looked like the delicately handsome young Milton, the scholarly genius "Lady of Christ's College" in old Unabridge. But I'm non-partisan in this mystery, save for the fatherless delivery of 100% love by my better half.

My nosey old friend Tessa, the prosecutor, will suggest that somewhat before the historic day hereabout known to anyone who knew my birthday following the Great Gloucestermas, Arthur Halymboyd—before his final departure from Moira's bed—had vaguely felt uneasy about Lance's crisp white presence around town as Dogtown's own "native scientific genius", for my future mother had innocently remarked more than once upon his remarkably evident polite culture, and his lithe gentlemanly beauty in white clothes on the tennis court, whereas the international lawyer himself was often absent on clandestine transatlantic business—though she believes that those two had never been introduced to each other.

If there could be a single keyword to Lancelot's oeuvre—rather than, say, Sacrifice or Experience—it might have been Offertory: the radical nexus of his noetical Theodynamics he quoted from the Athanasian Creed "taking manhood into God", as reciprocal incarnation.

Lancelot Dun began his religious devotion after his profession in science had personally yielded to his nearly congenital appreciation of the arts, especially the poetry of his time in the circle of his fellow Atlantean, T S Chittering (whose poems include the great one written from our very hill about the three reefs); but he soon found that he was less a poet himself than a Christian with his own aesthetic ideas about all the arts—which eventually formed a religious philosophy that I'm tempted to call the optimization of aesthetics. His catholic religion, he later wrote in his first book, "is a reappropriate version of the Faith in life and experience of the Faithful in every age, surely as Queen of all the Arts. . . . fresh patterns of practical action, and of inner experience, in the lives of even the most obscure Christians who continue to make up new and unique jewels, each one absolutely irreplaceable by any other one set in the Crown of Christ. . . . The Creeds, to be believed, must not be thought of as if they were solid, inert, unyielding platforms of abstract intellectual knowledge. . . . Instead, they have to be regarded as efficient springboards to fresh practical action . . . throughout every succeeding generation of human life."

Is it any wonder that I sympathetically volunteered to be his adult acolyte? His motto for the order, Metacosmesis Mundi Per Incarnationem, was as political as religious. It was a shield for Christian soldiers to carry forward the sacramental words and actions to sustain a gospel for our time at the altar, in the pulpit, and out into the modern world, without losing the precious history of our religious culture, which has served us in all weathers as toughly creased cortex for the oak still alive in all four seasons. As far as mundane hope and charity are concerned, I'm still his acolyte.

But a bitterly long winter of politically misunderstood Christianity is falling upon us with the election of a very competent DV actor of simpleminded goodwill who smoothly exploits personally suboptimized selfishness by calling it freedom. At the expense of social injustice he and his voters honor greed by calling it success. Individualism is the Protestican religion. Instead of being far along in the propagation of Father Dun's ideas in revisionary Christianity, we have the ubiquitous preachers of what he called the "extricationism" of saving individual souls from the world (who are generally unaware of the religious source of their political selfishness), and he is dead and all but forgotten. His former followers of the erstwhile Vine were scattered either by ecclesiastical impracticability or by shock and disillusion brought upon the Society's integrity by the misbehavior and financial disaster of the Father Economist. The Rev Christopher Lucey, the Order's one and only Member Regular living with the Father Superior at the Laboratory of Melchizedek and the Mesocosm, precipitated a lost cause probably for almost all the Members, and certainly for the few local friends who visited that monastery out of love for Father Dun or his liturgy, of course including me as quasi-faithful in my hope.

Indeed his death was the greatest lost cause I've ever experienced as the meliorist son of a Christian Mary whose life was an epitome of lost causes without the benefit of having known him or his radically unorthodox loyalty to the same Elizabethan Settlement to which she always returned from her adventures in the Protestican kind of private faith.

But there is one felicitous exception to the failure of M M P I. Father Lloyd Davy, a Member Secular of COV while a Tudor parish priest in Markland, the preordained successor to Father Dun as the

COV's Father Superior, a bachelor affable Ph D in philosophy from Unabridge, who loved to fish trout in northern freshwater streams, *did* carry forward the liturgical core of the Father Founder's theodynamics by taking it across the border to a Dominion's maritime diocese, stripped of Father Dun's least engaging fussiness in both dromena and legomena that were inessential to traditional act or meaning. Father Davy took advantage of being asked to join an official ecclesiastical committee meant to revise the offer to communicants, with the enthusiastic blessing of the liberal bishop, who'd already wanted a modern revision of the four-hundred-year-old Holy Eucharist rite, which would be carefully and lengthily tested at the altar in explanatory conferences as well as compared with the ongoing schedule of orthodox Holy Communion. Much of the ceremony would be reduced or eliminated, and the language of both Scripture and Prayer Book was to be taken from one or two of the Bible's best contemporary translations. I assume that vestments would be simplified, even for high mass.

I don't know how well this attempt to reconcile conservatives to this revision has fared—perhaps persisting for years at the dominant services; but the last I heard, a few years later, Father Davy was pleased by the outcome. To me it indicates Father Dun's at least indirect influence on a world greater than Dogtown's. . . . I only wish my mother could have had a church like that—Offertory, Consecration, Fraction, and Communion, to match one of her adored *preachers* of the Word!

2. Tessa's Précis of the Court's Second Day

Court of Love, our Queen calls it. Is that a euphemism? Or only half so? Can sudden desire turn to love in an hour—or perhaps in gratitude for a beatitude that forestalls natural neurological cinders? Or by ordinary chance in an extraordinary mood, more or less intempestively? Or love may simply be a word for the medium of anything like marriage. I should know better than she, considering the old impulsive intervals of my almost forgotten freedom.

I think that Arthur really loved Moira, at least before and maybe for some lonely time after the years of irregular liaison, and that she had reciprocated his love until he denied her the satisfaction of having with him at least the first of her three children— presumably in marriage. Yet at the same time she was probably not unaware that if she had her way it would preclude the secret dream of being in mutual love with a spiritual man of equivalent value but opposite qualities—the angelic scientist seen and sometimes heard in church, who was said to be headed for holy orders in England. Apparently she was *always* religious, though you wouldn't think so in Mrs Grundy's terms. But Moira-Mary, despite her liberal reputation, was always basically pious of the Pauline kind that "extricates" individual souls from the disordered real world—to use Father Duncannon's critical terminology a generation later for what's wrong with Christianity (if I understand the tracts of his Classic Order of the Vine).

Yet I gather that in Caleb's childhood there would be not a wisp of spiritual intellect in Tony Porter (a baptized Petrine), his mother's purely carnal and faithless pacifier—an unpaid "gigolo", she complained, the owner and operator of a taxi service (after many other occupations) who took his frequent pleasure as an unscrupulous connoisseur of female riders. For more than a few years of her otherwise celibate loneliness during Caleb's nonage in Unabridge, that "dark feline Loosey" was her erotic preoccupation. From what Caleb told me I suppose that by then she confessed to herself a shamefully asymmetrical passion for that Prince of Darkness as opposed to the earlier epiphany of Lancelot Duncannon at the 1934 Gloucestermas, when that holy man had seemed her final chance for redemption by reproduction. What was she thinking at the end of the day, purposely defenseless against nature, against God's will? She had given way to her fastidious urge, before it grew too late, just when God was growing impatient for the first of her three children, the purpose of love in all its rehearsals, whatever men think, and even when somehow impossible. So she thought in retrospect, I suppose, even at my own age now. Of course she'd loved Arthur Halymboyd before deceiving him with her preparation when she thought he might be her last acceptable chance to get what she wanted. The anagogical sensation was better than ever as she prayed for his absolute misconception—he who only a few days before (later understood as her sacrifice to God) had tenderly and passionately swept the vastation of her studio full of paintings, and was nearly able to resuscitate the smoked death of her beloved companion and protector the beautiful Jewish Shepherd dog she called Sycorax. His generous energy had lovingly softened her consciousness of that artistic metanoia at the midpoint of her early life.

The fire occurred just as she was about to convert her livelihood from the clever plastic art that had supported her to the insecure vocation of unencouraged poetry. Even as grief and fear had already begun to dissipate the faith hope and agape necessary to repair her disaster, left alone, her unpossessive soul was renewed by the virginal apparition of the holy man, as whiter yet than the cosmopolitan officer in a uniform that had caught her preoccupied eyes at the parade of heartrending animals on a famous holiday.

But a knight not to be dismissed from any woman's mind, regardless of what holiness transpired thereafter. Before the fall of darkness that personable Navy officer had bridged with an arch of charm and worldly competence, from terminus a quem to terminus ad quem, the fusion of beatitude embraced by Arthur and Lancelot. However more practiced Lieutenant Finn Macdane was in the art of love, it was not a measure of hers. It is not to be expected in my story that his contribution to Moira's spectrum of sensation was distinguished from each of theirs as her especially distinct afflatus in her long day of pleroma.

Yet he did ground the erotic lightning stroke aimed by Zeus. It was not simply an accidental joust with King Arthur and Sir Lancelot as intervened by a strange Celtic Norseman sometimes called Mac. He gleamed in summer uniform (but without his ceremonial sword) as white as the altar at Whitsuntide. In half an hour he became her knight errant, her valiant seagoing hero on technological quests beyond her ken. His steed for the day was a snug tugboat, the kind of civilian steamboat she said she liked the best. She was enchanted by his blond hair and blue eyes, his intelligent sympathy with her vitally significant disaster, which had emotionally culminated in the death of Sycorax, and his gentle manner of unevasive man-of-the-world response to her rapidly multiplying questions. His presence excited an unreserved curiosity that diverted objective information of many kinds from reversion to her overwhelming personal plight. Apparently there was no trace of the exhibitionism we've heard about that later evolved in her unclassified life. He must have been enthralled by her unfamiliar Bohemian habille, as well as by the sky-lighted ambience still redolent of burnt paint in the acrid atmosphere of a studio that served as her bedroom.

That is to say, their accidental meeting at midday was immediately exciting, and soon sufficiently frank, though he must have pretended not to notice evidence of a previous lover—who only recently, almost half a century later, I found to have been his much later friend Arthur Halymboyd. That came out in the trial. I'm afraid I dwelt too provocatively upon the scene as I thus reconstructed it. But I hope I've stirred the libido of all hands present. At least I found Rafe and myself unusually interested in each other's feelings at home last night. In words alone it was almost as if our courtroom play had verged exactly upon the kind forewarned by the police. But it may not be good for my professional reputation as a psychotherapist if I unnecessarily expatiated too much for the taste of some people we misguidedly invited to our outrageous Court of Love. I'm even a little uneasy about my next private conversation with our dear old judge. I can't quite firmly believe that she'll laugh about anything that pertains to her late lover. After all, she didn't recuse herself! The truth is that in my imaginative peroration I momentarily forgot about her own man's same heroic figure in very recent memory.

(Yet, if I do say so myself, I'm a pretty good female physiological psychologist of fiction, despite her and Caleb's doubts about my grasp even of Auto Drang's philosophy when I worked for that vilified analyst in my Ur-youth.)

Everyone knew that the late Finn Macdane was no stuffed shirt (to use Moira Mary Trevisa Tremont's term of contempt for many a well-dressed man of any profession). He was an individual who hated to kill an insect, if only to wash it down his kitchen sink alive; it troubled him to see any animal in a cage. Yet Fay called him a rogue Viking. He laughed at himself for daily rotating an assortment of different toothbrushes, she told me once when she was tipsy, according to his theory of hygiene, just as before quitting tobacco he had serially smoked a rack of differentiated pipes to keep them dry and complementary, as if they were golf clubs for a variety of strokes (though he had no use for that particular pastime). At the soda fountain in Pound's, where he first met Moira, he was favorably impressed by her unfashionable long hair, and skin without cosmetics.

He always had a book in his pocket and he didn't spend time in bars or nightclubs. His closest friends in the Navy were brilliantly unpopular Jews. Long after Hitler's war he traveled by train, if circumstantially possible, at a time when self-important individuals swaggered into airports. He never rode an escalator unless there was no alternative, glad to climb the stairs for exercise. He voted a straight Cratic ticket, often when he was the only one in a wardroom or B O Q [Bachelor Officer Quarters] to do so. Here in Dog-

town he read and sometimes studied the books or papers recommended by Caleb—and listened to him, a constructive crank if
there ever was one! I gather that Finn himself was a respected gentleman and scholar by international standards, despite an official
remark in his confidential service record that the Bureau of Domestic Investigation [B D I] listed him as a suspected "liberal Premature Antifascist".

As a retired Commander in the Reserve, but still an active private consultant to the Bureau of Ships, he was genuinely interested
in Caleb's extremely abstract (but "mathematically extremely
simple") Synectic Method of Diagnostic Correlation [S M D C],
"for possible computerized application in the relative evaluation of
individual ships (or other groups) and their management". This
serious attention to one of Caleb's fantasies surprised us all; and the
younger of that pair was seriously satisfied with the elder's pragmatic attention, though aware that Finn himself was unwilling to
devote the endless time it would take to write a treatise developing
the concept, even for a future project *non realisé*—as if he was a very
busy architect engaged in the design of a futuristic city and all it
takes to get one financed, governed, built, and inhabited. Caleb
once told me that he'd rather spend the time getting his Gilgamesh
realized by any tiny Abbey Theater. Besides, he said a naval application would be only a very special case. He claims that the
S M D C was so abstract that it could be useful for facts mixed with
fiction in almost any statistical matrix, and that therefore it could
be used in metaphysics! Fay confided to me that Finn was still
thinking pragmatically about S M D C at the time of his death. He
was less impressed by Caleb's isorectotetrahedral [IRTH] symbolism, in which she herself was philosophically interested.

In any case, though the jury's Scotch verdict was equally
divided after I had pleaded the cases for all three suspects (a k a
defendants), the consensus seems to have battened upon Caleb's fantastic insistence that the mystery's just a spurious superfecundation
not yet theoretically conceived in mathematical or molecular biology, but only slightly less possible than immaculate conception
with a trinity's participation—in fact, no less inventive than a
woman's imagination. Bastardy has never been broadly enough
studied by science, despite its overwhelming popularity in fiction
(where I find myself).

In my summation I mentioned Caleb as the "son" or "scion",
stifling my smiles as he watched for my terms, remembering our

many private conversations in which he'd called himself "by-blow
not whoreson" or "bantling" or "love child", if not "a harmless
little bastard". I made it clear to the court that his mother was the
only "victim" or "beneficiary" or "prize" of her "Pride and Joy".
But throughout this masque many of our metastatic terms were
properly understood in their proper contexts. More than once Her
Honor had to chide even me for malapropos solecisms, which I'd
purposely or inadvertently drawn upon for the purpose of tone.
This Court of Love amused no one more than us its unlawful
instigators.

For my brief on Commander Macdane I had summoned Caroline Chapman as proxy for her father in Cornucopia, our Controller,
to account for Caleb's shamrock paternity in Gloucestermas. He
also delights in the idea of triadic miscegenation as a metaphorical
expression of his own semi-person, as indicated by Father Duncannon and Arthur Halymboyd (as more fully represented in *Gloucesterbook* or *Gloucestertide*), together with the late Finn Macdane, as the
relevant personae of the present work-in-progress to be called
Gloucestermas in the trilogy embraced by Michael Chapman's
Gloucesterman, wherein that man's living triangles are never equilateral. At this controllable level Caleb has refused to choose one
father from a lineup on the beach.

But he is not the judge. And as the prosecutor I tried to shift
the burden of hypothesis to the absent Moira herself. But that
ghost wasn't alive to defend or confess herself, and there was not a
scintilla of evidence in all her remaining papers or my collected
obiter dicta—nor any possibility that she knew more than anybody
else about what went on in the confusion of inseminations in about
twenty-four hours of emotional agitation—and said potion was
finally absorbed the next morning without bygone sensation. I pled
for her the natural advantages of the female, an infamous thesis of
hers in later decades. She always after enjoyed her greater half of
Caleb's entelechy. He was her Honor Boy! But her great secret was
kept from him even when he babbled on his diaper pad after he'd
gleefully pissed in her eye. I'd had this anecdote from Caleb's godmother—the Bench itself—as a hint to alter my prosecutorial plan
from the unwarranted psychological deductions about three men
equally inscrutable to those who hardly had a set of bell curves to
distinguish one man from another at birth. The trial judge herself
has therefore ruled that only a mother—in the course of post-
partem time, without scientific assistance—is entitled to settle the

question, or at least to establish a bias, until the child (or subsequent children) justifies some definite hypothesis of normal paternity. Since our magistrate was the only one qualified for that position, and since she denied inequality of probability as to seminal
success, she declared that any pleading must be based upon both
figure and ground according to the argument or guess of the long-
lost mother, as the truth's only independent variable, to use Caleb's
jargon.

Naturally this begs the question—just as he hoped.

*

At the final recess (for coffee, lobster rolls, and wine, courtesy
Rafe Opsimath), I heard or overheard an encyclopedia of opinions,
including from some women gathered in the ladies room whom I
hardly know by sight, who were giggling or tittering in or about
the shadows. Other people stood on or off the platform, suppressing
the impulse to break into a blooming, buzzing, confusion of pruri-
ent interests. It made me feel like an embarrassed author who's
been reading aloud her frankly scandalous autobiography. So I
turned aside to engross Fay, as if to discuss legal precedents or other
arcane points of obscenity law as dispassionately as the author of a
microbiology textbook discussing solecisms of typography to be
corrected for the next printing.

Meanwhile, standing away from the podium by which our
queen, with a sigh of relief, had been seated as the bench of justice:

HECUBA: . . . It's how the three spasms do inside that counts,
like getting your bowels in an uproar before they can let go. I bet
the dewdrops get all mixed up in a soup, until one little squirt of
the mix wriggles all the way in while the others are still cranking
the separator for cream. You can't feel the final insinuation. The big
boys don't always win out. And the guy who buys the kid popcorn
never has a clue. It isn't the pillow of strength that wins the tide!

DEETA: No, it's not just a matter of luck! Without even thinking about it, a woman can influence her stars, no matter where the
moon is. One of them may have been a diviner. Or else she was. It
must have been the priest!

LILIAN: But it wasn't by magic. Think of it the other way:
she begot the baby she wanted first, but she had to pay for it by
never getting her other two kids. When you feel like it, it's better

to just let the men fight it like Darwin. Nowadays girls can have beatitudes galore without worrying about complications. The Paraclete was God's best medicine! Still, I think Deeta may be right.

BELLE: Anyway it's nice to be too old.

BENI: I'm the oldest one, but I have no opinion.

HECUBA: I haven't forgotten what incarnation is like. A trifecta must be delirious!

GRETTA [*to the best of my memory*]: I was afraid Tessa would call me to the box: After that Great Gloucestermas, when Moira got back from the Isle of Man, and I was still getting ready to graduate from high school, before and after the kid was born, she hired me to help her with housework. She was very generous when she couldn't afford to be. I loved her for opening my eyes to sex when no one else would. She never said anything to me about the father. All she talked about was the baby boy she almost lost. I had never heard of the Isle of Man. All I knew at the time was that she'd been there. She had a horribly long delivery at the hospital. Sometimes she called it God's punishment for her sins.

[BELLE (*aside*): Moira loved Dogtown, but she felt driven out of town a few years later by threatened danger to her baby from the sadistic chief of police she called a Fascist thug, who hadn't forgotten that she'd discovered him colluding with rum-runners and covering up a couple of murders that are officially unsolved to this day. No one doubted that the chief was behind her eventual confinement to the state mental hospital for what they called "indefinite observation". It was there that she demanded of the doctors her tubal ligation—for Caleb's sake, because she couldn't support more than one child, her one reason for continuing to live. The medics were apparently impressed by her educated self-awareness, and by her explanation of the charges against her as a suicidal patient persecuted by vindictive and narrowminded male authority. By then (after Caleb had been sent temporarily to a foster family) she had arranged to pull up stakes and taken him to Unabridge. It was a financially frightening time for everyone, even with Restoration and F D R's election. I hear she gained weight afterwards, but then she was a beautiful slim blonde in her own style—more like a classic Bohemian than either a fashionable flapper or an anachronistic Victorian.]

LILIAN: Too bad, this court is no romantic Parliament of Fowles—three eagles courting the formel, who then remains a virgin for a while to make up her mind about which one of them she had effectively lifted her tail to—if only to help guard an egg. In a real case like this all three eagles get a crack at it and fly away to look for other formels while their homunculi fight it as sport, sight unseen, without female quality control, which in our species usually admits only a single ticket to the mother's performance no matter what his odds in nestless jousting. And I don't believe that the woman can have any proprioceptive choice at any point of the gestation in a case like this. As far as the progeny is concerned it's the inside melee that determines the outcome! And that's neither F I F O or L I F O—first in or last in—to make it rational, seeing that the competition lasted for a day or so together in one black box!

HECUBA: No audit trail! I bet it was the Jew! Their circumspection is good.

DEETA: Maybe Caleb's right: it was a witchcraft tie!

HECUBA: A lot of people will commensurate with the poor bastard because he had a stirname that doesn't consist anywhere else in the world; but it well might be that Mr Karcist might need more names if it became known to farthering on his own part. I'll say no more. Let's balance desolations with desecrations. Might there not be three daughters who never knew him? Sometimes men get away as fast and loose as roving loins. What's good for the moose is good for the slander. But most of us allow them to wriggle out under the statue of imitations for our own good!

[TESSA (*aside*): I could have killed that woman for hinting at his past in Cornucopia. That preterite belongs in the Controller's other books. She's goodhumored, but she'll never make friends if she doesn't keep her mouth shut with that kind of gossip. She's intelligent and she means well, but she's talks too much. She admits to that. "I'm not at a loss for turds." she says. I'll have to spread it around that she drinks too much, so I can hope they'll think she was always a drunk. I notice that Lilian laughed and quickly changed the subject too!]

BELLE: I'm afraid I don't like the idea of fatherhood at all. Marriage is bad enough! No vows, no bastards! I saw enough of paternity when I was a daughter of the British Commonwealth.

3. Scotch Verdict: Caleb's Negative Trilemma

It's all over, ad hoc sine die—or whatever they said—with Rafe's cheerfully abundant party on the premises to dissolve the disappointment of any solemn truth—just as I had hoped. Directed verdict, sua sponte by a scientific judge; all my putative fathers acquitted in absentia nolo contendere, myself happily dismissed with the square root of minus one, as coefficient, making me a complex number. That's a thought! Therefore I am—by virtue of the fact that my trilemma was a mental trinity. It was fun to crow to Tessa that I'd told her as much from the very beginning—if she'd only listen to me! Half of my "genetic markers" are probably as indecipherable as cuneiformed isorectotetrahedrons, but in any case I'm the patient, not the doctor. The subject knows more than the object. Prosit! My case rests until science explains how I'm possible when all the corpses including mine would have to be available as facts! Fay doesn't seem to mind the time she spent by playing Tessa's long-simmered game as a posse comitatus à la Auto Drang's psychotypology! But the old girl has spared me the ignominy of an ordinary bastard vulnerable to physiological analysis! —That was very good wine. They say it's better for your health than Scotch.

Even Beni seemed to have forgiven me for being so evasive. In the end most of my friends are said to have given up on a favorite suspect, citing my godmother's principle of uncertainty in her concluding interpretation of the verdict. Hecuba winked and hugged me; Lilian kissed me while Gil Algo shook my hand. Caroline Chapman stepped forward with the Controller's compliments, nominating me for Noble's prize in Negative Capability!

. . . Of course this trial settled nothing except the imaginative intelligence of its briefs. It's been just the masque for a critic like me! But it reminded me of my mother's dream of the Brotherhood in a Peaceable Kingdom, because it was agape, after all, that intussuscepted this Court of Love as a Dogtown miracle play. Tim Scriabin came up to me afterwards and whispered thanks for loosening his writer's block against the true microtopopolis. He promised to keep his new novel totally fictional. That made me rather uneasy. I hope he's not interested in Gilgamesh! Fiorina said she was very sorry I quit my job at the Hall: the fishermen were rooting for me to save the waterfront from land-sharks. They're afraid Dexter is too friendly with Mooncusser.

It's hard to visualize, forty-five years ago, the tiny likes of an international lawyer, a Navy officer, and a religious physicist wrestling each other in a knot of three like competitive anacondas in a tunnel of mud! But I think each respected the other two enough to be glad as colleagues in the flurry—friends enough, curious enough, in deference to their rivals—"after you and you, sir"— to call it a draw without using a straw to pick. Let's just have a drink and *withdraw* to three cold feet on the joined legs of Manannan, our present chastity in common, no longer suitors of that target. Let her desire be our sacrifice to the gods!

I expect no deus ex machina. There was no Apollo to explain Karcism! But the tussle did entail demigods of Organization, Religion, and Constructors in their confrontation about a Christian woman as my nexus to the guiding humor from her own clandestine father, Captain Prosper Ozone, the Cathode King and Baron of New Albion. (It's possible, however, that her father really was the illustrious schooner captain Trevisa who bore her maiden name.) My trilemmata is only half of me in any case, naturally suggesting that she was three times as influential on me as any one important man—and so I believe as a function of love: intelligent love, brave love, talented love, even spiritual love in a single set of feminine chromosomes. If I were all hers I'd be an artist, not just a critic.

Yet her freely expressed criticisms of stupidity, malice, and willful ignorance sharpened my earliest notice of people and society as I learned by example the exchanges between subject and object, in looking, listening, and reading heard aloud.

It's no wonder that after this public catharsis, and Tessa's cheerful apologies, this negative trilemma has relieved me of any doubt about my intuitive wizardry. I now feel free to apply it where I left off in the vocation of my own ulterior Eigenschaft.

The key to which is the concept of suboptimization as an analytical device of great promise in almost any thought-experiment, perhaps even integrated with S M D C, C M S, the psychology of I E C, and tragedy (for which there is no acronym). And the key to those is what you might call the relativity between "subject" and "object". The subjects in my analogies are the points of view from which you consider whatever you establish, whatever it is that you're thinking about, while the object or objects thereby establish the relationship or relationships with subjects which are typically (but by no means only) the representations of a single suboptimized brain; and everything outside this imagined $\sqrt{-1}$ is its immediate environment in any number of dimensions that you wish to consider.

There is nothing uncommon or original in these comments. What can be remarkable about them is their pragmatic application to methodical studies of both real and imagined situations, especially when for purposes of efficiency or philosophy. That too is nothing new: it's simply a convenient method for connecting a purposeful concatenation and limitation of a certain idea by

subjective progression. It is best manipulated by assuming that
the initial idea or impression is not enough for mental satisfaction.
It is therefore considered a suboptimization of something more
comprehensive or otherwise better. It's a provisional optimization
of your subject.

But if thought continues to progress in size, shape, function,
value, beauty, truth, category, or number of dimensions, you realize
that you've reached another suboptimization. These steps may continue ad infinitum until you call it quits. If your conceptions
happen to progress regularly, without deformations, it will be like
blowing up a balloon with a series of breaths, one at a time.

But of course in ordinary life—if you need this methodology at
all—nothing is so simply that useful. In practice, more often than
not, there is a complex transfiguration at the instantaneous conversion from the optimized to the suboptimized (by your standards—
moral, technical, or philosophical), one after another until your
object is optimized, once and for all, in a particularly chosen subsystem of conscience. Naturally these are all matters of relativity.
Otherwise we could never stop an endlessly climbing and expanding chain of being from suboptimization to optimization often
enough for critics, as Anselm reasoned. But that's not the kind of
thing that I'm advising for the middle world of technology and
humanistic sensation.

Aside from opera, this method of criticism would be nonsense
for analysis of the arts. That goes without thinking. But it would
have been useful in building battleships. Nowadays it would help
immensely to clarify the universal waste of energy by owners and
operators of almost everything, warding off salesmen of suboopti-
mizing products in every trade, not the least of which is medical.

The acronym I E C [Immediate Exclusive Consciousness in
Chapman's *Gloucestertide*] led me into this eccentric path as a circling superficial reader of more than I could master as a doctor of
anything but my own I E C (at least as long as it lasts, or piece by
piece in random motion), usually with a sort of joy but always vulnerable to teasing if I talk about what drives me to audible speech
about what I've recorded only in diagrams even for myself. It's only
recently, as I told Fay when she mentioned her gradual loss of hearing, that I'm afraid of getting tongue-tied whenever I try too easily
to say what I mean, no matter how trivial. But of course I've just
been pronounced half trivial etymologically by our chief justice of
the Trivium itself in the liberal arts. . . .

Enter the ghost of Finn, to my good fortune! I began to hope for a wizard's wand of discussion about development of what I labeled Mini-Max Sub-Optimization [M M S O], at which he laughed as just another way of employing methods in systems theory. It was no surprise that he passed it off as nothing new. Wasn't cybernetics recognized as a subsumption of U S T? So with him I dropped the subject as that of a presumptuously clever child. For he was a battleship engineer who'd spent his career thinking all the time about adjudicating and balancing the components of military ship designs. Just as F D R worried about suboptimization in the allocation of people, funds, and materials—as well as strategies and tactics—among elements of the Navy, Army, and Air Force, for Finn himself, like naval architects before him, the ratios of suboptimizations were foremost in his own work, which consisted of constructive and operational suboptimizations according to ultimate purposes of each: viz weight, speed, stability, armor, personal defense, firepower, fire-control, cruising range, fuel capacity, air-defense, safety, damage control, personnel comfort, etc. Each of these required its own quality-control pyramid of suboptimizations—an almost enumerably increased complication to be integrated in the course of several years before and after launching. And obviously entire industries of prefabricate and supplies must be considered to get *U S S Guernsey* and her approximately identical sisters the benefit (over half a decade) of constructive efficiency elsewhere in the country. The Attic Greeks must have had difficulty enough in building their fleet of triremes!

Finn readily applied the same principles of commerce and warfare to those of suboptimizing the national infrastructure. He certainly didn't need any advice from a dilettante, though he didn't say so, in teaching me otherwise as a sympathetic friend. So for him the thing about I E C and its psychological ramifications was of little philosophical interest.

Fay had responded to my intimations of her opinion of M M S O for simple A D L or academic use, seeing that she's a very experienced godmother who happens to be a cultural anthropologist with a mind open to anyone's strange ideas. But she's obviously still occupied with her opus magnum, which presumably has little to do with contemporary technology like mine, which seems to me to be her only prejudice—though I'm not sure it didn't play a small part in her attraction to Finn as an alien Viking despite his modern military career.

So my M M S O must bide its time for me to work out a critical Weltanschauung, if not in some creative work of my own—fiction, nonfiction, or even drama! Anyway it should be a gambit for
edification in U S T.

First of all I must be sure of the ground I stand on, the functional "ego" or subjective ground from which one breaks out to
new attention from some Immediate Exclusive Consciousness or
other mental occupation. It's pretty obviously natural to begin with
an object that in turn becomes a subject of something greater,
unless you close your mind with perfect satisfaction, which will be
called the optimization of your object in whatever medium you are
thinking in—rational or emotional, real or imaginary, commonplace or exceptional; in time, space, or causality; in certainty or
speculation; as hierarchical or as democratic—at any level of finality, at any irregularity in successive shapes of topological expansion,
and always susceptible to overlapping shapes like those of complex
Venn diagrams in two or three or more dimensions.

You have to remember all this when you get more than a single
thermostat for your whole house in the winter if you care for energy
efficiency, as I do in this old bank building with dozens of rooms
and many shared spaces, windows and skylights, pretending it's a
closed system, while ignoring its effect upon the atmospheres of
Dogtown and the world! And it's easier to analyze the federal government strictly in terms of political power regardless of efficiency
or values. But I must devise a lucid paradigm that will easily suggest any useful train of M M S O thinking.

This method of analytical criticism is not regular or rhythmic
like the relationships of small and large sine waves in alternating
electrical current. Instead, typically, it consists of irregular concepts
irregularly related in irregular manners of thought springing from
a definite switch in the brain. Among other purposes it can clarify
one's linked-chain of vision or quantities: that is, say, personal
wealth or "the common good"; or your longevity as the sole purpose of an unpleasant time-consuming exercise that deprives you of
commensurate time for education or pleasure not yet enjoyed.

It probably depends on what happens, step by step, in your successive suboptimizations, either as personal feelings or as increasing
social sympathies. At every conversion from the experience of suboptimization that delivers you to the transitory wisdom of another
suboptimization—that is, unless you settle for the best, according

to your ultimate limit of interest—naturally there may be unintended consequence at the latest step in your opinions or consciousness, either at a pause or at some later time, when you resume with a new suboptimization.

If you've reconsidered your final optimization as too complex to analyze—or as too many options for the next step, like a concert of possible relationships in a cinema—you'll have to draw a diagram of new beginnings and start each one separately with its own M M S O if it's worth further pursuit as branch, twig, or foliage from the trunk of your original contemplation.

It all depends, at this stage, on efflorescence!

What I must do is get past all this theoretical dreaming without abstractions or charts. On that count I'm always guilty as charged!

I must boil all this foolish entanglement down to a paradigm for ordinary practical purposes. For me the simplest is always the hardest . . . like writing poetry!

Yet it may turn out that the most innovative use of M M S O's critical analysis will be in the anachronistic fourth dimension, when the succession of suboptimistic platforms changes not only in one or more shapes but in time, especially for budgeting and forecasting. I must work on that for simulations. Think of it, for example, as a series of matrices at intervals of time, like a sheaf of lengthening spreadsheets. In other words, a diachronistic map of past or future for various levels and departments of government!

They already call me the Scrutator, but an analytical critic is more than that, as an inspector general is more than an accountant—just as our Controller is my author—greater than He by whom nothing greater can be conceived. . . . Literature is larger than science—or at least as far as I like to believe. I can't write my own optimization. . . .

. . . Ah, if I tell my godmother about all this she'll want to say "Beware your confidence. . . . You already have too many acronyms. You may be adding to a house of cards. Keep your balance, dear Caleb!"

She may be right. I'm too complacent. It all depends. . . . Beware complacency. Beware half-education when dealing with fully educated systems. "Don't get too proud of yourself. Check your suboptimized tank of fuel!"

Trigonometry is my limit.

CODA

Agon

P M

▼ I'm sorry to be interrupting what may be the best time for your own work. And again, I apologize for breaking into your day at all when I phoned to ask for a reception.

▲ It's less disconcerting than your cryptic little inquiries posted a mile and a half across the inner harbor to check up on me. I thought that at last you were coming over to fire me! Short of that, what can I do to welcome you? —Let me take your coat. I've just made some coffee, but I don't stock sugar or cream.

▼ That's auspicious. I come in concord.

▲ Do you want to inspect the engine room? So far I'm satisfied with Mooncusser's janitorial service—at least after a few pointers from me. My logbook entries are always up to date by nine AM for your inspection there downstairs at any time thereafter. I think everything in the building is pretty much as the Commander left it, except perhaps for a few of my housekeeping idiosyncrasies up here. Otherwise he was a perfect man for me to emulate. —Have you had any complaints from the occupants?

▼ None at all! Everything seems to be running smoothly and efficiently. But I'm afraid I've been unintentionally rude. My mother and I are pleased with your management, and we've certainly found no fault with your landscape supervision over at our house, especially in the winter storms. She feels warm and secure. I'd hate to think that you and I have started out on the wrong foot together. I must admit that it's my fault, not Ma-mai's, who's finally been correcting some of my first impressions about your part in her intimate caucus, which has had nothing to do with business, much to do with politics. Shall we shake hands, for only the second time? —Good.

▲ It's time for me to correct my own faulty impressions. I'm not as surly as I probably sounded, and usually less unshaven than a castilian should be. I make it a point to look better as your mother's agent before I'm seen in public, even in the solemn corridors below.

▼ I've been too careless with my shorthand communications because a lot of unfamiliar things are required of the prodigal daughter trying to make amends for all sorts of distant neglect. But I'm very glad I got back to Dogtown in time for Ma-mai's Court. Now my plans have changed. I'm going to stay in her house. — Thanks, it smells good and strong. —Today I came over just to ask for a couple of voluntary favors.

▲ Glad to be of service, if possible.

▼ As to the first: it's been a week or more since Ma-mai and I started discussing with Mr Boxshaw what can be done to fix me up with my own quarters in the attic. I want a skylight as large and clear as possible, as well as a balcony, with a fire escape required by the building code for a separate apartment. And of course as many window views that I can have to see some landscape and seascape. —By the way, I'd never seen a snowscape on this cape before! I can't hope we get more snow. —First of all, Ma-mai sent me here to ask you over to look at Mr Boxshaw's plan. She says, in her own words, that you have been a dreamer of many mansions.

▲ That's true, but without poetic license—only as a free-handed draftsman with opinions and prejudices about practically anything brought up casually in soirees or seaside walks à deux—in short, an amateur critic of houses without knowing much about the residential building codes. Anyway I'm glad to see your mother at any time for any reason.

▾ That's very kind of you.

▴ But to the point, even sight unseen, I can suggest, if structurally possible in the existing attic, which I've seen only from outdoors, that you have windows on all four sides, making sure that from at least one position inside you can see both pairs of opposites when all doors are open, forming a rectangular cross of what used to be called railroad flats. That much a cat deserves!

▾ Sounds functional.

▴ Also, if we aren't at aesthetic odds, whether or not you change the exterior color of the house, don't trim it with white paint. But I may have already mentioned that crotchet of mine to your gentle mother more than once! Now that I've escaped public slavery, thanks to her, my landlady and godmother, I tend to speak too freely for no better reason than to rejoice at my liberty of speech.

▾ Well then, when I can be sure that Mr Boxshaw will be there. He seems awestruck by your reputation as a constructor of ideas. I don't think he'll have any strong aesthetic opinion. How about some time before Monday? I'll try to negotiate a time at less than half of your and Ma-mai's common inconvenience.

▴ It's always too early to predict and too late to repent, Wat Cibber would have said.

▾ Now for your advice about my surprise Christmas present for Ma-mai, which will be too technological for me by half. She probably won't refuse to use it if she knows you recommend it for her work. I'd like to get the same for myself. I'm talking about secretly buying a couple of those new so-called personal computers that seem to be getting half Atlantis so excited for writing as well numbering and recording. Sounds too good to be true—if you take time to learn the skill.

▴ That could be a godsend for her! A private cathode ray tube for our queen! Just what I've been thinking of for myself! But I haven't seen one yet. It looks like an ad for one that I see in your hand.

▾ Have you had your lunch? Can we talk about it now?

▴ By all means! But all I can tell you about PCs is the general concept of a desktop computer. Now that I don't have access to the small-scale computerized system we installed in Ibicity Hall, I haven't paid any attention to technical developments. The best place I know to learn about them is an OHM retail store just outside Unabridge Square. My car isn't very reliable. Can you drive us

down there, if you're free all afternoon? Afterwards, if we're too late
to avoid the worst traffic, we can have an early dinner somewhere
nearby. That way I can tutor you about as much as I can learn in
the new jargon.

▼ Do you really have that much time to spare! With parents
like mine I've always been very hesitant to intrude upon the silent
cogitation of elders.

▲ I happen to know that you're less than a year younger than I
am, and born in the same delivery room. This may be a good time
to dissipate the aura of nearly wordless misunderstandings. But in
any case it's a relief to find, if I hear you aright, that I haven't permanently displeased either the godmother or the godsister living
with Olympian scenery just over yonder ridge of granite. Please tell
me what you interpreted as my mein of resentment or aversion.

▼ At first I thought you might be a sort of lion's cub in my
mother's court.

▲ You mean because I was too playful?

▼ Not exactly. More like a pied piper that shouldn't be trusted
when he grows up. It was just that as a clever technocrat you
seemed to be a pundit of everything no one else knew, a presumptuous guest that Ma-mai didn't seem to see through. Full of unsubstantiated theories, full of criticisms. Too sure of yourself, when you
hardly knew the Greek alphabet and had to guess at Latin, which
you seemed to scorn as just the decadent medium for Virgil, who
was hardly worth more than his service to Dante! You were an Ion
who had dismissed Euripides as too decadent for Classic tragedy!
Furthermore, until Ma-mai disabused me, I thought you might
have taken a creative writing course!

▲ Fair enough. I do exaggerate now and then. Sometimes, over
the years, I'm inconsistent. Don't you think that might have
encouraged an enrichment of meanings, for lack of poesy, when I
didn't appreciate tragi-comedy. Have you never admitted opinions
remembered from the narrowminded depth of youth? You should
give me credit for rearranging my valences. Without redefining
tragedy I've become a comedian.

▼ They say women are allowed to change their minds. They
have the better negative capability.

▲ For my part, speaking of prejudices, I guessed that you were
a mirthless wine-taster, perhaps an aesthetic martinet, scornful of
her own beauty, naturally irritated by a guy who attended your

mother for the intellectual glory reflected from her unique reputation among the cognoscenti, or simply for the ordinary sympathy with which he buried her cat. I thought you were no less conscious of truly aristoi culture than you thought I pretended to.

▼ I'm simply peculiar, eccentric. Weird, like a harmless witch without a coven. You do have imagination!

▲ You now find that I was a seer through glasses as darkly as yours. If you don't mind a personal remark, I especially like to hear your level tones of speech, with diction as nice as your mother's. Which comports with your tasteful omission of cosmetics and high heels. You look like a dancer in comfortable clothes.

▼ Don't be needlessly polite.

▲ I'm sorry if this is taking too much liberty. It's simply because, as a mature lion, this may be my last chance at insubordination. If you take the l out of lion all you'll get is an 'ion.

▼ Hah, you have a laugh that's even nicer!

▲ So blarney isn't beneath you! Paracelsus says that no drug is without its poison. I'm uncertain about how to treat a godsister. —There!

▼ Your handshake is firm.

▲ I was led to believe that servomechanisms, not compliments, were your cups of tea. . . .

*

▼ They say that as a systems analyst you are a very keen critic of suboptimization.

▲ With you I now find nothing at all to criticize about my semi-hemi-demi-sister. Since I'm not doing the driving I can be objective from a very fair angle. At the same time I can see outside how well you drive on this infamous Felly, up over the Eisenhower Bridge three hundred feet above the estuary, while there's not too much competing traffic. I notice you don't gun up the accelerator to maintain unnecessary velocity up hill, but gather even more than maximum legal speed only when the momentum is safe and efficient. You're a rare bird! Does that observation betray my quasi-consanguinity?

▼ For me, driving men mild is instinctive. But I've read or heard more than one of your theories—

▲ Please, hypotheses!

▼ Don't be so modest! Let stand the hypothesis of pure tragedy, if you wish, but it's preposterous to bandy about critical terms like "suboptimization" before you define the system!

▲ It was in the management of my own Central Management System life that I got into the habit of using that word, but it pleased the ear of Finn Macdane in his discussion of obsolescent battleships and fleets.

▼ That reminds me of seeing *Gloucesterman* one summer when I was a little girl. —You see, some of your far-fetched analogies are interesting enough to give me pause. I'm downright curious about the nebulous claims you make for a mystical Synectic Method of Diagnostic Correlation [S M D C]. I'm also perplexed by your transcendentally symbolic Isorectotetrahedron in the Gilgamesh plays. But what I'd really like to know more about, and debate, is the apparent continuum of Dromenology, which seems to stretch from one end of anthropology to the other, including the arts, which I hear extends it ad infinitum! You must admit that you're a funny man!

▲ Well I must admit that's a theory still without much more than a genetic hypothesis that I abstracted from the books of an English woman overlooked by the male Classics industry almost as soon as she died. But it is meant, in my next tour of life, to explain the evolution of all culture, with the assistance, don't you see, of some foundation or university sustaining a collegium or network of enthusiastically openminded scholars willing to expatiate upon evidence for the idea. Guided by my ghost, they would reach out, with the prospect of grants and fellowships, to stimulate the mentality of extant professors in half a dozen different international departments. So even if you didn't call dromenology a half-baked conceit it would be extolling a pipe dream.

▼ That I won't probe further. Yet Ma-mai seems to think that some of your cathexes would be intriguing to someone she would classify as a sympathetically poetic psychologist.

▲ A what?

▼ Well, never mind now. I told you I'm really sorry for misjudging your authenticity. I often respect mad ideas. Maybe at least there *was* a cultural if not blood continuum between Uruk and Delphi, then from Delphi to Dante, and Dante to Dublin via Languedoc; from fertility dances to Bach's unaccompanied cello suites; or even directly from Homeric verse to your prosaic imagination of the Gilgamesh myth—if there really *can* be such tautology as fictitious myth!

▲ You're the only one who's ever understood me!

▼ But in the name near at hand of a genuinely anthropological philosophy (or philosophical anthropology)—I know you appreciate my mother as much as anyone does—can we talk right now about how I can keep her in a physical condition to deal with your rith and mitual in her conscientious summa? Even without your audacious (if not absurd) thema, she's already been overworked as culture's most prodigious student. Without saying so, she's now facing the absolute of time too soon to express all she has in mind—not like Mr Casaubon but like the Oxford History of the World!

▲ I'm very glad you appreciate your mother as much as I appreciate mine in another domain of originality.

▼ Too soon, in her remaining time, Ma-mai must complete with meticulous prose a vast chrestomathy—omitting only her study of such neognostic extrication as Alterian symbullisticism, which I join you in despising!

▲ God bless my luck! —Do I hear a little backhanded affinity on your part after all?

▼ My mother's worried about her mental faculties just when she needs them more than ever. She thinks even her nominally marginal time for A D L [Activities of Daily Living], not to mention her productive reading and writing, is flying faster through the calendar every day—meaning that her mind is getting slower. She laughs about that conundrum, saying that it reminds her of the young Einstein riding on a train when he hit upon Relativity just as he noticed that the landscape seemed stationary! But I know she's trying to conceal most of her apprehension about forgetting names and even words, sometimes even commonplace nouns, that are presumably still hidden in her underground word-hoard— though most of them are eventually recovered ad hoc in unexpected contexts. "Father Time doesn't compensate senescence for its dilapidation." she said this morning. "The collective entropy Caleb reminds us of is somber enough!"

▲ All the more reason to get her the PC, especially if OHM already has a few philological programs that eventually will save her various kinds of time in research and editing as well as typing.

▼ But I bet that like all busy old intellectuals she'll resist innovation of means because of the time it takes to learn how to use a machine rapidly. "I haven't got all day!" she'll say. "The 'Bega Press has been breathing down my dewlaps. You'd think the world's anthropologists were clamoring to see my criticisms of

them!" I'm sure she won't doubt the ophelimity of a desktop computer if you, the efficiency expert of this inefficient microtopopolis,
second my urging. But she'll still be weighing the odds against her
own capability to learn new habits soon enough to delay Father
Time.

▲ Don't worry. In a few days I'll find out what programs are
available; then you'll quickly learn how to use them in a few more.
Then you'll quickly teach her the basic procedures. Out of sheer
curiosity she'll have mastered what she wants by New Year's Day.
She's already used a similar keyboard on electric typewriters and her
so-called word-processor for millions of words!

▼ I'm afraid she'll be as cautious about the transition as about
everything we've seen in her jurisprudence. And maybe she'll want
to know *how* or *why* everything on the keyboard works!

▲ With our own head start before Christmas we'll have plenty
of time to anticipate her skepticism! All we may need today is our
credit cards. If you and I buy the same model you can wrap hers
with its own instruction manual and hide it for your Christmas tree
ahead of time, while we fool around secretly with ours. —Now
don't tell me you won't have a Christmas tree. She had one last year,
without an iconoclastic daughter! I helped her set it up!

▼ My God, you *are* useful. But I am *not* iconoclastic. That's
like calling me a bitch. I'm sentimental about certain symbols and
animals, especially when I'm overseas.

▲ No offense meant! At last you're revealing tidbits of your
natural kindness! —At any rate, you may fathom OHM's version of
expository English sooner than I do. Reading their manual will
probably be less exasperating than cascading telephone calls to
"Customer Service". —Hey, come to think of it, we might get a
discount if we buy the three PCs on one ticket. Unless the dealer
has all three PCs in stock they'll be shipped from their Old Homestead plant soon enough. I think it's too early in the PC market to
waste all the time it would take to study and compare the infant
competition. The machine's operating instructions and programs
that come with the machine, or follow later, are solecistically called
"software". They are copyrighted like books or music. . . .

*

▲ . . . Meanwhile try to get some hints of the conveniences
that your mother ought to have. Then make sure your mother

understands how easy it is to move any piece of text—as short as a single letter or as long as whole pages or chapters—anywhere forward or behind her place in a manuscript. She'll also see how quickly you can find any word or phrase or name that she may have already used—or the negative assurance.

▼ I hope you'll demonstrate every act you speak. I think we should get the printers and plenty of paper today.

▲ I'll be glad to catechize the godmother who delivered me into the world and soon afterwards into the church, though unable to follow up the oath she swore at the stoup. Serving your mother would be serving Athena, whose attic I gratefully occupy. Dogtown is my loft, where I now live in her Athenian attic! You can bear witness.

▼ I hope you serve her better than you served Liam Yeats your Homer! I don't think you interpreted the Four Faculties properly. You used his symbols for your own purposes, and made his heroes into your own stars. I looked into Chapman's Homer when I lived in Hume.

▲ That may be true to some degree, but, if so, it's literary evolution, even unto the latest fecundation! But you shouldn't hold against me what you think I thought at the age of twenty-four!

▼ I admit that you're free to play fast and loose with Gilgamesh, thus much nearer than us to the first dance around. Of course you enjoyed a leeway of two or three thousand years and all the ambiguities of several more millennia of languages to exploit. A little bird named Caroline told me you are now working on a play to rationalize your own cobweb between the first and third of your prosaic scripts. Myself, I'm especially hoping for an explanation of how your Nimrod had come to be two-thirds of a god. And, for that matter, where he and his Kassites came from in the first place. Not to mention the métier who must have manufactured Norkid's eyeglasses. But I like some of your ideas. —I don't mind your critical curiosity. It's better than being ignored with a spit and a grunt. By the way, you might have mentioned that Eber's people too are obviously questionable for biblical culture.

On the other hand, Keats would never have voted you the Academy Award for negative capability!

▲ Such ambivalent sticks and stones will break no bones! — But you can't much longer keep dodging my perfectly reasonable questions about yourself, at least in the name of your mother! I suppose keeping me in the dark with smokescreens is better than laying me off. Perhaps an irritating half-brother-once-removed who takes after his own mother's manners by butting into your family affairs *should* be rebuffed; but still, as your technological consultant, enthralled by your mother, I deserve to hear more about her daughter than the future quarters of the princess her daughter.

▼ What do you want to know. I'm not teasing you?

▲ You know perfectly well what I want to know, because you know that for all I know you may be a B D I agent on serendipitous leave, by the innocent name of Morgan, from investigation of Premature Antifascism in its latest version. —Seeing that you've obviously probed some aspects of my own ousia.

▼ Oh my God, has Ma-mai been talking to you? —I'll have to reveal a bit of my mysterious substance before the end of this excursion, but not while I'm trying to find a place to park and negotiate. —Meanwhile I hope we can find a good place to park near where you'll have been kind enough to direct us to a tap of beer where it is quiet enough to hear you tell me what a byte is, and a little—not too much—about an operating system. By the way, what's a macro?

▲ You don't have to learn that kind of my substance. —Listen to what's just occurred to me: couldn't I be more useful by helping your mother with a higher level of A D L in reading writing or arithmetic? In my own bachelor life they take far more time than progressive substance. Assistance in that kind of labor around here or in Unabridge, when I'm not needed in this castle's routine.

▼ You must be mad! I thought you were infinitely pressed for private time alone!

▲ So I am, for the most part. But right now I happen to be mulling all sorts of dramatic possibilities. I can do some of that on the hoof, or, accidentally among cloisters of unrelated knowledge— at my own pace, short of an urgency. I might need to borrow her car. I wouldn't do it for anyone one else. It's for my own benefit.

▼ It's certainly a far-fetched motive.

▲ Just for a while at least. As an occasional literary researcher or courier. I'd always spare some time for her because it would contribute to my truncated education.

▼ Where would that leave me? A princess twiddling her long braid like a superannuated princess waiting for a prince? I seem to have heard that some such canonized arrangement of A D L didn't work out well for you with the Father Superior when you were also doing stock exchange work for the Melchizedek as your regular job at the Laboratory. I doubt that it would please you for long to serve an irritable old genius known for demanding nothing less than mental telepathy for communication with any slow-witted servant who thinks at less speed than she does.

▲ That's slander! She's not like that at all!

▼ I dare say you weren't brought up within the family. Inside her study she sometimes bears no resemblance to her social self, especially when she's rightfully worried about her longevity. The more she loves one the more she shows her impatience. And I think she's fond of you already. —Actually she's more of a saint than a witch. I wouldn't want you to mar her appreciation of a godson like you. —Besides, I think you're too ignorant of foreign languages to do the translations that are sometimes important in her writing and citing.

▲ You may be right that I'm getting too close to your family. But I persist in intriguing curiosity about you its product.

▼ My own impression is that you are underestimating your own need for independent time to make up for what you've spent in serving secondary causes unworthy of your true vocation. But right now I'm more worried about what I can do to help Ma-mai. For the first time, as far as I can know, she's seriously thinking about her aging limits, especially in memory loss. She's admitted this disadvantage to me, and she's finally agreed to let me take her to a neurologist. At least we'll hear the medical opinion of a man who's unlikely to understand the especially excruciating depth of fear for an old lady who has no intention to settle for rest and recreation in extended longevity. He may rule out any irreversible difficulty.

▲ She probably should start building up a word-hoarde to preserve old ideas. I don't think her new ideas will be discouraged. Certainly her wisdom will continue to grow. I'm sure she doesn't have one of the syndromes that withered my mother's mental vitality at an earlier age.

▼ I hope you're right. She jokes about being a proverbial absent-minded professor when she can't immediately think of a famous proper name on the tip of her tongue. So far it always comes back to her in a few minutes, when we're talking about something else, or when I happen to be able to prompt it. Then she recalls it quite clearly—and probably most of what she ever associated with it.

▲ Probably it's not absolutely lost, as my mother's faculties were. Isn't it just a weakened and renewable connection rather than a final scission? It's said to be normal in old age. She's no older than many an effective politician. Experience is invaluable. She must have plenty of mnemonic devices in her study even without a PC.

▼ Maybe so. But she certainly *is* slowed up, just when she's most determined to work faster. That's what scares her. She's littering her study and kitchen table with slips of paper—I assume they're jots and tittles of memoranda: abbreviated reminders, even single words, maybe names or short quotations, or keys to new ideas that come to mind for future integration. Her desks didn't used to look disconcerted. In society her ideas and judgments still seem as unimpaired as they were at your trial, but in private she gropes slowly for words that used to fly as smoothly as her concatenated thoughts.

▲ Redburn would say that she's diving deeper for herself, necessarily leaving all the rest of organized life less attended.

▼ I hope you are right. That's rather comforting to hear you say.

▲ She's not grasping for straws. Aside from anchored love and personal sympathy, it takes certain old people too much energy to keep hold of the center when launching their final tangent. It's a matter of shaking off formerly useful distractions—such as the classify-and-sort problem! The re-classify and re-sort problem! A computer can't take care of your bookshelves, but it's worth the minimum effort to make it help postpone the struggle against cumulative desktop disorder that no number of servants could relieve you of. Accept a PC's help and curse the rest, unless you expect to count on a peacefully healthy unambitious retirement in pleasant society, contented with prizes and posthumous fame! —Of course all that advice won't keep *me* from postponing what I'm trying to accomplish, perhaps until it's too late!

▼ I won't comment on your aging prospects. My mother complains that she can no longer even manipulate analogies with the simplest algebraic ratios—she who used to address mathematicians at philosophical conferences! For pity's sake, she's only seventy-one! Furthermore she humorously mutters that in the kitchen she can't go through her solo breakfast routine without making at least one misstep in her immemorial rhythm for A D L—just because she gives a thought or two to something intended for segregated notation in another world. She's seriously worried about not being able to finish her summa. Anyway, it's the main reason I'm settling down with her in the creaking old house.

▲ Don't exaggerate the natural slowing down of aging capacitors and resistors in biological electricity. Get her a good copy machine. That may be almost as helpful as a computer. Think of all the great old savants and philosophers who've relied upon such devices as the *visual arrangement* of the books on their shelves, not just the books themselves. They must have had lots of secret methods to maintain what now seems preternatural memory. Besides, I'm sure that in household A D L your mother's often quite naturally preoccupied with the unique specific gravity of sentences she's about to form, or already carrying from her bed, perhaps with exciting new thoughts, while standing at the kitchen sink. Who in posterity would rather have had her more efficient with commonplace utensils? Probably many geniuses are absentminded at any age of their brain. In Dogtown we've often laughed with her when she apologetically uttered "I don't remember" in the most trifling context of conversation! Besides, nowadays we don't have to depend upon our own memory for almost anything that isn't as habitual as driving a car or washing dishes. As a matter of fact, Finn admired her efficiency. "It's wonderful that she's so fundamentally systematic!"

▼ I hear you. But anyway, please—my worry is just between us. Apparently we happen to share this mother, in a peculiar sense. You seem to sense better than anyone else why she's a miser of solitary time, and wants no time wasted in talk about it with me as something taken for granted. You've probably seen a lot of her when the work is going well and she's as sociable as a kindly grandmother. Of course it's not just a matter of living as long as possible. But I wish I'd been here to know Commander Macdane because I have a hunch that he was good for her life expectancy—even after we lost him. —The Court of Love seemed to find him one of your divinities. —No, I . . . I'm sorry. I didn't mean to joke about Dogtown's latest occult legend!

▲ Just don't call it a *myth*! I was a bit jealous of that father. But you were speaking about the goddess we both serve in the present tense. Please proceed confidentially.

▼ I keep thinking that Ma-mai is vaguely disappointed that I haven't come up with mnemonic tricks for her to search her own library and file cabinets for names and dates and quotations that she wouldn't have needed until recently as she approaches the all-important finishing touches of what's going to be a disputed masterpiece of anthropology "if only I can have enough *productive* time!"

That's an idiom I now often hear. She says that inconvenient petty time takes up more space in life than the time she lives for.

▲ Yes! I know how she despises the perversity of Axel and his kind!

▼ She can't help getting more and more irritable about all kinds of A D L, which includes medical appointments as well as eating even meals that are made for her. She'd rather ignore signs of cancer than get trapped in what doctors would expect to be a negative medical test. Anything that interrupts cerebral concentration! Even her favorite music. Now for the first time she makes fun of weakening legs that inhibit the choreography of private calisthenics that for many years have been unbegrudged as exercises well spent, like walking, as counterentropic time for mind and body.

▲ It's nice to see how well you seem to understand her.

▼ I've been away too long not to have been preconsciously aware of my intuitive duty as a gratefully liberated daughter. Nevertheless, I wouldn't confess to you my anxiety if it weren't that all of a sudden *she* seems alarmed by minor ailments she's never had before—such as tiny intermittent headaches on either side. The other day, when waking from nap, there was a pain she says felt like a thaw of her whole frozen right calf, not just a muscle spasm but a sort of electrical cramp in all the nerves and blood vessels, lasting a full five minutes! That seems serious. She's anything but a hypochondriac, and she's always been in vigorous good health for her age, a brisk long-distance walker, as you know. Until now I've never heard her actually complain about her own health, no matter how irritably or impatiently she put up with unnecessary A D L interventions or disruptive children. Do you think it's just an ordinary harbinger of aging, like what we all have ahead of us?

▲ I suppose so. If she hadn't been as psychosomatically robust as a scientific oak tree all these years, reading and writing as much as the Britannica, while anticipating all arguments for or against her humane ideas, engaging every student or scholar in any way curious about her unbounded variety of interests, her writings would not have had the specific gravity of a very rich fruit-cake that lasts for billions of bytes with a taste as fresh as cheesecake!

▼ What a silly gallant you are! Better not try that to her face.

▲ Well you know what I mean. I'm not a sumptuary poet!

▼ Not any kind of poet at all. But you should try to be, for Gilgamesh's sake!

▲ Give your mother the credit for the bravery and stamina that we can imagine she deserves from her academic wars. I'm sure she's always had to go out of her way to sustain male authority in her radical development of the best headway. As you should know, what I infer from a range of academic reading, colleagues (mainly men) who know her personally recognize her creative scholarship in their own citations, but most others in her field omit her in their societies of influential bibliography! You can't help admiring the subtly ironic humor with which she calmly exposes the weaknesses of their conventional positions. Yet apparently in the immense multilingual bibliographies of her own books many an author omitted from both her text and index is conscientiously listed as a matter of collegial courtesy.

▼ Or contempt?

▲ Except perhaps for a certain Tudor monk's history of Christian liturgy, her gracefully packed works of scholarship are the longest and most comprehensive of the researched kind that I have ever read. It will take a couple of more generations, if ever, for anthropologists to appreciate the philosophical value of her earlier paperbacks, which have been read far and wide by enthusiastic students and common readers of the polychromatic generation.

▼ My dear boy, I permit myself to accept my mother's Geisteswissenschaften praises. But how come you, without even a master's degree, think you know so much about the handicaps of academic women, passing judgment on their judges?

▲ Because I'm an expert in lost causes.

▼ Your condescendence isn't even self-conscious!

▲ Just poking at you.

▼ Someday you may find my name as a footnote for some pamphlet in the dustiest section of Dogtown history in a dusty shelf of the local rare-book trade.

Well our widow's royalties are still keeping bread on her table. Fortunately Ma-mai has admirers and allies at the Norumbega University Press, even though there are few fans among the big names of Anthropology Philosophy or History of Ideas inside the Garth. However, it might interest you to learn that, Press or no Press, she's been given pause to reconsider or add thoughts in consequence of her withdrawal to this town of dogs and gulls. That's why she's running late.

▲ I hope you're not blaming us for hindering the magnum opus!

▼ Among others, you and your phantom fathers. But one of them was all to the good for her—the one who was extolled by vociferous Hecuba as an extinquished man. Even if the tonic of your town turns out to have been nothing but a pinch of baking powder for her life-work, I think her suppressed grief for him was the only pressure that could have diverted her—before she was fully aware— from her supreme cathexis to such a therapeutic recreation as the three-day assize for that curiously inconsequential Court of Love. Commander Macdane seems to have been a man of many interests.

▲ And so he was. For me especially from years when the number of battleships was a measure of global seapower. But he was a great reader of history. I think he read as many books as she did, but mainly just for literary satisfaction. Aside from his professional journals, as far as I know he had nothing of his own in print. That's too bad because his knowledge and experience were apparently unlimited in scope. I thought he and your mother were of some- what complementary minds, like wave and particle at certain levels of energy. But only Father Duncannon would have matched her cre- ative intellect. As for King Arthur, he was too much of a specialist in the manipulation of market power to have cultivated more than a managerial soul.

▼ Anyway you've had the advantage of good odds!

▲ What generally surprises me is how your mother, all those years a student of culture and in its international currents, found time to nurse and teach you and your brother how to play and hunt for yourselves. She must have been a maternal lion conscious of the whole world's flora and fauna day and night!

▼ We weren't half grown but already interested in at least the whole savannah when my father left us, years before he died on his motorcycle. Ma-mai was extremely attentive to our official educa- tion. For the most part she was lucky enough to farm it out to pretty good public schools in college towns—though not so lucky on a few out-back plains. The rest of our training was her cool exam- ple, mainly in reading and music. Our maned father was a rarer presence, but still a huge influence of course. An even rarer presence after he founded another pride. Yet then she let him take us away for vacation trips or weekends. But all along she was very watchful of our health and extracurricular dangers. We had tutors or practice for things like music or tennis or dance, and foreign languages when we wanted them. She also encouraged us to join team sports.

▲ Sounds like a perfect childhood.

▾ Naturally she was too occupied with her own teaching jobs, as well as with personal studies, for much cuddling or companionship when we voluntarily outgrew the fireside stage. So we never had the kind of demonstrative love that you benefited from. Only now do I think I may be getting as close to her as I would have liked in my early days of kindly discipline and self-reliance. That's why I've decided to stay in Dogtown. Our early summers in that old house of my father's family are the happiest of my maternal memories. She was always a good mother, but I'm sure storge never came before everything else in her soul the way it did for your fantastic mother!

▴ Seeing that you know *I'm* an unwise childe, let me ask: Do you assume there's no uncertainty about your paternity?

▾ I doubt that anyone who knew Ma-mai in 1936, or later, could have even framed a silent hypothetical question of infidelity on the part of husband-adoring Fayaway Gabriel Morgan! She was still a young full-time nurse supporting my father, when he was a full-time graduate student who'd hardly even get up from his desk to empty the ice-chest water at home, to say nothing of cooking or housework! —So she told us as teenagers when she was angry at his self-centered paternity. Everything wasn't sweetness and light by that time. Then he was sometimes regarded as a la-de-da golden boy of a classically elite academic upper class. But she laughed about it as we grew older, until he was no longer alive.

▴ I'm lucky that I never had to suffer the rending of gods.

▾ But I never took sides after he was finally gone because I could see that she wasn't an ideal wife—though thank God for *that*! I loved and admired my father, who still unfairly favored me as his only daughter. But finally, as it's turned out, Ma-mai's as much my intellectual hero as yours. You must believe that. Now I'm a penitent daughter who left her here alone so long, having deprived her of grandchildren on my side—which I believe she'd half like to have had, at arm's length, without duties or moral responsibility, as long as they didn't take much time from her incessant reading and writing! She now all but confesses that both my brother and I were Adam's idea in the first place. . . . But wait! For God's sake: why in hell am I telling you all this? —She seems very pleased to have you take the place of Felixity. I believe that spayed Norseland Forest cat wanted to mother one of the squirrels!

Ma-mai has difficulty watching those acrobats now. If I can get her to take time off I'm going to drive her to the ophthalmic clinic where I got tested for my new glasses. But she's as canny as a cat that knows you're planning to take her to the vet. I think she needs cataract surgery. She already has blepharitis. But she wouldn't agree even to think about such an A D L interruption until there's a threat of something like a detached retina. All she says to some such prospect is "Wait until I've finished my book. Then I'll be ready for all kinds of medical polemics!"

▲ Maybe we should borrow a lion's cage. . . .

▼ She blames you and Finn Macdane with Systems Theory for making her slow down and revise or justify her final section, which is on philosophical anthropology.

▲ Or anthropological philosophy. To make fun of it, maybe?

▼ As long as she can see well enough to read everything worth writing on a new idea nobody can get her to skip even an undereducated amateur's one or two that her colleagues wouldn't deign to consider. —My father in Classical Studies, to the contrary, simply took it for granted that his own hypotheses, if not his theories, were the proper status quo in his arcane specialties, the only ones worth contemporary study until he gave notice in one of the journals.

▲ She may not love A D L, but it seems to me that she would never go to bed without washing all dirtied dishes. I think Finn loved her for that kind of self-discipline despite her aspirations. —By the way, just last week I noticed her hearing aid for the first time.

▼ She's never tried to look like anything but a fearless old maid. She had to give up her cello discipline when she began teaching anthropology, but she knows as much as there is to know about music history and theory. The other day when she was feeling good with after-supper wine she made me laugh with a vocal rendition of Pythia intoning to Ion that Apollo was his father: "*Music, my boy, is for life, and life is time; but so is reading for writing. Time for listening is the last straw. That good lord saved me from opera!*" She swears her hearing is not much worse than it was, except as a quick defense against nuisance phone calls.

▲ Your voice is as nice as hers.

▼ Not when I respond to Cans lying on the radio!

▲ They're what mortify our wailing wall. But my own voice never gets off the ground, except when I'm all by myself screeching at their menu.

▼ Then at least you and I can drink cheers to that. Caliban and Miranda!

A M

▼ I'd never had such clarity from Scotch as last night.

▲ It was meant for cheese with a landlady's taste.

▼ You have the stamina of Caliban. It was well worth risking your opinion of my immodesty.

▲ And for me the rewards of Ferdinand!

▼ Deserved for the virtuosity of Ariel.

▲ A princess the prize.

▼ I wasn't supposed to tell you this: Last night when I called Ma-mai to tell her that I wouldn't be home for breakfast she chuckled and said "It's about time to unveil yourself under the glass of our star chamber." Finn had that bed made to his specifications by a craftsman in Dogtown.

▲ I never would have thought of your Ma-mai as a Pandora! Who would have thunk it, my mother would have laughed!

▼ It emboldened me. —Your coffee's much better than yesterday's.

▲ I doubled its crescendo and decrescendo to keep you from going to sleep yet again. We are now well introduced, thanks to your transmogrification of attitude and amplification of liberty! —You purred like a panther. Perfect kinesthetic proprioception!

▼ At intervals. Twice you o'er-clouded moon and stars! I hope my skylight at home will be as transparent as yours.

▲ Shall we take turns in venue? Would the queen-mother approve of that?

▼ For the time being you'll be invited only when she's not home. I'm leery of having you two in the same house overnight. —Oh boy, poached eggs on buttered toast! That's ten times better than boiled eggs *followed* by the toast.

▲ I think our tastes congratulate each other from under the skin. So it's also about time you stopped teasing me about who you are in the web of society. I haven't wanted or dared to ask your mother point blank about the prodigal daughter who seems to have been away from home for many a year. But you *promised* me! Haven't I sung for my supper? After all, you've opened me your carnal existence under a night black sky—as well also when purpled, blue, white, and battleship gray as the earth continued its roll—between sleeping and waking (as when Liam Yeats dreams up poems); but so far only as a palpable succubus sans merci with gleaming skin in your secret time space and causality. I've made a few random or romantic guesses, but I don't know even enough to imagine a world you could breathe in.

▼ I know you're fishing for a lady's information more private than public. That's premature on our first day together, even though our whole coterie thinks it knows quite a bit about your derivation. Just because I've been enticed into pleroma it doesn't mean that you're yet my confessor. In the meantime I'll tell you semi-public truth, if that will keep you interested in my peculiar apparition.

▲ I thought you might be a poet!

▼ Merlin! That much clairvoyance penetrates my soft stone wall! Our beatitude of catapulsed atonement may give way to persistent inquisition in the Star Chamber. Next time will you take an oath here in the microcosm? Let there be *only three* of us here in D T to know that I'm a Shape Changer.

▲ I swear. Like mother, like daughter, when it comes to pseudonyms!

▼ But Ma-mai's pen name is only incidental, a consequence of harmless personal history, hardly secret. Mine is more functional than mere convenience. My perfectly legal duplicity is simple ambiguity. No pictures allowed! With an assumed moniker I am invisible to the world that knows me. For Dogtown citizens there's no correlation, which is just as I almost always want it. Whereas, according to what I've read, you've lived since gestation with an obscurely conjugated name oddly drawn from religion and magic, my pen name has flitted reasonably often before your literary eyes on periodical tables of contents for articles that you probably skipped in turning the pages that followed. There are many worthy names in the *New Uruk Review*. Judging by what you've revealed of yourself in words, by mouth or digitation, you're so uninterested in prosody that you've probably skipped whatever's registered with my by-line.

▲ Please stop tantalizing me! I'll look out the window while you tell me your anti-cryptic! I won't steal it, for God's sake! Even though I may disappoint your response as an ignoramus about what's half the rage among the literati—like postmodern poetry or French theories!

▼ Let disgust or gusto be yours on any vector. At our age we can't undo what we have done. —Kiss or curse, my fake name is Anetha.

▲ I've seen that name somewhere—but maybe not there. —A dancer? —Or choreographer? A Greek or medieval scholar? Some kind of critic?

▼ Sometimes they call me critic, sometimes poet.

▲ But Anetha *What?*

▼ That's my *surname*! Stop guessing, sweet detective—for better or for worse. My published name is Diatoma Anetha. My father's pet name when I was learning the Greek alphabet was his little Diatonic Anathema.

▲ The only poems I don't skip when they catch my eye! But not easy to understand. I don't have much time for homework.

▼ But the poems they print of my own are only occasional and short. I write reviews of books I'm qualified to appreciate or criticize, mainly concerned with literary history or its counterparts in Geisteswissenschaften that I know something about.

▲ Ah, ha! As I remember, those articles were in some way important and lucid. I must have missed others. I don't read every issue of the magazine when I'm too busy to keep up with Atlantean culture. . . . Tell me—

▼ Never mind all that now. It's a way to earn a living on other people's poetry or prose, animal vegetable or mineral. They put the bread and cheese on my quintessential table. In the old days Yeats would have called me a journalist—except when I'd have praised him. I try to negotiate a few of the literary wars between scholarship and the arts.

▲ What schools did you go to?

▼ Wisteria, and later Hume for Medieval History a few years after your time there. But I've traveled enough in time and space to qualify for judgment of a certain kind in other papers. Experience alone earns enough to allow charitable work for what I want to write as my own assignment, or for the best of samizdats.

▲ On any of my amateur themes perhaps?

▼ Possibly, in all innocence! I haven't learned enough about *you* since the Court. Poetry comes first, I'm afraid. I hope you'll complement me with prose. Everyone says you are prosaic with a vengeance. For which I'd like to complement you with some intertextual *dramatic* poesy. I know theatrical entrepreneurs and players who are starving for substantial action like yours on Off-Limeway stages, or alfresco bandwagons—something as prime and kinetic about the past as your ideas of fictive myth. Here and there I think you need imaginative verse to improve the literal prose!

▲ Of course I'm interested. There's great leeway in my idea of archeological theatrics in more than just the script—even opera!

▼ In consideration of which you could help *me.* I'd like to look to you for electromechanical understanding of angular geometry and kinematic physics that escaped my allegedly liberal education. I *do* realize that every skyscraper needs steel for bones!

▲ Your proprioception is obviously superb, so all we have to do is whirl arm in arm like an atom with particles *and* waves! You know the limits of my capability and I know the choice of yours. This day at Lauds in the Book of Hours we celebrate our uncelibation for the nonce! Can you give me a line or two of impromptu verse—let's say your impression of me as an orthogonal fanatic—just to prove to me that you're at least poetic enough to advance to the next intellectual level? You'll be compared with my sainted mother, who couldn't.

▼ Let's see: —In something . . . in something or other . . . as captivated catechized and complemented in communion, catapulsed and clarified with cries of Christ / converging concentrations of classic configurations for a confused career / that collapses into a crooning continuum of celestial catharsis. . . . See my alacrity with alliteration! Want me to whip up some wretched rhyme of repent and rue?

▲ Jesus Joseph and Mary, last night I heard no verses like that!

▼ Then you have a tin ear. But you weren't keeping everything to yourself.

▲ You're a congenital poet! Postmodern creative meter! Whatever your name, I don't remember seeing such a skillful stanza in the *N U R*.

▼ T'was saved for some critical cricket's cranium like yours.

▲ I'm sensitive in all my senses.

▼ I'm equally irritable.

▲ What in the sphere of fame are you working on now?

▼ I've agreed to take on a review of three or four rather new books more or less related to negative capability, simultaneity, and Copenhagen philosophy. I'd like to show how interesting it is to compare Liam Yeats and Nils Bohr, among others. It leads into the question of how much the subatomic conception of complementarity was anticipated by Keats or Coleridge or Kierkegaard in philosophical ideas in terms of subject and object. It's hard for me to express in words their common ground for phenomena.

▲ Without depending on poetic tropes, I hope!

▼ Yes, dear godbrother. I'll keep that temptation under control! —Or no. It's a matter of whether or not we can or cannot visu-

alize the prehension of a certain event or entity, perhaps expressed
in the four levels of meaning that were intrinsic to the medieval
meanings of language, such as Dante's, when not merged into literal unity. I'd like to discuss the proposition that mechanics like
you cannot banish the creative function of poetry from precise communication. Would you like to help me with that problem—if I
help you with yours?

▲ Yes indeed, dear girl! You are my second godsend from the
Morgan family! I'd love to reciprocate some more whenever there's
opportunity!

▼ It won't include cooking.

▲ In my present excitement, at times like this in the hours of
Tierce, now that we're clearheaded from healthy irrational passion,
in sublimely impersonal sunlight, before basic appetites recall the
energy of action: I'm sorry to know very little about the particle
and wave physics of Copenhagen, or quantum mechanics, or the
unending argument between Schrödinger and Heisenberg—still
less about the mathematics that keeps it alive in experimental
physics. In highest theory Alpha Einstein will still not accept
absolute indeterminism from Heisenberg or anyone else. I loved
Schrödinger for his energetically philosophical mind. . . . But I'll
go back and look again. This is a good incentive for me to consult
my latest unread books, to the extent I can do so without understanding his indispensable wave equation. I shudder to think of my
half-hearted untalented attempts at that kind of abstraction in my
youth, in favor of simply pragmatic systems requiring a very low
level of math simply as suggested by my own numerical experience
in managerial analysis and synthesis. Early on, with my right hand,
I punched out operating statistics with an old-time manual desktop
calculator. Eventually I had at my disposal, besides all the administrative systems, a mathematical programmer and a numerically
skillful secretary, the personal assistance I needed to develop all
kinds of business information. But all that hardly called for mathematical physics!

▼ Yes! *As for mathematics, servants can do that for us!* —I'd never
have taken on this literary task if I thought we should know the
metaphysics of it. Anyhow, I'll be picking only eisegetical
hermeneutics! I've gathered that you don't often scruple at that in
forming your opinions! More than science, what I'd like to have
from you is literate prose.

▲ I emphasize that I'm not a scholar of any department.

▼ That too is no surprise. I'll draw upon just a few of your eclectic interests. How much do you know about Mary Mitchell's romance with Wellingborough Redburn?

▲ Romance! My God, they saw each other only twice—once with her father and once at a picnic Pleasure Party, which happened to be right here on Cape Gloucester. A solid rock garden!

▼ That's why I call it romance. —Just what made it all the more romantic for a girl like me who'd spent most of her childhood vacations here. Romance of a certain kind! At college she was my optional hero. On the campus there was a monument to her outside the astronomy observatory in which she'd taught ladylike courses.

▲ So that's what excited your stargazing?

*

▼ Better than dreaming for an unenvisioned husband. She was famous as a woman for discovering a comet or comets missed by all the men before her time, including even her father the distinguished professor who'd encouraged her to use his own telescopes after discovering her extraordinary intellectual ability. She became internationally famous on her own as a professor in mathematical sciences, as well as a transatlantic leader in liberation movements.

▲ Redburn's first glimpse of her came before either of them was widely renowned. I think he immediately felt sorry for the liberty she lacked, even as he himself was feeling too tightly reencircled by the respectable society that he had eluded in his sea-loose youth—a freedom nearly always denied the peers of his heritage who complied with civilized society, and who probably for the most part would not even confess to themselves their envy of his footloose experience while he'd avoided the tawdry humiliation of whorehouses—though of course only a very few of them would ever have traded dangerous hard labor for the romance they presumed him to have enjoyed halfway around the world. Altogether conventionally forbidden the mystery of intimate experience with any class of males, even her intellectual peers, Mary Mitchell must have adjusted her psyche to Mrs Grundy's iron regime; and Redburn surely understood her deprivation better than she did. Maybe even the first meeting was deeper than mere sympathy on his part; but she may have dismissed the idea of Fayaway as romantic fiction, and no doubt much of the rest as customary euphemism in ordinary tales of callous adventures, without believing that it had anything to do with an author's mutual emotion. Yet maybe both were perspicacious enough to feel an elective affinity, though without certainty, at second meeting, when he was an honorably married man.

▼ All the more remarkable that in temperament and intellect she was academically and socially his superior while he was an autodidactic adventurer in secretly disreputable ideas! We hazard her thoughts, if not her feelings, only from his imagination of thoughts expressed in his words—I think among the best in his latterday flood of poems.

▲ As far as I know, she's never reflected in any of his stories. But maybe later in life, too late, his poetic afterthoughts were past the age of rueful wisdom. Or were they written in wan hope for what he had not sought at the time—perhaps in Europe, retrospectively wishful for her fully private company. . . . I've always thought he was a natural poet in impulse, but without the leisure early enough in independence to allow full expression of the urge like a gentleman of leisure with no economic impediment to his restless exuberance. —Of course he'd had enough of the thirty-two points in the compass, and of the angles in the sextant—though never a navigating officer—and even, I suppose, of Mary's fixed dots in the crowded sky.

▼ Can you say this "Pleasure Party" poem grew from thought before feeling? Would that mean that for herself, in his poem—in his imagination of her feelings—there was a striking revelation of himself as able to respond with empathetic enthusiasm to her inchoate desire. She had read his early books. She must have been erotically curious about Fayaway and his freedom in her apparently wanton culture.

▲ Could private intellectual excitement measure with great normal desire? So he wondered about her wonderment, raising himself to the caste of her imaginative frustration as they laughed and chatted—as they spoke in ideas—in the public picnic's open air, marveling at each other's absolute distinction from other acquaintances! For a few hours he forgets his pity for her and she forgets the limit of her uncertain gaiety and undefined hope.

▼ You're the male who should be writing the *N U R* article, seeing that he's the one guessing at her estimation of himself, according to his limited talent in a proper 19C Christianized style.

▲ You're the one who spent a year at the Divinity School. It wasn't just "The Bible-as-Literature" sort of thing there, was it?

Are you hinting at some moral restraint on Redburn's side that you definitely don't share at present, I'm glad to say?

▼ Maybe you take morality for granted as whatever's good and therefore harmless. I bet your mother did, in faith hope and charity. Redburn was no treacherous Tristram. At times I think of you as a questing Gawain—

▲ —but only in my own symbol-system! A man's a man for all that!

▼ You're man enough, my boy! But the device he carried inside his protective shield was the five fingers corresponding to the medieval five senses of both mind and body. In the legends did she realize that he was no Galahad or Parsival in motive, any more than she found in herself the original passion of Isolde?

▲ Am I to assure you that you're not—

▼ Who's talking about me, for God's sake! I'm talking about Redburn's poetic imagination of an inexperienced woman's brilliant imagination of a very different soul! For Miss Mitchell there's no pronounced spirituality on her hero's side of the subject—just the controlled complement of intellectual lust! Is that prosaically inconceivable?

▲ I suddenly see a finely threaded icicle of silver exposed by midday sunshine in your lustrous chestnut hair! I can only hope that your loosened braid won't cover *both* my ears to your annoyed contrarieties.

▼ There are really few of those. You're nice, and humorously irritating; but I'm getting seriously worried about meeting a deadline soon after Christmas. Bohr's "complementarity" is an exciting notion when set with contrariety, both terms for which, because of our language, are necessarily too poetic for certainty in the observations of science itself. Or so it seems to me. More than anything else right now I need your *impersonal* help to distinguish what I call true *dyadic esemplasy* from every sort of matching or pairing or coupling or ambiguating that drop trippingly from the tongue in sophisticated literary criticism, including those of Nils Bohr himself, even when substantiated in nature!

▲ Oh Thaley-whaley, honey cat, let me hug and squeeze and kiss you all over—my scintillating priestess of Delphi, princess of many brains and smoothly gleaming flat stomach! The joke's all on me, that I could be your tutor! I can only be your adoring student! The highest scientific definition of complementarity is the esemplasy of substance and system!

▼ At a time like this, must we deviate to mirth?

▲ When we're both in the same mood. I'd say it's equal, on the average.

▼ Please, Herr Schrödinger math-manqué, your balding pate is my new treasure too! But what I need from you first is a penciled sketch to inspire some verse about the nature of light in time, space, and causality!

▲ Let's cut to the chase, ignoring Einstein and Kant.

▼ Because you think I have the sword to cut it? . . . Then stick to quantum physics, if that will help me learn without knowledge of the learning existential enough for a comet-hunter's success in understanding a particular man. It's not simply that "Life drifts between a Fool and a Blind Man" on an Irish strand: it's a matter of reading in ordinary language what's sending you two unintelligible messages at once. Is that what we're talking about?

▲ Yes! Too many loosely matched dyads bandied about as complements are ad hoc analogies that exceed Bohr's plausibility outside the realm of physics. Almost any coupling or contrariety or dual partnership can be mistaken in a wink as the illustration of profound philosophy beyond the inconvenient pale of professional Western science—the very difficulties that you and I accept (at least speaking for myself) without having recourse to gnosticism or supernatural spirituality . . . or the Yin and Yang sort of thing that Bohr himself seriously considered.

▼ As long as we don't rule out the equal reality of subject and object!

▲ Of course not! That's our axiom already. But am I too brutal for you? I haven't yet seen your poems, and maybe I won't understand them without arduous study any better than I appreciate the Pleasure Party; but I already hazard enough of my canine clairvoyance to surmise that you're an adventurous poet who dispenses with the sentimentalities of sensation, or takes advantage of irresponsible ellipses to dodge what you can't figure out that you'd like to be able to say. In short, dear girl, are you really willing to assist the prospects of an imaginary theater framed with the allegorical equivalent of mathematical sentences?

▼ My dear boy, are we too far apart in gender, or too close in literal ambiguities, to illustrate what we're trying to define or exclude? I think we've now reached half the ambiguities of your thema, without melting the essential pièce de résistance!

▲ Let's see more of your dextrous handwriting. Does it help or

hinder our complementarity, if any, that I'm sinister? Our educations and reciprocal sensations seem to complement each other in a
certain way. We don't overlap in that regard. . . . But I wish we
could right now!

▼ Sir Gawain, much else remains for jousting.

▲ At middle age in the middle world, we must not count on
too much time for hopeful uncertainties.

▼ As we've seen, even scientific language can betray itself. In
his own lay tongue Nils Bohr struggled for precision in existing
words as his prolific thoughts and symbols were narrowed down in
the humanistic world. I wonder how far he raised and lowered the
tide of his lexicon.

▲ I don't know, but I doubt that he ever stayed too long in its
proper phase-state—solid, liquid, or gaseous.

▼ Of which I suppose you imply that the last is poetic!

▲ I wouldn't say that. Just that it's beyond me. I only mean
that it calls for too much space!

▼ Then you should pay more attention to your sententious
analogies in the form of ratios!

▲ But the more I expatiate with metaphor, the more I question prose as well as rhyme. Much as I admire Copenhagen genius
the more careful I am, in my radical objection to the bias in the
bifurcation of our English, as if every natural synthesis were essentially digital as one-and-two or zero-and-one.

▼ What was your best subject in school?

▲ Mechanical drawing.

▼ Artificers should major in that.

▲ I suppose your first grade was composition in ancient Greek.

▼ If you get sarcastic I'll rescind your liberty.

▲ All the more time to sit behind our bars and imagine the
story of Redburn and Mary when they met the second time. What
do you say?

▼ It was the singular double coordinate of an elliptical comet.

▲ You really should get serious about this if you want to maintain your rank in the intelligentsia. Each's one and only sojourn on
the Cape happened to be as invited guest to the elite picnic near the
top of Mount Azimuth, where it was still accessible by carriages to
ladies and gentlemen for whom the summit was too sweaty to
climb. By happenstance, these two itinerant lecturers, relaxing from
their respective apparitions in Dogtown before differently specialized audiences of Dogtown aristoi, were among the chosen picnic

guests of a scientific society founded by a descendant of Sir Anthony Bacon the First. This generous host of the picnic ironically dubbed a Pleasure *Garden* was wont to mention with a laugh that he was linear owner of the New Albion land grant, according to which he claimed all land westward from this New Armorica to Sir Francis Drake's New Albion, now called Cornucopia; but he also made it clear that he was still rightly enough in nearly full possession of South Parish land, as well as most of the private reality in the immediate vicinity of Dogtown's Acropolis. Not surprisingly, Mr Bacon was the philanthropist in supreme support of both the Atheneum Free Library and the Literary, Scientific, and Historical Lyceum, where the guest speakers had earned their respective honoraria. . . .

▼ This is much more than I knew. . . . Please go on. . . . Really, I'm not mocking you!

▲ You'd better not be, if you want me to help you with the question of "complementarity" in the case of this temporary pair.

▼ Well, let's see. . . . One of the speakers, of course, must have been talking about the Mediterranean's Old World art as appreciated by an autodidactic whalesman.

▲ At first, crowded delightfully al fresco around sumptuously served viands, these two guests of honor were continually interrupted in the personal conversation they tacitly craved. But at last, replete themselves with seafood delicacies and wine, they inconspicuously strolled away from the festivity's base to climb the final ascent, which was yet to be occupied by more than three or four of the present eaters, drinkers, or gaily faultless gentry.

▼ I can imagine what came next. The few who preceded or followed this couple seemed to spread and dissolve before their eyes and ears with the background of a harmless breeze like what we'd call a very low volume of white noise, carefully conscious of nothing but each other, without separating body from unrevealed soul.

▲ Was she conscious of her own visibility to others as a maiden lady admirably escorted by a comet without a tail who indicated their centripetal direction away from the festive magnet?

▼ I imagine they climbed through stunted pines up the spacious path, scarcely stumbling for his stabilizing touches, skirt plucked up now and then as any spinster would in being handed by a gentleman, slowly forestalling falls in suppressed haste, pausing to turn and face each other at the ends of certain humorous or pointed sentences, carried away in conventional behavior, but perhaps sometimes blushing at sensitive words—

▲ Till on the windswept summit, clear of all plants for a hundred and eighty degrees, gazing at the sky but speaking of less familiar cycloramas.

▼ Though ultimately preoccupied with hope for the personal information they almost evidently hoped to evoke by avoiding natural questions—yet all the while eagerly speaking of books they shared or declared. Even briefly mentioning politics?

▲ Careful not to take her hand as he led her over the smooth weather-rounded floor of rock warmed by the sun and sometimes lightly brushed by shadow motions drifting from a sparse parade of white islands at the heavenly level.

▼ I faintly remember having been taken up there in one of my childhood aestivations. So I think that as a granite-less islander of whale-bound Tasheto this woman must have paused to catch her breath, mentioning to him that she'd seen nothing like this in many a different insular landscape in Europe. Can't you envision them standing for a moment in unison, interrupting conversation about philosophy or literature, to admire or question what's spread out before them? Despite the personal intensity of their primary motives, to a remarkable degree let's say they both partook of informative catlike curiosity that requires no other incentive than casually unremunerative learning past the kitten phase. They wonder about what they can't see of the cape's furthest irregularities to the north and east, with its own islands, where fish and right whales were famously plentiful for mankind's direct or indirect consumption.

▲ I wouldn't have needed a chart to remember Cape Gloucester for the granite it is if I'd stood there for the first time, pointing at the Atlantic's landmarks from their vantage on its naked cap of weather-worn gray rock, as ironic for the city's picnic as a garden of smooth linearly fissured granite knobs or slabs, especially at one particular fissure in which you can easily imagine Abraham kindling the fire to sacrifice his son at the word of God! More distinctly than the few other cracks and crevices, until vaporized by the hottest summers, it's lined with lichen and narrowly bottomed with the kind of faded grass that's kindled by sparks from flint and steel in an iron age. Yet overhead hangs or floats the same old canopy of treacherous purple cliffs, beneath the same clouds that show pink linings of the wispy parade that sometimes harbingers the blows and floods of our vicious northeastern hurricanes.

▼ Let's get back to IRTH. Are you *trying* to be poetic?

▲ No, it's the prosaic way I think of you for lack of my own talent.

▼ Then what does Redburn think Mary may be hoping: Man and woman also parallel, even in her time known as electrical condensers—

▲ We now call them capacitors. I hope our circuit has enough personal capacitance in these tiny days of micro-electronics.

▼ —opposite each other as reservoirs of potential energy.

▲ Are you mocking my prose? Or just a silly idea of complementarity?

▼ Just what I can remember of the tenth-grade textbook. — Anyway, with unknown feelings, testing each other by sounds and gestures of encrypted hope based upon a mentality already reciprocated in those two exceptional brains, you'll say, the virginal body awakened to a melancholy frustration undoubtedly more important in her life than the unexpected sadness in this all but tested idea of complementary adventure!

▲ What I *do* say, at moments they looked away in parallel perspectives as instinctive behavior for communication of the sympathy divided by their abridged feelings of man and woman. At the same time, ignoring their opposition in gender, which is said by the Church to be complementary, and except for the momentary unison in which they gazed down and about Cape Gloucester, though without geographical familiarity, she dreamed or even recalled a fertile garden in Europa's liberally refined civilization. They glanced at each other with brave smiles, as if wishing they were cosmopolitan students, wordlessly nodding as fellow patriots of New Atlantis. As he guessed from the map he remembered on a wall in the Dogtown lecture hall, he could almost see beyond across the estuary that separated the mount from urban wards, the Purdeyville highlands to the last village—could almost imagine a few autumn-clothed peasants gleaning with song on a green carpet of wild Yankee strawberries sloping from the drumlin that surveyed Cachalot Point half a dozen miles from where he stood to the northern tip of Cape Gloucester.

▼ You've got a story there, my dear poet-manqué.

▲ It was something equivalent to that in Redburn's incubation of the poem, let's say.

▼ Then Mary must not have been surprised that he knew something about a fishing town that cursed whaling on the codfish banks of Vinland Bay.

▲ He was used to that mutual contempt of unenclosed seamen. He had put all that behind his education. His time for learning things he didn't know about *her* was drawing short. How to get her talking about her subjective self, about the meeting of their different minds?

▼ Or she, about how much to openly appreciate his unprecedented appreciation of her entire womanhood.

▲ So much for both to further say before the time is up, without the extended freedom of writing, since letters were barred by her father's guardianship and Redburn's marriage. There could be no communication to continue and ripen their ventured words unless they were destined by hopeless luck to cross each other's stars in a European museum.

▼ At any age, she was sure of her emotional fate. She wanted no lesser husband, I suppose.

▲ Yet if nothing else happens before they part you can hardly nominate them as one of Nils's complements—unless this perfect frustration was a rare proof of complementarity even as it might have been consummated like dual phenomena of quantum physics. It was a far cry from separating the dancer from her dance, though in the same real world of time space and causality. As far as abstract pattern is concerned, a philosophical incarnation of complementarity resembles for me the problem of terms like tragi-comedy, which isn't simple contrariety or antithesis in drama. Tim Hardy said "All comedy is tragedy, if you only look deep enough into it."

▼ Apparently you've had enough of such speculation!

▲ Are you taunting me? Redburn isn't even sure that she cares to visualize the coupling that surely somewhat differs from that of farm animals with very different feelings from those in mind at the consummation of an intellectual partnership.

▼ Sir Gawain, I am supposed to be clarifying a physicist's concept of cognitive esemplasy for common readers, whether or not erotic, in the world of non-fiction!

▲ Yes, my dear Diatoma. Animated conversation sequestered by pairs of mutually attracted genders does not necessarily indicate desire either for complemental action or for fused mentality. Two independent streams of experience are not simply coefficients. And two tidal currents meeting with a splash as opposites in the same estuary may affect nothing else in the several energies so encountered, leaving the agitated molecules and atoms intact, their essences undisturbed.

▼ That's said to be the way most men like it!

▲ Electrons without the waves. Fake atonement.

▼ As independent phenomena could they misunderstand each other at any angles? And explode?

▲ Back off! Beware specious examples of human complementarity! Start at the highest level of abstraction. Beside subject and object one must depend upon the other for manifestation. It's a dyad of matter and energy—say corpuscles and quantum energy, or particles and their system (not necessarily organic).

▼ Mary Mitchell had already said at large that "Every formula which expresses a law of nature is a hymn of praise for God." Does that, or does that not, sound potentially complementary to Redburn, the painfully secret agnostic or worse, to Mitchell, or to both, either before or after he mounted Azimuth with his Urania? Could you express all that as poetry?

▲ He seems to have anticipated more than one fallacy of misplaced concreteness before Alpha Whitehead recognized that semantic difficulty in his Anglo-Atlantean version of platonism. —Ye gods of nature and fiction, let there be light for Aristotelians to distinguish semantics from epistemology! What is substance, what is system? What is temperature, what is humidity?

▼ I thought they did in the Middle Ages. But without doubting supernatural Faith!

▲ I've never had time to read enough philosophy—mainly because I'm too slow at reading anything. But we have to explain what Bohr's "complementarity" meant in his own philosophical excursion from the physics he'd crucially advanced. How much of his amateur metaphysics was, like ours, merely metaphorical?

▼ So what?

▲ At times in later life he seems to belong as much with Coleridge and Kierkegaard as with his own Copenhagen physicists. Your problem is to separate the wheat from the chaff when it all looks like fodder. You might have to write an essay for every doublet you mention that doesn't echo physics at all. Or start by knowing how to classify and bundle them into categories that will at first only beg the question! But that itself may call for poetry, since most words have no fixed calibrations in etymological time, and more often than not are attenuated with imprecise ambiguities to start with.

▼ Except subject and object?

▲ Yes! And imagine the complexity of light itself when our

Double Digit Lights used to replicate each other like tall symmetrical mirrors on Pinnace Woe Island for the safety of landsmen at
sea in a chain of complements up and down the nation's rocky coast
of lighthouses! These two actually exchanged light when their
rotating beams swept across each other! Such complexity is left for
poetic language, without mentioning that waves of energy complement the photons! Without them both you see nothing.

▼ So that's the fate of Vinland's twin Phari! What else in the
world are you obfuscating now? Yin and Yang as well as lux and
lumen? Or some other eisegetical hypothesis of yours to challenge
poetry?

▲ Too easily one assumes that doublets in language are dyads
in phenomena, as I did at first. Apposites or opposites—whether or
not they are complementary in Nils's sense—are difficult enough to
demonstrate in manly words alone.

▼ Are you patronizing me, or Mary, the masculine superior by
birth?

▲ In this case, yes. Even as this year shrinks toward death I
have more experience with life than you have. Of course my experience may not be worth as much as yours. I don't yet claim even
the complementarity of roses and rhyme. Actually, as a poet you
no doubt can express better than I can what is to be said—once
you reach my age and understand what I'm about to say. But I'll
always be a step or two at my disadvantage in your education and
art, as well as in general sensitivity. Women of course are the
better people! Men and women can't be symmetrical, I'm glad to
say.

▼ Unless they're *first* complementary, with a single phenomenon in language. Then apart we are safe together. Say on, as rude
philosopher, not yet famous as psychologist or savant! May I quote
you before I catch you up in age? I admired your person more than
your wisdom—which may well have been faulty about a possibly
humorless virgin on Azimuth with her probably artless hero—so I
reserve the right of respectful ridicule!

▲ Sure, as long as I may admire your singular acuity, which is
superior to all known others, from capitol to toe. The aesthetics of
mathematical symmetry are not for the arts of a Muse. . . .

▼ It's snowing. I should go—

▲ If you'll just listen to what I hadn't noticed at first about
your thema: it helps me understand why A N W, your mother's

beloved mentor, so surprisingly called himself a platonist, when I'd always taken him to be in the Aristotelian hemisphere.

▼ I can't blame you for not having time to skim through the history of philosophy. Your career seems to have been about as abstractly nominalistic as any poor Benjamin Franklin could be without trivium, quadrivium, or poetic talent. I praise you almost as highly as your teasing mother did!

▲ Here's where I can help *you*—at least as a reciprocal literary warning. Like me, without mastering subatomic formulas and equations that call for quantum mechanics, you must narrow your tropology down to the least unreliable analogy in the observation of a phenomenal object that's otherwise unknowable without you and your experimental devices as the subject. Only then is the object realized, in your own language, testifying to knowledge in the realm of universal time space and causality. But when you reconstruct this thought-experiment by substituting an already known phenomenon for the one that was unknown, dispensing with quanta altogether, you find yourself simply with two phenomena in parallel: *a* is to *b* as *c* is to *d,* with no difficulty in exercising the literal syntax of complementarity between two subjects with two objects. You poets can ride lightshod over a good man's dual apparatus, resorting to imagination, when you're not on the road! Beware all metaphors stemming from loose language, often crossbred from radical or cladistical opposites. —For example, take the word *liberal*—

▼ Oh Gawain, you are too hard for a Muse like me.

▲ It's just a satyriasis attack.

▼ Down, Caleb, down! . . . Well, I suppose it's still too early for luncheon wine, so I'll listen while I heat more coffee. But don't go fast unless it's too lewd for the *N U R* crowd.

▲ All I'm saying is that the greatest Tudor Bishop for philosophy is properly classified as a nominalist only because he relied on God to complement his brilliant insight into perception—for lack of something to eliminate the need for quantum mechanics, as Einstein hoped to do, who asked a colleague "Do you really believe the moon is not there when you are not looking at it?"

▼ What great bishop are you talking about? You can't mean the lesser Father Duncannon without a see?

▲ No, but he might have been the first guy to understand what I'm ignorantly groping for! That's why he was never welcomed by our bishops. I mean the young Irish clergyman who spent four years in Atlantis trying to bring about the establishment of a Tudor college in Bermuda, before he went home and got to be a dean. Later he traveled in Europe and then settled down to his famous Tudor diocese at Cloyne.

▼ Berkeley! I've been there!

▲ Don't rub it in. Somehow, someday, I'll get across the Atlantic. Even if it's in my sixth decade! I still feel like Keats pressing his nose on the candy store glass.

▼ Well, what about the Irishman? Not that he was Hume's complement?

▲ No. God was Berkeley's complement, a divine surrogate for all the complements required alike for all phenomena in general, because neither divinity nor mortals were yet aware of the systemic nature of human perception as based upon human neurological experience rather than upon the suggestive promptings of preexistent forms.

▼ Wasn't he Locked out of Enlightenment?

▲ Certainly not by Merry Sterne over here. What I'm finally getting at, please, is not only that complementarity is a special case of duality but that duality is a special case of complementarity! We can't limit our speculations to duality in mating, or to Kierkegaard's ultimatum of Either/Or, nor to the digital language of computers; nor even to cranial lobes or the justice of scales. We've got to reckon on as many pony tails as there are nodal dimensions, at least up to the five fingers in my shield!

▼ Justice, Prudence, Temperance, Fortitude, and Obedient Reason they were called.

▲ Tri-partite options are enough for me—complex enough for each Idistic nodal point. Etymologically speaking, *conjugation* is too limited in conventional T S C, unless, with *ambiguity* and other solecisms, it's retrospectively redefined at the roots!

▼ Too late for a renaissance! But you're quite right to open the semantic question of dyadic *complementarity*, which denotes no such limitation. Think of polygamy!

▲ I'm interested in *trivial* complementarity! Bohr's mind seems as bicameral as his cranium, whether in quantum physics or exclusively on the dry land of what Einstein called the "real existence". Who needs quanta? the Dane might have asked after rising to molecular existence in both hands—if indeed he ever did—with the philosophical concept of your dyadic esemplasy, which might have anticipated him elsewhere three or four millennia before us. After all, it's known that Gilgamesh was two-thirds god and only one-third man.

▼ Please don't confuse yourself with your hero. Always ask your Creusa!

▲ Here's a useful paradigm for human biology: the body is an open system comprising three integrated subsystems of control— circulatory, endocrine, and nervous—all three complementary of each other, but collectively complementary with the body's total system. Think of this organism as analogically comparable with the quantum physics model with each of the subsystems as a particle, and the whole body as their source of energy.

▼ Yes: Or what if theoretical physics itself—bifurcated or x-furcated—comes up with a new energy-vector, or dimension, that supplants waves and quanta as the invisible catalyst of some kind, a sort of enzyme, to facilitate the metaphorical manifestation of relationships between subjects and objects? The word *complement* might apply to any number of subatomic components, limited, if at all, only by existence itself—like atmosphere as a function of temperature and humidity.

▲ Also: the unleavened bread, as an enzyme that catalyzes transubstantiation of the oblation! Enter Bishop Berkeley! . . . What an amazing brain you have, even though it's sometimes superciliously poetic! That was one of Father Duncannon's crucial postulates! . . . Let's fool around with some natural aspects of complementarity tonight! I'm willing to postpone triangulation. I'd rather help you think of ways to emphasize the *dyadic* in your thinking. So much is possible in my imaginary systems-mechanics that I can wave aside my trifling theories! They're nothing but leopard spots.

▼ When I was young they'd have called you a charming wolf.

▲ I won't have numerals or any other symbols to intrigue you with unless you grant me the fourth dimension.

▼ We'll have time at least to conjugate.

▲ I suggest that we should substitute for the general idea of complementarity some term that better limits what we mean in reality, without dependence upon invisible indeterminism or statistical uncertainty. Maybe it would help to study more of Coleridge and philosophers of his ilk.

And you'll promise right now to segregate and transfigure triads as merely chewing your cud? . . . But triangles are of special

interest to me if they're rectangular isosceles. Our Archangel con-
fines us to Pythagorean right triangles on the same plane. —I don't
entirely object, as long as I may ruminate with more dimensions
when you're not around.

▾ If that's all there is to your proviso, I don't see why I can't
restore your liberty and revert to my simple *cognitive* esemplasy and
deaphorize all the Karscististic opinions, so that we can get back to
ordinary expository journalism!

▲ Because *cognition* implies consciousness or information. I suspect that many of the literary complementarians are unaware of
both particles and waves, speaking tropologically, when they analyze neurological functions of mind.

▾ No wonder everyone curses you for antiplatonic abstractions! Just cut to the chase and tell me what term to use! All I ask
is a reasonable synecdoche! I'm not going to write a monograph for
specialists!

▲ I can't think of one at the moment. Come back tomorrow
for a very *very* early fast before breakfast-time and I may have a tale
to tell. Meanwhile I'll study Bohr, Coleridge, Keats, and
Kierkegaard for inspiration. —What I think you should realize and
tidy up for both journalists and poets to understand is that most
phenomena, as the Bishop might have written if he'd taken his philosophy a step or two more of deviation from theology about most
phenomena, unlike those of quantum physics or reified ambivalence and ambiguity, are far more complex than either/or, subject
and object, or the duplicity of sex—even of faith hope and charity—or contrariety, or positions in a spectrum. At least symbolically the Bishop did adumbrate the scientific discovery of an energy
unattempted yet in prose or rhyme.

▾ I think your metaphysics are as slippery as the forceps that
dragged you into the world.

▲ *Is.* —We may be able to devise a more poetic term than *complement* to abstract the concept of particles' need for energy. But you
poets have me at a disadvantage in common sense. You should
make allowance for a literal mind's Ionic struggles!

▾ Please, no more of your 'umble pie! Defer the comedy until
our next dalliance. In good faith, a certain single kiss of a certain
time and place may be one of my best ideas of what we're talking
about as the counterpart of lux and lumen in human light, not
unlike a solo dance. —Oh, my God, look at the time!

▲ I can see that the cat's beginning to twitch her tail with the suspicion that I'm trying to cage her! —Stay. We'll have lobster rolls and wine for lunch. There'll be no more lectures or lechery! Just highly respectful conversation.

▼ I'm sorry I can't stay all the way through the hour of Sext. Ma-mai might cut me out of her will. From now on she'll want me home every night by noon. —But the help I need most is about my present stumbling block in modern physics.

▲ I hereby renounce triads, quadratics, and pentagons.

▼ That's kind of you. But I hope you won't exclude the complex numbers I rely upon to read your mind.

▲ So I'll take down the physics books on that shelf when left to eat my lousy lonely lunch, looking for lovely analogies of proper puppy love. Next time, in turn, I hope you will start helping me revise the laborious prose wherever or everywhere it should energize as dramatic poetry.

▼ Of course, but I'm not assuming the greater responsibility of an editor by taking the blame for anything, probably because of your unconscious renitence to any psychoanalysis as the only child of an extremely feminine mother. Naturally you reacted with unusual interest in the mechanical drawing and architectural fascinations missing from her more emotional influence—e g, your fascination with guns and Big League baseball statistics.

▲ Here comes the usual lurking psychology! Just because she could never learn to drive a car without hitting something? Well, she could never afford to own one. —But you may be right about me at the quantum level. I'm sure it seems obvious to any old psychologist. In Montvert the village Scout Master was a Separatist Minister who was very kind to us. —It was he who taught me boxing—enough to make me dauntless among other kids. I was actually one of the flyweights in college for a while. No doubt that's because I had no da-da. Of course my skill was mainly defensive, based on pretty good footwork. Nothing is as exhausting as a few rounds in the ring!

▼ Gilgamesh, not you. I'm aware that you are or were an athlete. Your pentagonal silhouette is like Leonardo's sigil of Solomon. It's because I read and see a lot of plays that I'm your interested critic, and because I'm always looking for dramatic poesy. Your mother might have scorned my so-called modernism. But you'll read enough between the lines when you see my poems. I've never written a play myself. Feel free to disqualify me as, but only as, a theatrical complement.

▲ Never fear! From you I've already enjoyed—

▼ —the complement of raking me over the coals. —But I've been to many readings and rehearsals for things unattempted yet in prose or rhyme, and I've learned most of the pride and pitfalls by first second or third persons. Even at his peak in prose and rhyme Liam himself privately confessed that "poetry will remain a torture."

▲ For me it's theatricians in search of novelty who have the closest minds.

▼ With a little guile I'll lead them into your script as the makings of almost any theatrical genre for a composer with light fantastic toes as well as Weltschmerz.

▲ I abhor most of opera.

▼ It can be changed, ignored, or handed over to Holyrood and DV. It won't starve without us.

▲ All I want is a Tairov and an apron stage without proscenium.

▼ I could be your silent singer.

▲ I'd rather hear you talk. Or act. Or dance. —Better yet, let me be the silent partner, so I can watch you like a panther in his own territory.

▼ Yes, that would be a good story, but meanwhile I've got a lot of explaining to do for my article. I *do* need your help. Then I'll pay you back in the sweetest mask of prey. —So tomorrow please continue with your scientific coaching.

▲ Will it be okay if I start by making coherent what has already come to mind in my incoherent vagaries? You need a representative list of dyads to review, one by one, to accept, reject, or question, as relative to proper Bohrean complementarity. Ponder first the subjective/objective paradigm, and decide whether or not it's pertinent, literally or analogically. Take for instance, instead of Terpsichore in action, the volt and ampere of an electric watt—

▼ I suppose that's an example of what would naturally strike an Ion's mind!

▲ Or what you'd call the phenomenon when a curve ball is spinning halfway between pitcher and batter.

▼ I'm more familiar with back and front . . . Left and right. . . . Feeling and experience, which I know you know! . . . Middle-aged lad and ageless lass. . . .

▲ Yes, also: one that seems without the other! But lux and lumen is the classic case. More difficult is the simultaneous instant of conscious death. Epistemology and ontology for each of us at once together!

▼ But I can't bring myself to add Yin and Yang, or Alterian symbolism of any kind, even for the sake of wisdom! I'll turn the good real existence ones into poetry when I have time to spare, skipping all the other facile misconceptions and tautological fancies of the nominal pairs that you object to. There's no end to the conceivable candidates for yoking. The leitmotiv of my essay will suggest that the idea reflected by Liam Yeats and Nils Bohr accommodates a high level of analogical abstraction, though without trying to square a circle, unbeknownst to each other in exceedingly disparate professions. —Oh, I must get out of here before—

▲ You wonderful exciting boss! My Urania of all the arts. You are a world of special interests, with the pristine paps of Sheba's youth, canticles of spring wheat, clothed and unclothed! And at breakfast nobody but Athena could delight me more! Ecstasy leads me to the turbulent waters of unrequited romance when I see and feel so much of what's beautiful without you in words! I don't mind when you outwit me.

▼ Well there's a gleam in my eye for you too. Yet the O T says "do not stir or awaken love until it is ready". If one can hear thunder she is within striking distance of the lightning! Tomorrow I'll bring my sketchbook and show how you looked to me between times in penciled lines on a tumbled sheet. As a student you must have looked like a starving saint or a long-distance runner! Your face, thrown back, was what seemed to be the stirring recovery of a twisted lax-jaw smile. Your two purses of thunder were like Solomon's, a pair of nuggets waiting for the complement of your cryptic power.

▲ Though having a skylight, you had no mirror. You unfairly testified to my slightly aging fuselage of wrinkled skin, whereas I was honored with superlative views of the smoothly slender youth in your beautiful—

▼ —Stop! Caleb my dear, stop right there with the irony you cannot understand! *Please!* You'll make me weep for your sweet open-hearted friendship and goodwill! Let's wait a few more days before I come again. We must take it easy for a while—while we think things out. *Promise not to say I'm beautiful.* That word has been the curse of my life, as baby, as girl, as student, as woman, as happy fool, as sophisticated dolt! . . . I can't talk about it now. Maybe someday I will, perhaps when you're my priest. I wish you'd been my year-old godfather when *I* was baptised! . . . You may guess what I feel when I bring over my book—if I don't change my mind about ever acceding to that. I'm glad it's so hard to find in the rare-book market. . . .

▲ I hope it won't remain unopened at my gravestone.

▼ Keep taking me for the things you alone have taken me for—as what I feel you to have seen as good—perhaps more than I think you should have believed. For the present try to ignore what you wonder about beyond that pale. . . . I've never said anything like this to anyone else, even when I was a Petrine, even when I was in love . . . or especially when. . . . So there: speak to me as freely as you wish, praise me as much as you honestly can—only *don't say I'm beautiful*. I don't like to be told. I hate especially any repetition of the word. I try to avoid it even in my ordinary impersonal objective writing! I try to keep it out of my language . . . just the way you try to avoid the "he-or-she" as a third-person. (Under open duress to use it professionally I'm always tempted to substitute a math symbol in quotation marks, giving up on gender, as in "Either\Or"! Sometimes I think the word you've used is what drove me to the occult grammar of my poems, changing from oxygen to hydrogen to breathe in. Call me irascible, call me arrogant, call me haughty, call me selfish, call me devious, call me cold—but don't call me *that*! You are too imaginative to call me *that*! . . .

▲ . . . Why does *that* make you weep? Don't cry! . . . Take this napkin. . . . Poor Thalia, I call you by name for the first time, as a privilege, weeping with you face to face. . . . If it weren't for your few ambiguous qualifications and provisos about our accompaniment in the future I would be blind with tears of ignorant sympathy and despair for parallel lives of shared design.

▼ Oh, sweet knight, there's a gathering gleam in my eye too, of course! But right now why can't we just disregard this shameful weakness of mine—the only occasion, I suppose, since your rather unexpected homecoming to this provincial little city—as a lacuna in this purgatory of the comedy framed by our archangel Michael? He is *not* omnipotent! I have a will of my own, and so do you. Maybe it just needs your freewill to undo something in the past. I am not a kitten. . . . I'll gladly overturn his will whenever it opposes mine! So in this case it depends upon yours!

▲ Unless I oppose yours in what suddenly appears to be a frightening dilemma, I hope I don't absolutely need to understand your sadness.

▼ Then please proceed with the immediate scientific help I need for my feminine career. It reminds me of a skinny lone tiger cat, with large opal eyes separated from the starving horde, who gazed up at me for a whole minute without moving from his spot, seeming to know that I was on my way to Athens, sympathetically forgiving me for knowing that I couldn't take him home with me. He knew I had nothing for him in my backpack. If I hadn't already booked my berth I would have stayed to coax him to the animal rescue shelter that I'd already been looking for in vain to make a contribution. . . .

▲ . . . Now both of us are weeping.

▼ . . . Again I've changed my feckless mind. To ease your needless anxiety, I'll come back tomorrow, with both book and sketch pad after all. Meanwhile I'll have all night to ponder ways to make you understand what you may call just silly emotions. So read up on the physics!

▲ Okay: good, better, or best. . . . I'm not really interested in subatomic physics, or chemistry. I'm an engineer-manqué by temperament. I prefer the managerial kind of engineering. I'm sorry I don't know enough about the conception and delivery of modern physics. It started with Mark Planck in Berlin before W W 1. Father Duncannon studied under him for a while after he finished at V I P, long before he thought of taking vows. I wouldn't be surprised to know that in some indirect way physics played at least an allegorical part in the origin of his radical theodynamic Mass. When I was earnestly thinking of writing his biography I was too busy with shoes and ships and cabbages to do anything about it, not to mention the slow gestation of Gilgamesh.

▼ Well, for all the speculation about your Apollo, physics was never mentioned in our Court of Love. Your *autonomous* biography is what interests me. I now know you're crazy, which is what the Morgans named the house I live in now!

▲ I won't assist you an iota of what hasn't yet been known about me to your mother and her friends until you reveal a lot less than that about what other is known about you in other houses of the world.

▼ I'll sleep on that gentlemanly proposition. —But I've already hankered to see more private light. I've already promised to help you with theatrical poetics of your fictive myths. Many of Yeats's poems and plays were born with his intentions penciled in sketchy prose, as well of course as his shelf-ful of marvelous expository prose—

▲ Not counting diagrammatic explanations of his symbol-systems. His kind of mechanical drawing!

▼ Yes, you get my point. I don't disrespect your lack of poesy. You're still young enough for salvation.

▲ Madam, you are very kind to say so. God bless you for hoping to complement me. If you fail it will be because you can't make a silk purse out of a sow's ear!

▼ Or because I'm not on your level. Not because poetry isn't the highest art, the sine qua non of literature! So before we get down to earth let's get to work on my humble journalism, which has a deadline. I see that in my article I must pare down the meaning of "complement" with many more negatives than merely doubts, at least enough to deserve the philosophical respect of uncommon readers of common language! So far the best model I can imagine is one of Turner's paintings where I can see as "real existence" the integrated art of subject and object despite the uncertain law of uncertainty to make it visible. . . . Easy to think of as particles with waves—

▲ Forgive me for one last impenitent breach of your commandment: your taste for those pictures reminds *me* that whatever's *beautiful* as *I* define the word, is nothing stereotypical—first for person and second person only! I like Turner especially for the objects he chose to paint. My avidity for that—or anybody's—may be aesthetic waves of energy that make ordinary pixels of paint or photons the observed work of art. Of course there's a highly abstract adjective to serve everyone from Plato and the highest mathematicians to the lowest vernacular of drunken sailors, where the semantic competition is brutal; but my summons of your abject adjective, though lacking specificity, requires all four levels of meaning for expression, impossible to replicate anywhere but herein my T S C, where countless values intersect with each other in all five senses, like many dimensions radiating from a single isorectotetrahedron. *Your* phenomenon is posited by naked vision but sustained and amplified by every communication of heart and mind. To banish all that is to disappear.

▼ Well I *am* an apparition in your avid imagination. You forget that my tetrahedron is not an ideal IRTH. It's poorly shaped and measured as curving hypotenuses that almost continuously vary with mood and circumstance, each affecting the others, shrinking or inflating my capacity and character of worth from gem to needle, and even the average dimensions of yours are probably nicer than your orthogonal Muse's. Already you occupy most of the space in my solid geometry, because in it you come closest to what I've vaguely sought—all your comical blarney to the contrary notwithstanding! It's hard to believe that we haven't yet had more than twenty-four hours together! I must bethink myself, and you should do the same—you especially!

▲ But by no means do I renounce all the excitement and satisfaction a man could wish for in the flame of a meta-youth that can hardly notice cosmetics, coiffeur, couture, or even anatomic display, once an exciting mind has been discovered. How can I suppress the forbidden word that expresses every layer of the cake? I can't be content with suboptimized glorification! You are not as caged and innocent as Mary Mitchell, of course, but try to think of the horny-handed writer Redburn, not me, wanly idealizing the woman for himself the poet—as one "deep-diving original" to another in mind and body. Isn't it cruel to discourage a parfit gentil knight's Eureka every time he sees your face or other skin? Must I cultivate circumlocutions and code words readily regarded as allegorically parallel to some sort of invisible catalyst that enables the eye to see what's otherwise invisible in what we could call real existence?

▼ Dear Sir Caleb, it's too late now, but you *should* have been a poet! Your fantastic substitution for poetry touches my heart more than you can guess. It's a talent resembling satire. Yet I am honored to be its touching purpose. It makes up for magnificent stature and impressive power.

▲ Some meanings of words have been actually reversed in the decadence of our language over the centuries. At least among ourselves we need to keep alive at least the arcane ghosts of opposite or arcane words. But, though abused in the marketplace, the *b* is not one of them.

▼ And you, a conservative liberal, are very good at defending them, whether or not anyone but me notices your brave struggles in a language that won't stand still, taking from his incunabula a higher level of education than his mother's vehement interest in English.

▲ It leaves me all but incommunicado to any audience except you and yours.

▼ Don't be melodramatic! Sometimes poetry circumvents such sorrows. I hold art over precision. As an active admirer you must be less precise in expressing your singular whimsy.

▲ It was Bohr's difficulty to be understood even in the literature of his own science. . . . You know what? When we met yesterday morning you and I were both wearing button shoes—calibrated for defense. Now our feet are laced, each subjectively adjusted to the other's presence as they adjusted to the circumstances of pedal comfort. We aren't stupid twin lighthouses on the same insular ledge! Our continuum is sinuous. It runs from opposition to fusion, as in last night's mutuality raised to the power of ascending exponents!

▼ So you speak as I think of Abelard and Heloise. Were their passions worth what went wrong?

▲ Are you warning, or threatening, a post-romantic liaison of pain?

▼ Neither. I immediately bethought myself in horror. Instead I'm wondering if I'll be able to have a motherboard to provide a mythological database of Beatific romance! Is that possible to capture on a PC?

▲ Soon enough it probably will be. But for my sake I hope you don't ever analogize that couple with my legendary conception! In fact, my latest sudden ambition is to join you, after we joust a few more times, is to propose—

▼ Wait now! Hold your horses—

▲ —to assist you in an impersonally critical essay of the *N U R* kind, seeing that by your grand assertion it will steer clear of the anthropological and sociological positions—perhaps even some of your mother's—that otherwise would trepidate my gyroscopic *Eigenwert* for dromenology.

▼ Oh indeed! But first your exhilarating naked effrontery must afford me, your proposed literary partner, what that's all about, before admitting either of my names without protecting myself from ridicule for the hermetic obscurity of my provincial citation in cosmopolitan eyes.

▲ I'm telling you to avoid the very whiff of dromenology, or anything else of mine. All I can do for you is study a little about other people's physics without the math! Anything more than that, even as a sideline, might take us a quarreling lifetime, probably producing only on your part the futility of trying to work with a crazed technician.

▼ Well, in this instance, that's a relief! But I would love to help *you* in some way. Maybe with one of your other crotchets? After all, you're helping *me*!

▲ In due course, how about announcing and promoting the Synectic Method of Diagnostic Correlation? It's practicable, and not only for organized management, especially with computerized applications. It should be used even in teaching and academic administration. It ought to be welcomed for postmodern excitement!

▼ That's worse, I'm afraid! Instead, what could you and I have in common?

▲ I know! Or at least as I assume inamoration: *Poesy,* at the highest level of abstraction! —We are both *makers. Poets* of different kinds! Since a poet of any kind has always been a *maker,* we have made love of a certain kind, and we are both *makers* of various kinds—not ordinary discoverers or learners or brilliant teachers and scientists, not just priests who *make* the Mass—not just the leaders and organizers who *make* war—not just operators or practitioners—not *makers* of music or architects, or selectors of images, nor even simply makers of knowledge, or makers of machines, or chambermaids and bakers by metaphor—none of whom are necessarily more *creative* than skilled intelligent nurses at the hospital where Jack Keats worked!

▼ Or an unmarried black mother on the dole. I do respect some of your dicta. They make me try to hear of your mother as a poet. Your adventures in ideas also do make for truth as the reification of a million adjectives—if I excuse the collected notion of mud-baked bricks!

▲ I know I'm a technocrat with only a tiny job now, while unnecessarily mangling reified adjectives for my own amusement. But it's such a wonder that you understand so many of my otious hypotheses! Maybe I've instinctively touched upon what you make that are still unseen by me; and that you are cautiously admitting your part in the junction as not necessarily in sweetness and light. It would be a lot easier if I could sweep you off your feet! But it takes you as a witch to complement me with your broom.

▼ Have I already been bewitched myself? I admit I'm dazzled. But now I must stand up and leave you in doubt but not with disapprobation. I'll try to be less acerbic. Don't rush me. Give Mamai time to assimilate you in our nunnery. She's been under pressure to finish her penultimate draft, before she can muster up the energy to labor through all her meticulous editing. The book's as long as two volumes, you know. But soon I'll get her used to the godson hanging around more than ever without expecting her attention! I hope you'll soon be coming over for bed and breakfast to inspect the remodeled architecture every now and then. She does most of her research and writing later in the day or after dinner in the evening with her door shut. After the book's finished she'll probably accept a stint as visiting professor somewhere. Then, if I'm still tutoring you, I'll take you to Delphi for the certainly uncertain re-ionization of its comedy—the Euripides you've appointed as his best! By then you'll have earned a summer vacation away from Dogtown!

▲ I hope by then as your confessor I'll have gleaned and penetrated more than the odes you let get printed. By then you may have a poem for me alone, or at least a penciled sketch of its skeletal prose. By then I'd like to be the prompter for even later poems about your aversion to the adjective of the noun that Keats proclaims as the reification of everything that's true. By then there'll be no further need for either Sheets or Kelly on my shelf to meet the challenges of physics! By then instead of Virgil I'd like to have a carnal Beatrice to spin me down the dizzy vortex, and up again from Hell to pole star. —For by then, with luck, I shall see and feel a feral chestnut cat with lustrous longitudes of dark bronze threads as she watches me trying to decipher the sweeping twitches of her curled tail as it signals something meaningful only to herself—

▼ Stop it, Gilgamesh-manqué! You are an architect, not a troubadour. I don't need your kind of romantic efforts to inveigle me into the thorny rose garden. We are already there. You are a gardener, not a lark, and I am not a Belle Dame avec Merci. The substantial truth—not its abstraction—is that my heart has been reformed by your innovative gallantry. I like it, that you have reversed the process of seduction. In the old days at Hume, when we missed each other by only a few years—since I was a graduate student after my year in Europe—most girls I knew still wouldn't go all the way, despite their experimental sophistication. They still hoped for romantic wedding nights.

▲ But they knew the way, and the anatomy, better than some of the boys did. There was dangerously asymptotic liberty before separated shortcuts to the male goal. But before that, on the way to frustrations, at least if it seemed with exploration for love, they learned more about each other's selves from emotional conversation than from natural mating.

▼ That story wouldn't have been ours. It would have been too soon for me because it would have been too soon for you to have developed such learned ideas for a fascinating scutcheon inside and outside your shield. There would have been no nodular IRTH to symbolize the innumerable ideas inspired by our Controller's use of plane geometry inherited from Pythagoras!

▲ Nor you yourself perhaps still not wise enough to sit on a three-cornered stool as a Pythian capable of appreciating my peculiar attractions. Ergo, this is the best of all possible intersections, right here, right now, before you tire of my inamoration! I know it's a long shot, but try to remember that I have the advantage of not being a maestro in any one profession, or other experimental contraction!

▼ I'm not in the mood for nonsense. I admit I'm not often a playful cat. Let's be serious. It doesn't matter that you're not a genius or great leader.

▲ What a lovely compliment! But time enough. I'm afraid I iterate and reiterate my excitement about certain people and their attitude to jobs that I can only imagine as my own. You lead all the rest, and at just the best age!

▼ Listen, we are both in danger of ultimate giddiness at this very age of our seesaw's fulcrum. It's not entirely my heart and mind that make me suitable for you in body and soul: it's the sudden hope for what I hadn't known I needed to make me better than a typical so-called public intellectual perverted from the moral purity of art I once aspired to in Evelyn Dickinson's poems. I'm worthy enough in the common good of culture and its criticism, but at the expense of what I thought was potential originality.

▲ It's not too late to take vows of the purity you speak of. For that I can protect you.

▼ Perhaps, with your leverage.

▲ My own case is easier than yours, because I have no talent for anything but technics, as you might call it.

▼ That's what I like, without impugning your knighthood. But is it possible for equal wights with different histories to live for longer than passing the seesaw at ninety degrees? —See how you've poisoned my poetic mind with allegory fit for algebra? You see, that's *my* danger. Your danger is artificial poetry. There, now I've said it!

▲ Except as an artificer I could never be more than half-finished. That would still leave me with more than I'll properly have time to do. The best thing for us is to disprove with the substantial apparition of our Muses, to scientific satisfaction, that there is any such thing as human dyadic esemplasy. If I can't, we're shacked up together. But in any event it would take the two of us and no one else.

▼ Cautiously, I have no objection to your muddled drift. Shall we leave the outcome as theodicy? Thank God we're not still young! But you are not harmless.

▲ Neither are you. Something like incest!

▼ At our age? I'd rather die in suspense.

▲ We needn't test all the dichotomies. Obviously natural, for better or for worse.

▼ Or not at all. But seeing neither particles and feeling no waves I keep worrying about the figures in our sky. Just now I've been gazing up at the cube with rubber bands around it that I see on your shelf, wondering whether it's got something to do with the "Cubie" your mother was said to have called you at times. Does it by chance have anything to do with Gilgamesh stagecraft? The diagonal cracks make the corners look like the brown paperboard panels that architects make their models with. May I see it?

▲ Down here on the table. . . . Pick it up. —But be careful because it's hollow and as light as a scroll. . . . I'm surprised that you remember hearing that little second-hand bit about my infancy. . . . See, it shatters to pieces when I take off the crisscrossed rubber bands that hold it together.

▼ Like elastic belts circling each other to hold a square Humpty Dumpty together! . . . Oh, oh—not any longer! . . . —I'm sorry you had to demolish it just for me. You need some kind of reusable adhesive to use at all the seams. . . . I might have something at home that we could try. . . .

▲ My God, you're quick on the uptake! You're never impertinent! And a canny reader too, with the memory of a matriarchal elephant. I'll put it back together this afternoon when I have time. I haven't yet found a good way to demonstrate the assembly. . . . Look, I'll show you something interesting in solid geometry. While we're at it, wait another minute and help me marvel at the shocking discovery in my headlong misconception of that cube. I would never have hatched an unwelcome gem if I hadn't tried to socialize my isorectotetrahedrons—my IRTHs—as the rectilinear components of an organic monad propagated rather by triplicity as a functional alternative to duplicity, without forgoing the technological necessity of right angles. . . .

▼ Assuming, I suppose, in three dimensions, and maybe in time?

▲ Yes, symbolic representation of static or dynamic reality in a continuum of time space and causality. I overlooked a thing or two in my precipitous bottom-to-top induction from the simple equilateral Christian trinity (extracted from David's symmetrical star), which was too limiting for a paralleling railroad kid like myself, up to the isoceles right triangle. . . . Your mother once told me she had a daughter who was the best one in the family for math. That's why I was at first a little surprised to hear that you're a poet.

▼ Post hoc non propter hoc. I got interested in the Irish mathematician Sir Hamilton, who seems to have been the source of your little middle initial *i*. He was the one who led me back to Coleridge.

▲ I followed Coleridge back to his cavalry horse.

▼ The best of critics lead back from any head to tail. —I surprised my parents by doing what the teachers kept telling everyone to do. And because I wanted to wear glasses like Ma-mai's long before I needed them. As for numbers, I counted the books after father left. And I still remember that *one* plus *two* plus *three* plus *four* is *ten*! And that for a Pythagorean triangle *a*-squared plus *b*-squared must equal *c*-squared. Kids teased me for remembering theorems that I've long forgotten how to prove.

▲ I'd remember nothing that requires memorization unless I was forced to, because I associated it with my mother's vast memory of verse, therefore too unmanly to waste my time on. . . . A few decades later I happened to notice that if I made three more of my original IRTH I could make a cube, which interested me as a special case of my Synectic Method of Diagnostic Correlation when extended in the third dimension. . . .

▼ From Einstein and Yeats down, normal human beings have bifurcate brains. Your postmortem is going to be very interesting. . . .

▲ First I was dismayed to notice that when you turn an upright IRTH down—as I had always visualized it—its stabilized footing on the floor is an equilateral triangle—

▼ As any stagehand would have expected. . . .

▲ —and thus I was confronted with a classic pre-Socratic regular three-sided pyramid.

▼ Common enough in nursery schools. . . .

▲ Until I put four of them together to make the cube—which of course I couldn't see the hollow inside of. . . . How to shape that space? I made another hollow figure to fill that void—only to find that I then had four such faces to match for the lining of one more shape to fill the void, which I carelessly assumed would be one more tetrahedron. Instead it was that one there in your hands— much taller than the IRTHs!

▼ It took a big regular equilateral three-sided pyramid to complete the cube!

▲ This bloated alien core is my nemesis! A bloated pre-Socratic gem without a single right-angle! A quatrain of trinities. A purity of inhuman extrication from the complexity of culture in which we exercise the freewill God granted us to transcend his imagination! A spiritually static reaction to the entropy that forced us to think for ourselves!

▼ So we invented the rectangle!

▲ And I put twos and twos together to find that one more making the fifth in my shield of stupidity against analytical intelligence like yours! Instead I started with false induction—with monadic IRTHs as the beginning of synthesis when I knew perfectly well that the IRTH is only a special case of infinitely different shapes by unequal extensions such as those typified by Pythagorean planes in an irregular tetrahedron, dropping the *iso* in IRTH!

▼ Methinks thou chide thyself too greatly.

▲ Then I saw the cube as a special case of the rectangular parallelepiped. Thus my stupidity, for instance, in overlooking the affect of an IRTH as Gilgamesh's stage prop laid flat on its own *equilateral* face! —that is to say, instead of standing on two of the three congruent equilateral triangles. In other words, I was limiting to a single relative stasis the possible symbols for countless positions—even countless dimensions—in space, time, and causality [S T C]!

▼ So what? But I'll think on it, and let you know if this poet could have knotted your confession tighter—after she figures out what your prose is driving at.

▲ I'm ashamed for the inanity of having conceptually assembled four IRTH's into an unknowingly eviscerated cube—attempting to somehow integrate them geometrically with my truly functional S M D C, which is essentially rectangular in two or three dimensions as a matrix. It was wrong to put too much symbolic burden on a single IRTH! Simply for stability, as the builder of a quadrilateral ziggurat—geometrically similar to a distasteful Egyptian pyramid—Gilgamesh, for the path of least resistance to a human foot, would certainly have used IRTHs, if he could have baked his mud no more easily in a different shape, as his stumbling blocks (or monuments) simply for their symmetry, long before the Greek aesthetic prevailed in architecture.

▼ Poor playwright, don't laugh or cry. Mathematics has symmetry to turn triangles upside down. As far as misapprehensions are concerned I myself have plenty to confess to. Strangely enough before I knew you, in a published article I mistook Plato's Ion, the butt of Socrates's rhapsode (as the last in a string of rhetorical magnets), for the bastard Ion of Delphi—both of whom were inspired by Apollo, each in his own way. So I was coincidentally biased against you. How can I make up for that secret injustice? Isn't it enough that you've demonstrated your little IRTH a seminal contribution to civilization as a corollary to the Platonic "Realism" that he deplores as the exact reverse of the Platonic "Nominalism" that you've always clung to as what Alpha Einstein and all engineers and architects call *real* reality? In fact his IRTH, speaking more pragmatically than poetically, is the germ of the egg in this prosaic world. This little boy called his mother Theotokos. . . .

▲ Even as you jeer at me I continue to be astonished at your grasp of everything I think about! I have no more to teach you about physics. This Yin knows more than I do about geometry and all the arts, and apparently half of Yang. But my stimuli seem fair thema for the poetry intended to express more than half my amateur propositions. Instead of a gentleman's haughty condescension or retribution for your gracious tongue, right or wrong, you've doubled the exponent of my respect! Even in Bohr's own mind it was hard enough to distinguish ideas from phenomena when there was no doubt about the denotations of scientific language! Imagine the difficulties when he and his skeptical colleagues discussed the philosophical significance of his search for precisely real metaphorical reality on *both* sides of his dichotomies! For instance—his own tentative example of civilian complementarity—every radically individual human body has a front and a back! It's disappointing that he actually considered that even as a humorous analogy to a metaphor of his own physics! You would have instantly laughed at his preconscious version of poetry! If I'm a wandering ion searching your particularity, you are a photon at the Panopticon's center!

▼ In some ways you remind me of ill-fated George Bruno.

▲ Anyway, poets can get away with meretricious tricks. Coleridge says "The man's desire is for the woman, but the woman's desire is rarely other than for the desire of the man."

▼ I don't associate you with that male falsetto. For me, your self comes first.

▲ And I you—without detracting an iota from your gift! But it happens to remind me that you're an untrustworthy partner— getting up to go when you haven't yet told me anything like a curriculum vitae. It's still not fair, when you know too much of mine.

▼ Not enough of what's normal or curious in a man's middle years.

▲ All I know is that you're a nominally mature quasi-Lusitanian intellectual cat with chestnut-bronze hair sometimes anachronistically braided on the back of a classically lovely spine and flat stomach who delights in the negative capability defined by Keats, with the characteristic irritability of artists and the photon of my new light. Whence the history of this poetical apparition as far as others are concerned?

▼ For the present, nearly none of your business. I am called by others a commentator or critic in other categories, sometimes as a dogmatic Catholicat. Aside from nearly private poetry, I meow or hunt as a mild felion. I put charity and hope before faith. Sometimes I report or revile misguided canines in the jungle of journalism, which is what the late Liam would call dabbling in the devilish degradation of artificial articulation even in admirable acts of art. The only whole book of prose I ever published was about the problem of diverting opera from bourgeois entertainment to aboriginal art.

▲ Why didn't your mother ever mention this to me? Surely this isn't some weird mother-and-daughter sorcery. Any other pseudonyms in your lineage?

▼ I made her swear to secrecy. No one else in Dogtown knows the purely functional secret of my career. I need a secret homestead to complement the large world. Will you swear too?

▲ As faithfully as her oath at my baptism! But I didn't really need your mother's learning because my mother's modest education made me want to learn by myself.

▼ Well our mothers were unique friends. —Stop fishing for more familiarity this soon. Don't badger me!

▲ Oh oh: Swish goes the tail! There must be a tale to tell.

▼ I just need more time to think. We've both skipped our morning C N meditations. One of the reasons I've decided to stay at home is that for frustration of regular nullification I've missed the kind of inner world that Evelyn was so luckily stuck in. I don't want people here to connect me with the hurly-burly of social responsibilities. I want to be seen as a village spinster who doesn't encourage questions. They know I'm a Morgan. At least for a while. After supper I'll think of you. . . . In case you're wondering, I'm not married.

▲ I can say the same for myself.

▼ We'll never be close and dishonorable enough to reveal our mantras. Let that be our negative oath. It could be the negative germ of a long poem!

▲ No, please, make it a play, with enough poetry to bear the weight of skeletal prose! You can't make a silk purse out of a sow's bones!

▼ In one sense, all along we've made our knot: I'm dextrous and you are sinister! . . . I wish I had that lobster roll right now!

▲ I'm afraid the offer's expired. I can't keep postponing my entry to your log in the basement. . . . Instead, come to supper!

▼ Not tonight, my dear. I need a day or two of dreamy cogitation—not active indulgence. I'm going to spend the afternoon listening to Ma-mai's recording of Bach's cello suite. I'd like to be able to think of that as unending music despite cataracts between deep pools, interrupted cascades, caverns measureless to man, and dams to generate your goddam electricity! West against East. . . .

▲ It's snowing. Can you get home easily?

▼ I'm a veteran winter parker. This will be nothing like the High Sierra. . . . By the way, I think I was at Hume when Michael Chapman was thereabout, still holding forth in his tiny cult off campus. His lovely wife slowed him down with at least three children.

▲ Oh my God, we may both have a lot to evade in pillow talk! Did he ever finish his books? It wasn't easy for him to finish all he started.

▼ Not quite yet.

▲ Did you know his daughter works here at the Yard?

▼ She's at the point of my tail.

▲ There must be two ways *at once* to complement a tale. In the end that's what Nils was unconsciously leading up to when he approached the philosophical level of 4D abstraction. But it may demand poesy to explain that. He corrected himself about the head-and-ass of any old pig in ordinary life. . . . Unless I'm the one who's as careless as I was in solid geometry!

▼ Now you've given me to understand why the esemplasy of marriage doesn't belong in the category of complementarity! . . . I'm not so sure about your ion and photon poetry. . . . Then forget the metaphors of geometry. Let the IRTH rest as stagecraft! You're a madman. Write for the rare-book closet! Play for the door. —Unless you're willing to let me help.

▲ What do you think you've already been doing around the clock!

▼ I know a lot about what's missing. I know directors and choreographers.

▲ I bet you do! [*Aside.*]

▼ Your mother was braver than my mother but mine was luckier than yours.

▲ My father might have been even smarter than yours.

▼ But now we're in our own story. . . . Let your gyres and prisms float off on rafts of reason. Listen to Keats and me! Until you've bitten deeper into the apple of art, which for you is what everything else isn't—though for others it's much less of everything else because it's what God was willingly unable to create. That's what I'd call Anselm's secret Second Law, to account for the endless possibilities of what Auto Drang blessed as the ultimate expression of freewill. So did you, with the overweening audacity of youth, when you let Chapman print your half-baked theory of tragedy. . . . But I must say that I'm still intrigued about your Synectic Method of Diagnostic Correlation.

▲ If that's too abstruse, so be it! It can rub fiction with facts, like complex numbers. I was working on an essay to explain its possible applications to the military, as well as to business and politics and culture, including Church! That sounds more insolent than the absolute of tragedy, or the faulty symbol-system of IRTH, but I'm very careful to warn of its statistical requirements. It's pretty much limited to institutional organizations of some kind . . . or thoroughly imaginary matrices. It's essentially metabolic, and of course it's not unrelated to the parallelepipedics of IRTH discussions. But it does deal with organic reality.

▼ Ma-mai said it sounded like something for the habilitation of a German doctorate in sociology! But to me less suitable for dramatic poetry even than IRTH.

▲ Actually closer to poetry, insofar as it deals with organic life. Its metrics are up to you. But to be practicable it requires either a computer or an office full of Bartlebies with desk calculators and a faultless plethora of numbers with or without their semantics. The math is extremely simple: adding any number of columns and dividing by a hundred, side by side ad infinitum, to plot on charts and visualize as curves for purposes of functional interpretation. . . . If I hadn't preferred to stay immersed in the lost cause of my quasi-art I might have gotten rich by starting a company to develop S M D C as a computer consultant.

▼ Then I'd never have met you! Not worth it! . . . But you'd have had to persuade some firm or entrepreneur to invest in staff and paraphernalia. Even vulgar poetry would be easier to live on than your salesmanship!

▲ Yes, that's the rub. Anyway, it saved my half-soul from one more managerial enthusiasm!

▼ So Gilgamesh took its place? Less abstraction. At least it's not beautiful!

Did you really think I was a shrew?

▲ No, just a uniquely unconventional beauty; N.B., *noun*.

▼ I love you for that. Less abstraction! This present day has probably been too good to be true. Yet what follows is perhaps as likely for our joyful benefit as for sorrow. Now we'll have time for me to tell you all you want to know about my hesitations. Time enough to help each other's work, I earnestly hope.

This afternoon, when apart, our nullifications will bring us down to earth. Could it be that before an anabolic spring the only important secrets between us will be in sealed meditations?

▲ Yet it'll take very old age for us to exhaust the polar union of our *objective* thoughts! That's even more reason to love you than your purring.

▼ Before I go to sleep, I'll decide whether or not to come to see you as early as tomorrow morning. Don't call me first. Are we just the kittens of older cats? Down, dog, down! Not now!

▲ No cat is ever as enthusiastic as a dog! . . . Okay. I won't ask you to *really* love me this soon. I want to deliver to you, for poetical and critical advancement, the context and narrative of Gilgamesh's ventures between his Tower and his final Acts, as well

as a revelation of his mysterious Elamite origins. You are the object
of all my other subjects. By the way, I'm going to give you a
thermodynamic essay on how you can save a lot of fuel costs
for this whole building with a relatively small investment.
The Commander once asked me to think about it.
He was horrified by that old furnace, not to
mention all the unnecessary loss of heat
beneath this his highly efficient penthouse.
▼ I'm quite aware of your domestic
efficiency. It's a tragi-comedy.
▲ Take the el down, while
I go downstairs as usual.
Try to look like an
old-fashioned landlady
collecting rent.
▼ How can I, when I'm
smiling and purring?
—What do you
want for
Christmas?
▲ An
English-
to-Greek
dictionary.

|| : *dossim repetatur* : ||

EXODOS

ABOUT THE AUTHOR

Jonathan Bayliss (1926–2009) was a student at
Harvard, an electronics technician in the U. S.
Navy, a graduate teaching assistant at Berkeley, a
book buyer, an industrial administrator, a methods
and procedures analyst, a business consultant, a
computer systems architect, a corporate executive, a
municipal manager, a playwright, and a crypto-
novelist.